poison study

MARIA V. SNYDER

CW01084035

This edition published in Great Britain 2015
by Harlequin MIRA, an imprint of Harlequin (UK) Limited,
Eton House, 18-24 Paradise Road,
Richmond, Surrey, TW9 1SR

© Maria V. Snyder 2005

ISBN 978 1 848 45239 8

47-0613

MIRA Ink's policy is to use papers that are natural, renewable and recyclable products and made from wood grown in sustainable forests. The logging and manufacturing processes conform to the legal environmental regulations of the country of origin.

Printed and bound by
CPI Group (UK) Ltd, Croydon, CR0 4YY

poison study

'Yelena, I'm offering you a choice. You can either be executed, or you can be Commander Ambrose's new food taster. His last taster died recently, and we need to fill the position.'

I gaped at him, my heart dancing. He had to be joking. He was probably amusing himself. Watch hope and joy shine on the prisoner's face, then smash it by sending the accused to the noose.

I played along. 'A fool would refuse the job.' My voice rasped louder this time.

'Well, it's a lifetime position. The training can be lethal. After all, how can you identify poisons in the Commander's food if you don't know what they taste like?' He tidied the papers in the folder.

He was serious. My whole body shook. A chance to live! Service to the Commander was better than the dungeon and infinitely better than the noose. Questions raced through my mind: I'm a convicted killer, how can they trust me? What would prevent me from killing the Commander or escaping?

'What shall I tell the executioner?' Valek asked.

'I am not a fool.'

ACKNOWLEDGEMENTS

Without the support from my husband, Rodney, this book wouldn't exist. Thanks, dear, for all the printing, the copying, the critiquing, the willingness to be a single parent from time to time, for not complaining about conference fees, for being there when the rejections came in, and the million other things that I don't have room to list! To my children, Luke and Jenna, for understanding (most of the time) that I'm not playing on the computer (really, I'm not). To my parents, James and Vincenza McGinnis, thank you for always believing in me. To my sister, Karen Phillips, for reading the book and for giving me the support that only a sister can give. To Chris Phillips for his good ideas, and for putting up with all of us. And I can't forget the babysitters: Sam and Carole Snyder, Becky and Randy Greenly, Amy Snyder, Gregory Snyder, Melissa Read and Julie Read—without you I would still be on Chapter Two.

Many thanks go to my fellow Muse and Schmooze critique group members: Shawn Downs, Laurie Edwards, Julie Good, Lisa Hess, Anne Kline, Steve Klotz, Maggie Martz, Lori Myers, Kim Stanford, Jackie Werth, Michael Wertz, Judy Wolfman and Nancy Yeager. Without your help and support this book wouldn't have made it this far.

A heartfelt thanks to Helen French. She made the call I had been dreaming of, and her enthusiasm for this project has been wonderful. Thanks to Mary-Theresa Hussey, who has been an excellent editor. Thanks to my agents, Sally Wecksler and Joann Amparan-Close, for helping with the contract.

Very special thanks go to Alis Rasmussen, who took the time to read and critique my manuscript. Your advice was truly invaluable.

To my husband, Rodney, for all the support he has given, is giving and will give. I'm spoiled rotten.

In loving memory of Frances Snyder, Jeanette and Joseph Scirrotto.

'They would talk to you and make jokes while they were feeding you poison.'
—Kathy Brandt on chemotherapy; a good friend who lost the battle.

THE TERRITORY OF IXIA

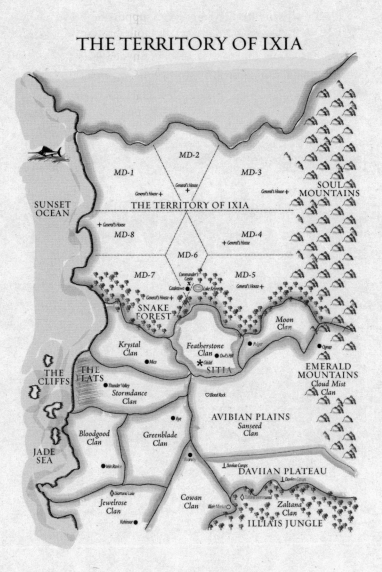

I

LOCKED IN DARKNESS that surrounded me like a coffin, I had nothing to distract me from my memories. Vivid recollections waited to ambush me whenever my mind wandered.

Encompassed by the blackness, I remembered white-hot flames stabbing at my face. Though my hands had been tied to a post that dug sharply into my back, I had recoiled from the onslaught. The fire had pulled away just before blistering my skin, but my eyebrows and eyelashes had long since been singed off.

"Put the flames out!" a man's rough voice had ordered. I blew at the blaze through cracked lips. Dried by fire and fear, the moisture in my mouth had gone and my teeth radiated heat as if they had been baked in an oven.

"Idiot," he cursed. "Not with your mouth. Use your mind. Put the flames out with your mind."

Closing my eyes, I attempted to focus my thoughts on making the inferno disappear. I was willing to do anything, no matter how irrational, to persuade the man to stop.

"Try harder." Once again the heat swung near my face, the bright light blinding me in spite of my closed eyelids.

"Set her hair on fire," a different voice instructed. He sounded younger and more eager than the other man. "That should encourage her. Here, Father, let me."

My body jerked with intense fear as I recognized the voice. I twisted to loosen the bonds that held me as my thoughts scattered into a mindless buzzing. A droning noise had echoed from my throat and grew louder until it had pervaded the room and quenched the flames.

The loud metallic clank of the lock startled me from my nightmarish memory. A wedge of pale yellow light sliced the darkness, then traveled along the stone wall as the heavy cell door opened. Caught in the lantern's glow, my eyes were seared by the brightness. I squeezed them shut as I cowered in the corner.

"Move it, rat, or we'll get the whip!" Two dungeon guards attached a chain to the metal collar on my neck and hauled me to my feet. I stumbled forward, pain blazing around my throat. As I stood on trembling legs, the guards efficiently chained my hands behind me and manacled my feet.

I averted my eyes from the flickering light as they led me down the main corridor of the dungeon. Thick rancid air puffed in my face. My bare feet shuffled through puddles of unidentifiable muck.

Ignoring the calls and moans of the other prisoners, the guards never missed a step, but my heart lurched with every word.

"Ho, ho, ho…someone's gonna swing."

"Snap! Crack! Then your last meal slides down your legs!"

"One less rat to feed."

"Take me! Take me! I wanna die too!"

We stopped. Through squinted eyes I saw a staircase. In an effort to get my foot onto the first step, I tripped over the chains and fell. The guards dragged me up. The rough edges of the stone steps dug into my skin, peeling away exposed flesh on my arms and legs. After being pulled through two sets of thick metal doors, I was dumped onto the floor. Sunlight stabbed between my eyes. I shut them tight as tears spilled down my cheeks. It was the first time that I had seen daylight in seasons.

This is it, I thought, starting to panic. But the knowledge that my execution would end my miserable existence in the dungeon calmed me.

Yanked to my feet again, I followed the guards blindly. My body itched from insect bites and from sleeping on dirty straw. I stunk of rat. Given only a small ration of water, I didn't waste it on baths.

Once my eyes adjusted to the light, I looked around. The walls were bare, without the fabled gold sconces and elaborate tapestries I had been told once decorated the castle's main hallways. The cold stone floor was worn smooth in the middle. We were probably traveling along the hidden corridors used solely by the servants and guards. As we passed two open windows, I glanced out with a hunger that no food could satisfy.

The bright emerald of the grass made my eyes ache. Trees wore cloaks of leaves. Flowers laced the footpaths and over-flowed from barrels. The fresh breeze smelled like an expen-sive perfume, and I breathed deeply. After the acidic smells of excrement and body odor, the taste of the air was like drinking a fine wine. Warmth caressed my skin. A soothing touch compared to the constantly damp and chilly dungeon.

I guessed it was the beginning of the hot season, which meant that I had been locked in the cell for five seasons, one season shy of a full year. It seemed an excessively long time for someone scheduled for execution.

Winded from the effort of marching with my feet chained, I was led into a spacious office. Maps of the Territory of Ixia and the lands beyond covered the walls. Piles of books on the floor made walking a straight line difficult. Candles in various stages of use littered the room, singe marks evident on several papers that had gotten too close to the candle's flame. A large wooden table, strewn with documents and ringed by half a dozen chairs, occupied the center of the room. At the back of the office a man sat at a desk. Behind him a square window gaped open, permitting a breeze to blow through his shoulder-length hair.

I shuddered, causing the chains to clatter. From the whis-pered conversations between prison cells, I had determined that condemned prisoners were taken to an official to confess their crimes before being hanged.

Wearing black pants and a black shirt with two red diamonds stitched on the collar, the man at the desk wore the uniform of an adviser to the Commander. His pallid face held no expression. As his sapphire-blue eyes scanned me, they widened in surprise.

Suddenly conscious of my appearance, I glanced down at my tattered red prison gown and dirty bare feet roughened with yellow calluses. Dirt-streaked skin showed through the rips in the thin fabric. My long black hair hung in greasy clumps. Sweat-soaked, I swayed under the weight of the chains.

"A woman? The next prisoner to be executed is a woman?" His voice was icy. My body trembled on hearing the word *executed* aloud. The calm I'd established earlier fled me. I would have sunk sobbing to the floor if the guards weren't with me. The guards tormented anyone who showed any weakness.

The man tugged at the black ringlets of his hair. "I should have taken the time to reread your dossier." He shooed the guards away. "You're dismissed."

When they were gone, he motioned me to the chair in front of his desk. The chains clanged as I perched on the edge.

He opened a folder on his desk and scanned the pages. "Yelena, today may be your lucky day," he said.

I swallowed a sarcastic reply. An important lesson I had mastered during my dungeon stay was never to talk back. I bowed my head instead, avoiding eye contact.

The man was quiet for a while. "Well-behaved and respectful. You're starting to look like a good candidate."

Despite the clutter of the room, the desk was neat. In addition to my folder and some writing implements, the only other items on the desk were two small, black statues glittering with streaks of silver—a set of panthers carved to lifelike perfection.

"You've been tried and found guilty of murdering General Brazell's only son, Reyad." He paused, stroking his temple with his fingers. "That explains why Brazell's here this week, and why he has been unusually interested in the execution schedule." The man spoke more to himself than to me.

Upon hearing Brazell's name, fear coiled in my stomach. I steadied myself with a reminder that I was soon to be out of his reach forever.

The Territory of Ixia's military had come to power only a generation ago, but the rule had produced strict laws called the Code of Behavior. During peacetime—most of the time, strangely enough for the military—proper conduct didn't allow the taking of a human life. If someone committed murder, the punishment was execution. Self-preservation or an accidental death were not considered acceptable excuses. Once found guilty, the murderer was sent to the Commander's dungeon to await a public hanging.

"I suppose you're going to protest the conviction. Say you were framed or you killed out of self-defense." He leaned back in his chair, waiting with a weary patience.

"No, sir," I whispered, all I could manage from unused vocal cords. "I killed him."

The man in black straightened in his chair, shooting me a hard look. Then he laughed aloud. "This may work out better than I'd planned. Yelena, I'm offering you a choice. You can either be executed, or you can be Commander Ambrose's new food taster. His last taster died recently, and we need to fill the position."

I gaped at him, my heart dancing. He had to be joking. He was probably amusing himself. Great way to get a laugh. Watch hope and joy shine on the prisoner's face, then smash it by sending the accused to the noose.

I played along. "A fool would refuse the job." My voice rasped louder this time.

"Well, it's a lifetime position. The training can be lethal. After all, how can you identify poisons in the Commander's food if you don't know what they taste like?" He tidied the papers in the folder.

"You'll get a room in the castle to sleep, but most of the day you'll be with the Commander. No days off. No husband or children. Some prisoners have chosen execution instead. At least then they know exactly when they're going to die, rather than guessing if it's going to come with the next bite." He clicked his teeth together, a feral grin on his face.

He was serious. My whole body shook. A chance to live! Service to the Commander was better than the dungeon and infinitely better than the noose. Questions raced through my mind: I'm a convicted killer, how can they trust me? What would prevent me from killing the Commander or escaping?

"Who tastes the Commander's food now?" I asked instead, afraid if I asked the other questions he'd realize his mistake and send me to the gallows.

"I do. So I'm anxious to find a replacement. Also the Code of Behavior states that someone whose life is forfeit must be offered the job."

No longer able to sit still, I stood and paced around the

room, dragging my chains with me. The maps on the walls showed strategic military positions. Book titles dealt with security and spying techniques. The condition and amount of candles suggested someone who worked late into the night.

I looked back at the man in the adviser's uniform. He had to be Valek, the Commander's personal security chief and leader of the vast intelligence network for the Territory of Ixia.

"What shall I tell the executioner?" Valek asked.

"I am not a fool."

2

VALEK SNAPPED THE folder closed. He walked to the door; his stride as graceful and light as a snow cat traversing thin ice. The guards waiting in the hall snapped to attention when the door opened. Valek spoke to them, and they nodded. One guard came toward me. I stared at him, going back to the dungeon had not been part of Valek's offer. Could I escape? I scanned the room. The guard spun me around and removed the manacles and chains that had been draped around me since I'd been arrested.

Raw bands of flesh circled my bloody wrists. I touched my neck, feeling skin where there used to be metal. My fingers came away sticky with blood. I groped for the chair. Being freed of the weight of the chains caused a strange sensation to sweep over me; I felt as if I were either going to float away or pass out. I inhaled until the faintness passed.

When I regained my composure, I noticed Valek now stood

beside his desk pouring two drinks. An opened wooden cabinet revealed rows of odd-shaped bottles and multicolored jars stacked inside. Valek placed the bottle he was holding into the cabinet and locked the door.

"While we're waiting for Margg, I thought maybe you could use a drink." He handed me a tall pewter goblet filled with an amber liquid. Raising his own goblet, he made a toast. "To Yelena, our newest food taster. May you last longer than your predecessor."

My goblet stopped short of my lips.

"Relax," he said, "it's a standard toast."

I took a long swig. The smooth liquid burned slightly as it slid down my throat. For a moment, I thought my stomach was going to rebel. This was the first time I had taken something other than water. Then it settled.

Before I could question him as to what exactly had happened to the previous food taster, Valek asked me to identify the ingredients of the drink. Taking a smaller portion, I replied, "Peaches sweetened with honey."

"Good. Now take another sip. This time roll the liquid around your tongue before swallowing."

I complied and was surprised to taste a faint citrus flavor. "Orange?"

"That's right. Now gargle it."

"Gargle?" I asked. He nodded. Feeling foolish, I gargled the rest of my drink and almost spat it out. "Rotten oranges!"

The skin around Valek's eyes crinkled as he laughed. He had a strong, angular face, as if someone had stamped it from a sheet of metal, but it softened when he smiled. Handing me his drink, he asked me to repeat the experiment.

With some trepidation, I took a sip, again detecting the faint orange taste. Bracing myself for the rancid flavor, I gargled Valek's drink and was relieved that gargling only enhanced the orange essence.

"Better?" Valek asked as he took back the empty cup.

"Yes."

Valek sat down behind his desk, opening my folder once more. Picking up his quill, he talked to me while writing. "You just had your first lesson in food tasting. Your drink was laced with a poison called Butterfly's Dust. Mine wasn't. The only way to detect Butterfly's Dust in a liquid is to gargle it. That rotten-orange flavor you tasted was the poison."

I rose, my head spinning. "Is it lethal?"

"A big enough dose will kill you in two days. The symptoms don't arrive until the second day, but by then it's too late."

"Did I have a lethal dose?" I held my breath.

"Of course. Anything less and you wouldn't have tasted the poison."

My stomach rebelled and I started to gag. I forced down the bile in my throat, trying hard to avoid the indignity of vomiting all over Valek's desk.

Valek looked up from the stack of papers. He studied my face. "I warned you the training would be dangerous. But I would hardly give you a poison your body had to fight while you suffered from malnutrition. There is an antidote to Butterfly's Dust." He showed me a small vial containing a white liquid.

Collapsing back into my chair, I sighed. Valek's metal face had returned; I realized he hadn't offered the antidote to me.

"In answer to the question you didn't ask but should have, this—" Valek raised the small vial and shook it "—is how we keep the Commander's food taster from escaping."

I stared at him, trying to understand the implication.

"Yelena, you confessed to murder. We would be fools to let you serve the Commander without some guarantees. Guards watch the Commander at all times and it is doubtful you would be able to reach him with a weapon. For other forms of retaliation, we use Butterfly's Dust." Valek picked up the vial of antidote, and twirled it in the sunlight. "You need a daily dose of this to stay alive. The antidote keeps the poison from killing you. As long as you show up each morning in my office, I will give you the antidote. Miss one morning and you'll be dead by the next. Commit a crime or an act of treason and you'll be sent back to the dungeon until the poison takes you. I would avoid that fate, if I were you. The poison causes severe stomach cramps and uncontrollable vomiting."

Before full comprehension of my situation could sink in, Valek's eyes slid past my shoulder. I turned to see a stout woman in a housekeeper's uniform opening the door. Valek introduced her as Margg, the person who would take care of my basic needs. Expecting me to follow her, Margg strode out the door.

I glanced at the vial on Valek's desk.

"Come to my office tomorrow morning. Margg will direct you."

An obvious dismissal, but I paused at the door with all the questions I should have asked poised on my lips. I swallowed them. They sank like stones to my stomach, then I closed the door and hurried after Margg, who hadn't stopped to wait.

Margg never slowed her pace. I found myself panting with the effort to keep up. Trying to remember the various corridors and turns, I soon gave up as my whole world shrank to the sight of Margg's broad back and efficient stride. Her long black skirt seemed to float above the floor. The housekeeper uniform included a black shirt and white apron that hung from the neck down to the ankle and was cinched tight around the waist. The apron had two vertical rows of small red diamond-shapes connected end to end. When Margg finally stopped at the baths, I had to sit on the floor to clear my spinning head.

"You stink," Margg said, disgust creasing her wide face. She pointed to the far side of the baths in a manner that indicated she was used to being obeyed. "Wash twice, then soak. I'll bring you some uniforms." She left the room.

The overpowering desire to bathe flashed like fire on my skin. Energized, I ripped the prison robe off and raced to the washing area. Hot water poured down in a cascade when I opened the duct above my head. The Commander's castle was equipped with heated water tanks located one floor above the baths, a luxury even Brazell's extravagant manor house didn't have.

I stood for a long time, hoping the drumming on my head would erase all thoughts of poisons. Obediently I washed my hair and body twice. My neck, wrists and ankles burned from the soap, but I didn't care. I scrubbed two more times, rubbing hard at the stubborn spots of dirt on my skin, stopping only when I realized they were bruises.

I felt unconnected to the body under the waterfall. The pain and humiliation of being arrested and locked away had been inflicted on this body, but my soul had long since been driven out during the last two years I had lived in Brazell's manor house.

An image of Brazell's son suddenly flashed before me. Reyad's handsome face distorted with rage. I stepped back, reflexively jerking my hands up to block him. The image disappeared, leaving me shaking.

It was an effort to dry off and wrap a towel around me. I tried to focus on finding a comb instead of the ugly memories Reyad's image called forth.

Even clean, my snarled hair resisted the comb. As I searched for a pair of scissors, I spotted another person in the baths from the corner of my eye. I stared at the body. A corpse looked back at me. The green eyes were the only signs of life in the gaunt, oval face. Thin stick legs looked incapable of holding the rest of the body up.

Recognition shot through me like a cold splash of fear. It was *my* body. I averted my eyes from the mirror, having no desire to assess the damage. Coward, I thought, returning my gaze with a purpose. Had Reyad's death released my soul from where it had fled? In my mind I tried to reconnect my spirit to my body. Why did I think my soul would return if my body was still not mine? It belonged to Commander Ambrose to be used as a tool for filtering and testing poisons. I turned away.

Pulling clumps of knotted hair out with the comb, I arranged the rest into a single long braid down my back.

Not long ago all I had hoped for was a clean prison robe before my execution, and now here I was sinking into the Commander's famous hot baths.

"That's long enough," Margg barked, startling me out of a light doze. "Here are your uniforms. Get dressed." Her stiff face radiated disapproval.

As I dried myself, I felt Margg's impatience.

Along with some undergarments, the food taster's uniform consisted of black pants, a wide red satin belt and a red satin shirt with a line of small black diamond-shapes connected end to end down each of the sleeves. The clothes were obviously sized for a man. Malnourished and measuring only four inches past five feet, I looked like a child playing pretend with her father's clothes. I wrapped the belt three times around my waist and rolled up the sleeves and pant legs.

Margg snorted. "Valek only told me to feed you and show you to your room. But I think we'll stop by the seamstress's first." Pausing at the open door, Margg pursed her lips and added, "You'll need boots too."

Obediently, I followed Margg like a lost puppy.

The seamstress, Dilana, laughed gaily at my appearance.

Her heart-shaped face had a halo of curly blond hair. Honey-colored eyes and long eyelashes enhanced her beauty.

"The stable boys wear the same pants and the kitchen maids wear the red shirts," Dilana said when she had stifled her giggles. She admonished Margg for not spending the time to find me better-size uniforms. Margg pushed her lips together tighter.

Fussing around me like a grandmother instead of a young woman, Dilana's attentions warmed me, pulling me toward her. I envisioned us becoming friends. She probably had many acquaintances and suitors who came to bask in her attentions like cave dwellers drawn to a blazing hearth. I found myself aching to reach out to her.

After writing my measurements down, Dilana searched through the piles of red, black and white clothing stacked around the room.

Everyone who worked in Ixia wore a uniform. The Commander's castle servants and guards wore a variation of black, white and red color clothes with vertical diamond-shapes either down the sleeves of the shirts or down the sides of the pants. Advisers and higher-ranking officers usually wore all black with small red diamonds stitched on the collars to show rank. The uniform system became mandatory when the Commander gained power so everyone knew at a glance who they were dealing with.

Black and red were Commander Ambrose's colors. The Territory of Ixia had been separated into eight Military Districts each ruled by a General. The uniforms of the eight districts were identical to the Commander's except for the color. A housekeeper wearing black with small purple diamond-shapes on her apron therefore worked in Military District 3 or MD-3.

"I think these should fit better." She handed me some clothes, gesturing to the privacy screen at the far end of the room.

While I was changing, I heard Dilana say, "She'll need boots." Feeling less foolish in my new clothes, I picked up the old uniforms and gave them to Dilana.

"These must have belonged to Oscove, the old food taster," Dilana said. A sad expression gripped her face for a moment before she shook her head as if to rid herself of an unwanted thought.

All my fantasies of friendship fled me as I realized that being friends with the Commander's food taster was a big emotional risk. My stomach hollowed out while Dilana's warmth leaked from me, leaving a cold bitterness behind.

A sharp stab of loneliness struck me as an unwanted image of May and Carra, who still lived at Brazell's manor, flashed before my eyes. My fingers twitched to fix Carra's crooked braids and to straighten May's skirt.

Instead of Carra's silky ginger hair in my hands, I held a stack of clothes. Dilana guided me to a chair. Kneeling on the floor, she put socks on my feet and then a pair of boots. The boots were made of soft black leather. They came up over my ankle to midcalf, where the leather folded down. Dilana tucked my pant legs into the boots and helped me stand.

I hadn't worn shoes in seasons and I expected them to chafe. But the boots cushioned my feet and fit well. I smiled at

Dilana, thoughts of May and Carra temporarily banished. These were the finest pair of boots I'd ever worn.

She smiled back and said, "I can always pick the right-size boots without having to measure."

Margg harrumphed. "You didn't get poor Rand's boots right. He's too smitten with you to complain. Now he limps around the kitchen."

"Don't pay any attention to her," Dilana said to me. "Margg, don't you have work to do? Get going or I'll sneak into your room and shorten all your skirts." Dilana shooed us good-naturedly out the door.

Margg took me to the servants' dining room and served me small portions of soup and bread. The soup tasted divine. After devouring the food, I asked for more.

"No. Too much will make you sick," was all she said. With reluctance I left my bowl on the table to follow Margg to my room.

"At sunrise be ready to work."

Once again I watched her retreating back.

My small room contained a narrow bed with a single stained mattress on a stark metal frame, a plain wooden desk and chair, a chamber pot, an armoire, a lantern, a tiny woodstove and one window shuttered tight. The gray stone walls were unadorned. I tested the mattress; it barely yielded. A vast improvement over my dungeon cell, yet I found myself somewhat dissatisfied.

Nothing in the room suggested softness. With my mind and eyes filled with Valek's metal face and Margg's censure, and the harsh cut and colors of the uniforms, I longed for a pillow or blanket. I felt like a lost child looking for something to clutch, something supple that wouldn't end up hurting me.

After hanging my extra uniforms in the armoire, I crossed to the window. There was a sill wide enough for me to sit on. The shutters were locked, but the latches were on the inside. Hands shaking, I unlocked and pushed the shutters wide, blinking in the sudden light. Shielding my eyes, I squinted beneath my hand, and stared at the scene in front of my window in disbelief. I was on the first floor of the castle! Five feet below was the ground.

Between my room and the stables were the Commander's kennels and the exercise yard for the horses. The stable boys and dog trainers wouldn't care if I escaped. I could drop down without any effort and be gone. Tempting, except for the fact that I would be dead in two days. Maybe another time, when two days of freedom might be worth the price.

I could hope.

3

REYAD'S WHIP CUT INTO my skin, slashing my flesh with a burning pain. "Move," he ordered.

I dodged ineffectively, hampered by the rope tied to my wrist, which anchored me to a post in the center of the room.

"Move faster, keep moving!" Reyad shouted.

The whip snapped again and again. My tattered shirt gave no protection from the stinging leather. A cool, soothing voice entered my skull. "Go away," it whispered. "Send your mind to a distant place, a warm loving place. Let your body go."

The silken voice didn't belong to Reyad or Brazell. A savior, perhaps? An easy way to escape the torment, tempting but I held out for another opportunity. Determined, I stayed, focusing on avoiding the lash. When exhaustion claimed me, my body began to vibrate of its own accord. Like an out-of-control hummingbird, I darted around the room, avoiding the whip.

★ ★ ★

I woke in darkness soaked with sweat, my crumpled uniform twisted tight around my body. The vibration in my dream replaced by a pounding. Before falling asleep, I had wedged a chair under the doorknob to prevent anyone from barging in. The chair rattled with each thud.

"I'm up," I shouted. The racket stopped. When I opened the door, Margg stood frowning with a lantern. I hastened to change my uniform and joined her in the hallway. "I thought you said sunrise."

Her disapproving stare seared my lips shut. "It *is* sunrise."

I followed Margg through the labyrinth of the castle's hidden hallways as the day began to brighten. My room faced west, shielding me from the morning sun. Margg extinguished the lantern just as the scent of sweet cakes filled the air.

Inhaling, I asked her, "Breakfast?" A hopeful, almost pleading, note crept into my voice, galling me.

"No. Valek will feed you."

The image of breakfast laced with poison did wonders for suppressing my appetite. My stomach tightened as the unwanted memory of Valek's Butterfly's Dust came to mind. By the time we had reached his office, I had convinced myself that I was about to collapse, soon to be vanquished by the poison if I didn't receive the antidote.

When I entered the room, Valek was in the process of arranging plates of steaming food. He had cleared off a section of the table. The displaced papers balanced in messy piles. He gestured to a chair; I sat, searching the table for the small vial of antidote.

"I hope you're…" Valek studied my face. I stared back, trying not to flinch under his scrutiny.

"It's amazing what a difference a bath and a uniform can make," Valek said, absently chewing on a slice of bacon. "I'll have to remember that. It might be useful in the future." Placing two plates of an egg-and-ham mixture before me, he said, "Let's get started."

Feeling dizzy and flushed, I blurted out, "I'd rather start with the antidote." Another long pause from Valek caused me to fidget in my seat.

"You shouldn't be feeling any symptoms. They won't arrive until later this afternoon." He shrugged and went to his cabinet. He used a pipette to extract a measure of the white liquid from a large bottle, and then locked the antidote back inside the cabinet. My interest in the location of the key must have been obvious because Valek used some type of sleight of hand to make the key disappear. Handing me the pipette, he sat down on the opposite side of the table.

"Drink up so we can start today's lessons," he said.

I squeezed the contents into my mouth, cringing at the bitter taste. Valek took the pipette from my hands and exchanged it for a blue jar. "Take a sniff."

The jar contained a white powder, resembling sugar but smelling like rosewood. Gesturing to the two plates cooling in front of me, Valek asked me to pick the one sprinkled with the poison. I sniffed at the food like a scent hound nosing for prey. A faint odor of rosewood emanated from the left plate.

"Good. Should you pick up that aroma from any of the

Commander's food, reject it. The poison is called Tigtus and a single grain of the powder will kill within the hour." Valek removed the tainted food. "Eat your breakfast." He indicated the other plate. "You'll need your strength."

I spent the remainder of the day smelling poisons until my head ached and spun. The multitude of names and aromas began to confuse me, so I asked Valek for some paper, quill and ink. He stilled.

"I don't know why you continue to surprise me. I should have remembered that General Brazell educates his orphans." Valek flung a book of papers, a quill and ink down in front of me. "Take them back to your room. We've done enough for today."

I silently cursed myself for reminding Valek why I had been the next person to be executed as I gathered the book and writing implements. Valek's hard, unforgiving expression revealed his thoughts. Taken off the streets, fed and educated by Brazell, I had repaid Brazell's kindness by murdering his only child. I knew Valek would never believe the truth about Brazell and Reyad.

General Brazell's orphanage was a topic of ridicule from the other Generals. They thought he had gone "soft" after the takeover of Ixia fifteen years ago. This impression suited Brazell. Seen as a kindly old benefactor, Brazell could continue unchallenged in his administration of Military District 5.

I hesitated at the entrance of Valek's office, noticing for the first time the three complex locks on the thick wooden door. Absently fingering the locking mechanisms, I lingered in the doorway until Valek asked, "Now what?"

"I'm not sure where my room is."

Valek spoke as if talking to a slow-witted child. "Ask the first housekeeper or kitchen maid you find, they're always scurrying about this time of day. Tell her you're in the west servant wing, ground floor. She'll show you."

The kitchen maid I snared into helping me was more talkative than Margg and I took full advantage of her good nature. She guided me to the laundry room to obtain some linens for my bed. Then I had her show me the way to the baths and the seamstress's work area. Dilana's piles of uniforms might come in handy someday.

In my room, I opened the shutters to let in the fading light from the setting sun. Sitting down at my desk, I wrote exhaustive notes on what I had learned that day, including a rough map of the servants' corridors. I considered more exploration of the castle, but Valek had been right, I needed my strength. I hoped I would have time to explore later.

During the next two weeks, the training proceeded in a manner so similar to the first day that I lapsed into a routine, arriving at Valek's every morning to train. After fourteen days of sniffing poisons, I found that my sense of smell had heightened. But then Valek announced I was strong enough to begin tasting poisons.

"I'll start with the deadliest one," he said. "If you don't die from it, the other poisons wouldn't kill you either. I don't want to waste all my time training you only to see you die in the end." He placed a slender red bottle on his desk. "It's nasty. Affects the body immediately." Valek's eyes lit up as he admired the poison. "It's called Have a Drink, My Love, or My Love for short because the poison has a history of being used by disheartened wives." He squeezed two drops of the poison into a steaming cup. "A larger dose would definitely kill you. With a smaller dose, there is a chance you'll survive, but you'll become delusional, paranoid and completely disoriented for the next few days."

"Valek, why do I have to taste My Love if it has immediate results? Isn't that what a food taster is for? I taste the Commander's food. I keel over, dead. End of the tale." I tried pacing around the room but kept tripping over stacks of books. Frustrated, I kicked two piles into their neighbors, scattering books into a messy heap on the floor. Valek's gaze pierced me, draining the odd feeling of satisfaction I had gotten from kicking the books.

"A food taster's job is much more complex than that," Valek explained, pulling his hair back from his face. "Being able to identify which poison taints the Commander's food can lead me to the poisoner." Valek handed me the cup. "Even if you only have a split second to shout out My Love before passing out, it would narrow down the list of suspects. There are a number of assassins who are partial to My Love. The poison is grown in Sitia, the southern lands. It was easy to obtain before the takeover. With the closure of the southern border, only a handful of people have enough money to purchase it illegally."

Valek went over to the mess on the floor and started restacking the books. His movements were so graceful that I wondered if he had been a dancer, but his words betrayed to me that his fluid gestures were those of a trained killer.

"Yelena, your job is very important. That's why I spend so much time training you. A shrewd assassin can watch a taster for several days to discover a pattern." Valek continued his lecture from the floor. "For example, the taster might always cut a piece of meat from the left side, or never stir the drink. Some poisons sink to the bottom of the cup. If the taster only sips off the top, then the assassin knows exactly where to place the poison to kill his intended victim." He finished picking up the books. The new piles were neater than the rest of the stacks on the floor. It seemed an invitation to Valek to continue straightening the books. He cleared a bigger path through his office.

"Once you drink the poison, Margg will help you to your room and take care of you. I'll give her your daily dose of Butterfly's Dust antidote."

I stared at the steam drifting from the tea. I picked up the cup, the heat warming my icy hands. When Margg entered the room, it felt as if the executioner had just mounted the dais, reaching for the lever. Should I sit down or lie down? I looked around the room, seeing nothing. My arms started to tingle as I realized I had been holding my breath.

I raised the cup in a mock salute, and then drained the contents. "Sour apples," I said.

Valek nodded. I had only enough time to put the cup on the table before my world began to melt. Margg's body undulated toward me. Her large head sprouted flowers from her eye sockets. A moment later her body filled the room as her head shriveled.

I sensed movement. The gray walls grew arms and legs that reached for me, trying to use me in their fight against the floor. Gray spirits rose from under my feet. They dived, poked and cackled at me. They were freedom. I tried to push the Margg thing away, but it clung and wrapped itself around me, digging through my ears and pounding on my head.

"Murderer," it whispered. "Sneaky bitch. You probably slit his throat while he slept. Easy way to kill. Did you enjoy yourself as you watched his blood soak the sheets? You're nothing but a rat."

I grabbed at the voice, trying to make it stop, but it turned into two green-and-black toy soldiers who held me tight.

"She'll die from the poison. If not you can take her," the Margg thing said to the soldiers.

They pushed me into a dark pit. I plunged into blackness.

The stench of vomit and excrement greeted me when I regained consciousness. They were the unmistakable odors of the dungeon. Wondering how I had ended up back in my old cell, I sat up. A surge of nausea demanded my attention. I groped around for the slop pot and encountered the metal leg of a bed, which I clutched as dry heaves racked my body. When they stopped, I leaned against the wall, grateful to be on the floor of my room and not back in the dungeon. Beds were a luxury not included with the subterranean accommodations.

Summoning the strength to stand, I located and lit my lantern. Dried vomit caked my face. My shirt and pants were soaking wet and smelled foul. The liquid contents of my body had collected in a puddle on the floor.

Margg took good care of me, I thought sarcastically. At least she was practical. If she had dumped me on the bed I would have ruined the mattress.

I thanked fate that I had survived the poison and that I had awakened in the middle of the night. Unable to endure the feel of my sodden uniform any longer, I made my way to the baths.

On my return, voices stopped me before I reached the hallway leading to my room. Extinguishing my lantern in one quick motion, I peeked around the corner. Two soldiers stood in front of my door. The soft light of their lantern reflected the green-and-black colors of their uniforms—Brazell's colors.

4

"SHOULD WE CHECK IF she's dead?" asked one of Brazell's soldiers. He held the lantern up to my door, his overloaded weapon belt jingling with the motion.

"No. That housekeeper checks every morning and gives her a potion. We'll hear about it soon enough. Besides, it stinks in there." The other soldier waved his hand in front of his face.

"Yeah. If the smell don't kill the mood, taking off her vomit-soaked uniform would make any man gag. Although…" The lantern soldier's hand briefly touched the manacles hanging from his belt. "We could drag her down to the baths, clean her up, and have some fun before she dies."

"No, someone would see us. If she survives, we'll have plenty of time to peel off her uniform. It'll be just like opening a present, and definitely more entertaining when she's awake." He leered. They laughed.

They continued down the hallway and were soon out of

sight. I clung to the wall and wondered if what I had just witnessed had been real. Was I still having paranoid hallucinations? My head felt as if it had soaked too long in a pool of water. Dizziness and nausea rippled through my body.

The soldiers were long gone before I worked up the nerve to go back to my room. I pushed the door wide and thrust my lantern in front of me, shining the light into every corner and under the bed. A harsh, acrid odor was the only thing to attack me. Gagging, I unlocked the shutters and threw them open, taking deep breaths of the cool, cleansing air.

I looked at the noxious puddle on the floor. The last thing I wanted to do was clean up the mess, but I knew I would never be able to sleep while breathing in that foul smell. After raiding housekeeping's supplies, and stopping for the occasional bout of nausea, I managed to scrub the floor without fainting.

Exhausted, I stretched out on the bed. It felt lumpy. I turned in my blankets, hoping to find a comfortable position. What if Brazell's soldiers came back? Asleep in bed, I would be an easy target. I had cleaned myself up so there was no need to drag me to the baths. The room smelled like disinfectant, and I had forgotten to put the chair under the doorknob.

Imagination kicked in, a vivid scene of me manacled to the bed, helpless while the soldiers stripped me slowly to heighten their anticipation and savor my fear.

The walls of my room seemed to thicken and pulse. I bolted out into the hallway, expecting to see Brazell's soldiers lurking around my door. The corridor was dark and deserted.

When I tried to reenter my room, I felt as if someone pressed a pillow against my face. I couldn't get my feet to move past the doorway. My room was a trap. The paranoia effect of My Love or common sense? I wondered. Indecision kept me standing in the hallway until my stomach growled. Guided by my hunger, I searched for food.

Hoping to find the kitchen empty, I was dismayed to see a tall man wearing a white uniform with two black diamonds printed on the front of his shirt mumbling to himself as he lurched around the ovens. His left leg didn't bend. I tried to sneak back out but he spotted me.

"Are you looking for me?" he asked.

"No," I said. "I was…looking for something to eat." I craned my neck back to see his face.

He frowned and shifted his weight to his good leg as he studied my uniform. Too thin for a cook, I thought, but he wore the proper clothes and only a cook would be up this early. He was handsome in a subtle way, with light brown eyes and short brown hair. I wondered if this was Dilana's Rand that Margg had talked about.

"Help yourself." He gestured toward two steaming loaves of bread. "You just won me a week's wages."

"Excuse me," I said while cutting off a large piece of bread. "How could I win you money?"

"You're the new food taster. Right?"

I nodded.

"Everyone knows Valek gave you a dose of My Love. I took a chance and bet a week's wages that you would live." He stopped to take three more loaves out of the oven. "A big risk, since you're the smallest and skinniest food taster we've ever had. Most everyone else had wagered that you wouldn't pull through, including Margg."

The cook rummaged through one of the cabinets. "Here." He handed me some butter. "I'll make you some sweet cakes." Grabbing various ingredients from a shelf, he proceeded to mix up a batter.

"How many food tasters have there been?" I asked him between bites of buttered bread. Working alone didn't seem to suit him. He seemed glad to have some company.

With his hands in constant motion, he said, "Five since Commander Ambrose has been in power. Valek loves his poisons. He poisoned many of the Commander's enemies, and he likes to keep in practice. You know, testing the food tasters from time to time to make sure they haven't grown lazy."

The cook's words crawled up my spine. I felt as if my body had liquefied and pooled into a giant mixing bowl. I was just a puddle of ingredients to be beaten, stirred and used. When the cook poured the batter onto the hot griddle, my blood sizzled along with the sweet cakes.

"Poor Oscove, Valek never liked him. Testing him constantly until he couldn't handle the pressure. The 'official' cause of death was suicide, but I think Valek killed him."

Flip. I stared as the cook deftly flicked his wrist, turning the cakes over. My muscles trembled in synch with the sound of frying sweet cakes.

Here I was worried about Brazell, when one misstep with

Valek and… Flip. I would be gone. He probably held a couple of poisons in reserve just in case he decided to replace the taster. Glancing over my shoulder, I imagined Valek coming into the kitchen to poison my breakfast. I couldn't even enjoy talking with a chatty cook without being reminded that tasting potentially poisoned food wasn't the only danger of my new job.

The cook handed me a plate loaded with sweet cakes, took three more loaves of bread out of the oven and refilled his bread pans with dough. Piping-hot sweet cakes were such a rare treat that I devoured them despite my unsettled stomach.

"Oscove was my friend. He was the Commander's best food taster. He used to come to my kitchen every morning after breakfast and help me invent new recipes. I have to keep things interesting or the Commander will start looking for a new cook. Know what I mean?"

I nodded, wiping butter off my chin.

He thrust out his hand. "My name's Rand."

I shook his hand. "Yelena."

I stopped at an open window on my way to Valek's office. The rising sun was just cresting the Soul Mountains to the east of the castle. The colors in the sky resembled a ruined painting, as if a small child had spilled water on the canvas. I let my eyes feast on the vibrant display of life as I inhaled the fresh air. Everything was in full bloom, and soon the cool morning breeze would warm to a comfortable level. The hot season was in its infancy. The days of sweltering heat and limp, humid nights were still a few weeks away. I had been training with Valek for a fortnight, and I wondered how long My Love had held me unconscious.

Tearing myself away from the window, I walked toward Valek's office, arriving at his door just as he was leaving.

"Yelena! You made it." Valek smiled. "It's been three days. I was beginning to worry."

I studied his face. He seemed sincerely glad to see me.

"Where's Margg?" he asked.

"I haven't seen her." Thank fate, I thought.

"Then you'll need your antidote," Valek said while moving back to his cabinet.

Once I swallowed the liquid, Valek headed toward the door. When I didn't follow, he gestured to me.

"I have to taste the Commander's breakfast," he said, setting a quick pace.

I huffed along behind him.

"It's time you meet the Commander and watch how food tasting should be done."

We turned into the main hallway of the castle. Valek didn't miss a step, but I stumbled and stifled a gasp. The famous tapestries from the King's era were torn and soiled with black paint. In Brazell's orphanage we had been taught that each tapestry represented a province of the old kingdom. Hand-quilted with gold threads during the course of many years, the colored silk pictures told a story about the history of each province. Now in rags, they still told a very powerful tale about the Commander's rule.

The Commander's disdain for the opulence, excesses and

injustices of the former ruler and his family was well known throughout Ixia. From monarchy to military, the changes in Ixia were severe. While some citizens embraced the simple but strict rules in the Code of Behavior, others rebelled by refusing to wear their uniforms, by not requesting permission to travel, and by escaping to the south.

Based on the offense, the insurgents' punishment matched exactly what was written in the Code. No uniform meant two days chained naked in the town's square. It didn't matter if the offender had a legitimate reason; the punishment was always the same. Ixia's people discovered that there wasn't going to be any guessing about their punishment. No bribing or good-old-boy networking either; the Commander meant business. Live by the Code or face the consequences.

I pulled my eyes away from the tapestries in time to see Valek disappear through an arched doorway decorated with lavish stonework. Splintered wooden doors hung crookedly on their hinges, but the intricate carvings of trees and exotic birds were still visible. Another victim of the takeover, and another reminder of the Commander's intent.

I stopped in amazement just past the broken doors. This was the castle's throne room. Inside was a sea of desks occupied by numerous advisers and military officers from every Military District in the Territory. The room hummed with activity.

It was hard to distinguish individuals in the commotion, but I finally spotted Valek's smooth stride as he went through an open door at the back of the room. Finding a path around the maze of desks took some time. When I arrived at the door, I heard a man's voice complaining about cold sweet cakes.

Commander Ambrose sat behind a plain wooden desk. His office was stark in comparison to Valek's and lacked personal decorations. The only object in the room that did not have a specific purpose was a hand-size statue of a black snow cat. The cat's eyes glinted with silver, and bright specks of the metal peppered the beast's powerful back.

The Commander's black uniform was perfectly tailored and immaculate, indistinguishable from Valek's except that the diamonds stitched on his collar were real. They twinkled in the morning light. The Commander's black hair was sprinkled with gray and cut so short that the strands stood straight up.

In Brazell's classroom, we had learned that the Commander avoided public appearances and having his portrait painted. The fewer people who knew what he looked like, the less his chances were of being assassinated. Some thought he was paranoid, but I believed that since he had gained power by using assassins and covert warfare, he was merely being realistic.

This was not the Commander I had envisioned: burly, bearded and weighed down with medals and weapons. He was thin, clean shaven, with delicate features.

"Commander, this is Yelena, your new food taster," Valek said, pulling me into the room.

The Commander's gold almond-shaped eyes met mine. His gaze had the sharpness of a sword point. It pressed against my throat and fastened me to the floor. I felt myself being drawn out and examined. When he looked over at Valek, I swayed with relief.

"From what Brazell's been hollering about, I expected her to breathe fire," the Commander said.

I stiffened on hearing Brazell's name. If Brazell was complaining to the Commander, I could be back in line for the noose.

"Brazell's a fool," Valek said. "He wanted the drama of a public hanging for his son's killer. I personally would have taken care of her immediately. It would have been within his rights." Valek slurped the Commander's tea and sniffed the sweet cakes.

My chest was tight. I was having trouble drawing in air.

"Besides, it's clearly written in the Code of Behavior that the next to be hanged gets the job offer. And Brazell was one of the authors." Cutting a piece of one sweet cake from the center and the other from the side, Valek put both pieces in his mouth, chewing slowly. "Here." He handed the plate to the Commander.

"Brazell does have a point," the Commander said. He picked up his tea and stared at the contents. "When does she start? I'm getting tired of cold food."

"A few more days."

"Good," the Commander said to Valek, then turned to me. "You arrive with my food and taste quick. I don't want to be looking for you. Understand?"

Feeling light-headed, I answered, "Yes, Sir."

"Valek, I'm losing weight because of you. Lunch is in the war room. Don't be late."

"Yes, Sir," Valek said and headed for the door. I followed. We wound our way through the tangle of desks. When Valek stopped to consult with another adviser, I glanced around. A handful of the Commander's advisers were women, and I noticed two female Captains and one Colonel. Their new roles were one of the benefits of the takeover. The Commander assigned jobs based on skills and intelligence, not on gender.

While the monarchy preferred to see women work as maids, kitchen helpers and wives, the Commander gave them the freedom to choose what they wanted to do. Some women preferred their former occupations, while others jumped at the chance to do something else, and the younger generation had been quick to take advantage of the new opportunities.

When we finally reached Valek's office, Margg was dusting around Valek's piles of papers on the table. It looked to me as if she was spending more time reading the papers than straightening them. Didn't Valek notice? I wondered what Margg did for Valek besides cleaning.

Margg turned a pleasant face to Valek, but as soon as he walked away she glared fiercely at me. Must have lost a lot of money betting against my survival, I thought. I smiled at her. She managed to control her outraged expression before Valek glanced up at us from his desk.

"Yelena, you look exhausted. You make me tired just looking at you. Go rest. Come back after lunch and we'll continue with your training."

I didn't really feel tired, but rest sounded like an excellent idea. As I moved along the hallway, Valek's comment wormed its way through my mind. My pace slowed and I dragged my feet toward my room. I was so preoccupied with the physical effort of walking that I bumped right into two of Brazell's guards.

"Lookie, Wren, I found our rat!" one guard exclaimed, grabbing my wrist.

Alert, I gaped at the green diamonds on the guard's uniform.

"Good for you," Wren said. "Let's show your catch to General Brazell."

"The General isn't fond of live rats. Especially this one."

The guard shook me hard. Pain coursed up my arm to my shoulder and neck. In a panic, I searched the hallway for help. It was deserted.

"That's right, he prefers them skinned alive."

I'd heard enough. I did what any good rat would do. I bit down on the guard's hand until I tasted blood. Yelping and cursing in surprise, his grip lessened. I jerked my arm out of his grasp and ran.

5

I WAS ONLY A COUPLE OF STEPS away from Brazell's guards when they recovered from their surprise and began to chase me. Being terrified and unburdened of weapons, I had a slight advantage. It wouldn't last. I was already puffing with the effort.

The corridors were mysteriously empty as I ran through them. If I did find someone, I wasn't really sure they would or could help me. Like a rat, my only hope of escape was to find a hole to hide in.

I ran without a plan, caring only about keeping ahead of the guards. The corridors blurred together until I imagined I was running in place and it was the walls that were moving. I slowed for a moment to get my bearings. Where was I?

The light in the hallway was waning. My pounding steps kicked dust up from the floor. I had headed toward an isolated part of the castle, a perfect place for a quiet murder. Quiet because I wouldn't have enough air in my lungs to scream.

I made a quick right turn into a corridor that led off into darkness. Momentarily out of the guards' sight, I pushed against the first door I encountered. Groaning and creaking, it yielded slightly under my weight, and then stuck tight. A gap big enough for my body, but not my head. Hearing the guards turn down the corridor, I threw myself against the door. It moved another inch. I tumbled headfirst into a dark room, and landed on the floor.

The guards found the door. I watched in horror as they tried to muscle it open. The gap began to expand. I scanned the room. My eyes adjusted to the gloom. Empty barrels and rotten sacks of grain littered the floor. A pile of rugs was stacked against the far wall below a window.

The door surrendered a couple more inches to the guards' efforts before lodging again. I stood, and stacked the barrels on top of the rug pile. Scrambling up them, I reached the window, only to discover it was too small for me to fit through.

The door cracked ominously. I used my elbow to shatter the windowpane. Pulling the ragged glass fragments out of the frame, I tossed them to the floor. Blood ran down my arm. Heedless of the pain, I jumped down, pressed myself against the wall next to the doorway, and fought to stifle the harsh sound of my breathing.

With a loud groan, the door stopped mere inches from my face as the guards stumbled into the storeroom.

"Check the window. I'll cover the door," Wren said.

I peeked around the edge. Wren's companion walked to the pile of rugs and barrels, crushing glass beneath his boots.

My plan wasn't going to work. Wren blocked my escape route. The broken window would only delay the inevitable.

"Too small, she's still here," the guard called from above.

My rough breathing had accelerated into fast gasps. I felt light-headed. The rat trap had sprung. I was immobilized in its metal jaws.

My thoughts jumbled into a cloud of images. I clutched at the door, trying not to fall. A buzzing sound burst uncontrolled from my throat. I was unable to suppress the drone. Trying harder only caused the sound to grow louder.

I staggered out from behind the door. With all the noise I made, the guards didn't even glance in my direction. They seemed frozen in place.

My lungs strained for air. On the verge of passing out, the buzzing then released me. The sound still rang in the room, but it no longer came from me.

The guards continued to be unresponsive. After taking several deep breaths, I bolted from the room. I wasn't going to waste time trying to understand. The buzzing sound followed me as I ran back the way we had come.

The loud hum ended as soon as I started seeing other servants hurrying through the hallway. Odd looks were cast my way. I realized I must be quite a sight. I forced myself to stop running as I tried to calm my hammering heart.

My throat burned from panting, my uniform was stained, pain throbbed in my elbow, and bright red beads dripped off my fingers. Looking at my hands, I saw deep cuts from handling the glass. I gazed at the blood on the floor.

Turning around, I saw a line of crimson drops disappearing down the corridor. I clutched my arms to my chest, but it was too late. I had left a blood trail, and there were Brazell's guards, like trained dogs, following it.

They were coming around the corner at the far end of the hall. Undetected so far, I knew any sudden movement would draw their attention. I joined a group of servants, hoping to blend in. Pain pulsated in harmony with my laboring heartbeat.

When I reached a turn, I risked a glance over my shoulder. The guards stood at the spot where my blood trail had ended. Wren gestured as he argued with his partner. I slipped around the corner unnoticed, then bumped right into Valek.

"Yelena! What happened to you?" Valek grabbed my arm. I winced. He let go.

"I…fell…on some glass." It was weak. I hurried to cover it. "I'm on my way to get cleaned up." As I began to walk past Valek, he grasped my shoulder, spinning me around.

"You need to see a medic."

"Ah…okay." I tried once more to get past Valek.

"The medic is this way." Valek pulled on my shoulder, forcing me to follow him back down the corridor toward the guards. Foolishly, I hoped they wouldn't see me, but as we walked past they smiled, falling into step behind us.

I glanced at Valek. There was no expression on his face. His grip on my shoulder tightened. Was Valek leading me to some secluded spot where the three of them could kill me? Should I make a break for it? But if Valek had wanted me dead, he had only to withhold the antidote to Butterfly's Dust.

When the hallway emptied of people, Valek let go of my shoulder and swung around to face the two guards. I stayed close behind him.

"Are you lost?" Valek asked the guards.

"No, sir," said Wren. A foot taller than Valek, his hands were the size of my head. "Just want to reclaim our prisoner." Wren tried to reach around Valek to grab me.

Valek deflected his hand. "*Your* prisoner?" Valek's voice sliced through the air like steel.

The guards looked at each other in disbelief. Valek had no weapons. While the other guard was shorter than Wren, he still outweighed the other two men. Identical cocky smirks touched both guards' faces. I wondered if sneering and glaring were part of their training. Rand the cook would probably bet a month's wages on Brazell's soldiers winning this argument.

"Actually, General Brazell's prisoner, sir. Now, if you would…" Wren gestured for Valek to step aside.

"Tell your boss that *Valek* doesn't appreciate having his new food taster chased through the castle. And that I would like her to be left alone."

The guards glanced at each other again. I was beginning to suspect they had only one brain to share between them. Regarding Valek with a more focused expression, they shifted their posture into a fighting stance.

"We have been ordered to bring the *girl* to the General. Not messages," Wren said, pulling his sword from his belt.

With the sound of ringing metal, the second guard flourished his weapon as well. Wren asked Valek to move aside once more. Faced with two swords, what could Valek do? Run for my life is what I would do, so I shifted my weight to the balls of my feet, preparing to flee.

Valek's right hand blurred into motion with two quick snaps of his wrist. It looked as if he had saluted both guards. Before the men could react, he was between them, too close for swords. He crouched low, put his hands on the floor and spun. Using his legs, Valek windmilled both guards to the ground. I heard a clatter of metal, a whoosh of air from Wren and a curse from the other before they both lay motionless.

Baffled, I watched Valek gracefully move away from his fallen opponents. He counted under his breath. When he reached ten, he bent over each man and removed a tiny dart from each of their necks.

"It's a dirty way to fight, but I'm late for lunch."

6

S T E P P I N G   O V E R   T H E   P R O N E   forms of the
sleeping soldiers, Valek took my injured arm and inspected it.
"Not as bad as it looks. You'll live. We'll see the Commander
first, then the medic."

Valek hurried me through the castle. My arm began to
throb. I lagged behind. The thought of facing the Commander's stony gaze dragged at my feet. Finding the medic, then
sinking into a hot bath was without a doubt more appealing.

We entered a spacious round chamber that served as the
Commander's war room. Slender, stained-glass windows
stretched from the floor to the ceiling and encircled three-
quarters of the chamber. The kaleidoscope of colors made me
feel as if I were inside a spinning top. Dizzy, I would have
stumbled except I caught a glimpse of something that rooted
me to the floor.

A long wooden table filled the center of the room. Sitting

at the head of the table with two guards standing behind him
was the Commander. His thin eyebrows were pinched together
in annoyance. A tray of untouched food sat by his side. Also
seated around the table were three of the Commander's
Generals. Two of the Generals were busy eating their lunch,
while the third's fork hovered in midair. I focused on the hand;
white knuckles equaled white-hot rage. With reluctance I met
General Brazell's gaze.

Brazell lowered his fork, his face taut. His eyes held lightning. I was the target, and like a rabbit caught in the open, I
was too frightened to move.

"Valek, you're…" Commander Ambrose began.

"Late," Valek finished for him. "I know. There was a slight
altercation," he said. He pulled me closer.

Intrigued, the other two Generals stopped eating. I flushed,
stifling a strong desire to bolt from the room. Having no
contact with any high-ranking officers, I recognized the
Generals only by the colors on their uniforms. My trip to the
Commander's dungeon was the first time I had been past the
borders of MD–5. Even during the first ten years I had lived
in Brazell's orphanage, I had only caught brief glimpses of him
and his family.

Unfortunately, after I had turned sixteen, the sight of Brazell
and his son Reyad became my daily nightmare. I had been flattered by the attention of my benefactor; his gray hair and short
beard framed a square-shaped, pleasant face that shouted re-
spectability. Stout and sturdy, he was the ultimate father figure
to me. Brazell told me I was the smartest of his "adopted"

children and that he needed my help with some experiments. I readily agreed to participate.

The memory of how grateful and naive I had been sickened me. It was three years ago. I had been a puppy. A puppy still wagging her tail as the bag's opening was tied shut.

Two years I had suffered. My mind recoiled from the memories. I stared at Brazell in the war room. His lips were pressed tight as his jaw quivered. He fought to contain his hatred. Faint with fatigue, I saw Reyad's ghost appear behind his father. Reyad's slashed throat hung open, and blood dripped down, staining his nightshirt. A distant recollection of a tale about murder victims haunting their killers until their business was settled filtered through my mind.

I rubbed my eyes. Did anyone else see the ghost? If so, they hid it well. My gaze slid to Valek. Was he haunted by ghosts? If that old story was to be believed, he would be swamped by them.

Worry that I might not be completely rid of Reyad pulsed through me, but not a trace of remorse. The only thing I was sorry for was not having the courage to kill Brazell when I had the chance. Sorry that I was unable to save my "sisters and brothers" at Brazell's orphanage from turning sixteen. Sorry that I was unable to warn May and Carra, and help them run away.

The Commander's voice brought my attention back to the war room.

"Altercation, Valek?" He sighed like an indulgent parent. "How many dead?"

"None. I couldn't justify the disposal of soldiers merely following General Brazell's orders to hunt down and kill our new food taster. Besides, they weren't very smart. Seems she was on the verge of giving them the slip when she ran into me. Good thing though, or I might not have found out about the incident."

The Commander studied me for a while before turning to Brazell.

It was all Brazell needed. Leaping from his chair, he shouted, "She should be dead! I want her dead! She killed my son!"

Valek said, "But the Code of Behavior…"

"Damn the Code. I'm a General. She killed a *General's* son and here she is…" Emotion choked off Brazell's voice. His fingers twitched as if he wanted to wrap his hands around my throat that instant. Reyad's ghost floated behind his father, a smirk on his face.

"It's a dishonor to me that she lives," Brazell said. "An insult. Train another prisoner. I want her dead!"

Instinctively, I stepped behind Valek. The other Generals were nodding their heads in agreement. I was too terrified to look at the Commander.

"He has a sound argument," the Commander said without a trace of emotion tainting his voice.

"You have never deviated from what's written in the Code of Behavior," Valek argued. "Start now and you'll begin a trend. Besides, you'll be killing the brightest food taster we've ever had. She's almost trained." He gestured to the tray of cold food beside the Commander.

I glanced around Valek to see the Commander's expression. Thoughtful, he pursed his lips while he considered Valek's argument. I crossed my arms, digging my fingernails deep into my flesh.

Brazell, sensing a change of heart, took a step toward the Commander. "She's smart because *I* educated her. I can't believe you're going to listen to this upstart, conniving, sneaky thief—" Brazell stopped. He had said too much. He had insulted Valek, and even I knew that the Commander had a special fondness for Valek.

"Brazell, leave my food taster alone."

My breath hissed with relief.

Brazell attempted to argue, but the Commander silenced him. "It's an order. Go ahead and build your new factory. Consider your permit approved." He dangled a carrot in front of Brazell. Was a new factory worth more than my death?

Silence followed as everyone waited for Brazell to comment. He gave me a look full of venom. Reyad's ghost grinned, and I guessed from his cat-that-got-the-rat smile that the permit approval was very important to Brazell. More important than he let on to the Commander. The rage and indignation over my missing the noose was genuine, but he could build his factory now, and then kill me later. He knew where to find me.

Brazell left the room without saying another word. The amused ghost mouthed the words "See you next time," before following his father.

When the other Generals started to protest the permit approval, the Commander listened to their arguments in silence. Momentarily forgotten, I studied the two Generals. Their uniforms were similar to the Commander's except that they wore black jackets with gold buttons. Instead of real diamonds on their collars, each General had five embroidered diamonds stitched on their coats over their left breasts. No medals or ribbons decorated their uniforms. The Commander's troops wore only what was needed for recognition and for battle.

The diamonds on the General sitting close to the Commander were blue. He was General Hazal in charge of Military District 6, just west of Brazell's MD–5. General Tesso's diamonds were silver for MD–4, which bordered to the north of Brazell's. If a district planned a big project, like building a new factory or clearing land for farming, a permit approved by the Commander was required. Smaller projects, like installing a new oven at a bakery or building a house within the district, only needed approval from that district's General. Most Generals had a staff to handle the processing of new permit applications.

It was apparent from the Generals' complaints that Brazell's permit was in the initial processing stages. Discussions with the bordering districts had started, but the Commander's staff had not yet reviewed and authenticated the factory's plans. Usually once the staff recommended approval, the Commander signed off on the application. The Code of Behavior only stated that permission must be received prior to building, and if the Commander wanted to bypass his own process he could do so.

We had been taught the Code of Behavior at the orphanage. Anyone wishing the honor of running errands into town had to memorize and recite the Code perfectly prior to gaining the privilege. Besides reading and writing, the education I had received from Brazell had also included mathematics and the history of Ixia's takeover by the Commander. Since the takeover, education was available to everyone and not just a privilege for the men of the richer classes.

My education, though, took a turn for the worse when I began "helping" Brazell. Memories threatened to overwhelm me. My hot skin felt tight. I trembled, forcing my mind to the present. The Generals had finished their rebuttal of the Commander's decision. Valek tasted the Commander's cold food, and pushed it closer to him.

"Your concerns are noted. My order stands," the Commander said. He turned to Valek. "Your food taster had better live up to your endorsements. One slip and you'll be training her replacement prior to your reassignment. You're dismissed."

Valek took my arm and steered me from the chamber. We walked down the hallway until the door of the war room clicked shut. Then Valek stopped. The features on his face had hardened into a porcelain mask.

"Yelena…"

"Don't say anything. Don't threaten or bully or intimidate. I've had enough of that from Brazell. I'll make every effort to be the best taster because I'm getting used to the idea of living. And I don't want to give Brazell the satisfaction of seeing me dead." Tired of examining Valek's every facial expression and straining to hear every small nuance in his voice for clues to his mood, I moved away from him. He followed me. When we reached an intersection, Valek's hand grasped my elbow. I heard him utter the word *medic* as he guided me to the left. Without once looking at his face, I let him steer me to the infirmary.

As I was led to an empty examining table, I squinted at the medic's all-white uniform. The only color on the uniform was two small red diamonds stitched on the collar. My mind was so muddled with fatigue that it took me some time to figure out that the short-haired medic was a female. With a grunt, I stretched out on the table.

When the woman left to get her supplies, Valek said, "I'll post some guards outside the door, in case Brazell changes his mind." Before leaving the infirmary, I saw him speak with the medic. She nodded and glanced toward me.

The medic returned with a tray full of shiny medical instruments that included a jar of a substance that looked like jelly. She scrubbed my arms with alcohol, making the wounds bleed and sting. I bit my lip to keep from crying out.

"They're all superficial, except this one," the medic said as she pointed to the elbow I had used to break the glass. "This wound needs to be sealed."

"Sealed?" It sounded painful.

The medic picked up the pot of jelly. "Relax. It's a new method for treating deep lacerations. We use this glue to seal the skin. Once the wound heals, the glue is absorbed into the body." She scooped out a large amount with her fingers and applied it to the cut.

I winced at the pain. She pinched my skin together, holding it tight. Tears rolled down my cheeks.

"It was invented by the Commander's cook, of all people. There are no side effects and it tastes great in tea."

"Rand?" I asked, surprised.

She nodded. Still holding the skin together, she said, "You'll need to wear a bandage for a few days and keep the cut dry." She blew on the glue for a while before releasing her grip. She bandaged my arm. "Valek wants you to stay here tonight. I'll bring you dinner. You can get some rest."

I thought eating might require too much effort, but when she brought the hot food, I realized I was starving. A strange taste in my tea caused me to lose my appetite in an instant.

Someone had poisoned my tea.

7

I WAVED DOWN THE MEDIC.

"There is something in my tea," I cried. I began to feel light-headed. "Call Valek." Maybe he had an antidote.

She stared at me with her large brown eyes. Her face was long and thin. Longer hair would soften her features, her short style merely made her resemble a ferret.

"It's sleeping pills. Valek's orders," she said.

I let out a breath, feeling better. The medic gave me an amused look before she left. My appetite ruined, I shoved the food aside. I didn't need sleeping pills to help me give in to the exhaustion that lapped up my remaining strength.

When I woke the next morning, there was a blurry white blob standing at the end of my bed. It moved. I blinked and squinted until the image sharpened into the short-haired medic.

"Did you have a good night?"

"Yes," I said. The first night in a long time free of nightmares, although my head felt as if wool had been shoved into it, and a rank taste in my mouth didn't promise for a good morning.

The medic checked my bandages, made a noncommittal sound and told me breakfast would be a while.

As I waited, I scanned the infirmary. The rectangular room held twelve beds, six on each side, and spaced so that they formed a mirror image. The sheets on the empty beds were pulled tight as bowstrings. Orderly and precise, the room annoyed me. I felt like rumpled bedding, no longer in control of my soul, my body, or my world. Being surrounded by neatness offended me, and I had a sudden desire to jump on the empty beds, knocking them out of line.

I was farthest from the door. Two empty beds lay between the three other patients and me on my side of the room. They were sleeping. I had no one to talk to. The stone walls were bare. Hell, my prison cell had more interesting decorations. At least it smelled better in here. I took a deep breath. The clean, sharp smell of alcohol mixed with disinfectant filled my nose, so different from the dungeon's fetid air. Much better. Or was it? There was another scent intermixed with the medical aroma. Another whiff and I realized that the sour odor of old fear emanated from me.

I shouldn't have survived yesterday. Brazell's guards had me cornered. There was no escape. Yet I had been saved by a strange buzzing noise that had erupted from my throat like an unruly, uncontrollable offspring. A primal survival instinct that had echoed in my nightmares.

I avoided thoughts about that buzz because it was an old acquaintance of mine, but the memories kept invading my mind.

Examining the past three years, I forced myself to concentrate on when and where the buzzing had erupted, and to ignore the emotions.

The first couple of months of Brazell's experiments had merely tested my reflexes. How fast I could dodge a ball or duck a swinging stick, harmless enough until the ball had turned into a knife and the stick into a sword.

My heart began to pound. With sweaty palms I fingered a scar on my neck. No emotion, I told myself sternly, flicking my hands as if I could push away the fear. Pretend you're the medic, I thought, asking questions to gain information. I imagined myself dressed in white, calmly sitting next to a fevered patient while she babbled.

What came next? I asked the patient. Strength and endurance tests, she answered. Simple tasks of lifting weights had turned into holding heavy stones above her head for minutes, then hours. If she dropped the stone before the time was up, she was whipped. She was ordered to clutch chains dangling from the ceiling, holding her weight inches above the floor, until Brazell or Reyad gave permission to let go.

When was the first time you heard the buzzing? I prompted the patient. She had released the chains too early too many times and Reyad became furious. So he forced her outside a window six floors above the ground, and let her hold on to the ledge with her hands.

"Let's try it again," Reyad said. "Now that we've raised the stakes, maybe you'll last for the whole hour."

The patient stopped speaking. Go on, tell me what

happened, I prodded. Her arms had been weak from spending most of the day hanging from the chains. Her fingers were slick with sweat; her muscles trembled with fatigue. She panicked. When her hands slipped off the ledge, she howled like a newborn. The howl mutated and transformed into a substance. It expanded out, enveloped and caressed her skin on all sides. She felt as if she was nestled in a warm pool of water.

Next thing she remembered she was sitting on the ground. She glanced up at the window. Reyad watched her with his face flushed. His perfect blond hair an unusual mess. Delighted, he blew her a kiss.

The only way she could have survived the fall was by magic. No. Absolutely not, she insisted. It had to have been some strange wind currents or landing the right way. Not magic.

Magic, a forbidden word in Ixia since Commander Ambrose came to power. Magicians had been treated like disease-riddled mosquitoes. They were hunted, trapped and exterminated. Any hint or suggestion that someone had magic was a death sentence. The only chance to live was to escape to Sitia.

The patient was growing agitated, and the other occupants of the room were staring at her... Me. Small doses, I told myself. I could handle the memories in modest quantities. After all, I hadn't been hurt by the fall, and Reyad was sweet to me for a while. But his kindness only lasted until I started failing his tests again.

To distract myself from the memories, I counted the cracks in the ceiling. I was up to fifty-six when Valek arrived.

He carried a tray of food in one hand and a file folder in

the other. I eyed the steaming omelet with suspicion. "What's in it?" I demanded. "More sleeping pills? Or another new poison?" Every muscle in my body had stiffened. I tried unsuccessfully to sit up. "How about giving me something to make me feel good for a change?"

"How about something to keep you alive?" Valek asked. He pulled me to a sitting position and offered a pipette filled with my antidote. Then he placed the tray of food on my lap.

"No need for sleeping pills. The medic told me you picked up on that taste last night." Valek's voice held a note of approval. "Taste your breakfast and tell me if you would allow the Commander to eat it."

Valek hadn't been exaggerating when he said I'd have no days off. Sighing, I smelled the omelet. No unusual odors. I cut the omelet into quarters, examining each for any foreign material. Taking a small piece from each section, I put them into my mouth one at a time and chewed slowly. Swallowing, I waited to discern any aftertaste. I sniffed the tea and stirred it with a spoon before sipping. Rolling the liquid over my tongue, I detected a sweet taste before I swallowed.

"Unless the Commander doesn't like honey in his tea, I wouldn't reject this breakfast."

"Then eat it."

I hesitated. Was Valek trying to trick me? Unless he had used a poison I hadn't learned, the breakfast was clean. I ate every morsel, and then drained the tea while Valek watched.

"Not bad," he said. "No poisons…today."

One of the medics brought another tray to Valek. This tray

held four white cups of an olive-colored liquid that smelled like mint. Replacing my breakfast tray with the new one, Valek said, "I want to go over some tasting techniques. Each of these cups contains mint tea. Taste one."

Clasping the closest mug, I took a sip. An overwhelming flavor of mint pervaded my mouth. I choked.

Valek grinned. "Taste anything else?"

I attempted another mouthful. The mint dominated. "No."

"All right. Now pinch your nose tight and try again."

After some fumbling with my bandaged arm, I managed to gulp the tea while holding my nose. My ears popped. I marveled at the taste. "Sweet. No mint." My voice sounded silly so I released my grip. Immediately, the mint eclipsed the sweetness.

"Correct. Now try the others."

The next cup of mint tea hid a sour taste, the third had a bitter flavor, and the fourth was salty.

"This technique works for any drink or food. Blocking your sense of smell eliminates all flavors except sweet, sour, bitter and salt. Some poisons are recognizable by one of those four flavors." Valek paged through his folder. "Here is a complete list of human poisons and their distinct tastes for you to memorize. There are fifty-two known poisons."

I looked through the inventory of poisons. Some of them I had already smelled. My Love was at the top. The list would have saved me from the dizziness, nausea, headaches and occasional delusional effects of the poison. I brandished the paper in the air. "Why didn't you just give me this list instead of making me sample My Love?"

Valek stopped paging through his folder. "What would you learn from a list? Kattsgut tastes sweet. What does that taste like? Honey sweet? Apple sweet? There are different levels of sweetness and the only way to learn them is to taste them yourself. The *only* reason I'm giving you this list is because the Commander wants you working as soon as possible." Valek snapped his folder shut. "Just because you aren't going to taste those poisons now doesn't mean you won't in the future. Memorize that list. Once the medic releases you from the infirmary, I will test your knowledge. If you pass, then you can start work."

"And if I fail?"

"Then I'll be training a new taster."

His voice was flat, monotone, but the force behind it caused my heart to lock.

Valek continued. "Brazell will be in the castle for another two weeks. He has more business to attend to. I can't have you guarded all day, so Margg is preparing a room for you in my suite. I'll come back later to see when you'll be discharged."

I watched Valek walk to the door. He glided across the room, balanced and athletic. I shook my head. Thinking about Valek was the absolute worst thing I could be doing. Instead, I focused on the list of poisons clutched in my hand. I smoothed the paper out and hoped my sweat hadn't smeared the ink. Relieved that the writing was legible, I began to study.

I barely noticed when the medic came to check on my arm. She must have taken the tray of teacups, because it disappeared from my lap. I had blocked out all the noise and commotion of the infirmary so that I jumped when a plate containing a round pastry was thrust under my nose.

The arm that held the plate led to Rand. His grin was gleeful.

"Look what I smuggled past Medic Mommy! Go ahead. Eat it before she comes back."

The warm dessert smelled like cinnamon. Melted white icing dripped down the sides, causing the cake to stick to my fingers when I picked it up. I examined the pastry closely, inhaling the aroma in search of a foreign smell. One small bite revealed multiple layers of dough and cinnamon.

"My God, Yelena, you don't think I'd poison it?" Rand's face was pinched tight, as if he was in pain.

Exactly what I'd been thinking, but admitting it to Rand would offend him. His motives for being here were unclear. Seeming nice and friendly, he could be holding a grudge over his friend Oscove, the previous food taster. But then again, he was a potential ally. Who better to have on my side? Rand, the cook, whose food I'd be eating on a daily basis, or Valek, the assassin, who had a nasty tendency of poisoning my meals?

"Occupational hazard," I tried.

He grunted, still put out. I took a big bite of the pastry.

"Wonderful," I said, appealing to his ego to give me another chance.

Rand's face softened. "Good, isn't it? My latest recipe. I take a long strip of pastry dough, cover it with cinnamon, roll it up into a ball, bake it, and then spread the icing on while it's hot. I'm having some trouble with the name though. Cinnamon cake? Ball? Swirl?" Rand stopped his rambling to find a chair.

After quite a bit of twisting to compensate for his unbendable left leg, he finally settled into a comfortable position.

While I finished the pastry, Rand continued. "Don't tell Medic Mommy I gave you that. She doesn't like her patients eating anything but a thin gruel. She says the gruel promotes healing. Well, of course it has an effect!" He threw his arms up, exposing several burn scars around his wrists. "It tastes so terrible that anyone would get better just to get a decent meal!"

The wild gesture caused the other patients to glance our way. Rand leaned in closer to me and asked in a quiet voice, "So, Yelena, how are you feeling?" He looked at me as though he was appraising a selection of meat, determining which one would make the best roast.

I was wary. Why would he care? "Gambling again?" I asked.

He leaned back. "We're always gambling. Gambling and gossiping is all we servants do. What else is there? You should've seen the commotion and betting that went on when you were spotted being chased by Brazell's goons."

Appalled, I said, "Nobody came to help me. The hallways were deserted."

"That would be involvement in a situation that doesn't affect us directly. Servants don't ever do that. We're like cock-roaches scurrying around in the dark." Rand's slender fingers waggled. "Shine a light…*poof!*" He flicked his long fingers for emphasis. "We disappear."

I felt like the unlucky cockroach that got caught by the light. Always scrambling to stay one step ahead while the shadow of a boot crept closer.

"Anyway, the odds were against you. Most lost big, while only a few—" Rand paused dramatically "—won big."

"Since you're here, I suppose you won big."

He smiled. "Yelena, I'm always going to bet on you. You're like one of the Commander's terriers. A tiny, yappy dog you wouldn't look at twice, but once it grabs your pant leg, it won't let go."

"Poison the dog's meat and it won't bother you anymore."

My sour tone deflated Rand's grin. "Trouble?"

Surprised that the castle's gossip network hadn't already started laying odds about Valek's test, I hesitated. Rand liked to talk, and he could get me in trouble. "No. It's just being the food taster and all…" I hoped that would satisfy him.

Rand nodded. He spent the rest of the afternoon alternating between reminiscing about Oscove and digressing about potential new recipes. When Valek appeared, Rand stopped talking, his face paled and he mumbled something about having to check on dinner. Lurching from his chair, he almost toppled in his haste to flee the room. Valek watched as Rand staggered out of the infirmary.

"What was he doing here?"

Valek's expression remained neutral, but the stillness of his body made me wonder if he was angry. Carefully choosing my words, I explained to him that Rand had come to visit.

"When did you meet him?"

A casual question, but again there was an undercurrent to his words. "After I recovered from My Love, I went in search of food and met Rand in the kitchen."

"Watch what you say around him. He's not to be trusted. I would have reassigned him, but the Commander insisted he stay. He *is* a genius in the kitchen. Some kind of protégé. He started cooking for the King at a very young age."

Valek stared at me with his cold blue eyes, warning me away from Rand. Maybe that's why Valek hadn't liked Oscove. Being allied with someone who had been loyal to the King could cast more suspicion on me. But letting Valek scare me off rankled. I stared back at him with, I hoped, an indifferent look.

Valek looked away. I was jubilant. In my mind, I had finally won a round.

"You leave the infirmary tomorrow morning." Valek was curt. "Get yourself cleaned up and report to my office to take the test. I won't think you're ready even if you pass, but the Commander ordered me to have you available by lunch." He shook his head in annoyance. "It's a shortcut. I hate shortcuts."

"Why? You won't have to risk yourself anymore." I regretted the words as soon as they had left my mouth.

Valek's gaze was lethal. "In my experience, shortcuts usually lead to death."

"Is that what happened to my predecessor?" I asked, unable to stifle my curiosity. Would Valek confirm or deny Rand's theories?

"Oscove?" Valek paused. "He didn't have the stomach for it."

8

WHEN I AWOKE THE NEXT morning, Valek's list of poisons was still clutched in my hand. I reviewed the poison inventory until the medic discharged me.

Bruised muscles protested every movement as I headed for the door. I should have been happy to leave the infirmary, but my nerves preoccupied me. My stomach felt as if it contained a live mouse, trying to chew its way out.

The guards stationed outside the infirmary door startled me. But they weren't wearing Brazell's colors, and I belatedly remembered that Valek had assigned them as protection until I reported to his office.

I glanced around to get my bearings, but had no idea which direction led to my room. I had been living in the castle for eighteen days, but I was still uncertain of its inner layout. The basic shape of the castle itself eluded me, having never seen it from the outside.

The prison carriage that had brought me to the castle had been a square box with airholes. I had refused to peer out like some caged animal. When I reached the castle, I squeezed my eyes shut in an attempt to block out the anguish of being chained, groped and dragged to the dungeon. I guess I could have focused on potential ways to escape, but I had accepted my punishment when I had killed Reyad.

As much as I hated to ask the guards for directions to my room, I had no choice. Wordlessly they guided me through the castle. One walked in front, the other followed. Only after the lead man inspected my room was I allowed inside.

My uniforms hung undisturbed in the armoire. But instead of being hidden inside a drawer, my journal lay open on the top of the desk. Someone had read my impressions of poisons and other information. The queasy feeling in my gut was replaced by a cold, hard sensation. The mouse had died, reflecting my sour mood perfectly.

I suspected Valek. He was bold enough to have gone through my personal papers. He had probably even reasoned that it was his duty to make sure I wasn't plotting something. After all, I was just the food taster, and not entitled to any privacy.

Grabbing the journal and uniforms, I left my room and headed for the baths. The guards waited outside while I soaked in the water. I took my sweet time. Valek and his test could wait; I wasn't going to carry out his orders like some idiotic drone.

Chased by Brazell's guards, finding poison in almost all of my meals, and being wagered on like some damn racehorse didn't cause me to be as angry as I was about Valek reading my journal.

Arriving at Valek's office, I cut off any smart remark he could make by demanding, "Where's your test?"

Amusement touched Valek's face. He rose from behind his desk. Sweeping his arm with a dramatic flourish, he indicated two rows of food and drinks on the conference table. "Only one item isn't poisoned. Find it. Then eat or drink your selection."

I tasted each item. I sniffed. I gargled. I held my nose. I took small bites. I spat. Some of the food had grown cold. Most of the meals were bland, making the poison easy to spot, while the fruit drinks masked the poison.

Finishing the last item, I turned to Valek. "You bastard. They're all poisoned." What a nasty trick; I should have suspected he would pull a stunt like that.

"Are you sure?"

"Of course. I wouldn't touch anything on that table."

Valek's gaze was stony as he walked toward me. "I'm sorry, Yelena. You've failed."

My heart plunged into my stomach. The dead mouse resuscitated and began to gnaw holes in my gut. I searched the table. What had I missed?

Nothing. I was right. I challenged Valek to prove me wrong.

Without hesitation he raised a cup. "This one is clean."

"Drink it." I remembered that cup. It was laced with a bitter poison.

Valek's hand wavered a bit. He sipped. I bit my lip. Maybe I was wrong. Maybe it was the cup next to it. Valek held my gaze as he rolled the liquid around his tongue. He spat.

I wanted to jump, to cheer, to dance little circles around him. Instead I said, "Blackberry poison."

"Yes," Valek said. He alternated between examining the cup in his hand and absentmindedly staring at the rows of cold food.

"I passed?"

He nodded, still distracted. Then he walked to his desk, and he gently placed the cup down. Shaking his head, he picked some papers up only to put them back unread.

"I should have known you would try to trick me."

My heated tone drew his eyes. I wished then that I'd remained silent.

"You're all fired up. And it isn't because of the test. Explain yourself."

"Explain? Why do *I* have to explain? Maybe *you* should explain why you read my journal." There, I'd said it.

"Journal?" Valek looked at me in amazement. "I didn't read anything of yours. But if I had, it would have been within my rights."

"Why?" I demanded.

An incredulous look settled on Valek's face. His mouth opened and closed several times before he was able to voice his thoughts. "Yelena, you confessed to murder. You were caught straddling Reyad's body with a bloody knife in your hand. I searched your file for a motive. There was none. Only a report that you refused to answer all questions."

Valek stepped closer. He lowered his voice. "Since I don't know what motivates you to kill, I can't predict if you'll do it again or what might set you off. I'm bound by the Code of Behavior, so I had to offer you the choice of becoming the new taster." He drew a deep breath and continued. "You'll be very close to the Commander on a daily basis. Until I can trust you, I'll be watching you."

My anger leaked away. Why should I expect Valek to trust me when I didn't trust him?

My composure returned. "How do I win your trust?"

"Tell me why you killed Reyad."

"You're not ready to believe me."

Valek averted his gaze to the conference table. I covered my mouth with my hand. Why had I used the word *ready*? Ready implied that he would believe me at some point. Pure wishful thinking on my part.

"You're right," he said.

We seemed to be at an impasse.

"I passed your test. I want my antidote."

Roused into action, Valek drew a dose, handing it to me.

"Now what?" I asked.

"Lunch! We're late." He hustled me out the door. I gulped the white liquid as we moved.

As we neared the throne room, the noise of many voices speaking at once echoed through the halls. Two of the Commander's advisers were arguing. Officers and soldiers clumped behind the two advisers. The Commander leaned against a nearby desk, listening intently.

The group debated the best way to locate and recapture a fugitive. The right side insisted upon using an oversupply of soldiers and tracking dogs, while the left claimed that a few clever soldiers would work. Brute force versus intelligence.

The exchange, while loud, lacked anger. The guards stationed around the room stood relaxed. Surmising that this type of debate was common, I wondered if the fugitive was a real person or just part of a hypothetical exercise.

Valek moved next to the Commander. I stood behind them. The debate made me squirm because I couldn't help imagining myself as the poor soul being hunted.

I pictured myself running through the woods, out of breath, and straining to hear the sounds of pursuit. Unable to blend into a town because a new face would alert the soldiers on patrol. Bored soldiers whose only job was to watch, who were familiar with the town's inhabitants.

Every citizen of the Territory of Ixia had a specific job. After the takeover, everyone had been appointed an occupation. A citizen was allowed to move to a different town or Military District, but proper forms were required. A completed transfer request needed approval from the supervisor, and proof that a position was being held at the new address. Without the proper documents, a civilian found in the wrong neighborhood was arrested. Visiting other districts was acceptable, but again only as long as the proper papers were obtained and shown to the soldiers on arrival.

While working in isolation with Brazell and Reyad, I had obsessively thought about escape. Thinking of freedom had been better than dwelling on my life as a laboratory rat. With no family or friends outside the manor to hide me, though, the southern lands were my best option, assuming I could penetrate the well guarded border.

I had created elaborate fantasies of stealing away to Sitia, finding an adoptive family and falling in love. Corny, sentimental rubbish, but it was my only elixir. Every day when the experiments began, my mind would focus on Sitia, finding bright colors, loving gestures and warmth. Holding those images in my mind, I endured Reyad's tests.

But even if I had been given the opportunity to escape, I don't know if I would have seized it. Although I remembered nothing of my birth family, I did have a family living within the manor house. The other lost children who had been taken in. My sisters. My brothers. My children. I learned with them, I played with them and I took care of them. How could I abandon them? To think of May or Carra taking my place was too much to bear.

I bit on my finger until I tasted blood, and dragged my thoughts back to the present. I had escaped from Brazell. He would leave the castle in two weeks and return home, probably to the next round of experiments with a different laboratory rat. My heart went out to her, whoever she was. Brazell was brutal. She was in for a rough time. But I had saved her from Reyad.

Pulling my hand away from my mouth, I inspected the bite mark. Not too deep, it wouldn't scar. I traced the network of semicircular scars that covered my fingers and knuckles. When I looked up, I caught Valek staring at my hands. I laced them behind my back.

The Commander raised his hand. Quiet descended in an instant. "Excellent points from both sides. We will put your theories to the test. Two teams." Pointing to the two main debaters, the Commander said, "You'll be the Captains. Assemble your team and organize a plan of attack. Recruit as needed. Valek will supply a fugitive from one of his men. You have a fortnight to prepare."

The noise level rose as the Commander headed toward his office with Valek and I close behind.

Valek shut the office door, muffling the commotion. "Is Marrok's escape to Sitia still bothering you?" he asked.

The Commander frowned. "Yes. Sloppy work, that pursuit. Marrok must have known you were in MD–8. You really need to train a couple of protégés."

Valek looked at him in mock horror. "But then I wouldn't be indispensable."

A quick smile graced the Commander's face, before he spotted me lingering near the corner. "Well, Valek, you were right about this one. She survived your test." Then to me, he said, "Come here."

My feet obeyed despite my hysterical heart.

"As my official food taster, you're to report to me with my breakfast. I'll give you my daily itinerary and expect you to be present at each meal. I will not accept tardiness. Understand?"

"Yes, Sir."

He glanced at Valek. "She looks fragile. Are you sure she's strong enough?"

"Yes, Sir."

The Commander appeared unconvinced. His golden eyes

tracked from me to Valek as he contemplated. I hoped with desperation that he wasn't looking for an excuse to fire me.

"All right. Since I missed lunch, Valek, you will join me for an early dinner. Yelena, you start as my food taster tomorrow morning."

"Yes, Sir," Valek and I said in unison. We were dismissed.

We returned to Valek's office to gather my extra uniforms and journal. Valek escorted me to his living quarters, located in the central part of the castle. As we traveled the main hallways, I noticed that the bright areas of stone on the wall outnumbered the darker zones. A vast array of paintings must have been taken down. We also passed several large, colorless rooms that had been redesigned as either offices or barracks.

It occurred to me that the Commander's functional style and stark standards had robbed the castle of its soul. All that remained was a dead stone building reassigned to purely utilitarian purposes.

I was too young to remember what life was like before the takeover, but I had been taught in Brazell's orphanage that the monarchy had been corrupt and its citizens unhappy. The takeover had been just that; to call it a war would be inaccurate. Most of the King's soldiers had switched loyalty to the Commander. They had been disgusted with promotions based on bribery and blood ties instead of hard work and skill. Orders to kill people for minor infractions because a member of the elite was angry caused sour feelings among the men.

Women had been recruited to the Commander's cause, and they made excellent spies. Valek assassinated the key supporters of the King. When the King tried to raise an army to fight the Commander's army, he had no defenders. The Commander captured the castle without a fight, and little blood was shed. Most of the nobility had been killed, but a few had escaped to Sitia.

Valek and I arrived at a pair of massive wooden doors, guarded by two soldiers. Valek spoke with the guards, instructing them that I was to be allowed access as needed. We entered a short hallway with two doors on opposite sides. Valek unlocked the door on the right and explained to me that the other led to the Commander's apartment.

Valek's living quarters turned out to be an expansive suite of rooms. Coming in from the gloomy hallway, I was struck by the brightness of the main, L-shaped living area. Windows as thin as a tiger's stripes allowed sunlight to pour in.

Piles of books occupied every corner and tabletop. Hand-size gray rocks, streaked with white, and multicolored crystals were scattered throughout.

Small black statues of animals and flowers glinted with silver. The statues dotted the room. Delicate and intricately detailed, they were similar to the panthers on Valek's office desk, and were the room's only decoration.

A considerable collection of weapons hung on the walls. Some of the weapons were old, dust-covered antiques that hadn't been used in years, while others shined. One long, thin knife still had fresh blood on the blade. The crimson liquid gleamed in the sunlight, causing a chill to snake through my body. I wondered who had been on the wrong end of that blade.

To the left of the entrance was a stairway, and three doors lined the right wall of the living area.

Valek pointed to the first door on the right. "That room is yours until Brazell leaves the castle. I suggest you get some rest." He picked up three books from an end table. "I'll be back later. Don't go out. I'll bring you dinner." Valek left, but then came back before the door shut. "Lock the door behind me. You should be safe here."

Safe, I thought, turning the bolt, was the last thing I could ever feel here. Anyone who knew how to pick a lock could sneak in, grab a weapon and have at me. I examined the swords on the wall, and sighed with some relief. The weapons were anchored securely. I tugged hard on a mace, just to be sure.

The clutter surrounding my door was thicker than around the other two, and I discovered why when I entered. Clean, box-shaped areas were outlined by the thick dust that still coated the floor, bed, bureau and desk. The room had been used for storage. Instead of cleaning it, Margg must have just moved the boxes out and considered her job done.

Margg's minimal work was a not so subtle hint of her vast dislike for me. Perhaps it would be best to avoid her for a while.

Inside the room, the bedding was filthy. A musty smell permeated. I sneezed. There was a small window, and after wrestling with the shutters, I managed to open it.

The furniture was made of expensive ebony. Intricate carvings of leaves and vines curled down chair legs and across drawers. When I wiped the dust off the headboard, I uncovered a delicate garden scene with butterflies and flowers.

After I stripped the bed of its dirty sheets and stretched out on the mattress, my impression of Margg as a harmless grump-with-a-grudge evaporated. At that moment I saw that a message had been written in the dust on the desk.

It read, "Murderer. The noose waits.

9

I VAULTED FROM THE BED. The message disappeared from view, but I didn't feel any better. Little darts of fear pulsed from my heart as my mind leaped from one horrible scenario to the next.

Was Margg warning or threatening me? Was she planning to earn the money she'd lost betting against me by turning me over to Brazell's goons for a fee?

But why warn me? I calmed myself. Once again I had overreacted. From what I'd seen and heard about Margg, her message was probably for the satisfaction of seeing me squirm. A peevish gesture because she was angry at having to do extra work for me. I decided it would be best not to give her any indication that I'd seen or had been affected by her childish note. Thinking back on it, I would bet that she had also read my journal, leaving it wide open on the desk just to annoy me.

Valek had suggested I rest, but I was on edge. I went into

Valek's living room. Margg's note had reminded me to stick to my instincts and not trust a soul. Then my worries would be minimized to tasting for poisons and avoiding Brazell.

If only it was that simple or I was that strong. Naiveté and blind trust may have been driven out of me by Brazell and Reyad, but deep down in the small corners of my heart I still clung to the hope that I might find a true friend.

Even a rat needs other rats. I could empathize with the rats. I, too, scurried around, looked over my shoulder and sniffed for poisoned traps.

Right now, I scrambled just to stay alive until the next day, but someday I would be searching for a way out. Knowledge was power, so I planned to sit tight, to listen and learn all I could. I started with Valek's living area. Lifting a rock off one of the tables, I began to pick my way through the clutter in his suite, surface snooping only because I suspected Valek would booby-trap his drawers.

I found a couple of texts on poisons that interested me, but their contents dealt mostly with assassination and intrigue. Some of the books had worn leather bindings and were written in an archaic language that I couldn't decipher. Valek was either a collector, or he had stolen the books from the dead King's library.

I was at the bottom of the stairs when I spotted a diagram of the castle's layout. It had been wedged into the corner of a picture frame hanging on the right wall of the staircase. Finally, something I could use. As I examined the map, I felt as if a translucent mask had been lifted off my face, allowing me to see the castle clearly.

Postponing my explorations of the rooms upstairs, I retrieved my journal. The map was displayed in full sight. Valek wouldn't be upset that I had seen it. He'd probably be happy that I didn't need to ask for directions every time I had to go somewhere new. I cleared a space on the couch, wormed into a comfortable position and began to copy the map.

I jerked awake. My journal slammed to the floor. Blinking in the candlelight, my eyes searched the room. I had been dreaming of rats. They had poured down from the walls, welled up from the floor and swarmed after me. A sea of biting rodents that seized clothes, skin and hair in their sharp little teeth.

A shudder shook my body. I lifted my feet off the floor as I scanned the room. No rats, unless I included Valek. He was halfway around the room, lighting the lanterns.

As I watched him finish, I thought about Valek being a fellow rat. No. Definitely not. A cat. And not just any ordinary, household cat, but a snow cat. The most efficient predator in the Territory of Ixia. Pure white, the snow cat was the size of two massive dogs fused together. Quick, agile and lethal, the snow cat killed before its prey even suspected danger. They stayed mostly in the north where the snow never melted, but had ventured south when food grew scarce.

No one in the history of Ixia had killed a snow cat. The predator either smelled, heard or saw the hunter before he could get close enough to strike with a handheld weapon. They bolted like lightning upon hearing the twang of a bowstring. The best the northern people could do was feed the cats, hoping to keep them on the snowpack and away from populated areas.

After lighting the last lantern, Valek turned toward me. "Something wrong with your room?" He picked up a tray and handed it to me.

"No. Couldn't sleep."

Valek snorted with amusement. "I see." He gestured toward the tray. "Sorry your dinner is cold. I was detained."

Automatically testing for poisons, I took a couple of small spoonfuls. I glanced at Valek to see if he was offended by the gesture. He was not. His face still held an amused expression. Between bites, I asked Valek if anyone else had a key to his suite.

"Just the Commander and Margg. Will that help you sleep better?"

Ignoring his question, I asked, "Is Margg your personal housekeeper?"

"Mine and the Commander's. We wanted someone we could trust. Someone instantly recognizable. She was with us before the takeover, so her loyalty is beyond doubt." Valek sat at his writing desk, but turned his chair to face me. "Remember when you were in the war room?"

Confused by the change in subject, I nodded.

"There were three Generals in the room. Brazell, you knew, but can you identify the other two?"

"Tesso and Hazal," I answered, proud that I had remembered.

"Can you describe them? Hair color? Eyes?"

I hesitated as I thought back. They had worn Generals' uniforms, and they had been eating lunch. I shook my head. "I think General Tesso had a beard."

"You identified them by their uniforms and didn't look at their faces. Correct?"

"Yes."

"That's what I thought. That's the problem with the uniform requirement. It makes a person lazy. A guard will see a housekeeping uniform and just assume that person belongs in the castle. It's too easy for someone to sneak about, which is why I keep the Commander surrounded at all times by loyal people. And why Margg is the only house-keeper permitted to clean the Commander's and my suites and offices."

Valek's tone made me feel as if I had been transported to a classroom. "Why not dismiss all the servants in the castle and use your own people?"

"Soldiers make up the majority of our army. Civilians who joined prior to the takeover were made advisers or given other prominent positions. Some of the King's servants were already on our payroll, and the others we paid double what they earned working for the King. Well-paid servants are happy servants."

"Does the entire castle's staff get paid?"

"Yes."

"Including the food taster?"

"No."

"Why not?" I hadn't even thought about receiving wages until Valek mentioned it.

"The food taster is paid in advance. How much is your life worth?"

10

NOT EXPECTING AN ANSWER, Valek swiveled back to his desk.

Ah, well, he had a point. I finished the cold food. When I set the tray aside to go to my room, Valek turned back to me.

"What would you buy with the money?"

A list rushed from my mouth, surprising even me. "A hair brush, nightclothes, and I'd spend some at the festival."

I wanted nightclothes because I was tired of sleeping in my uniform. I didn't dare sleep in my undergarments for fear I'd have to run for my life in the middle of the night. And the annual fire festival was approaching. It was sort of an anniversary for me. It had been during the previous fire festival that I had killed Reyad.

Although the Commander outlawed all forms of public religion, he encouraged the festivals as a form of boosting morale. Only two annual festivals were permitted.

I had been in the dungeon during the last ice festival, missing the indoor event where artists and craftsmen displayed their work. The ice festival was always held during the cold season when there was nothing to do but huddle by the fire and make crafts. It was a local event with each town hosting its own festival.

The fire festival was a massive carnival that traveled from town to town during the hot season. The festival began in the far north, where the warm weather lasted a few short weeks, and then wound its way south.

Traditionally, additional performances and contests were scheduled for the weeklong celebration at the castle in the middle of the hot season, and I was hoping I might be permitted to attend. Valek had indicated to me that he would be teaching me additional tasting techniques in the afternoons, but the rest of the time between meals had, so far, been mine.

I had always loved going to the fire festival. Brazell had given the children in his orphanage a small allowance so we could go each year. It had been the most anticipated event at Brazell's manor house. We would practice all year to qualify for the various contests, and save every penny possible for the entry fee.

Valek's practical voice interrupted my thoughts. "You can get some nightclothes from the seamstress, Dilana. She should have included them with your uniforms. As to the rest, you'll have to make do with what you can find."

Valek's words brought home the realities of my life; meaning fire festivals were not included. I might get a chance to see the festival, but I wouldn't be able to sample the spicy chicken steaks or taste the wine.

Sighing, I picked up my journal and went into my room. A dry, warm breeze caressed my face. I cleaned the rest of the dust, but I only wiped away half of Margg's message. She had been right in a way. The noose did wait for me. A normal life was not in my future. Her message would serve as a reminder to me to not get too comfortable.

I was either going to screw up and be replaced as the food taster, or I was going to foil an assassination attempt with my own death. I might not technically die from a broken neck, but the haunting image of an empty noose would always plague me.

The next morning I hovered outside Dilana's workroom. She sat in a small patch of sunlight, humming and sewing. Her golden curls gleamed. Unwilling to disturb her, I turned to go.

"Yelena?" she called.

I stepped back into view.

"My goodness, girl, just come in. You're always welcome." Dilana put her sewing down, and patted the chair next to her. When I joined her in the sunlight, she exclaimed, "You're as thin as my finest thread. Sit. Sit. Let me get you something to eat."

My protests didn't stop her from bringing me a large slice of buttered bread.

"My Rand sends me a steaming loaf of honey bread every morning." Her light brown eyes glowed with affection.

I knew she would stand over me until I took a bite. Not wanting to hurt her feelings, I suppressed my desire to taste the bread for poisons. Only when my mouth was full was she satisfied.

"How can I help you?" she asked.

Between bites, I asked about nightclothes.

"My goodness! How could I have forgotten? You poor dear." She bustled around the room, assembling quite a collection.

"Dilana," I said to stop her. "I only need a few things."

"Why didn't you come sooner? Margg should have said something to me." Dilana was genuinely upset.

"Margg," I began, then quit. I wasn't sure how Dilana felt about her.

"Margg's a mean old grump, a spiteful hag and an overgrown bully," Dilana declared.

I blinked at her in surprise.

"She instantly dislikes anyone new, and she's basically a plague on the rest of us."

"But she was nice to you."

"She hounded me for weeks after I first arrived. Then I snuck into her wardrobe and tightened all her skirts. It took her two weeks of physical discomfort to figure out what was happening." Dilana swooped down next to me, smiling. "Margg can't sew a stitch, so she had to tuck in her pride and ask for my help. Since then she's treated me with respect."

Dilana grabbed my hand in hers. "Unfortunately, you're her new target. But don't let her get to you. If Margg's nasty, be nasty right back. When she sees you're not easy prey, she'll lose interest."

I had trouble believing that this lovely woman was capable of such underhandedness, but her smile held a glimmer of mischief.

She draped a pile of nightclothes over my arms, and added an array of brightly colored ribbons.

"For the festival, my dear," she said, answering my quizzical look. "To augment your beautiful dark hair."

"Have you found a fugitive for the exercise?" the Commander asked Valek as soon as Valek arrived in his office for lunch.

I was tasting the Commander's food when Valek once again destroyed my tentative sense of well-being. Granted, I had been working as the official food taster for the last ten days, but my stomach had finally stopped its painful contractions whenever I was near the Commander.

"Yes. I know the perfect person for the job." Valek settled into the chair facing the Commander.

"Who?"

"Yelena."

"What!" Having given up all pretense of minding my own business, my exclamation echoed the Commander's.

"Explain," the Commander ordered.

Valek smiled at his reaction as though he knew all along what the Commander would say. "My people are trained to avoid capture. Assigning one of them wouldn't be fair to the search party. Therefore, we need a person not skilled in the art of evasion, but who is intelligent enough to bring some challenge to the exercise."

Valek stood to continue his lecture. "The fugitive needs an incentive for a good chase, yet must return to the castle. I can't use a real prisoner. None of the servants have any imagination. I briefly considered the medic, but she's needed here in case of emergencies. I was about to assign one of your soldiers when I thought of Yelena."

Valek gestured toward me. "She's smart." He counted with his fingers to emphasize his words. "She'll have an incentive to perform well, and an incentive to return."

"Incentives?" A frown creased the Commander's face.

"The food taster receives no wages. But for this extra job, and others like it in the future, she can be paid. The longer she evades capture, the higher the payment. As for the incentive to return, that should be obvious."

It was to me. The daily antidote to Butterfly's Dust kept me alive. If I didn't return to the castle by the next morning, they would be searching for a corpse.

"And if I refuse?" I asked Valek.

"I'll recruit one of the soldiers. But I'll be disappointed. I thought you would appreciate the challenge."

"Maybe I don't…"

"Enough." The Commander's voice was curt. "It's preposterous, Valek."

"That's the whole point. A soldier would make predictable moves. She's an unknown."

"*You* might outguess our fugitive, but the people I've assigned to the exercise aren't that quick. I'm hoping to find someone who can be trained as your assistant. I understand what you're waiting for, but I don't believe it'll happen anytime soon. We need someone now." The Commander sighed. It was the most emotion I'd witnessed from him. "Valek, why do you constantly undermine my orders to instruct an assistant?"

"Because so far I have disagreed with your choices. When the suitable candidate appears, then all efforts to train him will be fully endorsed."

The Commander glanced at the tray in my hands. Taking the food, he ordered me to fetch some hot tea. A thinly disguised ruse to be rid of me while they argued. I was more than happy to oblige.

On my way to the kitchen, I mulled over the possibility of playing fugitive for Valek. My first reaction had been negative; I didn't need any more problems. But as I contemplated the challenge of eluding searchers, combined with the chance to earn some money, the exercise started to look like an excellent opportunity. By the time I reached the kitchen, I hoped Valek would win. Especially since I would be outside the castle for a day, and any skills I learned from being a fugitive might prove useful in the future.

"Something wrong with lunch?" Rand asked, hurrying toward me, concern pulling the corners of his mouth tight.

"No. Just need some hot tea."

Relief softened his face. I wondered why he was so worried that lunch had been unsatisfactory. An image of a younger Rand rebelling against the Commander by ruining food as a form of sabotage entered my mind. I dismissed the thought. Rand wouldn't serve inferior food; his ego centered on his edible creations. There must be something else between him and the Commander. Uncertain that our new relationship would survive asking personal, perhaps sensitive, questions, I held my tongue.

I'd known Rand for almost two weeks now, but I still hadn't figured him out. His moods ran the gamut and changed without notice. Rand liked to talk. He dominated most conversations and asked only a few personal questions. I doubted he really heard my answers before he rambled on again.

"While you're here," Rand said, pulling a white cake from one of the cooling racks that hung on the wall like shelves, "can you try this? Let me know what you think."

He cut me a slice. Iced with whipped cream, the layers of vanilla cake were separated by a mixture of raspberries and cream.

I tried to mask that my first bite tasted for poison. "Good combination of flavors," I said.

"It's not perfect, but I can't pinpoint the problem."

"The cream is a little too sweet," I said, taking another bite. "And the cake is slightly dry."

"I'll try again. Will you come back tonight?"

"Why?"

"I need an expert opinion. It's my entry for the fire festival's baking contest. Are you going?"

"I'm not sure." When I had mentioned the festival the other night, Valek hadn't said that I couldn't go.

"A bunch of us from the kitchen are going. You can come with us if you want."

"Thanks. I'll let you know."

On my way back to the Commander's office, an unpleasant thought wove its way into my mind. I had been staying close to Valek because Brazell was still in the castle and wasn't slated to leave until after the festival. If I played fugitive, what would happen if Brazell found out? What if I accidentally encountered him at the festival?

Coming to the conclusion that I was safer within the castle walls until Brazell left, I decided to decline both Valek's and Rand's offers. But by the time I delivered the tea to the Commander, Valek had already won his argument. He quoted cash incentives to me before I could say a word.

The sum for remaining "free" for an entire day was a large amount.

"The exercise is scheduled to take place during the fire festival. A busy time for the soldiers. Should we postpone it until after?" Valek asked the Commander.

"No. The added commotion will increase the level of difficulty for our pursuers."

"Well, Yelena, that gives you only a few days to prepare. Fair enough, since some prisoners plan an escape route, while others see an opportunity and bolt. Are you interested in the challenge?" Valek asked.

"Yes." The word sprang from my gut before the rational

"no" in my mind could escape. "On the condition that Brazell not be informed of my participation."

"Isn't having a room in my personal suite an indication that I'm properly concerned with your well-being?" Valek's voice huffed. I realized that I had insulted him.

When I had offended Rand, I quickly tried to make amends. With Valek, I tried to think of another comment to annoy him further, but I couldn't produce one that quick.

"Speaking of Brazell," the Commander interrupted. "He gave me a gift. A new dessert that his chef invented. He thought I might like it."

Commander Ambrose showed us a wooden box full of thick, brown squares stacked on top of each other like tiles. They were smooth and shiny, but the edges looked as if they had been cut with a dull knife, ragged and shedding brown flakes.

Valek picked up a piece and sniffed it. "I hope you didn't try any."

"It's too blatant, even for Brazell, to be poisoned. But, no. I didn't."

Valek handed the container to me. "Yelena, take some pieces out at random and taste them."

I sorted through the squares and selected four. They were each about the size of my thumbnail and all four fit on the palm of my hand. If I hadn't been told they were a dessert, I probably would have guessed they were pieces of brown candle wax. My fingernail left an impression on the top, and my fingertips felt slightly greasy after handling them.

I hesitated. These were from Brazell, and I didn't remember his cook being especially inventive. I shrugged off my trepidation. I had no choice.

Thinking wax, I anticipated tasting wax. I bit into the hard cube expecting it to crumble between my teeth. It must have been the expression on my face that caused the Commander to rise, because I didn't say a word. The sensations in my mouth had me enraptured.

Instead of crumbling, the dessert melted, coating my tongue with a cascade of flavor. Sweet, bitter, nutty and fruity tastes followed one another. Just when I thought I could say it was one, I would taste them all again. This was unlike anything I had ever encountered. Before I knew it, all four cubes were gone. I longed for more.

"Unbelievable! What is it?"

Valek and the Commander exchanged puzzled looks.

The Commander said, "Brazell called it Criollo. Why? Is there poison in it?"

"No. No poisons. It's just…" The proper words to describe it failed me. "Try it," was all I could manage.

I watched the Commander's face as he bit into one of the squares. His eyes widened and his eyebrows arched in surprise. His tongue dashed along his lips and teeth as he tried to suck all the remaining flavor from them. He grabbed another piece.

"It's sweet. Different. But I don't taste anything unbelievable about it," Valek said, wiping the brown flakes from his hands.

It was my turn to exchange looks with the Commander.

Unlike Valek, he had an appetite for fine cuisine. He recognized excellence when he tasted it.

"I'll bet that little rat won't last an hour," Margg's muffled voice said through the kitchen door. I had been about to enter when I had heard her.

"I'll give fifty to one to anyone stupid enough to think the rat'll last the day. And one hundred to one to the sucker who thinks she won't be caught." After Margg called the odds, the room erupted with sounds of betting.

I listened with growing horror. Margg couldn't be talking about me. Why would Valek tell Margg about the exercise? It'd be all over the castle by tomorrow. Brazell would find out.

"I'll bet a month's wages that Yelena stays free all day," Rand's voice boomed out. The rest of the kitchen staff grew quiet.

My emotions seesawed from betrayal to pride. They were betting on me, and I couldn't believe Rand had bet a month's wages. He had more confidence in me than I did in myself. I tended to agree with Margg on this one.

Margg's laughter echoed on the tiled walls. "You've been in the kitchen too long, Rand. The heat's cooked your brain to mush. I think you're starting to like the little rat. Better lock up your knives when she's here or she may…"

"All right, that's enough," Rand said. "Dinner's over. Everyone out of my kitchen."

I moved down the hallway and out of sight. Since I had promised Rand I would taste his cake, I looped back to the kitchen after everyone had gone. Rand was sitting at one of the tables chopping nuts. There was a slice of his raspberry-and-cream cake on the table.

He pushed the plate to me. I tasted it.

"Much better. The cake is incredibly moist. What's different?" I asked.

"I added pudding to the batter."

Rand was unusually quiet. He didn't mention the betting. I wasn't going to ask.

He finished chopping the nuts. After cleaning up, he said, "I better get some sleep. We're going to the festival tomorrow night. Are you coming?"

"Who's going?" I stalled. I hated to miss out on the first night of the festival. Hated to let Brazell ruin the only fun I'd have. Although, if Margg was going as well, I'd stay with my original decision.

"Porter, Sammy, Liza and maybe Dilana." Rand's tired eyes lit up ever so slightly when he said Dilana's name. "Why?"

"When are you leaving?" Again my heart was ready to overrule the logical and safe choice.

"After dinner. It's the only time everyone is free. The Commander always orders an easy meal for the first night of festival so the kitchen staff can leave early. If you want to come, just meet us here tomorrow."

Rand headed to his rooms, which were adjacent to the kitchen, and I went back to Valek's suite.

The dark apartment was empty. Locking the door, I groped around and found some flint. As I lit the lanterns, I passed by Valek's desk and noticed a paper lying on top. Glancing around to make sure Valek wasn't hiding in the shadows, I looked at the sheet. Names had been written on it, and then scratched out. My name had been circled. Underneath was the comment that I would make a perfect fugitive for the exercise.

This was probably how Margg had known. I remembered seeing her reading papers in Valek's office before. Depending on how long these papers had been here, she could have known for a while. That woman was going to get me killed. If I survived long enough, I'd have to face her. Unfortunately, it would have to wait until after I played fugitive for Valek.

As for my escape plan, I searched through Valek's piles of books. I remembered seeing some appropriate titles, and I was rewarded by finding two on the techniques of pursuit, and one on the best ways to elude capture. Nobody said I couldn't do a little research. Borrowing Valek's texts, I took a lantern and retired to my room.

I studied the books until my vision blurred with fatigue. Changing into my new nightclothes, I extinguished the lantern and collapsed into bed.

I was jolted awake by the frightening awareness that someone was in my room. Instant, sweat-soaked fear gripped me. A black shape loomed over me. Yanked out of bed, I slammed into the wall. One, two, three gasps passed. Nothing more happened. The assault had stopped, but I remained pinned.

My eyes adjusted to the dark. I recognized my attacker's face. "Valek?

II

VALEK'S FACE, INCHES FROM mine, re-
sembled a statue, silent, cold and devoid of emotion. My door
had been left ajar, and even the faint glow of lantern light
slipping through the gap at the threshold couldn't lend his blue
eyes any warmth.

"Valek, what's wrong?"

Without warning, he released me. Too late I realized that
he had held me suspended above the floor. I landed in a heap
at his feet. Wordless, Valek left my room. I staggered upright,
feeling as if I had too many arms and legs, and managed to
catch up to him in the living room. He stood in front of his
desk.

"If this is about the books…" I said to his back, guessing
that he was angry with me for borrowing his manuals.

He turned. "Books? You think this is about books?" His
voice held amazement for a brief moment before it turned

sharp and cutting. "I've been a fool. All this time I admired your survival instincts and intelligence. But now…" He paused, and then looked around the room as if searching for the right words.

"I overheard some servants discussing you as the fugitive. They were placing wagers. How could you be so stupid, so indiscreet? I considered killing you now to save myself the trouble of hunting for your dead body later."

"I didn't tell a soul." I allowed anger to color my voice. "How can you think I would jeopardize my own life?"

"Why should I believe you? The only other person who knew was the Commander."

"Well, Valek, you're the spymaster. Couldn't someone have overheard the conversation? Who else has access to this room? You left your notes in full view on your desk." Before he could leap to another wrong conclusion, I hurried on. "They were conspicuous. If I noticed them with just a quick glance, then they begged for inspection to someone seeking information."

"What are you saying? Who are you accusing?"

A ridge of flesh grew above Valek's nose as his eyebrows pinched together. Alarm flashed across his face before being doused by his stone guise. His fleeting expression told me a great deal. Either Valek had been so convinced that I had gossiped to the servants that he hadn't considered other options, or he couldn't accept the possibility of a breach in his security. For once I had thrown him off balance, if only for a second. Someday I would dearly love to see him in an ungainly heap at my feet.

"I have my suspicions," I said. "But I'll accuse nobody without proof. It's unfair, and who would believe me?"

"No one." Valek snatched a gray rock from his desk and hurled it toward me.

Stunned, I froze as the stone whizzed past and exploded on the wall behind me. Gray debris pelted my shoulder and rained to the floor.

"Except me." He sank into a chair. "Either I'm addicted to risk or you're starting to make sense and we have a leak. An informer, a gossip, a mole. Whoever he is, we need to find him."

"Or her."

Valek frowned. "Do we play it safe and find another fugitive? Or cancel the exercise? Or continue as planned and make you both fugitive and bait? Enticing our spy to reveal himself." He grimaced. "Or herself."

"You don't think Brazell will come after me?"

"No. It's too soon. I don't expect Brazell to try to kill you before his factory is up and running. Once he gets what he wants, then it's going to get interesting around here."

"Oh good. I can barely stay awake now from all the boredom." My voice dripped with sarcasm. Only Valek would consider an attempt on my life a fascinating diversion.

He ignored my remark. "It's your choice, Yelena."

My choice wasn't contained in one of Valek's scenarios. My choice was to be someplace where my life wasn't in danger. My choice was to be where I didn't have an assassin for a boss, and some unknown person trying to make my already intense life even more complicated. My choice was freedom.

I sighed. The safer course of action was the most tempting, but it wouldn't solve anything. I had learned the hard way that avoiding problems didn't work. Run and hide were my trademark impulses, which only led to being trapped in a corner with no recourse other than to blindly strike out.

The results were not always favorable. The lack of control unnerving. My survival instinct seemed to have a mind of its own. Magic. The word floated at the edge of my mind. No. Someone would have noticed by now. Someone would have reported me. Or would he if that someone was Brazell? Or Reyad?

I shook my head, banishing the thoughts. It was in the past. I had more immediate concerns. "Okay. I'll dangle on the hook to see what fish swims out. But who's going to hold the net?"

"I will."

I let out a slow breath. The tight feeling around my stomach eased.

"Don't alter your plans. I'll take care of everything." Valek picked up the paper with my name on it. He dipped the corner of the page into a lantern, setting it on fire. "I should probably follow you to the fire festival tomorrow night. Unless logic has made you decide to turn down Rand's offer and stay in the castle." He let the burning paper float to the floor.

"How did you—" I stopped. I wasn't going to ask. It was well known that he didn't trust Rand, so I shouldn't be surprised that Valek had an informant in the kitchen.

Valek hadn't said I couldn't go. I made a sudden decision. "I'm going. It's a risk. So what? I take a risk every time I sip the Commander's tea. At least this time I might get a chance to enjoy myself."

"It's hard to have fun at the festival without money." Valek crushed the dying embers of the paper under his boot.

"I'll manage."

"Would you like an advance on your wage as fugitive?"

"No. I'll earn the money." I didn't want Valek to do me any favors. I was unprepared for thoughtfulness from him. For Valek to soften even a little might destroy our strange tug-of-war relationship, and I was reluctant for it to alter. Besides, thinking kind thoughts about Valek could be extremely dangerous. I could admire his skills, and be relieved when he was on my side in a fight. But for a rat to like the cat? That scenario ended only one way. With one dead rat.

"Suit yourself," Valek said. "But let me know if you change your mind. And don't concern yourself about the books. Read all the books you want."

Heading back to my room, I paused with my hand resting on the doorknob. "Thanks," I spoke to the door, unwilling to look at Valek.

"For the books?"

"No. The offer." My eyes traced the wood grain.

"You're welcome."

The castle hummed with activity. Smiling servants rushed through the corridors, laughter echoed off the stone walls. It was the first day of the fire festival, and the castle's staff hurried to complete their chores so they could attend the opening celebration. Their excitement was contagious, and even after a restless night of sleep, I was beginning to feel like a child again. Determined to push the ugly image of someone stalking me at the festival to a far, dark corner of my mind, I allowed myself to savor the anticipation of the evening's events.

I fidgeted through an afternoon lesson with Valek. He was trying to teach me how to spot a tail. It was mostly common-sense advice, and some techniques that I had already read about in one of his books, and my mind wandered. I wasn't planning on looking over my shoulder all night. Sensing my mood, Valek ended the session early.

Soon after, I grabbed a clean uniform and the colored ribbons Dilana had given me and headed toward the baths. At this time of day, the steaming pools were empty. I washed fast, and sank into one of the baths. Inching my way into the hot liquid, I let each muscle relax, oohing and aahing until the water reached my neck.

Only when the skin on my fingers began to wrinkle did I leave the water. I had been avoiding the mirror for a month. Now, curious, I scanned my reflection. Not as skeletal, although I needed to gain some more weight. My cheeks were hollow and my ribs and hipbones poked through my flesh. What had once been dull, uncombable black hair now shone. The scar on my right elbow had turned from bright red to a deep purple.

Swallowing, I looked far into the mirror. Had my soul returned? No. Instead, I saw Reyad's smirking ghost floating behind me, but when I turned around he was gone. I wondered what Reyad wanted. Revenge most likely, but how would you confront a ghost? I decided not to worry about it tonight.

Changing into a clean uniform, I braided the brightly colored ribbons into my hair, I let the ends fall past my shoulders and loosely down my back.

When I reported to the Commander to taste his dinner, I expected a tart comment on my unmilitary hairstyle. All I received was one raised eyebrow.

After dinner, I raced to the kitchen. Rand greeted me with a huge smile. The staff was still cleaning, so I helped scrub the countertops and floors to avoid the awkwardness of just standing around waiting. Rand reigned over an immaculate kitchen, and only when the kitchen was spotless was the staff dismissed.

While Rand changed out of his stained uniform, I watched a small group of people talking among themselves as they waited for him. I knew them all by sight and reputation, but hadn't spoken to any of them. Occasionally, one or two glanced warily in my direction. I suppressed a sigh, trying not to let their nerves bother me. I couldn't blame them. It wasn't a secret that I had killed Reyad.

Of the group, Porter was the oldest. He was in charge of the Commander's kennels. Another holdover from the King's reign, he had been deemed too valuable to be replaced. He scowled more than he smiled, and Rand was his only friend. Rand had told me stories about Porter in an "I can't believe anyone would believe such nonsense" tone of voice, but wild rumors that Porter had mental links with the dogs made him an outcast.

The uncanny way the dogs responded and understood Porter seemed abnormal. Almost magical. The suspicion of magic was enough for everyone to treat Porter like he had a contagious disease. Still no one had proof, and his rapport with the animals was useful. Something the Commander prized.

Sammy was Rand's fetch boy. A thin child of twelve, his sole purpose was to obtain anything Rand needed. I'd seen Rand yell at Sammy then hug him in the space of a heartbeat.

Liza was a quiet woman only a few years older than me. She was the castle's pantler, in charge of the pantry's inventory. Liza plucked at her uniform sleeve like she was nervous, but I guessed talking with Porter was better than being near me.

When Rand emerged from his rooms, we left the castle. Sammy raced ahead of the group, too excited to stay with us for very long. Porter and Liza continued their discussion, while Rand and I trailed behind.

The night air was refreshing. I could smell the clean scent of damp earth tinged with the distant aroma of wood smoke. It was my first trip outside in almost a year, and before we went past the gate in the immense, stone buttress that surrounded the castle complex, I peered back. Without a moon it was too dark to see any detail besides the few lighted windows and the towering walls. The complex appeared deserted. If Valek followed, I couldn't spot him.

When we cleared the gate, a breeze greeted us as the day's hot air cooled. I walked with my arms held slightly away from my body, allowing the air to flow past me. My uniform rippled in the wind and my hair blew. I inhaled, enjoying the fresh

evening scent. We walked through the grass field that surrounded the guard walls. No buildings were permitted within
a quarter mile of the castle. The town, once named for Queen
Jewel, was renamed Castletown after the takeover. Jewelstown
had been built by the King in the valley south of the castle
complex as a gift for his wife.

The fire festival's tents had been set up in the fields just west
of Castletown.

"Isn't Dilana coming?" I asked Rand.

"She's already there. Some big emergency came up this
afternoon. When the dancers opened the costume boxes
they discovered that some animal had eaten holes in all of
the outfits. They called Dilana to help mend them before
the opening ceremony." Rand laughed. "I bet the panic
that reigned after they opened the boxes would have been
fun to watch."

"Fun for you, but not for the poor woman in charge of
costumes."

"True." Now silent, he limped beside me. Because of our
slower pace, we fell farther behind the others.

"Where's your cake?" I hoped I hadn't ruined his good mood.

"Sammy ran it down this morning. The baking contest is
judged on the first day so they can sell the entries while they're
fresh. I want to check the results. How come you're not
entering any competitions?"

A simple question. One of many about the festival that I had
been avoiding with some success since Rand and I became
friends. At first I suspected his interest to be an attempt to gain

some insider information for the next round of betting. But now that the gambling was finished, I realized his interest was genuine.

"No money for the entry fees," I said. The truth, but not the entire story. I would need to completely trust Rand before I would tell him about my history with the fire festival.

Rand clucked his tongue in disgust. "It doesn't make sense not to pay the food taster. Otherwise, what better way to obtain information about the Commander than to bribe the taster?" He paused, then turned to me, his face serious. "Would you sell information for money?"

12

I SHIVERED AT RAND'S QUESTION.
Was he asking just to ask or was he offering to pay me for information? I imagined Valek's reaction if he discovered that I had taken a bribe. Having no money was better than facing his wrath.

"No. I wouldn't," I said.

Rand grunted. We walked in an unnatural silence for a while. I wondered if Oscove, the old food taster, had taken money for information. It would explain why Valek hadn't liked him and why Rand suspected Valek of killing Oscove.

"If you'd like, I'll pay the entry fee for you. Your help has been invaluable, and I've certainly won enough money on your resourcefulness," Rand said.

"Thanks, but I'm not prepared. It'd be a waste of money." Besides, I was determined to enjoy the festival without money just to prove to Valek that it could be done.

Despite promising myself I wouldn't, I glanced back over my shoulder. Nothing. I tried to convince myself that not seeing Valek was a good thing. If I could spot him, then anyone could. Still, the nagging feeling that maybe he had decided to let me take my chances wouldn't quit. Stop it, I told myself. Don't worry. Then again, I'd be an idiot to walk around the festival blind to danger.

I felt as if I balanced on a high wire, trying not to fall. Could I watch for trouble and have fun at the same time? I didn't know, but was determined to try.

"Which competition would you have entered?" Rand asked.

Before I could answer, he waved his hands in front of me. "No! Don't tell me! I want to guess."

I smiled. "Go ahead."

"Let's see. Small, thin and graceful. A dancer?"

"Try again."

"Okay. You remind me of a pretty bird, willing to sit on the windowsill as long as nobody comes too close, but prepared to fly away if somebody does. A songbird. Perhaps you're a singer?"

"You've obviously never heard me sing. Are all your guesses going to come with a lengthy discussion of my personality?" I asked.

"No. Now be quiet, I'm trying to think."

The glow from the festival was growing brighter. I heard the distant buzz of music, animals and people blended together.

"Long, thin fingers. Maybe you're a member of a spinning team?" Rand guessed.

"What's a spinning team?"

"Usually there's one shearer, one carder, one spinner and one weaver in a team. You know, sheep to shawl. The teams race to see who can shear a sheep's wool and turn it into a garment first. It's pretty amazing to watch." Rand studied me for a while. I began to wonder if he had run out of guesses.

"A jockey?"

"Do you really think I could afford to buy a racehorse?" I asked in amazement. Only the very wealthy citizens had horses to race for sport. The military used horses for the transportation of high-ranking officers and advisers only. Everyone else walked.

"People who own racehorses don't ride them. They hire jockeys. And you're the perfect size, so stop looking at me like I'm daft."

As we arrived at the first of the massive multicolored tents, our conversation ceased as we absorbed the frenzied activity and panoramic sights that assaulted us. When I was younger, I used to stand amid the chaos and feast on the energy of the fire festival. I had always thought the name of the festival was perfect, not because it occurred during the hot season, but because the sounds and smells pulsated like heat waves, making my blood sizzle and pop. Now, after spending close to a year in a dungeon, I felt the force slamming into me as though I were a brick wall. A wall whose mortar threatened to crumble from the overload of sensations.

Torches blazed and bonfires burned. We walked into a slice of captured daylight. The performance and competition tents were scattered throughout the festival, with small open stands tucked in and around them like children clinging to their mothers' skirts. From exotic gems to flyswatters, the merchants sold an array of goods. The aroma of food cooking made my stomach grumble as we passed several barbecue pits, and I regretted having skipped dinner in my haste to get here.

Entertainers, contestants, spectators and laughing children ebbed and flowed around us. Sometimes the press of people hurried us along from behind and sometimes we struggled to go forward. We had lost track of the others. If he hadn't linked his arm in mine, I probably would have been separated from Rand as well. Distractions peppered the festival. I would have followed the lively music to its source or lingered to watch a skit, but Rand was determined to see the results of the baking contest.

As we moved, I examined faces in the crowd, searching for green-and-black uniforms even though Valek had said Brazell wouldn't be a threat. I thought it prudent to avoid him and his guards altogether. Unsure of who I was looking for, I watched for unusual faces. It was the wrong way to detect a tail. Valek had taught me that the best agents were unremarkable in appearance and didn't draw attention to themselves. But I figured if a skilled spy followed me, my chances of spotting him or her was small.

We met up with Porter and Liza in a small tent filled with a sweet aroma that made my stomach ache with hunger. They were talking to a large man in a cook's uniform, but they stopped when we entered. Surrounding Rand, they congratulated him on his first-place win. The heavy man declared that Rand had broken a festival record by winning five years in a row.

While Rand examined the array of baked goods lining the

shelves, I asked the man who had won in Military District 5. I was curious if Brazell's cook had won with his Criollo recipe. The man's brow creased with concentration, causing his short, curly black hair to touch his thick eyebrows.

"Bronda won it with a heavenly lemon pie. Why?"

"I thought General Brazell's chef, Ving, might win. I used to work at the manor."

"Well, Ving won two years ago with some cream pie and now he enters the same pie each year, hoping it'll win again."

I thought it odd that he hadn't entered his Criollo, but before I could deduce a reason, Rand jubilantly swept us out of the tent. He wanted to buy everyone a glass of wine to celebrate his victory.

We sipped our wine and wandered around the festival. Sammy materialized on occasion from the crowd to report some wonder with great delight, only to rush off again.

Twice I spotted a woman with a serious expression. Her black hair was pulled into a tight bun. Wearing the uniform of a hawk mistress, she moved with the grace of someone used to physical exercise. The second time I saw her she was much closer, and I made eye contact. Her almond-shaped, emerald eyes narrowed, staring boldly back at me until I looked away. There was something familiar about her, and it was some time before I figured it out.

She reminded me of the children in Brazell's care, and was more similar to my own coloring than to the pale ivory complexion of most of the Territory's people. Her skin was bronze. Not tanned from the sun but a natural pigmentation.

Then our aimless group was snared in a flow of spectators heading into a big red-and-white-striped tent. It was the acrobatics tent, where trampolines, tightropes and floor mats were covered with brightly costumed men and women. They were all trying to pass the qualifying round. I watched as one man performed a beautiful series of flips on the tightrope, only to be disqualified when he fell during his solo tumbling run.

Out of the corner of my eye I saw Rand watching me. His expression triumphant.

"What?" I asked.

"You're an acrobat!"

"I *was* an acrobat."

Rand waved his hands. "Doesn't matter. I was right!"

It mattered to me. Reyad had tainted acrobatics. The time when I felt satisfaction and enjoyment from performing was gone, and I couldn't imagine getting any happiness from it now.

From the benches in the tent, our small kitchen group watched the contestants. Grunts of effort, sweat-soaked costumes and thumping feet made me long for the days when all that worried me was finding time to practice.

Four of us in Brazell's orphanage had taken up acrobatics. We had scavenged and begged for materials to set up a practice area behind the stables. Our mistakes sent us crashing to the grass until the stable master took pity on our bruised bodies. One day we arrived to find a thick coating of dung-scented straw carpeting our practice area.

Brazell's teachers had encouraged us to discover something we could excel in. While some found singing or dancing to be their calling, I had been fascinated by the acrobatic displays since my first fire festival.

Despite hours of practice, I failed during the qualifying round at my inaugural competition. The disappointment stabbed my heart, but I healed the ache with resolve. I spent the next year covered with black-and-blue marks, nursing sprains too numerous to count. When the festival returned, I passed the qualifiers and the initial round only to fall off the tightrope in the second. Each year I worked hard and advanced steadily. I won through to the final round the year before Brazell and Reyad claimed me as their laboratory rat.

Brazell and Reyad didn't allow me to practice acrobatics, but that didn't stop me from slipping away whenever Reyad was on some mission for his father. What did stop me was getting caught by Reyad a week before the festival, when he arrived home early from a trip. I was concentrating so hard that I failed to notice him astride his horse until I finished my tumbling routine. His expression, a mixture of anger and elation, caused the beads of sweat on my skin to turn into ice crystals.

For disobeying his orders, I was forbidden to go to the festival that year. And as an added deterrent to disobedience, I was punished for the duration of the festival. Each evening for five nights, Reyad forced me to strip. With a cruel grin on his face, he stared at me as I stood shivering despite the warmth of the night. He draped heavy chains from a metal collar around my neck to metal cuffs on my wrists and ankles. I wanted to scream, to beat him with my fists, but I was too terrified to anger him further.

Pleasure at my fear and humiliation made his face flush as he drove me with a small whip to perform acrobatics of his own devising. A lashing sting on my skin was the reprimand for moving too slow. The chains battered my body as they swung with my movements. Their weight dragged at my limbs, making each tumble an exhausting ordeal. The cuffs began to rub my wrists and ankles raw. Blood streaked down my arms and legs.

When Brazell participated in the experiments, Reyad meticulously followed his father's instructions, but when he was alone with me the indifferent exercises turned vicious. Sometimes he would invite his friend, Mogkan, to assist him, and they made my hell a contest to see who invented the best way to test my endurance.

I was in constant fear that I would madden Reyad enough to force him to cross the only line he seemed to have drawn. For all the torture and pain he inflicted, he never raped me. So I somersaulted and cartwheeled with chains just to keep him from crossing that line.

Rand's heavy arm fell across my shoulders. I flinched back into the present.

"Yelena! What's wrong?" Rand's eyes, full of concern, searched mine. "You looked like you were having a nightmare with your eyes open."

"Sorry."

"Don't apologize to me. Here…" He handed me a steaming meat pie. "Sammy brought these for us."

I thanked Sammy. When my attention focused on him, his eyes grew wide, and his young face whitened. He averted his gaze. Without thinking, I took a small bite and tasted for poison. Finding nothing, I ate and wondered what wild stories had been told about me to cause Sammy's fearful reaction. Children Sammy's age usually enjoyed scaring each other with imaginative horror tales.

We used to frighten ourselves at the orphanage after the lanterns had been blown out and we were in bed waiting for sleep. Whispered stories about monsters raging and magician's curses made us gasp and giggle. We told gruesome tales about the older "graduates" of the orphanage, who just seemed to disappear. No explanation was given to us of where they were working, and we never encountered any of them in town or in the manor house. So we created horrible scenarios about their fates.

How I missed those nights with the other children when I was finally able to rest after spending a day with Reyad. He had isolated me from the others. Taken from the girls' dorm, I had been given a small room next to Reyad's suite. At night, with my body aching and my spirits crushed, I would lie awake and recite those tales in my mind until I fell asleep.

"Yelena, we can go."

"What?" I looked at Rand.

"If this is upsetting you. We can go. There's a spectacular new fire dance."

"We can stay. I was just…reminiscing. But if you want to see the fire dance, I'll go along."

"Reminiscing? You must have hated being an acrobat."

"Oh no, I loved everything about it. Flying through the

air, the complete control over my body as I spun and twirled. The thrill of knowing I was going to land the perfect dismount before I even hit the ground." I stopped. The confusion on Rand's face made me want to laugh and cry at the same time. How could I explain to him that it wasn't the acrobatics that upset me but the events that they had triggered? Reyad's cruel punishment for practicing. Sneaking out to participate in the festival the following year, which had led to Reyad's death.

I shuddered. Those memories of Reyad were like a trap in the corner of my mind, and I wasn't ready to spring it. "Someday, Rand, I'll explain. But for now I would like to see the fire dance."

He hooked his arm around mine as our kitchen group left the tent and joined in the flow of people. Sammy raced ahead, shouting over his shoulder that he would save us some good seats. A drunken man bumped into me and I stumbled. He mumbled an apology and saluted me with his mug of ale. Trying to make a bow, he landed in a heap at my feet. I would have stopped to help him, but I was distracted by the appearance of blazing staffs of wood. I felt a pulsating rhythm vibrating through the soles of my feet as the fire dancers spun the flaming props around their heads and paraded into the tent. Amazed by the dancers' intricate movements, I stepped over the drunk.

But with the excitement and press of people through the entrance, Rand's grip was broken. I wasn't concerned until I found myself surrounded by four immense men. Two of the men wore blacksmith's uniforms, while the other two wore farmer's work uniforms. Excusing myself, I tried to slip past them, but they only pressed closer, trapping me.

13

TERROR WELLED IN MY THROAT; I was
in trouble. I screamed for help. A gloved hand clamped over
my mouth. Biting into the leather, I tasted ashes, but couldn't
reach skin. The blacksmiths grabbed my arms and pushed me
forward, while the farmers walked in front, blocking me from
sight. In all the commotion around the dance tent, nobody
noticed my abduction.

I struggled, dragged my feet and kicked. Their pace never
slowed. I was lugged farther away from the lights and safety of
the festival. Craning my neck, I looked for a way to escape.
The blacksmith next to me moved closer to block my meager
view. His thick beard was filled with soot and half of it had
been singed off.

We stopped behind a dark tent. The farmers stepped aside
and I saw a shadow pull away from the fabric.

"Did anyone notice? Did anyone follow you?" the shadow asked with a woman's voice.

"It went perfect. Everyone was focused on the dancers," the blacksmith with the leather gloves replied.

"Good. Kill her now," the woman ordered.

A knife flashed in Leather Gloves's hand. I renewed my struggle, managing to break free for an instant. But the farmers pinned my arms while Singed Beard grabbed my legs. They held me suspended above the ground. Leather Gloves raised his weapon.

"No knives, you idiot! Think of the bloody mess. Use this." She handed Leather Gloves a long thin strap. In a blink the knife disappeared. He wrapped the garrote around my neck.

"Nooo…" I screamed, but my protest was cut off along with my air supply as he tightened the strap. Intense pressure squeezed my neck. I jerked my limbs in vain. White dots swirled before my eyes. A faint buzzing sound dribbled from my lips. Too faint; the survival instinct that had saved me from Brazell's guards and Reyad's torture was too weak this time.

Over the roar of blood in my ears, I heard the woman say, "Hurry up! She's starting to project."

Ready to step off the edge of consciousness, a drunken voice said, "Excuse me, sirs, do you know where I can get a refill?"

The pressure on my neck lessened as Leather Gloves drew his knife. I let my body go limp and was rewarded by being dumped on the ground. The other three men stepped over me to face the intruder. Suppressing the urge to gasp for breath, I sucked in air with desperation. I muffled my efforts, unwilling to let anyone know I could still breathe.

From my new position, I saw Leather Gloves lunge toward the drunk. The clang of metal rang through the air as the knife stabbed into the man's pewter beer mug instead of his chest. With a hard jerk of his wrist, the mug blurred into motion. The knife flew through the air, imbedding into the fabric of the tent. Then the drunk struck Leather Gloves on the head with the mug. Leather Gloves crumpled to the ground.

The others, mere steps away when their companion went down, rushed the intruder. The farmers grabbed his upper arms and shoulders while Singed Beard punched him twice in the face. Using the farmers to support his weight, the drunk lifted both legs off the ground and wrapped them around Singed Beard's neck. With a loud snap, Singed Beard fell.

Still clutching his mug, the drunk swung it to the right into one farmer's groin. As the farmer doubled over, the drunk brought the mug up, smashing it into the farmer's face.

Then the intruder swept his beer mug to the left and slammed it into the other farmer's nose. Blood gushing, the farmer yelped in pain and released his grip on the drunk. The drunk launched a second blow to the farmer's temple. The farmer collapsed to the ground without a sound.

The fight had lasted seconds. The woman hadn't moved at all, her intent gaze had been focused on the skirmish. Recognizing her as the dark-skinned woman I had spotted twice before at the festival, I wondered what she would do now that her goons were beaten.

Regaining some strength, I contemplated my odds of reaching the knife in the tent before she did. The drunk wiped blood off his face. Bodies were littered around his feet.

I tried to stand on shaky legs. The woman's head snapped toward me as if she had forgotten I was there. Then she started to sing. Her sweet, melodious tune wound its way through my mind. Relax, it said, lie down, be still. Yes, I thought as I sank back down. My body mellowed. I felt as if she were tucking me into bed, drawing the blanket up to my chin. But then the blanket was yanked over my head, pushing against my mouth and nose, suffocating me.

I thrashed, wildly clawing my face to remove the imaginary blanket. Out of nowhere, Valek appeared before me, yelling in my ear, shaking my shoulders. Stupidly, belatedly, I realized he was the drunk. Who else but Valek could win a fight against four large men when armed only with a beer mug?

"Recite poisons in your mind!" Valek shouted.

I ignored him. Lassitude overcame me. I ceased fighting. All I wanted to do was sink into the darkness and follow the music to its depths.

"Recite! Now! That's an order!"

Habit saved me. Without thought, I obeyed Valek. Names of poisons marched through my mind. The music stopped. The pressure on my face eased, and I could breathe again. I gasped noisily.

"Keep reciting," he said.

The woman and the knife had disappeared. Valek pulled me to my feet. I swayed, but he steadied me with an arm on my shoulder. I clutched his hand for a second, suppressing the urge to throw myself sobbing into his arms. He had saved my life. When I regained my balance, Valek went back to the men. I knew Singed Beard was dead, but I was unsure of the others.

Valek turned one prone form over and cursed. "Southerners," he said with disgust. He moved around the others, feeling for pulses. "Two alive. I'll have them taken to the castle for questioning."

"What about the woman?" I croaked. Talking was painful.

"Gone."

"Will you search for her?"

Valek gave me a strange look. "Yelena, she's a southern magician. I took my eyes off her, so there's no way I can find her now."

He grabbed my arm and steered me toward the festival.

My muscles trembled as the shock of the attack worked through my body. It took a while for his words to sink in.

"Magician?" I asked. "I thought they were banished from Ixia." Killed on sight was more like it, but I couldn't bring myself to say those words aloud.

"Although very unwelcome, some visit Ixia anyway."

"But, I thought…"

"Not now. I'll explain later. Right now I want you to catch up with Rand and his friends. Pretend nothing has happened. I doubt she'll try again tonight."

The bright firelight stabbed my eyes. Valek and I stayed in the shadows until we spotted Rand near the acrobatics tent.

He was searching for me and calling my name. Valek motioned for me to join my friend.

I had taken only two steps when Valek said, "Yelena, wait."

I turned. Valek waved me closer. When I reached him, his hand reached toward my neck. I stepped back, but recovered and stood still. His hand brushed my skin as he pulled the garrote off my throat. He handed it to me as if it was a poisonous snake. Shivering in disgust, I flung it to the ground.

Rand's relief, when he saw me emerge from the crowd, rolled off him like a breaking wave. I hesitated. Why would he be so concerned? For all he knew, I had only been lost. I caught a sweet whiff of wine as Rand approached.

"Yelena, where have you been?" His words slurred.

I hadn't realized he had drunk that much wine, which would explain why he had been so desperate to find me. Alcohol poisoned the mind, exaggerated the emotions.

"The tent was too crowded. I needed some air." My voice caught on the word *air* as the horror of being strangled swept through me. I glanced back at the shadows. Was Valek still watching or had he gone to arrest those men? And where was the dark-skinned woman? Earlier, I had been so happy to get out of the castle, but now I wanted nothing more than to have strong stone walls around me, and to be safely back in Valek's suite. Now, *that* was an odd combination, the words *Valek* and *safe* in the same thought.

"I thought I'd catch up with you later," I lied to Rand as I scanned the festival crowd. I didn't enjoy deceiving him. After all, he was my friend. Maybe even a good friend who had been

concerned enough to search for me when I had been separated from him, and who probably would have been the only
person to be upset by my murder. Despite his fight on my
behalf, I was certain that Valek would have only been annoyed
at having to train a new food taster.

The fire dance had just ended and people poured from the
tent. The rest of the kitchen group waited outside. Dilana had
joined them. Rand dropped my arm like a lump of dough and
went over to her. She smiled at him, teasing him about chasing
after the food taster when he had promised to meet her.

Drunkenly, he begged for her forgiveness, explaining that
he couldn't afford to lose me since I had helped him win the
baking contest. She laughed. Throwing one of her heartwarming smiles my way, Dilana hugged Rand, and arm in arm they
headed back to the castle.

The rest of us followed. I found myself once again last in
the procession, but this time I had Liza as a companion.

She scowled at me. "I don't know what Rand sees in you,"
she said.

Not a friendly way to start a conversation. "Excuse me," I
said, keeping my tone neutral.

"He missed the fire dance looking for you. And ever since
you came around, the kitchen routine has been destroyed.
The staff's flustered."

"What are you talking about?"

"Before you showed up, Rand's mood swings were predictable. Cheerful and content when Dilana was happy and
the gambling was profitable, moody and sullen when they

weren't. Then…" Liza stressed the word. Her plain cornmeal face creased into an ugly expression, which she aimed at me. "You befriend him. He starts snarling at the kitchen staff for no reason. Even winning a big payoff, Rand's still depressed. It's frustrating. We've come to the conclusion that you must be trying to steal him away from Dilana. We want you to stop, leave him alone and stay out of the kitchen."

Liza had picked the worst time to accost me. Having just escaped a brush with death had put matters into perspective. I wasn't in the best frame of mind. Pure rage flared; I grabbed her arm and spun her around to face me. We stood nose to nose.

"*You* have concluded? The combined brainpower of the kitchen staff probably couldn't light a candle. Our *friendship* is none of your business. So I suggest you rethink your hypothesis. If there's a problem in the kitchen, then deal with it. You're wasting your time whining about it to me." I pushed her away. I could tell by her shocked expression that she hadn't expected such a fierce response.

Too bad for her, I thought as I hurried to catch up with the others, leaving her to walk alone. What did she want me to do? Had she assumed that I would meekly agree to stop talking to Rand just to smooth things in the kitchen? I wasn't going to let her unload her problems on me; I was already overloaded with my own. Like why would a magician from Sitia want to kill me?

At the castle, I said good-night to Rand and Dilana and rushed to Valek's suite. As much as I wanted to be inside, I cajoled one of the outer-door guards to check Valek's rooms for intruders before I went in. Murder attempts combined with an overactive imagination made me jumpy, fearing ambushes. Even sitting on the couch in the middle of the living room with every lantern blazing, I didn't feel safe until Valek arrived near dawn.

"Haven't you slept?" he asked. A fist-size, dark purple bruise on his jaw contrasted against his pale skin.

"No. But neither have you," I said peevishly.

"I can sleep all day. You need to taste the Commander's breakfast in an hour."

"What *I* need are answers."

"To what questions?" Valek began to extinguish the lanterns.

"Why is a southern magician trying to kill me?"

"A good question. The very same one I was going to ask you."

"How should I know?" I shrugged in frustration. "Brazell's guards I could understand. But magicians! It's not like I've been going around making southern magicians angry."

"Ahhh…that's a shame. Since you have a real talent for angering people." Valek sat at his desk and rested his head in his hands. "A southern magician, Yelena, a master-level southern *magician*. Do you know that there are only four master magicians in Sitia? Four. And since the takeover, they've stayed in Sitia. On occasion they send a minion or two with minor magical abilities into the Territory to see what we're up to. So far each spy has been intercepted and dealt with. Commander Ambrose will not tolerate magic in Ixia."

The magicians of the King's era had been considered the

elite. Treated like royalty, they had been quite influential with the King. According to the history of the takeover, Valek had assassinated every one of them. I wondered how, especially since he couldn't capture that woman tonight.

Valek stood up. He grabbed a gray rock off his desk. Tossing the stone from hand to hand, he paced around the living room.

Remembering Valek's near miss with the last rock he'd held, I pulled my feet off the floor and hugged my knees to my chest, hoping to make myself a smaller target.

"For the southerners to risk one of their master magicians, the reason has to be…" Valek shook the stone in his hand, searching for the right word. "Momentous. So why are they after you?" He sighed and sank down on the couch next to me. "Well, let's try to reason this out. You obviously have some southern blood in your heritage."

"What?" I had never thought about my heritage. I had been found on the street, homeless, and been taken in by Brazell. Speculation about my parents had only been on whether they were dead or had just abandoned me. I had no memories of my life prior to my arrival at the orphanage. Mostly, I had been thankful that Brazell gave me shelter. For Valek to make such a matter-of-fact statement stunned me.

"Your coloring is a bit darker than the typical northerner. Your features have a southern quality. Green eyes are very rare in the Territory, but are more common in Sitia." Valek misread my frozen expression. "It's nothing to be ashamed of. When the King was in power, the border to Sitia was open to commerce and trade. People moved freely between the regions, and marriages were inevitable. I would guess you were left behind right after the takeover when people panicked and fled south before we closed the border. It was complete mayhem. I don't know what they were expecting when the Commander came to power. Mass killings? All we did was give everyone a uniform and a job."

My mind reeled. Why hadn't I been more curious about my family? I didn't even know what town I had been found in. We had been told daily of our good fortune, reminded that we had food, clothes, shelter, teachers and even a small allowance. It had been repeatedly pointed out that many children with parents weren't as well off as we were. Was it a form of brainwashing?

"Well, anyway, I digress," Valek said into the silence. He stood and resumed his pacing. "I doubt it was missing family members. They wouldn't want to kill you. Is there anything else, besides murdering Reyad, that you did in the past? Witnessed a crime? Overheard plans for a rebellion? Anything at all?"

"No. Nothing."

Valek tapped the rock against his forehead. "Then let's assume this has to do with Reyad. Perhaps he was in league with some southerners and your killing him ruined their plans. Maybe they're scheming to retake Ixia. Or they think you know something about this plot. But I've heard nothing about Sitia attacking us. And why would they? Sitia knows the Commander is content to stay in the north and vice versa." Valek rubbed a hand over his face before continuing.

"Perhaps Brazell has gotten creative in his old age and hired southerners to kill you; thereby accomplishing his desire to see you dead without implicating himself. No. That doesn't make sense. Brazell would have hired thugs, no need for a magician. Unless he has connections I'm not aware of, which is highly doubtful." Valek looked around the room. Only half of the lanterns had been extinguished. Setting the rock down, he finished the job just as the timid predawn light started to brighten the room.

He stopped as if he had a sudden thought and scowled at me. "What?"

"Magicians will come north to smuggle one of their own kind to safety," Valek said. He studied me.

Before I could protest, he asked, "Then why kill you? Unless you're a Soulfinder, they wouldn't want you dead." Valek yawned and gently fingered the bruise on his face. "I'm too tired to think straight. I'm going to bed." He walked to the stairs.

Soulfinder? I had no idea what that was, but more important concerns needed to be addressed.

"Valek."

He paused with a foot on the first step.

"My antidote."

"Of course." He continued up the steps.

While he was upstairs, I wondered how many times in the future I would have to ask for the antidote. The knowledge that it was keeping me alive poisoned my mind as surely as the Butterfly's Dust poisoned my body.

As the early morning light brightened, I thought of my bed with longing. Valek could sleep, but I had to taste the Commander's breakfast soon.

Valek came downstairs. Handing me the antidote, he said, "You might want to wear your hair down today."

"Why?" I ran my fingers through my hair. The ribbons I had braided were torn and knotted.

"To cover the marks on your neck."

Before going to the Commander's office, I hurried to the baths. I had just enough time to wash and change into a clean uniform before I had to appear at breakfast. The garrote had left a bright red ring around my neck that I couldn't cover no matter how I styled my hair.

On my way to the Commander's office, I saw Liza. She set her mouth in a firm frown and looked away when she passed. Oh well, I thought, another person I'd angered. I regretted having taken my ire out on her, but I wasn't about to apologize. After all, she had started the argument.

Most mornings the Commander ignored my arrival. I would taste his breakfast, and then sort through his box of Criollo, randomly selecting a piece to verify that no one had poisoned it during the night. Each morning my mouth watered as I anticipated the taste of the bittersweet dessert. Its nutty flavor coating my mouth was the one pleasure I could look forward to during my day. I had argued with Valek that I should test it every time the Commander wanted some, but the Commander hoarded his supply. He rationed out one piece of Criollo after every meal. And I had heard through Rand that the Commander had already requested more from Brazell, along with a copy of the recipe from his cook, Ving.

Each morning after placing the Commander's breakfast tray on his desk, I would pick up his daily schedule and leave without a word being uttered. But this morning, when I set the tray down, he told me to sit.

Perched on the edge of the hard, wooden chair facing his desk, I felt a feather of fear brush my stomach. I laced my fingers tight together to keep my face impassive.

"Valek has informed me that you had an incident last night. I'm concerned that another attempt on your life will jeopardize our exercise." The Commander's golden eyes regarded me as he sipped his tea. "You have presented Valek with a puzzle, and he has *assured* me that keeping you alive will aid in a speedy resolution. Convince me that you'll be able to play fugitive without getting yourself killed. According to Valek, you failed to recognize him even after he bumped into you."

My mouth opened, but I closed it as I considered his words. A hastily explained or illogical argument would not sway the Commander. Also, I had been given an easy out. Why should I risk my neck for his exercise? I wasn't a skilled spy; I hadn't been able to identify Valek even when I knew he was following me. But then again it was my neck the murderous assailants were after. If I didn't try to draw them out on my own terms, they'd pick the time and location. I weighed the argument in my head, feeling as though I was forever on a tightrope, unable to decide which way led to the perfect dismount. Walking back and forth until some outside force came along to push me one way or the other.

"I'm new to the hunt-and-chase game," I told the Commander. "For someone untrained, trying to spot a tail in a noisy, crowded festival is a difficult task. It's like asking a child to run when she has just learned how to walk. In the woods, alone and trying to avoid everyone, picking up a tail will be easier and within my abilities." I stopped. No response from the Commander, so I continued, "If we can lure this magician out, maybe we can discover why she wants to kill me."

The Commander sat as still as a frog that watched and waited for a fly to come closer.

I played my last card. "And Valek has *assured* me he will be following."

My use of the Commander's word was not lost on him.

"We will proceed as planned. I don't expect you to get far, so I doubt we'll see this magician." He said the word *magician* as if it left a foul taste in his mouth. "I do expect you to keep quiet about this entire affair. Consider it an order. You're dismissed."

"Yes, Sir." I left his office.

I spent the remainder of the day collecting and borrowing provisions for the exercise, which was scheduled to begin the next morning at dawn. I visited Dilana's workroom and the smithy. Just mentioning Valek's name produced remarkable results from the blacksmiths, who hurried to procure the items I said Valek needed.

Dilana would have given me anything I requested. She seemed disappointed that I only wanted to borrow a leather backpack.

"Keep it," she had said. "No one has claimed it. It's been underfoot since I started."

I kept her company as she mended uniforms, told me the latest gossip and fussed about how I needed to eat more.

My last stop was the kitchen. With the hope of finding Rand alone, I waited until after the staff had cleaned up dinner. He was standing at a counter, working on menus. Each week's menus had to be approved by the Commander before Rand could give them to Liza, who made sure the required food and ingredients were available.

"You look better than I feel," Rand said in a soft tone. He held his head like a full cup of water, moving slowly as if to avoid spilling over. "I don't have anything for you to taste today. I haven't had the energy."

"That's okay." I noted his white face and the dark smudges under his eyes. "I won't keep you. I just need to borrow some things."

Interested, Rand almost returned to his jovial self. "Like what?"

"Bread. And some of that glue you invented. Medic Mommy used it to seal a cut on my arm. It's wonderful stuff."

"The glue! One of my best recipes yet! Did she tell you how I discovered it? I was trying to make an edible adhesive for this mammoth, ten-layer wedding cake and—"

"Rand," I interrupted, "I would love to hear the story, and you must promise to tell me another time. But we're both short on sleep."

"Oh, yes. You're right." He pointed to a stack of loaves and said, "Take what you need."

While I collected bread, he rummaged around in a drawer, then handed me a jar of white glue.

"It's not permanent. The glue will stick for about a week then it loses its grip. Anything else?"

"Um. Yes." I hesitated, reluctant to make my last request, which was my main reason for wanting to be alone with Rand.

"What?"

"I need a knife."

His head jerked. I could see a spark behind his eyes as the memory of how I had killed Reyad flashed through his mind. I saw the gears in his head turning as he weighed our fledgling friendship against this unusual request.

I fully expected him to question me as to why I needed a knife. Instead he asked, "Which one?"

"The scariest-looking one you've got.

14

THE NEXT MORNING, I headed out the south gate just as the sun crested the Soul Mountains. Soon a glorious sweep of sunlight rushed over the valley, indicating the start of the Commander's exercise. My heart pulsed with excitement and fear. A strange combination of feelings, but they fueled my steps. I scarcely felt the weight of my backpack.

I had worried that the items contained in my knapsack could be considered cheating. After much thought, I decided that a prisoner intent on escaping from the dungeon would save some of her bread rations, smuggle a weapon from the guard room and steal the other items from the blacksmiths. And if I was stretching things a bit, then so what. No one had told me I must flee with nothing.

My determination to "escape" had increased since the plan had first been proposed. The money was merely a bonus at this point. I wanted to prove the Commander wrong. The Commander, who thought I wouldn't get far, who had been concerned *my death* would jeopardize *his* exercise.

Before leaving the castle complex, I had stopped for a moment to view the main building in the daylight. My first impression was that a child had built the palace with his toy blocks. The base of the castle was rectangular. It supported various upper levels of squares, triangles and cylinders built atop one another in a haphazard fashion. The only attempts at symmetry were the magnificent towers at each corner of the castle. Streaked with brilliantly colored glass windows, the four towers stretched toward the sky.

The castle's unusual geometric design intrigued me, and I would have liked to view it from other angles, but Valek had instructed me to leave the complex at dawn as I only had an hour's head start. Then, the soldiers and dogs in pursuit would try to discover which gate I had exited, tracking me from there. Valek had taken one of my uniform shirts in order to give the dogs my scent. I had asked him who would taste the Commander's food while I was gone, and he'd given me some vague reply about having others trained in the art of poisoning who were too valuable to be used on a regular basis. Unlike me.

My southern route was an obvious direction, but I didn't plan to maintain it for long. I hoped the soldiers would assume I was headed straight for the border. The castle complex was in Military District 6 and quite close to the southern lands, wedged between MD–7 to the west and MD–5 to the east. The dead King, who had built the complex, had preferred the milder weather.

Alternating between jogging and walking, it wasn't long before I entered Snake Forest, avoiding Castletown. While studying some of Valek's maps the previous night, I had noticed that the forest surrounded Castletown on three sides. The northern district of the town faced the castle. Snake Forest also spread out to the east and west like a thin belt of green.

At the official southern border, Commander Ambrose's soldiers had cleared a hundred-foot-wide swath from the Soul Mountains in the east all the way to the Sunset Ocean in the west. Since the takeover it was a crime for anyone, Ixian or Sitian, to cross this line.

I jogged through the forest, making a conspicuous trail. Breaking branches and stomping footprints in the dirt, I remained southbound until I reached a small stream. My hour head start was almost up. I knelt by the stream's bank and reached into the water. Pulling out a handful of mud, I let the water drain through my fingers. I hunched over the stream and smeared the wet sediment on my face and neck. Since I had pulled my hair into a bun, I rubbed mud on my ears and the back of my neck. I hoped the men would guess I had knelt here for a drink. After stamping footprints near the stream's bank to mislead my pursuers into thinking I had walked into the water, I traced my route back until I found a perfect tree.

About six feet from my path, a Velvatt's smooth trunk rose high into the air. The first sturdy branch off the main trunk stretched fifteen feet above my head. Trying not to disturb the ground surrounding my scent path, I removed my backpack and pulled out one of the items I had borrowed from the blacksmiths. It was a small metal grappling hook. I tied it to the end of a long thin rope coiled inside my bag.

With my head start gone, a sudden image of guards and dogs exploding from the castle flashed through my mind. Hastily I threw the hook up to the branch. It missed. I caught it on the way down. Frantic, I threw the hook again. Missed. I calmed my raging pulse and focused on the task. The hook snagged the branch. Confident the hook was secure, I tied the extra line around my waist so it wouldn't drag and put on my backpack. Grabbing the rope with both hands, I pulled my weight off the ground and wrapped my legs around the slack.

It had been a long time since I had climbed this way. All the way up the rope, my arm, shoulder and back muscles complained over my year-long inactivity. Once I reached the top, I straddled the branch and repacked the rope and hook in my backpack.

A strong breeze blew from the west. Wanting to stay downwind of the dogs, I spent the next half hour climbing east through the trees until I was well away from my original path. For once, my small size and acrobatic abilities proved a benefit.

When I came across a Cheketo tree, I found a secure nook near the trunk and unslung my backpack. The Cheketo's leaf was the biggest that grew in the Snake Forest. Its circular-shaped green leaf, spotted with brown, was perfect for my needs. I sat still for a minute, listening for sounds of pursuit. Birds chirped and insects buzzed; I heard the quick rustling of leaves as a deer moved. I detected the faint baying of dogs, but it might have been just my imagination. There was no sign of Valek. But knowing him, he had to be close behind.

Taking Rand's glue from my pack, I stripped leaves off the tree. When I had enough, I removed my shirt and glued the leaves onto it. Feeling self-conscious in just my sleeveless undershirt, I worked fast.

I covered the shirt, then my pants, boots and backpack with leaves. Finally, I glued a large leaf onto my hair and two smaller ones onto the backs of my hands, leaving my fingers free to move. Rand's warning that the glue only held for a week passed through my mind, and I smiled as I envisioned his reaction when he saw me walking around the castle with leaves attached to my head and hands.

I didn't have a mirror, but I hoped I had camouflaged my entire body in green and brown. I wasn't concerned with the small black patches that might show through; it was the bright red of my uniform shirt that would immediately give me away.

Too nervous to stay in one place for long, I continued to climb east as fast and quiet as I could. My eastern direction wandered. Since I was unwilling to let my scent touch the ground, I had to detour either north or south on occasion. My grappling hook and rope were employed many times as I used them to bring branches within reach, or to swing from tree to tree. My muscles protested the abuse, but I ignored them. Laughing to myself whenever I overcame a difficult hurdle, I enjoyed the pure freedom of traveling above the ground. I grinned as I sweated through the entire morning. Eventually I knew I would have to head south again because that was the only place a fugitive could find safety and asylum.

Sitia welcomed the refugees from Ixia. Their government had

had an open relationship with the King, trading exotic spices, fabrics and foods for metals, precious stones and coal. When the Commander ceased trade, Ixia lost mainly luxury items while Sitia's resources became limited. Worry that Sitia would try to conquer the north for needed resources had dissipated when the Sitian geologists discovered that their Emerald Mountains, a continuation of the northern Soul Mountains, were rich in ores and minerals. Now, it seemed, Sitia was content to keep a wary eye on the north.

Soon my climb through the trees intersected a well-used path in the forest. I saw deep wagon ruts in the hard-packed dirt. The road was probably a part of the main east–west trading route, which turned north for a few miles to detour around Lake Keyra before resuming its easterly direction. The lake was just over the border of MD–5.

Settling on a sturdy branch within sight of the path, I leaned back on the tree's trunk, rested and ate my lunch while deciding where to go next. After a while, the soothing noises from the forest almost lulled me to sleep.

"See anything?" A male voice beneath me disrupted the quiet.

Startled, I grabbed the branch to keep from falling. Caught, I froze in shock.

"No. All clear," another man's voice replied from a distance. His tone was rough with annoyance.

There had been no barking to alert me; it must be the other team. I had been so worried about the dogs that I had forgotten about the smaller team. Too cocky, I thought. I deserved to be caught early.

I waited for them to order me down, but they remained quiet. Looking below, I searched the forest but couldn't locate them. Maybe they hadn't seen me after all. After a bit of rustling, two men emerged from the dense underbrush. They, too, wore green and brown camouflage, although their snug overalls and face paint were more professional than my glued-together ensemble.

"Stupid idea, coming east. She's probably at the southern border by now," Rough Voice grumbled to his partner.

"That's what the dog boys figured, even though the hounds lost her scent," said the second man.

I smiled. I'd outsmarted the dogs. At least I had managed to accomplish that much.

"I don't know if I follow the logic of going east," Rough Voice said.

The other man sighed. "You're not supposed to follow the logic. The Captain ordered us east; we go east. He seems to think she'll head deeper into MD–5. Familiar territory for her."

"Well, what if she doesn't come back? Another stupid idea, using the food taster," Rough Voice complained. "She's a criminal."

"That's not our concern. That's Valek's problem. I'm sure if she got away he would take care of her."

I wondered if Valek was listening. We both knew he wouldn't need to hunt me down; all he had to do was wait the poison out. I found the conversation helpful, especially the fact that it wasn't common knowledge that I'd been poisoned.

"Let's go. We're supposed to rendezvous with the Captain at the lake. Oh, and try to keep the noise down. You sound like a panicked moose crashing through the woods," the smarter man chided.

"Oh yeah. Like you could hear me over your specially trained 'woodland-animal footsteps,'" Rough Voice countered. "It was like listening to two deer humping each other."

The men laughed and in a wink disappeared into the underbrush, one on each side of the path. I strained to hear them moving but couldn't tell if they were gone. I waited until I couldn't bear the inactivity. The men had decided my next move. The lake was to the east. Climbing through the trees, I headed south.

As I worked my way along, an odd, creepy feeling burrowed its way into my mind. Somehow I became convinced that the men I had seen on the path were following me, hunting me. An uncontrollable urge to move fast pushed on me like a strong hand on the back of my neck, propelling me forward. When I couldn't stand it any longer, I threw all precautions of keeping hidden and quiet aside. I dropped to the ground and bolted.

When I burst into a small clearing in the trees, I stopped. The overpowering feeling of panic had disappeared. My sides stitched with pain. Dropping my pack, I collapsed onto the ground, gasping for breath. I cursed myself for such panicky behavior.

"Nice outfit," a familiar voice said. Dread and fear gave me the energy to jump to my feet.

No one in sight. Yet. I ripped open my backpack and pulled the knife. My heart performed somersaults in my chest. I turned in slow circles as I scanned the forest, searching for the voice of death.

15

LAUGHTER SURROUNDED ME. "Your weapon won't do you any good. I could easily convince you that it was your heart you want to plunge that knife into instead of mine."

I spotted her across the clearing. Clad in a loose, green camouflage shirt cinched tight at the waist and identical colored pants, the southern magician lounged against a tree with her arms crossed in front of her, her posture casual.

Expecting the southern magician's goons to attack me from the forest, I kept the knife out in front of me, turning in circles.

"Relax," the magician said. "We're alone."

I stopped circling but retained a firm grip on my weapon. "Why should I trust you? Last time we met, you ordered me killed. Even supplied that handy little strap." The sudden realization that she hadn't needed her thugs at all leaped into my mind. I began reciting poison names in my head.

The magician laughed like someone amused by a small child. "That won't help you. The only reason reciting worked at the festival was because Valek was there."

She stepped closer. I waved the knife in a threatening gesture.

"Yelena, relax. I projected into your mind to guide you here. If I wanted you dead, I would have pushed you from the trees. Accidents are less trouble than murders in Ixia. A fact you're well aware of."

I ignored her jibe. "Why didn't I have an 'accident' at the festival? Or at another time?"

"I need to be close to you. It takes a lot of energy to kill someone; I'd rather use mundane methods if possible. The festival was the first time I could get close to you without Valek nearby, or so I thought." She shook her head in frustration.

"Why didn't you kill Valek with your magic at the festival?" I asked. "Then I would have been easy prey."

"Magic doesn't work on Valek. He's resistant to its effects."

Before I could ask for more information, she hurried on. "I don't have time to explain everything. Valek will be here soon so I'll make this brief. Yelena, I'm here to make you an offer."

I remembered my last offer, to be the food taster or to be executed. "What could you possibly offer me? I have a job, color-coordinated uniforms and a boss to die for. What more could I need?"

"Asylum in Sitia," she said, her tone tight. "So you can learn to control and use your power."

"Power?" The word squeaked out of my mouth before I could stop it. "What power?"

"Oh, come on! How could you not know? You've used it at least twice at the castle."

My mind whirled. She was talking about my survival instinct. That strange buzzing that possessed me whenever my life was in serious jeopardy. My body numbed with dread. I felt as if she had just told me I had a terminal disease.

"I was working undercover nearby when I was overcome by your screaming, raw power. Once I was able to pinpoint the source to Commander Ambrose's food taster, I knew a rescue effort to smuggle you south would be impossible. You're either with Valek, or he's been one step behind you. Even now, I'm taking an extraordinary risk. But it's too dangerous to have a wild magician in the north. It's amazing you lasted this long without being discovered. The only choice left was termination. A task that proved more difficult than I'd first imagined. But not impossible."

"And now I'm supposed to trust you? Do you think I'd meekly follow you to Sitia like a lamb to the slaughter?"

"Yelena, if you weren't playing fugitive, which brought you out of the castle and away from Valek, you'd be dead by now."

I wasn't sure if I believed her. What would she gain by helping me? Why go to all this effort if she had the power to kill me? Something else must be motivating her.

"You don't believe me." She grunted in frustration. "Okay, how about a little demonstration?" She tilted her head to the side and pressed her lips together.

A searing, hot pain whipped through my mind like lightning. Wrapping my arms and hands around my head, I tried in vain to block the onslaught. Then a fist-size force slammed into my forehead. I jolted backward and fell to the ground. Sprawled on my back, I felt the pain disappear as fast as it had arrived. Through vision blurred with tears, I squinted at the magician. She still stood near the edge of the clearing. She hadn't touched me, at least not physically. The weight of her mental connection felt like a wool cap encompassing my skull.

"What the hell was that?" I demanded. "What happened to the singing?" I was dazed by her attack, the air on my body feeling as if it had liquefied, and when I moved to a sitting position the dense air swirled and lapped at my skin.

"I sang at the festival because I was trying to be kind. This was an effort to convince you that if I wanted you dead, I wouldn't be wasting my time talking to you now. And I certainly wouldn't wait until you were in Sitia." Her head cocked as if she listened to an invisible person whispering in her ear.

"Valek has dropped all pretense of stealth. He's traveling fast. Two men pursue him, but the men believe they're chasing you." She paused and her mouth settled once again into a hard line as she concentrated. "I can slow the men down, but not Valek." She focused her faraway gaze on me. "Are you coming with me?"

I couldn't speak. The thought that her idea of kindness was singing someone to death had left me quite distracted. I stared at her in complete astonishment.

"No." I had to force the word out.

"What?" It wasn't the answer she'd expected. "You enjoy being the food taster?"

"No, I don't, but I'll die if I go with you."

"You'll die if you stay."

"I'll take my chances." I stood, brushed the dirt off my legs and retrieved my knife. The last thing I wanted to do was explain to the magician about the poison in my blood. Why give her another weapon to be used against me? But with her mental link to me, I only had to think about the Butterfly's Dust and she knew.

"There are antidotes," she said.

"Can you find one before morning?" I asked.

She shook her head. "No. We would need more time. Our healers would need to understand where the poison is hiding. It could be in your blood, or in your muscles or anywhere, and they would need to know how it kills in order to banish it."

When she saw my complete lack of understanding, the magician continued, "The source of our power—what you call magic—is like a blanket surrounding the world. Our minds tap into this source, pulling a slender thread down to enhance our magical abilities, to turn them on. Every person has the latent ability to read minds and influence the physical world without touching it, but they don't have the ability to connect with the power source."

She sighed, looking unhappy. "Yelena, we can't have your wild power flaring uncontrolled. Without knowing it, you're pulling power. Instead of a thread, you're grabbing whole sections and bunching the power blanket around you. As you grow older you will have amassed so much power that it will explode or flame out. This flameout will not only kill you, it will warp and damage the power source itself, ripping a hole in the blanket. We can't risk a flameout and soon you'll be untrainable. That is why we have no choice but to terminate you before you reach that point."

"How long do I have?" I asked.

"One year. Maybe a little more if you can control yourself. After that you'll be beyond our help. And we need you, Yelena. Powerful magicians are scarce in Sitia."

My mind raced over my options. Her display of power had convinced me she was more of a threat than I had ever imagined and that I would be a complete idiot to trust her at all. However, if I didn't go, she'd kill me where I stood.

So I delayed the inevitable. "Give me a year. A year to find a permanent antidote, to find a way to escape to Sitia. A year free from worrying that you're plotting my death."

She stared deep into my eyes. Her mental touch pressed harder in my mind as she searched for a sign that I might be deceiving her.

"All right. One year. My pledge to you." She paused.

"Go on," I said. "I know you want to end this meeting with some kind of threat. Maybe a dire warning? Feel free. I'm used to it. I wouldn't know how to deal with a conversation that didn't include one."

"You put on such a brave front. But I know if I took another step toward you, you'd wet your pants."

"With your blood." I brandished my knife. But I couldn't keep a straight face; the boast sounded ridiculous even to my own ears. I snickered. She laughed. The release of tension made me giddy, and soon I was laughing and crying.

The magician then grew sober. Cocking her head again, she listened to her invisible companion. "Valek is close. I must go."

"Tell me one more thing."

"What?"

"How did you know I'd be the fugitive? Magic?"

"No. I have sources of information that I'm unable to reveal."

I nodded my understanding. Asking for details had been worth a try.

"Be careful, Yelena," she said, vanishing into the forest.

I realized that I didn't even know her name.

"Irys," she whispered in my mind, and then her mental touch withdrew.

As I thought about everything she had told me, I realized I had many more questions to ask her, all more important than who had leaked information. Knowing she was gone, though, I suppressed the desire to call after her. Instead, I dropped to the ground.

With my body shaking, I replaced my knife in the backpack. I pulled out my water bottle and took a long drink, wishing the container was filled with something stronger. Something that would burn my throat on its way down. Something to focus on besides the disjointed and lost feeling that threatened to consume me.

I needed time to think before Valek and the two men caught up with me. Taking out the rope and grappling hook, I searched once again for a suitable tree and reentered the forest canopy. Moving south, I let the physical effort of climbing keep my body busy while I sorted through all the information the magician had given me.

When I reached another path in the forest, I found a comfortable position on a tree branch within sight of the trail. I secured myself to the trunk of the tree with my rope. The magician had promised me one year, but I didn't want to tempt her with an easy target. She could change her mind; after all, what did I know about magicians and their pledges?

She claimed I had power. Magical power that I had always thought of as my survival instinct. When I had been in those dire situations, I had felt possessed. As if someone else more capable of dealing with the crisis took temporary control over my body, rescued me from death and then left.

Could the strange buzzing sound that erupted from my throat and saved my life really be the same as Irys's power? If so, I must keep my magic a secret. And I had to gain some control of the power to keep it from flaming out. But how? Avoid life-threatening situations. I scoffed at the notion of evading trouble. Trouble seemed to find me regardless of my efforts. Orphaned. Tortured. Poisoned. Cursed with magic. The list grew longer by the day.

I didn't have the time to resolve these complex issues that circled without end in my mind. Focusing my thoughts on the present, I studied the trail below. Small saplings threatened to retake the narrow forest path; it must have been one of the abandoned roadways used to trade with Sitia.

I waited for Valek. He would demand an explanation about my encounter with the magician, and I was ready to give one.

My only warning of Valek's arrival was a gentle rustling of the branch above mine. I looked up to see him uncoiling from the upper branch like a snake. He dropped soundlessly beside me.

Green camouflage seemed to be the outfit of choice today. Valek's was skintight and came equipped with a hood to cover his hair and neck. Brown and green paint streaked his face, causing the bright blue of his eyes to stand out in stark contrast.

I looked down at my own ragtag outfit. Some of the leaves had frayed at the edges, and my uniform had sustained many tears from climbing through the trees. Next time I planned to flee through the woods, I'd persuade Dilana to sew me an outfit like Valek's.

"You're unbelievable," Valek said.

"Is that good or bad?"

"Good. I assumed you would give the soldiers a good chase, and you did. But I never expected this." Valek pointed at my leaf-covered shirt and swept his arms wide, indicating the trees. "And to top it all off, you encountered the magician and somehow managed to survive." Sarcasm tinged Valek's voice during his last comment.

His way of asking for an explanation, I supposed.

"I don't know what exactly happened. I found myself tearing through the woods until I reached a clearing, where she was waiting. The only thing she told me was that I had ruined her plans by killing Reyad, and then pain slammed into my skull." The memory of her attack was still fresh in my mind, so I allowed the full horror of it to show on my face. If Valek ever suspected what had really happened, I wouldn't live the year the magician had granted me. And mentioning Reyad's name supported one of Valek's theories about why the magician was after me.

I took a deep breath. "I started reciting poisons. I tried to push the pain away. Then the attack stopped, and she said you were getting too close. When I opened my eyes she had disappeared."

"Why didn't you wait for me in the clearing?"

"I didn't know where she had gone. I felt safer in the trees, knowing you'd be able to find me."

Valek considered my explanation. I covered my nervousness by sorting through my backpack.

After a long while, he grinned. "We certainly proved the Commander wrong. He thought you'd be caught by midmorning."

I smiled with relief. Taking advantage of his good mood, I asked, "Why does the Commander hate magicians so much?"

The pleased expression dropped from Valek's face. "He has many reasons. They were the King's colleagues. Aberrations of nature, who used their power for purely selfish and greedy reasons. They amassed wealth and jewels, curing the sick only if the dying's family could pay their exorbitant fee. The King's magicians played mind games with everyone, taking delight in causing havoc. The Commander wants nothing to do with them."

Curious, I pushed on. "What about using them for his purposes?"

"He thinks magicians are not to be trusted, but I'm of two minds about that," Valek said. He gazed out over the forest floor as he talked. "I understand the Commander's concern, killing all the King's magicians was a good strategy, but I think the younger generation born with power could be recruited for our intelligence network. We disagree on this issue, and despite my arguments the Commander has—" Valek stopped. He seemed reluctant to continue.

"Has what?"

"Ordered that those born with even the slightest amount of magical power be killed immediately."

I had known about the execution of the southern spies and the magicians from the King's era, but imagining babies being ripped from their mother's arms made me gasp in horror. "Those poor children."

"It's brutal, but not that brutal," Valek said. A sadness had softened his eyes. "The ability to connect with the power source doesn't occur until after puberty, which is around age sixteen. It usually takes another year for someone other than their family to notice and report them. Then, they either escape to Sitia, or I find them."

His words had the weight of a wooden beam pressing down on my shoulders. I found it difficult to breathe. Sixteen was when Brazell had recruited me. When my survival instinct had started to flare, defending against Brazell and Reyad's torture. Had they been trying to test me for magic? But why didn't they report me? Why hadn't Valek come?

I had no idea what Brazell wanted. And knowing now about my power only added yet another way I could die. If Valek discovered my magic, I was dead. If I didn't find a way to go to Sitia, I was dead. If someone poisoned the Commander's food,

I was dead. If Brazell built his factory and sought revenge for his son, I was dead. Dead, dead, dead and dead. Death by Butterfly's Dust was beginning to look attractive. It was the only scenario where I would get to choose when, where and how I died.

I would have sunk into a deep, brooding bout of self-pity, but Valek grabbed my arm and put a finger to his green lips.

The distant sounds of hoofbeats and men talking reached my ears. My first thought was that it was an illusion sent by the magician. But soon enough, I saw mules pulling wagons. The width of the wagons filled the entire path, saplings and bushes thwacked against the wheels. Two mules pulled one wagon, and one man dressed in a brown trader's uniform led the team. There were six wagons and six men who conversed among themselves as they traveled.

From my post in the tree, I could see that the first five wagons were loaded with burlap sacks that might have been filled with grain or flour. The last wagon held strange, oval-shaped yellow pods.

Snake Forest was just bustling with activity today, I thought in wonder. All we needed was the fire dancers to jump from the trees to entertain us all.

Valek and I sat still in our tree as the men passed below us. Their uniforms were soaked with sweat, and I noticed a few of them had rolled up their pants so they wouldn't trip. One man's belt was cinched tight, causing the extra material to bunch around his waist, while another's stomach threatened to rip through his buttons. These poor traders obviously didn't have a permanent residence. If they had, their seamstress would never have permitted them to walk around looking like that.

When they were out of sight and hearing range, Valek whispered, "Don't move, I'll be back." He dropped to the ground and followed the caravan.

I fidgeted on my branch, wondering if the other two men Irys had said were tracking Valek would find me before he returned. The sun was disappearing in the west, and cooler air was replacing the day's heat. Muscles stiff from inactivity throbbed as the last of my energy faded. The strenuous day of climbing caught up to me. For the first time the possibility of spending a night alone in the forest made me apprehensive; I had never imagined staying free this long.

At last, Valek returned and waved me down from the tree. I moved with care, fumbling with the rope around my waist as my abused muscles trembled with fatigue.

He carried a small sack, which he handed to me. Inside were five of the yellow pods that had been stacked in the last wagon. I took one out. Now that I could see it up close, I noticed that the elongated, oval pod was about eight inches in length, with close to ten furrows running from one end to the other. It was thick around the middle. With two hands wrapped around its center, my fingers just overlapped.

I was amazed by Valek's ability to steal them in the daylight from a moving wagon. "How did you get these?"

"Trade secret," Valek said with a grin. "Getting the pods was easy, but I had to wait for the men to water their mules to look in the burlap sacks."

When I slid the pod back in with the others, I saw that in the bottom of the sack was a pile of dark brown pebbles. Reaching deeper, I pulled a handful into the waning light. They looked like beans.

"What's this?" I asked.

"They're from the sacks," he explained. "I want you to take these back to Commander Ambrose. Tell him I don't know what they are or where they came from and I'm following the caravan to see where they're going."

"Are they doing something illegal?"

"I'm not sure. If these pods and beans are from Sitia, then yes. It's illegal to trade with the south. One thing I do know, those men aren't traders."

I was about to ask him how he knew this, when the answer clicked in my mind. "Their uniforms don't fit. Borrowed maybe? Or stolen?"

"Most likely stolen. If you're going to borrow a uniform, I would think you'd find one that fits." Valek was quiet for a moment, listening to the sounds of the forest. I could hear the droning of the insects grow louder as the sun set.

"Yelena, I want you to find those two men you saw this afternoon, and have them escort you back to the castle. I don't want you alone. If the magician plans on attacking you again, she'll have to deal with two more, and I doubt she'd have the energy. Don't tell anyone about your tree climbing, the magician or the caravan. But give a complete report about everything to the Commander."

"What about my antidote?"

"The Commander keeps a supply handy. He'll give it to you. And don't worry about your incentive. You've earned every penny. When I get back, I'll make sure you get it. Now, I need to keep moving or I'll spend the rest of the night catching up to the caravan."

"Valek, wait," I demanded. For the second time today someone wanted to disappear before explaining everything to my satisfaction, and I was growing weary of it.

He stopped.

"How do I find the others?" Without the sun, my sense of direction failed. I wasn't sure if I could find my way back to the clearing, much less to the castle on my own.

"Just follow this path." He pointed in the direction the wagons had come from. "I managed to shake them off my tail before I caught up with you. The soldiers were heading southwest; they're probably staking out this trail. Technically, that's the best strategy."

Valek jogged away along the path. I watched him go. He moved with the light grace and speed of a deer, his muscles rippling under his formfitting camouflage.

When he was out of sight, I crunched my feet on the loose stones of the trail, making noise. Twilight robbed the trees of color as darkness descended. Uneasiness settled over me. Every rustle caused my heart to jump, and I found myself peering over my shoulder, wishing Valek was here.

A shout pierced the air. Before I could react, a large shape rushed me, tackling me to the ground.

16

"GOT YOU!" SAID THE MAN sitting on top of me.

Even with my face pressed into the stones, and my mouth full of dirt, I recognized his rough voice from earlier in the day. He yanked my arms behind me. I felt cold metal bite into my wrists as I heard the snap and clink of manacles.

"Isn't that a bit much, Janco?" asked Janco's partner.

Janco moved off me, and I was hauled to my feet. In the semidarkness, I saw the man that held me was thin, with a goatee. He wore his dark hair buzzed in the typical military style. A thick scar ran from his right temple to his ear. The lower half of his right ear was missing.

"She was too damn hard to find. I don't want her getting away," Janco grumbled.

His companion was about the same height but twice as wide. Thick, sculpted muscles bulged through his camouflage uniform. Small, damp curls clung to his head, and from this distance his eyes held no color except the black of his pupils.

I wanted to flee. It was almost dark; I was manacled and alone with two strange men. Logically, I knew that these were the Commander's soldiers, and they were professionals, but that didn't stop my pulse from racing.

"You made us look bad," Janco said. "Every soldier out here is probably going to be reassigned. We'll all be cleaning out latrines 'cause of you."

"That's enough, Janco," Colorless Eyes said. "*We* won't be scrubbing floors. We found her. And take a look at that getup. No one expected her to go camo, that's why she was so hard to find. But, still, the Captain's gonna shit when he sees this!"

"And the Captain's back at the castle?" I asked, trying to prompt them in that direction.

"No. He's leading a line farther southwest. We'll have to report to him."

I sighed at the delay. I had hoped for a quick trip back. "How about you send Janco here to find the Captain, while we head to the castle?"

"Sorry, but we're not permitted to split up. We're required to travel in pairs, no exceptions."

"Um…" Janco started.

"Yelena," I supplied.

"Why are you so anxious to get back?" he asked.

"I'm afraid of the dark."

Colorless Eyes laughed. "Somehow I doubt that. Janco,

take the cuffs off her. She's not going to run away. That's not the point of this exercise."

Janco hesitated.

I said, "You have my word, Janco. I won't run if you take off the manacles."

He grumbled some more but unlocked the cuffs. I wiped the dirt from my face. "Thanks."

He nodded, and then pointed to his partner. "He's Ardenus."

"Ari, for short." Ari extended his hand, giving me an honor. If a soldier offered his hand, he was acknowledging me as an equal.

I shook it gravely, and then the three of us headed southwest to find their Captain.

The trip to the castle was almost comical. Almost. If my stiff and sore muscles hadn't protested my every step, and if the bone-deep ache of pure exhaustion hadn't pulled at my body like a stone cloak, I would have been amused.

Janco and Ari's Captain fumed and blustered when we caught up with him. "Well, well, well. Look at what our two sweethearts finally found," Captain Parffet said. His bald head was beaded with sweat that rolled down the sides of his face, soaking his collar. He was old for a Captain, and I wondered if his surly disposition was the reason for his lack of promotion.

"I'm *supposed* to have the best scouts in Commander Ambrose's guard," Parffet shouted at Ari and Janco. "Maybe you can enlighten us as to which procedure you followed that took you over seventeen hours to find the bitch!" Parffet continued his verbal bashing. Even in the darkness I could see his face turning purple.

I tuned him out and studied his unit. A couple of faces smirked, agreeing with their Captain, some were resigned, as if used to his tantrums, and others wore bored and tired expressions. One man, who had shaved his entire head except for his bangs, stared with an uncomfortable intensity at me. When I made eye contact, he jerked his glance to the Captain.

"Nix, put the bitch in manacles," Parffet ordered, and the man with the bangs pulled metal cuffs off his belt. "I see our two prima donnas can't be bothered to follow this unit's standard procedures."

As Nix approached, I searched for a chance to slip away. My promise to Janco had only extended to a "hands free" trip back to the castle. Ari, sensing my frame of mind, placed a large hand on my shoulder, anchoring me to his side.

"We have her word, sir, that she won't run off," he said in my defense.

"Like that means anything." Parffet spat on the ground.

"She has given her word," Ari repeated. A low rumble in his voice reminded me of a huge dog growling a warning.

Parffet grudgingly allowed procedure to be modified, but savored his bad temper by harassing the rest of his soldiers into formation, initiating a fast march back to the castle.

I walked wedged between Ari and Janco like some prized trophy. Ari explained that the Captain didn't handle surprises well, and had been frustrated by my daylong romp in the forest.

"It doesn't help that we found you. He didn't promote us to his unit like the others. We were assigned by Valek," Janco said.

Parffet's mood turned blacker when the dog team overtook our procession. Chaos erupted as barking dogs and more guards tangled together. I experienced a moment of panic when the canines rushed me. As it turned out, they greeted me with wagging tails and licking tongues. Their pure joy was infectious. I smiled, and scratched their ears, stopping only when Parffet scowled and shouted for order.

The dogs wore no collars. The kennel master was part of the tracking team. The dogs reassembled on Porter's command, following his orders without fail. The commander of the dog team seemed disappointed that Porter's dogs hadn't found me first, but she took it with better grace than Ari's Captain had. She introduced herself as Captain Etta and walked beside me to ask questions about my "run." I liked her easy, respectful manner. Her mop of dark blond hair pushed the limits of military regulation.

I stuck to the truth as much as I could during our conversation. When it came to questions regarding where my scent had disappeared, I lied. I explained that I had walked northward in the water for a while before heading east.

Etta shook her head. "We were so focused on you heading south. Parffet was right to look east."

"My eventual destination was south, but I wanted to try and confuse the dogs before I turned."

"You succeeded. The Commander won't be pleased. Good thing Ari and Janco found you. Had you stayed out till morning, both teams would have been demoted."

The last two miles to the castle were a blur. Using every ounce of my dwindling energy to keep my feet moving forward, I concentrated all my strength on keeping up with the soldiers. When we stopped, it took me a moment to realize that we had entered the castle complex.

It was well past midnight. The noise of our arrival bounced and amplified off the silent stone walls. The dogs followed Porter to the kennels while the weary parade of soldiers trod up the steps toward the Commander's office. We finished our march among the empty desks of the throne room.

Lantern light blazed from the open door of the Commander's office. The two soldiers standing guard wore amused expressions, but remained quiet and still. Parffet and Etta shared a look of resignation before going in to report to the Commander. I found a chair and collapsed into it, accepting the risk that I might have difficulties regaining my feet.

Soon the Captains returned. Parffet's face was creased in a dark frown, but Etta's showed no emotion. They dismissed their units. I was summoning the energy to stand, when Etta came over and helped me to my feet.

"Thanks," I said.

"The Commander awaits your report."

I nodded. Etta left to rejoin her unit, and I headed toward the office. I hesitated in the doorway; I was used to the semi-darkness of the throne room, and the lantern light stung my eyes.

"Come in," Commander Ambrose ordered.

I stood before his desk. He sat immobile and impassive as always, his smooth, ethereal face barren of wrinkles. A stray thought plucked at my mind, and I wondered about his age. Gray streaks painted the Commander's short hair. His rank alone suggested an older man, but his slight build and youthful face made me guess his age was closer to forty. About seven years older than Valek, if my estimation of Valek's age was accurate.

"Report."

I described my actions for the day in detail, including my tree swinging and the magician. Giving the same version of my encounter with the southerner that I had told Valek, I concluded my report with the caravan and Valek's orders that I return. I waited for the Commander's questions.

"So Ari and Janco didn't capture you?" he asked.

"No. But they were the only ones who even came close. They passed right below a tree I hid in, and were skilled enough to track Valek for a while."

The Commander stilled for a moment. His golden eyes looked past me as he absorbed the information. "Where are the items Valek procured?"

I opened my backpack, and placed the pods and beans on his desk.

He picked up a yellow pod and rotated it in his hands before returning it. Grabbing a handful of beans, he hefted them, feeling their weight and texture. After sniffing one, he broke the bean in half. The inside was as unrevealing as the outside had been.

"They're not native to Ixia. They must be from Sitia. Yelena, take them with you and do some research. Find out what these are and where they're grown."

"Me?" Stunned, I had expected to dump them on the Commander and forget about them.

"Yes. Valek is constantly reminding me not to underestimate you, and once again you've proven yourself. General Brazell gave you a good education. I'd hate to see it go to waste."

I wanted to argue, but I was curtly dismissed. Sighing, I dragged my unwilling body to the baths. Painfully peeling off my leaf-covered clothes, I washed the mud from my face and neck before submerging into a steaming pool.

There, I luxuriated in the warmth, stretching my aching muscles under the hot water to loosen them. Hoping to dissolve some of the glue from my hair, I dipped my head back, pulled my bun apart and let the long black strands float on the surface. The gentle sounds of lapping lulled me.

Strong hands grabbed my shoulders. I jerked awake under the water. Liquid filled my mouth and nose. I pushed the hands away in a panic. They released their grip for a second. I began to sink. Instinctively, I clutched my unknown assailant's arms. Before I could curse my stupidity, I was yanked out of the bath and dumped onto the cold floor.

I sprang to my feet to meet the next assault. But there stood Margg with a disgusted expression anchored on her broad face. Water dripped from her hands and had soaked her sleeves. I shivered and pulled wet clumps of hair off my face.

"What the hell do you think you're doing?" I yelled.

"Saving your worthless life," she snarled.

"What?"

"Don't worry. I took no pleasure in it. Frankly, I would have rejoiced to see you drown. Justice finally served! But the Commander ordered me to find you and see to your needs." Margg grabbed a towel from the table and threw it at me. "You may have the Commander and Valek fooled into thinking you're smart. But how smart can you be to fall asleep in a deep pool of water?"

I tried to think of a rude retort, remembering Dilana's advice to be nasty right back. Nothing. My brain felt waterlogged with fatigue. The idea that Margg had just saved my life kept sloshing around in my head. It was such a foreign concept that I couldn't find a proper place to dock it.

Margg snorted, hatred oozing from her. "I followed my orders. Some might even agree that rescuing you was beyond the call of duty. So don't you forget it, rat."

She spun around to leave. Her skirts wrapped around her legs, and she stumbled through the door. So much for a dramatic exit, I thought as I toweled dry.

I felt no gratitude toward Margg for saving my life—assuming that was what she'd done. She might have pushed me under in spite, then "saved" me. And I didn't owe her a favor. She had left me in a puddle of my own vomit after I had taken My Love, had refused to clean out my room in Valek's suite, had written me a nasty message in the dust, and even worse, was probably leaking information about me to Brazell. If she had saved me from drowning, then, in my mind, it was a payback for some of those indiscretions, but not for all. As I saw it, she still owed me.

The hot soak helped restore some flexibility to my muscles.

I peeled the leaves from my hands. Although green still clung to parts of my hair, I thought with some artful braiding I might be able to hide it.

The walk back to Valek's suite seemed endless. In a zombie-like state of mind, I passed through countless hallways, intersections and doorways. My steps were fueled by the single-minded desire of getting to bed.

For the next few days I fell into a routine. I tasted the Commander's meals, went to the library for research and took a daily walk around the castle complex. My day as a fugitive had caused me to crave the outdoors, and if I couldn't swing through the trees, at least I could explore the grounds.

I used the map of the castle that I had copied in my journal to find the library. It was a multilevel suite of rooms, burgeoning with books. The smell of decay and dust floated in the air along with a sense of abandonment. I was saddened by the knowledge that this tremendous source of information was going to waste because the Commander discouraged his people from educating themselves beyond what was necessary for their jobs.

Within his military structure, a person was trained specifically for their position only. Learning just for the sake of learning was frowned on, and greeted with suspicion.

Once I had ascertained that the library was truly a forgotten place, I brought the pods and beans there instead of carrying the heavy books back to my room. I found a small nook tucked away in a corner. The nook had a wooden table which faced one of the large, egg-shaped windows that randomly perforated the back wall of the library. Sunlight streamed into the nook and, after clearing the table of dust, it became my work area.

Cutting one of the yellow pods in half, I discovered it was filled with a white mucilaginous pulp. A taste of the pulp revealed it to have a sweet and citrus flavor with a taint of sour, as if it was starting to rot. The white flesh contained seeds. I cleaned the pulp from the seeds and uncovered thirty-six of them. They resembled the beans from the caravan. My excitement diminished as I compared seed against bean in the sunlight. The pod seed was purple instead of brown, and when I bit into the seed, I spit it out as a strong bitter and astringent taste filled my mouth. Nothing close to the slightly tart and earthy taste of the brown beans.

Assuming that the pods were a fruit and the beans edible, I pulled out every botany book I could find in the library and piled them on my table. Then I went through the shelves again. This time, I grabbed any volume with information about poisons. A much smaller stack; Valek had probably taken the interesting ones back to his office. My third trip through the shelves was an effort to find books on magic. Nothing.

I paused by an empty shelf, an oddity in this tightly packed library, and wondered if it had contained manuals about magic. Considering how the Commander viewed magic, it was logical to destroy any pertinent information. On a whim, I explored the lower levels of the bookcase under the empty shelf. Thinking that a book from the empty shelf could have slid back behind the other books, I took out all the texts on the lower shelves.

My efforts were rewarded by the discovery of a slim volume entitled *Magical Power Sources.* I hugged the book to my chest as paranoia gripped me. Scanning the library, I made sure no one was there. With sweaty palms, I hid the book in my backpack. I planned to read it later, preferably in my room with the door locked.

Giddy with my illicit acquisition, I searched the various rooms of the library until I found a comfortable chair. Before dragging it back to my nook, I beat the dust from its purple velvet cushions. It was the most elegant seat I had seen in the castle, and I wondered who had used it before me. Had the dead King been a bibliophile? The considerable collection of books said as much. Either that or he had shown his librarian great favor.

I spent many hours in that chair reading through the botany books and discovering nothing. I planned to decipher the pod and bean puzzle while I researched information for myself. The tedious work was at least broken into small sessions by my tasting the Commander's meals and by my afternoon strolls around the castle.

It had been four days since the exercise, and that afternoon my walk had a purpose. I scouted for a place with a view of the east gate, but where I wouldn't be obvious to the flow of people passing through.

Valek still hadn't returned from his mission, and closing ceremonies had been performed the night before at the fire festival, ending the weeklong celebration. Rand, looking hungover, had informed me this morning that Brazell and his retinue would finally leave the castle, via the east gate, to go home. My desire to see Brazell's retreating back with my own eyes had driven me to seek the perfect position.

The barracks for the Commander's soldiers filled both the northeast and southwest corners of the castle complex. In the northeast barracks, the L-shaped building extended from the north gate to the east gate, and a large rectangular training area had been built next to the east leg of the building. There was a wooden fence around the yard and, when training was in progress, the fence attracted the castle's various residents to stop along it to watch the exercises. That afternoon I joined in with a group of observers, who not only had a clear view of the fighting drills, but the east gate as well.

Rand's information proved accurate. Soon I was rewarded by a parade of green-and-black–clad soldiers. I could see Brazell on his dappled mare, riding among his most trusted advisers, at the end of the procession. Brazell's retinue ignored the people around them.

As I watched Brazell's back, Reyad's ghost appeared next to me. He smiled as he waved goodbye to his father. A shudder vibrated down my spine. I glanced around. Did anyone else see him? The group of people that I had been standing with had dispersed. Had Reyad scared them off? But when I looked again, his ghost was gone.

A hand touched my arm. I flinched.

"Good riddance to that lot," Ari said, tilting his head toward the east gate. Seeing him for the first time in the sunlight, I noticed that Ari's eyes were such a pale blue that in the darkness his eyes had seemed to hold no color.

Ari stood with Janco on the other side of the fence. Both wore the sleeveless shirts and short pants that the soldiers liked to train in. Sweat-soaked and streaked with dirt, their faces and bodies sported new cuts and bruises.

"Bet you're as glad as we are to see them go," Janco said. Resting his wooden training sword on the fence, he rubbed the sweat off his face with the bottom of his shirt.

"Yes, I am," I said.

Looking toward the east gate, the three of us stood in companionable silence for a moment, watching Brazell's entourage disappear through the gate.

"We want to thank you, Yelena," Ari said.

"What for?"

"The Commander promoted us to Captains. He said you gave us a good report," Janco said.

Surprised and pleased that the Commander would heed my words, I smiled at them. I could see Ari and Janco shared a loyalty to one another, an obvious bond of friendship and trust. Three years ago, I had felt that kind of kinship with May and Carra at the orphanage, but Reyad had torn me away, and the empty space inside me still ached. Rand had given me friendship, but there was still a distance. I longed to connect with someone. Unfortunately, my life as the food taster made it impossible. Who would take the risk of connecting with me when my odds of living through the next year were little to none?

"We're scouting for the Commander's elite guard now," Janco said with pride in his voice.

"We owe you one. Anytime you need help, just let us know," Ari said.

His words gave me a bold idea. Brazell might be gone, but he was still a threat. I thought fast, searching for reasons why my plan wouldn't be to my benefit.

"I need help," I said.

Surprise flashed over their faces. Ari recovered first. "With what?" he asked warily.

"I need to learn how to defend myself. Can you teach me self-defense and how to use a weapon?" I held my breath. Was I asking too much? If they said no, I hadn't lost anything. At least I had tried.

Ari and Janco looked at each other. Eyebrows twitched, heads tilted, lips pursed and hands made small movements. I watched their silent conversation in amazement as they discussed my request.

"What kind of weapon?" Ari asked. Again that hesitation evident in his voice.

My mind raced. I needed something that was small enough to hide within my uniform. "A knife," I said, knowing I'd have to return Rand's to the kitchen.

More facial expressions were exchanged. I thought Ari might be agreeing, but Janco looked queasy, as if the idea didn't sit well with him.

Finally, I couldn't take it anymore. "Look," I said. "I'll understand if you refuse. I don't want to get you into trouble, and I know how Janco feels about me. I believe his exact words were: 'She's a criminal.' So, if the answer is no, that's fine with me."

They stared at me in astonishment.

"How did you—" Janco started to say, but Ari punched him on the arm.

"She overheard us in the forest, you dope. How close were you?"

"Fifteen feet."

"Damn." Ari shook his head, which caused his tight blond curls to bounce. "We're more worried about Valek. We'll train you if he doesn't object. Agreed?"

"Agreed."

Ari and I shook hands. When I turned to Janco, he seemed deep in thought.

"A switchblade!" he declared, grabbing my hand.

"What?" I asked.

"A switchblade would be better than a knife," Janco said.

"And where would I carry this…switchblade?"

"Strapped to your thigh. You cut a hole in your pants pocket. Then if you're attacked, you pull it out, hit the switch, and a nine-inch blade leaps to your disposal." Janco demonstrated the motion to me and mock stabbed Ari, who clutched his stomach dramatically and fell over.

Perfect, I thought. Thrilled by the idea of learning to defend myself, I asked, "When do we start?"

Janco scratched his goatee. "Since Valek isn't back we could start with some basic self-defense moves, nothing objection-able about that."

"Moves she could have learned by watching the soldiers train," Ari said, agreeing with his partner.

They decided. "Right now," they said in unison.

17

STANDING NEXT TO THE two oversize soldiers, I felt like a plum wedged between a couple of cantaloupes. Misgivings crept into my mind. The notion that I could defend myself against someone of Ari's build seemed ridiculous. If he wanted, he could pick me up and throw me over his shoulder, and there was nothing I could do about it.

"Okay. First, we'll start with some self-defense," Ari explained. "No weapons until the basic moves are instinctive. You're better off fighting hand to hand than wielding a weapon you don't know how to use. A skilled opponent would simply disarm you. Then your troubles would be doubled. Not only would you be under attack, but you'd have to counter your own weapon."

Ari leaned his practice sword next to Janco's, scanning the training yard. Most of the soldiers were gone, but small clumps of men still worked.

"What are your strengths?" Ari asked.

"Strengths?"

"What are you good at?"

Janco, sensing my confusion, prompted, "Are you a fast runner? That's a handy skill."

"Oh." I finally understood. "I'm flexible. I used to be an acrobat."

"Perfect. Coordination and agility are excellent skills. And…" Ari grabbed me around the waist. He threw me high into the air.

My limbs flailed a moment before instinct kicked in. Still in midair, I tucked my chin, arms and legs close to my body, executed a somersault to align myself, and landed on my feet, wobbling to regain my balance.

Outraged, I turned on Ari. Before I could demand an explanation, he said, "Another advantage of having acrobatic training is the ability to stay on your feet. That maneuver of yours could mean the difference between life and death. Right, Janco?"

Janco rubbed the vacant spot where the lower half of his right ear used to be. "It helps. You know who else would make a great fighter?"

Ari's shoulders sagged, as if he knew what Janco was going to say next and resigned himself to it.

Intrigued, I asked, "Who?"

"A dancer. With the proper training, the fire dancers at the festival could take on anyone. With a blazing staff spinning around, I wouldn't go against one with *any* weapon."

"Except a pail of water," Ari countered.

He and Janco then launched into an intense argument, debating the technical aspects of a fight against a fiery staff wielded by an enraged dancer. Although fascinated by the discussion, I had to interrupt them. My time was limited. The Commander's dinner would soon be served.

With only occasional sarcastic comments about fire dancers, Ari and Janco spent the remainder of my first lesson teaching me to block punches, then kicks, until my forearms were numb.

Ari halted the exercise when another soldier approached. His and Janco's relaxed postures tightened. They shifted to defensive stances, as Nix, the guard from Captain Parffet's unit, came closer. The skin on Nix's bald head was sunburned, and his thin fringe of black hair lay damply on his forehead. An overpowering stench of body odor preceded him, gagging me. His lean muscles reminded me of a slender coil of rope, dangerous when pulled tight.

"What the hell do you think you're doing?" Nix demanded.

"That's—what the hell do you think you're doing, *sir?*" Janco corrected him. "We outrank you. And, I think a salute would be a nice touch."

Nix sneered. "You'll lose your promotion when your boss finds out you're associating with a criminal. Whose brainless idea was it to make her into a more effective killer? When another dead body shows up, you'll be accomplices."

Janco took a menacing step toward Nix, but Ari's meaty hand on his shoulder stopped him. With undertones of a threat laced into his voice, Ari said, "What we do with our free time is none of your business. Now, why don't you shuffle off to Parffet. I saw him heading toward the latrines. He'll need you to wipe his ass soon. It's the one skill you're most suited for."

Nix was outnumbered, but he couldn't resist a parting shot. "She has a history of killing her benefactor. I'd watch my necks if I were you."

Ari's and Janco's eyes stayed on Nix's back until he left the yard. Then they turned to me.

"That's a good start," Ari said, ending the lesson. "See you tomorrow at dawn."

"What about Nix?" I asked.

"No problem. We can take care of him." Ari shrugged it off, confident in his ability to deal with Nix. I envied Ari's self-assurance and physical power. I didn't think I could handle Nix, and I wondered if there was another reason, besides killing Reyad, that made Nix hate me.

"I taste the Commander's breakfast at dawn," I said.

"Then right after."

"What for?" I asked.

"The soldiers run laps around the compound to keep in shape," Janco answered.

"Join them," Ari said. "Do at least five circuits. More if you're able. We'll increase the amount until you've caught up to us."

"How many laps do you run?"

"Fifty."

I gulped. As I returned to the castle, I thought of the work and time I would need to devote to training. Learning self-defense would require the same commitment I had applied to my acrobatics. I couldn't go halfway. It had seemed like a good idea at the time. I had been giddy with fairy-tale visions of easily fighting off Brazell's guards. But the more I thought about it, the more I realized this wasn't something to do on a whim.

I wondered if I would be better off spending my time learning about poisons and magic. In the end, all the physical training in the world wouldn't save me from Irys's magical powers.

My feet dragged on the ground, and my body felt as if it were pulling a wagon full of stones. Why couldn't I just go for it? Why was I constantly considering each option, searching both sides of an argument for gaps in the logic? Like somer-saulting on the trampoline, plenty of ups and downs but no forward motion. I longed for the days when a wrong decision wouldn't cost me my life.

By the time I reached the Commander's office, I had con-cluded that I had other enemies besides the magician, and being able to defend myself might save my life someday. Knowledge, whatever the form, could be as effective as a weapon.

Soon after I arrived, one of the tutors bustled into the office, dragging a young girl with him. At age twelve every child was assigned a profession based on their capabilities, and then they were sent to the appropriate tutor for four years to learn.

The tutor's red uniform had black diamonds stitched on the collar, making it the direct opposite of an adviser's black uniform. The girl wore the simple red jumper of a student. Her brown eyes were shiny with unshed tears. Her facial expressions alternated between terror and defiance as she battled to compose herself. I guessed she was about fifteen years old.

"What's the problem, Beevan?" the Commander asked, annoyance tainting his voice.

"This disobedient child is a constant disruption to my class."

"In what way?"

"Mia is a know-it-all. She refuses to solve mathematical problems in the traditional manner and has the gall to correct me in front of the entire class."

"Why are you here?"

"I want her disciplined. Whipped, preferably, and reassigned as a servant."

Beevan's request caused silent tears to spill down Mia's cheeks, although she maintained her composure, which was impressive for someone so young.

The Commander steepled his fingers, considering. I cringed for the girl, having her tutor bother the Commander for this dispute would not help her. Beevan must have gone over the training coordinator.

"I'll handle it," the Commander finally said. "You're dismissed."

Beevan wavered for a moment, opening and closing his mouth several times. His pinched expression revealed that this was not the response he had expected. Nodding stiffly, he left the office.

The Commander pushed his chair away from the desk and gestured to Mia to come around. Now eye level with her, he asked, "What's your side of the story?"

With a thin quavering voice, she answered, "I'm good with numbers, Sir." She hesitated as if expecting to be corrected for making a bold statement, but, when none came, she continued, "I was bored solving mathematical problems Tutor Beevan's way, so I invented new and faster ways. He's not good with numbers, Sir." Again she stopped, flinching as though she was anticipating a blow. "I made the mistake of pointing out his errors. I'm sorry, Sir. Please don't whip me, Sir. I'll never do it again, Sir. I'll follow Tutor Beevan's every command." Tears flowed down her bright pink cheeks.

"No, you won't," the Commander replied.

Terror gripped the girl's face.

"Relax, child. Yelena?"

Startled, I spilled some of his tea. I had been holding his tray. "Yes, Sir."

"Fetch Adviser Watts."

"Yes, Sir." I put the tray on the desk and hurried through the door. I had met Watts once. He was the Commander's accountant, who had given me the money I had earned playing fugitive. He was working at his desk, but immediately followed me back to the office.

"Watts, do you still need an assistant?" the Commander asked.

"Yes, Sir," Watts replied.

"Mia, you have one day to prove yourself. If you don't dazzle Adviser Watts with your mathematical skills, then you'll have to return to Beevan's class. If you do, then you can have the job. Agreed?"

"Yes, Sir. Thank you, Sir." Mia's pretty face was radiant as she trailed behind Watts.

I marveled at the Commander. Being compassionate, hearing Mia's side of the story, and giving her a chance, were the exact opposite of how I imagined the encounter would play out. Why would a man with such power take the time to go that extra step? He risked upsetting Beevan and the coordinator. Why would he bother to encourage a student?

His stack of reports reclaimed the Commander's attention, so I slipped out the door, heading toward the library to continue my research.

After a while, the sun began to set. I picked out a promising botany book to take with me as I was reluctant to have a lantern light betray my presence in the library.

The candlelight cast a dismal glow in the corridors. I watched my shadow glide along the walls as I headed for Valek's suite, wondering if I should move back to my old room in the servants' wing. Now that Brazell was gone, there was no logical reason for me to remain with Valek. But the thought of living in that small room, where I wouldn't have anyone to argue with or to discuss poisoning methods with, left a hollow feeling inside me. That same empty pang I'd been having on and off these last four days.

Only the cold darkness greeted me when I entered Valek's suite. My disappointment surprised me, and I realized I had been missing him. I shook my head at the foreign concept. Me? Miss Valek? No. I couldn't allow myself to think that way.

Instead, I focused on my survival. If I wanted to discover an antidote to Butterfly's Dust, paging through books on counteracting poisons while sitting in Valek's living room wouldn't be the smartest idea. Of course, the decision might not be mine to make. Once Valek found out Brazell had gone, he'd probably order me to move back anyway.

After I had lit the lanterns in Valek's suite, I relaxed on the couch with the botany book. Biology had never been a favorite subject of mine, and I soon found my mind wandering. My weak efforts to remain focused were lost to my daydreams.

A muffled slam brought my attention back to the present. It sounded like a book hitting the floor. I glanced down, but my volume remained in my lap, opened to a particularly boring passage about fruit trees. I scanned the living room to see if one of Valek's untidy piles of books had fallen over. Sighing at his mess, I couldn't tell if something had toppled or not.

A frightening thought crept into my mind. Maybe the noise had come from upstairs. Maybe it hadn't been a book but a person. Someone sneaking in to wait until I fell asleep to kill me. Unable to sit still, I grabbed a lantern and dashed into my room.

My backpack rested on the bureau. Rand hadn't asked for his knife yet, so I hadn't returned it. Pulling the blade from the pack, Ari's words about misusing a weapon flew through my mind. It was probably foolish to take the knife, but I felt more confident with it in my hand. Armed, I returned to the living room and considered my next move. Sleep would be impossible tonight until I investigated the upstairs rooms.

Blackness from above pressed down on my meager light as I ascended the staircase. Curving to the right, the stairs ended in a sitting room. Piles of boxes, books and furniture were scattered throughout the room in a haphazard fashion, casting odd-shaped shadows on the walls. I maneuvered with caution around the heaps. My blood slammed in my heart as I shone my lantern into dark corners, searching for an ambush.

A flash of light caused a yip to escape my lips. I spun, only to discover it was my own lantern reflecting in the tall thin windows that striped the far wall.

Three rooms were located to the right of the sitting chamber. A quick heart-pumping check of the box-filled rooms revealed they were empty of ambushers and identical to the three off the downstairs living area.

To the left of the upstairs sitting area was a long hallway. Doorways lined the right side of the corridor opposite a smooth stone wall. The hall ended in a set of locked double wooden doors. Carved into the ebony wood was an elaborate hunting scene. By the thin coating of white powder on the floor beneath the doors, I guessed this was the entrance to Valek's bedroom. The powder would show footprints, alerting Valek to an intruder. I breathed easier seeing the powder undisturbed.

As I systematically checked the remaining rooms along the corridor, the growing realization that Valek was a true pack rat struck me. I had always imagined assassins as creatures of the dark, traveling light and never staying in one place for too long. Valek's suite resembled the house of an old married couple who had filled their rooms with all the things they had collected over the years.

Distracted by these thoughts, I opened the last doorway. It took me some time to properly register what I saw. Compared to the others, the room was barren. One long table lined the back wall, centered under a large, teardrop-shaped window. Gray rocks streaked with white—the same stones I had been tripping over in Valek's living room and office for the past month and a half—were arranged by size on the floor.

A thick layer of dust scrunched under my boots when I walked into the room. On the table, carving chisels, metal sanding files and a grinding wheel occupied the only dust-free spots. Small statues in various stages of creation were interspersed among the tools. To my delight, I realized that the gray rocks, when carved and polished, metamorphosed into a beautiful, lustrous black, and the white streaks transformed into brilliant silver.

Setting the lantern on the table, I picked up a finished butterfly with silver spots sparkling from its wings. It fit into the palm of my hand. The detail was so exquisite that it appeared the butterfly might beat its wings and lift into the air at any moment. I admired the other statues. The same devoted care had been applied to each. Lifelike animals, insects and flowers lined the table; apparently, nature provided the artist's favorite subjects.

Stunned, I realized Valek must be the artist. Here was a side of Valek I never imagined existed. I felt as though I had intruded upon his most personal secret. As if I had uncovered a wife and children living up here in happy seclusion, complete with the family dog.

I had noticed the figurines on Valek's desk and, at least once a day, I glanced at the snow cat in the Commander's office, attempting to understand why he had selected that particular statue for display. I now understood its significance. Valek had carved it for the Commander.

The shuffle of feet made me whirl around. A black shape rushed me. My knife was yanked from my grasp and pressed against my neck. Fear clenched my throat tight, suffocating me. The familiar feeling triggered a sudden flashback of soldiers disarming and dragging me off Reyad's dead body. But Valek's face showed mirth instead of wrath.

"Snooping?" Valek asked, stepping back.

With effort, I banished my fear and remembered to start breathing again. "I heard a noise. I came to…"

"Investigate." Valek finished my sentence. "Searching for an intruder is different from examining statues." He pointed with the knife to the butterfly clutched in my hand. "You were snooping."

"Yes."

"Good. Curiosity is a commendable trait. I wondered when you would explore up here. Find anything interesting?"

I held up the butterfly. "It's beautiful."

He shrugged. "Carving focuses my mind."

I placed the statue on the table, my hand lingering over it. I would have enjoyed studying the butterfly in the sunlight. Grabbing the lantern, I followed Valek from the room.

"I really did hear a noise," I said.

"I know. I knocked a book over to see what you would

do. I didn't expect a knife, though. Is it the one missing from the kitchen?"

"Did Rand report it?" I felt betrayed. Why hadn't he just asked for it back?

"No. It just makes sense to keep track of large kitchen knives, so when one goes missing you're not surprised when someone attacks you with it." Valek handed the knife back. "You should return it. Knives won't help you against the caliber of people after you."

Valek and I descended the stairs. I lifted the botany book from the couch.

"What does the Commander think of the pods?" Valek asked.

"He thinks they're from Sitia. He returned them to me so I could discover what they are. I've been doing research in the library." I showed Valek the book.

He took it from me and flipped through the pages. "Find anything?"

"Not yet."

"Your actions as our fugitive must have impressed the Commander. Normally, he would have assigned this sort of thing to one of his science advisers."

Valek's words made me uncomfortable. I wasn't convinced that I could discover the origin of the pods and beans. The idea of failing the Commander made me queasy. I changed the subject. "Where did the caravan go?"

Valek paused, undecided. Finally, he said, "Brazell's new factory." If Valek had been surprised by his discovery, it didn't show on his face.

It occurred to me that despite all the discussion about Brazell's permit, I didn't know what he was planning to make. "What's the product?"

"It's supposed to be a feed mill." Valek handed the book back to me. "And I don't know why he would need those pods and beans. Maybe they're a secret ingredient. Maybe they're added to the feed to enhance the cow's milk supply. Then every farmer would buy Brazell's feed instead of growing his own. Or something along that line. Or maybe not. I'm not an expert." Valek pulled at his hair. "I'll have to study his permit to see what I'm missing. Either way, I assigned some of my corps to stake out the route and infiltrate the factory. At this point I need more information."

"Brazell left the castle this afternoon."

"I passed his retinue on my way back. Good. One less thing to worry about."

Valek crossed to his desk and began sorting through his papers. I watched his back for a while, waiting. He didn't mention my moving out. I finally worked up the nerve to ask. "Should I return to my old room now that Brazell's gone?" I berated myself for my choice of words. I should have been firmer, but it was too late.

Valek stopped. I held my breath.

"No," he said. "You're still in danger. The magician hasn't been dealt with yet." His pen resumed its course over the paper.

Strong relief flushed through my body like a hot wave, alarming me. Why did I want to stay with him? Remaining was dangerous, illogical, and, by every argument I could muster, the worst situation for me. The book on magic was still hidden in my backpack, which went with me everywhere because I feared Valek would pull one of his stunts and surprise me.

Damn it, I thought, angry at myself. As if I didn't have enough to worry about. I shouldn't miss Valek; I should try harder to escape. I shouldn't figure out the bean puzzle; I should sabotage it. I shouldn't admire and respect him; I should vilify him. Shouldn't, should, shouldn't, should. So easy to say but so hard to believe.

"Exactly how do you deal with a magician?" I asked.

He turned around in his seat and looked at me. "I've told you before."

"But their powers…"

"Have no effect on me. When I get close, I can feel their power pressing and vibrating on my skin, and moving toward them is like walking through thick syrup. It takes effort, but I always win in the end. Always."

"How close?" Valek had been in the castle both times I had unknowingly used magic. Did Valek suspect?

"I have to be in the same room," Valek said.

Relief washed through me. He didn't know. At least, not yet. "Why didn't you kill the southern magician at the festival?" I asked.

"Yelena, I'm not invincible. Fighting four men while she threw every ounce of her power at me was exhausting. Chasing her down would have been a fruitless endeavor."

I thought about what he said. "Is being resistant to magic a form of magic?" I asked.

"No." Valek's face hardened.

"What about the knife?" I pointed to the long blade hanging on the wall. The crimson blood gleamed in the lantern light. In the three weeks I'd lived in Valek's suite, it hadn't dried.

Valek laughed. "That was the knife I used to kill the King. *He* was a magician. When his magic couldn't stop me from plunging that knife into his heart, he cursed me with his dying breath. It was rather melodramatic. He willed that I should be plagued with guilt over his murder and have his blood stain my hands forever. With my peculiar immunity to magic, the curse attached to the knife instead of me." Valek looked at the weapons wall thoughtfully. "It was a shame to lose my favorite blade, but it does make for a nice trophy."

18

MY LUNGS BLAZED. Flushed and sweat-soaked, I lagged behind the main group of soldiers, my throat burning with every gasp. It was my fourth lap around the castle complex. One more to go.

I had hovered by the northeast barracks right after tasting the Commander's breakfast. When a large clump of soldiers ran past, I spotted Ari, who waved me to join in. I worried that the other guards would resent my presence, but there were servants, stable boys and other castle workers mixed in with the soldiers.

The first two laps quickened my pulse and shortened my breath. Pain began in my feet during the third lap and traveled up my legs by the fourth. My surroundings blurred until all I saw was the small patch of ground right in front of me. When I limped to my finishing point, ending my agony, I found a thick row of hedges and threw up my breakfast of sweet cakes. Straightening, I saw a grinning Janco give me a thumbs-up as he jogged by. He didn't even have the decency to look winded, and his shirt was still dry.

As I wiped vomit off my lip, Ari paused beside me. "Training yard, two o'clock. See you then," he said.

"But…" I said to nobody as Ari jogged away. I could hardly stand, I couldn't imagine doing anything more strenuous.

In the training yard that afternoon, Ari and Janco leaned against the fence watching two men sparring with swords. The loud ring of metal striking metal echoed. The fighters had drawn the attention of every soldier. I realized with surprise that one of the men was Valek. I hadn't seen him since early that morning, and I had assumed he was resting after being up late the night before.

Valek was liquid in motion. As I watched him, one word came to my mind: beautiful. His movements had the speed and cadence of a complex dance performance. In comparison, his adversary resembled a newborn colt, lurching and jerking his arms and legs as if this were his first time on his feet. Valek's smooth lunges and graceful parries disarmed his opponent in no time.

Pointing with his sword, he sent his beaten foe to a small group of men, and motioned for another to attack.

"What's going on?" I asked.

"Valek's challenge," Janco said.

"What's that?"

"Valek has declared a challenge to anyone in Ixia. Beat him in a fight with the weapon of your choice, or hand to hand,

and you can be promoted to his second-in-command." Ari gestured to Valek, now engaged in combat with a third man. "It's become a sort of graduation from basic training for the soldiers to fight Valek at least once, although you can try as many times as you like. The Captains watch the matches and recruit the more promising soldiers. And if you manage to impress Valek with your skills, he may offer you a post in his elite intelligence corps."

"How did you guys do?" I asked.

"Okay," Ari demurred.

"Okay!" Janco snorted. "Ari came close to beating him. Valek was pleased. But Ari would rather be a scout than a spy."

"I want all or nothing," Ari said with a quiet intensity.

We continued to watch. Ari and Janco made technical comments about the different fights, but I couldn't tear my eyes from Valek. With the sunlight glinting off his sword, he dispatched two more men. He tapped them with the flat of his weapon, just to let them know he had broken through their defenses without shedding any blood. The next opponent approached with a knife.

"Bad choice," Ari said.

Valek put down his sword and unsheathed his blade. The match was over in two moves.

"Valek excels in knife fighting," Janco commented.

The last challenger was a woman. Tall and agile, she wielded a long wooden staff. Ari called it a bow. She held her own against Valek, and their sparring lasted longer than any of the previous six fights. With a loud crack, her bow snapped in two, ending the match. As the crowd dispersed, Valek spoke with the woman.

"That's Maren," Ari said. "If she doesn't disappear into Valek's corps, you should ask her to teach you the bow. With your smaller size, it would extend your reach against a taller attacker."

"But you can't conceal a bow," I said.

"Not around the castle. But if you're hiking through the woods, you wouldn't look out of place holding a walking stick."

I looked at Maren and considered the possibilities. Would she agree to help me? Probably not. What would she stand to gain?

As if reading my thoughts, Ari said, "Maren's aggressive and encouraging. Every new female recruit gets her personal attention whether they want it or not. Since so many women fail due to the rigors of training, she tries to coach them through. We've more women in the guard now than ever because of her. We tried to get her to teach us—a bow would make a good weapon for a scout—but she has no interest in training men."

"But I'm not a new recruit, I'm the food taster. Why would she waste her time with me? I might be dead by tomorrow."

"Aren't we grumpy today," Janco said cheerfully. "Too much exercise this morning?"

"Shut up," I said. Unfazed, his grin only widened.

"All right, that's enough. Let's get started," Ari said.

I spent the rest of the afternoon learning to punch someone without breaking my hand and practicing the proper technique of kicking. The first two knuckles of both hands turned bright red as I punched into a training bag over and over. Mastering the front kick was a challenge since my stiff thigh muscles hindered my flexibility.

When Ari finally dismissed me, I aimed my battered body toward the castle.

"See you in the morning," Janco said with a gleeful sound in his voice.

I turned to tell him where to stick it and came face-to-face with Valek. I held my breath. He had been watching us. I felt self-conscious.

"Your punches are slow," he said. Taking my hand, he examined the bruises, which were starting to purple. "At least your technique is good. If you hold weights in your hands while you train, your punches will be much quicker without them."

"I can continue?" I asked in disbelief.

He still held on to my hand, and I couldn't summon the will-power to pull it back. The warmth of his touch coursed through my body, temporarily vanquishing my aches and pains.

With the memory of his stunning physical display fresh in my mind, I gazed at his strong face. His flashing and dangerous blue eyes had always taken my attention. I had learned to read his facial expressions as a survival tactic but I had never really looked at him in this way before. He was a study in contradiction. The man who carved delicate statues was also capable of disarming seven opponents without breaking a sweat. My interactions with Valek resembled a performance on the tightrope. One minute I was confident and balanced, and the next insecure and unstable.

"I think it's an excellent idea," he said. "How did you get the power twins to agree to teach you?"

"Power twins?"

"Combine Ari's strength with Janco's speed, and they would be unbeatable. But, so far, I haven't had to test my theory since they haven't tried to fight me together. No one said I couldn't have more than one second-in-command. You're not going to give me away, are you?"

"No."

Valek gave my hand a small squeeze, and then released his grip. "Good. They're probably the best instructors at the castle. How did you meet them?"

"They were the men who found me in the forest. The Commander promoted them, and I took advantage of their gratitude." My hand tingled where he had touched it.

"Opportunistic and underhanded, I love it." Valek laughed. He was in a good mood as he walked beside me to the castle. Probably a rush from beating so many opponents. Before we reached the east entrance, he stopped. "There's one problem."

My heartbeat increased to double time. "What?"

"You shouldn't train so visibly. Word spreads quickly. If Brazell finds out and makes a fuss, the Commander will order you to stop. And it'll make the Commander suspicious."

We entered the cool, dark air of the castle. It was a relief to be out of the hot sun.

"Why don't you make use of all those empty storerooms in the lower level of the castle? You can still run laps in the morning for exercise," Valek said.

Great, I thought sarcastically, jogging was the one aspect of training I would have been willing to give up. However,

Valek was right, working with Ari and Janco in the middle of the yard had already attracted negative attention. Mainly Nix, whose scowls and nasty glares burned on my skin.

Valek was quiet as we traveled through the castle. I was headed to the Commander's office to taste his dinner. He walked with me.

"Mentioning Brazell reminds me that I've been wanting to ask you about that Criollo that the Commander enjoys. Do you like the taste of it?"

I chose my words with care. "Yes, it's an excellent dessert."

"If you stopped eating it, how would you feel?"

"Well…" I hesitated, unsure where this conversation was leading. "Truthfully, I would be disappointed. I look forward to eating a piece every morning."

"Have you ever craved the Criollo?" Valek inquired.

I finally understood where his pointed questions were leading. "Like an addiction?"

He nodded.

"I don't think so, but…"

"But what?"

"I only eat it once a day. The Commander has a piece after every meal, including his evening snack. Why this sudden concern?" I asked.

"Just a feeling. It might be nothing." Valek was silent during the rest of the trip.

"Well, Valek, any new promotions?" the Commander asked as we entered his office.

"No. But Maren shows promise. Unfortunately she doesn't

want to be in my corps or even be my second. She just wants to beat me." Valek grinned, delighted by the challenge.

"And can she?" the Commander inquired. His eyebrows rose.

"With time and the proper training. She's deadly with her bow; it's just her tactics that need work."

"Then what do we do with her?"

"Promote her to General and retire some of those old windbags. We could use some fresh blood in the upper ranks."

"Valek, you never had a good grasp of military structure."

"Then promote her to First Lieutenant today, Captain tomorrow, Major the next day, Colonel the day after, and General the day after that."

"I'll take it under advisement." The Commander flashed me an annoyed glance. I was dawdling, and he had noticed.

"Anything else?" he asked Valek.

I finished tasting, placed the Commander's tray on the desk, and headed for the door.

Valek grabbed my arm. "I'd like to try an experiment. I want Yelena to taste the Criollo every time you do for a week, then the next week I'll taste it for you. I want to see if anything happens to her when she stops eating the dessert."

"No." The Commander raised a hand when Valek started to argue. "I recognize your concern, but I think it's misplaced."

"Humor me."

"We can try your experiment once Rand duplicates the recipe from General Brazell. Acceptable?"

"Yes, Sir."

"Good. I want you to join me in a meeting with General

Kitvivan. We're just starting the cooling season, and he's already worried about snow cats." The Commander's eyes found me. "Yelena, you're dismissed."

"Yes, Sir," I said.

After stopping at the baths to wash, I visited the kitchen to borrow a large sieve and bowl, which I carried to the library. The remaining four pods had turned brown and were starting to rot, so I opened them, scraped out the browning pulp and seeds into the colander, and placed it into the bowl. Its bottom and sides were suspended above the inside of the bowl by the metal handles. The strong odor from the seeds permeated the room. I set the bowl on the windowsill, and opened the window to air out the smell. My experiment wasn't based on any scientific research; I just wanted to see if the pulp would ferment. Maybe Brazell was using it to make some kind of alcoholic beverage.

My careful reading of the various botany books hadn't revealed anything useful so far. The poison books, while interesting, had made no mention of Butterfly's Dust. In four different volumes on poisons, I had discovered missing pages. Poking up from the binding were ragged edges where the paper had been ripped out. Valek had probably removed all pertinent information long ago in anticipation of the food tasters' keen interest in Butterfly's Dust.

Sighing, I piled the books at the end of my table. I knew Valek was attending the Commander's meeting, so I slid the book of magic out of my backpack. The silver lettering of the title glinted. My stomach knotted.

Opening the slim volume, I began to read a technical discussion of the source of a magician's power. Unable to understand all of the detailed descriptions, I only sensed that the power source blanketed the entire world, making it accessible from anywhere.

The magicians used this power in different ways, depending on their talents. Some could move objects, while others could read and influence minds. Healing, lighting fires and mental communication were also magical skills. Some could only do one thing, but the stronger the magician, the more the magician could do. A weaker magician could only read someone's mind, while a more powerful one could not only read but communicate and even control someone's mind. I shuddered at the thought of Irys controlling my mind.

But the magicians had to be careful when drawing power. By pulling on the source too hard or misusing it, a magician could cause creases that would set off a ripple effect. This effect, or warping, would concentrate power in certain areas and leave other places bare. Fluctuating unpredictably, another wave might reverse the amount of power available. In order to tap the power, the magicians would have to seek areas of power, but once they found a pocket, they wouldn't know how long it would remain.

The book chronicled a time when a strong magician had tapped into the source, pulling it toward him. Because he was so powerful he was able to control the blanket without causing an explosion. The other magicians were then uncovered. Stripped of their power, they united and searched for him.

Once found, and after a battle that left many dead, they tapped into his stolen source, and killed him. Eventually, the blanket had smoothed out and returned to normal, but that had taken over two hundred years.

Fingering the raised lettering on the cover, I now understood why Irys had been so determined that I should either be trained or be killed. When my magic reached a flameout, it would cause major ripples in the blanket of power. I sank deep into my chair, disappointed that the book hadn't contained magic spells or lessons. I had been hoping for an answer. Something along the lines of: this is why you have the power, here's how you use it, and while we're at it, this is how to conjure up the antidote to Butterfly's Dust.

It had been wishful thinking, plain and simple, dangerous for me to indulge in. Hope, happiness and freedom were not in my future. They had never been, not even as an ignorant child in Brazell's orphanage. While hoping for a normal life, I had been raised as a laboratory rat for his experiments.

I slumped in my chair until the sun set, allowing self-pity to run its course. When the muscles in my legs began to throb with inactivity, I stood and physically shook off my gloom. If I couldn't find the antidote in the books, I would find it another way. Someone had to know something. There had been food tasters on Commander Ambrose's staff for fifteen years. If no one could help me, then I would try another way, perhaps stealing the antidote or following Valek to its source. Skills I lacked, but I was determined to learn.

★ ★ ★

The next morning, prepared with an empty stomach, I joined in the flow of jogging soldiers. Ari and Janco breezed past me. Janco flashed a jaunty wave and mischievous smile. Later, when I heard heavy steps pounding behind me, I assumed Janco was up to no good.

I moved aside to let him pass, but the runner stayed close on my heels. I glanced back in time to see Nix thrust his arms out. His hands connected with my back. I fell forward, crashing to the ground. As Nix ran over me, his boot slammed into my solar plexus, knocking the wind out of me.

Pain bloomed in my chest. I gasped for breath while curled in a fetal position on the ground. Once I regained my wind, I pushed myself to a sitting position. The flow of soldiers remained unabated, and I wondered if anyone had witnessed what that bastard had done.

If he was trying to discourage me, he was going about it the wrong way. Nix had just increased my resolve to learn self-defense so I didn't fall victim to mongrels like him. I stood up and waited for Nix's next circuit, but he never came back.

Ari stopped. "What happened?"

"Nothing." Nix, like Margg, was my problem. If I didn't deal with him, he would never leave me alone. A tingle of doubt touched my stomach. It had been that kind of thinking that had landed me in the dungeon, awaiting execution.

"Your face is covered with blood," Ari said.

I wiped the blood on my sleeve. "I fell."

Before he could question me further, I changed the subject

by giving him something else to think about. I repeated Valek's advice about concealing our training sessions; Ari agreed that it was prudent to go "underground." He offered to scout out a suitable location.

"You're Maren, right?" I asked between gasps for air. I had been running laps for a week, and this morning I had timed my pace to run beside Maren.

She shot me a quick, appraising glance. Her blond hair was pulled back in a ponytail. Wide muscular shoulders atop a thin waist made her figure appear disproportionate. She moved with athletic ease, and I had to scramble to keep up with her long, loping strides.

"And you're the Puker," Maren said.

It was an insult aimed with a purpose; her interest in my response was keen. If she had wanted to dismiss me, she would have made her comment and sprinted away, not bothering to watch for a reaction.

"I've been called worse."

"Why do you do it?" Maren asked.

"What?"

"Run till you're sick."

"Five circuits were assigned. I don't like to fail." I received another measuring look. With my words coming out as huffs, I knew I wouldn't be able to maintain a conversation for long. "I watched you fight Valek. I've heard you're the best with a bow. I want to learn to use one."

Her pace slowed. "Who told you that?"

"Ari and Janco."

Maren snorted as if she thought a con artist had duped me. "Friends of yours?"

"Yes."

Her mouth formed a small *o* as she made a mental connection. "They found you in the forest. It's rumored they were training you to fight but you quit. Are they foisting you off on me?"

"The problem with rumors—" I panted "—is the difficulty in sorting the truth from the lies."

"And the reason I'm willing to donate my time?"

I had anticipated this question. "Information."

"About what?"

"You want to beat Valek, right?"

Her gray eyes focused on me like two sword points pressing against my skin.

With the last of my breath, I wheezed out, "Come to the east entrance of the castle this afternoon at two and I'll tell you." Unable to keep up with her any longer, I slowed down. She pulled ahead. I lost sight of her in the press of soldiers.

Throughout the rest of the morning, I replayed the conversation in my mind, trying to guess her response as I tasted the Commander's meals. At two o'clock, I waited in the castle's east doorway, chewing on my lip. Ari and Janco had spread a rumor that my training had stopped. I'd taken a considerable risk by indicating to Maren that this might not be true. When I spotted a tall figure carrying two bows heading in my direction, my anxiety eased a little.

Maren paused when she entered the corridor. She spotted me leaning against the wall.

Before she could comment, I said, "Follow me." I led her to a deserted hallway where Janco and Ari waited.

"I guess gossip is not to be trusted," Maren said to Ari.

"No. But there are certain rumors we would like to keep as is." A thinly disguised threat laced Ari's words.

Maren ignored him. "Okay, Puker, what's your information? And it better be good or I'm walking."

Ari's face reddened and I could see that he bit back a remark. Janco, as always, grinned in anticipation.

"Well, as I see it, the four of us can help each other out. Ari, Janco and I want to learn how to fight with the bow. You want to beat Valek. Working together, we may be able to achieve our goals."

"How's my teaching you going to help in a match against Valek?" Maren asked.

"You're skilled with the bow, but your fighting tactics need work. Ari and Janco can help you with that."

"One week of training and the Puker thinks she's an expert," Maren said to Ari with an incredulous voice. He remained mute, but his face darkened.

"I'm not an expert, but Valek is."

She shot me a cold stare. "He said that? About me?"

I nodded.

"So I teach bow, and Ari and Jan teach tactics. What's your contribution?"

I gestured to the four of us. "This. And…" I hesitated,

unsure if my next statement would have any sway. "I could teach you some flips, and help you to gain greater flexibility and balance that might benefit you in a fight."

"Damn." Janco was impressed. "She's got you there. And four does make for a better training group than three."

Annoyed, Maren shifted her focus to Janco. He smiled sweetly at her.

"All right, I'll try it on a temporary basis. If it doesn't work, I'm walking." Before anyone could interject, she said, "Don't worry. I may listen to the rumor mill, but I don't participate in it."

Once we shook hands on the arrangement, my apprehension dissipated. We showed her where we had been meeting for the last week.

"Cozy," Maren said as she entered our training room.

Ari had found an abandoned storeroom on the lower level in the deserted southwest corner of the castle. Two windows near the ceiling let in enough light to work by.

We spent the remaining time practicing the rudiments of bow fighting.

"Not bad, Puker," Maren said at the end of the session. "I see some potential."

When she picked up her bows to leave, Ari placed a large hand on her shoulder. "Her name's Yelena. If you don't want to call her by her name, then don't come back tomorrow."

I could see my astonished expression mirrored on Maren's face, but she recovered quicker than I did. Nodding curtly, she shook off Ari's hand and walked away. I wondered if she would join us again.

She returned the next day, and showed up without fail for the next two months as we trained together throughout the cooling season. The air held a fresh crisp scent, and true to the season's name, each day grew cooler than the last. The bright flowers of the hot season wilted while the trees turned orange, russet and finally brown. The leaves dropped to the ground and were blown away by the frequent rainstorms.

My research on the pods had stalled, but Valek appeared unconcerned by my lack of progress. On occasion he observed us training, and he would comment and make suggestions.

Nix continued to plague me during my morning run. He threw rocks, he spat on me and tripped me. I had to change my routine to avoid him by running laps around the outer wall of the castle complex. My defensive abilities were still in the beginning stages, and not sufficient for a confrontation with Nix. At least, not yet. There were advantages to running outside the complex. The smooth grass was softer on my feet than the dirt path inside the complex, and by jogging before dawn, I encountered no one, which added to the deception that I had quit training.

At the end of the cooling season, the hours of daylight shortened, and our training sessions ended with the setting sun. In the semidarkness of twilight I headed to the baths, moving with care to accommodate my bruised ribs. Janco, that annoying jackrabbit, had gotten through my defenses with his speedy little jabs.

As I approached the entrance to the baths, a large shadow detached from the stone wall. Alarmed, I stepped back into a fighting stance. Fear, excitement and doubt raced through my body. Would I need to defend myself? Could I do it? Should I run?

Margg's ample shape coalesced out of the shadows, and I relaxed a bit.

"What do you want?" I asked. "Are you running another errand for your master like a good doggie?"

"Better than being a rat caught in a trap."

I brushed past her. Exchanging insults, while enjoyable, was a waste of my time.

"Would the rat like some cheese?" she asked.

I turned. "What?"

"Cheese. Money. Gold. I bet you're the kind of rat that would do anything for a piece of cheese."

19

"WHAT WOULD I HAVE TO DO to get a piece of cheese?" I asked. I knew it! Margg was the one leaking information about me, and now she wanted to use me. Finally, some evidence.

"I have a source that pays well for information. It's the perfect setup for a little rat," Margg said.

"What kind of information?"

"Anything you might overhear while you're scurrying around the Commander's office or Valek's apartment. My contact pays on a sliding scale; the juicier the news, the bigger the chunk of cheese."

"How does it work?" My mind raced. Right now it was her word against mine. I needed proof I could show Valek. To be able to finger both Margg and her source would be a sweet treat.

"You give me the information," she said, "and I pass it

along. I collect the money, and give it to you, minus a fifteen percent fee."

"And I'm supposed to believe that you'd stick to fifteen percent cut of a total I'd be unaware of?"

She shrugged. "It's either that or nothing. I'd think that a half-starved rat like you would pounce on any morsel, no matter how small." Margg began to walk away.

"What if we went to your source together?" I suggested. "Then you'd still receive your fee."

She stopped. Uncertainty creased her fleshy face. "I'll have to check." She disappeared down the hallway.

I lingered outside the baths for a while, considering the possibility of following Margg around for a couple of days, but dismissed the idea. If her contact didn't like my suggestion, I'd scamper to Margg with my tail between my legs, begging for another chance. She'd enjoy that! Then I'd follow her. Revealing her as a traitor to Valek would be a pleasure.

My conversation with Margg had used up my bath time, so I headed to the Commander's office. When I arrived, Sammy, Rand's kitchen boy, hovered outside the closed door holding a tray of food. I could hear a muffled angry voice inside.

"What's going on?" I asked Sammy.

"They're arguing," he said.

"Who?"

"The Commander and Valek."

I took the tray of cooling food from Sammy. No reason we both had to be there. "Get going. I'm sure Rand needs you."

Sammy smiled his relief and sprinted through the throne

room. I'd seen the kitchen during dinnertime. Servers and cooks swarmed like bees with Rand directing the chaos. Barking orders, he controlled his kitchen staff like the queen bee of the hive.

Knowing the Commander disliked cold food, I stood close to his door, waiting for a break in the conversation. From my new position I could hear Valek clearly.

"Whatever possessed you to change your successor?" Valek demanded.

The Commander's soft reply passed through the wooden door as an indecipherable murmur.

"In the fifteen years I've known you, you've *never* reversed a decision." Valek's tone became more reasonable. "This isn't a ploy to discover your successor. I just want to know why you changed your mind. Why now?"

The response wasn't to Valek's liking. With a sarcastic jab in his voice, he said, "Always, Sir."

Valek jerked the door open. I stumbled into the office.

He wore a glacial expression. Only his eyes showed his fury. They were pools of molten lava beneath an icy crust. "Yelena, where the hell have you been? The Commander's waiting for his dinner." Not expecting an answer, Valek strode briskly through the throne room. Advisers and soldiers melted from his path.

Valek's anger seemed extreme. Everyone in Ixia knew that one of the eight Generals had been chosen as the Commander's successor. In the typical paranoid custom of the Commander's ruling, the name of the selected General was kept secret. Each General held an envelope that contained a piece of a puzzle. When the Commander died, they would assemble the puzzle to reveal an encrypted message. A key would be required to decipher the note. A key only Valek held. The chosen General would then have the complete support of the military and the Commander's staff.

The theory behind the puzzle was that secrecy would prevent someone from staging a rebellion in support of the chosen heir, since the heir was unknown. The added risk that the inheritor might be even worse than the Commander was another deterrent. As far as I could see, a change in the chosen General probably wouldn't affect day-to-day life in Ixia. We didn't know who had been originally selected, so the switch would have no bearing until the Commander died.

I approached Commander Ambrose's desk. He read his reports, unaffected by Valek's rage. I performed a quick taste of his dinner; he thanked me for the food then ignored me.

On my way back to the baths, I wondered if the information I had just overheard would fetch a decent price from Margg's contact. I quenched my curiosity; I had no desire to commit treason for money. I just wanted to get out of my present situation alive. And knowing Valek, I had no doubt that he would discover any clandestine meetings with Margg. For that reason alone, I had to prove that, no matter what Margg believed, I was not a spy. Just the mental vision of Valek's burning eyes focused on me sent a hot bolt of fear through me.

A long soak in the bath eased my sore ribs. As it was still early in the evening, I thought it prudent to avoid Valek for a while. I stopped in the kitchen for a late dinner. After helping myself to the leftover roast meat and a hunk of bread, I carried my plate to where Rand worked. He had an array of bowls, pots and ingredients messily spread out on his table. Dark smudges rimmed his bloodshot eyes, and his brown hair stuck straight out where he had run his wet hands through it.

I found a stool and a clean corner on Rand's table and ate my dinner.

"Did the Commander send you?" Rand asked.

"No. Why?"

"I finally received the Criollo recipe from Ving two days ago. I thought the Commander might be wondering about it."

"He hasn't said anything to me."

Two large shipments of Criollo, sans the recipe, had arrived for the Commander since Brazell had left the castle. Each time, the Commander had responded with a "thank you" and another request for the formula. As the quantity received had been plentiful, the Commander had given Rand some Criollo to play with. Rand hadn't disappointed. He had melted it, mixed it into hot drinks, invented new desserts, chipped it and remolded it into flowers and other edible decorations for cakes and pies.

I watched Rand stir a mahogany-colored batter with tight agitated movements. "How's it going?" I asked.

"Horrible. I have repeatedly followed this recipe, and all I've gotten is this awful-tasting mud." Rand banged the spoon on the bowl's edge to knock off the pasty residue. "It won't even solidify." He handed me a sheet of once-white paper smeared with brown stains and flour. "Maybe you can see what I'm doing wrong."

I studied the list of ingredients. It looked like a normal recipe, but I wasn't a cooking expert. Tasting, on the other hand, was becoming my forte. I took a scoop of his batter and slid it onto my tongue. A sickeningly sweet flavor invaded my mouth. The texture was smooth and the batter coated my tongue like Criollo, but it lacked the nutty, slightly bitter taste that balanced the sweetness.

"Maybe the recipe's wrong," I said, handing the sheet back to Rand. "Put yourself in Ving's position. Commander Ambrose loves Criollo, and you hold the only copy of the recipe. Would you give it away? Or would you use it to manipulate a transfer?"

Rand plopped wearily onto a stool. "What do I do? If I can't make Criollo, the Commander will probably reassign me. It'll be too much for my ego to stand." He attempted a weak smile.

"Tell the Commander that the recipe's a fake. Blame Ving for your inability to duplicate the Criollo."

Sighing, Rand rubbed his face in his hands. "I can't handle this type of political pressure." He massaged his eyelids with the tips of his long fingers. "Right now, I'd kill for a cup of coffee, but I guess wine will have to do." He rummaged around in the cabinet and produced a bottle and two glasses.

"Coffee?"

"You're too young to remember, but before the takeover, we imported this absolutely wonderful drink from Sitia. When the Commander closed the border, we lost an endless list of luxury items. Of all those, I miss coffee the most."

"What about the black market?" I asked.

Rand laughed. "It's probably available. But there's nowhere in this castle that I could make it without being discovered."

"I'll most likely regret asking you this, but why not?"

"The smell. The coffee's rich and distinct aroma would give me away. The scent of brewing coffee can weave its way throughout the entire castle. I woke up to it every morning before the takeover." Rand sighed again. "My mother's job was to grind the coffee beans and fill the pots with water. It's very similar to brewing tea, but the taste is far superior."

I sat up straighter on my stool when I heard the word *beans*. "What color are coffee beans?"

"Brown. Why?"

"Just curious," I said in a calm tone, but excitement boiled within me. My mystery beans were brown, and Brazell was old enough to know about coffee. Maybe he missed the drink, and planned to manufacture it.

My efforts to ferment the pod's pulp had resulted in a thin chestnut-colored liquid that tasted rotten. The purple seeds inside the pulp had been sopping wet, and covered with flies. I had closed the window and dried the seeds on the windowsill. As they dried, the seeds turned to brown and looked and tasted like the beans from the caravan. Thrilled to link the pods with the beans, my excitement had faded when I hadn't been able to learn anything further.

"Does coffee taste sweet?" I asked.

"No. It's bitter. My mother used to add sugar and milk to half of her finished pots, but I liked it plain."

My beans were bitter. I couldn't sit still any longer; I had to find out if Valek remembered coffee. I felt uncomfortable asking Rand, unsure if Valek wanted him to know about the southern pods.

After bidding farewell to Rand, who stared morosely into the failed batter as he drank his wine, I rushed back to Valek's suite. The sound of slamming books greeted my entrance. Valek stormed around the living room, kicking piles of books over. Gray rock debris littered the floor and clung to impact craters on the walls. He clenched a stone in each fist.

I had wanted to discuss my coffee hypothesis with him, but decided to wait. Unfortunately, Valek spotted me staring. "What do you want?" he snarled.

"Nothing," I mumbled and fled to my room.

For three days, I endured Valek's temper. He vented his ill humor on me at every opportunity. Thrusting the antidote at me, speaking curtly, if at all, and glaring whenever I entered a room. Weary of avoiding him and hiding in my room, I decided to approach him. He sat at his desk, his back to me.

"I may have discovered what those beans are." It was a weak opening. What I really wanted to say was, "What the hell's the matter with you?" But I thought a soft approach more prudent.

He swiveled to face me. The energy of his anger had dissipated, replaced by a bone-chilling cold. "Really?" His voice lacked conviction. The fire in his eyes had extinguished.

I stepped back. His indifference was more frightening than his anger. "I…" I swallowed, my mouth dry. "I was talking to Rand, and he mentioned missing coffee. Do you remember coffee? A southern drink."

"No."

"I think our beans might be coffee. If you don't know what coffee is, perhaps I should show them to Rand. If that's all right with you?" I faltered. My suggestion had sounded like a child pleading for a sweet.

"Go ahead; share your ideas with Rand. Your buddy, your best friend. You're just like him." Icy sarcasm spiked Valek's words.

I was stunned. "What?"

"Do as you like. I don't care." Valek turned his back on me.

I stumbled to my room, and then locked the door with shaky fingers. Leaning against the wall, I replayed the last week in my mind to see if there had been some clue to Valek's withdrawal. I could remember nothing that stood out. We had barely said a word to each other, and I had believed his anger had been directed toward the Commander—until now.

Maybe he had discovered my magic book. Perhaps he suspected I had some magical power. Fear replaced my confusion. Lying on my bed that night, I stared at the door. With every nerve tingling, I waited for Valek's attack. I knew I was overreacting, but I was unable to stop. I couldn't erase the way he had looked at me as if I was already dead.

Dawn arrived, and I moved through my day like a zombie. Valek ignored me. Even Janco's ever-present good humor couldn't snap me out of my funk.

I waited a few days before bringing the beans along to show Rand. He was in better spirits. A big smile graced his face, and he greeted me with an offer of a cinnamon swirl.

"I'm not hungry," I said.

"You haven't eaten in days. What's the matter?" Rand asked.

I dodged his question by asking about the Criollo.

"Your plan worked. I informed the Commander that Ving's recipe was wrong. He said he'd take care of it. Then he inquired about the kitchen staff: were they working well? Did I need more help? I just stared at him because I felt like I was in the wrong room. I'm usually greeted with suspicion and dismissed with a threat."

"That doesn't sound like a good relationship."

Rand stacked a few bowls and straightened a row of spoons. His smile faded. "My interaction with the Commander and Valek could be considered rocky at best. Being rather young and rebellious right after the takeover, I attempted every trick of sabotage possible. I served the Commander sour milk, stale bread, rotten vegetables and even raw meat. At that point, I was just looking to be a nuisance." He picked up a spoon and tapped it against his knee. "It became a battle of wills. The Commander was determined that I cook for him, and I was determined to either be arrested or be reassigned."

Thump, thump, thump went the spoon, and Rand continued his story, his voice husky. "Then Valek made my mother the food taster—that was before they implemented that damn Code of Behavior—I couldn't bear to have her taste the garbage I served the Commander." Old sorrows pulled at Rand's features. He twirled the spoon in circles between his fingers.

Words failed me. Dread crept up my spine as I contemplated the fate of Rand's mother.

"After the inevitable happened, I tried to run away, but they caught me just shy of the southern border." Rand rubbed his left knee. "They shattered my kneecap, hobbling me like some damn horse. Threatened to do my other leg if I ran again. And here I am." He snorted, sweeping all the spoons off the table. They clattered on the stone floor. "Shows you how much I've changed. The Commander's nice to me and I'm happy. I used to dream of poisoning the bastard, of taking that final step in our battle. But I have this weakness of caring for the food taster. When Oscove died, I promised myself never to care again." Rand pulled out a bottle of wine. "Only I failed. Again." He retreated to his rooms.

I hunched over the table, regretting that my comment had caused Rand pain. My pockets bulged uncomfortably with the beans. I shifted in my seat. Liza would have good cause when she blamed this mood swing on me. Valek's actions with Rand's mother seemed harsh from Rand's perspective, but when I thought about it from Valek's point of view, it made sense. His job was to protect the Commander.

I lived the next two days in a fog. Events blurred together. Tasting, training, tasting, training. Ari's and Janco's curses and attempts to rouse me remained unsuccessful. The news that I could start knife defense failed to produce any enthusiasm. My body felt as wooden as the bow I held.

When Margg materialized after one of my training sessions to inform me that a meeting with her contact had been scheduled for the following evening, it was with great difficulty that I summoned the strength to rally.

I thought out each possible scenario, and each combination of events kept leading me to one conclusion. Who would believe me if I reported the meeting? No one. I needed a witness who could also act as a protector. Ari's name sprang to mind. But I didn't want any suspicion to fall on him if something went wrong. It was also possible that Margg's contact had a boss, or a whole network of informers, and I could be getting in over my head. Dance as I might, there was but one course of action, and it led to but one person: Valek.

I dreaded the encounter. My interaction with him had dwindled to the silent awkward dispensing of my antidote every morning. But after tasting the Commander's dinner, I sought Valek out, my stomach performing flips. His office was locked, so I tried his suite. He wasn't in the living room, but I heard a faint sound from upstairs. A thin slash of light glowed under the door to Valek's carving studio. A metallic grinding noise raised goose bumps on my flesh.

I faltered at the entrance. This was probably the worst time to disturb him, but I was to meet Margg's contact the next day. I had no time to waste. Gathering courage, I knocked and opened the door without waiting for an answer.

Valek's lantern flickered. He stopped grinding. The wheel spun in silence, reflecting pinpricks of light that whirled along the walls and ceiling.

He asked, "What is it?"

"I've had an offer. Someone wants to pay me for information about the Commander."

He spun around. His face was half hidden in shadows, but it was as rigid as the stone he held. "Why tell me?"

"I thought you might want to follow along. This might be the one who has been leaking information about me."

He stared at me.

I wished then that I held a heavy rock, because I had the sudden desire to bash it on his head. "Espionage is illegal. You might want to make an arrest, or maybe even feed this leak some misinformation. You know, spy stuff. Remember? Or have you become bored with that, too?" Anger fueled my words.

I took a breath to launch into an attack, but it slid unvoiced past my clenched teeth. There was a slight softening in Valek's face. Renewed interest emanated from him, as if he had been holding every muscle taut and had just relaxed.

"Who?" he asked finally. "And when?"

"Margg approached me, and she mentioned a contact. We're meeting tomorrow night." I studied his expression. Was he surprised or hurt by Margg's treachery? I couldn't tell. Reading Valek's true mood was like trying to decipher a foreign language.

"All right, proceed as planned. I'll tail you to the rendezvous, and see who we're dealing with. We'll start by feeding this contact some accurate information to make you look reliable. Perhaps the Commander's change of successor would work. It's harmless information that will be made public anyway. Then we'll go from there."

We outlined the details. Even though I was placing my life

in danger, I felt cheerful. I had my old Valek back. But for how long? I wondered as wariness crept back in.

When we were through, I turned to go.

"Yelena."

I halted in the doorway, looking back over my shoulder.

"You once said I wasn't ready to believe your reason for killing Reyad. I'll believe you now."

"But I'm not ready to tell you," I said and left the room.

20

Damn Valek! Damn, damn, damn him! Gave me the cold shoulder for four days and then expected me to trust him? I'd admitted to murder. They'd arrested the right person. That was all he should care about.

Walking down the stairs in the darkness, I headed toward my room. I have to get out of this place, I thought with sudden intensity. The overwhelming desire to take off and damn the antidote was strong. Run away, run away, run away sang in my mind. A familiar tune. I had heard it before when I was with Reyad. Memories I had thought were tightly locked away now threatened to push free, seeping through the cracks. Damn Valek! It was his fault I couldn't suppress my memories any longer.

In my room, I locked the door. When I turned around, I spied Reyad's ghost lounging on my bed. The wound in his neck hung open, and blood stained his nightshirt black. In contrast, his blond hair was combed in the latest style, his mustache groomed to perfection, and his light blue eyes glowed.

"Get out," I said. He was, I reminded myself, an intangible ghost and not, absolutely not, to be feared.

"What kind of greeting is that for an old friend?" Reyad asked. He lifted a book on poisons off my nightstand, and flipped through the pages.

I stared at him in shock. He spoke in my mind. He held a book. A ghost, a ghost, I kept repeating. Reyad was unaffected. He laughed.

"You're dead," I said. "Aren't you supposed to be burning in eternal damnation?"

Reyad wasn't banished so easily. "Teacher's pet," he said, waving the book in the air. "If only you had worked this hard for me, everything would have been different."

"I like the way it turned out."

"Poisoned, pursued and living with a psychopath. Not what I would consider the good life. Death has its perks." He sniffed. "I get to watch your miserable existence. You should have chosen the noose, Yelena. It would have saved you some time."

"Get out," I said again, trying to ignore the touch of hysteria in my voice and the trickle of sweat down my back.

"You do know you'll never get to Sitia alive? You're a failure. Always were. Always will be. Face it. Accept it." Reyad rose from the bed. "You failed all our efforts to mold you. Do you remember? Remember when Daddy finally gave up on you? When he let me have you?"

I remembered. It had been the week of the fire festival, and Reyad had been so preoccupied with General Tesso's visiting retinue, especially Tesso's daughter, Kanna, that he hadn't bothered to check on me. Since I'd been meekly obeying his every command to gain some trust, he was smug in the assumption that he'd cowed me into submission. As a result, it was more than a month since he'd locked me into my tiny room that was next to his suite.

But the festival had once again tempted me into disobeying Reyad's instructions to stay away. The beatings and humiliations of the year before were insufficient to deter me this year. In fact, I felt a stubborn pride in refusing to be intimidated by him. I was terrified of getting caught, knew deep down in a small corner of my mind that I would get caught, but I threw all caution to fate. The fire festival was a part of me. The only time I tasted true freedom. Even though it was for but a few moments, it was worth the consequences.

My defiance added an edge to my acrobatic routines, making me bold and reckless. I sailed through the first five rounds with aplomb, dismounts steady, flips tight, energy level unlimited. I advanced to the final round of competition, which was scheduled for the last day of the festival.

I scrambled to put the finishing touches on my costume for the competition, while Reyad guided Kanna and a group of friends on a hunting party in the countryside.

I had scrounged around the manor for the preceding two weeks to acquire the necessary supplies for my attire. Now I stitched scarlet silk feathers onto a black leotard, and then outlined them with silver sequins. Wings tied to a harness completed the outfit, but I folded them small and flat so they wouldn't impede my motion. Braiding my hair into one long rope, I wound it tightly around my head and secured two flaming red feathers in the back. Pleased with the results, I arrived early at the acrobatics tent to practice.

When the competition started, the tent bulged with people. The crowd's cheers soon dimmed to a dull roar in my ears as I performed my routines. The only sounds reaching me were the thump of my hands and feet on the trampoline, the creaking of the tightrope as I launched myself in midair to execute a two-and-a-half twist and the crack of the slender rope when I landed on it without falling.

The floor routine was my last event. I stood on the balls of my feet at the edge of the mat, breathing deeply. The heavy earthy smell of sweat and the dry scratch of chalk dust filled my lungs. This was my place. This was where I belonged. The air vibrated like a thunderstorm poised to blow in. Energized as lightning, I started my first tumbling run.

I flew that night. Spinning and diving through the air, my feet hardly touched the ground. My spirit soared. I felt like a bird performing aerial tricks for sheer delight. At the end of my last run, I grabbed my wings with both hands. Pulling them open, I raised them over my head as I somersaulted and landed on my feet. The bright scarlet fabric of the wings billowed out behind me. The crowd's thunderous cheers vibrated deep in my chest. My soul floated with crimson wings on the updraft of the audience's jubilant praise.

I won the competition. Pure uncomplicated joy consumed me, and I grinned for the first time in two years. Face muscles aching from smiling, I stood on the platform to receive the prize from the Master of Ceremonies. He settled a bloodred amulet, shaped like flames and engraved with the year and event, on my chest. It was the greatest moment of my entire life—followed by the worst, as I spotted Reyad and Kanna watching me from the crowd. Kanna was beaming, but Reyad's expression was hard and unforgiving as suppressed rage leaked from his twitching lips.

I lingered inside the changing room until everyone had gone. There were two exits to the tent, but Reyad had positioned his guards at both. Knowing Reyad would take my amulet and destroy it, I buried it deep under the earthen floor of the room.

As I expected, Reyad grabbed me as soon as I stepped from the tent. He dragged me back to the manor. General Brazell was consulted. He agreed that I would never be "one of his group." Too independent, too stubborn and too willful, Brazell said, and gave me over to his son. No more experiments. I had failed. That night, Reyad just managed to control his temper until we were alone in his room, but once the door was closed and locked, he vented his full anger with his fists and feet.

"I wanted to kill you for disobeying me," Reyad's ghost said as he glided across my room. "I planned to savor it over a very long period of time, but you beat me to it. You must have had that knife tucked under my mattress for quite a while." He paused, creasing his brow in thought.

I had stolen and hidden a knife under Reyad's bed a year before, after he had beaten me for practicing. Why his bed? I had no real strategy, just a terrible foreboding that when I needed it, I would be in Reyad's room and not in my small room next door.

Dreaming of murder was easy; committing it was another story. Even though I'd endured much pain that year, I hadn't crossed the threshold of sanity. Until that night.

"Did something set you off?" the ghost asked. "Or were you procrastinating, like now? Learning to fight!" He chuckled. "Imagine you fighting off an attacker. You wouldn't last against a direct assault. I should know." He floated before me, forcing the memories out.

I flinched from him and from that night's recollection. "Go away," I said to the specter. Picking up the book on poisons, I stretched out on my bed, determined to ignore him. He faded slightly as I read, but brightened whenever I glanced his way.

"Was it my journal that set you off?" Reyad asked when my eyes lingered too long.

"No." The word sprang from my mouth, surprising me. I had convinced myself that his journal had been the final straw after two years of torment.

The painful memories flooded with a force that shook me and left me trembling.

After I had regained consciousness from the beating, I'd found myself sprawled naked on Reyad's bed. Flourishing his journal before me, he ordered me to read it, taking pleasure in watching the growing horror on my face.

His journal had listed every single grievance he had against me for the two years I'd been with him. Every time I disobeyed or annoyed him, he noted it, and then followed with a specific description of how he would punish me. Now that Brazell no longer needed me for his experiments, Reyad had no bound-aries. His sadistic inclinations and overwhelming depth of imag-ination were written in full detail. As I struggled to breathe, my first thought was to find the knife and kill myself, but the blade was on the other side of the bed near the headboard.

"We'll start with the punishment on page one tonight." Reyad purred with anticipation as he crossed to his "toy" chest, pulling from it chains and other implements of torture.

I flipped back to the beginning with numb fingers. Page one recorded that I had failed to call him *sir* the first time we met. And for lacking the proper deference, I would assume a submissive position on my hands and knees, and then be whipped. He would demand that I call him *sir*. With each lash, I would respond with the words, "More, *sir*, please." During the following rape, I would address him as *sir*, and beg him to continue my punishment.

His journal slipped from my paralyzed hands. I flung myself over the bed, intent on finding the knife, but Reyad, thinking I was trying to escape, caught me. My struggles were useless, as he forced me to my knees. With my face pressed into the rough stone floor, Reyad chained my hands behind my neck.

The anticipation was more frightening than the actual event. In a sick way, it was a comfort, because I knew what to expect and when he would stop. I played my part, understanding that if

I denied him his intended moves, I would only enrage him further.

When the horror finally ceased, blood covered my back and coated the insides of my legs. I curled into a ball on the edge of Reyad's bed. My mind dead. My body throbbing. His fingers were inside me. Where he would always be, he breathed into my ear as he lay beside me.

This time the knife was within my reach. My thoughts lingered on suicide.

Then Reyad said, "I guess I'll have to start a new journal."

I did not respond.

"We'll be training a new girl now that you've failed." He sat up, and dug his fingers deeper into me. "Up on your knees. Time for page two."

"No!" I screamed. "You won't!" Fumbling for a frantic second, I pulled the knife out and sliced at his throat. A surface cut only, but he fell back on the bed in surprise. I leaped onto his chest, slashing deeper. The blade scraped bone. Blood sprayed. A warm feeling of satisfaction settled over me when I realized I could no longer determine whose blood pooled between my thighs.

"So that's what set you off? The fact that I was going to rape you again?" Reyad's ghost asked.

"No. It was the thought of you torturing another girl from the orphanage."

"Oh, yes." He snorted. "Your friends."

"My sisters," I corrected. "I killed you for them, but I should have done it for me." Anger surged through my body.

I cornered him. My fists struck out even though I knew in a tiny part of my mind that I couldn't hurt him. His smug expression never changed, but I punched again and again until the first rays of dawn touched Reyad's ghost. He vanished from sight.

Sobbing, I sank to the floor. After a while, I became aware of my surroundings. My fists were bloodied from hitting the rough stone wall. I was exhausted and drained of all emotions. And I was late for breakfast. Damn Valek!

"Pay attention," Ari said. He jabbed me in the stomach with a wooden knife. "You're dead. That's the fourth time today. What's the matter?"

"Lack of sleep," I said. "Sorry."

Ari gestured me to the bench along the wall. We sat down and watched Maren and Janco, engaged in a friendly bow match on the far side of the storeroom. Janco's speed had overpowered Maren's skill, and she was on the retreat, backing into a corner.

"She's tall and thin, but she's not going to win," Janco sang. His words aimed to infuriate her—a tactic that had worked before. Too often, Maren's anger caused her to make critical mistakes. But this time, she remained calm. She planted the end of her bow between his feet, which trapped his weapon close to his body. Then she flipped over his head, landed behind him, and grabbed him around the neck until he conceded.

My bleak mood improved a notch watching Maren use

something I had taught her. The indignant expression on Janco's face was priceless. He insisted on a rematch. They launched into another rowdy duel. Ari and I remained on the bench. I think Ari sensed that I had no energy to continue our lesson.

"Something's wrong," he said in a quiet voice. "What is it?"

"I—" I stopped, unsure of my answer. Should I tell him about Valek's cold shoulder and change of heart? Or about my night-long conversation with the ghost of the man I'd murdered? No. Instead I asked him, "Do you think this is a waste of time?" Reyad's words about procrastination had held a ring of truth. Perhaps the time I spent training was merely a subconscious ploy to avoid solving my real problems.

"If I thought this was a waste of time, I wouldn't be here." A trace of anger colored Ari's voice. "You need this, Yelena."

"Why? I might die before I even have a chance to use it."

"As I see it, you're already good at running and hiding. It took you a week to get up the nerve to talk to Maren. And if it was up to you, she'd still be calling you Puker. You need to learn to stand and fight for what you want." Ari fidgeted with the wooden knife, spinning it around his hand.

"You hover on the edges, ready to take off if something goes wrong. But when you can knock the bow from Janco's hands, and sweep my feet out from under me, you'll be empowered." He paused, and then said, "If you feel you need to spend your time on something else, then do it…in *addition* to your training. Then the next time someone calls you Puker, you'll have the confidence to tell her to go to hell."

I was amazed at Ari's assessment of me. I couldn't even say if I agreed or disagreed with him, but I did know he was right about my compulsion to do something else. He didn't know what it was, but I did: find the antidote to Butterfly's Dust.

"Is that your idea of encouragement?" I asked in a shaky voice.

"Yes. Now quit looking for an excuse to stop training, and trust me. What else do you need?"

The quiet intensity of Ari's voice caused a chill to ripple up my spine. Did he know what I was planning, or was he guessing? My intentions had always been to get the antidote and run to Sitia. Run away, run away, run away. Ari had been right about that. But running south would require me to be in top physical condition, and to have the ability to defend myself from guards. However, I had been evading one important detail: Valek.

He would follow me to Sitia, and crossing the border wouldn't make me safe from him. Even Irys's magic couldn't protect me. He would consider my recapture or my death a personal responsibility. And that was what I'd been so afraid to face. What I'd been dancing around. I'd been concentrating on training so I wouldn't have to deal with the dilemma I feared I wasn't smart enough to solve. I had to enhance my strategy, to include not only obtaining the antidote, but dealing with Valek without killing him. I doubted Ari had the solution.

"You might beat Valek with these blows." Janco puffed while blocking Maren's bow. "He'll laugh himself silly at how pathetically weak they are, giving you the perfect opening."

Maren remained silent, but increased the pace of her attack. Janco backed off.

Janco's words stirred in my mind. An odd little long-shot plan began to take shape. "Ari, can you teach me how to pick locks?"

He considered my words in silence. Finally, he said, "Janco could."

"Janco?"

Ari smiled. "He seems harmless and happy-go-lucky, but as a boy he got into all kinds of mischief until he was trapped in a tight spot. Then he was given the choice of either joining the military or going to jail. Now he's a Captain. His biggest advantage is that no one thinks he is serious, and that's exactly what he wants."

"I'll try and remember that the next time he's cracking jokes and my ribs." I watched Maren beat Janco a second time.

"Best three out of five, my lady can not deny," Janco called tirelessly.

Maren shrugged. "If your ego can handle it," she replied, swiping at his feet with her bow. He jumped, avoiding her attack with an athletic grace, and lunged. The rhythmic crack of wood striking wood filled our practice room.

Ari stood, assumed a defensive stance, and somehow I found the energy to face him.

After the workout, the four of us were resting on the bench when Valek arrived. Maren shot to her feet, as if she thought being found sitting idle was a crime, but the rest of us kept our relaxed positions. I found it fascinating to watch the small changes in Maren's behavior whenever Valek was around. Her rough edge softened, she smiled more and tried to engage him in conversation or a match. Most of the time he would review fighting tactics with her, or conduct a practice, and she would preen like an alley cat attracting the biggest tom. But this time he wanted to talk to me. Alone. The others left the room. Maren shot me a dark look with the force of one of her bow strikes. I would pay for this tomorrow, I thought.

Valek paced. With an uneasy feeling, I hoped that he wasn't searching for a rock to throw.

"What's wrong?" I asked him. "Is it about tonight?" Excitement over exposing Margg soured to nervousness when I thought of the risk I'd be taking. The idea that this might be another waste of time surfaced. Damn Reyad's ghost! He was making me doubt everything. The leak impacted my life. Someone had tipped off those goons at the fire festival, and Irys had known I was in the forest. Margg needed to be plugged.

"No. We're all set for tonight," Valek said. "This is about the Commander." He paused.

"What about him?"

"Has he been meeting with anyone strange this week?"

"Strange?"

"Someone you don't know or an adviser from another Military District?"

"Not that I've seen. Why?"

Valek paused again. I could see his mental wheels turning as he considered whether or not to trust me. "Commander Ambrose has agreed to admit a Sitian delegation."

"That's bad?" I asked, confused.

"He hates southerners! They've requested a meeting with him every year since the takeover. And for the last fifteen years, the Commander has replied with a single word: no. Now they're due to arrive in a week." Valek's pacing increased. "Ever since you became the food taster and that Criollo showed up, the Commander has been acting different. I couldn't put my finger on it before, it was just a nagging feeling, but now I have two particular incidents."

"The change in his successor and now the southern delegation?"

"Exactly."

I had no response. My experience with the Commander had been the complete opposite of what I had expected from a military dictator. He considered other opinions, was firm, decisive and fair. His power was obvious; every command was instantaneously obeyed. He lived the spartan life that he endorsed. There was no fear in his advisers and high-ranking officers, just an unflappable loyalty and immense respect. The only horror story since the takeover that I'd heard was about Rand's mother. Of course, the assassinations before were infamous.

Valek stopped and took a deep breath. "I've misdirected some Criollo to our suite. I want you to eat a piece whenever he does. But you're not to tell anyone, not even the Commander. That's an order."

"Yes, sir," I replied automatically, but my mind reeled over his calling the suite "ours." Did I hear that right? I wondered.

"Keep your meeting with Margg tonight. I'll be there."

"Should I tell Margg's contact about the southern delega-tion?"

"No. Use the change of the Commander's successor. It's already floating around as a rumor, so you'll just confirm it." Valek strode from the room.

In case someone would discover our training room, I hid the practice weapons, removed all visible traces of our presence and locked the door. On my way to the baths, my thoughts dwelled on the meeting tonight. Distracted, I walked by an open doorway. An oddity. In this section of the castle, most of the doors led to storerooms and were kept locked.

Movement blurred to my left. Hands grabbed my arm and yanked me inside. The door slammed shut. Complete darkness descended. I was flung face-first against a stone wall. The air in my lungs whooshed out from the impact. I turned. My back to the wall, I gasped for breath.

"Stay put," a male voice growled.

I aimed a front kick toward the voice but met air. Laughter taunted. A candle was uncovered. The weak yellow glow re-flected off a long silver blade. Terrified, I traced the knife to the hand, then along the arm, and up to the face. Nix.

21

"WHY?" NIX PLACED THE candle among the cobwebs lacing the tabletop. "Why am I always the smartest one?" He stepped closer.

I kicked again, but he blocked it with ease.

"Why haven't my attempts to discourage you worked?" In the flicker of the candlelight he moved. The edge of his knife pressed against my throat. "Maybe I need to be more obvious?"

The smells of boiled cabbage and body odor penetrated my nose. Keeping my body still, I asked in the most neutral and unfrightened voice I could manage, "What's your problem?"

"My problem is that no one sees you as a threat. But I'm smarter than Ari, Janco and Maren. I'm even smarter than Valek. Aren't I?" When I failed to respond, Nix added pressure to the knife. "Aren't I?"

A thin line of pain burned across my neck. "Yes," I replied.

In the air behind Nix, Reyad's ghost coalesced out of the dust motes, sporting a smug smile.

"My boss wants you to stop training. I'm not allowed to kill you. Pity." Nix stroked my face with his free hand. "I'm here to warn you off."

"Parffet? Why would he care?" As I tried to distract him, my mind frantically shuffled through my brief sessions with Ari on knife defense. Damn, I thought, why hadn't I paid more attention?

"He doesn't care. The only thing dull-witted Parffet cares about is getting promoted. But General Brazell has a keen interest in your new hobby." Nix thrust his free hand between my legs, and leaned his body against mine.

For a terrified second, I froze. Panic erased all techniques of self-defense from my mind. A soft buzzing began to grow inside my head, but I stifled it, pushed it away, and it transformed into a simple musical scale of notes. Calm flowed. The necessary defense moves appeared before my eyes.

I moaned and rocked my hips, widening my stance.

Nix smiled with delight. "You're just the whore I thought you'd be. Now, remember, you're to be punished." His upper thigh replaced his hand. He began to tug at my belt.

I rubbed my knee between his legs then rammed it straight up into his groin. Grunting, Nix doubled over. I grabbed his blade with both hands to prevent it from biting farther into my throat. Ari's practical voice, "Better to cut your hands than your neck," echoed in my head even as I winced at the sharp pain. Focusing on the knife, I pushed the weapon from me. Nix stumbled back.

"Bitch!" He snarled and pulled his arm back to swing the knife.

As the blade swept toward me, I stepped in close to his body, so when I turned, my right shoulder brushed his chest. Using the edges of my opened hands, I struck his upper and lower arm. The combined force of my strike and his swing made Nix's arm go limp. The weapon clattered to the floor.

Grabbing his arm, I twisted it until the heel of his hand pointed toward the ceiling. Then I pivoted, placing my right shoulder under his elbow. With all my might, I yanked his hand down. I heard a loud crack followed by a scream as Nix's arm broke. Spinning around to face him, I punched him twice in the nose. Blood gushed out. While he was off balance, I kicked his kneecap, breaking it. Nix crumpled to the ground.

I danced around him, kicking him in the ribs. My blood hummed and sizzled. His weak attempts to block me only fueled my frenzy. In that state of mind, I might have killed him.

Reyad's ghost cheered me on. "That's it, Yelena," he urged. "Kill another man, and it's the noose for sure."

Somehow, his words reached the rational part of my mind, and I stopped, breathing hard. Nix was still. I knelt beside him and felt for a pulse. A strong throb met my fingertips. The relief that coursed through me vanished when Nix clutched my elbow.

I yelped and punched him in the face. His grip relaxed, and I pulled my arm free. Snatching the knife from the floor, I took Janco's often-repeated advice for self-defense: "Hit and git." I ran. But this time fear didn't follow me. I ran with imaginary scarlet wings flowing behind me.

Moving fast to ward off the shakes that threatened to over-power me, I reached the baths. They were empty at this time of day, so I hid Nix's knife under one of the towel tables. I checked the extent of my wounds in the mirror. The cut on my neck had stopped bleeding. But two deep gashes on my palms looked serious enough to require the medic's attention. There was also a wild, unrecognizable shine to my eyes, as if I had turned feral. I bared my teeth and thought, *Now who's the rat?* Pondering my next move, I wavered. The Commander expected me to taste his dinner, but I couldn't bleed all over his food. My initial surge of energy from the fight with Nix was waning. A wave of dizziness swelled. I headed toward the infirmary, hoping to reach it before I passed out.

Medic Mommy gave me a quick appraisal. She pointed to an examining table. I perched on the edge and held my hands out for inspection.

"How…" she started.

"Broken glass," I said.

She nodded, lips pressed tight in thought. "I'll get my med-kit."

I stretched out on the bed when she returned with her metal tray full of instruments. A jar of Rand's glue seemed out of place among the medical supplies, like a child's toy surrounded by adult paraphernalia. My hands had started to throb, and I dreaded the medic's ministrations. I turned my head in time to see Valek burst into the infirmary. Just what I needed, I thought, sighing. This had turned out to be one hell of a bad day.

"What happened?" Valek demanded.

I glanced at the medic.

She took my right hand and began to clean my wound. "Broken glass leaves jagged lacerations. These clean slices are obviously from a knife. I'm required to report it."

The medic had reported me to Valek and he wasn't going to leave without an answer. With resignation I focused on him, hoping to distract myself from the pain in my hands. "I was attacked."

"By who?" His tone sharp.

I cut my eyes at the medic, and Valek understood.

"Could you excuse us for a minute?" he asked her.

She pursed her lips as if considering his request. Her authority overruled Valek's for all medical situations.

"Five minutes," she ordered, and walked to her desk on the far side of the infirmary.

"Who?" Valek repeated.

"Nix, a guard in Parffet's unit. Said he worked for Brazell and warned me to stop training."

"I'll kill him."

The intensity of Valek's voice shocked and alarmed me. "No, you won't," I said, trying to sound firm. "You'll use him. He's a link to Brazell."

His hard blue eyes found mine and held my gaze, probing deep. "Where did he attack you?"

"A storeroom about four or five doors up from our training room."

"He's probably long gone by now. I'll send someone to the barracks."

"He won't be there."

"Why not?" Valek gave me a look that reminded me of the Commander. His eyebrows were raised in an effort to suppress his emotions, inviting me to continue.

"If he's not in the storeroom, he won't have gotten far. You might want to send a couple of men."

"I see." Valek paused. "So your training has been progressing to your satisfaction?"

"Better than expected."

Valek left the infirmary. Medic Mommy, the stoolie, returned to my side. Next time, I thought bitterly, I'll heal myself and avoid being betrayed by the medic. I still had a jar of Rand's glue in my backpack. How hard could it be to seal a couple of cuts?

I chewed on my lower lip while she finished cleaning and sealing my cuts. Wrapping bandages tightly around my hands, she gave me instructions that would allow them to heal: no immersion in water for a day, no lifting or writing for a week. And that meant no training for a while, I thought.

Valek's men entered. They dumped Nix onto another examining table. The medic shot me a quizzical expression, then she bustled over to Nix's groaning form, giving me the perfect opportunity to leave.

I hurried to the Commander's office, but Valek had beaten me there. He closed the door behind him as he joined me in the throne room.

"I've taken care of dinner," he said, guiding me back through the maze of desks. It was early evening, and only a handful of advisers were working.

"Find Margg and cancel tonight's meeting, then go back to our suite and get some rest," he said.

"Cancel? What for? It would look suspicious. I'll wear gloves to cover the bandages. It's cold enough at night; nobody will notice." When he didn't reply, I added, "I'm fine."

He smiled. "You should take a look at yourself in a mirror." He hesitated, his face creasing in indecision. "All right. We'll proceed as planned."

We stopped at the door to Valek's office. "I have some work to finish. Rest and don't worry. I'll be close by tonight." He inserted his key.

"Valek?"

"Yes."

"What will happen to Nix?"

"We'll patch him up, threaten him with years in the dungeon if he doesn't cooperate, and when he's done helping us, I'll reassign him to MD–1. Good enough? Or should I kill him?"

Military District 1 was the coldest, bleakest district in Ixia. The possibility of Nix falling prey to a snow cat brought a wicked grin to my face. "No. Reassignment's good. If I had wanted him dead, I would have done it myself."

Valek straightened his spine, snapping me a look. A combination of surprise, amusement and wariness over my comment flashed across his face before he reined in his emotions and was once again my stone-faced Valek.

I smiled my best Janco impression and headed down the hall.

Resting would have to wait since I had a number of errands to run before the evening's meeting. First, I needed a pair of gloves and a cloak. As the cooling season dwindled toward the cold season, the nights had turned sharp and brisk, coating everything in a blanket of ice so that the blades of grass sparkled like diamonds when touched by the morning sun.

Thanking fate that Dilana was still in her sewing room, I chatted with her about the latest gossip before I made my request.

"My goodness," she said, sounding like a worried matron. "You don't have any clothes for the cold!" She bustled about her stacks of uniforms. Her soft, honey-colored ringlets bounced with each movement. "Why didn't you come to me sooner?" she admonished.

I laughed. "I haven't needed them till now. Dilana, do you mother everyone in the castle?"

She stopped piling clothes to look at me. "No, dear, just the ones that need it."

"Thanks," I said in a tone of affectionate sarcasm.

By the time she was through outfitting me for the cold season, I was inundated with a heap of clothing. With all of the flannel undergarments, wool socks and heavy boots, I probably could survive on the pack ice for weeks. I stashed the pile into a corner of the room and asked Dilana to have someone deliver them to Valek's suite.

"Still there?" she asked with a grin.

"For now. But I think when things settle down, I'll be back in my old room." When, I thought sourly. It was more like *if.*

I selected a heavy black cloak from the stack, tucked black

wool gloves into its deep pockets, and then draped it over my arm. The cloak had two hand-size red diamonds stitched on the left breast and an oversize hood whose function was more to keep the rain off my face than to keep my head warm.

"I think you'll be there a long time," Dilana said.

"Why?"

"I believe Valek's sweet on you. I've never seen him take such an interest in a food taster before. He usually trains them and leaves them alone. If there was any potential for trouble, he would assign one of his sneaks to spy on the taster, but he wouldn't bother with him personally, let alone live with one!" Her face had the avid glow of a gossip at full steam.

"You're crazy. Deluded."

"In fact, he's never taken an interest in a woman before. I was beginning to suspect he might prefer one of his male sneaks, but now…" She paused dramatically. "Now, we have the lovely, intelligent Yelena to get Valek's cold heart pumping."

"You really should get out of your sewing room more. You need fresh air and a dose of reality," I said, knowing better than to believe a word Dilana said, but unable to control the silly little grin on my face.

Her sweet, melodious laughter followed me into the hallway. "You know I'm right," she called.

The only reason Valek was interested in me, I thought as I walked through the dim corridors, was because I was a puzzle for him to solve. Once he thought he had all the answers about the southern magician and Brazell, I'd be sent back to my room in the servants' wing. I couldn't let myself believe anything else. It was one thing for me to have a harmless in-fatuation that wouldn't have any influence on my plans. It wouldn't. Absolutely not. To think he felt the same toward me would be disastrous.

So I tried to convince myself that Dilana, although a sweet-heart, was a victim of her own overactive imagination and was mistaken. I tried very hard. I tried all the way to the kitchen. I tried when I saw Rand lurching around his ovens, reminding myself that Valek was ruthless, murdering dozens of people. The King's blood still adorned Valek's knife. Valek was deadly, moody and exasperating. But for some reason, I couldn't get that silly grin to go away no matter how hard I tried.

Draping my cloak over a stool, I helped myself to a late dinner. Rand finished spinning his pigs and pulled up a stool beside me. My mouth watered at the smell of roasting pork.

"What's the occasion?" I asked. Pork roast was a rare meal, requiring an entire day to cook and served only at special times.

"Generals coming to visit this week. All my special dishes have been requested. I've also been ordered to prepare a feast for next week. A feast! We haven't had one of those since…" He shook his head, pursing his lips. "Actually, we've never had one with the Commander in charge." Rand sighed. "I won't have any time to experiment."

"Would you have time to look at these?" Pulling a handful of the mystery beans out of my pocket, I handed them to Rand. I had been waiting for the perfect opportunity to show them to him. "I found them in an old storeroom, and I thought maybe they were your coffee beans."

He immediately ducked his head and took a deep sniff of the beans. "No, unfortunately not. I don't know what these are. Coffee beans are smooth and have a rounder shape. These are oval. See? And bumpy." Rand spread them out on the table and picked one up. He bit into it. Chewing, he cringed at the bitter taste. "I've never seen or tasted anything like this. Where did you find them?"

"Somewhere on the castle's lower level." Oh well, I thought, it had been worth a try. My disappointment pressed on my shoulders. I had hoped to solve this puzzle for Commander Ambrose, but it looked as though I had hit another dead end.

Rand must have sensed my frustration. "Important?" he inquired.

I nodded.

"Tell you what," he said. "Leave these here and after the feast I'll work on them for you."

"Work?"

"I'll try grinding, cooking and boiling the beans. Ingredients can change their flavor and texture when you add heat, and these might turn into something I recognize. All right?"

"I don't want to inconvenience you."

"Nonsense. I like a challenge. Besides, after the feast, it'll be back to my daily routine anyhow, and this will give me a project to look forward to." He funneled the beans into a jar, and placed it high on a shelf full of other strange edibles similarly encased in their own glass jars.

We discussed menu options for the feast until Rand needed to turn his pigs again. A quarter turn every hour, he said, reminding me that my time to meet Margg was fast approaching. A small pang of nervousness touched my stomach as I bade Rand good-night.

I stopped by the baths, intending to retrieve Nix's knife, but there were too many people there. Maybe being unarmed would be for the best, I told myself as I tried to calm the butterflies in my stomach. Maybe they would search me. If they found a weapon, I might be in more trouble.

Margg wore her usual expression of distaste when I met her just past the south gate of the castle complex. We exchanged insults by way of greeting and continued the walk into Castletown in silence. I hoped Valek was close behind, but I knew better than to glance over my shoulder and make Margg wary.

Stars decorated the night sky, and the full face of the moon shone brightly, casting shadows. The road to town was grooved with ruts from wagon wheels and worn smooth by the passage of many boots. I took a deep breath of the cool night air and felt a sense of renewal as the heavy scent of earth and dried leaves cleansed my lungs.

At the outskirts of town, I saw neat rows of four-story wooden buildings. I was struck by their symmetry. I had grown so accustomed to the wild, asymmetrical style of the castle, with its windows of every geometric shape, that the ordinary plainness of the town seemed bizarre. Even the placement of businesses among the residences had been planned in a logical manner.

The few townspeople that I spotted on the street walked

with a purpose. Nobody hung about, or talked, or looked as if they were out for a casual stroll. Nobody, except the town's guards.

Soldiers who had once played a major part in the takeover had been reassigned as policemen for the towns throughout the Territory of Ixia. Enforcing curfew and the dress code, they dealt justice in accordance with the Code of Behavior by checking papers, arranging transfers and making arrests. Every visitor to each town was required to report to the main station to complete the proper paperwork before seeking lodging.

Our meeting had been carefully scheduled to give us time to return to the castle before our presence on the street would be viewed with suspicion. The pairs of soldiers stationed on the streets followed us with their gazes. I felt my skin prickle under their scrutiny, and I had myself half convinced that they would swoop down on us at any moment.

In the middle of a street free from guards, Margg came to a stop at a house indistinguishable from its neighbors. She knocked twice on the door. After a pause, the door swung inward and a tall, red-haired woman in an innkeeper's uniform poked her head out. Glancing at Margg, she nodded in recognition. She had a sharp, sloping nose, which guided the movements of her head as she pointed her face at me. Her dark eyes rested upon me with an intensity that made me want to fidget. A bead of sweat trickled down my spine. Finally, she pulled her nose away to look down the street. Sniffing for a trap, I guessed. Apparently satisfied, she opened the door wider and let us in. Still no one spoke as we proceeded up three flights of steps.

The top floor of the house was ablaze with light, and I squinted in the harsh brightness. A profusion of candles ringed the room on multiple levels, heating the air with the smoky scent of apples. I glanced at the window. With the amount of light in the room, I was sure it would spill out into the street, but black curtains covered the glass and pooled on the floor.

Bookshelves, a desk and a scattering of comfortable armchairs led me to believe that the room was used as a study. The woman who had let us in sat behind the desk. Odd metal statues that resembled lanterns with rings around the top graced each side. Other strange and gleaming objects had been artfully arranged on shelves and tabletops. Some even hung from the ceiling. These spun in the air stirred by our passage.

The sharp-nosed woman didn't offer us a seat, so Margg and I stood before her desk. Most of her ruby hair was confined in a bun, but small, curly wisps had sprung free.

"The food taster," she said with a satisfied curl to her lip. "I knew it was only a matter of time before I had you in my employ."

"Who are you?" My bluntness informed her that I wouldn't tolerate games.

"You can call me Captain Star."

I looked at her innkeeper's uniform.

"I'm not part of Ambrose's military. I have my own. Has Margg explained how I work?"

"Yes."

"Good. This will be a simple exchange. This isn't a social call; I don't want gossip or hearsay. And don't inquire about my business or about me. All you need to know is my name. Agreed?"

"Agreed." Since I wanted to gain her trust, I wasn't about to cause any trouble, at least not yet.

"Good. What do you got?" With her nose leading the way, she leaned forward in her chair.

"The Commander has changed his successor," I said.

Star's body stilled as she absorbed this tidbit. I glanced at Margg, who looked shocked and annoyed that I had such interesting news.

"How do you know?" Star asked.

"I overheard the Commander and Valek talking."

"Ah, yes. Valek." Star tilted her nose at me. "Why are you living in his apartment?"

"None of your business," I said with a firm tone.

"So why should I trust you?"

"Because Valek would kill me if he knew I was here. You know it as well as I do. How much is my information worth?"

Star opened a black velvet purse and pulled out one gold coin. She tossed the coin to me like a master would throw a bone to a dog. I snatched it from the air, suppressing a wince. The cuts on my hands started to throb.

"Your fifteen percent." She sent one silver and one copper coin flying at Margg, who knew Star's ways, and caught them easily. "Anything else?" Star asked me.

"Not at this time."

"When you have something for me, tell Margg. She'll arrange another meeting."

Dismissed, I followed the silent Margg out of the house and down the street. Just as she guided me into a dark alley, Valek appeared out of the shadows. Before I could wonder why, he pulled me through a doorway and into a small room.

I was surprised and confused by his sudden arrival; I had thought he would wait a while before arresting Margg. She had followed me into the room, and stood with a sneering grin on her round face. It was the closest expression to pleasure that I had ever seen from her, and the opposite of what I had anticipated when she was caught as the leak. I tilted my head at Valek, hoping to prompt an explanation.

"I was right, Valek. She sold the Commander out for a gold coin. Check her pocket," Margg urged.

"Actually, Yelena came to me before the meeting. She believed she was going to expose *you*," Valek said to Margg.

Her gloating grin disappeared. "Why didn't you tell me?" she demanded.

"No time."

"Margg's not the leak?" I asked, still confused.

"No. Margg works for me. We've been feeding Star some rather unique information and hoping to find out who her other clients are. Star's been pestering Margg to get you involved, and I thought it would be a good opportunity to test your loyalty."

A complete understanding of Valek's ill temper snapped into my mind. He had expected me to betray him and the Commander. How could he have believed that? I wondered. Didn't he know me at all? Anger, disappointment and relief warred in my heart. I was unable to propel any words past my throat.

"I had hoped to send this rat back to the dungeon where

she belongs," Margg complained to Valek. "Now she'll still be scurrying around. Still a threat." Annoyed, she poked my arm with a meaty finger.

I moved. In a heartbeat I twisted her arm behind her back. She yelped as I raised her hand up high, forcing her to bend forward.

"I am *not* a rat," I said through clenched teeth. "I've proved my loyalty. You *will* get off my back. No more nasty messages in the dust. No more prying into my things. Or the next time, I'll break your arm." I shoved her hard as I released my grip.

She stumbled and landed on the ground in a heap. Pink-faced, she lurched to her feet. As she opened her mouth to protest, Valek stopped her with a glance.

"Well said, Yelena. Margg, you're dismissed," Valek said.

Margg's mouth snapped closed as she spun on her heel and left the room.

"She's not friendly," I said.

"No. That is precisely why I like her." He studied the door for a moment, then said, "Yelena, I'm going to show you something you're not going to like, but I think it's important that you know."

"Oh yeah? Like I enjoyed your test of faith?" Sarcasm rendered my voice sharp.

"I warned you that I tested the food taster from time to time."

Before I could reply, he stopped me. "Be quiet and stay close behind me." We went back out into the alley. Keeping in the shadows, we walked back to Star's house, where Valek guided me into a dark entrance within sight of Star's door.

"The person who has been leaking information to Star is due to arrive soon," Valek whispered close to my ear. His lips lightly rubbed my cheek. Shivers rippled down my spine at his touch, distracting me from what he had said.

The impact of Valek's words didn't hit me until I saw a lone figure with an uneven gait walking down the street.

22

I RECOGNIZED THAT STRIDE. My heart melted as I watched Rand limp to Star's house, knocking twice.

She admitted Rand into her home without a moment's hesitation. The faint thump of the closing door echoed hollowly in my chest.

"Another test?" I asked Valek with desperate urgency. "Is he working for you?" But I knew the answer deep in my soul, even before I saw the sad shake of his head. I felt empty, as if every emotion had been wrenched out of me. It was just too much. After Reyad's ghost, Nix's attack and Valek's test, I was mentally unable to handle another blow. I just stared at Valek with no thoughts, no feelings and no desires.

Valek motioned for me to follow him. I complied. We circled around to the back of Star's house. Entering the building to the left, we padded up three stories. The interior was dark and empty except for the top floor. One of Valek's men sat cross-legged with his back resting against the wall shared with Star's study. He wrote in a notebook, using a single candle as illumination.

Rand's voice could be heard clearly. Using hand signals, Valek communicated with the man. He gave the notebook to Valek and disappeared down the steps. Valek sat in the man's spot, and then tapped the floor next to him.

I crouched beside him, facing the wall. I had no desire to hear Rand's deceit, but I didn't have the willpower to leave. Valek pointed to an array of small holes in the wood. I peered through. All I could see was the back of a piece of furniture. I guessed that the holes were for listening purposes only. Squatting on the floor, I rested my forehead against the wall and closed my eyes as I eavesdropped on Rand's conversation.

"Generals are coming to town this week. That's nothing new, but the Commander ordered a feast, so something's up. Something significant. But I haven't been able to figure out what," Rand said.

"Let me know as soon as possible," Star replied. Then she paused. "Maybe Yelena knows what's going on."

My heart lurched when I heard my name. Run away, run away, run away, my mind screamed, but I only pressed my forehead harder on the wall.

"I doubt it. She was surprised when I mentioned the feast, so I didn't ask her. She might know more later this week. I'll try again."

"Don't bother. I'll ask her myself." The sleek tone of Star's voice implied that she had concealed this revelation until the time when exposing it would cause maximum damage.

"Yelena?" Rand sputtered. "Working for you? Impossible. That's not her style."

"Are you suggesting she's working for Valek?" Alarm tightened her voice.

Equally upset, I glanced at Valek. He shook his head, waving his hand in a "don't worry" gesture.

"No. She wouldn't." Rand had recovered. "I'm just surprised, but I shouldn't be. She could use the money, and who am I to think any less of her for it?"

"Well, you shouldn't be thinking of her at all. As I see it, she's disposable. The only concern I'll have when she dies is, who's going to replace her and how quickly can I bribe him?"

"Star, once again you've shown me in the most repulsive way that the sooner I pay off my debt to you the better. How much credit do I get for tonight's information?"

"Two silvers. I'll mark it in my book, but it won't make much difference."

"What do you mean?"

"Haven't you figured it out by now? You'll never pay off your debt. As soon as you get close, you always gamble yourself right down another hole. You're too weak, Rand. Too swayed by your own emotions. Easily addicted, and lacking in willpower."

"Oh, that's right. You *claim* to be a magician. Have you read my mind, Captain? 'Captain Star'—what a laugh! If you really had magic, Valek would have taken care of you long ago. I know you're not as smart as you claim." The heavy uneven tread of footsteps resounded through the wall as Rand started to walk away.

I was astounded. I had never heard Rand speak with such harsh sarcasm before, and more than that, if Star was a magician, I could be in serious danger. My mind spun, but it was all too complex to contemplate at this time.

"I don't need to read your mind," Star called after him. "All I have to do is review your history, Rand. It's all there."

Silence settled. The only noise coming from Star's study was the crinkle of papers being turned. Valek stood, pulling me up with him. His man had returned. Handing him the notebook, Valek descended the steps.

I followed Valek through the dark streets of Castletown. We kept to the shadows, avoiding the patrolmen. Once we had escaped the city's limits, Valek relaxed and walked beside me on the main road to the castle.

"I'm sorry," Valek said. "I know Rand was your friend."

His use of the past tense jabbed like a knife's point between my ribs.

"How long have you known?" I asked.

"I've suspected for the last three months, but only procured the hard evidence this month."

"What tipped you off?"

"Rand and his staff helped me with that poison test I gave you. He stayed while I laced the food with poison. I left that goblet of peach juice on my desk to keep it clean. It *was* a fair test. Blackberry poison was in that cup, but I didn't put it there." Valek paused, letting the information sink in.

"An interesting property of blackberries is that only when they're prepared in a special solution of grain alcohol and yeast and cooked with extreme care to the proper temperature are they poisonous. Most cooks, and certainly not their assistants, don't possess the skills or the knowledge to achieve that result." Valek sounded as if he admired Rand's ability to brew the poison.

The full understanding that Rand had tried to poison me almost knocked me off my feet. I stumbled as a surge of nausea boiled in my stomach. Dashing to the side of the road, I vomited into the bushes. Only when my body had ceased its convulsions did I realize Valek was supporting me. One of his arms was wrapped around my waist, while a cold hand pressed against my forehead.

"Thanks," I said, wiping my chin clean with some leaves. With trembling legs, I let Valek lead me to the castle. If he hadn't continued to support me, I would have curled up on the ground and called it a night.

"There's more. Do you want to hear it?" Valek asked.

"No." The truth, but as we drew closer to the outer wall of the castle complex, I made an ugly connection. "Did Rand set me up at the fire festival?"

"In a way."

"That's not an answer."

"The goons that nabbed you waited for you near the baking tent, so I suspected that Rand had told Star you would be there. But then he wouldn't let you out of his sight. It was as if he was protecting you. Remember how upset he was when he couldn't find you. How relieved he was when he spotted you alive and whole?"

"I thought he was drunk," I said.

"I suspect Rand is an unwilling participant. At the time of the poison test, he hardly knew you, but as your friendship grew, I imagine he finds himself in a difficult situation. He doesn't want to hurt you, but he needs to pay off his gambling debt. Star has an extensive organization, with plenty more thugs to replace the ones I took care of, thugs who would be willing to break a few bones for their boss. Does that make you feel any better?"

"No." My reaction to Rand's betrayal seemed extreme even to me, but I couldn't switch it off. It wasn't the first time someone had played false with me and it wasn't going to be the last. Brazell had deceived me. I had loved him like a father, and been loyal to him. In the end, it took almost a year of enduring his experiments before my feelings dwindled to the point where I could see him as he really was. But I had always known my young devotion to him was one-sided. Since he had never given me any reason to think he cared for me, his actions had been easier to stomach.

Rand's friendship, on the other hand, appeared genuine. I had begun to feel as if I had finally made a decent-size hole in the stone barricade I had built around myself. Big enough for me to slip through and enjoy our time together. Now the wall was crumbling. I felt stones pelting me and burying me deep beneath the rubble. How could I trust anyone again?

"Anything else you want to tell me?" I asked Valek as we

stopped a few feet short of the castle's south entrance. "Did Ari and Janco set me up for Nix's attack? Do you have another test of loyalty for me up your sleeve? Maybe the next time, I'll actually fail. A prospect that seems appealing!" I pushed away Valek's supporting arm. "When you warned me that you would test me from time to time, I thought you meant spiking my food. But it seems there is more than one way to poison a person's heart, and it doesn't even require a meal."

"Everyone makes choices in life. Some bad, some good. It's called living, and if you want to bow out, then go right ahead. But don't do it halfway. Don't linger in whiner's limbo," Valek said, his voice gruff. "I don't know what horrors you faced prior to your arrival in our dungeon. If I had to guess, I would think they were worse than what you have discovered tonight. Perhaps that will put things into perspective."

He strode into the castle. I leaned against the cold wall, resting my head on the unyielding surface. Maybe if I stayed here long enough, my heart would turn to stone. Then betrayals, tests of loyalties and poisons would have no effect on me. But the cold eventually drove me inside.

"Apply a force on the wrench. Not too much. You need a firm yet gentle touch," Janco said.

With healing hands still sore, I clumsily placed the tension wrench into the keyhole and applied pressure.

"Now use your diamond pick to lift the pin that's trapped by the tension, lift it until it breaks," he instructed.

"Breaks?" I asked.

"Reaches alignment. When you put a key into a lock, the metal ridges push the pins up so you can turn the cylinder and open the lock. The pins hold the cylinder in place. You'll need to do one pin at a time, and continue the pressure."

I slid the pick into the lock past the wrench. I maneuvered the pick, lifting each of the five pins. I could feel a tiny vibration in my finger joints as each pin broke with a subtle yet distinct click. When they were all aligned, the cylinder turned and the door unlocked.

"Good job! Damn, Yelena, you're a fast learner." Janco paused, his brow creased in concern. "You're not going to use this to do something stupid, right? And get us into trouble?"

"Define stupid," I said. When Janco's eyes widened, I added, "Don't worry. I'm the only one who would get into trouble."

He relaxed, and I practiced on another lock. We were in the lower level of the castle where no one would surprise us. It had been four days since the night I had learned about Rand. Valek's orders had been to act as if nothing had happened. He wanted to discover the full extent of Star's organization before exposing them. Valek was a true predator, I thought sourly, eyeing his prey before pouncing for the kill.

I knew I wasn't ready to play the friend to Rand, so I had been avoiding him, which wasn't hard to do. The castle crawled with Generals and their retinues, making every worker in the complex busy, including Rand.

Brazell was another reason I was glad to be out of sight. His black-and-green soldiers had infected the castle, and keeping away from them was becoming difficult. Although, I didn't mind hiding in Valek's suite. He had stolen a box of Criollo, and I was contented to munch a piece each time I tasted the Commander's food.

Ari, Janco and I had postponed our training sessions for the duration of the Generals' visit, but I had managed to rope Janco into teaching me to pick locks. Giving him the gold coin from Star had provided an added incentive. Valek had said I could keep it since working undercover wasn't part of the food taster's job. But the heavy weight of it in my pocket had been a constant reminder of Rand's treachery, so I decided to put it to good use.

"This last lock has ten pins. If you can open this one, you'll be able to handle all the pin-tumbler locks or key locks in the castle. Except the dungeon bolts. They're complicated, and it's not like we can practice on them." Janco's forehead furrowed. "You're not going to need that skill, are you?"

"I sincerely hope not."

"Good."

After several failed attempts, I managed to pop the lock open.

"Now you need to practice. The quicker you can spring a lock the better," Janco instructed. "I would let you borrow my picks, but I never know exactly when I might need them." He winked, a mischievous glint sparkling in his eyes. "So…" He pulled another set from his pocket. "I used that coin you gave me to buy a set for you." He handed me a black cloth case.

"That money was for you."

"Oh, there's plenty left. Even after I bought you this." He flourished an ebony-colored wooden rod as long as my hand.

It was decorated with a bright silver button, and silver symbols were engraved on the side.

"What's that?" I asked.

"Push the button," he said with glee.

I pressed down with my thumb, and started when a long gleaming blade shot out. It was a switchblade.

Amazed, I stared at my gifts. "Thank you, Janco. But why did you buy these for me?"

"Guilt, I suppose."

"Guilt?" Not the answer I had expected.

"I called you a criminal. I was once a criminal, but I've gone past it, and no one has held it against me. Besides, I have a terrible feeling you may need them. General Brazell's soldiers have been swaggering around the barracks, bragging about who is going to 'take out' Reyad's killer. They're quite imaginative, and I had to hold Ari back from challenging the lot a couple of times. Ten against one isn't good odds, even for Ari and me."

"I'll stay away from them," I said.

"Good. I'd better get moving. I've drawn the night shift. But, first, I'll escort you to your room."

"That's not necessary."

"Ari would kill me if I didn't."

We walked together toward Valek's suite. When we reached the corner before the main doors, Janco stopped just out of sight of the guards.

"Almost forgot," he said, reaching into his uniform pocket. He pulled out a sheath for the switchblade. "It goes around your right thigh. Remember to make a nice big hole in your pants pocket, so when you pull the weapon it won't get caught in the fabric."

He was about to leave when I stopped him. "Janco, what are these symbols?" I pointed to the silver markings on the handle of the knife.

Janco smiled. "They're the old battle symbols used by the King when he sent out messages and orders during war times. It didn't matter if the enemy intercepted them, because they were unintelligible to anyone who didn't know how to decipher them. Some of the soldiers still use them. They work well in military exercises."

"What do they say?"

His grin widened. "Too easy, Yelena. I'm sure you'll figure it out...eventually." Always the prankster, Janco laughed with delight.

"Come here," I said, "so I can punch you."

"I'd love to oblige you, my dear." Janco dodged beyond my reach. "But I'm late."

23

AFTER HIDING JANCO'S GIFTS deep in my uniform pocket, I went into Valek's suite. He was working at his desk, but he looked up as soon as I entered the room, giving me the impression that he had been waiting for me.

"Where have you been?" he asked.

"With Janco," I said. But I was wary. As long as I arrived at the scheduled times during the day, Valek didn't ask about what I did with my free time.

"Doing what?" Valek demanded, standing with his hands on his hips.

The comical image of a jealous husband popped into my mind. I stifled a smile. "Discussing fighting tactics."

"Oh." Valek relaxed his stance, but moved his arms awkwardly as if he felt he had overreacted and was trying to cover it up. "Well, that's all right. But from now on, I need to know where you are at all times, and I suggest you stay in the castle and keep a low profile for a while. General Brazell's guards have set a bounty on your head."

"A bounty?" Fear pulsed through my chest.

"It could be a rumor or just drunken soldiers' talk. But until they leave, I want you protected." Valek's tone was firm, but then he added, "I don't want to train another taster."

"I'll be careful."

"No. You'll be paranoid. You'll move in a crowd, keep to well-lit areas and you'll make certain to have an escort with you whenever you're walking down empty hallways late at night. Understood?"

"Yes, sir."

"Good. The Generals' brandy meeting is scheduled for tomorrow evening. Each General will bring a bottle of his finest brandy to share as they discuss Ixian business late into the night. You will be needed to taste the Commander's drinks." Valek lifted a box of eight bottles from the floor. They clinked musically as he set the carton on the table.

Pulling out a small drinking glass, he said, "I want you to sample each brandy once tonight and at least twice tomorrow, so you know how each tastes clean of poisons." He handed me the glass. "Each bottle is labeled according to the type of brandy, and which General brings it."

I grabbed a decanter at random. It was General Dinno's cherry brandy made in MD–8. Pouring a mouthful, I took a sip and rolled the liquid around my tongue, attempting to commit the taste to memory before swallowing. The strong alcohol burned down my throat, leaving behind a small fire in my chest. My face flushed with the heat.

"I suggest you use the 'slurp and spit' method so you don't get drunk," Valek said.

"Good point." I found another glass for spitting, and then worked my way through the remainder of the bottles.

On the day of the meeting, I tasted each brandy twice more in Valek's suite, and then tested myself with a third round. Only when I could pinpoint by taste alone which cordial belonged to which General was I satisfied.

That night, I waited for Valek to escort me to the war room. He came downstairs decked out in full dress uniform. Red braids draped his shoulders; medals were lined up six deep over his left breast. He oozed dignity, a man of stature. I would have been impressed, except for the uncomfortable and peevish look he wore. A petulant child forced to wear his best clothes. I covered my mouth, but was unable to block my laughter.

"Enough. I have to wear this damn thing once a year and, as far as I'm concerned, it's one time too many." Valek tugged at his collar. "Ready?"

I joined him at the door. The uniform enhanced his athletic body, and my thoughts drifted to how magnificent he would look with his uniform puddled around his feet.

"You look stunning," I blurted. Mortified, I blushed as a rush of heat spread through my body. I must have swallowed more brandy than I'd realized.

"Really?" Valek glanced down at his uniform. Then he set

his shoulders back and stopped yanking at his collar. His cross expression changed to a thoughtful smile.

"Yes. You do," I said.

We arrived in the Commander's war room just as the Generals assembled. The long, slender, stained-glass windows glowed with the weak light of the setting sun. Servants scurried around the circular chamber, lighting lanterns and arranging platters of food and drink. All military personnel were attired in their dress uniforms. Medals and buttons sparkled. I knew only three Generals by sight; the rest I deduced by the color of the diamonds on their otherwise black uniforms. Scrutinizing their faces, I memorized their different features in case Valek tested me later.

Brazell glared when I made eye contact. Adviser Mogkan stood next to him, and I shivered as Mogkan's eyes slid over me with cunning appraisal. When Brazell and Reyad had performed their experiments on me, Mogkan had always hovered nearby. His presence, sensed but unseen, had given me violent nightmares. Brazell's usual advisers were missing; I wondered why he had brought Mogkan instead.

The Commander sat at the tip of the egg-shaped conference table. His uniform was simple and elegant with real diamonds stitched onto his collar. The Generals, flanked by their advisers, seated themselves around the rest of the table. Valek's chair was to the Commander's right, and my stool was placed behind them, against the only stone wall in the room. I knew the meeting would last all night, and I was glad I would be able to rest my back. Another advantage to my position was that I wasn't in direct sight of Brazell. Although I could avoid seeing the poisonous looks he might flash my way, I couldn't hide from Mogkan's pointed stares.

The Commander pounded a wooden gavel on the table. Silence fell. "Before we launch into the scheduled topics," the Commander said, indicating the detailed agenda which had been distributed earlier, "I have an important announcement. I have appointed a new successor."

A murmur rippled through the war room as the Commander walked around the table and handed a sealed envelope to each General. Inside the envelopes were eight pieces to an encoded puzzle that would reveal the new successor's name when deciphered by Valek's key.

Tension permeated the room. I felt it pressing against me like an overfilled water-skin about to burst. A maelstrom of expressions, surprise, anger, concern and contemplation crossed the Generals' faces. General Rasmussen of MD–7 whispered into his adviser's ear, the General's cheeks turning as red as his hair and mustache. I leaned forward in my seat and saw Brazell struggle to keep his face neutral as delight tweaked at his features.

Instead of erupting, the tension simmered, and leaked away as the Commander ignored it by beginning the meeting. Items related to MD–1 were the first order of business, to be followed by each district in order. As a bottle of General Kitvivan's special white brandy slid around the table, the Generals discussed snow cats and mining rights.

"Come on, Kit. Enough about the cats. Just feed them up on the pack ice like we do, and they won't bother you,"

General Chenzo of MD–2 said in exasperation, running a meaty hand through his moon-white hair. His full mane stood out starkly against his tanned skin.

"Feed them so they'll get healthy and fat and start breeding like rabbits? We'll go broke supplying the meat," Kitvivan shot back.

My interest in the proceedings waxed and waned depending on the subject. After a while I began to feel light-headed and warm as the brandy influenced my body, since protocol dictated that I swallow when tasting for the Commander.

The Generals voted on various topics, but the Commander held the final vote. Mostly he ruled in favor of the majority. No one ventured a complaint when he didn't.

Commander Ambrose had lived in MD–3, scratching out a meager existence with his family in the foothills of the Soul Mountains. Nestled between the mountains and the ice pack, his home was atop a vast diamond mine. When the rich find had been discovered, the King had claimed the diamonds, and "allowed" the Commander's family to live there and work in the mines. He lost many family members to cave-ins, and to the damp and dirty environment.

As a young man seething at the injustices of the monarchy, Ambrose educated himself and began preaching about reform. His intelligence, bluntness and pervasiveness gained him many loyal supporters.

My mind focused back on the meeting when the Generals reached issues regarding MD–5. General Brazell caused a considerable stir. Instead of sliding around his best brandy, he sent a silver tray containing what looked like small brown stones. Valek handed one to me. It was a round drop of Brazell's Criollo.

Before protests about ignoring tradition could escalate, Brazell rose and invited everyone to take a bite. After a brief moment of silence, exclamations of delight filled the war room. The Criollo was filled with strawberry brandy. I gave the Commander the all-clear sign so I could savor the rest of my morsel. The combination of the sweet, nutty taste of the Criollo mixed with the smooth texture of the brandy was divine. Rand would be upset that he hadn't thought of mixing the two, I supposed, then regretted feeling sorry for Rand as I envisioned his deceitful face.

After the praise died down, Brazell made the announcement that the construction of his new factory was complete. Then he went on to more mundane matters of how much wool had been sheared and the expected output of the cotton plantations.

Military District 5 produced and dyed all the thread for Ixia, and then sent it to General Franis's MD–3 to be woven into fabric. Franis nodded his head in concern as he wrote down the figures Brazell quoted. He was the youngest of the Generals, and had the habit of tracing the purple diamonds on his uniform with a finger whenever he was concentrating.

I dozed on my stool as fuzzy thoughts gathered like storm clouds in my mind. Strange dreams about brandy, border patrols and permits swirled like snowflakes. Then the images turned bright and sharp as a picture of a young woman dressed in white hunting furs snapped into my mind.

She held a bloody spear high in the air in celebration. A dead snow cat lay at her feet. She slammed the tip of her weapon into the pack ice and drew a knife. Cutting a slash in the cat's fur, she used a cup to collect the blood that spilled out.

She exalted as she drank, scarlet rivulets spilling down her chin. I heard her thoughts clearly in my mind. "No one has managed this feat," she thought. "No one but I!" she shouted over the snow. Her exhilaration filled my heart. "Proof that I am a strong cunning hunter. Proof that my manhood was taken from me. Proof that I am a man. Men will not rule me any longer," she cried. "Become the snow cat to live with snow cats, become a man to live with men."

The hunter turned her face. At first, I took her to be the Commander's sister. They shared the same thin delicate features and black hair. She wore power and confidence like a cloak. Peering at my dreaming self, her gold almond-shaped eyes drove through me like a lightning strike. Sudden recognition that she *was* the Commander jerked me awake. My heart pounded and my head thumped and I realized I was staring directly into Mogkan's searing gaze. He smiled with satisfaction.

The Commander's reason for hating magicians was as clear to me as glass. He was a she, but with the utter conviction that she should have been born a man. That cruel fate had chosen to burden him with a mutation that he had to overcome. And the Commander feared that a magician might pull this secret from his mind. Pure foolishness, I thought, shaking my head to dismiss the whole crazy notion. Just because I had dreamed about a woman didn't mean that the Commander was one. It was absolute nonsense. Or was it?

Rubbing my eyes, I glanced around to see if anyone else had noticed that I had fallen asleep. The Commander stared off into the distance, and Valek sat stiff and alert, scanning the room, seeking something or someone. General Tesso had the floor.

Valek pulled his gaze back to the Commander, and bumped his arm in alarm. "What's going on?" he whispered urgently. "Where were you?"

"Just remembering a time long ago," the Commander said in a wistful voice. "More enjoyable than listening to General Tesso's excruciatingly detailed report on the corn harvest in MD-4."

I studied the Commander's features, trying to superimpose the woman from my dream. They matched, but that meant nothing. Dreams twisted reality and it was easy to envision the Commander killing a snow cat.

The rest of the meeting continued without incident, and I dozed on my stool from time to time, untroubled by strange dreams. When the Commander pounded his gavel, I was awake in an instant.

"Last item, gentlemen," the Commander announced. "A Sitian delegation has requested a meeting."

The room erupted with voices. Arguments sprang to life as if the Generals were picking up an old debate right where they had left off. They discussed trade treaties, and quarreled about attacking Sitia. Instead of trading for goods, why not take them? they argued. They wanted to expand their districts and gain more men and resources, ceasing all worries about Sitia attempting to attack Ixia.

The Commander sat in silence and let the flow of advice wash over him. The Generals settled enough to proclaim their beliefs about allowing the Sitians to come. The four northern Generals (Kitvivan, Chenzo, Franis and Dinno) didn't want to meet with the delegation, while the four southern Generals (Tesso, Rasmussen, Hazal and Brazell) favored a summit with the Sitians.

The Commander shook his head. "I acknowledge your opinions about Sitia, but the southerners would rather trade with us than attack us. We have more men and metal. A fact they are well aware of. To attack Sitia we would expend many lives and large sums of money. And for what? Their luxury items aren't worth the cost. I'm content with Ixia. We have cured the land of the King's disease. Perhaps my successor will want more. You'll have to wait until then."

A murmur rippled through the Generals. Brazell nodded in agreement, with his thin lips anchored in a predator's smile.

"I have already agreed to meet with the southern contingent," the Commander continued. "They're due to arrive in four days. You have until then to express your specific concerns to me before departing for your home districts. Meeting adjourned." The bang from the Commander's gavel echoed throughout the dead silent room.

The Commander rose and with his bodyguards and Valek close behind, he prepared to leave. Valek gestured for me to join them. I lurched to my feet. The full effect of the brandy I had consumed washed over me. Giddy, I followed the others from the room. An explosion of sound slipped through the door just before it closed behind us.

"That should stir things up a bit," the Commander said with a wan smile.

"I would advise against vacationing in MD-8 this year," Valek said sarcastically. "The way Dinno reacted to your announcement about the southern delegation I would expect him to pepper your beach house with sand spiders." Valek shivered. "A horribly painful way to die."

My skin crawled too, thinking of the lethal spiders the size of small dogs. Our procession continued in silence for a while as we headed back to the Commander's suite. My gait was unsteady. The stone walls blurred past me, as if they were moving and I was the one standing still.

Outside the Commander's suite, Valek said, "I'd watch out for Rasmussen too. He didn't take the news of the change in your successor well."

The Commander opened his door. I stole a quick glance inside his suite. The same plain utilitarian style that decorated his office and the rest of the castle was present. What had I expected? Maybe a splash of color, or something a bit more feminine? I gave my head a little shake to banish such absurd thoughts. The motion made my head spin, and I had to put a hand to the wall to keep myself from stumbling.

"I watch out for everyone, Valek. You know that," the Commander said before shutting the door behind him.

Upon entering our suite, Valek stripped off his uniform jacket and threw it on the couch. He pointed to a chair and said, "Sit. We need to talk."

I plopped into the chair and dangled a leg over the

armrest, watching Valek pace the room in his sleeveless undershirt and formfitting black pants. Imagining my hands helping to ease the tension in the long ropy muscles of his arms almost started a giggling fit. Brandy flowed through my blood, quickening my pulse.

"Two things were very wrong tonight," Valek said.

"Oh, come on. I just dozed for a minute," I said in my defense.

Valek shot me a quizzical look. "No, no. You did fine. I meant about the meeting; the Generals." He continued to pace. "First, Brazell seemed unusually happy about the change in successor and the Sitian delegation. He's always wanted a trade treaty, but he typically exercises a more cautious approach. And second, there was a magician in the room."

"What?" My breath locked. Had I been discovered?

"Magic. Very subtle, from a trained professional. I only felt it once, a brief touch, but I couldn't pinpoint the source. But the magician had to be in the room, or I wouldn't have felt it."

"When?"

"During Tesso's long-winded dissertation about corn." Valek's posture had relaxed a little, as if the act of talking out a problem helped him deal with it. "About the same time your snoring could be heard halfway across the room."

"Ha," I said rather loud. "You were so stiff at that meeting I thought rigor mortis had set in."

Valek snorted with amusement. "I doubt you could have looked any better sitting in that uncomfortable dress uniform all night. I imagine Dilana sprayed on extra starch with malicious glee."

Then he grew serious again. "Do you know Adviser Mogkan? He eyed you most of the evening."

"I know of him. He was Reyad's primary adviser. They also hunted together."

"What's he like?" Valek asked.

"Same kind of vermin as Reyad and Nix," I said. The words poured off my lips. I slapped both hands over my mouth, but it was too late.

Valek studied me for a moment. Then he said, "There were a number of new advisers at the meeting. I guess I'll have to check them out one by one. It seems we have a new southern spy with magic abilities." He sighed. "It never ends." He dropped onto the edge of the couch as weariness settled on him like a coating of dust.

"If it did, you'd be out of a job." Before I could stop myself, I squeezed behind Valek and started to massage his shoulders. The alcohol had taken complete command of my movements, and the tiny sober section of my brain could do nothing but yell useless admonishments.

24

VALEK STIFFENED UNDER my touch. Was he expecting me to strangle him? I wondered. As my hands kneaded his muscles, he relaxed.

"What would you do," I asked him, "if suddenly the world was perfect and you had no one to spy on?"

"I'd be bored," Valek said with amusement.

"Come on, seriously. A change in profession." I dug my thumbs into the muscle at the base of his neck. "A fire dancer?" A rush of warmth radiated as brandy pumped through my blood.

"No. An arms teacher?" Valek suggested.

"No. It's a perfect world. No weapons allowed." I moved my hands down his back. "How about a scholar? You've read all these books lying around, haven't you? Or are they just to make it difficult for someone to sneak in?"

"Books serve me in so many ways. But I doubt your perfect society would need a scholar on murder."

My hands paused for a second. "No. Definitely not."

"A sculptor? I could carve extravagant statues. We could re-decorate the castle and liven things up. How about you?" he asked as I pressed my fingertips into the small of his back. "What would you do?"

"Acrobatics." The word flowed without conscious thought. I had thought I left acrobatics behind with my fire amulet, but it seemed my excursion through the trees had reawakened my desire.

"An acrobat! Well, that explains a lot."

Aroused by my contact with Valek's sculpted body, I slid my hands around to his stomach. Reyad be damned. The brandy had relaxed me past fear. I started to unfasten Valek's pants.

He grabbed my wrists, stopping me. "Yelena, you're drunk." His voice was hoarse.

Valek released my hands and stood. I sat, watching him with surprise as he swooped down to lift me from the couch. Wordless, he carried me to my room and laid me on the bed.

"Get some sleep, Yelena," Valek said softly as he left the room.

My world spun as I stared into the darkness. Placing a hand on the cold stone wall next to my bed helped to steady my thoughts. Now I knew. Valek had no interest in me other than my job as the food taster. I had allowed myself to get caught up in Dilana's gossip and Maren's jealousy. The ache of rejection throbbing in my soul was my own fault.

Why hadn't I learned by now? People turned into monsters. At least the people in my experience. First Brazell, then Rand, although Reyad had stayed consistent. What about Valek? Would he transform into one or had he already? Like Star said, I shouldn't be thinking of him at all, not as a companion, and not to fill the dead place in my heart.

As if I could. I laughed. A drunken sound, tattered and ragged, the music of my thoughts. Look around you, Yelena, I chided myself. The poisoned food taster who converses with ghosts. I should be thankful that I breathed, that I existed. I shouldn't long for more than freedom in Sitia. Then I could fill the emptiness. Dismissing all sentimental, weak thoughts, I focused on the business of staying alive.

Escaping to Sitia would break no bonds with Valek. Once I obtained the antidote to Butterfly's Dust I could set my plans into motion. Determined, I reviewed lock-picking techniques in my mind until I fell into a deep alcohol-induced sleep.

I woke an hour before dawn with a pounding head. My mouth felt like an abandoned spiderweb. I imagined dust blowing from my lips with each exhaled breath. Moving with extreme care, I inched out of bed. Wrapping my blanket around my shoulders, I went to get a drink. Valek liked cold water and always kept a pitcher outside on the balcony.

The crisp night air blew away the lingering fuzziness of sleep. The castle's stone walls glowed, eerily reflecting the moonlight. I located the metal pitcher. A thin film of ice had formed on the top. Breaking it with a finger, I poured the water into my mouth, gulping.

When I tipped my head back for a second drink, I noticed a black spider-shaped object clinging to the castle wall above my head. With growing alarm, I realized the shape was de-scending toward me. It wasn't a spider but a person.

I searched for a hiding spot, but stopped when I realized that the intruder had probably already seen me. Locking myself in the suite and waking Valek seemed a better plan. But before I could enter the pitch-black living room, I hesitated. Inside, the intruder's dark clothes would be hard to see. A locked door no longer gave me a sense of security since my lock-picking lessons with Janco.

Cursing myself for leaving my switchblade inside, I moved to the far end of the balcony, clutching the water pitcher in my hand.

The wall climber jumped the remaining distance to the balcony floor. The effortless movement triggered recognition.

"Valek?" I whispered.

A bright flash of white teeth, then Valek removed a pair of dark glasses. The rest of his face was hidden behind a hood that covered his head and was tucked into a skintight body leotard.

"What are you doing?" I asked.

"Reconnaissance. The Generals tend to stay up late after the Commander leaves the brandy meeting. So I had to wait until everyone had gone to bed." Valek went into the suite. He removed his hood. Lighting the lantern on his desk, he pulled a paper from his pocket.

"I hate a mystery. I would have let the identity of the Com-mander's successor remain a secret, as I have for fifteen years, but tonight's opportunity was too tempting. With eight drunken Generals sleeping it off, I could have danced on their beds without waking them. Not one among them has any imagination. I watched all the Generals put their envelopes from the Commander right into their briefcases." Valek motioned for me to join him at the desk. "Here, help me decipher this."

He handed me a stiff piece of paper. A jumble of words and numbers were scrawled on it. He had copied the eight different pieces of the encrypted message by stealing into each General's room. I wondered why he was confiding in me. Too curious to question, I pulled up a chair to help him.

"How did you break the wax seal?" I asked.

"Rookie trick. All you need is a sharp knife and a tiny flame. Now read me the first set of letters." He wrote it down then reordered the letters until he had created the word *siege*. Opening a book, he flipped through the pages. Symbols like the ones on my switchblade's handle peppered the document. The page Valek stopped on was decorated with a large blue symbol that resembled a star in the middle of three circles.

"What's that?" I asked.

"The old battle symbol for *siege*. The dead King used these markings to communicate with his Captains during times of war. They were originally created hundreds of years ago by a great strategist. Read me the next set. They should be numbers."

I told him the numbers. He began to count the lines of text.

It occurred to me that I could borrow this book and figure out Janco's message on my switchblade. Eventually, my ass. Won't Janco be surprised.

When Valek reached that number, he wrote a letter down

on a clean page. After he had finished deciphering the message, Valek sat as still as a held breath. Unable to wait any longer I asked, "Who is it?"

"Guess," he said.

I looked at him. I was tired and hungover.

"I'll give you a hint. Who was the happiest about the change? Whose name keeps popping up during the most bizarre situations?"

Terror swept over my body like a cloak. If something happened to the Commander, Brazell would be in command. I would probably be his first order of business, and wouldn't live long enough to see any changes he might implement in Ixia.

Valek understood the look on my face. He nodded. "Right. Brazell."

For two days the Commander met with each General in turn. My brief and periodic interruptions to taste the Commander's food created uncomfortable moments of silence. The tension around the castle was palpable as the Generals' retinues snarled and fought with everyone.

On the third day, when I arrived to taste the Commander's breakfast, I found him absorbed in conversation with Brazell and Adviser Mogkan. The Commander's eyes were glazed, his voice a monotone.

"Get out of here!" Brazell barked.

Mogkan pushed me into the throne room. "Wait here until we summon you," he ordered.

I hesitated outside the door, uncertain if I should heed this unusual request. If it had come from Valek or the Commander I wouldn't have doubted, but being expected to follow Mogkan's orders rankled. My worries grew as I imagined Brazell attempting an assassination. I was about to search for Valek, when he burst into the throne room, his expression hard as he hurried toward the Commander's office.

"What are you doing out here?" Valek demanded. "Haven't you tasted his breakfast yet?"

"I was ordered to wait. He's with Brazell and Mogkan."

Sudden fear crossed Valek's face. He pushed past me into the office. I followed. Mogkan was standing behind the Commander with his fingertips pressing into the Commander's temples. When Valek appeared, Mogkan stepped away. He said smoothly, "You can definitely feel, Sir, that this is an excellent way to ease a headache."

Animation returned to the Commander's face. "Thank you, Mogkan," he said. Glaring at Valek's intrusion, he demanded, "What's so important?"

"Disturbing news, Sir." Valek stared daggers at Brazell and Mogkan. "I would like to discuss it in private."

The Commander rescheduled their meeting for later that day, then dismissed them.

"Yelena, taste the Commander's breakfast now."

"Yes, Sir."

Valek watched me taste the food. An intense expression lined his face, making me nervous. Did he think the food was tainted? I rechecked the cooling tea and lukewarm omelet, but detected no foreign substances. I placed the tray on the Commander's desk.

"Yelena, if I have to eat cold food again, I'll have you whipped. Understand?" The Commander's voice lacked passion, but the threat was genuine.

"Yes, Sir," I replied, knowing an excuse was useless.

"You're dismissed."

I fled from the office, barely noticing the bustling activity in the throne room. Walking past the entrance, I paused. "Hungry," said a flat voice in my head. My stomach growled; I was ravenous. I headed toward the kitchen.

When I rounded a corner, Adviser Mogkan stood there, blocking my path. He linked his arm through mine and guided me to an isolated section of the castle. Going with him seemed natural. I wanted to pull away. I wanted to be afraid, terrified even, but I couldn't produce the emotions. My hunger had dissipated. I felt content.

Mogkan steered me down a deserted corridor. A dead end, I thought, still unable to conjure a reaction. His silky gray eyes stared at me for a moment before he unhooked his arm from mine. His fingers traced the line of black diamonds down my uniform sleeve.

"My Yelena," he said possessively.

Fear blazed up my arm and exploded in my chest the second physical contact with Mogkan was broken. My emotional ennui had dissolved, but I couldn't move. The muscles in my body wouldn't obey my mind's frantic commands to fight.

A magician! Mogkan had power. He had used it during the brandy meeting, tipping Valek off. But further contemplation on this revelation was cut short when Mogkan stepped closer.

"Had I guessed you would cause such trouble I never would have brought you to Brazell's orphanage." He smiled at my confusion. "Didn't Reyad tell you that I found you?"

"No." My voice was husky.

"You were lost in the jungle, only six years old. Such a beautiful, bright child. Such a delight. I rescued you from the claws of a tree leopard because I knew you had potential. But you were too stubborn, too independent. The harder we tried, the more you resisted." Mogkan cupped his hand under my chin, forcing me to meet his gaze. "Even now, when I'm locked into you, you're still fighting me. I can command your body." He raised his left arm, and my own left arm mirrored his movement. "But if I tried to control both your mind and body, you would eventually thwart me." He shook his head in disbelief, as if the whole concept amazed him.

"Fortunately, subtle pressure is all that's required." He pulled his hand away, and then made a pinching gesture with his fingers and thumb.

My throat closed. I was unable to breathe. Powerless to defend myself, I sank to the ground. My mind's screaming went unvoiced. Logic grabbed the panic and wrestled it to the ground. Mogkan was using magic. Maybe I could block it before I passed out. I tried reciting poisons in my mind.

"Such strength," Mogkan said in admiration. "But it won't save you this time." He bent down and kissed me tenderly, almost fatherly, on the forehead.

Peace flowed through me. I stopped resisting. My vision blurred. I felt Mogkan take my hand, holding it in his own.

RECLINING AGAINST THE WALL, I clung to Mogkan's hand as the world faded around me. I felt an unwelcome jolt, then the tight blockage in my throat released. Gasping for breath, I came to my senses and realized I was lying prone on the floor. Next to me sat Valek atop Mogkan's chest. Valek's hands were wrapped around Mogkan's neck, but his eyes were on me.

Mogkan smiled when Valek stood and yanked him to his feet. "I hope you're aware of the penalty for being a magician in Ixia," Valek said. "If not, I'd be delighted to en-lighten you."

Mogkan smoothed out his uniform and adjusted his long dark braid of hair. "Some would say your ability to resist magic makes *you* a magician, Valek."

"The Commander thinks otherwise. You're under arrest."

"Then you're in for a big surprise. I suggest you discuss these false accusations with the Commander before you do anything drastic," Mogkan said.

"How about I kill you right now?" Valek stepped closer to him.

A hot, searing pain stabbed my abdomen. I yelped and rolled into a tight ball. The agony was relentless. Valek took another step. I screamed as fire blazed up my back and circled my head.

"Any closer, and she'll be a corpse," Mogkan said, a cunning sleekness in his voice.

Through eyes tearing with anguish, I saw Valek shift his weight to the balls of his feet, but he remained in place.

"Well, now. That's interesting. The old Valek really wouldn't have cared if I killed his food taster. Yelena, my child, I just realized how incredibly useful you are."

The intense pain was unbearable. I would have gladly died to escape from it. Before I passed out, my last glimpse was of Mogkan's back as he walked away unharmed.

I woke to blackness. Something heavy pressed against my forehead. Alarmed, I tried to sit up.

"It's all right," Valek said, pushing me down.

I touched my head and pulled off a damp cloth. Blinking in the light, I looked around at the familiar furniture of my own room. Valek stood next to me, a cup in his hand.

"Drink this."

I took a sip and cringed at the medicinal flavor. Valek insisted I finish it. When the cup was empty, he placed it on the night table.

"Rest," he ordered, then turned to leave.

"Valek," I said, stopping him. "Why didn't you kill Mogkan?"

He considered for a moment, tilting his head. "A tactical maneuver. Mogkan would have killed you before I could finish him. You're the key to too many puzzles. I need you." He strode to the door but paused at the threshold. His grip on the doorknob was hard enough to whiten his knuckles. "I've reported Mogkan to the Commander, but he was…" Valek's hand twisted on the knob, and I heard the metal crack. "Unconcerned, so I'll be guarding the Commander until Brazell and Mogkan leave. I've reassigned Ari and Janco as your personal bodyguards. Don't leave this suite without them. And stop eating Criollo. I'll taste the Commander's Criollo. I want to see if anything happens to you." Valek pulled the door shut, leaving me alone with my swirling thoughts.

True to his word and much to the Commander's annoyance, Valek didn't leave the Commander's side. Ari and Janco enjoyed a change in routine, but I made them work hard. Whenever I wasn't tasting the Commander's meals, I had Ari drill me with knife defense and Janco give me more lessons on picking locks.

The Generals' departure was scheduled for the next day, which meant it was time to do some of my own reconnaissance. It was early evening and I knew Valek would still be with the Commander until late. I told Ari and Janco that I was going to bed early, and bade them good-night at the threshold to Valek's suite. After waiting an hour, I slipped back into the hallway.

The corridors of the castle were not as deserted as I had

hoped, but Valek's office was located off the main through-way. I approached his door, scanning the hallway for activity. Seeing no one, I inserted my picks into the first of the three keyholes, but my nerves made popping the lock impossible. I took a couple of deep breaths and tried again.

I had two locks sprung when I heard voices approaching. Standing, I pulled the picks out of the keyhole and knocked on the door just as two men came into view.

"He's with the Commander," said the guard on the left.

"Thanks," I replied and started to walk in the opposite direction with my heart beating like a hummingbird's wings. I glanced behind me until they were gone, then raced back to Valek's office. The third lock proved to be the most difficult. I was covered with sweat by the time I popped it. I hurried into the room, locking the door behind me.

My first task was to open the small wooden cabinet that held my antidote. Perhaps Valek had locked the recipe in there. I lit a dim lantern to peer inside. Glass bottles of various shapes and sizes gleamed in the light. Most of the bottles were marked Poison. A growing sense of urgency consumed me as I searched. All I uncovered was a large bottle containing the antidote. I poured only a few doses into the flask I had hidden in my pocket, knowing that Valek would notice if I took too much.

After relocking the cabinet, I began a systematic search of Valek's files, starting with the desk drawers. Even though his office was strewn with books and maps, his personal dossiers were well organized. I found files on Margg and the Commander and was tempted to read them, but I stayed focused on finding any folder bearing my name or a reference to Butterfly's Dust. Valek had written many interesting comments about my tasting abilities in my personnel file, but there was no mention of the poison or the antidote.

When I finished with the desk, I moved to the conference table. Books on poisons were interspersed with files and other espionage documents. I sorted through the piles. My time was running out. I had to be back in Valek's suite before he escorted the Commander to his apartment.

I suppressed my disappointment as I finished with the table. There was still half of his office left to search.

I was halfway across the quiet room when I heard the distinct sound of a key being inserted into the lock. One click, then the key was withdrawn. I snuffed out the lantern as the second lock clicked open. Diving behind the conference table, I hoped the boxes piled underneath would hide me from view. Please, I prayed to the forces of fate, let it be Margg and not Valek. A third click made my heart squeeze.

The door opened and closed. A light tread of footsteps crossed the room. Someone sat at the desk. I didn't risk peeking, but I knew it was Valek. Had the Commander retired early? I reviewed my meager options: be discovered or wait Valek out. I eased into a more comfortable position.

A few minutes later, someone knocked on the door.

"Come," said Valek.

"Your, ah…package has arrived, sir," said a male voice.

"Bring him in." Valek scraped his chair on the stone floor.

I heard the rustle of chains and a shuffling step. "You're dismissed," Valek said. The door clicked shut. A familiar rancid smell of the dungeon reached my nose.

"Well, Tentil. Are you aware that you're next in line for the noose?" Valek asked.

My heart went out to the doomed prisoner. I knew exactly how he felt.

"Yes, sir," a voice whispered.

Pages crackled. "You're here because you killed your three-year-old son with a plow, claiming it was an accident. Is that correct?" Valek asked.

"Yes, sir. My wife had just died. I was unable to afford a nanny. I didn't know he had climbed under." The man's voice was pinched with pain.

"Tentil, there are no excuses in Ixia."

"Yes, sir. I know, sir. I want to die, sir. The guilt is too hard to bear."

"Then dying wouldn't be adequate punishment, would it?" Valek didn't wait for a response. "Living would be a harsher sentence. In fact, I know of a profitable farmstead in MD–4 that has tragically lost both the farmer and his wife, leaving behind three sons under the age of six. Tentil will hang tomorrow, or so everyone shall believe, but you will be escorted to MD–4 to take over the operation of a corn plantation and the job of raising those three boys. I suggest your first order of business should be to hire a nanny. Understand?"

"But…"

"The Code of Behavior has been excellent at ridding Ixia

of undesirables, but it is somewhat lacking in basic human compassion. Despite my arguments, the Commander fails to grasp this point, so I occasionally take matters into my own hands. Keep your mouth shut, and you will live. One of my associates will check on you from time to time."

I huddled behind the boxes, frozen in disbelief. Hearing Valek use the word *compassion* was as incomprehensible to me as the thought of Margg apologizing for her rude behavior.

There was another knock on the door.

"Come," Valek said. "Perfect timing as always, Wing. Did you bring the documents?"

I heard a rustle of papers. "Your new identity," Valek said. "I believe our business is concluded. Wing will escort you to MD–4." Chains clanked to the floor. "You're dismissed."

"Yes, sir," Tentil said. His voice cracked. He was probably overwhelmed. I knew how I would feel if Valek offered me a free life.

After the men left, a painful quiet descended. I feared the sound of my breath would give me away. Valek's chair scraped. Two faint thumps were followed by a loud yawn.

"So, Yelena, did you find our conversation interesting?"

I held still, hoping he was guessing. But his next statement confirmed my dismay.

"I know you're behind the table."

I stood. There was no anger in his voice. He lounged in his chair with his feet resting on the desktop.

"How did you…" I began.

"You favor lavender-scented soap, and I wouldn't be alive

today if I couldn't determine when someone had picked my locks. Assassins love to ambush, leaving dead bodies behind mysteriously locked doors. Fun stuff." Valek yawned again.

"You're not angry?"

"No, relieved actually. I wondered when you would search my office for the recipe to the antidote."

Sudden fury welled in my throat. "Relieved? That I might try to escape? That I rifled through your papers? You're that confident that I won't succeed?"

Valek cocked his head to one side, considering. "I'm relieved that you're following the standard steps of escaping, and *not* inventing a unique plan. If I know what you're doing, then I can anticipate your next move. If not, I might miss something. Learning how to pick locks naturally leads to this." Valek gestured around the room. "But, since the formula has not been written down and only I know it, I'm confident you won't find it."

I balled my hands into tight fists to keep them from wrapping around Mr. I-Know-Everything's superior neck. "Okay, so there's no chance for escape. How about this? You gave Tentil a new life, why not me?"

"How do you know I haven't already?" Valek put his feet on the floor and leaned forward. "Why do you think you were in the dungeon for almost a year? Was it only luck that *you* happened to be the next in line when Oscove died? Perhaps I was merely acting at our first meeting when I seemed so surprised that you were a woman."

It was too much to bear. "What do you want, Valek?" I

demanded. "Do you want me to give up trying? Be content with this poisoned life?"

"Do you really want to know?" Valek's voice intensified. He stood and walked over to me.

"Yes."

"I want you…not as an unwilling servant, but as a loyal staff member. You're intelligent, quick-thinking and becoming a decent fighter. I want you to be as dedicated as I am at keeping the Commander safe. Yes, it's a dangerous job, but, on the other hand, one miscalculated somersault on the tightrope could break your neck. That's what I want. Will you be able to give it to me?" Valek's eyes seared deep into mine, searching for an answer. "Besides, where would you go? You belong here."

I was tempted to concede. But I knew that if I wasn't poisoned or murdered by Brazell, the wild magic in my blood would eventually explode, taking me with it. The only physical mark I would leave on this world would be a ripple in the power source. Without the antidote, I was lost anyway.

"I don't know," I said. "There's too much…"

"That you haven't told me?"

I nodded, unable to speak. Telling him about my magical abilities, I thought, would only get me killed faster.

"Trusting is hard. Knowing who to trust, even harder," Valek said.

"And my track record has been rather horrendous. A weakness of mine."

"No, a strength. Look at Ari and Janco. They appointed themselves your protectors long before I assigned them. All because you stood up for them to the Commander, when their own Captain wouldn't. Think about what you have right now before you give me an answer. You have gained the Commander's and Maren's respect, and Ari's and Janco's loyalty."

"What have I earned from you, Valek? Loyalty? Respect? Trust?"

"You have my attention. But give me what I want, and you can have everything."

The next morning, the Generals prepared to leave. It took four hours for eight retinues to assemble. Four hours of noise and confusion. When everyone had finally passed through the outer gates, it seemed that the castle breathed a sigh of relief. In the wake of this sudden release of tension, servants and guards milled about. They grouped together in small clumps, taking a break before cleaning the eight guest suites. It was during this lull in activity that the Commander informed the rest of the castle staff that the Sitian delegation was scheduled to arrive the next day. His words struck like lightning. A flash of stunned silence was followed by a frenzy of activity as servants dashed off to make the proper preparations.

Although happy to see the backs of Mogkan and Brazell, I wandered listlessly about the castle. I hadn't given Valek his answer. To live, I had to go south, but without the antidote, I wouldn't survive. Dread filled my heart as the reality of my inevitable fate filled my mind.

The next day, my presence was required at the special greeting ceremony for the arriving southern delegation. Apprehension about seeing the Sitians unsettled my stomach. I felt as if someone were saying, "Yelena, take a good look at what you can't have."

Since the throne room had been converted into an office, the only place in the castle suitable for state affairs was the Commander's war room. Once again, Valek stood stiffly in his dress uniform on the Commander's right side, while I waited behind them.

My apprehension turned to awe as I felt the waves of nervous energy pulsing from the high-ranking officials and advisers selected to be a part of the ceremony. When the delegation was announced and invited to enter, I moved to get a better view.

The Sitians floated into the room. Their long, brightly colored, exotic robes draped to the floor, covering their feet. Wearing animal masks trimmed with bright plumes of feathers and fur, they stopped before the Commander and fanned out into a V-shape.

Their leader, wearing a hawk's face, spoke in formal tones. "We bring you greetings and salutations from your southern neighbors. We hope this meeting will bring our two lands closer together. To show our commitment to this endeavor, we have come prepared to reveal ourselves to you." The speaker and the four companions removed their masks in one rehearsed movement.

I blinked several times in astonishment, hoping that during the seconds of darkness everything would be set right. Unfortunately, my world had just mutated from bad to wretched.

Valek glanced at me with a resigned look as if he, too, couldn't believe this new turn of events.

The Sitian leader was Irys. A master-level magician stood a mere three feet before Commander Ambrose.

26

"Ixia welcomes you to our land, and hopes to make a fresh start," the Commander announced to the southern delegation.

As I waited behind the Commander, I wondered what would happen to the Sitians once Valek informed the Commander that Irys was a magician. Contemplating the mischief she might create before leaving the castle, I tried to envision a best-case scenario. I failed, realizing this was probably only the beginning of the end.

Valek watched thoughtfully as the southerners and the Commander exchanged more formal statements. I guessed from Valek's demeanor that Irys had not used her magic. After the official greeting ceremony concluded, the delegation was guided to their quarters to rest from their journey and to await the evening's feast. Protocol decreed that pleasantries and entertainment preceded hard-core negotiations.

Everyone, except the Commander and Valek, filed out of the war room. I started to leave, but Valek grabbed my arm.

"Okay, Valek, let's hear it. Some dire warning I presume?" the Commander asked, sighing.

"The Sitian leader is a master magician," Valek said, a hint of annoyance in his voice. He probably wasn't used to being sighed at.

"That's to be expected. How else could they know we're sincere about creating a trade treaty? We could have ambushed them instead. It's a logical move." Unconcerned, the Commander turned toward the door.

"She doesn't trouble you?" Valek asked. "She's tried to kill Yelena."

The Commander looked at me for the first time since we had entered the war room. "It would be unwise to kill my food taster. Such an act could be misinterpreted as an assassination attempt and halt negotiations. Yelena is safe…for now." He shrugged off any more thought of my future safety and left the war room.

Valek grimaced. "Damn."

"Now what?" I asked.

He kicked at one of the conference chairs. "I anticipated a magician with the southern delegation, but not *her.*"

He shook his head, as if to clear the frustration that gripped his voice. "I'll leave the power twins assigned to you while she's here. Although, if she's determined to get you, there's nothing they or I can do. I lucked out with Mogkan. I was just around the corner when I felt his power surge. Let's hope she behaves while she's a guest in our land."

Valek pushed the chair against the table with a loud bang. "At least I know where all the magicians are. Mogkan was the one I felt during the Generals' brandy meeting. And the southern master is now in the castle. Unless any more decide to show up, we should be safe."

"What about Captain Star?" I asked.

"Star's a charlatan. Her claims of being a magician are just a tactic for scaring her informers so they don't double-cross her." Valek sighed.

"Generals, Sitians and feasts increase my workload. Which reminds me, you need to stay for the entire feast tonight. A tiresome chore, but at least the food should be good. I've heard Rand wanted to use the Criollo for a new dessert, but the Commander refused his request. Another puzzle, since Brazell has been sending the stuff by the wagonload, and has promised to ship the dessert to all the other Generals. They were clamoring after it like it was gold."

I saw a flash in Valek's eye. "Any unusual symptoms, feelings or appetites since you stopped eating the Criollo?"

It had been three days since I had eaten a piece, and I couldn't recall any actual physical symptoms that might be linked to it. Eating it had lifted my spirits and given me a boost of energy. I longed for its sweet taste especially now that my chances for freedom had dwindled.

"A mild craving," I told Valek. "But nothing like an addiction. I find myself thinking about it from time to time, wishing for a piece."

Valek frowned. "It might be too soon. The Criollo could still be in your bloodstream. You'll inform me if something happens?"

"Yes."

"Good. I'll see you tonight."

Poor Valek, I thought, stuffed into his dress uniform three times in as many days. Elaborate decorations had been hung in the dining room for the feast. Crimson and black drapes hung along the walls, and red and gold streamers twisted and dipped from the ceiling. The room was ablaze with light. An elevated platform had been constructed to support a head table where the southern delegation, the Commander and Valek all wore their finest clothes. High-ranking officers and upper-level advisers were seated at round tables circling the room, leaving the middle empty. In the corner a twelve-piece band played sedate music, which was a surprise since the Commander frowned on music, considering it a waste of time.

I sat behind Commander Ambrose so he could pass his plate to me. As predicted, the food was marvelous. Rand had outdone himself.

My dark uniform blended in with the black drapes along the wall, and since I doubted anyone beyond the dais noticed I was there, I watched the others as I waited between courses. Ari and Janco sat next to each other at a table by the door. Attending their first formal function as Captains, they were clearly uncomfortable. Knowing them, I was sure they would rather be drinking beer with their comrades back in the barracks.

Irys and her retinue were seated to the Commander's left. Their formal robes had swirls of color and glittered in the firelight. Irys wore a diamond pendant shaped like a flower, which sparkled on her chest. She ignored my presence, which was fine with me.

After the servants cleared the meal from the tables, they extinguished half of the lanterns. The band quickened their tempo until a pulsating rhythm vibrated the glassware on the tabletops. Costumed dancers burst into the room, holding blazing staffs high above their heads. Fire dancers! They performed an intricate and complex routine. Watching them whirl and spin to the beat left me gasping for breath. I understood now why their festival tent had been so packed with enthusiastic fans.

At one point, Valek leaned back in his chair and said to me, "I don't think I would have made it past the audition, Yelena. I probably would have set my hair on fire by this point."

"What's a singed head for the sake of art?" I teased. He laughed. The mood of the room was energetic and elated. I hoped the Commander wouldn't wait fifteen more years before having another feast.

The dancers finished their second encore and exited the room. Irys rose to offer a toast. The Sitians had brought their finest cognac. Irys poured a glass for the Commander, Valek and herself. She didn't seem offended when the Commander's goblet passed to me.

I swirled the amber liquid and inhaled the sharp odor. Taking a small sip, I rolled the cognac around my tongue, then spat it onto the floor. Gagging and retching with the effort, I tried to expel every last bit of it from my mouth. Valek stared in alarm.

I choked out, "My Love."

Valek knocked over the other two glasses, spilling their contents on the table. As my body reacted to the poison, I watched Valek turn into a black ink spot, and the walls run with blood.

I floated on a crimson sea, colors dancing and whirling around my head. The sound of broken glass raining on stones created an odd melody in my mind. I drifted on a raft made of curly white hair, carried along by a strong current. Irys's soothing voice spoke amidst the tempest of colors, "You'll be fine, just hold on to your life raft. You can ride out this storm."

I awoke in my room. A dim lantern had been lit, and Janco sat in a chair, reading a book. This was much nicer than the last time I had tasted My Love. A soft bed was preferable to lying in a pool of my own vomit. Although this habit of waking in my room without knowing how I got here had to stop.

"Why, Janco, I didn't know you could read," I teased. My voice was hoarse, my throat sore and a dull ache resided deep in my head.

"I'm a man of many unknown talents." Janco smiled. "Welcome back."

"How long have I been out?"

"Two days."

"What happened?"

"After you turned into a madwoman?" Janco asked. "Or why you turned into one?"

I grimaced. "After."

"It's amazing how fast Valek can move," Janco said with admiration. "He pushed you out of sight onto the floor while corking the tainted bottle and using some sleight of hand to swap it for another. He apologized to everyone about being clumsy, and proceeded to pour three new glasses so that southern witch could make her phony toast. The whole incident was smoothed over so quick that only the people on the dais knew what really happened."

Janco scratched at his goatee. "Well, they and Ari. He had his eye on you all night, so when you went down, we were on our way. We slipped behind the head table during the toast and he carried you here. He'd still be here, but I forced him at knifepoint to get some sleep."

Ah, that explained my curly-haired raft. I sat up. The ache in my head intensified. A water pitcher rested on my night table. I poured a glass, draining it dry.

"Valek said you'd be thirsty. He's been here a couple of times, but he's been busy with the southerners. I can't believe that witch had the audacity to try to poison the Commander."

"She didn't. Remember? She poured three glasses from the same bottle. Someone else must have," I said. But the culprit eluded me as the effort of concentrating made my head pound.

"Unless she was going for a murder-suicide. A quick death instead of waiting in our dungeon to be hanged."

"Possible," I said, but I thought it unlikely.

"Valek must agree with you. The treaty discussions are proceeding as if nothing happened." Janco yawned. "Well, now that you're coherent again, I'll get some sleep. It's another four hours until dawn." Janco pushed me back down on the bed. "Get some rest. We'll be back in the morning."

He studied me, indecision creasing his face. "Ari said you screamed and raved a lot while he took care of you. In fact, he said that if Reyad was alive today, he'd gut the bastard without a moment's hesitation. I just thought you might want to know." Janco gave me a brotherly kiss on the forehead and left.

Oh great, I groaned. What else did Ari know? How would I be able to face him in the morning? Well, I thought, nothing I could do about it now. I tried to go back to sleep, but my empty stomach kept growling. All I could think of was food. I examined my hunger, trying to deduce if it was a mental command from Irys like Mogkan had done to me before, but I couldn't come up with a good reason why she would summon me.

Once I had decided to risk the trip, I strapped on my switchblade and made my way on wobbly legs to the kitchen, where I hoped to sneak in and grab some bread before Rand woke up to start his dough.

Slicing off a chunk of cheese to eat along with my loaf, I was about to leave, when Rand's door opened.

"Yelena," he said in surprise.

"Morning, Rand. Just stealing some food."

"I haven't seen you in weeks," he grumped. "Where've you been?" He moved toward the ovens. Opening the first black metal door, he stoked the embers of the fire and added more coal.

"I've been busy. You know. The Generals. The delegation. The feast. Which, by the way, was magnificent, Rand. You're a genius."

He perked up after I appealed to his ego. I resigned myself to the fact that, if I wanted him to think we were still friends, I would have to talk to him. I placed my breakfast on a table and pulled up a stool.

Rand limped toward me. "Someone said you were sick?"

"Yeah. Stomach bug. Haven't eaten in two days, but I'm better now." I gestured to the bread.

"Hold off, I'll make you some sweet cakes."

I watched him mix the batter, making sure he didn't slip in a poisonous ingredient. But after the cakes were under my nose, I dug into them with mindless abandon. The familiar scene of Rand making bread while I sat close by dissolved the awkwardness between us. We were soon chatting and laughing.

It wasn't until his questions turned pointed and specific that I realized Rand was pumping me for information about the Commander and Valek. I clenched my fork, stabbing it hard into my sweet cakes.

"Hear anything about this southern treaty?" Rand asked.

"No." My tone was harsh, and he looked at me with curiosity. "Sorry, I'm tired. I better get back to bed."

"Before you go, you might as well take these beans along." Rand pulled down the glass jar. "I've sautéed, ground, even boiled them, but they still taste unrecognizably terrible." He poured them into a bag, and went to check on his baking fires.

Watching him stir the glowing coals gave me an idea. "Maybe they're not to eat," I said. "Maybe they're a source of fuel." The southern pods had been delivered to Brazell's new factory. Perhaps he was using them to heat his ovens.

"Worth a try," Rand said.

I threw the beans into the hearth fire. We waited for a while, but there were no sudden flames or increase in temperature. While Rand switched his bread pans, I stared into the embers, thinking that as far as the mystery of the beans was concerned, I was out of options.

When Rand started again with his questions, I turned my eyes away from the oven's fire. Pressure knotted in my throat. "I'd better get going or Valek will be wondering where I am."

"Yes, by all means go. I noticed you and Valek have become close. Tell him, for me, not to kill anybody, will you?" Sarcasm rendered Rand's voice sharp.

I lost control and slammed the oven door shut. It echoed in the quiet kitchen. "At least Valek has the decency to inform me when he's poisoning me," I blurted out, but wished I could pull the words from the air and stuff them back into my mouth. Blaming my fatigue, my anger, or Rand for my outburst wouldn't erase what I had just said.

His facial expressions contorted and vacillated from surprise to guilt to anger. "Did Star tell you?" he demanded.

"Ah…" I was at a loss. If I said yes, he would find out from Star that I was lying, and if I said no, he would insist on knowing my source. Either way, he'd figure it out. I had just revealed Valek's entire undercover operation.

Fortunately, Rand didn't wait for me to answer before launching into a tirade. "I should have known she would tell you. She loves to play nasty head games. When you came along, I didn't want to know you. All I wanted was the heap of gold credit that Star offered to apply to my debt if I spiked Valek's test." Rand pounded the table. "Then my damn morals and your damn niceness complicated things. Selling information about you, then having to protect you without looking like I was protecting you made my life hell."

"Sorry for the inconvenience," I said. "I guess I should be grateful, poisonings and kidnappings aside." Sarcasm sharpened my voice.

Rand rubbed his hands over his face. His anger had dissipated. "I'm sorry, Yelena. I was backed into a corner and I couldn't get out without hurting someone."

I softened. "Why did Star want me poisoned?"

"General Brazell commissioned her. *That* shouldn't be a surprise."

"No." I thought for a moment, and then asked, "Rand, is there anyone who can help you get out of this mess? Maybe Valek?"

"Absolutely not! Why do you have such an elevated opinion of him? He's a murderer. You should hate him just for giving you Butterfly's Dust. I would."

"Who told you?" I demanded. "Who else knows? I thought only the Commander and Valek knew."

"Your predecessor, Oscove, told me why he never tried to run, and no, I haven't sold that information to anyone. I do have limits." He tugged at his apron. "Oscove's hatred of Valek rivaled my own, and I understood that, but your relationship with Valek…" Rand's furrowed brows spiked up toward his forehead.

"You're in love with him," he cried.

"That's preposterous," I shouted.

We gaped at each other, too stunned to say anything more.

Then a sweet, nutty aroma reached my nose. Rand, too, sniffed the air. I followed the scent to the oven where I had tossed the mystery beans into the fire. Opening the door, I was greeted by a strong puff of heavenly scent. Criollo.

27

"WHERE DID YOU FIND those beans?" Rand asked. "They're the missing ingredient to the Criollo recipe. I didn't think of roasting them to change the flavor."

"A storeroom downstairs," I lied. I wasn't about to tell him that Valek and I had intercepted them on the way to Brazell's new factory. Which, I now realized, was probably not producing feed but manufacturing Criollo.

"Which storeroom?" Rand asked, a hint of desperation in his voice.

"I don't remember."

"Try harder. If I can duplicate Ving's recipe for Criollo, then maybe I won't be transferred."

"Transferred? Where?"

"You mean Valek hasn't gloated over it by now? He's wanted to get rid of me since the takeover. I'm being sent to Brazell's

manor house, and Ving will come here. He won't last a week!"
Rand spat the words out with bitter force.

"When?"

"Don't know. I haven't gotten my transfer papers yet. So
there's some hope to stop it. *If* you can find me those beans."

He thinks we're still friends, I realized in amazement. Even
after admitting to poisoning me and accusing me of loving his
enemy, he believes I'll do it for him. I had no response. I
stalled. "I'll try," I said, then made a hasty exit.

The first flicker of dawn was cresting the Soul Mountains
as I arrived at Valek's suite unseen. The tall windows in the
living area faced east, and in the weak gray light I saw Valek's
profile as he sat on the couch, waiting for me.

"Back so soon?" he asked. "Too bad. I was just about to
organize a search for your dead body. What happened when
you knocked on the southerner magician's door to sacrifice
yourself? Did they kick you out, thinking you too half-witted
to waste their time on?"

I plopped on a chair to wait out Valek's sarcastic lecture. No
excuse I could offer would satisfy him. He was right, going
out alone had been a foolish thing to do, but logic and an
empty stomach were like oil and water, they didn't mix.

When he was quiet, I asked, "Are you done?"

"What? No rebuttal?"

I shook my head.

"Then I'm finished."

"Good," I said. "Since you're already in a bad mood, I
might as well tell you what happened while I was in the

kitchen. Actually two things: one bad, one good. Which would you like to hear first?"

"The bad," Valek answered. "That allows me the hope that the good will balance things out."

I braced myself and admitted to revealing his undercover operation. Valek's face hardened.

"It's your fault. I was defending you!" I blurted.

He paused. "In protecting my honor, you exposed months of work. I should be flattered?"

"You should," I said. I wasn't about to feel guilty. If he hadn't tested my loyalty with Star and then used me to further his investigation, he wouldn't be in this situation.

His shoulders drooped as he leaned back on the couch, kneading his temples. "I hadn't planned on making arrests till later this month. Better implement my cleanup plan before Rand has a chance to alert Star." Valek rubbed his eyes. "Still, this might be a benefit. I think Star's becoming suspicious. She hasn't been conducting any illicit business in her office. If I bring her in now, I might discover who hired her to poison the Sitian's bottle."

"Star? How?"

"She has a southern assassin in her employ. He would be the only one with the skill and the opportunity. I'm sure the poisoning wasn't a result of Star's personal political views. Her organization would do anything for anybody for the right price. I must find out who would risk so much to compromise the delegation."

He stood up, energized. "What's the good news?"

"The mystery beans are an ingredient in making Criollo."

"Then why did Brazell lie on his permit application? There's no law against manufacturing a dessert," Valek said, matching my leap of logic about the true nature of Brazell's factory.

"Perhaps because the beans are imported from Sitia," I theorized. "That would be illegal; at least until the trade treaty is finalized. Maybe Brazell's been using other southern ingredients or equipment as well."

"Possible. Which is why he was so eager to have a treaty. You'll have to take a good look around when you visit the factory."

"What?"

"The Commander has scheduled a trip to MD–5 when the southerners leave. And where the Commander goes, you go."

"What about you? You're going too, aren't you?" The panic welling in my throat made my voice squeak.

"No. I've been *ordered* to stay here."

"One, and two, and three, four, five. Keep fighting like this and you will die," Janco sang.

I was pinned against the wall. My bow clattered to the floor as Janco's staff tapped my temple, emphasizing his point.

"What's wrong? You're rarely *this* easy to beat." Janco leaned on his bow.

"Too distracted," I said. It was only a day ago that Valek had informed me of the Commander's plans.

"Then what are we doing here?" Ari asked. He and Maren had watched the match.

Still uncomfortable about what he might have heard when I was delusional, I had a hard time meeting Ari's gaze. "Next round, I'll try harder," I said as Janco and I caught our breath. Reviewing our fight, I asked Janco, "Why do you rhyme when you fight?"

"It helps keep my rhythm."

"Don't the other soldiers give you a hard time about it?"

"Not when I beat them."

We started another match. I made an effort to concentrate, but was beaten again.

"Now you're trying too hard. I can see you planning each offensive move," Janco said. "You're giving yourself away, and I'm there for the block before you even strike."

Ari added, "We drill for a reason. Offensive and defensive moves must be instinctive. Let your mind relax, but stay alert. Block out all distractions. Stay focused on your opponent, but not too focused."

"That's a contradiction," I cried in frustration.

"It works," was all Ari said.

I took a couple of deep breaths and cleared the distressing thoughts of my upcoming trip to Brazell's district from my mind. Rubbing my hands along the bow, I concentrated instead on the smooth solidness of the weapon. I hefted it in my grip, trying to make a connection, creating an extension of my thoughts through the bow.

A light vibration tingled through my fingertips as I traced the wood grain. My consciousness flowed through the bow, twisting and turning along the grain, and back along my arm. I possessed the bow and my body at the same time.

I moved into the third round with a sense of heightened

awareness. Intuitively, I knew what Janco was planning. A spilt second before he moved I had my bow up to block. Instead of scrambling to defend myself, I had more time to counter as well as block. I pushed Janco back. A beat of music pulsed in my mind, and I allowed it to guide my attack.

I won the match.

"Amazing," Janco shouted. "Did you follow Ari's advice?"

"To the letter."

"Can you do it again?" Ari asked.

"Don't know."

"Try me." Ari snatched his bow and assumed a fighting stance.

I rubbed my fingers along the bow's wooden grain, setting my mind back into its previous mental zone. It was easier the second time.

Ari was a bigger opponent than Janco. What he lacked in speed, he made up for in strength. I had to modify my defense by dodging his strikes or he would have knocked me off my feet. Using my smaller size to duck under one of his blows, I swept my bow behind his ankles and yanked. He dropped like a sack of cornmeal. I had won again.

"Unbelievable," Janco said.

"My turn," Maren challenged.

Again, I tuned in to that mental zone. Maren's attacks were panther-quick. She favored the fake jab to the face, which usually lured my guard up and away from protecting my torso, leaving it exposed for a body strike. This time, I was one step ahead of her, ignoring the fake and blocking the blow.

A clever opponent, she applied tactics instead of speed or

strength. She charged me. And I knew she planned to move to my side when I stepped up to engage her. Instead of moving up, I spun and tripped her with my bow. Pouncing on her prone form, I pressed my staff against her neck until she conceded the match.

"Damn!" she said. "When a student starts beating her teacher, it means she doesn't need her anymore. I'm walking." Maren strode from the room.

Ari, Janco and I looked at each other.

"She's kidding, right?" I asked.

"Blow to her ego. She'll get over it," Ari said. "Unless you start beating her every time you fight."

"Unlikely," I said.

"Very," huffed Janco, who was probably nursing his own bruised ego.

"That's enough fighting," Ari said. "Yelena, why don't you do some katas to cool down, and we'll quit for the day."

A kata was a fixed routine of different defensive and offensive blocks and strikes. Each kata had a name, and they grew more complex with each skill level. I started with a simple defensive bow kata.

As I moved I watched Ari and Janco become absorbed in conversation. I smiled, thinking that they bickered like an old married couple, and then concentrated on my kata. I practiced finding my mental fighting zone, sliding into and out of it while I performed the appropriate kata moves. Panting, I finished the routine, and noticed Irys watching me from the doorway with great interest.

She was wearing her hawk mistress uniform. Her hair had been tied back in accordance to Ixia's military regulations. She had probably walked through the castle unchallenged.

I glanced toward my "bodyguards." They were engrossed in their conversation, ignoring Irys and me. Uneasiness rolled in my stomach. I inched closer to my companions as she came into the room.

"Won't Valek sense your magic?" I asked her, gesturing to Ari and Janco.

"He's on the other side of the castle," she said as she stepped nearer. "But I did feel someone pulling power before we arrived. Two brief surges. So there is or was another magician in the castle."

"Wouldn't you know?" I asked in alarm.

"Unfortunately no."

"But you do know who it is? Right?"

She shook her head. "There are several magicians that have disappeared. They're either dead or hiding. And some keep to themselves and we never know about them. It could be anyone. I can only identify a magician if I have established a link with him or her, as I have linked with you." Irys examined the weapons lined against the wall.

"What's wrong with the Commander?" she asked. "His thoughts are practically dripping out of his head. He's so open, I could go in and extract any information I wanted if it weren't against our moral code of ethics."

I couldn't answer her. "What are you doing here?" I asked instead.

Irys smiled. She gestured to the bow in my hands. "What were you doing with that weapon?"

Seeing no reason to lie, I explained about my training.

"How did you do today?" she asked.

"I beat all three opponents for the first time."

"Interesting." Irys seemed pleased.

I glanced over at Ari and Janco, who were still involved in their conversation. "Why are you here?" I asked again. "You promised me a year." Then I had a sudden horrific thought. "Am I closer to flameout?"

"There's still time. You've stabilized for now, but how close are you to coming to Sitia?"

"The antidote is beyond my reach. Unless you can steal the information from Valek's mind?"

She frowned. "Impossible. But my healers say if you can filch enough antidote to last a month, there's a possibility we can remove the poison from your body. Come with us when we leave. I have an adviser just your size. She'll wear your uniform and lure Valek and his men away while you take her place. With a mask on, no one would know." Irys spoke with assurance. She was either unconcerned or unaware of the risks.

Hope bloomed in my chest. My heart raced. I had to calm myself with a cold reminder that Irys had said there was a possibility of removing the poison. In other words, no guarantees. The escape plan appeared straightforward, but I searched for loopholes anyway. I knew better than to fully trust her.

Deciding, I said, "Adviser Mogkan was here last week. Is he one of your spies?"

"Mogkan, Mogkan." She turned the name over her tongue.

"Tall with gray eyes and wears his long black hair in a single braid." I formed a picture of him in my mind. "Valek said he has power."

"Kangom! How unoriginal! He dropped from sight ten years ago. There was a big scandal about his alleged involvement with some kidnapping ring. Oh." Irys inhaled sharply and studied my face. Giving her head a tight shake, she asked with keen interest, "So where has he been hiding?"

"MD–5. Is he wanted?"

"Only if he becomes a danger to Sitia. But that explains why we've been picking up occasional flares of magic from that direction." She cocked her head as if straining to hear some faint music. "There is a faint flow of magic to the castle. It could be from Kangom…Mogkan, although it's highly unlikely. He doesn't have that kind of strength. It's probably just a tiny ripple in the power source, like a loop of thread hanging down. It happens from time to time. But I did feel someone pulling power recently." She paused, staring at me with her direct emerald gaze. "Are you coming with me?"

Mogkan's magic might not concern her, but it concerned me. There seemed to be a link between Mogkan's magic and the Commander's unusual behavior, but I couldn't quite grasp the reason why.

Undecided, I rolled it around my mind, much as I moved food in my mouth, tasting for danger. Running away had always been an automatic defensive move, and going south offered my best chance for survival. Months ago, I would have jumped at the offer, but now I felt as if I would be abandoning ship too soon, that there was a remedy yet to be discovered.

"No," I said. "Not yet."

"Are you crazy?"

"Probably, but I need to finish something first, then I'll keep my promise and come to Sitia."

"If you're still alive."

"Maybe you can help me. Is there some way I can shield my mind from magical influence?"

Irys cocked her head. "You're worried about Kangom?"

"Very."

"I think so. You're strong enough to handle it." She handed me the bow. "Do one of your katas, eyes closed, and clear your mind."

I started a blocking bow kata.

"Imagine one brick. Place the brick on the ground, and then make a row of them. Using imaginary mortar, build another row. Keep building until you have a wall as high as your head."

I did as she instructed, and heard a distinct tone as each brick was laid. A wall formed in my mind.

"Stop," she ordered. "Open your eyes."

My wall disappeared.

"Now block me!"

Loud music vibrated in my head, overwhelming me.

"Imagine your wall," Irys shouted.

My brick defense flashed complete in my mind. The music stopped midnote.

"Very good. I suggest you finish your business and escape south. With that kind of strength, if you don't achieve complete control of your magic, someone else might grab it and use it, leaving you a mindless slave." Annoyance quirked her face as she spun on her heel and left the training room.

The moment the door clicked into place, Ari and Janco ended their conversation and blinked as if they had just woken from a deep sleep.

"Done already? How many katas?" Ari asked.

I laughed and put my bow away. "Come on, I'm hungry."

When the Sitian delegation left three days later, I had a sudden panic attack. What the hell was I doing? My one perfect opportunity for escape had slipped away to the south, while I remained behind, preparing to leave for Brazell's manor. Irys had been right; I was crazy. My breath hitched every time I thought of the trip. The Commander's retinue was scheduled to depart in the morning.

I rushed around the castle, packing my own special provisions for the journey. Dilana's sorrowful face greeted me when I stopped by her room for some traveling clothes. Rand's paperwork had been finalized, she said. He was coming with us.

"I requested a transfer, but I doubt it'll be approved," Dilana said as she searched through her piles of clothing. "If only the lout had married me, then we wouldn't be in this predicament."

"There's still time to submit the application. If it's approved, you can travel to MD–5 for the wedding."

"He doesn't want to let anyone know how much he cares for me. He's worried that my safety might be used as leverage against him." She shook her head, refusing to be cheered even when I told her that the new trade treaty with Sitia would allow silk to be imported.

The southern treaty was a simple exchange of goods. Specific items were listed. Only merchants with the proper permits and licenses would be able to buy and sell these items at a fixed price. All caravans would be subject to inspection when crossing the Ixian border at the approved locations. Rand's cup of coffee was only a few months away, but I doubted he would brew some for me since I hadn't spoken to him since our argument in the kitchen. I couldn't get him more beans, and I couldn't explain why.

The morning of our departure was gray and overcast, hinting at snow. The cold season was beginning, which usually indicated the end of travel, not the onset of it. The snows would most likely keep the Commander's retinue at Brazell's until the thawing season. I shuddered at the thought.

Valek stopped me before I left our suite. "This is a very dangerous trip for you. Maintain a low profile and keep your eyes open. Question thoughts in your mind; they might not be your own." He handed me a silver flask. "The Commander has your daily dose of antidote, but if he *forgets* to give it to you, here's a backup supply. Tell no one that you have it, and keep it hidden."

For the first time, Valek trusted me. The metal flask felt warm in my hands. "Thanks."

A feather of fear brushed my stomach as I packed the flask into my backpack. Another danger I hadn't recognized. What else had I missed?

"Wait, Yelena, there's one more thing." Valek's manner and tone were strangely stiff and formal. "I want you to have this." He extended his hand. On his palm sat the beautiful butterfly he had carved. Silver spots on the wings glinted in the sunlight, and a silver chain hung from a small hole drilled into its body.

Valek looped the necklace around my neck. "When I carved this statue, I was thinking about you. Delicate in appearance, but with a strength unnoticed at first glance." His eyes met mine.

My chest felt tight. Valek acted as if he would never see me again. His fear for my safety seemed genuine. But was he worried about *me* or his precious food taster?

28

COMMANDER AMBROSE'S TRAVELING entourage consisted of nearly fifty soldiers from his elite guard. Some led the way, others walked beside the Commander and his advisers atop their horses. Guards also bracketed the small group of servants, who preceded the horses. The remaining soldiers followed behind. Ari and Janco scouted the Commander's planned route and were hours ahead of the procession.

We advanced at a brisk pace in the crisp morning air. The vivid colors of the hot season had long since drained from the forest, leaving behind a barren, gray-hued simplicity. I had tucked Valek's butterfly underneath my shirt, and found myself fingering the lump it made on my chest as we traveled. Valek's gift had caused my emotions to roil. Just when I believed I had figured him out, he surprised me.

Carrying a pack, I also held a walking staff that was a thinly disguised bow. A few of the guards cast suspicious glances my way, but I ignored them. Rand refused to meet my gaze. He stared straight ahead in stony silence. It wasn't long before he lagged behind; his leg prevented him from maintaining the pace.

After a stop for lunch, we continued until an hour before sunset. Major Granten, the official leader of the expedition, wanted to set up camp in the daylight. Spacious tents were raised for the Commander and his advisers, and smaller two-man tents were erected for the servants. I found I would share space with a woman named Bria, who ran errands and served the Commander's advisers.

I settled into the tent while Bria warmed herself by the fire. Lighting a small lantern, I pulled out the book on war symbols that I had borrowed from Valek. After we had deciphered the name of the new successor, I hadn't had a spare moment to interpret Janco's message on my switchblade. There were six silver markings etched into the wooden handle. I began with the top and worked my way to the bottom. My smile grew wider with each translation. Janco could be so annoying, but underneath he could be so sweet.

When Bria entered the tent smelling of wood smoke, I shoved the book into my pack.

Disturbing dreams made for a restless night. I awoke tired in the gray fuzz of dawn. With the amount of time the procession took to eat and reassemble, plus the shorter hours of daylight, I estimated the excursion to Brazell's manor house would take about five days.

On the second night of the trip, I found a note in my tent.

A request for a rendezvous. The next evening while the soldiers set up camp, I was to follow a small, northbound trail that intersected the main road just past our campsite. The message was signed Janco, in a lavish hand. I examined the signature in the fading light, trying to remember if I'd ever seen Janco's writing.

Genuine note or a trap? Should I go or should I stay in camp where it would be safe? I worried the question in my mind throughout the night and all through the third day on the road. What would Valek do in this particular situation? The answer helped me to form a plan.

When the signal to stop for the night sounded, I waited until everyone was occupied before leaving the clearing. Once out of sight, I swept off my cloak and turned it inside out. Before departing the castle I had procured gray cloth from Dilana, which I had then sewn into the inside lining of my cloak just in case I needed to hide in the winter landscape. I hoped the improvised ashen camouflage would be adequate in concealing my presence when I neared the meeting site.

I strapped my bow to my back, sheathed my switchblade on my right leg, then grabbed my rope and grappling hook from my backpack. I found the northern trail. Rather than walk down the narrow path, though, I sought a suitable tree and tossed my hook up into its branches. My first concern was the potential noise of my passage through the treetops, but I soon discovered that trees without leaves only creaked under my weight as I followed the trail.

Maneuvering close to the meeting site, I spotted a tall dark-haired man waiting at the prearranged location. He seemed restless and agitated. Too thin for Janco, I thought. Then the man turned in my direction. Rand.

What was he doing here? I circled the clearing. Discovering no threat lurking in the bushes, I climbed down to the path, leaving my rope hanging from the branch. I tucked my backpack behind the tree's trunk.

"Damn," Rand cursed. "I thought you weren't going to show." His haggard face had dark smudges under his eyes.

"And I thought Janco was supposed to be here."

"I wanted to explain, but there's no time, Yelena." Rand's haunted eyes bored into mine. "It's a trap! Run!"

"How many? Where?" I demanded, pulling the bow from my back. I scanned the woods.

"Star and two goons. Close. Leading you here was supposed to pay off my debt." Tears streaked Rand's face.

I spun on him. "Well, you did a good job. I see you're actually following through on this assignment." I spat the words at him.

"No," he cried. "I can't do it. Run, damn you, run."

Just as I moved to go, Rand's eyes widened with fright.

"No!" He shoved me aside. Something whistled past my ear as I fell to the ground. Rand dropped beside me, an arrow in his chest. Blood welled, soaking his white uniform shirt.

"Run," he whispered. "Run."

"No, Rand," I said, brushing the dirt from his face. "I'm tired of running."

"Forgive me, please." He clutched my hand as his eyes beseeched me through tears of pain.

"You're forgiven."

He sighed once, then stopped breathing. The shine in his brown eyes dulled. I pulled his hood over his head.

"Get up," a man's voice ordered.

I looked into the dangerous end of a loaded crossbow. Leaning on my bow, I rose. With my weight balanced on the balls of my feet, I rubbed my hands along the wooden staff, finding my zone of concentration.

"The area is secured, Captain," the man called out to the woods. "Don't move," he said to me, leveling his weapon at my chest.

Footsteps approached. The man took his eyes off me to look for his companions. I moved.

My first bow strike landed across his forearms. The crossbow sailed from his hands, firing into the woods. My second strike went to the back of his knees. I knocked his feet out from under him. Lying flat on his back, he blinked at me with a stunned expression.

Before he could draw breath, I slammed the point of my bow straight down onto his neck, crushing his windpipe.

A quick glance over my shoulder revealed Star and another man rushing into the clearing. Star shouted and pointed. Her goon drew his sword. I raced down the trail, his heavy footsteps thundering after me. When I reached my rope, I tossed my bow into the woods before scrambling up into the tree. The man's blade stabbed at my legs. Cloth ripped as his sword cut through my pants. The brush of cool steel on my thigh spurred me on.

He cursed as I leaped to the next tree. Moving fast, I swung through the treetops. When the sound of his crashing through the underbrush was far enough behind me, I found a good place to hide. Wrapping myself in my cloak, I hunkered down on a low branch and waited.

Star's thug barreled though the woods. Not far from my perch, he stopped to listen, searching the treetops. My heart raced. I muffled my heavy breathing with my cloak. Sword raised, he hunted for me.

When he was below me, I threw off my cloak and launched myself, hitting his back with my feet. We fell hard. I rolled away and stood before he could recover, then kicked his sword from his hand. He was faster than I had anticipated. He grabbed my ankle, yanking me down.

Next thing I knew, his weight pressed on top of me and his hands were wrapped around my neck. Banging my head on the hard ground, he muttered, "That's for giving me trouble." Then he pressed his thumbs deep into my throat.

Dazed and choking, I plucked at his arms before I remembered my switchblade. I fumbled in my pockets as my vision blurred, turning to snow. The smooth feel of wood greeted my fingertips. I grasped the handle, pulled it out and triggered the button.

The snick of the blade caused fear to flicker in his eyes. For a moment he stared straight into my essence. Then I plunged the knife into his stomach. With a low growl, he increased the pressure on my neck. Blood, hot and sticky, ran down my arms, soaking my shirt. Through dizziness and pain, I jerked the weapon out and tried again. This time, I pointed the tip of the blade up toward his heart. The man hunched forward, driving the knife in farther, and finally collapsed.

The dead man's weight impeded my starved lungs. Summoning my last bit of strength, I rolled his body off of me.

Dazed, I wiped my switchblade clean in the dirt, found my bow and went in search of Star.

Two men. I had just killed two men. A killing machine, I hadn't even hesitated. Fear and rage settled deep in my chest, forming a layer of ice around my heart.

Star hadn't gone far. She waited in the clearing. Her red hair blazed against the dark gray background of the forest dusk. Night would soon be on us.

She made a small noise of surprise when I stepped clear of the trees. Peering through the gloom, she studied the blood on my shirt. The wet material clung to my skin. When she saw I was unharmed, her sharp nose jerked her head around, searching for her goon.

"He's dead," I said.

The color drained from her face. "We can work this out." A pleading note entered her voice.

"No, we can't. If I let you walk away, you'll only return with more men. If I take you to the Commander, I'd have to answer for killing your thugs. I'm out of options." I stepped toward her, my body frozen with dread. The others I had killed in self-defense during the heat of battle; this would be difficult—this would be premeditated.

"Yelena, stop!" someone called from behind me. I spun.

One of the Commander's soldiers stood with a sword in his hand. As he moved closer, I judged the distance between us.

He must have recognized my battle stance because he stopped and sheathed his sword. Pulling the wool cap off his head, he let his black curls spring free.

"I thought you had orders to stay at the castle," I said to Valek. "Won't you be court-martialed?"

"And I thought your killing days were over," he replied as he examined the prone form of Star's thug. His crushed windpipe had suffocated him. "Tell you what. If you don't tell, I won't. That way we can both avoid the noose. Deal?"

I jerked my head at Star. "What about her?"

"There's an arrest warrant out for her. Did you even consider taking her to the Commander?"

"No."

"Why not?" Valek didn't try to hide his disbelief. "Killing isn't the only solution to a problem. Or has that been your formula?"

"*My* formula! Excuse me, Mr. Assassin, while I laugh as I remember my history lessons on how to deal with a tyrannical monarch by killing him and his family."

Valek flashed me a dangerous look.

I was on the edge. Changing tactics, I said, "My actions were based on what I thought you would do if you were ambushed."

He considered my words in silence for an uncomfortable length of time.

Star seemed horrified by our discussion. She glanced around as if planning her escape.

"You really don't know me at all," Valek said.

"Think about it, Valek, if I took her to the Commander and explained the details, what would happen to me?"

The sad knowledge in his face said it all. I would be arrested for killing Star's men, the food taster's job would pass on to the next prisoner awaiting execution and I would spend my last few days in a dank dungeon.

"Well, then, it was fortunate for both of you that I arrived," Valek said. He whistled a strange birdcall just as Star made her escape.

She dashed down the trail. I moved to follow, but Valek told me to wait. Two gray forms materialized from the dark forest on either side of the road. They grabbed Star. She yelped in surprise and anger.

"Take her back to the castle," Valek ordered. "I'll deal with her when I get back. Oh, and send a cleanup crew. I don't want anyone stumbling onto this mess."

They began to pull Star away.

"Wait," she said. "I have information. If you release me, I'll tell you who plotted to ruin the Sitian treaty."

"Don't worry." Valek's blue eyes held an icy glare. "You'll tell me." He was about to walk past her, when he paused. "However, if you want to reveal your patron now, then we can skip a painful interrogation later."

Star's nose twitched as she considered his offer. Even in this situation, she was still the shrewd businesswoman.

"Lying would only worsen your predicament," Valek warned.

"Kangom," she said through clenched teeth. "He wore a basic soldier's uniform with MD–8 colors."

"General Dinno," Valek said without surprise.

"Describe Kangom," I ordered, knowing that Kangom was another name for Adviser Mogkan, but unable to tell Valek how I had come by this information.

"Tall. Long black hair in a soldier's braid. An arrogant bastard. I almost kicked him out, but he showed me a pile of gold I couldn't refuse," Star said.

"Anything else?" Valek asked.

Star shook her head. Valek snapped his fingers. As the camouflaged men escorted Star back toward the castle, I said, "Could it be Mogkan?"

"Mogkan?" Valek looked at me as if I had sprouted antennae. "No. Brazell was far too happy about the delegation. Why would he jeopardize the treaty? That doesn't make sense. Dinno on the other hand was furious with the Commander. He probably sent one of his men to hire Star."

I tried to fathom the reason why Mogkan would endanger the treaty negotiations when trade with Sitia was to Brazell's benefit. Unable to deduce a logical answer, I wondered how I could convince Valek that Mogkan had hired Star.

I began to shiver. Blood soaked my uniform shirt and stained my hands. I wiped the blood on my ripped pants. Retracing my steps, I found my cloak, but before I could swing it over my shoulders, Valek said, "You better leave your clothes here. There would be quite a fuss if you showed up for dinner soaked with blood."

I retrieved my pack from behind the tree. Valek turned his back while I changed into a clean uniform. I wondered if he had any more sneaks in the woods as I wrapped my cloak around me.

We set out for the camp.

"By the way, nice work," Valek said as we passed the second dead body. "I saw the fight. I wasn't close enough to help. You held your own. Who gave you the knife?"

"I bought it with Star's money." A stretch of the truth, but I wasn't about to get Janco into trouble.

Valek snorted. "Fitting."

When we arrived, Valek melted into a group of soldiers while I rushed to the Commander's tent to taste his dinner. The entire Star episode had taken only an hour and a half, but my battered body felt as if I'd been gone for days.

As I sat by the campfire that night, my muscles trembled in reaction to the fight. Grief for Rand surprised me as melancholy thoughts filled my mind. The flames of the fire wiggled accusing red fingers at me. What do you think you're doing? they asked. Three men are dead because of you. How are you going to help anyone? Pure conceit, the flames admonished. Go south. Let Valek worry about the Commander and what Brazell's up to, you silly girl. The fire pulsed, making shooing motions at me.

I pulled my gaze away, blinking into the darkness. Was it my imagination or was someone trying to influence me? Summoning the mental image of my protective brick wall cooled some of the doubts, but not all of them.

Rand's disappearance wasn't noticed until the next morning. Thinking he had run away, Major Granten sent out a small search party, while the others continued deeper into Brazell's district.

The rest of the journey was uneventful except for the disturbing fact that the closer we drew to Brazell's manor house, the blanker the look grew on the Commander's face. He had ceased to give orders or to take an interest in the events surrounding him. The intelligent, piercing glint that had made his gaze lethal faded with each step, leaving only a vacant, dull expression in its place.

In contrast to the Commander, I was beginning to feel rather warm. My hands left slick prints on my bow as we neared Brazell's. I scanned the woods for an ambush as dread hovered behind me like a pair of hands waiting to wrap around my neck. The ground felt soft and sucked at my boots so that each step required an extra effort. Big mistake, big mistake, coming to Brazell's, I thought as my mind whirled on the edge of panic. To calm myself I imagined my brick wall, and focused my thoughts on survival.

An hour away from Brazell's, the rich aroma of Criollo hung heavy in the air. As a precaution, I slipped into the forest off the main trail and stashed my backpack in the crook of a tree, hiding my bow nearby. Taking only my picks from the bag, I pulled my hair into a bun, using the thin metal tools to hold it in place.

At the outer buildings of Brazell's manor our pace slowed. A collective sigh of relief rippled through the soldiers. They had safely delivered the Commander. Now they could rest in the barracks until it was time to return home.

I experienced the opposite of the soldiers' ease despite my

mental protection. I found it difficult to breathe as I followed the Commander and his advisers to Brazell's office. I heard the liquid slamming in my heart, and felt light-headed.

When we entered, Brazell rose from behind his desk, a large smile adorning his square face. Mogkan hovered behind Brazell's right shoulder. With my mental shield in place, I remained near the door, hoping to be inconspicuous. As Brazell recited a formal greeting, I surveyed his office. Lavish in its decoration, the room had a heavy, brooding feel. Black walnut wood framed hunting scenes, and crimson and purple velvet draped the windows. Brazell's oversize ebony desk seemed a barrier between his high-backed leather chair and the two overstuffed, velvet seats facing it.

"Gentlemen, you must be tired from your trip," Brazell said to the Commander's advisers as a tall woman entered the office. "My housekeeper will guide you to your rooms."

She motioned for them to follow her. As the advisers exited the room, I tried to slip out with them, but Mogkan grabbed my arm.

"Not yet," he said. "We have special plans for you."

Alarmed, I glanced at the Commander, sitting in one of the chairs. The abundant purple fabric of the cushion exaggerated his pale face and slight build. No expression touched his features; he stared into the distance. A puppet waiting for his master to pull the strings.

"Now what?" Brazell asked Mogkan.

"We put on a show for a few days. Take him to see the factory as planned." Mogkan gestured toward the Commander.

"Keep his advisers happy. Once everyone's hooked, then we don't have to pretend."

"And her?" Satisfaction bent the edges of Brazell's mouth.

I kept the picture of the brick wall in my mind.

"Yelena," Mogkan said, "you've learned a new trick. Red brick, how mundane. But…"

I heard a faint scraping noise like stone grinding on stone.

"Weak spots. Here and here." Mogkan pointed a finger in the air. "And I do believe this brick is loose."

Mortar crumbled. Small holes appeared in my mental wall.

"When I have a moment, I'll smash your defenses into dust," Mogkan promised.

"Why waste your time?" Brazell asked, drawing his sword. "Dead. Now." He advanced with murderous intent blazing in his eyes. I flinched back a step.

"Stop," Mogkan ordered. "We need her to keep Valek in line."

"But we have the Commander," Brazell whined like a child.

"Too obvious. There are seven other Generals to consider. If we kill the Commander while he's here they would be suspicious. You'd never become his successor. Valek knows this, so any threat to the Commander won't work." Mogkan turned his calculating eyes on me. "But who cares about a food taster? No one except Valek. And if she dies here, the Generals will agree that it was justified."

Mogkan leaned over the Commander, whispering in his ear. The Commander opened his briefcase, withdrew a flask and handed it to Mogkan. My antidote.

"Starting now, you'll come to me for your medicine," Mogkan said, smiling.

Before I could react, someone knocked on the door. Two soldiers entered the office without waiting for permission.

"Your escorts are here, Yelena. They'll take good care of you." Mogkan turned to the guards. "She doesn't need a tour. Our infamous Yelena has come home."

29

I SCANNED THE TWO MUSCULAR guards. Swords, short knives and manacles hung from their belts. They were well armed, and wore grim expressions of recognition. I was outmatched. I touched the familiar lump of the switchblade strapped to my thigh, but decided to wait until the odds were more in my favor.

The guards gestured for me to accompany them. I shot a final beseeching look at the Commander, but nothing so far had roused him from his oblivious stupor.

I felt a small surge of hope when the guards led me to a tiny, barren room in the guest wing instead of the underground cells in which Brazell housed his prisoners. Having spent a week in those dank, rat-infested chambers after I killed Reyad, I loathed the thought of ever going back.

After the door was locked behind me, I took comfort from removing the picks from my hair. The lock was a basic pin-

and-tumbler type, which would be easy to open. Before springing it, I slipped a small pick with a mirror on the end under the door. With the mirror, I spied a pair of boots standing on either side. Those overachieving guards had stationed themselves outside my room.

I went to the window. The guest wing was on the second floor. My view included the main courtyard. I could jump to the ground if I was desperate, but for now I would wait.

The next day, I was permitted out of my room only to taste the Commander's meals. After breakfast, Mogkan waved a small vial of antidote in front of my face.

"If you want this, you must answer a question," he said.

I steadied my nerves. With a calm voice, I replied, "You're bluffing. If you wanted me dead, I wouldn't be standing here now."

"I assure you, it's only a temporary condition." Anger burned in his eyes. "I'm merely offering you a choice. Death by Butterfly's Dust is a long, ugly and excruciating experience, while, say, slitting your throat is quick—a moment of pain."

"What's the question?"

"Where's Valek?"

"I don't know," I said truthfully. I hadn't seen Valek since the fight in the woods. Mogkan considered my answer. Taking advantage of his distracted state, I plucked the vial from his hand and drained it in a single gulp.

Mogkan's face reddened with fury. He seized my shoulders then shoved me toward the guards. "Take her back to her room," he ordered.

Once there, I wondered what mischief Valek was creating. I doubted he was sitting idle. Mogkan's questions on Valek's whereabouts confirmed my suspicions. Restless, I paced the small chamber, longing for a workout with Ari and Janco.

During my brief visits with the Commander over the next few days, I began to recognize that my presence was part of Mogkan's show. In order to keep the Commander's advisers from becoming suspicious, Brazell pretended the Commander was still giving orders. At one point, Brazell leaned close to the Commander as if they were having a private conversation, then proclaimed that, per Commander Ambrose's request, a factory tour would be scheduled for the next day.

I was allowed to join the group going to the plant. This surprised me almost as much as the fact that none of the Commander's advisers made a protest or comment about Brazell manufacturing Criollo instead of the livestock feed he had reported on his permit. They munched on bars of Criollo, content to nod and agree with Brazell that the factory was a marvelous invention.

As we walked through the building, sweltering heat pulsed from the gigantic roasters that were continuously fed with Sitian beans. Workers, streaked with sweat and black dust, shoveled coal into the massive fires under the ovens. Once roasted, the beans were conveyored to a large area where other workers cracked their shells with mallets, extracting a dark brown nib. Steel rollers crushed the nibs into a paste. The paste was spooned into a five-foot-wide metal container to which sugar, milk and butter were added. Using steel pitchforks, workers stirred these ingredients until the mixture became a smooth, thick liquid, which was then poured into square and rectangular-shaped molds.

A veritable shop of delightful smells and flavors, the place was, however, a joyless environment. The dour employees, uniforms soiled with Criollo and sweat, grunted and strained under the physical exertion. During the tour, I searched the various work areas for poisonous or addictive ingredients that might be slipped into the mix but found none.

When the group returned to Brazell's manor house, I watched the animated expressions on the advisers' faces leak away, leaving behind the same blank look that had taken over the Commander's face. Which meant that there must be a link between eating Criollo and succumbing to Mogkan's magic. Mogkan's show would end as soon as he had gained control of the advisers' minds, and when that happened my accommodations would change for the worse.

That night, under cover of darkness, I dropped my cloak out the window of my room and banged on the door, calling to the guards.

When the door opened, I declared, "I need a bath." Without waiting for a response, I strode with purpose down the hallway. The guards followed.

At the baths, one guard stopped me in the hallway while his companion looked around inside. Only when he was sure I would be alone did he nod and step back.

As I went through the entrance, I said in an authoritative voice, "I don't need an audience. Wait here, I won't be long."

To my delight they remained outside. I scurried to the far wall where, hidden from view, there was another entrance. The guards might work in the manor house, but I'd grown up here. With a child's curiosity and free time, I had been able to explore almost every corner of the house. Only Brazell's private suite, office and Reyad's wing had been off-limits. Unfortunately once I turned sixteen, Reyad's wing became my daily nightmare. Pushing away the thought, I concentrated on the present.

I pulled the handle of the door and encountered my first unwanted surprise. It was locked. No problem, I thought, reaching for my picks. The mechanism popped with ease, the door swung open, and I discovered a second nasty shock. One of the guards waited in the hallway.

He smirked. I rushed him. Using my momentum, I shoved him off balance and punched him in the groin. A dirty Valek move, but I didn't care as I raced down the corridor, leaving the guard far behind.

Slipping out the south entrance, I retrieved my cloak, and then headed west to find my pack and bow. Bright moonlight illuminated my path, and I could see where I was going; however, my true path was less evident. I knew I couldn't help the Commander from a locked room, but I was unsure what I could do from the outside. I needed to talk to Valek. Deciding it would be too risky to go to the barracks, I took to the treetops. Only Valek knew this trick. Once he learned of my escape, he would track me.

When I reached the open area reserved for the annual fire

festival's visit to MD–5, I stopped for the night. Shivering in my cloak, I huddled against a tree trunk, blowing clouds of steam from my mouth. Once, I heard the baying of dogs and distant shouts, but no one came close to my makeshift bed in the tree. Sleep eluded me; I was too cold and nervous. Instead, I envisioned the bright fabric of the festival tents in the clearing, hoping to warm myself by remembering the hot energy of the festival nights.

I imagined the big tops in their proper places. Dancers, singers and acrobats lined up in the middle of the clearing. Food stands huddled in and around the big tents, scenting the air with mouthwatering treats. I went to the festival every hot season when I had lived under Brazell's roof. It had been the highlight of my existence. Although my memories of those last two years, when I had been Reyad's laboratory rat, were dreadful.

Unable to resist, I climbed down from the tree and walked through my imaginary festival. I stopped where the acrobatics tent had stood, wondering if I could still perform the tumbling routine that had won me first place and the fire amulet. Without thought, I tossed off my cloak and started a warm-up. In the back of my mind, I knew I should be hiding, that it was stupid to be this exposed to discovery, but the desire to relive my one moment of true joy was too strong to deny.

Soon all thoughts of Brazell, Reyad and Mogkan were banished as I spun and soared through the air. My mind settled into the mental zone of pure concentration I used when I fought. I relished the release, brief as it might be, from my days of tension and threat.

As I performed my routine, I discovered that I could push my heightened awareness beyond my body to encompass the trees, even sense the animals in the forest. An owl, perched high on a branch, tracked the movements of a field mouse. A family of possums slipped without sound through the underbrush. A woman, crouched behind a stone, watched me.

Stealing into Irys's mind was as easy as slipping on a pair of gloves. Her thoughts flowed into my mind like silk. I reminded her of her younger sister, Lily, and she longed to be back home with her family, not sneaking around in cold, horrid Ixia. The situation in the north was getting dangerous; she would be safer in Sitia. But for how long? she wondered. As a master-level magician, she couldn't allow the abuse of power that she had felt emanating from this area to continue. Kangom, who called himself Mogkan, was producing Theobroma at alarming quantities. He had also rigged a way to intensify his power.

Irys's thoughts returned to me, and I felt a tug on our mental connection.

Yelena, what are you doing in my mind?

I'm not sure how I got here.

Haven't you figured it out by now? You're focusing your magic when you fight. That's why you instinctively anticipate your opponent's moves. I felt you at the castle when you were fighting your friends. Now that you have learned to harness your power, you have taken the next logical step by expanding it beyond the immediate area.

My surprise broke our link. I stopped, panting in the cold night air as Irys emerged from the woods.

"Does that mean I'm not going to flame out?" I asked.

"You've stabilized, but you won't get any stronger unless you receive the proper training. You don't want to waste your potential. Come south now; your pursuers are miles away."

"The Commander…"

"Is ensorcelled. Nothing you can do; his mind is probably gone. Mogkan has been feeding him Theobroma. I've smelled it since I arrived."

"Theobroma? Do you mean Criollo? The brown-colored sweet that Brazell's manufacturing."

"That sounds right. It opens a mind to magical influence. It relaxes the mental defenses, allowing easy access to someone's mind. We use it as a training tool in controlled situations where a fledgling magician is close to the subject. The Commander has a strong personality, very resistant to magical suggestion. Theobroma breaks down that barrier, which helps when a student is learning, but using it on the Commander to gain control of his mind is the same as rape." Irys pulled her cloak tight around her shoulders. "Even with Theobroma, a magician shouldn't be able to reach the Commander's mind from this distance, but Mogkan has. He has found a way to boost his power."

Irys rubbed her arms with her hands, trying to warm up. "I'm guessing Mogkan's visit to the castle was to lock himself into the Commander's mind so he could lead him out here."

"What can we do to break the lock?" I asked.

"Kill Mogkan. But it'll be difficult. He's very powerful."

"Isn't there another way?" I recalled my conversation in the woods with Valek about murder as a solution. *My* formula, he had said, and it still annoyed me. He'd probably never been in the lose–lose situation I was always finding myself in.

"Block Mogkan's power supply. That might work. He'll still have his magic, but it won't be enhanced."

"What would his extra power look like? How do we find it?"

"My guess would be that he's either recruited a number of magicians to pool their power, or he's devised a way to concentrate the power source without warping it." She paused, considering. "Diamonds."

"Diamonds?" A cold knot of anxiety churned in my stomach. There was so much I didn't know about magic.

"Yes. Very expensive, but they will gather and store power like a hot coal holds heat. He might be using diamonds to enhance his magic. He would need a man-size circle of diamonds, and that's not easily hidden. If we could find this circle I might be able to use it to block his power or, at least, redirect it long enough for you to awaken the Commander."

"What if the source is a group of magicians? How would I recognize them?"

"Unfortunately, Ixia doesn't have a uniform for magicians," Irys said, her voice sharp with sarcasm. "Instead of searching for them, look for an empty room with a wagon-wheel design painted on the floor. To link magical power, each magician must be perfectly aligned along the edge of a circle."

"I can search the manor, but I need help," I said. "I need Valek."

"You need a miracle," Irys replied with a wry twist to her lips.

"Can you direct Valek here?"

"He's already on his way. You two have forged a strong connection, although I don't know if it's of magical origin." Irys
pursed her lips. "I'd better go before Valek arrives. When and if
you discover the source of Mogkan's extra power, chant my name
in your mind. I'll hear your call because we, too, have created a
bond. Our mental link grows stronger each time we communicate. I'll try to help you with the Commander. But no promises.
I'm after Mogkan." She disappeared into the forest.

While I waited for Valek, I paced on the packed dirt and tried
to think of a way to find Mogkan's power source. Irys's words
about needing a miracle were, indeed, an understatement.

To distract myself, I focused on my surroundings. The tread
of many feet had rubbed out the grass and trampled the earth
until it was worn smooth and shiny. I remembered digging my
heels into this same hard dirt the last time I was here, when
Reyad dragged me to the manor house to punish me for disobeying him and winning the amulet. I had pressed that prize
so tight against my skin it had left a mark. Then I had hidden
it to keep it out of Reyad's cruel hands.

Two years had passed since I had buried my amulet.
Someone had probably discovered it by now. For an exercise,
I tried using my new magical skill. Directing my awareness
downward, I circled the clearing. I made many circuits and was
growing bored, when suddenly, the soles of my feet felt hot.
When I continued they cooled. I moved here and there until,
once more, heat stabbed my feet.

Taking my grappling hook from my pack, I dug at the

spot. My efforts revealed some fabric. I tossed my hook aside and clawed at the ground with my fingernails, uncovering my lost amulet.

It was dull and covered with dirt. The ribbon that held it was torn and stained. Pressing the flame-shaped amulet against my chest, I felt warmth emanating from it. I put it down to fill the hole, humming a tune. Cleaning the palm-size medal on my pants, I strung it onto the necklace chain with Valek's butterfly.

"Not the best hiding place. Wouldn't you agree?" Valek asked.

I jumped. How long had he been standing behind me?

"They're searching for you. Why did you run?" he asked.

I briefed Valek on the Commander, Mogkan, the factory and the advisers, hoping he would draw the same conclusions I had.

"So Mogkan is using Criollo to take control of their minds, but where's he getting the power?" Valek asked.

"I don't know. We need to search the manor."

"You mean, *I* need to?"

"No, *we*. I grew up there. I know every inch." The first place I wanted to look was in Reyad's laboratory wing. "When do we start?"

"Now. We have four hours till dawn. What are we looking for?"

When I explained that we were seeking either a circle of diamonds or a painted wheel, Valek's thin eyebrows puckered as if he wanted to question me about how I had come by this information. He held his peace and headed back toward the barracks.

I hid outside while Valek changed into his black skintight sneak suit. He brought me a dark-colored shirt to wear over my bright red uniform shirt, and carried an unlit bull's-eye lantern. My cloak would be too cumbersome for creeping through the halls, so I hid it in the bushes.

We found a back door near the servants' quarters. Valek lit the lantern. Pushing the slide almost closed, he allowed only a thin ray of light to escape. Inside the manor, I took the lead.

Reyad's suite was in the east wing on the ground floor, opposite the laboratory. The entire wing had been his, and there were a number of doors that he'd kept locked while I had been the resident laboratory rat.

Old horrors haunted me as we searched. My skin felt tight and hot. I recognized the faint acidic aroma of fear that mixed with the dust stirred by our footsteps. It was my smell. I had worn it like a perfume whenever Reyad dragged me to his test.

The thick air pressed down on me, filling my mouth with the taste of ashes and blood. I had bitten my hand without conscious thought. It was an old habit, a way to stifle my cries.

Exploring the laboratory room, the thin lantern's beam spotlighted instruments hanging from the walls and piled on the tables. Each revelation sent a cold numbing pulse through my body, and I shrank away from the large shadows of equipment unrevealed, unwilling to even brush against them. The room resembled a torture chamber rather than a place for experiments.

Feeling like an animal pierced in the metal jaws of a trap, I wanted to scream and bolt from the room. Why had I brought Valek here? Brazell's advisers were housed on the second floor. Mogkan's diamond device, if there was such a thing, was probably hidden near his room, not down here.

Valek hadn't said a word since lighting the lantern. In the hallway outside Reyad's bedroom, a physical force prevented me from entering. My muscles trembled. An icy sweat soaked my uniform. I waited at the door while Valek went in. I could see the dark malevolent shape of Reyad's sadistic "toy" chest lurking in a corner of the room. If I burned that chest to cinders, I wondered, would my nightmares cease?

"Not if I can help it," Reyad's ghost said, materializing beside me in the hallway.

I jerked back, hitting the wall. A yelp escaped my lips before I could shove my hand into my mouth.

"I thought you were gone for good," I whispered.

"Never, Yelena. I will always be with you. My blood has soaked into your soul. You have no chance of cleansing me away."

"I have no soul," I said under my breath.

Reyad laughed. "Your soul is drenched black with the blood of your victims, my dear, that is why you can't see it. When you die, that heavy blood-filled essence will sink to the bottom of the earth where you will burn in eternity for your crimes."

"From the voice of experience," I whispered with a rage that made my voice hiss.

Valek came out of Reyad's room. With a face pale as bone, he stared at me with a horrified expression so long that I wondered if he had been struck dumb. Finally, closing the door, Valek walked past the ghost without seeing him, then stopped at the next locked room, pausing a moment with his head bowed to press a hand to his forehead.

"*There's* someone who really needs to be haunted," Reyad said, stabbing a ghostly white finger at Valek. "It's a shame he doesn't let his demons bother him, because I know a certain dead King that would love to plague him." Reyad looked at me. "Only the weak invite their demons to live with them. Isn't that right?"

I refused to answer Reyad as I followed Valek. We continued our search but it was obvious that, other than the laboratory, the wing had been abandoned. There were three doors left.

While Valek picked the two locks, Reyad chatted on. "My father will soon send you to me, Yelena. I'm looking forward to spending eternity with you." He leered and wiggled his fingers at me.

But I was no longer interested in the ghost. The contents of the room before me riveted my attention. Inside, dozens of women and a few men flinched from the yellow beam of Valek's lantern. Greasy hair obscured their dirt-streaked faces. Rags clung to their emaciated bodies. None of them spoke or cried out. To my increasing horror, I realized they were chained to the floor. In circles. One outer circle and two inner rings with lines painted between them.

When Valek and I stepped into the room, the foul stench of unwashed bodies and excrement wafted through the air. Gagging, I covered my mouth. Valek moved among them, asking questions. Who are you? Why are you here? His queries were met with silence. Their vacant eyes followed his passage. They remained where they were chained, staring.

I began to recognize some of the grubby faces. They had lived in the orphanage with me. They were the older girls and boys who had "graduated" and were supposed to be employed throughout the district. The sight of one girl, her ginger hair dull and matted, finally made me cry out in pain.

Carra's soft brown eyes held no sign of intelligence as I stroked her shoulder and whispered her name. The free-spirited girl I had cared for in the orphanage had become a mindless, empty shell of a woman.

"My students," Reyad said. His chest puffed out in pride as he floated in the middle of the room. "The ones who *didn't* fail."

"What now?" I asked Valek with a shaky voice.

"You're arrested and thrown in the dungeon," Mogkan answered from the entrance.

Valek and I spun in unison. Mogkan loomed in the doorway, his arms folded across his chest. Valek charged him; fury blazed in his eyes. Mogkan stepped back into the hallway. I saw Valek stop just past the doorway and raise his hands in the air. Damn, I thought, racing to help him.

Mogkan stood like a coward behind eight guards. The tips of their swords were aimed mere inches from Valek's chest.

30

As sword points pricked my back, I watched Valek, expecting him to spring into action during the whole miserable trip to Brazell's holding cells. I waited for him to blur into motion as they stripped and searched us, enduring the humiliation of being prodded and poked by rough hands as they confiscated my backpack, switchblade and necklace. Losing my clothing didn't upset me as much as losing Valek's butterfly and my amulet.

I prepared for a sudden jailbreak when we were led down into the prison, and was still waiting as we were shoved into adjoining cells.

I held my breath as the heavy metal lock clanged shut on our underground chambers. The soldiers tossed our clothing in through the bars. Then they left, abandoning us to blackness. I fumbled with my uniform, trying to button my shirt in the dark.

Here I was again. A nightmare turned real as we went

through the guardroom, down one flight of steps, and into Brazell's small dungeon, which only contained eight cells, four on each side of a short corridor. Valek and I were in the two cells closest and to the left of the steps. A familiarly loud, rancid stench permeated the prison. The thick, silty air so overpowered my senses that it took me a while to realize we were the only occupants.

Unable to bear the sudden quiet, I asked, "Valek?"

"What?"

"Why didn't you fight the guards? I would have helped you."

"Eight men had drawn swords pointed at my chest. Any sudden movement and I would have been skewered. I'm flattered that you think I could win against those odds. Four armed opponents, maybe, but eight is definitely too many."

I could hear the amusement in Valek's voice.

"Then we pick the locks and make our escape?" My confidence was based on the fact that Valek was a master assassin and trained fighter, a man who wouldn't stay confined for long.

"That would be ideal, provided we had something to pick them with," Valek replied, dashing my hopes.

I searched my cell with my hands. Finding nothing but filthy straw, rat droppings and unrecognizable muck, I sank to the floor with my back against the one stone wall I shared with Valek.

After a long moment, Valek asked, "Was that your fate? If you hadn't killed Reyad, were you slated to be chained to the floor, mindless?"

The image of those captives burned in my mind. My flesh

crawled. For the first time, I was content to have failed Reyad's tests.

As I thought more about them, I remembered a comment Irys had made regarding a magician's ability to steal magic from others. Finally, the significance of the women and men sitting in circles hit me. Mogkan's extra power came from those chained captives. Brazell, Reyad and Mogkan must have screened the children of the orphanage for magical potential. Then, while experimenting on them, Mogkan had wiped their minds clean, leaving them mindless vessels from which to draw more power.

"I think Brazell and Reyad were determined to reduce me to that mental state. But I endured." I explained my theory about the captives to Valek.

"Tell me what happened to you," Valek said, his voice tight.

I paused. Then my tale flowed from my lips, in bits and pieces at first, but the words soon gushed with the same speed as the tears streaking down my face. I didn't spare him any details. I didn't gloss over the unpleasant parts. Telling Valek everything about my two years as a laboratory rat, Reyad's tortures and torments, the cruel games, the humiliations, the beatings, the longing to be good for Reyad, and, finally, the rape that led to murder, I purged myself of the black stain of Reyad. I felt light-headed with the release.

Valek remained silent throughout my disclosure, neither commenting nor questioning. Finally, with ice crystallizing in his voice he said, "Brazell and Mogkan will be destroyed."

Promise or a threat, I couldn't tell, but with all of Valek's force behind it, it was more than idle talk.

As if they had heard their names, Brazell and Mogkan stepped through the main door of the dungeon. Four guards holding lanterns escorted them. They stopped at our cells.

"It's good to see you back where you belong," Brazell said to me. "My desire to feel your blood on my hands has tempted me, but Mogkan has kindly informed me of your fate, should you not receive your antidote." Brazell paused, and smiled with pure satisfaction. "Seeing my son's killer writhing in excruciating pain will be better justice. I'll visit later to hear your screams. And if you beg me, I might put you out of your misery, just so I can breathe in the hot scent of your blood."

Brazell's gaze bored into Valek's cell. "Disobeying a direct order is a capital offense. Commander Ambrose has signed your death warrant. Your hanging is scheduled for noon tomorrow." Brazell cocked his head, appraising Valek like a thoroughbred. "I think I shall have your head stuffed and mounted. You'll make an effective decoration in my office when I become Commander."

Laughing, Brazell and Mogkan left the dungeon. The darkness that flowed in after them felt even heavier than before. It pressed against my chest, giving me a tight, panicky feeling around my ribs. I paced my cell. My emotions swung from sheer terror to overwhelming despondency. I kicked at the bars, threw straw into the air and pounded on the walls.

"Yelena," Valek finally said, "settle down. Get some sleep; you'll need your strength for tonight."

"Oh yeah, everyone needs to be well rested to die," I said,

but regretted my harshness when I remembered that Valek, too, faced death. "I'll try."

I lay on the foul straw, knowing it was futile to try and rest. How could anyone sleep her last hours away?

Apparently, I could.

I woke with a cry. My nightmare about rats melded with reality as I felt a warm, furry mass resting on my legs. Leaping to my feet, I kicked the rodent. It crashed into the wall and skittered away.

"Nice nap?" Valek asked.

"I've had better. My sleeping companion snored."

Valek grunted in amusement.

"How long was I out?"

"It's hard to tell without the sun. I'm guessing it's close to sunset."

I had received my last dose of antidote yesterday morning. That gave me until tomorrow morning to live, but the symptoms of the poison would take hold sometime tonight.

"Valek, I have a confess…" My throat closed. My stomach muscles contracted with such severity that I felt as if someone were trying to rip them from my body.

"What's the matter?"

"Stomach cramp from hell," I said, still gasping even though the pain had subsided. "Is this the start?"

"Yes. They begin slowly, but soon the convulsions will be continuous."

Another wave of agony hit, and I crumpled to the floor. When it passed, I crawled to my straw bed, waiting for the next assault. Unable to endure the anticipation in silence, I said, "Valek, talk to me. Tell me something to distract me."

"Like what?"

"I don't care. Anything."

"Here's something you can take some comfort from—there's no poison called Butterfly's Dust."

"What?" I wanted to scream at him, but a doubling-over, vomit-inducing convulsion hit, causing my abdominal muscles to feel as if they were being shredded with a knife.

When I was sensible again, Valek explained, "You're going to want to die, wish you were already dead, but in the end you'll be quite alive."

"Why tell me now?"

"The mind controls the body. If you believed that you were going to die, then you might have died from that conviction alone."

"Why wait until now to tell me?" I demanded, furious. He could have relieved my anguish.

"A tactical decision."

I bit back a nasty reply. I tried to see his logic; to put myself in his place. My training sessions with Ari and Janco had included strategy and tactics. Janco had compared sparring to a card game. "Keep your best moves close to your chest and only use them when you've nothing left," he had said.

An opportunity to escape might have presented itself during the day. In that case Valek wouldn't have to show his last card and tell me about the poison.

"What about the cramps?" I asked just as another one seized

my body. I rolled into a tight ball hoping to relieve some of the pain, but to no avail.

"Withdrawal symptoms."

"From what?"

"Your so-called antidote," Valek said. "It's an interesting concoction. I use it to make someone sick. As the potion wears off, it produces stomach cramps worthy of a day in bed. It's perfect for putting someone temporarily out of commission without killing him. If you continue to drink it, then the symptoms are forestalled until you stop."

Of all the books I had studied, I didn't recall reading about a tonic like that. "What's the name?"

"White Fright."

The knowledge that I wasn't going to die erased the frightened panic and helped me to endure the pain. I viewed each contraction as a step that must be taken in order for me to be free of the substance.

"What about Butterfly's Dust?" I asked.

"Doesn't exist. I made it up. It sounded good. I needed some threat to keep the food tasters from running away without using guards or locked doors."

An unwelcome thought popped into my head. "Does the Commander know it's a ruse?" If he did, Mogkan would also know.

"No. He believes you've been poisoned."

During the night, it was hard for me to remember that I had not been poisoned. Torturous cramps refused to release me. I crawled around the cell, retching and screaming.

I was vaguely aware, at one point, of Brazell and Mogkan gloating over me. I didn't care that they watched. I didn't care that they laughed. All I cared about was finding a position that would alleviate the pain.

Finally, I fell into an exhausted sleep.

I woke lying on the muck-covered floor of the cell. My right arm stretched through the bars. I marveled more over the fact that I clutched Valek's hand than the fact that I was alive.

"Yelena, are you all right?" The concern in Valek's voice was evident.

"I think so," I replied with a rasp. My throat burned with thirst.

A clank rang out as someone unlocked the prison door.

"Play dead," Valek whispered, releasing my hand. "Try to get them close to my cell," he instructed as two guards came into the dungeon. I yanked my Valek-warmed hand into the cell, and poked my ice-cold left hand out just as the men descended the stairs.

"Damn! The stench down here's worse than the latrine after a brew party," said the guard holding the lantern.

"You think she's dead?" the second guard asked.

With my face to the wall, I closed my eyes and held my breath as the yellow light swept my body.

The guard touched my hand. "Cold as snow-cat piss. Let's drag her out before she starts to rot. You think it smells bad now..." The snap of the lock was followed by a squeak of metal as the cell door opened.

I concentrated on being a dead weight while the guard

dragged me out by my feet. When the light moved away from me, I risked a peek. The guard with the lantern walked ahead to light the way, leaving my upper body in darkness. As we passed Valek's cell, I seized the bars with both hands.

"Ugh. Hold up, she's stuck."

"On what?" the lantern guard asked.

"I don't know. Come back here with that bloody light."

I released my grip, hooking my arm inside the cell.

"Back off," the lantern guard warned Valek.

His meaty hand tugged at my elbow. Then he grunted softly. I opened my eyes in time to see the lantern's light extinguish as it toppled to the ground.

"What the hell?" the other man exclaimed. He was still holding my feet. He backed away from Valek's bars.

I bent my legs, pulling my body close to his boots. He yelped with surprise when I grabbed his ankles. He tripped and fell back.

The sickening crunch of bone striking stone wasn't what I expected. His body went limp. I stood on shaky legs.

Hearing a thud and the jingle of keys, I turned back in time to see Valek lighting the lantern. The other guard was propped against the bars, his head cocked at an unnatural angle.

In the weak glow, I gazed at the prone form at my feet. The soldier's head had struck the edge of the bottom step. A black liquid began to pool around my boots. I had just killed another man. I began to tremble. A fourth man had died because of me. Had the robbing of my soul reduced me to a heartless killer? Did Valek feel any remorse or guilt when he took a life? I watched him through a veil of blood.

Efficient as always, Valek stripped the dead guards of their weapons.

"Wait here," he instructed. Unlocking the main door of the prison, he sprang through the entrance to the guardroom.

Shouts, grunts and the sound of flesh striking flesh reached my ears as I waited on the stairway. No remorse, no guilt, Valek did what he had to for his side to win.

When Valek motioned me to join him, I saw that blood had splattered on his face, chest and arms. Three guards, either unconscious or dead, were strewn about the room.

My backpack sat on a table, its contents scattered about. I stuffed everything back in while Valek tried to open the remaining locked door between freedom and us. Although meager, I wanted my possessions, including my butterfly and amulet, back. Once I wrapped the chain around my neck, I felt strangely optimistic.

"Damn," Valek said.

"What?"

"The Captain has the only key to this door. He will open it when it's time to change the guards."

"Try these." I handed Valek my picks.

He grinned.

While he worked on the lock, I found a pitcher of water and a wash barrel. The fear of being caught couldn't override the desire to rinse off my face and hands. But that was not enough. The need to rid myself of the stench of vomit and blood overpowered me. Soon, I was dumping buckets of water over my head until I was soaked through. I drained half the water pitcher before I thought to offer some to Valek. He stopped to drink, then continued to pick the lock.

Finally, it popped open. Valek peered out into the hallway. "Perfect. No guards." He pulled the door wide. "Let's go."

Taking my hand and a lantern, Valek turned away from our only escape, and led me back down into the prison, pausing to leave the door to the cells wide open as well.

"Are you insane?" I whispered as he dragged me toward the last cell. "Freedom's that way." I pointed.

He ignored me as he unlocked the door. "Trust me. This is the perfect hiding spot. The mess we left will soon be discovered, the open doors proof we've fled." Valek pushed me ahead of him into the cell. "Search parties will be sent out. When all the soldiers have left the manor, we'll make our move. Until then, we lay low."

Valek made a makeshift bed of straw in the far corner of the cell. After extinguishing and hiding the lantern, he yanked me down. I curled on my side with my back to him, shivering in my wet clothes. Valek pulled some straw on top of us and wrapped an arm around me. He drew me close. I stiffened at the contact, but his body heat warmed me, and I soon relaxed into his grip.

At first, every tiny noise made my heart race. But I shouldn't have worried; the commotion that ensued when our escape was discovered was deafening.

Angry and accusing voices shouted. Search parties were organized and dispatched. It was agreed that we had an hour head start, but Brazell and Mogkan argued on which direction we had taken.

"Valek's probably retreating west to well-known territory," Brazell stated with authority.

"South *is* the logical choice," Mogkan insisted. "We have the Commander; there's nothing they can do. They're running for their lives, not toward some strategic position. I'll take a horse and scan the forest with my magic."

Valek harrumphed in my ear, and whispered, "They actually think I would abandon the Commander. They have no concept of loyalty."

When the prison had been quiet and empty for a few hours, I grew bored and anxious to be gone. The door to the cells had remained wide open, allowing a faint light to illuminate our surroundings.

"Can we go now?" I asked.

"Not yet. I believe it's still daylight. We'll wait until dark."

To help pass the time, I asked Valek how he had become involved with the Commander. I thought it an unintrusive question, but he grew so quiet that I regretted asking it.

After a long pause, he spoke. "My family lived in Icefaren Province before it was renamed MD–1. A particularly harsh winter collapsed the building that housed my father's leather business, ruining all of his equipment. He needed to replace his equipment to stay in business, but the soldiers who came to our house to collect the tax money wouldn't listen to reason." Valek's arm tightened around me.

A minute stretched longer before he continued. "I was just a skinny little kid at the time, but I had three older brothers. They were about Ari's size and had his strength. When my father told the soldiers that if he paid the full tax amount he wouldn't have enough money left to feed his family—" Valek paused for several heartbeats "—they killed my brothers. They laughed and said, 'Problem solved. Now you have three less mouths to feed.'" The muscles on Valek's arm trembled with tension.

"Naturally, I wanted revenge, but not on the soldiers. They were only messengers. I wanted the King. The man who had allowed his soldiers to murder my brothers in his name. So I learned how to fight, and I studied the assassin's art until I was unbeatable. I traveled around, using my new skills to earn money. The royal upper class was so corrupt they paid me to kill each other.

"Then I was commissioned to kill a young man named Ambrose, whose speeches called for rebellion and made the royals nervous. He'd become popular, gathering large crowds. People started to resist the King's doctrines. Then Ambrose disappeared, hiding his growing army and employing covert operations against the monarchy.

"My payment to find and kill Ambrose was significant. I ambushed him, expecting to have my knife in his heart before he could draw breath to cry out. But he blocked the blow, and I found myself fighting for my life, and losing.

"Instead of killing me, though, Ambrose carved a C on my chest with my own knife. The same weapon, by the way, that I later used to kill the King. Then Ambrose declared himself my Commander, and announced that I now worked for him and no one else. I agreed, and I promised him that if he got me close enough to kill the King, I would be loyal to him forever.

"My first assignment was to kill the person who had paid me to assassinate Ambrose. Throughout these years, I've watched him achieve his goals with a single-minded determination and without excess violence and pain. He hasn't been corrupted by power or greed. He's consistent and loyal to his people. And there's been no one in this world that I care for more. Until now."

I held my breath. It had been a simple, innocent question. I hadn't expected such an intimate response.

"Yelena, you've driven me crazy. You've caused me considerable trouble and I've contemplated ending your life twice since I've known you." Valek's warm breath in my ear sent a shiver down my spine.

"But you've slipped under my skin, invaded my blood and seized my heart."

"That sounds more like a poison than a person," was all I could say. His confession had both shocked and thrilled me.

"Exactly," Valek replied. "You have poisoned me." He rolled me over to face him. Before I could make another sound, he kissed me.

Long suppressed desire flared to life as I wrapped my arms around his neck, returning his kiss with equal passion.

My response was a delightful surprise. I had feared, after Reyad's abuse, my body would clench tight in horror and revulsion. But the intertwining of our bodies linked our minds and spirits together.

The distant sound of music vibrated in the air. Pulsing, the magical harmony soon rose to a crescendo and encompassed us like a warm blanket. The prison cell and filthy straw dropped away from our awareness. Whiteness draped in snowy silk surrounded us. On this plane we were equals, partners. Our souls bonded. His pleasure was my ecstasy. My blood pumped in his heart.

Utter bliss came in short snatches, although, Valek and I were happy to try again. We had merged, our minds had become one. I drew in his essence, feasting on the feel of his body in mine, exhilarating in the caress of his skin against mine. He filled the hollow emptiness inside my heart with joy and light. Even though we lay in the grubby straw and faced an uncertain future, a deep hum of contentment vibrated throughout my body.

31

REALITY AND THE RANK ODOR of a decomposing animal intruded. Darkness had descended.

"Let's go," Valek said, pulling me to my feet.

"Where?" I asked, adjusting my uniform.

"The Commander's room, so we can take him back to the castle with us." Valek brushed the straw from his hair and clothes.

"Won't work."

"Why not?" Valek demanded.

"As soon as you touch him, Mogkan will know." I explained about Mogkan's link with the Commander and how he had established that connection using Criollo.

"How do we break the bond?" Valek asked.

It was time to tell him about my magic. I felt light-headed, as if I stood on the edge of the world. Taking a deep breath, I related the encounters and conversations I'd had with Irys, and how she might be able to help us.

Valek stood still for a full minute, while my heart thumped madly in my chest.

"Do you trust her?" he asked.

"Yes."

"Is there anything else you haven't told me?"

My head spun. So much had happened and we still needed to stop a powerful magician. Death was a real possibility. I wanted Valek to know how I felt.

"I love you."

Valek wrapped me in his arms. "My love has been yours since the fire festival. If those goons had killed you, I knew then that I would never be the same. I didn't want or expect this. But I couldn't resist you."

I molded my body to him, wanting to share his skin.

He took my hand. "Let's go."

We raided the guardroom for uniforms before slipping into the hallway. Wearing Brazell's colors of black and green, we hoped to avoid discovery as we stole through the manor.

Valek needed his bag of tricks, so we headed toward the barracks. While I retrieved my cloak, Valek slid inside the empty wooden building. The soldiers had gone to search for us.

I paced in the shadows of the building, chanting Irys's name in my mind. We needed a plan of attack. We had to move tonight.

Shouts and curses emanated from the barracks. Running inside, I found Ari and Janco with their swords drawn and pointed at Valek.

"Stop," I said.

Spotting me, Ari and Janco sheathed their weapons, smiling.

"We thought Valek had escaped without you," Ari said, giving me a bear hug.

"Aren't you supposed to be with a search party?" Valek asked as he pulled his black bag from under a bunk. He had changed into an ebony coverall with numerous pockets.

"We're too sick," Janco said, his best smirk in place.

"What?" I asked.

"The charges against you were obviously fabricated, so we refused to take part in the hunt," Janco said.

"That's insubordination." Valek extracted a long knife and some darts from his bag.

"That was the point. What's a fellow have to do around here in order to get arrested and thrown in the dungeon?" Janco asked.

I stared at Janco in amazement. They had been willing to risk a court martial in order to help me. He had meant what he had inscribed on my switchblade.

"Which direction did the search parties go?" Valek asked. He placed weapons in various pockets and strapped his sword and knife onto his belt.

"Mainly south and east, although a few small groups were sent west and north," Ari replied.

"Dogs?"

"Yes."

"And the manor?"

"Minimal coverage."

"Good. You're with us," Valek ordered them both.

They snapped to attention. "Yes, sir."

"Prep for covert ops, but keep the swords. You're going to need them." Valek finished dressing as Ari and Janco got ready.

"Wait," I said. "I don't want them getting into trouble." My heart started to skitter around in my chest and a nauseous wave threatened to send bile up my throat as fear of what we were planning to do overcame me.

Valek squeezed my shoulder. "We need their help."

"You're going to need more than that." Irys's voice came out of the darkness. Three men simultaneously drew their swords. When she stepped into the weak lantern light, Valek relaxed, but Ari and Janco brandished their weapons.

"At ease," Valek ordered.

Seeing their reluctance, I said, "She's a friend. She's here to help." I looked at her. "We discovered Mogkan's extra power source."

"What is it?"

I told her about the mindless captives and how they had been chained in circles, and then explained my theory that Mogkan had wiped their minds to seize their power. Horror and revulsion touched her face. Despite her rough exterior, her concern went deep. She managed to regain her no-nonsense frown, but Ari and Janco looked a little green, as if they were going to be sick.

"What's this all about?" Ari asked.

"I'll explain it later. Right now—" I stopped short. A complete plan of attack snapped into my mind, but it included Ari and Janco. I had been hoping to keep them safe, but Valek was right. We needed their help.

"I want you to protect Irys with everything you have. It's very important," I told my friends.

"Yes, sir," Ari and Janco said together.

Stunned, I stared at them. They had addressed me as *sir*, meaning they would follow my orders, even if it led to their death.

Valek's eyes drilled into mine. "You have a strategy?"

"Yes."

"Tell us."

Why, I thought as Valek and I crept through the silent empty halls of the manor, had I opened my mouth? *My* plan. What did I know? Valek, Ari and Janco had years of experience doing this nerve-racking, stomach-turning work, but everyone risked their necks following *my* plan.

In the dark corridor, I swallowed my fear and reviewed the strategy. At the Commander's door, we waited to give the others time to move into position. My short breaths seemed to echo off the walls, and I felt as if I was either going to scream or pass out.

After a few moments, Valek picked the lock and we slipped inside. He secured the door. Lighting a lantern, he moved toward the oversize four-poster bed. The Commander was stretched out on top of the bedding, fully clothed. His vacant eyes were open, staring at the ceiling. He made no acknowledgment of our presence.

I sat beside him and took his hand in mine. Following Irys's brief instructions, I imagined my brick wall, then expanded it until I had built a dome of brick that encompassed us both.

Valek pressed against the wall next to the door, waiting for Mogkan. His expression had hardened into his battle face. He was stone cold on the exterior, but I knew that a lethal, molten fury resided within.

It wasn't long before a key turned in the lock. Silence. Then the door burst open. Four armed guards rushed in. Valek had one down before the man could react. The ringing of swords filled the room.

Mogkan slinked into the chamber after his men had Valek fully engaged. Avoiding the fighting, he moved toward me. A condescending smile touched his lips.

"A brick igloo. How nice. Come on, Yelena, give me some credit. A stone fortress or a steel wall would have been more of a challenge."

I felt a solid blow strike my mental defenses. Brick crumbled. Patching holes as he hammered on my shield, I prayed with desperation that Ari, Janco and Irys had made it to the room where Mogkan kept the prisoners chained. Irys had explained that she needed to be there with them in order to block Mogkan's extra power. Even if she succeeded, I would still have to deal with Mogkan's own magic.

Halting his attack for a second, Mogkan jerked his head to the side, staring off into the distance. "Nice trick," he said. "Friends of yours? They're in Reyad's hallway, but unless they can fight their way through ten men, they won't make it to my children."

My heart sank. Mogkan resumed his onslaught with renewed determination. One guard out of four remained in battle with Valek. Hurry, I thought. My defenses weakened with each blow. I threw every ounce of strength into my wall, but it collapsed into a cloud of dust.

Mogkan's power gripped me like a giant's fist around my rib cage. I yelped in pain and dropped the Commander's hand. I stood on weak legs beside the bed just as Valek yanked his sword from the last guard's dead body.

"Stop or she dies," Mogkan ordered.

Valek froze. Three more guards hustled into the room, Brazell on their heels. They surrounded Valek. Taking his sword, they forced him to his knees with his hands on his head.

"Go ahead, General. Kill her," Mogkan said, stepping back to let Brazell pass. "I should have let you slit her throat the first day she arrived."

"Why listen to Mogkan?" I asked Brazell. "He's not to be trusted." Pain crawled along my spine as Mogkan turned his burning eyes upon me.

"What do you mean?" Brazell demanded. He gripped his sword as he glanced from me to Mogkan.

Mogkan laughed. "She's only trying to delay the inevitable."

"Like when you tried to delay the Sitian treaty negotiations by poisoning the cognac? Or were you aiming to stop the delegation altogether?" I asked him.

Mogkan's shock revealed his guilt. Although surprise touched Valek's face, he remained silent. His body tensed, ready to spring into action.

"That doesn't make sense," Brazell said.

"Mogkan wants to avoid contact with the southerners. They

would know about—" My throat closed. I clawed at my neck, unable to breathe.

Brazell turned on Mogkan. His square face creased with anger. "What have you been up to?"

"We don't need a treaty with Sitia. We were getting our supplies without any problems. But you wouldn't listen to me. You had to be greedy. After establishing a trade treaty it would only be a matter of time before we'd have southerners crossing the border, sniffing around, finding us." Mogkan showed no fear of Brazell, only anger that he had to explain his actions. "Now, do you want to kill her or should I?"

Spots spun in my eyes as my vision blurred. Before Brazell could answer, Mogkan staggered. His hold on me slipped slightly, releasing my airway. I gasped for air.

"My children!" Mogkan roared. "Even without them, I still have more power than you!"

Like a fish on a hook, I was yanked off my feet and hurled against the wall. My head banged on the stone. Pinned in midair, Mogkan's power pelted me. Each blow felt like a boulder crashing into me. This is it, I thought. Reyad was right; becoming the food taster had just delayed the inevitable.

Out of the corner of my eye, I saw Valek fighting his guards as he tried to reach Mogkan. Too late for me. With a final surge of strength, I mentally reached out. I hit an impenetrable barrier as I felt my consciousness drain. Blackness filled my world.

Then Irys's voice was there in my mind, soothing. "Here," she said, "let me help you." Pure power flowed into me. I reconstructed my mental shield and deflected Mogkan's on-slaught, pushing him back. He crashed into the opposite wall with a satisfying thud.

Confusion reigned in the Commander's chambers. Inex-perienced with magic as I was, I couldn't restrain Mogkan. He bolted from the room. With a knife in his hand, Valek fought three guards with swords. As I rushed to help Valek, Brazell grabbed my arm and spun me around to face him.

He raised his sword. Murder blazed in his eyes. I jumped back to avoid the first swing of his sword and bumped against the Commander's bed. I leaped onto the bed to avoid Brazell's next swing. I glanced down. The Commander's gaze was still fixed on the ceiling. Brazell's third swing severed one of the bedposts.

As I dived from the end of the bed to avoid another blow, I seized the post from the floor.

Now I was armed. The post wasn't balanced properly for a bow, but it was thick. Better than nothing.

Brazell was a powerful opponent. Each swing of his sword hacked chunks out of my weapon.

At first, he scoffed at my attempts to fight him. "What do you think you're doing? You're a skinny nothing. I'll gut you in two moves."

When I found my mental zone of power, he stopped wasting his breath. Even sensing his next attack, I still scram-bled to stay one step ahead of him. My wooden post was no match for his sword.

Reyad's ghost materialized in the room. He cheered his

father on, trying to distract me. His tactics worked. My back
hit the wall. Brazell's sword split my post in half.

"You're dead." With gleeful satisfaction, Brazell pulled his
sword back to slash at my neck. But I still held a part of the
wood. As his sword swung close, I deflected the weapon
downward with my broken post. The tip cut across my waist.
The sound of ripping fabric accompanied a line of fire across
my stomach. Blood soaked the ripped ends of my uniform
shirt.

Then Brazell made his first error. Thinking I was finished,
he relaxed his guard. But I was still on my feet. I raised my
weapon. With desperate strength, I struck him across the
temple. We crumpled to the floor together.

I gazed at the ceiling, trying to regain my breath. Valek
hovered over me. I shooed him away. "Find Mogkan." He disappeared from my view.

Once strength returned to my limbs, I examined my wound.
Running a finger along the gash, I thought all I needed was
some of Rand's glue.

Reyad's ghost floated over me, sneering. I couldn't bear
lying on the ground with him in the room. Cursing and
bleeding, I stood.

"You." I stabbed a bloody finger at him. "Go away."

"Make me," he challenged.

How could I fight a ghost? I moved into a defensive stance.
He scoffed. No, not a physical fight, a mental one.

I thought about what I had accomplished in the year and a
half since I had slit Reyad's throat. Overcoming my fears to make

friends. Confronting my enemies. Finding love. How I felt about myself. Who I was. I looked into the gilded floor-length mirror of the Commander's room. My hair was wild. My shirt soaked with blood. My face streaked with dirt. Almost the same reflection when I first became the food taster. But this time there was something different. The shadows of doubt were gone.

I peered deeper and found my soul. A little tattered and with some holes, but there all the same. It had always been there, I realized with a shock. If Reyad and Mogkan had truly driven it from me, I would be chained to a floor right now and not standing over Brazell's unconscious form.

I was in control. This new person in the mirror was free. Free of all poisons. I glanced at Brazell. He was still breathing, but I was in charge of him and of myself. In command. No longer a victim. No longer the rat caught in the metal jaws of a trap.

"Be gone," I ordered Reyad's ghost. His shocked expression gave me great joy as he vanished.

But joy was like a butterfly alighting on a hand; a brief rest before flying away.

"Janco's hurt." Irys's alarmed voice resounded in my skull. "We need a medic. Come now."

Using manacles from a dead guard's belt, I handcuffed Brazell to the heavy bed. Then I bolted from the room. I raced through the corridors. He can't die, I thought. Not Janco. I wouldn't be able to bear his death. Horrible scenarios played in my mind. I was so preoccupied that I rushed right toward Valek and Mogkan without even recognizing them.

They dueled with swords. The reason the scene had taken a while to clarify in my mind was because Mogkan had the upper hand. Valek's pale face was haggard. He swung his sword as if it was a dead weight. His natural grace had fled, and what remained were sporadic, jerky movements. Mogkan, on the other hand, was quick and competent, technically accurate, but lacking style.

My disbelief and concern grew as I watched the match. What was wrong with Valek? Was it Mogkan's magic? No, Valek was immune to it, I thought. Then realization dawned. Valek had said being close to a magician felt like wading in thick syrup. And Valek had fought seven guards in the Commander's room after spending the last two days in the dungeon without food or sleep. Exhaustion had finally caught up to him.

Mogkan's grin widened when he spotted me hovering nearby. He executed a lightning-quick feint, and then lunged. Valek's sword clattered to the floor as a crimson slash snaked up his arm.

"What an incredible day!" Mogkan exclaimed. "I get to kill the famous Valek and the infamous Yelena at the same time."

I triggered my switchblade. Mogkan laughed. He sent me a magical command to drop my weapon.

Just as my hand released the blade, I heard Irys's voice in my head. "Yelena, what's wrong? Did you find the medic?"

"I need help!" I cried in my mind. Power swelled inside me, pushing to break free. I aimed a finger of power toward Mogkan. His sword dropped from his hand. Terror gripped his face as the magic swaddled him like a baby, then tightened like a noose. He was paralyzed, rooted to the floor.

"You rat-spawned daughter of a demon!" Mogkan cursed. "You're a blight on this earth. An incarnation of hell. You're just like the rest of them. The Zaltana bloodline should be burned out, erased, exterminated…"

Mogkan raged on, but I ceased to listen. Valek picked up my switchblade. Mogkan's curses grew louder and more frantic as Valek approached him. A blur of movement, a shriek of pain, then Mogkan was finally silent. His body sank into a heap on the ground.

Valek handed me the bloody knife. With an exhausted bow, he said, "My love, for you."

32

I GASPED, REMEMBERING. "Janco!" Grabbing Valek's arm, I dragged him with me, explaining between huffs of breath. Still wearing Brazell's colors, although torn and bloodstained, we roused the medic, who, with peevish annoyance, fussed about protocol and proper authority until Valek drew his knife.

My stomach heaved when we entered Reyad's wing. The hallway leading to the captives' room was gruesome. Soldiers littered the floor, pieces of arms and legs were scattered about as if someone had hacked their way through them. The walls were splattered with blood and pools of scarlet dotted the floor.

The medic wanted to stop at the first man, but Valek yanked him to his feet. Stepping carefully around the bodies, we reached the doorway. Just inside, I saw Janco lying on his side with his head in Ari's lap. He was unconscious, which was a good thing since a sword had skewered his stomach, the bloody tip poking from his back. Ari's gore-splashed face held a grim expression. A crimson-coated ax, the weapon responsible for the carnage in the hallway, rested next to him. Irys sat cross-legged in the center of the circle of emaciated people. Her brow glistened with sweat. Her expression was distant. The chained women and men viewed the scene with dispassionate eyes.

The trip to the infirmary was a chaotic nightmare. Everything blurred together like a whirlwind until I found myself lying in a bed next to Janco, holding his hand. The medic did his best, but if the sword had pierced any vital organs or if there was internal bleeding, Janco wouldn't survive. Twice during the night Ari and I despaired that we would lose him.

My own wound had been cleaned and sealed with Rand's glue, but I hardly noticed or cared about the throbbing pain. I aimed all my energy and strength toward Janco, willing him to live.

Late the next day, I woke from a light doze.

"Sleeping on the job?" Janco whispered with a weak smile on his ashen face.

I breathed a sigh of relief. Surely if he was strong enough to insult me, then he was on his way to recovery.

Unfortunately, Irys couldn't say the same about the Commander. Four days after Mogkan's death, he still hadn't regained his spirit. His advisers had rebounded from their brief ensorcellment, and they had commandeered Brazell's manor while

waiting for the Commander to return. They assumed temporary control of the Military District. Messengers were sent
north to General Tesso of MD–4 and west to General Hazal
of MD–6, requesting their immediate presence. The Generals
would have the authority to determine what the next step
would be in case the Commander failed to revive.

Just as confusing was the fact that none of Brazell, Mogkan
and Reyad's victims woke to Irys's probing. She had tried to
enter their minds, to break through to where their self-aware-
ness was hiding. Irys reported that their minds were like abandoned houses, fully furnished, with embers still smoking in the
fireplace, but no one home.

Irys and I resigned ourselves to the knowledge that the
victims would live out their days unaware of their new comfortable surroundings in Brazell's guest wing. I mourned over
the loss of my friend Carra. Irys had sought out the rooms used
by the orphans, and reported that May was still there, alive and
well. I planned to visit with May as soon as Janco regained some
of his strength.

"It's obvious that the children in Brazell's orphanage were
kidnapped from Sitia," Irys explained, visiting me in the infirmary at Janco's bedside.

"Mogkan's ring of child thieves spaced their abductions far
enough apart to avoid detection. Magic is usually stronger in
women, and that explains why there are more girls. The kidnappers targeted bloodlines where magic was present, although
they took a gamble with children that young. There's no way
to be sure the power will develop. Mogkan and Brazell must

have planned this for a long time." Irys raked her fingers through her long brown hair. "Finding your family shouldn't be too difficult."

I blinked at her in shock. "You're joking. Right?"

"Why would I joke?" She was unaware of the emotional tailspin she'd caused me.

She was right, joking wasn't her style, so I thought for a moment. "Before he died, Mogkan said something about the Zaltana bloodline."

"Zaltana!" Wiping away her usual serious expression, Irys laughed. It was like the sun coming out after weeks of rain. "I think they did lose a girl. My goodness, you're in for a real surprise if you're part of the Zaltana clan. That would explain why you alone didn't cave in under Mogkan's spell."

Questions hovered on my lips. I wanted to know more about this family, but I didn't want to get my hopes up. There was the possibility that I wasn't a Zaltana. I guess I would find out when I reached Sitia. Irys wanted to start my magical training right away.

Uneasiness hovered in my chest whenever I thought of leaving Ixia. I changed the subject. "How's the Commander?"

Irys confessed her frustration. "He's different from the children. There's nothing in their minds, but he's retreated to a white place. If I can only find where he is, then I might be able to bring him back."

I considered this for a while, and thought back to a time in the war room when I had fallen asleep. "May I try?"

"Why not?"

I made sure Janco was comfortable and had everything he

desired. Irys accompanied me to the Commander's room. The bodies had been removed and someone had attempted to clean up. I perched on the edge of the Commander's bed and took his cold hand in mine. Following Irys's instructions, I closed my eyes, sending my mental awareness toward him.

My feet crunched on ice. A cold wind stabbed my face and filled my lungs with tiny daggers. Dazzling white surrounded me. Diamond dust or snowflakes, it was hard to tell. I walked for a while and was immediately confused by the sparkling blizzard. Stumbling through the storm, I fought to remain calm and to remind myself that I was not lost. Whenever I took a step forward, the icy wind drove me back.

I was about to admit defeat, when I remembered why I had thought I could find the Commander. Focusing on the scene of a young woman exalting over a slain snow cat caused the wind to stop and the blizzard to clear. I stood next to Ambrose.

She was dressed in heavy white hunting furs that resembled the skin of the cat.

"Come back," I said.

"I can't," she said, pointing into the distance.

Thin black bars surrounded us on all sides. A birdcage was my first impression, but upon closer scrutiny I could see that the bars were soldiers armed with swords.

"Every time I tried to leave, they pushed me back." Fury flamed in her face before dying into weary.

"But you're the Commander."

"Not here. Here I am just Ambrosia trapped inside my mistake of a body. The soldiers know about my curse."

I searched my mind for a reply. The guards didn't belong to Mogkan, they belonged to her. My eyes were drawn to the snow cat's carcass. "How did you kill the cat?"

Her face came alive as she recounted how she had bathed in snow-cat scent and spent weeks cloaked in snow-cat furs, pretending to be one of the animals until they allowed her to be part of their pack. In the end it was only a matter of time and the perfect opportunity to make the kill.

"Proof that I was really a man. That I had won the right to be a man."

"Then perhaps you need to wear your prize," I suggested. "Skins will not help you against that lot." I jerked my head at the ring of guards.

Comprehension widened the woman's golden eyes. She gazed at the slain cat, then morphed into the Commander. Her shoulder-length hair shortened into his buzz cut, fine lines of age growing on her face as he emerged. The white furs dropped to the ground as his wrinkle-free uniform materialized. He stepped away from the skins, kicking them dismissively.

"You shouldn't do that," I said. "She's a part of you. You might need her again."

"And do I need you, Yelena? Can I trust you to keep my mutation a secret?" the Commander asked with a fierce intensity.

"I came here to bring you back. Isn't that answer enough?"

"Valek swore me a blood oath of loyalty when I carved my initial on his chest. Would you do the same?"

"Does Valek know about Ambrosia?" I asked.

"No. You haven't answered my question."

I showed the Commander Valek's butterfly. "I wear this against my chest. I've pledged my loyalty to Valek, who is faithful to you."

The Commander reached for the butterfly. I stood still as he removed it from my necklace. He took a knife from the skins and sliced it across his right palm. Holding the pendant in his bloody hand, he extended the knife toward me. I held out my right hand, wincing as the knife bit into it. Our blood mixed as I shook his hand with the butterfly wedged between our palms. When he released his grip, Valek's gift was in my hand. I returned it to its proper place over my heart.

"How do we get back?" he asked.

"You're the Commander."

His eyes rested on the dead cat. Looking around at the ring of soldiers, he drew his sword. "We fight," he said.

I pulled the spear from the cat's side, and wiped the blood on the snow. Feeling the weight of the weapon in my grip, I swung it around in a few practice moves. It was lighter than a bow, and a bit off balance by the metal tip. But it would work.

We charged the men. The circle of guards tightened immediately around us. Back to back, the Commander and I fought.

The men were skilled, but the Commander was a master swordsman. He had bested Valek and killed a snow cat. It was like fighting with five more defenders by my side.

When I sunk the spear's tip into one guard's heart, he exploded into a shower of snow crystals that floated away with the wind.

Time slowed as I hacked at one man after another, until

finally time snapped to the present. I whirled around searching for an opponent only to discover that we had dispatched all the men. Snow swirled around us.

"Nice work," the Commander said. "You helped me rediscover my true self, killing off my demons." He took my hand and pressed it to his lips.

The wintry scene melted, and I found myself back on the bed, looking into the Commander's powerful eyes.

That night, Valek and I briefed the Commander on all that had happened since the Generals' brandy meeting. Valek had Brazell interrogated, and discovered that Brazell and Mogkan had been planning a coup for the past ten years.

"Brazell told me that Mogkan showed up at his manor with a group of children," Valek said. "He was looking for a place to hide and he struck a deal with Brazell to help Brazell become the next Commander. Once Mogkan achieved enough power to reach your mind from MD–5, they started feeding you Criollo, Sir."

"What about the factory?" the Commander asked.

"We have halted production," Valek said.

"Good. Salvage what equipment you can, then burn the factory and any Criollo to the ground."

"Yes, Sir."

"Anything else?"

"One more interesting item. Brazell said that once he and Mogkan had control of Ixia, they planned to take over Sitia."

The next day the Commander held court with Valek standing at his right side. Brazell was brought before him to face charges. As expected, Brazell was stripped of his rank and sentenced to spend the rest of his life in the Commander's dungeon.

Permitted a few last words, Brazell shouted, "You fools. Your Commander's a deceiver. You've been lied to for years! The Commander's really a woman dressed as a man!"

Silence blanketed the room, but the Commander's neutral expression never faltered. Soon laughter echoed off the stone walls. Brazell was hauled away amid cheers and jeers. Who would believe the ravings of a madman? Obviously, no one.

I thought about their jeers. They laughed not because the idea of a woman in power was so ridiculous, but because Commander Ambrose had a powerful presence. His frank and abrupt dealings were so honest and forthright that the thought of him deceiving anyone was laughable. And due to his beliefs and convictions about himself, even though I knew the truth, I could not think of him in any other way.

Later in the day, I went to visit the orphanage. I found May in the dormitory. This time, happy memories followed me as I walked through the rooms used by the orphans. When she saw me, May bounced off the bed and wrapped herself around me.

"Yelena, I thought I would never see you again," she gushed.

I squeezed her tight. When she pulled back, I smiled to see her crooked skirt and messy ponytail. As I braided her hair, May chattered about what had happened since I had left. Her excitement faded when she talked about Carra. And it was then that I could see how much she had grown.

When I finished her hair, she said, "We're going with you

to Sitia!" May spun in a circle, unable to remain still. She waved toward a suitcase on the floor.

"What?"

"That lady from the south told us that she would take us home. To find our families!"

A brief pang clenched my heart. Family had a different meaning to me. Valek, Ari and Janco felt like my family, and even Maren seemed like a grumpy older sister.

"That's wonderful," I said to May, trying to match her enthusiasm.

May stopped her dance for a moment. "There are so few of us left," she said in a sedate voice.

"Valek will make sure Carra and the others are taken good care of."

"Valek! He's *so* handsome." May laughed, and was so delightful I couldn't resist hugging her again.

Janco, on the other hand, greeted me with a gloomy face when I stopped to say goodbye. Irys, anxious to head south, wanted to be on the road in the morning.

Ari had taken over my role of nurse, and was sitting next to Janco.

"Whatever happened to 'Sieges weathered, fight together, friends forever'?" I asked him, quoting his message on my switchblade.

Janco's eyes lit up. "You little fox. Figured it out already, have you?"

I smirked.

"As soon as Janco's better, we're coming south," Ari said.

"And what would you do there?" I asked.

"Work on our tans," Janco said, smiling. "I could use a vacation."

"Protect you," Ari said.

"I don't need protection in the south," I said. "And I seem to remember that not long ago, I bested two of my instructors."

"She's cocky already." Janco sighed. "We can't go with her now, she'll be swaggering and boasting and generally obnoxious. It's bad enough I have to deal with that from Ari, I could never handle two."

"Besides," I said, "you'll be bored."

Ari grumped and crossed his massive arms, looking sour. "First sign of trouble, you send us a message and we'll be there. You got that?" Ari asked.

"Yes, sir," I said. "Don't worry about me, Ari. I'll be fine. And, I'll be back."

"You'd better," Janco said. "I want a rematch."

But I had spoken too soon about returning. Valek, Irys and I had discussed my future, but the Commander seemed to have other plans. Commander Ambrose called for a formal meeting that evening. With just Valek, Ari and Irys in attendance in Brazell's old office, the Commander agreed to honor the trade treaty, even though it had been enacted under Mogkan's influence. Then he told me my fate.

"Yelena," he began in a formal tone, "you have saved my life and, for that, I thank you. But you have magical abilities that are not tolerated in Ixia. I have no choice but to sign an order for your execution."

Valek placed a warning hand on Ari's shoulder to prevent him from charging the Commander. Ari stayed still, but his outrage was evident in his face. When the Commander held a paper out to Valek, coldness crept along my skin, leaving behind a numb feeling of dread.

Valek didn't move. "Sir, I've always believed that having a magician work for us would be beneficial and could have prevented this particular situation," Valek said. "We can trust her."

"A valid point." The Commander drew back his arm, resting it on the desk. "Even though we trust her, even though she saved my life, I must follow the Code of Behavior. To do otherwise would be a sign of weakness, something I can't afford right now, especially after this business with Mogkan. Plus, the Generals and my advisers will not trust her."

Once again the Commander extended the execution order to Valek. In my frantic mind I heard Irys telling me to flee. She would attempt to slow Valek down. No, I told her. I would see this to the end. I would not run away.

"I won't take it," Valek said in a flat voice. He betrayed no emotion.

"You would disobey a direct order?" the Commander asked.

"No. If I don't take the order, then I won't have to disobey it."

"And if I make it a verbal order?"

"I will obey. But it will be my very last task for you." Valek pulled a knife off his belt.

The ring of steel sounded as Ari unsheathed his sword. "You'll have to get through me first," he said, stepping in front of me. Ari had a better than average chance of beating Valek, but I knew he wouldn't win. And I didn't want him to try.

"No, Ari," I said. I pushed his sword arm down, and stood next to Valek. Our eyes met. I understood that Valek's loyalty to the Commander was without question. His blue eyes held a fierce determination and I knew in my soul that Valek would take his own life after he had taken mine.

The Commander gazed at us with a quiet consideration. I felt time freeze under his scrutiny.

"I've signed the order, per the Code," the Commander finally said. "I will assign someone else to carry it out. It may take a few days for me to find a suitable person." He looked at me and Irys. A hint that we needed to get on the road as soon as possible. "This order is valid in Ixia only. You're all dismissed."

The office emptied in a hurry. I was giddy with relief as Ari swept me into one of his bear hugs and whooped with joy. But then my heart seized with pain as I realized that I would be parted from Valek so soon after we had joined. After Irys and Ari left to organize the "escape," Valek pulled me aside. We kissed with passion and a desperate urgency.

After we drew apart to catch our breaths, I said, "Come with me." It wasn't a plea or a question. It was an invitation.

Valek's blue eyes closed with pain. "I can't."

I turned away, feeling like one of Valek's black statues, but he drew me back.

"Yelena, you need to learn, you need to find your family, you need to spread your wings and see how far you can fly. You don't need me right now, but the Commander needs me."

I clung to Valek. He was right, I didn't need him, but I wanted him to be with me forever.

We left that night. Irys led our ragtag group. Eight girls and two boys from Brazell's orphanage followed Irys through the forest toward the southern border. I took the rearguard position to make sure everyone stayed together, and to make sure no one tailed our group.

We hiked for a few hours until we found a suitable clearing to camp for the night. More than adequate provisions for our journey had been provided by Ari. I smiled, remembering his lecture to me about staying out of trouble. Just like an overprotective brother, he wasn't content until I promised to send him a message if I needed help. I would miss him and Janco dearly.

We set up six small tents in a circle. Irys amazed the children as she set fire to the kindling with a magical flourish. After everyone had gone to sleep, I sat by the fire, stirring the dying embers. Unwilling to join May in our tent, I gazed at the single flame that erupted when I poked at the fire. It danced by itself for an audience of one. I wondered for the hundredth time why Valek hadn't come to say goodbye, fingering my pendant.

I sensed movement. Jumping up, I drew my bow. A shadow detached from a tree. Irys had created a magical barrier around our tents. According to her, the barrier would deflect a person's vision, so all he would see was an empty clearing. The shadow stopped at the edge, unaffected by the magic, and smiled at me. Valek.

He held out a hand. I grasped his cold fingers with both

hands as he led me away from the tents and deeper into the forest.

"Why didn't you come before we left?" I asked him when we stopped at the base of a tree. The roots of the massive oak had broken through the ground, creating small protective hollows.

"I was busy making sure the Commander would have a hard time locating someone to carry out his orders." Valek grinned with vicious delight. "It's amazing how much work there is cleaning up after Brazell."

I thought about what that cleanup would entail. "Who is tasting the Commander's food?" I asked.

"For now, I am. But I believe Captain Star would make an excellent candidate. Since she knows who all the assassins are, I think her help will be invaluable."

It was my turn to smile. Star would do well if she passed the training. If.

"Enough talk," Valek said, guiding me down between the roots. "I need to give you a proper send-off."

My last night in Ixia was spent with Valek beneath the tree. The hours till dawn flew by. The rising sun intruded, waking me from a contented doze in Valek's arms, forcing me to face the day that I had to leave him.

Sensing my mood, Valek said, "An execution order hasn't kept us apart before. There are ways to get around it. We *will* be together."

"Is that an order?"

"No, a promise."

★ ★ ★ ★ ★

READ ON FOR AN EXTRACT FROM THE LATEST CHRONICLES OF IXIA NOVEL

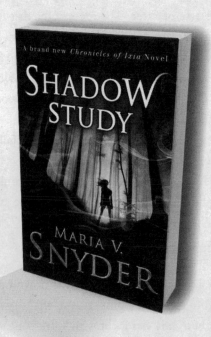

'A compelling new fantasy series'
—Rhianna Pratchett, *SFX* on *Poison Study*

1

YELENA

Ugh, mud, Kiki said as she splashed through another puddle. The wet muck clung to her copper coat and dripped
from her long tail. It packed into her hooves and coated the
hair of her fetlocks with each step.

Through our mental connection I sensed her tired discomfort. *Stop?* I asked. *Rest?*

No. Images of fresh hay, a clean stall and being groomed
formed in Kiki's mind. *Home, soon.*

Surprised, I glanced around the forest. Melting piles of snow
mixed with black clumps of dead leaves—signs that the cold
season was losing its grip. Rain tapped steadily on the bare
branches. The light faded, turning the already gray woods
leaden. For the past few hours, I'd been huddling under my
sopping-wet cloak, trying to keep warm. With my thoughts
fixed on my rendezvous with Valek, I'd failed to keep track
of our location.

I scanned the area with my magic, projecting my awareness out to seek life. A few brave rabbits foraged in the soggy
underbrush and a couple of deer stood frozen, listening to the
squishy plodding of Kiki's passage. No souls haunted these
woods. No humans within miles.

That wasn't a surprise. This remote area in the northeastern Featherstone lands had been chosen for that very reason. After Owen Moon ambushed us about four years ago, Valek and I had decided to move to a less well-known location near the Ixian border.

I leaned forward in the saddle. We were getting close and my wet cloak no longer pressed so hard on my shoulders. At this pace, we'd reach our cozy cottage within the hour. Valek's involvement with our friend Opal's rescue from the Bloodrose Clan and the aftermath had kept him busy for months. Finally we would have a few precious days all to ourselves before he reported back to the Commander. He should already be there waiting for me. Visions of sharing a hot bath, snuggling by a roaring fire and relaxing on the couch once again distracted me.

Kiki snorted in amusement and broke into a gallop. Behind the clouds the sun set, robbing the forest of all color. I trusted Kiki to find the path in the semidarkness as I kept a light magical connection to the wildlife nearby.

In midstride, Kiki jigged to the right. Movement flashed to the left along with the unmistakable twang of a bow. Kiki twisted under me. I grabbed for her mane, but a force slammed into my chest and knocked me from the saddle.

Hitting the ground hard, I felt all the air in my lungs whoosh out as pain erupted. Fire burned with each of my desperate gasps. Without thought, I projected again, searching for the... person who had attacked me. Despite the agony, I pushed as far as I could. No one.

Kiki, smells? I asked. She stood over me, protecting me.

Pine. Wet. Mud.

See magician?

No.

Not good. The person had to be protected by a magical

null shield. It was the only way to hide from me. Null shields blocked magic. At least it also prevented the magician from attacking me with his or her magic since it blocked magic from both sides of the shield. But it wouldn't stop another arrow. And perhaps the next one wouldn't miss.

I glanced at the shaft. The arrow had struck two inches above and one inch to the left of my heart, lodging just below my clavicle. Fear banished the pain for a moment. I needed to move. Now.

Rolling on my side, I paused as an icy sensation spread across my chest. The tip had been poisoned! I plopped back in the mud. Closing my eyes, I concentrated on expelling the cold liquid. It flowed from the wound, mixing with the blood already soaked into my shirt.

Instead of disappearing, the poison remained as if being refilled as fast as I ejected it. With pain clouding my thoughts, the reason eluded me.

Kiki, however, figured it out. She clamped her teeth on the arrow's shaft. I had a second to realize what she planned before she yanked the arrow from my chest.

I cried as intense pain exploded, blood gushed and metal scraped bone all at once. Stunned, I lay on the ground as black and white spots swirled in my vision. On the verge of losing consciousness, I focused on the hollow barbed tip of the arrow coated with my blood, reminding me of the danger. I remained a target. And I wasn't about to make it easy for my attacker to get another shot.

Fix hole, Kiki said.

I debated. If I healed myself now, then I'd be too weak to defend myself. Not like I was in fighting condition. Although I still had access to my magic, it was useless against arrows and, as long as the assassin hid behind the null shield, I couldn't touch him or her with my magic, either.

Kiki raised her head. Her ears cocked. *We go. Find Ghost.*

I groaned. How could I forget that Valek was nearby? *Smart girl.*

With the arrow still clutched in her teeth, Kiki knelt next to me. Grabbing her mane, I pulled myself into the saddle. Pain shot up my arms and vibrated through my rib cage when she stood. She turned her head and I took the arrow. It might give us a clue about the assassin's identity.

I crouched low over Kiki's back as she raced home. Keeping alert for another twang, I aimed my awareness on the surrounding wildlife. If the animals sensed an intruder, I'd pick up on their fear. A sound theory, except I'd been in contact with the deer when the arrow struck. I'd be impressed by the assassin's skills if I wasn't in so much pain.

It didn't take long for us to reach our small stable. The main doors had been left open. A warm yellow glow beckoned. Kiki trotted inside. The lanterns had been lit and Onyx, Valek's horse, nickered a greeting from his stall. Kiki stopped next to a pile of straw bales. Relieved to be safe, I slid onto them then lay down.

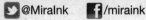

magic study

Talk ceased the minute we entered. All eyes focused on me. My skin crawled. I felt as if they were examining every inch of my face, my clothes and my muddy boots. From their expressions, I gathered I wasn't meeting expectations. I stifled the desire to hide behind Irys. Regret that I hadn't asked Irys more questions about the Zaltanas thumped in my chest.

At last, an older man stepped forward. 'I'm Bavol Cacao Zaltana, Elder Councilman for the Zaltana family. Are you Yelena Liana Zaltana?'

I hesitated. That name sounded so formal, so connected, so foreign. 'My name is Yelena,' I said.

A young man a few years older than I pushed through the crowd. He stopped next to the Elder. Squinting hard, his jade-eyed gaze bore into mine. A mixture of hatred and revulsion creased his face. I felt a slight touch of magic brush my body.

'She has killed,' he called out. 'She reeks of blood.'

Also by New York Times bestselling author
Maria V. Snyder

from
MIRA INK™

The Chronicles of Ixia

POISON STUDY
MAGIC STUDY
FIRE STUDY

STORM GLASS
SEA GLASS
SPY GLASS

The Insider Series

INSIDE OUT
OUTSIDE IN

from
MIRA BOOKS

Avry of Kazan series

TOUCH OF POWER
SCENT OF MAGIC
TASTE OF DARKNESS

www.mirabooks.co.uk/mariavsnyder

magic study

MARIA V. SNYDER

MIRA Ink is a registered trademark of Harlequin Enterprises Limited, used under licence.

Published in Great Britain 2015
by MIRA Ink, an imprint of Harlequin (UK) Limited,
Eton House, 18-24 Paradise Road,
Richmond, Surrey, TW9 1SR

© Maria V. Snyder 2006

ISBN 978 1 848 45240 4

Harlequin (UK) Limited's policy is to use papers that are natural, renewable and recyclable products and made from wood grown in sustainable forests. The logging and manufacturing processes conform to the legal environmental regulations of the country of origin.

Printed and bound by CPI Group (UK) Ltd, Croydon, CR0 4YY

MIX
Paper from
responsible sources
FSC
www.fsc.org   FSC™ C007454

THE TERRITORY OF IXIA

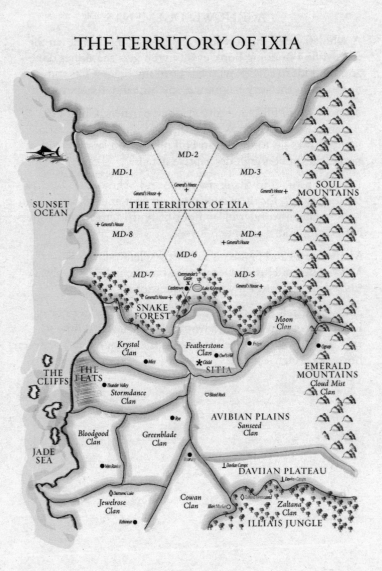

ACKNOWLEDGEMENTS

A wholehearted thank-you to the one who holds down the fort while I'm doing book events, who gets the dishes done and the kids to soccer, who has been my biggest fan and supporter from the very beginning, my husband, Rodney.

To my Seton Hill University critique partners, Chun Lee, Amanda Sablak, Ceres Wright, thanks for all the help. Also many thanks go to my Seton Hill mentor, Steven Piziks. I hope you find enough descriptive details!

I couldn't forget to thank my Muse and Schmooze critique group for their continued support and guidance. Your help has been wonderful, and our biannual retreats and coffee-bar conversations are much loved.

Many thanks and praise go to my excellent editor, Mary-Theresa Hussey. Despite her busy schedule, she always finds time to answer my million questions.

And a heartfelt thanks to Susan Kraykowski and her horse Kiki. Without them both, I wouldn't have learned how to ride, and I wouldn't have discovered the unique bond between horse and rider.

To my children, Luke and Jenna,
a constant source of inspiration and love.
You both are truly magical.

In loving memory of Anthony Foster.

I

"WE'RE HERE," IRYS SAID.

I looked around. The surrounding jungle bulged with life. Overgrown green bushes blocked our path, vines hung from the tree canopy, and the constant chatter and trill of jungle birds beat at my ears. Small furry creatures, who had been following us through the jungle, peeked at us from their hiding spots behind huge leaves.

"Where?" I asked, glancing at the three other girls. They shrugged in unison, equally confused. In the thick humid air, their thin cotton dresses were soaked in sweat. My own black pants and white shirt clung to my clammy skin. We were tired from lugging our heavy backpacks along snake-thin jungle paths, and itchy from hosting unnameable insects on our skins.

"The Zaltana homestead," Irys said. "Quite possibly *your* home."

I surveyed the lush greenery and saw nothing that resembled a settlement. During the course of our travels south, whenever Irys had declared that we had arrived, we were usually in the midst of a small town or village, with houses made of wood, stone or brick, hemmed in by fields and farms.

The brightly dressed inhabitants would welcome us, feed us and, amid a cacophony of voices and spicy aromas, listen to our story. Then certain families would be summoned with great haste. In a whirlwind of excitement and babble, one of the children in our party, who had lived in the orphanage in the north, would be reunited with a family they hadn't known existed.

As a result, our group had grown ever smaller as we'd traveled farther into the southern land of Sitia. Soon, we had left the cold northern air far behind, and were now cooking in the steamy warmth of the jungle with no sign of a town in sight.

"Homestead?" I asked.

Irys sighed. Wisps of her black hair had sprung from her tight bun, and her stern expression didn't quite match the slight humor in her emerald eyes.

"Yelena, appearances can be deceiving. Seek with your mind, not your senses," she instructed.

I rubbed my slick hands along the grain of my wooden staff, concentrating on its smooth surface. My mind emptied, and the buzz of the jungle faded as I sent out my mental awareness. In my mind's eye, I slithered through the underbrush with a snake, searching for a patch of sunlight. I scrambled through the tree branches with a long-limbed animal with such ease that it felt as if we flew.

Then, above, I moved with people among the treetops. Their minds were open and relaxed, deciding what to eat for dinner, and discussing the news from the city. But one mind worried about the sounds from the jungle below. Something wasn't right. Someone strange was there. Possible danger. *Who's in my mind?*

I snapped back to myself. Irys stared at me.

"They live in the trees?" I asked.

She nodded. "But remember Yelena, just because someone's mind is receptive to your probing doesn't mean you're permitted to dive into their deeper thoughts. That's a breach of our Ethical Code."

Her words were harsh, the master level magician scolding her student.

"Sorry," I said.

She shook her head. "I forget that you're still learning. We need to get to the Citadel and begin your training, but I'm afraid this stop will take some time."

"Why?"

"I can't leave you with your family like I did for the other children, and it would be cruel to take you away too soon."

Just then, a loud voice from above called out, "Venettaden."

Irys swung her arm up and mumbled something, but my muscles froze before I could repel the magic that engulfed us. I couldn't move. After a frantic moment of panic, I calmed my mind. I tried to build a mental wall of defense, but the magic that ensnared me knocked down my mental bricks as fast as I could stack them.

Irys, however, was unaffected. She yelled into the treetops. "We're friends of the Zaltanas. I'm Irys of the Jewelrose Clan, Fourth Magician in the Council."

Another strange word echoed from the trees. My legs trembled as the magic released me and I sank to the ground to wait for the faintness to pass. The twins, Gracena and Nickeely collapsed together, moaning. May rubbed her legs.

"Why have you come, Irys Jewelrose?" the voice above asked.

"I believe I may have found your lost daughter," she replied.

A rope ladder descended through the branches.

"Let's go, girls," Irys said. "Here, Yelena, hold the bottom while we climb."

A peevish thought about who would hold the ladder for me flashed through my mind. Irys's annoyed voice admonished me in my own head. *Yelena, you will have no trouble getting into the trees. Perhaps I should have them raise the ladder when it's your turn to climb, as you might prefer to use your grapple and rope.*

She was right, of course. I had used the trees to hide from my enemies in Ixia without the convenience of a ladder. And even now, I'd enjoyed an occasional "walk" through the treetops to keep my skills honed.

Irys smiled at me. *Perhaps it's in your blood.*

My stomach filled with unease as I remembered Mogkan. He had said I was cursed with Zaltana blood. I'd no reason to trust the now dead southern magician, though, and I'd been avoiding asking Irys questions about the Zaltanas so I wouldn't get my hopes up about being a part of their family. Even while dying, I knew Mogkan would have been capable of pulling one last spiteful trick.

Mogkan and General Brazell's son, Reyad, had kidnapped me along with over thirty other children from Sitia. Averaging two children a year, they had brought the girls and boys north to Brazell's "orphanage" in the Territory of Ixia for use in their twisted plans. All of the children had the potential of becoming magicians because they had been born to families with strong magic.

Irys had explained to me that magical powers were a gift, and only a handful of magicians came from each clan. "Of course, the more magicians in a family," Irys had said, "the greater chance of having more in the next generation. Mogkan took a risk kidnapping children so young; magical powers don't manifest until a child reaches maturity."

"Why were there more girls than boys?" I had asked.

"Only thirty percent of our magicians are males, and Bain Bloodgood is the only one to achieve master level status."

As I steadied the rope ladder that hung from the jungle's canopy, I now wondered how many Zaltanas were magicians. Beside me, the three girls tucked the hems of their dresses into their belts. Irys helped May start up the rope rungs, and then Gracena and Nickeely followed.

When we had crossed the border into Sitia, the girls hadn't hesitated to exchange their northern uniforms for the bright multicolored, cotton dresses worn by some of the southern women. The boys switched their uniforms for simple cotton pants and tunics. I, on the other hand, had kept my food taster's uniform on until the heat and humidity had driven me to purchase a pair of boy's cotton pants and a shirt.

After Irys disappeared into the green canopy, I set my boot on the bottom rung. My feet felt as if they were swollen with water, weighing me down. Reluctance clung to my legs as I dragged them up the ladder. In midair, I paused. What if these people didn't want me? What if they didn't believe I was their lost daughter? What if I were too old to be bothered with?

All the children who had already found their homes had been immediately accepted. Between the ages of seven and thirteen, they had been separated from their families for only a few years. Physical resemblances, ages, and even names had made it easy to place them. Now, we were down to four. The identical twins, Gracena and Nickeely were thirteen. May was the youngest at twelve, and I was the oldest of the group at twenty.

According to Irys, the Zaltanas had lost a six-year-old girl over fourteen years prior. That was a long time to be away. I was no longer a child.

Yet I was the oldest one who had survived Brazell's plans and remained whole. When the other kidnapped children reach maturity, those who had developed magical powers had been tortured until they surrendered their souls to Mogkan and Reyad. Mogkan had then used the magic of these now mindless captives to enhance his own, making the children nothing more than living bodies without souls.

Irys bore the burden of informing the families of these children, but I felt some guilt by being the only one to survive Mogkan's efforts to capture my soul. The effort, though, cost me a great deal.

Thinking about my struggles in Ixia led to thoughts of Valek. An ache for him chewed at my heart. Hooking an arm around the ladder, I fingered the butterfly pendant he had carved for me. Perhaps I could devise a way to return to Ixia. After all, the magic in my body no longer flared out of control, and I would much rather be with him than among these strange southerners who lived in the trees. Even the name of the south, Sitia, felt thick as rancid syrup in my mouth.

"Yelena, come on," Irys called down to me. "We're waiting."

I swallowed hard and ran a hand over my long braid, smoothing my black hair and pulling out the few viney tendrils that clung to it. Despite the long trek through the jungle, I wasn't too tired. While shorter than most Ixians at five feet four inches, my body had transformed from emaciated to muscular during my last year in Ixia. The difference had been in my living arrangements. From starving in the dungeon to tasting food for Commander Ambrose, my situation had improved for my physical well-being, but I couldn't say the same for my mental well-being during that time.

I shook my head, banishing those thoughts and concentrating on my immediate circumstances. Climbing up the rest of the ladder, I expected it to end at a wide branch or a platform in the tree like a landing on a staircase. Instead, I entered a room.

I looked around in amazement. The walls and ceiling of the room were formed by branches and limbs that had been roped together. Sunlight leaked in between the gaps. Bundled sticks had been worked into chairs that had cushions made of leaves. The small room held only four seats.

"Is this her?" a tall man asked Irys. His cotton tunic and short pants were the color of the tree's leaves. Green gel had been combed into his hair and smeared over all his exposed skin. A bow and a quiver of arrows hung over his shoulder. I guessed he was the guard. Why, though, would he need a weapon if he were the magician who had frozen us? Then again, Irys had deflected that spell with ease. Could she turn aside an arrow as well?

"Yes," Irys said to the man.

"We've heard rumors at the market, and wondered if you would pay us a visit, Fourth Magician. Please, stay here," he said. "I'll get the Elder."

Irys sank into one of the chairs, and the girls explored the room, exclaiming over the view from the single window. I paced the narrow space. The guard seemed to disappear through the wall, but upon investigation, I discovered a gap that led to a bridge also made of branches.

"Sit down," Irys said to me. "Relax. You're safe here."

"Even with that heartwarming reception?" I countered.

"Standard procedure. Unaccompanied visitors are extremely rare. With the constant danger of jungle predators, most travelers hire a Zaltana guide. You've been edgy and defensive ever since I told you we were headed to the Zaltana's village."

Irys pointed at my legs. "You're in a fighting stance, prepared for attack. These people are your family. Why would they want to hurt you?"

I realized that I had pulled my weapon off my back, and was clutching it in the ready position. With effort, I relaxed my posture.

"Sorry." I threaded the bow, a five-foot wooden staff, back into its holder on the side of my backpack.

Fear of the unknown had caused me to clench. For as long as I could remember in Ixia, I had been told my family was dead. Lost to me forever. Even so, I used to dream of finding an adopted family who would love and care for me. I had only given up that fantasy when I had been turned into Mogkan and Reyad's experiment, and now that I had Valek, I felt I didn't need a family.

"That's not true, Yelena," Irys said aloud. "Your family will help you discover who you are and why. You need them more than you know."

"I thought you said it was against your Ethical Code to read someone's mind." I rankled at her intrusion on my private thoughts.

"We are linked as teacher and student. You freely gave me a pathway to your mind by accepting me as your mentor. It would be easier to divert a waterfall than to break our link."

"I don't remember creating a pathway," I grumbled.

"If there was a conscious effort in making a link, it wouldn't have happened." She watched my face for a while. "You gave me your trust and your loyalty. That was all that was needed to forge a bond. While I won't pry into your intimate thoughts and memories, I can pick up on your surface emotions."

I opened my mouth to reply, but the green-haired guard returned.

"Follow me," he said.

We wound our way through the treetops. Hallways and bridges connected room after room high above the land. There had been no hint of this maze of dwellings from the ground. We didn't see or meet a soul as we passed around bedrooms and through living areas. From glimpses into the rooms, I saw they were decorated with items found in the jungle. Coconut shells, nuts, berries, grasses, twigs and leaves were all artfully arranged into wall hangings, book covers, boxes and statues. Someone had even fashioned an exact replica of one of those long-tailed animals by using white and black stones glued together.

"Irys," I said, pointing to the statue, "what are those animals?"

"Valmurs. Very intelligent and playful. There are millions of them in the jungle. They're curious, too. Remember how they spied on us from the trees?"

I nodded, recalling the little creatures that never stood still long enough for me to study. In other rooms, I spotted more animal replicas made from different colored stones. A hollowness touched my throat as I thought of Valek and the animals he carved out of rocks. I knew he would appreciate the craftsmanship of these stone statues. Perhaps I could send one to him.

I didn't know when I'd ever be able to see him again. The Commander had exiled me to Sitia when he had discovered I possessed magical powers. If I returned to Ixia, the Commander's order of execution would be in effect, but he had never said I couldn't communicate with my friends in Ixia.

I soon found out why we hadn't encountered anyone on our journey through the village. We entered a large, round common room where about two hundred people gathered. It appeared the entire settlement was here. People filled the benches of carved wood that circled a huge fire pit made of stone.

Talk ceased the minute we entered. All eyes focused on me. My skin crawled. I felt as if they were examining every inch of my face, my clothes and my muddy boots. From their expressions, I gathered I wasn't meeting expectations. I stifled the desire to hide behind Irys. Regret that I hadn't asked Irys more questions about the Zaltanas thumped in my chest.

At last, an older man stepped forward. "I'm Bavol Cacao Zaltana, Elder Councilman for the Zaltana family. Are you Yelena Liana Zaltana?"

I hesitated. That name sounded so formal, so connected, so foreign. "My name is Yelena," I said.

A young man a few years older than I pushed through the crowd. He stopped next to the Elder. Squinting hard, his jade-eyed gaze bore into mine. A mixture of hatred and revulsion creased his face. I felt a slight touch of magic brush my body.

"She has killed," he called out. "She reeks of blood."

2

A COLLECTIVE GASP SOUNDED from the crowd of Zaltanas. Abhorrence and outrage gripped the now hostile faces in the room. I found myself behind Irys, hoping to block the negative force emanating from so many eyes.

"Leif, you always tend toward the dramatic," Irys admonished the young man. "Yelena's had a hard life. Don't judge what you don't know."

Leif wilted before Irys's gaze.

"I reek of blood, too. Do I not?" she asked.

"But you're the Fourth Magician," Leif said.

"So you know what I've done and why. I suggest you find out what your sister has had to deal with in Ixia before you accuse her."

His jaw tightened. The muscles on his neck pulled taut as he swallowed what might have been a reply. I risked another peek around the room. Now contemplative, worried and even sheepish looks peppered the group. The Zaltana women wore sleeveless dresses or skirts and short-sleeved blouses with bright flora patterns on them. The hemlines reached to their knees. The men of the clan wore light-colored tunics and plain pants. All the Zaltanas were barefoot, and most had lean builds and bronze skin.

Then Irys's words sank in. I grabbed her arm. *Brother? I have a brother?*

One side of her mouth quirked up. *Yes. A brother. Your only sibling. You would have known this if you hadn't changed the subject every time I tried to tell you about the Zaltanas.*

Great. My luck was holding steady. I had thought my troubles were over when I had left the Territory of Ixia. Why should any of this surprise me? While all the other Sitians lived in villages on the ground, my family resided in the trees. I studied Leif, searching for a resemblance. His stocky muscular build and square face stood out compared to the rest of the lithe clan. Only his black hair and green eyes matched my own features.

During the awkward moments that followed, I wished for an invisibility spell, and reminded myself to ask Irys if there were such a spell.

An older woman about my height approached us. As she neared she shot Leif a powerful glance, and he hung his head. Without warning, she embraced me. I flinched for a heartbeat, uncertain. Her hair smelled like lilacs.

"I've wanted to do this for fourteen years," she said, hugging me tighter. "How my arms have ached for my little girl."

Those words transported me back in time, shrunk me down into a six-year-old child. Wrapping my arms around this woman, I bawled. Fourteen years without a mother had made me believe I could be stoic when I finally met her. During the journey south, I had imagined I would be curious and unemotional. *Nice to make your acquaintance, but we really need to get to the Citadel.* But I was woefully unprepared for the torrent of emotions that racked my body. I clung to her as if she alone kept me from drowning.

From a distance, I heard Bavol Cacao. "Everyone get back to work. The Fourth Magician is our guest. We need a proper feast for tonight. Petal, make up the guest rooms. We'll need five beds."

The buzz of voices filling the common area disbursed. The room was almost empty when the woman—my mother—released me from her arms. It was still difficult to match her oval face to the title of "Mother." After all, she might not be my real mother. And if she were, did I have the right to call her by that name after so many years away?

"Your father will be so pleased," she said. She pulled a strand of black hair from her face. Streaks of gray painted her long braids, and her pale green eyes shone with unshed tears.

"How do you know?" I asked. "I may not be your—"

"Your soul fits the void in my soul perfectly. I've no doubt you're mine. I hope you'll call me Mother, but if you can't you can call me Perl."

I wiped at my face with the handkerchief Irys handed me. Glancing around, I looked for my father. Father. Another word that threatened to ruin what little dignity I had remaining.

"Your father's out collecting samples," Perl said, seeming to read my mind. "He'll be back as soon as word reaches him." Perl turned her head. I followed her gaze and saw Leif standing near us; his arms crossed over his chest and his hands bunched into fists. "You've met your brother. Don't just stand there, Leif. Come give your sister a proper greeting."

"I can't stand the smell," he said. He turned his back on us and stalked away.

"Don't mind him," my mother said. "He's overly sensitive. He had trouble dealing with your disappearance. He was blessed with strong magic, but his magic is…" She paused. "Unique. He can sense where and what a person has been doing. Not specifics, but general feelings. The Council calls on him to help solve crimes and disputes, and to determine if a person is guilty or not." She shook her head. "Those Zaltanas with magical powers have unusual abilities. What about you, Yelena? I feel the magic coursing through you." A brief smile touched her lips. "My own limited ability. What is your talent?"

I glanced at Irys for help.

"Her magic was forced from her and was uncontrolled until recently. We have yet to determine her specialty."

Color drained from my mother's face. "Forced?"

I touched her sleeve. "It's all right."

Perl bit her lip. "Could she flame out?" she asked Irys.

"No. I have taken her under my wing. She has gained some measure of control. Although, she must come to the Magician's Keep so I can teach her more about her magic."

My mother grabbed my arms hard. "You must tell me *everything* that has happened to you since you were taken from us."

"I…" A trapped feeling seized my throat.

Bavol Cacao stepped to my rescue. "The Zaltanas are honored that you have chosen one of ours as your student, Fourth Magician. Please let me escort your party to your rooms so you may freshen up and rest before the feast."

Relief coursed through me, although the determined set to

my mother's jaw warned that she was not yet finished with me. Her grip tightened when Irys and the three girls moved to follow Bavol Cacao to our rooms.

"Perl, you'll have plenty of time to spend with your daughter," he said. "She's home now."

She released me, stepping back. "I'll see you tonight. I'll ask your cousin, Nutty, to lend you some decent clothes for the feast."

I grinned as we worked our way to the guest rooms. With all that had happened today, my mother had still managed to notice the clothes I wore.

The feast that night began as a sedate dinner, but then transformed into a party despite the fact that I might have offended my hosts by first tasting the many fruit dishes and seasoned cold meats for poisons before I ate. Old habits die hard.

The night air filled with the scent of burning citronella mixed with a damp earthy smell. After the meal, various Zaltanas pulled out musical instruments made of bamboo and twine, some jumped up to dance and others sang with the music. All the while, petite furry valmurs swung from the ceiling rafters and hopped from table to table. Some of my cousins had made pets of them. Splashes of black and white and orange and brown sat on their shoulders and heads. Other valmurs tumbled in the corners or stole food from the tables. May and the twins were delighted with the animals' long-tailed antics. Gracena tried to tempt a little tan-and-gold valmur to eat from her hand.

My mother sat next to me. Leif hadn't come to the feast. I wore a bright yellow and purple lily-patterned dress that Nutty had loaned me. The only reason I wore the obnoxious thing was to please Perl.

I thanked fate that Ari and Janco, my soldier friends from

Ixia, weren't here. They would be rolling with laughter to see me wearing such a gaudy outfit. But oh, how I missed them. I changed my mind, wishing they were here; it would be worth the embarrassment just to see the glint in Janco's eyes.

"We need to leave in a few days," Irys said to Bavol over the din of voices and music. Her comment caused a mood-dampening ripple in those around us.

"Why do you have to leave so soon?" my mother asked. Dismay creased her eyebrows tight together.

"I need to get the other girls home, and I've been away from the Citadel and the Keep for too long."

The tired sadness in Irys's voice reminded me that she hadn't seen her family for nearly a year. Hiding and spying in the Territory of Ixia had drained her.

Our table was quiet for a while. Then my mother brightened. "You can leave Yelena here while you take the girls home."

"It will be out of her way to come back for Yelena," Bavol Cacao said.

Mother frowned at him. I could see her thoughts whirling behind her eyes. "Aha! Leif can take Yelena to the Citadel. He has business with the First Magician in two weeks."

Emotions rolled through my chest. I wanted to stay, but I feared being separated from Irys. They were my family, yet they were strangers. I couldn't help being wary; it was a skill learned in Ixia. And traveling with Leif seemed as unpalatable as drinking a wine laced with poison.

Before anyone could agree or disagree, Mother said, "Yes. That will do." She ended all discussion on the matter.

The next morning I had a small panic attack when Irys pulled on her backpack. "Don't leave me here alone," I pleaded.

"You're not alone. I counted thirty-five cousins and a whole mess of aunts and uncles." She laughed. "Besides, you should spend some time with your family. You need to learn not to distrust them. I'll meet you at the Magician's Keep. It's within the Citadel's walls. In the meantime, keep practicing your control."

"Yes, sir."

May gave me a big hug. "Your family is so much fun. I hope my family lives in the trees, too," she said.

I smoothed her braids. "I'll try to visit you sometime."

Irys said, "May might be at the Citadel's school this cooling season if she can access the power source."

"That would be great!" May cried out with delight. The twins both gave me a quick hug.

"Good luck," Gracena said with a grin. "You're going to need it."

I followed them down the rope ladder and into the cooler air of the jungle floor to say goodbye. Watching Irys and the girls fight their way through the tight trail, I kept my eyes on them until they were out of sight. In their absence, my body felt paper-thin and in danger of being shredded by the light breeze.

In order to delay my return to the treetops, I studied my surroundings. The jungle's canopy above showed no evidence of the Zaltana dwellings, and the thick vegetation all around prevented me from seeing too far in any direction. Even with the loud clamor of insects, I could hear the faint sound of water rushing and lapping nearby. But I couldn't push past the growth to find the source.

Frustrated, sweaty and tired of being a meal for every mosquito, I gave up and climbed the rope ladder. Back in the warm and dry forest canopy, and among the labyrinth of rooms, I quickly became lost.

Unrecognizable faces nodded or smiled at me. Others frowned and turned away. I had no idea where my room was, or what I was supposed to be doing and I didn't want to ask. The thought of telling my mother my life story was unappealing. Inevitable, I knew, but too much to bear at this moment. It had taken me almost a year to trust Valek with my history—how could I divulge my struggles to someone I'd just met?

So I wandered here and there, searching for a view of the "river" I had heard on the jungle floor. Large expanses of green filled every vista. Several times, I spotted the gray smoothness of a mountainside. Irys had told me the Illiais Jungle grew in a deep valley. Tucked into the crooks of the Daviian Plateau's edge, the odd-shaped jungle was below the plateau's rim, leaving only one side open for travelers.

"Very defensible," Irys had said. "It's impossible to scale the walls to reach the plateau."

I was fooling around and testing my balance on a rope bridge when a voice startled me and I had to grab the handrail.

"What?" I tried to reestablish my footing.

"I said, what are you doing?" Nutty stood at the end of the bridge.

Sweeping an arm out, I said, "Taking in the view."

I could tell by her dubious expression that I hadn't convinced her. "Follow me if you want to see a real view." Nutty bounded away.

I scrambled to keep up with her as she took shortcuts through the tree branches. Her thin arms and legs reached and grabbed vines with such flexibility that she reminded me of a valmur. When she entered a spot of sunlight, her maple-colored hair and skin glowed.

I had to admit there was one good thing about staying in the south. Instead of being the only person with tan skin, I finally looked as if I belonged. Living in the north with the pale-skinned Ixians for so long, though, had not prepared me for such a variety of brown skin tones. Much to my embarrassment, I had found myself gawking at the deeper mahogany skin colors when we had first entered Sitia.

Nutty stopped suddenly, and I almost knocked into her. We stood on a square platform in the tallest tree in the jungle. Nothing blocked the view.

An emerald carpet stretched out below us, ending at two sheer rock faces that angled toward each other. Where the two cliffs joined, a vast waterfall poured forth, ending in a cloud of mist. Beyond the top edge of the rock cliffs, I saw a flat expanse. A mixture of tans, yellows, golds and browns painted the smooth landscape.

"Is that the Daviian Plateau?" I asked.

"Yep. Nothing lives there but wild prairie grass. They don't get a lot of rain. Beautiful, huh?"

"An understatement."

Nutty nodded, and we stood for a while in silence. Finally, my curiosity broke the lull in conversation. I asked Nutty questions about the jungle, and eventually wove the conversation around to the Zaltana family.

"Why do they call you Nutty?" I asked.

She shrugged. "My real name is Hazelnut Palm Zaltana, but everybody's called me Nutty since I was little."

"So Palm is your middle name."

"No." Nutty swung down over the edge of the platform

and into the tree branches that supported it. The leaves shook and after a moment, she climbed back. She handed me a group of brown nuts. "Palm, as in palm tree, is my family's name. Zaltana is the clan name. Everyone who marries us has to take that name, but within the clan there are different families. Here, crack them like this…" Nutty took one of the nuts and banged it on a nearby branch, revealing an inner nib.

"Your family is Liana, which means 'vine.' Yelena means 'shining one.' Everyone is either named after something in the jungle or their name means something in the old Illiais language, which we're forced to learn." Nutty rolled her eyes in exasperation. "You're lucky you missed that." She poked me with a finger. "And you missed having to deal with obnoxious older brothers, too! I once got into trouble for tying mine up in a vine and leaving him hanging… Oh, snake spit! I forgot. Come on." She hurried back through the trees.

"Forgot what?" I asked, scrambling after her.

"I was supposed to take you to your mother. She's been looking for you all morning." Nutty slowed only slightly to negotiate a rope bridge. "Uncle Esau's back from expedition."

Another family member to meet. I considered "accidentally" losing her. But remembering the hostile glares that I had received from some of my cousins, I stayed with Nutty. When I caught up to her, I grabbed her arm.

"Wait," I panted. "I want to know why so many Zaltanas frown at me. Is it the blood smell?"

"No. Everyone knows Leif can see gloom and doom in everything. He's always looking for attention." She gestured at me. "Most of them think you're not really a Zaltana, but a spy from Ixia."

3

"YOU'RE JOKING RIGHT?" I asked. "They don't really believe I'm a spy."

Nutty nodded. Her ponytails, one on each side of her head, bobbed in contrast to her serious face. "That's the gossip. Although, no one would dare breathe a word of that to Aunt Perl or Uncle Esau."

"Why would they think such a thing?"

Her light brown eyes widened as if she couldn't believe my stupidity. "Look at your clothes." She gestured at my black pants and white shirt. "We all know northerners are forced to wear uniforms. They say if you were truly from the south, you wouldn't want to wear pants ever again."

I glanced at Nutty's orange skirt. The hem was tucked up into her brown fur belt and she wore a pair of short yellow pants underneath.

Ignoring my stare, she said, "And you carry a weapon."

That much was true. I had my bow with me in case I found a place to practice, but, so far, the only space big enough had been the common room and that was always too crowded. Now was probably not the best time to tell Nutty about the switchblade strapped to my thigh.

"Who's been saying these things?" I asked.

She shrugged. "Different people."

I waited. The silence drove the information out of her.

"Leif's telling everyone that you don't feel right to him. He says he would know his own sister." She fidgeted with her sleeve, rolling up the bright cotton fabric. "Sitians are always worried that the Commander will attack us someday, and we think northern spies are gathering information on our ability to defend ourselves. Even though Leif tends to over-react, his magic is strong, so almost everyone believes you're a spy."

"What do you think?"

"I don't know. I was going to wait and see." She looked down at her bare feet. They were tanned and callused.

Another reason I stood out among the Zaltanas. I still wore my leather boots.

"That's very smart," I said.

"Do you think so?"

"Yes."

Nutty smiled. Her light brown eyes lit up. I noticed a sprinkle of freckles across her small nose. She continued to lead the way to my mother.

As I followed, I thought about the accusations that I was an Ixian spy. I wasn't a spy, but I couldn't say that I was a true southerner, either. And I wasn't sure I wanted to be called a Sitian. My reasons for being in the south were twofold: to avoid being executed and to learn how to use my magic. Meeting my family had been a bonus, and I wasn't going to let some petty rumors ruin my time here. I decided to ignore any more sidelong glances for now.

There was no ignoring my mother's fury, though, when Nutty and I reached her residence. Every muscle in her thin arms and long neck was pulled taut. Waves of unspoken anger pulsed from the petite woman.

"Where have you been?" she demanded.

"Well, I saw Irys off, and then…" The explanation seemed weak in the face of her outrage, so I stopped.

"You've been gone from me for fourteen years, and we have only two weeks together before you go again. How could you be so selfish?" Without warning she crumpled into a chair as if all her energy had been pulled from her.

"I'm sorry…" I started.

"No, I'm sorry," she said. "It's just that your speech and manners are so foreign. And your father's back and anxious to see you. Leif's been driving me crazy, and I don't want my daughter to leave here feeling like she's still a stranger."

I hugged myself, feeling guilty and inadequate. She was asking for a great deal; I was sure to fail her in some way.

"Your father wanted to wake you in the middle of the night. I made him wait, and he's been searching the homestead all morning," Perl explained. "I finally sent him upstairs with something to do." She swung her arms wide. "You'll have to forgive us if we go too fast for you. Your arrival was so unexpected and I should have insisted you stay with us last night, but Irys warned us not to smother you." She took a deep breath. "But it's killing me. All I want to do is wrap you in my arms." Instead, her arms dropped into her lap, resting on the blue-and-white fabric of her sleeveless dress.

I couldn't reply. Irys had been right; I needed time before

I would feel comfortable with the whole family dynamic, but I could also empathize with my mother. Each day, I missed Valek more than the day before. Losing a child had to be much worse.

Standing by the door, Nutty pulled at her ponytails. My mother seemed to realize she was there. "Nutty, can you fetch Yelena's things from the guest quarters and bring them here?"

"Sure thing, Aunt Perl. I'll have them here faster than a curari bat can paralyze a valmur." In a flash of orange, Nutty was gone.

"You can stay in our extra room." My mother pressed her hand to her throat. "It's your room actually."

My room. It sounded so normal. I had never had a place of my own before. I tried to imagine how I might have decorated it and made it my own, but I came up with a blank. My life in Ixia hadn't included special items such as toys, gifts or art. I stifled a bark of laughter. My only private room had been my dungeon cell.

Perl jumped from her seat. "Yelena, please sit down. I'll get us some lunch. You have no meat on your bones." As she hurried away, she called toward the ceiling, "Esau, Yelena's here. Come down for tea."

Alone, I glanced around the sitting area. The warm air smelled faintly of apples. The couch and two armchairs appeared to be made from ropes woven together, yet they were hard to the touch. The furniture was unlike the other Zaltana chairs I had seen, which were constructed with branches and sticks tied together.

I settled into an armchair; the red leaf-patterned cushions crunched under my weight, and I wondered what had been stuffed inside them. My gaze lingered on a black wooden bowl on a small glass-topped table in front of the couch. The bowl looked to be hand carved. I tried to relax, which worked until I saw a long counter against the back wall.

Stretching across the length of the countertop was a series of odd-shaped bottles connected by loops of tubes. Unlit candles sat under some of the containers. The configuration reminded me of Reyad's lab. The memory of his collection of glass jars and metal instruments unnerved me. Visions of being chained to a bed while Reyad searched for the perfect torture device caused sweat to roll down my neck and my heart to squeeze. I berated myself for my overactive imagination. It was ridiculous that a similar contraption could make me recoil after two years.

I forced myself closer. Amber liquid pooled in a few bottles. I picked up one and swirled the contents. A strong apple scent filled my nose. The memory of swinging and laughter floated into my mind. The image disappeared when I focused on it. Frustrated, I set the bottle down.

The shelves behind the table were lined with rows of more bottles. The contraption looked like a still for making alcohol. Perhaps the liquid was an apple brandy like General Rasmussen's of Military District 7 in Ixia.

I heard my mother return, and turned around. She held a tray full of cut fruit, berries and some tea. Placing the lunch on the small table before the couch, she gestured for me to join her.

"Found my distillery, I see," she said as if every Zaltana had one in their living room. "Smell anything familiar?"

"Brandy?" I guessed.

Her shoulders drooped just a bit, but her smile didn't waver. "Try again."

Putting my nose over one of the amber-filled bottles, I inhaled. The scent blanketed me in feelings of comfort and safety. It also choked and smothered. Memories of bouncing mixed with the image of lying on my back, clawing at my throat. I suddenly felt light-headed.

"Yelena, sit down." My mother's hand was on my elbow, guiding me to a chair. "You shouldn't have breathed in so deeply. It's very concentrated." She kept her hand on my shoulder.

"What is it?" I asked.

"My Apple Berry perfume."

"Perfume?"

"You don't remember." This time her disappointment showed as her smile faded from her lips. "I wore it all the time when you were a child. It's my best-selling perfume—very popular with the magicians at the Keep. When you disappeared, I couldn't wear it anymore." Her hand touched her throat again as if she were trying to block either her words or emotions.

With the word "magicians" my windpipe tightened. The scene of my brief abduction at the Fire Festival the previous year played in my mind. The tents, the darkness and the smell of Apple Berry mixed with the taste of ashes and the image of Irys ordering four men to strangle me to death.

"Does Irys wear your perfumes?" I asked.

"Oh, yes. Apple Berry is her favorite. In fact, she asked me last night to make her more. Does the scent remind you of her?"

"She must have worn it the first time we met," I said, choosing not to say more. If it hadn't been for Valek's timely arrival, Irys would have succeeded in killing me. It was ironic how both my relationships with Irys and Valek began badly.

"I have found that certain smells are linked to specific memories. It's something Leif and I have been working on as part of his project with First Magician. We've created a variety of scents and odors that we use to help victims of crime remember. These memories are very powerful, and they help Leif get a clearer picture of what happened to them." She moved away from me. Sitting down, she spooned fruit into three bowls. "I had hoped the Apple Berry would trigger your memories of us."

"I did get something, but…" I stopped, unable to put the brief impressions into words. I quelled my growing aggravation at being unable to recall anything from my six years of living here. Instead, I asked, "Do you make many perfumes?"

"Oh, yes," she said. "Esau brings me wonderful flowers and plants to use. I enjoy making new perfumes and scents."

"And she's the best in the land," a booming male voice said behind me. I turned to see a small, stout man enter the room. His resemblance to Leif was unmistakable.

"Her perfumes have been worn by Master Magicians, as well as the Queen and Princess of Ixia when they were alive," Esau boasted. He grabbed my wrists and pulled me upright. "Yelena, my child, look how you've grown." He squeezed me in a bear hug that lasted several seconds.

A strong odor of earth filled my nose. He released me, sat down with a bowl of fruit in his lap and a cup of tea in his hand before I could react. Perl handed me the other bowl as I resumed my seat.

Esau's uncombed gray hair fell to his shoulders. As he ate, I saw that the lines on his hands were stained dark green.

"Esau, have you been playing with that leaf oil again?" Perl asked. "No wonder you took so long to come down. Trying to scrub it off so you wouldn't smear it everywhere."

I could tell by the way he ducked his head without responding that this was an old argument. Esau stared at me in silence, squinting and cocking his head from side to side as if deciding on something. His complexion resembled tea without the milk. Deep lines etched his forehead and fanned out from his eyes. He had a kind face used to laughing and crying.

"Now I want a report on what you've been doing all these years," Esau said.

I suppressed a sigh. No more chances to avoid it. Used to obeying orders in the north, I told them about growing up in General Brazell's orphanage in Military District 5. I glossed over the unpleasant years when I had reached maturity and become Reyad and Mogkan's laboratory rat. My parents were distressed enough just hearing about their plans to use their kidnapped victims' magical power to help Brazell overthrow the Commander; I saw no reason to tell them the brutal details of how they had erased the southern children's minds.

When I mentioned becoming Commander Ambrose's food taster, I failed to tell them that I had been in the Commander's dungeon awaiting execution for killing Reyad. And after I had spent a year there, I had been given the choice of the noose or the poison taster's position.

"I bet you were their best taster," my father said.

"What a terrible thing to say," Perl admonished. "What if she were poisoned?"

"We Lianas have a great sense of smell and taste. The girl's here and safe, Perl. If she wasn't good at detecting poisons, I doubt she would have lasted this long."

"It's not like someone was trying to poison the Commander all the time," I said. "Only once, really."

Perl's hand flew to her neck. "Oh, my. I bet it was his pet assassin that tried to poison him. That loathsome creature."

I stared at her uncomprehending.

"You know, his spy, Valek? Every Sitian would love to see that man's head on a pike. He murdered almost the entire royal family. Only one nephew survived. Without Valek, that usurper would have never gained power and upset Sitia's good relationship with Ixia. And those poor northern children who are born with magic. Slaughtered by Valek in their cribs!"

While she shuddered with revulsion, I gaped. My fingers sought the chain around my neck, and found the butterfly pendant Valek had carved for me. I squeezed it. Guess I wouldn't be telling her about my relationship with him. And I decided not to enlighten her about the Commander's policy on Ixians discovered with magical abilities. Not as gruesome as killing babies, but usually ending in death for the unfortunate man or woman. Valek had not been a fan of that policy, but he wouldn't disobey an order from the Commander. Perhaps, in time, Valek would help the Commander see the benefits of having magicians on his staff.

"Valek isn't as horrible as you think," I said, trying to redeem his reputation. "He was instrumental in uncovering Brazell and Mogkan's plans. In fact, he helped to stop them." I wanted to add "he saved my life twice," but the twin grimaces of loathing on my parents' faces stopped me.

So much for my effort. He was *the* villain of Sitia, and it would take more than words to change his status. I couldn't say I blamed my parents. When I had first met Valek, I feared his reputation, having no clue about the fierce loyalty, sense of fairness and willingness to sacrifice himself for others that lurked beneath his reputation.

I thanked fate when Nutty barged in with my backpack swinging from her hands.

Esau took it from her. "Thanks, Nut," he said, tugging one of her ponytails.

"Welcome, Saw." She punched him lightly in the stomach, and then danced out of reach as he swung to grab her. Sticking her tongue out at him, she skipped toward the door.

"Next time, Nut, I'm going to crack you."

Her laugh echoed. "You can try." And she was gone.

"Let me show you to your room," Esau said to me.

As I turned to follow him, Perl said, "Yelena, wait. Tell me what happened to Brazell's plans?"

"Thwarted. He's in the Commander's dungeon."

"And Reyad and Mogkan?"

I took a breath. "Dead." I waited for her to ask me who had killed them, and I wondered if I would tell her about my role in both of their deaths.

She nodded with satisfaction. "Good."

Esau and Perl's living quarters had two floors, and instead of a ladder or staircase to connect them, Esau used what he called a lift. I had never seen anything like it before. We stood in a closet-size room. Two thick ropes went through holes in the floor and ceiling. Esau pulled on one of the ropes, and the wooden room rose. I put my hand on the wall, but the motion was smooth. Eventually, we ascended to the second floor.

Esau poked his head back into the lift when I failed to follow him out. "Like it?" he asked.

"It's great."

"One of my designs. Pulleys are the key," he explained.

"You won't find many in the Zaltana homestead. The others are slow to change, but I've sold a ton at the market."

"Does Perl sell her perfumes at the market, as well?" I asked as I stepped onto the landing.

"Yep. Most of the Zaltanas either sell or exchange goods at the Illiais Market. It's open all year. My inventions and Perl's perfumes have provided us with a plentiful source of income." Esau talked as we walked down the hallway. "A group of Zaltanas will make a trip to the market when enough items have been made or when a special order's due. We aren't the only ones who sell there either, so if we want something, we'll go and buy. Unfortunately, not everything we need can be found in the jungle. Like your mother's glass bottles and the hardware for my chairs."

"You designed the rope furniture, too?"

"Yep. Except they're not ropes. They're lianas." When understanding failed to brighten my face, he explained, "Vines from the jungle."

"Oh."

"The lianas are a constant source of trouble. Probably why they're our family name." Esau grinned. "They grow everywhere, and they can pull trees over. We have to keep them trimmed or cut them down. One day, instead of burning them, I took a bunch home and tried working with them." Esau pulled back a cotton curtain that covered an entrance on the right side of the hallway. He gestured for me to precede him into a room.

"The vines become very strong when dried. While they're pliable, they can be woven into almost anything."

At first, I thought we had entered a storeroom. The air held a slight musty odor, and rows and rows of shelves holding glass containers of every size obscured the walls. The bottles were filled with various tinted substances. Only when I pulled my gaze away from the colorful collection did I see a small bed made from lianas and a wooden bureau.

Esau ducked his head. He ran a green-stained hand through his hair. "Sorry. I've been using this room to store my samples. But I cleaned off the bed and desk this morning." He pointed to a Blackwood desk tucked into a corner.

"It's fine," I said, trying to mask my disappointment. I had been hoping that this room would help me remember something, anything of my life before Brazell's orphanage.

Laying my backpack on the bed, I asked, "What other rooms are up here?"

"Our bedroom and my workroom. Come on, I'll show you."

We continued down the hall. There was another curtained doorway on the left, which led to a big bedroom. This room had a large bed with a purple flowered quilt, two end tables and shelves filled with books instead of containers.

Esau pointed to the ceiling, which was made of leather hides stretched over branches. "I coated it with oil so the rain runs off," he explained. "No water drips in here, but it does get hot."

Hanging from the middle of the ceiling was a large flower-shaped fixture made of wood planks. Ropes wrapped around the base, crossed the ceiling and trailed down the walls. "What's that?" I asked.

He smiled. "Another invention. Pulleys again and some weights make the flower spin, cooling the room."

We went out into the hallway. Across from Esau's bedroom was another bedroom. A plain single bed, dresser and nightstand were neatly arranged inside. No decorations, inventions or other signs of its occupant were evident.

"Leif lives at the Magician's Keep most of the year," Esau said.

We continued down the hall, which ended in a spacious room. I grinned as I looked around. Esau's workroom was stuffed full with plants, containers, piles of leaves and tools. Shelves groaned under the weight of many jars filled with strange items and various liquids. Walking into the room without bumping a shin seemed impossible. The clutter reminded me of Valek's office and apartment. While Valek had books, papers and rocks piled everywhere, Esau had invited the jungle to reside with him.

I stood in the doorway for a moment.

"Come in, come in." He walked past me. "I want to show you something."

Taking my time, I threaded my way toward him. "What do you do here?"

"This and that," he said as he searched through a pile of papers on a table. "I like to collect samples from the jungle and see what I can cook up. Found some medicines. Found some foods. Flowers for your mother. Aha!" He held up a white notebook. "Here."

I took the book, but my attention was on the room as I searched for something familiar. The words "my mother" had triggered the feeling of doubt that had plagued me since my arrival at the Zaltana homestead. Finally, I asked Esau the same question I had asked Perl. "How do you know I'm your daughter? You seem so certain."

Esau smiled. "Look in that book."

I opened the cover. On the first page was a charcoal drawing of a baby.

"Keep turning."

The next page had a drawing of a small child. As I turned the pages, the girl grew from a child to an adolescent into someone I recognized. Me. A hard knot gripped my throat as tears threatened to gush from my eyes. My father had loved me even when I was gone and I couldn't even remember anything from my time here. The pictures showed my childhood as it should have been, living here with Esau and Perl.

"It's really fun to flip through the book fast. Watch yourself grow twenty years in a few seconds." Esau took the sketchbook from my hands, and held it open. "See? This is how I know you're mine. I drew your picture every year after your birth, and even after you disappeared." He turned to the last page and studied the portrait there. "I wasn't too far off. It's not perfect, but now that I've seen you I can make corrections."

He tapped the book on his chest. "When you first disappeared, your mother carried this book with her, looking through the pictures all day long. Eventually she stopped, but after a couple years, she saw me drawing another picture, and she asked me to destroy it." Esau handed the book to me. "I told her she would never see it again. As far as I know, she hasn't. So let's keep it between us for now. Okay?"

"Sure." I gave each page my full attention. "This is wonderful."

All doubts of my lineage vanished as I took note of the details that my father had put into these pictures. In that moment I knew I was part of the Zaltana clan. A feeling of relief washed through me. I vowed to try harder to make a connection with my parents. Leif, though, was another story.

"You should show your sketchbook to Leif," I said, giving the book back to Esau. "Maybe then he would believe I'm his sister."

"Don't worry about Leif. He doesn't need to see a picture. He knows who you are. It's the shock of your arrival that's thrown him off balance. He had a difficult time with your disappearance."

"Oh, yes. I forgot; I've had it so easy in the north."

Esau grimaced, and I regretted my sarcasm.

"Leif was with you the day you were taken from us," he said in a quiet voice. "You had begged him to take you down to play on the jungle floor. He was eight, which may sound young, but Zaltana children are taught to survive in the jungle as soon as they can walk. Nutty was climbing trees before she took her first steps; it drove my sister crazy."

Esau sat in one of his vine chairs and weariness seemed to settle on him like a coating of dust. "When Leif came home without you, our concern was minimal. A lost child had always been found within an hour or two. After all, the Illiais Jungle isn't that big. Predators are not as active during the daytime, and at night we have a few tricks to keep them from our homestead. But we grew more frantic as the day wore on and we still hadn't located you. You had disappeared so completely that everyone thought you had been caught by a necklace snake or a tree leopard."

"Necklace snake?"

He grinned, and an appreciative glint flashed in his eyes. "A green-and-brown predator that lives in the trees. Sometimes fifty feet long, it loops its body over the branches, blending in with the jungle. When its prey comes close, it wraps itself around the victim's neck and squeezes." Esau demonstrated with his hands. "Then it swallows the body whole and feeds on the carcass for weeks."

"Not pleasant."

"No, and it's impossible to see what is inside the snake unless you kill them. But their hides are too thick for arrows, and it's suicide to get close to one. Same with the tree leopard. The cat drags its kill into its den, another unapproachable site. In the end, only Leif believed that you were still alive. He thought you might be hiding somewhere, playing a game. As the rest of us grieved, Leif searched the jungle for you day after day."

"When did he finally stop?" I asked.

"Yesterday."

4

No wonder Leif was so angry. Fourteen years spent searching, and I hadn't had the decency to let him find me. He alone had believed I was still alive. I regretted every harsh thought I had entertained about him. Until he showed up at the door to Esau's workroom.

"Father," Leif said, ignoring me. "Tell that girl, if she wants to go to the Citadel, I'm leaving in two hours."

"Why so soon?" Esau asked. "You're not due for two weeks!"

"Bavol has received a message from First Magician. Something has happened. I'm needed right away." Leif's chest seemed to inflate with his own sense of importance.

I suppressed the desire to jab him in his solar plexus and knock some of his ego out of him.

When Leif turned on his heel and left, I asked Esau, "Is there anyone else going to the Citadel in the next couple weeks?"

He shook his head. "It's a long journey. Many days' walk. And most Zaltanas prefer the jungle."

"What about Bavol Cacao? Isn't he our Councilman at the

Citadel? Doesn't he have to be there?" Irys had explained that the Council consisted of the four Master Magicians plus a representative from each of the eleven clans. Together they ruled the southern lands.

"No. The Council disbands during the hot season."

"Oh." It was hard to believe they were just starting their hot season. Coming from Ixia during its cold season, the whole southern territory felt as if it were already scorching.

"Can you give me directions?" I asked.

"Yelena, you'll be safer with Leif. Come now, let's pack. Two hours isn't…" Esau stopped, and shot me a glance. "Is that backpack all you have?"

"And my bow."

"Then you need some provisions." Esau began to search his room.

"I don't—" My words were cut short as he handed me a book. It was white like his sketchbook, but inside were drawings of plants and trees with written descriptions beneath.

"What's this?" I asked.

"A field guide. I planned to reteach you how to survive in the jungle, but this will have to do for now."

I found a page with an illustration of an oval-shaped leaf. The instructions below the picture explained that boiling the Tilipi Leaf in water would make a draught that would reduce a fever.

Next, Esau gave me a set of small bowls and some bizarre-looking utensils. "That guide is of little use without the proper equipment. Now let's find your mother." He paused and sighed. "She is not going to be happy."

He was right. We found her working at her distillery and fussing at Leif.

"It's not my fault," Leif said. "If you want her to stay so badly, why don't you take her to the Citadel? Oh, that's right—*you* haven't set your precious little feet on the jungle floor in fourteen years."

Perl spun on Leif with a bottle of perfume clenched in her hand poised to throw. He stepped back. When she spotted Esau and me standing in the doorway, she went back to filling the bottle.

"Tell that girl I'll be at the bottom of the Palm ladder in two hours," Leif said to Esau. "If she's not there, I'm leaving without her."

When Leif left the room, the silence continued to thicken.

"You'll need some food," my father said, retreating into the kitchen.

Bottles clinking, my mother approached. "Here," she said. "Two bottles of Apple Berry for Irys, and a bottle of Lavender for you."

"Lavender?"

"You loved it when you were five, so I took a chance. We can experiment later and find something else if you'd like."

I opened the cap and sniffed. Again, I experienced no memories of being five, but the scent made me remember the time I had hidden under a table in Valek's office. I had been searching for the recipe to the antidote for Butterfly's Dust, the so-called poison in my body that had been Valek's way to keep me from escaping. Thinking I had needed a daily dose of the antidote to stay alive, I had been intent on finding the cure. Valek had come back early, and discovered me because I had used lavender scented soap.

I still favored the scent. "This is perfect," I said to Perl. "Thank you."

Unexpected fear flared in Perl's eyes. She clamped her lips and clasped her hands. Taking a deep breath, she declared, "I'm coming with you. Esau, where's my pack?" she asked him as he returned with an armload of food.

"Upstairs in our room," he said.

She rushed past him. If he was surprised by her sudden decision, it didn't show in his expression. I added the bread and fruit he had brought to my pack, and I wrapped the perfume bottles in my cloak. During the journey south, my cloak had been too hot to wear, but it had made a soft place to sleep when we had camped along the road.

"The food will only last so long, and you'll probably need more clothes while you're at the Citadel," Esau said. "Do you have any money?"

I fumbled in my pack. Needing money for food and clothes still seemed odd to me. In the north, we had been provided with all of our basic necessities. I pulled out the bag of Ixian gold coins that Valek had given to me before we parted.

Showing one to Esau, I asked, "Will these work?"

"Put that away." He closed my hand around the coin. "Don't let anyone see that you have them. When you get to the Citadel, ask Irys to exchange them for Sitian money."

"Why?"

"You might be mistaken for a northerner."

"But I am—"

"*You are not.* Most southerners are suspicious of people from Ixia, even the political refugees. You are a Zaltana. Always remember that."

A Zaltana. I worked the name around my mind, wondering if just saying the name would make me one. Somehow I knew it wasn't going to be that easy.

Esau went over to a desk and rummaged through the drawers. I put away Valek's money. With my father's supplies and food, my pack bulged. I made an attempt to organize the contents. Would I need my rope and grapple? Or my northern uniform? While I hoped that I wouldn't have cause to use them, I couldn't bring myself to part with them just yet.

Metal rattled. Esau returned with a handful of silver coins. "It's all I could find, but it should be enough until you get to the Citadel. Now go up and say goodbye to your mother. It's getting late."

"Isn't she coming with us?"

"No. You'll find her on the bed." He said those words with a mixture of resignation and acceptance.

I pondered his words as I pulled the lift up. I found her curled up in a ball on top of the quilt in her bedroom. Perl's body shook as tears soaked into her pillow.

"Next time," she sobbed. "Next time I'm going with Leif to the Citadel. Next time."

"I would like that," I said. Remembering Leif's comment on how she hadn't left the jungle in so long, I added, "I'll come home and see you as soon as I can."

"Next time. I'm doing it next time."

Having decided to delay the trip to the Magician's Keep, Perl calmed. Eventually, she unfurled and stood, smoothing her dress and wiping tears from her cheeks. "Next time, you'll stay with us longer."

It sounded like an order. "Yes, Per... Mother."

The creases of worry disappeared from her face, revealing her beauty. She hugged me tight and whispered, "I don't want to lose you again. Be very careful."

"I will." I meant it. Some hard-learned habits couldn't be broken.

* * *

There were only a few exits to the jungle floor. Each exit was named after a family whose residences were nearby. I reached the room that had the Palm ladder. Just as I swung a leg onto the first rung, I heard Nutty's voice. I had already said goodbye to my parents and Bavol Cacao, but hadn't been able to find Nutty anywhere.

"Yelena, wait," Nutty said.

I stopped, looking up in time to see her swinging through the door. She clutched a mass of colorful cloth in one fist.

"I made these—" she paused to catch her breath "—for you."

The light yellow skirt—subdued by Zaltana standards—was printed with small buttercups, and the shirt was a solid coral color. I eyed the skirt with suspicion. Nutty laughed.

"Look," she said, pulling the skirt apart. "See? It looks like a skirt, but it's really pants. You'll be awfully hot in those black trousers when you cross the plains." She held the waistband up to me as if judging the length. "And this way, you won't stand out so much."

"Clever girl," I said, smiling.

"You like?"

"I like."

She seemed pleased with herself. "I knew it."

"Can you make me some more? Perhaps you can send them with Bavol when he comes?"

"Sure."

I removed my backpack, and searched for some money. "How much?"

Nutty shook her head. "When you get to the Illiais Market, buy some cloth from Fern's stand. Then have her send it to me. I'll need three yards for each set of clothes. I'll make as many as you want."

"But what about wages for your efforts?"

Her ponytails flew as she swung her head no again. "Zaltanas do not charge family. Although..." Her brown eyes glinted. "If anyone should ask who designed your clothes—feel free to give them my name."

"I will. Thanks." I folded my new outfit and stuffed it into my backpack. Then Nutty hugged me goodbye.

The warmth from her body clung to me as I climbed down the ladder. It lasted until the first cold sneer from Leif drove it away.

He waited for me on the jungle floor. Leif had changed into traveling clothes that consisted of a tan cotton tunic, dark brown pants and boots. He carried a large leather pack on his back and a machete hung from his thick belt.

"Keep up or be left behind," he said to the air above my head. Turning his broad back to me, he took off at a brisk clip.

I knew I would soon tire of looking at his back, but, for now, the pace he set was a welcome chance to stretch my legs.

Without another word uttered between us, we traveled on a narrow path through the jungle. Sweat soon soaked my shirt, and I found myself glancing up in search of necklace snakes. Esau had also mentioned tree leopards. I decided I would search Esau's field guide for a picture of the predators when I had some time.

Various birds sang and whistled and animal cries echoed through the leafy canopy. I wanted to know the names of these creatures, but I guessed Leif would ignore my questions.

He stopped once, taking a machete from his belt. Without

thought, I grabbed my bow. Snorting in derision, he merely hacked at a small sapling.

"Strangler fig," he huffed over his shoulder.

I made no reply. Should I be honored that he had finally chosen to talk to me?

Leif didn't wait for a response. "A parasite. The strangler fig uses another tree to reach the sunlight. Once there it grows bigger, eventually strangling and killing its host." He pulled the fig's branches away from the tree. "A process I'm sure you're very familiar with." He tossed the plant onto the ground and marched on.

Not a lesson on jungle life, but a jab at me. I contemplated tripping him with my bow. It would be a petty, mean-spirited thing to do. Tempting, but I threaded my staff into its holder on my pack instead.

We arrived at the Illiais Market just as the sun began to set. The collection of bamboo structures had thatched roofs and bamboo shades for walls. Some of the "walls" had been rolled up to allow customers to browse and the light breeze to cool.

Leif and I had been walking downhill, and the trail ended at the market, which stood in a clearing at the edge of the jungle. The mammoth trees of the tropical forest no longer dominated the landscape. Beyond the clearing, I could see woodland that looked similar to the Snake Forest in Ixia.

"We'll camp here tonight and leave at first light," Leif said before heading toward one of the stands.

I had thought that with the setting of the sun, the market would close. Instead, a vast array of torches was lit, and business continued unabated. The sounds of bartering could be heard above the general buzz of a hundred or so customers talking, calling to children and hurrying from stand to stand carrying packages.

Some of the shoppers wore the familiar dress of the Zaltanas, but I also saw a number wearing green leggings and tunics that were the dress of the forest dwelling Cowan Clan. When we had traveled from Ixia, Irys had taught me to recognize the different clans by their clothing.

I also spotted a few women wearing the traditional shimmering silk pants, short beaded tops, and sheer veils of the Jewelrose Clan. The Jewelrose men even sported beads and jewels on their long tunics that hung down to the knees of their pants. When Irys had explained her clan's customs to me, I couldn't imagine Irys wearing anything but the simple linen shirt, pants and wide belt that she always donned.

I wandered through the market, marveling at the variety of goods available for sale. Practical items like food and clothing sat side by side with jewelry and handcrafts. A pine scent from the torches dominated, but it didn't take long for me to discern the smell of roasting meat. I followed the mouthwatering aroma to a fire pit. A tall man covered with sweat spun the meat that sizzled in the flames. His white apron was streaked with soot. I bought some hot beef from him to eat right away and some smoked jerky for later.

Trying to ignore the pointed stares of the other shoppers, I searched the market for Fern's stand, vowing to change into Nutty's clothes as soon as I found some privacy. Soon a table piled high with bolts of cloth attracted my attention. As I looked through the prints, a small dark woman with large eyes peeked out from behind the collection.

"May I help you?" she asked.

"Are you Fern?"

Her eyes widened in alarm as she nodded.

"Nutty Zaltana sent me. Do you have any solid colors?"

From underneath the table, Fern pulled bolts of plain cloth and added them to the table. Together we matched up colors and patterns for three outfits.

"Are you sure you don't want this Illiais print?" Fern held up a loud pink-and-yellow flowered pattern. "Solid colors are usually worn by the Zaltana men. This print is very popular with the girls."

I shook my head. Just as I began to pay her for the cloth, I spotted a material that matched the colors of the forest. "Some of this, too," I said, pointing to the green pattern. When we had settled up, I asked her to send the fabric to Nutty, but I found room for the forest print in my pack.

"Who should I say is sending it?" Fern asked; her quill poised above the parchment.

"Her cousin, Yelena."

The quill froze in midair. "Oh, my," she said. "The lost Zaltana child?"

I gave her a weary half smile. "Not lost, nor a child any longer."

Strolling past a few more stands, I stopped at a table displaying statues of jungle creatures. They were constructed of small multicolored stones glued together. I selected a black-and-white valmur statue and bought it for Valek. Not quite sure how I would send it to him, I wrapped the gift in my new green fabric.

Campfires began to blaze behind the market. Commerce slowed as the shop owners rolled the bamboo shades down, closing their stands. Customers either headed into the surrounding forest or toward one of the camps. I spotted Leif seated next to one of the fires. He held a bowl in his lap while he talked to the three young Zaltana men seated near him. Through the shimmering air above the fire, I saw him smile and laugh. His whole face transformed in that instant. Scowl lines smoothed. Cheeks lifted, erasing the impact of his serious face and softening his square jaw. He looked ten years younger.

Remembering that Esau had said Leif had been eight when I was kidnapped, I realized now that my brother was only two years older than me. He was twenty-two instead of my original guess of thirty.

Without thought, I moved to join him. In a heartbeat, the merriment dropped from his face. He scowled with such fierceness that I stopped in my tracks. Where was I to sleep that night?

Someone touched my shoulder. I spun.

"You're welcome to stay at my fire," Fern said. She pointed to a small blaze behind her stand.

"Are you sure? I might be a spy from Ixia." I tried to joke, but the words came out harsher than I had wanted.

"Then you can report to your Commander that I make the finest cloth of all the clans. And if he wants a new uniform made from my famous Illiais print, just have him send me an order."

I laughed at the image of the impeccable Commander Ambrose draped in gaudy hot-pink and yellow flowers.

As the first rays of sunlight touched the straw roofs of the market, I waited for Leif to continue our journey. Fern had been a kind host, treating me to dinner and showing me where I could change in private. As it turned out Nutty was her best customer, supplying all the Zaltanas with clothes.

I fidgeted in the warm morning air, trying to get used to the extra fabric around my legs. The hem just covered the tops of my soft leather boots. Fern had assured me that my boots would blend in better once I reached the Citadel. Only the jungle and forest clans preferred mud between their toes.

Finally, Leif appeared. Refusing to acknowledge my presence, he started down a forest path. After a couple of hours, I grew tired of following him in silence. I pulled my bow and began executing blocks and jabs as I walked. I concentrated on the feel of the wood in my hands, setting my mind into that mental awareness that Irys had claimed was my way of tapping into the magical power source.

To practice control of the magic, I projected my awareness out. At first, I encountered a cold stone wall. Confused, I retreated until I realized the barrier was Leif's mind; closed and unyielding. I shouldn't have been surprised.

Skirting his presence, I sought the calm forest surrounding us. I crept with a chipmunk, looking for nuts. I froze with a young deer, hearing the sound of footsteps. My mind touched different creatures as I reached out. Gradually, I projected my awareness farther and farther away, seeing how far I could go.

Behind me, I could still feel the people at the market, five or six miles away. Thrilled, I pushed ahead to see if a town was close by. At first, I touched only more animals, but just as I was about to pull back, my mind touched a man.

Careful to avoid breaking the Ethical Code, I skimmed the surface of his mind. He was a hunter, waiting for prey, and he wasn't alone. There were many men around him. They crouched in the bushes just off the trail. One sat on a horse with his weapon poised for an attack. I wondered what they hunted. Curiosity made me dip a little deeper into the man's thoughts. An image of his prey appeared, snapping me back to my body.

I stopped.

I must have gasped, because Leif turned and stared at me. "What are you doing?" he demanded.

"The forest. Men."

"Of course. The woods are full of game," he explained as if talking to a simpleton.

"Not hunters. Ambushers. Waiting for us."

"AMBUSHERS? DON'T BE ridiculous," Leif said. Amazement colored his voice. "You're not in Ixia anymore."

"Why would a hunting party hide so close to the path?" I asked, ignoring his tone and hoping that logic would prevail.

"Animals use the forest trails. It's easier than fighting through the underbrush." Leif started to walk away. "Come on."

"No. You're leading us into a trap."

"Fine. I'll go without you."

When he turned his back again, I was gripped with rage. "Do you think I'm lying?" The words growled from between my teeth.

"No. I think you're suspicious of everything and everyone, just like a northerner." His mouth twisted as if he wanted to spit.

"You think I'm a spy," I snapped at him in frustration. "I'll lower my defenses. Project your mind out and see for yourself that I'm not here to spy on Sitia."

"I can't read minds. In fact, no *Zaltana* can."

I ignored the jab. "Can't you at least sense who I am?"

"Physically you're a Zaltana. But just because Irys claims you survived Mogkan's efforts to wipe your mind doesn't mean it's true." Leif pointed an accusing finger at me. "You could be a pawn, an empty vessel that has been provided with a northern host. What better way to have eyes and ears in the south?"

"Ridiculous."

"No. It's not. You've revealed yourself," Leif said with a quiet intensity. Then his eyes dulled and turned vacant as if he peered into another world. "I taste strong loyalty and longing for Ixia emanating from you. You stink of blood and pain and death. Anger and passion and fire buzz around you like a haze." His gaze refocused on me. "My sister would be reveling in her freedom, and wrapped with hatred for her captors. You have lost your soul to the north. You are not my sister. It would have been better if you had died than return to us tainted."

I took a deep breath to calm the sudden fury that threatened to take control. "Wake up, Leif! What you dreamed of finding in the jungle didn't factor in reality. I'm not that innocent six-year-old. I endured more than you can imagine and fought hard to keep my soul." I shook my head. I was *not* going to explain myself to this stubborn fool. "I know who *I* am. Perhaps *you* need to reevaluate your expectations of me."

We stood for a moment, glaring at each other. Finally, I said, "You're walking into an ambush."

"I'm walking *to* the Citadel. Are you coming?"

I weighed my options. If I used my grapple and rope to climb into the trees, I could travel through the forest canopy and move past the ambush while remaining near the trail. But what about Leif; my brother who acted like my enemy? He had his machete. Did he know how to use it in a fight?

What if he were injured in the ambush? It would be his own fault. We were brother and sister by blood alone, and I couldn't imagine Leif and me ever being close. Still, a pang of regret touched my heart. Esau and Perl wouldn't want to see Leif hurt. Then I realized Leif was a magician. Could he defend himself with his magic? I shook my head. I didn't know enough about magic to even contemplate what could be done with it.

"I would have never guessed a hunting party could frighten a northerner away." Leif laughed as he set off down the trail.

That did it. I unslung my backpack and found my switch-blade. Cutting a small slit along the outer seam of my new pants, I strapped the thigh-holder to my leg. I pulled apart my single braid, and wrapped my hair up into a bun using my lock picks to hold it in place. Now dressed for a fight, I slipped my pack over one shoulder, and raced after Leif.

As I caught up with him, he gave me an amused grunt. With my five-foot bow in hand, I set my mind into my mental fighting zone. The zone was a concentration technique that allowed me to anticipate my opponent's moves as I fought. This time, I focused on the trail ahead.

The men were poised and ready, six on each side of the road. I knew the instant they heard us, but they waited. They wanted to surround us, attacking only when we had walked into the middle of their group.

I had other plans. Just before we reached the ambush, I dropped my pack to the ground and called, "Wait up!"

Leif spun around. "What now?"

"I think I heard some—"

A shout filled the forest. Birds darted into the sky with a flurry of wings. Men exploded from the bushes with their swords in hand. But the element of surprise was mine. I knocked aside the swords of the first two men who rushed me. Slamming my bow hard against their temples, I sent them to the ground.

As a third man approached, I swept his feet out from under him. Two more men rushed me, I stepped up to engage them, but they jumped to the sides of the trail. My confusion lasted until I felt a deep rumbling through the soles of my boots. Looking up I saw a broad-chested horse charging down the path toward me. I dove out of the way just as a flash of steel bit into my upper left arm. Furious, I attacked the man closest to me, jabbing my bow into his nose. Blood gushed as he cried out in pain.

"Stop her," the man on horseback ordered.

I searched for Leif. He stood in the middle of the road surrounded by four armed men. An astonished look creased his face, but otherwise he appeared unharmed. His machete lay at his feet.

Outnumbered, I had only seconds left. The horseman had turned his steed around, preparing for another charge. The man with the broken nose lay on the ground. I stood on his chest and threatened his neck with the end of my bow.

"Stop or I'll crush his windpipe," I yelled.

The young man halted his horse. But as the others backed away, staring at me in disbelief, he raised his sword into the air.

"Surrender or I'll kill your brother," he said.

How did he know Leif was my brother? I looked at Leif, considering. The point of a guard's sword balanced mere inches from Leif's heart. Fear had bleached my brother's face. Served him right. The soldier under my feet wheezed.

I shrugged. "Seems we're at an impasse," I said to the horseman.

"Indeed." He paused. "What say we stand down and discuss the situation?"

I began to agree when the rider snapped his fingers. I sensed movement, but before I could swing around, I heard a horrible thud, felt a crushing pain at the base of my skull, then nothing.

My head pulsed with pain as if someone were beating two mallets on the sides of my skull. I opened my eyes for a second, but squeezed them shut again. Bobbing brown hide filled my view, causing nausea. As I fought to keep the contents of my stomach in place, I realized I had been hung upside down and was being moved. I risked another peek and confirmed my suspicion that I had been thrown over the back of a horse. I vomited.

"She's awake," said a male voice.

Thank fate the horse stopped.

"Good. We'll stop and make camp here," said the horseman.

I felt a hard push in my side, and I dropped to the ground. A jolt shot through my body on impact. Stunned, all I could do was hope nothing had been broken.

As the sunlight faded, I heard the rustle of men working. When I tried to squirm into a more comfortable position, I started to panic. I couldn't move very well. Then I recognized the familiar stomach clenching sound of manacles clamped on my wrists and ankles. Upon inspection I noticed a foot long chain hanging between the metal cuffs on my wrists. It took a considerable effort not to scream and flail at my re-straints. A few deep breaths calmed my speeding heart and frantic mind.

I assessed the damage to my body. Aside from some bruised muscles, I couldn't feel any broken bones, although my upper left arm burned from the sword cut. I hadn't noticed the pain during the fight and, even now, it seemed a mere nuisance compared to the pounding in my skull. So I lay still and bided my time.

By full dark, the noises of setting up the camp had been replaced by the quiet murmur of voices. When the pain in my head died down to a dull ache, I tried to move again, and succeeded in turning onto my back. My view of the stars was soon obscured by a man's face looking down at me. Small close-set eyes peered around a many-times-broken nose. Moonlight glinted off his sword, allowing me to see that the tip hovered above my throat.

"Make trouble and I'll skewer you with me blade," the man said with a sick smile. "And I'm not talking about me sword." To prove his point, he sheathed his weapon.

I decided not to make trouble. At least not yet. The guard seemed satisfied with my silence. He crossed his thick muscled arms over his chest, staring at me. I could feel my switchblade holder on my thigh. Whether or not it still held my weapon was another matter, and I couldn't risk checking it while under guard. Instead, I surveyed the area to get my bearings.

My attackers had camped in a clearing. Men surrounded a bright fire, cooking something that smelled like meat. A single tent had been erected. Leif and the horseman were not in sight, but the horse was tied to a nearby tree. I counted ten men in the clearing, including my guard. There might have been more inside the tent. Either way, too many for me to fight.

I tried to sit up. The world spun, and my stomach heaved until there was nothing left inside.

A guard came toward me from the campfire. He was an older man with short gray hairs bristling from his scalp. He held a cup in his hand, which he handed to me. "Drink this," he ordered.

The warm scent of ginger floated from the liquid. "What is it?" My voice rasped.

"It doesn't matter." My guard took a step closer to me, raising his fist. "You do what Captain Marrok says."

"Easy, Goel, she has to be able to walk tomorrow," Captain Marrok said. Then to me, "Your brother made it from some leaves he had in his pack."

Leif was alive. My relief surprised me.

"It's to make your head feel better," the Captain said when my lips hesitated on the rim of the cup. A hint of kindness touched his blue-gray eyes, but he didn't let the feeling alter his stern expression.

Why poison me now when they could have killed me before? Perhaps Leif wanted me dead?

"Drink it or I'll force it down your throat," Goel said.

I believed Goel, so I took a small sip, testing for poisons. It tasted like sweet ginger mixed with lemon juice. Feeling a little better from the one taste, I gulped the rest.

"Cahil said to move her closer to the fire. It's too dark back here. I've assigned four-hour buddy shifts for tonight," Captain Marrok said.

Goel grabbed me under the arms and pulled me to my feet. Preparing for another round of nausea, I braced myself, but nothing happened. My stomach settled, and my head cleared enough for me to wonder how I was supposed to walk with such a short chain between my manacled ankles. At least my wrists and ankles weren't connected together.

The problem was solved when Goel lifted me over his shoulder. When he dropped me near the fire, the other men ceased their conversation. One man glared at me above the bloody bandage that he held to his nose.

Marrok gave me a plate of food. "Eat. You'll need your strength."

The guards all laughed. It was a humorless, frightening sound.

I debated whether or not to eat the meat and cheese bread. It had been only a few minutes since I had emptied my stomach on the ground, but the inviting smell of grilled meat made the decision for me. After tasting for poisons, I gobbled the meal.

With my headache gone, and my body somewhat revived from the food, I contemplated my situation. My biggest question was why had Leif and I been captured, and by whom. Goel still hovered nearby so I asked him.

He backhanded me across my face. "No talking," he ordered.

My cheek stung as unbidden tears welled. I hated this Goel.

I spent the next hours in silence, using the time to search for a way to escape. My backpack wasn't anywhere in sight, but, across the fire, a heavyset man tried to spar another guard with my bow. Sweating with profusion, the big man inexpertly hacked at the other's practice sword and was beaten with ease.

After watching the bout, I decided that these men had to be soldiers even though they wore plain homespun civilian clothes. Their ages ranged from mid-twenties to late-forties, maybe even fifty. Mercenaries, perhaps? Captain Marrok's command of these men was obvious.

So why had they attacked us? If they needed money, they could have taken what they wanted and been on their way. If they were killers, I would be dead by now. That left kidnapping. For a ransom? Or for something worse?

A shudder shook my shoulders when I thought of my parents receiving word that I had disappeared again and I promised myself that I wouldn't let it go that far. Somehow, I would escape, but I knew it wouldn't be under Goel's zealous watch.

I rubbed my neck. My hand came away sticky with blood. Exploring with my fingertips, I found a deep gash at the base of my skull and a smaller cut above my left temple. I tapped my bun and moved my hand away with what I hoped was a casual motion. My lock picks were still holding up some of my hair, and I prayed Goel didn't see them.

A possible means of escape was within reach. I just needed some time unguarded. Unfortunately, it didn't look like that would happen any time soon; two men came out of the tent and headed straight toward me.

"He wants to see her," one man said as they hauled me to my feet.

They dragged me toward the tent. Goel followed. I was pulled inside and dumped on the floor. When my eyes adjusted to the dim candlelight, I saw the young horseman sitting at a canvas table. Leif, unchained and unharmed, sat beside him. My backpack was on the table, and my possessions had been spread out.

With effort, I stood. "Friends of yours?" I asked Leif.

Something hard connected with the side of my head, slamming me back to the ground. Leif half rose from his seat, but settled when the horseman touched his sleeve.

"That was unnecessary, Goel," the horseman said. "Wait outside."

"She spoke without permission."

"If she fails to show the proper respect, you may teach her some manners. Now go," ordered the horseman.

I struggled to my feet again. Goel left, but the other two guards remained by the door. By now my patience was gone. If I were quick enough, I might be able to wrap the foot of chain hanging between my wrists around the horseman's neck.

As I was gauging the distance, the horseman said, "I wouldn't try anything stupid." He lifted a long, broad sword from his lap.

"Who the hell are you and what do you want?" I demanded.

"Watch your language or I'll call Goel back," he replied with a smile.

"Go ahead, call him back. Take my manacles off and let us have a fair fight." When he didn't reply, I added, "Guess you're afraid I'd win. Typical ambusher mentality."

He looked at Leif in amazement. Leif stared back with concern, and I wondered what had gone on between them. Friends or foes?

"You failed to mention this bravado. Of course," he turned back to me, "it could all be an act."

"Try me," I said.

The horseman laughed. Despite his full blond beard and mustache, he still looked younger than I. Maybe seventeen or eighteen years old. His eyes were a washed-out blue, and his shoulder-length blond hair had been pulled back into a ponytail. He wore a simple light gray tunic. Even from this distance, I could tell that his shirt's fabric was finer than the guards' clothes.

"What do you want?" I asked again.

"Information."

I gaped at his unexpected answer.

"Oh, come on," he said. "Don't play the simpleton with me. I want military statistics on Ixia. Troop size and location. Strengths. Weaknesses. How many weapons? Valek's precise location. Who and where his other spies are. That type of information."

"Why would you think I know all this?"

He glanced at Leif, and sudden understanding flooded my mind. "You think I'm a northern spy." I sighed. Leif *had* set me up. That's why the horseman knew Leif was my brother. Leif's fear and shock during the ambush had all been an act. He had no business with the First Magician. No wonder he hadn't said a word since I had arrived in the tent.

"All right, since everyone believes I'm a spy, I guess I should act like one." I crossed my arms to achieve a defiant posture. The clang of the manacles didn't help the image, but I sallied forth anyway. "I'm not telling you southern scum anything."

"You'll have no choice."

"Then you're in for a surprise." Meaning I didn't have the answers he sought. If he had wanted to know the Commander's favorite food, I'd be happy to oblige.

"I could have Goel torture the information out of you," he said. "He would enjoy that. But that's rather messy and time-consuming. And I always consider facts divulged under stress to be suspect."

The horseman rose from his chair, and walked around the

table, coming closer to me. He clutched his sword in his right hand, trying to be intimidating. He was about seven inches taller than me and he had tucked his dark gray pants into knee-high black leather riding boots.

"You're the one in for a surprise, because I'm going to bring you to the Magician's Keep where First Magician will peel your mind like a banana, exposing the soft center where all the answers lie. Your brain gets a little mashed in the pro-cess—" he shrugged his shoulders as if unconcerned about this detail "—but the information is always accurate."

Real fear brushed my skin for the first time since I had awakened a prisoner. Perhaps I'd made a mistake in playing the spy. "I don't suppose you would believe me if I said I didn't have what you wanted?"

The horseman shook his head. "The proof of your loyal-ties is in your backpack. Ixian coins and your northern uni-form."

"Which really proves I'm *not* a spy, because Valek would never recruit someone stupid enough to carry her uniform on a mission," I said in frustration, but regretted having men-tioned Valek's name. A "she-just-gave-herself-away" look flashed between the horseman and Leif.

I tried to stall for time. "Who are you and why do you want this information?"

"I'm King Cahil Ixia. And I want my throne."

6

KING OF IXIA? THIS young idiot was claiming to be a king?

"The King of Ixia is dead," I said.

"I'm well aware that your *boss,* Valek, murdered the King and all his family when Commander Ambrose took control of Ixia. But he made what will soon prove to be a fatal mistake." Cahil jabbed his sword into the air. "He didn't count the bodies, and the King's six-year-old nephew was smuggled to the south. I'm the heir to the Ixian throne and I plan to claim it."

"You'll need more men," I said.

"How many more?" he asked with considerable interest.

"More than twelve." My best guess of the number of men in the camp.

He laughed. "Don't worry. The Commander's military and corps of assassins are enough of a threat to Sitia to provide me with plenty of followers. Besides—" he thought for a moment "—once I deliver you to the Citadel, and show them that I've uncovered a dangerous spy, they'll have no choice but to support my campaign against Ambrose. I'll have the whole Sitian army at my command."

He failed to impress me. Instead, he reminded me of a boy playing with toy soldiers. I did a quick mental calculation. Cahil was a year older than me, making him twenty-one.

"So you're taking me to the Citadel?" I asked.

He nodded. "There, First Magician will reap the information from your mind." He smiled as a greedy glint sparked in his eyes.

Somehow, I had missed the connection of the Magician and the Citadel the first time Cahil had mentioned it. The reference to them mashing my brains must have thrown me off.

"I'm going to the Citadel anyway. Why all the trouble?" I unfolded my arms, showing the manacles.

"You are masquerading as a student. Unfortunately, the Magicians take their Ethical Code very serious, and won't interrogate you unless you're caught doing something illegal. Without my intervention, they would have invited you in, and taught you all the secrets of Sitia."

So I was to be his proof. He wanted to show them that he had saved the Sitians from a menacing criminal. "Okay. I'll go with you to the Citadel." I offered my wrists. "Remove these, and I won't give you any trouble."

"And what's to stop you from running off?" he asked. There was a hitch of disbelief in his voice.

"My word."

"Your word means nothing," Leif said.

His first verbalization of the night, and I felt a strong urge to quiet him with my fist. I stared at him, beaming the promise of a future confrontation.

Cahil appeared unconvinced.

"How about the twelve men you have guarding me?" I asked.

"No. You're my prisoner. You should be dressed as such." Cahil waved his hand, and the two guards by the tent's entrance grabbed my arms.

Meeting over. I was dragged from the tent and dumped by the fire, where Goel resumed his hawklike guard. Cahil had left me no choice. I would *not* arrive at the Citadel as his prize.

I lay there, watching and listening to the men as a simple plan formed in my mind. When the camp settled in for the night, two men relieved Goel. I feigned sleep, waiting until the second shift of men had enough time to grow bored.

Magic was the only weapon I had left; yet I was uncertain of my strength and abilities. What I planned to do could be considered a direct violation of the Magicians' Ethical Code, but, at this point, I didn't care. I would have preferred to fight, but I was out of options and time.

Breathing deep, I tried to project my awareness out. Without the aid of my bow, I failed miserably. I couldn't focus. Not wanting to risk any big movements, I rubbed my thumbs along my fingertips. The skin contact helped to center my mind until I could push it away from me.

I had hoped my guards would be drowsy, but one whistled under his breath and the other reviewed military tactics in his head, although I could feel the desire for sleep pulling at their minds.

I used that desire. I gave a mental command to sleep, and crossed my fingers. My knowledge of magic was very limited; I had no idea if it would work. At first, resistance pushed back. I tried again. Soon, the two men sank to the ground, but still remained awake. I had wanted to be subtle, but the night was running out. Sleep, I ordered with force, and they fell over.

The chains clanked when I sat up. Pressing them to my beating chest, I scanned the slumbering men. I had forgotten about the noise. Since I could only use one hand and my mouth, picking the manacles' locks would be difficult and loud, so I revised my plan. Perhaps I could send all the men into a deep sleep where noise would not rouse them.

I projected my awareness, touching each man's mind, putting them into a heavy, dreamless slumber. Cahil slept on a cot in the tent. While I would have enjoyed rifling through his mind, I settled for sending him into an unconscious state. Leif's magical protection prevented me from affecting him. I hoped he was a heavy sleeper.

Working with my diamond pick in one hand and with the tension wrench between my teeth, I managed to pop the locks on my wrist manacles after a fifth attempt. The sky began to brighten a shade. My time was slipping away. I crept into the tent to retrieve my backpack, stuffing my belongings into it. I made more noise then I wanted, but my instincts told me that full dawn would waken the men. As I fled, I grabbed my bow from beside the guard who had claimed it.

Running through the forest, I noticed that the darkness faded with every stride. My thoughts turned sluggish, and I huffed for breath as weakness pulled at my legs. Using magic on the men had drained my energy.

I scanned the treetops, looking for a big leaf variety with lots of branches. Spotting a tree with potential, I halted and took my grapple and rope from my backpack.

By the time I managed to hook a branch, my arms felt like rubber. I had to smile at the irony of my situation, though, as I pulled myself up the rope. This was the third time I had used the treetops for escape, and the climb was becoming almost routine. But the distant shouts of angry men spurred me on.

When I reached the top, I reeled in my rope, and then scrambled to a higher limb for more cover. I wrapped Fern's green cloth around me as I sat with my back to the trunk, my knees drawn to my chest. Leaving a gap to see through, I settled in for a long wait. I hoped my strength would return soon.

Hearing a commotion, I imagined the scene going on at Cahil's camp. The reprimand of the guards who fell asleep during their watch; the discovery that my backpack and effects were missing. I trusted that made Cahil pause, knowing that I had stood only a few feet from him and let him live.

My position in the tree was closer to the camp than I had wanted. Searchers with drawn swords came into view sooner than I had anticipated. I froze in my green cocoon.

Goel led the men. He stooped to inspect a bush, and then called, "This way. She's not far. The sap's still sticky."

Rivers of sweat ran down my skin. Goel was a tracker. I moved my hand, finding the slit in my pants. My switchblade hadn't been confiscated. Grabbing the smooth wood of the handle made me feel a bit better.

He stopped at the bottom of my tree. I shifted my weight forward and crouched on the branch, preparing to flee if needed.

Goel examined the ground around the base of the trunk. His eyes slid up into the branches. My breath locked as cold fear splashed through me. I realized I had made a grave mistake.

A predatory smile spread across Goel's lips. "Found you."

7

I YANKED MY FOREST CAMOUFLAGE off my back and shook the material out like a sheet.

"There she is," one of Goel's men cried out, pointing up at me.

Releasing the fabric, I let it float down toward the men. The second the material obscured their view, I launched myself through the treetops, scrambling with a sudden spur of energy from branch to branch in an effort to get myself higher and farther from Goel and his men.

"Hey!" someone yelled from below.

"Stop her!"

I kept moving, hoping that Goel couldn't track me through the trees. My mistake had been to forget that Cahil had searched through my backpack. He knew I carried a grapple and rope. With a good tracker and the hint of my trick, it hadn't taken them long to find me.

Curses and yelling followed below me. I focused all my efforts on finding branches that would hold my weight, and getting away. Once my mind calmed enough for rational thought, I realized I was making a racket. Goel and his men could track me by listening to the rattle of the leaves and the snapping of branches. All they had to do then was wait for me to fall, or exhaust myself.

Once I slowed down, taking care not to make any noise, I could hear the men on the forest floor. They called my position to each other, closing in.

"Hold up!" a voice said right below me.

My muscles jerked in shock.

"She stopped."

I kept climbing. My progress was a nerve-racking snail's pace, but quiet.

"We have you," Goel called. "Come down now and I'll only hurt you a little."

I bit back a sarcastic reply to his "generous" offer. Instead, I continued to move through the trees. The men remained silent, and soon I had no idea where they were. I paused on an upper branch to search for some sign of them, but saw nothing but a sea of green leaves.

Then my imagination kicked in. I felt trapped. My face burned with the sudden belief that Goel's eyes were on me. Panic pumped in my heart until I remembered the instruction Irys had given me back in the jungle—seek with your mind, not with your eyes. Using my magic still wasn't instinctive.

Taking a deep breath, I pulled my bow, concentrated on the smooth wood against my fingers, and projected my awareness down to the forest floor.

The men had spread out. They searched a wide area to my right. I couldn't sense Goel below. With a sick feeling crawling along my skin, I swept the treetops. Goel had climbed into the canopy. He followed the trail I had left in my haste. Black thoughts of inflicting pain colored his mind.

When he reached the place where I had begun to travel with more care, I waited. He hesitated for a heartbeat, but spotted another sign, continuing on toward my location.

It was only a matter of time before Goel found me. I considered using my magic to force him off my trail. Could I make him fall asleep? Probably, but Goel would eventually wake up and track me down. I could try prompting him into forgetting who he searched for, but for that I would need to delve deep into his mind and such an effort would drain my remaining strength.

Think. I had to take Goel out. Unless Cahil had another tracker, my chances of escaping improved without Goel on my tail. A plan began to form in my mind. I slid my bow back through its holder on my pack.

Keeping light contact with Goel's mind, I picked up the pace and continued on my route for a while, making sure to leave a trail. When I reached a small clearing in the forest, I swung down to the ground, landing with a hard jolt. Leaving nice deep boot prints, I walked across the clearing, and broke through the underbrush on the other side.

Now came the hard part. Retracing my path, I returned to the tree from which I had jumped. The grapple would leave marks, so I used it to throw the rope over the tree branch, and then I shimmied up. Hopefully, the rub marks on the branch would make it appear that I had gone down to the clearing, not up. Then I looped the rope and hung it around my shoulder and torso so my hands were free.

Goel was now close enough to hear me. I made a small

grunt like I had hit the ground hard. With the utmost care, I climbed higher in the tree. Goel came into sight. I froze.

He inspected the branch I had used to drop into the clearing. He leaned over and peered at the forest floor.

"So me prey has gone to ground," Goel said to himself.

He swung down and crouched by my marks. His thoughts focused on how much he would enjoy torturing me. Sleep, I projected into his mind. Sleep. But he was wide-awake and the command raised immediate suspicions. He stood and glanced around the clearing.

Damn. That wasn't working. Don't look up; I projected as I moved to a lower branch. The leaves shook, but Goel didn't notice. Triggering my switchblade, I cut a three-foot section of rope. I wrapped the ends around my hands as Goel turned back to examine my tracks.

I jumped, landing behind him. Before he could move, I looped the rope I held around his throat. I spun. My backpack touched his back, and the rope was now over my shoulder. I dropped to one knee, forcing Goel to bend backward over me. In that position only his fingertips could reach me. Instead, he yanked at the garrote around his neck.

Just when I thought he was unconscious, his head bumped mine, and I felt his full weight on my back. He did a backward somersault over me. I saw his boots hit the ground in front of me.

Damn. Goel knew some self-defense techniques. He straightened and wrenched the rope right out of my hands.

"Got anything else?" he asked. His voice rasped from my strangulation attempt.

I pulled my bow from my back. He drew his sword.

He smiled. "Little girl. Little weapon." Goel pointed to himself. "Big man. Big weapon."

I shifted into a fighting stance, balancing my weight on the balls of my feet. He wasn't going to intimidate me. If I could disarm my friend Ari, who had twice Goel's muscle mass, and Ari's partner, Janco, who was rabbit fast, I could take on Goel.

Sliding my hands along the wood of my weapon, I reestablished my mental link with Goel. When he lunged, I knew it before he moved. I stepped to the side, turning sideways so his sword missed my stomach. In a stride, I was in close. I slammed my bow into his temple. He crumpled to the ground, unconscious.

Thanking fate that Goel hadn't called for his men, I searched his pack. I found brass knuckles, a small whip, a black club, an assortment of knives, a gag, manacles, keys and my camouflage material.

If I killed Goel, I would be doing the south a favor. A shame that Goel's death wouldn't go well in my "I'm not a spy" defense. So I dragged him to a tree and propped him into a sitting position against the trunk. The manacles had just enough chain for me to lock his hands behind the tree. I shoved his gag into his mouth, fastening the strap around his head.

I took my camouflage material and the manacles' keys from his pack. Then I hid his pack and sword in the bushes. Pausing a moment to regain my focus, I sought Goel's men with my mind. Satisfied that they were far enough away, I mentally scanned the forest for Cahil's campsite. Once I knew in which direction to go, I set out.

I couldn't leave Goel to die. Yet, if I released him, he would only track me down. I could find someone to direct me to the Citadel, and hope the few hours it took Cahil to find Goel would be enough time for me to stay ahead of them. That had been my intent when I had first escaped. But now that rankled. It would be the actions of a criminal or a spy, and I wasn't guilty. I *wouldn't* run away.

Perhaps I could use my magic and trick Goel into losing my trail. Then I could follow Cahil, keeping a close eye on him. But would he continue to the Citadel without me as his prisoner? I didn't know.

A sudden intense desire for Valek was swept through my body. Discussing military tactics with him had always helped me work out a problem. I thought about how Valek would handle this situation and, soon after, a rough plan formed.

"You lost her," Cahil repeated. He frowned as he stared at the faces of the four unhappy men who stood in front of him. "Where's Goel?" he asked.

A mumbled reply.

"You lost him, too?" Outrage gripped Cahil's face.

The men cringed and stammered.

I suppressed the urge to laugh out loud. My position near his campsite afforded me a clear view of Cahil and his men, while I remained hidden under my camouflage. I had used the waning daylight and the clamor of the search party's arrival to move closer to the clearing.

"You're a bunch of bumbling fools. Searching a prisoner for weapons and anything that would help an escape, is standard procedure." Cahil glared at his men. "A *complete* and *thorough* search. You don't stop because you found one weapon." Cahil stared at his men until they fidgeted. "Captain Marrok?"

"Yes, my lord." Marrok snapped to attention.

"If Goel doesn't return by first light, I want you to lead a search party to find him. He's our best chance of recovering that spy," Cahil ordered.

"Yes, sir."

Cahil stalked off to his tent. When he was gone, I could see the grim faces of his men as they stood around the campfire. The smell of roasting meat made my stomach complain. I hadn't eaten all day, but I couldn't risk making any noise. With a sigh, I squirmed into a comfortable position, settling in for a long wait.

Keeping alert proved difficult once the men had gone to sleep. Captain Marrok posted two guards, who circled the campsite. Using magic had drained me and I fought my heavy eyelids until I gave up and dozed for a while. The dream image of Goel's hands on my neck jerked me awake in the middle of the night.

The guards were on the far side of the camp. I used my magic to send the sleeping men into a deeper slumber. The guards, though, fought hard. The image of the harsh punishment their comrades had received for falling asleep on guard duty the night before kept them vigilant. So I tried the "don't look" command as I crept toward Cahil's tent.

Upon reaching the back wall of the tent, I triggered my switchblade and cut a slit in the fabric. Then I entered the tent through that small opening.

Cahil was asleep. Leif looked like he hadn't heard my entrance. Curled up on his side with one arm dangling over the edge of the cot, he appeared to be sleeping. Cahil lay on his back, his arms crossed over his stomach. His long sword rested on the floor within Cahil's reach. I moved the weapon away before I sat on his chest.

The instant he awoke, I had my blade pressed against his throat. "Quiet or I'll kill you," I whispered.

His eyes widened. He tried to move his arms, but my weight pinned them down. Cahil could muscle me off, but I pushed the blade's point into his skin. A drop of blood welled.

"Don't move," I said. "Your sword is out of reach. I'm not that stupid."

"So I'm learning," he whispered.

I felt him relax.

"What do you want?" Cahil asked.

"A truce."

"What kind?"

"You stop trying to drag me to the Citadel in chains and I'll accompany you there as a fellow traveler."

"What do I get out of the deal?"

"You get Goel back and my cooperation."

"You have Goel?"

I dangled the manacles' keys over his face.

"How can I trust you when your brother doesn't trust you?"

"I'm offering a truce. So far, I've had two opportunities to kill you. You're a real threat to Ixia. If I were a true spy, your death would make me famous in the north."

"And if I renege on this truce?"

I shrugged. "I'll escape again. But this time, I'll leave Goel's dead body behind."

"He's a good tracker," Cahil said with pride.

"Unfortunately."

"If I say no to your offer?"

"Then I'm gone, leaving you to find Goel."

"Dead?"

"Yes." I bluffed.

"Why come back? You took care of Goel. He was the only threat to you."

"Because I want the chance to prove that I'm not a spy," I said with frustration. "I'm a Zaltana. And I'm not going to run like a criminal, because I'm not guilty. But I don't want to be your prisoner. And…" I couldn't explain anymore. I sighed. He was right. If my own brother didn't trust me, why should Cahil? I had gambled and lost.

Time for plan B. I would run. My safest course would be to find Irys. I withdrew my switchblade from Cahil's throat. After a full day on the lam without food or sleep, a bone-deep fatigue overcame me. I jumped off of Cahil.

"I'm not going to kill anybody." I backed toward the slit I had cut in the tent, keeping my eyes on Cahil.

When I turned to find the rip in the fabric, a sudden wave of dizziness overcame me, and I stumbled to the ground. The tent spun and I lost consciousness for a mere moment as all my energy fled. I regained my wits in time to see Cahil pick up my switchblade.

8

CAHIL MOVED AWAY AND lit the lantern on his bedside table. He examined my switchblade in the candle-light.

"My lord?" a voice called through the door.

I braced myself, preparing to be accosted and manacled by a rush of guards.

"Everything's fine," Cahil called.

"Very good, sir."

I heard the guard move away and I looked at Cahil in surprise. Perhaps he wanted me to tell him where Goel was before he "reclaimed" me. I sat up and glanced at Leif. His eyes were closed, but I didn't know if the light and Cahil's voice had roused him.

"These markings are very familiar," Cahil said, referring to the six symbols engraved on the handle of my switchblade. "My uncle's secret battle codes, I believe." His gaze returned to me.

His sleep-tousled hair reinforced my first impression of his youth, but a sharp intelligence danced in his eyes.

I nodded. The codes had been used by the King of Ixia to send secret messages to his captains during battles.

"It's been so long," Cahil said. A brief sadness pulled at his face. "What do they mean?"

"It says, 'Sieges weathered, fight together, friends forever.' It was a gift."

"Someone in the north?"

Loneliness touched my heart as I thought of what I had lost by coming south. My fingers sought the lump under my shirt, Valek's butterfly. "Yes."

"Who?"

An odd question. Why would he care? I searched Cahil's face for some sign of duplicity, and found only curiosity. "Janco. One of my self-defense teachers." I grinned at the memories of Janco singing his rhymes and knocking aside my attacks. "Without him and Ari, I wouldn't have had the skills to escape you and take on Goel today."

"They taught you well." Cahil ran a hand along his neck, smearing the drop of blood.

He seemed deep in thought as he turned my switchblade in his hands. He pushed the blade into the handle then triggered it. The snick from the weapon made me flinch.

"Well made," he said.

Cahil stepped toward me. I scrambled upright and stood in a defensive stance. Even though I was light-headed and weak, I contemplated my chances of getting away. Instead of threatening me, Cahil retracted the blade and gave me the switchblade. I looked at the weapon in my hand with a tired astonishment.

"A truce, then," he said. "But any trouble and I'll have you in chains." Cahil gestured to a corner of the tent. "You're exhausted. Get some sleep. We have a long day tomorrow." Placing his sword back within reach, Cahil lay down on his cot.

"Do you want to know where Goel is?" I asked.

"Is he in any immediate danger?"

"Unless there are poisonous or predatory animals in this forest."

"Then let him sweat out the night. Serves him right for being caught." Cahil closed his eyes.

I glanced around the tent. Leif hadn't moved since I had arrived, but his eyes were open. He made no comment as he rolled over to his other side, turning his back on me. Again.

I sighed, wondering how much he had heard, and found I was too tired to care. With weariness dragging at my limbs, I spread my cloak on the floor, blew out the lantern and collapsed on my makeshift bed.

The next morning, Leif left the tent without saying a word. Cahil told me to stay inside while he made a show of the fact that Goel hadn't returned.

I heard Cahil question the guards of the previous night.

"All was quiet, my lord," one man replied.

"Nothing unusual?" Cahil asked.

"Just your light, sir. But you said—"

"What if I'd had a knife at my throat, Erant? Would you have believed what I said?"

"No, sir."

"How did you know, then, that I wasn't in trouble?"

"I didn't, sir. I should have checked," Erant said, sounding miserable.

"Should haves lead to death. In war, you don't get a second chance. In a battle with the north, they won't send an army against us. They'll send one man. Without vigilance, we'll all be killed in our sleep."

Someone scoffed. "Surely one man can't get by us."

"How about a woman?" Cahil asked.

"No way," a guard said amid cheers of assent.

"Then explain this. Yelena," Cahil called. An immediate silence filled the forest. "Join me, please."

I didn't like being part of Cahil's lesson, but he was right. An assassin trained by Valek would have had no trouble taking out his guards. I stepped from the tent, holding my bow in case anyone decided to rush me. The morning sun shone in my eyes as I squinted to examine Cahil's men.

Surprise, anger and disbelief peppered their faces. Captain Marrok drew his sword. Leif was nowhere in sight.

"Everything wasn't fine last night, Erant," Cahil said. "Next time, make sure."

Erant hung his head. "Yes, sir."

"Yelena will be traveling with us to the Citadel. Treat her as a comrade," Cahil ordered.

"What about Goel?" asked Captain Marrok.

Cahil looked at me. "Tell him where Goel is."

"You'll keep Goel on a leash?" I asked. There was no doubt in my mind that Goel's desire for revenge would cause trouble. I shuddered at the thought of being at his mercy.

"Captain Marrok, explain the situation to Goel. Before you free him, make sure he gives his word not to harm Yelena."

"Yes, sir."

"Unless I give him permission," Cahil added, staring at me. "Trouble will get you in chains. Treason will get you Goel."

A rumble of appreciation rolled through Cahil's men. His

little show had earned him points in their minds. I gave him a bored look. I had been threatened many times before and had learned that the men who didn't make verbal threats were the most dangerous. With that thought, I searched the camp-site for Leif. Perhaps he had returned home now that I had delivered myself to Cahil.

I gave Marrok the key to the manacles and instructions as to where to find Goel and his pack. As the Captain left to free him, the rest of the guards began breaking down the camp-site. Cahil's men kept a wary eye on me. A couple of hostile glares were thrown my way, especially when they discovered the rip in the tent's fabric.

While waiting for the Captain and Goel to return, I sorted and organized my backpack. I combed and braided my hair, then twisted the long braid up into a bun, using my lock picks to hold the hair in place. It never hurt to be prepared. Cahil might trust me not to cause trouble, but he still believed I was a northern spy.

Goel returned with Marrok and Leif. I was surprised to see Leif, but not surprised by the seething glower on Goel's face. His cheeks had deep red marks where the gag's strap had pressed into his skin. His hair and clothes were unkempt. Wet-ness stained his pants and his skin was blotchy from multiple mosquito bites. Goel gripped his sword, starting toward me.

Captain Marrok intercepted Goel and pointed across the clearing to a bedroll still lying on the ground. Goel sheathed his sword and headed to the sleeping mat, shooting me a look of venom.

I resumed breathing. Once the camp was packed, Cahil mounted his horse and led us to the forest trail. I stayed close to Marrok in case Goel forgot his promise again.

The Captain grinned at me and said, "Watch now."

Cahil clicked at his horse as he tapped his heels into the animal's sides. The horse increased its stride, and the men began to jog.

"Keep up," Marrok said.

I hadn't run laps since training with Ari and Janco, but I had found some time to exercise while traveling south. Matching Marrok's pace, I asked, "Why does he make you run?"

"Keeps us battle ready."

I had more questions, but I saved my breath, concentrating instead on staying with Marrok. By the time we reached the next campsite, my field of vision had shrunk to a small area on the Captain's back. My efforts to stay in shape hadn't been enough. When we stopped, I labored for air, sucking in huge mouthfuls. Leif, too, seemed winded. Hasn't run with his friends for a while, I thought peevishly.

Once the camp was erected, Cahil offered to let me sleep in the corner of his tent again. There, I collapsed to the ground without bothering to spread my cloak. In the morning, I ate a light breakfast.

The next three days mirrored the first day of traveling with Cahil, but by the end of the fourth day, I wasn't as exhausted. I could eat dinner, and even stayed by the fire for a while. Goel glared at me whenever I met his eye, so I ignored him. Leif pretended I didn't exist.

I began to think the forest was endless. Day after day we covered many miles, yet met no one on the trail, nor saw any sign of a village. I suspected Cahil avoided the towns. I couldn't be sure if it was for my benefit or his.

Eventually, the men got used to my presence. They bantered and kidded with each other, and practiced sword fighting. The wary glances disappeared, and my arrival at the campfire no longer caused an immediate hush. I found it interesting that the men always sought Captain Marrok's approval prior to doing anything.

After we'd been traveling for seven days, Captain Marrok surprised me. Some of the guards were performing self-defense drills, and he invited me to join them.

"We could use the practice against that staff of yours," he said.

I agreed, showing the men some basic defense moves with my bow. While they used their wooden swords, I demonstrated the advantages of having a longer weapon. My participation in the practice drew Cahil's attention. He usually showed no interest in the training sessions, preferring instead to talk to Leif about his quest to conquer Ixia, but now he approached to watch.

"Wood against wood is fine for practice, but wood against steel is no contest in a real fight," Cahil said. "A sharp sword would reduce that staff to splinters."

"The edges are the sword's danger zone. The trick is to avoid the edges," I said.

"Show me." Cahil drew his sword.

The thick blade extended about three and a half feet from the hilt. An impressive weapon, but heavy. Cahil would need two hands to wield it, slowing him down.

I concentrated on the feel of the bow's wood in my hands, setting my mind into my mental fighting zone.

He lunged forward. Surprised by his quickness, I jumped back. Cahil held the sword one-handed, and I found myself on the defensive. He had some skill with his weapon, but not much. When he swung the massive blade, I dodged, stepped in close, and struck the flat of his sword with my bow. The next time he swung I hit his hand. When he lunged, I kept my bow horizontal and brought it down on the flat tip of the blade, deflecting the weapon toward the ground. My counterstrikes wouldn't disarm him, but all the while, I kept moving, forcing Cahil to chase me.

When he grabbed his sword with both hands, I knew he was beginning to tire. It was just a matter of time before he made a tactical error.

Our match lengthened. His men cheered for him, urging him to take me out. They didn't notice the sheen of sweat on Cahil's forehead, or hear the rasp of his breath.

Soon enough, he swung too wide. I ducked in close, and tapped my bow on his ribs. "Have I proven my point?" I asked, dancing past his next attack.

Cahil stopped. "It's getting late. We'll have to finish this later," he said. Sheathing his sword, he marched off to his tent.

Practice was over. His men were quiet as they put away their equipment.

I sat by the campfire, waiting until Cahil had a chance to cool down. Captain Marrok sat next to me.

"You proved your point," he said.

I shrugged. "With a lighter sword, Cahil would have won."

We stared at the flames in silence.

"Why does he carry that sword?" I asked Marrok.

"It was the King's. We managed to smuggle it south with Cahil."

I studied Marrok. His face had that worn leather look of a man who has been around for a long time and seen it all. I realized his skin was tanned from the sun and wasn't a natural pigmentation. "You're from the north."

He nodded and gestured to the men. "We all are."

I studied the men. They were a mixed crew of dark- and light-skinned. And I remembered that, before the takeover, the border between Ixia and Sitia had been just a line on the map, and people from both countries mingled freely.

Marrok continued, "We're the soldiers who weren't important enough to assassinate, nor willing to switch our loyalties to the Commander. Goel, Trayton, Bronse and I were all part of the King's guards." Marrok shoved a twig into the fire. Sparks flew up into the night sky. "We couldn't save the King, but we saved his nephew. We raised him, and taught him everything we know. And," he stood, "we plan to give him a kingdom." Marrok barked orders to the men, and then headed to his bedroll.

Weariness settled over me. My eyes grew heavy and I dragged myself to my corner of the dark tent.

Just before I fell asleep, the tent brightened. I felt a presence near me. My eyes snapped open. Cahil loomed over me with his sword in his hand. Anger pulsed from him in waves.

I STOOD SLOWLY AND STEPPED back from Cahil.

"You humiliated me in front of my men," he said in anger.

"You asked me to show you how a bow could defend against a sword. I was only doing what you wanted."

"It wasn't an honest match."

"What?"

"Leif said you used magic during the fight. That you made me tired."

I suppressed my anger and looked Cahil straight in the eye. "I did not."

"Then what did?"

"Do you really want to know why you lost?" I asked.

"Do you really have an answer?" he countered.

"You need to get off your horse and run with your men. You don't have the stamina for a long fight. And find a lighter sword."

"But it was my uncle's."

"You're not your uncle."

"But I'm the King, and this is the King's sword," Cahil said. His brows creased together. He seemed confused.

"So wear it to your coronation," I said. "If you use it in battle, you'll be wearing it to your funeral," I said.

"You believe I'll be crowned?"

"That's not the point."

"What *is* the point?"

"I would have beaten you with my bow. That sword is too heavy for you."

"I always win against my men."

I sighed. Of course his men wouldn't beat him. I tried another tactic. "Have you been in a battle?"

"Not yet. We're in training. And besides, a King doesn't risk himself during a battle. I stay in the base camp and direct the combat."

His comment didn't sound right to me, but, then again, I had no experience with warfare. Instead, I said, "Think about it, Cahil. Your men raised you. They want to reclaim the throne. But do they want it for you or for themselves? Exile in the south isn't as glamorous as being the King's guards."

Cahil snorted with disdain, shaking his head. "You know nothing. Why would you care? You're a spy. You're just trying to confuse me." He returned to his cot.

Cahil was right. I didn't care. Once we reached the Keep and I proved my innocence, I wouldn't have to bother with him again. Leif, on the other hand, had interfered with me one too many times.

I scanned the tent. My brother's cot was empty.

"Where's Leif?" I asked.

"Gone."

"Where?"

"I sent him ahead to notify the Keep of our arrival. Why?"

"Family business." I spat the words out.

Cahil must have seen the murderous glint in my eyes. "You can't hurt him."

"Oh, yes, I can. He's caused me a lot of trouble."

"He has my protection."

"Is that one of the benefits of being a member of your quest for the north?"

"No. When we captured you and Leif, I gave him my word that no harm would come to him in exchange for his full co-operation in dealing with you."

I blinked at Cahil. Had I heard him right? "But Leif set me up."

"No, he didn't."

"Why didn't you tell me before?"

"I thought letting you believe you had been betrayed by your own brother would demoralize you. However, it seems to have had the opposite effect."

Cahil's plan might have worked if Leif and I had had a re-lationship. I rubbed my face as I tried to decide if knowing the truth changed my opinion about Leif.

Sitting on the edge of his cot, Cahil studied me in silence.

"If Leif didn't set me up, then who did?"

Cahil smiled. "I can't reveal my sources."

Leif had managed to convince many Zaltanas that I was a spy, so the entire clan was suspect. Anyone at the Illiais Mar-ket could have overheard our destination, as well.

I couldn't worry about it now, but I wouldn't forget it, ei-ther. "You said you sent Leif to the Keep," I said. "Will we be there soon?"

"Tomorrow afternoon; about an hour after Leif arrives. I

want to make sure we're met by the right people," Cahil said. "An important day, Yelena. Better get some sleep." He blew out the lantern.

I reclined on my cloak, wondering about the Citadel and Keep. Would Irys be there by tomorrow? Doubtful. I stretched my awareness out, seeking Irys but only encountering wild-life. Without Irys at the Keep would the First Magician peel away the layers of my mind? Apprehension churned inside my stomach. I would rather face Goel than the unknown. Even-tually, though, I slept.

Dark dreams of Reyad swirled in my mind.

"Same story, Yelena," Reyad's ghost said, laughing and taunting. "No options. No friends. But you have a knife. Again."

An image of Reyad wrapped in blood-soaked sheets flashed in my dreams. The killing wound in his neck was the result of my desire to protect myself and the other kidnapped chil-dren from torture and mindless slavery.

"Will you cut another's throat to save yourself?" he asked. "How about your own?"

I woke to the sound of crying and realized with horror that my face was wet. Brushing away the tears, I resolved not to let my doubts plague me. Reyad's ghost might haunt my dreams, but I wouldn't allow him to haunt my life.

Morning dawned with the smell of sweet cakes, and I joined the men by the fire for breakfast. After we ate, Cahil's men packed up the camp. Their mood was light and their banter friendly, so I was caught off guard when I felt a hand on my shoul-der.

Before I could move, the grip tightened, causing pain. I turned my head. Goel stood behind me.

He dug his fingers deeper into my flesh as he whispered in my ear. "I promised not to hurt you while we traveled to the Citadel. Once there, you're mine."

I rammed my elbow into Goel's stomach. He grunted. I stepped forward and knocked his hand off my shoulder with my arm as I spun. Facing him, I asked, "Why warn me?"

He drew in a deep breath and grinned. "Your anticipation will make the hunt more exciting."

"Enough talk, Goel. Let's do it now."

"No. I want time to play. I have all kinds of games planned for when I have you, my sweet."

My body shook with an icy chill of revulsion. Goose bumps covered my skin. It was a sensation I never thought I would feel in the sweltering south.

"Goel, help take down the tent," Captain Marrok ordered.

"Yes, sir." Goel walked away, glancing back at me with a smirk on his face and a promise in his eyes.

I let my breath out slowly. This didn't bode well.

When the men finished breaking camp, Cahil mounted his horse and we set off through the forest. After several hours, the trees thinned as the trail ascended a hill. At the top of the rise, a vast valley, bisected by a long dirt road, spread out in front of us. Farm fields etched geometric shapes on the left side of the road. An immense plain dominated the landscape on the right side. Across the vibrant valley was another ridge, and I could just make out a white fortress spanning its crest.

"Is that the Citadel?" I asked Marrok.

He nodded. "Another half day's march." His gray eyes slid to the right as if searching for something.

I followed his gaze and watched the long grass stalks sway in the breeze. "Daviian Plateau?"

"No. That's farther southeast," Marrok said. "This is the edge of the Avibian Plains. The plain is huge. It takes ten days to cross it."

"My cousin mentioned traveling through a plain on the way to the Citadel, but we're really just skirting it."

"Crossing Avibian is a shortcut. Zaltanas will cross, but everyone else avoids contact with the Sandseed Clan who calls the plains home. Taking the forest route is the long way, but it's safe."

I wanted to ask more, but Cahil increased the pace as we descended into the basin. He was either eager to reach the Citadel or anxious to put the plains behind him.

We passed laborers working in the farm fields, and a caravan of merchants with their horse-drawn wagons loaded with goods. Nothing but the tall grass moved in the plains.

The Citadel grew massive in appearance as we traveled closer. We stopped only once to water the horse and the men.

When we reached the towering gates, I was awed by the sheer size of the outer bulwark. Green veins streaked the white marble walls. I ran a hand along them, finding it smooth and cool despite the blistering heat. I had thought it was hot in the forest, but that had been nothing compared to being fully exposed to the searing sun.

The two guards at the Citadel's open gates approached Cahil. After a brief conversation, Cahil led us into a courtyard. I squinted in the bright sunlight. The majestic sight before me took a while to sink in. An entire town resided within the Citadel's outer walls. All the structures were made of the same white marble with veins of green that comprised the outer wall. I had visualized the Citadel as one large building, like the Commander's castle in Ixia, but this was far beyond anything I could have imagined.

"Impressed?" Marrok asked.

I closed my mouth and nodded. Our party began to walk through the streets and I realized the place was deserted. "Where is everyone?" I asked Marrok.

"The Citadel's a ghost town during the hot season. The Council is in recess, the Keep is on holiday and only a skeleton crew tends the crops. Everyone who can flees to the cooler climates, and those who are left retreat inside at mid-afternoon to avoid the sun."

I didn't blame them. My scalp felt as if it were on fire. "How much longer?" I asked.

"Another hour," Marrok said. "See those four towers?" He pointed to the east. "That's the Magician's Keep."

I stared at their height, wondering what dwelled in those lofty chambers.

We trudged on through the empty streets. The road surface alternated between packed dirt and cobblestones. I spotted dogs, cats and a few chickens crouched in bits of shade. When we neared a large square structure with multiple tiers, Marrok said, "That's Council Hall where the Sitian government has its offices and conducts meetings."

The building had long steps that stretched the entire length beneath the first floor and led up to a grand entrance. Jade colored columns bracketed the doorway. A group of people huddled in the Hall's shadow. They approached us as we walked past. A strong odor of urine emanated from them. Filth matted their hair and covered their tattered attire.

One man reached out with a soot blackened hand. "Please, sir, spare a coin?"

Cahil's men ignored them and kept walking. The group followed along, determined.

"Who are…?" I started to ask, but Marrok didn't slow. I tried to catch up, but a small boy pulled on my arm. His brown eyes were rimmed with sores and streaks of dirt lined his cheeks.

"Lovely lady, please. I'm hungry," the boy said. "Spare a copper?"

I glanced around for Marrok. He was half a block away. I couldn't understand why this boy needed money, but I couldn't refuse those eyes. I dug into my pack and pulled out the Sitian coins Esau had given me. I dumped all of them into his palm.

Kneeling down to his level, I said, "Share these with your friends. And take a bath. Okay?"

A joyful expression lit his face. "Thank—"

Before he could finish we were engulfed by a strong stench as the others surrounded us. They grabbed my arms, pulled at my clothes and yanked on my backpack. I saw the boy pocket the coins and slid out of the melee between the others' legs. The putrid smell of so many unwashed bodies made me gag.

"Lovely lady. Lovely lady," filled my ears until their words were cut off by the clatter of hooves on the cobblestones.

"Get away from her," Cahil yelled. He brandished his sword in the air. "Go. Or I'll cut you in half."

In a heartbeat, the crowd disappeared.

"Are you all right?" Cahil asked.

"Yes." I smoothed my hair and reshouldered my pack. "What was that about?"

"Beggars. Filthy street rats." A look of disgust darkened his face. "It was your fault. If you hadn't given them money, they would have left you alone."

"Beggars?"

My confusion seemed to amaze Cahil. "Surely you know what beggars are?" When I didn't answer, he continued, "They don't work. They live on the streets. They beg for money for food. You had to see them in Ixia," he said with frustration.

"No. Everyone in Ixia has a job. Basic necessities are provided to all by the Commander's military."

"How does he pay for it?"

Before I could answer, Cahil's shoulders drooped. "With my uncle's money. He has probably drained the treasury dry."

I bit back my reply. As far as I was concerned, better to have the money helping people than covering the floor of some treasury.

"Come on." Cahil took his foot out of the stirrup, reached down, and held out his hand. "We need to catch up to the others."

"On the horse?" I asked.

"Don't tell me they don't have horses in the north."

"Not for me," I said as I placed my foot in the stirrup and grabbed his arm. He pulled me into the saddle. I sat behind him, not sure what to do with my arms.

Cahil turned slightly. "For who then?"

"The Commander, Generals and high-ranking officers."

"Cavalry?" Cahil asked.

He was fishing for information. I suppressed a sigh. "Not that I saw." The truth, but I ceased to care if he believed me or not.

Cahil craned his head around and studied my face. A wave of heat enveloped me; I suddenly felt too close to him. His eyes sparked a bluish-green color like the water in the sunlight. And

I found myself wondering why he wore a beard in such a hot climate. I imagined Cahil without his beard. He would look younger, and it would be easier to see his smooth, tanned skin and hawklike nose.

When he turned back, I shook my head. I wanted nothing more to do with him.

"Hold on," he said. Then he clicked his tongue.

The horse began to move. I clutched Cahil's waist as I bounced in the saddle. The ground seemed so far down and looked so hard. I fought to keep my balance as we caught up to his men. When we passed them, I relaxed, assuming he would stop and let me off. But we kept going, and the men ran behind.

As we wound our way through the Citadel, I focused on the horse beneath me, trying to find a rhythm for my body to match the horse's like Cahil seemed to be doing. He crouched above the saddle, while my legs pounded the leather. I concentrated on the horse's movement and suddenly found myself looking out of the horse's eyes.

The road wrapped around like I was inside a bubble. I could see far forward as well as to each side, and almost all the way behind. The horse was hot and tired, and he wondered why there were two people on his back. Peppermint Man was the only one who usually rode him. But sometimes Straw Boy took him out for exercise back home. He longed for his cool quiet stall filled with hay and a bucket of water.

Water soon, I thought to the horse. I hoped. *What's your name?* I asked.

Topaz.

I marveled at our communication. Contact with other animals had only given me a glimpse through their eyes and a hint of their desires. I never had an actual conversation with an animal before.

My back began to ache. *Smoother?* I asked. Topaz changed his gait. Cahil grunted in surprise, but I exhaled with relief. It was as if I rode on a sled down a snow-covered hill.

With the new gait, we moved faster, and the men fell farther behind us. Cahil tried to slow Topaz down, but the horse was determined to get his water.

We reached the base of a tall tower and stopped in the shade. Cahil jumped down from the horse and inspected Topaz's legs.

"I've never seen him do that before," Cahil said.

"Do what?"

"He's a three-gaited horse."

"Meaning?"

"Meaning he knows how to trot, canter and gallop."

"So?"

"So that wasn't one of his gaits. Some horses can do up to five, but I'm not even sure what that was."

"It was smooth and fast. I liked it," I said.

Cahil looked at me with suspicion.

"How do I get down?" I asked.

"Left foot in the stirrup. Swing your right leg back around to the left, then hop off."

I landed on wobbly legs. Topaz swung his head and looked at me. He wanted water. I took one of Topaz's water bags off the saddle and held it open for him. Cahil narrowed his eyes at me, then at his horse.

"Is this Magician's Keep?" I asked to distract Cahil.

"Yes. The entrance is around the corner. We'll wait for my men, then go in."

It didn't take long for his men to catch up. We walked to the Keep's entrance, where high scalloped arches framed the massive marble doors. Pink columns supported the arches that spanned two stories. The gates stood open, and we entered without any resistance from the guards.

Inside was a courtyard and beyond that was a collection of buildings. Another city within the city. I couldn't believe the sizes and colors. A patchwork of different-colored marble formed the structures. Statues of various animals peeked out from corners and roofs. There were gardens and lawns. My eyes were relieved to view the greenery after enduring the white glare of the Citadel's walls.

I could see that the Keep's thick outer wall formed a rectangle that enclosed the entire area. A tower occupied each of the four corners.

Directly opposite the entrance, two figures stood on the steps that led up to the largest structure. Small blocks of peach marble dotted the predominately yellow-colored building. As we drew closer, I realized the figures were Leif and a tall woman. She wore a sleeveless midnight-blue dress that fell to her ankles. Her feet were bare and her white hair was cropped close to her head. Sunlight disappeared into her almost black skin.

When we reached the base of the steps, Cahil handed the horse's reins to Marrok. "Take him to the stables and then unpack. I'll meet you in the barracks."

"Yes, sir," Marrok said, turning to go.

"Marrok," I said. "Make sure you give Topaz some milk oats."

He nodded and moved on.

Cahil squeezed my arm. "How do you know about milk oats?"

I thought fast. "Cahil, I've been traveling with you for over a week I've helped feed him." True to a point, but I didn't think it would be a good idea to tell Cahil that his horse had asked me for some milk oats. And I was certain he didn't want to know that his own horse called him Peppermint Man.

"You're lying. Milk oats are a special treat that the Stable Master bakes. *He* feeds them to the horses, no one else."

I opened my mouth to reply, but a strident voice interrupted, "Cahil, is something wrong?"

Together we glanced at the woman. She and Leif were descending toward us.

"Nothing's wrong," Cahil said.

They stopped a few steps above us.

"Is this her?" the woman asked.

"Yes, First Magician," Cahil said.

"Are you certain about her allegiance to Ixia?" she asked.

"Yes. She carries an Ixian uniform and has Ixian coins," Cahil said.

"Her loyalty and longing for Ixia tastes thick like a rancid soup," Leif said.

The woman stepped closer to me. I looked into her amber eyes. They were shaped like a snow cat's and were just as lethal. Her gaze expanded, encompassing me and my world disappeared as the ground turned to rippling amber liquid. I began to sink. Something circled my ankles, and then pulled me under the surface. My clothes were stripped away, then my skin, then my muscles. My bones dissolved until there was nothing left but my soul.

IO

SOMETHING SHARP SCRATCHED my soul, searching for vulnerable spots. I pushed away the intrusive object and began to build a wall of defense in my mind. This magician would not reach me.

Bricks formed and stacked, but they crumbled at the edges. Holes drilled through as I struggled to stay ahead of First Magician. I poured all my strength into that wall. I patched the holes. I added another wall within the first. But the bricks disintegrated and collapsed.

Damn it! No! I scrambled for a while, but it was just a matter of time. In the end, I let the wall dissolve. But, with a sudden rush of energy, I created a curtain of green-veined marble, cutting her off.

I pressed myself to the smooth stone and held on with all my might. Exhaustion pulled at my mind. In pure desperation, I used the last of my power, calling for help. The marble transformed into a statue of Valek. He looked at me in concern.

"Help," I said.

He wrapped his strong arms around me, pulling me close to his chest. "Anything, love."

With nothing left, I clung to him as darkness descended.

I awoke in a narrow room; my head throbbing. Looking up at the ceiling, I realized that I was on a bed. It had been pushed against a wall under an open window. When I moved to sit up, my stiff legs protested. I felt raw and violated as though someone had scrubbed off my skin. My throat blazed with thirst. A pitcher of water sweated on a night table, an empty glass beside it. I poured a large drink and downed the cool liquid in three gulps. Feeling a little better, I examined the room. An armoire stood along the opposite wall with a full-length mirror on the right and a doorway on the left.

Cahil appeared in the doorway. "I thought I heard you."

"What happened?" I asked.

"First Magician tried to read your mind," Cahil said. He looked embarrassed. "She was extremely annoyed by your resistance, but she did say you weren't a spy."

"Peachy." Sarcasm rendered my voice sharp. I crossed my arms over my chest. "How did I get here?"

Splotches of red spread on his cheeks. "I carried you."

I hugged myself. The thought of being touched by him made my skin crawl. "Why did you stay?"

"I wanted to make sure you were all right."

"*Now* you're concerned about me? I find that hard to believe." I stood on sore legs. They felt as if I had run too many laps, and my lower back ached. "Where am I?"

"In the student's quarters. Apprentice wing. You've been assigned these rooms."

Cahil retreated into the other room. I followed him into a

small sitting area with a large desk, a couch, table and chairs and a marble fireplace. The walls were made of light green marble. My pack rested on the table with my bow.

There was another door. I crossed the room and opened it. Beyond the threshold was a garden courtyard with trees and statues. Through them I could see the setting sun. I stepped outside, glancing around. My rooms were at the end of a long one-story building. No one was in sight.

Cahil joined me outside. "The students will be back at the start of the cooling season." He pointed to a path. "That leads to the dining hall and classrooms. Want me to give you a tour?"

"No," I said, going back into the sitting room. I turned around in the doorway. "I want you and your toy soldiers to leave me the hell alone. Now you know I'm not a spy, stay the hell away from me." I closed the door and locked it, leaving Cahil outside. Just to be safe, I wedged a chair under the door-knob.

I curled up on the bed. The desire to go home racked my body. Home to Valek. To his strength and his love. Just that brief contact with him made me miss him even more. His absence left an emptiness that burned deep inside me.

I wanted to leave Sitia. I had gained enough control of my magic to avoid a flameout. I didn't need to be here with these horrible people. All I had to do was head north, and I would reach Ixia's border. I planned the journey in my mind, making a list of provisions, and even considered horse-napping Topaz to make my escape. When the room grew dark, I fell asleep.

When the sun woke me, I rolled onto my other side, weighed my chances of escaping the Keep without anyone knowing, and realized I knew nothing of the layout of the

Keep. I could make a reconnaissance of the area, but I had no desire to see anyone or be seen. So, I stayed in bed all day and went back to sleep that night.

Another day passed. Someone rattled the doorknob then knocked, calling out to me. I shouted for them to go away, and was content when they did.

Eventually, I lay in a stupor. My mind floated and reached some creatures in the garden. I flinched away from even that light contact, seeking a peaceful place.

Then I found Topaz. Peppermint Man had come to visit, but the horse wondered where Lavender Lady was. I saw a picture of me in Topaz's mind. Lavender Lady must be the name he had given me. It was funny that Topaz called me Lavender Lady. Traveling with Cahil left little time for bathing, but I had managed to find some privacy to freshen up and apply a few drops of my mother's Lavender perfume.

Go smooth and fast, Topaz thought.

Would you take me far away to the north? I asked.

Not without Peppermint Man. Smooth and fast with you both. I am strong.

You are very strong. Perhaps I'll stay with you.

No, you won't, Yelena. You've sulked enough, Irys's voice said in my mind. Her contact was like a thick cool salve rubbed on an open wound.

I'm not sulking.

Then what would you call it? Irys demanded with annoyance.

Protecting myself.

She laughed. *From what? Roze barely got through.*

Roze?

Roze Featherstone, First Magician. And she's been in a rage ever since. You've weathered worse things, Yelena. What's the real problem?

I felt helpless and alone with no one to watch my back. But I buried that thought deep, unwilling to share it with Irys. Instead, I ignored her question. Knowing my mentor was back, I rallied. She was the only person I could trust in the Keep.

I'm coming with some food. You will *let me in and you* will *eat.* Irys ordered.

Food? Topaz thought hopefully. *Apple? Peppermints?*

I smiled. *Later.*

My stomach grumbled. As I moved to sit on the edge of the bed, a wave of dizziness overcame me. I had lost track of the days and I was weak from hunger.

Irys came as promised, carrying a tray laden with fruit and cold meats. She also brought a pitcher of pineapple juice and some cakes. As I ate, she told me about her trip to May's home. May was the last of the kidnapped girls to find her lost family.

"Five sisters just like her," Irys said, shaking her head.

I grinned, imagining May's homecoming. Six girls squealing with delight, laughing and crying as they all talked at once.

"Their beleaguered father wanted me to test all the girls for magical potential. May has some, but I want her to wait another year before coming to the school. The others were still too young." Irys poured two cups of juice. "I had to cut my visit short when I felt your call for help."

"When Roze was invading?"

"Yes. I was too far away to assist you, but it seems like you managed on your own."

"Valek helped me," I said.

"That's impossible. *I* couldn't reach you. Valek's not a magician."

"But he was there and I drew on his strength."

Unwilling to believe me, Irys shook her head.

I thought about how Irys had found me in the north. "You felt my power when I was in Ixia," I said. "It's the same distance for Valek to reach me."

She shook her head again. "Valek is resistant to magic so I think you used his image as a shield against Roze. When I felt you last year, you had no control over your powers. Uncontrolled bursts of magic cause ripples in the power source. All magicians, anywhere in the world can feel that, but only Master Magicians will know from which direction it comes."

That worried me. "You felt my call for help when you were at May's home, though. Was I out of control to be able to reach you at that distance?" Loss of control led to flameout, which led to death for the magician and damaged the power source for all magicians.

She looked startled. "No." She frowned and stared at the wall, considering. "Yelena, what have you been doing with your magic since I left you?"

I told her about the ambush, the escape and the truce with Cahil.

"So you put *all* of Cahil's men into a deep sleep?" she asked.

"Well, there were only twelve. Did I do something wrong? Have I broken your Ethical Code?" There was so much I didn't know about magic.

Irys snorted, reading my mind. *And you wanted to run away with a horse.*

"Better than staying here with Cahil and Leif," I said aloud.

"Those two." Irys frowned again. "The Master Magicians had a discussion with both of them. Roze is furious that they misled her about you. Cahil actually had the audacity to demand a Council session in the middle of the hot season. He'll just have to wait until the cooling season. Perhaps he'll get on the agenda, or perhaps not." Irys shrugged, seeming unconcerned.

"Would the Sitians go to war for Cahil?" I asked.

"We have no quarrel with the north, but no love for them either. The Council has been waiting for Cahil to mature. If he develops the charisma and strong leadership abilities, his plans to take back Ixia may be supported by the Council." She cocked her head to the side as if considering the prospect of going to war.

"The trade treaty is the first official contact we've had with Ixia in fifteen years," she explained. "It's a good beginning. We have always been worried that Commander Ambrose would try to take over Sitia as he did in the north, but he seems content."

"Would a Sitian army prevail against the north?"

"What do you think?"

"Sitia would have a difficult time. The Commander's men are loyal, dedicated and well trained. To lose a battle, they would either need to be vastly outnumbered or be vastly outsmarted."

Irys nodded. "A campaign against them would have to be launched with the utmost care, which is why the Council is waiting. But that is not my concern today. My priority is to teach you magic, and discover your specialty. You're stronger than I thought, Yelena. Putting twelve men to sleep is no easy task. And having a conversation with a horse..." Irys pulled her hair back from her face and held it behind her head. "If I hadn't been listening in, I wouldn't have believed you."

Irys rose and began to pile the dishes onto the tray. "What you did to Cahil's men would normally be considered a breech of the Ethical Code, but you acted in self-defense, so it was acceptable." She paused for a moment. "What Roze did to you was a clear violation of our ethics, but she thought you were a spy. The Code doesn't apply to spies. All Sitians are united in their intolerance for espionage. The Commander gained power by infiltrating the monarchy and using assassination, so Sitia worries when a spy is uncovered that the Commander is trying to collect enough information to launch another takeover."

Picking up the tray of dirty plates, Irys said, "Tomorrow, I will show you the Keep and start your training. There are candles and flint in the armoire if you need a light, and there's firewood behind the building for when it gets cold. I've assigned you to the apprentices' wing because you're too old for the first-years' barracks. And I think by the start of school, you'll be ready to join the apprentice class."

"What's the apprentice class?"

"The Keep has a five-year curriculum. Students start the program about a year after they reach maturity. Usually around the age of fourteen their magic has grown to a point where they can direct it. Each year of the Keep's curriculum has a title. First year, novice, junior, senior and apprentice. You'll be at the apprentice level, but your schooling will be different since you need to learn about our history and government." Irys shook her head. "I'll figure it out before classes start. You'll probably be with students from different levels, depending on the subject. But don't worry about that now. Why don't you unpack and make yourself at home."

Her words reminded me that I had something for her in

my pack. "Irys, wait a moment," I said before she could leave. "My mother sent you some perfume." I dug into my bag. By some stroke of luck, the bottles hadn't been damaged during the trip to the Citadel. I gave Irys the Apple Berry perfume, and put my bottle of Lavender on the table.

Irys thanked me and left. After she was gone, the room felt empty. Taking everything out of my backpack, I hung my old uniform in the armoire and decorated the table with the valmur statue I had bought for Valek, but the rooms still seemed bare. I would ask Irys to exchange my Ixian money. Perhaps I could purchase a few things to brighten up the place.

I found Esau's field guide at the bottom of my pack. Taking a candle into the bedroom, I read his book until my eyes grew heavy. From his vast notes, it seemed that almost every plant and tree in the jungle had a reason for existing. I caught myself wishing there was a page in his guide that had my picture on it with the reason for my existence written underneath in Esau's neat hand.

In the morning, Irys scrunched up her nose when she entered my rooms. "Perhaps I'll show you the bathhouse first. We'll send your clothes to the laundry and get you some fresh ones."

I laughed. "Bad?"

"Yes."

Irys and I went to another marble building with blue columns all around. The bathhouse had separate pools for men and women. Washing the road grime from my skin felt wonderful. The laundry mistress took my tattered and stained clothes. Nutty's outfit, my white shirt and black pants all needed mending.

I borrowed a light green cotton tunic and khaki-colored pants. Irys told me the Keep had no particular dress code for classes and everyday events, but special functions required an apprentice robe.

After I combed and plaited my hair, we walked to the dining room for breakfast. Gazing around the Keep, I could see a pattern in the inner layout. Paths and gardens wound their way past marble buildings of various size and shape. Barracks and student housing ringed the main campus. The stables, laundry and kennels lined the back wall of the Keep. Horses grazed in a large fenced pasture next to an oval training yard.

I asked Irys about the four towers.

"The Master Magicians live in them." She pointed to the one in the northwest corner. "That one is mine. The one in the northeast corner near the stables is Zitora Cowan's, Third Magician. The southwest one is Roze Featherstone's, and the southeast one is Bain Bloodgood's, Second Magician."

"What if you have more than four Masters?"

"In the history of the Magician's Keep, we have never had more than four. Less, yes, but never more. It would be a wonderful problem to have. The towers are huge so there would be plenty of room to share." She smiled.

Three people sat in the dining room. Rows and rows of empty tables lined the long room.

"When school starts, these tables will be filled with students, teachers and magicians. Everyone eats here," Irys explained.

She introduced me to the two men and one woman eating breakfast. Gardeners on break, they were just a small part of the vast force needed to tend the landscaping.

We ate, I pocketed an apple for Topaz and Irys took me to

her chambers. After climbing what seemed like a million steps and passing ten levels of rooms, we emerged at the top. The circular room's windows stretched from floor to ceiling. Curtains, long and lacy, blew in the hot breeze. Colorful cushions and couches in blues, purples and silver decorated the bright area. The place was ringed with bookshelves, and the air held a fresh citrus scent.

"My meditation room," Irys said. "The perfect environment to draw power and to learn."

I walked around, looking outside. She had a magnificent view of the Keep and, through the northeast facing windows, I could see rolling green hills pockmarked with small villages.

"That's part of the Featherstone Clan's lands," Irys said, following my gaze. She gestured to the center of the room. "Sit down. Let's begin." Irys sat on a purple cushion, crossing her legs.

I perched on a blue pillow across from her. "But my bow…"

"You won't need your bow. I'll teach you how to draw your power without relying on physical contact. The power source surrounds the world like a blanket. You have the ability to take a thread from this cloth, pull it into your body and use it. But don't take too much or you'll bunch up the blanket, warping the source and leaving some areas bare and others with too much power. It's rumored that there are places where there are holes in the blanket, areas of no power, but I haven't found any."

I felt her power spread from her like a bubble. She raised her hand and said, "Venettaden."

The power slammed into me. My muscles froze solid. I stared at her in a growing panic.

"Push it away," she said.

I considered my brick wall, but knew it was no match for her strength. Once again, I drew down my marble curtain and severed the flow of power. My muscles relaxed.

"Very good," she said. "I took a line of power and shaped it into a ball. Then, using a word and a gesture, I directed it toward you. We teach the students words and gestures for learning purposes, but really you can use anything you want. It just helps focus the power. And after a while you won't need to use the words to perform the magic. It becomes instinctive. Now, your turn."

"But I don't know how to pull a thread of power. I just concentrate on the feel of my bow's wood and then my mind somehow detaches and I project it out to other minds. Why does that work?"

"The ability to read thoughts is another thread of power linking two minds, forging a connection. Once the link is made, it remains there and reconnecting is easy. For example, consider the link between us, and between you and Topaz."

"And Valek," I said.

"Yes, Valek, too. Although with his immunity to magic, I think your link with him must be on a subconscious level. Have you ever read his thoughts?"

"No. But I haven't tried. Somehow I always knew what he was feeling."

"A survival instinct. That makes sense, considering his position in Ixia, and since he decided if you would live or die on a daily basis."

"That survival instinct saved me a few times," I said, remembering my troubles in Ixia. "I would find myself in a tight spot, and suddenly it seemed another person had taken control of my body and impossible things would happen."

"Yes, but now you have control and you can *make* those things happen."

"I'm not so sure—"

Irys raised her hand. "Enough of that. Now concentrate. Feel the power. Pull it to you and hold it."

I took a deep breath, and closed my eyes for good measure. Feeling a little silly, I focused on the air around me, trying to sense the blanket of power. For a while nothing happened. Then, I felt the air thicken and press against my skin. I willed the magic to gather closer. Once the pressure grew intense, I opened my eyes. Irys watched me.

"When you release it toward me, think of what you want the power to do. A word or gesture will help and can be used as a shortcut for the next time."

I pushed the power, and said, "Over."

For a moment nothing happened. Then Irys's eyes widened in shock, and she fell over.

I ran to her. "I'm sorry."

She peered up at me. "That was odd."

"Odd how?"

"Instead of pushing me over, your magic invaded my mind, giving me a mental command to fall." Irys settled herself back on the pillow.

"Try again, but this time think of the power as a physical object like a wall and direct it toward me."

I followed her directions, but the results were the same.

"It's an unorthodox method, but it works." Irys tucked a loose strand of hair behind her ear. "Let's work on your defenses. I want you to deflect my power before it can affect you."

In a blur of motion she aimed a ball of energy toward me. "Teatottle."

I jumped back and put my hands up, but I wasn't fast enough. My world spun. Streaks of color swirled around me before I could position my defenses. I was flat on my back, looking up at the sloped ceiling of the tower. An owl slept on a nest in the rafters.

"You need to keep your defenses up at all times," Irys said. "You don't want to be caught unaware. But then again…" Irys smoothed her shirt. "You kept Roze from going deep into your mind."

I shied away from that subject. "What does Teatottle mean?" I asked.

"It's a nonsense word," Irys said. "I made it up. No sense alerting you to what I planned to do. I use those words for attacks and defensive moves. But for practical matters like fire and light, I use real words."

"I can make fire?"

"If you're strong enough. But it's tiring work. Using magic is draining, some types more than others. You seem to be able to connect with other minds without a lot of effort," Irys said. "Perhaps that is your specialty."

"What do you mean by specialty?"

"Some magicians can only do certain things. We have magicians who can heal physical injuries and others who can help with mental trauma. Some can move large objects like statues, while others can light fires with minimal effort." Irys played with the tassels on her cushion. "Sometimes, you'll find someone who can do two or three things, or a hybrid talent like Leif who can sense a person's soul. For you, we've discovered that not only can you read minds, but you can also influence a person's or animal's actions. A rare talent. That's two abilities."

"Is that the limit?" I asked.

"No. Master Magicians can do everything."

"So why is Roze called First Magician and you're Fourth?"

Irys gave me a tired smile. "Roze is stronger than I am. We can both light fires. While I can only make a campfire, she has the ability to set a two-story structure ablaze."

I thought about what she had said. "If a magician only has one talent, what do they do when they finish their training?"

"We assign magicians to different towns and cities, depending on what is needed. We try to have a healer in every town at all times. Other magicians cover several towns, traveling from place to place to help with projects."

"What would I do?" I asked, wondering if a useful place for me existed. But, at the same time, I wasn't sure if I wanted a useful place in Sitia.

Irys laughed. "It's too soon to tell. For now you need to practice collecting power and using it. And practice keeping up your defenses."

"How do I keep my wall up without draining myself?"

"I imagine my defensive wall, which resembles this tower room. I make it solid and strong, and then I make it translucent so I can see out of it, and then I don't think about it anymore. But when magic is directed toward me, my barrier solidifies and deflects the attack before my consciousness is even fully aware of it."

I followed her instructions and created an invisible barrier in my mind. Irys tested it at unexpected times throughout the morning and it held. The rest of the time I practiced gathering magic, but, no matter how hard I tried, my magic could only affect two things. Irys and the owl sleeping in the rafters.

Irys's patience amazed me, and, for the first time since

coming to Sitia, I felt hopeful that mastering my powers might be within my abilities.

"That was a good start," Irys said as lunchtime neared. "Go eat, and then rest this afternoon. We'll work in the mornings and you can practice and study at night. But tonight you need to see the Stable Master and pick out a horse."

Did I hear her right? "A horse?"

"Yes. All magicians have horses. Occasionally you'll be needed somewhere fast. I had to leave my horse, Silk, here during my mission in Ixia. When you called for help, I had to borrow a horse from May's father. How else do you think I got here so fast?"

I hadn't even thought about it. I had been so wrapped up in my own misery at the time. Following Irys's directions, I located the dining hall. I ate lunch then went back to my rooms where I collapsed into bed and fell asleep.

That night after dinner, I sought out the Stable Master. I found him at the end of a row of stalls, cleaning a leather saddle. A small stocky man, his wild brown hair fell past his shoulders like a horse's mane. When he glared up at me, I suppressed my smile.

"What do you want? Can't you see I'm busy?" he asked.

"I'm Yelena. Irys sent me."

"Oh, right, the new student. I don't know why Fourth Magician couldn't wait until everyone's back to start your lessons," he muttered to himself as he put the saddle down. "This way."

He led me past the stable. Topaz poked his head out of his stall.

His big brown eyes looked hopeful. *Apple?* he asked.

Irys had been right. I reconnected with Topaz without any

conscious effort. Or had he connected with me? I would have to ask her about that. I gave him the apple in my pocket.

The Stable Master turned around. "You just made a friend for life," he said, snorting in amusement. "That horse loves food. I never saw a horse take such pleasure in eating before. You can train him to do just about anything for a peppermint."

We went past the hay barn to the pasture. The Stable Master leaned against the wooden fence. Six horses grazed in the field.

"Pick one out. Makes no difference which one, they're all good. I'll go find your instructor."

"You don't teach?" I asked before he could go.

"Not in the middle of the hot season when everyone but me is gone," he said with annoyance. "I'm too busy mucking out stalls and fixing tack. I said to wait, but Fourth Magician wanted it right away. Good thing one of my instructors came back early." He mumbled some more as he headed toward the stable.

I studied the horses in the field. Three were dark brown like Topaz, two were black, and one was copper with white on the legs from the knees down. Knowing nothing of horses, I guessed it would come down to color. The copper-and-white horse looked over at me.

Like her, Topaz said. *She go smooth and fast for Lavender Lady.*

How do I get her to come over? I asked.

Peppermints. Topaz looked lovingly at a leather bag hanging near his stall. The Stable Master had disappeared. I went back to the stable. Taking out two mints, I gave one to Topaz, and took the other back to the field.

Show Kiki peppermint.

I held out the mint. Kiki glanced at the other horses, and

then moved toward me. When she came closer, I could see she had a white face with a patch of brown around her left eye. Something about her eyes seemed strange. It wasn't until she sucked the peppermint from my palm that it struck me. Her eyes were blue. I had never seen that before, but that didn't mean much. I knew next to nothing about horses.

Scratch behind ears, Topaz suggested.

The mare's long copper ears were cocked forward. I stood on tiptoes and rubbed my fingernails behind them. Kiki lowered her head and pressed it against my chest.

"What do you think, girl?" I asked out loud. I couldn't hear her like Topaz. While rubbing her ears, I pulled a thread of power and projected my mind to her. *Be with me?*

She nudged me with her nose. *Yes.*

I felt Topaz's pleasure. *We go smooth and fast together.*

I jumped when I heard the Stable Master behind me.

"Found one already?" he asked.

I nodded without looking at him.

"That one came from the plains," he said. "Good choice."

"She must pick another," said a familiar voice.

I turned. Dread curled in my stomach. Cahil stood next to the Stable Master.

"And why would I listen to you?" I demanded.

He smirked. "Because I'm your instructor."

II

"NO," I SAID. "YOU WILL *not* be my instructor."

"No choice," said the Stable Master. He glanced at Cahil then me, looking puzzled. "There's no one else and Fourth Magician insists you start right away."

"What if I help you muck out the stables and feed the horses? Will you have time to teach me then?" I asked the Stable Master.

"Young lady, you already have plenty to do. You'll be mucking and caring for your own horse, as well as studying your lessons. Cahil's been a stable rat since he was six. No one, other than me…" He grinned. "…knows more about horses."

I planted my hands on my hips. "Fine. As long as he knows more about horses than he does about people."

Cahil cringed. Good.

"But I keep this horse," I said.

"She's a walleye," Cahil said.

"A what?" I asked.

"She has blue eyes. That's bad luck. And she's been bred by the Sandseed Clan. Their horses are difficult to train."

Kiki snorted at Cahil. *Mean Boy.*

"A silly superstition and an unfair reputation. Cahil, you should know better," the Stable Master said. "She's a perfectly good horse. Whatever's going on between you and Yelena, you'll have to work it out. I've no time to babysit." With that, he stalked away, once more muttering to himself.

Cahil and I glared at each other for a while until Kiki nudged my arm, looking for peppermints.

"Sorry, girl, no more," I said, holding out my empty hand. She tossed her head, and resumed grazing.

Cahil stared at me. I crossed my arms over my chest, but they seemed an inadequate barrier between us. I would have preferred thick marble walls. He had exchanged his traveling clothes for a plain white shirt and tight-fitting jodhpurs, but he still wore his black riding boots.

"You'll have to live with your decision about the horse. But if you're going to fight me every time I try to teach you something, let me know now, and I won't waste my time."

"Irys wants me to learn, so I'll learn."

He appeared satisfied. "Good. First lesson starts now." He climbed over the pasture's fence. "Before you learn how to ride a horse, you must know everything about your horse from the physical to the emotional." Cahil clicked his tongue at Kiki, and when she ignored him, he approached her. Just as he came up beside her she turned, knocking him over with her rump.

I bit my lip to keep from laughing. Every time he tried to get near, Kiki either moved away or bumped into him.

His face red with frustration, Cahil finally said, "The hell with this. I'm getting a halter."

"You hurt her feelings when you said she was bad luck," I explained. "She'll cooperate if you apologize."

"How would you know?" Cahil demanded.

"I just know."

"You didn't even know how to dismount a horse. I'm not that stupid," he said.

When he started to climb over the fence, I said, "I know the same way I knew Topaz wanted milk oats."

Cahil stopped, waiting.

I sighed. "Topaz told me he wanted the treat. I connected with his mind by accident, so I asked him to go smoother because my back hurt. It's the same with Kiki."

Cahil pulled at his beard. "The First Magician said you had strong magical abilities. I guess I should have known it before, but I was too focused on the spy thing." He looked at me as if noticing me for the first time.

For a second, I thought I witnessed cold calculation slide through Cahil's blue eyes, but it disappeared, leaving me to wonder if I had seen anything at all.

"Her name's Kiki?" he asked.

I nodded. Cahil returned to Kiki and apologized. I felt a sudden peevish annoyance. He should have been apologizing to me for all the pain he had caused. Spy thing, my ass.

Push Mean Boy? Kiki asked.

No. Be nice. He's going to teach me to care for you.

Cahil gestured for me to join him near Kiki. I clambered over the fence. As Kiki stood her ground, Cahil pointed to and lectured about the different parts of her body. Starting with her muzzle, he didn't stop until he had lifted her right back hoof and showed me the underside.

"Same time tomorrow," he said, ending the lesson. "Meet me in the stable. We'll go over horse care."

Before he could head back to the barn, I stopped him. Now that my annoyance that he was my instructor was gone, I wondered why he was here. "Why are you teaching me? I thought your campaign for the Ixian throne would take up most of your time."

Well aware of how I felt about his quest, Cahil studied me, seeking for signs of sarcasm.

"Until I receive the full support of the Sitian Council, I can only do so much," he said. "Besides, I need money to pay for my expenses. Most of my men are employed at the Keep as guards or gardeners, depending on what's needed." He wiped his hands on his pants, staring at the horses in the pasture. "When the Keep is on hiatus during the hot season, I focus all my efforts on gathering support. This season I thought I would finally get the Council's backing." Cahil looked at me. "But that didn't work out. So I'm back to work and back to begging the Council to put me on their agenda." He frowned and shook his head. "Tomorrow, then?"

"Tomorrow." I watched Cahil as he walked to the stable. He had been counting on catching an Ixian spy to influence the Council. I wondered what he would try next.

Kiki nudged my arm and I scratched behind her ears before I returned to my rooms. Rummaging around for some paper, I sat at my desk and drew a crude sketch of a horse. I labeled the parts that I could remember. Topaz and Kiki helped me with the rest.

The connection I had formed with the two horses was odd yet comforting. It was as if we were all in the same room, doing different tasks and minding our own business and having our own private thoughts. But when one of us would "speak" directly to the other, we would "hear" it. I only had to think about Kiki and her thoughts would fill my mind. The same was true with Irys. I didn't need to pull power and project it to Irys. All I needed to do was think about her.

Over the next week, my days fell into a pattern. Mornings spent with Irys to learn about magic, afternoons spent napping, studying and practicing my self-defense techniques. Evenings were spent with Cahil and Kiki. As I moved throughout the campus, I kept a wary eye out for Goel. I hadn't forgotten his threat.

Not long into my magical training, Irys began testing me for other abilities.

"Let's see if you can start a fire," Irys said one morning. "This time, when you pull in the power, I want you to concentrate on lighting this candle." She placed a candlestick in front of me.

"How?" I asked, sitting up. I had been reclining on the pillows in her tower room, thinking about Kiki. It had been a week, and I still hadn't ridden her. So far, Cahil had spent every lesson teaching me about horse care and tack. What an annoying man.

"Think of a single flame before you direct your magic." Irys demonstrated. "Fire," she said. The candle flared and burned before she blew it out. "Your turn."

I focused on the candle's wick, forming a flaming image in my mind. Pushing magic toward the candle, I willed it to light. Nothing happened.

Irys made a strangled sound and the candle burned. "Are you directing your magic to the candle?"

"Yes. Why?"

"You just ordered me to light the candle for you," Irys said in exasperation. "And *I* did it."

"Is that bad?"

"No. I hope you know how to light a fire the mundane way, because, so far, it seems that's not part of your magical skills. Let's try something else."

I tried to move a physical object with no success. Unless making Irys do it for me could be considered a magical skill.

She raised her mental defenses, blocking out my influence. "Try again. This time focus on keeping control."

As I pulled in power, Irys threw a pillow at me. The pillow struck me in the stomach. "Hey!"

"You were supposed to deflect it with your magic. Try again."

By the end of the session, I was glad Irys had chosen a pillow. Otherwise, I would have been covered with bruises.

"I think you just need to practice your control," Irys said, refusing to give up. "Get some rest. You'll do better tomorrow."

Before leaving, I asked something that had been on my mind for several days. "Irys, can I see more of the Citadel? And I need to exchange my Ixian coins for Sitian so I can buy some items and clothes. Is there a marketplace?"

"Yes, but it's only open one day a week during the hot season." She paused for a moment, considering. "I'll give you market days off. No lessons. You can explore the Citadel or do whatever you want. It'll be open in two days. In the meantime, I'll exchange your money."

Irys couldn't pass up the opportunity to lecture me on spending money wisely. "Your expenses are covered while you're in the Keep. But once you graduate, you'll be on your own. You'll earn wages as a magician, of course," Irys said. "But don't give your money away." She smiled to ease the reprimand. "We don't like to encourage the beggars."

The image of the dirty little boy rose in my mind. "Why don't they have any money?" I asked.

"Some are lazy, preferring to beg instead of work. Others are unable to work because of physical or mental problems. The healers can only do so much. And some gamble or spend their money faster than they can earn it."

"But what about the children?"

"Runaways, orphans or the offspring of the homeless. The hot season is the worst time for them. Once school starts and the Citadel is populated again, there are places they can go for food and shelter." Irys touched my shoulder. "Don't worry about them, Yelena."

I mulled over Irys's comments on my way back to my rooms.

That evening, while teaching me to saddle and bridle Kiki in her barn stall, Cahil asked, "What's gotten into you? You've been snapping at me all night."

Lavender Lady upset, Kiki agreed.

I sucked in a deep breath, preparing to apologize, but an unbidden torrent of words poured from my mouth instead. "You want Ixia so you can be king. So you can collect taxes, sit on a throne and wear a crown of jewels while the people suffer like they did under your uncle. So your henchmen like Goel can kill innocent children when their parents can't pay the taxes for your fine silk clothes, or so they can kill the parents, leaving their offspring homeless and beggars." My outburst ended as fast as it had begun.

Cahil gaped in shock, but recovered fast. "That's not what

I want," he said. "I want to help the people of Ixia. So they have the freedom to wear whatever clothes they want instead of being forced to wear uniforms. So they can marry whomever they want without securing a permit from their district's General. Live wherever they want, even if it's in Sitia. I want the crown so I can free Ixia of the military dictatorship."

His reasons sounded superficial. Would the people be any freer with him as their ruler? I didn't believe his answer was the real reason. "What makes you think the Ixian people want you to free them? No government is perfect. Did it ever occur to you that the Ixians might be content under the Commander's rule?" I asked.

"Were you content with your life in the north?" Cahil asked. An intensity held his body rigid while he waited for my response.

"I had unusual circumstances."

"Such as?"

"None of your business."

"Let me guess," Cahil said with a superior tone.

I clutched my arms to keep from punching him.

"A kidnapped southerner with magical abilities? That is unusual. But do you think you were the first person that Fourth Magician had to rescue? Northerners are born with magical powers, too. My uncle was a Master Magician. And you *know* what the Commander does to anyone found with power."

Valek's words echoed in my mind. Anyone found in the Territory of Ixia with magical power was killed. Magicians might be hunted in Ixia, but the rest of the citizens had everything they needed.

"We're not that different, Yelena. You were born in Sitia and raised in Ixia, and I'm an Ixian raised in Sitia. You have returned home. I'm only trying to find mine."

I opened my mouth to reply, but snapped it shut when Irys spoke in my mind. *Yelena, come to the infirmary right away.*

Are you all right? I asked.

I'm fine. Just come.

Where's the infirmary?

Have Cahil show you. Then her magical energies withdrew.

I told Cahil what Irys required. Without hesitation, he removed Kiki's saddle and bridle. We hung them in the tack room before we headed for the center of the Keep. I had to jog to keep up with him.

"Did she say what this was about?" he asked over his shoulder.

"No."

We entered a one-story building. The marble walls were a soothing pale blue, resembling ice. A young man in a white uniform moved about the lobby, lighting lanterns. The sun's rays had begun to disappear for the day.

"Where's Irys?" I asked the young man.

He looked puzzled.

Cahil said, "Fourth Magician."

"She's with Healer Hayes," he said, and when we failed to move, the man pointed to a long corridor. "Down the hall. Fifth door on the left."

"Few call her Irys," Cahil explained as we hurried down the empty hallway.

We stopped at the fifth one. The door was closed.

"Come in," Irys called before I could knock.

I opened the door. Irys stood next to a man dressed in white. Healer Hayes perhaps. A figure lay under a sheet spread over a bed in the center of the room. Bandages shrouded the face.

Leif hunched in a chair in the corner of the room, looking

horrified. When he spotted me, he asked, "What's she doing here?"

"I asked her to come. She may be able to help," Irys said.

"What's going on?" I asked Irys.

"Tula was found in Booruby near death. Her mind has fled, and we can't reach her," Irys explained. "We need to find out who did this to her."

"I can't feel her," Leif said. "The other Master Magicians can't reach her. She's gone, Fourth Magician. You're just wasting time."

"What happened?" Cahil asked.

"Beaten, tortured, raped," the healer said. "You name something horrible, and it's probably been done to her."

"And she was fortunate," Irys said.

"How can you call that fortunate?" Cahil demanded. His outrage evident in the sudden tautness of his shoulders, the strident tone in his voice.

"She escaped with her life," Irys replied. "None of the others were so lucky."

"How many?" I asked, not really wanting to know, but unable to stop the words.

"She is the eleventh victim. The others were all found dead, brutalized in the same manner." A look of disgust etched Irys's face.

"How can I help?" I asked.

"Mental healing is my strongest power, yet you reached the Commander and brought him back when I couldn't," she said.

"What?" Cahil cried. "You helped the Commander?"

His outrage focused on me. I ignored him.

"But I knew the Commander. I had an idea of where to look," I said to Irys. "I'm not sure I can help you."

"Try anyway. The bodies have been discovered in different towns throughout Sitia. We haven't been able to find a reason for the killings and we have no suspects. We need to catch this monster." Irys pulled at her hair. "Unfortunately, this is the kind of situation you will be asked to deal with when you become a magician. Consider this a learning experience."

I moved closer to the bed. "May I hold her hand?" I asked the healer.

He nodded and pulled the sheet back, revealing the girl's torso. Between the blood-soaked bandages, her skin looked like raw meat. Cahil cursed. I glanced at Leif; his face remained turned to the wall.

Splinted with pieces of wood, each of the girl's fingers must have been broken. I gently took her hand, rubbing my fingertips along her palm. Pulling a thread of power, I closed my eyes and projected my energy to her.

Her mind felt abandoned. The sense that she had fled and would never come back filled the emptiness. Gray intangible ghosts floated in her mind. Upon closer examination, each specter represented Tula's memory of a specific horror. The ghosts' faces twisted with pain, terror and fear. Raw emotions began to sink into my skin. I pushed the ghosts away, concentrating on finding the real Tula who was most likely hiding some place where her horrors couldn't reach her.

I felt a sensation along my arms as if long grass tickled my skin. The clean earthy scent of a dew-covered meadow lingered in the air, but I couldn't follow the source. I searched until my energy became depleted and I could no longer hold the connection.

At last, I opened my eyes. I sat on the floor with the girl's hand still clutched in mine. "Sorry. I can't find her," I said.

"I told you it was a waste of time," Leif said. He rose from his corner. "What did you expect from a northerner?"

"You can expect me not to give up as easily as you have," I called before he stalked out of the room.

I frowned at his retreating form. There had to be another way to wake Tula.

The healer took the girl's hand from mine and tucked it back under the sheet. I remained on the floor as he and Irys discussed the girl's condition. Her body would heal, they thought, but she would probably never regain her senses. It sounded as though she would be mindless like the children Reyad and Mogkan had created in Ixia when they had siphoned their magical power, leaving behind nothing but empty soulless bodies. I shivered at the memory of how the two evil men had tried to break me.

I brought my mind back to Tula's problems. How *had* I found the Commander? He had retreated to the place of his greatest accomplishment. The place where he felt the happiest and in the most control.

"Irys," I interrupted. "Tell me everything you know about Tula."

She considered for a moment. I could see questions perched on her lips.

Trust me, I sent to her.

"It's not much. Her family operates a profitable glass factory right outside Booruby," Irys said. "This is their busy season, so they keep the kilns going all the time. Tula was to keep the fire hot during the night. The next morning when her father came out to work, the coals were cold and Tula was gone. They searched for many days. She was finally found twelve days later in a farmer's field barely alive. Our healer in

Booruby tended her physical wounds. But her mind was un-reachable, so they rushed her here to me." Irys's disappoint-ment shone on her face.

"Does Tula have any siblings?" I asked.

"Several. Why?"

I thought hard. "Any close to her age?"

"I think a younger sister."

"How much younger?"

"Not much. A year and a half maybe." Irys guessed.

"Can you bring her sister here?"

"Why?"

"With her sister's help, I might be able to bring Tula back."

"I'll send a message." Irys turned to the healer. "Hayes, let me know if Tula's condition changes."

Hayes nodded and Irys marched out the door.

Cahil and I followed. He said nothing as we left the infir-mary and stepped into the twilight. With the sun almost gone, the air cooled and a faint breeze touched my face. I sucked in the freshness, trying to dilute the bitter smell of the girl's hor-ror.

"Pretty bold," Cahil said, glancing at me. "To think you can reach her when a Master Magician could not." Cahil strode away.

"Pretty stupid," I called after his retreating form. "To give up before all possible solutions have been tried."

Cahil continued to walk without acknowledging my com-ments. Fine. He had given me another reason to prove him wrong.

12

DREAMS OF TULA'S HIDEOUS ordeal swirled in my mind that night. Over and over, I fought her demons until, at last, they transformed into my own demon's mocking face. Vivid memories of my own torture and rape at Reyad's hands haunted my sleep. I awoke screaming. My heart hammered against my chest. My nightshirt was drenched with sweat.

I wiped my face, focusing on reality. There had to be a way to help Tula. Wide-awake, I dressed and went to the infirmary.

In Tula's room, Healer Hayes slumped half-asleep in a chair. He straightened when I stepped closer to the bed.

"Something wrong?" he asked.

"No. I wanted to…" I cast about for the right explanation. "Spend some time with her."

He yawned. "Can't hurt, and I could use some rest. I'll be in my office at the end of the hall. Wake me if anything changes."

I sat in Hayes's chair and held Tula's hand. Reestablishing our link, I was once again inside her vacant mind. The ghosts of her horrors flickered past. I studied them, looking for weakness. When Tula came back, she'd have to deal with each of these ghosts, and I planned to help her banish them.

Irys woke me the next morning. I had rested my head on the edge of Tula's bed.

"Have you been here all night?" she asked.

"Only half." I smiled, rubbing my eyes. "I couldn't sleep."

"I understand all too well." Irys smoothed the sheets on Tula's bed. "In fact, I can't stay here doing nothing. I'm going to fetch Tula's sister myself. Bain Bloodgood, Second Magician has agreed to continue your training while I'm gone. He usually teaches history, and likes to lecture about famous and infamous magicians." Irys smiled. "He'll give you a ton of books to read, and will quiz you on them, so be sure to finish each of your assignments."

Hayes entered the room. "Anything?"

I shook my head.

When he started to change Tula's bandages, Irys and I left the room.

"I'm leaving this morning," Irys said. "Before I go, I'll introduce you to Bain."

I followed her from the infirmary. We headed toward the large building with the peach-and-yellow marble blocks that was located across from the Keep's entrance.

The structure housed offices for the Keep's administrative staff. It contained various-size conference and meeting rooms, and an office for each Master Magician. According to Irys, the Masters preferred to meet with outsiders and officials in these rooms rather than in their towers.

Irys led me into a small meeting room. Four people huddled over a map that was spread open on a conference table. Other maps and charts were hung on the walls.

Of the four, I recognized Roze Featherstone and Leif. Roze wore another long blue dress and Leif wore his customary scowl. Beside them stood an elderly man in a navy robe and a young woman with braided hair.

Irys introduced me to the man. He had curly white hair that stuck out at odd angles.

"Bain, this is Yelena, your student for the next week or so," Irys said.

"The girl you rescued from the north?" He shook my hand. "Strange mission that."

A failed mission, Roze's cold thoughts stabbed my mind. *Yelena should have been killed, not rescued. She's too old to learn.*

Yelena's linked to me. She can hear your thoughts. Irys's annoyance was clear.

Roze gazed at me with her amber eyes. *I don't care.*

Unflinching, I stared back. *Your mistake.*

Irys stepped between us, breaking our eye contact. "And this is Zitora Cowan, Third Magician," Irys said, gesturing to the young woman.

Zitora's honey-brown braids hung to her waist. Instead of shaking my hand, she hugged me.

"Welcome, Yelena," Zitora said. "Irys tells us you may be able to help us find Tula's attacker."

"I'll try," I said.

"Tula's from my clan, so I would appreciate whatever you can do to help her." Zitora's pale yellow eyes shone with tears. She turned away.

"As you can see," Bain said, indicating the room's contents, "we are trying to deduce the methods and means of this killer.

A very cunning and shrewd fellow. Unfortunately, that's all we know. Perhaps fresh eyes can spot something we missed." Bain pointed to the map on the table.

"She shouldn't be here," Leif said. "She knows nothing about this."

Before Irys could speak in my defense, I said, "You're right, Leif, I haven't dealt with this before because a horror like him would not have survived in Ixia for long."

"Why don't you just run back to your precious Commander and your perfect Ixia and keep your nose out of our troubles?" Leif spat the words at me.

I drew breath to counter, but Irys put a warning hand on my sleeve.

"Yelena and Leif, that's quite enough," Irys said. "You're wasting time. Catching this killer is imperative."

Chastised, I peered down at the map on the table. The Sitian lands were divided into eleven territories, one for each clan. City and town locations were marked, as well as the places where the other girls had been found. Some towns had two victims, while others had none. I failed to see a pattern.

"The only consistency has been in the victims," Bain said. "All are unmarried females fifteen to sixteen years old. All were missing for approximately twelve to fourteen days. All were taken during the night. Some were stolen right from the very bedrooms they shared with siblings. And no witnesses. None."

My initial gut feeling indicated that magic had been involved, but I didn't want to say as much in front of four Master Magicians.

"We have considered a rogue magician," Irys said. "And while we have confirmed the alibis of the magicians who have graduated from our school, we are unable to question those who have one-trick powers."

"One-trick?" I asked.

"There are some who have just enough magic to do one thing like light a candle, but are unable to use magic for anything else," Irys explained. "One-tricks do not come to the Keep, but they normally use their gift in beneficial ways. Some, though, do use their ability for crime. Mostly petty. It's possible this killer's one-trick is to turn himself invisible, or be able to walk without making a sound. Something that gives him the upper hand when kidnapping a girl."

Irys's face hardened into an expression of serious determination. A look I recognized with a queasy feeling deep in my stomach. She had worn it when she had tried to kill me in Ixia.

"But only for the moment," she vowed.

"We have not ruled out a rogue magician," Bain said. "History is full of them. And I include recent history." He nodded to me. "Some day, you must tell me of the misdeeds of Kangom in Ixia, and how he met his end. I wish to add his folly to the history books."

Confused at first, it took me a moment to remember that Kangom had changed his name to Mogkan upon fleeing to Ixia.

"Speaking of books," Bain said to me, "I have some for you in my office." He turned to Roze. "Are we finished here?"

She gave a curt nod.

The other magicians made to leave, but Zitora stayed by the table, tracing a finger over the map of Sitia.

"Irys?" she asked. "Did you mark Tula's location?"

"No." Irys picked up a quill and dipped it into a bottle of

red ink. "With all the commotion, I forgot." She placed a mark on the map and stepped back. "I'll be back in ten days. Please send word if something happens. Yelena, keep practicing your control."

"Yes, sir," I said.

Irys smiled then left the room. I glanced down at the map to see how far Booruby was from the Citadel. The red ink had not yet dried. Tula's town resided on the western edge of the Avibian Plains. I had thought Captain Marrok exaggerated when he had said the plains were huge, but the map showed that the plains dominated the eastern Sitian landscape.

When my eye caught the other red marks, I must have made a sound because Zitora clutched my arm.

"What is it?" she asked.

"A pattern. See?" I pointed to the map. "All the marks are near the border of the Avibian Plains."

The others returned to the table.

"Fresh eyes," Bain said, nodding to himself.

"It's obvious, now that the map's been updated," Roze said. Annoyance made her voice sharp.

"Did anyone search the plains when the girls went missing?" I asked.

"No one goes into the plains," Zitora said. "The Sandseed Clan doesn't like visitors, and their strange magic can befuddle the mind. It's best to circumvent them."

"Only the Zaltanas are welcomed by the Sandseeds," Roze said. "Perhaps Yelena and Leif could visit and determine if anything is amiss."

"No need to rush," Bain said. "Better to wait until Irys returns with Tula's sister. If Tula awakes and identifies her assailant, we would have the advantage."

"What if another girl goes missing in the meantime?" Leif asked. His scowl had deepened, and he seemed upset either by the thought of another victim or the prospect of traveling with me again.

"Then, welcome or no, we will send armed searchers into the plains," Bain said.

"But you might be too late," I said.

"We have some time." Zitora pulled at one of her braids. "That was another pattern we were able to discern. He has the victims for two weeks and then waits four weeks before claiming a new one."

The thought of another victim filled me with dread and led to a horrible scenario. "What if he comes to the Keep to finish what he started? Tula could be in danger!"

"Let him come." Roze's voice turned icy with determination. "I *will* take care of him."

"First we would have to apprehend him." Bain tapped the table with a bony finger. "We must post guards in Tula's room."

"But it's the hot season, and we're short-handed," Zitora said.

"I will tell Cahil to assign some of his men," Roze said. "He owes me."

"Get them right away, Roze," Bain said. "Not a moment to lose. Come now, Yelena, we have work to do."

Bain led me out of the room and down the hallway.

"Nice observations, young lady. I see why Irys chose not to kill you."

"Has Irys ever chosen to kill?" I asked. Cahil's comment that I had not been the first person Irys had rescued from Ixia weighed on my mind.

"Unavoidable at times. Nasty choice overall, but Irys is well suited to that role. She has a unique ability to cease a heart without pain or fear. Roze has the skill, too, but she's much too harsh. She works best with criminals and their ilk. Leif helps her with those unfortunate criminal investigations. During his schooling at the Keep, the Masters determined that would be the best use of his unusual power. Zitora, on the other hand, would die rather than harm another. I have never met a sweeter soul."

Bain stopped to unlock a door. He gestured for me to precede him into his office. Entering the room, I was greeted by a riot of color, a jumble of contraptions and shelves upon shelves of books.

"And you, sir?" I asked. "What place do you hold in this group of magicians?"

"I teach. I guide. I listen." He stacked books into a pile. "I answer questions. I let the younger magicians go on missions. I tell stories of my eventful past." Bain smiled. "Whether or not my companions wish to hear them. Now, we'll start you with these few books."

He handed me the stack. I counted seven texts. Few? Obviously, my definition of few was different than his. At least most of the books were slim.

"Tomorrow is market day. An extra day for study." Bain's voice held a touch of reverence. To him it seemed an extra day to study was similar to receiving a pouch of gold. "Read the first three chapters in each book. We'll discuss them the day after tomorrow. Come to my tower after breakfast."

He bustled around a table, looking for something. He pulled a leather pouch from beneath an immense tome. "Yours from Irys."

The pouch jingled as I opened it. Irys had exchanged my Ixian coins for Sitian.

"How do I find the market?" I asked.

Bain rummaged around his desk until he found a sheet of paper. It was a map of the Citadel.

"Use this." Bain pointed to the market square located near the center of the Citadel.

"May I keep this?"

"Yours. Now, go. Read." With the indulgence of a father sending his child off to play, he shooed me out the door.

I read the book titles as I made my way back to my rooms. *The Source of Magic; Magical Mutations; The History of Sitian Magic; Master Level Magicians Throughout the Ages; Misuses of the Power Source; The Magician's Ethical Code,* and *Windri Bak Greentree: A Biography.*

I had to admit the titles seemed fascinating, so I started my reading assignments as soon as I reached my rooms. The afternoon flew by, and only the incessant growling of my stomach made me stop to find some food.

After dinner, I visited the stables. Topaz and Kiki's heads appeared over their stall doors the moment I arrived.

Apples? Both horses looked hopeful.

Have I ever come without? I asked.

No. Lavender Lady nice, Topaz said.

I fed Topaz and Kiki their apples. After wiping apple juice and horse slobber from my hands, I realized Cahil was late. Deciding not to wait for him, I took Kiki's bridle and riding saddle from the tack room.

Practice? Kiki sounded as bored as I by the repetitive lessons.

How about a walk? I asked.

Fast?

No. Slow and steady so I don't fall off.

I bridled and saddled Kiki without incident, surprising my-self with how much I had learned.

Before I could mount, Cahil arrived, his face red, and his beard matted with sweat. He looked as though he had run to the stables. I wondered how far he had run, which led me to wonder where he lived in the Keep, which led me, ultimately, to wonder about his childhood. What had it been like to grow up in the Magician's Keep without any family?

Cahil, oblivious to my curiosity, inspected every inch of Kiki's tack. Probably searching for a mistake. I smiled in sat-isfaction when all he found was a crooked stirrup.

"All right then, since she's saddled, why don't you try mounting?" Cahil said, reminding me to always mount on the horse's left side.

I placed my left foot in the stirrup and grabbed the saddle. When he moved to give me a boost up, I stopped him with a look. Kiki stood at sixteen hands, tall for a horse, but I wanted to mount her without help. Pushing off with my right foot, I launched myself up and swung my leg over the saddle.

Once settled, I looked down at Cahil from what now felt like an uncomfortable height. From this vantage point, the ground at his feet seemed to transform from plush grass to hard and unyielding earth.

Cahil lectured about the reins and the proper way to hold them, and how to sit in the saddle. "If you think you're going to fall, grab her mane. Not the saddle."

"Why not?"

"You could pinch a finger. Don't worry. You won't hurt the horse."

Cahil continued to lecture about the correct way to steer

the horse and the best way to give stop and go commands. He also repeated his advice to grab Kiki's mane if I felt myself falling at least a half dozen more times. Eventually, I tuned him out, gazing around the pasture from my new perspective. I admired the way the sun reflected off a stallion's coat near the far fence, until a change in Cahil's tone caused Kiki's ears to cock forward.

"...listening to me?" Cahil demanded.

"What?"

"Yelena, this is very important. If you don't know how to—"

"Cahil," I interrupted. "I don't need commands. All I have to do is ask Kiki."

He stared at me as if I had spoken another language.

"Watch." I held the reins in front of me as Cahil had instructed. Kiki's left ear cocked back, the other pointed forward. She turned her head slightly to the left so she could see me fully.

Walk around the pasture? I asked her. *Near the fence.*

Kiki started to move. Her steps rocked me from side to side. I let her find the path as I enjoyed the view.

As we circled the pasture, I heard Cahil yell, "Heels down! Straighten up!"

Eventually, we moved out of his sight.

Fast? Kiki asked.

Not yet.

A glint of sunlight and a blur of motion from outside the fence caught my eye. Kiki shied, turning sharply to the right. I flew left.

Bad smell. Bad thing.

Instinctively, I grabbed her mane, stopping my fall. My

right leg stretched across the saddle as I hung from Kiki's side, clutching her coarse brown hair.

Kiki's muscles bunched and she danced to the side. I caught a glimpse of what had startled her. *Stop. A man.*

She held still, but her legs trembled in terror. *Bad man. Shiny thing.*

I yanked myself upright in the saddle. *Bad man. Run.*

13

KIKI TOOK OFF.

I held on to her mane, and tried to stay in the saddle. After a few strides, I looked behind just in time to see Goel's sword flash in the sunlight.

When Cahil saw us racing across the pasture, he raised his arms and shouted. "Whoa! Whoa!"

Kiki galloped straight for him, her mind so focused on survival that I had to wait for Goel's scent to disappear before she would respond to my calming thoughts.

Man gone. It's okay, I said to her. I patted her on the neck and whispered the same thing into her ear. She settled and halted mere inches from Cahil.

"At least you stayed on the horse." He grabbed Kiki's reins. "What happened?"

I jumped down from the saddle and examined Cahil. He didn't look surprised. In fact, he seemed mildly amused.

"What do you think happened?" I countered.

"Kiki spooked at something. I told you horses are skittish, but you had to go off before you were ready."

Something in Cahil's eyes made me suspicious. "Did you send Goel to ambush me?" I demanded.

"Goel?" Cahil seemed taken aback. "No, I—"

"You set that up. You wanted Kiki to panic."

Cahil frowned. "I wanted you to learn. Horses are prey animals and will react to the slightest noise, scent or movement long before any logic can kick in. And if you'd fallen, you would know it's not terrible. Then you wouldn't be afraid to fall or bail off a horse when you need to."

"How nice for you that you've already forgotten I've fallen off a horse. Actually, shoved off a horse. *Your* horse to be exact. It's a memory I wish I could forget so easily."

Cahil had the decency to look contrite.

"So sending Goel was a lesson?" I asked. "I don't believe it, Cahil. He was armed."

Fury flashed across Cahil's face. "I asked Erant to help me. Goel is supposed to be guarding Tula. I'll deal with him."

"Don't bother. I can take care of Goel. At least *he* had the decency to warn me of his plans. Unlike others." I glared at Cahil, snatched the reins from his hands and strode back to the stable with Kiki. It had been a mistake to go to my lesson unarmed. I had foolishly assumed Goel wouldn't try to attack me while I was with Cahil. Lesson learned. Cahil should be proud, even if it wasn't the lesson he intended.

The next morning, I set out to find the market. I kept a wary eye on the people in the streets of the Citadel. All seemed headed toward the center square. Amazed by the number of people crowding around the market stands, I hesitated. I didn't want to push my way through them, yet I needed to shop.

I spotted a few of the Keep's workers, and had decided to ask one of them for assistance when I felt a tug on my sleeve. Spinning around, I reached for my bow on my backpack. The small boy flinched. I recognized him as the beggar I had given my Sitian coins to on my first day in the Citadel.

"Sorry. You startled me," I said.

He relaxed. "Lovely Lady, can you spare a copper?"

Remembering what Irys had said about the beggars, I thought of an idea. "How about you help me and I'll help you?"

Wariness filled his eyes. In that instant he seemed to grow ten years older. My heart broke, and I wanted to empty my purse into his hands. Instead, I said, "I'm new here. I'm look-ing to buy paper and ink. Do you know a good merchant?"

He seemed to catch on. "Maribella's has the finest statio-nery," he said, his eyes alight. "I'll show you."

"Wait. What's your name?"

He hesitated, and then lowered his eyes to the ground. "Fisk," he mumbled.

I dropped to one knee. Looking him in the eyes, I offered my hand. "Greetings, Fisk. I'm Yelena."

He grasped my hand with both of his, his mouth agape with astonishment. I guessed he was close to nine years old. Fisk recovered with a shake of his head. He then led me to a young girl's table at the edge of the square. I purchased writing paper, a stylus and some black ink, then gave Fisk a Sitian copper for his help. As the morning wore on, Fisk guided me to other stands for more supplies and soon other children were "hired" to help carry my packages.

When I finished shopping, I surveyed my entourage. Six

grubby children smiled at me despite the heat and searing sun. I suspected that one boy was Fisk's younger brother; they had the same light brown eyes. The other two boys may have been his cousins. Greasy strands of hair hid most of the two girls' faces so it was impossible to tell if they were related to Fisk.

I realized then that I was reluctant to return to the Keep.

Sensing my mood, Fisk asked, "Lovely Yelena, would you like a tour of the Citadel?"

I nodded. The midday heat had emptied the market, but as I followed the children through the deserted streets, a feeling of unease settled over me. What if they were leading me into a trap? My hand sought the handle of my switchblade. Concentrating, I pulled a thread of power and projected my awareness.

My mind touched life all around me. Most of the Citadel's citizens resided inside, their thoughts focused on finding a cool spot or a quiet activity while they waited for the sun to set. No threats. No ambushes.

I heard the sound of water before I saw the fountain. With squeals of delight, the children put down my packages and ran to the spray. Fisk stayed by my side, though, taking his role as tour guide seriously.

"That's the Unity Fountain," he said.

A circle of waterspouts surrounded a huge stone sphere with large holes spaced evenly across its surface. Nestled inside the sphere, I could see another smaller sphere with holes of its own. The deep green color of the fountain wasn't veined like the marble of the Citadel's walls, yet the stone hinted that it held something else within.

"Marble?" I asked Fisk.

"Jade mined from the Emerald Mountains. This is the largest piece of pure jade ever found. It took a year to get it here and, because jade is so hard, it took over five years to carve it with diamond-tipped chisels. There are eleven spheres and all of them were carved inside that one stone."

Amazing. I moved closer to the fountain so I could see the other spheres. The cool mist felt good against my hot skin.

"Why eleven?" I asked.

Fisk stood next to me. "One sphere for each clan. And one waterspout for each clan. Water represents life," he explained. "See the carvings on the outer circle?"

I risked getting soaked to examine the intricate lines on the fountain.

"Mythical creatures. Each represents one Master Magician. Ying Lung, a sky dragon for First Magician; Fei Lian, a wind leopard for Second; Kioh Twan, a unicorn for Third; and Pyong, a hawk for Fourth."

"Why those creatures?" I asked, remembering that Irys had worn a hawk mask when she had visited Ixia as part of the Sitian delegation.

"When magicians reach the Master level, they endure a series of tests." Fisk sounded as if he quoted a schoolbook. "During that time, they travel through the underworld and meet their guide. This creature not only shows them through the underworld, but guides them throughout life."

"Do you believe that?" It sounded like a fairy tale to me. When the Commander had taken power in Ixia, superstitions and religious beliefs had been discouraged. If anyone still believed, they kept quiet and worshipped in secret.

Fisk shrugged. "I know something happens to the Magicians during the test because my father's seen it. He used to work at the Keep."

A hardness settled on Fisk's face, so I didn't ask any more questions. But I wondered about the creatures. Irys had disguised herself as a hawk mistress in Ixia. She wore the proper uniform to blend in with the Ixian. Perhaps she also worked with the Commander's hawks.

"It's good luck to drink from the fountain," Fisk said. Then he ran to his friends who played in the water, opening their mouths to catch the spray.

After a moment's hesitation, I joined them. The water tasted fresh as if laced with strong minerals like an elixir of life. I drank deeply. I could use a little good luck.

When the children finished playing, Fisk led me to another fountain. This one was carved from rare white jade. Fifteen horses frozen in motion circled a large spout of water.

Although Fisk didn't complain, I could see that the heat had finally worn him out. Still, when I offered to carry my purchases back to the Keep, all the children refused, saying they would take them as promised.

On the way back, I sensed Topaz's worry the moment before I saw Cahil rounding the corner. My parade of children stepped to the side of the road as Cahil advanced, stopping Topaz in front of us.

"Yelena, where have you been?" he demanded.

I glared at him. "Shopping. Why? Do you have another surprise test for me?"

He ignored my question, staring instead at my companions. The children shrank against the wall, trying to make themselves as small as possible.

"The market has been closed for hours. What have you been doing?" he asked.

"None of your business."

His gaze snapped to me. "Yes, it is. This is your first trip into the Citadel alone. You could have been robbed. You could have gotten lost. When you didn't come back, I thought the worst." Cahil's eyes slid back to the children.

"I can take care of myself." I glanced at Fisk. "Lead on," I said.

Fisk nodded and started down the street. The other children and I followed him.

Cahil snorted and dismounted. Taking Topaz's reins, he walked beside me. But he couldn't remain quiet.

"Your choice of escorts will lead to trouble," he said. "Every time you go into the Citadel, they'll descend on you like parasites, sucking you dry." Loathing filled his face.

"Another lesson?" I asked, not hiding my sarcasm.

"Just trying to help." Anger tightened his voice.

"You can stop. Stick to what you know, Cahil. If it doesn't involve horses, then I don't need your assistance."

He let his breath out in a long huff. From the corner of my eye, I saw him swallow his temper. Impressive.

"You're still mad at me," he said.

"Why would I be?"

"For not believing you about being a spy."

When I didn't say anything, he continued, "For what happened with First Magician. I know it must have been awful—"

"Awful!" Stopping in the middle of the street, I rounded on Cahil. "What do you know? Has she done it to you?"

"No."

"Then you have no idea what you're talking about. Imagine being helpless and stripped bare. Your thoughts and feelings exposed to a ruthless intimate scrutiny."

His eyes widened in shock. "But she said you fought her off. That she couldn't fully read you."

I shuddered at the thought of Roze going deeper, understanding why Cahil had claimed that her interrogation left some people with mental damage.

"It's worse than being raped, Cahil. I know. I've suffered both."

He gaped. "Is that why?"

"What? Go ahead. Ask." I wasn't about to spare him to make him feel better.

"Why you stayed in your room those first three days?"

I nodded. "Irys told me I was sulking, but I couldn't stand the thought of anyone even looking at me."

Topaz put his head over my shoulder. I rubbed my cheek on his soft face. My anger at Cahil had blocked out the horse's thoughts. Now I opened my mind to him.

Lavender Lady safe. Topaz's pleasure filled my mind. *Apple?*

I smiled. *Later.*

Cahil watched us with a strange expression on his face. "You only smile at the horses."

I couldn't tell if he was jealous or sad.

"What Roze…I…did to you. Is that why you keep everyone at arm's length?" Cahil asked.

"Not entirely. And not everyone."

"Who else do you smile at?"

"Irys."

He nodded as if he had expected that answer. "Anyone else?"

My fingers touched the bump my chest made by the butterfly pendant under my shirt. Valek would get more from me than a smile. But I said, "My friends in the north."

"The ones who taught you to fight?"

"Yes."

"How about the person who gave you that necklace?"

I jerked my hand away. "How did you know about my necklace?" I demanded.

"It fell out while you were unconscious."

I frowned, remembering Cahil had carried me to my room after Roze's interrogation.

"Guess I shouldn't have reminded you about that," he said. "But I was right about it being a gift, wasn't I?"

"It's none of your business. Cahil, you're acting like we're friends. We're not friends."

The children waited for us at an intersection. I started toward them.

Cahil caught up. We walked on in silence. When we reached the Keep, I took my packages from the children and paid them each two coppers.

I grinned at Fisk, and then glanced at Cahil, feeling self-conscious about my smiles.

"See you on the next market day," I said to Fisk. "And tell your friends they'll each get an extra copper if they show up clean."

He waved. I watched the group of children disappear; they probably knew all the back alleys and secret ways inside the Citadel. That knowledge might be useful one day. I would have to ask Fisk to show me.

Having grown up in the Citadel, Cahil probably knew the shortcuts, too, but I wouldn't ask him. Not when he had such a dour expression.

"What now?" I asked.

He sighed. "Why do you always have to make things so difficult?"

"You started this. Remember? Not me."

He shook his head. "Why don't we start over? We've been at odds from the start. What can I do to receive one of your rare smiles?"

"Why do you want one? If you're hoping that we'll become friends and I'll confide in you all the military secrets of Ixia, don't bother."

"No. That's not what I want. I want things to be different between us."

"Different how?"

Cahil looked around as if searching for the right words. "Better. Less hostility. Friendlier. Conversations instead of arguments."

"After what you put me through?"

"I'm sorry, Yelena." The words tore from his throat as if it pained him to say them. "I'm sorry I didn't believe you when you said you weren't a spy. I'm sorry I asked First Magician to—" he swallowed. "To rape your mind."

I turned my face away from him. "That apology is weeks old, Cahil. Why bother now?"

He sighed. "Plans are being made for the New Beginnings feast."

Some hitch in Cahil's voice caused me to look at him. He wrapped and unwrapped Topaz's leather reins around his hands.

"It's a feast to celebrate the beginning of the cooling season and the new school year. A chance for everyone to get together and start anew." Cahil's blue eyes searched mine. "In all these years, I have never wanted to take anyone with me. I never had anyone who I wanted to have by my side. Yet when I overheard the cooks discussing the feast's menu this morning, your image filled my mind. Come with me, Yelena?"

CAHIL'S WORDS STRUCK ME like a physical blow. I jerked back a step.

His face saddened at my reaction. "I guess that's a no. We'd probably just fight all night anyway." He began to walk away.

"Cahil, wait," I said, catching up to him. "You surprised me." An understatement for sure.

I had believed that the only thing Cahil wanted from me was information about Ixia. This invitation might still be a ploy, but for the first time I saw a softness behind his eyes. I put my hand on his arm. He stopped.

"Does everyone go to this New Beginnings feast?" I asked him.

"Yes. It's a good way for the new students to meet their teachers, and a chance for everyone to get reacquainted. I'm going because I'll be teaching the senior and apprentice classes about horsemanship."

"So, I'm not your first student?"

"No, but you've been my most stubborn one." He smiled ruefully.

I smiled in return. Cahil's eyes lit up.

"Okay, Cahil, in the spirit of this New Beginnings feast, let's start over. I'm willing to accompany you to the feast as the first step in our new *friendship*." Besides, the thought of going alone to meet my fellow students seemed daunting.

"Friendship?"

"That's all I can offer."

"Because of the person who gave you that butterfly pendant?" he asked.

"Yes."

"And what did you give him in return?"

I wanted to snap that it was none of his business, but I controlled my temper. If we were going to be friends, he needed to know the truth. "My heart." I could have added my body, my trust and my soul.

He looked at me for a moment. "Guess I'll have to be content with friendship." He grinned. "Does this mean you won't be so difficult anymore?"

"Don't count on it."

He laughed and helped me carry my market purchases back to my rooms. I spent the rest of the night reading the chapters Bain had assigned, stopping on occasion to think about Cahil's new role as friend in my life.

I enjoyed my fascinating mornings with Bain Bloodgood. Sitian history extended back for centuries. The eleven Sitian clans fought with each other for decades until Windri Greentree, a Master Magician, united them and formed the Council of Elders. I realized to my dismay, and to Bain's delight, that

I had a great deal of study ahead of me to learn the full history. And their mythology alone, populated with creatures, demons and legends, would take years of lessons to know them all.

Bain also explained the structure of the school. "Every student has a magician as a mentor. That mentor oversees the student's learning. He teaches. He guides. He schedules classes with other magicians who have more expertise in certain subjects."

"How many students are in each class?" I asked.

Bain swept his hand through the air, indicating the room, empty except for us. We sat in an open circular chamber at the base of his tower. Books lined the walls in neat piles, and writing projects covered each of Bain's four ink-stained worktables. The metal rings of Bain's astrolabe glowed in the morning sunlight.

I perched on the edge of his wide desk. Small writing tools and piles of papers rested on the top in an organized arrangement. A white seashell appeared to be his only decoration. Sitting across from me, Bain wore a deep purple robe that drank in the light. His diverse collection of robes amazed me. So far, he was the only magician I'd seen that wore a formal robe on a daily basis.

"We are a class," he said. "There can be up to four students, but no more. You will not see rows upon rows of students listening to a lecturer in this school. We teach using hands-on learning and small groups."

"How many students does each mentor have?"

"No more than four for those who have experience. Only one for the new magicians."

"How many do the Master Magicians teach?" I was dreading the day when I would have to share Irys.

"Ah…" He paused. For once Bain seemed at a loss for words. "The Masters do not mentor students. We are needed in Council meetings. We aid Sitia. We recruit prospective students. But occasionally a student comes along that piques our interest."

He gazed at me as if deciding how much he should tell me. "I have grown weary of Council meetings. So I have transferred all my energies to teaching. This year I have two students. Roze has chosen only one since she became First Magician. Zitora has none. She is adjusting; she only became a Master last year."

"And Irys?"

"You're her first."

"Just me?" I asked in amazement.

He nodded.

"You said Roze chose one. Who?"

"Your brother, Leif."

Evidence that the Keep prepared for an invasion of returning students mounted as the week progressed. Servants scurried to air out rooms and dorms. The kitchen buzzed with activity as the staff prepared for the feast. Even the Citadel's streets hummed with life as residents returned. In the evenings, laughter and music floated on the cooling air.

As I waited for Irys to return from fetching Tula's sister, I spent my mornings with Bain, my afternoons studying and my evenings with Cahil and Kiki. My riding had advanced from walking Kiki to trotting, a bone-jarring gait that left me stiff and sore at the end of the day.

Every night I sat with Tula, connecting with her and lending her my support. Her mind remained vacant, but her brutalized body healed by leaps and bounds.

"Do you have healing powers?" Hayes asked me one night. "Her physical progress has been amazing. More like the work of two healers."

I considered his question. "I don't know. I've never tried."

"Perhaps you've been helping her heal without realizing it. Would you like to find out?"

"I don't want to hurt her," I said.

"I won't let you." Hayes smiled as he picked up Tula's left hand. The splints on her right hand were gone, but the fingers on her left were still swollen and bruised. "I have only enough energy to mend a few bones a day. Usually we let the body heal on its own. But for serious injuries, we speed up the process."

"How?"

"I draw power to me. Then I focus on the injury. Skin and muscles disappear before my eyes, revealing the bones. I use the power to encourage the bone to mend. It works the same for other injuries. My eyes will only see the wound. It is truly wonderful."

Hayes's eyes glowed with purpose, but when they shifted to Tula they dimmed. "Unfortunately, some injuries just can't be healed, and the mind is so complex that any damage is usually permanent. We have a few mind healers. Fourth Magician is the strongest of these, but even she can only do so much."

As Hayes focused on Tula, I felt the air around me thicken and pulsate. Drawing a breath became an effort. Then Hayes closed his eyes. Without thinking, I linked my mind with his. Through him I saw Tula's hand. Her skin became translucent, showing the battered pink fibrous muscles attached to the bones. I saw strands of power, thin as spiderwebs, wrapped around Hayes's hands. He wove the webs around the crack in Tula's bone. As I watched, the crack disappeared and then the muscles healed.

I broke the mental connection to Hayes and looked at Tula. The bruises had faded from her now straight index finger. The air thinned as the power faded. His forehead shone with sweat and his breath puffed from the effort he'd just expended.

"Now, you try," he said.

I moved closer to Tula and took her hand from Hayes. Holding her middle finger, I rubbed it lightly with my thumb as I pulled power to me, revealing the bone. Hayes gasped. I paused.

"Go on," he said.

My strands of power were rope thick. When I applied the strands to the bone, they wrapped around it like a noose. I pulled back, fearing her finger would snap in half.

Placing her hand back on the bed, I looked at Hayes. "Sorry. I don't have full control of my magic yet."

He stared at Tula's hand. "Look."

Both fingers appeared to have been healed.

"How do you feel?" he asked.

Using magic usually left me tired, but I really hadn't used any. Or had I? "About the same."

"Three healings and I need to nap." Hayes shook his head. His dark hair fell into his eyes. He swiped his bangs back with an impatient hand. "You just mended a bone effortlessly. Fate be with us," he said. Awe and fear roughened his voice. "Once you have full control, you may be able to wake the dead."

15

FEAR SURGED THROUGH ME, leaving my muscles trembling.

"No," I said to Hayes. "You must be mistaken. No one can wake the dead."

Hayes rubbed a hand over his tired eyes, reconsidering.

"Perhaps I spoke rashly," he agreed. "Only one person in our history could revive the dead." He shuddered. "And the results were truly horrible."

I wanted to ask more questions, but Hayes bolted toward the door, insisting he had work to do.

Feeling odd and unsettled, I peered at Tula's motionless form. Through her blanket and skin, I could see each of her injuries. It seemed now that I had learned this new ability, I couldn't turn it off. The fractures, sprains, bruises all pulsed with an urgent red light. The more I studied the light the more it drew my mind in, and I felt Tula's physical pain soak into me. In sudden agony, I collapsed onto the floor.

Curling into a ball, I squeezed my eyes shut. A small part

of me knew the pain was imaginary, but, in panic, I still tried to push the torment away. I pulled power from the source. Magic filled me. The buildup crackled across my skin like fire. I released the power.

My scream resounded through the room as cool relief swept through me, quenching my pain. Drained of energy, I remained on the floor, panting.

"Yelena, are you all right?"

I opened my eyes. Hayes hovered over me in concern. I nodded. "Tula?"

He left my side. "She's fine."

I sat up. The room spun for a moment but I forced myself to focus.

"What happened?" Hayes asked.

I wanted to say that I had lost control, to explain that my old survival instincts had kicked in, reacting to the pain without conscious thought. But it hadn't felt quite like that, and to admit that I had lost control would be dangerous. Uncontrolled magicians could damage the power source and the Masters would be forced to kill me. Instead, I clamped my lips together, trying to bring some order to my jumbled thoughts.

Before I could speak, Hayes said, "You healed her other two fingers."

He stood next to Tula's bed, and held her left hand up. Hayes inspected her fingers before laying her arm across her stomach.

Then he turned to me with a frown. "You shouldn't have tried that without me. No wonder you screamed. You gathered too much power and had to release it." Hayes gestured to my prone form. "A beginner's mistake, and now you're exhausted. You really need to work on your control."

While helping me to my feet, Hayes's frown softened into what might have been relief. "You have the ability to heal, but need guidance. I misjudged you at first, thinking you might be a Soulfinder." Hayes huffed out a laugh. "Next time, wait for me. Okay?"

Not trusting myself to speak, I nodded.

Hayes guided me toward the door. "Get some rest. You'll probably be weak for a few days."

As I shuffled to the apprentice's wing, I replayed the events in my mind, and by the time I collapsed into my bed, I managed to almost convince myself that Hayes's explanation was correct. Almost.

Fatigue dogged me all through the next day. Bain's morning lesson passed in a blur. Instead of reading, I napped the afternoon away, and fought to stay awake while riding Kiki that night. Cahil's bellowing eventually pierced the fog in my mind.

"Yelena!"

I looked at him as if seeing him for the first time that evening. Coated with dirt and horse hair, his once-white cotton shirt clung to his muscular frame. Annoyance creased his forehead. His mouth moved in speech, but it took me a moment to discern his words.

"…distracted, exhausted, and you're going to get hurt."

"Hurt?" I asked.

"Yes, hurt. When you fall asleep in the saddle and slide off the horse." Cahil controlled his frustration, but I could see by the way he pumped his clenched fists that he wanted to shake some sense into me.

Lavender Lady tired. Kiki agreed. *Forgot apples.*

"Yelena, go home." Cahil took Kiki's reins to hold her steady while I dismounted.

Home? Unbidden, the image of my small room in the Commander's castle jumped into my mind, followed by the memory of Valek's smiling face. I could use some of his energy right now.

"Are you all right?"

I gazed into Cahil's light blue eyes. They were pale in comparison to Valek's vibrant sapphire color. "Yes. I'm just a little tired."

"A little?" Cahil laughed. "Go get some sleep; I'll take care of Kiki. You'll need your energy for tomorrow night."

"Tomorrow?"

"The New Beginnings feast. Remember?"

"I didn't realize it was so soon."

"Prepare yourself for an invasion of students and magicians. Come morning, our peace and quiet will be gone."

Cahil led Kiki toward the stable. I promised her extra apples before our next lesson as I headed to my rooms.

Apprehension about the feast, though, gnawed through my fatigue even as I climbed into bed. Half-asleep, the shock of realizing that I didn't own the proper attire for a feast nearly jolted me awake. What did one wear to a feast anyway? Would I have to don my formal apprentice robe? I wondered, then sighed. Too tired to worry about things like clothes, I rolled over. More important worries such as the need to take control of my magic pushed out all others.

A frenzy of activity filled the campus the next morning. I skirted groups of people carrying parcels as I walked to Bain's tower.

Opening the door to his study, I started to ask Bain about the arriving students, but stopped when I saw he had two visitors.

From behind his desk, Bain gestured me in. "Yelena, these are my students. Dax Greenblade, a fellow apprentice, and Gelsi Moon, a novice." With an open hand, he pointed to each in turn.

They nodded in greeting. Their serious expressions looked out of place on such young faces. I guessed that Dax was eighteen years old, while the girl must have been about fifteen.

"Have you chosen another student, Master Bloodgood?" Gelsi asked. She tugged absently on the white lace at the end of her sleeve. Violet and white swirls patterned both her blouse and long skirt.

"No, Yelena is working with another," Bain said.

I had to suppress a grin as each relaxed. Dax flashed me a smile.

Gelsi, though, seemed intrigued with me. "Who is your mentor?" she asked.

"Irys…ah…Master Jewelrose."

The two students seemed as surprised as I had been when Bain told me about Irys.

"What's your clan?" Gelsi asked.

"Zaltana."

"Another distant cousin of Leif's?" Dax asked. "You're a little old to start training. What strange power do you have?"

His tone implied curiosity and humor, but Bain said, "Dax, that's inappropriate. She's Leif's sister."

"Ahhhh…" Dax studied me with keen interest.

"Do we have a lesson this morning?" I asked Bain.

The magician perked up at my question. He instructed Dax

to go unpack, but he asked Gelsi to remain. Her heart-shaped face paled for a moment before she steadied herself, smoothing her shoulder-length copper curls.

"I fear Irys will be back soon and reclaim you," Bain said to me with a smile. "Gelsi's focus for this semester is to learn how to communicate magically with other magicians. Irys has told me this is your strongest ability. Therefore, I would like your assistance with introducing this skill to my student."

Gelsi's eyes widened. Her long thick eyelashes touched her brows.

"I'll do what I can," I said.

Bain rummaged through one of his desk's drawers and pulled a small burlap sack from it. He set the bag on the desk and opened it, taking out two brown lumps.

"We'll use Theobroma for the first lesson," he said.

The lumps triggered memories of my time in Ixia. Theobroma was the southern name for Criollo, a delicious sweet that had the unfortunate effect of opening a person's mind to magical influences. General Brazell had used the nutty flavored dessert to bypass the Commander's strong will so Brazell's magician, Mogkan could gain control of the Commander's mind.

Bain handed me one of the Theobroma pieces and he gave the other to Gelsi. Then he told us to sit in the two chairs that faced each other. While I would have enjoyed eating the mouth-coating sweet, I thought it unnecessary.

"Can we try without it first?" I asked.

Bain's bushy gray eyebrows rose as he considered my question. "You don't need it to make an initial connection?"

I thought about the different people and horses I had linked with. "So far, no."

"All right. Yelena, I want you to try to connect with Gelsi."

Dredging some energy from my tired body, I pulled a thread of power and directed it to the girl, projecting my awareness to her. I sensed her apprehension about working with this strange woman from Ixia in her mind.

Hello, I said.

She jumped in shock.

To help her relax I said, *I was born in the Illiais Jungle. Where did you grow up?*

Gelsi formed an image of a small village wrapped in fog in her mind. *We reside in the foothills of the Emerald Mountains. Every morning our house is enveloped in the mist from the mountains.*

I showed her my parents' dwelling in the trees. We "talked" about siblings. A middle child, Gelsi, had two older sisters and two younger brothers, but she was the only one in her family to develop magical powers.

Bain watched us in silence, then he interrupted, "Break the connection now."

Sapped of energy, I dragged my awareness back.

"Gelsi, it is your turn to make contact with Yelena."

She closed her eyes, and I sensed her seeking my mind. All I would need to do was tug on her awareness.

"Do not help her," Bain warned me.

Instead, I kept my mind open, but she failed to reach me.

"Not to worry," Bain consoled her. "The first time is the hardest. That is why we use Theobroma."

Bain's gray eyes studied me with kindness. "We will try again another time. Gelsi, go unpack and get settled."

After she left Bain's tower, he said, "No doubt you wore yourself out yesterday. Hayes mentioned something to me. Tell me what happened," he instructed.

I told him about the pain and the power. "It seems I don't

have full control yet," I offered, waiting to see if he would chastise me. If my actions had truly been an uncontrolled burst, I knew the other Master Magicians would have felt it. And certain that Roze would have acted without hesitation on that knowledge.

"A lesson learned," Bain said. "Repairing injuries takes immense effort. Enough for today. I'll see you tonight at the feast."

The feast! I had forgotten. Again. "What should I…" I stopped, feeling awkward and silly to be asking about clothing.

Bain smiled in sympathy. "No expertise in that matter," he said, seeming to read my mind. "Zitora will enjoy helping you. She's at loose ends this year and will welcome some company."

"I thought she was busy with Council business."

"She is, but she's transitioning from five years of being a student to being on her own. Having no time to be a mentor doesn't mean she won't have time to make a friend."

I left Bain's tower and headed toward Zitora's in the northeast corner of the Keep. Lively groups filled the campus walkways and people hurried past me in every direction. My quiet walks through the Keep were at an end, yet I felt energized by all the activity.

Zitora greeted me with a bright smile that only dimmed when we discussed Tula's condition. Talk eventually turned to the upcoming festivities, and I inquired about appropriate dress.

"The formal robes are only for the boring school functions," Zitora said. "Do tell me you have something pretty to wear."

When I shook my head, she transformed into a mother hen and set about finding me some clothes.

"Thank fate you're my size," Zitora said with glee.

Despite my protests, she dragged me up two flights to her bedroom and loaded my arms with dresses, skirts and lacy blouses. Zitora propped her hands on her hips, considering my boots. "Those will not do."

"They're comfortable and I can move easily in them," I said.

"A challenge then. Mmm. I'll be right back."

She disappeared into another room, while I waited in her bedroom on the third floor of her tower. Soft pastel paintings of flowers hung on the walls. Oversize pillows graced her canopy bed. The room oozed comfort like open arms wrapping me in a hug.

With a triumphant shout, Zitora sauntered into the room, a pair of black sandals raised high for admiration.

"Rubber soles, soft leather and a small heel. Perfect for dancing all night long." She laughed.

"I don't know how to dance," I said.

"Doesn't matter. You have a natural grace. Watch the others and follow." Zitora added the sandals to the top of my pile.

"I really can't take all of this." I tried to give the clothes back. "I came for advice, not your entire wardrobe." I planned to go to the market. With the return of the Citadel's residents, the shops remained open every day.

She shooed me away. "Hardly made a dent in my armoire. I'm a collector of clothes. I can't pass a dress shop without finding something I must have."

"At least let me pay—"

"Stop." She raised her hand. "I'll make it easier for you. Tomorrow I'm leaving on a mission for the Council, and—much to my chagrin—I will have an escort of four soldiers. Irys and Roze can gallivant all over Sitia by themselves, and they're assigned all the fun, secret missions. But the Council worries about me. So I'm limited to escorted missions." She huffed with frustration. "I've seen you practicing with your bow near the stable. How about I exchange my clothes for some lessons in self-defense?"

"Okay. But why didn't you learn how to defend yourself while a student here?"

"I hated the Master of Arms," she said with a deep frown. "A bully who turned the teaching sessions into torture sessions. He enjoyed inflicting pain. I avoided him at all costs. When the Masters realized I had strong powers, they focused more on my learning."

"Who's the Arms Master?"

"One of the northerners with Cahil. Goel's his name." Zitora shuddered with revulsion. "Although he wasn't as bad as the Master test…" She paused as a cringe of horror crossed her face. Then she jerked her head as if dislodging unwanted memories.

"Anyway, Roze offered to teach me, but I'd rather have you as my instructor." She flashed me a conspiratorial smirk.

Having agreed to the exchange, I maneuvered down Zitora's tower steps with the bundle of her clothes heaped in my arms. So burdened, I headed toward my rooms. On the way, I wondered about the Master test. Fisk, the beggar boy had also mentioned it. I would have to ask Irys.

The courtyard across from my quarters buzzed with students. A few boys tossed a ball, while others lounged on the grass or talked in groups. Hampered by Zitora's clothes, I fumbled at my door.

"Hey, you!" someone called.

I looked around and spotted a group of girls gesturing at me.

"The first year barracks are that way." One of the girls with long blond hair pointed. "This is for apprentices only."

"Thanks, but this is my room," I called, turning back.

I managed to get the door open before I felt a prickle of power along my spine. Tossing the clothing on to the floor, I spun around. A group of students stood mere inches from me.

"You don't belong here," said the long-haired girl. A dangerous shine lit her violet eyes. "You're new. I know everybody, and new students go to the first-year barracks. You have to *earn* a room here."

Persuasive magic emanated from her. A strong desire to pack my belongings and move to the first-year dorms coursed through my mind and pressed against my body. I deflected her magical command by strengthening my mental defenses.

She grunted in outrage. A look passed among her companions. Power built as they readied to join in. I braced for another attack, but before they could use their combined power, another voice cut through the throng.

"What's going on here?"

The power dissipated in a stiff wave as Dax Greenblade pushed his lean muscular body through the group, staring down at the others with his bottle-green eyes. In the sunlight, his honey-brown skin made his face appear older.

"She doesn't belong here," the girl repeated.

"Yelena is Fourth Magician's student," Dax said. "She's been assigned to this wing."

"But that's not fair," the girl whined. "You have to *earn* the right to be here."

"And who's to say she hasn't?" Dax asked. "If you believe Fourth Magician is in error, I suggest you take it up with her."

An uncomfortable silence followed before the group returned to the courtyard. Dax stayed beside me.

"Thanks," I said. The group huddled in a tight pack, casting nasty looks my way as they talked. "Guess I haven't made any friends."

"Three points against you, I'm afraid. One." Dax held up a long slender finger. "You're new. Two. Fourth Magician's your mentor. Any student selected by a Master is guaranteed to be the subject of jealousy. If you're looking for friends, I'm afraid Gelsi and I are your only choices."

"What's the third point?"

He smiled sardonically. "Rumors and speculation. The students will dig up every bit of information they can on you and why you're here. It doesn't matter if the information is true or not. In fact, the stranger the tidbits the better. And I have a feeling from what I already heard your tidbits are quite juicy and should inflame the gossip all the more."

I studied his face. Lines of concern creased his forehead, and I saw no signs of deceit. "Tidbits?"

"You're Leif's lost sister, you're older than all the students and you're extremely powerful."

I looked at him in surprise. Me? Powerful?

"I didn't come over to help you. I came to protect them." He inclined his head toward the group in the courtyard.

Before I could comment, Dax pointed to a room, five doors down from mine. "Come anytime for any reason. Gelsi is in the novice barracks near the west wall."

Dax waved goodbye and strode toward his room. The group's hostility transferred briefly to his back before returning to me. I closed my door.

Great. Day one and already the outcast. But did I care? Here to learn and not to make friends, I thought it wouldn't matter once lessons started. By then, the students would be too busy to pay any attention to me.

I sorted through Zitora's clothes, choosing a long black skirt and a red-and-black V-neck blouse. The shirt had two layers of material. A pattern of fine black lace over red silk.

I tried on the outfit. Deciding to leave my bow behind during the feast, I cut a slit in one of the skirt's pockets for quick access to my switchblade. The sandals were a little big, so I poked another hole in the strap.

Until I looked at myself in the mirror I hadn't realized I wore Commander Ambrose's colors, the same combination as my northern uniform. I considered another outfit, even tried on different clothes, but felt the most comfortable in my first choice.

Pulling my hair from its braid, I scowled at the limp mess. The year before I had cut out the snarls and tangles, and now the ends had grown in ragged. My black hair now reached past my shoulders. It would need a good trim and washing.

I changed back into my day clothes and left my rooms to feed the promised apples to Topaz and Kiki. Conversation in the courtyard ceased as I emerged. Ignoring them, I set out for the stable. I would stop by the baths on my return.

The time for the feast came quicker than I expected. Once again, I stood in front of the mirror in my bedroom, assessing my clothing with a critical eye. I pushed a stray curl from my face.

An assistant at the baths had fussed over my awkward attempts to cut my own hair. She had commandeered my scissors and proceeded to trim the ends, then had rolled my hair with hot metal tubes.

Instead of being pulled into a bun, my hair now fell to my shoulders in big soft curls. I looked ridiculous. But before I could rearrange it, someone knocked on my door.

I grabbed my bow and peeked out the window. Cahil waited outside. His hair and beard appeared white in the moonlight.

Opening the door, I said, "I thought we agreed to meet…" I gaped.

Cahil wore a long silk tunic of midnight-blue. The collar stood up and silver piping followed the edge of the fabric to form a vee far enough below his throat to allow a glimpse of his muscular chest. The piping also went across his shoulders and dropped down the outside seam of his full sleeves. A silver mesh belt studded with gemstones cinched the tunic around his narrow waist. His trousers matched his shirt, and, once again, silver piping traced the outside seam of his pants, carrying my eyes down to a pair of polished leather boots. Royalty incarnated.

"I pass your rooms on the way. Seemed silly not to stop," Cahil said.

He squinted into the lantern light that glowed behind me, and I realized he couldn't see my openmouthed stare.

"Ready?" he asked.

"Give me a moment." Returning to the sitting area, I gestured Cahil toward a chair as I went into my bedroom, where I secured my switchblade then smoothed my skirt. With no time to fix my hair, I settled for tucking it behind my ears. Curls! Living in Sitia had made me soft.

Cahil smiled broadly when he saw me in the light.

"Don't laugh," I warned.

"I never laugh *at* a beautiful woman. I'd much rather laugh and dance *with* her."

"False flattery won't work on me."

"I meant every word." Cahil offered his arm. "Shall we?"

After a slight hesitation, I linked my arm in his.

"Don't worry. I'm only your escort tonight. I would offer to protect you from the drunken attentions of the other men, but I know all too well that you're quite capable of holding your own. You're probably armed. Right?"

"Always."

We walked in companionable silence. Groups of students and other couples headed in the same direction soon joined us. Lively music pulsed through the air, becoming louder as we approached.

The dining room had been converted into a ballroom. Orange, red and yellow velvet streamers twisted along the ceiling and draped the walls. Laughter and conversation competed with the music as some people drank and ate, while others danced on the wooden dance floor. Everyone appeared to be wearing their finest clothes. The room sparkled with jewelry in the candlelight.

Our arrival went unnoticed. But as Cahil pulled me through the crowd toward the back of the room, a couple of surprised glances marked our passing.

A jolt snapped through me as we cleared the crowd and I spotted Leif. I hadn't seen him since Irys had left, and I had assumed since he had graduated from the Keep he was no longer involved with the students or classes. But there he stood, next to Roze and Bain. Cahil aimed for them.

I almost fainted when Leif smiled at me as we approached, but when he recognized me it turned into a scowl. I wondered what I would have to do to get a true smile from Leif. Dismissing the thought, I didn't want to earn his goodwill, and

I certainly didn't need it. Now, if I could keep saying that over and over in my mind, I might just start to believe it.

When we joined the group, Bain complimented my hairstyle, while Roze ignored me. Our group only truly came alive when Zitora joined us.

"Perfect! Absolutely perfect!" Zitora exclaimed over my outfit.

The talk soon turned to Council business and Cahil pressed Roze to get him on the agenda. Having no interest in discussing politics, my attention wandered as I scanned the crowd. I saw only a few of Cahil's men. They wore dress uniforms and stood awkwardly to the side as if on duty instead of being there for pleasure. Perhaps they were.

I watched the dancers for a while. They circled the floor in pairs. After eight beats, they stopped and then took four steps into the center, then four steps back and continued around the circle. The pattern was then repeated. Similar to some of my self-defense katas, the dance resembled a prescribed set of moves.

Dax and Gelsi appeared. Bain's students greeted the three Master Magicians with a stiff formality. Gelsi wore a soft green gown that shimmered in the lantern light. The gown's color matched her big eyes. Studded with gold buttons, Dax's red shirt had a mandarin collar. Gold piping lined the outside seam of his black pants.

"Hey, we match," Dax said to me. I could just hear him over the music. "Would you like to dance?"

I glanced at Cahil, debating with Leif. "Sure."

Dax smiled and pulled me into an opening on the dance floor. Watching had been easier than doing, but with Dax's steady guidance, I soon caught the rhythm.

As we circled the floor, Dax said, "Remember when I said you had three points against you?"

I nodded.

"Now there are five."

"What now?" I asked in exasperation. It was hard to believe I'd had time to make anyone else mad.

"You came to the feast on Cahil's arm. Everyone will assume two things. One. That you're his girlfriend. And two. That you're an Ixian sympathizer, which is the greater of the two evils."

"Well, they would be wrong. Who comes up with all these points and assumptions?" I demanded.

"Not me, that's for sure," Dax said. "If I were in charge, we'd have more desserts at dinner, more feasts and much more dancing."

We danced for a while in silence. I mulled over the implications and decided not to waste my time worrying about what everyone else thought, or to bother attempting to change their perceptions. My time at the Keep was just a stopover. Let them wonder. My nervousness about the evening dissipated with my decision. I smiled at Dax.

"You have a mischievous glint. What are you planning?"

"Only five points against me?" I narrowed my eyes in mock concern. "Such a small number. I say we try for eight or ten."

A wolfish grin spread across Dax's face. "My lady, you are far too modest. You're more than capable of handling fifteen or twenty."

I laughed with genuine pleasure. Dax and I twirled around the dance floor for a few more songs before rejoining the group. Cahil met our return with a sour look. Before he could say anything or go back to debating with Leif, I grabbed Cahil's hand and pulled him toward the dancers.

"Tonight is not for business," I said as we followed Dax and Gelsi around the floor. "Tonight is for fun. Dancing instead of fighting."

He laughed. "You're right."

The evening flew by as I danced with Cahil, Dax and Bain. Even the Stable Master swung me around for a rowdy foot-stomping song. If Cahil hadn't insisted, I wouldn't have stopped to eat.

Irys's arrival should have made the evening perfect, but I could see exhaustion etched in her face. Wearing a simple light blue gown instead of traveling clothes, she must have taken the time to bathe and to decorate her regal bun with rubies and diamonds before coming to the feast.

"Is everything okay? Did you find Tula's sister?" I asked.

Irys nodded. "Her sister, Opal, is with Tula now." She gave me an odd look.

"Should we try to help Tula tonight?"

Irys shook her head. "Let Opal spend some time with her sister. It's the first she's seen her since Tula was kidnapped." Again, Irys flashed me that strange look.

"What then? There's something you're not telling me."

"I warned Opal of Tula's condition—both mental and physical." Irys rubbed a hand along her cheek. "But when we arrived, it seemed a miracle had occurred." Irys peered with a deep intensity into my eyes.

"Is Tula awake?" I asked in confusion. Irys's news contradicted her body language.

"No, her soul is still in hiding, but her body is completely healed."

16

"HOW?" I ASKED IRYS. Hayes had said he could only heal a few bones at a time. Perhaps another healer had come to help him with Tula.

"You tell me," Irys demanded. "What did you do that day? Hayes has been in a state ever since. He's terrified of you."

"Me?"

Bain came to my temporary rescue. "Perhaps you ladies would like to go outside."

I looked around. Several people had stopped talking and gawked at us.

"I forget myself," Irys apologized to Bain. "Now is not the time to discuss this."

She headed toward the buffet. Everyone returned to their conversations. But she wasn't finished with me.

Yelena, she said in my mind. *Please tell me what happened with Tula.*

Sudden dread churned in my stomach. Was Irys upset because I had lost control of my magic and had accidentally healed Tula, or because I could have jeopardized Tula's life? With reluctance, I told her everything that had happened that day in Tula's room.

You were in pain and you pushed the pain away from yourself? Irys asked.

Yes. Did I do something wrong?

No. You did something impossible. I thought you tried to heal her, which would have been dangerous, but it sounds as if you assumed her injuries and then healed yourself.

I stared at Irys with pure amazement. She sat across the room, eating her dinner.

Could you do it again? she asked.

I don't know. It must have been an instinctive reaction.

There is only one way to find out. I felt Irys's weary sigh. *For now, I want you to get a good night's rest. Meet me in Tula's room tomorrow afternoon.* Irys broke her magical connection to me.

Confusion creased Cahil's face, and I realized he had been watching me. "What's the matter?" he asked. "Shouldn't Fourth Magician be pleased that you healed that girl? That would mean... Oh, my sword!" He gaped.

Before I could press him for details, the music stopped.

"Midnight," Bain declared. "Time to go. The students have a full day tomorrow." His delighted anticipation of a full day of learning caused a ripple of smiles around him.

Obediently, everyone streamed out into the darkness, heading off to dorms and apartments. As he passed, Dax caught my eye. He grinned and held up seven fingers. I looked forward to hearing from him about my additional two points of gossip-inspiring behavior.

Cahil walked me to my rooms. He was unusually quiet.

Finally, I couldn't stand it anymore. "Oh, my sword what?" I demanded.

"I realized something," he said, trying to shrug me off.

Not content with his vague answer, I prompted, "Which was…"

"If I told you, you would be angry. I don't want to end the evening with a fight."

"And if I promised not to get upset?"

"You would anyway."

"Tomorrow, then?"

"Ask me the next time we're fighting."

"What if we don't fight?"

Cahil laughed. "With you, there is always a next time."

Then with a speed that surprised me, he grabbed me around the waist and pulled me in for a quick kiss on the cheek before releasing me.

"Till tomorrow," he said over his shoulder as he strode away.

It was only after watching him disappear into the darkness that I realized I stood with my switchblade clutched in my right hand. But I hadn't triggered the blade. The south was making me soft. First curls, now this. Shaking my head, I opened my door.

At Tula's room the next afternoon, I had to squeeze my way in. Tula's bed occupied the center. Leif and Hayes stood on the right side of her bed, and Irys and a young girl stood on the left. Tula's guard, one of Cahil's men, looked uncomfortable wedged in a corner.

Hayes paled when I looked at him. Irys introduced me to Opal, Tula's sister. Opal's long brown hair was pulled into a ponytail, and her red-rimmed eyes looked swollen from crying.

I hadn't expected an audience. "Irys," I said. "I need to spend some time with Opal before I can try to bring Tula back."

Leif muttered something about grandstanding on his way out, and Hayes just aimed for the door.

"Do you need me?" Irys asked.

"No."

"We don't have much time," Irys warned as she left the room.

She didn't need to remind me that Tula's attacker still roamed free, possibly hunting for another victim. However, I knew in my heart that if I rushed this, I wouldn't succeed.

I asked Opal to tell me about her sister. In halting sentences, the young girl told me only a couple stories of their childhood.

"Tula once made me a large glass tiger to protect me from nightmares." Opal smiled at the memory. "It worked and the tiger looked so lifelike that Tula started making other glass animals." She glanced from her sister's still form to the guard in the corner.

Opal seemed hesitant and distracted by her sister's condition. So I changed the subject and asked about her trip to the Citadel.

Her dark brown eyes widened. "Fourth Magician woke us all up in the dead of night."

At the word dead, the young girl glanced with dread at Tula.

"I was barely awake. Before I knew it, I was on the magician's horse, riding flat out for the Keep." Opal clutched her arms to herself. "When Tula was found, the healers rushed her to the Citadel. My parents had to find people to work the kilns and take care of us before they could follow her. They're on the road somewhere." Opal began to ramble. "We didn't pass them. They don't know I'm here. It's my first trip away from home, and we stopped only to eat. I slept in the saddle."

That would explain Irys's exhaustion. Even today she had dark circles under her eyes. That also explained why Opal seemed so distressed. I switched tactics and invited Opal to take a walk. She appeared reluctant to leave her sister until I assured her that Tula would be fine.

I showed her the campus. The air temperature felt comfortable. With warm afternoons and chilly evenings, the weather during the cooling season was my favorite.

Eventually, we wandered out into the Citadel. I guided Opal toward the market. Fisk appeared with a ready smile and led us to a dress shop. I bought Opal a change of clothes and Fisk played tour guide for her.

When Opal seemed more relaxed, my questions about Tula grew more specific. As she remembered more stories, I pulled a thread of magic and linked my mind with Opal's, witnessing her memories as she spoke. I smelled the hot furnace of their family's glass factory, and felt the coarse sand in my hands.

"Tula and I used to hide from Mara, our older sister. We had found the perfect spot. Mara still doesn't know where it is," Opal said, smiling.

The image of an awning of tree limbs and sun-dappled grass filled Opal's mind as the cool scent of moist earth reached my nose.

"That's it." I grabbed Opal's arm. "Hold that place in your mind. Concentrate on it."

She did as I asked. I closed my eyes and put myself into the memory. Blades of grass brushed my arms as I lay in the small hollow behind a row of overgrown bushes. The smell of sweet honeysuckles hung heavy in the fresh air. Dewdrops sparkled in the morning sunlight. Instinctively, I knew this place hid Tula's soul.

"Come on." I pulled Opal toward the Keep, waving good-bye to Fisk. A guard stood outside Tula's door. He nodded to us as we went inside.

"Shouldn't we wait for Fourth Magician and the others?" Opal asked.

"No time. I don't want to lose the image." I took one of Tula's hands and held my other out to Opal. "Take my hand. Now, I want you to imagine yourself in your hiding spot with Tula. Close your eyes and really concentrate. Can you do that?"

Opal nodded, her pale face drawn.

I linked with Tula. The ghosts of her horrors still floated in the emptiness, but they seemed less tangible than before. Connecting with Opal, I followed the smell of honeysuckles and dew through Tula's mind.

The ghosts thickened with a sudden fury, flying at me, blocking my passage. The air pressed and clung like molasses. I pushed past them only to be ensnared in a row of thorn bushes. My clothing snagged on branches and the barbs dug into my skin.

"Go away," Tula called. "I don't want to come back."

"Your family misses you," I said.

Vines began to wrap around my arms and waist, anchoring me.

"Go away!"

I showed her Opal's memories of what her family suffered when Tula had disappeared.

The thorny bushes thinned a bit. Through their branches I spotted Tula curled up in her childhood hiding spot.

"I can't face them," Tula said.

"Your family?"

"Yes. I've done…things. Terrible things so he wouldn't hurt me." Tula shuddered. "But he hurt me anyway."

The vines climbed up my arms and circled my neck.

"Your family still loves you."

"They won't. He'll tell them what I did. They'll be disgusted. I was his slave, but I didn't try hard enough for him. I couldn't get anything right. I didn't even die for him."

I controlled my anger; my desire to slaughter the beast would have to wait. "Tula, *he* is the disgusting one. *He* is the one who should die. Your family knows what he did to your body. They only want you back."

She drew her body into a tighter ball. "What do you know? You know nothing about what I went through. Go away."

"You assume too much," I choked out as the vines around my throat squeezed tight. I struggled to breathe. Could I face my own horrors again? To find this monster, I would. I opened my mind to hers and showed her Reyad. His delight in torturing me. My willingness to make him happy so he wouldn't harm me. And the night I slit his throat after he had raped me.

Tula peeked at me through her arms. The vines lessened the pressure. "You killed your torturer. Mine is still out there, waiting."

I tried again. "Then he is free to make someone else his slave. What if Opal is his next victim?"

Tula jumped up in horror. "No!" she screamed.

I linked Opal's mind with ours. For a moment, Opal stood stunned, blinking in surprise. Then she ran to Tula and hugged her. Together they wept. The vines withdrew, and the bushes died away.

But this was just the beginning. The grassy hollow soon faded and Tula's ghosts hovered around us.

"There are too many," Tula said in defeat. "I will never be rid of them."

I drew my bow from its holder on my back and broke it into three pieces. Handing one to Tula and the other to Opal, I said, "You're not alone. We'll fight together."

The ghosts attacked. They were tenacious and quick. I swung at them over and over until my arms felt like lead. A few of Tula's horrors disappeared, others shrank, but some seemed to grow as they fought.

My energy drained at an alarming pace. I felt my bow become stuck inside one of the ghosts. The spirit expanded and consumed me. I screamed as the pain of being whipped racked my body.

"You're weak. Tell me you'll obey and I'll stop," a voice whispered in my ear.

"No." Near panic I reached out for help. A powerful presence formed and handed me a full-size bow that pulsed with energy. Strength returned to me and I beat at the horror until it fled.

We had repelled the attack, but I could see that Tula's ghosts prepared for another.

"Tula, this is merely the first battle in an ongoing war. It will take time and effort to be free of your fears, but you'll have plenty of help from your family. Are you coming with us?" I asked.

She bit her lip, gazing at the piece of bow in her hands. Opal added her bow to Tula's. Tula clutched them both close to her chest. "Yes. I'll come."

Tula's mind filled with memories of her life. Vertigo twirled in my stomach as I broke my mental links with Tula and Opal. Relief descended, and I sank into blackness.

When I came to my senses, I felt hard stone against my back. For the third time I had collapsed on Tula's floor. This time I had no hope of moving. My energy was completely depleted. After a while I noticed that someone gripped my hands. Strong fingers wrapped around mine, encompassing them with warmth.

With effort I opened my eyes to see who held me. Then I closed them tight. I must still be asleep. But after hearing Irys's insistent calls, I looked again. And there sat my brother, holding my hands and sharing his energy with me.

17

WEARINESS LINED LEIF'S FACE. "You're in big trouble," he said.

His words didn't seem malicious, just factual, and, as expected, past his shoulders, I saw Irys, Roze, Hayes and Bain all frowning at me. Leif released my hands, but remained on the floor beside me.

Roze eyed him, her displeasure evident in the tight twist of her lips. "You should have let her die," she scolded him. "One less magician to taint our land with her incredible stupidity."

"A little too harsh, Roze," Bain said. "Though I agree about the stupidity. Child, why did you try that alone?" Bain asked.

I couldn't even speak in my defense for I hadn't the energy to form words, let alone try and explain myself.

"Cocky and stupid," Roze said for me. "Since she cured Tula of her physical injuries, she must have believed she was an all-powerful magician and could do anything. The fool will probably be asking to take the Master level test next." Roze snorted with disgust. "Maybe she'll feel differently after we assign her to the first year's barracks. There she can learn the basics of magic while scrubbing the floors, like every new student."

I glanced at Irys. Roze's punishment sounded horrible. Irys said nothing. Disapproval pulsed off her. I braced for an outburst.

Instead, Opal called, "Tula's awake!"

I closed my eyes in relief as everyone focused on Tula. When I opened my eyes, the magicians had all disappeared from my view.

"You're still headstrong and reckless; an out of control strangler fig," Leif said. "I guess Ixia didn't change everything about you." He stood on shaking legs, and I watched him join the others by Tula's bedside.

I puzzled over his comment. Good or bad? I couldn't decide. But then Roze's harsh voice jarred me out of my reflection. She bombarded Tula with questions about her attacker, but Tula wouldn't answer. I cringed, knowing that Tula wasn't up to Roze's interrogation. Thank fate, Hayes intervened.

"Give her some time," he said.

"There is no time," Roze replied.

A thin raspy voice asked, "Who are all these people? Where's Yelena? I can't see her."

"She's here," Opal said. "She's just exhausted from helping you, Tullie."

"Hayes, get some assistants and go dump the fool girl into another room," Roze instructed. "She's done enough damage for one day."

When Hayes moved to obey, Tula said, "No. You leave. All of you. I won't tell you anything. Yelena stays with me. I'll talk to her."

A mummer of irritation and discussion rumbled through the magicians before Roze agreed with reluctance to bring a bed in for me. Hayes and Irys hoisted me off the floor and dropped me without fanfare onto the mattress. Irys still hadn't said a word, and her silence scared me.

"Child," Bain said to Tula. "I understand your fear. You have awakened to a room full of strangers." He then introduced everyone in the room. "First Magician and Leif are the ones you need to tell about your abduction. They will find your kidnapper."

Tula pulled the sheet up to her chin. "I'll tell Yelena. No one else. She'll take care of him."

Roze's harsh laughter scraped in my ears. "She can't even talk! If your attacker walked into this room, he would kill you both." She shook her head in disbelief. "You're not thinking clearly. I'll be back in the morning, and you *will* talk to me. Come, Leif." Roze strode out the door with Leif on her heels.

Hayes shooed everyone else out. As the door closed, I heard Bain tell Irys to assign an extra guard for the evening. A good idea. If Goel came in, I couldn't prevent him from carrying out his promises to torture me.

Apprehension about being so helpless crawled along my spine. A similar situation that haunted Tula. One of her many ghosts was being at the mercy of another. Her promise to tell me everything weighed on my mind; I had just gotten rid of my own ghost. Though, I hated to admit, Reyad still retained some power. Whenever I had doubts, he seemed to enjoy visiting my nightmares. Or did he cause them? Or did I invite him?

To distract myself from such troublesome thoughts, I tried to muster some energy to talk to Tula, but exhaustion claimed me instead and I sank into a deep dreamless sleep.

★ ★ ★

I felt a little better in the morning, but had only enough strength to sit up in bed. At least I could ask Tula how she felt.

She closed her eyes. Pointing to her temple she said, "Come."

I sighed with regret. "I don't have the energy to link our minds, Tula."

"Perhaps I can help," Leif said from the doorway.

"No! Go away." Tula shielded her face with her arms.

"If you don't talk to me, First Magician will come and take the information she needs from you," Leif explained.

Tula peeked out at me in confusion.

"It won't be pleasant," I said. "It's almost as bad as what your attacker did to you. I know."

Leif averted his eyes. I hoped he felt guilty. Studying him closer, I wondered why he had aided me the day before. What had happened to his smirk? Where was his derision and condescension? I realized I barely knew this man.

Not wanting to guess his motives anymore, I demanded, "Why did you help me?"

A scowl gripped his face, but, with a sigh, he smoothed his features, shuttering his emotions. "Mother would kill me if I had let you die," he said.

He turned to Tula, but I refused to let him get away with such a flippant response. "What's the real reason?"

Hatred blazed in Leif's jade eyes, but a second later his posture softened, as if someone had blown out a candle. He whispered, "I couldn't bear to do nothing and lose you again."

Then, his mental defenses dropped and I heard his thoughts. *I still hate you.*

His trust surprised me, though his petulant comment failed

to concern me. An emotion, even hatred, was better than apathy. Could this be a first step in bridging the distance between us?

"What did he say?" Tula asked.

"He wants to help you," I said. "Tula, this is my brother. Without him we wouldn't have gotten you back. If you want me to find your attacker, I'll need his strength."

"But, he'll see. He'll know about…" Tula squeezed her arms together.

"I already know," Leif said.

He pulled Tula's arms away from her face with a gentleness that amazed me. I thought back to my mother's comments about Leif's magic. She had said he helped with crimes, sensing a person's guilt and history. Now, as I watched him with Tula, I wanted to know more about him and how he used his magic.

"We need to find him and stop him from hurting another girl," Leif explained.

She swallowed and bit her lip before nodding. Leif stood between our beds, took Tula's hand, and reached for mine. I reclined on the mattress and grabbed his hand. Then, using his energy, I formed a mental link with Tula.

In her mind, the two of us stood by a gray stone furnace. Leif's power roared around us like the fire under the kiln.

"I was here, putting coal into the furnace. It was close to midnight when…" She clutched her apron. Black soot streaked the white fabric. "A dark cloth wrapped around my face. Before I could scream, I felt a sharp stab in my arm. Then…then…" Tula stopped speaking.

On our mental stage, she stepped toward me. I hugged her trembling body, and within the space of a breath I became Tula, witnessing my own abduction.

Numbness spread from the stab wound, freezing my muscles. Dizziness was the only indication I'd been moved. Time passed. When the cloth was removed from my face, I was lying inside a tent. Unable to move, I stared up at a lean man with short brown hair that was streaked with gold. He wore only a red mask. Strange crimson symbols had been painted all over his sand-colored skin. He held four wooden stakes, rope and a mallet. Feeling returned to my limbs.

"Tula, no. I can't," I said in my mind. I knew what horrors threatened to come. I lacked the strength to endure them with her right now. "Just show him to me."

She froze the image of the man so I could study the symbols. The circular patterns resided within bigger patterns of animals. Triangles traced down his smooth arms and legs. Though thin, he radiated power.

A complete stranger to Tula, everything about him seemed foreign to her. Even the harsh way he pronounced her name, emphasizing the la, sounded odd. But he knew her. Knew the names of her sisters and parents. Knew how they melted sand, working it into glass.

Then, in a whirl of sound and color, she showed me the man at different times. She wasn't permitted to leave the tent, but whenever he entered or left, Tula caught a glimpse of the outside, a tease of freedom. Long thick grass filled the whole view.

When he came to her, he always wore a mask. Letting the numbness in her body wear off before beating or raping her. Letting her feel the pain he applied with seeming reverence. After he finished the torture, he took a thorn and scratched her skin.

Puzzled at first by this action, Tula soon learned to dread and to crave the ointment he would rub into the thorn's bleeding gash. It was the numbing lotion that would paralyze her, taking away all her pain and any chance she might have to escape.

The ointment, though, had a strong crisp scent, similar to the sharp smell of alcohol mixed with a citrus perfume. The aroma remained around me like a poisonous fog as Leif's energy waned. He broke the magical connection to Tula.

"That smell…" Leif said as he perched on the edge of my bed. "I couldn't get a good whiff. All my effort went into keeping you and Tula connected."

"It's horrible," Tula said, shuddering. "I shall never forget it."

"What about those symbols?" I asked Leif. "Did you recognize them?"

"Not really. Though there are some clans that use symbols for rituals."

"Rituals?" Dread coiled in my stomach.

"Wedding ceremonies and naming rituals." Leif scowled in concentration. "Thousands of years ago, magicians used to perform intricate rituals. They believed that magical power came from a deity, and if they tattooed their bodies and showed the proper respect, they would be granted greater power. Now we know better. I've seen some symbols painted on faces and hands before, but not like the ones on Tula's attacker."

Leif pulled his black hair back behind his head with both hands. With his elbows jutting out past his face, his posture seemed so familiar. I felt like I could transport back to a time when my concerns only focused on what game to play next. The faint childhood memory dissolved with my efforts to concentrate on it.

Tula covered her eyes, silent tears spilling down her cheeks. Reliving the kidnapping and the torment had to be grueling.

"Get some rest," Leif told her. "I'll come back later. Perhaps Second Magician will know something about those symbols." He left the room.

The morning's events had drained my own small supply of energy. I knew words would give no comfort to Tula, so I was relieved when Opal came in. Seeing her sister's concern, Tula sobbed loudly, and Opal crawled into the bed with her, held Tula close and rocked her like a baby. I fell asleep listening to Tula purge her body of the masked man's poison.

We had visitors throughout the rest of the day. Cahil came, smelling of the barn.

"How's Kiki?" I asked, missing her. Even though my connection with her remained, I couldn't produce enough power to hear her thoughts.

"A little agitated. All the horses are. The Stable Master's been in one of his tempers. Horses take their cues from people's emotions. If a rider is nervous, then the horse will be, too." Cahil shook his head. "I still have a hard time believing you can communicate with them. Guess today is just one of those days where my notions are proven wrong."

"Why's that?"

"I thought you were an overconfident braggart when you said you could help Tula. But you did it." Cahil studied me.

I conceded the overconfidence title. My rescue of Commander Ambrose's soul had seemed easy in comparison to Tula's, but I had forgotten that Irys had been with me in the Commander's room, and it had been his superior fighting skills and determination that had gotten us free of his demons.

"You almost killed yourself saving Tula, though," Cahil said. "Was it worth the risk to prove me wrong again?"

"My motivations weren't selfish," I snapped at him. "I

wanted to help her. I understood what she's been through and I knew she needed me. Once I had an idea about how I could find her, I didn't stop to think. I just reacted."

"And the danger to yourself never entered your mind?"

"Not this time." I sighed at his aghast expression.

"You have put yourself in danger for others before?"

"I *was* the Commander's food taster." This was common knowledge, unlike my role in stopping Brazell.

Cahil nodded. "A perfect position to overhear the Commander's plans. He used you as a shield. You should want to help overthrow him. Why do you hold such loyalty for him?" Frustration roughened his voice.

"Because of my position, I saw through his reputation. I witnessed kindness and a deep concern for his people. He didn't abuse his power, and, while he is far from perfect, he always stayed faithful to his beliefs. Reliable and true to his word, you never had to guess at hidden meanings or suspect duplicity from him."

His stubbornness refused to soften. "You've been brainwashed, Yelena. Hopefully, you'll regain some sense after living in Sitia for a while." Cahil left without waiting for a reply.

Our conversation had drained me. I drifted in and out of an uneasy sleep the rest of that afternoon. The masked man invaded my dreams, hunting me through a thick jungle.

Toward evening Dax Greenblade surged into the room, energizing the air.

"You look like hell," he said to me in a low voice. Tula and Opal had fallen asleep in Tula's narrow bed.

"Gee, Dax, don't coat it with honey. Tell me what you really think," I said.

He covered his mouth to mute his laughter. "I figured I'd

hit you while you were down, because once you hear the rumors that have been flying through the campus like bare feet on hot sand, your ego will think it's a compliment." In a grand gesture, Dax swept his arms into the air. "You have become a legend!"

"A legend? Me?" Disbelief colored my voice.

"A scary legend," he amended, "but a legend all the same."

"Come on! How gullible do you think I am?"

"Simple enough to think you can find someone's consciousness alone." Dax waved a hand over my bed. "Although, it's not so stupid if this was an attempt to get out of class. But if you see your fellow students scurrying to get out of your way, now you know why. Here comes Yelena, the all powerful Soulfinder!"

I threw my pillow at Dax. His magic brushed my skin as the pillow veered to the right and struck the wall with a soft thump before sliding to the floor. I glanced at the girls. They appeared to be asleep.

"Now you're exaggerating," I said.

"Can you blame me? Cursed with the ability to read and speak archaic languages, Master Bain has me translating ancient history. Very dry and dull." Dax retrieved my pillow and even fluffed it before returning it to me.

When Leif entered the room carrying a large square box, Dax leaned close to me and whispered, "Speaking of dull…"

I suppressed a chuckle. Dax left as Leif began to unpack small brown vials. The clink of glass woke Tula and Opal. Tula eyed the bottles with obvious alarm.

"What are those?" I asked Leif.

"Scent vials," he said. "Each one contains a specific odor. Mother and Father helped me make these. Smells trigger memories, which aid me in finding criminals. But I figured I could use this kit as a start in determining the ointment that Tula's attacker used."

Interested, Tula tried to sit up. Opal got off the bed to help her. Leif rummaged through his collection of about thirty vials until he had lined up ten of them.

"We'll try these first." He uncorked one and passed it under my nose. "Breathe normally."

I wrinkled my nose and sneezed. "No. That's awful."

A small smile touched Leif's face as he put that vial away.

"Leif?" Tula asked. "What about me?"

He hesitated. "You've done so much already; I didn't want to exhaust you."

"I want to help, too. Better than lying here doing nothing."

"All right." He had us sniff three more vials. Tula and I each smelled different ones, and then we took a break for dinner.

"Too many scents will give you a headache, and you won't be able to tell the difference between them after a while," he explained.

Leif spent the evening with us. My interest began to wane, but he kept at it even when he neared the bottom of the box. I was on the edge of sleep when a sharp odor jolted me.

Leif held an uncorked bottle. Tula cowered in her bed, her hands raised as though she tried to deflect a blow. Leif squinted in confusion.

"That's it," I cried. "Can't you smell it?"

He passed the vial under his nose, breathing in the pungent scent. Then he shoved the cork back in, flipped the bottle over, and read the label. He stared at me in shock.

"It makes perfect sense!" His mouth opened in horror.

"What?" I demanded. "Tell me."

"It's Curare." When he saw my confusion he continued, "Comes from a vine that grows in the Illiais Jungle. It paralyzes the muscles. It's great for numbing toothaches, and for relieving minor pain. To freeze a whole body, the medicine would have to be very concentrated." Leif's eyes flashed in dismay.

"Why are you so upset?" I asked. "Now you know what it is. Isn't that good?"

"Curare was rediscovered just last year. Only a handful of Zaltanas know about its properties. Our clan likes to know everything about a substance before selling it to others."

Understanding flooded my mind. Leif believed that the red-painted man could be from our clan.

"Who found the Curare?" I asked.

Still upset, Leif turned the vial in his hands.

"Father," he said. "And the only person I can think of who has the skills to concentrate the Curare enough to paralyze a whole body, is Mother."

18

I SAT UP IN BED. "Leif, you don't really believe…" I couldn't bring myself to conjecture aloud. To say that Esau and Perl, our parents, might have some connection to this horrid murderer.

Leif shook his head. "No. But someone close to them, perhaps."

Another dreadful thought came to mind. "Are they in danger?"

"I don't know." Leif began to pack his scent vials into their box. "I need to talk to our clan leader. Somehow, the Curare must have been stolen. That one of our clan is…" Seeming lost for words, Leif banged the box's top down. "Compromised? Saying we have a spy sounds too dramatic even for me." Leif gave me a rueful grin. "I doubt our leader will even believe me." He grabbed his kit and rushed from the room.

Tula, who had remained quiet during our conversation, asked, "Could Ferde…" She swallowed. "Could my attacker be from the Zaltana Clan?"

"Ferde? Is that his name?"

She covered her face with a hand. "No. That's just what I named him. I hid that from you. I was embarrassed." She stopped and took a deep breath, glancing at her sister.

Opal yawned and said she needed to get some sleep. She kissed Tula on the cheek and pulled the covers up to Tula's chin before leaving.

After a few moments of silence, I said, "You don't have to explain."

"I want to, talking helps. Ferde is short for Fer-de-lance. A poisonous viper that hunts for prey by seeking heat. We used to get them in our factory all the time. They were drawn to the kilns. One killed my uncle. Anytime one of us would go out to the factory, my mother would say, 'Be careful. Don't let Ferde get you.' My older sister and I used to scare Opal by telling her Ferde was coming for her." Tula made a small sound as tears tracked down her face. "I have to apologize to Opal for being so mean. It's funny…" She choked out. "I was the one taken by Ferde, but if I'd had a choice, I would have rather been bitten by the real snake."

I couldn't find any words of comfort for Tula.

Later that night, Bain arrived. He carried a lantern, and Dax, ladened with a large leather-covered book and rolls of paper, followed him into the room. Yet another roll of paper was tucked under Bain's arm. He lit the lanterns in the room until the air blazed with candlelight. Bain wore the same purple robe he had worn the day before. Without preamble, he spread the paper across my bed. My stomach clenched when I looked at the scroll. The symbols I had seen tattooed on Ferde's body covered the parchment.

Bain watched my reaction closely. "These, then, are the right symbols?"

I nodded. "Where..?"

Bain took the book from Dax, and for once the young man's face held a serious expression.

"This ancient text written in the Efe language tells of magic symbols from long ago. It reports that these symbols were so powerful that they could not be drawn in the book, for to do so would call the power. But, fortunate for us, they describe them in detail. And fortunate, too, Dax was able to translate the Efe language into these." Bain gestured to the paper.

"That's some progress," I said.

Dax flashed a smile. "My talents are *finally* being used for a good cause."

Bain gave Dax a stern look. Dax sobered.

"The order of the symbols is very important," Bain explained, "for they weave a story. If you can tell us where they were on the killer's body, we might be able to discern what motivates him."

I studied the sheet, trying to remember where Ferde had painted the markings on his body. "There are some patterns on him that aren't on this paper," I said.

"Here," Tula said. Her eyes were closed. Even though her arm trembled, she held out her right hand. "I know them by heart."

Bain handed her the paper as Dax put his rolls on the floor. Unrolling one, he began to sketch an outline of a man on the sheet with a slender piece of charcoal. Tula stared at the symbols for a moment then she recited their order. Starting with Ferde's left shoulder; she worked her way across his body to his right shoulder, then continued left to right like lines of words in a book.

When Tula came to a symbol that wasn't on Bain's sheet, I drew it on a piece of scrap paper for Dax. Even though my drawings looked clumsy compared to his, he was able to duplicate my efforts on his paper.

Tula stuttered in embarrassment when she reached Ferde's groin. Bain squeezed her hand and made a comment about how the man must have suffered for his art. A single chuckle burst from Tula. By her expression, I knew the brief laugh had surprised her. I suppressed a smile; Tula had started on the long road of recovery.

Tula had memorized the symbols on her attacker's back. I cringed, remembering that she had spent almost two weeks as his prisoner. She also recalled other things about him—the scars on his ankles, the size of his hands, the red dirt under his fingernails, the shape and soft fabric of his red mask, and his ears.

"Why his ears?" Bain asked.

Tula shut her eyes and, even though her voice quavered, explained that each time he had staked her to the ground and thrust deep inside her, he turned his head to avoid looking into her eyes. To block out the pain, Tula focused on his ear. The first time he raped her, Tula bit him on the right ear. She recalled feeling a moment of satisfaction when the hot metallic taste of his blood filled her mouth.

"A tiny victory for me," Tula said then shuddered so fiercely her bed shook. "I never did it again."

Dax, who had been drawing Tula's every description from his spot on the floor, smoothed his horrified expression before giving her his sketch.

After some minor corrections, Tula handed the paper to Bain. "That's him," she said.

The effort had sapped so much of her strength that Tula fell asleep before Dax could gather his supplies.

I touched Bain's sleeve. "Can I ask you something?"

The magician glanced at his apprentice.

"I'll wait for you in your tower," Dax said to him. He left.

"You can always ask. No need to get permission, child."

I shook my head at the endearment. With only a bit of my strength returning, I felt ancient. I had no energy to correct him, though I doubt it would do me any good. He tended to call everyone child, even Irys, and she was twice my age.

"Irys hasn't come to visit. Is she still angry with me?"

"I would not use the word angry. Furious or livid comes closer to the truth."

My face must have reflected my terror because Bain laid a soothing hand over mine.

"You must remember that you are her student. Your actions reflect her skills as a teacher. What you did with Tula was extremely dangerous. You could have killed Tula, Opal, Leif and yourself. You did not consult Irys or seek her help, relying solely on yourself."

I opened my mouth to defend myself, but Bain raised a forestalling hand. "A skill, I am sure, you learned in Ixia. No one to help you. No one to trust. You did what you had to do to survive. Am I not correct?" Bain didn't wait for my reply. "But you are not in the north anymore. Here you have friends, colleagues and others to guide you and to help you. Sitia is very different from Ixia. No one person rules. We have a Council that represents our people. We debate and decide together. This is something you need to learn, and Irys needs to teach you. When she understands why you acted as you did, she will not be so upset."

"How long will that take?"

Bain smiled. "Not long. Irys is like the volcanoes in the Emerald Mountains. She might emit some steam, spit some lava, but she is quick to cool. She probably would have visited today, but a messenger arrived from Ixia this afternoon."

"A messenger?" I tried to get out of bed, but my legs wouldn't hold my weight. I ended up on the floor.

Bain *tsked* at me, calling Hayes to help me into bed.

When Hayes left, I asked again, "What messenger? Tell me."

"Council business." The magician made a shooing motion with his hand as if the entire topic bored him. "Something about an Ixian ambassador and his retinue requesting permission to visit Sitia."

An Ixian ambassador coming here? I mulled over the implications, as Bain, anxious to translate the killer's tattoos, hastened to leave the room.

"Bain," I called as he opened the door. "When are the Ixians coming?"

"I do not know. I am sure Irys will tell you when she comes."

When. At this point, I felt *if* was the better word. Waiting for her became intolerable. I hated just lying there, being so helpless. Irys must have sensed my agitation.

Yelena, I heard her voice in my mind. *Relax. Conserve your strength.*

But I need—

To get a good night's sleep. Or I shall tell you nothing. Understand?

Her firm tone left me no chance to argue. *Yes, sir.*

I tried to settle my mind. Instead of obsessing about when the northern delegation would arrive, I thought about who Commander Ambrose would send as his ambassador. He wouldn't risk one of his generals; sending an aide seemed more logical.

Valek would be my choice, but the Sitians wouldn't trust him, and he would be in too much danger. Cahil and his men would try to kill him for assassinating the former King of Ixia.

But would they succeed? That would depend on how many attacked him at one time.

I imagined Valek countering strikes with his typical grace and speed, but huge green leaves began to obscure the image in my mind. The leaves blocked my view and soon vegetation surrounded me. I fought my way through the dense jungle, searching for Valek. My pace increased as the awareness of being chased pressed on my back. Glancing over my shoulder, I spotted a long tan snake with red markings slithering after me.

Catching glimpses of Valek through the trees, I shouted and called to him for help. But thick vines from the jungle had ensnared his torso and legs. He hacked at them with his sword, but the vines continued to wrap around him until they covered his arms, as well. I pushed toward him, but a sharp pinch in my thigh stopped me.

The viper had wrapped around my leg. His fangs dripped Curare. Blood welled from the two small holes in my pants. The drug spread through my body. I screamed until the poison froze my voice.

"Yelena, wake up."

Someone shook my shoulder hard.

"It's just a dream. Come on, wake up."

I blinked at Leif. A frown anchored his face. His short black hair stuck out at odd angles, and he had dark smudges under his eyes. I glanced at Tula. Propped up on one elbow, she looked at me with concern in her brown eyes.

"Is Valek in trouble?" she asked me.

Leif's gaze jumped to Tula. "Why are you asking about him?" he demanded.

"Yelena was trying to help him when she was bitten by the snake."

"You saw it?" I asked.

She nodded. "I dream of the snake every night, but Valek's new. He must be from your dreams."

Leif turned back to me. "You know him?"

"I…" I closed my mouth. Choosing my words with care, I said, "As the Commander's food taster, I saw him every day."

Leif blinked. The red flush of annoyance drained from his face. "I know nothing about your life in Ixia," he said.

"That was entirely your choice."

"I don't think I could stand the extra guilt." Leif turned his face away, staring at the wall.

"You shouldn't feel any guilt now that you know I was kidnapped. There was nothing you could do," I said, but he refused to meet my questioning gaze.

"Isn't she your sister?" Tula asked into the silence. She wrinkled her nose, squinting in confusion.

"It's a long complicated story," I said.

Tula settled her head on the pillow, and then squirmed around under the covers as though she were seeking a more comfortable position. "We have plenty of time."

"We have no time," Irys said from the doorway. "Leif, are you ready?"

"Yes."

Irys took a step inside the room. "Then go help Cahil with the horses."

"But I was going to—"

"Explain what is going on," I demanded, sitting up.

"No time. Bain will fill you in."

Irys and Leif turned to leave.

Fury bloomed in my chest. Without thought, I pulled power and directed it toward them. "Stop."

They both froze in place until I released them. I slumped in bed. My outburst had sapped what little strength I had.

Irys returned to my bedside. An odd mixture of anger and admiration on her face. "Feeling better?"

"No."

"Leif, go," Irys said. "I'll catch up in a moment."

He shot me a rueful glance on his way out. Leif's way of saying goodbye, I guessed.

Irys perched on the edge of my bed and pushed me back onto the pillow. "You'll never get better if you keep using magic."

"I'm sorry. I just can't stand being so—"

"Helpless." A wry smile bent Irys's mouth. "It's your own fault. At least, that's what Roze keeps telling me. She wants me to assign you to a season of kitchen duty as punishment for rescuing Tula."

"She should be rewarded, not punished," Tula said.

Irys held her hand up. "Advice I won't be taking. In fact, I believe that your current situation is bad enough that you'll think twice next time you're tempted to use more magic than you can handle. And being stuck here while Cahil, Leif and I travel to the Avibian Plains to visit the Sandseed Clan is sufficient punishment."

"What happened?" I asked.

Irys softened her voice, her words just louder than a whisper. "Last night Leif and I asked Bavol, the Zaltana's Councilman about the Curare. It did come from your parents. They made a large batch and had it delivered to the Sandseed Clan."

My heart skipped a beat. "Why?"

"According to Bavol, Esau had read about a substance that paralyzes muscles in a history book about the nomadic tribes of the Avibian Plains. So, Esau traveled to the Sandseed Clan and found a healer named Gede who knew a little about this substance. In the Sandseed Clan, information is orally passed down from one healer to the next, and sometimes knowledge is lost. Esau and Gede searched the jungle for the Curare vine and, once found, they had Perl help them extract the drug. It's a time-consuming process so Gede returned to the plains, and Esau promised to send him some Curare as a gift for helping him." Irys stood. "So, now we are going to find out what Gede did with his Curare since Councilor Harun Sandseed didn't know."

"I must come!" I struggled to sit up, but my arm refused to hold my weight.

Irys watched me impassively. When I stopped, she asked, "Why?"

"Because I know the killer. I've seen him in Tula's mind. He might be with the clan."

She shook her head. "We have Dax's drawing and Leif caught a glimpse of the man when he helped you connect your mind to Tula's." Irys reached out and smoothed my hair from my face. Her hand felt cool against my hot skin. "Besides, you're not strong enough. Stay. Rest. Grow strong again. I have a great deal to teach you when I return." She hesitated, then leaned over and kissed me on the forehead.

My protests froze on my lips. My reason for being at the Keep was to learn, and already I felt as if I had gone off course, but visiting the Sandseeds could be an educational experience. Why wasn't anything simple?

Irys reached the door when I remembered to ask her about the Ixian delegation.

Pausing at the threshold, she said, "The Council has agreed

to a meeting. The messenger left this morning to deliver our reply to Ixia."

She shut the door, leaving me to ponder all that she had told me.

"Ixia," Tula said with wonder. "Do you think Valek will escape the vines and come with the delegation?"

"Tula, that was a nightmare."

"But it seemed so real," she insisted.

"Bad dreams are ghosts of our fears and worries, haunting us while we sleep. I doubt Valek is in trouble."

My thoughts, though, lingered on the image of Valek trapped. It had seemed real. I gritted my teeth in frustration and impatience. Irys had been right, lying here unable to do anything was far worse than scrubbing the kitchen.

Taking some deep breaths, I calmed my mind, cleansing out my worries and irritation. I focused on my last night with Valek in Ixia. A cherished memory.

I must have drifted off to sleep because I felt Valek's presence. A strong cloud of energy surrounded me.

You need help, love? he asked in my dream.

I need you. I need love. I need energy. I need you.

His regret pulsed in my heart. *I can't come. You already have my love. But I can give you my strength.*

No! You'll be helpless for days! The image of Valek tangled in vines leaped into my mind.

I'll be fine. The power twins are with me. They'll protect me. Valek showed me an image of Ari and Janco, my friends in Ixia, guarding his tent. They camped in the Snake Forest, participating in a military exercise.

Before I could stop him, power washed over me, soaking into my body.

Good luck, love.

"Valek," I yelled out loud. He disappeared.

"What was that?" Tula asked.

"A dream." But I felt rejuvenated. I stood on my now steady legs, marveling.

Tula stared. "It wasn't a dream. I saw a light and—"

I made a sudden decision and bolted for the door. "I have to go."

"Where?" Tula demanded.

"To catch up with Irys."

19

T H E   T W O   M E N   G U A R D I N G   our room jumped in surprise when I sprinted out the door. I raced toward the stable before my mind could slow me down with logic, but I arrived too late. The yard was empty.

Kiki poked her head out of her stall. *Lavender Lady better?*

Yes, much better. I stroked her nose. *I missed the others. When did they leave?*

Some chews of hay. We catch up.

I studied Kiki's blue eyes. She presented an interesting idea. Even if I had caught up to Irys before they left, there was no guarantee that she would have let me go with them to the Avibian Plains.

Kiki pawed the ground with impatience. *Go.*

I thought fast. Perhaps it would be better if I followed Irys and Leif to the plains, revealing myself only when we traveled too far for her to send me back to the Keep.

I need supplies, I told Kiki. On the way to my room, I made a mental list of everything I would need. My backpack and bow, my switchblade, my cloak, some clothes and food. Money perhaps.

After gathering what I could from my room, I locked the door, turned to go and bumped into Dax.

"Look who's vertical," he said. A wide smile spread across his lips. "I don't know why I'm surprised. After all, you are a living legend."

Shaking my head, I said, "Dax, I don't have time to exchange barbs with you."

"Why?"

I paused, realizing that taking off on my own would be yet another black mark against me. An Ixian decision. But getting information from the Sandseeds was too important for me to worry about the consequences. I told Dax about my plans. "Can you tell Second Magician where I've gone? I don't want Bain combing the Keep for me."

"You're on the fast path to expulsion," Dax warned. "I've lost count of points against you." He paused, considering. "Doesn't matter now. How long of a head start do you want?"

I glanced at the sky. Midafternoon. "Till dark." The timing still left Bain a slight chance to send someone to retrieve me, but I hoped he would wait until the morning.

"Done. I'd wish you good luck, but I don't think it would help."

"Why not?"

"My lady, you make your own luck." Then he shooed me away. "Go."

I hurried to the kitchen and grabbed enough bread, cheese and dried meat to last for ten days. Captain Marrok had said the Avibian Plains were vast and it took ten days to cross them. If the Sandseed Clan lived on the far side, I would have enough food to reach them, and I hoped I could buy more for the return trip.

With my thoughts focused on supplies, I raced toward the barn. As I approached, Kiki snorted in agitation, and I opened my mind to her.

Bad smell, she warned.

I spun in time to see Goel rush me. Before I could react, the point of his sword stopped mere inches from my stomach.

"Going somewhere?" he asked.

"What are you doing here?"

"Little birdie told me you flew the coop. It wasn't hard to track you."

The guards outside Tula's room must have alerted Goel. I sighed. My distraction while collecting supplies had made me an easy target.

"Okay, Goel. Let's make this quick." I took a step back and reached for my bow, but Goel moved forward. The point of his sword cut through my shirt and pricked my skin just as my hands found the smooth wood of my staff.

"Freeze!" he shouted.

I huffed more in annoyance than fear. I didn't have time for this. "Too scared for a fair fight? Ow!" The sword's tip jabbed into my stomach.

"Drop your bow to the ground. Slowly," he ordered.

He nudged his sword tip deeper when I hesitated. In slow motion, I pulled my bow from its strap, keeping Goel's attention on me because out of the corner of my eye I saw Kiki open the latch on her stall's door with her teeth.

The door thumped open. Goel turned his head at the noise. Kiki spun, aimed her hind legs. I scurried back a few paces.

Not too hard, I told her.

Bad man. She kicked him.

Goel flew through the air and slammed against the pasture's wooden fence. Then he crumpled in a heap. When he didn't move, I approached and felt for a pulse. Still alive. I had mixed feelings about his survival. Would he ever give up or would he keep coming after me until he had caught me or until I had killed him?

Kiki interrupted my thoughts. *Go.*

I retrieved her tack and began to saddle her. As I tightened the girth straps around her chest, I asked, *Could you always open your door?*

Yes. Fence, too.

Why don't you?

Hay sweet. Water fresh. Peppermints.

I laughed and made sure to take some mints from Cahil's supply, packing them into my bag. I hooked five feed bags and water bags for her onto the saddle along with my own food and water skins.

Too heavy? I asked.

She looked at me with scorn. *No. Leave now. Topaz scent going.*

I mounted. We left the Magician's Keep and headed through the Citadel. Kiki stepped with care as she walked along the crowded streets of the market. I spotted Fisk, my beggar boy, carrying a huge package for a lady. He smiled and tried to wave. His clean black hair shone in the sun and the hollow smudges under his eyes were gone. A beggar no longer. Fisk found a job.

When we passed under the massive marble arches that marked the gateway of the Citadel, Kiki picked up her pace, breaking into a gallop. The view sped past as we traveled along the main valley road that led from the Citadel to the forest.

Harvest activity buzzed in the fields to our right. On the left, the Avibian Plains flowed out to the horizon. The colors of the tall grasses had transformed from the greens and blues of the hot season into reds, yellows and oranges as though someone had taken a giant paintbrush and swabbed large bands of color across the landscape.

The plains appeared deserted, and I saw no signs of wildlife. Only the colors rippled in the wind. When Kiki turned to enter the plains, I spotted a faint trail cutting through the grass.

The long blades rubbed against my legs and Kiki's stomach. Kiki relaxed her pace. I touched her mind. We were on the right path, and the strong scent of horses filled her nose. She picked out each one by their smell. *Silk. Topaz. Rusalka.*

Rusalka?

Sad Man's.

Confused at first, it took me a moment to realize Sad Man was Kiki's name for Leif. From what I had gathered from Kiki, when a horse meets someone for the first time their immediate impression becomes that person's horse name and they relayed it to other horses. Apparently it doesn't change. To the horses, it made sense. They gave us names just like we had given them names.

Other horses? I asked.

No.

Other men?

No.

Surprised that Cahil hadn't taken some of his men with him, I wondered why. Cahil had skirted the plains on our trip to the Citadel, afraid of the Sandseeds even when traveling with twelve men. I guess he felt safer having a Master Magician accompany him. Either that, or Irys had insisted he leave his watchdogs at the Keep.

As we advanced farther into the plains, I realized that the surrounding grassland hid many things. Despite appearing flat, the terrain rolled like a messy blanket. I looked back the way we had come and couldn't see the farmland. Clusters of gray rocks peppered the plains, an occasional tree rose up from the grass, and I glimpsed field mice and small animals darting away from Kiki's hooves.

We passed a strange crimson-colored rock formation. White veined the single stone, whose top tier loomed above my head. The thick squarish profile of the structure reminded me of something. I scanned my memory and realized the rock resembled a human heart. The fact that I had recalled my lessons surprised me. Biology at Brazell's orphanage had been my least favorite subject. The teacher had delighted in making his students sick to their stomachs.

When the light over the plains began to fade and the air chilled, the thought of spending a night in such an exposed place made me uneasy.

Catch up? Kiki asked.

Are we close?

The pungent smell of horses mixed with a thin scent of smoke. Through Kiki's eyes, I could see a distant fire.

They stop.

I weighed my options. A night alone or the possibility of facing Irys's anger if I joined her. Not used to sitting in the saddle for more than an hour, my legs and back ached. I needed a break. Kiki, though, could travel much longer. Pulling power, I projected my awareness, feeling for the overall mood of the campsite.

Cahil gripped the handle of his sword; the wide-open sky alarmed him. Leif lounged on the ground almost asleep. Irys—

Yelena! Her outrage seared my mind.

Decision made. Before she could demand an explanation, I showed her what had happened between Valek and me.

Impossible.

The word triggered a memory. *You said the same thing when I reached out to Valek to help me against Roze's mental probing. Perhaps there is something connecting us that you haven't encountered?*

Perhaps, she conceded. *Come, join us. It's too late to send you home. And you can't go back to the Keep without me to help you against Roze's wrath.*

With that sobering thought, I told Kiki to find the campsite. She felt glad, though, when we reached Topaz. He grazed with the other horses near the camp.

I removed Kiki's tack, rubbed her down and made sure she had enough food and water. Reluctance and sore muscles made my movements slow.

When I finally joined Irys in the small clearing where they had stopped for the night, she only asked me if I needed dinner. I glanced at the others. Leif stirred a pot of soup cooking over the flames. He wore a neutral expression. Cahil's hand now hovered near his sword handle; he seemed more relaxed about the night sky. He grinned when he met my gaze. He was either glad about my arrival, or was anticipating the entertainment from the reprimand I was certain to receive from Irys.

Instead, Irys lectured Cahil and me on the proper way to interact with the Sandseed Clan members.

"Respect of the elders is a must," she said. "All requests are to be made to the elders, but only after they invite us to speak.

They don't trust outsiders and will watch for any sign of disregard or any indication that you are spying on them. So don't ask questions unless given permission and don't stare."

"Why would we stare?" I asked.

"They don't like to wear clothes. Some members will dress when outsiders are visiting, but others won't." Irys smiled ruefully. "Also they have a few powerful magicians. They aren't Keep trained, they teach their own. Although a few of their younger magicians have come to the Keep, seeking to enhance their knowledge. Kangom was one of these, but he didn't stay at the Keep for long." Irys frowned.

Unfortunately, I knew where he had gone from there. He changed his name to Mogkan and started kidnapping children, smuggling them into Ixia.

Before Cahil could voice his questions about Mogkan, I asked Irys, "What about the Sandseed magicians that stay with the clan?"

"They call them Story Weavers," Irys explained. "They hold the clan's history. The Sandseeds believe their history is a living entity, like an invisible presence that surrounds them. Since the clan's story is always evolving, the Story Weavers guide the clan."

"How do they guide them?" Cahil asked with concern.

"They mediate disputes, help in decision making, they show the clan members their past and aid them in avoiding the same mistakes. Very similar to what the Master Magicians do for the people of Sitia."

"They soothe a troubled heart," Leif said, staring into the flames. "Or so they claim." Then he stood abruptly. "The soup's done. Who's hungry?"

We ate in silence. After we arranged sleeping areas for the

evening, Irys informed us that we would be on the road for one more night before we reached the clan's dwellings.

Cahil wanted to make a night watch schedule. "I'll take the first shift," he offered.

Irys just looked at him.

"It makes sense," he said in his defense.

"Cahil, there is nothing to fear. And if trouble heads in our direction, I will wake you long before it arrives," Irys said.

I hid my smile as I watched Cahil pout. I wrapped my cloak around me against the cold night air and lay on the soft sandy ground of the clearing. I checked with Kiki. *Everything okay?*

Grass sweet. Crunchy.

Bad smells?

No. Nice air. Home.

I remembered now that Kiki had been bred by the Sandseeds. *Nice to be home?* I thought of Valek in the Snake Forest, and hoped he had regained some of his strength.

Yes. Nicer with Lavender Lady. Peppermints? Hopeful.

In the morning, I promised.

I gazed up at the night sky, watching the stars dance while waiting for sleep. Kiki's view of life sounded right. Good food, fresh water, an occasional sweet and someone to care for. That's what everyone should have. A simplistic and unrealistic view I knew, but it soothed me.

My thoughts, though, drifted into strange dreams. I ran through the plains, searching for Kiki. The knee-high grass grew until it reached above my head and impeded my forward motion. I pushed through the sharp blades, trying and failing to find a way out. My foot snagged on something and I fell. When I rolled over, the grass transformed into a field of snakes and they began to wrap around my body. I struggled until they immobilized me.

"You belong with us," a snake hissed in my ear.

I jerked awake in the weak light of dawn. My ear tingled from the dream snake, and I shivered in the cold morning air, trying to shake off the horror of my nightmare.

Irys and the others milled around the small fire. We ate a breakfast of bread and cheese and saddled our horses. My muscles had stiffened during the night, and they protested each movement. By midmorning, the sun warmed the land and I shed my cloak, stuffing it into my backpack.

As we traveled, the soft ground turned into hard stone and the grasses thinned. Small sandstone outcroppings sprinkled the area. By lunch the outcroppings rose higher than our heads, and I felt as if we rode inside a canyon.

During a brief stop, I noticed streaks of red on a pair of sandstone pillars some distance away. "Tula's attacker had something red under his fingernails," I told the others. "Could it be from here?"

"It's possible," Irys agreed.

"We should get a sample," Leif said. He rummaged in his pack until he found a short glass vial.

"We need to keep going." Irys squinted at the sun. "I want to find a campsite before dark."

"Go. I'll catch up," Leif said.

"Yelena, help him, make sure it's the color you remember," Irys ordered, then turned to Cahil before he could voice the objections behind his frown. "Cahil, you stay with me. If Yelena can find us hours after we left the Citadel, she'll have no problem catching up today."

Irys and a still scowling Cahil mounted their horses and

headed toward the sun, while Leif and I found a path to the pillars. They were farther away than I had thought. Then, it took us longer than we had anticipated to collect a sample. The streaks turned out to be a layer of red clay. The exposed clay had hardened, and we chipped through it to reach the softer material underneath. We placed both the hard chips and soft clay into the vial.

By the time we returned to our starting point, the sun hovered halfway to the horizon. Kiki found Topaz's trail, and we nudged the horses into a run.

I felt unconcerned when the sky began to darken. Topaz's pungent scent filled Kiki's sensitive nose, which meant we were getting close. But when full dark descended and I could not see a fire, I began to worry. When the moon rose, I halted Kiki.

"Are we lost?" Leif asked. He had been following me without comment since we had discovered the trail. I could just make out his annoyed frown in the faint moonlight.

"No. Kiki says Topaz's scent is strong. Perhaps they decided to travel longer?"

"Can you reach Irys?" Leif asked.

"Oh, snake spit! I forgot!" I took a deep breath and gathered a string of power, chastising myself for failing to remember my magic again. I wondered when using magic would become instinctive.

I felt a surprising rush of power. The source seemed concentrated in this area. Projecting my awareness, I searched the surrounding land. Nothing.

Alarmed, I extended my reach, seeking further. Then I realized that my mind hadn't even touched field mice or any other creatures. I stopped in frustration. If I could connect to

Valek in the Snake Forest, I should be able to find Irys; after all, her horse had just passed this way.

Topaz smell always strong, Kiki agreed.

Always?

Yes.

"Well?" Leif asked with impatience.

"Something's wrong. I can't find Irys." I told him what Kiki had just said.

"But that's good, right?"

"There should have been a gradual buildup of scent from faint to sharp. Instead, it's been the same since we found their trail." I turned in a circle; magic pulsed in the air all around us. "Someone is trying to trick us."

"Finally!" A deep voice barked from the darkness.

Kiki and Rusalka reared in surprise, but a soothing strand of magic calmed them. I pulled my bow and scanned the few faint shapes I could see in the weak light.

"Not very quick, are you?" the voice taunted from my left.

I spun Kiki around in time to see a man coalesce out of a blue ray of moonlight. Tall enough to meet my gaze without having to look up, the naked man's skin was indigo and hairless. His bald head gleamed with sweat and I could see strength coiled in his powerful muscles. But his round face held amusement, and I sensed no immediate threat from him. Pure magical energy emanated from him, so I thought he might be influencing my emotions.

I drew my bow. "Who are you and what do you want?" I demanded.

Bright white teeth flashed as he smiled. "I am your Story Weaver."

20

I GLANCED AT LEIF; his alarmed expression had turned to fear. Color leaked from his face as he looked from me to the large indigo-colored man. The man's painted skin and lack of clothes made me think of Tula's attacker, but his body was more muscular and scars crisscrossed his arms and legs. But no tattoos.

With my mental barrier in place, I held my bow ready, but the man stood relaxed. I would be relaxed, too, if I had access to the amount of magical power within his control. He had no need to move; he could kill us with a word. Which begged the question, why was he here?

"What do you want?" I asked.

"Go away," Leif said to the man, "you cause only trouble."

"Your stories have tangled and knotted together," Story Weaver said. "I am here as a guide to show you both how to untangle them."

"Banish him," Leif told me. "He has to obey you."

"He does?" That seemed rather easy.

"If you wish me to leave, I will go. But you and your brother will not be allowed to enter our village. His twisted soul causes us pain and you are linked to him."

I stared at the Story Weaver in confusion; his words didn't make sense. Friend or foe?

"You said you were here to guide. Guide us where?"

"Banish him now!" Leif yelled. "He will deceive you. He's probably in league with Tula's kidnapper and is trying to delay us."

"Your fear remains strong," Story Weaver said to Leif. "You are not ready to face your story, preferring instead to surround yourself with knots. Some day, they will strangle you. Your choice was to decline our help, but your tangles threaten to squeeze the life out of your sister. This must be corrected." Extending his hand to me, he said, "You are ready. Leave Kiki and come with me."

"Where?"

"To see your story."

"How? Why?"

Story Weaver refused to answer. He radiated calm patience as if he could stand there with his arm extended all night, waiting.

Kiki looked back at me. *Go with Moon Man,* she urged. *Hungry. Tired. Want Topaz.*

Smell? Bad? I asked.

Hard road, but Lavender Lady strong. Go.

I returned my bow to its holder and dismounted.

"Yelena, no!" Leif cried. He clutched Rusalka's reins tight to his chest.

I paused in shock. "That's the first time you've called me by my name. *Now* you care what happens to me? Sorry, it's too late in the game for that to work. Frankly, I don't want to deal with your troubles. I have enough of my own. And we have to find Tula's attacker before he takes another, so it's imperative that we meet with the clan elders. If this is what I need to do, then so be it." I shrugged. "Besides, Kiki told me to go."

"And you would listen to a horse instead of your brother?"

"Until now *my brother* has refused to acknowledge any connection with me since I have arrived in Sitia. I trust Kiki."

Leif snorted in exasperation. "You spent your life in Ixia. You know nothing of these Sandseeds."

"I learned who to trust."

"A horse. You're a fool." He shook his head.

There was no sense telling him about how I had trusted an assassin, a magician who had tried to kill me twice and two soldiers who had jumped me in the Snake Forest. All four now dear to my heart.

"When will I be back?" I asked Story Weaver.

"With the sun's first ray."

I unsaddled Kiki and gave her a quick rubdown while she ate some oats. Then I exchanged her feed bag for water. She drained it, and I placed the empty sacks near her tack.

Apprehension about this strange trip began to crawl along my stomach. *Wait for me?* I asked Kiki.

She snorted and whacked me with her tail, moving away to search for some sweet grass to graze on. Ask a dull-witted question.

I met Leif's stony gaze for a moment, then walked over to Story Weaver. He hadn't moved. Kiki had called him Moon Man. Before I took his hand, I asked, "What's your name?"

"Moon Man will do."

I studied his colored skin. "Why indigo?"

A slow grin spread over his lips. "A cooling color to help soothe the fire between you and your brother." Then, a sheepish look. "It is my favorite."

I laid my hand in his. His palm felt like velvet. His warmth soaked into my bones and flowed up my arm. Magic shimmered and the world around us melted. I began to uncoil, feeling my body loosen and elongate as if it transformed into a string. The individual strands that entwined within my life's story began to separate and diverge so I could see the many events that had formed my life.

Some of my history was familiar; I sought the pleasant memories, watching them as if I stood outside a window.

This is why you need me, Moon Man's voice floated through the scene before my eyes. *You would stay here. My job is to guide you to the proper thread.*

Memories blurred around me. I closed my eyes as the visions swirled. When the air settled once more, I opened them.

I sat in the middle of a living area. Couches constructed of lianas and a glass-topped table surrounded me. A young boy about eight or nine years old reclined across from me on the wooden floor. He wore a pair of green short pants. With his hands behind his head and his elbows jutting out, he stared at the leaf-covered ceiling. About ten bone dice littered the ground between us.

"I'm bored," the boy said.

The appropriate response popped into my mind. "How about Onesies? Or Two Through the Skull?" I scooped up the dice and shook them.

"Baby games," he said. "Let's go down to the jungle floor and explore!" Leif jumped to his feet.

"I don't know. How about we go swinging with Nutty?"

"If you want to play silly baby games with Nutty, go ahead. I'm going to explore and probably make a big discovery. Maybe I'll find the cure to the rotting disease. I'll be famous. They'll probably elect me the next clan leader."

Not wanting to miss any important discoveries and ensuing fame, I agreed to go with him. With a quick call to our mother, we left our tree dwelling and climbed down the Palm ladder into the cooler air of the jungle's floor. The soft ground felt spongy under my bare feet.

I followed Leif through the jungle, marveling at the youthful energy pumping through my six-year-old body. A part of me knew the truth, that I was older and not really here, that this was a vision. Yet I found I didn't care, and I cartwheeled down the jungle path just for fun.

"This is serious," Leif scolded. "We're explorers. We need to collect samples. You gather some leaves while I search for flower petals."

When he turned his back, I stuck my tongue out at him, but I grabbed some tree leaves all the same. A quick movement among the branches distracted me. I froze, scanning the area. Clinging to a sapling hung a young black-and-white valmur. Brown eyes bulged from its small face, peering at me.

I smiled and whistled at the creature. It scampered a bit higher, then turned its gaze back to mine and flicked its long tail. The animal wanted to play. I followed, copying its movements through the jungle. We climbed vines, swung and dodged around the big buttress roots of a Rosewood Tree.

I stopped when I heard a distant voice. Straining to listen, I heard Leif calling for me. I would have ignored him, playing was more fun than collecting leaves, but I thought he said something about a Ylang-Ylang Tree. Mother would bake us star fruit pies if we brought her Ylang-Ylang Flowers for her perfumes.

"Coming," I shouted, jumping down to the jungle floor. When I turned to wave goodbye to the little valmur, it startled and dashed high up into the Rosewood Tree. A feeling of unease settled over me like a mist. I searched the nearby branches, looking for necklace snakes—the main predator of valmurs. With my gaze focused on the tree canopy, I almost tripped over a man.

I jumped back in surprise. He sat on the ground with his right leg splayed out and the other tucked in close. His hands gripped his left ankle. Torn and stained with dirt and sweat, his clothing hung in tatters. Leaves and tendrils clung to his black hair.

The adult part of my mind screamed. Mogkan! Run! But my young self remained unafraid.

"Thank fate!" Mogkan cried as relief smoothed the worry from his face. "I'm lost. I think I broke my ankle. Can you help?"

I nodded. "I'll go get my brother—"

"Wait. Just help me up first."

"Why?"

"To see if I can walk. If my ankle is really broken, you'll have to get more help."

My adult consciousness knew he lied, but I couldn't prevent my child self from stepping closer. I reached out a hand; he grasped it then yanked me down. In one swift motion he grabbed me and muffled my cry with a damp cloth. He pressed it tight against my mouth, forcing a sweet aroma into my nose.

The jungle spun around me. Stay awake! Stay awake! I yelled to my body, but the blackness crept closer.

Struggling in Mogkan's arms, my adult self knew what would happen next. Mogkan would take me to Ixia, and I would be raised in the orphanage of Reyad's father, General Brazell, so when I reached maturity they could try to take the magic out of me as if milking a cow. All so Mogkan could increase his magical powers and help Brazell take over control of Commander Ambrose and Ixia. Even knowing the ending didn't make me feel any better about my abduction.

Leif's face in the bushes was the last thing my young self saw before the darkness claimed me. And that was truly horrifying.

The vision faded. I stood with Moon Man on a dark plain. "Did Leif really see what happened to me?" I asked Story Weaver.

"Yes."

"Why didn't he tell our parents?" They could have sent a rescue party, or tried to get me back. Better for them to know their child's fate than to guess and wonder for years.

As I thought about Leif, my resentment grew. He had robbed me of the chance to have a childhood, to have a bedroom and loving parents, to learn about the jungle with my father and distill perfumes with my mother, to swing through the trees with Nutty and to play games instead of memorizing Ixia's Code of Behavior.

"Why?" I demanded.

"That is a question you must ask him."

I shook my head. "He must have hated me. He was glad to see me kidnapped. That explains his anger when I returned to Sitia."

Moon Man said, "Hate and anger are some of the emotions that strangle your brother, but not all. The easy answer is never the right answer. You must untangle your brother before he chokes himself."

I thought about Leif. He had helped me with Tula, but he could have lied when he told me why, just like he had lied to our parents for fourteen years. My interactions with him since my return to Sitia had almost all been unpleasant. And the single memory I now owned of Leif before my time in Ixia made my blood boil with fury. Perhaps if I had more memories of my childhood.

"Why can't I remember my life before Mogkan kidnapped me?" I asked.

"Mogkan used magic to suppress all your memories, so you would believe him and stay in the orphanage."

That made sense. If I had remembered a family, I would have tried to run away.

"Do you want those memories back?" he asked.

"Yes!"

"Promise you will help your brother and I will unlock them."

I considered his offer. "How do I help him?"

"You will find a way."

"Cryptic, aren't we?"

He smiled. "The fun part of my job."

"What if I refuse to help him?"

"That is your decision."

I huffed in frustration. "Why do you care?"

"He sought relief from his pain in the Avibian Plains. He tried to kill himself. His need for help drew me to him. I offered my services, but fear twisted his heart and he refused. His pain reaches me still. A job unfinished. A soul lost. While there is time left, I will do what I can even if I have to bargain with a Soulfinder."

21

"SOULFINDER?" FEAR BRUSHED up my spine. "Why do I keep hearing that name?" I asked Story Weaver. We still stood on the featureless expanse. Not unlike the surface of a frozen pond.

"Because you are one," he said in a plain, matter-of-fact tone.

"No," I protested, remembering the loathing and horror that had crossed Hayes's face when he had first mentioned that title to me. He had talked about waking the dead.

"I will show you."

The smooth plain under our feet turned transparent and, through it, I saw my Ixian friend, Janco. His pale face grimaced in pain as his blood gushed from the sword lodged in his stomach. The scene switched to Commander Ambrose lying motionless on a bed; his eyes vacant. Then I saw my own face as I stood over an unconscious General Brazell. My green eyes took on a sudden intensity as if I'd had an epiphany. A brief image of Fisk, the beggar boy, carrying packages and smiling.

Then a picture of Tula, lying broken on her bed. The images faded as the ground returned.

"You have found five souls already," Moon Man said.

"But they weren't—"

"Dead?"

I nodded.

"Do you know what a Soulfinder is?" he asked.

"They wake the dead?" When he raised an eyebrow without commenting, I said, "No, I don't."

"You need to learn."

"And telling me would be too easy. Right? Takes all the fun out of being a mysterious Story Weaver."

He grinned. "What about my bargain? Childhood memories for your help with Leif."

Just hearing his name sent waves of anger through my body. My reasons for coming to Sitia had been so simple. First for survival, fleeing the Commander's order of execution. Second had been to learn how to use my magic and meet my family. Perhaps along the way I might develop a kinship with this southern world. Or perhaps not.

My plans had seemed straightforward, then my road kept dipping and turning and I kept getting caught in its traps. Now I felt mired in mud in the middle of nowhere. Lost.

"Your path is clear," said Moon Man. "You need to find it."

And the best way to find something you had lost was to return to the last place you remembered having it. In my case, I needed to start at the very beginning.

"I promise to try to help Leif," I said.

Smells and softness flooded my mind as memories of my childhood came to life. Apple Berry perfume mixed with the musky scent of earth. Laughter and the pure joy of swinging through the air followed an argument with Leif over the last mango. Playing hide-and-seek with Leif and Nutty, crouching on branches to ambush Nutty's brothers during a mock battle. The sharp sting of hazelnuts on my bare arms as her brothers discovered our hiding spot, launching an attack. The slap of mud as our clan leader dug a grave for my grandfather. The sound of my mother's soothing voice as she sang me a lullaby. The lessons with Esau on different species of leaves and their medicinal properties.

All the happiness, sadness, pain, fear and thrills of childhood came rushing back. I knew some would fade with time, but others would stay with me forever.

"Thank you," I said.

Story Weaver inclined his head. He held out a hand and I grasped it. The dark plain faded and shapes grew from the ground. Colors returned as the sun's first light crested the horizon.

I blinked, trying to orient myself. The clearing where I had left Kiki and Leif had changed. Large circular tents ringed a huge fire pit. Brown animal shapes had been painted on the white canvas of the tents. Dark-skinned people milled about the roaring fire. Some cooked while others tended children. Some wore clothes while others wore nothing. The clothes were all made of white cotton. The women wore either sleeveless dresses that reached to their knees or a tunic and short pants like the men.

Near the fire, Irys and Cahil sat cross-legged with two older men and a woman. They were intent on their discussion and didn't see me. I couldn't spot Leif or his horse, but Kiki stood next to one of the tents. A woman wearing short pants groomed her. Her brown hair bobbed to her neck.

I jumped when I realized Moon Man no longer stood beside me. In fact, I couldn't see him anywhere in the small village. Perhaps he'd gone into one of the tents.

Not wanting to interrupt Irys, I checked on Kiki. She whickered at me in greeting. The woman stopped brushing the dust off her coat. She studied me in silence.

Who's this? I asked Kiki.

Mother.

"Is this your horse?" the woman asked. The inflection in her voice rose and fell with each word, and there was a slight pause between them.

I reviewed Irys's lecture about the Sandseeds from the night before. The woman had spoken first so I guessed it would be all right to answer her. "I'm hers."

She snorted a short laugh through her nose. "I raised her, taught her and sent her on her journey. It's a pleasure to see her again." She kicked at her saddle on the ground. "She doesn't need this. She will float under you like a gust of wind."

"That's for me." And for our supplies.

Another huff of amusement. She finished brushing her. Kiki turned her blue eyes toward her and understanding flashed on the woman's face. She whooped and jumped up on Kiki's back.

Have fun, I told Kiki as she raced through the tall grass.

"Is that wise?" Cahil asked. He watched Kiki disappear over a hill. "What if that woman doesn't come back?"

"I don't care if she comes back or not." I shrugged, looking past Cahil. Irys and the three Sandseeds stood next to the fire. They were still in deep conversation. One of the men gestured in what appeared to be anger.

"You don't care if she steals Kiki?"

Instead of trying to educate Cahil on my relationship with Kiki, I searched his face. Tension had pulled his eyes into an intent expression. His gaze darted around the campsite as if he expected to be attacked.

"What's been going on?" I asked him, tilting my head toward Irys.

"Last night, we made camp and waited for you and Leif. *I* worried when you failed to catch up, but Irys seemed amused. Then this group of Sandseeds arrived at our site. These are the clan leaders. They travel from village to village, settling disputes, bringing news and goods. It's very convenient that they found us. I think they're hiding something."

Cahil's frown reminded me of my brother. "Where's Leif?"

Worry lined his face. "*They* said he went back to the Keep. Why would he do that?"

Because he, too, felt afraid. But, I said, "He probably wanted to get the red soil samples to Bain."

Cahil appeared unconvinced. Before I could ask more questions, Irys ended her conversation and moved to join us.

"They're upset," she said.

"Why?" I asked.

"They think we're accusing them of giving the Curare to Tula's attacker. And Cahil's attempts to recruit them to his cause have inflamed them." Irys scowled at Cahil. "I thought you wanted to come along so you could see another part of our culture. Your selfish obsession to raise an army has jeopardized our mission."

Cahil didn't look remorseful. "I wouldn't have to raise an army if the Council supported me. You—"

"Silence!" Irys sliced her hand through the air and I felt a brush of magic.

Bright red blotches grew on Cahil's cheeks as he tried to speak.

"Despite all my diplomatic training, I can't get them to tell me anything. Cahil has offended them. They will now talk only to you, Yelena."

"Should we plan our escape route now?" I asked.

She laughed. "We'll push Cahil into their path to slow them down."

Cahil shot Irys a venomous glare.

"You have a slight advantage, Yelena," she said. "I might be a Master Magician and member of the Council, but you're a blood relative. In their eyes, a relative is more important than a Master." Irys shook her head in frustration.

"Relative?" I asked.

"About five hundred years ago a group of Sandseeds decided to move into the jungle. The Sandseeds are wanderers by nature, and there have been many groups that have broken from the main clan to find their own way. Most don't stay in communication with the main clan, but some, like the Zaltanas, do. Just try and discover some information without implying that these Sandseeds are involved. Choose your words carefully."

Irys must have read the skepticism on my face because she added, "Consider it your first lesson in diplomacy."

"Seeing how well you did with them, I'm surprised that I don't feel more confident."

"Avoid sarcasm."

"How about coming with me? So when I start to say something stupid you can wave your hand and silence me, too."

A sardonic smile flashed on her face. "I've been asked to leave and to 'take that annoying puppy' with me. You're on your own. I won't be able to reach your mind through this bubble of Sandseed magic, so we'll meet you at the edge of the Avibian Plains next to Blood Rock."

Irys formed an image in my mind of that white-veined structure that Kiki and I had passed two days ago.

Cahil waved his arms and tapped his throat. Irys sighed again. "Only if you promise not to talk about armies until we're back at the Citadel."

He nodded.

"Yelena, I'll let you release his voice," she said.

Another lesson. I calmed the nervous thoughts about my meeting with the elders before I opened my mind to the magic. Magical energy pulsed all around me, but I saw a thin thread of power wrapped around Cahil's throat. Pulling the power to me, I unlocked his voice.

"Well done," Irys said.

Cahil's ears were still bright red, but he had the sense to speak in an even tone. "If I may point out the obvious," he said. "Leaving Yelena alone is dangerous."

"I don't have a choice," Irys said. "I could force them to tell me what they know, but the Sandseeds would consider that an act of war. Then you'll never get your army, Cahil; because we'll be too busy trying to prevent the Sandseeds from taking a blood vengeance from everyone in Sitia." She turned to me. "Yelena, good luck. We'll have a lot to discuss when you catch up with us. Cahil, go saddle Topaz." Irys strode away, whistling for her horse.

A stubborn expression gripped Cahil's face, and he crossed his arms over his chest. "I should stay. Someone needs to watch your back. Basic military tactics. Always have a partner."

"Cahil, there is so much magic in the air around here that

the Sandseeds could close my windpipe and there isn't a damn thing you or I could do about it."

"Then come with us."

"What about Tula or the killer's next victim? I have to try."

"But the risk—"

"Living is a risk," I snapped at him. "Every decision, every interaction, every step, every time you get out of bed in the morning, you take a risk. To survive is to know you're taking that risk and to not get out of bed clutching illusions of safety."

"Your view of life doesn't sound comforting."

"It's not supposed to. That's the whole point." Before Cahil could launch into a discussion on philosophy, I tried to shoo him away. "Get going before Irys loses her patience with you again." I swept my hand through the air as Irys had done.

He grabbed my wrist. "No, you don't!" He held my hand for a moment. "If the Sandseeds hurt you, they'll see some of my blood vengeance. Be careful."

I pulled my hand away. "Always."

All those worried thoughts about offending the Sandseeds came flooding back as I watched Irys and Cahil ride away. I reviewed Irys's last-minute instructions about dealing with the clan elders. I glanced around, wondering what I should do.

The Sandseeds worked in their temporary village with a calm efficiency. My hunger flared when I caught a whiff of roasting meat, and I realized I hadn't eaten since we had stopped for lunch the day before. I laid my pack next to Kiki's saddle and rummaged for something to eat, but sitting down proved to be a bad decision as exhaustion pulled at my body. I let my new memories of childhood circle in my mind, and I contented myself with reliving some of them. Using the saddle as a pillow, I stretched out on the grass, not bothering to spread my cloak. Strange that I felt so safe here.

But I wasn't safe from my nightmares. Hunted by a slithering mass of snakes, I scrambled through the jungle. They wrapped around my ankles, yanking me down. Unable to move, they sank fangs, dripping with Curare deep into my flesh. "Come with us," the snakes hissed.

"Cousin?" a timid voice asked.

I awoke with a loud cry. A petite woman with large eyes stepped back in alarm. Her brown hair was streaked with yellow and tied back with a leather cord. Stains lined the white fabric of her dress.

"The elders will see you now."

I peered at the sky, but sheets of clouds obscured the sun. "How long was I asleep?"

The woman smiled. "All day. Follow me please."

I looked at my bow, knowing it would be an insult to bring it, yet wanting it anyway. With reluctance, I left it on the ground and followed the woman. Questions swirled in my mind as we passed the tents, but I bit my lip to prevent myself from voicing them. Wait, wait, I thought, quelling my impatience. Unfortunately, diplomacy was a dance I needed to learn.

The woman stopped at the largest tent. The animal patterns almost covered the white fabric. She swept back a panel and gestured for me to enter. I stepped into the tent, waiting in the muted light for my eyes to adjust.

"You may approach," said a male voice from the far side of the tent.

I surveyed the interior as I crossed to the back. Maroon and tan rugs woven with intricate geometric patterns covered the floor of the round tent. I spotted some sleeping mats and colorful pillows on the left. Bigger pillows on the right surrounded a low table, and candleholders with long red tassels hung from the ceiling.

Sitting cross-legged in a row on an ebony-and-gold mat were two men and a woman. One I recognized. Moon Man smiled at me from between the man and woman. His skin was now painted yellow. Wrinkles creased the face of the other man, and the woman's hair was peppered with gray. Both wore red robes.

I halted in shock as the sudden image of my red prison robe, tattered and bloody, rose in my mind. I hadn't thought of that garment since Valek offered me the option of being executed or becoming the Commander's food taster. I had cast it aside and accepted the Ixian uniform without a backward glance. Odd that I should think of it now. Or had Story Weaver pulled those thoughts from my mind? I peered at Moon Man with suspicion.

"Sit," said the woman. She gestured to a small round rug on the floor in front of them.

I settled into the same position as my hosts.

"A Zaltana who has traveled far. You have returned to your ancestors to seek guidance," the man said. His dark eyes brimmed with knowledge and his gaze pierced my soul.

"I seek understanding," I said.

"Your journey has twisted and bent. Your journey has stained you with blood and pain and death. You must be cleansed." The man nodded to Story Weaver.

Moon Man rose. From under the mat, he pulled a scimitar. The sharp edge of the long blade gleamed in the candlelight.

22

MOON MAN ADVANCED. He rested the curved blade of the scimitar on my left shoulder with the sharp edge dangerously close to my neck.

"Are you ready to be cleansed?" he asked.

My throat tightened. "What? How?" My mouth stumbled over the words. All logic fled.

"We take the stains of blood, pain and death from you. We take your blood and cause you pain. You will atone for your misdeeds with your eventual death and be welcomed into the sky."

One word cut through the jumble of fear in my mind. Sudden clarity focused my thoughts. I stood with deliberate care, trying not to jostle the weapon, and stepped back. The blade remained poised in midair.

"I have no misdeeds to atone for. I hold no remorse for my past actions and, therefore, do not need to be cleansed." I braced for their reaction. Diplomacy be damned.

Moon Man grinned and the two elders nodded in approval. Confused I watched him replace the scimitar under the mat and settled back into his position. "That is the correct response," he said.

"What if I had agreed?"

"Then we would have sent you away with only a few cryptic remarks to puzzle over." He laughed. "I must admit I am slightly disappointed. I worked all afternoon on those remarks."

"Sit," the woman ordered. "What do you seek to understand?"

I chose my words with great care as I sat on the mat. "A beast has been preying on young women throughout Sitia. To date, he has killed ten and injured one. I want to stop him. I seek to understand who he is."

"Why come to us?" the woman asked.

"He has been using a certain substance as a weapon. I'm concerned that he might have stolen it from one of your clan members." I waited, hoping the word "stolen" would not imply guilt.

"Ah, yes, this substance," the old man said. "A blessing and a curse. A package from Esau Liana Sandseed Zaltana arrived at one of our villages near the Daviian Plateau. That village was raided soon after by the Daviian Vermin." The old man spat on the dirt floor. "Many things were stolen in that raid."

His scorn for these Vermin was obvious, but I asked anyway. "Who are these Vermin?"

The elders tightened their jaws, refusing to reply.

Frowning, Moon Man explained them to me. "They are young men and women who have rebelled against our traditions. They have broken from the clan and settled on the Plateau. The Plateau does not give up its bounty without a fight. The Vermin prefer to steal from us rather than work to grow their own food."

"Could one of them be the monster I seek?"

"Yes. They have perverted our art of magic weaving. Instead of benefiting the clan, they seek to increase their power, enriching only themselves. Most of them do not have the gift, but there are a few who are very powerful."

Moon Man's fierce expression gave me a mental image of how he would look when swinging his scimitar in battle. I held a picture of Ferde, Tula's attacker, in my mind.

"Is he one of them?" I asked. Moon Man's magic coursed through me.

Moon Man grunted, then growled deep in his throat. Looking at the elder man, he said, "They are practicing the old evil. We must stop them."

Horrified, the man replied, "We will try again to pierce their magic screen. We will find them." He stood with grace and dignity, bowed once to me, then gestured to the woman. "Come. We must make plans."

They left the tent. Moon Man and I remained. "The old evil?" I asked.

"An ancient horrible ritual of binding a victim's soul to you, then killing him. When the victim dies, his magic flows into you, increasing your strength. The red markings on that beast are part of the ritual." Moon Man's brow furrowed for a moment before his eyes widened with concern. "You said one woman was injured. Where is she now?"

"In the Magician's Keep."

"Guarded?"

"Yes. Why?"

"The one you seek will not be in the Daviian Plateau; he will be in the Keep, waiting for another chance to take her life. He can not bind another soul until she dies."

"I must go back." I jumped up from the small mat intent on leaving.

Moon Man grabbed my shoulder and turned me to face him. "Do not forget your promise."

"I won't. Tula first, then Leif."

He nodded. "May I ask another favor?"

I hesitated. At least, he didn't want a promise. "You can ask."

"When your training with Master Irys is complete, will you return to me so I may teach you the magical arts of the Sandseeds? It is part of your heritage and of your blood."

The proposition sounded appealing, but would be yet another curve in my journey. At this rate, I doubted I would even finish my training. If history served as guidance, my future tended to go in unanticipated directions. "I will try."

"Good. Now go!" He bowed to me, then shooed me from the tent.

A frenzy of activity encompassed the camp. Dismantled tents littered the ground as the clan members prepared to leave. Twilight crept closer as I searched for my pack. I found Kiki instead. She was saddled and ready to go. Her shorthaired "mother" offered her reins to me.

As I took the leather straps, she said, "Do not sit on the saddle. Crouch over it and shift your weight forward. And she will fly home for you."

"Thank you." I bowed.

She smiled. "You are well matched. I am pleased." With a final pat to Kiki's neck, the woman turned to join the clan in their packing efforts.

I mounted Kiki, and tried to follow her directions. We would lose the light soon. Kiki turned her head to the left, peering at me with a blue eye.

Catch Topaz? Silk? she asked.

Yes. Let's fly!

Kiki moved. The long grasses blurred past my feet until I could no longer see them in the darkness. I held my position as we traveled over the plains. It felt as if I rode on top of a wind storm rather than a horse.

When the moon reached its apex, I felt the Sandseed's magic thin, then disappear. No longer surrounded by their power, I used my magic to search for Irys.

I'm here, she said in my mind and I saw through her eyes that they had made camp by Blood Rock.

Wake Cahil, I told her. *We have to return to the Keep as fast as we can. Tula's still in danger.*

She is well guarded.

He has powerful magic.

We're on our way.

I sent my awareness toward the Keep, hoping to warn them. My mind touched Hayes dozing in his office. He flinched away from me in horror and raised a stronger barrier. The other Master Magicians' defenses were as well constructed as the towers in which they slept. Growing weary with the effort, I pulled back.

Kiki overtook Irys and Cahil on the Citadel road just as the sky began to lighten. I had only a moment to wonder how she had managed a two day journey in one night before we sped past the others.

Need rest? I asked her, glancing behind in time to see Irys and Cahil wave me on.

No.

But my legs burned as if they were on fire. I aimed blue cooling thoughts at them, and they numbed.

We were within sight of the marble gates of the Citadel when all desire to rest fled my mind. A sudden and intense feeling of terrified helplessness pressed on my body. Tula. I launched my awareness toward the Keep, searching for someone, anyone to warn. The guards with Tula didn't have any magic. While I could read the minds of non-magicians, they had no power to "hear" me. Desperate, I kept hunting.

My mind found Dax. He was in the middle of a practice bout, learning to parry and lunge with a wooden sword.

Tula, I screamed in his mind. *Danger! Get help!*

He dropped his sword in surprise and was whacked in the ribs by his opponent.

Yelena? He spun around, looking for me.

Tula's in danger! Go. Now, I ordered. Then my connection to him severed. It felt as if someone had drawn a stone curtain down between us.

Time slowed to drips of molasses as we entered the Citadel and navigated the busy streets. It seemed as if the entire population walked in the streets. Their unhurried pace clogged the roadway.

The air sparked with the perfect cooling season temperature. And a perfect contrast to the fire in my heart. I wanted to scream at the crowd to move. Kiki, sensing my urgency, stepped up her pace and nudged the dawdlers out of our way.

A few curses followed us. Kiki startled the guards at the Keep's entrance when she refused to stop. She headed straight to the infirmary and even climbed the stairs, stopping only when we had reached the door.

I slid from her saddle. Racing toward Tula's room, I feared the worst when I spotted her guards lying in the corridor. I jumped over them and burst into her room. The door slammed against the wall. The noise echoed off the cold marble, but failed to rouse Tula.

Her lifeless eyes stared at nothing. Her bloodless lips were frozen in a grimace of horror and pain. My fingers sought a pulse; her skin felt icy and stiff. Black bruises ringed her neck.

Too late, or, was I? I placed my hand on her throat, pulling power to me. In my mind's eye, I saw her crushed windpipe. She had been strangled. I sent a bubble of power to reinflate it, sending air into her lungs. I focused on her heart, willing it to pump.

Her heart beat and air filled her lungs, but the dullness refused to leave her eyes. I pushed harder. Her skin warmed and flushed. Her chest rose and fell. Yet, when I stopped, her blood stilled and she failed to take another breath.

He had stolen her soul. I couldn't revive her.

A heavy arm rested on my shoulder. "There is nothing more you can do," Irys said.

I glanced around. Behind me stood Cahil, Leif, Dax, Roze and Hayes. They crowded the small room and I hadn't even noticed their arrival. Tula's skin cooled under my fingers. I pulled my hand away.

A sharp, bone-crushing exhaustion settled over me. I dropped to the floor, closed my eyes and rested my head in my hands. My fault. My fault. I should never have left her.

The room erupted with sound and activity, but I ignored them as tears poured down my face. I wanted to dissolve into the floor, mixing myself with the hard stone. A stone had a single purpose: to be. No complicated promises, no worries and no feelings.

I lowered my cheek to the smooth marble. The cold stung my fevered skin. Only when the noise in the room faded did

I open my eyes. And saw a scrap of paper lying under Tula's bed. It must have fallen off when I had tried to put life into her body. I reached for it, thinking it had been Tula's.

The words written on the paper cut through the fog of my grief like Moon Man's scimitar.

The note said: *I have Opal. I will exchange Opal for Yelena Zaltana at the next rising of the full moon. Send Tula's grief flag up First Magician's tower as a sign of agreement and Opal will not be harmed. More instructions will follow.*

23

"WE'LL SEND TULA'S grief flag up, but we're not exchanging Yelena for Opal," Irys insisted. "We have two weeks until the full moon. That should give us enough time to find Opal."

Again, loud arguments echoed through the magician's meeting room. Zitora had returned from her mission for the Council so all four Master Magicians were there, as well as Tula's family, Leif, and the Captain of the Keep's guard.

Leif had tried to ask me about the Sandseeds before the meeting started, but I cut him off with an angry response. I still couldn't look at him without seeing his eight-year-old face in the bushes, watching my kidnapping and doing nothing.

The events that had occurred after I discovered the ransom note felt as if they happened in a dream. Once everyone settled down, the killer's movements prior to attacking Tula were uncovered.

He obtained a position with the Keep's gardeners. Unfortunately, the people he worked with couldn't agree on his facial features and Bain had drawn four completely different men from their descriptions. They also failed to remember his name.

With ten magical souls, Ferde obtained enough power to equal a Master Magician. He concealed his presence in the Keep with ease and confused those he worked with.

Tula's guards were shot with tiny darts dipped in Curare. They could only recall seeing one of the gardeners delivering some medicinal plants to Hayes before their muscles froze. The fact that Ferde had infiltrated the Keep had put the Keep's guards in serious trouble.

"He was living in the Keep and we had no clue," Roze said. Her powerful voice rose over the din. "What makes you think we can find him now?"

Tula's mother and father drew in horrified breaths. They had arrived the day before. The news of her passing had shocked them to their core. I could see in their drawn faces and in their haunted gazes that knowing the same man held Opal made their lives a living nightmare. Just like mine.

"Give him Yelena," Roze said into the now quiet room. "She was able to animate Tula. She has the power to handle this killer."

"We don't want anyone else harmed," said Tula's father. He wore a simple brown tunic and pants. His large hands were rough with calluses and burn scars; evidence of a lifetime of working with molten glass.

"No, Roze," Irys admonished. "She doesn't have full control of her magic yet. Probably the main reason he wants her. If he stole her magic, think how powerful he would then be."

Bain, who had translated the markings on the killer's skin, told the group in the meeting room that the purpose of the man's quest was written in his tattoos. Bain's information matched what Moon Man had told me.

Ferde performed an ancient Efe binding ritual that used intimidation and torture to turn a victim into a willing slave. When all free will had been surrendered, the victim was murdered and her soul's magic was directed into Ferde, increasing his own power. He had targeted fifteen- and sixteen-year-old girls because their magic potential was just beginning.

Sour bile churned in my stomach as I listened to Bain's explanation. Reyad and Mogkan's tactics in Ixia to increase Mogkan's magic had been sickeningly familiar. Although, they hadn't raped or killed their thirty-two victims, they tortured their souls from them, leaving them mindless. Just as horrible.

Ferde had gained eleven souls. According to the ritual, the twelfth soul must go to him willingly. No kidnapping for the final ritual, which, when completed, would give him almost unlimited power.

Debate on why Tula survived the initial attack led to a guess that Ferde had been close to being discovered and fled before finishing the ritual.

"Yelena should be protected at all times," Irys said. Her words brought me back to the meeting. "If we can't find him, we'll set up an ambush near the exchange site and apprehend him that way."

The magicians continued to argue. It seemed as if I would have no say in the plans. It didn't matter. I would either find Ferde or be at that exchange site. I had failed Tula; I wasn't going to let Opal suffer the same fate.

A messenger from the Council arrived as the meeting ended. He handed Roze a scroll. She read it then thrust the paper at Irys in what appeared to be disgust. Irys's shoulders drooped when she scanned the document.

What else has gone wrong? I asked her.

Another situation to deal with. This one is not life threatening, though, just bad timing, she said. *At least this will be another chance for you to practice your diplomacy.*

How?

An Ixian delegation is expected to arrive in six days.

So soon? I had thought the messenger with the Council's reply had just left.

Yelena, it's been five days. It's a two-day ride to the Ixian border and a half a day to the Commander's castle.

Five days? So much had happened in those five days that I felt as if I lived one endless day. Difficult, too, to believe I had been living in Sitia for only two and a half seasons. Almost half a year gone in what seemed like a fortnight. My ache for Valek hadn't dulled, and I wondered if meeting the northern delegation would cause me to miss him more.

I followed the others from the room. In the hallway outside, Zitora linked her arm in mine.

"I need some help," she said, guiding me from the Keep's administration building, and toward her tower.

"But I need to—"

"Get some rest. And *not* go searching the Citadel for Opal," Zitora said.

"I will, anyway. You know that."

She nodded. "But not tonight."

"What do you need?"

A sad smile touched her face. "Help with Tula's flag. I believe asking her parents would only increase their grief."

We entered her tower and climbed two flights of stairs to

her workroom. Comfortable chairs and tables littered with sewing and art supplies filled the large chamber.

"My seamstress skills are limited," Zitora said. She moved around the room, adding fabric and thread to the one empty table near the chairs. "But not for the lack of practice. I can sew and embroider, but I'm better at drawing. When I have the time, I've been experimenting with painting on silk."

Satisfied with her collection, Zitora dug through another pile of cloth and pulled out a sheet of white silk. She measured and cut off a five-foot-by-three-foot rectangle.

"The background will be white for Tula's purity and innocence," Zitora said. "Yelena, what should I put in the foreground?" When she saw my confusion, she explained, "A grief flag is our way of honoring the dead. It's a representation of the person. We decorate it with the things that made up a person's life, and when we raise the flag high, it releases their spirit into the sky. So what would best represent Tula?"

My thoughts went immediately to Ferde. A poisonous snake, red flames for pain and a jar of Curare all came to mind. I scowled, unable to imagine Tula's spirit free. She had been trapped in the blackness of Ferde's soul because of my stupidity.

"He's a cunning demon, isn't he?" Zitora asked, as if reading my mind. "To have the boldness to live in the Keep, to have the skill to kill under our roof and to have you blame yourself for it. A masterful trick, I'd say."

"You're starting to sound like a certain Story Weaver I know," I said.

"I'll take that as a compliment," Zitora replied. She sorted through colorful squares of silk. "Let's see. If you had listened to Irys and remained behind, the killer would have gotten Tula *and* you."

"But I had gotten my energy back," I said. Irys had thought it best not to mention Valek's help.

"Only because you wanted to follow Irys." Zitora raised a thin eyebrow.

"But I wouldn't have gone with Ferde willingly."

"Truly? What if he had promised not to kill Tula in exchange for you?"

I opened my mouth, then closed it, considering. She had a point.

"Once you say the words or move with intent, it's done. What follows after will not change that, and he would have killed Tula anyway," Zitora said. She lined the colored squares along the table's edge. "If you had stayed behind, you would both be gone, and we wouldn't have the information from the Sandseeds."

"Are you trying to make me feel better?"

Zitora smiled. "Now, what should we put on Tula's flag?"

The answer came to mind. "Honeysuckles, a single drop of dew on a blade of grass and glass animals."

Opal had told me about Tula's glass animals. Most of them Tula had either sold or given away as gifts, but Tula kept a small collection of them near her bed. The unwelcome thought of what we would sew on to Opal's flag rose in my mind. I suppressed it, squashing the image into a small corner of my brain. I would not let Ferde murder Opal.

Zitora drew shapes on the silk and I cut them out. When the pile met her approval, we arranged them on the white silk. Honeysuckles bordered the flag, while the blade of grass rose in the center surrounded by a ring of animal sculptures.

"Beautiful," Zitora said. Her eyes shone with grief. "Now comes the tedious part—sewing all these bits of cloth onto the background!"

I threaded needles for her, the extent of my sewing ability. After a while, she told me to go back to my room and get some sleep.

"Don't forget about our agreement," Zitora called as I started down the steps.

"I won't."

Now that she was back, I could begin teaching her some self-defense. With my thoughts preoccupied with scheduling her training, I was startled by two guards who waited for me outside Zitora's tower.

"What do you want?" I demanded, pulling my bow.

"Orders from Fourth Magician. You're to be protected at all times," said the larger of the two men.

I huffed with annoyance. "Go back to the barracks. I can take care of myself."

The men grinned.

"She told us you would say that," the other man said. "We follow *her* orders. If our unit fails to protect you, we'll be assigned to clean chamber pots for the rest of our days."

"I could make your job very difficult," I warned them.

The stubborn stiffness of their shoulders never softened.

"There is nothing you can do that's worse than cleaning chamber pots," said the large man.

I sighed; giving them the slip to search for Opal would be hard. Which was probably why Irys had assigned them to me. She knew that I would go hunting as soon as I could.

"Just stay out of my way," I growled.

I turned my back on the guards and headed for the apprentice's wing. The dark campus seemed to mourn, and an uneasy quiet filled the air. The raising ceremony for Tula was scheduled for dawn.

Then life would continue. I would have my afternoon lesson with Irys. Cahil had already reminded me of our evening ride. I would attempt to keep my promise to Moon Man. All these events would occur despite the threat to Opal. Or should that be in spite of the threat?

My guards refused to let me enter my rooms until one of them searched for intruders. At least they remained outside afterward and didn't insist on staying with me. But Irys had informed them that I would attempt to "escape," because when I looked out my bedroom window, I saw one of the guards standing there. I closed and locked the window shutters.

The guards blocked both exits. I could see Dax's grin in my mind, knowing he would delight in telling me the gossip and rumors from the other students about my protectors.

I sat on the bed in annoyance and sealed my fate. The soft comfort of my pillow called to me. I would rest only a moment, clearing my head so I could plan a way to lose my two shadows.

During the next five days, I had only one successful escape. The morning after I had helped Zitora with Tula's grief flag, I stood next to Irys for Tula's raising ceremony.

Tula's body had been wrapped in white linen strips and covered with her flag. The leader of the Cowan clan spoke kind words over her body as her parents wept. All four Master Magicians attended. Zitora soaked a handkerchief with her tears, but I clamped down on my emotions and focused on Opal, hardening my resolve to find her.

Tula's body was to be taken home and buried in her family's graveyard. But, according to Sitian beliefs, during this farewell ceremony her spirit transferred to the flag. The people surrounding me believed that when this pennant of white silk fluttered above Roze's tower, Tula's spirit would be re-leased into the sky.

But I knew better. Tula's spirit was trapped inside Ferde and only his death would release her. For me, Tula's flag not only signaled Ferde that we had agreed to his exchange, but also symbolized my determination to find and stop him.

The morning after Tula's ceremony, I led my guards to the baths. The pools and changing rooms bustled with students getting ready for classes, and despite the assortment of wary looks aimed my way, I managed to pay a few novices to cre-ate a diversion near the back entrance.

The ruse worked. I dashed out of the baths and out of the Keep before the soldiers at the gate could recognize me. The guards stationed at the Keep's gate monitored who came in, and, unless there was a crisis, they only paid a passing interest to those who left.

Once out of sight, my first task included finding Fisk and his friends. The market was just stirring to life. Only a few customers wandered through the stands at this early hour. I found Fisk playing dice with a group of children.

He ran over to me. "Lovely Yelena, how can I assist you today?" His smile lit up his face.

The other children surrounded me, waiting for instructions. They appeared clean and cared for. They earned money for their families, and I thought that once I finished this ugly business with Ferde, I would give them more help. I remembered to tell them about the Keep's need for another gardener, though, and was rewarded to see one girl run home to tell her father.

"I need guides," I told Fisk. "Show me all the shortcuts and hidden areas of the Citadel."

While they took me through back alleys and forgotten

quarters, I questioned them about the people. Anybody new? Anybody acting strange? Had they seen a young, frightened girl with a man? They regaled me with wild stories, but the information was not what I needed. As we moved, I searched the surrounding homes with my magic, seeking Opal, or the wisp of someone else's magic, or anything that might give me a clue as to her whereabouts.

The day was well spent and only my hunger could stop me. Fisk led me to the best meat griller in the Citadel's market. As I ate the juicy beef, I decided I would continue my search late into the night and then find a place to sleep. I would have plenty more days to spend hunting Opal.

At least that had been my intention until Irys and my guards ambushed me. Hidden behind a shield of magic, she prevented me from sensing them until too late. The instant the two soldiers grabbed my arms; she seized control of my body, pushing aside what I had thought to be a strong mental barrier. The full power of a Master Magician reduced my own defenses to dust. Unable to move or to talk, I stared at her in complete surprise.

Even though I had missed Irys's morning lesson and blocked her efforts to find me with her magic, I thought she would understand my mission. I was unprepared for the severity of her anger.

My guards, looking grim and scared, clung to me.

You will not *leave the Keep again. You will not lose your guards again. Or I will lock you in the Keep's prison. Understand?*

Yes. I'm—

I'll be watching.

But—

Irys severed our mental connection with a head aching abruptness. Yet her magic still gripped my body.

"Take her back to the Keep," Irys ordered the guards. "Take her to her rooms. She may leave them only for lessons and meals. Do not lose her again."

The guards flinched under her searing gaze. The larger one picked me up and threw me over his shoulder. I suffered the indignity of being carried through the Citadel, across the Keep's campus and dumped onto my bed.

Irys didn't relinquish control of my body until the next morning, although I still felt a band of her magic wrapped around my throat. By then, I was ready to throttle anyone who dared to get in my way. Avoided as if I carried a disease, I could only vent my ill humor on the guards as they escorted me through the campus.

After three days of this hell, I stood next to Irys in the great hall of the Council building, waiting for the Ixian delegation to arrive. Irys had used my lesson time to lecture me on proper Sitian protocols and diplomacy. She had refused to let me talk to her about anything other than the lecture topic. My frustration at not knowing about the search for Opal seized my chest like a vise.

The great hall was decorated with large silk banners representing each of the eleven clans and each of the Master Magicians. Hung from the ceiling, these colorful banners flowed down three stories of marble walls until they reached the floor. Tall slender windows separated the banners, allowing the sunlight to stripe the floor with gold. The Council members wore formal robes of silk, embroidered with silver thread. Irys and the other Masters wore their ceremonial robes and masks.

I remembered Irys's hawk mask from when she had visited

the Commander in Ixia, and I looked at the others with interest. Roze Featherstone, First Magician wore a blue dragon mask. Bain Bloodgood, Second Magician had donned a leopard skin mask. And a white unicorn covered Third Magician, Zitora's face.

According to Fisk, these animals acted as the magicians' guides through the underworld and throughout their life. They had found them while enduring the Master level test, which, from the little bits of information I could gather, seemed a horrible ordeal.

Cahil had donned the midnight-blue tunic with the silver piping that he had worn to the New Beginnings feast. The color complemented his blond hair and he looked regal despite his hard expression. Present to assess his enemy for weakness, he promised to keep quiet and not draw attention to himself; otherwise, the Council members would have banned him from the greeting ceremonies.

Fidgeting, I twisted the wide sleeves of my formal apprentice robe around my arm. Pale yellow in color, the hem of the plain cotton garment touched my feet and revealed the black sandals Zitora had given to me. I plucked at the skin on my neck and pulled at the robe's collar.

What's wrong? Irys asked. Her rigid posture radiated disapproval.

It was the first time since my house arrest that she had mentally communicated to me. I wanted to ignore her. My anger at her punishment still sizzled in my blood. Even now, Irys's magic wrapped around my neck. She hadn't been kidding when she had said she'd be watching. The power I would need to remove her magic would exhaust me, and I didn't possess enough nerve to provoke her again.

Your leash chafes. My thoughts were cold.

Good. Maybe now you'll learn to listen and to think before you act. To trust others' judgments.

I've learned something.

What?

The harsh tactics of the Commander are not unique to Ixia.

Oh, Yelena. Irys's stiff demeanor melted. The hard band of magic around my throat disappeared. *I'm at my wit's end. You're so focused on action. You have a single-minded determination that barrels through situations. You've been lucky so far, and I don't know how to make you understand that if Tula's killer absorbs your power, he will be unstoppable. Sitia will be his to rule. This goes beyond you and your desire for revenge. This affects us all. All options must be carefully considered before any action is taken. That is the Sitian way.*

She shook her head, sighing. *I have forgotten that you're a grown woman. Once you have complete control of your magic and when this killer is found, you can do as you like, go where you please. I had hoped you would have become a part of our efforts to keep Sitia a safe and prosperous place to live. But your unpredictability will only jeopardize our community.*

Irys's words cut through my anger. To be free to do anything I wanted seemed a foreign concept. The first time in my life that I had been offered such a choice.

I envisioned traveling all over Sitia with Kiki and with no worries or promises to keep. To be unconnected. Moving from one town to the next, experiencing the culture. Or climbing through the jungle with my father, learning about the medicinal properties of some leaf. Or sneaking into Ixia to meet with Valek. She presented an attractive option.

Perhaps I would take her up on it, but not until *after* I captured Ferde and fulfilled my promise to Moon Man.

Deciding I would try harder to work in the Sitian way, I said, *Irys, I would like to help find Opal.*

Sensing my intentions, she turned to me and studied my expression. *There's a meeting scheduled after the formalities with the Ixians. You're welcome to come.*

I smoothed out the sleeves of my robe as the row of trumpet players sounded the arrival of the northerners. An immediate hush fell over the great hall as a stately parade of Ixians entered the room.

The Ambassador led the procession. The tailored cut of her black uniform lent her an air of importance. Two diamonds sparkled from her collar. The Commander must have shown her great favor in allowing her to wear the precious stones for this mission. Her long straight hair was fading toward gray, yet her almond-shaped eyes held a powerful vitality.

Sudden recognition pierced my heart.

24

I QUICKLY SCANNED THE rest of the Ambassador's retinue, searching for the person who had to be there. Her aide, walking one step behind her, wore the same uniform as the Ambassador except the red diamonds on his collar had been stitched with thread. His bland face was unremarkable, so I moved my gaze to the others.

Some of the guards looked familiar, but two captains near the middle caught my eye. Ari's massive muscles strained the seams on his uniform. His tight blond curls looked almost white in the sunlight. His face remained impassive when he glanced at me, but I could see two red blotches spreading on his cheeks as he fought to keep from smiling.

Janco sauntered next to him, looking much healthier than when I had said goodbye to him in Ixia. Then his pale face had been tight with pain and he hadn't the strength to stand. The results of defending Irys against Mogkan's men. Now he moved his lean build with an athletic grace and his skin was tanned. Straight-faced, he peered at me, but I could see pure mischievous glee dancing in his eyes.

It was wonderful to see them, but I kept searching. Clutching my butterfly pendant through my robe, I scrutinized all the guard's faces. He *had* to be here. If the Commander was here, posing as the Ixian Ambassador, then Valek *had* to be close by.

But Valek didn't know about Commander Ambrose's secret. Only I knew about what the Commander called his mutation, having been born a woman with a man's soul. Since Valek didn't know the Ambassador was the Commander, he probably would be with whoever was posing as the Commander in Ixia.

Unless the Commander had sent Valek on another mission, or, even worse, maybe Valek still hadn't recovered from giving me his strength. Maybe he had been injured while weak. Or dead. Horrible scenarios chased through my mind as the delegation exchanged formal greetings.

I willed the pleasantries to move faster. My need to question Ari and Janco about Valek grew with every second.

With my thoughts on Valek, I found my eyes lingering on the Ambassador's aide. His straight black hair fell to his ears and clung limply to his head. A soft fat nose sat above colorless lips and a weak chin. He appeared to be bored as he scanned the Councilors and magicians in the room with no hint of intelligence in his blue eyes.

Our gazes met for a moment. Sapphire-blue lightning struck my heart. That rat. I wanted to slug Valek and kiss him at the same time.

His expression never changed. He gave no sign of having seen me at all as his attention refocused on the Councilors. I could hardly bear the rest of the meeting.

Too impatient to wait until the meeting concluded, I tried

to link with Valek's mind. I encountered a formidable barrier stronger than any of the Master Magicians'. Valek sensed the magic and glanced at me.

When the introductions and formalities came to an end, the Ixian delegation was served refreshments and every one milled about in small groups.

I headed for Ari and Janco, who stood near the Ambassador as if they had metal rods strapped onto their backs, but Bavol Cacao, my clan leader, stopped me.

"I have a message from your father," Bavol said. He handed me a small scroll.

I thanked him. This was only the second time I had talked to him since he had arrived at the Citadel. He had delivered the clothes Nutty had sewn for me. Even though I wanted to talk to my friends, I inquired after the clan.

"Dealing with the usual petty problems, and trying to combat some fungus that is eating through the wood on a few walls." He smiled. "I've no doubt that Esau'll figure it out. Now if you'll excuse me, I need to check to make sure the Ambassador's suite is ready."

Before Bavol could walk away, I touched his sleeve. "What does the suite look like?" I asked him.

Puzzled, he said, "Our most opulent chambers. The Citadel's guest suites have every convenience. Why?"

"The Ambassador doesn't like opulence. Perhaps you could have some of it removed? Simple elegance would suit her better."

Bavol considered. "She's a cousin of Commander Ambrose. Have you met her?"

"No. But I know most Ixians agree with the Commander's dislike for extravagance."

"Your concern is noted. I'll see to the changes." Bavol hurried away.

I broke the wax seal on the scroll. Unrolling the paper, I read the note then closed my eyes for a moment. In my mind's eye I saw my story line twist into a big complicated noose-like knot. According to the letter, Esau and Perl were on their way to the Keep to visit me. They planned to arrive five days before the full moon.

Who else could come? If I had gotten a message from the underworld announcing Reyad and Mogkan's arrival, I wouldn't have been surprised.

Tucking the note away, I shook my head. I had no control over these events and I would deal with my parents when they arrived. I approached the Ixians. The Ambassador chatted with Bain, Second Magician.

Her gold eyes flicked to me and Bain stopped speaking to introduce us. "Ambassador Signe, this is Apprentice Yelena Liana Zaltana."

I clasped her cool hand in the Ixian greeting, and then bowed formally in the Sitian salutation.

She returned the bow. "I have heard much about you from my cousin. How are your studies progressing?"

"Very well, thank you. Please extend my best wishes to Commander Ambrose," I said.

"I will." Signe turned toward her aide. "This is Adviser Ilom."

I held my face in a neutral expression as I shook his limp hand. He mumbled a greeting then ignored me as someone not worth his time or attention. I knew Valek had to be acting, yet his complete disregard made me worry if his feelings for me had changed.

I didn't have much time to brood, though. When Bain led Signe and Ilom to meet another Councilor, Ari grabbed me in a quick bear hug.

"What's with the dress?" Janco asked.

"Better than that wrinkled uniform," I countered. "And is that gray hair in your goatee?"

Janco smoothed a hand over his facial hair. "A little present from my run-in with a sword. Or should I say from when the sword had a run-in with me?" His eyes lit up. "Want to see the scar? It's cool." He started pulling his shirt out of his pants.

"Janco," Ari warned. "We're not supposed to be fraternizing with the Sitians."

"But she's not Sitian. Right, Yelena? You haven't gone south on us, have you?" Janco's voice held mock horror. "Because if you have I can't give you your present."

I took my switchblade out, showing the inscription to Janco. "What about 'Sieges weathered, fight together, friends forever'? Does that change if I become an official southerner?"

Janco rubbed the hair on his chin, considering.

"No," Ari said. "You could change into a goat and it would still apply."

"Only if she made us some goat's cheese," Janco said.

Ari rolled his light blue eyes. "Just give her the gift."

"It's from Valek," Janco said, digging into his pack. "Since he was unable to accompany the delegation."

"Suicide," Ari said. "The Sitians would execute Valek if they caught him in their lands."

Concern for Valek coursed through me, and I glanced around the hall, looking to see if anyone else had recognized him. Everyone seemed to be engaged in conversation except

Cahil. He stood alone, watching the Ixians. He met my gaze and frowned.

At Janco's triumphant grunt I turned back to my friends. Once I saw what Janco had in his palm, all thoughts about Cahil disappeared. A black stone snake with glints of silver twisted four times around his fingers. The snake's scales had been carved with a diamond pattern along its back, and two tiny sapphires gleamed from its eyes. One of Valek's carvings.

"It's a bracelet," Janco said. He took my hand and slipped the snake over it until it fit onto my forearm. "It was too small for me," Janco joked. "So I told Valek he should give it to you. Looks like it fits you perfectly."

I marveled at my gift. Why had Valek chosen a snake? Apprehension coiled in my stomach.

"Things have been quiet since you left," Ari said. "Even though we're not part of his corps, Valek made Janco a fox statue and a horse for me. They're the nicest things we own."

We talked until Ari and Janco had to follow the Ambassador to her suite. They told me they would have rotating shifts to guard Signe and Ilom and would have some time to talk to me again. I offered to show them around the Citadel and perhaps the Keep.

Irys found me before I left the great hall and she accompanied me through the Citadel's streets to the meeting to discuss the ongoing efforts to find Opal. My ever-present guards, who had been discreet during the ceremonies, followed us.

"Janco looks great," Irys said. "That was a quick recovery from such a severe injury. I'm glad."

Irys's words reminded me of something Story Weaver had said. With all the commotion surrounding Opal and the delegation, I hadn't discussed Moon Man's claims with her.

"Irys, what is a Soulfinder? My—"

Don't say anymore aloud, Irys's voice admonished in my mind. *That's not something you want anyone to overhear.*

Why not? Why all the fear? My hand sought Valek's bracelet. I twisted it around my arm.

She sighed. *Sitian history is full of wonderful and brave magicians, who have joined the clans together and stopped the wars. Unfortunately, those tales aren't told in the taverns and to the children. The tales of the few magicians who have caused harm seem to be the ones whispered by the fireside. With Mogkan's corruption and now this beast that has Opal, I don't want rumors and stories to circulate about a Soulfinder.*

Irys fiddled with the brown feathers on her hawk mask that she carried. *About a hundred and fifty years ago, a Soulfinder was born. He was considered a gift from the underworld. His strong magic affected people's souls, healing both emotional and physical pain. Then he discovered he could pluck a soul from the air before it could float to the sky, waking the dead.*

But something happened. We don't know what, but he became bitter and he went from helping people to using them. Keeping the souls for himself, he woke the dead without their souls. These emotionless creatures followed his orders and had no remorse for their actions. That ability is considered an aberration and is against our Ethical Code. With his soulless army, he had control of Sitia for many many dark years before the Master Magicians could stop him.

Before I could ask for details, Irys continued her story. *Yelena, you have all the abilities of a Soulfinder. When you breathed for Tula, you shocked me and alarmed Roze. That's why I was so harsh with you about losing your guards. I had to show Roze I could control you. But today you made me realize that was wrong. It was probably the same type of panicked response that pushed the*

Soulfinder over the edge. We need to discover the extent of your abilities before we categorize you. Who knows? You could be a Master Magician.

I laughed, thinking of how easy it had been for Irys to ambush me and break through my magical defenses. "Highly doubtful," I said. And also doubtful was Moon Man's claims that I was a Soulfinder. Tula's soul was stolen. I could breathe for her, yet I couldn't wake her without it. I shared some abilities with a Soulfinder, but obviously not all.

As we drew closer to the Keep's entrance, I noticed a small beggar wearing a dirty cloak huddled by the wall, shaking a cup. Annoyed that I was the only one to notice, I walked over and dropped a coin into the cup. The beggar looked up, and I saw a flash of Fisk's smile before he hid his face again.

"We have news about the one you seek. Come to the market tomorrow."

"Hey, you! Stop bothering the lady," said one of my guards.

I spun to glare at the guard. When I turned back, Fisk was gone.

I mulled over Fisk's message. My first instinct involved ditching my guards tomorrow and meeting with him, an Ixian response, but I decided to try the Sitian approach and see what the others had found regarding Opal.

Leif leaned over a table in the meeting room, studying a map. He greeted my arrival with a surprised expression, but I refused to acknowledge him and had to suppress a sudden fury that welled in my throat. I had no idea how I would fulfill my promise to Moon Man when all I wanted to do was shake Leif and demand an explanation.

Irys broke the silence and filled me in on the group's efforts so far. They had divided the Citadel into sections and one magician was assigned to search each quarter. Councilor Harun, the Sandseed's Councilman, had taken his people to hunt for Opal in the part of the Avibian Plains that bordered the Citadel. No clues had been found.

"We'll send guards to search every building in the Citadel," Roze said, sweeping into the meeting room with Bain on her heels.

"Which will cause Opal's immediate death," I said.

Roze sneered at me. "Who invited you?" She gave Irys a poisonous glare.

"She's right, Roze," Irys said. "News of the searches would spread like a barn fire and he would be alerted."

"Does anyone have a better idea?"

"I do," I said into the silence.

All eyes turned toward me. Roze's gaze froze my blood.

"I have friends in the Citadel who can get information without calling attention to themselves. Seems they might have already learned something, but I need to meet them at the market tomorrow." Under my sleeve, I twisted Valek's snake around on my wrist, waiting for their response.

"No," Roze said. "It could be a trap."

"Now *you're* concerned for my welfare? How touching. Although I think jealousy is the real emotion," I shot back.

"Ladies, please," said Bain. "Let us focus on the task at hand. Do you trust this source, Yelena?"

"Yes."

"It would not look unusual for Yelena to go to the market to shop. Her guards would be with her," Irys added.

"The guards would scare away my source," I said, which was true enough for my purposes. "Also my source might lead me somewhere, so I'll have to move quick."

"But you'll need protection. We could disguise your guards," Irys offered.

"No. They're not the protection I need. I can defend myself against a physical threat, but I need to defend against a magical one." Irys was a powerful ally.

Irys nodded, and we made plans for the next day.

After the meeting, I went to the dining room to grab something to eat and I picked up a few apples for Kiki and Topaz. My guards continued to follow me, and it felt odd how I had grown used to their presence. At least I didn't need to worry about Goel trying another surprise attack. Especially when I had so many other things to occupy my thoughts.

I hadn't been able to ride since my house arrest, and, even if I couldn't leave the Keep, at least I could practice riding. Kiki's mother had sneered at my saddle, so I wanted to learn how to ride bareback. Besides, it could be a useful skill to learn. In an emergency I wouldn't have time to saddle her.

And I needed the distraction. Bad thoughts of losing my guards and sneaking into a certain Adviser's room in the Citadel's guest quarters kept surfacing. I drowned the dangerous impulse. I wouldn't risk Valek's life for my own selfish reasons. Pulling up my sleeve, I examined Valek's gift in the late afternoon sunlight, running a finger along its back. The bracelet even felt like a snake, although its body language seemed to indicate a protective rather than an aggressive stance.

Again, I wondered at his choice. Perhaps he had somehow witnessed my nightmares about snakes, but why make one as a present? Wouldn't a mongoose make a better gift?

Kiki waited for me by the pasture's gate. She nickered in greeting, and I fed her an apple before climbing over the fence. My guards took up positions outside the gate, close but not too close. They were learning.

As Kiki ate, I checked her over. She had nettles snarled in her tail, and dried mud on her belly and caked around her hooves.

"Didn't anyone groom you?" I asked aloud, *tsking*.

"She wouldn't let anyone near her," Cahil said. He held a bucket of brushes and combs over the rail. "Seems only you can do the honors."

I took the handle. "Thanks." I pulled out a currycomb and began to loosen the mud on her coat.

Cahil rested his arms on the fence. "Saw you talking to the northerners today. You know some of them?"

I glanced at Cahil. A serious expression gripped his face. So his timely arrival with the supplies hadn't been a coincidence. He had waited to ambush me with questions about the Ixians.

Choosing my words with care, I said, "Two of the guards are my friends."

"The ones who taught you how to fight?" Cahil tried to sound casual.

"Yes."

"What division do they belong to?"

I stopped brushing Kiki and stared at him. "Cahil, what do you really want to know?"

He stammered.

"You're not thinking of jeopardizing the delegation are you? Planning to sabotage the meetings? Or are you more interested in ambushing them on their way back to Ixia?"

He opened his mouth, but no words came out.

"That would be unwise," I continued. "You'll make both Sitia and Ixia your enemy, and besides…"

"Besides what?" he demanded.

"The Commander's elite guards surround the Ambassador. It would be suicide to make a kidnapping attempt."

"Aren't you just full of wisdom today," Cahil said with a sharp jab of sarcasm. "Your concern for the welfare of my men is truly heartwarming. Are you sure you're not just protecting your northern friends? Or perhaps protecting your heart mate?"

He had to be guessing. I called his bluff. "What are you ranting about?"

"I was watching you when the delegation arrived. Although your face never moved, I saw your hand fly to that butterfly pendant under your robe. I know the one who gave that to you is here. In fact, he gave you another gift today."

I turned back to work on Kiki, hiding my face from Cahil. "If you know so much then why are you asking *me* questions?"

"Who is he?" When I refused to answer, Cahil continued, "It's the man who's missing half of his right ear. The one who gave you the snake."

Cahil wore such a smug expression that I laughed. "Janco? We bicker like brother and sister. No. He was just delivering the gift."

"I don't believe you."

I shrugged. "Here." I handed a wire brush to Cahil. "You can get the nettles out of her tail." When I saw him hesitate, I added, "Don't worry, she won't kick you."

We worked for a while in silence.

Cahil, though, wasn't content with the quiet. "You're happier now that your northern friends are here."

"I missed them," I agreed.

"Would you want to go back to Ixia?"

"Yes. But that's impossible because I'm a magician." And there was a signed order for my execution, but I thought it prudent not to mention that.

"Nothing's impossible." Cahil finished Kiki's tail and began combing her mane. "When I gain control of Ixia and free the people, you would have a place by my side if you chose to accept it."

Avoiding his unspoken question, I gave him a dubious look. "Do you still believe Sitia will support you even after they've been making nice with the northern delegation?"

With the passion of a mystic, Cahil said, "All my life I have been told I would rule Ixia one day. Every lesson, every interaction and every emotion was tailored to that single purpose. Even the Council encouraged me to plan and train and wait for the perfect moment to attack." Cahil's blue eyes radiated such a pure intensity that I almost stepped back.

"Then the north agrees to a trade treaty and they visit Sitia." He spat the words out. "Suddenly the Commander is the Council's friend, and my reason for existing is no longer supported. The Council has failed to realize that the Commander is deceiving them, and when he tips his hand, I'll be there. I have many loyal followers who are equally unhappy about the Council's dalliances with the north."

"You're going to need a trained military if you plan to go against the Commander's forces," I said. "And if Valek—"

"What about Valek?" Cahil grabbed my arm. His fingers pressed my bracelet into my skin. I winced in pain.

Kiki cocked an ear. *Kick?*

No. Not yet.

"If Valek discovers what you're planning, he'll stop you before you can rally your men."

"Do you really think he can stop me?" he asked.

"Yes." I pulled my arm out of Cahil's grasp, but he caught my wrist with his other hand and yanked my sleeve up with his free hand, exposing the snake circled around my arm. Before I could stop him, he let go of my sleeve and tugged my collar down. My black stone butterfly pendant swung free. The silver spots on its wings glinted in the sunlight, matching the silver on the snake's body.

"And you would know," Cahil said, releasing me. His face took on a stunned expression as he made a sudden realization.

I staggered back.

"As the Commander's food taster, you worked with Valek every day. He had to teach you about poisons and poisoning techniques." He stared at me in revulsion. "Marrok told me that when the royal family members were assassinated, the assassin would leave behind a black statue that glittered with silver. It was the assassin's calling card. Only after the Commander took control of Ixia was Valek named the assassin."

I returned to brushing Kiki. "That's a big leap in logic, Cahil. Based on a bedtime story, which I'm sure gets more interesting with each telling, and a couple of trinkets. Valek is not the only person who carves things out of those rocks. Think about that before you leap to conclusions."

Refusing to meet Cahil's gaze, I put the grooming equipment back into the bucket and led Kiki to her stall. By the time I finished filling her water pail, Cahil had gone.

My guards trailed me to the baths, and stayed outside while I washed off the horse hair and dust that coated my skin. The sun had set by the time we reached my rooms. I waited outside, shivering in the cold night air while one guard searched inside. Given the all clear, I entered my dark living room. I shuttered and locked my windows against the chilly wind, then lit a fire in the hearth.

"That's better," said a voice that set my soul on fire.

I turned. Valek lounged on a chair with his booted feet propped up on the table.

25

VALEK HELD THE VALMUR statue I had bought for him long ago, admiring it in the firelight. He wore a simple black shirt and pants. The clothes did not appear to be as tight fitting as his hooded sneak suit, but seemed snug enough not to impede his movements.

"How did you—"

"Fool your guards? They're not very good. They forgot to check the ceiling for spiders." Valek grinned. His angular face softened.

Startled, I realized he wasn't in disguise. "This is dangerous."

"I knew falling for you was dangerous, love."

"I meant coming to Sitia. Being here in the Magician's Keep with guards just outside my door." I gestured wildly.

"It's only dangerous if they know I'm here. According to them, I'm just Ambassador Signe's lowly and dull-witted aide." Valek stood; his movements liquid. The black fabric of his clothes clung to his lean build. He stretched his arms out to the side. "See, I'm not even armed."

He made a weak attempt to look innocent, but I knew better. "Should I guess how many concealed weapons you have or should I strip search you?"

"A strip search is the only way to be absolutely certain." Valek's deep blue eyes danced with delight.

I took three steps and was wrapped in his arms, where I belonged. No confusion here. No worries here. No troubles here. Just Valek's scent, an intoxicating combination of musk and spice.

During our short trip to the bed, I found two knives strapped to Valek's forearms, darts and other throwing implements tucked inside his belt, a switchblade strapped to his right thigh and a short sword in his boot.

I knew more weapons hid within his clothes, but once I touched his skin, the game ceased to matter as we became reacquainted. With his body next to mine, I felt all the empty places inside me fill with his essence. Home.

It wasn't until deep into the night that we stopped to talk. Lying next to him under the blanket, I thanked him in a low voice for the snake bracelet and told him about Tula, Opal and the reason for the guards.

"And you said it was dangerous for me," Valek said, pointing out the irony. "Good thing I'm here. You'll need backup that can't be influenced by magic."

Valek's immunity to magic could be considered another concealed weapon. Hope of recovering Opal unharmed bloomed in my chest for the first time since her capture. "How can you provide backup? You're supposed to be with the Ambassador."

He grinned. "Don't worry. I've got that covered. This is not the first time, nor will it be the last time, I've been in Sitia.

Keeping tabs on our neighbors has always been one of my duties as security chief. Fun stuff."

"Until you're caught," I said. My mood soured, but Valek seemed unaffected by my comment.

"There's always that chance. Part of the allure, I suppose." He nuzzled my neck and sighed with regret. "I better get back. It'll be dawn soon." He rolled out of bed and began to dress. "Besides, I don't want to be here when your boyfriend arrives."

"Who?" I sat up.

"The blonde that follows your every move with his lovesick eyes," Valek teased.

"Cahil?" I laughed, dismissing him. "He thought Janco was my heart mate. I think you should feel more jealousy toward my horse. She's the one who has stolen my heart."

Valek stilled as the amusement dropped from his face. "What's his name?"

"*Her* name is Kiki."

He shook his head. "Not the horse. The blonde."

"Cahil."

"Cahil Ixia? The King's nephew? He's alive?" Valek seemed confused.

"I thought you knew," I said.

I had imagined Valek had let Cahil live once he had reached Sitia. But now Cahil's comment about Valek forgetting to count the bodies when he had assassinated the royal family came to mind. With a growing horror, I realized my mistake.

"Valek, don't kill him."

"He's a threat to the Commander." A dead flatness covered Valek's eyes. He wore his stone face. Unyielding. Uncompromising.

"He's my friend."

Valek's cold killer's gaze met mine. "The second he becomes more than a potential threat, he's dead."

Valek had pledged to protect the Commander, and only his love for me kept him from assassinating Cahil that night. Valek's loyalty was without fail. If the Commander had given him a direct order to kill me, Valek would have. Lucky for us that the Commander hadn't given Valek that order.

"I'm glad the Commander is safe within Ixia's borders." Valek's face softened and he laughed. "He's taking a vacation. He's the only person I know who thinks hunting sand spiders is relaxing."

"Aren't you worried he'd get stung?" My skin crawled just thinking about the poisonous spiders. They were the size of a small dog and jumped with a lethal quickness. But then I remembered that the Commander was really in the Citadel's guest quarters.

"No. I still can't beat the Commander in a knife fight. His skills are more than adequate to handle a sand spider. Plotting royalty is another matter, though. I'll have to keep an eye on this Cahil."

I knew it was a matter of time before Valek found out about Cahil's plans to regain his kingdom. Then what would I do? Those thoughts reminded me about something Cahil had said that hadn't sounded right.

"Valek, did you used to leave your carvings behind when you assassinated someone?"

"Have you been listening to Sitian rumors?" He smiled.

I nodded. "But I don't necessarily believe all that I hear."

"Good. Although, I'm embarrassed to admit that one is true. I was young, cocky and stupid, enjoying being known as the Death Artist. I even started leaving a carving before I began a job, letting my victim find it." Valek shook his head at the memory. "That nonsense almost got me killed, so I stopped it altogether."

Valek finished dressing. "I'll be at the market today in case anything happens."

He kissed me and I clung to him for a moment, wishing we could run away and forget about soul-stealing magicians and Cahil. But that wasn't for us. Dealing with poisoners, schemers and killers seemed to be our lot in life. Besides, we would probably grow bored living in safety without any problems to worry about. But still I wished for it.

With reluctance, I let Valek go. He nodded toward the door. I opened it and distracted the guard. When I returned to the living room, the heavy darkness pressed on my skin as the icy air soaked into my bones. Valek was gone.

Irys and I walked to the market that morning. The bleak, overcast sky reflected my mood. I huddled in my cloak. It was the first time I needed to wear it during the daytime.

People crowded the market. They hurried to get their shopping done before the dark rain clouds that hovered on the horizon could descend on the Citadel.

I made a few small purchases before I felt a familiar tug on my sleeve. Fisk stood next to me. He flashed me a smile. His face no longer held the gauntness of malnutrition, and I could see his busy gang of children carrying packages for the shoppers.

"You wanted to find a strange man living with a young girl?" he asked.

"Yes. Have you seen them?"

He grinned, holding out his hand. "Information costs money."

"I see you're branching out into a new trade. Very wise," I said as I handed him a Sitian copper. "But watch who you deal with. Some won't take kindly to your inquiries."

He nodded with understanding and I saw a wisdom far beyond his nine years in his light brown eyes. I suppressed a sigh. In Ixia, Fisk's intelligence would be encouraged. He would grow up to be an Adviser or a high-ranking officer, but in Sitia he had grown up on the street, begging for food and money. But not anymore.

I smiled. "What do you know?"

"I'll show you." Fisk pulled on my hand.

Irys, who had remained silent during our exchange, asked, "Can I come with you?"

Fisk ducked his head, looking at the ground. "If it pleases you, Fourth Magician," he mumbled.

A wry grin touched Irys's face. "So much for my disguise."

Fisk glanced up in surprise. "Only the beggars who work near the Council's Hall would recognize you, Fourth Magician. With not much to do all day, they study the Council members. It's a game to be the first to recognize one of the Master Magicians."

Irys considered Fisk's comments. He squirmed under her scrutiny until he couldn't stand it any longer and turned away from her stare.

"Come. This way," he said.

We followed him through the Citadel. Cutting across back alleys and empty courtyards, I wondered if Valek followed us. The residents seemed intent on their chores and hardly noticed our passage.

Fisk stopped before we reached an open plaza. A large jade statue of a tortoise with intricate carvings on its shell occupied the middle of the square. The dark green turtle shot water out of its mouth and into a pool of water.

Pointing to a building on the opposite side of the plaza, Fisk said, "On the second floor lives a man with red lines on his hands. He's new and no one knows him. He wears a cloak that hides his face. My brother has seen a young girl enter the building, carrying packages."

I looked at Irys. *Was this quarter searched with magic?* I asked her with my mind.

Yes. But not by a Master.

She stretched out her awareness and my mind's eye went with her. Our minds touched a young woman nursing a baby on the first floor. Her thoughts on getting the baby to nap after he'd eaten his fill. Another woman on the third floor worried about the possibility of rain. We could feel no one on the second floor, but Ferde's magic matched Irys's in strength and he would not be easy to detect.

I could push harder, but he would know we were here, Irys said. *I will come back with some reinforcements.*

Who?

Roze and Bain. Together we should be able to subdue him. And once he's unconscious, he'll be easier to transport to the Keep's prison.

Why unconscious?

A magician is helpless when unconscious.

Sleeping? I asked in alarm.

No. Only if it's a drugged sleep or you get knocked out.

What happens once he wakes? Won't he be able to use his magic to escape?

The Keep's prison cells contain a power loop. If a magician tries to

use magic within the cell, the loop absorbs the magical power and directs
it back into the cell's defenses until the magician is exhausted.

Fisk, who had been staring at us in fascination, cleared his
throat. "Do you think the one you seek is living here?"

"Could the young girl your brother saw be the one with
the baby?" Irys asked Fisk.

He shook his head. "That's Ruby. Sometimes she hires me
to watch Jatee."

I grinned. "You're turning into quite the entrepreneur."

"I bought my mother a new dress," he said with pride.

Rain began to fall as we made our way back to the market.
With a wave, Fisk joined his friends and disappeared. The market emptied as the vendors packed up their wares. One woman
bumped into me in her haste to get out of the rain. She
shouted an apology, but never slowed her pace. Rumbles of
thunder echoed off the hard marble walls of the Citadel.

I'll find Roze and Bain. You return to the Keep, Irys instructed.

But I want to be there when you search that building.

*No. Stay at the Keep, Yelena. He wants you. And if something goes
wrong and he threatens to hurt Opal, you know you'll give yourself
up. It's too dangerous.*

I wanted to argue. But Irys was right, and, if I followed her
despite her instructions, she wouldn't trust me again.

Irys headed toward the Council Hall to find Roze, who had
an appointment with the Ixian Ambassador. A meeting I
would have loved to eavesdrop on. The arrogant Master Magician against the powerful Commander.

The rain began to fall in sheets, soaking my cloak. When I
tucked my cold, wet hands into the pockets, my fingers
touched paper. I couldn't remember putting anything there. I
hadn't worn my cloak since coming to Sitia, although, I had

used it to sleep when we had camped on the Avibian Plains. Perhaps the paper contained a cryptic message from Story Weaver. I laughed; it seemed to be something he would enjoy doing, leaving a puzzling note in my cloak. However, the mystery would have to wait until I found some shelter from the rain.

My guards waited at the Keep's entrance. They followed me as I headed toward my room. After they searched the interior, I invited them inside, but they declined, citing some military regulation.

After I started a roaring fire and hung up my sodden cloak, I extracted the paper. It *was* a message for me. My hands turned to ice as I read the words, and even the heat from the hearth couldn't warm them up.

"What does the message say?" Valek asked, coming from the bedroom.

I had ceased to be amazed by his abilities. Dripping wet, he must have come in through the bedroom window past one of my guards.

He plucked the paper from my hand. "She had some rudimentary skills. Probably a pickpocket hired to give you this note. Did you get a good look at her face?"

I made the belated connection between the woman who had bumped into me in the market and the message. "No. Her hood covered most of her head."

Valek shrugged, but his gaze pierced me after he scanned the note. "Interesting development."

Yes, Valek *would* think this turn of events interesting. However, I found myself conflicted.

"Seems the killer is one step ahead of the magicians," he said. "He knows they won't exchange you for Opal. So he has taken matters into his own hands. How important is Opal's life to you?"

Valek had, as usual, gotten to the heart of the matter. Ferde's note specified a location and a new date for the exchange. Three nights before the full moon, which was four days from now. I guessed that he needed some time to get me ready for the Efe ritual. My skin crawled with dread and I forced horrible images of being raped and tortured from my mind.

I could tell Irys and the others. They would set a trap for Ferde. But they wouldn't let me near the site, so the trap was bound to fail.

Or I wouldn't tell Irys about the note and would go to the meeting site alone. Irys's warnings of what would happen if Ferde absorbed my magic filtered through my mind. He would then be powerful enough to control Sitia.

Let Opal die to save Sitia? I had promised myself that I wouldn't let that happen to her. And what would stop Ferde once Opal died from tricking another magician into giving him her soul? Nothing.

I would need to keep this new situation tucked deep beneath my surface thoughts. Irys had been true to her word to not pry into my mind, but with the fate of Sitia at stake, I wouldn't be surprised if she broke her promise.

My gaze met Valek's. Magic couldn't detect him.

"Her life is important," I said, answering his question. "But capturing the killer is vital."

"What do you need, love?"

26

VALEK AND I MADE SOME initial plans for rescuing Opal. When he returned to the Ixian delegation, I felt a renewed sense of purpose. The next day I used my free time to practice controlling my magic and to do some physical training in preparation for my encounter with Ferde.

Irys, Roze and Bain had raided the apartment where, according to Fisk, the man with the red hands lived. The rooms were empty, and, by the mess that was scattered on the floor, the occupants had left in a hurry. Either someone had tipped him off, or he had felt the Masters' approach. A dead end either way, which made Valek and my plans critical.

I also began demonstrating self-defense techniques to Zitora, finally keeping my side of our bargain to trade the Third Magician's pile of clothes for defense training. The review helped in my training, as well.

The rain from the day before puddled in the training yard, and splattered us with mud as we worked on basic self-defense techniques. A apt student, Zitora quickly grasped the concepts.

"I pull my wrist out of your grasp through your thumb?" Zitora asked.

"Yes. It's the weakest part." I grunted as she yanked her arm from me. "Perfect. Now I'll show you how to not only free your wrist, but twist your hand so you can grab your attacker's arm and break it."

Her eyes lit up with glee and I laughed. "Everyone thinks you're so sweet and nice. I almost feel sorry for the first person to try and take advantage of that. Almost!"

We worked for a while until her moves became more instinctive.

"That's a good start," I said. "Those moves will help you against someone stronger than you, but if you go against a well-trained opponent, you'll have to use different tactics."

Zitora looked past my shoulder and her tawny eyes grew wide. "You mean *I* could take on someone like *him?*"

I turned. Ari strode into the training area with Janco at his heels. Wearing his sleeveless training shirt and short pants, his powerful physique was apparent. While Janco might be leaner than his partner, I knew his speed could match Ari's strength. They carried bows and broad smiles. My Keep guards looked queasy and undecided. I waved them off.

"Yes," I said to Zitora. "With the proper training, you could escape from him. You wouldn't last in a sparring match, but that's not what self-defense is all about. Remember what I told you? Hit and—"

"Git!" Janco added. "Run like a bunny with a wolf on its tail. I see you're passing our wisdom on, Yelena." Janco turned to Zitora, and said in a conspiratorial whisper, "She was trained by the very best instructors in all of Ixia."

"Another rule of self-defense is never believe everything

you hear," Ari said when Zitora appeared to be impressed by Janco's words.

"How did you get past the Keep's guards?" I asked Ari.

He shrugged his massive shoulders. "The guard asked for our names and our reason for visiting. We told him and he went into the guardhouse to consult with someone. When he came out he told us where to find you."

There must be a magician posted at the gate who could communicate by magic to others in the Keep. That was good to know.

"Can we join you?" Janco asked. "I learned a few new self-defense moves. They're nasty, too!"

"We were just finishing up," I said.

Zitora wiped her face with a towel. "I need to get cleaned up before my Council meeting." She hurried off with a wave.

"Are you too tired for a match?" Janco asked. "I want to make sure you're at your best when I beat you." He smiled sweetly.

"He's been getting into trouble all day," Ari said. "Too much time spent standing around, guarding Ambassador Signe and Adviser Ilom as they sat through one meeting after another."

"Boring!" agreed Janco.

The fact that Valek had managed to fool Ari and Janco with his Ilom disguise made me feel a little better about his presence in Sitia.

"I could be half-asleep and still beat you, Janco," I countered with my own boast.

He spun his bow and stepped back into a fighting stance. I picked my bow up and set my mind into my zone of concentration. I attacked.

"Good to know you're keeping fit," Janco puffed. He retreated a few feet, but counterattacked with determination. "She's strong and spry, but can she fly?" Janco chanted.

I smiled, realizing how much I had missed his fighting rhymes. A second before he moved, I knew that he would feint high to draw my guard up so he could strike my exposed ribs. My failure to take the bait and to counter the rib strike shocked Janco into silence. Laughing, I drove him back, swept his feet out from under him, and scooted back to avoid the splash of mud when he dropped into a puddle.

Wiping his eyes with the back of his hand, Janco said, "Gee, Ari, and *you* were worried about *her.*"

"She's learned a new trick since coming to Sitia," Cahil said. He was leaning on the training yard's fence, and must have watched the match.

Ari's posture turned defensive and alert as Cahil moved to join us. Armed with his long sword, Cahil wore a loose sand-colored tunic and brown pants.

After I introduced Cahil, Ari still didn't relax. He kept a wary eye on him. I hoped Ari and Janco didn't recognize Cahil's name. Names of the dead King's family were not mentioned in the Commander's history books of the takeover, and if the older citizens of Ixia remembered, they kept it to themselves.

"What trick?" Janco asked.

"A magic trick. She anticipated your every move by reading your mind. Devious, isn't she?" Cahil asked.

Before Janco could respond, I said, "I didn't read his mind. I kept my own mind open and picked up on his intentions."

"Sounds like the same thing to me," Cahil countered. "Leif was right when he accused you of using magic to beat me that time we sparred in the forest. Not only devious, but a liar, too."

I placed a hand on Ari's arm to keep him from throttling Cahil. "Cahil, I didn't need to read your mind. Truth is you're not as skilled as Ari and Janco. In fact, they taught me to find that zone of concentration, or else I never would have the chance to win against them. There is only one person I know who could take them on and win without any help," I said.

Janco considered. "One?" He scratched at the scar in his right ear, thinking.

"Valek," Ari said.

"Oh, yes. The infamous Valek. I'm sure his lover *would* think that highly of him. Or should I call you his spy?" Cahil stared at me in challenge.

"I think you should leave. Now," Ari said. His voice rumbled close to a growl.

"This is my home. Thanks to Valek. You leave," Cahil said to Ari, but his eyes never left my face.

Janco stepped between us. "Let's see if I have this right," he said to Cahil. "Yelena beats you, so you want a rematch, but you think she'll use her magic instead of her fighting skills to win. That's quite the quandary." Janco pulled at his goatee. "Since *I* taught her everything she knows, and I don't have any magic, thank fate, how about you fight me? Your long sword against my bow."

"*You* taught her everything?" Ari asked.

Janco waved away his comment. "Details, details. I'm thinking big picture here, Ari."

Cahil agreed to the match. With a confident expression, Cahil assumed a fighting stance then attacked. Janco's bow blurred and he unarmed Cahil within three moves. His mood didn't improve when Janco told Cahil he needed to use a lighter sword.

"She helped you," Cahil said to Janco. "I should know better than to trust a bunch of northerners." Cahil stalked away with the promise of a future encounter flaming in his eyes.

I shrugged his comments off. Cahil wouldn't ruin my time with my friends. Challenging Janco to another match, I swung my bow toward him, but he blocked it with ease and countered with one of his lightning-fast jabs.

The three of us worked together for a while. Even connected to my mental zone, Ari still beat me twice.

Ari grinned. "I'm trying not to project my intentions," he said after dumping me in the mud.

The daylight disappeared in a hurry. Tired, covered with layers of mud and sweat and smelling as if I could attract dung beetles, I longed for a bath.

Before Ari and Janco headed back to the Citadel, Ari put a large hand on my shoulder. "Be extremely careful. I don't like the way Cahil looked at you."

"I'm always careful, Ari." I waved and aimed my sore body toward the bathhouse.

The cooling season was ending; I could see the Ice Queen constellation glittering in the clear night sky. The half-moon glowed like a jewel. Only six days until the full moon. I shivered in the cold air. The puddles would be frozen by morning.

My thoughts lingered on Cahil and how fast our relationship had changed back to those first days when he had believed I was a northern spy. A full circle. I reached for my snake bracelet, spinning it around my arm.

Only when I noticed that the campus seemed strangely empty and quiet did I look around for my guards. Used to their presence, it took me a few moments before I realized that they no longer followed me.

Pulling my bow, I searched for attackers. I saw no one. I drew power to project my awareness out, but a bug bit me on the neck, and, distracted, I slapped at it. My fingers found a tiny dart. The hollow metal end dripped with my blood.

I lied to Ari. I wasn't careful. I had trusted my guards to keep me safe. Hundreds of excuses for my lapse churned through my mind as the world around me began to spin. No one to blame but myself.

Unfortunately this acknowledgement of my own stupidity didn't prevent the blackness from claiming me.

27

A SHARP PAIN AND A BURNING numbness in my shoulders roused me from sleep. With a rank taste in my dry mouth, I glanced around. Nothing looked familiar. And why was I standing? Not standing, but hanging. Looking up, I spotted the reason for my position. My wrists were manacled to the ends of a long chain that hung from a thick wooden beam in the ceiling. Once I put my weight on my feet, the pain in my shoulders eased somewhat.

Studying my surroundings, I saw rusted shovels and dirt encrusted hoes lining the wooden walls. Spiderwebs clung to dull-edged scythes. Dust coated the tools. Sunlight filtered in through small cracks and holes, illuminating what I guessed to be an abandoned shed with a muted light.

My confusion about how I had gotten here disappeared the moment I heard his voice behind me.

"We'll start your lessons now." Goel's satisfied tone caused my stomach to lurch.

"Turn around and see what I have planned for you," he said.

My skin prickled with fear, but I forced my face into a neutral expression before I spun. A smirk lit Goel's face as he gestured to a table on his right. Weapons and exotic instruments of torture covered the top. A wagon containing an empty burlap sack was to the left of Goel. The structure was bigger than I had thought. The shed's door loomed behind him, appearing impossibly far to me, but in reality only ten feet.

Goel followed my gaze and smiled. "Bolted and locked. We're in a forgotten place far away from the Keep." He picked up a small black leather whip that had metal spikes on the ends.

The Keep! I pulled some power to me and projected a desperate mental call. *Irys.*

"How're the ribs?" I asked, trying to distract him.

He frowned and touched the side of his chest. "That horse is gonna make a tasty stew." He smacked his lips. "But that's later." He raised the whip.

Yelena! Thank fate you're alive. Where are you? Irys's worried voice sounded in my mind.

A shed somewhere.

Goel stepped closer to strike me with the whip. I kicked him in the stomach. He jumped back more from surprise than pain.

"Me mistake," he said, retreating to his table. "Not to worry. I'll fix." He picked up a dart, dipping it in a vial of liquid.

The sleeping potion. I thought fast.

I need more information. Is Ferde with you? Irys asked.

Not Ferde. Goel.

Goel?

No time. I'll explain later.

Goel loaded the dart into a hollow pipe. He aimed. I laughed. The pipe wavered as he squinted at me in confusion.

"I can't believe it," I said.

"Believe what?" He lowered the weapon.

"That you're afraid of me. No, not afraid. Terrified." I laughed again. "You can't beat me in a fair fight so you ambush and drug me. And even when I'm chained, you're still scared."

"Am not." He exchanged the pipe for a pair of manacles then dove for my feet.

I struggled, but he outweighed me. In the end, my ankles were manacled together. Goel then staked the six-inch chain between the cuffs to the floor. No more kicking, but I remained awake, and I had another trick. Magic. My mind raced through options.

I could try and freeze the muscles in his body, but I didn't know how. Goel chose another whip from his table. This one was longer with braided leather and small metal balls tied into the fringes on the end.

His arm blurred. I projected a confusing array of images into his mind.

Goel lost his balance and fell to the ground. "Huh?" He seemed confused.

As he regained his feet, I caught a slight movement behind Goel. The bolt moved and the knob turned. The door burst open with a rush of light. Two figures stood in the doorway. They pointed their swords at Goel's heart. Ari and Janco.

"Yelena, are you all right?" Ari asked. His eyes never left Goel's surprised face.

Janco came over and inspected the chains. "Keys?" he asked Goel, who pressed his lips together. "Guess I'll have to do it the hard way." Janco pulled his lock picks from his pocket.

My first rush of relief at seeing my friends cooled. This rescue wouldn't stop Goel from trying again. Even if he was arrested for kidnapping, Goel would harbor his grudge until freed and years from now, I might be in the exact same position. *I* had to deal with him. He needed to know that he couldn't win against me.

I shook my head at Janco. "I've got the situation under control. Go back to the Keep, I'll meet you there."

Janco stared at me in astonished silence. Ari, though, trusted me. "Come on, she doesn't need our help." Ari sheathed his sword.

Janco recovered. He flashed me one of his mischievous grins. "I'll bet you a copper that she'll be free in five minutes," he said to Ari.

Ari grunted in amusement. "A silver on ten minutes," he countered.

"I'll bet you both a gold coin that she kills him," Valek said from behind them. They moved aside and he entered, still dressed in his Adviser Ilom disguise. "The only way to take care of your problem. Right, love?"

"No killing," I said. "I'll manage."

"He's my man. I'll handle this," Cahil said from the doorway.

Valek spun, but Cahil just stared at him for a moment before coming inside. "Goel, stand down," Cahil ordered.

Valek disappeared from sight. The crowded shed seemed to shrink in size and, by this point, I wouldn't be surprised to see Irys and the other Masters following Cahil. We could all have a festival.

During the conversations and arrivals, Goel's face had transformed from stunned to horrified and finally settled into stubborn determination. "No," he said to Cahil.

"Goel, you were right about her. But this isn't the way to deal with her. Especially not with her two henchmen nearby. Release her."

"I don't take orders from you. Everyone else can pretend you're in charge. I won't."

"Are *you* challenging my authority?" Cahil demanded.

"You don't have any authority with me," Goel shot back.

Cahil's face turned bright red as he sputtered. "How dare—"

"Gentlemen!" I shouted. "You can fight it out later. Everyone leave. Now! My arms are killing me."

Janco pulled Cahil from the shed. Ari shut the door. Goel stood there blinking in the sudden darkness.

"Where were we?" I prompted.

"You can't expect me..." He gestured toward the door.

"Forget about them. You have more to worry about in here than outside."

He sneered. "You're not really in the position to be boasting."

"And you don't fully understand what it's like to go against a *magician*."

The sneer faded from his lips.

"You think I'm just some girl to be taught a lesson. That I should fear you. You're the one who needs the lesson." I gathered power to me and reached my awareness out to Goel's.

The word "magician" had only caused a brief feeling of doubt in Goel's mind. *After all,* he thought, *if she was a good magician, she wouldn't have been so easy to catch.*

"A momentary lapse," I said. Since he had no magical power, he couldn't hear my thoughts, but I might be able to control him. I closed my eyes and projected myself into Goel, taking the chance that if I could do it with Topaz I should be able to do it with a person.

He jumped as if struck by lightning when I entered his mind. Although glad that my transfer worked, being closer to Goel's slimy thoughts made me wish for Topaz's clean mind.

When I focused Goel's eyes on me, I understood why he thought so little of me. My hair hung in messy clumps. The combination of closed eyes, dirt-streaked face and mud covered clothes made me seem pathetic. A helpless figure in need of a bath.

I felt his panic when he realized he had lost control of his body. He could still think, see and feel. I marveled at his physical strength, but I encountered some difficultly moving his body around. The proportions felt strange and balancing his body took a concentrated effort.

He tried to regain control, but I pushed his weak efforts aside. I searched for the key to the manacles and found them in his pack under the table. Then I unlocked and removed the manacles from my body's feet. Supporting myself with one of Goel's arms, I unlocked the wrist cuffs. I grabbed my body before it could fall to the ground and lifted it up.

It felt light as a pillow. My body breathed and blood pulsed. I carried it and laid it gently on the ground near the door. Using Goel's thumb, I raised my left eyelid. Although my body lived, the spark of life was gone. Unnerved I stood and backed away.

When the feeling of utter helplessness overcame Goel, I let him experience that sensation for a long while. Picking up a knife from the table, I cut a shallow line along his arm. I felt his pain from the cut, but it was muted and distant. Resting the tip of the blade on his chest, I wondered if I plunged the knife into his heart, would I kill us both?

An interesting question that would have to be answered at another time. Kicking off his boots, I snapped the manacles around Goel's ankles then I shortened the chain hanging from the overhead beam before locking his wrists into the cuffs. I savored the combination of fear, discomfort and chagrin that coursed through his mind before I projected myself back toward my own body.

The shed spun for a moment when I opened my eyes. Fatigue coursed through my limbs. I stood in slow motion, but managed a smug smile at Goel's new predicament. As I headed for the door, I thought I probably wouldn't have discovered that magical skill working with Irys or the other magicians. And what exactly had I done? Transferred my magic? My will? My soul? I shied away from those disturbing thoughts. Taking control of someone's body and forcing him to move must be in violation of the Ethical Code. But when Goel kidnapped me he became a criminal. The Ethical Code didn't apply to him. I almost laughed. I guess I should be grateful Goel attacked me. Now I knew another defensive magical move.

Ari and Janco waited for me in the overgrown field that surrounded the shed. I saw a dilapidated fence and a collapsed barn and guessed we stood on an abandoned farm outside the Citadel. Valek and Cahil hadn't waited for me.

Ari smiled as Janco slapped a silver coin into his huge hand.

"Your problem?" Ari asked me.

"I left him hanging."

"What took you so long?" Janco complained.

"I wanted to prove my point. Where's...ah, Adviser Ilom and Cahil?"

"Why the sudden concern for Ilom?" Janco asked with mock sincerity. "He's a grown man with surprising abilities.

That stuffy old bore appeared out of nowhere, did a dead per-fect impression of Valek's voice and disappeared as if by magic. The man's a genius! I should have known he would come along. Valek wouldn't miss all the fun."

The smile dropped from Ari's face. "Valek's going to get caught. Cahil made a beeline for the Citadel, probably to tell the Council members about Valek."

"Great disguise, though," Janco said. "He had us fooled."

"Cahil already suspected Valek was here," I said, shivering in the cold morning air. Now he knew for certain. "I'm sure Valek can handle it." My tired mind, though, couldn't produce a good solution.

Ari went over to the shed and picked up my backpack from where it leaned against the side. "I thought you might need this." He handed it to me.

I found my cloak inside. Wrapping the warm garment around me I moved to sling the pack onto my back, but Ari took it from me.

"Let's go," Ari said.

He and Janco led me through the fallow fields. We passed an empty farmhouse.

"Where are we?" I asked.

"About two miles east of the Citadel," Ari said.

I stumbled just at the thought of walking two miles. "How did you find me?"

"We followed your guards last night to make sure they knew what they were doing. By the time we realized they had been hit, you had disappeared," Ari said.

Janco grinned. "The magicians were frantic. Search parties were sent." He shook his head as if amazed by the uproar. "We had no idea what they would find in the dark. We just hoped they wouldn't ruin the trail. Once the sun was up, it took us no time to follow the tracks. Goel used a wagon to wheel you out of the Keep and Citadel."

I thought of the burlap sack lying in the wagon. Goel must have hidden me in that sack.

"I guess Cahil followed us," Janco said. Scratching his scar, he added, "Of course, you didn't want our help. Now I have to go beat up some soldier just to keep my ego intact."

As we reached the east gate of the Citadel, I spotted a commotion near the guardhouse. A loose horse was giving the guards some trouble. Kiki.

She stopped when we crossed through the gate. *Lavender Lady tired. Need ride.*

How did you find me?

Follow scent of Strong Man and Rabbit Man.

She referred to Ari and Janco. I apologized to the gate's guards about Kiki's disruption. Ari helped me onto her back and gave me my pack.

"We'll catch up with you later," Ari promised.

Before Kiki and I headed toward the Keep, I thanked my friends.

"For what? We didn't do anything," Janco grumbled.

"For caring enough to follow my guards. And the next time, I might need the help."

"There better not *be* a next time," Ari said, giving me a stern look.

"How touching," Janco said, pretending to wipe his eyes. "Get going, Yelena. I don't want you to see me cry." He faked a sniffle.

"I'm sure your ego can handle it," I said. "Or will you need to beat up some trainees to feel like a man again?"

"Very funny," he said.

I waved and asked Kiki to take me home. On the way, I connected to Irys and updated her on what had happened. She promised to send some guards out to arrest Goel.

If I don't make it to my room, I'll be asleep in the barn, I said, yawning. I felt her hesitate. *Now what?*

Your parents arrived this morning.

Oh, no!

Oh, yes. Esau is here with me, but when your mother found out you were missing, she climbed a tree and we can't convince her to come down. She's hysterical and won't listen to us. You'll have to talk to her.

I sighed. *I'm on my way. Where is she?*

Perl was in one of the tall oak trees next to the pasture.

Kiki took me to the base of the tree. A handful of orange and brown leaves still clung to the branches. I spotted my mother's green cloak near the top. I called to Perl, telling her I was fine. "You can come down now," I said.

"Yelena! Thank fate! Come up here where it's safe," she said.

I resigned myself to the fact that getting Perl down would be difficult, and took off my cloak and backpack, dropping them to the ground. Even standing on Kiki's back, I still had to stretch to reach the lowest branch. My mother's climbing ability was impressive.

As Kiki grazed, I hauled myself higher, climbing until I reached my mother. I settled on a branch below her, but she appeared next to me in an instant, hugging me tight. When her body started shaking with sobs, I had to grab the tree's trunk to keep us both from falling.

I waited for her to calm before gently pulling her away. She sat next to me, leaning against my shoulder. Her face was streaked with dirt where her tears had mixed with the dried mud on my clothes. I offered the one clean spot on my shirt, but she shook her head, taking a handkerchief from her pocket. Her dark green cloak had many pockets, and the garment had a slim tailored cut, eliminating the bulky excess of material. It wouldn't make a good blanket, but it was perfect for keeping warm while traveling through the tree tops.

"Is this one of Nutty's designs?" I asked her, fingering the cloth.

"Yes. Since I hadn't left the jungle in fourteen years…" She gave me a rueful smile, "I needed something for the cooler weather."

"I'm glad you came," I said.

Her smile fled. A look of terror touched her eyes before she took a few deep breaths. "Your father gave me some Eladine to keep me calm during the trip, and I was doing so well, until…" She put a hand to her neck, grimacing.

"Bad timing," I agreed. "But I'm fine, see?" I held out an arm. My mistake.

She gasped, staring at the bloody bruises around my wrist. I pulled my sleeve down to cover them.

"They're just scratches."

"What happened? And don't sugarcoat it for me," she ordered.

I gave her a condensed version with only a slight dusting of sugar. "He won't be bothering me again."

"It won't happen again. You are coming home with us," she declared.

After this morning, I wanted to agree. "What would I do there?"

"Help your father collect samples or help me make perfumes. The thought of losing you again is too much to bear."

"But you have to bear it, Mother. I'm not going to run or hide from difficult or dangerous situations. And I've made some promises to myself and others. I have to see things through, because if I ran away, I couldn't live with myself."

A breeze rustled the leaves, and the sweat on my skin felt like ice. My mother pulled her cloak tight. I could sense her emotions as they twisted into knots around her. She was in a strange place, dealing with the realization that her daughter would willingly put herself in harm's way for others, and she could lose her again. She struggled with her fear, wanting nothing more than the safety of her family and the familiarity of home.

I had an idea. "Nutty's cloak reminds me of the jungle," I said.

She glanced down at the garment. "Really?"

"It's the same color as the underside of an Ylang-Ylang Leaf. Remember that time when we were caught in a sudden downpour on our way home from the market, and we huddled under a big Ylang-Ylang Leaf?"

"You remembered." She beamed.

I nodded. "My childhood memories have been unlocked. But I wouldn't have them now, if I hadn't taken a risk and followed Irys to the Avibian Plains."

"You've been to the plains." The horror on her face transformed to awe. "You're not afraid of anything, are you?"

"During that trip, I could list at least five things I was afraid of." Especially getting my head chopped off by Moon Man's scimitar, but I was smart enough not to tell *that* to my mother.

"Then why did you go?"

"Because we needed information. I couldn't let my fear stop me from doing what I needed to do."

She considered my words in silence.

"Your cloak can protect you from more than the weather," I said. "If you fill the pockets with special items from home, you can surround yourself with the jungle whenever you're feeling overwhelmed or afraid."

"I hadn't thought of that."

"In fact, I have something you can put into your pocket now that will remind you of me. Come on." Without waiting to see if she followed, I climbed down. I hung from the lowest branch before dropping to the ground.

As I searched my backpack, I heard a rustling and I looked up in time to see my mother shimming down the tree's trunk. I found my fire amulet in one of the pack's pockets. Considering my recent run of troubles, the amulet would be safer with my mother.

"I won this during a time in my life when fear was my constant and only companion." I handed it to her. It was the first place prize for an acrobatic competition at Ixia's annual Fire Festival. What followed after was the worst time of my life, but I would have competed for the amulet again, even knowing the outcome.

I handed the amulet to my mother. "This is one of only four items I hold dear. I want you to have it."

She examined the fire amulet. "What are the other three?"

"My butterfly and snake." I pulled out my necklace, and I showed her my bracelet.

"Did someone make those for you?"

"Yes. A friend," I said before she could ask more.

She raised a slender eyebrow, but only asked, "What's the last thing?"

I rummaged in my pack while I decided if my mother

would be shocked to know I held a weapon dear. Far from being the perfect daughter, I figured she wouldn't be surprised at all. Handing her my switchblade, I explained what the silver symbols on the handle meant.

"Same friend?" she asked.

I laughed and told her about Ari and Janco. "They're more like older brothers than friends."

My mother's smile felt like the sun coming out after a storm. "Good to know there are people in Ixia who care about you." She tucked my fire amulet into a pocket of her cloak. "Fire represents strength. I will keep it with me always."

Hugging me tight for a moment, Perl pulled away and declared, "You're freezing. Put your cloak on. Let's get inside."

"Yes, Mother."

Esau and Irys waited for us in the Keep's guest quarters on the west side of the campus. I endured a bone-crushing hug from my father, but had to decline an invitation to dinner with my parents. My desire for a bath and sleep overrode my hunger. I had to promise to spend most of the next day with them before they allowed me to leave.

Irys accompanied me to the bathhouse. Dark smudges lined her eyes and she looked as tired as I felt. She seemed in a contemplative mood.

"Did you use magic on your mother?" she asked.

"I don't think so. Why?"

"She seemed at peace. Perhaps you did it instinctively."

"But that's not good. I should have complete control. Right?"

"I'm beginning to think that not all the rules apply to you, Yelena. Perhaps it was your upbringing or the fact that you started controlling your magic at an older age that has made your powers develop in an unusual way. Not to worry, though," she added when she saw my expression. "I believe it will be to your benefit."

Irys and I parted at the baths. After a long hot soak, I dragged myself to my rooms. My last thought before drifting off to sleep was to marvel over the fact that Irys had trusted me enough not to assign more guards to me.

It seemed a mere moment that I had sunk into a dreamless slumber when Irys's mental call woke me. I squinted in the bright sunlight, trying to orient myself.

What time? I asked her.

Midmorning, Irys said.

Morning? That meant I had been asleep since yesterday afternoon. *Why did you wake me?*

An emergency Council session has been called, and your presence is required.

Emergency session?

Goel was murdered, and Cahil is claiming Adviser Ilom is Valek in disguise.

28

GOEL MURDERED? VALEK CAUGHT?
My groggy mind couldn't quite understand Irys's comment
and her attention pulled away before I could question her. I
changed as fast as I could and ran toward the Council Hall.

Did Valek kill Goel? And if Valek really was in custody, he
just gave the Sitians one more reason to execute him. Should
I act surprised by Valek's presence or admit I knew about him?
Would I be considered an accomplice to Goel's murder? Perhaps they suspected me. I only told Irys where to find him; I
hadn't mentioned the others to her.

Questions without answers swirled in my mind. I paused
before the steps to the Council Hall, smoothed my braid, and
adjusted my clothes. I wore one of the new shirts and
skirt/pants that Nutty had sewn for me. Glancing at my surroundings, I checked to make sure no one had followed me.
Irys trusted me to take care of myself. I couldn't let her down.

The Council's members, four Master Magicians, a handful
of the Keep's guards, and Cahil had assembled in the great hall.

The noise of their various arguments reached deafening levels, and I spotted Cahil gesturing wildly to the Sandseed's Councilman. Cahil's flushed face contorted in anger as he replied.

Roze Featherstone, First Magician pounded a gavel to bring order to the meeting. Conversations ceased as the Councilors took their seats. The decorations from the greeting ceremony had been removed, and a U-shaped table had been brought in. Roze and the other three Magicians sat at the bend, while the clan Elders sat along the straight sides. Six on one side, five on the other with Cahil taking the sixth seat. A wooden podium had been placed in the middle of the U. I stood with the Captain of the guard and his men near the side wall, hoping to blend in with the white marble.

"Let us address the matter of Lieutenant Goel Ixia," ordered Roze.

I glanced at Irys in surprise.

All the northern refugees are given Ixia as their clan name, Irys explained in my mind. *Cahil is considered their clan leader. It is an honorary clan and title. He has no lands and no power to vote in the Council.*

That explained Cahil's resentment toward the Council and his continuing frustration of not getting their support for his campaign against the Commander.

"Lieutenant Ixia was found dead in a fallow field east of the Citadel in Featherstone Clan lands," Roze recited. "The healers have determined that he was killed with a sword thrust through his heart."

Murmurs rippled through the Council members. Roze stopped them with a cold stare. "The weapon was not found at the scene, and a search of the surrounding fields is currently in progress. According to Fourth Magician, Yelena Liana Zaltana was the last person to see him alive. I call her to the witness stand."

Sixteen pair of eyes turned toward me. Hostile, concerned and worried expressions peppered the group.

Don't worry, Irys said. *Tell them what happened.*

I walked to the podium, guessing that was the witness stand.

"Explain yourself," Roze demanded.

I told them about the kidnapping and my escape. A collective gasp sounded when I explained about taking control of Goel's body. Whispers about the Ethical Code started to spread.

Irys stood and said, "There is nothing illegal about using magic to defend yourself. In fact, she should be commended for extracting herself without harming Goel."

The Council members asked an endless amount of questions about Goel's motives. Only after the guards that had been assigned to protect me confirmed they had been drugged did the Council run out of inquiries.

"You left Goel chained in the shed, and that was the last time you saw him?" Roze asked.

"Yes," I said.

"She's telling the truth." By Roze's sour expression, I knew that statement had been hard for her to say. "The investigation into Goel's murder will continue. Yelena, you may sit down." Roze gestured to a bench located behind her and the other Master Magicians. "That leaves us with the other matter. I call Cahil Ixia to the witness stand."

As I moved toward the bench, I passed Cahil. His blue eyes held a hard determination and he refused to meet my gaze. I sat on the edge of the wooden bench, and, even though I braced myself for his accusations, Cahil's words made my heart squeeze with fear.

"—and compounding Valek's deception is the fact that his soul mate and master spy is Yelena Zaltana."

The room erupted with a cacophony of voices. Roze pounded her gavel, but no one listened. I felt the force of her magic when she ordered everyone silent. She held them quiet for only a moment, but it was enough to get her point across.

"Cahil, where is your evidence?" Roze asked.

He motioned to one of the Keep's guards. The guard opened a door in the back wall and Captain Marrok and four of Cahil's men entered the hall, dragging Adviser Ilom with them. Ilom's arms were manacled behind his back and the four guards had their swords pointed at him. Ambassador Signe and a handful of Ixian soldiers followed the grim procession.

I strained to catch Valek's eye, but he looked at the Council members with an annoyed frown.

Ambassador Signe was the first to speak. "I demand an explanation. This is an act of war."

"Cahil, I told you to release the Adviser until this matter was settled," Roze said. Fury flared in her amber eyes.

"And let him escape? No. Better to bring him here and unmask him in front of everyone." Cahil strode to Ilom and yanked on his hair.

I cringed, but Ilom's head jerked down as he cried out in pain. Undaunted, Cahil pulled Ilom's nose then clawed at the flesh under his chin. Ilom yelped and blood welled from the scratches on his neck. Cahil stepped back astounded. He reached toward Ilom's face again, but Marrok grabbed him and held him. Cahil's mouth hung open with astonishment.

"Release the Adviser," Roze ordered.

Ilom's manacles were removed as Cahil, his face red with rage, and his men were escorted from the room. The session ended and Roze rushed to make amends and apologize to the Ambassador and Ilom.

I stayed on the bench, watching as Signe's anger and Ilom's pout transformed into more agreeable expressions by Roze's words. I was afraid to call attention to myself, hoping no one would remember Cahil's other accusations about me.

Cahil's shock over Ilom had matched my own. Even knowing his tricks, Valek continued to surprise me. I scanned the Ixian guards, and, sure enough, one blue-eyed soldier looked mighty pleased with himself. Ilom probably dressed as a guard when Valek disguised himself as the Adviser, and they probably switched places when Valek needed to sneak around Sitia.

Eventually, the Council members and Ixians began to leave. Irys joined me on the bench.

Tell Valek to leave, Irys said. *The danger is too great.*

You know.

Of course. I expected him to be with the delegation.

It doesn't bother you that he's here. That he might be spying on Sitia.

He's here for you. And I'm glad you had some time together.

But what if he killed Goel?

Goel was a danger to you. While I would have preferred to arrest him, I'm not upset by his demise.

"Go get something to eat. You look a little pale," Irys said.

"That's just great. I went from having none to having *two* mother hens."

Irys laughed. "Some people just need the extra help." She patted my knee and went in search of Bain.

Before I could leave, though, I saw Bavol Zaltana heading toward me. I waited for him.

"Ambassador Signe requests a meeting with you," Bavol said.

"When?"

"Now."

Bavol led me out of the great hall. "The Ambassador has been assigned some offices so she can conduct business while a guest here," Bavol explained as we walked through the Council Hall.

The entire Sitian government was housed in the vast building. Offices and meeting rooms hummed with the daily tasks of running a government. An underground record room stored all the official documents, although the local records remained at each clan's capitol.

I wondered about the Sandseed's moving capitol. Did they haul their records with them as they traveled throughout the plains? Remembering Irys's lecture about the Sandseeds, I realized they kept a verbal record, telling history through the Story Weavers. An image of Moon Man painted blue and sitting in the Council's underground room caused me to smile.

Bavol gave me a questioning glance.

"I was thinking of the record room," I said. "Just trying to imagine how the Sandseed Clan reports information to the Council."

Bavol grinned. "They have always been difficult. We indulge their…unusual ways. Twice a year, a Story Weaver comes to the Council and recites the clan's events to a scribe. It works, and keeps peace in our land. Here we are." Bavol gestured to an open door. "We will talk again later." Bavol dipped his head and shoulders in a half bow and left.

The invitation had not included Bavol. I walked into a receiving area. Adviser Ilom sat behind a plain desk. The scratches on his neck had stopped bleeding. Two soldiers guarded a closed door.

Ilom stood and knocked on the door. I heard a faint voice, and Ilom turned the knob. "She's here," he said, then pushed the door wider and gestured me inside.

I entered Ambassador Signe's office, noting the simple functional furniture and lack of decorations. Guards stood behind her, but she dismissed them. None of the soldiers had been Valek, and I wondered where he had gotten to. Ari and Janco were probably off-duty.

"You caused a considerable stir last night," Signe said when we were alone.

Her powerful eyes scanned me. I marveled at her appearance. She had the same delicate features as the Commander, yet the long hair and the thin lines of kohl around her eyes transformed his face into her ageless beauty.

"I hope your sleep wasn't interrupted," I said, sticking to a diplomatic approach.

She waved away comment. "We're alone. You may speak freely."

I shook my head. "Master Magicians have excellent hearing." I thought about Roze, she would consider eavesdropping on the Ambassador to be her patriotic duty.

Signe nodded in understanding. "Seems the Wannabe King has gotten hold of some *wrong* information. I wonder how that happened."

"A miscommunication between several parties."

"There will be no more false accusations?" Signe asked.

Her gaze pierced me as if she held a knife to my throat. She wondered at my ability to keep her disguise a secret.

"No." I showed her my palm, pointing to the scar she had

made when I promised not to reveal the Commander's secret to anyone. Not even to Valek.

That thought reminded me of Irys's suggestion that Valek leave Sitia. I pulled my butterfly pendant out. "Some rumors tend to smolder, and it would be best to make certain there is no fuel left to ignite another fire."

Signe had to know about Valek. "I will take that under advisement. However, I had another matter to discuss with you." Signe pulled a sheet of parchment from her black leather briefcase. She rolled it up, and held it in her hand.

"The Commander has sent a message for you. He has thought in depth about your last conversation with him. He decided that the advice presented was valid and would like to thank you for the suggestions." Signe handed me the paper roll.

"An invitation to come visit us when your magical training is complete. We are planning on returning to Ixia in a week's time," she said. "Your response is required before we leave."

A dismissal. I bowed to the Ambassador and left her office. I puzzled over her words as I headed toward the Keep. The Commander had signed an order of execution, visiting Ixia would be suicide.

I waited until I had a warm fire lit in my rooms before unrolling the Commander's message. Staring at the dancing flames, I contemplated Commander Ambrose's offer. I held the order for my execution in my hands. But tossing it into the fire would not be a simple act. A brief note had been written on the document.

Prove my loyalties to Ixia and the order would be nullified. Show the benefits of having a magician working for Ixia to the Ixian generals and an adviser's position would be mine. Do these things and I could return to Ixia. Return to my friends. Return to Valek.

Without knowing it, Cahil had seen my possible future when he had called me a master spy at the Council's session.

29

I GAZED AT THE FIRE AS MY conflicting emotions, my conflicting loyalties and my conflicting desires all burned and danced in my chest, mimicking the flames. Coming no closer to a decision, I hid the execution order in my backpack. It might be better to think about it later.

Remembering my promise to my parents, I headed toward the dining hall, hoping I would find them eating lunch. Along the way, I encountered Dax.

"Yelena," he said, falling in step with me. "Haven't seen you in days."

"I'm sure you're just dying to tell me all the campus gossip about me. Right?"

"I *do* have a life. Maybe I've been too busy to listen to rumors," he huffed, pretending to have hurt feelings.

I looked at him.

He sighed. "Okay, you win. I'm bored out of my skull. Second Magician is busy playing detective, and Gelsi is neck-deep in some project and I never see her anymore." Dax paused dramatically. "My life is so boring that I have to live vicariously through your adventures."

"And since the rumors are so accurate—"

"Your adventures have turned into legends." He swept his arms wide, laughing. "So where are you off to now? Going to slay a dragon? Can I tag along as your lowly squire? I'll polish your staff of power every night with my shirt. I promise."

"I'm glad my problems are keeping you entertained," I said with some sarcasm. "I'm searching for my...ah, for the Tree King and his Queen. We're going to plan our attack against the evil Tree Varmints who have assembled an invisible army in the Keep."

Dax's eyes lit up. "I heard about the Tree Queen's adventures this morning."

The game soured. I didn't want to hear the students' gossip about my mother. Before Dax could elaborate, I invited him to tag along.

I found my parents in the dining hall and we joined them. While we ate, Dax's presence worked to my advantage. The topic of conversation stayed on school and horses and mundane matters, giving my parents no chance to question me about the Council session. And when my mother offered to distill a special cologne for Dax, I knew she was glad I had found a Sitian friend.

After saying goodbye to Dax, I went to the guest quarters with my parents. As Perl brewed some tea in the small kitchen, I asked Esau about the Curare. Irys had told him about the drug when she feared Ferde had kidnapped me.

He ran a calloused hand over his face. "I never thought it would be used like that," he said, shaking his head. "When I discover something new, I always experiment with it until I know all the side effects and know how the substance could be used or abused. Then I weigh the good against the bad. Some discoveries never see the light of day, but for others, even though they might not be perfect, the benefits outweigh the risks."

Esau stopped speaking when Perl entered the room carrying a tray of tea. The warning in my father's eyes told me that my mother didn't know about Ferde's gruesome use of the Curare.

She served the tea and sat close to me on the couch. She had worn her cloak during lunch, but had removed it when we entered their suite.

"What happened at the Council's session?" she asked me.

I gave them a watered-down version of Cahil's accusations against Adviser Ilom. Perl's hand flew to her neck when I mentioned Valek's name, but she relaxed when I told her Cahil had been proven wrong. Neglecting to mention Cahil's claims about my involvement with Valek, I informed them about Goel's murder.

"Good," Perl said. "Saves me the effort of cursing him."

"Mother!" I was astonished. "Can you do that?"

"Perfumes and scents are not the only things I can concoct."

I looked at Esau. He nodded his head. "Good thing Reyad and Mogkan were already dead. Your mother has quite the imagination when she's angry."

I wondered what other surprises I would discover about my parents. Changing the subject, I asked about their journey to the Keep and about the Zaltana family, spending the day with them as promised.

When the hour had grown late, Esau offered to escort me to my rooms. At first I declined. I hadn't been assigned guards since the episode with Goel. When he insisted and when Perl frowned, I remembered her comment about curses and not wanting to be a target of her ire, I agreed.

The campus atmosphere hung silent and empty. Moonlight glistened off the ice-coated trees. Only four more days until the full moon. My hand found Valek's snake and I twisted the bracelet around my arm.

When we were halfway to my rooms Esau said, "I need to tell you another thing about Curare."

"There's more?"

He nodded. "The stinging nettle plant was the reason I sent the shipment of Curare to the Sandseeds before I finished all my experiments on the drug. The plant grows in the Avibian Plains and the sting causes unbearable pain for many days. It's usually the children who wander into a patch without realizing it. In low doses, Curare is excellent for numbing the wound. It had never occurred to me that someone would use high doses of Curare to paralyze the entire body." Esau frowned, running a hand through his shoulder length gray hair. "Later I discovered another side effect that seemed minor at the time. But now..." Esau stopped and turned to me. "At high doses the Curare will also paralyze a person's magical abilities."

I felt the blood drain from my face. That meant Curare could render even a Master Magician completely helpless. Tomorrow night was the time of the secret exchange. Since I had taken over Goel's body with my magic, I planned to take over Ferde's, believing that, even if I was incapacitated by the drug, I could still use my magic. It now seemed imperative that I avoid getting shot with Curare.

My father must have seen the horror in my eyes. "There is an antidote of sorts," he said.

"Antidote?"

"Not a complete reversal, but it does free the magic and return some feeling, although it creates some new problems." Esau shook his head in frustration. "I haven't been able to experiment with it fully."

"What is it?"

"Theobroma."

That explained the new problem. Eating the brown sweet would open my mind to magical influences. My mental defenses would not work against another magician, even one weaker than me.

"How much Theobroma would I need?" I asked my father.

"A lot. Though, I could concentrate it," he mused.

A chill wind blew through me, shivering I pulled my cloak tighter as we continued our walk.

"It wouldn't taste as good, but it would be a smaller quantity," Esau said.

"Can you do it by tomorrow afternoon?" I asked.

He stared at me. A worried concern filled his kind eyes.

"Are you going to do something that I shouldn't tell your mother about?"

"Yes."

"Important?"

"Very."

My father considered my request. When we arrived at my rooms, he gave me a hug. "Do you know what you're doing?"

"I have a plan."

"Yelena, you managed to find your way home despite the odds. I'll trust that you'll prevail again. You'll have the antidote by tomorrow noon."

He stood in my doorway like a protective bear while I

searched inside. Satisfied that I was safe, he said good-night and headed back to the guest quarters.

I lay in bed and mulled over the information Esau had given me. When my shutters swung wide, I sat up, grabbing my switchblade from under the pillow. Valek climbed through the window with a lithe grace, dropping without a sound onto my bed. He locked the shutters then joined me.

"You need to leave. Too many people know you're here," I said.

"Not until we find the killer. And besides, the Commander ordered me to protect the Ambassador. I would be remiss in my duties if I left."

"What if she ordered you home?" I turned so I could see his face.

"The Commander's orders overrule all others."

"Valek, did you—"

He stopped my question with a kiss. I needed to discuss many things with him. Goel's death and the Commander's offer. But once his body molded to mine and his musky scent reached my nose all thoughts of murder and intrigue evaporated. I pulled at his shirt. He smiled with delight. Our time together was limited and I didn't want to waste the night on words.

When I woke in the semidarkness of sunrise, Valek was gone. But I felt energized. My rendezvous with Ferde was scheduled for midnight so I reviewed the plan as I went through my day.

Irys had wanted me to try to move objects again with my magic for my morning lesson. I had yet to manage that skill. But I asked if we could work on strengthening my mental defenses. If I had to resort to using Esau's antidote, I wanted to be able to produce a strong enough barrier that might block his magic even while under the influence of the Theobroma.

Before dismissing me for the day, Irys asked, "Are you still feeling tired from your encounter with Goel?"

"A little. Why?"

She gave me an ironic smile. "You've been pestering me about the search for Opal every day for the last week. Yet no questions today."

"I assumed you would tell me any news."

"We've reached a milestone!" Irys declared. "You're learning to trust us." Then the humor in her eyes dulled. "No news. We don't think they are in the Citadel or the plains so now we're widening the search area."

Feelings of guilt squeezed my chest as I hurried to find my father. I had wanted to work with Irys and the others, but now I planned to meet Ferde with just Valek backing me up. Granted Valek equaled four armed men, but I hadn't confided our plans to her. A true Sitian would present the information to the Council.

But why didn't I trust Irys? Because she wouldn't let me go to the rendezvous. The danger to Sitia was too great, but trying to ambush Ferde wouldn't work without me there. Irys believed they would find him eventually and sacrificing Opal was a small price to pay for Sitia. I believed that risking all was the only way to stop him. Knowing the risks, and trying to minimize them would be the key.

Irys didn't believe in my abilities to capture Ferde, but I had kept Roze, the most powerful magician in Sitia, from extracting my innermost thoughts, I had healed Tula's body and found her consciousness, I had taken over Goel's body and would soon have an antidote to Curare.

Trust needed to go both ways. Loyalty, too. Did I feel any loyalty? To Irys, yes. But to Sitia? I couldn't say.

Even if we succeeded in rescuing Opal and capturing Ferde, Irys would cease my lessons. That grim thought led me to contemplate my future and the Commander's offer.

Irys would sever our relationship, and I would have no obligations to Sitia. I could tell the Commander about Cahil and his plans to build an army to overthrow Ixia. Cahil, that weasel, had no qualms about telling the Council of my connection with Valek.

My father waited for me outside the guest quarters. He had concentrated the Theobroma into a pill the same size and shape as a robin's egg.

"I coated it with a gelatin that will keep it from melting," Esau explained.

"Melting?"

"How would you eat it if you're frozen with Curare?" When my eyes widened in sudden understanding, he said, "You can hold this pill between your teeth. If you're pricked with the Curare just bite down on it and try and swallow as much as you can before your jaw muscles become paralyzed. Hopefully the rest will melt and slide down your throat."

Before learning about this antidote my main goal had been to not get hit with Curare at all. If I willingly went to Ferde, he shouldn't need to use it. Or so I'd hope. Esau's pill made me even more confident about the rendezvous tonight, and he had given me an idea. I borrowed a few other items from my father.

I spent the remainder of the afternoon practicing self-defense with Zitora, and after dinner with my parents I went to the barn. Everything about the day seemed odd as if I did things for the last time. Perhaps the feeling was due to the fact that my life would be different after tonight.

Kiki sensed my mood. *Lavender Lady sad.*

A little. I led Kiki from her stall and groomed her. Usually I talked to her, but tonight I worked in silence.

I go with Lavender Lady.

Surprised, I stopped brushing. I had thought my connection with Kiki only involved emotions and simple communication. She discerned my feelings, and possessed certain instincts like when I had been threatened by Goel, but until now I had believed she didn't know why.

It would be suspicious if I take you.

Take me to smelling distance. Lavender Lady needs me.

I pondered her words as I put the grooming brushes away. Cahil hadn't come to the barn for my lesson. I wasn't surprised. Guess I would practice on my own. But how to get onto Kiki's back without a saddle or a boost up?

Grab mane. Hop. Pull.

Kiki, you're full of advice tonight.

Smart, she agreed.

As we rode around the pasture, I realized the value of her offer. I would take her along and let her graze in the plains. The exchange site was set at the only location in the plains that I knew, Blood Rock. My skin crawled when I contemplated how Ferde had gotten that information.

Ferde's image and thoughts still frequented my nightmares, and I wondered if I had inadvertently formed a mental connection with his mind. His desire to possess me haunted my dreams. I no longer ran from the snakes. Instead, I waited for their tight embrace, welcoming the oblivion of their bites. My dream actions became as disturbing as Ferde's.

Kiki switched to a trot, jarring me from my thoughts. I concentrated on maintaining my balance. When my legs and back began to ache, she stopped.

After giving Kiki a quick rubdown, I led her back in her stall. *See you later,* I said, heading toward my rooms to prepare for the exchange. My confidence soured to nervousness as the darkness advanced over the sky.

Trust, Kiki said. *Trust is peppermints.*

I laughed. Kiki viewed the world through her stomach. Peppermints were good; therefore, trusting another was also good.

Valek waited for me in my rooms. His stiff expression resembled a metal mask. A cold sheen covered his eyes; his killer's gaze.

"Here." He handed me a black turtleneck shirt and black pants. "They're made of a special fabric that will protect you from airborne darts from a blow gun, but won't stop a dart if you get jabbed by one."

"These are great," I said, thanking him. At least I wouldn't be surprised, and hopefully, once Ferde was close enough to jab me, I would have the upper hand.

The new clothes hung on my small frame. I rolled up the sleeves and added a belt to keep the pants from falling down.

A brief smile touched Valek's lips. "They were mine. I'm not the best seamstress."

I packed my backpack with care, taking only critical supplies, which included the Theobroma, the items Esau gave me, my grapple and rope, an apple and my bow. Ferde hadn't specified to come unarmed. My lock picks went into my hair, and I strapped my switchblade onto my thigh through the hole cut into my pant's pocket. Valek had thought ahead. He might not be the best with a needle and thread, but he knew the art of combat like no other.

We reviewed our plan and I told him about Kiki.

"Sneaking through both the Keep's and Citadel's gates without a large animal is hard enough, love," Valek said.

"I'll manage. Trust me."

He gave me a flat stare, showing no emotion.

"I'll take Kiki out to the plains and give you time to get through the Citadel's gate before heading toward the meeting site," I said. "Once Opal is out of harm's way and Ferde is visible, that's the sign to move in."

Valek nodded. "Count on it."

I put on my cloak and left. Four hours remained until midnight. A few people moved about the campus. The torches along the walkways had been lit and students hurried through the cool night air, heading to an evening class or to meet up with friends. I was a stranger among them. A shadow, watching and yearning to join them, wishing that my worries only focused on studying for one of Bain Bloodgood's history quizzes.

Kiki waited for me in her stall. I opened the door and let her out. Getting onto her back with a cloak and loaded backpack became an impossible task. I pulled a step stool over and used it.

Need practice, Kiki said. *No stool in wild.*

Later, I agreed.

Kiki glanced back at Irys's tower as we started toward the Keep's gate. *Magic Lady.*

The guilt I had suppressed about not telling Irys about the exchange threatened to break free. *She won't be happy.*

Kicking mad. Give Magic Lady peppermints.

I laughed, thinking I would need more than peppermints to repair the damage.

Peppermints sweet on both sides, Kiki said.

Cryptic horse advice? *Are you sure Moon Man isn't your father? Moon Man smart.*

I pondered her words, trying to decipher the true meaning. Before we reached the Keep's gate, I pulled a magic thread to me and projected my awareness. Two guards watched the gate. Bored, one guard thought of the end of his shift with longing; the other considered what he would eat for a late dinner. A magician dozed on a stool. I sent the magician into a deeper slumber, and using the guard's desires, I encouraged them to focus on something other than the horse and rider passing beneath the gate. As one soldier scanned the sky to see how far the South Star had moved, the other rummaged around the guardhouse looking for something to eat. Both failed to notice us and we soon passed out of sight.

Kiki walked quietly through the Citadel. No farrier would go near a sandseed horse, the breed's strong disdain for metal shoes was well-known. Four guards watched the Citadel's gates. Once again, I distracted the guards as we crossed. When we were out of sight of the gate, Kiki broke into a gallop and we headed into the Avibian Plains. When we could no longer see the road or the Citadel, Kiki slowed to a walk.

My thoughts returned to Kiki's words about peppermints. For the plan to work tonight, we each had to do our part. Both sides needed to be sweet. She had also claimed trust equaled peppermints. Did she refer to Irys instead of Valek?

The answer bloomed in my mind. I didn't know whether to feel smart for figuring out Kiki's advice, or feel like a simpleton for having a horse tell me the right thing to do.

Irys, I called in my mind.

Yelena? What's the matter?

I took a deep breath, steadied my nerves, and told her my plans. Silence, long and empty, followed my confession.

You'll die, she finally said. *You're no longer my student. I'll link with the other Master Magicians and we will stop you before you get to him.*

I expected her response. Her anger and immediate censure were the reasons I hadn't wanted to tell her about the exchange. *Irys, you told me I would die before. Remember when we first met in Ixia's Snake Forest?*

She hesitated. *Yes.*

I was in an impossible position. My magical powers were uncontrolled, you were threatening to kill me and I had been poisoned by Valek. Each course of action from that point seemed to lead to my eventual death. But I asked you to give me some time, and you did. You hardly knew me, yet you trusted me enough to let me figure a way out. I might not know the ways of Sitia, but I'm an old hand at dealing with impossible situations. Think about that before you call the others.

Another long painful silence. I withdrew my connection to Irys, needing to focus my attention on tonight's task. Kiki stopped within a mile of Blood Rock. I sensed the Sandseed's subtle magic. The protection lacked the strength of the one that covered their camp, but it resembled a thin web, waiting to catch its prey unaware. A magician with the proper magical defense in place could avoid detection by the Sandseeds, but if the clan intensified their power, they would then sense the magician's presence. Their magic would attack the interloper. I breathed a small sigh of relief, knowing Valek's immunity would make him undetectable.

I slid off Kiki's back. *Stay out of sight,* I told her.

Stay in wind. Keep smell strong, Kiki instructed.

I hid in the tall grass, giving Valek time to catch up. Kiki had reached this point in an hour, but it would take him an extra hour to get into position. When I felt I had waited long enough, I started walking toward Blood Rock, trusting that Valek would approach the exchange site from the opposite direction.

Rabbit, Kiki said. *Good.*

I smiled. She must have flushed a bunny from its burrow. The moon's bright light shone on the long stalks of grass. A slight breeze blew and I watched as my moon's shadow skimmed over the rippling surface.

Irys's voice reached my mind. *You're on your own.* Then her mental connection with me severed, destroying our student mentor link. My head throbbed with the sudden emptiness.

My heart squeezed out little spikes of panic. I calmed my nerves with the reminder that both Valek and Kiki trailed me.

When I drew closer to the meeting point, I stopped and took off my cloak. I rolled the garment up and hid it in a clump of tall grass. Pulling Esau's Theobroma pill from my pack, I placed it between my back teeth. My mouth felt awkward, and I hoped I didn't accidentally bite into the pill.

I continued onward. The dark shape of the rock filled the land before me. Rays of moonlight filtered through the clouds as I peered into the semidarkness, searching for some sign of Ferde and Opal.

Relief poured through my body when I saw Opal step out from behind Blood Rock. She hurried toward me, and only when she left the shadows could I see the terror on her face. Her eyes looked swollen; her pale skin blotchy from crying. I scanned the area with my magic, feeling for Ferde as my gaze hunted for him.

Opal threw herself into my arms, sobbing. Too easy. Wouldn't he want my promise to go with him before releasing her? The girl hugged me so tight she pinched my skin. Ferde still didn't appear. I pulled her away, planning to guide her back to the Citadel.

"I'm so sorry, Yelena," she cried and ran away.

I spun around, expecting Ferde to be standing there gloating. No one. Confused, I moved to follow Opal but my feet would not obey me. Stumbling, I fell as my body lost all sensation.

30

I LAY ON THE GROUND AS THE paralysis swept through my body with amazing speed. I had only a second to realize that I'd been hit with Curare before the drug froze all my muscles. Only a second to bite down on the Theobroma pill before my jaw seized, swallowing just a drop of the antidote.

Lying on my side, I saw Opal in the gray moonlight, running toward the Citadel. My helpless position was the direct result of my appalling overconfidence. By focusing on the danger from Ferde either from his magic or from the Curare, I didn't prepare for an attack by Opal. She had jabbed me, apologized and run off.

A muted fear pulsed in my body. The Curare seemed to dull my emotions as well as my magic. I felt as if I wore a heavy wet woolen cap around my head.

Behind me, I heard the slight crunch of footsteps coming closer. I waited for Valek. Would he pounce when Ferde drew closer to me?

The footsteps stopped and my view changed. Without feeling anything, I was pulled over onto my back. My head spun for a moment before I could focus on the night sky. I couldn't move my gaze, but I could still blink. I couldn't speak, yet I could breathe. I couldn't move my mouth or tongue, but I could swallow. Odd.

When a face entered my view, I remembered to be scared again. Until surprise eclipsed my fear for a moment. A woman with long hair peered down at me. She wore a robe and I could see faint lines had been drawn or tattooed on her neck. When she flaunted a knife and brought the metal tip close to my eyes, the air suddenly seemed thick and hard to draw into my straining lungs.

"Should I kill you now?" she asked. Her accent sounded familiar. She cocked her head to the side in amusement. "No comment? Not to worry. I won't kill you now. Not when you won't feel any pain. You need to suffer greatly before I'll end your pain for good."

The woman stood and walked away. I searched my memory. Did I know her? Why would she want to kill me? Perhaps she worked with Ferde. Her language matched his, but without the lilt.

Where was Valek? He should have witnessed my predicament.

I heard a rubbing sound and a thump then a strange disorientation made me realize that the woman dragged me. My world tilted and straightened. She brandished a rope, and I guessed by the brief glimpses and sounds that she had pulled me onto a cart and was tying me to it. She jumped off, and, after a moment, I heard her call to a horse.

The creaking of the wheels and steady clomping of the

horse were the only indication that we moved. From the swish and whack of grass, I guessed we were headed deeper into the Avibian Plains. Where was Valek?

I worried and waited and even slept. Every time some of the melting Theobroma reached the back of my throat, I swallowed. Would I get enough to counteract the Curare? By the time the woman stopped, a pale sheen of dawn had wedged into the night sky. Feeling began to return to my limbs. I moved my tongue, trying to swallow more of the Theobroma.

Pain flared in my wrists and ankles. My hands and feet were stiff and cold. I had been tied spread eagle on the hard cart. My ability to connect with the power source started to wake when the woman climbed onto the cart. My thoughts scattered when I saw her holding a long thin needle. I banished the fear and drew power to me.

"Oh, no you don't," she declared then jabbed me with the needle. "We need to reach the Void before I let you feel. Then you can feel cold steel slicing into your skin."

I thought that this would be an excellent time for Valek to arrive. But, when he failed to appear, I said, "Who..." before the drug numbed all my muscles.

"You don't know me, but you knew my brother very well. Don't worry; you'll know the reason for your suffering soon enough." She hopped off the cart and the familiar sounds of movement started again.

Anytime now Valek, I thought. But as the sun progressed through the sky, my hopes for a rescue faded. Something must have happened to keep Valek from following me. Perhaps Irys's message last night about being alone had been a warning.

Various horrible scenarios about Valek played in my mind. To distract myself, I wondered about Kiki. Was she near?

Would she follow my scent? With my magic ability paralyzed, would she know I needed her help?

The sun hovered above the horizon when the cart stopped again. A burning sensation in my fingertips meant the Curare started to wear off. Soon enough cramps, pain, and cold air wracked my body. I shivered and gulped the rest of Esau's antidote, preparing for another jab. But it didn't come.

Instead, the woman climbed onto the cart and stood over me. She spread her arms wide. "Welcome to the Void. Or in your case, welcome to hell."

In the fading light, I saw her gray eyes clearly. The strong features of her face reminded me of someone, but I couldn't think. My head ached and my mind felt dull. I reached for a thread of power, but found dead air. Nothing.

A smug smile spread on the woman's lips. "This is one of the few places in Sitia where there is a hole in the blanket of power. No power means no magic."

"Where are we?" I asked. My voice sounded rough.

"The Daviian Plateau."

"Who are you?"

All humor dropped from the woman's face. She appeared to be around thirty years old. Her black hair reached past her waist. She rolled the sleeves up on her sand-colored cloak, revealing the purple animal tattoos that covered her arms.

"You haven't figured it out? Have you killed that many men?"

"Four men, but I'm not averse to killing a woman." I gave her a pointed stare.

"You're really not in the position to be bragging or boasting." She pulled her knife from a pocket of her cloak.

I thought quick. Of the four, Reyad was the only one I

knew well, the others I had killed in self-defense. I didn't even know their names.

"Still don't know?" She moved closer to me.

"No."

Rage flamed in her gray eyes. That expression jolted my memory. Mogkan. The magician that had kidnapped me and tried to rob me of my soul. He was known as Kangom in Sitia.

"Kangom deserved to die," I said. Valek had made the killing blow, but Irys and I had first caught the magician in a web of magical power. I had not included him in my count, but I admitted being responsible for his death.

Fury twisted the woman's expression. She drove her knife into my right forearm, and then pulled it out just as fast. Pain exploded up my arm. I screamed.

"Who am I?" she asked.

My arm burned, but I met her gaze. "You're Kangom's sister."

She nodded. "My name's Alea Daviian."

That was not one of the clan names.

She understood my confusion and said, "I used to be a Sandseed." She spat the clan name out. "They're stuck in the past. We are more powerful than the rest of Sitia, yet the Sandseeds are content to wander the plains, dream and weave stories. My brother had a vision on how we could rule Sitia."

"But he was helping Brazell to take over Ixia." I found it hard to follow her logic when my blood poured from the stab wound.

"A first step. Gain control of the northern armies then attack Sitia. But you ruined that, didn't you?"

"Seemed like a good idea at the time."

Alea sliced her knife along my left arm, drawing a line from my shoulder to my wrist. "You'll learn to regret that decision before I cut your throat just like you did to my brother."

Pain coursed through my arms, but a strange annoyance that she had ruined Valek's special shirt tugged at my mind. Alea raised the knife again, aiming for my face. I thought fast.

"Are you living in the plateau?" I asked.

"Yes. We broke from the Sandseeds and declared a new clan. The Daviians will conquer Sitia. We will no longer have to steal to survive."

"How?"

"Another member is on a power quest. Once he completes the ritual he will be more powerful than all four Master Magicians together."

"Did you kill Tula?" I asked. When she squinted in confusion, I added, "Opal's sister."

"No. My cousin had that pleasure."

Alea had a family connection to Ferde. He must be the one on the quest, which led me to the question. Who was Ferde targeting for the final ritual? It could be any girl with some magical abilities and he could be anywhere. And we only had two days to find him.

I pulled against the ropes with the sudden need to move.

Alea smiled in satisfaction. "Not to worry. You won't be around for the cleansing of Sitia. However, you will be around for a little longer." She pulled out her needle and jabbed into the cut on my arm. I yelped.

"I don't like wasting your blood on this wagon. We have a special frame set up so I can collect your red life and make good use of it." Alea hopped off the cart.

The Curare began to dull the pain in my arms, but full paralysis didn't grip my body. Esau's antidote must be working. The presence of Void meant I didn't have to worry about my mind being open to magical influences. However, being tied to the cart and unarmed, I didn't know if my body would be in any condition to fight Alea.

Searching for my pack and bow would reveal to her that I could move. So I clamped my teeth down to keep them from chattering and to remind myself to stay still.

I heard a thump and the cart tilted. My feet now pointed toward the ground as my head came up. With this new angle, I could see a wooden frame just a few feet away. Made of thick beams, the frame had manacles and chains hanging from the top with some type of pulley rigged to them. Under the frame lay a metal basin. I guessed that the victim stood in the basin.

Beyond the frame spread the vivid colors of the flat Daviian Plateau. The patchwork of yellows, tans and browns seemed so soothing in comparison to the torture device.

My heart began beating in a fast tempo. I kept my eyes staring straight ahead when Alea came into view. A few inches taller than me, Alea's chin reached my eye level. She had removed her cloak and revealed her blue pants and short-sleeved V-neck blouse that had white disks sewn onto it, making it look as if she wore fish scales. A leather weapon belt circled her waist.

"Feeling better?" she asked. "Let's make sure." She poked the tip of her blade into my right thigh.

Concentrating so hard on not reacting, I took a moment to realize the thrust hadn't hurt. The tip of Alea's knife had hit my switchblade holder. Still strapped to my thigh, I wondered if the weapon remained inside it. Alea considered my expression for many frantic heartbeats. If she suspected I could move, then all would be lost.

"Your clothes are strange," she said finally. "They're thick and resist my knife. I will remove them and keep them. They would make a fine reminder of our time together."

She stepped over to the frame and grabbed the manacles that hung down, pulling. The wheel on the pulley spun and let more chain through until the cuffs reached my cart.

"You're too heavy for me to lift. Good thing my brother added that pulley so I can easily yank you into place." She unlocked the metal cuffs and opened them wide.

My time to act approached. If she was smart, she would secure my wrists in the cuffs before untying my feet. Once my arms were locked into the frame, I would be helpless again. I would only have a brief window of opportunity. And I planned to risk everything on a guess.

She leaned over with her knife and cut the rope holding my right arm to the side of the cart. I let it drop to my side as if it were a dead weight, hoping she would untie my other arm before fastening them. Instead, Alea put her knife in her belt and reached for my arm.

I plunged my hand into my pocket and grabbed for my switchblade. Alea froze for a moment in shock. My fingers found the smooth handle and I almost laughed aloud with relief. Yanking the weapon out, I knocked aside her arm and triggered the blade.

She drew her knife. Before she could step back, I plunged my blade into her lower abdomen. Grunting in surprise, she aimed her weapon at my heart. She staggered a bit as she leaned forward to strike, and I felt cold steel bite deep into my stomach. Alea fell, sitting hard on the ground. She hunched over my switchblade.

I gasped for breath, trying to keep from passing out. Pain flamed up my back and gripped my insides like a tight vise.

Alea pulled my blade from her guts and dropped it onto the ground. Crawling over to her cloak, she retrieved a vial of liquid from one of the pockets. She opened it, dipped her finger in, and rubbed the liquid into her stab wound. Curare.

Lurching to her feet, she walked back to me. She studied my condition in silence. The Curare she had used must have been diluted in order for her to move.

"Take my knife out to free yourself and you will bleed to death," she said with grim satisfaction. "Leave it in and you will eventually die. Either way you're in the middle of the plains with no one to help you and no magic to heal you." She shrugged. "Not what I had planned, but the results will be the same."

"What about your problem?" I asked, huffing with the effort.

"I have my horse and my people close by. Our healer will cure me and I will be back in time to watch your final moments." She moved past the cart. After some rustling and grunting, she clicked at her horse, and I heard the familiar thumping of hooves.

As my vision began to blur I had to agree with Alea. My position hadn't improved, but at least I'd denied her the satisfaction of torturing me. The intense pain made concentrating difficult. Do I pull the knife? Or keep it in?

Time passed and I drifted in and out of consciousness. I roused when the drum of a galloping horse reached my ears. I hadn't made my decision and Alea was returning to gloat.

Closing my eyes to avoid seeing her smug expression, I heard a whinny. The sound soothed my pain as if I'd been dosed with Curare. I opened my eyes and saw Kiki's face.

My prospects looked better, but I wasn't sure I could communicate with Kiki.

"Knife," I said aloud. My throat burned with thirst. "Get me the knife." Looking over to my switchblade on the ground, I then stared at Kiki. I let my eyes and head move from one to the other. "Please."

She turned an eye in the right direction. Then walked over and grasped the handle with her teeth. Smart, indeed.

I held out my free hand and she placed the weapon in my palm. "Kiki, if this works out," I said, "I'll feed you all the apples and peppermints that you want."

Fresh waves of pain coursed through my body as I twisted to cut the rope around my left wrist. When the strands severed, I fell to the ground, but had enough sense to land on my elbows and knees, keeping the knife from plunging deeper into my stomach. After an eternity, I reached back and cut the rope around my feet.

I probably would have curled up on the ground and given in to the release of unconsciousness, but Kiki huffed at me and nudged my face with her nose. Looking up, I thought her back seemed as unattainable as the clouds in the sky. No step stool in the wild. I laughed, but it came out as a hysterical cry.

Kiki moved away. She returned with my pack in her mouth, setting it down next to me. I gave her a wry smile. Whenever I rode her, I always had my pack with me. She probably thought I needed my backpack to climb onto her back. Pawing with impatience, she pushed the pack closer to me. I had mentioned apples. Perhaps she wanted the one inside.

I opened it. Smart girl. I found the Curare that I had forgotten about. Planning to use the drug against Ferde, I had packed one of Esau's vials. I rubbed a tiny drop into my wound. The drug soothed my pain. Sighing with relief, I tried to sit up. My arms and legs felt wooden and heavy, but they moved the right ways. The Theobroma in my body kept the Curare from freezing all my muscles. It was an effort to put my backpack on. Fear of Alea's return motivated me, and I stood on wobbly legs.

Kiki bent her front legs down to her knees. I looked at her askance. No step stool? She whickered with impatience. I laced my fingers in her mane and swung a leg over her back. She lurched to her feet and broke into a smooth ground-eating stride.

I knew the instant we left the Void. Magic encompassed me like a pool of water, but I soon felt drowned by the amount. An unfortunate side effect of the Theobroma opened my mind to the magical assault. On entering the Avibian Plains, the Sandseed's protective spells rushed me. Unable to block the magic, I fell.

Strange dreams, images and colors swirled around me. Kiki spoke to me with Irys's voice. Valek steeled himself as a noose wrapped around his neck. His arms tied behind his back. Ari and Janco huddled by a fire in a grassy clearing, alarmed and uneasy. They had never been lost before. My mother clung to the upper branches of a tree as it swung wildly in a storm. The smell of Curare filled my nose and Theobroma coated my mouth.

Alea's knife had been driven deeper into my abdomen when I had hit the ground. In my mind's eye, I saw the torn muscles, the tear in my stomach with blood and acid gushing out. Yet I couldn't focus my magic to heal the wound.

Valek's thoughts reached me. He fought the soldiers around him with his feet, but someone pulled on the rope and it tightened around his neck.

Regret pulsed in his heart. *Sorry, love. I don't think we're going to make it this time.*

31

NO! I YELLED TO HIM. *Stay alive. Think of something!*

I'll stay if you will, he countered.

Damn frustrating man. In exasperation, I gathered the twisting images and magic that threatened to overwhelm me. I wrung them and wrestled the magic. Images swirled around me like snowflakes in a blizzard. Theobroma coursed through my blood and enhanced my perceptions, making the magic tangible. The threads of power slipped through my hands like a coarse blanket.

Sweating and panting with the effort to hold on to the magic, I yanked Alea's knife from my stomach and pulled magic toward the wound. Laying my hands over my abdomen, I covered the warm torrent of blood with power.

Concentrating, I sent my mind's eye toward the damage. I grabbed a thread of the magic swirling around me and used it to stitch closed the rip in my stomach. I repaired my torn abdominal muscles and knitted my skin together. A quick glance at my stomach revealed an ugly red ridge of puckered flesh that caused a sharp stab of pain whenever I drew breath. But the wound was no longer life threatening.

I kept my end of the bargain. I desperately hoped Valek kept his. Exhaustion tugged at my consciousness, and I would have fallen asleep, but Kiki nudged me.

Come, she said in my mind.

I opened my eyes. *Tired.*

Bad smell. Go.

We were out of the Void, but we must be close to Alea's people.

Grab tail, she instructed.

Clutching the long strands of her tail, I pulled myself into a standing position. Kiki knelt, and I mounted her back.

She took off, breaking into her gust-of-wind gait. I hung on and tried to stay awake. The plains blurred past as the sun set. The icy air bit at my skin.

When she slowed, I blinked, trying to focus on my surroundings. Still in the plains, but I saw a campfire ahead.

Make noise. Not scare Rabbit.

Rabbits? Sudden hunger made my stomach growl. I did have an apple, but I'd promised that to Kiki.

She snorted in amusement, whinnied and stopped. I glanced past her head and saw two men blocking the path. The moonlight shone off their swords. Ari and Janco. I called to them and they sheathed their weapons as Kiki drew closer.

Rabbit? Not Rabbit Man?

Too quick for a man.

"Thank fate!" Ari cried.

Seeing how I drooped over Kiki's neck, Ari pulled me off and carried me to their campfire, setting me down as if I was as fragile as an egg. The sudden wish that Ari was my real brother overcame me. Even as an eight-year-old, I'd bet Ari never would have let me be kidnapped.

Janco feigned boredom. "Going off and getting all the glory again," he said. "I don't know why we even bothered to come to this crazy land. Your trail marks didn't even have the decency to go anywhere but in circles," he grumped.

"Don't like being lost, Janco?" I teased.

He harrumphed and crossed his arms.

"Don't worry. Your skills are still keen. You're in the Avibian Plains. There's a protective magic here that confuses the mind."

"Magic," he spat. "Another good reason to stay in Ixia."

Ari sat me by the fire. "You look terrible. Here." He wrapped my cloak around my shoulders.

"Where—"

"We found it in the plains," Ari explained. Then he frowned. "Valek had asked us to back him up last night. We followed him, but they ambushed him at the Citadel's gates."

"Cahil and his men," I said.

He nodded then began inspecting the cuts on my arms.

"How did they know where to find him?" I asked.

"Captain Marrok is a tracker of some renown," Ari said. "Seems he had dealings with Valek before. He is the only soldier to have escaped from the Commander's dungeon. He must have been waiting for the perfect opportunity." Ari shook his head. "Valek's capture presented a dilemma."

"Help Valek or help you," Janco said.

"I think he suspected something might happen to him and didn't want you unprotected. So we stuck to the plan and followed you." Ari handed me a jug of water.

I gulped the liquid.

"Not that we did any good," Janco huffed. "When we reached the meeting site, the horse and cart were gone and we figured we would track you. She had to stop sometime. But—"

"You lost your way," I finished for him. Ari probed the deep gash on my right forearm. "Ow!"

"Hold still," Ari said. "Janco, get my med kit from my pack—these cuts need to be cleaned and sealed."

If I'd had any energy, I could have healed the wounds on my arms with magic. Instead, I endured Ari's administrations and admonishments. When he pulled out the pot of Rand's sealing glue, I asked him about the Commander's new chef to distract myself from the pain.

"Since Rand never made it to Brazell's for the transfer of cooks, the Commander promoted one of Rand's kitchen staff." Ari frowned.

I grimaced as Ari applied the glue to my cut more from remembering Rand than from the burning in my arm. Rand had lost his life protecting me, but I wouldn't have been in danger if he hadn't set me up for an ambush in the first place.

"The food hasn't been the same," Janco said with a sigh. "Everyone is losing weight."

When Ari finished wrapping my arms, he pulled something from the fire. "Janco got a rabbit." He broke off a piece and handed it to me. "You need to eat something."

That reminded me. "Kiki needs…" I moved to stand up.

Janco waved me down. "I'll take care of her."

"Do you—"

"Yeah, I grew up on a farm."

I had gnawed every bit of meat off the rabbit's bone when Janco came back covered with horsehair. He seemed to be in a better mood. "She beautiful," he said about Kiki. "I've never had a horse stand so patiently to be rubbed down and she wasn't even tied!"

I told him about the honor she gave him by changing his name from Rabbit Man to Rabbit. "Unprecedented."

He gave me an odd look. "Talking horses. Magic. Crazy southerners." He shook his head.

He might have said more, but I could no longer stay awake.

The next morning, I told my friends about Alea and the clan on the plateau. They wanted to go after her, but I reminded them about Valek and the need to find Ferde. My heart lurched when I thought of Valek. Even with a night of sleep, I still didn't have enough energy to find out what had happened to him.

The rest had roused me. "We need to get to the Citadel," I said, standing.

"Do you know where we are?" Ari asked.

"Somewhere in the plains," I said, shouldering my backpack.

"Some magician you are," Janco said. "Do you even know which direction the Citadel is?"

"No." Kiki came and stood next to me. I grabbed her mane. "How about a boost?" I asked Janco.

He muttered under his breath, but offered his linked hands for my boot. When I had settled onto her back, I looked down at him. "Kiki knows where to go. Can you keep up?"

He grinned. "This rabbit can run."

Ari and Janco packed their gear and we set off at a trot. All those laps around the Commander's castle had kept them in top physical condition.

We reached the road, and I heard Janco curse and grumble

about being lost only a mile away. When we approached the Citadel's gates, we encountered the four Master Magicians. They all sat on horseback. A well-armed Calvary team accompanied them.

I smiled at Roze Featherstone's look of astonishment, but sobered at Irys's cold stare.

"Why are you here?" I asked.

"We were coming to either rescue you or kill you," Zitora said. She flashed Roze an annoyed glance.

I met Irys's gaze, questioning. She turned away and blocked my efforts to reach her mind. Even though I had known she would shun me for going off alone, her actions still tore at my heart.

Not bothering to conceal the satisfaction in her voice, Roze said, "Because of your dangerous disregard for the well-being of Sitia, you have been expelled."

The least of my worries. "Is Opal safe?" I asked the magicians.

Bain Bloodgood nodded. "She told us a woman held her. Was she connected to the killer?"

"No. We still need to find Ferde. He doesn't want me. He must have taken someone else. Has anyone been reported missing?"

My announcement caused a considerable stir. Everyone had assumed that Ferde was holding Opal. Now they needed to change tactics.

"We've been searching for him for two weeks," Roze said, putting a stop to the chatter. "What makes you think we can find him now?"

"The last victim would not have been kidnapped," Bain said. "Let us go back and discuss this. Yelena, you will be safest in the Keep. We will talk about your future when this whole mess is resolved."

The Magicians headed toward the Keep. Ari, Janco and I followed. I thought about Bain's comment. My future would be nothing without Valek. I caught up to Bain and asked about him.

Bain gave me a stern look, and I felt his magic press against my mental barrier. I relaxed my guard and heard his voice in my mind.

Best not to talk aloud about this, child. Cahil and his men captured him two nights ago, but Cahil would not release Valek to the Councilors or Master Magicians.

I felt Bain's disapproval over Cahil's actions. And I had to quell my desire to find Cahil and skewer him with his own sword.

Cahil tried to hang Valek yesterday at dusk, but Valek escaped. Bain seemed impressed. *We have no idea where he is now.*

I thanked Bain and slowed Kiki, letting the others go ahead. I savored my relief that Valek was alive. When Ari and Janco caught up to me, I relayed the information to them.

When we reached the Council Hall, Ari and Janco headed toward the guest quarters. Kiki picked up her pace and we joined the others.

I thought about where Valek might have gone. Back to Ixia seemed the safest and most logical course, but I knew Valek would stay nearby until Ferde was caught. That led me to consider who would be Ferde's next victim. He had been working in the Keep where there were many young female magicians just learning to control their magic. Since the full moon would rise tomorrow night, he would probably need a few days to prepare. The Master Magicians couldn't locate him with magic, but they might be able to contact the girl with him. But how to find her?

Just past the Keep's gate, the Master Magicians dismounted, handed their horses to the guards and started for the Keep's administration building. I followed, but Roze stopped me at the base of the steps.

"You're confined to your quarters. We will deal with you later," she promised.

I had no intention of obeying her, but I knew they wouldn't let me into the meeting room. So before Bain could mount the steps to the building, I touched his arm.

"The killer probably seduced one of the young first-years to come with him," I told him. "If everyone takes a barrack you can find out who's missing and try to communicate with her."

"Excellent," Bain said. "Now go rest, child. And do not worry. We will do all that we can to find the killer."

I nodded. Fatigue wrapped around me like a stone cloak, and Bain's order to rest made sense. Before heading toward my rooms, I made a slight detour to the Keep's guest suite.

My father answered the door. He crushed me in his muscular arms. "Are you all right? Did my pill work?"

"Like a charm." I kissed him on the cheek. "You saved my life."

He ducked his head. "I've made some more for you just in case."

I smiled with gratitude. Looking past his shoulder, I asked, "Where's Mother?"

"In her favorite oak tree by the pasture. She was doing so well until…" He gave me a sardonic grin.

"I know. I'll find her."

★ ★ ★

I stood at the bottom of the oak, feeling as if I'd been run over by a horse. "Mother?" I called.

"Yelena! Come up! Come up where it's safe!"

No place is safe, I thought. The events of the last two days began to overwhelm me. Too many problems, too much riding on me. My encounter with Alea proved that, even when I felt confident that I could take care of a situation, I really didn't know what I was doing. If Alea had checked me for weapons, I would be standing ankle deep in my own blood.

"Come down. I need you," I cried. I sank to the ground and wrapped my arms around my legs as tears poured from my eyes.

With a rustle and creak of branches, my mother appeared beside me. I transformed into a six-year-old child, flung myself into her arms and sobbed. She comforted me, helped me to my room, gave me a handkerchief and a glass of water. Tucking me into bed, she kissed me on my forehead.

When she went to leave, I grabbed her hand. "Please stay."

Mother smiled, took off her cloak, and lay next to me. I fell asleep in her arms.

The next morning she brought me breakfast in bed. I protested about the extravagance, but she stopped me. "I have fourteen years of mothering to catch up on. Indulge me."

Even though the plate was loaded with food, I ate every bit and drained the tea. "Sweet cakes are my favorite."

"I know," she replied with a smug smile. "I asked one of the servers in the dining hall, and she remembered that every time they cooked sweet cakes your eyes would light up." She took the empty tray. "You should go back to sleep." Perl went into the other room.

I could have easily complied, but I needed to find out if the others had discovered who was missing. Unable to stay in bed, I decided to get a quick bath before finding Bain.

"Come to our suite when you're done at the bathhouse," Perl said. "Once your father told me what's been going on with this killer and the Curare, I thought of something that might help you. It may have aided you yesterday," she huffed. "I'm not a delicate sapling. You and Esau don't need to keep things from me. And that includes Valek." She put her hands on her hips, wrinkling the smooth lines of her blue-green dress.

"How—" I sputtered.

"I'm not deaf. The dining hall buzzed with conversation about you and Valek. And Valek's escape from Cahil!" She put a hand to her throat. But then she took a deep breath.

"I know I tend to overreact about some things and go running for the trees." She smiled ruefully. "Valek has the most horrible reputation, but I trust you. When you have some time, you need to educate me about him."

"Yes, Mother," I said and also promised to stop by their suite after my bath.

It was the middle of the morning so the bathhouse was almost empty. Washing, I thought about how much I would tell my mother about Valek. When I finished drying off, I changed and headed toward the guest suite.

Dax intercepted me. His usual jovial face was taut with worry, and the dark smudges under his eyes made it look as if he hadn't slept in a while.

"Have you seen Gelsi?" he asked.

"Not since the New Beginnings feast." So much had happened since that night. The semester had not gone as I had imagined. Nothing since coming to Sitia had gone as I had imagined. "Wasn't she working on some special project for Master Bloodgood?"

"Yes. She was experimenting with the Bellwood plant. But I haven't seen her in days and I can't find her anywhere."

His words struck me like Alea's knife. I gasped.

"What?" His green eyes widened in alarm.

"Plant? Where? With who?" The questions tumbled from my mouth.

"I already checked the greenhouses many times. She worked with one of the gardeners. Maybe we could ask him?"

Him. My heart twisted. I knew who Gelsi was with.

32

"ME? BUT I'VE NEVER LINKED with Gelsi." Dax's drawn face took on a wild fearful expression.

I had taken Dax back to my rooms. We sat together on the couch. "Don't worry. I've only worked with her once, but you've known her for a year. I'll find her through you." I hoped. "Relax," I instructed. I took his hand in mine. "Think of her." Finding a thread of magic, I reached toward his mind.

A horrible vision of Gelsi, bloody and terrified, filled my mind. "Dax, don't imagine where she might be. Think of her at the New Beginnings feast."

The image transformed into a smiling young lady wearing a soft green gown. I felt Dax's thrill when he held her hand and guided her while they danced. I sent my magic to Gelsi, trying to see Dax from her mind.

She gazed up at him. They had always danced together at the feast, but this time felt different. Her skin tingled where he had touched her, and a warmth pulsed in her chest.

Gelsi, I called, pulling her into the memory.

What a lovely evening, she thought. *How things have changed. Dax seemed distant after that night. Preoccupied.*

Gelsi, where are you? I asked.

Shame flared. *I've been a fool. No one must know. Please tell no one.* Fear trembled through her mind.

You were deceived by a cunning sorcerer. No one will hold that against you. Where are you?

He will punish me.

She tried to pull away. I showed her Dax's concern for her. His hunt through the Keep. *Don't let your captor win,* I pleaded.

Gelsi showed me a bare room. She was naked and tied to metal spikes that had been driven into the wooden floor. Strange symbols had been painted on the floor and walls. Pain throbbed from between her legs and the multiple cuts along her arms and legs burned. He hadn't needed to drug her with Curare.

I loved him, she said. *I gave myself to him.*

Instead of the wonderful loving experience she had expected, Ferde tied her down, beat her and raped her. Then he bled her, collecting the blood in an earthen bowl.

Show me where you are, I instructed.

Beyond the room was the living area and outside I could see a courtyard with a white jade sculpture of fifteen horses.

Have faith, I said. *We'll be there.*

He'll know. He has surrounded the neighborhood with a magical shield, he knows when someone passes through and if he feels threatened, he'll complete the ritual.

Doesn't he need to wait until the full moon tonight?

No.

The note left by Alea had originally set the exchange for the full moon so everyone had not only assumed Ferde sent the note, but that the phase of the moon was critical for the ritual.

He had to move many times, Gelsi said. *I had thought it exciting. I didn't know he was the one the Masters were searching for. He led me to believe he was on a secret mission for the Master Magicians.*

We'll find a way, I promised.

Hurry.

I withdrew my awareness and sat back. Dax stared at me in horror, he had been able to see and hear our conversation.

"She will need you when this is over," I told him.

"We need to tell the Masters—"

"No." My mind raced through options.

"But he's strong. You heard Gelsi. He has a shield," Dax said.

"All the more reason to go alone. They have been searching for him and he knows them. I think I can get through undetected."

"How?"

"There's no time to explain. But Gelsi will need you close by. Can you meet me in the market in an hour?"

"Of course."

I jumped up and started gathering supplies.

Dax hesitated at the door. "Yelena?"

I looked at him.

"What happens if you don't stop him?" Fear shone in his green eyes.

"Then we find Valek. Otherwise, Sitia will be Ferde's."

Dax swallowed his fright and nodded before leaving. I packed my equipment and changed my clothes. Dressed in a plain brown tunic and pants I would blend in with the regular citizens of the Citadel. Covering my disguise with my cloak, I stopped at my parent's suite on the way out.

Leif sat with them in the living room. I ignored him. "Father, do you have those extra pills?" I asked, hoping he knew I wanted the Theobroma.

He nodded in understanding and went to retrieve them. While I waited, Mother remembered her little invention she had told me about. She handed me a strange device made of tubes and rubber and explained how to work it.

"Just in case," she said.

"This is great," I said. "You were right about it being useful."

She beamed. "That's what every mother wants to hear."

Leif had said nothing, but I could feel his penetrating stare as if he tasted my intentions.

Esau handed me the pills. "Are you coming to lunch with us?"

"No. I have something I need to do. I'll catch up with you later," I said, giving my father a hug and my mother a kiss on her cheek.

A queasy feeling rolled in my stomach. Perhaps I should tell the Master Magicians about Ferde and Gelsi? After all, it had been only pure chance that saved me from Alea. I was still discovering what I could do with my magic. And now that I had been expelled, would I be able to fully explore my potential?

My mother stopped me just past the door.

"Here," she said, handing me my fire amulet. "I think you need this. Remember what you endured to win it."

I opened my mouth to protest, but she shook her head, "I want it back." She squeezed me in a tight hug for a moment.

Examining the scarlet prize in the sunlight, I marveled at Perl's empathy. I tucked the amulet into my pocket and set a brisk pace for the Citadel.

After I had passed the Keep's gate, I heard pounding foot-steps behind me. I whirled, drawing my bow. Leif halted a few feet away. His machete hung from his belt, but he made no move to grab it.

"Not now, Leif," I said, turning, but he clasped my shoul-der and spun me around to face him.

"I know where you're going," he said.

"Bully for you." I shrugged his hand off. "Then you know time is of the essence. Go back to the Keep." I started to walk.

"If I do, I'll tell the Masters what you're doing."

"Truly? You're not very good at telling."

"This time I won't hesitate."

Seeing the stubborn set to his broad shoulders, I stopped. "What do you want?"

"To come along."

"Why?"

"You'll need me."

"Considering how helpful you were in the jungle four-teen years ago, I think I'm better off on my own." I spat the words at him.

He cringed, but the obstinacy remained in his face. "Either include me in your plans, or I'll follow you and ruin them."

I clamped down on my sudden rage. I didn't have time for this. "Fine, but let me warn you that you're going have to let me inside your mind in order for you to get through Ferde's shield."

His face paled, but he nodded and fell into step with me as I hurried to the market. Dax waited there. I left Leif with him and hunted for Fisk. He helped a woman barter for a bolt of cloth, but he finished as soon as he recognized me.

"Lovely Yelena, do you need help?" he asked.

I told him what I needed.

He smiled and said, "Sounds like fun, but—"

"It's going to cost me," I finished for him.

He raced off to gather his friends.

Once Fisk had assembled about twenty children, I explained my plan to them. "Make sure you don't go within a block of the courtyard until you hear the signal. Understand?" I asked. The children nodded. When I felt satisfied they knew what to do, Fisk's friends scattered and went to get into position. Fisk led Leif and me toward the white jade statue. Dax waited in a side alley far enough away not to touch Ferde's shield, but within sight of the second-story windows.

I kept my mind open, seeking for the edge of Ferde's magical barrier. About half a block away from the courtyard, Leif touched my arm, stopping me.

"It's just ahead," he whispered.

"How do you know?"

"I feel a wall of fire. Don't you?"

"No."

"Then it's good that I came."

I glared, but had no reply. Fisk watched us, waiting for our signal.

This was not the time for a fight. I looked at Leif. "You have to open your mind to me," I told him. "You have to trust me."

He nodded without hesitating. "Do it."

I pulled power to me, spinning it around me like a huge curtain. Reaching out, I made contact with Fisk's mind. "Think of your parents," I instructed, hoping this would work.

The young boy closed his eyes and imagined his parents. I linked to their minds through Fisk then reached for Leif's.

Leif's mind resembled a black labyrinth of pain. Guilt, shame and anger twisted together. I understood why Moon Man wanted to help him, but I felt a mean satisfaction at Leif's remorse.

Pushing his dark thoughts aside, I replaced them with Fisk's father's concerns about finding work and supporting his family. I pulled in Fisk's mother's thoughts about her sister's ailing health into my own mind. Holding their personalities and thoughts in Leif's and my mind, I gave Fisk the signal.

He barked like a dog. Soon other barks echoed on the marble walls in reply. Fisk's friends would begin the distraction, playing tag and running in and out of the courtyard and Ferde's magical shield as many times as they could.

I took Fisk and Leif's hands and the three of us continued on to the courtyard. As we crossed the barrier, I felt the probing heat of an annoyed and powerful magician. He scanned our thoughts, determined we were one of the local beggar families and dismissed us.

When we reached the statue, I released Fisk's parents. They would have an unusual story to tell their friends about how they had felt as if they were in two places at once.

"That's half the battle," I said to Leif.

He wouldn't meet my eyes. His face was flushed with shame. Irritated, I snapped, "Now is not the time for this."

He nodded, but still wouldn't meet my gaze. Fisk ran off to join his friends in the game, giving us a few more minutes to get into the house.

We approached the house from a side street. The door was locked. I pulled my diamond pick and my tension wrench from my backpack and began working on the lock. Once I had aligned the pins, the lock's tumbler turned and the door swung inward. I heard a surprised huff from Leif. Then we stepped inside the foyer and closed the door. I shoved my picks into my pocket.

Walking without sound, we entered a living area. The normal furniture and decorations seemed out of place. I guess I had expected something wild and weird; something that reflected a killer's mind.

Leif held his machete and I gripped my bow, but I knew they would not protect us. Magic filled the house. It pressed against my skin and I started to sweat. The sounds of the children faded and we heard the light tread of feet from the floor above us.

Connecting with Gelsi's mind, I saw Ferde approach her. He held a brown stone bowl and a long dagger. He wore his red mask and nothing else. She had been fascinated with the tattoos and symbols on his sculpted physique, but now she eyed them with revulsion.

I'm downstairs, I told her. *What's he going to do?*

He wants more blood. Wait or else he will kill me if he hears you.

I had to physically hold on to Leif when Gelsi started moaning with pain. Handing him one of Esau's Theobroma pills, I motioned that he should put it into his mouth. I placed my pack on the floor and quietly removed Perl's device from my backpack.

With my bow in one hand and the device in the other, I waited at the bottom of the staircase with Leif. Finally, we heard Ferde moving again.

He's gone, Gelsi said with relief.

My stomach tightened with apprehension. I pulled power to me to strengthen my mental defenses. A mistake. Ferde felt the draw and I could sense his growing alarm.

"Now," I whispered to Leif. We rushed up the stairs, taking them two at a time.

Ferde waited for us on the landing. We skittered to a stop on the top step. An amused smile quirked Ferde's lips before he pressed them together with concentration. Revulsion and terror welled up my throat at the sight of him, and I thought I would vomit as Tula's horrible memories filled my mind.

The wave of his magic crashed against us. I grabbed the railing to keep from plummeting down the stairs. Leif jerked beside me but remained upright. Was that it? I glanced at Ferde. His eyes were closed. Moving toward him, I raised Perl's device.

"Yelena, stop," Leif said. His voice sounded odd.

I looked at Leif in time to see him swing his machete. Jumping back, I dropped Perl's device and blocked Leif's weapon with my bow.

"What are you—" I tried to ask, but with the pill between my teeth made it hard to talk.

Leif spat his pill out and moved to strike again. "When those men took my perfect baby sister, I thought I would reclaim my parents' undivided attention." Leif's machete sliced toward my neck.

I ducked. Had his shame and guilt all been an act? Was he working with Ferde this whole time? Pushing aside my stunned disbelief, I jabbed him in the stomach with the end of my bow. He hunched over and grunted. Magic pressed on my skin and Leif straightened with renewed vigor. But who's magic?

"Instead, I had to compete with a perfect ghost," Leif said and attacked.

Chunks of wood flew through the air as I blocked his wide

blade. It was only a matter of time before he would destroy my bow and I was running out of room in the narrow landing. There was a hallway to my left, and an open doorway on my right.

"Mother refused to leave our house, and Father was never home. All because of you." Leif puffed with effort. "And you stayed away just to spite me. Didn't you? You're my strangler fig, and now it's time to chop you down."

Ferde had disappeared. I felt Gelsi's brief cry of alarm as Ferde entered her room. He planned to finish the ritual while Leif kept me occupied. And it was working.

With a loud crack, my bow splintered in two. Leif advanced and I formed a magical shield, but he walked right through. As a last-ditch effort I sent out my mental awareness, entering his dark mind.

Hate and self-loathing filled his thoughts. I felt another presence in Leif's head. Ferde had Story Weaver abilities and he had brought out all of Leif's raw emotions and used them against me.

As Leif sliced his machete toward me, I stepped to the left, bringing my awareness back. I couldn't defend myself physically while mentally gone; I just wasn't that strong. Leif pulled his weapon back and thrust at me again. I had nothing left to defend myself. Perl's device was out of reach.

Gelsi's pleas for help burned through my thoughts like a hot poker, energizing me. I projected myself into Leif's mind, taking control of his body like I had done with Goel. Halting the tip of his machete a mere inch from my stomach, I made Leif step back.

Pushing through the darkness of Leif's mind, I found the young boy who had watched his sister being kidnapped; untainted with the feelings of guilt and hate. At that moment he held only curiosity and disbelief. Two emotions that Ferde wouldn't be able to use against me. I sent Leif into a deep dreamless sleep. He crumpled to the floor as I went back to my body. Stopping Ferde was paramount; I would deal with Leif later. I hoped.

Picking up Perl's device, I sprinted down the hall, searching for Gelsi. Only the last door on the left had been closed. Locked. I yanked my picks out and unlocked the door. My fastest time yet. Janco would be proud.

The door swung inward and I stumbled into the room. Ferde had his hands around Gelsi's throat. I watched in horror as all animation left her face. Her eyes turned sightless and flat.

Ferde shouted and thrust his fists toward the ceiling in celebration.

33

TOO LATE. WITH MY HEART sinking, I watched Ferde rejoice. But then I saw a strange shadow rise from Gelsi's body. Before logic could overrule, I dove. Knocking Ferde aside, I inhaled this shadow, gathering Gelsi's soul inside me. It felt as if the world paused for a moment so I could tuck her into a safe corner of my mind. Then, *snap*. Movement resumed and I fell on top of Ferde. Perl's device flew from my hand. It landed next to the wall.

After a brief struggle, Ferde pinned me to the floor, sitting on my stomach. "That's my soul," he said. "Give it back."

"It doesn't belong to you."

Yelena? I felt Gelsi's confusion in my mind.

Hold on, I told her.

Ferde reached toward my neck. I grabbed his hands, and using his forward momentum I pushed him further off balance with my left knee. I planted my left foot on the floor and twisted my hips, rolling him off me. I jumped up and assumed a fighting stance.

Ferde smiled and regained his feet with a panther-quick grace. "We are well matched. But I think I have the advantage."

I braced for an attack, but he didn't move. His red tattoos began to glow until they burned my eyes. He caught my gaze with his own, staring at me with his dark brown eyes.

Ferde's face transformed into Reyad's. My world spun and I found myself back in Reyad's bedroom in Ixia, tied to the bed and watching Reyad dig through his chest of torture devices. After an initial moment of panic and fear that I would be forced to relive Reyad's torture, the scene jumped ahead to Reyad's stunned expression as hot blood gushed from his throat, soaking me.

You are a killer, too, Ferde said in my mind. Images of the other men I had killed flashed by. *You have the power to collect souls without the need for symbols and blood. Why do you think Reyad still haunts you? You have taken his soul, your first of many more. I see the future and yours doesn't improve.*

The images spun dizzyingly and Irys's cold eyes stared at me as I watched Valek swing from a noose. Leif's hatred pounded in my mind along with Cahil's desire to have me executed. The Commander smiling in satisfaction at my trial for committing espionage, because he had gotten what he wanted from me and now I would no longer be a problem for Ixia.

Look at what the Master Magicians did to that Soulfinder long ago, Ferde said.

A man who had been chained to a post was set on fire. His screams of pain vibrated in my mind. Ferde held that image until the man's skin had burned away. I struggled to regain control over my mind, but Ferde's magic equaled a Master and I couldn't push him away.

The Soulfinder only wanted to help, bringing the dead back to life for their family and friends. It wasn't his fault they were different when they awoke, Ferde said in my mind. *Panic and fear of the unknown condemned him just like the Council will condemn you, too. All that I have shown you will be your fate. I see it in your story threads. Moon Man isn't your true Story Weaver, I am.*

His logic was persuasive. He understood my desire to find my place. It was next to him. Soulfinder and Soulstealer.

Yes. I'll change your story and the Council won't burn you alive. Just give me Gelsi's soul.

A small corner of my mind resisted, yelling for action. *Stealing souls is wrong,* I said. *I shouldn't.*

Then why have you been gifted with the ability if you're not supposed to use it? Ferde asked.

I should use it to help people.

That's what the other Soulfinder wanted to do. See what happened to him.

Focusing my thoughts became difficult. Ferde's control began to spread and soon he would take Gelsi from me.

Give me the girl. If I pull her from you, you will die. You'll be the first victim of my new administration. Your parents will be the next two.

Images of Perl being mutilated and Esau being hacked into pieces filled my mind. Blood splashed as I watched in helpless horror.

Save them and you can have complete freedom for the first time in your life.

His strong spell enticed me. I found myself agreeing with him. Freedom. Ferde sent a wave of pleasure through my body. I moaned as an intoxicating mix of joy and gratification flushed through me. I wanted to give Gelsi to him. But he went too far when my soul filled with contentment. Because I already owned that feeling whenever Valek held me in his arms.

I swayed on my feet and sweated with the effort to keep Ferde from taking Gelsi. He had realized his mistake and launched a mental attack to get her soul. Wrapping my arms tight around my chest, I collapsed to the ground. Fire burned inside me. Tears and sweat stung my eyes, but I spotted Perl's device nearby before pain twisted my body. All I needed was a second.

Trouble, love? Valek asked.

I need your immunity to magic.

Yours.

A resistance to magic, unlike any barrier I could form, grew in my mind, blocking Ferde's control. I opened my eyes.

"You almost had me," I said to Ferde. I picked up Perl's device and stood on unsteady legs.

Ferde's surprise didn't last long. "No matter. The effort to repel me has weakened you."

In two strides, he closed the distance between us. His hands wrapped around my throat. He was right. While I didn't have the power to stop him, I could do something else. As his thumbs pressed into my windpipe, I lifted Perl's device.

Black and white spots began to dance in front of my eyes. Before Ferde could react to my movement, I aimed the nozzle at him and pumped the rubber ball, spraying Curare into his face. Invented to apply perfume, Perl's little device worked like a charm.

Ferde's face froze in horror. I pushed his hands away and he fell to the ground.

There will be others, was Ferde's last thought before the drug paralyzed his body and his magic.

Once satisfied that he was frozen, I entered his mind. Trapped within the darkness were all the souls he had stolen. I released them into the sky. Feeling a rush of movement, I briefly joined the freed souls, soaking in their happiness and joy, then I returned to my body.

Without a moment to lose, I scooted over to Gelsi. Resting the tips of my fingers on her neck, I concentrated on her injuries and repaired them, including the cuts along her arms and legs.

Go back, I told Gelsi.

She had huddled in my mind, frightened and confused during the battle with Ferde, but now she understood. Her body bloomed with life, and she drew in a long shaky breath.

I cut her bonds with my switchblade, and, after spitting out the soggy Theobroma pill, I lay next to her, feeling exhausted and spent. She clung to me. My throat blazed with each lungful of air.

After a long while, I summoned the energy to stand, pulling Gelsi with me. We found Gelsi's clothes and I helped her into them. Before guiding her down to the living room to rest on a comfortable couch, I waved a hand out one of the second-story windows. Dax would be here soon.

"I will be expelled," she whispered.

I shook my head. "You'll be smothered with concern and understanding. And given all the time you need to recover."

Once Dax arrived to take my place next to Gelsi, I went back up to the landing where I had left Leif. Reluctance pulled at my legs. It felt as if they had been pricked with Curare.

I didn't have the strength to untie his twisted thoughts. My promise to Moon Man would have to wait a while longer. I drew Leif into a lighter sleep so he would rouse after I left. Ferde's last comment had made me realize that I still had some unfinished business to attend to.

Dax had a protective arm around Gelsi when I went downstairs.

"I sent a message to Master Bloodgood. The Masters are on their way with a battalion of guards to take Ferde to the Keep's prison," Dax said.

"Then I better go. I'm *supposed* to be confined to my quarters."

Dax shook his head. "Second Magician knows what you did."

"All the more reason not to be here when they arrive."

"But—"

I waved and hurried out the door, slinging my backpack over one shoulder. Since I had been expelled from the Keep's program, I knew I would soon be kicked out of my rooms. I planned to be long gone before giving Roze the satisfaction of evicting me.

Fisk ran over to me when I crossed the courtyard.

"Did we help?" Fisk asked. "Is everything okay?"

"You did great." I rummaged in my pack and handed Fisk all the Sitian coins I had. "Distribute these to your troops."

He smiled and dashed away.

A bone-deep weariness settled on me as I made my way through the Citadel. My surroundings blurred and I walked in a daze. When I passed the Council Hall, the group of beggars, who always hovered near the steps, began to follow me.

"Sorry. I can't help you today," I called over my shoulder. The group returned to the Hall, but one persisted. I turned around. "I said—"

"Lovely lady, spare a copper?" the man asked.

Dirt streaked his face and his hair hung in greasy clumps. His clothes were torn and filthy, and he smelled like horse manure. But he couldn't disguise those penetrating sapphire-blue eyes from me.

"Can't you spare a copper for the man who just saved your life?" Valek asked.

"I'm broke. I had to pay off the distraction. Those kids don't work cheap. What—"

"Unity fountain. A quarter hour." Valek returned to the steps and joined the other beggars.

I continued toward the Keep, but once I was out of sight of the Council Hall, I took a side street and headed to the Unity Fountain. The jade sphere with its holes and other spheres nestled inside it shone in the sunlight. The water spray from the circle of waterspouts sparkled in the cool air. My relief from knowing that Valek was unharmed warred with my concern that he should be far away from the Citadel.

A quick movement in a shadow caught my attention. I wandered over to the dark recess of a doorway and joined Valek, embracing him for a fierce moment before pulling back.

"Thank you for helping me against Ferde," I said. "Now go home before you get caught."

Valek smiled. "And miss all the fun? No, love. I'm going with you on your errand."

I could only produce a muted surprise. Valek and I didn't have a mental connection like the one I'd had with Irys, yet he knew my thoughts, and, when I had needed his help, he had always been there.

"There's no way I can convince you to go to Ixia?" My brief spurt of energy on seeing Valek safe faded.

"None."

"All right. Although I reserve the right to say, 'I told you so' should you get captured." I tried to say it in a stern tone, but my battered and tired soul was so filled with relief that Valek was coming with me that the words turned playful.

"Agreed." Valek's eyes lit up, anticipating the challenge.

34

VALEK AND I DECIDED ON the best course of action, and arranged to meet again at the edge of the Avibian Plains.

When I reached the Keep, I went straight to my rooms to pack. While I determined what to take along, someone knocked on my door. Out of habit I looked for my bow before realizing it had been destroyed by Leif. Instead, I grabbed my switchblade.

I relaxed a bit when I opened the door. Irys stood there, looking hesitant. Stepping back, I invited her in.

"I have some news," Irys said. When I just stared at her, she continued, "Ferde has been taken to the Keep's cells, and the Council has revoked your expulsion. They want you to stay so you can fully explore your magical abilities."

"Who would teach me?"

Irys glanced at the ground. "It would be your choice."

"I'll think about it."

Irys nodded and turned to go. Then stopped. "I'm sorry,

Yelena. I had no trust in your abilities and yet you achieved what four Master Magicians could not."

There was still a faint link between us, and I felt Irys's uncertainty and her loss of confidence. She questioned her ability to handle future difficult situations. She felt her beliefs on what was needed to solve a problem had been proven wrong.

"In this situation, magic was not the solution," I told her. "It was the lack of magic that allowed me to beat Ferde. And I couldn't have done that without Valek."

She considered my words for a moment and seemed to make a decision.

"I propose a partnership," Irys said.

"A partnership?" I asked.

"I believe you no longer need a teacher, but a partner to help you discover just how strong a Soulfinder you are."

I winced at the title. "Do you think I'm one?"

"I've suspected, but didn't want to really believe it. An automatic response just like your cringe just now. And, it seems I need some guidance. I've found that the Sitian way is not always appropriate. Perhaps you could help me with that?"

"Are you sure you would want to learn the 'rush into a situation and hope for the best' method?"

"As long as you want to discover more about being a Soulfinder. Is it really against the Ethical Code? Perhaps the Code needs to be updated. And could you be considered a Master, or would you have to take the Master's test first?"

"The Master test? I've heard some horror stories." My throat began to tighten. I swallowed with some difficulty.

"Rumors, mostly. To discourage the students so that only those who feel confident in their abilities will be brave enough to ask to take the test."

"And if they're not strong enough?"

"They won't succeed, but they'll learn the full extent of their powers. This is better than being surprised later."

Irys fell silent. I felt her mind reaching toward mine. *Do we have a deal?* she asked in my mind.

I'll think about it. A lot has happened.

So it has, she agreed. *Let me know when you're ready.* Irys left my rooms.

I closed the door. My mind shuffled through the possibility of exploring my powers versus the risk of being condemned as a Soulfinder. Despite having to worry about poison in the Commander's food, I began to think life in Ixia had been easier. After my errand, as Valek so casually called it, I had some choices on where to go next. Nice to have choices. Again.

I moved through my rooms, checking if I missed anything. I had packed the valmur statue for Valek, the rest of my Sitian coins, my northern uniform and an extra set of clothes. My armoire remained filled with my apprentice's robes and a couple of Nutty's skirt/pants. Papers and books piled on my desk, and the room smelled of Apple Berry and Lavender. My stomach squeezed with longing and with a sudden realization. These rooms in the Keep had turned into my home, despite my resistance.

Shouldering my pack, I felt the weight of it drag on me as I left. Stopping at the Keep's guest quarters on my way, I visited my parents. I could hear Esau in the kitchen and Perl had a strange expression on her face. Her hand touched her neck so I knew something had upset her. She made me promise to stay for tea, pulling my backpack off, and she hovered over me until I sat in one of the pink overstuffed chairs.

Calling to Esau to bring another cup, Perl perched in the seat next to me as if she would spring into action should I decide to leave. Esau brought in the tea tray. She jumped up and handed me one of the steaming cups.

Seeming to be satisfied that I was anchored to my chair, at least until I finished the tea, Perl said, "You're leaving. Aren't you?" She shook her head before I could answer. "Not that you would tell me. You treat me like a delicate flower. I'll have you know that the most delicate flowers often produce the strongest scent when crushed." She stared at me.

"I have some unfinished business to attend to. I'll be back," I said, but the weak response failed to soothe her.

"Don't lie to me."

"I wasn't lying."

"All right. Then don't lie to yourself." She eyed my bulging pack that she had set on the floor. "Send us word when you're settled in Ixia, and we'll come visit," she said in a matter-of-fact tone. "Though, probably not until the hot season. I don't like the cold."

"Mother!" I stood and almost spilled my drink.

Esau nodded, seeming nonplussed by the topic of our conversation. "I'd like to find the Mountain Laurel that grows near the ice pack. I read somewhere that the plant can cure Kronik's Cough. Be interesting to find out."

"You're not concerned that I might return to Ixia?" I asked my parents.

"Considering the week you had," my father said, "we're just happy you're alive. Besides, we trust your judgment. "

"If I do go to Ixia, will you promise to visit often?"

They promised. Not wanting to prolong the goodbyes, I snatched my pack and left.

★ ★ ★

Apple? Kiki asked with a hopeful tone.

No, but I'll get you some peppermints. I went into the barn's tack room to search for the bag of candy. I took two and returned to Kiki.

After she sucked the candy down, I asked her, *Ready to go? Yes. Saddle?*

Not this time. The Keep provided tack for the students, but it was understood that once a student graduated, he bought his own equipment.

I pulled the step stool over and Kiki snorted. *I know. I know,* I said. *No step stool in wild. But I'm tired.*

In fact, what little energy I had left leaked away with an alarming speed. Kiki and I didn't encounter any trouble at either the Keep's or the Citadel's gates. We took the road through the valley for a while. I refused to look back at the Citadel. I planned to come back, didn't I? Today wouldn't be the last time I saw the pastel colors of the sunset reflected in the white marble walls. Right?

As the light faded from the sky, I heard the pounding of hooves on the road behind me. Kiki stopped and spun to face the newcomer.

Topaz, she said with pleasure.

Though by the molten anger and murderous expression on Cahil's face, I knew this encounter would be far from pleasant.

"Where do you think you're going?" he demanded.

"That's not your concern."

Cahil's face turned a livid red as he sputtered in astonishment. "Not *my* concern? Not *my* concern?"

I saw him rein in his temper. Then in a deadly rumble, he

said, "You're the heart mate of the most wanted criminal in Sitia. Your whereabouts are of the utmost concern to me. In fact, I'm going to personally see to it that I know exactly where you are at all times." He whistled.

I heard a rush of movement and turned in time to see Cahil's men move into defensive positions behind me. Trying to conserve my strength, I hadn't scanned the road ahead with my magic. Hadn't believed I would need to. Silly me.

Did you smell them, Kiki? I asked.

No. Upwind. Go past?

Not yet.

Looking back at Cahil, I demanded, "What do you want?"

"Playing the simpleton to delay the inevitable, Yelena? I guess it has worked for you in the past. You certainly played me for a fool," he said with an eerie calmness. "Convincing me *and* First Magician that you weren't a spy, using your magic to make me trust you. I fell for it all."

"Cahil, I—"

"What *I* want is to kill Valek. Besides getting revenge for the murder of my family, I will be able to show the Council my abilities and they will finally support me."

"You had Valek before and lost him. What makes you think you can kill him this time?"

"Your heart mate will exchange his life for yours."

"You're going to need more men to capture me."

"Truly? Take another look."

I glanced over my shoulder. Cahil's men had kept their distance from Kiki's hindquarters, but, even in the twilight, I could see that each one held a blowpipe to his mouth, aiming at me.

"The darts are treated with Curare," Cahil said. "An excellent Sitian weapon. You won't get far."

Fear replaced annoyance as my heart rate increased. I had some Theobroma in my pack, but I knew if I tried to take it off my back, I would become a pin cushion for Cahil's men.

"Will you cooperate or do I need to have you immobilized?" Cahil sounded as if he asked if I would like some tea.

Ghost, Kiki said.

Before I could understand what Kiki meant, Valek sauntered into our group from the tall grass of the plains. Everyone froze for a second in shock. Cahil gaped.

"That's an interesting choice, love," Valek said. "You'll need some time to think it over. In the meantime…" Valek held his arms away from his body as he moved closer to Cahil. He had changed from his beggar disguise into the plain brown tunic and pants that the local citizens wore. He appeared to be unarmed, but I knew better, and, it seemed, so did Cahil who transferred Topaz's reins to his left hand and pulled his sword.

"Let's see if I have this right," Valek continued, seeming unconcerned about Cahil's sword a few feet away. "You want revenge for your family. Understandable. But you should know that the royal family is not *your* family. One thing I have learned over the years is to know my enemy. The royal bloodline ended the day the Commander took control of Ixia. I made sure of that."

"You lie!" Cahil urged Topaz forward, lunging at Valek with his sword.

Stepping to the side with grace and speed, Valek avoided being trampled and cut.

When Cahil turned Topaz for another charge, I said, "It makes sense. Valek wouldn't leave a job unfinished."

He pulled back on the bridle, stopping in disbelief. "Your love for him has damaged your senses."

"And your hunger for power has affected your intelligence. Your men are using you, yet you refuse to see the obvious."

Cahil shook his head. "I won't listen to any more lies. My men are loyal. They obey me or else they will be punished. Goel's death helped me to reinforce that lesson."

I recognized that flatness in his pale blue eyes. "*You* killed Goel."

He smiled. "My men have pledged their lives to me. I committed no crime." He brandished his sword. "Ready," he called to his men. "Aim and—"

"Think about this before you gloat about *your* men, Cahil. They look to Captain Marrok for approval before following your orders. They gave you a sword that was too heavy for you, and failed to properly train you with it. You are supposed to be related to the King, who was a powerful magician. Why don't you have any magic?"

"I—" Cahil hesitated.

His men glanced at each other in either consternation or confusion. I couldn't tell, but it broke their concentration. And in that moment, Valek leaped onto Kiki's back behind me. She took off into the plains without being told. I grabbed her mane as Valek's arms encircled my waist, and Kiki broke into her gust-of-wind gait.

I heard Cahil yell fire, and thought I heard the whiz of a dart near my ear, but we were soon out of range. Kiki traveled twice the distance of a normal gallop without any obvious effort. When the moon had reached its apex, Kiki slowed then stopped.

Smell gone, she said.

Valek and I slid off her back. I inspected her for injuries before she snorted with impatience and moved away to graze.

I shivered in the cold air, searching my body for darts before wrapping my cloak tighter. "That was close."

"Not really," Valek said, pulling me toward him. "We distracted the men so when Wannabe King gave the order they didn't have time to aim."

Valek felt warm even though he wasn't wearing a cloak. Seeming to read my thoughts, he said, "I'll share yours." He smiled with a mischievous delight. "But first you need a fire, food and some sleep."

I shook my head. "I need you." It didn't take me long to convince him. Once I had divested him of his clothes, he elected to join me in my cloak.

I woke to the delightful smell of roasting meat. Squinting in the bright sunlight, I saw Valek crouched near a fire. He had set up a spit of meat over the glowing embers.

"Breakfast?" I asked as my stomach rumbled.

"Dinner. You've slept all day."

I sat up. "You should have woken me. What if Cahil finds us?"

"Doubtful with all this magic in the air." Valek peered into the sky, scenting the wind. "Does it bother you?"

I opened my mind to the power surrounding us. The Sandseed's protective magic tried to invade and confuse Valek's thoughts, but his immunity deflected the strands of power with ease. The magic seemed indifferent to my presence.

"No." I told Valek about my distant relationship to the Sandseed clan. "If I came close to their village with the intent to harm them, I think the protection would attack me." Then I thought about Moon Man's magical abilities and his scimitar. "Either that or one of their Story Weavers would."

Valek considered. "How long will it take us to reach the Daviian Plateau?"

"It depends on Kiki. If she decides to use her gust-of-wind gait, we could be there in a few hours."

"Gust-of-wind? Is that what you call it? I've never seen a horse run that fast before."

I mulled over Valek's comment. "She only does it when we're in the plains. Perhaps it's connected to the Sandseed's magic."

Valek shrugged. "Faster is better. The faster we can take care of Alea, the better."

But exactly how we would take care of Alea remained the real question. I knew she would be a threat to me if she had survived her injury, yet I didn't want to kill her. Perhaps turning her over to the Sandseeds would be enough. I thought about Moon Man's remarks about the Daviian Vermin, and realized that Ferde's comment about the existence of others might not have been about Alea coming after me, but about the other Daviians.

Valek pulled the meat from the fire and handed the spit to me. "Eat. You need your strength."

I sniffed the unidentifiable lump. "What is it?"

He laughed. "You're better off not knowing."

"Poisons?"

"You tell me," he teased.

I took an experimental bite. The juicy meat had an odd earthy taste. Some type of rodent, I thought, but no poisons. When I had finished my supper, we began to pack up our meager supplies.

"Valek, after we deal with Alea, you must promise to return to Ixia."

He grinned. "Why would I do that? I'm beginning to enjoy the climate. I might build a summer home here."

"It's that cocky attitude that got you into trouble in the first place."

"No, love. It was you. If you hadn't gotten yourself captured by Goel, I wouldn't have tipped my hand to the Wannabe King."

"You didn't tip your hand. I'm afraid I did that when I was fighting with Cahil."

"Defending my honor again?" he asked.

Back in Ixia, I had inadvertently exposed one of his under-cover operations by standing up for him. "Yes."

He shook his head in amazement. "I know you love me, so you can stop proving it. I really don't care what Wannabe King thinks of me."

I thought about Cahil. "Valek, I'm sorry for believing you killed Goel."

He waved away my apology. "You would have been right. I went back to take care of him for you, but he had beaten me to it." Valek's angular features grew serious. "The Wannabe King remains a problem."

I nodded. "One that *I'll* deal with."

"Now who's cocky?"

I started to protest, but Valek stopped me with a kiss. When he pulled away, I noticed that Kiki's head was up and her ears pointed forward.

Smell? I asked her. Then I heard the sound of hoof beats, heading toward us.

Rusalka, Kiki said. *Sad Man.*

My first reaction was annoyance that Leif had followed us. But the thought that, if he could find us, then so could Cahil filled me with apprehension.

Anyone else? I asked.

No.

Valek disappeared into the tall grass just as Leif's horse seemed to materialize from a cloud of dust.

Leif's green eyes were wide with shock. "She's never done that before."

My annoyance transformed to amusement. Rusalka's black coat gleamed with sweat, but she didn't appear to be stressed.

"I call that Kiki's gust-of-wind gait," I told Leif. "Is Rusalka a sandseed horse?"

He nodded. Before he could say another word, I saw a blur of motion to his left as Valek leaped out of the grass and knocked Leif from his horse. They landed together with Valek on top of Leif's chest. He held Leif's machete to Leif's throat as my brother struggled to get his breath.

"What are you doing here?" Valek asked.

"Come. To find. Yelena," Leif said between gasps.

"Why?"

By this time, I'd recovered from my surprise. "It's all right, Valek. He's my brother."

Valek moved the blade away, but remained on top of him. Leif's face twisted into an expression of astonished terror.

"Valek? You have no smell. No aura," Leif said.

"Is he a simpleton?" Valek asked me.

I grinned. "No." I pulled Valek from Leif. "His magic can sense a person's soul. Your immunity must be blocking his power." I bent over Leif and examined him, looking for broken bones with my magic. I didn't find any serious injuries.

"Are you all right?" I asked Leif.

He sat up and glanced nervously at Valek. "That depends."

"Don't worry about him, he's overprotective."

Valek harrumphed. "If you could keep out of trouble for one day, protecting you wouldn't be so instinctive." He rubbed his leg. "Or so painful."

Leif had recovered from his shock and stood.

My annoyance returned. "Why are you here?" I asked.

He looked at Valek then at the ground. "It was something Mother said."

I waited.

"She told me that you were lost again. And only the brother that had searched for you for fourteen years could find you."

"*How* did you find me?"

Leif gestured a bit wildly at his horse. "Kiki had found Topaz in the plains, so I thought, since Rusalka was bred by the Sandseeds, I asked her to find Kiki. And... And..."

"She found us very fast." I mulled over what Leif had said about our mother. "Why does Perl think I'm lost? And why send you? You weren't any help the last time." Now, I had to suppress the urge to punch him. He had almost killed me with his machete at Ferde's house.

Leif cringed with guilt. "I don't know why she sent me."

I was about to tell him to go home, when Moon Man walked into sight. "A good guy," I said to Valek before he could attack him.

"This seems to be quite the meeting place," Valek muttered under his breath.

When Moon Man came closer, I asked, "No mysterious arrival? No coalescing from a sunray? Where's the paint?" The scars on his arms and legs stood out against his dark skin, and he wore a pair of short pants.

"It is no fun when you already know those tricks," Moon

Man said. "Besides, Ghost would have killed me if I had suddenly appeared."

"Ghost?" I asked.

Moon Man pointed to Valek. "Kiki's name for him. It makes sense," he said, seeing the look of confusion on my face. "To magical beings, we see the world through our magic. We see him with our eyes, but cannot see him with our magic. So he is like a ghost to us."

Valek listened to Moon Man. Although expressionless, I could tell by the rigid set to Valek's shoulders that he was prepared to strike.

"Another relative?" Valek asked.

A broad smile stretched Moon Man's lips. "Yes. I am her mother's uncle's wife's third cousin."

"He's a Story Weaver, a magician of the Sandseed clan," I explained. "And what are you doing here?"

Moon Man's playfulness faded from his face. "You are on *my* lands. I could ask you the same thing, but I already know why *you* have come. I came to make sure you keep your promise."

"What promise?" Leif and Valek asked at the same time.

I waved the question away. "I will, but not now. We need—"

"I know what you intend to do. You will not succeed with that unless you untangle yourself," Moon Man said.

"Me? But I thought you said…" I stopped. He had made me promise to untie Leif, but then I remembered that Moon Man had said our lives twisted together. But what did helping Leif have to do with going after Alea? "Why won't I succeed?" I asked.

Moon Man refused to answer.

"Do you have any more cryptic advice?" I asked.

He held out his hands. One toward Leif and the other to me.

Valek huffed in either amusement or annoyance, I couldn't tell, but he said, "Looks like a family affair. I'll be close by if you need me, love."

I studied Leif. His reaction to the Story Weaver the last time we had met him had been one of fear. Now, he stepped forward and grabbed Moon Man's hand, shooting me a look of stubborn determination.

"Let's finish this," Leif said, challenging me.

35

I SLID MY HAND INTO MOON Man's. My world melted as the warm magic of the Story Weaver took control of my senses.

We traveled to the Illiais Jungle to the place Leif had hidden while watching Mogkan kidnap me over fourteen years ago. The three of us viewed the events through Leif's eyes and felt his emotions. In essence, becoming him.

A mean approval that Yelena got what she deserved for not staying close to him spiked Leif's heart. But when the strange man put her to sleep, and pulled his pack and sword from under a bush, sudden fear of getting taken by the man kept Leif in his hiding place. He stayed there long after the man had carried his sister away.

Moon Man manipulated the story's thread for a moment, showing Leif and me what would have happened if Leif had tried to rescue me. The ring of steel rolled through the jungle as Mogkan pulled his sword from its scabbard and stabbed Leif in the heart, killing him. Remaining hidden had been a good decision.

The story then changed and focused on Perl and Esau's despair and anger when Leif had finally told them that I was lost. Leif believed he would be in worse trouble if he had told them the truth and they knew he hadn't done anything to stop the man. Leif had been convinced that the search parties would find the man and his sister. Already he felt jealous of the attention she would get for just being rescued.

When the search parties failed to find her, Leif began his own quest. He knew they lived in the jungle, keeping out of sight just to spite him. He had to find her, and maybe his mother and father would love him again.

As the years passed, his guilt drove him to attempt suicide, and, eventually, the guilt transformed into hatred. When she finally came back into their lives stinking of blood and of the north, he wanted to kill her. Especially when he saw for the first time in fourteen years the pure joy on his mother's face.

Cahil's ambush, while unexpected, gave Leif a receptive audience about the need to get rid of the northern spy. But watching her get hurt caused a small rip of concern in his black cloak of hate.

Her escape from Cahil was proof he had been right about her, but then she came back, insisting she wasn't a spy and therefore would not run away like one. Roze then confirmed her claims, puzzling Leif.

His confusion and conflicting emotions only grew when he saw her try to help Tula. Why would she care about another? She hadn't cared about him or how he suffered while she was gone. He wanted to keep hating her, but when she struggled to bring Tula back, he couldn't bear the guilt if he stood by and did nothing again.

When they traveled to the plains and Story Weaver approached, Leif had known his sister would discover the truth about him. He ran, unable to face the accusations that would fill her eyes. But when he calmed, he thought, would the truth be that difficult for her? She weathered so much in Ixia. Perhaps she could overcome this hurdle, too.

But after she had returned from the plains, Leif knew it was impossible. Her anger and censure flamed on her skin. She didn't want him or need him. Only his mother's pleas that he help his sister made him seek her out.

Story Weaver let the strands of the tale fade. The three of us stood on that dark plain I remembered from my last encounter with Moon Man. His coloring matched a ray of moonlight. Leif glanced around with wonder.

"Why did Mother ask you to help me rescue Gelsi?" I asked Leif.

"She thought I could assist you in some way. Instead, I had tried to—"

"Kill me? You can join the 'I Want to Kill Yelena Guild.' I hear they have six members in good standing. Valek is president since he had wanted to kill me twice." I smiled, but Leif stared at me with guilt in his eyes. "It wasn't you. Ferde tapped into your memories and used them."

"I did want to kill you before you helped Tula." Leif hung his head.

"Don't feel ashamed for having those feelings and those memories. What happened in the past can't be changed, but they can be a guide for what happens in your future."

Moon Man radiated approval. "We could make a Story Weaver out of you if you were not already a Soulfinder." He flashed me a wide smile.

"Truly?" How many people would I need to hear it from

before I believed it or felt it? Perhaps it would be best not to declare myself a Soulfinder and just be regular old Yelena.

Moon Man raised an eyebrow. "Come visit me when you are ready."

Then the world spun and I shut my eyes against the feelings of vertigo. When they stopped, I opened them, finding myself back in the plains with Leif. Moon Man was talking to Valek.

I digested what happened on the stony plain. Leif had been in the process of untying himself. His road had smoothed when he made the decision to help me with Tula. So why had Moon Man asked me to help him? I looked for the Story Weaver, but he had disappeared.

Then the answer came to me, and, along with it, my own guilt. Without truly understanding Leif, I had treated him badly, holding the actions of an eight-year-old boy against a grown man and failing to see how he tried to amend them.

Leif watched me.

"How come they never schedule a New Beginnings feast when you really need to start over?" I asked.

Leif smiled at me. The first genuine one since I had returned from Ixia. It warmed me to the core of my soul.

"That's okay. I don't dance," he said.

"You will," I promised.

Valek cleared his throat. "Touching as this is, we need to go. Your Story Weaver is providing us with some soldiers to aid against Alea's people. We're to rendezvous with them at dawn. I take it your brother…"

"Leif." I filled in.

"…is coming along?"

"Of course," Leif said.

"No," I said at the same time. "I don't want you to get hurt. Mother wouldn't like it."

"And I wouldn't be able to face her wrath if I didn't stay and help." Leif crossed his arms over his chest. His square jaw set into a stubborn line.

"Your mother sounds like a formidable woman," Valek said into the silence.

"You have no idea," Leif replied with a sigh.

"Well, if she's anything like Yelena, my deepest sympathies," Valek teased.

"Hey!"

Leif laughed and the tense moment dissipated.

Valek handed Leif his machete. "Do you know how to use it?"

"Of course. I chopped Yelena's bow into firewood," Leif joked.

"You took me by surprise. I didn't want to hurt you," I shot back.

Leif looked dubious.

"How about a rematch?"

"Anytime."

Valek stepped between us. "I'm beginning to wish that you were an orphan, love. Can you both manage to focus on the task at hand without trying to catch up on fourteen years of sibling rivalry?"

"Yes," we said in unison, properly chastised.

"Good. Then let's go."

"Where?" I asked.

"In keeping with his cryptic nature, all your Story Weaver said was, 'The horses know where to go.'" Valek shrugged.

"It's certainly not a military strategy *I* would use, but I've learned that the south uses its own strategy. And, strangely enough, it works."

The horses did know where to go, and, as the sun rose over the plains, we encountered a group of Sandseed soldiers on a rocky outcropping surrounded by tall grass. A dozen men and six women dressed in leather armor and equipped with either scimitars or spears waited. They had painted red streaks on their faces and arms, creating an impressively fierce countenance.

There were no other horses. Valek and I jumped off Kiki and Leif dismounted Rusalka to join us. The two horses began to graze. I shivered in the cold morning air, feeling naked without my bow, wishing I had another weapon besides my switchblade.

Moon Man greeted us. He had dressed like his clansmen, but he was armed with his scimitar and a bow. The bow he held was no ordinary staff of ebony wood. It had been carved with symbols and animals, revealing a gold-colored wood under the black surface. And I felt that, if I could just stare at it long enough, the carvings may reveal a story. I shook my head, trying to stay focused on Moon Man's words.

"I sent a scout last night," Moon Man said. "He found the blood-letting apparatus in the Void just as Yelena described. Then he tracked the Daviian Vermin to a campsite about a mile east of that location. We are on the edge of the plains about two miles north of that site."

"We'll wait until dark and launch a surprise attack," Valek said.

"That will not work," Moon Man said. "The Vermin have

a shield that will alert them to intruders. My scout could not get too close to their camp for fear of discovery." Moon Man appeared to scan the horizon. "They have strong Warpers, who can hide their whereabouts from our magic."

"Warpers?" Leif asked.

Moon Man frowned. "Magicians. I refuse to call them Story Weavers for they manipulate the threads for their own selfish desires."

I glanced at the group of Sandseeds, noting again the array of weapons. "You don't plan to use your magic?"

"No."

"And you don't plan to take prisoners?"

"That is not the Sandseed way. The Vermin must be exterminated."

I wanted to neutralize the threat of Alea, but I didn't want to kill her. Esau's vial of Curare still remained in my backpack. Perhaps I could paralyze her and take her back to the Keep's cells.

"How are you going to prevent the Daviians from using their magic?" Valek asked.

A dangerous glint flashed in Moon Man's eyes. "We move the Void."

"You can do that?" I asked, surprised.

"The blanket of power can be repositioned only with the utmost care. We will center the blanket's hole directly over the Vermin's camp and then we will attack."

"When?" Valek asked.

"Now." Moon Man walked over to his soldiers.

"I'd hoped to use the Sandseeds as a distraction," Valek said to me in a low whisper. "This will work. Once Alea is dead, we leave. This isn't our fight."

"I think capture and incarceration would be a harsher punishment for her," I said.

Valek studied me for a moment. "As you wish."

Moon Man's group shouted a war cry, then disappeared into the tall grass. He came back to us. "They will position themselves around the camp. The signal to attack will be when the Void is in place. You are to come with me." He glanced at the three of us. "You need weapons. Here."

He tossed his bow to me. I caught it in my right hand.

"That is yours. A gift from Suekray."

"Who?"

"A horsewoman of our clan. You must have made an impression on her. Her gifts are as rare as the snow. Your story is etched into it."

Mother, Kiki said with approval. And I remembered the short-haired Sandseed woman who had taken Kiki for a ride the day I had met with the elders.

I marveled at the bow. The balance and thickness felt perfect in my hand, and, despite the carvings, the black wood remained smooth and strong. By the time I pulled my eyes from the beauty of the bow, I saw that Valek clutched a scimitar and Leif wielded his machete.

"Let us go."

I took off my cloak and made a few quick preparations before we followed Moon Man into the tall grass.

From our position near the Daviian camp, I could see some activity around their tents and campfire. The air hovering over their site seemed to shimmer and it distorted the images of the people inside as if a massive pocket of heat had been trapped over them.

The grasses of the plateau grew in small clumps and had turned brown from lack of rain. I crouched with Valek behind a small bush. Leif and Moon Man were five hundred feet to our right huddled in a slight depression. I wondered how the other Sandseeds had fared in finding hiding spots. The Daviians had chosen a wide-open area for their camp and cover was minimal.

I felt the hair raise on my arms as power pressed against my skin. Seeking out with my awareness, I felt Moon Man and three other magicians tug the blanket of power. They applied equal pressure so the blanket would not gather in one location, but would move smoothly. Their magical abilities impressed me, and I thought, if I did stay in Sitia, the Sandseeds would make powerful teachers.

The Void's arrival felt like all the air had been sucked out of my lungs. My awareness of my surroundings reduced to the mundane senses of sight, smell and sound. Before I could adapt to my magical loss, another war cry sounded. The signal to attack the camp.

I jumped to my feet and followed Valek toward the camp. And stopped dead in my tracks when the scene in front of me registered in my mind.

The Daviians shield had been destroyed and, with it, the illusion. Instead of a few people milling about the campfire, there stood over thirty. Instead of a handful of tents, there were rows and rows of them. Granted most of the Vermin stared in shock at the loss of their magic, but we were outnumbered four to one.

Too late to retreat. We had the element of surprise and nineteen battle-thirsty Sandseeds, who cut wide bloody swaths through the Daviians. I could see Moon Man's bald head above the fighting, and Leif's powerful strikes kept a couple

Daviians busy. Valek shot me a grim look. Find Alea, he mouthed to me before joining in the fray.

Great, I thought, edging around the outskirts of the battle. Find Alea in this mass of confusion. I ducked as a Daviian swung his scythe at me. I swept his feet from under him and hopped onto his chest before he could raise his long weapon. Ramming the end of my bow into his neck, I crushed his windpipe.

I paused for a heartbeat. He was the first person I killed since coming to Sitia. I had hoped never to take a life again, but if I wanted to survive this melee, I couldn't afford to be compassionate.

Another Daviian attacked. My melancholy thoughts disappeared as I defended myself and searched for Alea. Dodging and fighting, I lost all track of time as the series of matches began to blur together. In the end, Alea found me.

Her long black hair had been pulled back into a knot and she wore a simple white tunic and pants that were splattered with blood. She held a bloody short sword in each hand. Alea smiled at me.

"I planned to find you," she said. "How nice that you saved me the trouble."

"That's just how I am, always thinking of others."

She crossed her swords in a mock salute and lunged. I stepped back, and brought my bow down on the top of her blades, deflecting them toward the ground. She took a step forward to regain her balance just as I shuffled closer to her. We touched shoulders. Our weapons pointed down.

But mine remained on top. I yanked the bow up, hitting her in the face. She yelped as blood gushed from her nose. My strike failed to stop her, and she tried to swing her swords toward my stomach. I moved next to her; too close for large weapons. We dropped them.

I triggered my switchblade as she pulled a knife from her belt. She turned and stabbed at me. I blocked her blade with my arm. Pain burned as the knife bit into my flesh, but the move allowed me to grab her hand. I pulled her toward me and sliced her forearm with my blade then released her.

Alea staggered back in confusion. I could have plunged my knife into her stomach, killing her. Her expression turned to horror as she realized what I had done.

My switchblade had been treated with Curare. All I had needed to do was prick her skin with the tip of the weapon. When she fell to the ground, I stood over her.

"It's not fun being helpless. Is it?" I asked.

I looked around. Valek had maneuvered himself so that he stayed between me and the Daviians, keeping the others from interfering with my fight with Alea. Leif fought a short distance away, hacking with his machete. I couldn't see the other Sandseeds, but I spotted Moon Man just as he took a man's head off with his scimitar. Yuck.

Moon Man sprinted for us. "Time to retreat," he called.

"Next time," I said to Alea. "We'll finish this."

Then the Void moved and the magic came back for half of the campsite, creating a diversion. We were bathed in power, and I felt Moon Man encompass us in a shield of protective magic as we began our retreat. Valek, though, paused over Alea's still form. He knelt beside her, picked up her knife, and said something to her.

Before I could call to him, he cut her throat in one smooth move. It was the same lethal strike that he had delivered to her brother, Mogkan.

When Valek caught up to me he said, "We can't afford to play favorites."

★ ★ ★

We raced back toward the plains. The Vermins ceased chasing us at the border of the Avibian Plains, but we kept our pace until we reached the rocky outcropping where Kiki and Rusalka waited.

"No doubt they will move their camp farther into the plateau," Moon Man said. The effort of running had not winded him, although his skin gleamed with sweat. "I will need to bring more soldiers. To have deceived my scout and me means their Warpers are more powerful than we suspected. I must consult with the elders."

Moon Man inclined his head in farewell and I soon lost sight of him in the grass.

"What now?" Leif asked.

I met Valek's gaze. What now, indeed.

"You go home and so will I," I said to Leif.

"You're coming with me to the Keep?" Leif asked.

"I…" Back to the Keep and to the feelings of isolation? Back to being feared for my abilities? Or back to spy on Sitia so I could eventually return to Ixia? Or just being on my own, exploring Sitia and spending time with my family?

"I think you're afraid to go back to the Keep," Leif said.

"What?"

"It will be much easier for you to stay away, and not have to deal with being a Soulfinder, being a daughter and being a sister."

"I'm not afraid." I had tried to find a place in Sitia, but I kept getting pushed away. How many hints did I need? I wasn't a glutton for punishment. What if they decided that a Soulfinder equaled evil and they burned me alive for violating their Ethical Code?

"You *are* afraid." Leif challenged.

"Am not."

"Are too."

"Am not."

"Then prove it."

I opened my mouth, but no sound came out.

Finally, I said, "I hate you."

Leif smiled. "The feeling is mutual." He paused for a moment. "Are you coming?"

"Not now. I'll think about it." It was a delay tactic and Leif knew it.

"If you don't come back to the Keep, then I'll be right. And every time you see me, I'll be insufferably smug."

"And how's that different from now?"

He laughed and I could see the young carefree boy he had been in his eyes. "You've only had a small glimpse of how insufferable and annoying I can be. As the older brother, it's my birthright."

Leif mounted Rusalka and galloped away.

Valek and I walked with Kiki toward the north. Toward Ixia. He held my hand and I felt content as my thoughts mulled over the last few hours.

"Valek. What did you say to Alea?"

"I told her how her brother had died."

I remembered how I had trapped Mogkan with magic, immobilizing him so Valek could cut his throat. Alea died the exact same way.

"We had no time to take Alea with us, love. I wasn't going to let her have another chance to hurt you."

"How do you always know when I need you?"

Valek's eyes flamed with an intensity that I had rarely seen.

"I know. It's part of me like hunger or thirst. A need that must be met to survive."

"How do you do it? I can't connect my mind to yours with my magic. And you don't have magic. It should be impossible."

Valek remained quiet for a moment. "Perhaps, when I feel your distress, I relax my guard and allow you to connect with me?"

"Perhaps. Have you ever done that for anyone else?"

"No, love. You're the only one who has caused me to do the oddest things. You have truly poisoned me."

I laughed. "Odd, eh?"

"It's a good thing you can't read my mind, love."

A sapphire-blue fire smoked in his eyes, and I noticed a tightening in his lean muscles.

"Oh, I know what you're thinking." I stepped into his arms, putting my hands under his waistband to where his thoughts had traveled, making my point.

"I can't. Hide. From you," Valek panted.

I heard Kiki snort and move away as my world filled with the feel and smell and taste of Valek.

Valek and I spent the next several days walking the plains and enjoying being together without any worries or problems hovering over our heads. We would discover small caches of food and water along our path. And while I didn't have the feeling that someone watched us, I felt that the Sandseeds knew where we were, and the provisions were their way of extending their hospitality to a distant cousin.

Eventually, we left the plains. Skirting east of the Citadel, we headed north through the Featherstone clan's lands. Careful to travel at night and hide during the day, it took us three days to reach the Ambassador's retinue.

I had lost track of the days and been surprised to see their camp, but Valek had known they would be about a half-day's walk to the Ixian border. After determining where the Sitian "spies" hid, Valek changed into his Ilom disguise, and slipped into the camp in the middle of the night. I waited and approached the next day. There was no reason for me to hide, and, if I went back to Ixia, the Sitian spies could report back to the Keep and the Council that I had left.

The Ixians had begun to pack up their equipment when I rode in on Kiki. One tent still stood, but Ari and Janco rushed over to greet me before I could reach it.

"Didn't I tell you, Ari? She's come to say goodbye after all. And you were pouting and miserable for days," Janco said.

Ari just rolled his eyes, and I knew if anyone was miserable it was Janco.

"Or have you decided that you can't bear to be parted from us and are going to disguise yourself as a soldier and come back to Ixia?" Janco's smile was hopeful.

"Beating you in a bow fight every day is really tempting, Janco."

He scoffed. "I know your tricks now. I won't be so easy to beat."

"Are you sure you want me to come? I have a tendency to cause trouble."

"That's what I'm counting on," Janco said. "Life has been *so* dull without you."

Ari shook his massive head. "We don't need any more trouble. The diplomatic niceties started falling apart between the Ambassador and the Sitian Council toward the end. Before we left, one of the Councilors had accused the Ambassador of bringing Valek to Sitia to assassinate the Council."

"Not good," I said. "The Sitians are constantly worried the Commander will want to take control of their lands. And I would be, too, knowing that Valek possessed the skills to assassinate the Councilors as well as the Master Magicians, creating enough chaos so there is little resistance to an Ixian attack."

I shook my head, sighing. The Ixians and Sitians viewed the world so differently. They needed someone to help them understand each other. A strange feeling churned in my stomach. Fear? Excitement? Nausea? Perhaps all three; it was hard to tell.

"Speaking of Valek," Janco said, "I take it he's well?"

"You know Valek," I said.

Janco nodded, grinning.

"I'd better talk to the Ambassador." I slid off Kiki. Before I could move, Ari's large hand grabbed my arm.

"Just make sure you say goodbye to Janco," Ari said. "You think he's annoying when he's in a good mood; he's worse when he's in a bad mood."

I promised Ari, but as I walked to the Ambassador's tent, that odd feeling in the pit of my stomach became almost painful. Goodbye seemed so final.

One of the two guards outside the tent ducked inside to announce me. He came out and held the flap for me to enter. Ambassador Signe sat at a canvas table, drinking tea with Valek still dressed as Adviser Ilom. Signe dismissed him and I caught a look and the word "tonight" from Valek before he left the tent.

Bypassing the pleasantries, Signe asked, "Have you decided if you're going to visit us?"

I took the Commander Ambrose's order of execution from my pack. My hand trembled slightly and I took a breath to steady my nerves. "With this unfortunate clash of opinions between Ixia and Sitia, I believe you both will need a liaison. A neutral party who knows both countries and can facilitate negotiations, assisting them in understanding each other better." Meaning I wouldn't spy for Ixia, but I offered to help. I handed Signe the order. The Commander must decide what to do with it.

And there he stood in Signe's uniform, studying me with his powerful gold eyes. I blinked several times. The transformation from Signe to Commander Ambrose was so complete that I could only see a faint resemblance to the Ambassador in his face.

The Commander rolled up the execution order and tapped it on his palm as his gaze grew distant. Considering all the options, I thought, he never made a hasty decision.

"A valid point," he said.

He stood and paced the small area. I saw a bedroll on the floor behind him and a lantern. The tent and table appeared to be his only luxuries.

Commander Ambrose stopped then tore my execution order into small pieces, sprinkling them onto the ground. Turning, he held out his hand to me. "Agreed, Liaison Yelena."

"Liaison Yelena Zaltana," I corrected as we shook hands.

We discussed the Commander's plans for Ixia and how he wanted to expand trade with Sitia. He insisted I finish my magical training before becoming the official liaison. Before I left, I witnessed Ambassador Signe's return. It was then that I felt, for a brief moment, that two souls resided within one body.

That would explain why he had been so successful at keeping his secret.

I mulled over the interesting idea to keep my mind off the startling fact that I was going to return to the Keep. The Ambassador's retinue finished packing. I told Ari and Janco that I would see them again.

"Next time, your ass is mine," Janco sang.

"Keep your skills sharp," Ari ordered.

"It was bad enough having two mothers, now I have two fathers," I teased.

"Send word if you need us," Ari said.

"Yes, sir."

I headed south as the Ixians traveled north. Pulling a thread of magic, I projected my awareness. One of the Sitian spies followed me in hopes that I would meet up with Valek. I sent the man a confusing array of images until he lost all sense of what he was supposed to do.

Remembering Valek's promise, I didn't travel too far. I found an empty wooded area between two farms and set up a small campsite. As the sunlight faded, I projected my awareness into the surrounding woods. A few bats began to wake and a couple rabbits crept through the underbrush. All was quiet except for the steady approach of Cahil and his men.

He didn't try to mask his movements. Bold and cocky, Cahil left his men guarding the edge of the wood while he continued toward me. I sighed, more annoyed than scared, and reached for my bow.

I glanced around. Nowhere to hide on the ground, although the tree canopy might offer some protection. It might work except Marrok waited with Cahil's men. And I was certain the Captain's tracking skills had led Cahil to me. I would have to resort to using magic in my defense. Projecting, I reached toward Cahil's mind.

His emotions boiled with hate, but he had tempered them with a cold calculation. He stopped at the edge of my camp and inclined his head. "May I join you?"

"It depends on your intentions," I said.

"I thought you could read my intentions." He paused. "I see you have decided to stay in Sitia. A bold move considering the Council will know about your involvement with Valek."

"I'm not a spy, Cahil. And the Council needs a liaison with Ixia."

He barked out a laugh. "You're a liaison now? That's funny. Do you really think the Council will trust you?"

"Do you think the Council will go to war for a commoner?"

Cahil sobered for a moment. He glanced over his shoulder in the direction where his men waited. "I will find out the truth about that. But it really doesn't matter to me anymore. I've decided to take matters into my own hands."

Even though he hadn't moved, I could feel a renewed sense of threat from him. "Why are you telling me this? You know you can't get to Valek through me. Besides, he's back in Ixia by now."

He shook his head. "As if *I* would believe *you*. A beautiful day for riding and you stop here?" He gestured to the surrounding woods then took two steps toward me. "I'm here to give you a warning." Another step.

I brandished my bow. "Stop right there."

"You once said you thought Goel was decent for warning

you about his intentions. I thought I would do the same. I know I can't beat you or Valek—even my men don't have a chance—but someone, somewhere has that ability. I'll swear I'll find him and, together, we'll make it our mission to see you and Valek dead." With that, Cahil spun around and headed for his men.

I didn't relax my grip on my bow until Cahil mounted Topaz and rode away. His men followed behind, running to keep up. As I broke my connection with Cahil's mind, I dipped into Marrok's mind. He was scared and worried about Cahil's odd behavior. That made two of us.

That night, my campfire seemed lonely until Valek arrived. He appeared by the fireside, warming his hands over the flames. I decided not to ruin our last night together by telling him about Cahil's visit.

"Forgot your cloak again?" I asked.

He smiled. "I like sharing yours."

Long after the fire had died, I fell asleep wrapped in Valek's arms. When the sun intruded, I burrowed deeper under my cloak.

"Come with me," Valek said.

It wasn't a plea or an order. An invitation.

Regret ached in my heart. "I still have much to learn. And when I'm ready, I'll be the new liaison between Ixia and Sitia."

"That could lead to serious trouble," Valek teased.

"You would be bored if it was any other way."

He laughed. "You're right. And so was my snake."

"Snake?"

He pulled my arm out to expose my bracelet. "When I

carved this, my thoughts were on you, love. Your life is like this snake's coils. No matter how many turns it makes, you'll end up back where you belong. With me." His sapphire eyes held a promise. "I'll look forward to your first official visit. But don't wait too long. Please."

"I won't."

After another kiss, Valek rose and, as he dressed, I told him about Cahil.

"Many have tried to kill us. All have failed." He shrugged. "We've thrown him a curve. Either he'll sulk over his lack of royal blood and disappear, or he'll make himself believe we lied and will have a renewed determination to attack Ixia, which should make life interesting for the new liaison."

"*Interesting* isn't the word I would use."

"Make sure you keep a close eye on him." Valek smiled ruefully. "I have to go, love. I promised the Ambassador I would catch up to her at the border. If there is going to be any trouble from the Sitians it would be near there."

I regretted my decision to stay the moment he left and utter loneliness overcame me. But Kiki's cold nose against my cheek intruded on my morose thoughts.

Kiki stay with Lavender Lady, she said. *Kiki help.*

Yes, you're a big help.

Smart.

Smarter than me, I agreed.

Apple?

You've grazed all night. How can you still be hungry?

Always room for apple.

I laughed and fed her an apple before we began our two-day trip back to the Keep.

★ ★ ★

When I arrived at the Keep's gate, the guard instructed me to go directly to the Master's meeting room. As I gave Kiki a quick rubdown at the stables, I wondered what had been going on in my absence.

Students hurried from one building to the next as an icy wind blew through the campus. They gave me only a fleeting surprised glance before increasing their pace. The gray sky darkened and sleet cut through the air. An ominous start to the cold season. I pulled my hood up to protect my face.

I had arrived in Sitia at the beginning of the hot season. The two seasons I had lived here felt more like two years.

When I entered the conference room, three neutral expressions and one livid greeted my arrival. Roze threw a ball of furious energy at me. It hit me square on the chest, and I stumbled back before deflecting her attack. Pulling power to me, I projected my awareness toward her. Her mental defenses were impenetrable, but I aimed lower. Through her heart and into her soul. A much more vulnerable spot.

Now, now, I said. *Play nice.*

She jumped. *What? How?*

I have found your soul, Roze. It's dark and nasty in here. You've been hanging around those criminal types too long. You better change your ways or this soul won't fly to the sky.

Her amber eyes burned into mine with all the hate and loathing she could muster. Underneath, though, she was terrified. Hate and loathing didn't bother me, but fear was a powerful emotion. Fear causes the dog to bite and Roze was one bitch.

I released her. Roze sputtered and glared at me with a poisonous gaze. I stared back with calm patience. Eventually, she stormed from the room.

"So it is true," Bain said into the sudden silence. "You *are* a Soulfinder." He seemed more thoughtful than scared.

"What made her so upset?" I asked.

Irys gestured for me to sit down. I sank into one of the plush chairs.

"Roze thinks you and Valek are part of a plot to assassinate the Council." Before I could respond, Irys went on, "There's no proof. But what is more alarming is Ferde's escape from the Keep's cells."

I jumped to my feet. "Ferde escaped? When? Where?"

Irys exchanged a knowing glance with Bain. "I told you she had nothing to do with his release," she said to him. Then to me, "We're not sure when. He was discovered missing this morning." Irys gave me a wry grin. "We think Cahil rescued him."

"Cahil?" Now I was confused.

"He is gone. Captain Marrok was found brutally beaten. Once Marrok regained consciousness, he told us Cahil had tortured him until Marrok had told him the truth." Irys stopped, shaking her head in astonishment.

"That Cahil doesn't have royal blood," I said.

"You knew?" Zitora asked. "Why didn't you tell us?"

"I suspected. But Valek just confirmed my suspicions."

"Marrok told us that Cahil's mother had died in childbirth and he was the son of a soldier slain during the Ixian take-over. When they fled to Sitia, they took him along," Irys explained.

"Where is he now?" I asked.

"We don't know," Irys said. "And we don't know what his plans are now that he has learned the truth, and why he took Ferde with him."

So much for Valek's sulk-and-do-nothing theory about Cahil's reaction to his origins. "I guess, we'll just have to find him and ask," I said.

"But not yet," Irys said, and sighed. "The Council is a mess. Since you released all those souls, Ferde is weak and will be unable to do any magic for quite some time. And…" She hesitated, and I had the unpleasant feeling that I wasn't going to like what she said next. "They want you to explore your Soulfinder capabilities and perhaps become a Council Adviser."

Discovering my abilities matched my own wishes, but if I wanted to be a neutral liaison, I couldn't be attached to the Council in any capacity.

"They don't need a Council Adviser," I said. "They need a liaison with Ixia."

"I know," Irys said.

"We should go after Ferde and Cahil today."

"I know. You'll just have to convince the Council of that."

I stared at Irys. My Story Weaver had to be laughing his blue ass off right now. My future appeared to be a long twisted road fraught with knots, tangles, and traps.

Just the way I liked it.

★ ★ ★ ★ ★

Read on for a sneak peak at Maria V Snyder's
fantastic new Chronicles of Ixia novel

SHADOW STUDY

1

YELENA

Ugh, mud, Kiki said as she splashed through another puddle. The wet muck clung to her copper coat and dripped from her long tail. It packed into her hooves and coated the hair of her fetlocks with each step.

Through our mental connection I sensed her tired discomfort. *Stop?* I asked. *Rest?*

No. Images of fresh hay, a clean stall and being groomed formed in Kiki's mind. *Home, soon.*

Surprised, I glanced around the forest. Melting piles of snow mixed with black clumps of dead leaves—signs that the cold season was losing its grip. Rain tapped steadily on the bare branches. The light faded, turning the already gray woods leaden. For the past few hours, I'd been huddling under my sopping-wet cloak, trying to keep warm. With my thoughts fixed on my rendezvous with Valek, I'd failed to keep track of our location.

I scanned the area with my magic, projecting my awareness out to seek life. A few brave rabbits foraged in the soggy underbrush and a couple of deer stood frozen, listening to the squishy plodding of Kiki's passage. No souls haunted these woods. No humans within miles.

That wasn't a surprise. This remote area in the northeastern Featherstone lands had been chosen for that very reason. After Owen Moon ambushed us about four years ago, Valek and I had decided to move to a less well-known location near the Ixian border.

I leaned forward in the saddle. We were getting close and my wet cloak no longer pressed so hard on my shoulders. At this pace, we'd reach our cozy cottage within the hour. Valek's involvement with our friend Opal's rescue from the Bloodrose Clan and the aftermath had kept him busy for months. Finally we would have a few precious days all to ourselves before he reported back to the Commander. He should already be there waiting for me. Visions of sharing a hot bath, snuggling by a roaring fire and relaxing on the couch once again distracted me.

Kiki snorted in amusement and broke into a gallop. Behind the clouds the sun set, robbing the forest of all color. I trusted Kiki to find the path in the semidarkness as I kept a light magical connection to the wildlife nearby.

In midstride, Kiki jigged to the right. Movement flashed to the left along with the unmistakable twang of a bow. Kiki twisted under me. I grabbed for her mane, but a force slammed into my chest and knocked me from the saddle.

Hitting the ground hard, I felt all the air in my lungs whoosh out as pain erupted. Fire burned with each of my desperate gasps. Without thought, I projected again, searching for the... person who had attacked me. Despite the agony, I pushed as far as I could. No one.

Kiki, smells? I asked. She stood over me, protecting me.

Pine. Wet. Mud.

See magician?

No.

Not good. The person had to be protected by a magical

MARIA V. SNYDER

null shield. It was the only way to hide from me. Null shields blocked magic. At least it also prevented the magician from attacking me with his or her magic since it blocked magic from both sides of the shield. But it wouldn't stop another arrow. And perhaps the next one wouldn't miss.

I glanced at the shaft. The arrow had struck two inches above and one inch to the left of my heart, lodging just below my clavicle. Fear banished the pain for a moment. I needed to move. Now.

Rolling on my side, I paused as an icy sensation spread across my chest. The tip had been poisoned! I plopped back in the mud. Closing my eyes, I concentrated on expelling the cold liquid. It flowed from the wound, mixing with the blood already soaked into my shirt.

Instead of disappearing, the poison remained as if being refilled as fast as I ejected it. With pain clouding my thoughts, the reason eluded me.

Kiki, however, figured it out. She clamped her teeth on the arrow's shaft. I had a second to realize what she planned before she yanked the arrow from my chest.

I cried as intense pain exploded, blood gushed and metal scraped bone all at once. Stunned, I lay on the ground as black and white spots swirled in my vision. On the verge of losing consciousness, I focused on the hollow barbed tip of the arrow coated with my blood, reminding me of the danger. I remained a target. And I wasn't about to make it easy for my attacker to get another shot.

Fix hole, Kiki said.

I debated. If I healed myself now, then I'd be too weak to defend myself. Not like I was in fighting condition. Although I still had access to my magic, it was useless against arrows and, as long as the assassin hid behind the null shield, I couldn't touch him or her with my magic, either.

Kiki raised her head. Her ears cocked. *We go. Find Ghost.*

I groaned. How could I forget that Valek was nearby? *Smart girl.*

With the arrow still clutched in her teeth, Kiki knelt next to me. Grabbing her mane, I pulled myself into the saddle. Pain shot up my arms and vibrated through my rib cage when she stood. She turned her head and I took the arrow. It might give us a clue about the assassin's identity.

I crouched low over Kiki's back as she raced home. Keeping alert for another twang, I aimed my awareness on the surrounding wildlife. If the animals sensed an intruder, I'd pick up on their fear. A sound theory, except I'd been in contact with the deer when the arrow struck. I'd be impressed by the assassin's skills if I wasn't in so much pain.

It didn't take long for us to reach our small stable. The main doors had been left open. A warm yellow glow beckoned. Kiki trotted inside. The lanterns had been lit and Onyx, Valek's horse, nickered a greeting from his stall. Kiki stopped next to a pile of straw bales. Relieved to be safe, I slid onto them then lay down.

Kiki nudged my arm. *Lavender Lady fix hole.*

After Ghost comes. I suspected I would drop into an exhausted sleep once I healed the injury and I knew Valek would have questions.

She swished her muddy tail and stepped away. *Ghost.*

Valek appeared next to me. His confusion turned to alarm as his gaze swept my blood-soaked shirt. "What happened?"

No energy for a detailed explanation, I filled him in on the basics and handed him the arrow.

All animation dropped from Valek's angular face. Fury blazed in his sapphire-blue eyes as he examined the weapon. For a moment, I remembered our first meeting when he offered me the job of the food taster. Poisons had brought us

MARIA V. SNYDER

together at that time, as well. But I'd never expected it to last. Then I'd wanted nothing more than to escape from him as quickly as possible.

Clear liquid dripped from the hollow shaft. He sniffed it. "Did you expel all the poison?"

"I think so." Hard to tell for sure, but I wouldn't add more fuel to his anger. Valek's hard expression already promised murder.

He smoothed the hair from my cheek. "How bad is it?"

"Not as bad as it looks. Now go, before the assassin gets away." I shooed.

"I'm not leaving you unprotected."

Kiki huffed and flicked her tail, splattering mud on Valek's black pants. I yanked my switchblade from its holder, triggering the blade. "I'm far from unprotected. Douse the light before you go."

"All right. I'll station Onyx outside the stable. Stay here." Valek opened Onyx's stall and the black horse trotted out. After he extinguished the lantern, Valek disappeared into the blackness.

I lay there listening for any sounds. My shoulder and left arm throbbed. Each inhalation caused a sharp stab of pain in my chest. To ease the discomfort, I pulled a thin thread of magic from the blanket of power that encompassed the world. A mental picture of the injury formed when I focused on the wound. My clavicle had been broken. The arrow had sliced through my muscles on impact, and the metal barbs in the arrow's head had ripped chunks of skin when Kiki had yanked it out. Lovely. I used the ribbon of power to lessen the pain— a temporary measure.

Once more sending my awareness into the surrounding forest, I kept a light contact with the nocturnal creatures. Too bad my bat friend was hibernating over the cold season. His unique senses would have helped with finding the assassin in the dark. The wildlife conducted their nightly hunt of food and showed no signs of agitation—not even from Valek. His immunity to magic prevented me from keeping track of him. I hoped he stayed sharp.

As time passed without incident, I wondered who had attacked me. That line of thought didn't go far as all I could deduce at this point was the person was a magician who had the power to form a null shield, who favored a bow and arrow, and who might have an affinity with animals. Either that or he/she was really quiet and had masked his/her smell.

Unfortunately, pondering why I was attacked generated a longer list. As the official Liaison between the Commander of the Territory of Ixia and the Sitian Council, I'd created at least a dozen political and criminal enemies in the past six years. As the heart mate of Valek, the infamous Ixian assassin, for the past eight years I'd been a target for anyone who hated Valek, which included most of Sitia and probably hundreds of Ixians. As a magician and Soulfinder, I made many people nervous, worrying that I'd turn rogue. These people were under the mistaken impression that I could create a soulless army when in fact all I did was find lost souls and guide them to either an eternity of peace in the sky or an eternity of suffering in the fire world, depending on their deeds while alive.

A slight squish jolted me from my thoughts. Careful of my injury, I sat up and swung my legs over the bales of straw. Then I slid off. Better to stand and fight than be caught lying down. The darkness outside was one hue lighter than inside due to the faint moonlight. It illuminated just enough to see shapes.

I kept alert for any movement, peering through the door. When Kiki stepped between me and the entrance, I startled. Even though she was sixteen hands high she could be really quiet. Her back was taller than me and she blocked my view.

Granted, I reached only five feet four inches, but she was a big girl like most Sandseed horses.

A few more squishes set my heart to beat in double time. I tightened my grip on my switchblade.

Ghost, Kiki said, moving away.

I sagged against the bales. A Valek-shaped shadow strode into the stable. He lit the lantern. One look at his grim expression and I knew he'd lost the assassin's trail.

"The guy's a pro," he said. "He used magic to erase his footprints. They just stopped. And without leaves on the bushes, it's harder to track him, especially at night. I'll go out again in the daylight."

"He? How do you know?"

"Big boots, deep prints. We can discuss it later. Let's go inside and take care of you."

"Kiki first." And before he could argue, "She saved my life. If she hadn't moved, the arrow would have pierced my heart."

Valek's shoulders dropped. Knowing I wouldn't leave, he worked fast. He removed her saddle and knocked the dried mud off her legs and stomach. After he cleaned out her hooves, she walked into her stall and munched on hay.

"Guess she's happy enough," Valek said, tossing the pick into a bucket. "Now, let's get you warm and dry, love."

I removed my muddy cloak and left it on the bales before I wrapped my right arm around Valek's shoulders. He wanted to carry me, but I worried he might jar the broken bone out of alignment and I wouldn't have enough strength to heal it.

The sharp pain returned by the time we reached the house. I made it as far as the couch. A bright fire burned in the hearth and a bottle of wine sat on the end table with two glasses and a plate of cheese. Valek must have arrived a few hours before me.

Tilting my head at the food, I said, "That's lovely."

"We'll indulge after you're healed and rested. Do you want to change first?"

Just the thought of moving my left arm hurt. "No."

"Then what are you waiting for?"

"A kiss. I haven't seen you in months."

Valek transformed when he smiled. The sharp angles of his face softened and warmth radiated from him. He leaned forward and pressed his lips to mine. Before I could deepen the kiss he pulled back.

"No more until you're better."

"Meanie."

"Yelena." His stern tone would have made my mother proud.

"All right." I reclined on the couch and closed my eyes.

Reaching for the power blanket, I gathered a thick thread of magic. I wound this ribbon around my broken clavicle, fusing the two pieces back together. A second thread knitted the muscles and a third replaced skin. The effort exhausted me. Drained dry, I passed out.

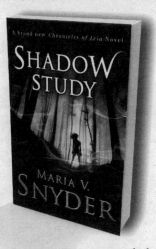

THEY DESTROYED HER WORLD. BUT SHE'S THEIR ONLY HOPE...

Avry's power to heal the sick should earn her respect in the plague-torn land of Kazan. Instead she is feared and blamed for spreading the plague.

When Avry uses her forbidden magic, she faces the guillotine. Until a dark, mysterious man rescues her from her prison cell. His people need Avry's magic to save their dying prince.

Saving the prince is certain to kill Avry. Now she must choose—use her healing touch to show the ultimate mercy or die a martyr to a lost cause?

www.mirabooks.co.uk

fire study

'You need my permission to exit the Keep,' Roze said.
'This is *my* domain. I'm in charge of all magicians,
including you, Soulfinder.' Her hands smacked her chair's
arms. 'If *I* had control of the Council, you would be
taken to the Keep's cells to await execution. No good has
ever come from a Soulfinder.'

The other Masters gaped at Roze in shock. She remained incensed. 'Just look at our history. Every Soulfinder has craved power. Magical power. Political power.
Power over people's souls. Yelena will be no different.
Sure now she plays at being a Liaison and has agreed to
my training. It's only a matter of time.'

Looking over her shoulder, she gave me a pointed stare.
*Keep out of Sitia's affairs. And you might be the only
Soulfinder in history to live past the age of twenty-five.*

Go take another look at your history books, Roze, I said. *The
demise of a Soulfinder is always reported along with the death
of a Master Magician.*

Roze ignored me as she left the meeting room.

fire study

MARIA V. SNYDER

Published in Great Britain 2015
by MIRA Ink, an imprint of Harlequin (UK) Limited,
Eton House, 18-24 Paradise Road,
Richmond, Surrey, TW9 1SR

© Maria V. Snyder 2008

ISBN 978 1 848 45241 1

Harlequin (UK) Limited's policy is to use papers that are natural, renewable and recyclable products and made from wood grown in sustainable forests. The logging and manufacturing processes conform to the legal environmental regulations of the country of origin.

Printed and bound by
CPI Group (UK) Ltd, Croydon, CR0 4YY

MIX
Paper from
responsible sources
FSC
www.fsc.org FSC C007454

THE TERRITORY OF IXIA

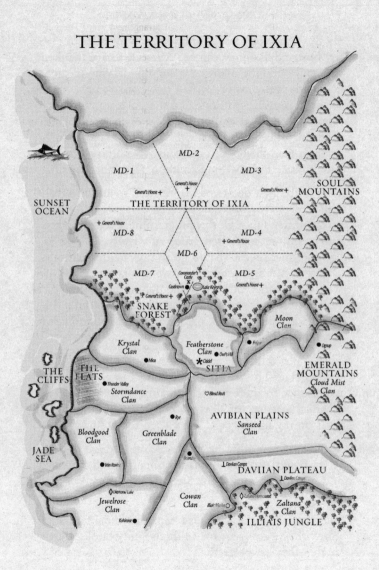

ACKNOWLEDGEMENTS

By this time you all should know how wonderful my husband, Rodney, can be. After all, I have thanked him and listed the many ways he supports me in the acknowledgements of my first two books. However, the writing wouldn't get done and the holes in plot logic wouldn't get filled without him. So once again, thanks go to him, because I don't ever want to take him for granted. And thanks also go to my two little sparks who fire my imagination—my children, Luke and Jenna.

One of the best decisions I've made is to attend Seton Hill University's graduate writing programme. Through this programme, I've learned so much and met a talented group of writers. Thanks to them all, and special thanks go to my critique partners, Diana Botsford, Kimberley Howe and Jason Jack Miller, who helped me with this book. Kim, I hope this reads better than the ingredients on a frozen dinner! I would also like to thank my Seton Hill mentor, David Bischoff.

First drafts of novels can be pretty rough, but my editor, Mary Theresa Hussey, has the knowledge and experience to wade in and guide me to calmer waters. Thanks, Matrice, for all your hard work and the smiley faces on my manuscript. They keep me going!

Thanks go to Catherine Burke, Selma Leung, Anna Baggaley, and Belinda Mountain for all their help and support in getting the Study series noticed in the UK.

Many thanks to Henry Steadman, who did a fantastic job with the cover art for all three Study books. I love them—they are perfect!

Researching for a book is always fun, and this time I enrolled in a glass-blowing class. My appreciation for glass art rose considerably as I struggled to craft simple items from molten glass. Thanks go to my teacher and glass artist, Helen Tegeler, whose patient instruction not only added to my know-ledge of glass for this book, but made the experience a blast.

And, finally, heartfelt thanks go to my army of Book Commandos! They're out in the trenches promoting and recommending my books to all who will listen, affixing stickers, and handing out bookmarks. Thanks to my Aunt Bette, whose efforts in the field earned her the rank of General. The Commander would be proud.

To my parents, James and Vincenza,
for your constant support and encouragement
in all my endeavours. You sparked the fire.

I

"**That's pathetic, Yelena**," Dax complained. "An all-powerful Soulfinder who isn't all-powerful. Where's the fun in that?" He threw up his long thin arms in mock frustration.

"Sorry to disappoint you, but *I'm* not the one who attached the 'all-powerful' to the title." I pulled a black strand of hair from my eyes. Dax and I had been working on expanding my magical abilities without success. As we practiced on the ground floor of Irys's Keep tower—well, mine too, since she has given me three floors to use—I tried not to let my own aggravation interfere with the lessons.

Dax was attempting to teach me how to move objects with magic. He had rearranged the furniture, lined up the plush armchairs in neat rows and turned the couch over on its side with his power. My efforts to restore Irys's cozy layout and to stop an end table from chasing me failed. Though not from lack of trying—my shirt clung to my sweaty skin.

A sudden chill shook me. Despite a small fire in the hearth, the rugs and the closed shutters, the living room was icy. The white marble walls, while wonderful during the hot season, sucked all the heat from the air throughout the cold season. I imagined the room's warmth following the stone's green veins and escaping outside.

Dax Greenblade, my friend, tugged his tunic down. Tall and lean, his physique matched a typical Greenblade Clan member. He reminded me of a blade of grass, including a sharp edge— his tongue.

"Obviously you have no ability to move objects, so let's try fire. Even a baby can light a fire!" Dax placed a candle on the table.

"A baby? Now you're really exaggerating. Again." A person's ability to access the power source and perform magic manifested at puberty.

"Details. Details." Dax waved a hand as if shooing a fly. "Now concentrate on lighting this candle."

I cocked an eyebrow at him. So far, all my efforts on inanimate items were for naught. I could heal my friend's body, hear his thoughts and even see his soul, but when I reached for a thread of magic and tried to use it to move a chair, nothing happened.

Dax held up three tan fingers. "Three reasons why you should be able to do this. One, you're powerful. Two, you're tenacious. And three, you've beat Ferde, the Soulstealer."

Who had escaped, and was free to start another soul-stealing spree. "Reminding me of Ferde is helping me how…?"

"It's *supposed* to be a pep talk. Do you want me to list all the heroic deeds you've—"

"No. Let's get on with the lesson." The last thing I wanted was to hear Dax recite the latest gossip. The news about my being a Soulfinder had spread through the Magician's Keep like dandelion seeds carried by a strong wind. And I still couldn't think about the title without a cringe of doubt, worry and fear touching my heart.

I pushed all distracting thoughts aside and connected to the power source. The power blanketed the world, but only magicians could pull threads of magic from it to use. I gathered a strand to me and directed it to the candle, willing a flame to form.

Nothing.

"Try harder," Dax said.

Increasing the power, I aimed again.

Behind the candle, Dax's face turned red and he sputtered as if suppressing a cough. A flash seared my eyes as the wick ignited.

"That's rude." His outraged expression was comical.

"You wanted it lit."

"Yeah, but I didn't want to do it for you!" He glanced around the room as if seeking the patience to deal with an unruly child. "Zaltanas and their weird powers, forcing *me* to light the candle. Pah! To think I wanted to live vicariously through your adventures."

"Watch what you say about my clan. Or I'll…" I cast about for a good threat.

"You'll what?"

"I'll tell Second Magician where you disappear to every time he pulls one of those old books off his shelf." Bain was Dax's mentor, and, while the Second Magician delighted in ancient history, Dax would rather learn the newest dance steps.

"Okay, okay. You win and you've proved your point. No ability to light a fire. I'll stick to translating ancient languages."

Dax made a dour face. "And you stick to finding souls." He teased, but I sensed an undercurrent to his words.

His uneasiness over my abilities was for excellent reasons. The last Soulfinder was born in Sitia about a hundred and fifty years ago. During his short life, he had turned his enemies into mindless slaves and almost succeeded in his quest to rule the country. Most Sitians didn't react well to the news about another Soulfinder.

The awkward moment passed as a mischievous glint lit Dax's bottle-green eyes. "I'd better go. I have to study. We have a history test tomorrow. Remember?"

I groaned, thinking of the large tome waiting for me.

"Your knowledge of Sitian history is also pathetic."

"Two reasons." I held up my fingers. "One, Ferde Daviian. Two, the Sitian Council."

Dax gestured with his hand.

Before he could say anything, I said, "I know. Details, details."

He smiled and wrapped his cloak around him, letting in a gust of arctic wind as he left. The flames in the hearth pulsed for a moment before settling. I drew closer, warming my hands over the fire. My thoughts returned to those two reasons.

Ferde was a member of the unsanctioned Daviian Clan, who were a renegade group of the Sandseed Clan. The Daviians wanted more from life than wandering the Avibian Plains and telling stories. On a power quest, Ferde had kidnapped and tortured twelve girls to steal their souls and increase his magical power. Valek and I had stopped him before he could complete his quest.

An ache for Valek pumped in my heart. I touched his butterfly pendant hanging from my neck. He had returned to Ixia a month ago, but I missed him more each day. Perhaps I should get myself into a life-threatening situation. He had a knack for showing up when I most needed him.

Unfortunately, those times were fraught with danger and there hadn't been many chances to just be with each other. I longed to be assigned a boring diplomatic mission to Ixia.

The Sitian Council wouldn't approve the trip until they decided what to do with me. Eleven clan leaders and four Master Magicians comprised the Council, and they had argued about my new role of Soulfinder all this past month. Of the four Masters, Irys Jewelrose, Fourth Magician, was my strongest supporter and Roze Featherstone, First Magician, was my strongest detractor.

I stared at the fire, following the dance of flames along the logs. My thoughts lingered on Roze. The randomness of the blaze stopped. The flames moved with a purpose, divided and gestured as if on a stage.

Odd. I blinked. Instead of returning to normal, the blaze grew until it filled my vision and blocked out the rest of the room. The bright patterns of color stabbed my eyes. I closed them, but the image remained. Apprehension rolled along my skin. Despite my strong mental barrier, a magician wove magic around me.

Caught, I watched as the fire scene transformed into a lifelike picture of me. Flame Me bent over a prone body. A soul rose from the body, which I then inhaled. The soulless body stood and Flame Me pointed to another figure. Turning, the body stalked the new person and then strangled him.

Alarmed, I tried to stop the fire vision to no avail. I was forced to observe myself make more soulless people, who all went on a massive killing spree. An opposing army attacked. Fire swords flashed. Flames of blood splattered. I would have been impressed with the magician's level of artistic detail if I hadn't been horrified by the blazing carnage.

In time, my army was extinguished and I was caught in a net of fire. Flame Me was dragged, chained to a post and doused with oil.

I snapped back to my body. Standing next to the hearth, I still felt the web of magic around me. It contracted and tiny flames erupted on my clothes.

And spread.

I couldn't stop the advance with my power. Cursing my lack of fire skill, I wondered why I didn't possess this magical talent.

An answer echoed in my mind. *Because we need a way to kill you.*

I stumbled away from the blaze. Sweat poured down my back as the sound of sizzling blood vibrated in my ears. All moisture fled my mouth and my heart cooked in my chest. The hot air seared my throat. The smell of charred flesh filled my nose and my stomach heaved. Pain assaulted every inch of my skin.

No air to scream.

I rolled around the floor, trying to smother the fire.

I burned.

The magical attack stopped, releasing me from the torment. I dropped to the floor and breathed in the cool air.

"Yelena, what happened?" Irys touched an icy hand to my forehead. "Are you all right?"

My mentor and friend peered down at me. Concern lined her face and filled her emerald eyes.

"I'm fine." My voice croaked, setting off a coughing fit. Irys helped me sit up.

"Look at your clothes. Did you set yourself on fire?"

Black soot streaked the fabric and burn holes peppered my sleeves and skirt/pants. Beyond repair, I would have to ask my cousin, Nutty, to sew me another set. I sighed. I should just order a hundred of the cotton tunics and skirt/pants from her to save time. Events, including magical attacks, conspired to keep my life interesting.

"A magician sent me a message through the fire," I explained. Even though I knew Roze possessed the strongest magic in Sitia, and could bypass my mental defenses, I didn't want to accuse her without proof.

Before Irys could question me further, I asked, "How did the Council session go?" I hadn't been allowed to attend. Although the rainy weather wasn't conducive for walking to the Council Hall, it still rankled.

The Council wanted me well-versed in all the issues they dealt with on a daily basis as part of my training to be a Liaison between them and the Territory of Ixia. My training as a Soulfinder, though, remained a subject the Council hadn't agreed on. According to Irys's theory, my reluctance to begin learning could be the cause of the Council's indecision. I thought they worried I would follow the same path as the Soulfinder from long ago once I discovered the extent of my powers.

"The session…" Her lips twisted in a wry smile. "Good and bad. The Council has agreed to support your training." She paused.

I steeled myself for the next bit of news.

"Roze was…upset about the decision."

"Upset?"

"Fiercely opposed."

At least now I knew the motive behind my fire message.

"She still thinks you're a threat. So the Council has agreed to let Roze train you."

I scrambled to my feet. "No."

"It's the only way."

I bit back a reply. There were other options. There had to be. I was in the Magician's Keep, surrounded by magicians of various skill levels. There had to be another who could work with me. "What about you or Bain?"

"They wanted a mentor who was impartial. Out of the four Masters, that left Roze."

"But she's not—"

"I know. This could be beneficial. Working with Roze, you'll be able to convince her you're not out to rule the country. She'll understand your desire to help both Sitia and Ixia."

My doubtful expression remained.

"She doesn't like you, but her passion for keeping Sitia a safe and free place to live will override any personal feelings."

Irys handed me a scroll, stopping my sarcastic comment on Roze's personal feelings. "This arrived during the Council session."

I opened the message. In tight-printed letters was an order from Moon Man. It read, *Yelena, I have found what you seek. Come.*

2

THE MESSAGE I HELD WAS typical for Moon Man, my Sandseed Story Weaver and friend. Cryptic and vague. I imagined he had written the note with a devilish grin on his face. As my Story Weaver, he knew I sought many things. Knowledge about Soulfinders and finding a balance between Sitia and Ixia resided at the top of my list. A quiet vacation would be nice, too, but I felt certain he referred to Ferde.

Ferde Daviian, the Soulstealer, and killer of eleven girls had escaped from the Magician's Keep cells with Cahil Ixia's help. After the Council failed to recapture him, they debated for an entire month about how to find them both.

My frustration mounted with every delay. Ferde was weak from when I had pulled the souls—his source of magical power—from him during our fight. But all it would take was another girl's murder for him to regain some of his strength. So far, no one had been reported missing, but the knowledge that he remained free clawed at my heart.

To avoid imagining the horror Ferde might cause, I focused

on the message in my hand. Moon Man hadn't specified to come alone, but I dismissed the notion to tell the Council as soon as the thought formed in my mind. By the time they decided what to do, Ferde would be long gone. I would go without informing them. Irys would call it my rush-into-a-situation-and-hope-for-the-best method. With only a few minor mishaps, it had worked in the past. And at this point, rushing off held more appeal.

Irys had moved away when I unrolled the message, but, by the way she held herself so still, I knew she was curious. I told her about the note.

"We should inform the Council," she said.

"So they could do what? Debate every possible issue for another month? The message invited me. If I need your help, I'll send for you." I sensed her resolve softening.

"You should not go alone."

"Fine. I'll take Leif with me."

After a moment's hesitation, Irys agreed. As a Council member, she wasn't happy about it, but she had learned to trust my judgment.

My brother, Leif, would probably be as glad as I was to get away from both the Keep and the Citadel. Roze Featherstone's growing animosity toward me put Leif in a difficult situation. Apprenticed to Roze while training at the Magician's Keep, he had become one of her aides upon graduation. His magical skill of sensing someone's emotions helped Roze determine a person's guilt in a crime, and his magic also aided victims in remembering details about what had happened to them.

Leif's first reaction to my reappearance in Sitia after a fourteen-year absence had been immediate hatred. He had convinced himself that my kidnapping to the Territory of Ixia had been done to spite him and my return from the north had been an Ixian plot to spy on Sitia.

"At least we should tell the Master Magicians about Moon Man's message," Irys said. "I'm sure Roze would like to know when she can begin your training."

I frowned at her, and considered telling her about Roze's petty fire attack. No. I would deal with Roze on my own. Unfortunately, I would have plenty of time with her.

"We're having a Masters meeting at the administration building this afternoon. It will be the perfect time to inform them about your plans."

I scowled, but she remained steadfast.

"Good. I'll see you later," she said.

Irys sailed out of the tower before I could voice my protest. I could still reach her with my mind, though. Our minds always remained linked. The connection was as if we both stood in the same room. We each had our own private thoughts, but if I "spoke" to Irys, she would hear me. If she did probe into my deeper thoughts and memories, it would be considered a breach in the magician's Ethical Code.

My horse, Kiki, and I shared the same connection. A mental call to Kiki was all that was needed for her to "hear" me. Communicating with Leif or my friend Dax proved more difficult; I had to consciously pull power and seek them. And, once found, they had to allow me access through their mental defenses and into their thoughts.

Although I possessed the ability to take a shortcut to their thoughts and emotions through their souls, the Sitians considered the skill a breach of the Ethical Code. I had scared Roze by using it to protect myself against her. Even with all her power, she couldn't stop me from touching her essence.

Anxiety rolled in my stomach. My new title of Soulfinder didn't sit well with me, either. I shied away from that line of speculation as I wrapped my cloak around me before leaving the tower.

On my way across the Keep's campus, my attention returned to my musings about mental communication. My link with Valek couldn't be considered a magical connection. To me, Valek's mind was unreachable, but he had the uncanny ability to know when I needed him and *he* would connect with me. He had saved my life many times through that bond.

Turning Valek's snake bracelet around my wrist, I pondered our relationship until a biting wind laced with icy needles drove away all warm thoughts about him. The cold season had descended on northern Sitia with a vengeance. I shuffled through slushy puddles and shielded my face from the sleet. The Keep's white marble buildings were splattered with mud and looked gray in the weak light, reflecting the miserable day with perfection.

Spending most of my twenty-one years in northern Ixia, I had endured this type of weather for only a few days during the cooling season. Then the cold air would drive the dampness away. But, according to Irys, this horrid mess was a typical Sitian day during the cold season, and snow was a rare event that seldom lasted more than a night.

I trudged toward the Keep's administration building, ignoring the hostile stares from the students who hurried between classes. One of the results of capturing Ferde had been the immediate change in my status from an apprentice of the Keep to a Magician's Aide. Since Irys and I had agreed to a partnership, she offered to share her tower. I had accepted with relief, glad to be away from the cold censure of my fellow students.

Their scorn was nothing in comparison to Roze's fury when I entered the Masters' meeting room. I braced myself for her outburst, but Irys jumped from her seat at the long table and explained why I had come.

"…note from a Sandseed Story Weaver," Irys said. "He may have located Ferde and Cahil."

The corners of Roze's mouth pulled down with disdain. "Impossible. Crossing the Avibian Plains to return to his clan in the Daviian Plateau would be suicide. And it's too obvious. Cahil is probably taking Ferde to either the Stormdance or the Bloodgood lands. Cahil has many supporters there."

Roze had been Cahil's champion in the Council. Cahil had been raised by soldiers who had fled the takeover in Ixia. They convinced Cahil that he was the nephew of the dead King of Ixia and should inherit the throne. He had worked hard to gain supporters and attempted to build an army to defeat the Commander of Ixia. However, once he discovered he was really born to a common soldier, he rescued Ferde and disappeared.

Roze had encouraged Cahil. They held the same belief that it was just a matter of time before Commander Ambrose set his sights on conquering Sitia.

"Cahil could bypass the plains to get to the plateau," Zitora Cowan, Third Magician, offered. Her honey-brown eyes held concern, but as the youngest of the four Master Magicians her suggestions tended to be ignored by the others.

"Then how would this Moon Man know? The Sandseeds don't venture out of the plains unless it's absolutely necessary," Roze said.

"That's what they want us to believe," Irys said. "I wouldn't put it past them to have a few scouts around."

"Either way," Bain Bloodgood, Second Magician, said, "we must consider all options. Obvious or not, someone needs to confirm that Cahil and Ferde are not in the plateau." With his white hair and flowing robes, Bain's appearance matched what I had assumed to be a traditional magician's uniform. Wisdom radiated from his wrinkled face.

"I'm going," I declared.

"We should send soldiers with her," Zitora said.

"Leif should go," Bain added. "As cousins of the Sandseed, Yelena and Leif will be welcomed in the plains."

Roze ran her slender fingers along the short white strands of her hair and frowned, appearing to be deep in thought. With the colder temperatures, Roze had stopped wearing the sleeveless dresses she preferred and exchanged them for long-sleeved gowns. The deep navy hue of the garment absorbed the light and almost matched her dark skin. Moon Man had the same skin tone, and I wondered what color his hair would be if he hadn't shaved it off.

"I'm not sending anyone," Roze finally said. "It's a waste of time and resources."

"I'm going. I don't need your permission." I stood, preparing to leave.

"You need my permission to exit the Keep," Roze said. "This is *my* domain. I'm in charge of all magicians, including you, Soulfinder." Her hands smacked her chair's arms. "If *I* had control of the Council, you would be taken to the Keep's cells to await execution. No good has ever come from a Soulfinder."

The other Masters gaped at Roze in shock. She remained incensed. "Just look at our history. Every Soulfinder has craved power. Magical power. Political power. Power over people's souls. Yelena will be no different. Sure now she plays at being a Liaison and has agreed to my training. It's only a matter of time. Already…" Roze gestured to the doorway. "Already she wants to run off before I can begin lesson one."

Her words echoed through the stunned silence. Roze glanced around at their horrified expressions and smoothed the wrinkles from her gown. Her dislike of me was well-known, but this time she had gone too far.

"Roze, that was quite—"

She raised her hand, stopping Bain from the rest of his lecture. "You know the history. You have been warned many, many times, so I will say no more about it." She rose from her seat. Towering a good seven inches above me, she peered down. "Go, then. Take Leif with you. Consider it your first lesson. A lesson in futility. When you return, you'll be mine."

Roze made to leave, but I caught a thread of her thoughts in my mind.

…*should keep her occupied and out of my way.*

Roze paused before she exited. Looking over her shoulder, she gave me a pointed stare. *Keep out of Sitia's affairs. And you might be the only Soulfinder in history to live past the age of twenty-five.*

Go take another look at your history books, Roze, I said. *The demise of a Soulfinder is always reported along with the death of a Master Magician.*

Roze ignored me as she left the meeting room, ending the session.

* ★ ★

I went to find Leif. His quarters were near the apprentice's wing on the east side of the Keep's campus. He lived in the Magician's building, which housed those who had graduated from the Keep and were now either teaching new students or working as aides to the Master Magicians.

The rest of the magicians who had also completed the curriculum were assigned to different towns to serve the citizens of Sitia. The Council tried to have a healer in every town, but the magicians with rare powers—like the ability to read ancient languages or find lost items—moved from place to place as needed.

Magicians with strong powers took the Master-level test before leaving the Keep. In the past twenty years, only Zitora had passed, bringing the number of Masters to four. In Sitia's history, there never had been more than four Masters at one time.

Irys thought a Soulfinder could be strong enough to take the Master's test. I disagreed. They already had the maximum, and I lacked the basic magical skills of lighting fires and moving objects—skills all the Masters possessed.

Besides, being a Soulfinder was bad enough, having to endure and fail the Master test would be too much to bear. Or so I guessed. The rumors about the test sounded horrific.

Before I even reached Leif's door, it swung open and my brother stuck his head out. The rain soaked his short black hair in an instant. I shooed him back as I hurried into his living room, dripping muddy slush onto his clean floor.

His apartment was tidy and sparsely furnished. The only hint of his personality could be gleaned from the few paintings that decorated the room. A detailed rendering of a rare Ylang-Ylang flower indigenous to the Illiais Jungle, a painting of a strangler fig suffocating a dying mahogany tree and a picture of a tree leopard crouched on a branch hung on his walls.

Leif scanned my bedraggled appearance with resignation. His jade-colored eyes were the only feature that matched my own. His stocky body and square jaw were the complete opposite of my oval face and thin build.

"It can't be good news," Leif said. "I'd doubt you would brave the weather just to say hello."

"You opened the door before I could knock," I said. "You must know something's up."

Leif wiped the rain from his face. "I smelled you coming."

"Smelled?"

"You reek of Lavender. Do you bathe in Mother's perfume or just wash your cloak with it?" he teased.

"How mundane. I was thinking of something a little more magical."

"Why waste the energy on using magic when you don't have to? Although…"

Leif's eyes grew distant and I felt the slight tingle of power being pulled.

"Apprehension. Excitement. Annoyance. Anger," Leif said. "I take it the Council hasn't voted to make you Queen of Sitia yet?"

When I didn't answer, he said, "Don't worry, little sister, you're still the princess of our family. We both know Mother and Father love you best."

His words held an edge, and I remembered it hadn't been long since he had wanted to see me dead.

"Esau and Perl love us equally. You really do need me around to correct your misconceptions. I've proved you wrong before. I can do it again."

Leif put his hands on his hips and raised one dubious eyebrow.

"You said I was afraid to come back to the Keep. Well—" I spread my arms wide, flinging drops of water onto Leif's green tunic "—here I am."

"You are here. I'll grant you that. But are you unafraid?"

"I already have a mother and a Story Weaver. *Your* job is to be the annoying older brother. Stick to what you know."

"Ohhh. I've hit a nerve."

"I don't want to argue with you. Here." I pulled Moon Man's note from my cloak's pocket and handed it to him.

He unfolded the damp paper, scanning the message. "Ferde," he said, coming to the same conclusion. "Have you told the Council?"

"No. The Masters know." I filled Leif in on what had happened in the meeting room, omitting my "exchange" with Roze Featherstone.

Leif's wide shoulders drooped. After a long moment, he said, "Master Featherstone doesn't believe Ferde and Cahil are going to the Daviian Plateau. She doesn't trust me anymore."

"You don't know that for—"

"She thinks Cahil is headed in another direction. Normally she would send me to determine his location and send for her. Together, we would confront him. Now I get assigned the wild-valmur chase."

"Valmur?" It took me a moment to connect the name with the small, long-tailed creature that lived in the jungle.

"Remember? We used to chase them through the trees. They were so fast and quick, we never caught one. But sit down and hold a piece of sap candy and they'll jump right into your lap and follow you around all day."

When I failed to respond, Leif cringed with guilt. "That must have been after…"

After I had been kidnapped and taken to Ixia. Although I could imagine a young Leif scampering through the jungle's canopy after a fleet-footed valmur.

The Zaltana Clan's homestead had been built high in the tree branches, and my father had joked that the children learned to climb before they could walk.

"Roze could be wrong about Cahil's intentions. So pack some of that sap candy. We might need it," I said.

Leif shivered. "At least it will be warmer in the plains, and the plateau is farther south."

I left Leif's quarters, heading to my tower to pack some supplies. The sleet blew sideways and tiny daggers of ice stung my face as I hurried through the storm. Irys was waiting for me in the receiving room just past the oversize tower entrance. The flames in the hearth pulsed with the rush of cold air slipping around the doors as I fought to close them against the wind.

I hustled to the fire and held my hands out. The prospect of traveling in such weather was unappealing.

"Does Leif know how to light fires?" I asked Irys.

"I think so. But no matter how skilled he is, wet wood won't ignite."

"Great," I muttered. Steam floated from my soaked cloak.

I draped the soggy garment around a chair then dragged it closer to the fire.

"When are you leaving?" Irys asked.

"Right away." My stomach grumbled and I realized I had missed lunch. I sighed, knowing dinner would probably be a cold slice of cheese and mushy bread.

"I'm meeting Leif in the barn. Oh snake spit!" I remembered a couple of commitments.

"Irys, can you tell Gelsi and Dax I'll start their training when I get back?"

"What training? Not magic—"

"No, no. Self-defense training." I pointed to my bow. The five-foot-long staff of ebony wood was still threaded through its holder on my backpack. Drops of water beaded and gleamed on the weapon.

I pulled it free, feeling the solid weight of the staff in my hands. Underneath the ebony surface of the bow was a gold-colored wood. Pictures of me as a child, of the jungle, my family, and so on had been etched into the wood. Even Kiki's loving eyes had been included in the story of my life. The bow moved smoothly in my hands. A gift from a master craftswoman of the Sandseed Clan who had also raised Kiki.

"And Bain knows that you won't be at his morning lesson," Irys said. "But he said—"

"Don't tell me he assigned homework," I pleaded. Just thinking about lugging the heavy history tome made my back hurt.

Irys smiled. "He said that he would help you catch up on your studies when you return."

Relieved, I picked up my pack, sorting the contents to see what other supplies we would need.

"Anything else?" Irys asked.

"No. What are you going to tell the Council?" I asked.

"That Roze has assigned you to learn about your magic from the Story Weavers. The first documented Soulfinder in Sitia was a Sandseed. Did you know that?"

"No." I was surprised but shouldn't have been. After all, what I knew about Soulfinders wouldn't fill a page in one of Master Bain's history books.

When I finished packing, I said goodbye to Irys and muscled my way through the wind to the dining hall. The kitchen staff always had a supply of travel rations on hand for the magicians. I grabbed enough food to last us a week.

As I drew closer to the stables, I could see a few brave horse heads poking out of their stalls. Kiki's copper-and-white face was unmistakable even in the murky half-light.

She nickered in greeting and I opened my mind to her.

We go? she asked.

Yes. I'm sorry to take you out on such a horrible day, I said.

Not bad with Lavender Lady.

Lavender Lady was the name the horses had given me. They named the people around them just like we would name a pet. I had to smile, though, remembering Leif's comment about my bathing in the pungent herb.

Lavender smell like... Kiki didn't have the words to describe her emotions. A mental image of a bushy blue-gray lavender plant with its long purple cluster of flowers formed in Kiki's mind. Feelings of contentment and security accompanied the image.

The main corridor of the stable echoed as if empty despite the pile of feed bags nearby. The thick supporting beams of the building stood like soldiers between the stalls and the end of the row disappeared into the gloom.

Leif? I asked Kiki.

Sad Man in tack room, Kiki said.

Thanks. I ambled toward the back of the barn, inhaling the familiar aroma of leather and saddle soap. The dry smell of straw scratched my throat and clung to the earthy scent of manure.

Tracker, too.

Who?

But before Kiki could answer I spotted Captain Marrok in the tack room with Leif. The sharp tip of Marrok's sword was aimed at Leif's chest.

3

"STAY BACK, YELENA," Marrok ordered. "Answer me, Leif."

Leif's face had paled, but his jaw was set in a stubborn line. His gaze met mine, questioning.

"What do you want, Marrok?" I asked.

The bruises on Marrok's face had faded, but his right eye was still puffy and raw despite Healer Hayes's efforts to repair his broken cheekbone.

"I want to find Cahil," Marrok said.

"We *all* want to find him. Why are you threatening *my* brother?" I used a stern tone to remind Marrok that he now dealt with me. Having an infamous reputation had a few advantages.

Marrok looked at me. "He works with First Magician. She's in charge of the search. If she has any clue as to where to find Cahil, she'll send Leif." He gestured to the bridles in Leif's hands. "On a day like today, he's not going to the market or out for a pleasure ride. But he won't tell me where he's going."

It continued to amaze me just how fast news and gossip traveled through the Keep's guards.

"Did you ask him before or after you pulled your sword?"

The tip of Marrok's blade wavered. "Why does it matter?" he asked.

"Because most people are more willing to cooperate if they don't have a weapon pointed at their chest." Realizing that Marrok was a career soldier who did most of his talking with his sword, I switched tactics.

"Why didn't you plan to follow Leif?" Marrok's tracking abilities had impressed the horses so much that they had given him the name Tracker.

Marrok touched his cheek and winced. I could guess his thoughts. Marrok had followed Cahil with the utmost loyalty, but Cahil had beaten and tortured him to find out the truth about his common heritage, leaving Marrok for dead.

The soldier sheathed his sword in one quick motion as if he had made a decision. "I can't follow Leif. He would sense me with his magic and confuse my mind."

"I can't do that," Leif said.

"Truly?" Marrok rested his hand near his sword, considering.

"But I can," I said.

Marrok's attention snapped back to me.

"Marrok, you're hardly fit for travel. And I can't let you kill Cahil. The Sitian Council wants to talk to him first." *I* wanted to talk to him.

"I don't seek revenge," Marrok said.

"Then what do you want?"

"To help." Marrok gripped the hilt of his weapon.

"What?" Leif and I said at the same time.

"Sitia *needs* Cahil. Only the Council and the Masters know he doesn't have royal blood. Ixia is a real threat to Sitia's way of life. Sitia needs a figurehead to rally behind. Someone to lead them into battle."

"But he aided in Ferde's escape," I said. "And Ferde could be torturing and raping another girl as we speak!"

"Cahil was just confused and overwhelmed by learning the truth of his birth. I raised him. I know him better than anyone. He probably already regrets his rashness. Ferde is most likely dead. If I get a chance to talk to Cahil, I'm positive he would come back without a fight, and we can work this out with the Council."

Power brushed me.

"He's sincere about his intentions," Leif said.

But what about Cahil's intentions? I had seen him be ruthless and opportunistic in his quest to build an army, but never rash. However, I had only known him for two seasons. I considered using magic to see Marrok's memories of Cahil, but that would be a breach in the magician's Ethical Code unless he gave me his consent. So I asked for it.

"Go ahead," Marrok said, meeting my gaze.

Pain lingered in his blue-gray eyes. His short gray hair had turned completely white since Cahil's attack.

Granting me permission was enough to convince me of his sincerity, but despite his good intentions he still wanted to build an army and attack Ixia. And that ran counter to what I believed. Ixia and Sitia just needed to understand each other and work together. A war would help no one.

Do I leave Marrok here to influence the Council toward an attack, or take him with me? His skills as a tracker would be an added benefit.

"If I allow you to come with us, you must obey *all* my orders. Agreed?" I asked.

Marrok straightened as if he stood in a military formation. "Yes, sir."

"Are you strong enough to ride?"

"Yes, but I don't have a horse."

"That's all right. I'll find you a Sandseed horse. All you'll need to do is hold on." I grinned, thinking of Kiki's special gust-of-wind gait.

Leif laughed and his body relaxed with the release of the tension. "Good luck convincing the Stable Master to loan you his horse."

"What do you mean?" I asked.

"Garnet is the only other horse in the Keep's stables bred by the Sandseeds."

I wilted in defeat just thinking about the stubborn, cranky Stable Master. Now what? No other horse breed would be able to keep up with us.

Honey, Kiki said in my mind.

Honey?

Avibian honey. Chief Man love honey.

Which meant, if I offered to bring some Avibian honey back for the Stable Master, he might lend me his horse.

We left the Citadel through the south gate and headed down the valley road. Farm fields peppered with corn stubble and wagon ruts swept out from the right side of the road. The Avibian Plains dominated the left side.

The long grasses of the plains had turned from yellow and red to brown in the cold weather. The rains created extensive puddles, transforming the rolling landscape into a marshland and scenting the air with a damp smell of earthy decay.

Leif rode Rusalka, and Marrok had a death grip on Garnet's reins. His nervousness affected the tall horse, who jittered to the side at every noise.

Kiki slowed so I could talk to him. "Marrok, relax. I'm the one who promised to bring back a case of Avibian honey plus clean the Stable Master's tack for three weeks."

He barked out a laugh but kept his tight grip.

Time to switch tactics. I reached for the blanket of power hovering over the world and pulled a thread of magic, linking my mind with Garnet's. The horse missed Chief Man and didn't like this stranger on his back, but he settled when I showed him our destination.

Home, Garnet agreed. He wanted to go. *Pain*.

Marrok's rigid hold hurt Garnet's mouth, and I knew Marrok wouldn't relax even if I threatened to leave him behind. Sighing, I made light contact with Marrok's mind. His worry and fear focused more on Cahil than on himself. His apprehension came from not feeling in control of the powerful horse underneath him despite the fact that he held Garnet's reins. And also from not being in charge of the situation, having to take orders from *her*.

A dark undercurrent to his thoughts about me pulled a warning bell in my mind, and I would have liked to explore deeper. He had given me permission to see his memories of Cahil, but he hadn't given me carte blanche to probe. Instead, I sent him some calming thoughts. Even though he couldn't hear my words he should be able to react to the soothing tone.

After a while, Marrok no longer held himself so rigid, and

his body moved with Garnet's motion. When Garnet felt comfortable, Kiki turned east into the plains. Mud splashed from her hooves as she increased her pace. I gave Leif and Marrok the signal to let the horses have control.

Please find Moon Man. Fast, I said to Kiki.

With a slight hop, she broke into her gust-of-wind gait. Rusalka and Garnet followed. I felt carried by a river of air. The plains blurred under Kiki's hooves at a rate about twice a full-speed gallop.

Only Sandseed horses could achieve this gait, and only when they rode in the Avibian Plains. It had to be a magical skill, but I couldn't tell if Kiki pulled power. I would have to ask Moon Man about it when we found him.

The plains encompassed a massive section of eastern Sitia. Located to the southeast of the Citadel, it stretched all the way to the base of the Emerald Mountains in the east, and down to the Daviian Plateau to the south.

On a normal horse, it took about five to seven days to cross the plains. The Sandseeds were the only clan to live within the borders, and their Story Weavers had shielded their lands with a powerful protective magic. Any stranger who ventured into the plains without Sandseed permission became lost. The magic would confuse the stranger's mind and he would travel in circles until he either stumbled out of the plains or ran out of water and died.

Magicians with strong powers could travel without being affected by the magic, but the Story Weavers always knew when someone crossed into their land. As distant cousins of the Sandseeds, the Zaltana Clan members could also travel the plains unharmed. The other clans avoided the area altogether.

Since Marrok rode on a Sandseed horse the protection didn't attack him and we were able to ride all night. Kiki finally stopped for a rest at sunrise.

While Leif collected firewood, I rubbed the horses down and fed them. Marrok helped Leif, but I could see exhaustion etched in his pale face.

The rain and sleet had slowed during the night, but gray clouds sealed the sky. Our campsite had plenty of grass for the horses. It was on a high spot in the plains next to a rocky out-cropping with a few scrub trees growing nearby, and was a solid place for us to stand without sinking ankle-deep into the mud.

Our cloaks were soaked, so I tied my rope between two trees to hang the wet garments. Leif and Marrok found a few dry branches. Making a tent of the twigs, Leif stared at the wood and small flames sprang to life.

"Show-off," I said.

He smiled as he filled a pot with water for tea. "You're jealous."

"You're right. I am." I growled in frustration. Leif and I were both born to the same parents, yet we had different magical powers. Our father, Esau, had no overt magic, just a flair for finding and using the plants and trees of the jungle for food, medicines and his inventions. Perl, our mother, could only sense if a person had magical abilities.

So how did Leif get the magical abilities to light fires and sense a person's life force while I could affect their souls? With my magic, I could force Leif to light a fire, but couldn't do it on my own. I wondered if anyone in Sitian history had studied the relationship between magic and birth parents. Bain Blood-good, Second Magician, would probably know. He owned a copy of almost every book in Sitia.

Marrok fell asleep as soon as we finished eating our breakfast of bread and cheese. Leif and I remained by the fire.

"Did you put something in his tea?" I asked.

"Some fiddlewood bark to help him heal."

Wrinkles and scars lined Marrok's face. Through the yellowed bruises along his jaw, I spotted some white stubble. His swollen eye oozed blood and tears. Red streaks painted his right cheek. Healer Hayes hadn't allowed me to help with Marrok's recovery. He had only let me assist with minor injuries. Another who feared my powers.

I touched Marrok's forehead. His skin felt hot and dry. The fetid smell of rotten flesh emanated from him. I reached for the power source and felt the Sandseeds' protective magic watching me for signs of threat. Gathering magic, I projected a thread to him, revealing the muscles and bone underneath Marrok's skin. His injuries pulsed with a red light. His cheekbone had been shattered and some bone fragments had gotten into his eye, affecting his vision. Small dark growths of an infection dotted the ruined area.

I concentrated on the injury until his pain transferred to my own face. A sharp needle of pain stabbed my right eye as my vision dulled and tears welled. Curling into a ball, I pushed against the onslaught, channeling the magic from the power source through my body. The flow chugged, and I strained. All of a sudden the current of magic moved with ease as if someone had removed a beaver's dam, washing away the pain. Relief swept through me. I relaxed.

"Do you think that was a good idea?" Leif asked when I opened my eyes.

"The wound was infected."

"But you used all your energy."

"I…" I sat up, feeling tired but not exhausted. "I—"

"Had help," a voice snapped out of nowhere.

Leif jerked upright in surprise, but I recognized the deep masculine tone. Moon Man appeared next to the fire as if he had formed from the rising heat and ashes. His bald head gleamed in the sunlight.

In deference to the chill, Moon Man wore a long-sleeved tan tunic and dark brown pants that matched the color of his skin, but no shoes.

"No paint?" I asked Moon Man. The first time I had met him he had coalesced out of a beam of moonlight covered only with indigo dye. He had claimed to be my Story Weaver and proceeded to show me my life's story and unlocked my childhood memories. Six years of living with my mother, father and brother had been suppressed by a magician named Mogkan so I wouldn't long for my family after Mogkan had kidnapped me.

Moon Man smiled. "I did not have time to cover my skin. And it is a good thing I came when I did." His tone conveyed his displeasure. "Or you would have spent all your strength."

"Not all," I countered, sounding like a belligerent child.

"Have you become an all-powerful Soulfinder already?" He widened his eyes in mock amazement. "I will bow down before you, Oh Great One." He bent at the waist.

"All right, enough," I said, laughing. "I should have thought it through before healing Marrok. Happy now?"

He sighed dramatically. "I would be content if I thought you learned a lesson and would not do it again. However, I am well aware that you will continue to rush right into situations. It is weaved into your life's pattern. There is no hope for you."

"Is that why you sent for me? To tell me I'm hopeless?"

Moon Man sobered. "I wish. We had heard that the Soul-stealer had escaped from the Magician's Keep with Cahil's help. One of our Story Weavers scouting in the Daviian Plateau sensed a stranger traveling with one of the Vermin."

"Are Cahil and Ferde in the plateau?" Leif asked.

"We think so, but we want Yelena to identify the Soul-stealer."

"Why?" I asked. The Sandseeds didn't waste time on trials and incarceration. They executed criminals on capture.

However, the Daviian Vermin had been very hard to find, and they had powerful magicians. The Vermin were a group of Sandseed youths who had become discontented with the Sandseed lifestyle of keeping to themselves and limiting contact with the other clans. The Vermin wanted the Sandseed Story Weavers to use their great powers to guide all of Sitia and not just the inhabitants of the plains.

They had broken from the Sandseed Clan and settled in the Daviian Plateau, becoming the Daviian Clan. The plateau's dry and inhospitable soil made farming a nightmare, so the Daviians stole from the Sandseeds, and earned the nickname of Vermin. The Sandseeds also referred to the Vermin's magicians as Warpers, since they used their magic for selfish reasons.

"You need to identify the Soulstealer because he may have harvested more souls, and only you can release those souls before we kill him," Moon Man said with a flat and emotionless voice.

I grabbed his arm. "Have you found any bodies?"

"No. But I am concerned about what we will discover when we raid their camp."

The horror of the last two seasons threatened to overwhelm me. Eleven girls mutilated and raped by Ferde so he could steal their souls and gain more magical power. Valek and I had stopped him before he could collect the final soul. If he had succeeded, Sitia and Ixia would now be his to rule. Instead, I had released all those souls to the sky. To think that he might have started again was unbearable.

"You've found their camp?" Leif asked.

"Yes. We put our lives on hold," Moon Man said. "The warriors of the clan have done a complete sweep of the plateau. We found a large encampment on the southern edge near the border of the Illiais Jungle."

And close to my family. I must have gasped because Moon Man touched my shoulder and squeezed.

"Do not worry about your clan. Every Sandseed warrior is ready to attack if the Vermin show any signs of departing their camp. We will leave when the horses are rested."

I paced around the campfire, knowing I should get some sleep but unable to still my racing thoughts. Leif groomed the horses and Marrok slept. Moon Man reclined next to the fire, staring at the sky.

Marrok woke as the sky darkened. His eye had stopped weeping blood, and the swelling was gone. He probed his cheek with a finger. Amazement lit his face until he spotted Moon Man standing next to him. He jumped to his feet and pulled his sword, brandishing the weapon at the Story Weaver. Even armed, Marrok looked slight next to the muscular Sandseed, who towered six inches over him.

Moon Man laughed. "I see you are feeling better. Come. We have plans to make."

The four of us sat around the fire while Leif made dinner. Marrok settled next to me, and from the corner of my eye I could see that whenever Marrok touch his cheek, he stared at Moon Man with a fearful fascination. And his right hand never strayed far from the hilt of his sword.

"We will leave at dawn," Moon Man said.

"Why does everything have to start at dawn?" I asked. "The horses have good night vision."

"That will give the horses a full day to recover. I will be riding with you on Kiki. She is the strongest. And once we reach the plateau, there will be no rest stops until we join the others."

"And then what?" I asked.

"Then we will attack. You are to stay close to me and the other Story Weavers. The Soulstealer will be protected along with the Warpers. Once we break through the outer guards, then the hard part begins."

"Dealing with the Warpers," I said.

He nodded.

"Can't you move the Void again?" Leif asked.

The Void was a hole in the power blanket where no magic existed. The last time the Sandseeds had uncovered a Vermin hideout, it had been protected by a shield of magic that created an illusion. The camp appeared to be occupied by only a few warriors. When the Sandseeds had moved the Void over the Vermin, the illusion was broken. Unfortunately, the encampment held four times the number of soldiers, and we had been vastly outnumbered.

"They are aware of that trick and will be alerted to our presence if we try to move the power blanket," Moon Man said.

"Then how are you going to beat the Warpers?" I asked, worried. If the Vermin had access to magic it would be a difficult battle.

"All the Sandseed Story Weavers will link together and form a strong magical net that will seize them and prevent them from using their magic. We will hold them long enough for you to find the Soulstealer."

Breaking his silence, Marrok asked, "What about Cahil?"

"He helped the Soulstealer escape. He should be punished," Moon Man said.

"The Council wants to talk to him," I said.

"And then *they* will decide what to do with him," Leif added.

Moon Man shrugged. "He is not a Vermin. I will tell the others not to kill him, but in a large battle it might be hard."

"He's probably with the Daviian leaders," Marrok said.

"Marrok—you and Leif find Cahil and take him north of the fighting and I'll rendezvous with you after the battle."

"Yes, sir," Marrok said.

Leif nodded, but I could see a question in his eyes.

Problem? I asked in his mind.

What if Cahil convinces Marrok not to take him back to the Council? What if they join together and I'm outnumbered?

Good point. I'll ask Moon Man to—

Assign one of my warriors to stay with Leif, Moon Man said.

I jerked in surprise. I hadn't felt Moon Man draw power to link with us.

What else can you do? I asked.

I am not telling you. It would destroy my mysterious Story Weaver persona.

★ ★ ★

The next morning we saddled the horses and made our way south toward the plateau. Even with the weight of two riders, Kiki easily carried us. Stopping only once for a warm dinner and sleep, we reached the border in two days. At sunset on the second day, we stopped to rest the horses at the edge of the plains.

The flat expanse of the plateau stretched to the horizon. A few brown clumps of grass clung to the sunbaked surface. While the plains had a few trees, rolling hills, rocks and sandstone protrusions, the plateau had bristle bushes, coarse sand and a few stunted spine trees.

We had left the cold, cloudy weather behind. The afternoon sun had warmed the land enough for me to take off my cloak, but as the light slipped into the darkness, a cool breeze stirred to life.

Moon Man left to find his scout. Even at this distance from the Vermin camp, it was too risky to make a fire. I shivered as I ate my dinner of hard cheese and stale bread.

Moon Man returned with another Sandseed.

"This is Tauno," Moon Man said. "He will show us the way through the plateau."

I peered at the small man armed with a bow and arrows. Only an inch taller than me, he wore short pants despite the chilly air. His skin had been painted, but in the dim light I couldn't discern the colors.

"We will leave when the moon is a quarter up," Tauno said.

Traveling at night was a good idea, but I wondered what the warriors did during the day. "How do the Sandseeds stay hidden in the plateau?" I asked.

Tauno gestured to his skin. "We blend in. And hide our thoughts behind the Story Weavers' null shield."

I looked at Moon Man.

"A null shield blocks magic," Moon Man explained. "If you were to scan the plateau with your magic, you would not sense any living creature behind the null shield."

"Doesn't using magic to create the shield alert the Vermin?" I asked.

"Not when it is done properly. It was completed before the Story Weavers left the plains."

"What about the Story Weavers behind the shield? Can they use magic?" Leif asked.

"Magic can not penetrate the shield. It does not block our vision or hearing, just protects us from being discovered by magical means."

As we prepared to travel, I thought about what Moon Man had said, and realized that there were many things I still didn't know about magic. Too many. And the thought of learning more with Roze quelled my curiosity.

When the moon had traveled through a quarter of the black sky, Tauno said, "It is time to go."

The muscles along my spine tightened in apprehension as Moon Man settled behind me on Kiki's saddle. What if my lack of magical knowledge caused me to endanger our mission?

No sense worrying about it now. I pulled in a deep breath, steadied my nerves and glanced at my companions. Tauno sat with Marrok on Garnet's back. From the pained expression on Marrok's face, I knew he wasn't happy about sharing his mount with a Sandseed warrior. And to make it worse, Tauno insisted on being in front and holding Garnet's reins.

To stay behind the null shield, our path through the plateau had to be precise. Tauno led us. The soft crunch of the horses' hooves on hard sand was the only sound.

The moon crawled along the sky. At one point I wanted to yell out and urge Kiki into a gallop just to break the tension that pressed around us.

When the blackness in the sky eased in the east, Tauno stopped and dismounted. We ate a quick breakfast and fed the horses. As the day brightened, I saw how well Tauno blended in with the plateau. He had camouflaged himself with the plateau's colors of gray and tan.

"We walk from here," Tauno said. "We will leave the horses. Take only what you need."

The clear sky promised a warm day so I removed my cloak and stowed it in my backpack. Dry air laced with a fine grit blew, scratching at the back of my throat. I decided I needed my switch-blade. Strapping the sheath around my right thigh, I removed the weapon and triggered the blade. I treated the tip of the blade with some Curare. The muscle-paralyzing drug would come in handy if Cahil wouldn't cooperate. After I retracted the blade, I positioned the weapon in its holder through a hole in my skirt/pants pocket. I wrapped my long black hair into a bun and used my lock picks to keep the hair in place. Finally, I grabbed my bow.

Dressed for battle, though, didn't mean I was prepared for battle. I hoped I would be able to find Cahil and Ferde and take them without killing anyone. But the grim knowledge that I would kill to save myself formed a knot in my throat.

Tauno scanned our clothes and weapons. Leif's machete hung from his waist. He wore a green tunic and pants. Marrok had strapped his sword onto his belt. The dark brown scabbard matched his pants. I realized that we had all dressed in the colors of the earth, and, while we didn't blend in as well as Tauno, we wouldn't stand out either.

We tied our packs and supplies onto the horses' saddles, then left the horses to graze on what little grass they could find, and walked south. The plateau appeared deserted. The need to search the area with magic crept along my skin, and I tried to ignore the desire. Connecting with the life around me had become almost instinctive and I felt exposed and out of sorts by not knowing what breathed nearby.

Taking a circuitous path, Tauno eventually stopped. He pointed to a cluster of spine trees. "Just beyond that copse is the camp," he whispered.

I searched the plateau. Where was the Sandseed army? The earth undulated as if the sand had liquefied. The waves on the ground grew. I clamped a hand over my mouth to stifle a cry of surprise. Row upon row of Sandseed warriors stood. Camouflaged to match the sand, they had been lying on the ground in front of us and I hadn't noticed them.

Moon Man smiled his amusement at my dismay. "You have been relying on your magical senses and have forgotten about your physical senses."

Before I could respond, we were joined by four Sandseeds. Though they dressed the same as the warriors, these Sandseeds held themselves with authority. They issued orders and power radiated from them. Story Weavers.

A male Story Weaver handed Moon Man a scimitar. His sharp gaze pierced me as he studied my features. "This is the Soulfinder?" Doubt laced his words, but he spoke softly. "She is not what I expected."

"What did you expect?" I asked.

"A large dark-skinned woman. You look like you could not survive a sandstorm let alone find and release a soul."

"It's a good thing you're not my Story Weaver. You're easily distracted by the pattern of the cloth and can't see the quality of the threads."

"Well done," Moon Man said to me. "Reed, show us the camp."

The Story Weaver led us to the trees. Through the spiky needles on the branches, I saw the Daviian camp.

The air shimmered around the camp as if a bubble of heat had gotten trapped near the ground. A large cook fire burned in the central area. Many people scurried about either helping with breakfast or eating it. Tents fanned from the area, extending out until they reached the edge of the plateau.

Squinting in the sunlight, I looked beyond the encampment's border. Just the tops of the trees in the Illiais Jungle were visible. They reminded me of a time when I had stood on a platform built near the peak of the tallest tree in the jungle and had seen the flat expanse of the plateau for the first time. The sheer rock drop-off into the jungle had appeared to be an impossible climb. So why set up camp there? I wondered.

Moon Man leaned next to me. "The camp is an illusion."

"Do you have enough warriors to attack?" I asked, thinking the illusion hid many more Vermin.

"Every one."

"All—" The Sandseeds yelled a battle cry and dashed toward the camp.

Moon Man grabbed my arm, pulling me with him. "Stay with me."

With Leif and Marrok right behind us, we followed the Sandseeds. When the first warriors crossed into the illusion, they disappeared from sight for a moment. The sound of rushing water reached my ears as the chimera dissipated.

I blinked a few times to adjust my vision to what the Daviians had concealed. The central fire remained the same. But instead of many Vermin around the flames, there stood only one man. The rest of the camp was empty.

4

WHEN THE ILLUSION disappeared, so did the expanse of tents and all the Daviians. The lone man standing by the fire collapsed before the Sandseed warriors could reach him.

Evidence that a large army had camped here was imprinted on the ground. Although, by the time the Sandseed leaders restored order to the milling warriors, many of the Daviian tracks had been ruined.

And the only witness had taken poison.

"One of their Warpers," Moon Man said, nudging the corpse with his bare foot. "He held the illusion and killed himself once it broke."

"If you can clear the area, I might be able to tell you where they've gone," Marrok said.

The Sandseed warriors returned to the copse of spine trees. Moon Man and I stayed by the fire as Marrok and Leif circled the camp. Marrok looked for physical evidence while Leif used his magic to smell the intentions of the Daviians.

I projected my mental awareness as far as I could. If I sought a specific person, then I could reach them from far away, but with a general search my magic could only extend about ten miles. I reached no one in the plateau, and the bounty of life in the jungle was too overwhelming to sort out.

When they had finished their circuit, Marrok and Leif returned. Their glum expressions reflected bad news.

"They've been gone for days. The majority of the tracks head east and west," Marrok reported. "But I found some metal spikes with rope fibers in the ground near the edge of the plateau. A few Vermin could have climbed down into the jungle."

I touched Leif's arm. "The Zaltanas?"

"If the Vermin can even find our homestead among the trees, they're still well protected," he said.

"Even from one of the Warpers?" I asked.

Leif blanched.

"Are the ropes still there?" I asked Marrok.

"No. The others must have waited and either cut the rope or taken it along with them," Marrok said.

"Do you know how many went down?" Moon Man asked.

"No."

Leif said, "There were so many scents and emotions mixed together. The need for stealth and urgency predominated. They moved with a purpose and felt confident. The eastern group, though, had the most men and they…" Leif closed his eyes and sniffed the breeze. "I don't know. I need to follow their trail for a while."

Marrok led Leif to the eastern tracks. I asked Kiki and the other horses to come to us. While waiting for them, Moon Man and the other Story Weavers split the warriors into two groups, and sent two scouts, one to the west and the other to the east.

But what about those that went down the rope to the jungle? What about Cahil and Ferde? Were they even with the Daviians? And, if so, which way had they gone?

When the horses arrived, I grabbed my pack off Kiki's saddle. Opening it, I pulled my rope out and headed for the rim of the plateau. I found one of the metal spikes Marrok had mentioned and tied the end of the rope to it. On my belly, I inched closer to the edge until I could see down into the jungle.

The sides of the cliff appeared to be smooth, with no handholds in sight. I tossed the rope over, but knew it wouldn't reach the bottom far below. The end stopped a quarter of the way down. Even with a longer rope, the climb looked dangerous. Water sprayed out of fissures in the rock face about halfway down. The stones below glistened.

I considered the descent. A desperate person might attempt it, but Leif's assessment of the Vermin hadn't included desperation.

Moon Man waited for me by the horses.

"When the scouts return, we will set out," he said.

A notion that had been bothering me finally clicked. "Your people have swept the plateau and have been watching the camp. How could the Vermin slip away without you knowing?"

"A few of their Warpers had been Story Weavers. They must have learned to make a null shield."

"That would only hide their presence from a magical search. What about seeing them?"

Before Moon Man could answer, a shout rang out. Leif, Marrok and the scout ran toward us.

"Found a trench," Marrok panted.

"Heading east then north." The scout gestured.

"Ill intent," Leif said.

North toward the Avibian Plains. Toward the Sandseeds' un-protected lands because their warriors were here in the plateau. Every one.

Moon Man covered his face with his hands as if he needed to block out the distractions and think.

The second scout arrived from the west. Puffs of sand from his passage reached us before he did.

"Another trench?" Marrok asked.

"The trail ends. They doubled back." The scout reported.

Moon Man dropped his hands and began shouting orders, sending the warriors northeast at a run, ordering the Story Weavers to make contact with the people who stayed behind on the plains.

"Come on," he said, turning to join the others.

"No," I said.

He stopped and looked back. "What?"

"Too obvious. I don't think Cahil would go along with that."

"Then where did he go?" Moon Man demanded.

"The bulk of the Daviians went east, but I think a smaller group either went west or south."

"My people are in trouble," Moon Man said.

"And so are mine," I replied. "You go with your warriors. If I'm wrong, we'll catch up with you."

"And if you are right, then what?"

Then what, indeed. There were only three of us.

"I will go with you," Moon Man said. He called one of the

Story Weavers and a touch of magic pricked my skin as they linked their minds.

Not wanting to intrude on their mental conversation, I focused on finding Cahil. I examined the edge of the plateau. A branch from one of the tall jungle trees reached toward the cliff. I could use my grapple and rope and hook it—

No, Leif said in my mind. *Suicide.*

I frowned at him. *But I could swing—*

No.

Nutty could do it. Our cousin climbed trees as if valmur blood coursed through her veins.

You're not Nutty.

I reluctantly abandoned that course of action. Even if I could swing to the tree, I doubted anyone else would follow me. Then I would be alone. I berated myself for being worried about being on my own: living in Sitia had made me soft.

It has made you smarter, Leif said. Then he added, *not much smarter, but we can still hope for improvement.*

"Where to?" Tauno asked as he joined our group.

I looked at Moon Man.

He shrugged. "He is better at scouting than fighting. We will need him," he said with certainty.

I sighed at the implication. "West."

Perhaps we would find a better way down into the jungle or, failing that, we would follow the plateau's edge west toward the Cowan Clan's lands. Once in Cowan land, we would turn south into the forest then loop east into the Illiais Jungle. And hope we weren't too late.

We mounted the horses. Tauno and Marrok once again led us. The point where the Daviians had turned around was obvious even to me. The hard-packed sand had been scuffed where they stopped, and only flat unblemished sand continued westward.

Tauno halted the horses and waited for more instructions.

"A ruse. I can smell deceit and smugness," Leif said.

"Why so smug?" I asked. "Laying a false trail is a basic strategy."

"It could be Cahil," Marrok said. "He tends to think he is smarter than everyone. Perhaps he thought this would fool the Sandseeds into sending half their warriors in the wrong direction."

I projected my magical awareness over the smooth sand. A few mice skittered into the open, searching for food. A snake curled on a warm rock, basking in the afternoon sun. I encountered a strange dark mind.

I withdrew my awareness and scanned the plateau. Sure enough there was a small area a few feet away where the sand looked pliant, as if it had been dug up and packed back down. I slid off Kiki and walked over to the patch. The sand felt spongy beneath my boots.

"A Vermin must have buried something there," Marrok said.

Tauno snorted with disgust. "You have probably found one of their waste pits."

With Moon Man still on her back, Kiki came closer. *Smell damp,* she said.

Bad damp or good damp? I asked.

Just damp.

Taking my grapple out of my pack, I started to dig. The others watched me with various expressions of amusement, distaste and curiosity.

When I had dug down about a foot, my grapple struck something hard. "Help me clear the sand."

My reluctant audience joined me. But eventually we uncovered a flat piece of wood.

Marrok rapped his knuckles on it and proclaimed it the top
of a box. Working faster to remove the sand, we sought the
edges. The round lid was about two feet in diameter.

While Tauno and Moon Man discussed why the Vermin
would bury a circle box, I found the lip and pried the top up.
A gulp of air almost sucked the lid back down.

Everyone was stunned into silence. The lid covered a hole
in the ground. And, judging by the pull of air into its depths,
a very deep hole.

5

THE SUNLIGHT ILLUMINATED a few feet of the hole. Below the lip a couple rough steps had been cut into the sandstone.

"Can you sense anyone in there?" Leif asked.

Pulling a thread of power, I projected into the darkness. My awareness touched many of those dark minds, but no people.

"Bats," I said. "Lots of bats. You?"

"Just smug satisfaction."

"Could this be another false trail?" Marrok asked.

"Or a trap?" Tauno asked. He glanced around with quick furtive movements as if worried the sand would erupt with Vermin.

"One of us needs to go inside and report back," Moon Man said, looking at Tauno. "I knew we would need a scout."

Tauno jerked as if he had stepped on a hot coal. Sweat ran down his face. He swallowed. "I will need a light."

Leif retrieved his saddlebags and removed one of his cooking sticks. "This won't burn long," he said. He set the end on fire and handed the stick to Tauno.

With the flaming stick to lead the way, the Sandseed scout crawled into the opening headfirst. Tempted to link my mind with his to see what he found, I forced myself to focus instead on the ground beneath my feet, trying to discover a sign of life that would indicate the end of the cave.

The jungle's pulse throbbed in my soul, but I couldn't tell if it came from an opening below the ground or just from being so close to it on the plateau.

Waiting proved difficult. I imagined all types of hazards in Tauno's way and was convinced he had fallen and broken a leg or worse when he appeared at the hole's opening.

"The steps lead to a big cavern with many tunnels and ledges. I spotted a few footprints in the dirt, but had to come back before my light died," Tauno said. "I also heard water gurgling nearby."

Now we knew. Vermin had gone through the cave.

"Leif, what do you need to make a light last longer?" I asked him.

"You're not thinking about going in there, are you?" Marrok asked, sounding horrified.

"Of course. You want to find Cahil, don't you?"

"What makes you so certain he went that way?"

I looked at Leif. Together we said, "Smug satisfaction."

While Leif and Tauno returned to the Daviian camp for firewood, Moon Man and I discussed what to do with the horses. We would need Marrok's tracking skills and Tauno's keen sense of direction to find our way through the cavern. Leif and I needed to take Cahil back to the Council, so that left Moon Man.

"I am not staying behind," Moon Man said.

"Someone needs to feed and water the horses," I said.

Kiki snorted at me. I opened my mind to her.

Don't need, she said. *We wait then go.*

Go where?

Market. An image of the Illiais Market formed in my mind. As the main southern trading post for Sitia, the market was tucked between the western edge of the Illiais Jungle and Cowan Clan lands.

How do you know about the market? I asked.

Know land like know grass.

I smiled. Kiki's concise view of life kept surprising me with its many layers of emotion. If I could view the world the same way, I knew it would make my life easier.

Moon Man had been watching me. "Perhaps Kiki should mentor you."

"On what? How to become a Soulfinder?"

"No. You *are* a Soulfinder. She can help you *be* a Soulfinder."

"More cryptic Story Weaver advice?"

"No. Clear as air." Moon Man drew a deep breath and grinned at me. "Let us get the horses ready."

We removed their bridles and reins and packed the tack into their saddlebags. When Leif and Tauno returned, we sorted our supplies, distributing them among our packs and repacking the rest into the saddlebags. The horses would keep their saddles on, but we made sure nothing would hang down or impede their motion.

My pack weighed heavier than usual, but I had an uneasy intuition we might need a few of the items inside.

When we were ready, Leif lit the firewood torches dipped in the plant oil he had stored in Rusalka's saddlebags. He left most of his odd concoctions and medicines behind, boasting he could find anything we needed in the jungle.

"*If* we find a way out," Marrok muttered. "What will we do if we become lost in the caves?"

"That will not happen," Moon Man said. "I will mark our way with paint. If we can not find our way through, we will return to the plateau. The horses will wait until Yelena tells them to go."

Moon Man wrapped his muscular arm around Marrok's shoulders. Marrok tensed as if he expected a blow.

"Trust yourself, Tracker. You have never been lost," Moon Man said.

"I have never been inside a cave."

"Then it will be a new experience for both of us." Moon Man's eyes glinted with anticipation, but Marrok hunched his back.

I wasn't a stranger to small dark places. Before becoming the Commander's food taster, I had spent a year in the Commander's dungeon awaiting execution. While I wasn't anxious to return to a confined space, I would push past my nerves to recapture Ferde.

"There are a few caves in the jungle," Leif said. "Most of them are used as dens by the tree leopards and are avoided, but I've explored some." His gaze met mine and, by the sad smile, I knew he had searched those caves looking for me.

Tauno and Marrok each held a torch. With Tauno leading the way, I followed, crawling headfirst through the small opening. Leif was close behind, then Marrok and finally Moon Man.

The torchlight illuminated the three-foot-wide tunnel. Shovel marks scraped the rough walls, indicating the space had been dug. The steps turned into bumps that helped slow our progress as we slid down the sloped passageway. I coughed as the dust of our passing mixed with the steady flow of cool damp air.

When we reached the cavern, the tightness around my ribs eased. Tauno's light reflected off stones resembling teeth. A few of these hung from the ceiling and others rose from the ground as if we stood inside the mouth of a giant beast.

"Don't move," Marrok ordered as he examined the floor.

Shadows danced on the pockmarked walls as Marrok searched for signs. Deep wells of blackness indicated other tunnels, and small puddles of water peppered the floor. Dripping and running water filled the air with a pleasant hum that countered the unpleasant wet mineral smell mixed with a sharp animal musk.

Moon Man hunched his shoulders and short breaths punctuated his breathing.

"Is something wrong?" I asked him.

"The walls press on me. I feel squeezed. No doubt my imagination." He went to mark the tunnel to the surface with red paint.

"This way," Marrok said. Amplified by either the stone walls or by fear, his voice sounded louder than usual. He showed us a series of ledges descending down a chute.

The smell rising from the chute turned sharp and rank. I gagged. Tauno climbed down. The ledges turned out to be large chucks of rocks stacked crookedly on top of one another. In certain places he hung over the side and dropped down. We followed and with some mumbling and cursing we caught up to Tauno.

He waited on the last visible ledge. Beyond him, the chute ended in a pit of blackness. Tauno dropped his torch. It landed on a rock floor far below.

"Too far to jump," Tauno said.

I pulled the grapple from my pack and wedged the metal hooks into a crack, glad I had decided to bring it along. Tying the rope onto the hook, I tested the grapple's grip. Secure for now, but Moon Man braced himself and gripped the rope when Tauno swung over the edge and descended.

Moon Man's forehead dripped with sweat despite the cool air. His uneven breathing echoed off the walls. When Tauno reached near the bottom, Moon Man released the rope. The grapple held Tauno's weight. He jumped the last bit and picked up the torch, exploring the area before giving us the all-clear signal. One by one we joined him at the bottom of the chute. We left the grapple in place in case we needed to return.

"I have some good news and some bad," Tauno said.

"Just tell us," Marrok barked.

"There is a way out of this chamber, but I doubt Moon Man or Leif will fit." Tauno showed us a small opening. The torch's flame flickered in the breeze coming from the channel.

I looked at Leif. Even though Marrok was taller than him, Leif had wide shoulders. How had Cahil and Ferde fit through? Or had they traveled a different way? It was hard to judge size based on a memory. Perhaps they hadn't encountered any trouble.

"First explore the tunnel. See what's on the other side," I instructed.

Tauno disappeared into the hole with a quick grace. Leif crouched next to the opening, examining it.

"I have more plant oil," Leif said. "Perhaps we can grease our skin and slide through?" He stepped back when Tauno's light brightened the passageway.

"It gets wider about ten feet down and ends in another cavern," Tauno said. Black foul-smelling muck covered his feet. When questioned about the mud, he wiggled his toes. "The source of the stench. Bat guano. Lots of it."

Those ten feet took us the longest to traverse. And I despaired at the amount of time we used to squeeze two grown men through a narrow space. It might be impossible to catch up with Cahil and the others. And Moon Man's panic attack when he had become wedged for a moment had set everyone's mood on edge.

Standing ankle deep in bat droppings, we made for a miserable group. My dismay reflected in everyone's face. And it wasn't due to the putrid and acidic smell. Leif's shoulders were scratched raw and bloody, and the skin on Moon Man's arms looked shredded. Blood dripped from his hands.

Moon Man's breathing rasped. "Go back. We should…go back." He panted. "Bad idea. Bad idea. Bad idea."

I suppressed my worries about Cahil. Connecting with the power source, I gathered a fiber of magic and sought Moon Man's mind. A claustrophobic fear had pushed logic and reason aside. I probed deeper into his thoughts to find the strong unflappable Story Weaver, reminding him of the importance of our journey. A Sandseed Story Weaver would not let himself panic. Moon Man's breathing settled as calm reclaimed his emotions. I withdrew from his mind.

"I am sorry. I do not like this cave," Moon Man said.

"No one does," Leif muttered.

Keeping my thread of magic, I focused on Moon Man's arms. Large chunks of his skin had been gouged out. My upper limbs burned with pain as I concentrated on his injuries. When I could no longer endure the stinging fire, I used magic to push it away from me. I swayed with relief and would have fallen to the floor if Leif hadn't grabbed me.

Moon Man examined his arms. "I could not lend you my strength this time," he said. "Your magic held me immobile."

"What's this?" Leif asked.

He raised my hand into the light. Blood streaked my skin, but I couldn't find any damage. When I had helped Tula, one of Ferde's victims and Opal's sister, Irys had speculated that I had assumed her injuries then healed myself. I guessed it had been the same with Marrok's crushed cheek. But seeing the physical evidence turned Irys's theory into reality. I stared at the blood and felt light-headed.

"That's interesting," Leif said.

"Interesting in a good way or bad?" I asked.

"I don't know. No one has done that before."

I appealed to Moon Man.

"A couple Story Weavers have the power to heal, but not like that," he said. "Perhaps it is something only a Soulfinder can do."

"Perhaps? You don't know? Then why have you led me to believe you know everything about me?" I demanded.

He rubbed his newly healed arm. "I am your Story Weaver. I do know everything about you. However, I do not know everything about Soulfinders. Do you define yourself strictly by that title?"

"No." I avoided the title.

"Well then," he said, as if that settled the matter.

"Let's go," Marrok said through his shirt. He had covered his nose and mouth to block the smell. "The Daviians' trail through this muck is easy to follow."

With Marrok in the lead, we stepped with care. About halfway through the bats' cavern, I sensed an awakening. Sending a thin tendril of power, I linked with the dark minds above me as they floated toward a collective consciousness. Their need for food pushed at me, and, through them, I felt the exact location of each bat, of each wall, of each exit, of each rock, and each figure below. They launched.

"Duck!" I yelled as the cloud of flying creatures descended.

The drone of beating wings reached a crescendo as black bodies flew around us. The air swirled and filled with bats. They deftly avoided knocking into us or each other as they headed toward the exit, seeking the insects and berries of the jungle.

My mind traveled with them. The instinctual exodus of thousands of bats flying through the tight tunnels of the cave was as organized as a military attack. And like any well-planned event, it took time for all the bats to leave.

The muscles in my legs burned when I finally straightened. The flapping and fluttering sounds echoed from the tunnels then faded. I looked at my companions. No one appeared to be hurt, although a few of us were splattered with dung.

Marrok had dropped his torch, and his arms covered his head. He puffed with alarm.

"Captain Marrok," I said, hoping to calm him. "Give me your torch."

My order pierced his panic. He picked up the unlit stick. "Why?"

"Because the bats have shown me the way out." I cringed as my hand closed on the muck-covered handle. "Leif, can you relight this?"

Leif nodded. Flames grew. When the torch burned on its own, he asked, "How far to the jungle?"

"Not far." I led the group, setting a quick pace. No one complained. All were as eager as I to exit the cave.

The sound of rushing water and a glorious freshness to the air were the only signs we had reached our destination. The day had turned into night while we had traveled through the cave.

From the bats, I knew water flowed along the floor of the exit and dropped down about twenty feet to the jungle. The waterfall splashed onto a tumble of rocks.

The others followed me to the edge of the stream. We doused the torches and waited for our eyes to adjust to the weak moonlight. I scanned the jungle below with my magic, searching for signs of an ambush and for tree leopards. Necklace snakes were also a danger to us, but the only life I touched were small creatures scurrying through the underbrush.

"Prepare to get wet," I said before wading into the cold knee-deep water.

My boots filled immediately as I sloshed to the edge. There were plenty of rocks below to climb on, but they were either under the water or wet. I eased off my backpack and threw it down, aiming for a dry spot on the rocky bank.

"Be careful," I instructed.

I turned around and crouched, leaning into the force of the water. Keeping my face above the stream, I stuck my feet over the edge and felt for a foothold. By the time I reached the bottom, my clothes were soaked. At least the water had washed away the foul-smelling dung.

Once everyone climbed down, we stood dripping and shivering on the bank.

"Now what?" Leif asked.

"It's too dark to see trail signs," Marrok said. "Unless we make more torches."

I looked at our ragtag group. I had a dry change of clothes in my backpack, but Tauno and Moon Man had nothing with them. The bank was big enough for a fire. "We need to dry off and get some rest."

"You need to die," a loud voice said from the jungle.

6

ARROWS RAINED DOWN. Tauno cried out as one pierced his shoulder.

"Find cover," Marrok ordered. An arrow jutted from his thigh.

We scrambled for the underbrush. Moon Man dragged Tauno with him. Marrok fell. An arrow whizzed by my ear and thudded into a tree trunk. Another slammed into my backpack before I dived under a bush.

I scanned the treetops with my magic, but couldn't sense anyone.

"Null shield," Moon Man shouted. "No magic."

Marrok lay in the open, unmoving. Arrows continued to fly, but they missed him. He stared at the sky.

"Curare!" I yelled. "The arrows are laced with Curare."

The ambushers wanted to paralyze us, not kill us. At least not yet. The memory of being completely helpless from the drug washed over me. Alea Daviian had wanted revenge for her brother's death, so she had pricked me with Curare and carted me to the plateau to torture and kill me.

Leif yelped nearby. An arrow had nicked his cheek. "Theo-broma?" he asked before his face froze.

Of course! My father's Theobroma, which had saved me from Alea. I ripped open my pack, searching for the antidote to Curare. The rain of arrows slowed, and a rustling noise from above meant our attackers were climbing down. Probably to take better aim. I found the brown lumps of Theobroma and put one into my mouth, immediately chewing and swallowing it.

Moon Man cursed and I broke cover to run to him. An arrow hit my back. The force slammed me to the ground. Pain rippled through my body.

"Yelena!" Moon Man grabbed my outstretched arm and pulled me to him.

"Here." I panted as the Curare numbed the throb in my lower back. "Eat this."

He ate the Theobroma lump without a moment's hesitation. An arrow's shaft had pinned his tunic to a tree.

I lost feeling in my legs. "Are you hit?"

He ripped his shirt free and examined the skin along his right side. "No."

"Pretend to be," I whispered. "Wait for my signal."

Sudden understanding flashed in his deep brown eyes. He broke the shaft off the arrow that had missed him, and swiped blood from my back. Lying down, he held the shaft between two bloody fingers of his left hand which he placed on his stomach, making it look like the arrow had pierced his gut. His right hand gripped his scimitar.

Men called as they reached the jungle floor. Before they could discover me, I put my right hand into my pant's pocket, palming the handle of my switchblade. Numbness spread throughout my torso, but the Theobroma countered the Curare's effects to a point where limited movement remained. Even so, I lay still, pretending to be paralyzed.

"I found one," a man said.

"Over here's another."

"I found two," a rough voice right above me said.

"That's the rest of them. Make sure they're incapacitated before you drag them out. Dump them beside their companion in the clearing," said a fourth voice.

The rough-voiced man kicked me in the ribs. Pain ringed my chest and stomach. I clamped my teeth together to suppress a grunt. When he grabbed my ankles and hauled me through the bushes and over the uneven stones of the bank, I was a bit glad for the Curare in my body. It dulled the burning sting as the left side of my face and ear were rubbed raw by the ground.

The Curare also dulled my emotions. I knew I should be terrified, yet felt only mild concern. Curare's ability to paralyze my magic remained the most frightening aspect of the drug. Even though the Theobroma counteracted it, Theobroma had its own side effect. The antidote opened a person's mind to magical influence. While I could use magic, now I had no defense against another's magic.

Marrok still lay where he had fallen. The loud scrape of Moon Man's weapon on the ground reached me before he was dropped beside me.

"His fingers are frozen around the handle," one of the men said.

"A lot of good it will do him," another joked.

Listening to their voices, I counted five men. Two against

five. Not bad odds unless my legs remained numb. Then Moon Man would be on his own.

Once the men brought Leif and Tauno to the bank, the leader of the attackers dropped the null shield. It felt as if a curtain had been yanked back, revealing what lurked behind. All five men's thoughts were open to me now.

Their leader shouted orders. "Prepare the prisoners for the Kirakawa ritual," he said.

"We should not feed these men to it," Rough Voice said. "We should use their blood for ourselves. You should stay."

My gaze met Moon Man's. We needed to act soon. I suppressed the desire to make mental contact with the Story Weaver. Their leader had to be a strong Warper to have created such a subtle null shield. There was a chance he would "hear" us.

The crunch of gravel under boots neared. My stomach tightened.

"I have orders to bring the woman to Jal," the leader said from above me. "Jal has special plans for her."

Without warning, the arrow in my back was yanked out. I bit my tongue to keep from yelling. The leader knelt next to me. He held the arrow, examining the weapon. My blood stained the smooth metal tip. At least the tip wasn't barbed. Strange I should worry about that.

"Too bad," Rough Voice said. "Think of the power you could have if *you* performed Kirakawa on her. You might become stronger than Jal. *You* could lead our clan."

My lower back pulsed with pain. The Theobroma was working. Another minute and I should regain the use of my legs.

"She is powerful," the leader agreed. "But I do not know

the binding rite yet. Once I bring her to Jal, I hope to be rewarded and allowed to ascend to the next level."

He smoothed tendrils of hair from my face. I made a conscious effort not to flinch as his fingers caressed my cheek.

"Are the rumors true? Are you really a Soulfinder?" he whispered to me. He stroked my arm in a possessive way. "Perhaps I can siphon a cup of your blood before I deliver you to Jal." He reached for the knife hanging from his belt.

I moved. Pulling my switchblade from my pocket, I triggered the blade and rolled over, slicing his stomach open. But instead of falling back in surprise, he leaned forward and wrapped his hands around my neck.

A blur of motion beside me, and Moon Man leaped to his feet, swinging his scimitar in a deadly arc through Rough Voice.

I struggled with the leader. His weight trapped my arms. The pressure from his thumbs closed my windpipe. He attempted to connect with my mind, and would have succeeded with his magical attack if the Curare on my switchblade hadn't worked so fast to paralyze his power.

One problem remained. Trapped under the frozen Vermin, I couldn't breathe.

Moon Man, I called. *Help!*

One minute. The clang of weapons split the air.

I'll be dead in a minute. Just push him off. A brief flurry of steel hitting steel was followed by silence. The man on me fell to the side. I freed my arms and pried his hands from my neck.

Moon Man reengaged in the battle. He fought three men. One man's decapitated head rested next to me. Lovely.

My short blade wouldn't last against their long scimitars and my bow was in the jungle with my pack. Gathering power, I sent a light touch to one man's mind. Relieved he wasn't a Warper, I sent him puzzling images to distract him.

He dropped out of the fight with Moon Man and stared at my approach with a baffled expression. The man raised his sword a second too late. I stepped close to him and nicked his arm with my switchblade, hoping Curare still clung to my blade. Unable to use his sword, the man dropped his weapon and lunged. His intent to subdue me rang clear in his mind, but I deepened my mental connection and forced him to sleep.

With only two attackers left, Moon Man had both their heads off in short order. He strode over to the man sleeping at my feet and raised his scimitar.

"Stop," I said. "When he wakes, we can question him about Cahil's plans."

"The other?"

"Paralyzed."

Moon Man rolled the leader over. The blood from his stomach wound had pooled on the rocks. After touching the man's neck and face, Moon Man said, "He is gone."

The cut was deeper than I thought. A felt a tinge of guilt as I scowled at the body. The leader probably had more information than the other man.

"It is a good thing. He was a Warper. We would not have gotten anything from him except trouble."

I looked at the scattered carnage. The headless bodies cast macabre shadows in the pale moonlight. The side of my face and the wound in my back throbbed. The cool night air felt icy on my wet clothes. Tauno and Marrok both needed medical attention, and we couldn't go anywhere until the Curare wore off. And the thought of spending the night surrounded by corpses…

"I will take care of them," Moon Man said, reading my thoughts. "And I will build a fire. You take care of the wounded. Including you."

Pulling the arrows from Marrok's thigh and Tauno's shoulder, I gathered power but couldn't assume their injuries. The Curare in their bodies blocked my magic. An interesting discovery. It seemed when under the influence of the drug, a person couldn't do magic or be affected by it.

I mulled over the implications as I searched in my pack. Finding a few lumps of Theobroma, I gave it to Moon Man to melt over the fire and feed to our paralyzed companions. From my own experience with Curare, I knew the drug didn't affect the body's ability to swallow, breathe and hear. So I told them what I planned to do.

The last of my energy faded after healing my own wound. I curled into a ball on the ground and fell asleep.

When I woke, watery streaks of color painted the sky. Moon Man sat cross-legged next to a fire, cooking a divine-smelling hunk of meat. My stomach grumbled in anticipation.

I checked on the others. Marrok, Leif and Tauno still slept. Leif's cut had scabbed over, but I would need to heal Marrok's and Tauno's wounds. Moon Man had tied the Daviian prisoner's arms and legs with some jungle vines even though the Vermin remained unconscious.

Moon Man gestured for me to join him. "Eat first before you heal them." He handed me a sliver of meat speared on a stick. When I sniffed at the offering, he said, "Do not analyze it. It is hot and nourishing. That is all you need to know."

"Why do *you* get to decide what I need to know? Why can't you just give me the information I ask for?" My frustration extended beyond the mystery meat.

"That would be too easy."

"What's wrong with easy? I can understand if the most stressful aspect of my life was worrying about Bain's next history test, but lives are at stake. Ferde could be stealing another's soul and I might have the power to stop him."

"What do you want? For me to tell you to do this or do that and wa-lah!" Moon Man flourished his hand in the air. "Instant success!"

"Yes. That is exactly what I want. Please, tell me."

A thoughtful expression settled on his face. "When you were training to be the Commander's food taster, would you know what the poison My Love tasted like if Valek had just described it to you?"

"Yes." There was no mistaking the sour-apple taste.

"Would you trust your life on that knowledge? Or others?"

I opened my mouth to reply but paused. Now I couldn't remember the poisons I hadn't tasted or smelled. But I'll never forget the tartness of My Love, the rancid orange flavor of Butterfly's Dust, and the bitter thickness of White Fright.

"I'm talking about magic. Testing food for poisons is different."

"Is it?"

I pounded my fist on the ground. "Do Story Weavers sign a contract or make a blood oath to be difficult and stubborn and a pain in the ass?"

A serene smile spread on his face. "No. Each Story Weaver chooses how he will guide his charges. Think about it, Yelena. You do not respond well to orders. Now eat your meat before it gets cold."

Stifling my desire to fling the food into the fire and prove the insufferably smug Story Weaver right about my inability to take orders, I bit off a large chunk.

Spiced with pepper, the oily meat tasted like duck. Moon Man fed me two more pieces before he would let me return to the sleeping men and heal them. Tired, I snoozed by the fire.

When everyone had roused and gathered around the campfire to eat, we discussed our next move.

"Do you think they would set more ambushes in the jungle? Leave more Warpers in our path?" I asked Moon Man.

He considered my question. "It is possible. They left one at the camp who sacrificed himself. This one was supposed to come back. Our spies have determined the Daviian Vermin have about ten Warpers—eight now. Two are very powerful, and the rest have various lesser talents."

"The ambush leader had enough magic to create and hold a null shield."

Moon Man turned the meat roasting over the fire. "A valid and alarming point. Which means they might have been performing Kirakawa for some time."

"What's Kirakawa?" Leif asked.

"It is an ancient ritual. It has many steps and rites. When done correctly, it transfers the life energy of one person to another. All living beings have the ability to use magic, but most cannot connect to the power source. A person performing Kirakawa will either increase their magical power or gain the ability to connect with the power source, and therefore become a Warper.

"Their leader mentioned levels and a binding rite. They are probably using the Kirakawa to grant certain members magical abilities and increase certain Warpers' powers. Their leader would not want all the clan members to be equally powerful."

"How is the Kirakawa different than the Efe ritual Ferde used?" Leif rubbed the cut on his cheek.

"The Efe ritual binds a person's soul to the practitioner, increasing their power. While blood is needed, it isn't the medium holding the power in Efe. The soul carries the power. And the person performing the ritual must be a magician."

"It sounds like anyone can use this Kirakawa to gain power," Leif said.

"*If* they knew the proper steps. With the Kirakawa, the victim's soul is trapped in blood. It is gruesome, too. The victim's stomach is cut open and the heart is removed while the victim is still living. The Kirakawa is also more complex than the Efe ritual."

"Could any magician use Efe? Or just the Soulstealer?" I asked.

"A Soulfinder could, but no one else. Is that a straight enough answer for you, Yelena?"

I didn't dignify his comment with a reply. Instead, I asked about Mogkan, Alea's brother. In Ixia, he had captured over thirty people, turning them into mindless slaves so he could siphon their power and augment his own. Valek and I had eventually stopped him from gaining control of Ixia, which explained Alea's desire for revenge.

"Mogkan tortured them both physically and mentally until they could no longer bear to be aware of their surroundings. They retreated within themselves and just became a conduit for him to exploit. Their magic remained in their bodies."

The implications over the different ways for people to abuse power raced through my mind. "Going back to the Kirakawa. If the Daviian Vermin have been performing it for a while, then they could have more than eight Warpers."

Moon Man nodded. "Many more."

Paranoia sizzled up my spine. Convinced Warpers surrounded us, my desire to return my friends to the safety of the plateau pressed between my shoulder blades.

However, if the Daviians wanted to find more victims for their ritual, the Zaltana Clan teemed with people and magicians. With the Warpers using a null shield, the clan would have no warning. Fingers of desperate fear squeezed my stomach as the images of my mother and father being mutilated filled my mind.

7

"HOW DO YOU COUNTER the null shield?" I asked Moon Man, failing to keep the panic out of my voice. The jungle around us darkened and I imagined predators lurking behind every tree and bush. Only the small fire we huddled around gave off any light.

"Magic cannot pierce the shield, but find a way around the shield's edges and you can use your magic."

"What are the shield's dimensions?"

"Depends on the strength of the builder. The one we used in the plateau was as tall as a man astride a horse, and as wide as thirty men. But we had four Story Weavers combine their powers to build it. For one Warper, the shield would have to be smaller."

I looked up at the trees. The ambush had come from above. Would they use the same tactic for another ambush? No. If the first attempt hadn't worked, then a different strategy would be used. Being higher than your target had many advantages, and if I climbed into the tree canopy, I might be able to get past the edges of another null shield and discover where another ambush lurked.

Knowing my next move helped to dampen my terror for my family. I made contact with Kiki, projecting my awareness up toward the plateau.

Any trouble? I asked.

No. Bored, she replied. *Go?*

Yes. I'll meet you at the Illiais Market rendezvous location.

I then told my plan to the others.

"Not without me," Leif said. "I grew up in the jungle. I know every leaf and tree." His body stiffened with determination.

"That is why you need to stay with them. To show them the way to the homestead. To help them avoid predators."

Leif crossed his arms over his broad chest. But he knew I made sense, so he couldn't argue.

"I need to question our prisoner before I go. There could be a chance the other Vermin might not be targeting my family."

The man groaned and blinked at me when I woke him from his deep sleep. Moon Man had been right to tie his arms. There hadn't been enough Curare left on my blade to paralyze him.

The Vermin's tunic and pants had been ripped, and I glimpsed portions of blackish-red tattoos on his brown skin. Moon Man reached over and ripped the man's right sleeve off.

The Story Weaver pointed to the symbols on the man's arm. "He has made the proper blood sacrifice to prepare for the Kirakawa ritual. That ink in his skin has been mixed with blood." Moon Man's shoulders dropped as if he grieved. "The Sandseeds were wise to banish the old rituals."

"You were misguided and fooled into following the teachings of Guyan," the prisoner said. "Not wise but weak and

pitiful, giving up your power to become docile pathetic Story
Weavers instead of—"

Moon Man grabbed the man by the throat and lifted him
off the ground. *Docile* and *weak* were not words I would have
used to describe the Story Weaver.

"Where did you get the instructions?" Moon Man asked,
shaking him.

The man smiled. "I am not telling you."

"Instructions?" I asked.

"The details for the old rituals had been lost to time. At one
point in history, we knew how to perform many different
rituals to increase our power. Our clan passes information
down to our children through teaching stories. Once Guyan
became our leader, the evil ones who knew the required steps
were killed. The information should have died with them." He
dropped the Daviian to the ground.

I remembered Dax reading a bunch of ancient tomes when
we had tried to interpret Ferde's tattoos to discover why Ferde
had been raping and killing those girls.

"There were a few books in the Magician's Keep. A
Sandseed might have written the instructions and symbols
down before they died. Perhaps there is another copy that the
Vermin are using." I turned to the man. "I guess you're not
going to tell us what the Vermin's plans are either?"

He met my gaze and sneered. It was all I needed. My family
could be in danger. I sent a rope of power toward his mind
and rifled through his thoughts and memories, extracting the
information I needed. I suppressed the pang of guilt and my
recollections of when Roze Featherstone had tried to examine
my mind in a similar fashion. She had thought I was a spy from

Ixia, and the Ethical Code didn't apply to spies or criminals. I could argue the same in my defense. Did that make me the same as Roze? Perhaps. The thought made me uncomfortable.

Besides a few horrid memories of watching an initial level of the Kirakawa ritual, the man knew almost nothing. Ordered to stay behind and ambush anyone who came out of the caves, his small unit had scheduled a rendezvous with the larger jungle group at a later time. Where and when the meeting would be, he had no idea. And, more important, he didn't know what the others planned to do.

He had a few tidbits of information. I confirmed that both Cahil and Ferde had come this way and they traveled with a group of twelve Vermin.

"Fourteen is not enough to win in an attack on the Zaltanas," Leif said, pride in his voice.

I agreed. "But winning isn't everything."

My anxiety to leave increased a hundredfold. A group of Vermin had entered the jungle and my clan could be in trouble. Images of my father and mother being captured and staked to the ground replayed in my mind. The thought of my cousin Nutty climbing without care through the trees and falling into a trap, hurried my preparations.

I shouldered my pack, threading my bow through its holder. "What about our prisoner?" I asked Moon Man.

"I will take care of him."

"How?"

"You do not want to know."

"Yes, I do. I want you to tell me everything!"

Moon Man sighed. "The Vermin were once a part of the

Sandseed clan. They are our wayward kin, and they are infest-
ing the rest of Sitia. How we deal with them is in accordance
to our laws, and it is the proper way to take care of Vermin."

"And that would be?"

"You exterminate them."

A protest perched on my lips. What about those members who
might have been misguided? But my question remained
unvoiced. Now wasn't the best time to argue crime and punishment.

Instead, I gazed at the tall trees, looking for a way up into
the canopy, wishing I hadn't left my grapple and rope in the
cave. I found a long vine and used it to climb into the higher
branches. After a moment to reorient myself—the Zaltana
homestead was to the west—I swung over to the next tree.

I kept my magical senses tuned to the life around me,
seeking the Daviians and other predators as I traveled toward
home. The web of branches and crowded trees slowed my
progress. After a few hours, my sweat-soaked clothes were
ripped, and my skin burned and itched from innumerable cuts
and insect bites.

Resting on the branch of a hawthorn tree, I scanned the area
between me and Moon Man. There was no sign of any intelligent life so I linked my mind with Moon Man's and Leif's.

You will be safe to travel to this area, I said, picturing the small
clearing below. *Stay there until I contact you again.*

They agreed.

After I rested, I pushed my way through the jungle's canopy,
staying alert to any sign of the Daviians. The rhythm of
climbing from tree to tree combined with the steady pulse of
the jungle's undisturbed life force. When an out-of-tune

presence plucked at my senses, my energies focused on the distant ripple. Engrossed, I concentrated on discovering the source. A man in the tree canopy. Before I could determine if he was friend or foe, my left hand grasped a smooth and pliant branch. Surprised, I jerked my awareness back and my mind connected with a hunter lurking in the trees.

The leaves rustled with movement. The terrifying rasp of a stirring snake surrounded me. The limb under my feet softened. I scrambled for a solid branch, and touched nothing but the snake's dry coils. The necklace snake's coloring blended with the jungle's greenery so well that I couldn't determine where the rest of it lay.

I closed my eyes and projected into the snake's mind. It had looped part of its body between two branches, creating a flat net now closing around me. Pulling my switchblade from my pocket, I triggered the blade.

When the heavy coils of the snake dropped onto my shoulders, I knew I had mere seconds before the predator would wrap around my throat like a necklace and choke me to death. I sensed satisfaction from the snake as it moved to tighten its hold.

I stabbed my knife into the snake's thick body. Would the Curare on the blade affect the creature? Mild pain from the thrust registered in the snake's mind, but it considered the wound minor.

The snake contracted around me, trapping my legs and left arm. I realized the necklace snake held me aloft. If I cut through its coils, I would plummet to the ground.

Another loop brushed my face as the snake tried to

encircle my neck. I pushed it away with my free arm. A coil slid up my back.

Deciding the odds of surviving a fall were better than dying by strangulation, I stabbed my blade in the nearest coil with the intention of sawing through it. Before I applied more pressure, the creature stopped.

Perhaps Curare had paralyzed the snake. I pulled the blade out and the snake resumed its tightening. The Curare hadn't worked. But when I reinserted the knife, the creature paused. Odd. I must have found a vulnerable area. We were at an impasse.

Through my link with its mind, I sensed the snake's hunger warring with its desire to live. I tried to control the predator's will, but our minds were too incompatible. Even though I could feel its intentions, I couldn't direct its movements.

I wanted to avoid killing the snake, but I could see no other way. Once dead, I should be able to cut my way back into the trees.

"Hello. Is someone in there?" a man's voice asked.

My struggle with the snake had seized all my attention. Cursing myself for forgetting the man, I directed my mind into the tree canopy and encountered the well-protected thoughts of another magician. But Warper or Story Weaver, I couldn't tell.

"Has the snake got your tongue?" He laughed at his own joke. "I know you're there. I felt your power. If you don't belong in the jungle, I'll gladly let the snakes have you for dinner."

"Snakes?" I asked. His speech patterns sounded familiar. Not Daviian. Not Sandseed. I hoped Zaltana.

"Your necklace snake has sent a call for help. You might kill this one and untangle yourself, but by then its kin will be here to finish the job."

I scanned the jungle canopy and, sure enough, I felt five other snakes moving toward me.

"What if I do belong in the jungle?" I asked.

"Then I'll help you. But you'd better make a strong case. Strange things have been happening lately."

I thought fast. "I'm Yelena Liana Zaltana. Daughter of Esau and Perl and sister to Leif."

"Common knowledge. You have to do better."

Soul mate to Valek, the scourge of Sitia, I thought, but knew that wouldn't help my case. I searched my mind for a bit of information only the Zaltanas knew. The problem was, since I had been raised in Ixia, I knew only a few things about my lost clan.

"I could send you on a wild-valmur chase, but wouldn't it be easier if I gave you a piece of sap candy?" I held my breath, waiting.

Just when I was convinced I would have to cut my way out of the snake before its brothers arrived, a low drumbeat throbbed. More beats followed. The vibrations pulsed through the snake.

The snake relaxed. A gap appeared above my head and a green painted face smiled down at me.

He extended his hand, which was also camouflaged. "Grab on."

I clasped his wrist. He pulled me from the snake's net and onto a solid branch. Relief puddled in my knees and I had to sit down.

The man's clothes matched the jungle's colors and patterns. He placed a leather drum on the branch and played another song. The snake unraveled and disappeared into the jungle.

"That should hold them off for a while," he said.

From his clothes and dyed-olive hair color, I knew the man had to be a Zaltana. I thanked him for helping me.

His answering nod reminded me of someone. "Who are you?" I asked.

"Your cousin, Chestnut. I was out on patrol when you were here the last time so I didn't get a chance to meet you."

After living in Ixia for fourteen years, I had finally returned to a home I hadn't known existed. It had been such an emotional whirlwind, and I had met so many cousins, aunts and uncles it was unlikely I would have remembered him even if I had been introduced to him.

Seeing no sign of recognition on my face, he added, "I'm one of Nutty's brothers."

Nutty's stories about her siblings had been humorous and I remembered a game I used to play with her against her brothers before my kidnapping.

"How did you control the snake?" I asked.

"I'm a snake charmer," he said as if the title explained everything. But when I failed to respond, he said, "It's part of my magic. The necklace snakes are very hard to spot. Not only do they blend in so well, but also they mask their life energy. Even if you're able to sense the other jungle animals you probably wouldn't feel the snakes. Not until it was too late." He rubbed his hands together in appreciation. "They usually hunt alone, but if one gets into trouble it can call to the others with a low sound we can't hear. My magic allows me to locate the snakes and hear their calls. And my drum is my way to talk to them. It doesn't work on the other animals." He shrugged. "But I keep the snakes away from our homestead."

"You were out on patrol when you heard my snake?" Funny how I had become possessive of the creature that had tried to squash and eat me.

"Yes. Although, when I left this morning, I had hoped to find more than snakes." He gave me an odd look. "I guess I just did. Why are you here, Yelena?"

"I'm following a group of people who had been living in the plateau," I said. "They came through here. Has anyone seen them?" But what I really wanted to ask was had they attacked the clan? Were my mother and father okay?

"Seen? No. Strangers are in the jungle, but we can't find them and…" He paused, probably considering what information he should divulge. "Perhaps it would be best for you to talk to our clan elders. Are you alone?"

"No. My brother and some Sandseeds are traveling with me."

"In the trees?"

"On the ground." I told Chestnut about the attack and how I had been acting as a scout for our group.

Chestnut accompanied me to the Zaltana homestead. It contained a vast network of living, sleeping and cooking areas connected by bridges and suspended above the ground. Hidden by the thick jungle vegetation, the homestead was hard to find, but once inside the complex, I continued to be amazed the tree canopy could camouflage such a collection of rooms.

Built of wood, the floors of the buildings were anchored to wide branches. Ivy grew on the outside of all the walls to hide their shape. Almost all of the furniture was constructed of wood, and rope hammocks provided comfortable places to sleep. Handcrafts made of jungle items like seeds and sticks decorated the various rooms, including animal sculptures created by colored pebbles glued together.

The main throughway of the homestead tended to be common areas of each of the families within the clan. The living and sleeping quarters branched off from the public rooms.

Besides being extensive, the homestead was also well defended. The Zaltana magicians kept a vigilant watch for any strangers.

After our arrival, Chestnut hurried to find the clan elders and I scanned the path back to Moon Man. Once I was certain that the way was clear, I made contact with the Story Weaver's mind.

Come, I told him. *Come quickly.*

We are on the way, he replied.

I raced to my parents' suite. A few surprised glances and quizzical calls followed me as I dashed toward the Liana quarters, but I ignored them.

My mother, Perl, paced the living room. The air smelled like ginger and cinnamon, but her perfume distillery set up on the long table against the back wall appeared to be empty.

"Yelena!"

She flew into my arms. A few inches shorter than me, the slender woman clutched me as if to keep from falling.

"Mother. What's the matter?" I asked.

"Esau," she said, and cried.

I suppressed the urge to shake her as she sobbed in my arms. Instead, I waited for the flow of tears to subside before I pulled her away and looked into her light green eyes. "What about Father?"

"He's missing."

8

I RESISTED THE URGE to use magic to calm my
mother. Many horrible scenarios played in my mind before she
settled enough to tell me the details. My father had been
expected back from an expedition yesterday and had failed to
return.

"There was a clan meeting," Perl said between sobs. "A
couple of scouts had gotten lost, and he went to find them."

"Lost scouts?"

She gave me a watery smile. "Some of the newer ones will
lose their way. Esau always finds them. No one knows the
jungle as well as he does."

"Maybe one of the scouts was hurt," I said, hoping to calm
her and to stop myself from imagining Esau being a victim of
the Kirakawa ritual. "Why was he expected yesterday?"

"Another clan meeting. The jungle creatures have been
restless and disturbed and we can't pinpoint why. When the
two scouts failed to return, the clan decided everyone should
stay close to our homestead. Each night we gather in the

common room to make sure everyone is safe. Esau was only supposed to be gone a few hours." Tears tracked down her cheeks.

Her face reflected the hours of worry and fear. Her long hair had more gray than black. I couldn't leave her alone, yet I needed more information.

"I have to talk with the clan elders," I said. "You can come along only if you promise not to get too upset."

She agreed, but uncertainty filled her eyes. Her hand went to her throat. Maybe taking her with me was a bad idea. Perhaps Nutty could stay with her?

Perl stiffened as if with a sudden realization. "Wait," she said before bolting toward the lift.

As I watched her pull the ropes and ascend to the second floor of the apartment, my heart filled with dread. Esau had invented that lift, using vines from the jungle and a pulley system. I wouldn't be able to forgive myself if anything happened to him.

Panic made me fidget, and just as I was about to call out to Perl to hurry, the lift moved. My mother had splashed water on her face and had tied her hair back. She also wore my fire amulet around her neck. I smiled.

"For strength," she said, and she met my gaze. This time only stubborn resolve radiated from her. "Let's go."

I thought about the fire amulet as we made our way to the homestead's meeting room. Winning an acrobatic contest during an Ixian fire festival, I had achieved a moment of pure joy in the midst of hell. Reyad—one of my captors, the first man I'd killed—had tried to keep me from participating, and I was severely punished for my disobedience, but I knew I would do it again. I now realized the stubborn streak from both my parents had kept me fighting despite Mogkan and Reyad's efforts to control me.

Our clan name might be Zaltana, but our family name was Liana, which meant vine in the old Illiais language. Those vines grew everywhere in the jungle, pulling down trees in their search for the sun. When cut and dried, the vines turned rock hard.

Looking at the firm set of my mother's shoulders, I knew she had reached the point where she would no longer bend to her emotions, but do what was needed to help find her husband.

The common room was the largest area of the homestead. Big enough to hold the entire clan, the round area had a stone fire pit at its center. The black ashy remains of the fire drifted in the sunlight, streaming from the smoke hole in the room's wooden ceiling. Benches made of branches and hardened vines ringed the pit. The scent of many perfumes lingered in the air and I remembered the first time I stood here.

The entire clan had filled the room then. Curious to see the lost child returned from—according to their viewpoint— the dead, they peered at me with a mixture of hope, joy and suspicion. My hopes for an uneventful reunion dissolved when my brother declared to all that I reeked of blood.

Chestnut interrupted my reminiscence by introducing me to the clan elders. "Oran Cinchona Zaltana and Violet Rambutan Zaltana."

They bowed in the formal Sitian greeting. Their dark faces creased with worry. These two dealt with the day-to-day problems of the clan when our clan leader, Bavol, was at the

Citadel. Missing scouts plus unexpected guests equaled big problems.

"Your friends have reached the palm ladder," Violet said. "When they climb up, they will be escorted here." A slight smile flickered across her face.

Relieved they had arrived safely, I projected my awareness to encourage Leif to hurry. When Leif opened his mind to me, his annoyance was clear.

You should have taken me with you to search for the Vermin, he said. Leif's muscles ached from the day-long march through the jungle. The trails tended to get overgrown quite fast in the steamy warmth, and Leif had had to cut a path for the others with his machete.

We can fight about it later, I said. *Right now I need you here.*

I can't leave Tauno.

Leif and Marrok had reached the tree canopy, but through Leif's eyes I saw Tauno frozen about halfway up the rope ladder, clutching the rungs with a death grip.

I moved my awareness to Tauno. Although he couldn't hear my words in his mind, I sent him calming emotions, reminding him how he had climbed down from rocks in the blackness of the cave. I chased his memory of that descent and realized why he hadn't been frightened then.

Close your eyes, I instructed.

He did. Tauno relaxed his hold and climbed the ladder.

I pulled away and reconnected to Leif. *Hurry.*

By the time Leif and the others joined us, I felt my desire for action pushing out, threatening to explode. I updated the clan elders on what I knew, but the only information that Oran and Violet added was the direction that the lost scouts had been assigned. South and east, and Esau had gone east first to find them.

"It has to be the Daviians," I said. "We have to rescue them before they can do any part of the Kirakawa ritual."

"Let's go." Leif held his machete tightly, a fierce countenance on his square face.

"You do not know for sure if the Vermin have your father," Moon Man said. "Or where they are. Or how many Warpers there are. Or how well defended they may be." The words tumbled out in a rush. Moon Man's eyebrows pinched together, reflecting his obvious discomfort with being surrounded by walls.

"All right, Mr. Logic. How do you propose we get this information?" I asked.

"Marrok and Tauno will search for trail signs and report back."

"Where?" I asked.

"To the east."

"And stumble into the same ambush as my father? They'll be caught and killed," I countered. "It's too risky to send people out there. The jungle is the perfect setting for ambushes. Unless—" A sudden idea circled in my mind. I thought it over, looking for any holes. If the Daviians hid behind a null shield, no magic could pierce it, but mundane physical things like sound and light would.

"Unless," Leif prompted.

"Unless we could get a bird's-eye view," I said.

"They probably have men stationed in the trees," Marrok said. "Isn't that how the scouts would have been captured?"

"Actually I was being literal. I could link with one of the birds in the jungle and see out through its eyes."

"You will not see much during the daytime," Moon Man said. "The Vermin will be well camouflaged. In the night, they will need a small fire and the moon to perform even the first level of the Kirakawa ritual."

A cold wave of dread washed over me. "The moon rose last night."

"Too soon. They need time to properly prepare themselves."

"For someone who claims the old rituals have been lost, you certainly know a lot about them," Marrok said. Accusation laced his voice.

"The specifics of the ritual have been forgotten, but some knowledge about them has been included in our teaching stories," Moon Man replied, meeting Marrok's stare. "It keeps us from making the same mistakes over and over and over again."

A warning to Marrok or just cryptic Story Weaver advice, I couldn't tell. Marrok rubbed his healed cheek. He tended to stroke the spot whenever he was upset or frightened. The wounds from Cahil's beating went deeper than shattered bone fragments. Broken trust was harder to fix than bones. I wondered if Marrok would change his opinion about Moon Man if he knew the Sandseed had helped repair his injuries.

"Can a bird see at night?" Leif asked, bringing our attention back to the problem at hand.

"There'll be light from the fire," Marrok said.

"But what about guards in the trees or outside the firelight?" Tauno asked. "We need to know how many Vermin are there."

I considered the difficulties and a solution flew into my mind. "Bats."

Tauno hunched over. "Where?"

"I'll link with the bats to find the Vermin. Their fire should attract insects the bats like to eat," I said.

"Can we afford to wait until dark?" Leif asked. "What if Yelena can't locate them with the bats? Then we will have wasted time that could have been spent searching for Father."

"Yelena will find them," my mother said. She had kept her promise and controlled her emotions during our discussion. Her confidence in me was heart-warming, but I still worried. Three lives were at stake.

"What happens when we find the Vermin?" Marrok asked.

"An army of Zaltanas could capture them," Leif said.

"That might or might not work," Moon Man said. "It will depend on how many Warpers they have with them."

"No. It's too risky." Oran Zaltana broke the silence he had held during our discussion. "I won't send clan members until we know what and who we're dealing with."

I glanced at the floor beneath the ceiling's smoke hole. The patch of sunlight had shifted. It would be dusk in a couple hours. "Let's find the Vermin first and determine their strength. Everyone else should eat and rest. It might be a long night."

When we filed out of the common room, Chestnut touched my arm. He had stood apart from our group as we talked. His dark brown eyes showed concern. "Esau is my favorite uncle. Let me know if I can help."

"I will." I followed Leif and Perl back to her apartment. She made us sit down on the couch Esau had built from vines. The leaves in the cushions crackled under my weight. Perl went into the kitchen and fetched a tray of food and tea. Our mother hovered over us until we ate. I pushed the fruit and cold meat past my numb lips and chewed without tasting.

Eventually fatigue from climbing through the jungle caught up to me and I dozed on the couch. Nightmares about serpents coiling around my body plagued my sleep as they hissed in my ear.

"—wake up. It's getting dark," Leif whispered.

I blinked in the gray light. Perl, curled in a ball, dozed on one of the armchairs. Moon Man stood near the door to the apartment.

I woke my mother. "Can you fetch the clan elders? We'll need to make plans once I've found Esau."

She hurried out the door.

"Where do you want to go?" Leif asked.

"Upstairs, to my old room," I said and headed for the lift.

Leif and Moon Man joined me in the closet-size lift. Two thick ropes went through holes in the ceiling and floor. Moon man bent over to fit. His breath came in uneven huffs and he muttered about Sandseeds, the plains and suffocating.

Leif and I pulled on the ropes and the lift began to move. We ascended to the upper level and walked down the hallway. My room was on the right. Pulling back the cotton curtain, I let Leif and Moon Man precede me into the small clutter-filled space.

A few years after my kidnapping, Esau had started using the area for storage. Fourteen years of collecting jungle samples had resulted in rows and rows of shelves filled with glass containers of every size and shape. The only places free of the assortment were a small bed and a wooden bureau.

Wanting to focus all my energy on linking with the bats, I stretched across the bed. "Try to keep all distractions away from me and be ready to help."

Leif and Moon Man signaled their understanding. Both had enough magical energy I could draw from if needed. I tried to keep the horrible thoughts about Esau's plight in the back of my mind as I projected my awareness toward the mouth of the cave. The bats would soon be leaving their roost in search for food.

My mind met the dark consciousness of the bats. They didn't perceive the world by sight, but by sensing objects and movement around them. Unable to direct them to where I wanted to go, I flew with them, my mental perception floating from one bat to another, trying to make sense of my location in the jungle. The flutter of wings and hum of insects cut through the silent night air.

Even though the bats had spread over many miles, they remained connected to each other, and I soon had a detailed mental image of the jungle. It was a bird's-eye view without colors—just shapes, sizes and movement. In my bat mind, the trees and rocks were not visual, but in scapes of sound.

The straight walls of the Zaltana homestead felt odd to the bats. They avoided the clan's dwellings, but I jumped over to the minds flying east of the homestead.

Frustrated because I couldn't affect their movements, I had to wait and watch until one bat found a small campfire. I channeled my awareness on the bat as it dived and flew through the hot rising air, snatching the insects that danced above the light.

Instinctively avoiding the creatures below, the bat stayed high in the air. I used the bat's senses to determine the number of Vermin. Three around the fire, two crouched in the trees and four stood guard outside the camp. A pair of tents were close to the fire. Three unmoving forms lay flat on the ground next to them. Alarmed, I focused my attention on them until I felt their chests rise and fall.

When I had the exact location of the Vermin's camp in my mind, I withdrew from the bat's consciousness.

"There are nine of them," I said to Leif and Moon Man. "I don't know how many are Warpers."

"We should have enough Zaltana magicians to overpower them," Leif said. "If we could surprise them, it would give us the advantage. Can you form a null shield?" Leif asked Moon Man.

"No. That is not one of my skills."

I sat up. A wave of dizziness crashed into me and I hunched over until the feeling passed. Linking with the bats had used my energy. Moon Man put a steadying hand on my elbow and his strength coursed through me.

I thought about what Leif said. If we attacked with a large group, the Vermin would know we were coming, and they would either flee and hide again, or fight back. Either way they would have time to kill their prisoners. The element of surprise was key, but how to achieve that?

"Could Tauno shoot the guards with Curare-laced arrows and immobilize them?" Leif asked. "Or could we blow treated darts through reed pipes?"

"Too many trees," Moon Man said.

"It would be hard in the dark," I agreed. "We could get close and jab them."

"But what about the guards in the trees? Getting close without alerting them is a difficult if not impossible maneuver," Leif said.

If I'd had the ability to control the bats, I could use them as a distraction. We needed something else to cause a commotion. I followed the logic and found an answer.

Leif, sensing my mood, smiled. "What are you scheming, little sister?"

WE DIDN'T HAVE MUCH TIME to waste. Leif, Moon Man and I rushed down to my parents' living area. Perl had returned with Oran and Violet.

"Did you find them?" Perl asked.

"They're about three miles southeast of us."

"We'll need some magicians and soldiers," Leif told Oran.

"How many are there, and what do the Vermin plan to do?" Oran asked me.

"Nine. And it doesn't matter what they plan. The Vermin have Esau and your scouts. We need to rescue them!"

Oran hemmed and hawed. "We should consult Councilman Bavol—"

"Bavol's at the Citadel. It will take weeks to get a reply." I suppressed the desire to wrap my hands around Oran's thin neck.

"We can't leave our homestead unprotected," Violet said. "We'll call a meeting and request a few volunteers."

Sitians! I thought in exasperation, couldn't do anything

without consulting a committee. "Fine. Call your meeting. Do whatever." I shooed Oran and Violet out the door.

"Yelena—" my mother began.

"You can scold me later. We're leaving now."

Leif and Moon Man looked at me as if waiting for orders. "Get Tauno and Marrok. I'll catch up to you at the base of the ladder."

"Where are you going?" Leif asked.

"To get our distraction."

They hurried from the room and I was about to follow when my mother grabbed my arm.

"Just a minute," she said. "There are only five of you. What are you planning? Tell me now or I'm coming along."

That Liana stubbornness radiated from her and I knew her threats weren't idle. I sketched a brief outline of my plan.

"That won't work without some help," she said.

"But I'm going to—"

"Need more incentive. I have just the thing. Go. I'll meet you at the base of the ladder." Perl rushed off.

After a few minutes of frantic searching, I found what I needed. By the time I slid down the ladder, the others were ready. Shafts of bright moonlight pierced the darkness of the jungle floor, giving just enough light to make out the shadowy shapes of the tree trunks.

I told Tauno and Marrok how to approach the Vermin camp and guards and instructed them on where to position themselves nearby. "No noise. Keep your distance. Wait for my signal before attacking."

"Signal?" Marrok asked. His face hardened into grim determination, but uncertainty lurked behind his eyes. Even though Cahil had issued orders to his men, Marrok had really been the one in charge.

"Something loud and obnoxious," I said.

Marrok frowned. "This isn't the time to joke."

"I wasn't joking."

After a mere moment's hesitation, Marrok and Tauno set off. Moon Man stared after them. "What about us?"

There was a faint rustling from above as someone took hold of the rope ladder. A few heartbeats later, Chestnut joined us on the jungle floor. He wore a dark-colored tunic and pants, and his drum was tied to his belt. The green paint and dye had been washed from his hair.

"I'm glad I could help," Chestnut said. "But you need to know I've never done this before."

"Done what?" Leif asked. "Yelena, what's going on?"

"I'm hoping Chestnut will be able to call a few necklace snakes to join the Vermin's party."

"Ah. Your distraction," Moon Man said.

"How close do you need to be?" I asked Chestnut.

"Probably within a mile, but it'll all depend on how many snakes are around." He hesitated. "I'm used to chasing them away, not calling them. What if it doesn't work?"

As if on cue, the rope ladder swung with the weight of another person. Perl descended. She moved as graceful as liquid, and I would have bet Nutty hadn't been the only Zaltana child to drive her parents crazy by learning to climb before she could walk.

"Here." My mother handed me ten grape-size capsules and several straight pins. "Just in case your first plan fails."

"What if the second plan fails?" Leif asked.

"Then we'll storm the camp and hope for the best. Come

on." I put the capsules in my pocket, put the pins through my shirt so they didn't stick me, adjusted my pack so its weight rested between my shoulder blades, and pulled my bow.

"Be careful," Perl said.

I hugged her before setting off. While I had told Marrok and Tauno to take a wider more circuitous path to the Vermin, I wanted to lead the three men straight toward them. Once again I made a light mental connection to the bats flying above us. Guided by the bats' shape map of the jungle, I moved with ease through the tight trail even though the tree canopy blocked the dim moonlight in places.

The jungle's night sounds echoed in the damp air. A howler bat cried in a loud staccato. Valmurs climbed and swung through the trees. The rustle and shake of branches and bushes hinted at the unseen activity of other night creatures.

About a mile from the Vermin camp, I halted. Chestnut leaned his forehead on a nearby tree and power brushed my skin.

"There is only one snake nearby," he said. "He is waiting for the men in the trees to stumble into his trap. Necklace snakes are not active hunters. They prefer to lie in wait, using the element of surprise." Chestnut looked at me. "And I don't want to teach them how to hunt."

"That is a good point," Moon Man said.

"Now what?" Leif asked.

"I'm thinking," I said.

"Think faster," Leif urged.

One snake wasn't enough. Time for Perl's suggestion. I handed everyone two capsules and a pin. "Get as close to the guards as you can. Poke a small hole in the capsule and squirt the liquid near them. Don't get it on you," I instructed.

"Why not?" Leif asked.

"You'll have a necklace snake trying to mate with you."

"Gee, Yelena. I'm so *glad* you're home," Leif grumbled. "It's good to know Mother is doing something useful with her time."

"I thought your mother made perfumes," Moon Man said.

"It all depends on how you look at it," Chestnut said. "To a male necklace snake, that stuff *is* a perfume."

"There are six guards. Moon Man, Leif and I will each spray two," I said. Taking off my pack, I stashed it behind a tree. "Chestnut, you stay back here. Can you keep the snakes from grabbing us when they come?"

"I'll try. They have an excellent sense of smell so get clear once you spray that stuff."

"What about the guards in the trees?" Leif asked.

"Aim high and be quiet about it."

Leif muttered to himself as the three of us fanned out to approach the Vermin guards. Chestnut stayed behind to communicate with the predators while we moved into position. Once our distraction arrived and the guards became busy dodging amorous snakes, Leif and Moon Man would find Marrok and Tauno and await my signal. I would spy on the Vermin in the camp.

I crept through the trees, seeking a sign of the guards. I disconnected with the bats and reached out with my mental awareness, searching for the Vermin.

Beyond the outer guards, I knew the camp held six people, three Daviians and three Zaltanas, yet I couldn't detect them, which meant someone had erected a null shield. At least one of the Vermin was a Warper and he could be performing one of the Kirakawa rites while we snuck around in the dark. It was then I realized the sounds from the jungle had ceased.

My heart drummed a faster beat as my stomach cramped with fear. A presence hovered above me and I connected with a man crouched in the lower branches of a tree. His mind was alert for signs of intruders, but he hadn't detected me. Poking a hole in one capsule, I sprayed the liquid along the tree's trunk, and then slipped away.

Five minutes later, I found my second guard. She failed to notice my approach and I squirted some of Perl's snake perfume on the bushes near her. I hoped she would rub against them at some point.

As I retreated, I tripped over a buttress root and fell. I turned over on my back in time to see her aim an arrow at me.

"Freeze," she shouted. "Hands up."

So much for being quiet. I raised my hands and cursed myself for not reestablishing my link with the bats. Through their eyes, I never would have tripped.

She called to another guard.

"Stand up slowly," she ordered. "Leave your weapon."

My bow rested on the ground within reach.

She stepped closer and peered at me in the semidarkness. The guard gasped and said, "Soulfinder."

I rolled as her weapon twanged and snatched my bow. The arrow stuck the dirt. I jumped to my feet, swinging my staff in a wide arc. The end of my weapon caught her behind her ankles. I yanked her feet out from under her. She went down with a loud oath. The black shape of her partner grew bigger as he ran toward us. Great.

The air filled with a strange rasp as if a person had pulled a rope from a wooden holder very fast. The noise grew louder and came from all directions. The three of us stopped. All thoughts of fighting banished as we searched for the source of the sound.

A necklace snake slithered past my legs. It aimed for the female guard and wrapped around her with amazing speed. All my preconceptions about a slow-moving creature dissipated.

The other guard looked at his partner and bolted. Another snake slid after him. The vibrations of the necklace snakes and Chestnut's drum thrummed in my chest.

I projected into Chestnut's mind for an update. He kept the creatures from going after us, but he didn't know how long he could maintain control.

Faster is better, he said.

Right. I switched my awareness to Moon Man. He and Leif had marked the other four guards. They waited with Marrok and Tauno for my signal.

Running toward the campfire, I avoided snakes, terrified guards and broke through the null shield. I stumbled for a moment as an array of thoughts and emotions washed over me. The air was charged with magic and fear. My panic pressed on my back, but I forced myself to slow down.

When I reached the edge of the Vermin camp, my blood turned to ice. Three men pulled out the stomach of one of the prone forms on the ground. The Vermin turned their attention to me, their surprise evident in their openmouthed gapes. I had moved without realizing it and stood in the middle of their camp, screaming at them to stop.

10

WE BLINKED AT EACH OTHER for a stunned moment. Blood and gore dripped from the Vermin's hands. The three men then returned to their macabre task, ignoring me. Astonished, I moved toward them, raising my bow to strike when a blistering force slammed into me from behind as if I'd been struck with a red-hot iron pan.

I hit the ground hard. My bow flew from my grasp. My breath whooshed out. Searing pain clung to my back; I rolled over, convinced my clothes were on fire. Gasping for air, I thrashed on the ground until I spotted what had attacked me. I froze in horror. The Vermin's campfire had grown to three times its previous size. A man stood in the midst of the roaring bonfire.

The man stepped from the burning wood. Scorched black from head to toe, small flames clung to him like feathers. He advanced toward me. I broke my paralysis and scrambled away from him. He stopped. A trail of fire linked him with the campfire.

"Did I surprise you, my little bat?" the man asked. "Counted nine when there really were ten. Hot little trick."

He knew my consciousness had flown with the bats. But *who* was he?

I scanned the surrounding jungle, looking for my backup. Leif and my friends were at the edge of the clearing. Their arms and hands were raised as if they protected their faces from a searing wind. Sweat and soot stained their clothes and they averted their gazes from the man.

"No help from them, my little bat. They will burn if they come any closer."

I tried to project into the flaming man's mind, but his mental defenses proved impenetrable, a Warper of incredible strength. Running out of options, I glanced behind me and caught sight of my bow.

The blazing Warper pointed and a line of fire appeared between me and my weapon. I jumped to my feet. The heat singed the hair in my nose. The moisture evaporated from my mouth. I tasted ashes. A wall of hot air pushed against me and the Warper was before me. Yet his connection with the burning wood remained.

"Fire is your downfall, little bat. Can not call it. Can not control it."

My body roasted as if I had been staked to a spit over a giant campfire. I cast my awareness into the jungle, hoping to find help. Nothing but the panicked thoughts of my friends and one curious necklace snake nearby.

Just when I thought I would faint, he extended his hands and a bubble of cool air caressed my skin. The break from the heat was an intoxicating relief. I swayed.

"Take my hands. I will not burn you. Travel with me through the fire."

"Why?"

"Because you belong to me."

"Not good enough. Many others have made that claim."

"I need you to complete my mission."

"Which is…?"

The flames on his shoulders pulsed in amusement. He laughed. "Nice try. Take my offer or I will burn you and your friends into a pile of ash."

"No."

Flaring brightly, the flames jumped in size before he shrugged. "No matter."

The cold air disappeared and I gasped. The heat's intensity robbed my lungs of air.

"I need only wait until you go to sleep, little bat. Then I will take you."

My throat strained as my vision scrambled. Sleep was a nice way of describing the process of suffocation. It was a strange notion, but it gave me an idea.

With my last bit of energy, I grabbed a capsule from my pocket and crushed it in my hand. The sticky liquid coated my palm, dripping down my arm. My legs buckled as I collapsed to my knees. The last thing I remembered before the world melted was a brown and green coil reaching for me.

I woke, shivering. Chestnut's concerned face peered at me. He waved a large leaf, fanning me with cool clean air. Exhaustion lined his brown eyes.

"I guess that's one necklace snake who'll go away hungry," Chestnut said.

"What do you mean?" I asked, wincing at the sharp pain in my throat. When I tried to sit, I realized we were on a tree branch.

Chestnut helped me. "If you died, I told the snake he could eat you." He smiled.

"I'm sorry to disappoint him."

"No matter. Perhaps we'll have some extra Vermin to feed him." His grin faded.

I jerked as my memory returned. "The Fire Warper! My father! The others! What—"

Chestnut raised his hand. "When the snake grabbed you and pulled you into the trees, he distracted the Warper long enough for Leif to break through the wall of heat. With Moon Man's help, Leif was able to quench the link between the main fire and the Warper." Chestnut glanced away. "The Warper disappeared." He shuddered. "The remaining Vermin ran off, with Moon Man, Tauno and Marrok chasing after them."

"And Leif?"

"Below with your father."

Before I could ask, Chestnut said, "He's fine. Although I fear Stono will not live to see the dawn."

Sudden purpose energized me. "Help me get down."

My limbs trembled as I slid and crashed through the lower branches. I hit the ground hard, but didn't stop until I stood next to Leif. He had Stono's head in his lap. My gaze shied away from the gruesome mess that used to be Stono's stomach. My father and the other scout lay on the ground next to them, unmoving—still paralyzed by the Curare. I couldn't see my friends.

"Where are the others?" I asked.

"They haven't returned," Chestnut said. He sank to the ground next to Leif and took Stono's left hand in his own.

"At least he isn't feeling any pain," Leif whispered. Streaks of soot and sweat lined Leif's face. Burn holes peppered his clothes. He reeked of smoke and body odor.

I knelt beside Leif. I put two fingers on Stono's neck and felt a tentative heartbeat. Stono groaned and his eyelids fluttered.

"He's not paralyzed like the others so the Kirakawa ritual could work," I said.

"Can you save him?" Leif asked.

Stono's wounds were fatal. I hadn't healed anyone with such extensive damage before. Tula's windpipe had been crushed when she was killed. I was able to repair the damage, but couldn't "wake" her without her soul. Why not? According to Roze's fire scenario, I had the power to create a soulless army.

"Yelena." Leif's impatience cut through my musings. "Can you save him?"

Would I be able to save myself once I assumed his injuries? I drew in a shaky breath. Only one way to find out.

Closing my eyes, I pulled power and wrapped thick strands of magic around my stomach. I reached for Stono and forced myself to examine the bloody distended mass, seeing his wounds through my magic. His wounds pulsed with an urgent red glow as I focused on them.

Without warning, Stono's heart stopped its labor and his soul rose from his body. Instinct drove my actions as I breathed in his soul from the air and tucked it into a safe corner of my mind. I ignored his confused thoughts, concentrating on his injuries. My stomach exploded with the pain of a million sharp knives digging deep into my guts. Clutching my abdomen, I curled into a ball. Blood coated my hands, arms, and pooled on the ground. The air filled with the hot stench of body fluids.

I struggled to push the pain away, but it clung to me, eating its way through my spine and toward my heart. Leif's voice battered at my ears. He wanted something. Annoyed by his persistence, I transferred my attention to him for a moment. His energy flooded my body. We stopped the advance of pain, but we couldn't conquer it. It was only a matter of time before our strength failed and we would lose the battle.

Moon Man's resigned voice sounded in my mind. *I can not leave you alone. What made you believe you could counter the power of the Kirakawa ritual on your own?*

I didn't—

Know? Think? Does it matter now?

Moon Man's blue energy added to Leif's and together the three of us banished the pain.

I reached for Stono and laid my hand on his smooth stomach. *Go back,* I instructed his soul. A tingling sting pulsed down my arm. When I felt his gasp for breath, I pulled my hand back.

Too exhausted to move, I fell asleep where I lay.

At one point a hand shook me into semiconsciousness.

"Theobroma?" Leif asked, his voice a distant call.

My tired thoughts slogged through a fog. "Pack," I muttered.

"Where?"

Leif shook me again. I batted at his arms, but he wouldn't stop.

"Where?"

"Backpack. In jungle. Snake."

"I'll go," Chestnut said.

His retreating footsteps lulled me back to sleep.

I woke choking on a foul-tasting liquid. Coughing, I sat up and spit.

"You still need to drink the rest," my father said.

He offered me a cup.

"What is it?" I clasped the mug. The green-colored contents smelled like swamp water.

"Soursop tea. Restores the body's strength. Now drink."

I grimaced and put the cup to my lips, but couldn't produce the nerve to consume it.

Esau sighed. Blood and dirt matted his shoulder-length gray hair. He looked older than his fifty years. Weariness pulled at his broad shoulders. "Yelena, I would like to get home. And your mother must be having fits by now."

Good point. Cringing at the rancid flavor, I gulped the tea. My raw throat burned as I swallowed the liquid, but, after a few moments, I felt more awake and energetic.

The sun loomed high in the sky and the clearing was empty. "Where is everyone?" I asked.

Esau grunted. "I'll tell you on the way home." He stood.

Spotting my backpack nearby, I checked through the contents before shouldering the pack. My bow rested on the ground next to a wide scorch mark. I hefted the weapon, running my hands along the ebony wood. It appeared to be unharmed. A nice surprise since, during the skirmish, I had thought the Fire Warper had reduced my bow to a pile of ash.

A hot flush of fear raced over my skin when I thought of the Fire Warper. I had never encountered magic like his. I had been completely unprepared to fight him, and I couldn't think of anyone in Sitia who could match his power. But what about in Ixia? My thoughts turned to Valek. Would his immunity to magic save him from the Fire Warper's flames? Or would he be consumed?

"Come on, Yelena," Esau said.

I shook off my morbid thoughts and followed my father from the clearing. He set a quick pace, and, once I caught up to him, I asked him what had happened after I had fallen asleep.

He huffed in amusement. "Passed out, you mean?"

"I had just saved Stono's life. And yours, too."

Stopping, Esau grabbed me in a tight hug. "I know. You did good."

He released me just as fast as he had seized me and continued through the jungle. I hurried after.

"The others?" I asked.

"You were asleep for a full day. We thought it best for Leif and Chestnut to take Stono and Barken back to the homestead. The Sandseeds and the other Ixian fellow never came back."

I stopped. "They could be in trouble."

"Two Sandseed warriors and a swordsman against three Daviians? I doubt it."

"How about against three Vermin with Curare?"

"Ah, hell!" Esau spit. "I wish I had never discovered that

foul substance!" He pounded his fists on his thighs. "I had hoped the supply they stole from the Sandseeds would be almost gone by now."

"You extracted the drug from a vine in the jungle?"

"Yes."

"So how do they know how to make more?" I wondered out loud.

"And where are they making it?" Esau glanced around. "Maybe in the jungle. I'm going to cut down every single Curare vine and burn it," Esau vowed.

I put a hand on my father's arm. "Remember why you searched for it. There're plenty of good uses. Our immediate concern should be for Moon Man and the others. I'm going to try to contact him."

Gathering power, I projected my mind into the surrounding jungle. My awareness touched a variety of life. Valmurs swung through the tree canopy, birds perched on branches, and other small creatures scurried through the underbrush. But I couldn't locate Moon Man's cool thoughts.

Did the Vermin have him hidden behind a null shield? Was he dead? I searched for Tauno and Marrok, also to no avail.

My father said, "Let's go home and figure out a way to find them. *All* of them, including the Curare-making Vermin."

He reminded me of the other Vermin guards we had sprayed with the snake perfume. "We can question the Daviian guards. Are they at our homestead?"

Esau tugged on his stained tunic as if deciding how to tell me something unpleasant. "When you were picked up by that snake, the creature wasn't happy to discover you weren't a female snake. So in order for Chestnut to keep you from being

devoured, he had to concentrate all his efforts on saving you."
He paused.

"And that means…?"

"He lost control of the other snakes."

"The guards are dead?"

"An unfortunate development, but there is an upside," Esau
said.

"Which is?"

"Now there are four very full necklace snakes who won't
be bothering the Zaltanas for a long while."

I washed as much dried blood and sticky gore from my body
as I could in the small stream flowing underneath my clan's
homestead. My mother would worry and fuss over my disheveled appearance despite the fact I would be standing before her
safe and sound.

Climbing the ladder into the tree canopy, I mulled over
recent events. There might be a group of Daviian Vermin
working in the jungle, gathering vines and distilling Curare. I
had no idea where Ferde and Cahil had gone or where my
friends had disappeared to. And there was a Fire Warper on
the loose who could possibly jump out of any campfire in Sitia.
My life in Ixia as the Commander's food taster sounded like a
vacation in comparison.

Why had I wanted to leave Ixia? An order for my execution for being a magician had been one compelling reason to
escape to Sitia. That and wanting to meet my family, whom I
had no memories of until Moon Man unlocked them. Well,
I'd met my parents and the execution order had been revoked.
The thought of returning to Valek and Ixia tempted me.

I reached the top of the ladder and arrived into a small receiving room made of branches tied together. Esau hadn't waited. The Zaltana guard stationed there informed me my father would meet me in my parents' living quarters.

Walking toward their apartment, I marveled at the ingenuity and craftsmanship of the vast complex of living areas built above the jungle floor. The Zaltanas were resourceful and determined and stubborn. All traits I had been accused of possessing.

I wondered if those qualities would be enough to counter the Fire Warper. Did I have the experience or magical knowledge to find Moon Man, recapture Ferde and stop the Vermin from killing more people?

The daunting and overwhelming to-do list would not deter me from making the attempt or die trying. But how many would be hurt or killed in the process because of me?

II

I NEVER REACHED my parents' suite. My cousin Nutty intercepted me en route, relaying a message to go to the common room. She scrunched up her face and tsked over my ripped and stained clothes.

"I have a change in my pack," I told her.

"Let's see then." She held out her long thin arms, waiting.

Knowing it was useless to argue with her, I opened my bag and showed her the other set of skirt/pants and cotton top she had sewn for me. I thought a lifetime's worth of events had happened since then, but in reality it had only been two seasons.

Nutty examined the clothes with a dismayed purse to her full lips. "You'll need some new ones. I'll make them for you." With a slight nod of farewell, she hopped up into the tree branches with the grace and speed of a valmur, disdaining the practical rope bridge.

"Oh, snake spit," she called from above. "I'm supposed to fetch Uncle Esau and Aunt Perl." She changed directions and disappeared through the trees.

I reached the common room. Oran, Violet, Chestnut and the two scouts stood together. My strong relief over the absence of a fire in the central pit alarmed me. If I was afraid of a simple hearth fire, what would I do when faced with the Fire Warper again? I avoided thinking about that scenario and focused my attention on the matter at hand.

When he saw me, Stono sat down. His face drained of color, and I worried he would faint. He muttered a thank-you to the floor, evading my gaze. Oran and Violet continued to question Chestnut on the necklace snakes.

Chestnut stammered and fidgeted. "I wanted to help."

"You didn't have our permission," Oran said. "And now how many are dead?"

"Six," Chestnut said in a quiet voice.

"Good for you, Chessie," Stono said. "I wish you had killed them all. Pulled out their guts and strangled them with it!" Stono's eyes lit with murderous intensity.

The elders rounded on Stono. Shock mirrored on their faces.

Violet recovered first. "Stono, you've had a difficult time. Why don't you go and get some rest," she ordered.

He stood on trembling legs and shuffled a few steps, but paused next to me.

"I'll kill the snake that tried to eat you if you want," he whispered in my ear. "Let me know what I can kill for you."

I turned to protest, but he moved away.

"What did he say?" Oran asked.

What, indeed? An offer of revenge on a snake or something more disturbing. "He said he would like to help me."

"Not without *our* permission." Oran puffed up his chest with importance.

"You can't just use our clan members as your personal army. Taking Chestnut into an unknown, dangerous situation that could have killed him was wrong."

I had had enough of Oran Cinchona Zaltana. Stepping close to him, I said, "Could have, but didn't. If we had waited for *your* permission, you *would have* lost three clan members. And I wouldn't debate too long on how you're going to search for a possible nest of Vermin living in *your* jungle. If you wait too long, they're liable to multiply."

"What are you talking about?" Violet asked.

It was then that Esau and Perl joined us. Having heard my warning, Mother touched her throat, and my father's grim expression deepened.

"Father, could you inform the elders about the potential threat? I have other business to attend to," I said.

"Where are you going?" Perl asked.

"To find my friends."

I found Leif in our parents' quarters. He was sound asleep on the couch and it occurred to me that I didn't know if he had his own rooms within the Zaltana homestead. Esau had knocked down the wall to Leif's room to expand his work area. Unwilling to bother my brother, I tiptoed past him and went up to my room. Soon the sun would set and I wanted to fly with the bats.

Lying down on my narrow bed, I felt sleep pull at me. I resisted, thinking of Moon Man. He had helped me and Leif in healing Stono. Perhaps the effort had exhausted him and rendered him unable to respond to my search.

As the light dimmed, I drew magic from the power source

and projected my mind into the jungle. Finding the collective consciousness of the bats, I joined in their nightly hunt for food.

I floated from one bat to another, sensing the space below and around. On the lookout for any fires or signs of people, I coasted through the air, feeling the sun leave the sky. I wondered how the bats could know the size and shapes of their surroundings without seeing them. Was it a skill I could learn? My magic let me feel living beings, but I couldn't sense anything from the lifeless objects in my path.

The bats invaded every section of the Illiais Jungle. Nestled below the Daviian Plateau, the jungle wasn't large. Two days of hard walking would see a person from one end to the other. The Illiais Market marked the western border of the jungle. A few bats swooped close to the market campfires, but they avoided the gritty air and noisy crowds of people.

I pulled my awareness back. Having found no physical signs of Moon Man or the others in the jungle, I decided Leif and I would travel to the market tomorrow. The market was the rendezvous location we had set back on the plateau. If Moon Man followed the Vermin from the jungle, he would eventually look for us there. I hoped.

When I awoke the next morning, a group of people were in my parents' living area, all engaged in animated conversation.

"It's your turn. I delivered a wagonload of pummelo fruit last time," Nutty said to Chestnut. "See?" She held up her right hand. "I still have the blisters."

"I'm not stupid. They're from staying up all night finishing the clothes you owe Fern," Chestnut retorted. "It's your turn to go to the market."

"You can't go collecting every single Curare vine, Esau. It will take you seasons," Perl said. "And what about the Vermin? If they caught you again—" Perl's hand flew to her throat as if she tried to block the emotion welling from her heart.

"I'm not worried about that," Esau said. "I'm worried about what they can do with the Curare!"

"Curare can be countered with Theobroma," Leif said to Esau. "We just need to make sure everyone has enough with them."

"Is not my turn," Nutty said.

"Is too," Chestnut countered.

"Yelena!" Nutty cried, spotting me. "I've made another pair of skirt/pants for you." She held a light blue-and-yellow print.

"Thanks," I said. "You don't have to go to the market, Nutty. I'll deliver the clothes for you. And Leif, Theobroma is good at regaining movement, but it leaves you helpless against a magical attack. Father, can you find a way to get the Theobroma to work against Curare without the side effects? That would be more helpful than tearing down every vine. Besides, I couldn't find any signs the Vermin are collecting vines right now, but I think sending out well-armed scouts to search the jungle from time to time would be a good idea."

"Yelena's here," Leif said. "Problems solved," he teased.

"I'll have an easier time with the Theobroma than convincing Oran and Violet to send out reconnaissance teams," Esau said. "They want to huddle in our homestead and hide!"

"I'll handle Oran and Violet," Perl said.

Her face had set in a determined frown, which she then turned on me. "You're leaving us already?"

"We need to rendezvous with our horses and our other team members," I said.

"Are they at the market?" Leif asked with a hopeful note in his voice.

"Too many people for me to determine. In any case we need to look for signs of Ferde and Cahil." They could be anywhere by now and doing unspeakable things. I shuddered as the image of Stono's ruined stomach rose in my mind.

"Not without breakfast." Perl hurried toward the kitchen.

"I'll go get the dresses." Nutty bounded away.

"I'd better get my pack ready." Leif smiled. "Never a dull day with you, little sister."

"What do you need?" Esau asked me.

"I'm running out of Theobroma and Curare."

He went into the lift to ascend to the second floor. Chestnut looked around at the suddenly quiet room. He fidgeted, avoiding my gaze and I realized he wanted to talk about something other than whose turn it was to go to the market.

"Now's the time," I said. "Once everyone comes back…"

"I can't…" He moved his hands as if he wanted to pull his thoughts from the air. "I'm having trouble getting past…" Wrapping his arms around his body, Chestnut rocked with frustration. "How can you be so calm? Standing there, making plans, barking out orders. Six people have died. Stono came back from the dead and now he's different—"

"Different? How?"

"It's probably nothing. He's had a shock, but he's harsher

somehow." Chestnut shook his head. "That's not the point. Six people killed by necklace snakes. That's the point."

I understood his problem. "You've never lost anyone to a snake before?"

"No one. I know it's not a terrible death. At least they're dead before they get swallowed. I've always been kind of curious…" He cringed with guilt.

"Curious to see a snake devour its prey and you feel responsible for not stopping the snakes?"

"Yes." The word hissed out.

"Think of what would have happened if the snakes had released the Vermin."

"You and Stono would have died."

"I'm not happy about the death of six people either, but, considering the alternative, I can rationalize it in my mind." A shiver raced over my skin. As long as I didn't think about it too much. "You asked how I can be so calm. I don't have time not to be. I would like to grieve and worry and carry on, but that doesn't get results."

"And results are important. Right, Yelena?" Leif asked as he entered the room. "One of the foremost things the First Magician taught me when I arrived at the Keep was to leave all sentimentality behind. Roze believes she was given the gift of magic to use for a purpose and she can't let guilt and remorse keep her from achieving that purpose." Leif rubbed his chin as his face settled into a thoughtful expression. "You're a lot like her."

"I am not," I said.

"It was a compliment. You're both intelligent. You're doers. Natural leaders."

I disagreed. I didn't conduct myself like Roze. She was a tyrant who thought she knew everything and didn't stop to consider other options or other people's views. I wasn't like that. Was I?

"Although *she* has a bad temper," Leif said. "She was wrong about Ferde and Cahil's direction. She's not going to be happy about it."

"That I would agree with," I said.

"Agree with what?" Esau asked. His arms brimmed with containers.

Nutty arrived with her stack of clothes, then Perl returned with a tray full of fruit and tea. By the time we ate, the morning hours were gone.

"We better go. It'll be a hard push to get to the market before dark," Leif said.

"Yelena, you have to come back and have a proper visit," my mother instructed. "Perhaps when your life settles down." She thought for a moment, and added, "Perhaps you can make some time to visit. I don't see things settling down for you for a long while."

"Do you know this from your magic?" I asked.

"No, dear. From your history." A smile quirked her lips before Perl's stern mother expression returned long enough for her to lecture me on being careful.

With our backpacks loaded, Leif and I climbed down the ladder to the jungle floor. He set a quick pace and I hurried after him. When we stopped for a short rest, I tossed my heavy pack down and rubbed my sore back. Now I could sympathize with a pack horse…. Kiki!

"Leif, does this trail stay wide until the market?"

"As long as no trees have fallen over recently. The Zaltanas keep this pretty clear. Why?"

"The horses."

He smacked his forehead with a hand.

I reached out with my mind and searched for Kiki's thoughts.

She hid with Garnet and Rusalka in the forest west of the market.

Late, she said in my mind. *Dirty. Hungry.*

Come meet us on the jungle trail? We'll get to the market faster. Groomed faster.

She agreed. Leif and I continued to hike for a while in silence. The insects' droning grew louder as the sunlight began to wane.

"I keep forgetting you can communicate with horses," Leif said. "I think you might be the first one in Sitian history."

"Are you sure?"

"All the Keep's students had to learn about past magicians and their powers, but Master Bloodgood would know for sure."

Bain Bloodgood, Second Magician, was a walking, talking history book. My list of questions grew longer each day. I had so much to learn about magic and history. The sheer amount overwhelmed me at times, and reminded me how unprepared I was.

And how did I end up with these Soulfinder powers? Both my parents hadn't enough power to be invited to the Keep so I hadn't inherited them. Sheer dumb luck?

Leif interrupted my thoughts. "Do you know anyone else who can talk to horses?"

"The Stable Master has said he knows the horses' moods and

intentions, but he doesn't hear their words in his mind per se." And he had looked at me as if I had grown wings when I mentioned it to him.

"How about in Ixia?"

I considered. When the Commander had taken control of Ixia over sixteen years ago, he had ordered Valek, his chief of security, to assassinate all the magicians. Then, whenever an Ixian developed the ability to use magic—usually after puberty—Valek would assassinate the person if they hadn't already escaped to Sitia. No magicians in Ixia, but my thoughts did linger on Porter, the Commander's kennel master. He had an uncanny knack with the dogs, and he hadn't needed leashes or a whistle to get them to obey him.

"Perhaps one other," I said. "Though he would never admit to it—that would be a death sentence."

"Maybe we could help smuggle him to Sitia."

"I don't think he would want to come."

"Why not?" The idea shocked Leif.

"I'll explain later." I didn't have the energy to educate Leif about the Commander's politics. Raised in Sitia, Leif believed Ixia equaled a horrible place to live. That with Ixia's strict Code of Behavior, uniform requirement and having to obtain permits to marry or move to another house, the citizens had to be extremely unhappy. Ixia wasn't perfect, but there were benefits to living there. For me, Valek was one.

I missed seeing him every day, missed discussing poisons and fighting tactics and missed having a soul mate who knew what I needed before I did. I sighed. Better to have an immunity to magic like Valek than to be this feared Soulfinder. A Soulfinder, and completely useless against a Fire Warper.

The Commander's views on magic didn't seem so extreme now. Magic was messy. And what the Vermin had done to increase their powers remained more horrible than anything I had witnessed in Ixia.

"Leif, what about that Fire Warper?" I asked. Since the incident in the jungle, I hadn't had time to discuss it with him. "Have you seen a magician step from a fire before?"

"No. Roze Featherstone can make huge fires that'll consume whole buildings, but she'll burn if she gets too close to one. Since you've come home, I've been seeing all types of strange magic. You bring out the best and the worst in people," Leif tried to joke.

I failed to be amused. "The Vermin are using old magical rituals. Do you know anything about them?"

"The Sandseed Story Weavers' powers are legendary. They used to be called Efe Warriors. I had thought the stories of these Warriors were exaggerated." Leif paused for a moment. "Until now. Two thousand years ago, well before the Sitian clans united, the Efe Tribe dominated the others. Using blood magic, the Efes had no rivals. The other clans would give them whatever they wanted. Food, gold or sacrifices, hoping to placate them. A disagreement erupted between the Efe rulers and a civil war started. The ensuing battle flattened the Daviian Mountains."

"Mountains?"

"Now a plateau."

"Oh my."

"Right. After that a new leader named Guyan took control of the tribe's survivors. He declared he would plant the seeds for a new tribe in the sands that fell when the mountains were destroyed. That's how they got the name Sandseed and their magicians were then called Story Weavers."

The rumble of hooves interrupted Leif's tale. Kiki's face was a welcome sight, although her blue eyes looked tired and mud covered her copper-colored coat. Garnet and Rusalka hadn't fared any better.

Leif and I fed and watered the horses. I wanted to groom them and let them rest, but Leif insisted we get to the market first.

"Too many predators at night," Leif said. "The horses will attract every tree leopard in the jungle."

Market not far, Kiki said. *Jungle smells…odd.*

We mounted and galloped toward the market. Being with us, the horses didn't have to hide and we groomed them near the Zaltana campfire behind the market buildings as the sun began to set. Many clans had built permanent sites for their members to stay while trading or purchasing goods.

The Illiais Market did not close until late into the evening hours. An array of torches was lit to allow business to continue, although the commotion of customers bidding, arguing and shopping quieted in the evenings.

After the horses were settled, I strolled quickly through the collection of bamboo buildings topped with thatched roofs. Most of the owners had the bamboo shade walls down to block the cold night breeze. When I had been here before, it had been the beginning of the hot season, and the shades had been rolled up to help cool the workers.

Scanning the people at the market, I searched for Moon Man. I stopped a few customers and asked if anyone had seen my friends. One stand owner recalled spotting some men running through the market a few days ago, but he couldn't describe them.

My imagination kicked in and visions of Moon Man, Tauno and Marrok staked to the ground for the Kirakawa ritual filled my mind. Hidden behind a null shield, I wouldn't be able to find them, and every minute we delayed was another minute for Cahil and Ferde.

Focusing on the task at hand, I breathed in the market's smells to ease the tightness in my chest. The exotic spices offered by the Greenblade Clan mixed with the smell of roasting meat. My stomach growled with hunger. Before I could stop to eat, I delivered the package of clothes to Fern. The small woman huffed with relief.

"I thought Nutty wouldn't have them done in time," she exclaimed from behind a table piled with bolts of cloth.

"I thought you sold fabric," I said.

"I'm expanding my business. Nutty's getting quite the reputation."

"Is that good or bad?" I asked.

"Both. A few of the Greenblade women have gotten tired of their plain green tunics and leggings and wanted a more colorful wardrobe. They've been buying every single one of Nutty's shirts, dresses and skirt/pants. I supply the cloth and we split the profits. However, the clan elders are not too happy about the break with tradition."

As a forest-dwelling clan, the Greenblades usually wore the colors of the forest. I glanced around and, sure enough, spotted a few women wearing Nutty's bright cotton creations. I had assumed they were Zaltanas, but upon closer examination, I could see the lighter maple coloring of the Greenblade's skin.

In Ixia, I knew which Military District someone lived in by

the color of their uniform. Here, it was all a matter of knowing how each clan preferred to dress. Interesting.

"Yelena, do you need some new material?" Fern asked. She pulled out a bolt of fabric from under her table. "I just finished this beautiful green pattern. See?" She held it up to the torch-light. "Just a hint of gold woven through the fabric. Matches your eyes perfectly."

I laughed. "You're quite the saleswoman. But Nutty just made me another outfit."

Undaunted, Fern found another bolt. The rich gold color caught my attention as soon as she spread it out. "This would be for the shirt." She watched me for a moment. "Should I send this to Nutty for you?"

"You're evil," I said.

She grinned. "I'm only thinking about what's best for my customers."

"And your cash box."

A predatory smile flashed on her face. I paid her for the material and left before she could convince me I needed another set. I bought some Avibian honey for the Stable Master before buying some grilled beef to eat as I searched through the other market stands. Items displayed for sale or trade included handcrafts, clothing, fruit and baked goods.

I stopped for a minute to examine an intricate silver ring that held a black moonstone. Putting it down, I dismissed the thought of purchasing the ring. Only a few coins remained of the money I had earned as a Magician's Aide.

Besides, I already wore a butterfly pendant and snake bracelet. Both had been carved and gifted to me by Valek. I fingered the pendant on my chest, wondering about Valek.

Was he in his carving room, creating another animal statue? Perhaps he was discussing military tactics with Ari and Janco or dueling with Maren. She had taught me how to fight with a bow, and Maren's own skills had improved. Perhaps she was with Valek right now, working on some complicated project that required them to be together every day. Maybe Valek would forget about me. Be content to have Maren by his side.

No. I forced myself to ignore those thoughts. I had plenty to worry about without creating phantom worries. Determined, I headed back to our campsite. Perhaps another magical sweep of the area would reveal Moon Man and the others to me.

Leif and I waited another day for some sign of Moon Man. I prowled around the market, cursing under my breath. Each minute we delayed reduced the possibility of recapturing Cahil and Ferde. I scanned the forest with my magic, connecting with the woodland creatures. The area remained serene. Undisturbed.

That night we discussed our next move. Sitting by the fire, I stared at the flames. My bow was within reach, but I didn't believe the weapon would do much damage against the Fire Warper.

"We should go back to the Citadel," Leif said. "That makes the most sense."

"What about the Sandseeds? They left their clan unprotected in the plains. They might need help, and we should tell them about Moon Man and Tauno."

"Tell them what? That we lost them? I'd rather tell them Tauno is afraid of heights and Moon Man is claustrophobic."

And I would rather have them with us. Delaying the decision, I said, "Our direction of travel is the same for either the Citadel or the plains. Tomorrow we'll go north."

Leif agreed. He spread his bedroll by the fire and lay down. Using Kiki's saddle as a pillow, I put my cloak on and tried to get comfortable on the cold ground next to Leif.

"You should move closer to the fire. You'll freeze," Leif said.

"I'm fine."

He was quiet for a while. "Perhaps Moon Man and the others are lost."

"Doubtful. If they were lost in the jungle, I would have found them."

"Marrok's afraid of getting lost," Leif said in a soft voice. "And you're afraid of—"

"Leif, go to sleep. We have a long day tomorrow." I rolled over, turning my back to him. I didn't want him to put a name to my fear. Naming it made it true.

Cold and uncomfortable, I tossed and turned, trying to sleep. Disturbing dreams of fire and death invaded my mind. Flames would spark in a benevolent dream, here and there until they multiplied and consumed the picturesque scene, burning the images into a storm of black ash. I woke coughing on imaginary smoke, my body coated with sweat.

To avoid the nightmares, I watched the moon rise above the forest's trees. When Ferde had been on his soul-stealing rampage, the Master Magicians and I theorized the timing of his ritual murders were linked to the phases of the moon. We were wrong. He just needed enough time to torture his victims into submitting their wills to him so he could steal their souls when they died. The old Efe symbols and ritual he used to collect their souls would have made him the most powerful magician in Sitia if he been able to gather all twelve of them.

Valek and I had stopped him from absorbing Gelsi's soul and

completing the ritual, but now he was free to try again. And Cahil helped him. How could he? I couldn't really believe Cahil would get involved after witnessing what Ferde did to those girls. But he had assisted with Ferde's escape from the Keep's protective cells, and now traveled with him. Was he that greedy for power? He could no longer claim the Ixian throne. Did he want to rule Sitia instead?

I studied the moon. Waxing toward full, the bright disk lit the landscape. I wondered about the moon's power and why certain things like the Kirakawa ritual needed the moon's presence to work. I could feel the invisible layer of power blanketing the sky, but I felt nothing from the moon.

In a subtle flicker of the light, Moon Man coalesced out of a blue shaft of moonlight as if he had been summoned by my thoughts. He stood next to our fire without clothes or his weapon.

Are you a dream? I asked him.

Deep lines of exhaustion etched his face, but he managed a weary smile and said, *Perhaps I have always been a dream. What do you think?*

I think I'm too tired to discuss Story Weaver philosophy with you right now. And if you're not real, then, at least, make yourself useful and tell me where you really are!

I am here. Moon Man slumped to his knees.

12

I JUMPED TO MY FEET and ran to Moon Man's prone form by the campfire. Wrapping my cloak around Moon Man's muscular shoulders, I shared energy with him.

"Are you all right? What happened? Where are the others?" I asked.

"Everyone is fine. I will explain later." He pulled the edge of my cloak closer to his face.

"Will you? Or will you just spout some vague details in typical Story Weaver style?"

He answered with a soft snore.

I suppressed the desire to share more power with him and wake him. Sleep was the best way for Moon Man to recover his strength after using magic. Unfortunately, I couldn't sleep. I grabbed an extra blanket from Leif's saddlebags and spread it over Moon Man. My cloak didn't seem adequate protection for him against the chilly night air. Despite my reluctance, I added some logs and coaxed the fire into a warm blaze.

As I stared at the dancing flames, I wondered what other

surprises waited for me. The answers would be revealed in time, but my ability to deal with them remained uncertain.

Even with the loud calls of shoppers and stand owners from the bustling market, Moon Man didn't wake until the sun reached its apex. By the time the Story Weaver finished eating the meal Leif had thoughtfully prepared for him, my impatience had built up enough energy that I could probably scale a smooth tree without the aid of a rope.

"Tell us everything," I demanded before he could swallow his final bite.

He smiled at my agitation. Weariness still pulled at his features, but his eyes sparked with an amused glint.

"And don't try any of that cryptic Story Weaver mumbo jumbo or I'll…"

"What?" Moon Man asked.

"I'll hurt you. Bad. So talk."

Moon Man glanced at Leif.

My brother shrugged. "I've seen her swinging that stick around. Now, if you had your scimitar…"

"Too risky," Moon Man said. He saw the rising fury in my eyes and wisely began telling us what had happened.

"After you and Leif distracted the Fire Warper, we chased the Vermin through the jungle. And would have caught them if you had not needed my help." Moon Man aimed a pointed stare at me. "How is the scout?"

"Alive and well," I said.

"Back to his old self?"

I hesitated, but I wouldn't let Moon Man change the subject. "He's fine. Continue your story."

"Helping you drained all my energy and I needed to rest for a while," Moon Man said. "Marrok tracked the Vermin to the Illiais Market and then north to the city of Booruby. It is a thriving place and we lost the Vermin's trail. Too many people."

He shuddered. The motion reminded me of Leif's claim that Moon Man was claustrophobic. The city was the complete opposite of the wide open space of his home in the Avibian Plains. Located at the northern tip of the Cowan Clan's lands, Booruby's eastern side bordered the plains, and was too far for my magic to reach.

"Where are the others?" Leif asked.

"We rented a room at one of the inns. I left Tauno and Marrok there to hunt down any information about the Daviians while I rejoined you."

Leif looked around the campsite. "How, exactly, did you get here?"

Moon Man grinned. "A secret Story Weaver power."

"You used the moonlight," I said.

He beamed his approval. "I came through the shadow world. Moonlight reveals the world of shadows, allowing access."

"Is that where you showed me the story of my life?" I asked, remembering the dark plain that had transformed into visions of my childhood.

"Yes. It is a place where I unravel story threads to help others learn from their past as they weave their future."

"Is it a physical place?" I had been there twice. The second time Moon Man had brought Leif and me to untangle our knots of hostility and anger toward each other. Each time, though, I had felt intangible, as if my body had turned into smoke.

"It exists in the shadows of our world."

"Can anyone with magical powers get into the shadow world?"

"So far, only Story Weavers have the ability. But I am waiting to see if there is another who is brave enough to claim that gift." His eyes met mine, and I caught a glimpse of shadows. I looked away.

Breaking the silence, Leif said, "However you arrived, you still need to work on your transportation skills. Maybe next time you can bring some clothes along with you."

Leif and I bought Moon Man a tan-colored tunic and pants, and we purchased supplies for the trip. Packing the saddlebags, I readied the horses. Moon Man would ride Garnet until we reached Booruby.

We went north, taking a well-used path through the forest. I scanned our surroundings with my magic, but thought the odds of being ambushed remained low because of all the other caravans and travelers crowding the trail. Leif also used his magic to smell the intentions of the Vermin, but he couldn't discern anything.

Once we reached Booruby, we would find the others and decide our next move. I brooded over the fact we had lost the Vermin and worried about which direction Cahil and Ferde had gone. Back to the plains or plateau? Or engaging in another scheme to gain power?

Ferde had kidnapped Tula from her home in Booruby. His only victim found alive, Tula had been sent to the Magician's

Keep. I healed her body and found her soul only to lose both to Ferde. Guilt welled in my throat. His freedom ate at my heart.

I tightened my grip on the reins, causing Kiki to snort in agitation.

Sorry. I relaxed. *I was thinking about Ferde and Cahil.*

Peppermint Man like apple, Kiki said, referring to Cahil.

Why do you say that? I knew Kiki loved apples.

He black apple. No one wants.

I saw an image of rotting apples on the ground.

Bad. But good come.

Kiki showed how the seeds inside grew roots and became a tree after the apple decayed. *Are you saying a good thing might come from Peppermint Man? Or if he dies, it would be beneficial?*

Yes.

Cryptic horse advice? Well now I could die happy—I'd heard it all.

Two days later, we reached Booruby. Clusters of wooden and stone houses marked the outskirts of the city. The forest thinned. And the clear air fogged to a haze of smoke, coal dust and sawdust that hovered over the main street's buildings. The thick air assaulted us with the smells of garbage mixed with human waste. People bustled along the walkways and wagons full of goods choked the roads. Stores and stands had been wedged between factories and business offices.

Moon Man's alarmed face showed his discomfort as we maneuvered our horses through the crowded streets. He led us to the Three Ghosts Inn. The stone-faced building leaned its narrow four-story height against its neighbor. Through a tight alley, we led the horses to an empty stable just big enough to hold six horses.

The stalls were clean and had fresh straw and water. A stable boy soon joined us as we took off the horses' saddles. The quiet boy helped us groom and feed them. He shot me a shy smile when I tipped him.

We had passed a number of inns on our way into the city. "Why this inn?" I asked Moon Man as we carried our bags through the alley.

"I liked the name. Although…" He paused as if deep in thought.

"Although?" I prompted.

"I have not encountered the three ghosts. Perhaps you will have better luck."

I laughed. "You don't really believe in ghosts?"

Moon Man stopped and I bumped into him. He turned around, revealing his shocked expression. "How can *you* not? They are lost souls. You can help them find their way. Like you did for Reyad."

I put a hand out to steady myself. "Reyad was…" The man I had killed in Ixia. The reason I had been awaiting execution before Valek offered me the food taster's job. "How did you—"

"Story Weaver, remember? I know all the threads that are woven into your life."

"But I thought his ghost had been my imagination. A manifestation of my fears. Why haven't I seen any others? If I can help them, why aren't they all around me?"

"Perhaps they are and you do not wish to see them."

"This is weird," Leif said.

I agreed with him. My skin crawled with goose bumps, imagining being surrounded by invisible ghosts.

"I could teach—"

"Let's get inside." I cut off Moon Man's offer. Of all the things I wished he would teach me, seeing ghosts wasn't high on my list.

"Yes, let's. I'm hungry." Leif patted his stomach.

We entered into a common area. Wooden tables and long benches scarred with hard use lined the slender room. A fire crackled in the stone hearth, but the area was empty.

"Dinner's a few hours off," a woman said. She leaned from a doorway near the back wall. Spotting Moon Man, she smiled and walked toward us. "Mr. Moon! I'm so glad you're back. Your friends left this morning, but I suspect they'll be coming back for dinner. Mr. Tauno loves my vegetable stew."

The woman's steel-gray hair was pulled back into a bun. Small wisps of hair framed her oval face. Her fair skin caused me to wonder if she was a refugee from Ixia. When the Commander had launched his campaign to take over Ixia, many Ixians fled to Sitia before the Commander closed the border.

The innkeeper scanned Leif and me with bright intelligence in her sky-blue eyes. Her gaze lingered on my hands before returning to Moon Man.

"Will you be needing another room?" she asked.

"Yes. Mrs. Floranne, this is Yelena and Leif."

She wiped her hands on her apron before shaking our hands. "I'll be showing you to your rooms, then."

We followed her up the stairs. Stopping on the third floor, she led us down the slim hallway. She opened the second door on the left.

"This'll be Miss Yelena's room. Will Mr. Leif be staying with you, Mr. Moon, or do you need another room?"

Sweat beaded Moon Man's face and he glanced around the tight hallway as if seeking a way out.

"Leif can stay with me," I said, spotting two beds inside the tiny room.

Disapproval radiated from Mrs. Floranne's stiff demeanor, but before she could comment I added, "He's my brother."

Her face softened and she relaxed. "I'll be ringing the bell when dinner's ready. Don't be late." She left us alone.

Leif stifled a giggle. "Interesting place you found here, Mr. Moon."

"If Leif had been my lover instead of my brother, would she have let us stay together?"

"I do not know," Moon Man said.

"Perhaps the ghosts dislike improper behavior," Leif said, laughing.

Moon Man went to his room down the hall to check if Tauno or Marrok had left us a message. I mulled over Leif's comment as we put our few belongings on the beds.

"Is it considered improper if Valek and I…? You know."

"Yelena," Leif said with mock indignation. "Don't tell me you and Valek—"

"Just answer the question."

"Some clans like the Bloodgood Clan are very strict and require a couple to be married before living together. Others, like the Zaltanas, prefer a couple to marry, but don't get upset if they're not. Then there are the Sandseeds who don't even believe in marriage. They just do what they want." He spread his arms wide. "With their aversion to wearing clothes, I don't understand why the Sandseed Clan isn't overrun with children."

"We are careful with our seeds of life," Moon Man said from the doorway. "I did not find a note. Do you want to take a walk through the city? I need…" His gaze traveled around the room. "It is better for me outside."

Leif licked his lips. "I don't know. I don't want to miss dinner. That vegetable stew'll be smelling good."

"Do not worry. We will hear the bell. The entire city knows when the Three Ghosts Inn is having dinner."

We left the inn and wandered through the streets. I used my magic at different locations to find a sign of the Vermin, but there were just too many people around. Their thoughts and emotions crashed against me, and I blocked them out to avoid being overwhelmed. Leif, too, was inundated with smells. We searched the city and listened for any snippets of information.

A sparkle drew my gaze. Rows and rows of glass animals were displayed inside a store window. The beautiful jewel colors of the statues radiated as if a fire had been captured within their cores. They reminded me of Tula. She had sculpted animals with glass from her family's factory. Had she created these animals? Was this her family's store?

I peered through the window but couldn't see past the display. Should I go in and ask? Perhaps her family wouldn't want to see me again. Considering what had happened to Tula and her sister, Opal, I wouldn't blame them for hating me. After all, the only reason Opal had been kidnapped after Tula had died had been to exchange her life for mine. At the time, I had thought Ferde held Opal, but it had been Alea Daviian, seeking revenge for the death of her brother, Mogkan. Another man whose death I had been part of.

In Ixia, Mogkan had been power-hungry. He had taken control of not only Commander Ambrose's mind, but the minds of thirty innocent people. He deserved to die, but Alea had failed to see it my way, and now she was also dead. I sighed. I should stay far away from Opal and her family.

Death followed me. And perhaps ghosts as well? Was Alea or Mogkan's ghost haunting me? I held my hands out and turned in a circle, spinning my arms. Nothing.

Leif and Moon Man were engaged in a debate half a block away. I stepped toward them.

"Yelena!" a voice called from behind.

A woman carrying a small crate hustled along the sidewalk. A white kerchief covered her hair, and, even though soot smudged her face and hands, I recognized Opal's bright smile and I couldn't resist giving her a quick hug.

"What are you doing here?" she asked.

"I have some business." Before she could ask what kind, I hurried on. "Is this your family's store?" I pointed to the glass shop.

"Oh no. Our factory is on the east side of town, practically in the plains. We sell our glassware through a bunch of stores in Booruby. You have to come visit us!" She twisted her hands together. "That is, if you want to." She averted her face. "I mean after what I did…"

Opal yanked her focus from the ground and met mine with a sudden intensity. The shy, uncertain girl who had come to the Keep transformed in front of my eyes. "Let me make it up to you. You *will* come visit."

"You did nothing wrong," I said with conviction. "You have nothing to make up for."

"But I pricked you with Curare!"

"Alea forced you. And I must admit, that was a pretty good trick." I had thought once Opal was freed, the danger was gone. A near fatal mistake.

"But—"

"You can't let the past ruin your future. Let's call it even and start anew."

"Agreed. Can you come to dinner this evening?" she asked. Then her mouth dropped in shock and she stepped back.

Moon Man loomed behind me, blocking the sunlight.

"You'll not be missing dinner," Leif said, copying Mrs. Floranne's lilt.

Opal relaxed a bit when she saw Leif. "You can come too. And...your friend?"

I understood Opal's fear. At first glance, Moon Man resembled Ferde. But Opal had only gotten a brief glimpse of Ferde through her sister's memories so she could not really compare the two. I introduced her to the Story Weaver.

"I think I should wait for Tauno and Marrok to return," Moon Man said. "You and Leif go. I will see you later tonight."

Moon Man raised his eyebrows, giving me a signal. I opened my mind to him.

Perhaps her family will have some information about the Vermin. Ask them.

Yes, sir, I replied.

He flashed me a smile before he left. Opal hurried into the store to finish her deliveries. While Leif and I waited for her,

I returned to examining the glass animal statues in the window. Leif joined me.

"Look at how they glow!" he said. "Which one would you pick? The snake?"

"No. I've had my fill of snakes. I like the horse, but the eyes are the wrong color. They should be blue."

Leif laughed. "You're biased. I'd buy the tree leopard. The detail is amazing. I wonder how the artist is able to get the leopard's green and yellow pattern just right."

"The pattern is inside." Opal exited the store. "There's a thin layer of clear glass on the outside."

"Did Tula make these?" I asked.

Sadness welled in her eyes. She blinked back tears. "No. Tula's are too precious to sell."

"Opal, I'm—"

"Don't say it," she said. "Starting anew, remember?"

"Yes."

"Good. Let's go." Opal led the way.

I worried the girl's parents wouldn't be so forgiving, but they greeted us warmly. Their house and glass factory had been built on the edge of the city, surrounded on three sides by the Avibian Plains. The location explained why Ferde had chosen Tula. Keeping the kilns hot, Tula had been in the factory all night alone where no one could witness her abduction.

Opal guided us on a tour of her family's business and we met her remaining sister, Mara, and her younger brother, Ahir. The promised meal consisted of beef stew served in a bowl made of bread.

"Less to wash," Opal's mother, Vyncenza, said with a grin.

Leif sat next to Mara and flirted with her. He even joined

her in the kitchen to help clean up. I couldn't blame him, the beautiful loose curls of her golden-brown hair hung past her shoulders. Kindness radiated from big tawny eyes, and she listened to Leif's tales with rapt attention.

While the others cleared the table, Opal's father, Jaymes, regaled me with stories about his business and his family.

"...she wasn't paying attention and set fire to her mother's apron! It was another four seasons before we would let Tula handle a punty iron again." He laughed and launched into another one.

When he had run out of anecdotes, I asked him about news from Booruby.

"The Cowan elders are always arguing about how many trees to cut down, and now they want to start taxing the sand I import for my glassware." He tsked over the prospect. "Rumors about the other clans have always been good fodder for the gossips. This year's is about those Daviians. Everyone's worried about them, but the magicians have Tula's killer in jail and I'm sure the Sandseeds will take care of the rest. They always do."

I agreed, but my mind snagged on the fact that he still believed that Ferde was locked away. Not good. Why hadn't the Council informed the populace? Probably to avoid frightening them. Ferde was still weak, and they had hoped to recapture him by now. Should I tell Jaymes? He had two other daughters. The people should also be told about the Vermin's Kirakawa ritual. They could help find the Vermin and keep their families protected. But would they panic and hinder our efforts instead?

It was a difficult choice to make on my own and the

benefits of having a Council to vote on important issues became clearer to me. No one member could be held responsible for a bad judgment.

Delaying a decision, I asked him if his children still worked alone at night.

"No. No. I work the entire night shift. We've learned our lesson and won't be caught unaware again."

"Good. Keep vigilant. The Cowan Clan leaders are right to be worried about the Daviians."

Opal returned, giggling. Water splotched her long skirt and she tucked a few stray strands of damp hair back under her kerchief.

"Water fight," she said. And before her father could scold, she added, "Mama started it!"

He sighed but didn't appear to be too upset. Opal grabbed my hand, wanting to give me a tour of the house. The room she shared with her sister resided on the second floor of the stone house. The air smelled of honeysuckles. Hanging over the one empty bed was Tula's grief flag. The white silk banner had been part of her funeral ceremony. The Sitians believed that once raised, the flag released Tula's soul into the sky. Having freed Tula's soul from Ferde, I knew the Sitian custom just helped comfort the families.

"Why is the flag hung over her bed?" I asked.

"It's to keep her spirit from returning to earth," Opal answered. "All the things that she might want to come back for are under the flag. She can't see them there."

I looked under the banner and spotted a small shelf filled with glass animals. The figurines were lifelike and well-made but had not captured the inner fire like the ones I had seen earlier.

"Tula gifted a couple statues and sold many others, but those she kept for herself. I tried to copy her, but mine come out differently. I have only sold a few." She shrugged.

"You made the ones in the store window. Didn't you?"

"Yes." Again she made a dismissive shrug. "The store owner is a kind woman. She knew I was coming today and put them in the window. My animals are dull in comparison to Tula's."

"Opal, they're stunning. How did you get them to glow?"

She pressed her hands over her heart as if she couldn't believe what she heard. "You see the light?"

"Of course. Doesn't everyone?"

"No!" she cried. "Only I see it—and now you!" She twirled with delight.

"And Leif. He saw it also."

"Really? How odd. No one else in my family or my friends can see the inner light. They all think I'm daft, but they humor me anyway."

"How do you make them?"

She explained the process of glassblowing to me. More detail than I needed, but I understood the basics.

"Usually you shape animals from solid glass, but, when I try it, the animals resemble blobs. To make a tumbler or vase, you have to blow an air bubble into the glass. I can't do that either. I turn purple trying to get a starter bubble but have never accomplished it. However once I fail to make the bubble, I shape the piece so I don't waste the glass. That's when I get results. Not only does my animal look real, but a spark remains inside even when the piece has cooled."

I thought for a moment. "But eventually the middle would cool. What keeps it glowing?"

She threw her arms out in a frustrated gesture. "I don't know. I put my heart into these."

The answer popped into my mind. "Magic."

"No. Master Jewelrose has tested me. I didn't have enough power to stay at the Keep."

I smiled. "She should test you again." Dax's taunt about weird powers replayed in my mind. If Opal had been born a Zaltana, the test would have been different. "You have enough power to capture fire inside your statues."

"Why can't anyone else see it?"

"Perhaps a person has to have some magical ability to see the fire," I theorized. "If that's the case, you need to sell these at the Citadel's market where there are many magicians."

She pursed her lips in thought. "I obviously don't meet a lot of magicians. Can you take one of my statues along and test your theory?"

"On one condition."

"Anything!"

"That you let me pay for it so I can keep it."

"You don't have—"

I put my hand up, stopping her. "You said anything."

She laughed. "Okay, but I'll charge you the wholesale price. I know just the piece to give you, too. It's in the factory."

Opal dashed down the steps and flew out the door. The cold rush of night air reminded me that we needed to get back to the inn. I thanked Opal's parents for the meal. They told me Leif had gone with Mara to the factory.

I found Opal there. She handed me a package. Wrapped

with layers of cloth to protect the glass, the fist-size parcel fit neatly in my hand.

"Open it later," she said. "I had another one in mind for you, but this one…called. Crazy. I know."

"I've heard stranger things. I'll write you a letter when I get back to the Keep and let you know how the experiment went." I gently placed Opal's package in my backpack, slung the straps back over my shoulders then paid her for the statue. "Do you know where Leif is?" I asked.

She blushed. "I think he's sweet on Mara. They're in the back in the mixing room. She's *supposed* to be measuring sand."

I wove my way through the kilns, workbenches and barrels of supplies. The hot air baked into my skin. Light gray smoke rose from the burning coals and flowed through the chimneys to vent outside. Opal's family used a special white coal mined from the Emerald Mountains to heat their kilns. Cleaner than the black variety, the white coals burned hot enough to reach the two thousand degrees needed to melt the sand ingredients.

In the back room, a table filled with mixing bowls lined the far wall. Leif and Mara leaned over a deep bowl, but they were looking at each other instead of the concoction. The cloth masks used to prevent them from breathing in the fine particles hung around their necks.

I paused before interrupting them. Mara's hands were coated with sand, and granules peppered Leif's hair. He looked younger and his face shone with delight. It was a side of Leif I hadn't seen before, and I wondered if he had someone he cared about back at the Keep. I realized I knew nothing about certain parts of Leif's life.

Taking a few steps backward, I moved from their sight. I called Leif's name loud enough for them to hear me over the noise of the kilns. He now stood away from Mara when I came into view, the sand gone from his hair.

"It's getting late. We need to get back."

Leif nodded but didn't move. I understood the hint and left.

Outside the factory, a strong breeze hustled the clouds overhead. Shafts of moonlight poured from the sky between the breaks. When Leif joined me, we headed back to the inn. He was quiet.

"Do you want to talk about it?" I asked.

"No."

After several steps, he asked, "Did you learn anything about the Vermin from Jaymes?"

"The city is worried about them, but there is no information on where they might be if they're even here at all." I told him about Opal's glass animals, and he seemed intrigued by the magical element.

"Did you tell Mara about Ferde's escape?" I asked.

"No. I just told her to be extremely careful."

We walked for a while in silence. The air bit through my shirt and I wished I had my cloak. Booruby resided on the edge of the temperate zone with warm afternoons followed by cold nights.

"I like her," Leif said, breaking the quiet. "I haven't liked anyone before. Too busy and too worried about you to care for another. I couldn't keep you safe. I didn't lift a finger to help you. Finding you became more important than living my own life."

"Leif, you were eight years old and would have been killed if you had tried to stop Mogkan from kidnapping me. You did the right thing."

"Getting killed would have been easier. No guilt. No worries. No fear. Caring for someone is terrible and wonderful. I don't know if I have the strength to do it for another. How do you deal with it?"

"I focus on the wonderful parts and suffer through the terrible parts, knowing it will end eventually."

"Did you like Valek as soon as you saw him?"

"No. In the beginning our relationship was purely business." The first time I had met Valek he had offered me the choice of going to the noose or becoming the next food taster. My family knew I had been the Commander's food taster, but not why. Someday I would tell them about Reyad's torture.

"When did your feelings change?"

That was a harder question. "I guess the first time he saved my life." I told Leif about the Ixian fire festival and how Irys had hired four goons to kill me because my uncontrolled magic could flame out and ruin the power source.

"So the first time you met Master Jewelrose, she tried to kill you? And you told me before Valek had wanted to kill you twice. Gee, Yelena, you're not a people person, are you?"

"There were other circumstances," I said in my defense.

"It all sounds too complicated. I shouldn't get involved with Mara."

"That would be taking the easy road. Safe yet dull. Why do you like her?"

"She smells like the jungle on a perfect day. It's a light whiff of the Ylang-Ylang flower combined with the sweet aroma of living green and a touch of the nutty earthy essence. It's a scent you can wrap around yourself and feel at peace. Only those dry and sunny days will produce that smell, and they are as rare as a solid-white valmur." Leif took a deep breath. "She has a soothing, contented soul."

"Sounds like she might be worth the effort. There might be plenty of rainy days, but those perfect ones will make all the memories of rain disappear."

"Is this from experience?"

"Yes."

We reached the Three Ghosts Inn and entered the building. Moon Man and Tauno sat at one of the tables in the common area. Customers filled the room.

Tauno held a bloody cloth to his temple and his split lower lip bled.

"What happened?" I asked when we joined our friends. "Where's Marrok?"

Tauno's face was glum. He glanced at Moon Man as if seeking the Story Weaver's permission.

"We found the Vermin," Tauno said. He winced. "Or I should say they found us. A group of five soldiers with the Soulstealer and Cahil. They surrounded us, dragged us into a building and threatened to kill us. Cahil drew Marrok away and they had a private discussion. They laughed and left together, seeming the best of friends." Tauno put a hand to his ribs and cringed with pain. "The others descended on me and I have no memory except waking in the empty building."

"When did this happen?" I asked.

"This morning."

"I am glad he is alive, but I wonder why they did not kill him," Moon Man said.

Contemplating the situation, I said, "Taking a captive through crowded streets would be difficult. If they wait until

nightfall to perform Kirakawa on him they risk being discovered."

"So why not just kill him?" Moon Man asked.

"Because they want us to know they have Marrok," Leif
said.

"As a hostage?" Moon Man asked.

"No. Marrok left with Cahil. They're flaunting the fact that
Marrok is now with them," I said. "And they know everything
he knows. Including our present location."

13

"Do you think they will attack us here?" Leif asked.

I glanced at the fire warming the inn's common room. Would the Fire Warper risk being seen by the other guests?

"They could watch the building and follow us, waiting until we get to a secluded spot to attack," Moon Man said.

"That's a happy thought," Leif muttered.

I reached out to Kiki. She dozed in the stable but roused at my light mental contact. If Vermin skulked around the inn, she and the other horses would be upset.

Smell? I asked.

Night. Straw. Sweet hay, she said.

All good for now.

Kiki help? Watch. Listen. Smell for you.

What if you get tired?

Rusalka. Garnet. Take turns.

Good idea. I'll come and open the doors.

Lavender Lady stay. Kiki do.

I smiled, remembering how she had unlatched her stall door in the Keep's stable when Goel had attacked me. One of Cahil's men who held a grudge, Goel hadn't seen her. Probably hadn't known what hit him until he regained consciousness among the broken boards of the pasture's fence.

"…Yelena? Hello?" Leif poked my arm.

"I'm here."

"What are we going to do?" Leif asked me.

"It's too late to go anywhere else. Kiki and the horses will watch the outside of the building and alert me if anyone approaches."

"Ooh, guard horses. How quaint." Leif pointed to the hearth. "What if Mr. Fire Warper decides to jump out of the fire? I don't think Mrs. Floranne will be serving him a bowl of her stew."

"Can we douse the fire?" I asked.

"No," Leif said. "The inn will get too cold and Mrs. Floranne won't have hot coals for breakfast."

"Leif, do you always think with your stomach?" I asked.

"Is there any other way?"

I sighed. "We'll post a watch inside. Moon Man, how many entrances to this building?"

"Two. The main one leading to the street, and one in the back through the kitchen."

"How about upstairs? Is there another staircase in the kitchen?"

"Yes, but we can secure the door into our hallway."

"Good. We'll each take a two-hour watch. I need to rest after I heal Tauno's injuries so I won't take the first shift. Moon Man can start, followed by Leif, me and Tauno."

We left Moon Man in the common room. I helped Tauno to his room. Stiff and sore, he moved with care. When he was comfortable on the bed, I pulled a string of power and examined the damage. Aside from two broken ribs, his other wounds were minor. Staring at his injuries until they transferred to me, I hunched over with the pain and then pushed it away.

Tauno squeezed my hand in thanks before falling asleep. I trudged to my bed, not as exhausted as I had been in the past. Perhaps my healing skills improved with practice. Or had I grown used to relying on my magic?

"Yelena, wake up." Leif shook my shoulder.

I peered at him through heavy eyes. He placed the lantern on the table.

"You're the one who set the schedule. Come on." He pulled the blanket off me. "Most commanders don't take a turn guarding the troops. They get a good night's sleep so they can make the right decisions in the morning."

I sat on the edge of the bed, rubbing my eyes. "I'm not a commander and we're not a troop."

"I disagree. You've been leading the way. You're the one who knows what you're doing."

"I—"

Leif put his fingers on my lips. "Don't say it. I like—no—need to believe that you know what you're doing. Makes it so much easier to follow your instructions, especially when I'm acting as bait for a fifty-foot-long snake."

"Fine. I have things well in hand. I don't need much sleep because I have all the steps we need to take already planned out. Happy now?"

"Yes." Leif stretched out on his bed.

I picked up the lantern. "Sweet dreams."

"They will be now."

The hallway of the inn was dark and quiet. I checked the door leading to the kitchen stairs. It remained locked tight. Good. Descending into the common area, I thought about Leif's comments. I might be the one making the decisions, but I didn't believe I had enough knowledge to be a commander. Gut instinct still propelled my actions.

Valek had taught me about strategy and clandestine operations, and my Ixian friends, Ari and Janco, had taught me to fight. Late-night sessions with Janco were the reason I could pick locks. However, my magical training with Irys had been interrupted by Ferde's quest for power.

There could be a magical way to find Ferde and counter a Fire Warper, but since I hadn't read all those books about magic and history, and I hadn't explored my powers to find their limits, he was the test I hadn't studied for, the quiz I was bound to fail. Out of my depth.

The empty common room echoed with my footsteps. I made a circuit of the area to check for intruders before I set the lantern down and went outside to visit the horses. The cold air stabbed through my cloak.

Kiki stood in the alley next to the inn. Her dark coat blended with the shadows, but the white blaze down her face reflected the moonlight.

Smells? I asked, reaching up to scratch behind her ears.

Fresh. No bad.

Any trouble?

She snorted with amusement. *Two men. Woman.*

She replayed the memory of two men robbing a woman.

They had been so preoccupied with searching her packages they failed to notice Kiki's quiet approach. Quiet, because Kiki, like all the Sanseed horses, refused to wear metal horseshoes.

Kiki had spun and used her back legs with expert precision. The men landed half a block away, and the woman, after staring wide-eyed at Kiki, took off in the opposite direction. I wondered why the lady had been out so late.

She'll probably spread rumors about being rescued by a ghost horse, I said to Kiki. *Maybe they'll change the inn's name to Four Ghosts.*

I like ghosts. Quiet.

You see ghosts?

Yes.

Where?

Here. There. Places.

Here? I looked around. The empty street seemed deserted. *I don't see any.*

You will. She nuzzled my cloak, sniffing the pockets. *I like peppermints, too.*

I gave her the mints. *Care to elaborate on the ghost issue?*

No.

She retreated down the alley and I returned to the inn. The lantern's flame flickered as I made another sweep of the kitchen and rooms upstairs before settling down near the hearth. Embers glowed within the remains of the fire. Suppressing my apprehension, I added a few logs to coax the coals into a small fire to heat water for tea. Such a diminutive blaze shouldn't be big enough for the Fire Warper.

Perhaps the size of the fire equaled the size of the Fire Warper. The image of a foot-tall Fire Warper leaping from the hearth caused me to laugh, but knowing he needed only one flame to start a fire ruined my good humor.

Searching my pack for tea leaves, I found Opal's package. Curious to see which glass animal had called to her, I unwrapped the thick cloth. A charcoal-gray bat with green eyes came to life in my hands. I almost dropped the piece in surprise, but even with its wings outstretched the palm-size creature didn't take flight. Opal's magic—not life—glowed from the core of the bat. Closer examination revealed flecks of silver along the bat's body and wings.

An invigorating tingle swept up my arm. I mulled over the benefits of being a creature of the night. Could I locate Marrok or Cahil now while the city slept? Drawing power, I projected my mind and encountered a confusing array of dream images. Once again too many people for me to sort through. I pulled back.

The water bubbled. With reluctance, I returned the statue to my pack and found the tea. Over my steaming cup, I watched the miniature fire. I considered making an attempt to contact Bain Bloodgood. The Second Magician might have some advice on how I could find one soul among so many.

The Citadel was three days away by horseback. Too far for me to project in normal circumstances. Desperation increased my distance, but then I had no control of direction. Also, Bain would be asleep, his mental defenses impenetrable. I decided to wait until the morning to try.

The desire to sleep dragged at my body. I made several rounds of the room just to stay awake. When seated, my attention lingered on the fire's dancing flames. They pulsed in a rhythm that matched my heartbeat. The flames' movements appeared choreographed, as if they tried to communicate something to me. Something important.

I knelt near the fire. Fingers of orange and yellow beckoned. *Come*, they invited. *Join with us. Embrace the fire.*

I inched closer. Waves of heat caressed my face.

Come. We need to tell you…

What? I leaned in. Flames crackled, sap hissed and boiled and the harsh scent of burning hair billowed.

"Yelena!"

Moon Man's voice drenched me with cold reason. I scurried away from the hearth, stopping when I reached the far side of the room. Chills raced over my skin and I shivered.

"Thanks," I said to him.

"I thought something was not right." Moon Man descended the rest of the way down the stairs. "I woke feeling as if the threads of my blanket had ignited."

"It's a good thing you did."

"What happened?"

"I'm not sure." I wrapped my cloak tighter. "I thought I saw souls in the fire."

"Trapped?"

I barked out a laugh. If I had said that to anyone else, they would have believed I was a raving lunatic. Moon Man wanted details. Details I couldn't provide.

"I think they wanted me to join them."

He frowned and stared at the hearth. "You should not be left alone with a fire. I will finish Tauno's shift."

"Finish?" I glanced out the window. The curtain of darkness

had thinned. I had lost track of the time, and failed to wake Tauno for his turn. Not a good sign.

"Go get some sleep. We will need to make plans when you wake."

The deafening peal of Mrs. Floranne's bell jarred me from sleep. Leif sat on the edge of his bed with his head between his hands, blocking out the noise. With silence came relief and he dropped his arms.

"She'll be ringing that again if we don't get down to breakfast soon," Leif said.

All the motivation I needed. I kicked off my blanket and followed Leif from the room. We joined Moon Man and Tauno in the common area. The crowded inn buzzed with conversation. Mrs. Floranne poured tea while her staff served breakfast. The smell of sweet syrup wafted through the air.

The good night's sleep reflected in Tauno's face. The swelling was gone and the bruises faded from bright red to a light purple smudge. He moved without wincing in pain.

We ate our breakfast of honey, eggs and bread and discussed our next move.

"We should search the city," Leif said. "Quarter by quarter until we either find them or determine they're not here."

"It would take a long time." Moon Man spooned a glob of eggs onto a slice of bread.

"They are gone," Tauno said.

I stopped eating. "How do you know?"

"They mentioned leaving Booruby."

"Why didn't you tell us last night?" I stabbed my eggs with my fork.

"I was distracted by the pain and did not remember the comment until now."

"Would it have made a difference?" Leif asked.

I thought it over. Tauno had been in bad shape. But with no fatal injuries, I could have left him here and…what? Scanned the surrounding forest with my magic? I didn't know which direction they had gone and they had almost a full day of travel.

"Probably not," I sighed. "Tauno, do you remember anything else? Did they say where they were going?"

"The need to hurry was all I sensed. Perhaps that is why I was not killed. They did not have enough time."

"The best strategy would have been to keep us in the dark about Marrok, wondering if he is dead or alive and what he told them." I sipped my tea. "However, Cahil likes to feel superior and probably believes letting us know Marrok has betrayed us would make us doubt our instincts and slow us down."

Cahil had tried that tactic with me before. When he had thought I was a spy from Ixia, he had ambushed me in the forest. Then, he wanted me to believe Leif set me up to demoralize me. It hadn't worked. And it wouldn't work now.

If anything, I was more determined to find them. Even though we had lost their trail. My appetite gone, I pushed my plate away.

"What's next?" Leif asked.

The door to the common room banged open. Marrok stood in the threshold with a bloody sword in his hand.

The four of us jumped to our feet. Breakfast forgotten, we pulled our weapons as the conversation in the inn's common room dwindled into a deadly silence.

"Come on." Marrok gestured from the doorway with his sword. "Let's go before they catch up."

"Who?" I asked.

"Cahil and his…his…friends." Marrok spit the words out. "I escaped." Horror bleached his face, and blood dripped from a cut on his throat. "I've lost them, but they know we're here."

"How many?" I demanded.

Marrok straightened. "Seven."

"Armed?"

"Swords, scimitars and Curare."

"How soon?"

Marrok glanced over his shoulder and froze. He dropped his sword. It clattered on the stone floor. A big hand shoved him, pushing him to the ground.

Behind Marrok, Cahil, Ferde and five Vermin streamed into the common room.

14

WITH THEIR WEAPONS pointed toward us the Vermin and Cahil fanned out in front of the door. Two Vermin had scimitars, two had swords and one held a blowpipe to his lips.

"Everyone just stay calm," Cahil ordered. His long broadsword made an impressive threat. The people in the common room stayed in their seats. Mostly merchants and salesmen, there wasn't a soldier among them.

Marrok remained on the floor. A Vermin stood over him with the tip of his scimitar pointed at Marrok's throat.

I glanced at Tauno. "You said they were gone."

His face had paled and, although he held his weapon, he hadn't nocked an arrow. Moon Man eyed the Vermin as if judging the distance between their necks and his scimitar. Leif's machete glinted in the sunlight from the open doorway.

"Change of plans," Cahil said.

Cahil had let his blond hair grow past his shoulders and it was unbound. Besides that, he remained the same. Same gray traveling clothes, same black riding boots, same washed-out blue eyes and same hate-filled expression on his bearded face.

"My friend wanted to exchange Marrok for Yelena." Cahil inclined his head to Ferde.

I noted his use of the word *friend*. How could he call that creature his friend?

The Soulstealer's plain homespun tunic and pants hid most of the red tattoos covering his body. With a scimitar in one hand and a blowpipe in another, he looked at me with cold calculation. Despite his lean and powerful build, I sensed his magic remained weak. Yet a bite of fear nipped my stomach.

"I hope you have a few more Warpers with you," I said to Cahil. "The Soulstealer is no condition to fight three magicians."

"I may have failed in my power quest," Ferde said. "However, I now serve another who has learned blood magic."

The sound of roaring flames reached me before the heat. A quick look over my shoulder confirmed the blaze in the hearth had grown. Terror boiled in my throat, prompting me to act before the Fire Warper appeared.

Pulling power, I sent a thread to Moon Man. *Take out the man with the blowpipe. I'll take Ferde.* He agreed. *Leif,* I said, *attack the man over Marrok then keep Cahil busy.*

When? Leif asked.

"Now." I shouted and projected my awareness into Ferde's mind, bypassing his mental defenses and seizing control of his body. It was a self-defense move I had learned when Goel had captured me. Chained and left with no recourse except using my magic, I had sent my soul into Goel's body.

Once Ferde realized I had invaded, he concentrated all his energy on ejecting me. I ignored his efforts. He threatened to kill me the same way he had murdered his other victims.

Memories stabbed; sounds of their screams pounded; the smell of rancid blood pierced and visions of mutilations assaulted. His black desires of power and dominance through torture and rape revolted me.

To stop him, I harvested his soul and wrung it, exposing his deep fears and the events that had caused his addiction to power. The favorite uncle who had tied him down and sodomized him. The older sister who had tormented him. The father who had belittled him. The mother he had trusted and confided in. The mother who had sent him back to live with his uncle as punishment for lying.

A Story Weaver may have helped Ferde untie the knotted strands of his life, but I wrenched them apart, broke the threads. He became the helpless victim again. I examined his memory for every bit of detail, looking for information about the Daviian Vermin. When I finished, I peered through his eyes.

My body lay on the ground, comatose. Moon Man fought a Vermin. They maneuvered around a headless body. Cahil hacked at Leif, whose machete was no match against Cahil's longer sword. Leif would soon be forced to surrender. Tauno stood in the same spot as if rooted to the floor. Marrok had regained his feet and sparred with one of the Vermin near another body. The people in the inn had organized a bucket brigade to dump water on the fire.

Even though my time with Ferde felt like a lifetime, only seconds had passed. I raised the blowpipe in the Soulstealer's hand and aimed. First Cahil. Reloading, I shot each Vermin with a Curare-laced dart, ending the fight.

Water wasn't going to stop the Fire Warper, but with his cohorts neutralized, he conceded the fight. "Next time, my little bat." The fire died with a hiss and puff of oily smoke.

I returned to my body. My limbs felt as if they weighed a thousand pounds each. Leif helped me to stand on weak legs.

Mrs. Floranne came over. She clutched her apron between her hands and worried at the fabric. "What should we be doing?"

"Send someone to fetch the city guards. We'll need help transporting the prisoners to the Citadel," I said.

She sent the stable lad.

"Have they all been hit with Curare?" Leif pointed to the prone figures.

I looked at Ferde. He had collapsed in a heap on the floor. "All but one. I've examined his soul, and he won't be giving us any more trouble."

"For how long?"

"Forever."

"Do you think that was wise?" Moon Man asked. His scimitar dripped with blood and gore, and lacerations crisscrossed his chest. "You could have achieved the same result without damaging his mind."

"I—"

Leif jumped to my defense. "Hold on, Mr. Let's-extermi-nate-all-the-Vermin Man. Given the chance you would have decapitated him. Besides, he deserved it. And it doesn't matter anyway; Roze would have done the same thing to him once he arrived at the Citadel. Yelena just saved time."

Small darts of fear pricked my heart. Leif's words repeated

in my mind. *Roze would have done the same.* He was right. Numbness spread throughout my body. I hadn't even stopped to consider the implications before acting.

Don't get in my way; I'm the all-powerful Soulfinder. Disgust coursed through me. History books hadn't been kind to Soulfinders. The vision of Flame Me being burned at the stake rose in my mind. Perhaps the Councilors and Roze were right to fear me. After what I had just done to Ferde, I feared I might turn into a power-hungry despot.

"We need to leave as soon as possible," Moon Man said.

We had assembled in the inn's common room again. The city guards had taken Cahil and the others into custody yesterday. We had spent the day explaining to the city officials about Cahil's group; an afternoon's worth of discussion to convince them to send the prisoners to the Council. Leif and Marrok would accompany the city guards to the Citadel this morning. I intended to go with Moon Man and Tauno to the Sandseed homeland in the Avibian Plains.

"You're worried about your clan," I said.

"Yes. Also I think we need to learn more about the Kira-kawa, the Fire Warper and your abilities before we have another run-in with the Vermin."

"But your clan has forgotten the details. How are you going to learn more?" Leif asked.

"We can consult Gede. He is another Story Weaver, but he is also a descendant of Guyan and may have more information." Moon Man stole my ginger muffin and ate it.

Although I was curious to know more about how Guyan had reunited the Sandseeds after their civil war with the Efe

Warriors, Moon Man's comments reminded me I needed to try to contact Irys and let her know what had happened.

We finished breakfast and made arrangements to leave. Moon Man and Tauno would get the horses ready while Leif and I tried to communicate with Irys.

We returned to our room. I lay on my bed.

"Do you think you can reach her from this distance?" Leif asked.

"I hope to, but I may need a boost of energy."

Leif sat on the edge of my bed. Closing my eyes, I drew power to me and projected my awareness toward the Magician's Keep in the Citadel. I bypassed the chaotic jumble of minds in the city and reached for the wide-open fields marking the eastern border of the Greenblade Clan's lands. The few livestock I encountered hunched against the damp wind.

Pushing past the barren farmland, I aimed for the white marble walls of the Citadel. But my mind stretched thin as if it had turned to taffy. Leif's warm hand encompassed mine and a surge of strength pushed my awareness further, but I couldn't reach those walls. The effort left me drained.

Leif gave my hand a squeeze before he stood. He searched through his pack and before I could ask, he handed me a yellow leaf rolled like a scroll.

"Eat it," he said. "It'll give you energy."

I sniffed. The leaf smelled like spearmint and rosemary. An odd combination. As I crunched the leaf, the bitter mint taste dominated and it shredded like paper in my mouth. "Yuck. What is it?"

"A baka leaf. One of Father's discoveries."

After a while, I felt better. We packed our bags and joined

Moon Man and Tauno in the stables. The four of us mounted. Leif and Marrok rode together on Rusalka and headed toward the city's garrison. Marrok would borrow one of the guard's horses for the trip to the Citadel.

The rest of us went east through Booruby's crowded streets. Tauno shared Kiki's saddle with me, and Moon Man rode Garnet.

When we reached the Avibian Plains, the horses broke into their gust-of-wind gait. We traveled until the sun set then halted to rest. Our stopping point was a bleak section of the plains. A few stalks of grass clung to the sand, and no trees or firewood were in sight. Tauno reconnoitered the area as soon as he dismounted.

Moon Man and I tended the horses. Once they were fed, watered and rubbed down, Moon Man removed the oil nuts Leif had given to him. One of my father's finds, the oil nuts would burn long enough to heat water for stew. The night air smelled damp, hinting at rain.

After arranging the fist-size lumps into a circle, he lit the nuts on fire by striking two stones together to make a spark. I guessed Story Weaver powers didn't include lighting fires. Interesting.

Tauno returned with a couple rabbits he had shot with his bow and arrow. He skinned the animals and added the meat to the stew.

After dinner I asked Moon Man about Guyan. "What happened between the Efe rulers?"

"Just over two thousand years ago, the Efe Tribe was a peaceful nomadic people, following the cattle and the weather." Moon Man reclined against Garnet's saddle, warming to his tale. "Before becoming an official member of the tribe, the young people would make a year-long pilgrimage and bring back a new tale for the tribe. It is said that Hersh was gone many years, and, when he returned, he brought back knowledge of blood magic.

"At first he taught a few Efe magicians, called Warriors, how to boost their powers. Little rites requiring a drop of their own blood. The extra power would dissipate when the task was completed. Then Hersh showed them how to mix their blood with ink and inject it into their skin. Now the power did not dissipate and they became stronger Warriors. Soon they discovered using another's blood was even more potent. And heart's blood, taken from the chambers of the heart was incredibly empowering."

Moon Man shifted his weight and stared into the black sky. "The problem with using blood magic is it becomes addictive. Even though the Efe Warriors were powerful, they wanted still more. They did not kill their own clan members, but sought victims from neighboring clans. No longer content to follow the cattle and forage for food, they stole what they needed from others.

"This abuse continued for a long time. And would have continued if an Efe named Guyan had not stopped the Warriors. He kept his magic pure. Sickened by the horrors he witnessed, Guyan organized a resistance. The details of the battle are lost to time, but the amount of magic pulled from the power blanket was enough to knock over the Daviian Mountains and shred the blanket of power. Guyan organized what was left of the clan, and established the role of Story Weavers, who helped mend the people and the power." Moon Man yawned.

I compared his story to what I had learned about Sitian history. "Can you really mend the power source? I read a history where a magician had bunched the power around himself, and it took two hundred years for it to smooth out."

"Guyan was the first Weaver," Tauno said. He hadn't moved a muscle during Moon Man's story. "Guyan's incredible powers could mend the power source, a skill not seen in another since."

Moon Man agreed. "The blanket is not perfect. There are holes, tears and thin patches. There might come a point in time where it will be worn away and magic will be a story of the past."

A loud pop sounded from the campfire. I jumped. The last of Leif's oil nuts sputtered and died, leaving the three of us in darkness. Tauno offered to take the first watch as Moon Man and I readied for bed.

I lay awake shivering in my cloak, thinking about the power source. Finding out about those holes called Voids had been a nasty surprise. Alea Daviian had dragged me into an area without power to torture and kill me. Being unable to access my magic, I had felt quite helpless. The fact I had been tied to a cart had reinforced my complete lack of control. Alea erred by not searching me for weapons, and I had used my switchblade to escape.

Alea had also wanted to collect my blood and I wondered if she'd planned to perform the Kirakawa ritual on me. I supposed I wouldn't ever know. I couldn't ask a dead woman. Or could I? An image of invisible spirits hovering over me filled my mind and I felt as if a layer of ice coated my skin.

The next morning we ate a cold breakfast of jerked beef and cheese. Moon Man estimated we would reach the Sandseeds' main camp by late afternoon.

"I tried to reach the elders," Moon Man said. "But there is a strong barrier of protective magic tenting the encampment. Either my people managed to fight off the Vermin and this new shield is a safeguard against another attack, or the Vermin have taken control and are defending themselves."

"Let's hope for the first one," I said.

We mounted and rode for most of the day, stopping only once to rest the horses. Before we reached the point where we would be visible to the Sandseeds' camp, we halted. Tauno would scout the camp and report back.

Taking off his bow and arrows, Tauno doused himself and his clothes with water then rolled in the sandy soil. Granules clung to his skin. He blended in so well with the surroundings, he soon vanished from our sight.

I paced and fretted while Moon Man appeared serene.

"Worrying can not change anything," he said to my unspoken question. "I would rather conserve energy for when we can do something."

"You're right, of course, but on occasion logic does *not* win against emotions."

He shrugged. I resisted thinking worrisome thoughts and focused instead on what I could do.

Smells? I asked Kiki.

Sweet. Home, she replied. *Itchy.*

Clumps of mud clung to her copper coat. I rummaged in my pack until I found the currycomb. I was still combing Kiki when Tauno returned.

"The camp is secure. If we leave now we can get there before dark," Tauno reported.

As we prepared to go, he told us what he had seen. "Everything looked normal. Yanna washed clothes and Jeyon skinned a hare. I crept closer and saw the elders arguing over the fire. The children at their lessons. The youths practicing with their wooden swords. Many heads drying in the sun."

"Heads?" I asked.

"Our enemies," Moon Man replied in a matter-of-fact tone as if decorating with decapitated heads was a normal occurrence.

"It is a good sign," Tauno said. "It means we have won the battle."

Yet Tauno didn't look happy. "Did you talk to anyone?" I asked.

"Yes. Jeyon signaled to me everything was fine. I did not want to waste the daylight finding out the details." He peered at the sky. "A hot meal by a warm fire will be most welcome."

I agreed. Tauno joined me on Kiki's back, and Moon Man mounted Garnet. In high spirits we joked and raced to the Sandseeds' camp.

The gray twilight waned as the white tents of the camp became visible. Many Sandseeds had gathered near the fire. A few stirred the contents of large cooking pots, and, by the heady aroma, I guessed venison stew bubbled inside. Yum. Others waved to us as we approached. We slowed the horses.

The air shimmered with the rising heat. I scanned the area with my magic, but felt only the strong protection Moon Man had mentioned. The magic didn't feel like an illusion, but my experience was limited.

When we crossed the magical barrier, I braced myself. Even Tauno gripped my waist tighter. But the scene didn't change. The Sandseeds stayed the same. Three men and two women came over to us as we stopped the horses while the rest resumed their evening's work.

The women's faces appeared to be strained with either worry or grief. There must have been Sandseed casualties. The Sandseed men grabbed the horses' bridles. An odd thing to do, considering they had trained the horses to keep still. Kiki reared. I held her mane as she jerked away from the Sandseeds' grasp.

Bad smell, she said.

Firelight flashed on steel. I turned in time to see a mass of well-armed Daviian Vermin erupting from the tents.

15

TAUNO'S BOWSTRING TWANGED and I yelled, "Go! Go! Go!" Kiki was free, but two Sandseeds held tight to Garnet's bridle. A quick glance to the side revealed ten feet separated us from the fastest Vermin.

I pulled my staff from my pack as Kiki turned. She used her rear legs to keep the Vermin occupied while I brought my bow down on the temple of a Sandseed holding Garnet. A pang of regret touched my heart as the man crumpled to the ground. He had probably been forced to ambush us. But I didn't let the feelings stop me from attacking the second man clutching Garnet.

"Go! Go! Go!" I yelled again.

Even with Moon Man's scimitar, Tauno's arrows and my bow, the Vermin outnumbered us. It was only a matter of time before they would overrun us. In a flurry of hooves and steel and shouts, the horses headed away from the Sandseed camp, breaking into their gust-of-wind gait.

We had ridden through most of the night to get as far away from the Vermin as possible. The horses slowed. Heads down, they panted. Their coats gleamed with sweat. Only a couple dark hours remained. Dismounting, we removed their saddles. While I walked the horses to cool them down, Moon Man and Tauno searched for wood and game.

No one said a word. The shock of the attack had yet to wear off and the vivid memory of it played over and over in my mind. The ramifications alone were too awful to consider right now.

We ate another rabbit stew in silence. I thought about our next move.

"The elders…" Moon Man's voice seemed loud in the thick night air.

"Are still alive," Tauno said. "For now."

"Would they kill them?" A shudder gripped my body at the thought of all those drying skulls.

"The trap was sprung. They have no need for them," Moon Man replied then seemed to reconsider his words. "They might keep them as slaves. The Vermin are lazy when it comes to domestic tasks."

"And they're just busy beavers when it comes to ritual killings and gaining power," I said. "Lucky us." The scene once again flashed in my mind. "Do you think some of your people escaped?"

"Perhaps. They would have left the plains, though." Moon Man considered. "The Sandseeds no longer control the protective magic over the Avibian Plains. To stay within its borders would be too dangerous for them. Right now, the Vermin are using the protection to keep their presence a secret, but now that we have fled, I believe they will use it to find us. Perhaps to attack us with magic."

"Then we shouldn't linger long. Is there any way to know if they find us?"

"We can create a barrier to alert us to an attack and maybe deflect an initial foray."

"We should saddle the horses in case we need to make a quick exit." I stood.

"That would be prudent." Moon Man helped me with the horses.

Kiki snorted in annoyance when I tightened her straps.

Tired, she said. *Don't need. Smell good.*

For now. If the smells turn bad, we can leave faster. I fed her some peppermints and scratched behind her large ears. She sighed and her eyes drifted shut.

After the horses were ready, the three of us sat in a circle around the fire.

"Maybe we should douse the flames." Worried that the Fire Warper would sense me through the blaze, I hadn't used my magic near a fire.

Moon Man dumped water onto it. Puffs of gray smoke rose into the air.

"Yelena, I want you to pull threads of magic and I will do the rest," Moon Man instructed.

Concentrating, I gathered strands of power. Moon Man plucked the strands from me and weaved them into a net around us. Tauno's pinched and sullen expression reflected his discomfort. As the only one without magic, he didn't have the ability to see the protection building around us.

When Moon Man finished, I disconnected from the power source, feeling drained of energy. The net pulsed with magic even though we no longer fueled it. I wondered why it still worked. In all my past efforts, the power dissipated as soon as I stopped using magic. Except for my mental connections with Kiki and Irys, every time I wanted to heal or project I had to consciously draw from the power source. Yet the Sandseeds had their protection, and there were other lingering spells.

An image of the knife in Valek's suite came to mind. When Valek had assassinated the King of Ixia, the King cursed him, vowing his blood would stain Valek's hands forever. Since magic doesn't work on Valek, the curse transferred to the knife instead. The King's blood still clung to the blade and remained as wet and bright as the day the King had been killed.

I asked Moon Man how the protective net stayed active.

"Mostly we channel the magic through us. But there are times when you can loop the power back to the source. It can be very difficult to do, and, by having you draw the power, I could save my energy for knitting it together and redirecting it back to the source. Large-scale protection like the one covering the Avibian Plains and the Sandseeds…"

A hitch of emotion stopped his words. He closed his eyes and swallowed his grief before he continued. "Huge magical loops require an immense effort by many magicians, but can be effective for a long time. The protection we just created will last for a few hours before dissipating. Enough time to give the horses a chance to rest."

"And then what?" I asked, but he looked at me. Leif's comments about my role as commander flittered through my mind. I answered my own question. "We leave the plains. Head toward the Citadel and let the Council know what's been going on with the Vermin."

"Hopefully they will already know. The Sandseed survivors would have gone to the Citadel." Moon Man scowled. "If there were any."

Waiting for the horses to regain some of their strength proved to be difficult. Our protective net flashed whenever the Vermin's magic scanned the area. So far the net hid us from the Vermin, but each encounter weakened the fibers.

The desire to flee and the need to sleep battled within me. I wanted to stay awake in case the Vermin attacked, but I dozed off and on until the sky brightened with the rising sun.

The few hours before dawn had been enough time for the horses. We mounted and headed northwest, riding hard. During our rest breaks, Moon Man searched for any sign the Vermin's magic had found us. I projected my awareness to learn if they physically pursued us. In our haste, we left a physical trail even my untrained eyes could follow.

A couple hours short of the Avibian border, we stopped for a longer rest. Moon Man proclaimed the Vermin had lost us, and I couldn't sense anyone nearby.

Since we had been traveling together for fifteen days, we automatically attended our chosen tasks, even with the Daviian threat hanging over our heads.

By the time I had finished rubbing down the horses and seeing to their needs, I smelled rabbit stew cooking on the fire.

Tauno sat next to the pot. His shoulders hunched as if a great weight pressed down on him, and his attention remained fixed on the ground. He hadn't uttered more than a few words since yesterday. Perhaps he felt guilty and responsible for leading us into an ambush. I debated discussing it with him, but considered he might be more comfortable talking to Moon Man. I wondered if Moon Man was his Story Weaver. Every Sandseed had a Story Weaver to guide and advise them throughout their lives.

I glanced around, realizing Moon Man hadn't returned from collecting firewood even though a pile of branches rested near the cook fire.

"Tauno, where's Moon Man?" I asked.

Tauno didn't even lift his head when he said, "He was called to the shadow world."

"Called? Does that mean another Story Weaver survived the Vermin attack?"

"You will have to ask him."

"When will he be back?"

Tauno ignored the rest of my questions. Frustrated, I circled the area, searching for Moon Man, and found his clothes in a heap on the ground. I moved to return to the fire and bumped into him.

I jerked back in surprise. Moon Man seized my upper arms to keep me from falling.

"Where have you been?" I asked.

He peered at me with an alarming intensity. Blue fire flecked his brown eyes. I tried to move, but he wouldn't let go.

"They are dead," he said with a flat voice. "Story Weavers and Sandseeds gone. Their souls haunt the shadow world."

His grip on my arms tightened. "You're hurt—"

"You can help them."

"But I don't—"

"Selfish girl. You would rather lose your abilities than use them. And that is what will happen. You will become a slave to another."

His words slapped me in the face. "But I've been using them all along."

"Anyone can heal. You, though, hide from your real power and others suffer for it."

Stung and hurt, I tried to break loose, but his hold wouldn't release. In order not to injure him, I projected into Moon Man's mind. Thick ropes of gray power surrounded him. The shadow world still held his mind. My efforts to cut the ties failed.

"The shadow world calls."

Moon Man began to fade. My body became translucent. He planned to take me with him to a place where I feared I couldn't access my magic. Reaching into my pocket, I pulled my switchblade and triggered the blade. I slashed him across his stomach. Moon Man shuddered and let go. He collapsed to the ground, curling into a ball on his side.

I looked at Moon Man's still form. The gray power had vanished, but I wasn't sure of his mental state. Perhaps the shock and grief had been too much for him. Difficult to believe. He had been a calm and steady presence all along.

I knelt next to him. The blood from his wound soaked his shirt. Drawing power, I focused on his stomach. The cut pulsed with a red light and a line of pain formed on my own stomach. I huddled on the ground, concentrating on the injury. My magic repaired the damage.

When I finished, Moon Man grasped my hand. I tried to pull free, but he squeezed. My body jerked as the image of headless bodies slammed into my mind. They crowded close, enveloping me with the reek of dead flesh as they demanded revenge. Another jerk and the scene of a massacre flooded my senses. The burning stench of body fluids and death stung my nose as blood soaked into the sand. Mutilated bodies were strewn in a haphazard, irreverent manner and left for the vultures to find.

Moon Man sat, and I tried to break his hold. His gaze met mine.

"Is that what you saw in the shadow world?" I asked.

"Yes." Horror filled his eyes as the gruesome images replayed in his mind.

"Give the memories to me." I felt his reluctance. "I will not forget them."

"Will you help them?"

"Can't you?"

"I can only help the living."

"Are you going to tell me how or spout some cryptic bullshit?"

"You do not want to learn. You have refused to see what is all around you."

"You didn't answer my question."

Pain creased his face and the light in his eyes dulled. He would be unable to function with the dreadful knowledge of how his people suffered.

"Give them to me. I'll try to help them, but not right now." I mentally added soothing-the-dead-Sandseeds to the end of my long list of things to do. After I dealt with the Fire Warper, which should be a breeze. While I was lying to myself, I included flying and turning stones into gold to my list. Might as well think big.

Moon Man released the emotional turmoil of his visions. He wouldn't forget the images, but they would no longer strangle him. I gathered his grief and guilt and anguish to my soul. So much carnage and blood. All to boost the Vermin's power. So many dead. Too many. How to soothe those victims? Stopping the Vermin from increasing their strength might work. What if they tried again? Perhaps destroying the power blanket to keep everyone from using magic would work. A drastic and desperate measure that might not even be possible.

Letting go of my hand, Moon Man stood.

"What you said about my future. Is it true?" I asked.

"Yes. You will become a slave to another." The discussion over, Moon Man returned to the campfire.

We ate the stew in silence. Packing up, we mounted and spurred the horses toward the Avibian border. When we reached the road located between the plains and the fields of the Green-blade Clan's lands, we turned north toward the Citadel and slowed the horses to a walk. At this late hour, the road was empty.

Being out of the plains gave us at least an illusion of safety, but I wanted to ride a little farther before we stopped for the night.

The next three days dragged. With hardly a word spoken between the three of us, an awkward hush resulted as we traveled to the Citadel. Moon Man's comment about my future repeated in my mind, grating on my nerves like a high-pitched squeal. I wanted to know who would force me to be a slave and when, but I knew Moon Man would reply with a cryptic remark and I wouldn't be smart enough to figure it out. The air turned cold and damp as we went farther north, and one night sleet pelted us, making our ride miserable.

Seeing the welcome sight of the white marble walls of the city on the third day, I spurred Kiki into a gallop. Gone from the Keep for eighteen days, I missed Irys, my old mentor who answered my questions with a refreshing directness, and my friends at the Magician's Keep.

After crossing the south entrance gate of the outer wall, we walked the horses through the streets of the Citadel. Puddles of icy muck peppered the walkways. Citizens hurried through the intermittent rain, and the grayness cast a mournful facade over the expanse of marble buildings. The smell of wet wool clung to the air. We aimed for the Council Hall, which was located with the other government buildings in the southeast quadrant of the Citadel.

Home? Kiki looked with longing at the four towers of the Keep.

Soon, I said. *Rest here for now.* A stable for the Councilors had been erected behind the building. *At least you'll be out of the rain.* Once Kiki and Garnet were settled, we entered the hall.

A guard informed us a Council meeting had just finished and we should go in before the Councilors left for the day. Entering the Great Hall, I spotted Irys talking to Bain Bloodgood, Second Magician. Groups of Councilors and aides formed small knots and the noise of their discussions filled the room. By the harsh tones and strident voices, I sensed the discussion hadn't gone well and an undercurrent of fear trembled against my skin.

Moon Man and Tauno went directly to their Councilman, Harun Sandseed. I hung back, not wanting to interfere with the Sandseeds. Irys hurried toward me. She wore her stern Fourth Magician expression. She was worried. I scanned the clumps of Councilors with more care and I discovered the reason for her concern.

Cahil stood with Roze Featherstone and another Councilor. He laughed and talked as if he belonged there.

16

I MOVED TO CONFRONT Cahil. He should be in the dungeon for aiding and abetting a murderer, not standing in the middle of the Great Hall having a conversation with Roze. My alarm increased when I saw a few Vermin inside the Hall.

Irys had other plans. She grabbed my arm and pulled me aside.

"Now is not the time," she said, appealing to me.

"What is going on?" I demanded.

Irys glanced around the room. A few Councilors stood close enough to overhear us, so she switched to our mental communication.

Cahil claims he's been on an undercover mission this whole time, she said. *He says that he didn't free Ferde.*

Why would anyone believe that? I asked.

Because Roze corroborated his story.

A lightning strike of shock ripped through my body. I hoped I misunderstood her. But her grim expression didn't change.

It gets worse, she said. *Cahil says he caught Marrok rescuing Ferde and, after interrogating him, Cahil discovered Ferde was on his way to rendezvous with others. Cahil followed the Soulstealer to discover what they plotted.*

That's ridiculous. We know Cahil beat Marrok to find out about his birth parents.

It's Cahil's word against Marrok's at this point because there is no evidence to say who freed Ferde. Especially since Ferde can't be questioned. Irys frowned. *We'll talk about your actions later, but whatever you learned from Ferde's mind can't be used as evidence.*

Why not?

Because you were emotionally involved with the Soulstealer and your impartiality is suspect. I know—she went on, sensing my protest—*it isn't right, but when the Council discovered what you had done to Ferde, it confirmed their fears about you being a Soulfinder and validated Roze's warnings.*

I sighed. It had confirmed my fears, too. *Where's Ferde now?*

In the Citadel's jail, waiting for the Council to decide what to do with him. Although I think executing him would be a kindness.

Her censure hurt and guilt welled. I forced my thoughts away from Ferde and concentrated on Cahil. There had to be a way to show the Council the truth about his involvement. *Where's Marrok? What has he said?*

Marrok is being held for questioning. He claims he didn't free Ferde. He had no motive. But Cahil says Marrok wanted to frame him for the escape so Marrok could lead Cahil's men. And also that Marrok lied to him, and Cahil really has royal blood.

My mind spun. Cahil had an answer for everything. *So why was Cahil traveling with Ferde?*

He says it was part of the undercover mission. Once he caught up with Ferde, he convinced Ferde he wanted to be a part of their plans.

While he traveled with the Daviians, Cahil says he recruited them to switch sides. She gestured to the Vermin in the room.

Did he mention the Vermin using blood magic and the Fire Warper?

No. He didn't, but Leif tried. Leif attempted to discredit Cahil and many of the Councilors thought he exaggerated about the Daviians. Unfortunately, Leif's reputation for seeing doom and gloom in everything worked against him.

Did Cahil say what the Vermin plan to do? Half of me didn't want to hear Irys's response. I steeled myself.

According to Cahil, the Daviians' leaders are in league with the Commander of Ixia. Together they plan to assassinate the Council and Master Magicians and, in the ensuing chaos, the Daviians will offer to help Sitia battle the Ixians. But there won't really be a war and the Daviians will eventually turn Sitian's government into a dictatorship.

Exactly what the Council feared since the Commander took over Ixia, and, combined with the resultant bad feelings from the Ixian Ambassador's visit, the Councilors were primed for Cahil's lies. So now it seemed Roze was right to warn the Council about the Commander. And I had no evidence to prove them wrong.

What about my training? I asked.

I didn't think Irys could look any more upset, but she managed to deepen her scowl. *The Council has given Roze permission to "assess" your involvement in these events and to determine what risk you pose to Sitia.*

I'm sure that would be impartial. Do I have any say in this?

No. But the other Masters will be there as witnesses. All except me. My objectivity is considered compromised by our friendship.

Moon Man and Tauno finished their conversation with Harun. They came toward us.

Did you hear about the Sandseed massacre? I asked Irys.

Yes. Horrible news, and it gave Cahil more proof of the Daviian threat. The Council is preparing the Sitian army for war.

I didn't even have to ask. Irys saw the question in my eyes.

War against the Daviians and against Ixia.

So much for my job as Liaison. War between Sitia and Ixia was the one thing I had hoped to avoid. There had to be more going on with the Daviian Vermin, though. I knew the Commander would never team up with them. They used blood magic, and he wouldn't condone the use of any magic. Besides, he could attack Sitia without the Vermin's help. Again, I had no proof.

Moon Man and Tauno joined us.

"There are about a dozen Sandseed survivors," Moon Man said. "They came to the Citadel and are staying here for now. Only one Story Weaver besides me survived. It is Gede, and he is the one we need to talk to about the Fire Warper."

Irys said, "Who—"

Moon Man kept talking. "You said Master Bloodgood has a few books about the Efe, right?"

"Yes," I said.

"We should examine them. Gede and I will come to the Keep tomorrow morning." Moon Man turned and walked away.

I watched his back, feeling uneasy. His whole attitude toward me had changed since he had tried to drag me into the shadow world. He acted as if he had given up on me.

"That was rather abrupt," Irys said.

"He's been through a lot."

"And so have you. Tell me about this Fire Warper. Leif had only sketchy details."

I reported all our adventures to her as we left the Council Hall and headed toward the Keep.

The next morning we assembled in Bain Bloodgood's study. Occupying the entire second floor of his tower, Bain's office was ringed with bookcases. They had been built around the long thin windows and every shelf overflowed with texts. A desk, a few wooden chairs and a ratty armchair looking as old as Bain resided in the center of the room. The sharp tang of ink permeated the air. Ink stained the desk's top and Bain's fingers. And the only space on the floor without a pile of books was a foot-wide path from the door to the desk.

The tension in the room pressed on my skin. Moon Man had folded his large frame into one of the chairs. He appeared uncomfortable and he glanced with longing outside. I shared his discomfort. The room felt crowded and tight even for me. Bain sat behind his desk, with Dax Greenblade standing next to him. Dax was Bain's apprentice and he had the unique talent of being able to read ancient languages. His help in finding Ferde and rescuing Gelsi had been vital.

Irys stared at the other Sandseed Story Weaver with ill-concealed dislike. Gede had arrived with Moon Man and he had pushed his way into the room as if he belonged there. He carried his bulk with authority and appeared to be taller than he was. It wasn't until he stood next to Irys that his true height was revealed. He matched Irys's five feet eight inches.

"Those books belong to me," Gede said.

Silence met his statement. Dax glanced at me. Incredulity flashed in his bottle-green eyes.

"My ancestor labored to banish all the knowledge about the blood magic, yet there they sit—" he gestured to the two open books on Bain's desk "—for anyone to pick up and read."

Irys said, "I doubt anyone but Master Bloodgood and Dax can read or understand the language—"

Gede cut her off. "It is all you need. One person to read it, to get ideas and to experiment with the knowledge. Blood magic is like no other—once you start you can not stop."

"It appears the Vermin have discovered the information without these books," I said.

"How do you know?" Gede asked. He peered at Dax with open suspicion. "Perhaps someone has been feeding them information."

I stepped in front of Gede before Dax could defend himself. "Not from here. Besides, having these books might prove to be an advantage. Your ancestor Guyan defeated the Efe and perhaps the books contain information about how to counter the Vermin's blood magic and to defeat the Fire Warper."

"All the more reason to give them to me," Gede said. "The Sandseeds will deduce a way to oppose the Daviians. After all, they are our problem."

"Not anymore. They've gone beyond your problem," Bain said. "We will keep the texts here. You're welcome to study them with us."

But Gede wouldn't back down on his claim and Bain refused to give in. Eventually Gede rose to leave. He paused before me and scanned me with cold calculation in his dark eyes.

"Did you know Guyan was a Soulfinder?" Gede asked me.

Surprised, I said, "No. I thought he was the first Story Weaver."

"He was both. You know nothing about Soulfinders." He

glared at Moon Man. "Your education is pathetic. I can teach you how to be a true Soulfinder."

My heart jumped in my chest. The prospect of learning more about Soulfinders both thrilled and terrified me.

Gede must have seen the indecision on my face. "You do not need these books to defeat the Fire Warper."

Too good to be true, I knew there had to be a catch. "I suppose you'll guide me with some cryptic nonsense."

"Bah!" Again Gede shot Moon Man an annoyed look. "There is no time for that. Interested?"

Logic warred with emotion. "Yes." Emotion won.

"Good. I am staying in the Citadel's guest quarters. Come at twilight. The moon should be up by then." Gede swept out of the room, with Moon Man trailing behind him.

Irys raised one slender eyebrow at me. "I don't—"

"Think it's the best decision." I finished for her. "Think I should rush into the situation and hope for the best."

She smoothed out the sleeves of her tunic, giving me a wry look. "No. I don't trust him."

I lingered outside Roze's tower, debating. This meeting with her, Bain and Zitora could be a trap. She could either trick me into confessing to conspiring against Sitia, or it could be my chance to redeem myself. Nice to have choices.

Bain opened the door and said, "Come in, child. It is cold outside."

Decision made, I followed Bain into Roze's home. A huge fire crackled and popped, spitting out sparks, which would have burned the threadbare carpet if Roze hadn't doused the errant embers with her magic. With the memory of her fire attack seared in my mind, I chose a hard wood chair as far from the hearth and from her as possible.

Spartan and bare, the room lacked the cozy comfort of Irys's living area and the scholarly smell of Bain's study. Zitora, Third Magician, perched on the edge of her seat, another straight-backed chair without cushions. She kept her gaze on her hands. They were laced together in her lap. Bain occupied the only comfortable seat. Overstuffed and worn thin, the chair's fabric was close to tearing, and by the annoyed frown on Roze's face whenever she glanced at Bain, I guessed he had taken her favorite spot.

"Let's get this over with," I said into the awkward silence.

"Nervous?" Roze asked.

"No. I have a meeting in an hour and I need to wash my hair."

Roze drew a breath.

"Ladies, please. This is difficult enough as it is," Bain said. "Put your differences aside and let us assess the situation."

Roze kept her comment to herself. Impressive. She gave Bain a stiff nod. He smoothed the wrinkles in his robe before continuing. "Yelena, you have shredded Ferde's soul."

"I—"

"No commenting until I am finished."

The stern tone in Bain's voice raised the hair on my arms. He was the second most powerful magician in the room. "Yes, sir."

Satisfied, Bain resumed his lecture. "Your rash actions have set off a ripple of discontent within the Council. First you acted without their permission. Second, your ability to shred a soul alarmed the Councilors, including me. You have lost their trust, and therefore the information you uncovered through Ferde is invalid."

I tried to meet Zitora's gaze, but she averted her face.

"You are hereby ordered to stay out of Sitian affairs while we deal with this new Daviian threat. Roze has agreed to let you work with Gede to discover the extent of your powers and we will reassess how you can aid our efforts in the future." Bain gestured for me to comment.

Protests pushed in my throat, but I swallowed them down as I wrestled my thoughts into a logical response. This meeting was an ambush. They didn't want to question me, just dictate to me.

"What about Cahil? You can't believe him?" I appealed to Bain.

"There is no proof he lied. First Magician supports him."

"He's always been selfish," Roze said. "He wants only one thing. To aid the Daviians against Sitia runs counter to his desire. He needs our help to launch his campaign to claim Ixia. A country in the midst of a civil war wouldn't be able to aid him at all."

Roze's reasonable logic worried me more than her anger. "How about the Fire Warper?"

A bright fireball erupted from the fire, and hovered above us. I squinted into the harsh light. The heat of the flames fanned my face. Roze curled her fingers into a fist and the fire ball disappeared. Opening her hand, she gestured and snuffed out the hearth fire, casting us into cold semi-darkness.

"I'm First Magician for a reason, Yelena. My command of fire is my best ability. You need not fear the Fire Warper. *I'll* deal with him." Flames ignited. Once again heat and light emanated from the hearth.

I couldn't suppress my skepticism.

"Do you really think I would let the Daviians and this Fire Warper take control of Sitia? They wouldn't take proper care of my country. No. I will do all I can to keep them from power, including protecting you from the Fire Warper."

Now she was outright scaring me. "You want me dead."

"True. You're a threat to Sitia, but there is no proof. I can't obtain the Council's support to have you executed. But once I have evidence, you're mine."

This was more like the Roze I knew and hated. We glared at each other.

Bain cleared his throat. "Child, by listening to the Council and working with Gede Sandseed you will regain the Council's trust."

Learning about my powers was what I had desired all along. Ferde was no longer a threat and the Council knew about the Daviians. If they wished to believe Cahil, why should I care? The Commander's army would prevail against Cahil. I had sought to avoid a war, but I held no sway within the Council. Why couldn't I be selfish for once and stay out of politics while I explored my powers?

I agreed. But the slight rush of relief failed to ease the pang of doubt. Moon Man's comment about becoming a slave to another echoed in my mind.

I returned to my rooms in Irys's Keep tower. She had given me three of the ten floors to use. I trudged up the steps, anxious, worried and frustrated. Roze's boast she could handle the Fire Warper had better be true. Bain's Efe books described power symbols and blood rituals, but he had discovered nothing to counter them. And there was no mention of a Fire Warper.

Dax had translated the bulk of the books, but a few chapters remained. He planned to spend the afternoon working on them. My worry also stemmed from a comment Dax had made about Gelsi. Bain's other apprentice, Gelsi, had been Ferde's last victim, but I stopped him in time and revived her body and returned Gelsi's soul.

When I had inquired about her, Dax's vague response caused me to question him further.

"To tell the truth," Dax had replied, "she's different than before."

"Different how?" I had asked.

"She's harsher. Unhappy." He moved his arms in a gesture of futility. "She no longer enjoys life. She's more preoccupied with death. It's hard to explain. Master Bloodgood is working with her. We hope it's a condition she can work through and not—" Dax shrugged "—permanent. Maybe you can talk to her?"

I promised to visit her. Thinking back, I had returned two people's souls to bodies that had been dead. Gelsi and Stono. And both came back changed. Were their altered personalities due to something I did when I held their souls? My anxiety grew over what I might discover about my Soulfinder abilities with Gede.

Uneasiness soured my stomach, and I remembered the attack Roze had sent me where Flame Me made a soulless army. While it didn't apply to Gelsi and Stono, I recalled Stono's offer to kill for me.

With those morbid thoughts, I reached my rooms. Even though I had three levels, I only possessed enough furniture to occupy one. An armoire, a desk, a single bed and night table looked lonely in the round room. I would need to do some shopping when I had the time. Right now finding souls took priority over finding curtains. Then I could be Yelena, the all-powerful Curtainfinder. Able to decorate a room in one hour.

I laughed out loud.

"What's so funny?" a heart-melting voice asked from behind me.

Valek leaned in the doorway, his arms crossed over his chest as if he visited me every day. Dressed as one of the Keep's servants, he wore a gray tunic and pants.

"I was thinking about curtains." I moved toward him.

"Curtains are funny?"

"In comparison to all my other thoughts, yes, curtains can be amusing. But you, sir, are the best thing that's happened to me all day, all week and, now that I think about it, all season." Two steps and I was wrapped in his arms.

"That's the best welcome I've had all day."

I could only imagine what he had been up to. His ability to get into any building undetected made him the most feared man in Sitia. And his immunity to magic terrified the Master Magicians. He was Commander Ambrose's best weapon against them.

"Do I want to know why you're here?" I asked.

"No."

I sighed. "Should I know why you're here?"

"Yes. But not now." He leaned over and his lips met mine, and it no longer mattered why.

The late-afternoon sun woke me and reminded me about my meeting with Gede. I nudged Valek awake. We huddled under the blankets against the icy air.

Valek moved to get up. "I'll make a fire—"

"No!" I grabbed his arm, stopping him.

He peered at me with concern. I marveled at the rich sapphire color of his eyes and how they contrasted with his pale skin.

"You'll need to reapply your skin-darkening makeup," I said, brushing a black strand of hair away from his face.

He held my hand. "Nice try, but you *are* going to tell me why you don't want a fire."

"Only if you tell me why you're here." I countered.

"Agreed."

I filled him in on the series of events with Cahil, Ferde and the Fire Warper.

"It's ridiculous to think the Commander is working with these Vermin." Valek looked thoughtful. "So the Wannabe King has chosen to ignore the truth about his birth. You got to admit his ability to dupe the entire Council is impressive."

"Not the entire Council. Irys doesn't believe Cahil and I'm sure there are others." I waved my hand in a shooing motion. "Doesn't matter. It's not my concern. I've been told to be a good little student and mind my own business."

Valek snorted. "Like *you* would listen to them."

"I agreed."

He laughed long and hard. "You. Not. Get involved." Valek paused to catch his breath. "You've been in the midst of trouble ever since you became the Commander's food taster, love. You would never walk away."

I waited until he wiped the tears from his cheeks. "This is different. Then I didn't have a choice."

"Oh? And you have a choice now?"

"Yes. I'll let the Council deal with these Vermin and I'll stay out of trouble."

"But you know they can't counter them."

"They don't want my help."

Valek sobered and a hard edge glinted in his gaze. "What happens when the Vermin win?"

"I'll stay with you in Ixia."

"What about your parents? Leif? Moon Man? Irys? Do they come with you? And what happens when these Warpers with their incredible blood magic decide to follow you to Ixia? What choice will you have then?" He studied my face. "You can't let your fear of the Fire Warper stop you from—"

Annoyed, I snapped. "The Council has stopped me. They're the ones who are against me." Besides, I didn't want to think about my family—they were all grown people able to look after themselves. Then why did guilt tug at my heart and doubt squeeze my chest?

"You just said there're a few Councilors on your side. Once the Council hears Marrok's evidence tonight, they'll believe you about the Wannabe King."

"How did you know about Marrok?" Irys had just told me this morning. I had insisted on attending Marrok's questioning, but she said the session was closed, for Councilors only.

Amusement returned to Valek's face. "Servants. Their information network is far superior to a corps of trained spies." In an offhand way, he added, "I'll tell you about the session later tonight."

"You rat! It's a closed meeting. Only you would try to pull it off."

"You know me, love."

"I know. You crave a challenge and you're cocky."

He grinned. "I wouldn't call it cocky. A certain amount of

self-confidence is needed, especially for my line of work." He turned serious. "And for yours."

I ignored the implication. "Speaking of work, we made a deal. Why are you here?"

He stretched his arms over his head and yawned, pretending to consider my question.

"Valek," I warned, poking him in the ribs. "Tell me."

"The Commander sent me."

"Why?"

"To assassinate the Sitian Council."

17

I GAPED AT VALEK. Assassinating the Council would help the Vermin and support Cahil's claims. "You're not—"

"No. It's the wrong thing to do right now. The Commander based his decision on the state of Sitian affairs before these Vermin showed up. He allowed me a degree of flexibility on this mission. We need to find out what's going on. The Council meeting tonight might reveal crucial information."

"We?"

"Yes. *We*."

I sighed. I was disobeying direct orders from the Master Magicians and the Council again, getting involved with Sitian affairs. Would I ever agree with their decisions or was I deep down an Ixian just pretending to be impartial? Perhaps my session with Gede would be useful. I needed guidance as well as information.

Valek and I agreed to meet back in my room later tonight. He left.

Apprehension swirled around me like a thick fog as I dressed and walked to the Citadel's guest quarters. The small clouds in the sky darkened as the light faded. The streets hummed with people finishing up their tasks for the day. Lamplighters began lighting the vast network of street lanterns. The main thoroughfares would be lit, but the back alleys would remain dark.

My concern grew as I passed a number of Vermin saunter-ing along the streets as if they owned the place. I avoided their gazes and wondered how the Council could be so swayed by Cahil's words. Perhaps a Warper had influenced them with magic, making them more agreeable.

The Citadel's guest quarters were located in a building behind the Council Hall and next to the stables. The two-story struc-ture housed many apartments and I peered through the gloom, trying to determine which one Gede occupied. A shadow moved next to an entrance. Moon Man stepped from a pool of darkness.

"This way," he said.

No emotion showed on his face. Gone was his sense of mischievousness and the spark of amusement in his eyes. I missed them.

"Moon Man, I—"

"You must not keep Gede waiting," he said in a flat voice. "Your Story Weaver is ready for you."

He ushered me inside, closing and locking the door behind us. Heat pressed against my skin as if I stood in an oven. A roaring fire blazed in the hearth, illuminating the living area. All the furniture had been pushed against the walls. Gede sat cross-legged on a mat in front of the fire. A few Sandseeds sat in the cleared space in the center of the room.

"Come. Sit." Gede pointed to a mat in front of him.

I hesitated.

"You are the Soulfinder. You should not be afraid of fire. Sit or learn nothing."

Removing my cloak and pack, I placed them by the entrance. I longed to pull my bow from its holder but ignored the desire. Instead, I joined Gede on the floor. Sweat ran down his round face. His skin appeared black in the firelight. A trick of the light revealed an intricate tattoo design connecting the scars on his bare arms. But when I blinked, the design was gone.

"As a Soulfinder you can examine a soul, twist it, hold it and return it. You can send your soul to others. And you can project your soul to the other worlds, and return without any harm being done to your body," Gede instructed.

"The other worlds?"

"The fire world, the sky and the shadow world. You know about the shadow world from Moon Man. Moonlight is the gateway to the shadow world. The sky is the final resting place of our essence. The fire world is what some call the underworld. What it is supposed to be under, I have no idea. But that is where the Fire Warper lives. And where you must go."

"Why? Why must it be me?"

Gede's disappointment was evident by the sagging of his shoulders. "You are the Soulfinder. The Fire Warper's soul is there."

The heat from the room baked into my body. My shirt clung to my back. "How do I get there?"

"Through the fire."

When I didn't say anything, Gede continued. "Only you can go in and leave without being harmed. The Warpers have been feeding this creature with souls from the Kirakawa ritual. His strength grows."

The flames in the fire pulsed with an urgency. They swelled to man-size. I looked at Gede in alarm, but he appeared serene.

"He waits for you. Go to him," Gede said.

I stood. "No. I'm not ready. I don't even know how to fight him. With magic?"

Gede sneered with disdain. "You have no idea, do you? All the better."

Confused, I glanced between Gede and the fire, expecting the Fire Warper to step from the conflagration.

"He comes for you. If you will not go on your own, then I will provide an incentive." He snapped his fingers. "Moon Man, show your pupil what she needs to do."

Moon Man strode toward the blaze. The flames reached out to him. He extended his hands and the fingers of fire wrapped around his arms.

"No," I yelled. "Get back." I grabbed Moon Man's shoulders and pulled to no avail.

The tendrils of fire advanced and crawled over my hands. A burning excitement tingled and souls writhed in agony within the depths of the blaze. Caught between worlds. Hundreds of them. They dragged us toward them.

My first instinct had been to resist, but their need for freedom, for relief clawed at my body. I needed to help them. Leaning with Moon Man, I pushed forward. The fire burned on my skin, but the pain stayed bearable and a cooling relief lurked on the other side. If I could just get through.

A hand tugged on my shoulders. I tried to shake the person off. "It's okay. They need me."

An arm from outside the fire world circled my neck and

squeezed. My hands still clutched Moon Man's shoulders, trapped in the fire world. "No. Stop. I must…"

The souls ceased their pleading and flinched. "Wait." The word wheezed from my lips as I strained for air. But they hid and cowered. "I've come to help—"

"But who will help you, my little bat?" the Fire Warper asked.

I lost my grip on the Story Weaver. Without the breath to speak, I projected, *Do something!* into Moon Man's mind.

I can not. I have no power here.

The fire world blurred into a blob of orange and yellow. I plucked at the arm around my neck, but my hands weighed a hundred pounds. The blob transformed into black.

I woke. Lying on my back, I squinted and blinked until my eyes adjusted to the darkness. The cold air moved like silk over my hot body. My head throbbed and the skin on my hands and arms sizzled with pain. I drew a thread of magic and used it to soothe my head and heal the blisters.

"How about helping me," Leif said. He held out his arms. They had been scorched.

Leif sat next to me. We were in an alley in the Citadel. Concentrating, I pulled power and healed his burns. My energy sapped, I leaned back against a wall as a wave of dizziness made my head spin.

"What happened?" My voice croaked as pain ringed my neck.

"I had business in the Citadel tonight and thought I'd wait for you by the guest quarters. Out of nowhere Valek appeared." Leif paused, but when I failed to explain, he continued. "He muttered a comment about a Council meeting and asked where you were. By the firelight blazing through the windows, it wasn't hard to figure out. Valek picked the lock and we peeked in time to see you and Moon Man hug the fire."

He wiped soot from his face with a sleeve. "Valek attacked the Sandseeds inside and yelled for me to get you. Gede screamed for me to leave you alone, that you need to learn. Valek's scarier than Gede, so I listened to him, but I couldn't pull you away from the fire. I choked off your air until you passed out. Carried you out here."

I touched my neck. "Did you do the same for Moon Man?"

"He was too far in. I couldn't reach him." Leif's voice cracked with anguish. "Does the Fire Warper have him?"

"I don't know. It was strange. I'm not certain what just happened." My brain felt overcooked and logic stuck to the sides of my skull like a burnt crust. I needed another opinion. "Where's Valek?"

"Disappeared. But he left your cloak and pack. And orders." Leif smiled ruefully. "We are to leave the Citadel as soon as possible."

"Did he say why?"

"No. Just to meet him about two miles south of the Citadel."

I stood, wrapped my cloak around me and shouldered my pack. My legs protested the weight. "Let's get our horses and supplies from the Keep."

Leif shook his head. "He said not to return to the Keep for *any* reason."

I mulled over the implications. Valek had been in the closed Council session where they questioned Marrok. Evidence must have been gleaned, but obviously not in our favor. So much for my promise to visit Gelsi.

★ ★ ★

We fled the Citadel and camped in a farm field west of the main road. With no supplies, and me refusing to let Leif light a fire, a miserable night loomed. We huddled in the dark.

Leif muttered over Valek's reason for sending us here. I cursed my own stupidity; I didn't have to wait for Valek. I could contact Irys myself.

I asked Leif to keep watch.

"Better than freezing to death," he said.

Lying on the hard ground, I projected my thoughts. Irys's tower sparked with life. And instead of finding the Master Magician sleeping, she was bent over a handful of books in her study. Because of the bond we shared, her thoughts were open to me.

Irys, I said in her mind.

Yelena! Thank fate! Are you okay?

I'm fine.

Where are you?

I don't know if I should answer. What happened at the Council session?

A long pause. *Marrok confessed.*

To what? He didn't do anything.

To freeing Ferde and conspiring against Sitia.

Stunned, my mind blanked for a moment. *What…what was his motive?*

Just like Cahil said. Marrok wanted to get Cahil arrested and be in charge of Cahil's men. But…

Go on, I urged.

There's a new wrinkle. Marrok conspired to team up with Ferde and the Daviians to provoke a war with Ixia.

Why is that new? We already know the Daviians want war.

The new part is Marrok named accomplices. Another pause. *You and Leif.*

My body numbed. *Unbelievable. Someone must have forced Marrok to confess. It's all a lie. Did you feel any magic being used? How can the Council swallow that?* The thoughts tumbled one after another.

Unless you have some proof otherwise, the Council has signed an arrest warrant for you and Leif. They wish to capture you so you can be safely executed.

I almost laughed at the words *safely* and *executed* said together. The whole situation was ridiculous.

I'm not supposed to be telling you this either. I could be incarcerated in the Keep's dungeon if the Council finds out. Bain and I are already being watched for disagreeing with them. They've gone quite mad.

That's putting it mildly.

What are you going to do? Irys asked.

There has to be a reason the Council has gone mad. Discovering the reason should be next. Guess I really was going to stick my nose in Sitia's business. Nothing like having a warrant for your execution to get a girl motivated.

But all the clans will be alerted to your arrest warrant, and there's already talk of a reward. There's no safe place for you in Sitia.

I'll figure something out, and I think it's best if I don't contact you again for a while. You're already under suspicion. I don't want to compromise you any further.

Good point. Be very careful, Yelena.

I'll try. But you know me.

Yes, I do. So I'll say it again. Be very careful.

I pulled my awareness back, breaking our connection. Exhaustion dragged at my body and I would have drifted to sleep if Leif hadn't bumped my arm.

"Oh, no you don't, little sister. You were gone a long time. Tell me what's happening."

I filled Leif in on the details and managed to shock him into a rare silence.

"So what do we do now?" Leif finally whispered.

"We wait for Valek."

Valek arrived near dawn. He rode Kiki and had Rusalka in tow. The saddlebags bulged with supplies. Fatigue lined his face.

He peered at me. "You know?"

"Yes."

Valek dismounted. "Good. Saves time. The Citadel and Keep are crawling with soldiers looking for you."

"How did you get the horses out then? A secret spy maneuver?" Leif asked.

"No. A distraction at the Keep's gate, and I bribed the guards at the Citadel's south entrance."

Leif groaned. "Now they'll know where we are."

"I want them to think you went south. But you should get as far away from here as possible."

"And go where?" Leif asked.

"Ixia."

"Why would we do that?" Leif's jaw set into a stubborn line.

Danger flashed in Valek's eyes, but he bit back a sarcastic reply. "Things are happening too fast right now. We need to regroup and plan. We need reinforcements."

Valek made sense. Ixia was the only place where we would be safe.

"We should go now," I said.

"I'll meet you at the Commander's castle." Valek handed me Kiki's reins.

She nudged my arm, but I ignored her. "You're not coming with us?"

"No. I still have a few of my corps inside the Citadel. They need to be informed about what's happening. I'll join you at the castle afterward."

Before he could go, I pulled him aside. We embraced.

"Stay safe," I ordered.

He smiled. "I'm not the one getting pulled into fires, love."

"How did you know I was in trouble?"

"After I heard the Council agree to your execution, I had an odd notion the Council was the least of your worries."

"Thank you for saving me."

"You keep things interesting, love. It would be boring without you."

"Is that all I am to you? An amusement?"

"If only it was that simple."

"I guess I'm no longer retired." I managed a tired smile.

Valek kissed me goodbye. "Take a roundabout route to Ixia. The borders north of the Citadel will probably be watched."

"Yes, sir."

Valek left and the air turned cold. I shivered. Kiki nipped at my sleeve and I opened my mind to her.

I stay with Lavender Lady. Keep warm.

I'm glad you're here, I said. I checked my pockets for a treat. No luck.

Ghost put peppermints in bag.

I laughed. Kiki always knew where to find the mints. I marveled that Valek had taken the time to include treats in his packing. The horses' name for him was perfect, though. He appeared and disappeared as if he were a true ghost.

"Which way?" Leif asked.

Good question. Valek said to go around. The best direction would be to head northwest through the fields of the Stormdance Clan's lands. Then head north toward Ixia, skirting the Featherstone lands surrounding the Citadel. I outlined my plan to Leif.

"Lead on." Leif's resignation tainted his voice. "I've never been to Ixia."

Throughout the day, our passage through the fields hadn't drawn any notice, but we still felt exposed by the daylight. Leif and I decided to do the bulk of our traveling during the night. After a short break for dinner, we rode through the dark hours. Between galloping, walking and resting, the horses made progress toward our goal.

We found an apple orchard as the sun dawned. Kiki sniffed around the neat rows of trees, but they had been picked clean of apples. Nothing grew in this area during the cold season. Deciding to camp within the shelter of the orchard, we found a site hidden from the few surrounding farmsteads.

"Have we crossed into Stormdance lands?" I asked Leif as I pulled Kiki's saddle off her back.

"Not yet. See that ridge?" He pointed to the northwest.

"Yes."

"That's their border. Stormdance lands are mostly shale.

They have a few farms in the eastern portion of their territory, but the west side is just sheets of shale on top of rock. The storms blown in from the Jade Sea have carved fantastic sculptures along their coast, but no one lives there. They only go to the coast to dance." Leif sat down and assembled sticks for a fire.

I plopped next to him. Saddle sore and drained of energy, I delayed grooming the horses. "Why do they dance?"

"It's how they harness the power from the storms. They capture the storm's force in glass orbs. It's a dangerous dance, but the risk is worth it. If they're successful, they protect our land. Instead of being lashed with gale-force winds and soaked with heavy rains, Sitia receives a mild rain. The added benefit is the Stormdancers can use those orbs to fuel their factories."

I gestured for more information.

"Haven't you paid attention in class?"

"My lessons kept getting interrupted by mundane things like chasing after a Soulstealer. I'll try harder in the future to ignore such events."

"Boy, you're grumpy when you're tired." Leif started a small fire and poured water into his cooking pot. "This container was made by the Stormdance Clan. They smelt ore to manufacture different metal items, including Sitian coins. They also produce parchment and make ink from indigo plants they grow on their eastern farms."

I mulled over Leif's lecture. Buying goods at the market, I hadn't stopped to consider who might have made them. In Ixia, every Military District had a particular product or service contributing to the Territory which could be used for barter and trade. It appeared Sitia worked the same way, although the

Stormdancers were a new twist. I wondered if they could harness the power of the blizzards blowing down from the northern ice pack. Life in MD-1, MD-2 and MD-3 turned into a struggle for survival during the cold season.

Would Commander Ambrose consider lifting his ban on magicians to alleviate the storms? He had grown up in MD-3, working in the diamond mines so he was no stranger to the incapacitating snowstorms. Even Valek, who had lived in MD-1, had seen his father's leather business destroyed by the heavy snow.

I thought about the chain of events that had started with the collapse of Valek's father's roof. He didn't have enough money to replace his equipment, feed his family and pay taxes to the King. When Valek's father asked the soldiers, who had come to collect the taxes, for an extension, they had killed three of his four sons. That act sent Valek on a mission of revenge against a King who allowed his soldiers to murder innocent children. Becoming the best assassin in Ixia, Valek eventually joined forces with Ambrose. Together they had defeated the King and gained control of Ixia.

If the roof hadn't collapsed, I wondered if the King would still be in power or if Ambrose would have found another assassin to help him. Would I even be here?

I shied away from those thoughts and focused on our present situation. Leif and I needed to guard our small camp. He manned the first shift while I tried to sleep.

The fire had been doused as soon as our meal was cooked. The smoke drifted on the breeze. Dreams swirled in my mind like sparks rising from a hot fire. The dizzying images slowed for a moment, and each time I glimpsed a horror. Stono's twisted stomach transformed into a necklace snake. Blood rained in the Illiais Jungle. Severed heads floated over the sands of the plains. And fire danced on my skin. The hot prick of each flame both seared and excited me.

I jerked awake. My skin tingled. Afraid to go back to sleep, I sent Leif to bed.

Uneasy sleep came in fits during the next two days. We kept out of sight, used small fires to cook meals before we extinguished the flames, and shivered on the cold, hard ground. On the third day, we crossed into the Krystal Clan's lands and turned north for the Ixian border.

Located directly west of the Featherstone Clan and the Citadel, the rolling terrain of the Krystals' land was dotted with clumps of pine trees. Quarries stretched between the wooded areas. The Krystal Clan mined marble for buildings and exported the high-quality sand needed by the glassmakers in Booruby, leaving behind deep pits gouged into the ground.

We avoided the bustle of activity around the quarries and journeyed through the pine forests. Another day of travel would get us to the Ixian border. Our approach to the boundary needed to be considered with care. Sitian soldiers could be waiting to ambush us. And if we managed to get through, I would need to choose the right words when addressing the Ixian guards. Or risk being arrested by them.

In the end, all the planning, all the time and energy Leif and I had spent finding the perfect spot to cross the border without alerting the Sitians was for naught. Just as we made our way into the hundred-foot-wide swatch of cleared land that was the official neutral zone between Ixia and Sitia, two riders on horseback bolted from the pine forest and into the borderland.

Two things happened that made the riders' presence go from bad timing to a deadly coincidence. Their horses headed straight toward us, and a whole squad of Sitian solders erupted from the woods in armed pursuit.

18

ONLY ONE OPTION REMAINED. We spurred our horses toward the border, hoping the Ixian guards would listen to our story before killing us. The unwelcome riders drew up beside us as we entered Ixia's Snake Forest. They kept pace as we penetrated deep within the forest before stopping.

As expected, the Sitian soldiers hadn't followed us into Ixia.

"Stay where you are," a voice ordered from the woods. "You are surrounded."

I knew the Ixians would be quick to find us. Just not this quick. I had chosen midmorning to cross into Ixia to avoid the changing of the guards. At this time, there was only one team of soldiers on duty.

"Drop your weapons and dismount," the unseen guard said.

Topaz. Garnet, Kiki said. She whinnied a greeting.

Cahil's horse? I pulled my bow and rounded on the riders, ignoring the orders from the guards. Two men sat on Topaz and Moon Man rode Garnet. "What? How?"

With shaking hands, one of the riders on Topaz pulled

back his hood, revealing his pale face before collapsing. Tauno held him tight.

"Marrok! What—" An arrow struck a tree next to me.

"Drop your weapons and dismount. Or the next arrow goes into her heart!" the Ixian shouted.

I tossed my bow to the ground and gestured to the others to follow. Tauno slid off Topaz, lowered Marrok down, then removed his bow and arrows. Moon Man frowned but released his scimitar before getting off Garnet. Leif tossed his machete next to my staff.

"Step away from the weapons and raise your hands."

We did as instructed. I made sure to step closer to Marrok. An arrow had pierced his side.

The ring of Ixian soldiers closed in. I counted four men and two women. Armed with crossbows and swords, they advanced on us.

"Give me one good reason why I shouldn't send you back to the squad of southerners?" asked an Ixian captain.

His uniform was mostly black except for a row of yellow diamond shapes down his sleeves and pant legs. We had crossed into Ixia's MD-7.

"Because it wouldn't be diplomatic to turn away a Sitian delegation," I said.

The captain laughed. "Delegations come with *honor* guards not *fleeing* guards. Want to tell me another one?"

"I'm Liaison Yelena Zaltana. I'm here to speak with the Commander even though my visit is not sanctioned by the Sitian Council."

"Yelena? The ex-food taster who saved the Commander?" the captain asked.

"Yes."

"But you have magic. Why would you want to come back to Ixia? I could kill you now and be considered a hero."

"I see your reputation has preceded you," Leif said, grinning. I hoped his good humor was relief over seeing Moon Man alive and well and not over the death threat to me.

I frowned at him. Leif didn't understand just how precarious a situation we were in. The captain's boast had merit. I was quite sure the rumors about the order for my execution had traveled throughout Ixia, while the fact that the Commander had ripped up those orders when I agreed to be a Liaison probably had not.

Especially since everyone in Sitia and Ixia believed the Commander had stayed behind in Ixia when the Ixian delegation visited Sitia a couple months ago. The Commander had been disguised as Ambassador Signe, and *she* had no authority to cancel an execution order.

Because of the edict that magicians were not allowed in Ixia unless invited, and any Ixians discovered with magical powers were put to death, I had one volatile situation on my hands.

While killing us wouldn't be easy, the captain had what amounted to standing orders to execute us on the spot. If he succeeded, though, he would have to face Valek. I shied away from that line of thought.

Instead, I said, "The Commander has appointed me as a Liaison with the Council. I am a neutral third party so I would *not* come with an honor guard of Sitians. I come with friends. Those guards had been chasing him." I gestured to Marrok's prone form. "I *need* to discuss something important with the Commander right away."

The captain's crossbow wavered. He appeared to be considering my answer. I pulled a thread of magic and skimmed his mind, touching only on his surface thoughts and emotions.

His ambition warred with his intelligence. Tired of guarding the border, the captain wanted a promotion and reassignment. Killing these southern magicians would give him enough recognition to become a major. But what if Yelena told the truth? The Commander wouldn't be happy to have his Liaison killed. Still, bringing a magician close to the Commander would be dangerous. What if Yelena lied and planned to assassinate him?

I nudged his thoughts to trust us and to believe that if he led us to his commanding officer, he would be doing a commendable deed.

"You will accompany me and my squad," the captain said. "We will confiscate your weapons and horses, and you will obey all orders. Any trouble or signs of revolt and you will be incapacitated." He signaled for a few of his soldiers to approach us. "Search them. What about him?"

I looked at Marrok. "Let me attend to his wounds, Captain…"

"Nytik." Again the captain signaled to one of his soldiers. "Lieutenant, search him for weapons."

After the lieutenant secured Marrok's sword, he gave me permission to examine him. The arrow had pierced Marrok's right side, missing his ribs. There wasn't much blood and the arrow hadn't gone deep. Why was Marrok unconscious?

Accessing my magic, I scanned the rest of his body. He had been beaten. Two ribs and his collarbone were broken. A mass of bruises covered his body and his jawbone was cracked.

"Leif, I'm going to need some help." Healing the extensive

damage in Marrok's body would exhaust me and I needed to reserve some energy in case Captain Nytik changed his mind.

"A poultice?" Leif knelt next to me.

"No. His story threads are frayed." Moon Man placed his large hand on Marrok's forehead.

I glared at Moon Man. "Stay away from him. Leif, let's deal with the physical injuries first."

Moon Man retreated. Leif and I drew power from the source. With my brother's help, I assumed his injuries and repaired them. When Marrok woke, Leif gave him water and a sustaining tonic to revive him.

I questioned him on what had happened and why he was here, but Marrok just stared at me with a wild, unconnected look in his eyes. Worried about his mental state, I projected my awareness into his thoughts.

A cacophony of images flooded his mind. Memories and emotions and secret thoughts were exposed, unlocked and left to run amok, as if someone had taken a library full of books and torn and scattered them all around the room. The sheer amount of disarray overwhelmed Marrok. He could no longer bring two thoughts together to form a coherent sentence.

And there in the middle of the mess, gleefully shredding what remained of Marrok's mind, was Roze Featherstone, First Magician.

She turned to me. *There you are. I knew I'd find you in here if I looked hard enough. Now I can discover where you've been hiding.*

She advanced, but I held my position. *I'm not a memory, Roze. You won't be able to extract anything from me.*

I wouldn't be so sure. Too much confidence can be a weakness.

You tried twice before and failed. I'm feeling pretty certain about my prediction. Why did you destroy Marrok's mind?

She glanced around at the chaos. *He's a criminal. And you shouldn't be so shocked. It's no different than when you destroyed the Soulstealer's mind.*

I ignored the jab. *Marrok isn't a criminal and you know it. Did you force him to make a false confession?*

He was honest, unlike you. You've been lying to us and to yourself, thinking you can be a benefit to Sitia. Now the Council knows the danger and I have permission to eliminate the threat you pose.

Again I failed to be impressed with her boast. *How did Marrok and the others find us?*

Roze smiled. *You'll have to figure that out on your own.*

Are you trying to tell me I have a spy in my midst?

Dishonest people tend to find each other, Yelena. It's the price you pay for associating with the criminal element. Frankly, I was surprised the Council hadn't given me permission to neutralize you before. After all, how can they trust the heart mate of the most feared man in Sitia? Think about it. How could you be a Liaison when it's obvious where your loyalties lie? First sign of trouble and you're running for home. I will tell you one thing. You won't be safe in Ixia.

I didn't say anything, but she laughed. *I have found what I needed. Good luck trying to put the pieces of Marrok's mind back together.*

She faded from his consciousness. Standing in the middle of the destruction she had left behind, I knew restoring order would be an impossible task. I returned to my body. There was nothing I could do.

Roze had the Council's support against me. If I hadn't known any better, the web of lies Cahil spun made complete sense. Roze even made sense. If she was as dedicated to Sitia as she claimed, then her efforts to discredit me were valid. Why trust me? I'm a Soulfinder, the one type of magician with an evil history. It would take a major effort and physical evidence to counter Cahil now.

"Moon Man, how did you find us?" I asked.

"Logic. I knew you would go to Ixia and I knew you would not cross the Avibian Plains in order to go around Featherstone lands. So that left west. Tauno found your trail in the Krystal lands."

It was too much of a coincidence. "But Leif saw you disappear into the fire. And what about Marrok and the horses? How did you get them?" He had help and must have been sent by Cahil or Roze. Moon Man worked for them now.

"Gede pulled me from the fire. Marrok had been dumped in the infirmary and left unguarded. The horses came when we needed them."

It still sounded too easy. "Why did Gede insist I go into the fire?"

"You will have to ask him. He is your Story Weaver now. I can not guide you." His tone held sadness.

"Why did you go into the fire, Moon Man?" Leif asked.

"Gede is the only surviving leader of my clan. I follow his orders."

"Even when your life's at stake?"

"Yes. Loyalty to one's clan comes before personal safety."

"Like being bait for a necklace snake?" Leif gazed at me.

"Exactly," Moon Man said.

"Can your man walk?" Captain Nytik asked. He had been standing nearby, watching us with distaste creasing his forehead. "We need to get moving."

Marrok couldn't walk, but he could ride. Kiki and Topaz's heads were together. I connected to Topaz, and asked, *Go home? Miss Peppermint Man?*

No. Stay.

Why? Topaz had been with Cahil for a long time.

Bad smell. Blood.

I turned to the captain. "He'll sit on his horse."

With the lieutenant in the lead, Moon Man, Leif, Tauno and I followed. The captain and his remaining soldiers formed a rear guard. We traveled north through the Snake Forest. On a map, the forest resembled a thin rope of green that undulated along the entire east-west border from the Jade Sea to the Emerald Mountains. After a half day of travel, we arrived at a guard station and barracks.

Another round of explanations had to be endured before we could care for the horses and eat lunch. We sat in the middle of the guard house's dining area surrounded by fifty suspicious soldiers who shot us hard glances between bites of food. Moon Man guided Marrok with a gentle patience. Basic skills like eating and caring for himself would all have to be relearned.

During our cold meal of venison jerky and bread, I explained to my companions about Ixia's uniform system. "Everyone who lives in Ixia must wear a uniform. The standard colors for the shirts, pants and skirts are black and white, but each Military District has its own color. We're in MD-7, which is governed by General Rasmussen, who reports to the Commander. Rasmussen's color is yellow and you'll see a line of yellow diamond shapes somewhere on the uniforms." I gestured to the guards around us. Their uniforms matched the captain's, but the rank insignia on their collars were different.

"A cook's uniform is all white with diamonds printed side by side across the shirt. The color of the diamonds tells you which district the cook works in. Red is the Commander's color."

"Who's that?" Leif pointed to woman heading our way. She wore all black, but had two red diamonds stitched onto her collar. Her blond hair was pulled into a tidy bun. She held two bows in her hands.

"She's an adviser to the Commander." I stood and grinned.

She tossed me my bow. I caught it. The noise in the room ceased the instant it hit my hand.

"Okay, Puker, let's see if you've been practicing," she said with an exultant yet predatory glint in her eyes.

"*Adviser* Maren, didn't your mother teach you it's not nice to call people names?" I hefted my bow. "Especially not *armed* people."

She waved away my comment. "We'll deal with the niceties later. Stuck in this backwoods, I haven't had a decent bow fight in a long time. Come on!" She beckoned me to follow as she threaded her way through the dining room.

"Should we be worried?" Leif asked.

"She taught me all her tricks, but I've learned a few new ones since our last fight. This should be...interesting."

"Play nice," Leif said.

I navigated through the quiet room. It erupted with sound as soon as I left. A mass of soldiers followed me outside.

Maren stretched her muscles before picking up her bow. Tall and lean, she made a formidable opponent. She swung her six-foot staff with deft hands. At a slight disadvantage, my bow measured only five feet. I removed my cloak and rubbed my hands along the smooth wood of my weapon, setting my mind into the zone of concentration I used when fighting. Not quite magical in origin, this mental state kept my mind open to my opponent's intentions.

As soon as I was ready she attacked with two quick strikes toward my ribs. I blocked both, countering with a strike to her arms. The fight began in earnest.

The rhythmic crack of our weapons filled the air. I ducked a temple strike and thrust the end of my bow staff toward her stomach. She stepped back and attempted to trip me with her bow. I jumped and did a front kick in midair, hitting her shoulder. Maren retreated a few steps before coming at me with a series of jabs.

"Did you get tired of losing to Janco all the time and request a transfer?" I asked, knocking her bow aside and executing a flurry of temple strikes. Maren had been a captain in the Commander's Special Forces, along with my friends Ari and Janco.

"I was promoted," she said. She met my assault and feinted to the right.

Sensing her intentions, I ignored the feint and stopped the blow to my head just in time. "Promoted to adviser? Sounds shady. Bribe anyone I know?"

"Once I beat Valek, I could choose any job in Ixia."

I froze for a moment in surprise and she hit my upper arm, knocking me over. I rolled, avoiding her jabs, but she pressed her advantage. Two moves later, she sat on my chest and pressed her bow to my neck. The crowd of soldiers cheered.

"Concede?"

"Yes."

She grinned and pulled me to my feet. "Rematch?"

"Give me a minute." I brushed the dirt from my clothes.

"What's with the skirt?"

"It's not a skirt. See?" Pulling the fabric apart, I revealed the pants.

She snorted with amusement. "We need to get you back into uniform, Yelena."

Her use of my proper name meant that I had at least impressed her with my fighting skills. Which reminded me of her comment that had thrown me off guard. "What's all this about *you* beating Valek? You're adequate with a bow, but, come on, Valek?"

Valek had issued a challenge to everyone in Ixia. Beat him in a fight with the weapon of your choice and win the right to become his second in command. Many soldiers had tried and failed to win the right.

"Adequate?" She laughed. "I guess *when* I beat you again, you'll up it to decent."

"That's *if* you beat me, and you haven't answered my question."

"I had help. Happy now? Valek never said we had to beat him one on one. Three of us got together and we won the right to pick any position in Ixia. I chose to become an adviser for the Commander. I'm in MD-7 on a temporary assignment to deal with some—" she glanced at the soldiers "—issues."

Three against one was still good odds for Valek. I wondered who the other two were, and the answer came to me. "Please don't tell me Ari and Janco were your partners."

Her chagrined expression confirmed my guess.

"Janco was insufferably smug before. There'll be no living with him," I said.

"Valek's challenge has been modified. Since Janco and Ari have been promoted to Valek's seconds, if other soldiers want to claim the second positions they must beat Ari and Janco, but no more than six can attack at one time. Valek's seconds should be able to handle three each. If a soldier wishes to fight Valek alone, he must beat one of us to have the chance."

"Having Janco in charge when Valek's away is a scary state of affairs."

"Not as scary as when you're begging for mercy." Maren swung her bow.

I blocked and countered. Soon we were engaged in another brisk fight. But this time I stayed focused. I swept her feet out from under her and stepped on her bow before she could roll away. I won the match and received a few cheers from my brother, who had joined the audience. Moon Man and the others stood apart. He watched me with no expression on his face.

"Tie breaker?" Maren didn't wait for an answer. Round three began.

We fought until we reached an impasse.

Leif's voice interrupted us before we started another match. "As much as I enjoy watching my sister get beaten, we really need to talk to the Commander. You're wasting time."

Maren studied Leif with a dubious expression. "I don't see a family resemblance."

I introduced my brother to Maren. "Although I hate to admit it, Leif's right. We need to go."

Maren shook her head. "General Rasmussen wants to talk with you first. These soldiers have orders to keep you here until he gives you permission to leave."

"But I've explained—"

"Everything but exactly what you need to discuss with the Commander."

"That's classified."

"That's what I was afraid of." Maren leaned on her bow. "The general has become…cautious in his advancing years. *He* won't let you leave unless you tell him the reason you came to Ixia."

From her choice of words, I could tell there was more to the story. She worked for the Commander but was helping the general, and probably reporting every bit of information to Valek.

"We'll talk to the general then," I agreed.

"Great. I'll schedule an audience with him tomorrow."

"Tomorrow? We have pressing business."

"I'm sorry. The general retires early. He'll see no one tonight."

Leif opened his mouth to protest. I touched his arm, stopping him. Maren and I had dueled the afternoon away, and I suspected she had a good reason for it.

"All right. We'll wait until tomorrow. How long will it take us to get to the manor? Perhaps it would be best to leave tonight?"

"No. It would be *best* to leave in the morning. It's a half-day's ride." Maren led us to a brick cottage with a stable nearby. "You can stay in our guest quarters. This location is a popular spot for travelers from MD-6 to stop."

The castle complex was located in the southern end of MD-6. Two-and-a-half days' ride directly north of Sitia's Citadel. I found it interesting the two centers of political power remained physically close while their governing styles were worlds apart.

We entered the cottage. Although the furnishings in the

main room were sparse, it looked comfortable enough. Guards stationed themselves outside, but one lieutenant followed us in.

"Beds! They have beds with feather mattresses," Leif called from a bedroom.

"There is wood in the back, and you can dine with the soldiers for your evening meal. I'll let the general know when you're arriving." Maren left with the Lieutenant close on her heels, but two guards remained positioned by the front door.

A quick peek out the side and back windows revealed the presence of more guards. We were surrounded. I thought about Maren's comments. A few of the things she said didn't add up. I wondered what she planned to do. All I knew were my plans, and they didn't include visiting the general.

I joined my traveling companions in the bedroom. Moon Man sat next to Marrok, who lay on his back, staring at the ceiling. Tauno perched on the edge of a chair.

Leif had stretched out across one of the beds. A sigh of contentment escaped his lips. "I haven't slept in a bed since… since…I can't even remember!"

"Don't get too comfortable," I said.

He groaned. "Now what?"

I put a finger over my lips then pointed to my forehead. *Too many ears around*, I said in his mind.

What's going on? he asked.

We are not going to waste time with the general, Moon Man said.

I scowled at him in surprise, forgetting that he could link his mind to ours.

Since you have chosen Gede as your guide, I had to channel through Leif.

I ignored Leif's confusion. *Unchannel then. This is a private conversation.*

Moon Man remained quiet for a while. *I will withdraw.*

Care to tell me what that was about? Leif asked.

I filled him in on my conversation with Roze. *Moon Man's a spy.*

No way. You can't believe that.

Are you saying Roze is lying?

No. I'm saying maybe you're overreacting. Moon Man admitted Gede is his boss. Their clan was decimated by the Vermin so Gede and Roze want the same thing. Gede probably sent Moon Man to keep an eye on you.

And that's different than spying how?

He's probably here to protect you. To keep you safe until your name can be cleared.

It would be nice just to ask him, but I'm sure he has a vague non-answer already prepared.

That's harsh, Yelena. He has witnessed the massacre of his clan. Although, I do wish for the old Moon Man back, Leif said. *I'll take his teasing, cryptic advice and mysterious arrivals over his somber demeanor any day.*

My brother put another pillow under his head. *Looks like we'll be in Ixia for a while. Leif Liana Ixia has a nice ring to it. If they don't execute me for being a magician, perhaps I can find a job at an Ixian apothecary. Do they have uniforms for an apothecarist?*

We're going back to Sitia.

To certain death? No thank you. Perhaps the Commander will need one of my tisanes?

We need to talk to the Commander and rendezvous with Valek. I hoped.

Surrounded by guards. Remember?

That's right. We're outnumbered. It's a shame we don't have magic to help us. A mage could put the guards to sleep. Or better yet we could use Curare. Too bad I don't have any blowpipes in my backpack.

Sarcasm is an ugly trait, little sister. You should avoid it.

And you give up too easy. And trust too easy, but I wouldn't say it to him.

I blame the feather mattress. It has sucked all my motivation. If there is a comfortable bed in my apartment above my apothecary shop, I will be quite content living in Ixia.

Leif. I warned.

All right. All right. I'll make you a few blowpipes just in case we can't put everyone to sleep. He grumbled to himself as he rolled out of bed and went over to his pack.

I debated what I should tell Tauno and Moon Man. As long as we didn't have a fire, I could warn them about my plans. And I wanted them with me so I could keep an eye on them.

"We should go to bed early tonight," I said to them. "To *rest* for *tomorrow*."

They appeared to understand my hint. Once the Ixian soldiers had gone to bed, we would make our escape.

I planned to be at the Commander's castle before the MD-7 guards realized we had gone. Approaching the main gate of the castle complex without an Ixian guide would create instant suspicion, but that was a problem I would deal with when it arose.

After having dinner with the soldiers, I eyed our new set of guards with care, trying to size them up. I knew Tauno and Moon Man wouldn't pass for Ixian, so either Leif or I would have to wear a uniform and pose as a soldier until we reached the Commander. Ideally, I should disguise myself, but at five feet four inches tall, I doubted I would find a uniform that fit.

Not bothering to build a fire, we retired early. I slept for a few hours. The luxury of being in an actual bed made it difficult to rouse. But I forced myself to get up and woke the others, gesturing for quiet.

Leif didn't have the skills to put our guards to sleep, but he could complement my energy. I held his hand and projected my awareness to the circle of soldiers. Three men and one woman stood watch. Reaching farther, I connected to the horses in the stable.

Ready? I asked Kiki.

Yes.

The two stable lads slept on bales of hay, content to have horses in their stables. To them the musky smell of horse, manure and straw equaled a feather bed.

I swept the barracks with my mind, seeking trouble. At two hours past midnight, the garrison was calm. Since I couldn't put the entire garrison into a deep sleep, I hoped we were far enough away not to wake them. I returned to the sleeping lads and sent them into a heavy slumber.

The guards who ringed our quarters proved resistant to my mental suggestion. Their Ixian training fought my magic and I feared I would have to resort to using the Curare. Before I broke the connection, one of the guards jerked in surprise as a sharp point jabbed his neck. His vision spun as the drug entered his blood. I pulled away before the man passed out.

Leif released my hand.

"Time to go," I said, moving fast. We had help and my heart soared. One person always knew when I needed him. I threw open the door, expecting Valek, but found Maren instead. She dragged one of the guards into the guest quarters, and was soon followed by three others who each carried in a prone form, dumping them onto the floor.

Her companions wore MD-7 uniforms.

"Guess we had the same idea. My men will pose as your guards while we head toward the castle," she explained.

"Will they be out long?" I poked one of the men on the floor with the toe of my boot.

"A good six hours. I used Valek's sleeping potion on them." She smiled with a mischievous glint in her gray eyes.

"*Adviser* Maren, you aren't doing a little moonlighting with Valek's corps now, are you?" I tsked with mock concern. "How did you know when to strike?"

Maren gave me an odd look. "When the horses left the stable, I thought you might be ready to go."

"Are you coming with us? Can you ride?"

"Yes. I have a horse nearby. I need to return to the general's manor house before you're discovered missing. I'll take you to MD-6's border and introduce you to the soldiers at the way station there. They will take you to the Commander's castle. Your weapons are outside. Let's go."

Leif, Moon Man, Tauno and I carried our saddles until we were far enough away to risk the noise. Moon Man and Marrok rode on Topaz. Marrok still couldn't speak, but he mounted when Moon Man asked him to.

Maren proved to be an adept rider and we covered the distance to MD-6 in record time. Before she alerted the way-station guards, I asked her, "What will happen when General Rasmussen finds out we escaped?"

"Once you're with the Commander, he can't admit to trying to delay you, because he'll have to answer why. He'll probably have his people keep the whole incident quiet. Valek will most likely let him believe he got away with it. Until Valek needs something from him." Another predatory grin spread on her face.

Our transfer to MD-6 and into the hands of General Hazel's soldiers proceeded with quick efficiency. The new guide wore a captain's uniform with blue diamonds instead of Captain Nytik's yellow.

In fact, the whole trip to the Commander's castle went smoothly. Admitted into his complex without any trouble, I should have savored those few quiet hours. Because after we met with Commander Ambrose, nothing went right.

19

AFTER OUR ARRIVAL at the castle complex, we waited in the outer courtyard. We received many curious glances from the castle's denizens, and I knew the servants would soon be gossiping and laying bets about who we were and why we had come. They probably didn't recognize me without my food taster's uniform on.

Grooms from the stable appeared to take the horses. I wanted to stay with Kiki, but we were instructed to enter the castle to await a meeting with the Commander.

My companions exclaimed over the odd-shaped structure. With its multiple levels of unusual geometric shapes, the castle resembled a child's toy. Balanced on the rectangular base, the other floors of the castle were a combination of squares, triangles and even cylinders built on top of one another in a haphazard fashion. On some levels all three shapes could be found. The windows of the building also reflected the architect's fondness for geometry, including octagons and ovals.

It had been a year since I last saw the castle. Once part of my everyday routine, I had grown used to its strange style. Now, the sight of the structure jolted me and unease fluttered through my body.

The four towers at the corners gave the viewer some sense of symmetry. They rose a few stories higher than the main building and colored glass decorated their windows. I paused. The Magician's Keep also had four towers in the corners and I wondered about the similarity.

A servant led us to an austere waiting room with minimal comforts. Served refreshments, I automatically tested the drink for poisons, surprising Leif when I gargled the juice. He had been staring at the blank walls, probably wondering where all the legendary paintings and gilded mirrors had gone to. I assumed the Commander had destroyed all the treasures from the King's era, but, remembering a comment Cahil had made to me about the amount of money needed to support Ixia, I wondered if Commander Ambrose had traded them for services instead.

"Did you live here?" Leif asked.

I nodded. "For two years." One of them in the dungeon. Not many people in Sitia knew about Reyad. I preferred to keep the details of that time to myself. However, most Ixians were aware I killed Reyad.

"Where did you stay?"

"I had a room in Valek's suite."

Leif shot me an incredulous look. "Boy, you worked fast."

"And you assume too much." One day I would tell Leif and my parents about my ordeal, but not today.

Leif grew thoughtful. Tauno napped in one of the wooden chairs. I marveled at how the Sandseed could wedge himself into a small space and still look comfortable. During our time together, he had adapted to being within walls.

Moon Man, on the other hand, fidgeted in his chair. I couldn't determine if his discomfort grew from being in a confined space or from my hostility. He claimed I had a new Story Weaver. It was an easy way for him to avoid telling me the truth.

Knowing we were headed toward Ixia, Cahil must have planned Marrok's escape. The Sitian guards who chased them were probably part of the ruse, too.

I longed to pace the room. The wait stretched as long as a necklace snake. There was nothing to avert me from my list of worries. Valek remained near the top. Where was he? By this time, he should be back in Ixia. Thoughts circled in my mind. To distract myself, I sat in one of the hard chairs near the only window. Outside, a portion of the barracks and practice yard where the Commander's soldiers lived and trained was visible, reminding me of Ari and Janco, my soldier friends who, according to Maren, were now Valek's seconds in command.

I stood, desiring action. Perhaps I should just go to the Commander's office. I knew how to get there, and I hated this unsettled sensation sloshing in the pit of my stomach. Why was I so on edge?

Understanding crashed through me and I needed to sit down again. Inside these walls I had always been a prisoner. Either by the bars of the dungeon or by the belief I had ingested a poison called Butterfly's Dust, knowing I couldn't get far without the daily antidote keeping me alive. And all the logic in the world couldn't convince my body I was free.

Finally, an adviser arrived to lead us though the main corridors of the castle. Leif gasped in surprise when we entered the main hall. Greeted by the sight of the silk and gold tapestries hanging in tatters, I sympathized with my brother's reaction. Black paint stained the once famous quilts that had symbolized each province during the King's era. They now represented the takeover. The old provinces had been torn apart and borders redrawn into eight neat Military Districts.

Commander Ambrose's disdain for opulence, excess and greed was evident in every part of the stone building. Stripped of the trappings of royalty, the castle had been robbed of its soul, and reassigned as a basic utilitarian structure.

The transformation of the throne room was another example of his disregard. Instead of lavish decorations and thick carpets, the room buzzed with the activity of numerous advisers and military officers from every Military District in Ixia, with no sign of a dais or throne in sight. With desks wedged in tight together, getting the five of us through the room turned into an exercise in agility as we threaded our way toward the back.

The Commander's office matched the rest of the castle. Stark, neat and organized, the room lacked personality but reflected its occupant perfectly.

Wearing a tailored black uniform with real diamonds glittering from his collar, Commander Ambrose stood when we entered. I studied his clean-shaven face as I introduced him to my companions, detecting only a faint resemblance to Ambassador Signe. As if they were truly cousins instead of the same person.

The power of his gaze, though, remained the same. My heart flipped in my chest when he focused his gold-colored eyes on me.

"This is an unexpected visit, Liaison Yelena. I trust you have a good reason for bypassing standard protocol," he said, raising a single slender eyebrow.

"An excellent reason, sir. I believe Sitia will try to mount an offensive against you."

The Commander glanced at my companions as he considered my words. More gray had infiltrated his black hair, which had been cropped so short it looked as if Kiki had grazed on it.

Walking to his office's door, the Commander called to one of his men.

"Adviser Reydon, please escort our guests to the dining hall for lunch and then to the guest suite." He turned to the others. "The Liaison will dine with me and meet up with you later."

Leif looked to me for guidance. I opened my mind to him. *Do you want us to stay?* he asked.

I don't think you have a choice.

He isn't my Commander. I don't have to listen to him.

A childish, stubborn remark. Perhaps Leif felt left out. *Be a good guest and do as he says. I'll let you know what happens.*

You sure you don't need backup? This guy creeps me out.

Leif, I warned.

He left the office with obvious reluctance, shooting me an annoyed frown before following the adviser.

When the room emptied, the Commander gestured for me to sit in the chair in front of his desk. Unnerved, I perched on the edge.

He served me a cup of tea before settling behind his desk. I sipped the drink with care, testing for poisons. In command of a powerful military and with eight ambitious generals to oversee, the Commander needed a food taster on his staff.

"Why have you come?" he asked.

"I told you. Sitia plans—"

He stopped me with a dismissive wave. "You know that's old news. Why are you *really* here?"

"To ask you to delay a first strike."

"Why?"

I paused, gathering my thoughts. Only logic would persuade the Commander. "The Sitian Council has had a dramatic change of opinion from wanting to trade and communicate with you to being terrified of you."

"Yes. They're very unstable."

"But not *that* unstable. They're being influenced."

"With magic?" The Commander said the word as if it pained him.

General Brazell and Mogkan—my kidnappers—had used magic and Theobroma on him to gain control of his mind despite his ban on magicians. Though his firm censure softened, the Commander still viewed magicians as untrustworthy. Consenting to let me act as Liaison for Ixia had been his first and only concession.

Valek had theorized the Commander feared magicians, but I believed it had more to do with what the Commander referred to as his mutation. Born with a female body, he believed his soul was a man's and he worried a magician would expose him. But from my interaction with him when he had been disguised as the female Ambassador Signe, I had sensed the presence of two souls within his body.

Standing in front of him, I suppressed the desire to project into his mind, avoiding even a surface sweep. It would be a serious breach of protocol. Besides, it felt wrong.

"Magic could be a factor, but there could be another reason or even a person influencing them. At this point I don't know, but I want to find out. If you kill them all, you might not solve the problem and those who replace them will be worse," I said.

"Sounds rather vague. Perhaps you have more information on this?" The Commander flourished a scroll then handed it to me.

I unrolled the parchment. Each word I read increased my concern and outrage.

"And if you notice——" he leaned over and tapped the bottom "——it's signed by all the Councilors, but it's lacking two Master Magicians' signatures. Curious."

Curious wouldn't be the word I would use. *Disastrous* sounded more fitting. I worried about Irys and Bain. If the Council tried to coerce their signatures, what had happened to them by refusing? I focused on the paper in my hand. Fretting wouldn't help Irys and Bain.

In short, the letter warned the Commander about my renegade status and suggested my treasonous companions and I be killed on sight. Probably the reason Roze had been confident I wouldn't be safe in Ixia.

"They seek to undermine your credibility all the while planning to attack me. Do they think I'm a simpleton?" He relaxed back in his chair and sighed. "Explain to me exactly what's going on."

"If I knew exactly, then I wouldn't have sounded so vague." My turn to sigh. I wiped a hand over my face, thinking how best to tell the Commander about Cahil. Did I mention the Fire Warper or not? I had no idea what role he played in all this. Exactly the problem.

So I explained about Ferde's escape with Cahil's help and how Cahil had turned it all around to implicate Marrok, Leif and me.

"Sounds like assassinating the Council would be a good deed for Sitia," the Commander said.

"That would give Cahil and his cohorts evidence they were right to suspect you. Sitia would rally behind them in support. Valek agrees with me. He hasn't targeted the Council yet. He's on his way here."

If the Commander was surprised, he didn't show it. "So you already delayed my preemptive strike. Yet you have no proof."

"None. That's why I wanted you to wait before launching another attack. We need more information. Valek and I—"

The office door opened. Star came into the room, carrying a tray of food. The Commander's food taster froze in shock when she recognized me. My own pulse skipped when I saw my old uniform being worn by her. And not just any woman, but the former Captain Star, who had been the leader of a successful black market and racketeering ring before Valek uncovered her operation.

Star stared daggers at me. Her goon's unsuccessful attempt on my life had led to her capture. Already warned about Valek's setup, Star could have disappeared into her own underground network. Instead, she had let petty vengeance rule her and now she tasted food for the Commander.

"At least you survived the training," I said to her.

She looked away. The long red curls of her hair had been tied into a sloppy knot, and her prominent nose led the way as she walked. Putting the tray onto the Commander's desk, she performed a fast taste and left. Even though two lunches had been set on the tray, she tested only the one.

I eyed my food. Star seemed surprised at my presence, but that could have been an act. She could still be nursing her desire for revenge. The Commander handed me a plate. Not to appear rude, I took a tentative bite of the meat pie, chewing slowly and rolling the food around my tongue. The beef was flavored with rosemary and ginger and lacked poisons. At least, I couldn't taste the poisons I remembered. I lost my appetite when I remembered Moon Man's comment about learning by doing and how easy it was to forget dictated information.

We talked about minor things while eating. When I complimented his new chef on the lemon-wedge dessert, he told me Sammy now held the position.

"Rand's fetch boy?" I asked. He was thirteen years old.

"He worked with Rand for four years and it became evident only he knew all the ingredients in Rand's secret recipes."

"But he's so young." The kitchen during meal times had been a cacophony of ordered chaos guided by Rand's firm hand.

"I gave him a week to prove he could do it. He's still there."

I had forgotten age didn't matter to the Commander. He could have forced Sammy to divulge the recipes, but he respected ability over experience or gender. My young friend, Fisk the beggar boy turned entrepreneur, would have flourished in Ixia.

When we finished lunch, the Commander moved the tray aside and repositioned his snow cat statue. Glints of silver sparked from the black stone. The single piece of decoration in the room, the cat was one of Valek's carvings. Killing a snow cat was considered impossible. The citizens of Ixia avoided the

lethal creatures living on the northern ice pack. The cat's pre-
ternatural ability to escape death made it feared.

Commander Ambrose was the only person to successfully
hunt and kill one, and in doing so, he proved to himself that
despite his mutation he could infiltrate a man's world just as
he had lived among the snow cat's world. He believed his
female body had just been a disguise for his soul. Only the
Commander and I knew about his hunt and dual personalities.
He had sworn me to secrecy when I had rescued him from
Mogkan's mind control.

"Before Star came in with lunch you mentioned getting
more information about the Sitian Council. Now that you're
a wanted criminal, how do you plan to achieve that?" the
Commander asked.

"I had hoped to infiltrate the Citadel and talk to one of the
Councilors. But I fear the Master Magician's magic would
discover me, so now I want to borrow Valek and a few of his
men. They could assist us in contacting the Councilor."

"Which one?"

"Bavol Cacao Zaltana, my clan's Councilman. He has been
my strongest supporter and if you see by his signature…" I
picked the Sitian letter up and pointed to his name. "He didn't
include his family name, Cacao, in his signature, so it's not an
official inscription. I believe it's a message to me that he can
be approached."

The Commander stared across the room as if considering
my words. After a while, he brought his attention back to me.
"You want me to risk my chief of security to help you gain
information. All the while I'm to do nothing and hope the
Sitians don't attack before you discover what's going on?"

"Yes." Although, the way the Commander said it made the situation sound terrible. There was no sense sugarcoating it. And the last thing I wanted was to put Valek or anyone else at risk. But it had to be done.

The Commander rested his chin on his folded hands. "The information isn't worth the risk. I could wait to see what develops with the Council and then decide how to handle it."

"But—"

A warning flashed in his eyes. "Yelena, why would you care what happens to the Council? They have turned their backs on you. You can't go back to Sitia. You would provide the most help here with me as my adviser."

An unexpected offer. I considered. "What about my companions?"

"Magicians?" A small crease of distaste pinched his forehead.

"Two."

"They could be part of your staff if you want. But they can *not* use their magic against any Ixians without *my* permission."

"What about *my* magic? Would you place the same restrictions on me?"

The Commander's gaze didn't waver. "No. I trust you."

I froze for a moment in shock. His trust was an honor, and, considering the recent reaction from the Sitian Council about me, the temptation to become his adviser warred with my emotions. It would probably be easier to stay and help defeat Cahil from this side of the border.

"Don't answer right away. Talk to your companions. I should have news from Valek soon. We'll meet again then. In the meantime, do you need anything?"

I thought about our dwindling supplies. If we left, we would need more provisions. "Could you exchange Sitian coins for Ixian?" I rummaged in my pack, placing various loose objects on his desk to get them out of my way.

"Give them to Adviser Watts. You remember my accountant?"

"Yes." The covering on Opal's bat had come undone and was all over the bottom of my pack. I removed the glass animal and freed it from the wrapping. The Commander gasped.

His focus was riveted on the statue in my hand; his fingers poised as if to snatch the bat.

"May I see?" he asked.

"Sure."

With a snap of motion, he plucked the statue from my palm. He spun the bat, examining it from every possible angle. "Who made this?"

"My friend, Opal. She's a glass artist in Sitia."

"It glows like there is molten fire on the inside. How did she make it?"

Trying to comprehend his words, I stared. He saw the inner glow. Impossible. Only magicians could see the light.

The Commander had magical powers.

20

THE GLASS BAT GLOWED for the Commander. I had theorized only magicians could see the inner light. But I could be wrong. Maybe I hadn't tested the bat on enough people. If the Commander had magical power, his magic would have raged uncontrolled and flamed out by now, killing him. The Masters in Sitia would have felt him long ago. Irys would have sensed it when she stood next to him.

Shaking those ridiculous thoughts out of my mind, I answered the Commander's questions about glassmaking.

"But what causes it to glow?"

I knew if I said *magic*, he would drop it as if burned. Instead, I told him the internal workings were a family secret.

He passed the glass bat to me. "Extraordinary. Next time you see your friend, please ask her to make one for me."

I found the coins I had been searching for, and repacked my bag. Only when I had slung my pack onto my shoulders did I realize I forgot to rewrap the bat.

The Commander picked up the coins, walked to his office

door and opened it. Summoning Adviser Watts, he asked him to exchange my money and to show me to the guest area.

Dismissed, I followed Watts into the throne room, holding the bat in my hand. The adviser noticed the creature when handing me the Ixian coins.

"Sitian art?" he asked.

I nodded.

"Not a bad likeness, but rather dull. I thought the Sitians had more imagination than that."

I mulled over the Commander and Adviser Watts's comments as I followed Watts through the castle. Still unable to bend my mind around the Commander's ability to see the glow, I had to postpone further ruminations when I entered the guest suite.

Leif peppered me with a million questions the moment I stepped through the door. The guest quarters were rather lavish by Ixian standards. The main room contained a comfortable sofa and soft chairs as well as a number of desks and tables. A faint odor of disinfectant scented the air. Four bedrooms branched off from the living area, two on each side. Sunlight streamed in through the circle of windows in the back wall, warming the empty room.

I stopped Leif's questions with a look. "Where are the others?"

He pointed to the second door on the right. "They're all resting. Moon Man and Marrok are in the big room next to Tauno's."

Double doors marked the entrance to Moon Man's room.

"Which one is mine?"

"Second door on the left, next to me."

I went into my room. Leif trailed along like a lost puppy. A simple layout of a bed, armoire, desk and night table all made of oak decorated the small interior. The bedding looked fresh and inviting. I stroked the soft quilt. The air smelled of pine. The lack of dust made me remember Valek's housekeeper, Margg. She had plagued my existence when I first became the food taster, refusing to clean my room and writing nasty messages in the dust. I hoped I wouldn't run into her during this trip.

Leif's questions began again, and I filled him in on what had happened in the Commander's office, neglecting to mention his ability to see the bat's glow. I wasn't convinced that the Commander had magic, and certainly wouldn't try to persuade Leif or anyone else.

"Black and red really aren't my colors. Which Military District has green? Maybe I can open my shop there," Leif said.

Leif's joke wasn't as funny now. "MD-5 is green and black. General Brazell used to govern the district, but now he's in the Commander's dungeon." I wonder who was promoted.

"What are we going to do next?"

"I don't know."

Leif pretended to be shocked. "But you're our fearless leader. You have it all planned out. Right?"

I shrugged. "I'm going to take a long hot bath. How's that?"

"Sounds good. Can I come?"

"As long as you promise not to spend all day in there." I gathered some clean clothes.

"Why would I?"

"You thought the feather mattress was a luxury. Wait until you see the Commander's baths."

* * *

The hot water soaked my aches away.

Leif joined me in the corridor with a contented smile on his face. "I won't have any trouble adjusting to life in Ixia. Those pools and the overhead duct, pouring water…amazing. Does every town have a similar bathhouse?"

"No. Only the Commander's castle has such luxury. It's a holdover from the King's regime. The Commander usually disdains the extravagance, yet it remains."

During my soak, I had thought long and hard about our situation and the Commander's offer. The temptation to stay tried to overpower my logic, but I knew we needed to return to Sitia. The Sandseed clan had already been destroyed by the Vermin, and Cahil and the Fire Warper remained a problem.

How I would deal with them continued to be a mystery. Not being able to trust Moon Man, Tauno or Marrok, left Valek, Leif and me against the Daviians, the Fire Warper, Cahil and his army.

And what would happen if I revealed Cahil's involvement with the Vermin? The Council trusted him. I would need to convince them of his deceit. I would need hard evidence to gain their trust. Evidence I lacked.

In fact, the more I thought about the whole situation, the less confident I felt about my ability to find a solution.

When Leif and I returned to the guest suite, Moon Man and Tauno waited for us in the living room.

"How's Marrok?" I asked Moon Man.

"Better."

"Can he talk?"

"Not yet."

"Soon?"

"Perhaps."

I stared at him. He answered in typical Story Weaver fashion. Refraining from shaking information out of him, I asked, "Have you learned anything while working with Marrok?"

"I have seen bits and pieces. Marrok's feelings of betrayal are making it difficult for me to get through to him. He does not trust me." Moon Man's eyes met mine and I could see his unspoken words.

"Trust has to go both ways."

"It is not a lack of trust which causes me to keep my silence. It is a lack of acceptance on your part."

"And you're afraid of what you might discover once you accept your role in all this, aren't you?" Leif asked me.

A knock at the door saved me from having to reply to Leif's question. One of the housekeeping maids handed me a message from the Commander. We were invited to dine with him in his war room.

"You don't have an answer for me. Do you have an answer for the Commander? Are you going to stay and be his adviser?" Leif asked when the maid left.

"Actually Leif, I don't have any answers. I've no idea what I'm doing or going to do." I went into my room and shut the door.

The Commander's war room was located in one of the four towers of the castle. With long stained-glass windows reflecting the lantern light, the circular chamber reminded me of the inside of a kaleidoscope.

Our conversation followed mundane topics while we ate

spiced chicken and vegetable soup. Leif wolfed his food with obvious relish, but I took my time, sampling all the dishes with care. A few guards stood near the Commander. Star hovered close by, ready to taste the Commander's food whenever a new course was served. Moon Man and Tauno remained quiet during dinner.

We discussed the new general in MD-5. Colonel Ute from MD-3 had been promoted and transferred. The Commander thought it best an officer from outside the district be in charge. In other words, a loyal person who had not been tainted by General Brazell's attempt to become the new leader of Ixia.

When the subject turned to General Kitvivan's worry over the upcoming blizzard season, I told the Commander about the Stormdance Clan and how they handled the storms from the sea.

"Magicians could harness the power of the blizzard," I said, "saving the people in MD-1 from the killing winds. Then you could use the power for General Dinno's sawmills in MD-8." Dinno used the wind to fuel his mills, and calm days hurt production.

"No. The matter of magicians and magic in Ixia will *not* be discussed," the Commander said.

His stern tone had once intimidated me, but not this time. "You want me to be your adviser, yet you won't consider using magic for the good of your people. I'm a magician. How can I be an effective adviser to you?"

"You can advise me on how to counter the magicians in Sitia. I'm not interested in what magic can do for Ixia." He made a cutting motion with his hand. End of discussion.

I wouldn't let the subject drop. "What happens when one

of your generals becomes ill or injured and I can save their life with my magic?"

"You don't. If they die, I'll promote another colonel."

I considered his answer with mixed feelings. I knew his firm style of governing was inflexible. The Code of Behavior's strict list of proper Ixian conduct left no room for debate. However, I hoped once he saw the benefits of magic to his people, he might relax his views.

As if reading my mind, the Commander said, "Magic corrupts. I've seen it before with the King's magicians. They start out wanting to help and performing great deeds, but soon the power consumes them and they hunger for more despite the cost. Consider what has occurred to Moon Man's clan. Frankly, I'm surprised something like that hasn't happened sooner."

"My clan will repopulate," Moon Man said. "I have no doubt."

"And I have no doubt if these Vermin of Sitia are conquered, it's only a matter of time before another magician wishes to take over the current government. The talent to control another's mind and body is intoxicating and addicting. Better to ban magic and eliminate magicians altogether."

I wondered if the Commander's views would change if he knew he might possess the skill to access magic. My thoughts returned to Opal's bat and his ability to see the glow, mulling over the implications.

"Better to kill people the old-fashioned way," Leif said, his voice indignant. "You're saying that taking over a government with poisons, knives and swords is *much* better than using magic. Frankly, I see no difference."

"Magic forces a person to do things they don't want to. It controls their will." The Commander leaned forward; his eyes lit with an intense passion.

Leif quailed under the Commander's scrutiny, but he continued with his debate. "And your Code of Behavior doesn't force people to do things they don't want? Everyone in Ixia *wants* to wear uniforms? They *want* to obtain permission to marry or move to another district?"

"Small inconveniences to live in an area where there is no hunger and no corruption. To know exactly where your place is in society and what is expected from you. Being rewarded for your abilities and efforts instead of getting privileges because of who you were born to or what gender you are."

"But the reward for having magical abilities is death," Leif said. "I'm sure the families of those potential magicians don't feel the loss of their loved one as inconvenient. Why not send them to Sitia instead?"

"Send them so they could be used against me?" The Commander's voice reflected his incredulity. "That would be poor military strategy."

Leif remained quiet.

"No government is perfect," the Commander said, relaxing back into his chair. "The loss of a few personal freedoms has been embraced by most of Ixia, especially those who suffered under the King's corruption. However, I know the younger generation is feeling restless and I will have to address that issue fairly soon." He stared at Leif as if contemplating the future. "Yelena, I see your intelligence is a family trait. I hope you both decide to stay."

A determined line formed along my brother's jaw. Leif

could be stubborn and perhaps he viewed changing the Commander's mind about magicians as a challenge.

A messenger arrived and handed a scroll to the Commander. After reading the message, he stood. "Please enjoy the rest of your dinner. I have some matters to attend to." He left, taking his guards and Star with him.

Before Star followed him, she flashed me a calculating look.

The Commander's opinions about magic and magicians replayed in my mind as we returned to the guest suite. Although I agreed with Leif that Ixians with magical powers should not be killed, I also felt magic corrupted. Even Roze, the most powerful magician in Sitia, had been affected. To fear my potential as a Soulfinder was one thing, to support Cahil was another.

When we arrived at our quarters, I pulled Leif into my room.

"What's the matter?" he asked.

"I want to contact Irys. See what's going on in the Citadel."

"What I want to know is what's going on with *you?*"

"What do you mean?"

"Since crossing the border, you have changed, treating Moon Man like a traitor and not trusting anyone. If you decide to stay as the Commander's adviser, *you'll* be a traitor to Sitia. What happened to Liaison Yelena? The neutral third party?"

"To be a Liaison, I need to have support of *both* parties. Are you going to help me contact Irys or lecture me?"

Leif grumbled and pouted but agreed to share his energy. I lay on the bed and drew power, projecting my awareness south to the Keep. Bypassing the busy thoughts of the Citadel's inhabitants, I searched the campus for Irys. I couldn't find her within her tower, but I sensed a faint echo as if the scent of her soul remained behind after she had left the room. Odd.

I moved on to the Keep's other towers, hoping Irys was visiting with another Master. Zitora's thoughts were walled off from intruders. Bain's tower had that same odd feeling as Irys's, and the cold barrier of Roze's mind slammed into me. I bounced off and retreated, but an icy wind sucked me back toward her. This time her barrier was down, and cold fingers clamped around my awareness, pulling me into her mind.

Searching for someone? Roze asked.

I refused to answer.

You make it so easy, Yelena. Roze laughed. *I knew you would contact Irys. You won't be able to talk to her, I'm afraid. The Council decided Masters Irys and Bain were engaged in treasonous activities. They're currently in the Keep's cells.*

21

HOW DID YOU MANAGE to frame two Master Magicians, Roze? I said, suppressing my shock and outrage.

They refused to sign the letter to the Commander, and they have been stalwart defenders of you and your brother. She said the word *brother* with heated contempt. *They doubted Cahil's word. Cahil, who single-handedly increased the strength of our army with Daviian Warriors.*

Those Warriors are not there to help you. They're there to use you.

I'm not going to take advice from you. Roze tightened her grip on my consciousness. *A simpleton who's about to lose her mind.*

She peeled the layers of my consciousness away with a knife made of ice. Cold stabbed deep into the core of my thoughts, attempting to expose what I kept hidden.

Thinking of becoming an adviser to the Commander, what a laugh. After I'm done with you, you won't be able to advise a baby on how to suck its thumb.

Unable to pull away, I panicked. Leif's energy poured into me, but I still couldn't break free. Flayed by her arctic magic, I remained helpless.

Valek was in Sitia to assassinate the Council. Hmm…most interesting, she said.

Desperate and knowing I couldn't sever her hold, I reached closer to her, searching for a part of her I could control. Her soul. I tugged at the ghostlike force, smelling its rotten stench, and feeling it fray as if her soul was splitting into multiple personalities.

Roze jolted in horror and expelled me from her grip. As I escaped, her words reached me.

Try to rescue Irys and Bain. Come to the Citadel. We're ready for you. Roze yanked a defensive wall between us, breaking our link.

I returned to my body, feeling exhausted and weak.

Leif loomed over me. "What happened? I lost you."

"I got caught by Roze…" My thoughts returned to what she had said about Irys and Bain.

"And?"

"And, I broke free before she could dissect *all* my thoughts."

"What did she find out?"

I told him she knew about the Commander's offer and about Valek being in Sitia.

He creased his thick eyebrows as he considered. "Knowing about Valek could be a good thing. The Council can take measures to protect themselves in case Valek comes back."

"*If* Roze warns them. Their deaths may be exactly what she wants."

"No. Roze wants what is best for Sitia. She's a strong-willed person and many Councilors are swayed by her arguments, but I don't believe she would use murder or magic to get her way."

I shook my head. After the attack, I knew she would resort

to both to get what she wants. "You were her student. Of course you still hold charitable thoughts for her."

"I know her better than you." Leif's voice huffed with anger. "I've worked for her and with her for nine years. Her methods can be harsh, but her concern is *always* for Sitia. She has *always* supported Cahil's desire to become King of Ixia. In her mind, your Soulfinder abilities are a threat to Sitia. And I'm starting to agree with her." Leif stormed from the room.

I wondered what had really upset Leif. In my opinion, Roze was a murderer. She didn't kill the body, but she destroyed minds without any remorse. Look at Marrok. But then again I had done the same thing with Ferde. At least, I admitted to being a killer. Was I any better? No.

My mind sorted through all the information from Roze. Rescuing Irys and Bain became a priority. I needed eyes and ears inside the Citadel's walls, and a way to get messages inside the Keep. All without being seen or without risking anyone else. Magic was no longer an option. If I projected my awareness near the Keep, Roze would catch me again. Mundane methods remained my only recourse.

A plan formed, making my heart buzz with the possibilities. If I hadn't been so drained of energy, I would have started preparations that night. Instead, I mapped out the steps I needed to take to return to Sitia.

I hovered at the entrance to Dilana's workroom. The Commander's seamstress sat in a pool of early-morning sunlight, humming to herself as her deft fingers repaired a pair of pants. Her soft curls glowed like fresh honey. I hesitated, not wanting to disturb her.

My need for information, though, spurred me into the room. She glanced up in surprise and my heart stopped. I braced myself for her reaction, guessing hate and anger ranked at the top of her list.

"Yelena!" She jumped to her feet. "I heard you were back." She pulled me into a warm hug then released me for inspection. "You're still too thin. And what's this you're wearing? The material is far too light for Ixia's weather. Let me get you some proper clothes and something to eat. I have a fresh loaf of cinnamon bread." She moved away.

"Dilana, wait." I grabbed her arm. "I ate breakfast and I'm not cold. Sit down. I want to talk to you."

Her baby doll's beauty hadn't dimmed with time or grief, but I could see a touch of sadness in her eyes despite her smile.

"It's so good to see you again." She rubbed a hand along my arm. "Look at how tan your skin is! Tell me what you've been doing in Sitia besides sunning yourself."

I laughed at the fantasy of me lounging in the sun, but sobered. She wanted to avoid the subject. Avoid the reason I thought she might hate me. But I couldn't go on without saying anything. "Dilana, I'm sorry about Rand."

She waved the comment away. "No need. The big oaf got himself mixed up with Star and her nefarious deeds. Not your fault."

"But he wasn't her target. I was and—"

"He saved you. The dumb ox died a hero." She blinked back tears threatening to spill over her long eyelashes. "It's a good thing we didn't get married or I'd be a widow. No one wants to be a widow at twenty-five." She took a deep breath. "Let me get you a slice of bread."

Dilana left before I could stop her. When she returned with a plate, she had regained her composure. I asked her about the latest gossip.

"Can you believe Ari and Janco are working with Valek? They were in here last month trying on their new uniforms and preening in front of the mirrors."

"Do you know where they are?" I asked.

"Some mission with Valek. I had to make a sneak suit for each of them. I used up all my black fabric to cover Ari's muscles. Can you imagine that big lunk sneaking around?"

I couldn't. Ari didn't strike me as the assassin type. He was more of a one-on-one fighter. Same with Janco. He wouldn't feel right killing someone without a fair fight. So why *were* they with Valek?

Dilana continued to chat. When the subject returned to uniforms, I asked her about getting an adviser's uniform. "The Commander has asked me to stay and I feel like I stand out in these Sitian clothes." Not an outright lie, yet a pang of guilt twinged in my chest.

"Even though coral is a beautiful color on you, you'll be warmer in a uniform." Dilana bustled over to her piles of clothes. She picked out a black shirt and pants. Handing them to me, she shooed me behind the changing screen. "Try them on."

I fingered the two red diamonds stitched on the shirt's collar. The last time I had stood here, I had been exchanging my red prison gown for the food taster's uniform. When I pulled my shirt off, I saw my snake bracelet. Round and round, it hugged my arm. I suppressed the sudden laughter bubbling in my throat. I've come full circle, but this time I put on an adviser's uniform. It fit better than my food taster uniform, molding to my body like a second skin. The Commander wanted me to help him, while the Council wanted me dead. About a year ago, the opposite had been true. This time I allowed the hollow snort of laughter to escape my lips.

"Something wrong?" Dilana asked.

I stepped out. "The pants are a little big."

She grabbed the waistband and pinched the material together, marking it with chalk. "I'll have these fixed by lunch."

I changed, thanked her and headed out to visit Kiki and the horses. The Commander's stables were located next to the kennels. The animals shared a training ring and there was a pasture for the horses along the castle's walls.

Kiki dozed in her immaculate stall. I checked on the other horses. Their coats gleamed in the sunlight. They seemed content and well cared for. I complimented the stable boys and girls, who nodded and resumed their work. Their demeanor reminded me of adults and I wondered if they had any fun.

On my way back to the castle, I spotted Porter, the Commander's Kennel Master. His dogs never wore leashes and their obedience to him was uncanny. I paused and watched him work with a litter of puppies. He had hidden treats in the training yard and taught the pups how to find them. Being puppies, they frequently forgot what they were supposed to do, but once Porter caught the attention of a dog, he touched its nose and said, "Go find."

Energized with its mission, the puppy scented the air and made a beeline for a treat. Impressive. Porter noticed me watching and gave me a curt nod. He had been good friends with Rand, and I recalled a conversation I had had with Rand about Porter.

Rand hadn't believed the rumors about Porter's magical connection with the dogs. Since there was no proof, Rand stayed true to their friendship when everyone else avoided contact with the Kennel Master. As long as Porter continued to be useful and did not draw attention to himself, his job for the Commander was secure.

I wondered about the magic, though. If he had magic and could use it without getting caught, then there might be others in Ixia doing the same thing. Porter had worked for the King many years before the Commander's takeover, giving him plenty of time to learn how to use and hide his power. Perhaps communicating with the dogs was all he could do.

One way to find out. I pulled a thread of power and made a mental connection with one of the puppies. Her energy and enthusiasm jumped from one smell to another. When I tried to communicate with her, she either ignored me or didn't hear me. Her nose filled with the scent of soft laced with a sharp hint of squish, and she dug into the ground seeking a worm. When a voice of warmth and caring called, she left her task and ran toward Porter.

He gave all the puppies a rawhide stick to chew and filled the row of bowls with water. I moved my awareness to him, sensing his surface thoughts. They were focused on the tasks for the day, yet uneasiness lingered. *Why was she here? What does she want?*

To help Ixia, I said in his mind.

He jerked as if bitten in the leg and glared at me.

You hear me, don't you? The rumors are true.

He strode toward me. I checked the empty yard. Although I knew how to defend myself, his tall muscular frame reminded me that, despite the gray hair, Porter remained a formidable opponent. He stopped mere inches from me.

"You're here to help Ixia?" Porter growled. If he had hackles they would have been raised. "You can help by leaving us alone."

He didn't mean him and the dogs. I caught a brief image of other Ixians.

"There must be something I can do?"

"Like you did for Rand? No, thank you. All you'll do is get us killed." He turned away, but his words, *or enslaved*, reached me.

A cold splash of fear drenched me. Was there someone in Ixia using magicians against their will? Why was I surprised? Magic and corruption went hand in hand. Would it corrupt me as well? I'd been using my magic without stopping to think about the consequences. Connecting with Porter could get him killed, and I did it just to satisfy my own curiosity. If I was so blasé about using magic now, how would I view it in the future? Would I crave it like an addiction? I began to think it would be better not to use magic at all.

Before I could return to the castle, I heard Kiki's whinny. I hurried back to the stables, but Kiki had already opened the door and met me in the walkway.

Foot hurt, she said.

She followed me to the training yard and bent her front right hoof back for me to inspect the underside. A rock was lodged in her frog.

When did this happen?

Night. Didn't hurt then.

Out in the sunlight, she didn't appear to be as well groomed as I had thought.

She snorted. *Lavender Lady take care.*

You wouldn't stand for the stable boy?

Too rough. Wait for you.

You're spoiled rotten.

I left Kiki in the yard, and fetched my pick and brushes.

She lifted her leg and I dislodged the stone then pulled the shedding blade through her copper hair. After a while, I removed my cloak. When I finished, clumps of horse hair clung to my sweaty clothes.

You're beautiful and I need a bath, I said to her. *Pasture or stall?*

Stall. Nap time.

And what about your snooze before I groomed you?

Pre-nap.

Ah, the life of a horse. I made sure her bucket held fresh water. On my way out, I bumped into Porter.

"You're good with that horse," he said.

I waited, sensing he had more to say.

"Maybe you *can* help us." He scanned the area. A few lads worked nearby. He lowered his voice. "There's a meeting tonight in Castletown. Forty-three Peach Lane rear door. Come during dinner. Don't let anyone know where you're going."

22

HE STRODE AWAY. TONIGHT I had planned to be on my way to Sitia. A visit to Porter would delay me, but it seemed too important to ignore.

After my jaunt to the stables, I arrived back at the doors of the guest suite at the same time as a messenger. The Commander wanted us to meet him in the war room this afternoon. Inside, Tauno paced the living area like a trapped animal, prowling next to the windows.

"Why don't you go outside?" I suggested to him. "The soldiers run laps around the castle complex for exercise. You can join them if you want."

He stopped in surprise. "I can leave this room without being escorted by an adviser?"

"The advisers are a courtesy provided by the Commander to help you find your way around the castle. If you go out on your own, you'll get some suspicious looks, but as long as you stick to common areas, no one will bother you. Just make sure you're back for the meeting." I told them about the message.

Moon Man sat next to Marrok on the couch. Marrok stared at us with an intense expression as if he tried to decipher our conversation.

"Interesting how you see the advisers as a courtesy, while Tauno sees them as guards," Moon Man said.

I ignored the Story Weaver's comment and gave Tauno directions to find his way outside. Even with my assurances, he still pulled the door open as if he expected to be accosted.

"Has Marrok said anything yet?" I asked.

"No, but he is understanding more and more. Unlike you."

I scowled. "What is that supposed to mean?"

Moon Man refused to answer. My plan to leave my companions in Ixia so I could travel faster through Sitia became more appealing as time went on. The Commander would keep an eye on them and I wouldn't have to worry about being betrayed.

I looked around the room. "Where's Leif?"

"In his room," Moon Man said.

Judging by the monosyllable response through Leif's door, I guessed he was still upset with me. I told him about the meeting then retired to my room.

A quiet group followed me to the Commander's war room. Tauno had returned, seeming more settled since he had burned off some of his energy. Moon Man's calm demeanor returned, and Leif frowned at the world at large and me in particular. My brother knew how to pout.

The Commander had a surprise waiting for us. Valek, Ari and Janco sat around the circular table. My emotions flipped to joy at seeing them.

"Valek was just informing me on the state of affairs in Sitia," the Commander said. "Continue."

"I found the situation to be rather ah…unique." Valek leaned back in his chair. He scanned my companions with a thoughtful purse of his lips. The sharp features of his angular face would soften only when he smiled.

"Unique is putting it mildly," Janco said. He rubbed the scar where the bottom half of his right ear used to be. A sure sign of his worry.

"Try alarming," Ari added.

Panic began to simmer under my heart. Ari tended to counter Janco's exaggerations with cool logic. His steadying presence helped keep Janco in check. Opposite in appearance, Janco's wiry build reflected his quick wit and lightning-fast fighting style, while Ari's strength could outmuscle most others.

"Alarming would work," Valek agreed. "Taking out the Council wouldn't result in better leaders. In fact, it would have inflamed the citizens to all-out war. And they have some new players who could potentially tip the battle in their favor."

"Players? Try creepy men. Scary magicians. Evil demons." Janco shuddered.

Valek shot Janco a warning look. "I need to obtain more information before I can assess the true nature of the threat and determine the best way to counter it."

"Why have you returned?" the Commander asked.

Another glance from Valek, but this time he aimed it at me. "I require more help. Things were getting a little too hot even for me."

So much for my plans to travel to Sitia alone.

The room fell quiet as Commander Ambrose considered. "What do you need?"

"A few more men, Yelena and her brother."

I had suspected Valek would want me. By Leif's grunt of shock, I knew his surprise matched my own when hearing his name.

"She hasn't agreed to be an adviser yet so I can't order her to assist you," the Commander said.

"Then I will have to ask." Valek looked at us.

"Yes," I said the same time Leif said no.

"I'm a Sitian, remember? I can't aid Ixia in overthrowing Sitia," Leif said.

"I don't want to take control of Sitia," the Commander said. "I just don't want them to invade us and I will take preventative measures to stop them."

"By helping us, you will also help your country," Valek said.

"We can do it on our own. We don't need you or Yelena." Leif turned to me. "You could never have been a true Liaison, little sister. Ever since we've been in Ixia, you have revealed your true loyalties."

Outraged, I asked, "Is that what you believe?"

"Look at the evidence. At the first sign of trouble, you run for Ixia. We could have returned to the Citadel, and explained everything to the Council."

His accusations stabbed me as if he held a knife.

"The Council will not believe us. I told you what Irys said."

"But what if you lied? You know I don't have the power of mental communication on my own. You don't trust us so why should we trust you?"

First the Council had turned on me and now my brother.

"Believe what you want, then. Valek, can we do without him?"

"We can."

The Commander stared at Valek. "You *will* tell me your plans before you disappear again."

"Yes, sir."

"Good. You're all dismissed." The Commander stood.

"What about us?" Leif gestured to Moon Man and Tauno. "Can we return to Sitia?"

"Consider yourselves a guest of Ixia until this unfortunate incident is resolved," Valek said.

"What if we no longer wish to be guests?" Moon Man asked.

"Then you will be our first prisoners of war and your accommodations will not be so luxurious. It's your choice." The Commander left.

Leif glared at me and I wanted to laugh. His current reaction mirrored the first encounter I had had with him after fourteen years of being apart. Another full circle. I felt dizzy. Perhaps this was a sign I should stay in this spot to avoid having to exert time and effort to go around again.

Valek turned to Ari and made a slight movement with his hand.

Ari nodded and stood; his blond curls bounced with the motion. "We will be happy to escort you to your quarters."

A gamut of emotions flowed over my former companions' faces as they followed Ari from the room. Leif barely contained his fury, Tauno looked worried and Moon Man appeared thoughtful.

Janco brought up the rear of the procession. He flashed me an inviting smirk. "Training yard, four o'clock."

"You need more lessons?"

"You wish."

My smile faded when the door closed. Valek remained on the far side of the table, his face serious. I felt awkward and uncertain.

"Is it that bad?" I asked.

"It's a situation I've never encountered before. I'm worried."

"About Ixia?"

"About you, love."

"Me?"

"I've always been amazed at how you can draw unwanted attention and ire from powerful people. This time, though, you managed to get a whole country upset. If I was the Commander, I would wait out the political strife in Sitia and then offer you to the victors in trade for Ixia being left alone."

"Good thing you're not the Commander."

"Yes. And we should leave Ixia before the Commander figures it out. What were you planning?"

I tried to look innocent. "Me? You're the one with the plan."

"And the adviser uniform you had Dilana size for you? You weren't thinking of sneaking off to Sitia without me, were you?"

Another betrayal. "Did she tell you?"

"I had ripped a hole in my favorite pants. When I dropped them off, she asked me to deliver your uniform and gifted me with a leer. I would guess the servants were already betting how soon one of them would spot us together." He sighed. "If only intelligence information worked through my corps as efficiently as gossip flowed through the servants, then my problems would be minimal."

In one fluid motion, Valek stood. He walked over to me, his smooth stride graceful as a panther. Powerful energy coiled in his body. He leaned on my chair's arms, bringing his face inches from mine. His black hair hung to his shoulders; his expression was lethal. "I'll ask you again. Your plans include me, correct?"

I slumped deeper into my chair.

"Yelena?" His voice warned.

"You said you had never encountered this situation before. It's an unknown. I don't want to risk…"

"What?"

"Risk losing you. With your immunity I can't heal you!"

"I'm willing to take the chance."

"But I'm not willing to let you."

"Sorry, love, that's not your decision. It's mine."

I grumbled. Events had spiraled out of my control. Again. I just spun in circles and never gained any ground.

"Okay, I promise not to go to Sitia without you." Which didn't include my meeting tonight with Porter.

"Thank you." Valek brushed his lips on my cheek. A tingle sizzled up my spine.

"What about your plan?" I tried to stay on topic, but I lost my motivation once Valek's musky smell enveloped me.

"This *is* my plan."

He moved closer and kissed me. Warmth spread throughout my body. The panic clutching my throat eased. I pushed away my worries and focused on Valek, wrapping my arms around him. But the feel of his muscles through his shirt wasn't enough. I yanked at it, wanting to touch his skin, wanting to wear his skin.

He pulled away, straightening. "In the war room, love? What if someone comes in?"

I stood and removed his shirt. "Then they'll have a good story to tell."

"Good?" He adopted the pretense of being offended.

"Prove me wrong."

His eyes lit with the challenge.

Valek and I ended up underneath the war room's round table. Lying together, I felt safe for the first time in weeks. We discussed the events in Sitia.

"I could hardly move within the Citadel," Valek said. "The air was so thick with magic I felt like I swam in syrup."

"But you weren't detected."

Valek's immunity to magic remained a powerful weapon. Without it, I couldn't have defeated Ferde.

"No. Although it was only a matter of time. With that many—what do you call them?—Warpers, my presence would have eventually caused a noticeable dead zone."

I considered how fast things had changed in the Citadel. Twenty-two days ago Moon Man had speculated the Daviians had eight Warpers, but once he realized they were performing Kirakawa we knew the actual number of Warpers could be much higher, depending on how many victims they had used. And how far along in the ritual they were. Plus only a victim with magical powers could make a Warper.

If they had been preparing for this offensive for a while, then who were the victims? They wouldn't have used clan members and the Sandseed Clan would have noticed if a couple of their Story Weavers went missing. So would the other clans. Unable to deduce an answer, I put the question to Valek.

"They're probably targeting the homeless. Who would miss a few beggars in a big city? No one."

"What about the need for magicians?"

"The first year after a magician reaches adolescence is a difficult and vulnerable year. Half the people don't even realize they can access the power source, and the other half don't have a clue how to use it. The Warpers could be hunting the streets, looking for someone in that precarious situation."

My conviction to stop using it became stronger the more I learned about magic and how others exploited it.

Valek and I mapped our return to Sitia and planned how to contact Bavol Zaltana.

"I'll leave Ari and Janco here. They won't be happy, but security around the Citadel is too tight and we're better off just going ourselves. Two of my corps have already been caught inside." Valek sat up with reluctance. "I have some business to attend to. I'll meet you in my suite later tonight and we can finalize our time schedule. I'll have your belongings delivered there."

I should retrieve my pack, but realized I had no desire to see Leif or the others. But I remembered something. "Why did you want Leif to come with us?"

He shook his head. "You wouldn't have agreed anyway."

"To what?"

"To letting Leif get caught and using your mental connection to him to find out what's going on in the Keep. But now you're mad at him—"

"No. He would be killed. I'm not *that* angry with him." Besides, if I used my magic anywhere near the Citadel, all the preparation in the world wouldn't be able to help me.

"She's quick and fast, but she can't get past," Janco sang as he blocked my rib strikes.

"You need to work on your rhymes. Either that, or I'm

getting better." I faked a temple strike and swept his feet out from under him. Before I could press my advantage, he rolled away and regained his feet.

"You hesitated," Ari said from the sidelines. "Too busy talking."

I renewed my attack and Janco countered with ease. We fought in the soldier's training yard, which had been filled with the sounds of practice until Janco and I started this match. We had attracted quite a crowd.

"Can't talk and fight. So much for being polite." Janco spun his bow. His weapon blurred.

I backed up and blocked the flurry of hits, keeping pace with his attack until he changed the rhythm. I missed a connection. The air exploded out of my lungs as Janco landed a solid blow to my solar plexus. I bent over, coughing and gasping for breath.

"Funny," Janco said. He smoothed his goatee with a hand. "You're usually not this easy to beat. Have I succeeded in hiding my thoughts?"

Once I regained my composure and straightened, he smiled sweetly at me. The last time we had fought in Sitia, he had found out about my zone of concentration, a semimagical state allowing me to notice my opponent's intentions when I sparred with them. This time I had tried to fight him without setting my mind into that zone.

"No. You're still self-centered and overly cocky," I said.

"They're fighting words."

"Do you need more time to rest? Now you're management, you probably need to expend extra energy moving that paunch."

He swept his bow toward my legs in response and we engaged in another match. I lost again, but kept challenging him until we were both sweat soaked and exhausted.

"Your fighting improved as the matches went on," Ari said. "But it wasn't your best." He looked at me as if waiting for an explanation.

I shrugged. "I was trying something different."

"It's not working. Better go back to your old style."

"I like her new style." Janco piped in. "It's good for my ego."

Ari frowned and crossed his massive arms over his chest.

"Life or death, Ari, and I'd go back to using all my tricks. Don't worry."

He seemed mollified, and I hadn't lied. When push came to shove, I knew I would fall back on using my magic. Another problem. Magic made me lazy and when I encountered a bad situation, I reached for it without thought. I needed to improve my other skills, because magic wouldn't help me against the Fire Warper.

I changed the subject and asked my friends about their new jobs. Janco regaled me with the story of their battle against Valek. Every time Ari shook his head, I knew Janco had exaggerated a detail.

"What is it like being second in command of Ixia's intelligence network?" I asked.

"I don't like all this sneaking around," Ari said. "There's a lot more going on in Ixia than I thought. And there's so much to do. Valek is the king of delegating."

"I'm getting to use my lock-picking skills." Janco grinned. Pure mischievousness danced in his eyes. "And the information we've discovered. Did you know General Dinno has—"

"Janco," Ari warned. "We enjoy the work. It's just not what we had expected."

"Nothing is," I said.

My bones ached with fatigue. I waved goodbye to Ari and Janco and headed toward the baths. Before joining my friends in the training yard, I had retrieved my pack and stashed it in the changing room. After a long soak, I dried and dressed in my adviser's uniform in preparation for the meeting with Porter. I rationalized I would draw less attention wearing a uniform than my Sitian clothes.

I cut a hole in the pant's pocket and strapped my switchblade to my right thigh. Not wanting to show up armed with my bow, I felt it prudent to have a knife on me just in case. Braiding my hair into one long braid, I let it hang between my shoulder blades.

Although my stomach grumbled with hunger, Porter had instructed me to come during dinner. His timing made sense, as most of the castle's inhabitants would be busy either serving dinner or eating it. And Castletown should be relatively quiet.

I stopped beside the pasture on my way out, checking to see if anyone followed me. A few servants hustled between buildings, but no one paid me any attention. The cold hung in the air as if waiting for a breeze. I fed Kiki and the other horses some apples.

Smells? I asked Kiki.

Big snow.

When?

Half moon.

Three days. Valek and I would need to leave sooner than planned.

Kiki come?

Of course, and Garnet, too.

She sighed with contentment as I scratched behind her ears. When I felt certain no one watched me, I headed toward the south gate. I joined in with a group of town residents returning home for dinner. With my Ixian wool cloak covering my adviser's uniform, I blended right in. My group hurried over the grass field surrounding the walls. The Commander had ordered all buildings within a quarter mile of the castle be destroyed when he had gained power. He also renamed Jewelstown, named in honor of the former Queen Jewel to the rather unoriginal Castletown.

Once we reached the edge of town, the group dispersed as the others headed for their homes. The symmetry of the town with its neat rows of wooden buildings conflicted with the asymmetrical style of the castle complex. The logical array of businesses interspersed among residences made navigating the town easier. Each district had a name matching the merchandise sold there. Peach Alley would be located in the Garden District.

A few townspeople bustled about, all intent on some errand. I walked as if I had a purpose so I didn't attract unwanted attention from the town's guards, who watched the streets.

The colors of the buildings thinned toward gray as the sun set. My perceptions shifted, and I felt as if I had entered into a colorless shadow world. The buildings transformed into a watery representation of a town populated with ghosts.

I stumbled over some unseen curb and snapped back to the real world. Dismissing the strange spell, I rationalized hunger as the culprit. I picked up my pace, determined to find the right address before the lamplighters came out. Peach Lane seemed devoid of life, and only when I went around to the back alley did I see signs of habitation.

A glow of firelight came from number forty-three. Keeping to the shadows, I approached the back door. I pulled a thread of magic and scanned the area. Inside the house I felt Porter waiting with two young girls. They were nervous about being found, but I didn't sense any duplicity.

I paused as the realization of how much I depended on my magic dawned on me. Not only with searching for attackers, but with Kiki, too. Could I completely stop using my magic? It would be much harder than I thought.

The door opened right after my light tap, as if Porter had been hovering near it. He pulled me into the room and closed it behind me.

"Did anyone see you?" he asked.

"No." I looked around the room. Small and tidy, the sitting area had a couch, a chair and three dogs getting nervous attention from the girls. The girls perched on the edge of the couch with their backs straight. They wore students' uniforms, which consisted of a simple jumper made of red linen. White-faced, their gazes jumped between Porter and me.

"You said I could help you?" I asked.

"We're taking a big chance trusting you." Porter picked up a half-chewed roll of rawhide from the floor. He clutched the dog's treat in his hands as he stared at me. "You must promise not to tell Valek or anyone else about all this."

"I can't promise until I hear what 'all this' is."

The rawhide popped and cracked in Porter's hands. He glanced at the girls and sighed. His wide shoulders drooped with the release of his tension, and he gestured to the empty chair. "Have a seat. This is going to take a while."

As soon as I sat down, one of the dogs came over and put

his head in my lap. Peering at me from between his gray shaggy hairs, he pleaded for attention. I stroked his smooth head and scratched behind his ears. The dog's tail thumped on the floor. The smell of wet dog and wood smoke mixed into a stuffy odor.

Porter tapped the roll on his leg as he talked. "I've set up a network of people throughout Ixia to help me in smuggling children out of the country."

I leaned forward in alarm, thinking about Mogkan's kidnapping ring and how he had taken children from Sitia to Ixia to abuse them for his own purposes. "Children?"

"They seem like children to me." Porter gave the two girls a grandfatherly smile. "Adolescents who have just discovered their magical powers." He pointed to the couch. "Young people like Liv and Kieran. I've been helping them to escape to Sitia before their powers are known to others. But I believe something has gone wrong."

"What?" I prompted when Porter appeared to be lost in his own thoughts.

"I was in MD-7 last month. General Rasmussen has a nice wolfhound I wanted to breed with my bitch. While there, one of my contacts who works in the general's stables told me the last person I sent through the network never arrived. And two others he had sent on never made it to the border contact. They have all disappeared."

My stomach twisted around my heart. "Do you think Valek has killed them?"

"I don't know and I can't risk asking around. If my network has been compromised then I won't be able to send Liv and Kieran. Eventually they'll get reported."

I hadn't thought it possible, but the girls' faces turned whiter. Considering Porter's story, I said, "Tell me how your network operates."

"I have four contacts from here to the border. A few people know about my underground efforts and they'll send their son or daughter to me as an apprentice. The Commander gives me complete management of his kennel and no one pays too much attention to my students. They come and go as part of their animal husbandry training. It's risky, being this close to Valek, but then I usually know where he is and can send my charges when he's gone on business." Porter paced. "It's too risky to have a guide with them, so I instruct the person how to find the first contact and then he sends them on until they get to the border contact, who takes them into Sitia. They have transfer papers with them if they're stopped by the guards. If they had gotten caught, I would have been arrested by now." His erratic movements showed his frustration.

"How can I help?"

He stopped. "I wanted you to go along with Liv, and maybe find out what's happening to my charges. With that adviser's uniform you can go anywhere in Ixia without permission."

"No. Too dangerous for Liv. The best thing to do would be for me to disguise myself as a student and go through your network alone."

Porter's eyebrows spiked up in surprise. "You would do that for us?"

"Yes. Unfortunately though, it will have to wait."

The ability to connect with the power source began at the onset of puberty. A person typically had a year before anyone else noticed and reported them, and another three to four years to learn how to harness their power. A fledgling magician's power, when uncontrolled, could flame out and warp the blanket of power that covers the world, causing trouble for magicians everywhere. And the stronger the magician, the bigger the flameout. One-trick power similar to Opal's ability to capture magic in molten glass tended to be unconscious and didn't require formal training.

"How long do the girls have?" I asked.

"A year at most for Liv. Kieran is younger so she could last up to two years, but I'd rather they both be gone as soon as possible. I can hide them here if we're desperate. I've had some refugees who didn't have time to work in the kennel," Porter said.

"Give me a couple months. Sitia's not the best place to be sending anyone right now. Once I settle another matter, I'll come back and help you. For now, I can teach the girls how to tame their powers enough so they don't give themselves away."

Relief shone on Liv and Kieran's young faces. I worked with them for the next hour. Irys would be proud over how much I remembered from her guidance. A finger of dread stabbed my guts with the thought of Irys. I hoped she was still alive.

After my session, the girls left Porter's together while I waited for them to be well away before I left. The need to begin my journey back to Sitia pressed on my mind as I worried about Irys and Bain locked in the Keep's cells.

I made a quick sweep of the area outside Porter's door with my magic. The activity around the houses seemed muted as everyone finished their daily tasks. No one lurked in the alley.

With a wave goodbye, I exited Porter's. I stood outside and

let my eyes adjust to the darkness. When the shadows grew less black, I strode toward the street.

About halfway there I felt a presence behind me. I spun, grabbing for my switchblade. Something jabbed me in the neck and I saw Star lower a thin pipe.

I yanked the dart out of my throat. "How?"

"Some great magician you are," Star said. "Missing my own tiny talent."

My world spun and I stumbled. Star caught me, but I had no energy to fight her off. "What?"

She cradled me in her arms. "Valek's goo-goo juice. Relax, Yelena. Star's going to take *good* care of you."

My last coherent thought focused on how her sinister expression didn't match her soothing words.

23

THE WORLD STIRRED. MY thoughts scattered and failed to connect. Warm hands guided me. Whenever the hands pulled away, the ground swelled and I tumbled off my feet.

I thought about the lack of fear for only a moment before the air spun around my head. Lying down felt best. I sensed movement and smelled horses.

Inside my chicken crate, I wondered what I was supposed to be doing. Important things? My mind chased the thought until the sunlight lit the dust motes. I studied the flecks floating above me. The flecks transformed into daggers. I wanted to knock them away. My hands stayed glued to my back. A leather strap lodged in my teeth. The problem disappeared with the sun.

Time ebbed and flowed. My crate opened. It closed. Faces peered. Mouths talked. Words chimed in my ears. Some like *eat*, *drink* and *sleep* I understood. Others resembled a baby's babble. Goo-goo. Goo-goo. A prick on my arm or neck or back. The air filled with colors. My crate bobbed on an invisible sea.

A small lucid part of me wanted action. Freedom. Majority ruled and I let the world slide by me content in my crate. My crate. My crate. I giggled.

The fire woke me. A finger of flame poked. I jerked away, no longer inside my crate. My thoughts congealed into a coherent whole. The air became invisible, revealing my surroundings. I braced for another prick. When none came I focused. The booted feet of a couple guards stood near me. I lay on my side in front of a campfire. Darkness pressed against the firelight, and my hands were tied behind my back.

Actual conversation reached my ears. The baby babble was gone. But for how long? I coaxed my mind to think, but my thoughts remained sluggish.

A man's voice. "Should not do this," he said. "She should stay under until we reach our destination. Jal is the only one strong enough to counter her power."

A familiar voice said, "I made a promise to her. I want her to know who has her, and what we plan to do to her."

Footsteps approached and I tried to put a name to the familiar voice. My mind churned as if mired in river mud.

"Take the gag off," Familiar Voice said from behind me.

One of the guards removed the leather strap. A mixture of pain and relief flowed into my cracked lips. I licked them, tasting blood. Other aches and cramps woke. Only the sight of a pair of black riding boots covered with dust could distract me from my medley of aches.

My gaze followed the boots up to jodhpurs that disappeared under a gray riding cloak. I squinted in the firelight, hoping the person in front of me was an illusion.

The cocky smirk caused my heart to stutter. And when he

kicked me in the ribs, I knew all hopes for a pleasant reunion were gone. I coughed and wheezed as the pain shot through my body.

"That's for hitting me with Curare!" He kicked me again. "And that's just because I can."

His words sounded thin and distant, reaching me through my efforts to reclaim my breath. He loomed over me. When the sharp pain dulled to a loud throb, I struggled to a sitting position. I glanced around. Four guards stood a few feet away and I counted three Daviian Vermin nearby, but I couldn't tell if they were Warpers or not.

"Cahil," I said between gasps. "You're still…scared. Of me."

He laughed. The washed-out blue of his eyes sparked with amusement.

"Yelena, you're the one who should be scared." He crouched down.

We were face-to-face. He held a dart between us. A drop of clear liquid hung from the end. Fear coiled in my stomach as I smelled the sweet odor. Curare. I tried not to let my terror show on my face.

"*I* allowed you this brief moment of lucidity. Listen closely. Remember what I said to you the last time we were together?"

"When you wanted to exchange me for Marrok?"

"No. When I promised to find a person who could defeat you and Valek. I've met with success. In fact, you have already had an encounter with my champion."

"Ferde?" I played the simpleton to prolong the conversation, hoping my slow mind would produce a plan for escape.

"Act the fool, but I know better. My champion makes you sweat with fear *and* desire. The Fire Warper has been called to this world with one mission. To capture you. And you're powerless against him." Pure satisfaction shone on Cahil's face. "I will deliver you to Jal and the Fire Warper. Jal will perform the Kirakawa ritual's binding ceremony on you, taking your powers as the Fire Warper claims your soul."

My mind buzzed with the need to stop him yet produced nothing intelligent. I couldn't even connect with the power source. "And what do you get, Cahil?"

"I get to witness your death and watch your heart mate suffer before he meets the same end."

"But Jal gains power. Do you really believe Jal will let you rule? And what about the Fire Warper? Do you think he'll be content to go back after his task is complete?"

"He has come asking for you. Once he has you, he'll go back. Then Jal rules Sitia, and I rule Ixia."

I saw a faint trace of uncertainty in Cahil's eyes. My mind pulled free from the mire of the goo-goo juice and I made a connection. "Before you said you called him. Now you say he has come. Which one is it?"

"It doesn't matter."

"Yes it does. If you called him, you have control over him."

He shrugged. "Jal will deal with him. As long as I have Ixia. I don't care."

"You should care. The need for power is addicting. Ask your Daviian friends about the history of the Sandseed Clan and the Daviian Mountains. Then you'll realize Jal won't be content with just ruling Sitia. Once your usefulness is gone, you will be too."

"You're just trying to trick me. I know better than to listen to you."

He tried to stab the dart into my throat. I fell back and pulled power as Cahil pinned me with his weight. With no time to think, I focused the magic on my neck as he jabbed the dart into my skin. Closing my eyes, I treated the area as I would an injury. In my mind's eye, I saw the Curare as a pulsing red light, spreading through my throat. I used power to push the liquid back through the tiny hole in my skin. It trickled down the side of my neck.

My gaze met Cahil's when I opened my eyes. He stared at me with a mixture of triumph and hatred.

Hoping he hadn't seen the drug run out, I said, "Pay close attention, Cahil. You'll see the truth." I acted as if I had been paralyzed, unfocusing my eyes and letting my body go slack.

He grunted and stood. "I've seen the truth. That's why I want you dead."

The Vermin joined him next to the fire, and I watched them from the corner of my eye.

"I felt magic. Brief. Did she use her power on you?" one of the Vermin asked Cahil.

"No. I got her in time."

They discussed their plans for leaving in the morning.

When the others moved to set up camp, Cahil said, "I should kill her now."

Alarmed replies told him it would be imprudent. For the first time ever, I agreed with the Vermin.

"Jal needs her and we do not wish to infuriate the Fire Warper," another said.

"Why should *I* care about infuriating the Fire Warper?" Cahil asked. "*I'm* in charge. He should answer to *me*. He should worry about infuriating *me*, especially after the fiasco in the jungle."

Soothing words were muttered.

"Put her back in the box," Cahil finally said. "Secure it, just in case we encounter trouble."

Two of the Vermin lifted me. I concentrated on being a dead weight. My hands were tied and I couldn't use magic without alerting them. I knew one of the three was a Warper but was unsure about the other two. At this point I needed more information. I decided to wait for a better opportunity and hoped I would get one.

The Vermin climbed onto a cart, dropped me into a crate and shut the lid. In the darkness the sound of metal latches being closed grated on my skin. I bit down on a cry of dismay when the snap of three locks sounded. The coffin-shaped crate seemed to press into me, and I drew in a couple of calming breaths. My gaze found the small slit between the boards, allowing air to come in. And light. The faint flicker of firelight seeped through the cracks.

I wiggled into a more comfortable position. My mind raced over my limited options. Magic remained my only weapon. The desire to project my awareness and scan my surroundings pulled at me, but I knew if they discovered I wasn't drugged, all possibility of escape would be gone. Would the Warper feel my power while he slept? Could I put the Vermin and Cahil into a deep sleep? I would still be locked in a box, but I could call someone to break me out.

Who? Only a fellow magician could hear my mental call, and I had no idea where I was. If I was lucky enough to find a local citizen, perhaps I could discover my location.

Unable to plan a course of action, I marveled over my ability to push the drug out of my body. Had I known I possessed that skill, I wouldn't be in this situation. And my problems with Curare, sleeping potion and goo-goo juice were solved. Although it was hard to celebrate when locked in a box.

Ever since I went to Sitia, all I wanted was to learn about magic, to discover the extent of my powers and be reacquainted with my family. Events conspired against me and I had hardly had time to catch my breath, let alone spend time exploring my magic.

Pushing the Curare out of my body was a new wrinkle. My abilities only affected living things, since my magic didn't move the drug; it must have made the muscles in my body do the work.

Desperation and raw instinct had gotten me this far. I hoped it would carry me through, and as much as I disliked using it, magic was unavoidable. If I was lucky enough to survive this, I planned to retire as a Soulfinder and limit my magic to only communicating with Kiki. I wondered if she knew I'd been taken. Did Valek know? And what about Star's role in all this?

Too many questions without answers swirled in my mind. Eventually, my thoughts bounced back to the need to do something soon, because I sensed being delivered to the Fire Warper would be the ultimate end.

"Let's get moving. If we push, we can reach the Avibian border by sundown."

Cahil's voice woke me from a light doze. A few disorienting seconds passed before I remembered my predicament and his words sank in. Shock followed understanding. We were in Sitia. I must have been under the influence of the goo-goo juice for days. Where was Valek? So much for my promise not to go to Sitia without him.

"Should we check on her?" a voice with an Ixian accent asked.

"No. She's under Curare now. She can't do anything besides breathe until the potion wears off," Cahil answered. "Finish feeding the girls. We'll let the juice wear off before we prepare them for the ritual."

The girls? I peered through one of the slits in my crate. Another crate lay beside mine. My stomach turned to ice. How many and could I help them? I suppressed a hollow laugh. Here I was trying to save others while locked in a box.

Two lids slammed then the crate lurched forward. The sound of trotting horses added to the rumble of the wagon. We were on our way.

My body went through a gamut of emotions as the day passed. Sometimes terrified, sometimes hopeful and sometimes bored, I even listed an inventory of woes. Thirsty, hungry, aching ribs, numb hands, sore muscles and a burning cramp between my shoulder blades. With the noise of our travel masking my movements, I attempted to alleviate some of my misery. I squirmed and wiggled until I managed to squeeze my body and legs through my arms. The benefits of keeping limber and being small became apparent as I succeeded in bringing my tied hands to the front of my body. I almost groaned aloud when cool relief spread over my back.

Having my hands in front allowed me to explore. I patted my right thigh, checking for my switchblade. No luck. Even the holder had been removed. I stared at the knots on the leather straps binding my hands and pulled at them with my teeth. I untied a few before the wagon stopped, but I decided to keep working, risking discovery.

"We'll camp here," Cahil said. "When you're done setting

up, let the girls out. They should be lucid by now and you can get them ready for the Kirakawa tomorrow."

"What about the Soulfinder?" one of the Vermin asked.

"Drakke will give her another dose tonight. Too much Curare could stop her heart," Cahil replied.

I listened to the sounds of the men in the camp as I continued to gnaw and pull at my bindings. The smell of roasting meat stole into my crate. My stomach grumbled with alarming loudness. After a while, two crates were opened and two scared voices asked questions. By the brief flash of a red jumper through the slits in my box, I guessed the girls were the students from Ixia. Liv and Kieran. My heart went out to them.

Again I wondered how the Vermin and Cahil had managed to smuggle us all out of Ixia. Perhaps the Vermin had posed as traders taking a wagonload of goods across the border.

I caught glimpses of the camp. A tent had been erected and I counted four guards and three Vermin. Some of the guards I recognized as Cahil's men, while two looked unfamiliar. All were armed with swords or scimitars. I searched for some sign of my backpack. The limited view hindered me, although I guessed my pack would be found with Cahil.

The daylight faded, and I renewed my efforts on the leather strips around my wrists. Each shrill scream from one of the girls spurred me on. I ignored the pain, the smell of fear and the metallic taste of blood as I yanked at the knots. Cahil had mentioned a ritual tomorrow. Tonight would be my only chance to escape.

The last knot proved impossible to untie, but my spit had soaked the leather enough to give a little when I moved. I pulled my hand through the last loop, scraping off a layer of skin in the process. Panting with relief, I relaxed and waited for my crate to open.

My plan was simple, with as much chance for failure as for success. Time moved at a glacial pace. Years crept by. When the rasp and click of the lock finally sounded, I laced my hands behind my back and froze.

A soft yellow glow of firelight reflected off the Vermin who opened my crate. He lifted the lid up with one hand and reached toward me with the other. He held a tiny dart between his finger and thumb.

I moved.

Grabbing his hand in both of mine, I yanked him toward me, unbalancing him. He grunted with surprise. His weight came forward. I bent his hand back and shoved the dart into the Vermin's shoulder. Letting go of his hand, I covered his mouth to stifle his yell.

Mere seconds later the Curare paralyzed his muscles. The lid rested on his back and his body leaned on my chest. Knowing I probably had seconds before someone discovered us, I pulled the rest of him inside my box. An awkward, difficult maneuver to do while trying to keep the lid from slamming down.

Once the Vermin joined me, I wriggled from under his body and lifted the lid to peek out. The guards remained by the fire, but the other two Vermin were out of sight. The two girls had been stripped and tied down by the fire. Bloody cuts lined their arms and legs. There was nothing I could do for them right now. One problem at a time.

I slid down to the end of my crate and considered my options. Try to sneak out of the box and slip into the night or just shove the lid up and make a run for it?

What I really needed was a distraction, but that involved magic. By the time they figured out the magic came from me, I would be gone. I hoped.

A flicker of black above the campfire gave me an idea. Pulling a strand of power as thin as a spider's silk, I projected my mind toward the bat. He flew through the hot, insect-filled air rising from the flames. I tapped into the collective consciousness of his fellow bats and sent them all an image. An image of insects covering the men below. Large juicy crawling things. Easy picking for a mass of hungry bats.

Black shapes swooped down from the sky. The guards yelled and swung their arms around. Cahil and the Warper exited the tent to investigate. The Warper yelled about magic, but his words were cut off as the bats attacked.

I pushed the lid wide and hopped out. After a quick glance to make sure no one had noticed me, I stepped off the wagon and bolted for the darkness, keeping the wagon between me and the campfire.

I encountered the third Vermin who had been tending the horses. Prepared for my approach, he had pulled his scimitar. With a gesture of his weapon magic slammed through my mental defenses and my body froze. Another Warper. I cursed as he called for his companions. Then I realized he didn't have control of my mind. I projected to the two horses.

Tired, sore and unsettled by the smell of blood, the horses welcomed my contact. I appealed to them for help.

Bad men want to hurt me, I said in their minds.

Kick?

Please.

The one horse backed up. With a blur of motion, the

Warper went flying. As soon as the man's head slammed into the ground, he lost consciousness, releasing his magical hold on me.

Thank you. I ran.

Kick others?

Sounds of pursuit drew closer. The bats had lost their insect image when I switched my efforts to the horses.

If you can, I said, increasing my speed. Shouts of surprise reached my ears. I glanced over my shoulder. Four figures still chased me. The terrain remained flat and featureless, as if part of the Avibian Plains. A black bulge in the distance looked promising. Perhaps it was a cluster of trees.

The men gained on me. My hopes to reach cover faded with every step.

I pulled power and planned to baffle my pursuers' minds, betting my life on the pure conjecture that I possessed the ability to project confusing images into four minds in rapid succession.

A figure on horseback approached from the left, aiming for me. I caught a glint of moonlight off a sword. My options dwindled to either bewildering the men or stopping the horse.

My chances of success went from doubtful to none when a cold sting pricked my back.

24

I DIVED TO THE GROUND, rolling into a ball. The power I had drawn to confuse my pursuers I now applied to the area turning numb on my back. In my mind, I saw the Curare spreading through my muscles, seeking my bloodstream. I swept at it, using my magic like a broom and guiding the substance to the hole. A warm wetness spread on my shirt.

The effort left me weak, and I debated the merits of pretending to be paralyzed. The ground vibrated with the drumming of hooves. The animal cut between the guards and me. An unexpected sound of steel hitting steel rang in the cool night air. I crouched.

The horse made a quick turn and came back. Recognition shot through me. I knew that gait. I jumped to my feet.

"Yelena!" Valek threw me my bow.

I caught it in midair. Kiki spun and Valek slid off her back. The rapid clash of blades followed as Valek engaged four men in a sword fight. I hurried to join him before the remaining

Vermin and Cahil caught up. Four against one was pushing it for Valek. He would be outnumbered against six.

With the occasional kick from Kiki, Valek and I fought side by side. Cahil and the Warper hung back. I strengthened my mental defenses, sensing the Warper would try a magical attack.

Once Valek cut a guard's arm in half, we pressed our advantage. As the man fell to the ground yelling with pain, Cahil ordered the remaining men to disengage. They stepped back. Valek shot me a questioning look.

"The girls are still at the camp," I said.

He nodded and we stalked the retreating men.

The Warper threw his arms up and yelled, "Inflame."

Power pressed on my skin. With a whoosh of hot air, the guard on the ground burst into flames. Valek and I jumped away. The man screamed and writhed. He stilled as the intense heat consumed him. Acrid puffs of charred flesh reached us, and I covered my nose.

"Come! Find your soul mate!" The Warper's voice cut through the roaring fire.

A man's form coalesced from the pulsing flames.

"What's going on?" Valek asked.

"Let's go." I scrambled onto Kiki's back, Valek right behind me. Kiki took off.

"What about the girls?"

Guilt stabbed my heart. "Later."

I let Kiki decide our direction. Eventually we came to a farmhouse, modest in size and surrounded by precise flower beds. Kiki stopped at the stable and Valek slid off.

Where are we? I asked Kiki.

Ghost's house. Good hay. Nice lad.

I eyed the wooden structure with sudden distrust. *Ghosts are here?*

Kiki snorted and nudged Valek. *Ghost.*

Moon Man had explained to me Valek's immunity to magic made him appear as a ghost to magical creatures.

I looked at him. "Summer home? Isn't it a little dangerous?"

He smiled. "Safe house for my corps. A base of operations."

"How convenient."

The stable was empty. Valek helped me remove Kiki's saddle and groom her, delaying the inevitable conversation.

I sagged with fatigue, but needed to know what he had been doing while I was in my box. "How did you find me? And your timing was impeccable as always."

Valek pulled me into his arms. I molded to him, seeking warmth and comfort. My body shook with a delayed reaction. The horror of the Warper setting his own man on fire replayed in my mind.

"You're welcome, love. I had wanted to sneak in and unlock you tonight, but you had other plans. I should have been more prepared, but when I saw him poke you last night, I thought for sure you would be out of it." He pulled me away. "Let's go inside. I need a drink."

The interior of the farmhouse lacked the homey warmth of its exterior. Spartan and utilitarian, Valek's operatives obviously didn't entertain guests here. Valek lit a few lanterns, but I refused to let him build a fire. We huddled together on the couch, sipping brandy.

"General Kitvivan's white brandy?" I asked.

"You remembered!" Valek seemed surprised.

"There are tastes and smells that call certain memories.

White brandy reminds me of the Commander's brandy meeting."

"Ah, yes. And after having to taste all those brandies for the Commander, you drunkenly tried to seduce me."

"And you refused." I couldn't pinpoint a specific time or event when Valek's feelings for me had changed. He had shocked me with his declaration of love in Brazell's dungeon.

"I wanted to accept. But I didn't know if your desire was from your heart or from the brandy. You might have regretted it later."

The image of Valek wearing his dress uniform recreated the desire to seduce him again, but we had much to discuss.

"Enough small talk. Tell me everything," I ordered.

He sighed. "You're not going to like it."

"Compared to what I've just been through these last— what? Three days? I don't even know. It can't be that bad."

"I knew you were swimming in some very dangerous waters," he said, "but I hadn't known they extended so deep."

"Valek, get to the point."

He fidgeted. Fear brushed my heart. Something horrible had happened. I had never seen him fidget before. He stood and started prowling the room. His liquid movements were soundless.

"Five days ago you were taken—"

"Five days!" So much could have happened in that time. My thoughts went to Irys and Bain. They could be dead.

Valek put up his hand to forestall my questions. "Let me finish first. You were kidnapped by Star, and the reason she was able to smuggle you so far south, was because…I let her." He paused to let his words sink in.

I stared at him in astonishment. "You set me up?"

"Yes and no."

"You need to do better than that."

"I knew Star would want to exact some type of revenge on you. She has kept in contact with the underground network, and I allowed her because then I could learn who the new players were. With the Code of Behavior, there will always be a black market for illegal goods and forged papers. I like to keep tabs on the network to make sure things don't go too far, like when Star hired assassins to ruin the Sitian trade treaty. And when—"

"Get to the point."

"Star knew you would be at Porter's safe house—"

"Porter set me up?"

"I don't think so. Are you going to let me tell you or not?" He put his hands on his hips in annoyance.

I gestured for him to go on.

"I've known about Porter's rescue operation for a couple years and have allowed it to continue. However, recently, his charges have been disappearing and I've been wondering why. But that wasn't the reason I watched the house. I had followed Star and three of her men there, and was shocked to see you walk blindly into her trap. Didn't you even see her?"

"She used a subtle kind of magic."

"I haven't felt her, and I've been working with her for a while."

I thought back to the night I had been captured. The only odd event had been when my perception had altered for a moment before returning to normal. Perhaps she had affected my vision somehow. "You didn't pick up on my magic, either. And it flared out of control a couple times within the castle."

"I will keep it in mind," Valek said with an icy tone. "Star's

motives for ambushing you, I understood. The surprise arrived
when she and her friends also targeted the girls. I needed to
know where they were taking you."

I mulled over his explanation. "You could have helped me
that night, but instead decided to wait?"

"A calculated risk. I wanted to discover the extent of her operation and why she kidnapped the girls. I had no idea you
would end up across the border and in the Wannabe King's
hands."

Valek knelt in front of me, and would have taken my hands
in his had I not kept my arms crossed. Anger simmered deep
within me. I had lost five days. Five days for the Fire Warper
to grow stronger.

"This wouldn't have happened at all if you told me about
your meeting with Porter," he said.

"A *calculated* risk. Like it or not, I'm a magician, and if there's
a way to help my colleagues I'm going to try. I wasn't going to
tell the Commander's magician killer about it." Still, a small,
guilt-inducing thought about killing magicians being preferable
to using them to increase the Fire Warper's power pulsed in my
mind.

Valek sank back onto his heels. His expression hardened into
his metal mask. "Magician killer? Is that what you think of
me?"

"That *is* one of your duties for the Commander. I know
how you operate. You like to stalk your prey before you
pounce. Allowing Porter's network to continue is part of
your modus operandi."

His expression turned flat and emotionless; my anger had
ruled my tongue. My fury, though, remained.

I changed the subject. "How did Star get us into Sitia?"

As if reporting to the Commander, Valek said, "Put you into crates, stacked boxes of goods on top, and dressed as traders. They had the proper papers. The border guards did a cursory check and off you went." He paused as extreme irritation flashed through his eyes. "The border guards will be taken to task and retrained."

Valek stood. "I was going to suggest we get a few hours' sleep and try to rescue those girls. But since *I'm* the magician killer, I guess I won't concern myself about their fate." He left the room.

25

THE LIFE DRAINED from the room after Valek's departure. I blamed fatigue for my harsh words, but knew it was wrong. I had lost control of events the moment we crossed into Ixia. But the real truth was I had never had control. From the instant the Fire Warper stepped from the fire in the jungle, I'd been ruled by fear. Which had kept me alive, so far, but it had certainly made a mess of things. Valek was just the latest in a long list.

I sighed. There was a good reason for the fear. The Fire Warper's power surpassed my own, and I didn't think a bucket of water would douse him. Curling up on the couch, I made plans to free those girls. I couldn't counter the Warper, but at least I could try to stop the Vermin from gaining more power.

But what about the next shipment of young magicians from Ixia? From what Valek told me, I guessed Star had tapped into Porter's network, kidnapping his charges and selling those adolescents for the Vermin to use in the Kirakawa ritual.

After a few hours of restless sleep, I went to the stables. Kiki dozed in her stall, but she woke to my call.

Do you have enough energy for a trip? I asked.

Yes. Where?

Back to where you found me.

Bad smell.

Yes, but I need to go back and pick up their scent. They've probably moved into the plains by now.

We go fast.

That's what I'm counting on. Not bothering to saddle her, I hopped onto her back. All I had was my bow. I glanced at the farmhouse. If I had apologized to Valek, he would have come with me, but I wasn't ready to admit I needed to apologize. At least he would be safe for tonight.

We were soon near the border of the Avibian Plains. Evidence of the Vermin's campsite littered the ground, and from the number of items left behind, it appeared Cahil had left in a hurry. Only a few hours of darkness remained.

Kiki, which way? I asked.

She headed south, and I let her choose her speed. She trotted until we reached the plains, then broke into her gust-of-wind gait. The air sped past my ears as the ground blurred. She didn't maintain the pace for long, slowing when the smell of wood smoke and horses strengthened.

The Vermin's magic waited on the plains. Unlike the Sand-seeds' net of protection, the Daviians preferred to lay traps, which would spring on the unsuspecting victim. Kiki sensed these hot spots and avoided them.

A faint glow of firelight shone through Kiki's eyes. We stopped and I was considering my next move when Kiki reared and danced to the side. The sizzling odor of blood burned in Kiki's nose. She would have bolted, but I steadied her with a soothing hand while my mind turned numb with shock.

They hadn't waited for the next moon. Guilt slammed into me. I hunched over Kiki's back, rocking with anger and frustration.

Girls hurt? Kiki asked.

Yes.

Go. Stop.

What? But she didn't wait. She galloped toward the camp.

Kiki!

Help. Fix. She ran through the camp. Rearing and jumping as if crazed with fear.

Her sudden arrival surprised everyone. The guards scattered and dodged her flailing hooves and my bow. Kiki knocked down Cahil's tent, kicked the wagon over and sent the horses running.

I froze in horror when I spotted the two Warpers stooped over the still forms of Liv and Kieran. Blood coated the Warpers' arms up to their elbows. They each cradled a fist-size lump of meat in their hands, lovingly stroking the object. I gasped with recognition. They each held a human heart. Liv and Kieran's hearts.

Kiki knocked me to my senses when she dumped me onto the ground. I gained my feet, ready for an attack, but the Warpers remained engrossed in their ritual.

Help, Kiki ordered as she made another loop of the camp.

I glanced at the fire. No Fire Warper yet. I mentally kicked myself for even worrying about him, and drew a thick strand of power. The Vermin defensive magic tried to clamp down on my connection, but I had pulled such a fat rope it failed to cut even a thread.

I launched my awareness at the Warpers. A fog of magic surrounded them. Instinctively, I knew in order for them to consume and maintain the power, they had to milk the blood from the hearts and inject it into their skin.

The Kirakawa ritual had its own power and I couldn't interfere with the Warpers. Their black lust for magic sickened me and for a moment my vision filled with blood.

But a movement from the corner of my eye caught my attention. Liv's ghost stood next to her dead body and she gestured to me, thumping her heart with a fist. I squinted at the apparition. Her ghost or her soul? When I understood her motions, I cursed myself for my stupidity.

I couldn't affect the ritual, but there was one thing only I could do. Concentrating on the girls' hearts, I reached for their souls. The ritual had trapped them within its chambers. I inhaled their essence, leaving behind dead flesh. The Warpers wouldn't gain any power tonight.

Kiki slowed near me. I grabbed her mane and hauled myself onto her back. Within two strides she moved into her special gait.

When we reached the edge of the plains, I asked Kiki to stop so I could release the girls' souls. The sun began to rise, casting long shadows on the ground. I wished I had known the girls better so I could make Sitian grief flags for them. The occasion called for the fanfare of raising their flags to memorialize the girls' short lives.

Without silk or a flagpole, I settled for expressing my deep regret for not saving them. They felt content and relieved to be free. But what else could they say while I held their souls?

A vile thought occurred to me. I wondered if my powers

were enhanced while they remained with me. Could I counter
the Fire Warper if I increased my strength? Shuddering in revulsion for just thinking about it, I released their souls to the
sky. They rushed from me. A lingering tingle of joy vibrated
inside me before my body sagged with fatigue.

I arrived at Valek's safe house without any memories of the
trip. Kiki headed for the stable and I summoned enough energy
to give her a good rubdown. The stack of hay bales outside
her stall appeared to be too inviting for me to pass. I lay down
on top of them and fell asleep.

An army of flaming soldiers chased me. My legs refused to run
any faster as the burning men advanced. Leif rushed to my aid
but, as soon as he drew near me, he burst into flames. Only Valek
remained. He stood amid the conflagration, untouched by the
searing heat. A block of ice, he seemed indifferent to my plight.

"Sorry, love." He shrugged. "Can't help you."

"Why?"

"You won't let me."

The fire soldiers closed in until a circle of fire surrounded
me. Tongues of flames licked at my clothes then grabbed the
fabric.

"Yelena!"

Bright yellow and orange danced along my cloak. Their
movements held my attention in a bizarre fascination as they
consumed my clothes.

"Yelena!"

Cold water splashed on me, followed by a drenching deluge.
Steam hissed. I yelled and woke, choking on the water. Valek
stood next to me. He held an empty bucket.

"What?" I sat up. My clothes and hair were soaking wet. "What was that for?"

"You were having a nightmare."

"And shaking me awake seemed too tame?" He was still angry.

Valek didn't answer. Instead, he pulled me to my feet and pointed to the figure-shaped scorch mark on the topmost hay bale. The place where I had slept.

"You were too hot to touch," he said in a deadpan.

I shivered. If Valek hadn't been here, what would have happened?

"I take it your rescue attempt last night has angered some powerful people? I saw you and Kiki create chaos in the camp, ruining my plans yet again. What else did you do?"

Valek hadn't gone to bed. He had left to help the girls. Kiki and I could have gone with him. Together we might have reached the camp in time to save Liv and Kieran. Guilt balled in my chest, souring my mood. I hadn't managed to do anything right. I didn't find Cahil and Ferde in time. The Sandseed Clan was gone. Irys and Bain were locked up. I had upset my friends and my brother. And Valek.

He stared at me with his flat expression, giving nothing away. An invisible wall grew between us. Mine or his? I told him about the girls' souls and how I had removed the power from the ritual.

"I should have let you kill Cahil," I said.

If the change in subject surprised him, he didn't allow it to show on his face. "Why?"

"It would have prevented all this."

"I think not. Cahil's involvement is recent. These Vermin

are prepared. They've been planning this move for a while. Cahil wants you dead and wants his throne. I believe the whole Kirakawa ritual sickens him."

"He helped with the kidnapping."

"Because he wanted you. He wasn't at the camp last night. He's probably heading to the Citadel."

"How do you know?"

Valek gave me a tight, joyless smile. "When you stormed the camp, I stole into the tent, intending to put the Wannabe King out of my misery. I had a few seconds to determine he was gone before the tent collapsed on me."

I suppressed a chuckle. From the annoyed frown, I knew Valek wouldn't appreciate it.

"But I found that." He gestured to the floor. My backpack rested against Kiki's stall door.

A happy cry escaped my lips and I knelt down to check the contents. Before I dug into the pack, I looked up to thank Valek, but he was gone. I considered finding him to explain, but I wasn't ready to breach the wall surrounding me. Inside my little cocoon, I could pretend the Fire Warper's threat to the people I loved didn't exist.

My pack still held my switchblade, my Sitian clothes, my lock picks, vials of Curare, lumps of Theobroma, jerky, tea and Opal's glass bat. The glow from the statue seemed brighter.

The intricate swirls of liquid fire drew my gaze. I marveled at Opal's talent. The whirlpool of light in the core of the bat transformed into a snake. The roar of a kiln beat at my ears. Hands wielded a pair of metal tweezers to shape the thin glass body before it cooled. The thoughts of the glassmaker reached me. Opal's thoughts.

She dripped water on a groove in the glass near the end of the pole. The snake cracked off. Using thick mittens, she picked up the piece and put it into another oven to cool slowly. This one was not as hot as the first.

Opal, can you hear me? I asked.

No response.

When my awareness returned to the bat in my hand, I knew I had reached Booruby with my mind without expending a lot of energy. Booruby! A six-day ride south of here. I hadn't been able to reach Bain from Booruby and I had been closer. What would happen if Irys held the snake? Would we be able to communicate over vast distances without sapping our strength? My mind raced with the implications.

The cold air intruded on my excitement. My wet hair felt icy in the breeze, and I remembered Kiki mentioning snow. We were north of the Avibian Plains, but I had no idea if the farmhouse resided in the Moon Clan's lands or Featherstone's. Either way, by the time the storm reached us, it would turn to rain and sleet. And by looking at the gray wall of clouds advancing from the west, it wouldn't be long before the storm hit.

I shouldered my pack and went inside. Valek had lit a small fire in the living room. His soft tread padded on the floor above me. Probably planning to sleep after being up all night.

Hesitating on the threshold of the room, I debated. My cloak was soaked. I needed the fire to dry it and I wanted to warm myself.

In the end, I changed into Sitian clothes, hung my cloak by the hearth and filled a pot for tea. I heated the water, but avoided looking directly into the fire. Feeling uneasy, I chewed a piece of jerky and drank the tea as far away from the flames as I could get. Unable to stay in the room any longer, I wanted to run upstairs to Valek. Instead, I grabbed a blanket off the couch and ran to the stables, joining Kiki.

She snorted in amusement when I made a bed of straw in her stall. I filled two buckets with water and put them next to me.

If I start to smoke, pour these on me, I said to her. *I don't want to set fire to the barn.*

Soon after I laid down, an odd melody of sleet drummed on the slate roof. The whistle of wind through the rafters augmented the beat. Lulled to sleep by the storm's music, I slept without dreams.

The arrival of a strange horse woke me and Kiki the next morning. At least I hoped the weak storm light meant the beginning and not the end of the day.

Valek led in a black horse with white socks. With its long legs and sleek body, the animal was built like a racehorse. Pulling a thread of power, I linked my mind with the new arrival.

He felt uncomfortable in this new barn. Strange smells. Strange horse. He missed his stall and friends.

Smells here are good, I said in his mind. *You'll make new friends. What's your name?*

Onyx.

I introduced him to Kiki.

Valek tied Onyx to a hitch. "We need to leave for the Citadel." He saddled Onyx. "This weather is good cover."

My heart twisted with pain. He had gotten his own horse so he didn't have to sit with me on Kiki. "How far?"

"Two days. I have another safe house about a mile north of the Citadel. We can set up operations there."

We worked in complete and utter silence.

The next two days felt more like ten. With the nasty weather, Valek's cold shoulder and my anxiety to hurry, I would have preferred spending the time in the Commander's dungeon.

Our arrival at the safe house seemed a relief until the necessity of planning our actions made our strained relationship almost unbearable. I remained stubborn, believing the distance between us would make it easier for me to make life-threatening decisions.

After we settled into the cottage, I headed for the Citadel. The weather again promised rain, lending a bleakness to the landscape. Bare trees and brown hills seemed muted and barren of life. I knew if I swept the area with my magic, I would feel the small stirrings of creatures, waiting for the warmth. But the risk of using magic this close to the Keep was too high.

Disguised as a Featherstone clanswoman, I wore a long-sleeved linen dress underneath a plain sand-colored cloak. Although I left my bow behind, I had access to my switchblade. My hair was pulled into a stylish knot favored by the Featherstones and held in place by my lock picks.

Valek had styled my hair. He worked in a cold and efficient manner, making it easier for me not to grasp his hands and pull him close. His deft fingers twisted the strands of my hair expertly, and a strange vision of fire melting his arms to stumps rose in my mind.

I banished the image and put my hood over my head. The

north gate of the Citadel wasn't as busy as I had hoped. In fact, once inside, only a few people walked the streets. They hunched over their packages and stared at the ground. The weather could be a factor, but the rain had ceased. The streets should be teeming with citizens hurrying to the market before the next squall.

Even the beggars were few and far between. Most of them wore expressions of worry as they glanced around, and none approached me.

The Citadel's white marble walls looked dingy and dull. The green veins resembled streaks of dirt and the whole town felt as if a layer of grime coated it. The grunge had built up in the cracks, and soaked into the foundations. The shine was gone from the town. And it wasn't due to the weather.

I missed a step when the first Daviian Vermin came into my sight. But soon they were everywhere. Hunching over, I mimicked the citizens' posture, searching for an alley or side street free of Vermin. Blood throbbed in my ears. The Vermin's gazes burned into my soul. When I entered a shortcut to the market, my legs wobbled with relief. But I kept out of view until I had studied the center square, watching the people scurrying around the market's stands. The sense of fear even diluted the usual heady smell of spices and roasting meat.

The concentration of citizens meant more Vermin. I waited until I spotted my target and then joined the shoppers. When I drew beside a young boy of ten, I had to suppress a smile as I listened to him barter with the stand owner.

"Four coppers, take it or leave it," Fisk said, sounding like an adult.

"I can't feed my family for that!" the owner countered. "Since you're my friend, I'll take seven coppers."

"Belladoora is selling them for four."

"But look at this quality. Hand embroidered by my own wife. Look at the detail!" He held up the fabric.

"Five, and not a copper more."

"Six, and that's final."

"Good day, sir." Fisk walked away.

"Wait," the stand owner called. "Five then. But you're stealing the bread out of my children's mouths." He grumbled some more while wrapping the fabric in paper, but he smiled when the boy paid him the money.

I followed Fisk to his client. The woman paid him six coppers and he handed her the package.

"Excuse me, boy," I said. "I'm in need of your services."

"What can I do for you?" he asked. Then his eyes flew wide with shock before worry touched them. He glanced around with small furtive movements. "Follow me."

He led me to a tight alley and into a dark dwelling. I stood in the blackness while Fisk lit a few lanterns. Thick curtains hung over the windows and only a few chairs decorated the barren room.

"This is where we meet," Fisk said.

"We?"

He smiled. "The Helpers Guild members. We plan our day, divide up the money, and exchange gossip about our clients."

"That's wonderful." Pride at what Fisk had accomplished filled my heart. The grubby beggar boy I had met on my first Citadel visit had transformed into a productive member of his family.

Fisk's own pride showed in his light brown eyes. "It's all because of you, my first client!"

Instead of begging for money, now Fisk and the other beggar children helped shoppers find good deals, carried packages and would do just about anything for a small fee.

His grin dropped from his face. "Lovely Yelena, you shouldn't be here. There's a reward for your capture."

"How much?"

"Five golds!"

"Is that all? I thought it would be more like ten or fifteen," I teased.

"Five is a lot of money. So much I wouldn't trust my own cousin not to turn you in. It's dangerous for you here. For everyone."

"What's been going on?"

"These new Daviian Clan members. They have taken over. At first it was just a couple of them, but now the streets are filled. Ugly rumors about their involvement with the Sandseed genocide has everyone frightened. People living in the Citadel have been questioned, and certain beggars have disappeared. Whispers about how the Council members have lost control have spread, yet they are preparing for a war."

Fisk shook his head. He had wisdom beyond his years. I mourned the loss of his childhood. Being a child of beggars had robbed him of fun, wonder and the ability to make mistakes without fatal consequences.

"How about the Keep?" I asked.

"Locked down. No one enters or leaves except under the Daviians' armed escort."

The state of affairs was worse than I had anticipated. "I need you to get a message to one of the Councilors for me."

"Which one?"

"My kinsman, Bavol Zaltana. But I don't want you to write anything down. It must be a verbal message. Can you do it?"

Fisk frowned, considering. "It will be difficult. The Councilors all have an escort while out in the Citadel, but perhaps I could set up a distraction..." He rubbed his hands along his arms as he contemplated the task. "I can try. No promises. If it gets too hot, I'm out of there. And it's—"

"Going to cost me. And you must not repeat the message to anyone."

"Agreed."

We shook hands on the deal. I told Fisk my message. He left to recruit a couple helpers. I returned to the market to purchase a few items and to eat, killing time without appearing to be.

My gaze kept returning to the Keep's towers. Located within the Citadel's marble walls, the Magician's Keep occupied the northeastern section. Unable to suppress my desire to see the pink-pillared entrance gates, my path led to the Keep.

Instead of appearing warm and inviting, the cold stone seemed impenetrable and daunting. I longed to make contact with my friends and colleagues inside. Where were Dax and Gelsi? Had they been allowed to continue their studies? I felt blind and cut off, frustrated and lost. As if I had been exiled and would never see them again.

Daviian guards stood next to the Keep's guards. Feeling too exposed, I returned to Fisk's meeting room to await the boy's return. Time crept along in mind-numbing increments. A small tan spider built its elaborate web in the corner of the room. To help the spider, I hunted for an insect to place on the sticky strands.

Fisk arrived as I stood on a chair, attempting to nab a moth. He puffed out his chest and declared the mission a success. "Councilor Zaltana said he would meet with you tonight in his home." Fisk deflated a bit with his next remark. "He warned his residence is guarded by a Warper. What's a Warper?"

"A Daviian magician." I considered the complication. "What time?"

"Anytime, but if you're out on the streets after midnight, the guards will arrest you. I would suggest after the evening meal. There is usually a flurry of activity as the shops close and everyone heads home." Fisk sighed. "It used to be a good time to beg. People would feel guilty passing by a child without a home when they had a warm comfortable bed waiting for them."

"Used to be, Fisk. That's in the past. I bet you have a nice home, now."

His posture straightened. "The best! Which reminds me. You had better leave before my helpers come back. We meet in the morning and again in the late afternoon."

I paid Fisk, thanking him for the help. "If you ever get caught, don't hesitate to tell them about me. I don't want you to be hurt because of me."

Fisk gave me a confused frown. "But you could be taken and killed by the Daviians."

"Better me than you."

"No. Things are bad and getting worse. If you're killed, I have a horrible feeling life wouldn't be worth living."

★ ★ ★

Fisk's dire comments followed me as I traveled through the Citadel. Keeping to the back alleys, I hid behind buildings until the streets filled with residents hurrying home, just as Fisk had predicted. I joined the flow, blending in as the sky grew dark and the lamplighters began their evening chore. When I passed Bavol's dwelling, I slowed long enough to determine his house was empty.

I made another loop around the street to make sure, then slipped behind the building. Using my picks, I unlocked the back door and startled a woman.

"Oh my!" She dropped a rake. It clattered on the edge of the stone heath, and the fire she had been stirring to life dimmed.

"I didn't mean to startle you," I said, thinking fast. "I have an urgent appointment with Councilman Zaltana."

"I don't remember him telling me about a guest. And certainly no guest would come creeping in the back door!" She swept up the iron rake and hefted it in her big hands. She wore a type of loose tunic the Zaltanas preferred, but it was hard to see in the semidarkness.

I chanced it. "We just set the meeting today. It's regarding *clan* business."

"Oh my." She bent and raked at the coals. When a flame ignited, she used it to light a lantern. She peered at me through the glow. "Goodness, child. Come in then. Shut the door. This is all highly unusual, but I don't know why I'm surprised. These are unusual times."

The woman bustled and fussed about the kitchen, claiming the Councilman would soon be home and would want his supper. I helped her by lighting the lanterns in the dining room and living room. Bavol's home was decorated with jungle art and valmur statues. A pang of homesickness struck me.

When I heard someone at the front door, I hid in the kitchen.

"His guard dog doesn't come in the house," the woman said. "The Councilman won't allow it. The day that dog is allowed in will be the end of the Sitian Council."

But would the Warper use his magic to scan the interior? Would I feel the power? I hovered by the back door just in case.

The woman said, "Call me Petal, child," and invited me to join them for supper. She shooed away any protests about my limited time. "Nonsense, child. Let me tell the Councilman you're here."

"Ah, Petal," I said, stopping her. "Perhaps it would be best if you just asked him to come in here? Dogs have very acute hearing."

She tapped a finger to her forehead and then pointed to me before leaving. Bavol came into the kitchen with Petal on his heels. He greeted me with a tired smile.

"Smart to come before me," he said in a soft voice. He rubbed at the dark smudges under his eyes. Worry lines etched his face and he stood as if he strained under a heavy weight. "If you're discovered…" He sank down to perch on an edge of a stool. "You can't stay long. If they hear or see anything out of the ordinary, the Warper will barge in and I *will* tell him everything."

His matter-of-fact statement about his response to the Warper sent a ripple of fear through my body. What were the Warpers doing to gain information and cooperation?

"I'll be quick then. Why did the Council allow the Daviians to come?"

Alarm flashed on Bavol's face and he clamped his hands together in his lap. "Petal, could you please get me a glass of whiskey?"

She eyed him with annoyance. Even though she stirred her stew pot on the other side of the kitchen, she had been leaning toward us, trying to listen to our conversation.

With a huff of indignation, Petal left the kitchen.

Bavol closed his eyes for a moment and grimaced. But when he focused on me, his old confident self returned.

"We should have let them die," he said.

26

"LET WHO DIE?" I ASKED, but Bavol ignored me.

"At first the Daviians required minor things from us to keep them alive. A vote one way or another. The requests became more frequent and alarming. Visitors grew in numbers and the next thing we knew we had agreed to everything."

"Keep who alive?"

"We made a mistake, but you're here now. Perhaps it's not too late."

"Bavol, I don't—"

"The Daviians have our children."

I stared at him for a moment in stunned silence. "How?"

Bavol shrugged. "Does it matter how? Our families live with our clans most of the year. We're not home to protect them."

"Who do they have?"

"My daughter, Jenniqilla. She disappeared from the Illiais Market. I've been instructed not to tell anyone. But from the other Councilors' faces I knew the Daviians had gotten to everyone. Eventually, we talked about it amongst ourselves. All the Councilors with children had one taken. For the others, the Daviians kidnapped Councilor Greenblade's husband, and Councilor Stormdance's wife."

"Where are they keeping them?"

"If I knew I wouldn't be here talking to you," he snapped.

"Sorry." I considered the implications. Petal returned with two glasses of whiskey and handed one to me. She went back to stirring her pots.

"When?" I asked, thinking about Valek's comment that the Vermin had been planning this before Cahil had gotten involved.

"Fourteen days ago," Bavol whispered.

I thought back. Fourteen days seemed like fourteen years when I sifted through everything that had happened. The Vermin had grabbed the Councilors' families right after I fled the Citadel. It wasn't Roze influencing the Council after all.

"Do the Master Magicians know?"

"Master Bloodgood and Master Jewelrose suspected when we wrote the letter to the Commander. Master Featherstone interpreted their refusal as an act of treason. And the Daviians forced us to agree with her and sign their arrest warrant and help incarcerate them in the Keep. They cooperated," Bavol added when he saw my concern. "It's a shame Master Cowan is still too young to exert much influence on Master Featherstone."

"Do you think Roze is working with the Daviians?"

"No. She would be horrified to know they are making the decisions. We are voting with her, so she is content and the Daviians are offering her support in her campaign against the Commander."

"Couldn't she learn of your dilemma from your thoughts?"

Bavol's gaze snapped to me. "That would be a serious breach

of the Magician's Ethical Code. Master Featherstone would never resort to invading our private thoughts."

I had a difficult time believing in Roze's high moral standards, but I possessed no evidence to the contrary.

"Should I set an extra place for dinner?" Petal asked.

Bavol and I both shook our heads no. His anxious expression reminded me I needed to leave soon. She tsked and carried a stack of plates from the kitchen.

Finding and rescuing the Council's family members became a priority. There was one way I could discover where they were being held, but I would have to use magic.

"Bavol, I may be able to find your daughter through you. But I can't do it in the Citadel. Is there any chance you can leave?"

"No. My guard is with me always."

"Could you slip out the back door?"

"I have to make contact with my guard every hour. It is the only way he will give me any privacy."

"What about when you're sleeping?"

"He sits in the living room. Petal doesn't know about it, since she retires so early and sleeps like a log. I haven't been able to sleep since Jenniqilla's capture. I'm up before the sun and can send him back outside."

"It will have to be during the night, then. I'll make arrangements. Just don't be surprised if you have company in your bedroom tomorrow evening. And leave the back window open."

"That's Petal's room," he said.

"Perhaps you can make sure she remains asleep?"

He sighed. "I long for the simpler days. Never again will I complain about Councilor Sandseed's stubbornness or Councilor Jewelrose's petty problems."

"Dinner's ready," Petal called.

"You should go," he said.

"Do you know any way I could get into the Keep?"

"The emergency tunnel. But I don't know if it has collapsed or been sealed up. The magicians dug it when they first constructed their Keep, during the clan wars long ago. I hadn't known it existed until recently. Second Magician mentioned it to me a few days before they arrested him and Fourth Magician."

"Are Bain and Irys still being held in the Keep's cells?"

"As far as I know."

"Did Bain tell you where the tunnel is located?"

"He said something about the east side of the Keep, and about how it was big enough for a horse." Bavol stood. "We have lingered too long. I expect to hear from you again. Stay safe." He went into the dining room.

I waited a moment, then opened the back door. Peeking out, I scanned the dark alley. It appeared to be deserted, but without my magic, I couldn't be sure. I risked it and left Bavol's. The Citadel's quiet streets alarmed me. Only a few people walked on the roads, and most of them were Vermin. Even the taverns remained dark and desolate.

My chances of getting through the north gate undetected didn't seem likely. I considered going to one of the inns, but the Vermin could have people there watching for strangers. The longer I stayed on the street increased the danger of being caught.

In desperation, I found a house with an outside staircase reaching the ground of a narrow alley. Climbing up to the top of the steps without making too much noise, I stood on the handrail and reached for the edge of the roof. I discovered a problem with marble buildings as I tried to use the wall to push myself onto the roof. My foot slipped and I just managed to regain my balance and avoid plummeting four stories to the ground.

In the end, I employed my acrobatic training and made a leap of faith onto the roof. Good thing these same marble walls were thick enough to mask the sound of my thud.

I lay on the flat roof, gasping, glad Valek hadn't been here to see my awkward ascent. His ability to scale the Commander's castle walls was now more impressive. I wondered if he would be worried when I failed to come back. Perhaps it was for the best that I had stayed too long with Bavol. Multiple trips through the gate would arouse suspicion.

The night air turned cold. I huddled in my cloak and slept. Dreams of fire haunted me. No matter where I ran to or where I hid, the flames always found me. Always.

I woke sweat soaked in the morning light, achy and feverish. The prospect of climbing down from the roof unseen and finding Fisk was as appealing as taking a cold bath. At least descending proved easier than ascending the roof. I made it down the stairs and into the alley without incident. Although the thumping in my head failed to stop.

Bleary-eyed and tired, I searched for Fisk at the market. Remembering his meeting room, I hid nearby and waited for him.

The group of children who left the building caused me to smile. So intent on their day's work, they moved with purpose and carried themselves with a businesslike air. After they disappeared from sight, Fisk appeared beside me.

"Did something happen?" he asked.

"Nothing bad. I have another job for you." I told him what

I needed and he thought he could help me. "I don't want anyone to get into trouble, though."

"Don't worry, you picked a good night."

"Why is it good?"

"It's Midseason's Night. We celebrate the midpoint of the cold season. Gives everyone something to look forward to." Fisk grinned. "Doesn't Ixia have something similar?"

"Yes. They hold an annual Ice Festival. People display their handcrafts and get together to exchange ideas. I just hadn't realized we were this far into the season."

"The celebration's bound to be quieter this year, but there should be enough activity to hide ours." This time Fisk's smile held a hint of mischievousness, reminding me of Janco.

I'd bet Janco had been pure trouble as a kid. At least I hadn't upset him and Ari before leaving Ixia. Then again, since I hadn't brought them along, they could be annoyed with me, too.

We made plans for the evening and Fisk told me of a place where I could stay to wait for the night. After he left, I walked over to the Council Hall. I made a loop around it while trying not to appear as if I held any special interest in the square structure. The activity on the wide steps leading to the first floor was busy. The Councilors' offices, the great hall, record room, library and Citadel's jail all resided inside. My interest lay in the record room. Information from all the clans had been stored there, and I wanted to find any mention about the magician's emergency tunnel within the records. Or perhaps the library would have some reference to the Keep's layout?

Bain's private stash of books most likely contained the information I needed. The irony of my situation was not lost on me. The Second Magician had told Bavol about the tunnel's existence because he knew Bavol would be the first person I would contact. What Bavol had thought was an interesting tidbit of information turned out to be a message for me.

The lack of details remained a problem. East side of the Keep and big enough for a horse didn't give me much to go on.

The flow of people in and out of the Council Hall stayed steady. However, a few Vermin hung about and I decided not to risk my life for research.

When I headed back toward the market, a strange feeling touched my back as if a thousand little spiders crawled up my spine in unison. Turning a corner, I glanced to the side. A male Daviian walked a small distance behind me. He wore red pantaloons and a brown hooded short cape. When I rounded another corner, he remained on my tail.

His scimitar glinted in the sunlight. I entered the market. Pausing at a vegetable stand, I hoped the Vermin would pass me, but he leaned on a lamppost. Small darts of panic began to pierce my heart. If the Daviian was a Warper, I wouldn't be able to lose him.

Joining with a group of women, I stayed with them as they shopped. The man kept pace with us. I needed a distraction and fast.

One of the women in the group paid for a beaded necklace. She had been rather loud and full of opinions as we went from stand to stand, and she made her annoyance over my unwanted presence clear to me.

When the stand owner handed her the wrapped package, I leaned over and whispered to her, "He sold that very same necklace to my friend for two silvers last week."

The woman had just paid four silvers. As predicted, she loudly demanded the same price and the confused seller tried to reason with her. The ensuing argument drew a considerable crowd and I squeezed between them, hoping to lose the Daviian.

No luck. He caught sight of me and followed. A few shoppers temporarily blocked his way, and I ducked under one of the market stands.

Not the best decision, but I had run out of options. I hunched under the table. A purple cloth had been draped over it and the material hung to the ground. A few bolts of fabric and a box of buttons had been stored underneath.

I wondered when it would be safe to leave. Popping up just as the Vermin walked by wouldn't be ideal, so I squirmed into a more comfortable position to wait.

The purple fabric pulled aside. I froze.

A man's face peered through the opening. "Your friend's gone. It's safe to come out."

He backed away when I started to move. "Thanks," I said, brushing the dirt off my cloak.

"Attracting *their* attention is never a good thing," the man said. His round face held a serious expression. "People tend to disappear around here. Especially those with five golds on their head."

I calmed my furious heartbeat. The stand owner knew I hid under his table and he hadn't reported me. At least not yet. Perhaps he wished to strike a bargain? Something like six golds to keep quiet.

"Don't worry. You're a friend to Fisk and his guild. And just the fact the Daviians would be willing to pay five golds for your capture means you, of all people, scare them. I hope for the sake of my family the reason you scare them is because you can do something to bring our normal lives back."

"I scare them," I agreed, thinking about the Sitian Council and how terrified they had been over me being a Soulfinder. "But I don't know if I can restore your old way of life. I'm only one person."

"You have Fisk's help."

"Until my money runs out."

"True. That little scamp, forcing me to make an honest living!" The man paused and considered. "Aren't there any others to help you?"

"Would you help me?"

He blinked in surprise. "How?"

"Not all these Vermin are Warpers. They carry scimitars and spears, but look around you—they are outnumbered."

"But their Warpers have powerful magic."

"You don't have any magicians? No one has escaped from the Keep? No one has come from the other clans?"

His eyes lit with understanding. "But they're scattered around the Citadel. They hide in fear."

"A concerned citizen needs to convince them to act despite their fear, to organize them and, when the time is right, to lead them."

"You can do that. You're the Soulfinder."

I shook my head. "My presence would jeopardize the efforts. I'm needed elsewhere. If you're determined, you will find the right person."

The man smoothed out the fabric on his table. He appeared deep in thought. "Merchants come and go from the Citadel all the time…caravans of goods…"

"Just be very careful." I started to walk away.

"Wait. How will we know when the time is right?"

"I have a bad feeling that you won't be able to miss it."

After the day settled into night, I met up with Fisk and his uncle. People walked the streets in good humor despite their Vermin watchers and the late hour. While Fisk went to prepare for later, I led his uncle onto the roof.

Once we ascended, we traveled over the roofs of the Citadel to Bavol's dwelling. If they weren't out celebrating, the other residents had already gone to bed. I pulled the rope Fisk had bought for me from my pack, and secured it around the chimney before tossing the end over the side.

The glow from the lamplights didn't reach the back alley, so I hoped Bavol had remembered to open the back window. Clutching the rope, I shimmied down the side of the house and was relieved to find the window open. I climbed into Petal's room with the utmost care. Inside the room, I stilled and listened to her breathing, steady with the occasional snore. I yanked on the rope, then held it stable while Uncle slid down. He joined me in the room with a thump. We both froze until Petal resumed her even breathing.

Bavol, awake and ready, waited for us in his room. Uncle slipped into bed, pulling the blankets up to his neck and the Councilor came with me to the back window. Living in the jungle canopy all his life, Bavol had no trouble ascending the rope. I followed.

Traveling over the rooftops proved to be ideal. Eventually, we climbed down to the ground. When we came within sight of the north gate, we found a place to hide. No traffic.

I worried, and the longer the gate remained empty the greater my fear.

As I tried to decide if we should risk crossing through, a group of obviously inebriated men and women approached. With loud voices, a few of the group decided they wanted to go outside the Citadel, and a discussion ensued, leading to a fight.

When the guards became entangled in the brawl, Bavol and I slipped through the gate unnoticed. Once out of sight of the guardhouse, we ran. Our time was limited.

We reached Valek's cottage and I hoped we would be far enough away from the Citadel and the Warpers.

Kiki whinnied in her stall and I opened my mind to her.

Lavender Lady safe, she said with contentment. *Ghost upset.*

I'll talk later. No time right now. I hustled Bavol into the cottage. Valek sat on the couch, his expression set into cold fury.

I ignored his anger. He of all people should know the nature of this operation lent itself to unforeseen circumstances. However, I knew why Bavol's face blanched when he spotted Valek on the couch.

"You set me up," he said, taking a step back.

"Relax, Bavol. If Valek was going to assassinate the Council, you would be dead by now. He's helping me."

Valek snorted. "I am? Funny how I forgot. Or is it because someone forgot about me?" Sarcasm spiked each word.

Again, I ignored his fury and filled him in on what Bavol had told me. His face lost some of his ire as he considered the new information.

"Bavol, sit down. Close your eyes. Think of your daughter," I ordered.

When he settled on the couch, I reached for power. Touching the source caused a sudden rush of relief. I hadn't used magic in two days and reconnecting felt like being wrapped tight in my mother's arms.

I projected my awareness to Bavol. His loving thoughts dwelled on his little girl. She appeared to be around eight years old. Strands of gold streaked her long brown hair and a spattering of freckles dotted her warm maple-colored cheeks. A beautiful child, she twirled with delight after being presented with a piece of sap candy.

Through Bavol, I reached toward Jenniqilla. Within the memory, her happiness over the candy matched her joy over spending time with her father. I pushed past the memory and tried to find the girl.

She missed her father with a painful desperation. Cold and hungry, she wanted her father and mother more than food or heat. She rocked back and forth, trying to soothe the child in her arms. The two-year-old boy's crying had set off a chain reaction among the children in the room. A woman paced with a year-old baby girl and the man tried to cajole another two-year-old.

The gloomy light in the wooden room came from small cracks between the gray boards. The area contained no furniture and only two slop pots had been placed behind a ripped screen. From the harsh acidic smell, the pots hadn't been emptied in a while. A coating of grime clung to Jenniqilla's skin and she promised herself she would never fuss at her mother about bathing again. An icy chill seeped into her legs and back from the dirt floor.

Jenniqilla, I said in her mind. *Where are you?*

She glanced around, wondering if someone had called her name. Seeing no one, she continued to sing to Leevi.

I'm your cousin, Yelena. I need to know where you are so I can help you and the others.

She remembered how her second cousin was taken long ago, but had returned. *If she got away, than I can, too,* she thought.

Jenniqilla was too young to access the power source. She couldn't communicate with me directly, but she felt the intentions of my power. She remembered her kidnapping. Somehow, she had lost sight of her mother at the market. As she wandered around, searching for Mama a man dressed in the loose tunic of the Sandseed clan picked her up. Before she could yell, he clamped a sweet-smelling rag over her mouth and nose.

Jenniqilla woke inside a box and cried for Mama. A man banged on the wood and threatened to kill her if she didn't shut up. She felt movement and when the box stopped and opened, the same Sandseed man pulled her out and brought her to an old dilapidated barn smelling of rot. Within the barn was another structure. This one smelled like sawed wood and had shiny locks on the door.

When they shoved her through the door, dark shapes moved in the corners. Distraught and confused, she cried. A woman materialized from one of those black forms and took Jenniqilla into her arms. After she had quieted, the woman, Gale Stormdance, explained to her why they all were there.

Ask Gale where you are, I encouraged Jenniqilla.

But Gale wasn't sure. "I think somewhere in Bloodgood's lands," she said. Her face grew thoughtful, and I projected myself toward her and encountered a magical defensive barrier.

She stared at Jenniqilla in shock but lowered her defenses tentatively.

I'm here to help, I said to Gale, explaining who I was and how I had found her.

Thank goodness, she said. *I've been hoping a Keep magician would look for us. Why did it take so long?*

I updated her on what I knew, then asked her again about her whereabouts.

I only had a brief glimpse. I sensed her frustration.

Visualize the area around the barn for me.

Forest-covered hills loomed behind the barn and a large stone farmhouse was located to the right. Something odd had caught her eye on the left. A glint of sunlight off a crimson-colored pond. The shape, though, had been stranger than the color. Her mind sifted through all the panic and fear of being hauled out of a crate and taken inside to find the required image.

A diamond, she exclaimed. *The pond is shaped like a diamond.*

It was a start. I thanked her for her help and promised to find them.

I pulled away from Gale, away from Jenniqilla and back to Bavol. A thin filament looped around my mind as I returned to Bavol. As if another power had caught me in a parasitic embrace.

Through Bavol's confused mind, I returned to my body. Valek had disappeared and the smell of smoke burned my nose. I rushed to the window.

The stable was on fire.

27

"Kiki!" I screamed, running. The image of her trapped in her stall and engulfed by flames filled my vision.

A voice yelled my name.

A black horse stood in the pasture.

A Daviian Warper coaxed the blaze higher. Brighter. Hotter. It didn't matter.

The parasite in my mind had gained control.

I ran straight into the stable, diving into the fire.

The heat burned my face and seared the inside of my nose. Flames danced with delight on my cloak, eating the fibers in gleeful disregard. The soles of my boots melted. The smoke robbed air from my lungs. My throat closed.

Hot knives of pain stabbed into my skin. Layers burned off in sheets of torment. The sound of boiling blood sizzled in my ears.

Pleasure followed pain and the colors of my world turned from white-hot and blinding yellow into bloodred and ice-black.

I marveled at my surroundings. Lit with a soft gray light, the flat world extended for miles in every direction. With reluctance, I glanced at my body, expecting to see a burnt corpse, but was surprised to find no damage. A weightless feeling tingled, and my arms and legs were slightly transparent.

A ghost perhaps? Was I in the shadow world? Then where were the others? All the Sandseeds who waited for me. Perhaps they had been a figment of Moon Man's imagination.

A soft laugh sounded beside me.

"You don't see them because you have chosen *not* to see them," a voice said.

A voice I feared more than anything. The Fire Warper stood next to me. He had lost his cloak of flames and appeared as an ordinary man. Broad shouldered with short dark hair, he stood as tall as Moon Man. His skin gleamed as if carved from coal.

He raised his arm to me. "Go ahead, touch it. It's not hard."

I hesitated. "You read my mind?"

He laughed again. "No. I read the question in your eyes. Despite your fear, you're curious. An admirable trait."

The Fire Warper stroked my arm with his fingertips. I jerked away.

"So afraid of being burned. I knew I needed a big fire to attract my little bat. It wasn't that bad, was it?"

"Bad enough." Caught here with him, my fear turned to resignation.

He seemed delighted with my response. Gesturing around, he said, "So what do you think of my fire world? Rather dull?"

"Yes. I thought it would be…" I scanned the featureless plain, with black ground and crimson sky.

"Hotter? Filled with burning souls? That you would be welcomed by your old tormentor, Reyad, for an eternity of rape and torture?"

"Filled with souls," I agreed. Drawn into the fire before, I had seen others.

"That's because you were with Moon Man. He has *chosen* to see those unfortunate souls. They've all lived colorful stories of life. You block them from your mind. Unwilling to see and unwilling for Moon Man to show you."

"I saw them in the shadow world, and relieved him of those painful images," I protested.

"Really? Do they haunt your dreams? Are you working with Moon Man to soothe them?" He paused and, when I didn't answer, he smiled. "Of course not! You have locked them away just like you have pushed Moon Man and your brother out of your life. Soon Valek will follow."

"At least they'll be safe."

"No one is safe."

Tired of his wordplay, I asked him what he wanted.

The amusement dropped from his face in an instant. "The sky."

I stared at him.

"I rule the fire world. I now have control over the shadow world, thanks to those Daviian magicians. And even though the shadow world is a borderland between fire and sky, I still can't access the sky."

"Why?"

"Because once I rule the sky, I can return to the living world."

Horror rolled through me. "What's in the sky?"

"The source of all magic."

I didn't quite understand. All magicians had access to the power source. Would he block others from using it?

"You know so little of magic," he said. His expression was incredulous.

I peered at him. His face had changed from smooth to covered with burn scars. His skin rippled as if melting.

"Why do you need me?"

"You're the only one who can get me into the sky."

"And why would I do that?"

"Because this is what I'll do to your family and friends."

He touched my arm. Burning pain seared up my shoulder and encompassed my head. My eyes turned hot and dry. The other occupants of the fire world became visible through a shimmering veil of heat.

Souls writhed in pain, dancing as if flames clinging to a log. Twisting and contorting, their misery pulsed off them in waves. The force of their emotions slammed into me. I stepped back into the Fire Warper's embrace.

He pointed to the different souls. "A few belong here, like Hetoo and Makko. Others were sent by the Daviians to feed me. Increased my power so much I can travel into the shadow world and steal more souls." He dragged me through the sea of suffering. "Your brother would add nicely to my collection. His magic is strong. Moon Man." He savored the Story Weaver's name. "Would bring me a cooling blue power. Combined, your mother and father would give me a boost. But I'll let them *all* live if you help me."

"If I help you, you'll be able to rule the living world, so how does that save them?"

"I'll show them special favor."

I knew they wouldn't agree. Yet spending eternal life in complete misery wasn't an attractive alternative.

The Fire Warper released me. The souls faded from sight and the dull plain reappeared.

"Much better, isn't it?" he asked.

"Yes."

"This could be your eternity. It's not very interesting, but it is safe. However…"

I leaned forward.

"You could live in the sky. It's peaceful and filled with contentment and joy."

"Until you join them."

"I only need to use them for a while. Once I've returned to the living, I will let you preside over their happiness."

An appealing prospect, except he had changed his story and I knew then I couldn't trust anything he said or promised. Being dead hadn't released me from my responsibilities at all. Perhaps if I went into the sky, I could tap into the power source and stop him.

"What would I have to do?" I asked.

"You need to find a soul on its way to the sky and follow it."

"What about you?"

"I'll be with you."

I looked at him in confusion.

"When you go to the sky, you'll be able to explore all aspects of magic. But to get there, you need to draw a soul to you. You know how to do that. Once you have the soul, step into the fire. Come to me and together we will go to the sky," he explained.

"But I'm dead already. Why can't I take one of the souls that doesn't belong here?"

He shook his head. "You must come under your own volition. You're not dead. I pulled you from the flames before they could consume your body. Besides, all these souls belong here. They don't deserve to be in the sky."

Another contradiction. I didn't know what to believe. And his motives were unclear, so I asked him, "Why do you want to go back to the living world?"

His burned face creased with anger. Fire erupted on his shoulders. "He sent me here to spend an eternity in misery. But *his* descendant released me, fed me power in exchange for knowledge and obedience. My master is strong, but not that strong. I have exceeded my savior's power. Now I want to regain my life that had been stolen from me."

"Who sent you here?"

"An Efe traitor named Guyan. Now do we have an agreement? If not, then you will remain here." He shrugged as if my decision didn't concern him too much.

Guyan's name was familiar to me. He was Gede's ancestor. So my new Story Weaver was in league with the Fire Warper. Perhaps Gede was also their leader Jal. I would have to remember that tidbit the next time I had a lesson scheduled with Gede. I choked out a laugh. At this point, there would be no future sessions for me.

I scanned the flat plain, peering into the red-tinged light. A gray shape swooped from the air. It dived and danced over a figure. I moved closer. The shape was a bat. But there weren't any insects or sources of heat to warrant its actions. Yet it picked and yanked at the figure. Another torture on the poor soul?

"What do you see, Yelena?" the Fire Warper asked. "Your future?"

"Perhaps." I turned away.

"Will you come back?"

"Yes."

He held out his hand. I grasped it. My world melted in a blaze of heat and cooled just as quickly in a swirl of ash and smoke. I lay among the ruins of the stable. Charred beams rested in crooked angles, twisted pieces of blackened metal littered the floor, and the scorched smell of burnt leather hung in the air.

I stumbled from the still-warm pile of wood. Singed holes peppered my clothes and soot streaked my skin. My cloak was gone. The hair on my arms had been burned away. I reached for my head, stopping when I encountered half-burnt stubble instead of hair.

My ruined boots crunched on the remains of the stable and shuffled through ash-filled puddles as I walked out, seeking Kiki. No response to either my mental or physical calls.

A loud bang sounded behind me and I turned to see Valek standing in the doorway of the cottage.

I laughed at his expression of complete and utter surprise. Then my legs turned to liquid as I realized what I would really lose when I kept my promise to the Fire Warper. My efforts were so focused on trying to protect him—protect everyone— I hadn't considered the cost of keeping them safe. I fell.

He was beside me in an instant. Caressing my face with a feather-light touch, he looked uncertain.

"Are you real?" he asked. "Or just some cruel joke?"

"I'm real. A real simpleton, Valek. I should never have said…I should never have done…" I drew in a deep breath. "Forgive me, please?"

"Would you promise never to do it again?" he asked.

"Sorry, I can't."

"Then you certainly are real. A real pain in the ass, but that's who I fell in love with." He pulled me close.

I clung to him with my ear pressed against his chest. The beat of his heart, steady and solid, comforted me. His soul, nestled within its chambers, was unreachable with my magic, but he had given it to me freely.

"Why were you so determined to push me away, love?"

"Fear."

"You've faced fear before. What's different?"

Good question. The answer horrified me. All this time I believed I wanted to protect my friends and family from the Fire Warper. "I'm afraid of my magic." The words tumbled from my mouth, breaking through the invisible barrier I had built between us. "If I harvested enough souls, I know I would possess ample power to defeat *all* the Warpers, including the Fire Warper. That's tempting. Tempting enough to want to protect *you* from *me*."

Valek pulled back and tilted my head so he could meet my gaze. "But all you need to do is ask. We wouldn't hesitate to give you our souls to defeat the Warpers."

"No. There has to be another way."

"And that would be...?"

"When I figure it out, you'll be the first to know." Before he could comment, I added, "You never answered me. Am I forgiven?"

He sighed dramatically. "You're forgiven. Now come inside, you reek of smoke."

Valek helped me to my feet. I swayed on unsteady legs for a moment. "Where's Kiki?"

"Once you disappeared into the stable, she ran off and hasn't come back."

I wanted to find her and reassure her, but my body lacked the energy.

We walked to the cottage. The bright light of midday burned in the sky. I could no longer think of the sky without remembering my deal with the Fire Warper. Unease wrapped around chest.

"Where's Bavol?" I asked to distract myself.

"The Daviian Warper captured him while I tried to douse the fire. Will they kill him?"

"No. They need him and all the Councilors for a while to keep up the pretense that the Council and Master Magicians are in charge."

"How long will it last?"

"Not very."

"Will they come after us here?"

The Fire Warper had gotten what he wanted. "No. But we need to retake control."

"We, love? I thought you could handle this by yourself."

Dealing with the Fire Warper was my task, but, for the rest, I required assistance. "I was wrong."

Valek heated water and filled the cast-iron tub. He removed my pile of burnt clothes. By the time I finished bathing, he had brought me a clean outfit.

"What's this?" He held Opal's glass bat.

I told him about my visit with Opal. "As a fellow artist, what do you think of the construction?"

Valek examined the statue, turning it this way and that. "It's an accurate reproduction. The coloring matches one of the smaller jungle bat species. It's sticky with magic. I feel it, but can't see it. Can you?"

"The inside glows as if molten fire has been captured by ice."

"That would be something to see, then."

Thinking about what the Fire Warper had done to show me his world, I touched Valek's shoulder and opened myself to him, letting him see the bat through me.

"Ahh...spectacular. Can everyone see this?"

"Only magicians." And the Commander, I thought.

"Good. That lays *that* debate to rest. I am *not* a magician."

"Then what are you? You're not a regular person either."

Valek pretended to be mortified.

"Come on," I said. "Your skills as a fighter have an almost magical air. Your ability to move without sound and blend in with shadows and people seem extraordinary. You can communicate with me over vast distances, but I can't contact you."

"An anti-magician?"

"I suppose, but I'd bet Bain could find it in one of his books." I told Valek about the tunnel and about the Councilors' families, describing the pond to him.

He considered. "That sounds like Diamond Lake in the Jewelrose lands. It's near the Bloodgood border. The Jewelrose Clan had built a series of lakes that resemble shapes of jewels and the water reflects the colors."

"Why red?"

"Because the Jewelrose Clan is famous for cutting rubies into diamond shapes. The Commander even has a six-carat ruby on a ring, but he had stopped wearing it after the takeover. I wonder..." Again, Valek's gaze grew distant.

"What?"

He looked at me as if deciding whether to tell me something important. "Have you shown your bat to the Commander?"

"Yes."

"And?"

I hesitated. I had promised the Commander to keep what he called "his mutation" a secret. Would telling Valek about the bat break that confidence?

"I know about the Commander, love. How could you believe that I spent the last twenty-one years with him and *not* know?"

"I…"

"After all." Valek made a scary face. "I am the anti-magician!"

I laughed. "Why didn't you tell me?"

"For the same reason you didn't." He wrapped my bat and placed it back into my pack.

"The Commander saw the glow. I think his body contains two souls, but I have no idea how or why it's magical. And if he does have magic, why didn't he flame out after puberty?"

"Two? Ambrose's mother died during his birth and there was some confusion. The midwife insisted a boy had been born, but later his father held a baby girl. They searched for evidence of a second child but found nothing. They chalked it up to the midwife being upset about losing her patient. Ambrose used to blame this invisible twin whenever he was in trouble, which from his stories was quite often. His family indulged him when he began wearing boy's clothes and calling himself Ambrose. It seemed mild in comparison to a few of his other antics."

"Was his mother a magician?"

"She was considered to be a healer, but I don't know if she healed with magic or with mundane remedies."

Valek drained the tub while I attempted to do something with my ruined hair. Some sections remained long, while others had been burnt to stubble.

"Let me, love." Valek removed the brush from my hands. He rummaged around the bath area until he found his razor. "Sorry, nothing else will work."

"How did you get so good with hair?"

"Spent a season working undercover as Queen Jewel's personal groomer. She had beautiful, thick hair."

"Wait, I thought all the Queen's servants had to be women."

"Good thing no one thought to look up my skirt." Valek grinned with impish delight as he cut my hair. Large chunks floated to the ground. I stared at them, trying to convince myself losing my hair didn't matter. Especially not when I considered I wouldn't need it in the fire world.

After he finished, Valek said, "This will help with your disguise."

"My disguise?"

"Everyone's looking for you. If I disguise you as a man, you'll be much harder to find. Although…" He studied my face. "I'll use a little makeup. Being a man won't draw unwanted attention unless they notice you don't have any eyebrows."

I touched the ridge above my eyes with my fingertips, feeling smooth skin. I wondered if they would grow back. Again, I dismissed the notion. It wouldn't matter in the end.

"What should we do first? Try to find the tunnel to the

Keep, if it even exists. Or go and rescue the Councilors' families?" I asked.

"We should—" Valek sniffed the air as if he smelled a dangerous scent. "Someone's coming."

28

HE SIGNALED ME TO WAIT and left without a sound. I grabbed my switchblade and crept through the living room. A murmur of voices filtered in from the kitchen. The door flew open as soon as I reached it. I brandished my knife at the hulking figure in the doorway.

"What happened to your hair?" Ari demanded. "Are you all right?"

Janco followed him in. "Look what happens when you sneak off without us!"

"I'd hardly call being captured and taken to Sitia inside a box sneaking off," I said.

Janco cocked his head this way and that. "Aha! You look just like a prickle bush in MD-4. If we buried you up to your neck, we could—"

"Janco." Ari growled.

"If you gentlemen are finished, I'd like to know why you disobeyed my orders," Valek said.

Janco smiled one of his predatory grins as if he had anticipated this question and already composed an answer. "We did *not* disobey any of your orders. You said to keep an eye on Yelena's brother, the scary-looking big guy and the others. So we did."

Valek crossed his arms and waited.

"But you didn't specify what we should do if our charges came to Sitia," Ari said.

"How could they possibly escape the castle and get through the borders?" The expression on Valek's face showed his extreme annoyance.

Glee lit Janco's eyes. "That's a very good question. Ari, please tell our industrious leader how the Sitians escaped."

Ari shot his partner a nasty look, which didn't affect Janco's mood in the least. "They had some help," Ari said.

Again, Valek said nothing.

Ari began to fidget, and I covered my mouth to keep from laughing. The big man resembled a ten-year-old boy who knew he was about to get into a lot of trouble. "We helped them."

"*We?*" Janco asked.

"I did." Ari sounded miserable. "Happy now?"

"Yes." Janco rubbed his hands together. "This is going to be good. Go on, Ari. Tell him why—although, I think they magiked him." He waggled his fingers.

"They didn't use magic. They used common sense and logic." Valek raised an eyebrow.

"There're strange things going on here," Ari said. "If *we* don't put it right, then it'll spread like a disease and kill us all."

"Who told you this?" I asked.

"Moon Man."

"Where are they now?" Valek asked.

"Camped about a mile north of here," Ari said.

The drumming of horses reached us before Valek could comment. Through the window, I saw Kiki followed by Topaz, Garnet and Rusalka.

"How did they find us?" Icy daggers hung from Valek's voice.

Janco seemed surprised. "They didn't know where we were going. I told them to wait for us."

"Isn't it frustrating when no one obeys your orders?" Valek asked.

We went outside. Tauno rode on Kiki and she came straight to me. She bumped my chest with her nose. I opened my mind to her.

Don't go into fire again, she said.

I didn't reply. Instead, I scratched behind her ears as Tauno slid off her back. He greeted me with a cold look and returned to the others. Leif, Moon Man and Marrok lingered near their horses while they talked to Ari and Janco.

From Leif's various frowns and Tauno's scorn, I knew they remained angry with me. I couldn't blame them—I had acted badly. Liveliness lit Marrok's face and I hoped Moon Man had been able to weave his mind back into a coherent whole.

Everyone went inside, but I stayed behind, taking care of the horses as best as I could with half-burnt brushes and scorched hay. Part of the pasture's fence had caught fire and collapsed. I stared at the gap, knowing the well-bred Sandseed horses didn't need a fence and Onyx and Topaz would stay with them. However, I attempted to fix the broken section. And kept at it while the sun set and the night air turned frosty. Kept working even when the horses decided it was too cold in the open and left the pasture to find warmth under a copse of trees nearby.

Valek arrived. I pounded on a post with a heavy rock. He halted my swing and removed the rock from my hand.

"Come inside, love. We have plans to discuss."

Reluctance pulled at my feet as if I walked through thick, sticky mud.

The living-room conversation died the moment I entered. Moon Man looked at me with sadness in his eyes and I wondered if he knew about my deal with the Fire Warper or if he was disappointed by my actions.

A fire had been lit. I sat down next to it, warming my frozen and bleeding fingers, no longer afraid of the flames. The trapped souls within the fire twisted. Their pain and presence were clear and I wondered how I had been able to ignore them before.

I averted my gaze. Everyone stared at me. Ari and Janco had gained their feet and held their bodies as if ready to spring into action.

"Did I pass your test?" I asked. "By not diving into the flames."

"That's not it," Janco said. "You have a rather ugly bat clinging to your arm."

Sure enough, a hand-size bat peered at me from my upper left arm. His eyes glowed with intelligence; his claws dug into my sleeve. I offered a perch and he transferred his weight to the edge of my right hand. Carrying him outside, my efforts to release him failed. He didn't want to leave. Settling on my shoulder, he seemed content so I returned inside.

No one commented on my new friend. In fact, Leif regarded the bat with an intensely thoughtful expression.

The others waited. A moment passed until I realized they waited for me to begin. To make the decisions. To set events into motion. Even after leaving them as prisoners of the Commander, they still looked to me. And this time, instead of backing down and pushing them away, I accepted the responsibility. Accepted the fact that they might be hurt or killed, and understood my life would be given in exchange for keeping the Fire Warper from returning.

"Leif," I said.

He jumped as if bitten.

"I want you and Moon Man to get into the Council Hall's library and find everything you can about a tunnel into the Keep." I explained Bain's comments. "Moon Man can disguise himself as a Vermin and hopefully you won't be caught. Do not use magic at all from now on. It will only draw them to you."

Moon Man and Leif nodded.

"Marrok?"

"Yes, sir."

"Are you able to fight?"

"Ready, willing and *able*, sir."

I paused, swallowing a sudden knot in my throat. By their determined expressions, I knew they were *all* willing. At least Valek's smug smile was better than hearing him say, *I told you so*.

"Good. Marrok and Tauno will accompany Valek and me. We'll go south to rescue the hostages."

Ari cleared his throat as if he wanted to protest.

"I haven't forgotten about you two. I need you to go into the Citadel and help organize the resistance."

"Resistance?" Valek asked. "I hadn't heard."

"I put an idea into a merchant's head, and, I think if Ari and Janco disguised themselves as traders, they could move about the Citadel. Ari will have to dye his hair. Oh, and find a boy named Fisk. Tell him you're my friend and he'll help you make contacts."

"And when and where, Oh mighty Yelena, do we resist?" Janco asked.

"At the Keep's gates. As for when, I don't know, but something will happen and you'll know."

Janco and Ari exchanged a look. "Gotta love the confidence," Janco said.

"And when do we start, love?"

"Everyone get a good night's sleep and we'll begin preparations in the morning. We'll leave early. Do you have enough disguises for four of us or do we need to get supplies? Money?"

Valek smiled. "You mean raid some laundry lines? Steal a couple purses? No. My safe houses are well stocked with all types of items."

Leif was the only one to be alarmed by his statement.

The room erupted with the noise of multiple conversations. Plans were made and actions decided. Tauno's unhappiness at being separated from Moon Man became apparent. He asked why we wanted him. I explained about needing a good scout.

"What about Marrok?" he asked.

"We need him just in case they've moved the captives. He can track them to the new location." Also I wanted to talk to Marrok and find out why he had accused Leif and me of helping Ferde escape.

The next morning, my group saddled the horses. Since we wouldn't be crossing the Avibian Plains, Valek rode Onyx,

Tauno sat on Garnet and Marrok rode Topaz. Valek had used his skills to transform us into members of the Krystal Clan. We wore the light gray tunics and dark woolen leggings that the clan preferred, which matched the short hooded capes and black knee-high boots.

Before we left, Leif handed me a bunch of his herbs. "Since you can't use your magic, you might want to have them. There are directions on how to use each one inside the packet."

"Leif, I'm—"

"I know. Truthfully, I didn't like the distrustful and mean person you became in Ixia. The fire brought my real sister back. So be careful, as I'd like to keep her around for a while."

"You take care, too. Don't get caught. I wouldn't want to tell Mother about it. She wouldn't be pleased."

Leif looked at Ari and Janco. They fought over who would drive the wagon and who would guard. "Do they always argue?"

I laughed. "It's part of their appeal."

Leif sighed. "I'm amazed we made it to Sitia without being discovered." He paused and considered. "I think I'm actually going to miss them."

"I always do."

We set a time and place for everyone to rendezvous, knowing the cottage would no longer be safe. I said goodbye to Leif and the others and we headed west, hoping to reach the Krystal Clan's border by nightfall. We would follow the border south to the Stormdance lands. Then cross through Stormdance and Bloodgood before reaching Jewelrose's border.

Should anyone stop us on the road, we concocted a cover story. We were delivering samples of quartz to the Jewelrose

Clan. Irys's clan cut and polished gems and stones of all types. They designed and produced almost all the jewelry in Sitia.

Disguised as a man, I used the name Ellion, and asked everyone to call me by that name.

The day turned warm in the bright sunshine and we set a quick pace. Valek hoped the temperate weather would draw people onto the roads.

"Why?" Tauno asked.

"Then we will be one of many instead of the only ones," Valek explained. They rode together and talked about how best to find the barn that held the Councilors' family members.

Kiki stayed beside Topaz. She had missed his company and I wondered if Cahil mourned the loss of his horse. They had been together since Cahil was young. My eyes rested on Garnet. I cringed when I imagined facing the Stable Master's wrath. Garnet had been with us so long and I had lost the Avibian honey I had bought to appease the Stable Master. He would make me clean tack and scrub stalls for weeks. I snorted with amusement. I had found one positive thing about spending eternity with the Fire Warper: no mucking out.

And no bat. My new friend hung from the edge of my hood. His weight rested comfortably in the small of my back. He seemed content to sleep away the daylight hours with me.

Marrok remained quiet throughout the day, but I wanted to know what had happened to him at the Citadel.

"Cahil tricked me," he said when I asked. "I fell for his lies about remaining with Ferde to discover the extent of the Daviians' operations. Applauded his plan to lure Ferde back to the Citadel. Commiserated over your ill-timed interference.

He convinced me to confess and name you and Leif as accomplices. It would help him persuade the Council to attack Ixia. He promised…" Marrok paused, rubbing a hand along his right cheek. "After I confessed, he turned on me. A mistake I paid for…" He shuddered. "Am still paying for."

"Betrayals are brutal," I agreed.

Marrok looked at me in surprise. "Don't you think leaving us in Ixia was a betrayal?"

"No. That wasn't my intention. I wanted to protect you and was honest with all of you from the start. I just wasn't honest with myself. A mistake."

"You're still paying for?" Marrok smiled. The gesture smoothed out the lines of worry and time on his rugged face, erasing years from his age.

"Yes. It's the problem with mistakes, they tend to linger. But once we're done with the Vermin and Cahil, I will have paid for all my mistakes. In full."

Marrok gave me a questioning glance, but I didn't want to elaborate. Instead, I asked, "Do you remember your rescue from the Citadel?"

He grinned ruefully. "Sorry, no. At the time, I was in no condition to think. Moon Man is a wonder. I owe him my life." He glanced around then lowered his voice. "Being here without him, I feel…fragile. And that's hard for an old soldier to admit."

We rode the rest of the way in silence. Around midnight we set up camp. Funny how we automatically attended to the chores without discussion. Tauno hunted for rabbits and I cared for the horses. Valek searched for firewood and Marrok prepared the meal.

"I'm used to soldiers' rations on the road, so don't expect this to taste like Leif's," Marrok said as he dished out his version of rabbit stew.

The stew tasted a little bland but filled our stomachs. After dinner, we arranged our sleeping mats and set a watch schedule. I shared a blanket with Valek, wanting to be near him. I clutched him tight.

"What's the matter, love," he whispered in my ear. "You're rarely this quiet."

"Just worried about the Councilors' families."

"I think we have things well in hand. Between my sleeping potion for the guards, your Curare for the Warpers and the element of surprise, we should rescue them in no time."

"But what if one of the captives is sick? Or dying? If I use my magic, I risk letting the Vermin know where I am and what I've been doing."

"Then you'll have to decide what is more important—one person's life or the success of the mission for Sitia's future. It's pointless to worry. Instead, use your energy to decide how you would react to each contingency you can imagine. It's more prudent to prepare for all possibilities than fret."

He was right. Eventually, I slept.

Shadows haunted my sleep. They roamed the shadow world, lost and afraid. Whenever the bright heat would appear, they hid and waited for the hot hunter to dissipate. Each time, the hunter captured more of them in his net of fire. They didn't understand why he came and they knew nothing about the bridge to the sky. They clung to this world, desiring revenge and justice. The shadows needed a guide to convince them to let go and to show them the way.

★ ★ ★

"Ellion…Ellion…Yelena! Wake up."

I pushed the arm away, wanting to roll over. "Tired," I mumbled.

"Yes, we *all* are. But it's your turn," Valek said.

I blinked. My eyelids would not stay open.

"There's a pot of tea on the fire." When I failed to move, Valek pushed me off the mat and curled in my place under the covers. "Ahh. Still warm."

"You're evil," I said, but he feigned sleep.

We had been on the road for the past four days, riding every minute we could to turn a seven-day journey into five days. And since Tauno had left before dinner to scout the area ahead, we had one less to guard the camp.

My bat swooped over the rising heat of the fire. He'd been staying with me during the day and hunting food at night. I longed to fly with him, soaring over the ground.

Tauno returned the next morning to report no signs of activity along our path to the Jewelrose border. "There is a good site to camp about two miles south of the border," he said. "I will join you there." He left.

I wondered what had kept him awake. Unlike Tauno, I had had a few hours' sleep last night. Perhaps I shouldn't complain anymore.

We packed and followed Tauno's trail. Another uneventful day and we found the camp location without any problems. Tauno reappeared with dinner hanging from his belt.

"I discovered the location of the barn," he said, while butchering the rabbits. "It is four miles west of here in a little hollow."

Valek quizzed him for the details. "We'll have to strike in the dark," he said. "We'll go after midnight, leave the horses in the trees and then attack."

Tauno agreed. He cubed the meat and dropped it into the pot. "I will sleep, then."

While Marrok stirred the stew, Valek prepped the reed pipes and I saddled the horses. Garnet sighed when I cinched his straps tight.

"It's not far," I said aloud. "Then you can rest."

I joined Marrok and Valek where they sat by the fire. They ate their stew and I filled a bowl for me. The broth tasted better; there was a hint of spice.

"This is good," I said to Marrok. "I think you're getting the hang of it. What did you add?"

"A new ingredient. Can you tell what it is?"

When I sampled another spoonful, I rolled the liquid around my mouth before swallowing. The aftertaste reminded me of Rand's favorite cookie recipe. "Ginger?"

Valek dropped his stew. He jumped to his feet but stumbled. A look of horror creased his forehead. "Butter root!"

"Poison?"

"No." He sank to his knees. "Sleeping draft."

29

VALEK COLLAPSED ONTO the ground. But just before he closed his eyes, he winked at me. I glanced around. Marrok hunched over his bowl, appearing to be asleep. A bone-deep fatigue spread throughout my body, but I remained awake. Perhaps I hadn't swallowed enough butter root.

Not wanting to be caught "aware," I pulled my switchblade and hid the weapon in the palm of my hand with my thumb resting on the button. Slumping over, I let my upper body fall to the side. The stew spilled off my lap and onto the ground, soaking into my pants. Great.

I feigned sleep. My muscles stiffened and the cold seeped into my skin. Trying not to shiver, I strained to hear any noise to give me a hint of what was going on.

The horses whinnied in alarm and I opened my mind to Kiki for the first time in days, hoping the tiny use of my magic wouldn't alert anyone.

Bad smell, she said. *Quiet Man tied reins.*

Quiet Man?

She huffed and showed me an image of Tauno.

Why would he do that?

Ask Garnet.

Where did you go today, Garnet? I asked.

See people. Smell fear.

I cut off the connection when voices approached.

"So easy! All the talk about the Soulfinder and the Ghost Warrior and look at them! Sleeping like babies," a male voice said.

"Trust is a powerful ally. Right, Tauno?" a female voice asked. She had the same lilt as a Sandseed.

Was Tauno in league with them? Or had they captured him today and forced him to help them?

"Yes. And trust is blind. No one suspected me even after the ambush in the plains." He laughed. "Trust is for stupid people. Even the Sandseed Elders had no idea. My ability to find the Daviian camps amazed them."

They chuckled, enjoying themselves. Anger seethed in my blood. Tauno could *trust* I would make him regret his actions.

As they decided what to do, I counted four distinct voices. Two men and one woman plus the traitor Tauno. They planned to use Marrok to appease the Council, and bring me to their leader, Jal.

"Kill the Ghost Warrior," one of the Vermin ordered. "Make sure you cut his throat and collect his blood. It will be just revenge for Alea and her brother."

I waited. Arms wrapped around my chest and another set around my ankles. They lifted me off the ground.

"Now!" Valek yelled.

I triggered my switchblade and yanked my knees toward my

chest, pulling the surprised Vermin holding my feet into my knife. Hot blood gushed onto my hands. I wrenched the blade out of his stomach before the other Vermin dropped me onto the ground. I scrambled to my feet as he pulled his scimitar.

Switchblade against scimitar. Bad odds. And I had used the Curare on my weapon on the first man. This wouldn't be a long fight. I glanced at Valek. He fought Tauno and the woman. His sword against their spears. Better odds. I hoped I could last long enough for Valek to help me.

"Drop your weapon," the Vermin ordered me.

When I didn't obey, the man swung and I dodged to the side. He lunged. I backed away. He swiped at my neck. I ducked. He hacked and I danced.

Winded with the effort, the Vermin said, "You will not be harmed if you surrender."

After another attack, I realized what he was doing. "You're not allowed to kill me," I said. "Jal wants me alive so he can feed me to his pet Fire Warper!"

My smugness infuriated him. He increased the pace of his swings. Bad decision.

"I can still hurt you. Bleed you. Torture you."

His blade sliced through my cape. I stepped back as blood welled from the slash along my arm. Really bad decision. He advanced. I retreated. His scimitar found more open areas and soon my arms and legs were crisscrossed with bleeding cuts. I felt light-headed and my feet moved with an unusual slowness. My energy drained at an alarming rate.

My bat appeared. He flew at the Vermin, diving and pulling his hair. The Vermin flailed his arms, giving me an opening, but my switchblade felt so heavy and my body reacted too slowly. The Vermin must be a strong Warper. He had weakened my mental defenses without my notice.

The Warper stared at the bat and the poor creature crashed to the ground.

"Is that all you have?" he asked. "What about your great soul magic? I think the Fire Warper will be disappointed." He shrugged. "Orders are orders."

He swung his weapon. My arms moved, but couldn't block the hilt of his scimitar from striking my temple.

My vision blurred as I crumpled to the ground. The world spun. I rolled away from the Warper. When I reached Kiki's hooves, I let the blackness claim me.

A hammer pounded on the side of my skull. Wake up, it pounded. Open your eyes. More hammering. I refused. The next time, a dull throb intruded on my oblivion. Come on, it pulsed. Open your eyes. Please.

I woke, feeling like a cutting board. My arms and legs burned with pain and my head hurt. Valek hunched over me, pouring water on my cuts, inflaming them.

"Ow! Stop that," I said.

"Finally," he said. But he didn't stop. He dabbed at them, cleaning the lacerations, and sat back on his heels. "That'll have to do for now. Come on. We need to go."

When I failed to move, he pulled me into a sitting position. A wave of nausea swelled.

"Here." He thrust red leaves into my hands. "I found them in your saddlebags. The note said to eat them for head pain."

I chewed one. My stomach settled, but my sight remained blurry. I peered into the semidarkness, assuming the fuzzy white blob in the sky meant the moon had risen. Had I slept all day? Valek's words finally sank in.

"Go where?" I asked.

Valek yanked me to my feet. "We need to find the barn."

My thoughts still moved as if coated with sap. "Barn?"

Valek shook the rest of the canteen's water onto my shorn head. A jolt went through me when the cold breeze hit my wet skull.

"When the Vermin don't come back with us, the others will know something has happened and will either kill their hostages or move to another location." Valek ennunciated each word as if speaking to a simpleton. "Here." He handed me a set of clothes. "Hurry."

I changed. The carnage around our campsite made me sick and I sucked on another red leaf. Valek had killed the woman and Tauno. Traitor! Marrok remained where he had fallen asleep. And the Warper lay on his side. His head looked misshapen, as if kicked by a horse.

Kiki? I asked.

Bad man. No one hurt Lavender Lady.

Thanks.

Peppermints?

When we're done. And apples, too!

I wore my coral-colored shirt and matching skirt/pants. They reflected the moonlight. No hope for me to blend in. Valek dressed in the Warper's clothes and he applied makeup to match the Warper's skin tone. Fear twirled up my spine as I figured out what he planned. At least, I wasn't going to be bait for a necklace snake. This time.

We untied the other horses. The smell of blood made them skittish, and they were happy to leave despite being tired. Valek and I rode Kiki and Onyx while leading the others. We traveled the four miles to the barn in silence. Approaching the edge of the woods with care, I strained to see a sign of the Vermin hideout. An eerie red glow shimmered above Diamond Lake. The small structure looked deserted, but after a moment, the figures guarding the doors became visible.

"Which horse?" I asked.

"Onyx. Kiki is too well-known."

I dismounted and told the horses to stay in the woods until I called.

"Take off your cape," Valek said. "Lie in front of me." He took his foot from the stirrup.

I pulled myself up and lay across the saddle. He handed me my switchblade. The weapon had been cleaned and the blade was retracted.

"It's been primed with Curare." Valek grabbed the reins with his left hand and held a scimitar in his right.

"Pretend to be unconscious," he ordered as he clicked at Onyx.

We entered the open area, hopefully appearing as the Warper coming back with his prize.

Feigning to be a dead weight, I bounced on Onyx's saddle. The motion made me nauseous. A whoop of joy cut through the air as we neared. I prepared for Valek's signal.

"Where are the others?" a male voice asked.

"They're coming," Valek said in a rough tone.

"Finally! We have her!" another man said as he tugged my legs. "Help me."

Valek slid off on the opposite side of the saddle, keeping Onyx between him and the Vermin.

Another person joined in pulling me off. "We'll keep her

asleep until she reaches Jal. Get the wagon, you'll leave to-night," the man ordered. He cradled me in his arms.

"Where is Jal?" Valek asked.

The man froze and I risked a peek. The tip of Valek's scimitar touched the Vermin's neck. Although armed with his own scimitar and a spear strapped to his back, the Vermin's hands held me.

"At the Magician's Keep. Go ahead and find Jal. Just make sure to take *her* with you." The man tossed me at Valek and yelled for help.

At that close distance, even Valek couldn't dodge out of the way. I hit him in the chest. We tumbled to the ground, but I kept going until I cleared his body. Jumping to my feet, I spun in time to see Valek rolling away to avoid being sliced by the Vermin's blade.

Four more Vermin with weapons drawn ran toward us.

I triggered my switchblade and threw it at the Vermin at-tacking Valek. He grunted when the blade nicked his shoulder, but he didn't stop. However, the Curare on my blade spread throughout his body and paralyzed his muscles. I grabbed the man's spear. Valek regained his feet and his weapon.

A mere second later, the others reached us.

Events blurred into one long fight. I used the spear's length to my advantage, keeping the scimitars from reaching me. After a fake to the midsection, I swept my opponent's feet out from under him. I didn't hesitate to plunge the tip of the spear into his neck. His soul rose from his body and hovered above it. Should I help his soul?

Before I could decide, another man approached. But he stopped and I felt strands of magic tug at my spear. A Warper who could move objects. The spear flew from my grasp, turned and pointed straight at me.

"Jal wants me alive." I reminded him.

He advanced. "Why not use your power to stop me? Afraid the Fire Warper will tell Jal what you're doing?"

"Give the man a prize. Your intellect is truly amazing."

The spear's tip came closer and poked me in the hollow of my throat. "Surrender or I'll skewer her," the Warper called to Valek.

Valek disengaged, his gaze questioning.

"He won't do it," I said to Valek.

"You are right. How about surrender or I will set the barn on fire?" The Warper pointed to the building. "Do you want to be responsible for the deaths of ten children?"

30

"No! Don't," I yelled. "Let the children go and I'll come with you."

"I know you will," the Warper said. "I am more concerned about the Ghost Warrior." He looked at Valek. "Put your weapon down."

Valek placed his scimitar on the ground, but as he straightened, he flicked his hand twice. A small dart pricked the Warper's neck. The man jerked in surprise.

"Move," Valek ordered.

I twisted, avoiding the spear's thrust, but I wasn't fast enough to stop the sharp edge from cutting a gash across my neck. A line of stinging pain registered in my mind. It was forgotten as soon as I saw the Warper turn. Fire erupted under the barn's door. He collapsed beside his colleague, finally overcome by Valek's sleeping potion.

Smoke reached my nose, igniting memories of dread and fear.

"Valek, go!" I waved him on and whistled for the horses. They came and I raced toward the barn. *Kiki help!* I said.

Valek had gotten the burning door opened, but flames crept toward the roof. Topaz and Onyx shied away from the acrid smoke, but Kiki and Garnet braved the heat.

"Tell them to move to the left side," I yelled to Valek over the roar.

He sprinted through the opening and I led Kiki and Garnet to the right side. I waited for two horrible seconds then banged on the barn's wall.

Kiki. Garnet. Kick. I dived to the side. The animals aimed their back hooves and punched a hole in the wall with their powerful legs.

When the opening was big enough for the adults, I stopped the horses. Pulling a few splintered boards clear, I looked inside and called to the captives. Even with the bright firelight, the room was obscured by smoke. But a person grabbed my hand. I pulled coughing children through the hole, counting them as they came out.

The smoke thickened and the inferno advanced.

When Councilor Greenblade's husband crawled out with a small child clinging to his back and a baby clutched to his chest, my count totaled ten children and one adult.

"Where's Gale?" I asked.

Hacking with the effort to expel the smoke from his lungs, he pointed through the opening. "Collapsed." He wheezed for air. "Couldn't take…them all."

I moved to go in, but he pulled me back.

"Roof." He coughed.

We shooed the children away from the barn mere moments before the roof buckled with a shower of sparks and an explosion of sound.

I counted children again. Ten. One adult. No Gale. No Valek. He was still in the barn!

Horror and anguish twisted around my throat and shredded my heart. I bolted toward the blazing building. The heat rolled off the structure, pushing me back. Roof beams had fallen on top of the Vermin. The flames lapped at their bodies and sucked their souls into the inferno.

A porthole into the fire world opened in front of me. I could have grabbed one of the Vermin's souls and returned to the Fire Warper. But I wasn't ready. I had a few more things to accomplish and a few goodbyes to make before I embraced the fire.

Then I would crave the fire. Living in this world without Valek held no appeal for me.

The blaze raged all night. By morning it settled into a large smoldering heap. Still too hot for me to search among the ruins for some sign of Valek or Gale. Instead, I led the children over to Diamond Lake to get cleaned up and tried to ignore the grief burning inside me.

Councilor Greenblade's husband, Kell, helped feed the children and tend their wounds. Kiki and Garnet drank from the lake, and I washed the soot from their coats. The water was clear. The red color came from the bottom of the lake as if someone had painted the rocks and gravel. Perhaps they had. After all, it was a man-made lake.

When everyone's needs were met, we headed back to the campsite. We found Marrok engaged in the grim task of burying bodies.

"Guess I slept through the battle," he said. "Did we win?" He inclined his head to Tauno. "Or lose?"

"Both," I said. My anguish over Valek threatened to push from my throat. I bit down hard on my lip, tasting blood.

"Care to explain?"

I filled him in on what had happened. He accepted Tauno's betrayal with a cynical snort and a wry twist of the lips that reflected his black thoughts about trust.

After I finished, he said, "At least your little friend is all right."

"Friend?"

He pointed to a nearby tree. "I thought he was dead, but when I went to pick him up he flew off. Scared the heck out of me."

I went over. My bat hung upside down on a low branch. The creature opened an eye halfway then closed it again, contented. Somehow I had created an emotional link with the bat that was similar to my link with Kiki.

Contemplation about my affinity for animals would have to wait, though. More pressing matters needed to be addressed—finding Valek's body, for one. But I said, "We have to find a safe place for the Councilors' family members."

Bavol Zaltana's daughter, Jenniqilla, pulled at my cape. "I want to go home," she said. Although happy to be free, sadness touched her eyes and weariness lined her young face.

I crouched down next to her. "I know, but I need you to pretend you're still a hostage for just a little while longer. It's really important. Can you help us out?"

Determination filled her eyes, reminding me of Fisk. I assigned all the older children small jobs, and they moved about with a renewed sense of purpose.

"What about me?" Kell Greenblade asked.

The Greenblade lands were east of Bloodgood's. "Do you know anyplace where we can hide all of you?"

He gazed off into the distance. Tall and wiry, he resembled my friend, Dax, another member of his clan. I hoped Dax and Gelsi were all right, and the thought of them being the next victims of the Kirakawa ritual made me restless to get moving.

Kell sensed my mood. His attention focused on me. "My sister has a farm outside of Booruby that could hold all of us."

"In the Cowan Clan's lands?"

"Yes." He tsked. "She married a flatlander, but he's a good man and will help us."

I looked at the ragtag group of children. Booruby was farther east than I had wanted to travel and it would be a slow trip.

Kiki nickered at me. *Get wagon*, she said.

The wagon was burned in the fire.

I felt her huff of impatience. *Horses run off. Take wagon.*

Where are they?

Stuck. Come. Kiki flicked her tail.

Marrok came with me. We mounted Kiki and she went southwest through a small wood.

What about Onyx and Topaz? I asked her.

I felt her sorrow. *Can't smell.*

We reached the wagon. When the fire had erupted, the panicked horses had bolted through the woods until the cart wedged between two trees. The animals had calmed, but their raised heads and alert ears meant they felt unsafe.

The wagon had been filled with empty coffin-shaped crates, but we found a toolbox underneath the floor. Getting the wagon free was difficult and time-consuming.

While fixing the broken wheel, Marrok lost his patience and

shooed me away. "You're rushing and making it worse. Go take a walk, Yelena. This is a one-person job anyway."

When I hesitated, he added, "Go look for him or you won't find peace. And we won't either."

Being busy had been good. Walking through the quiet forest, there was nothing to distract me from my flaming thoughts. No respite from the wrenching pain deep inside me. It felt as if I had swallowed a red-hot coal.

The barn's ashy remains drifted in the air. Only a few beams at the edge of the structure retained their shape. Everything else had been reduced to gray and white cinders. Smoke curled from a few hot spots, but otherwise a pine-scented breeze blew the acrid fumes away.

The crunch of my boots on the residue echoed a lonely and final sound in my ears. All hope disappeared when I found Valek's knives. Blackened and misshapen, the blades were half-melted. I collapsed to my hands and knees and sobbed, turning the ash under me into slurry. Gasping, ribs aching and throat raw, I tried to expel the smoldering sadness within, only stopping when all moisture was gone from my body. I sat back on my heels and wiped my face, smearing soot and tears.

Once my breathing returned to normal, I scooped up a handful of the ash near Valek's weapons and let the wind scatter them. Soon, love. I'll join you soon. The knowledge of our reunion in the other world was my only comfort.

Eventually I returned to Marrok. He had fixed the wheel. After looking at my face, he squeezed my shoulder. I had washed off the dirt, but I knew my eyes were red and puffy from crying.

Marrok steered the wagon, but finding a road around the wood used up our remaining daylight.

By the time we returned to the camp, Kell had settled the children next to the fire. I wanted to wake everyone and get moving, but Kell convinced me the children would be upset by being roused and hidden in those crates at night. After recalling my own horrible experience with the boxes, I agreed.

If Valek hadn't shot the Warper, I would have been shoved inside one of those crates. The Councilors' families would still be hostages, but Valek and Gale would still be alive.

I stared at the sleeping children. Jenniqilla had a protective arm over Leevi and the baby curled next to him, sucking on his thumb even while asleep. In that state, they embodied innocence and peace and joy and love. Valek had known the risk when he went into the barn and he hadn't hesitated. I would have done the same. Eleven living beings for one unselfish act. Pretty good odds.

Even with the wagon, the trip to Booruby lasted four days. Four days of worry, frustration, hunger, sleepless nights and noise. By the time we arrived, I had a new appreciation for parents, and was as glad to see Kell's sister as she was to see us. She wrapped Kell in a tight embrace for many heartbeats. I bit my lip and turned away. My empty arms ached.

Located about two miles south of Booruby, the farmstead appeared to be isolated from its neighbors, but her husband was quick to usher us inside. The children were fed their first hot meal in weeks. Marrok and I made plans to return to the rendezvous location to join the others. I kept my mind focused on action; otherwise, I knew I would surrender to the grief consuming me from the inside out.

We would risk crossing through the western edge of the

Avibian Plains. Garnet and Kiki's gust-of-wind gait would make up for the time lost traveling to Booruby.

Before leaving, Kell asked me, "How will I know when it's safe for the children to return home?"

I considered. "If everything works out, you will receive a message."

"And if it doesn't work out?"

Emotion choked his words, reminding me that his wife was one of the Councilors. If I failed, she would be among the first of many casualties.

"If you don't hear anything after fourteen days, that means the Daviians are in charge. Send the children to their homes and hope."

"Hope for what?"

"Hope a person in the future will be strong enough to rebel against the Daviian Vermin. And win."

Kell looked doubtful. "We have four Master Magicians and a Soulfinder, yet they still managed to take control."

"It has happened before. One person *can* bring peace to Sitia."

I didn't add that the man had leveled the Daviian Mountains in the process. But it did lead me to wonder if the Sandseeds' legendary warrior had had help. My mind reviewed Moon Man's story about the origins of the Sandseed Clan and I remembered the warrior's name was Guyan. Guyan had imprisoned the Fire Warper, and his descendant, Gede, had freed him. A complete circle.

Marrok and I said goodbye to Kell and the children. We traveled northwest, planning to skirt Booruby on our way to the plains. My little bat hung from Kiki's mane and didn't appear to be bothered by the jostling motion.

Our plans changed when I spotted Opal's family's glass factory in the distance and I had a sudden idea.

Before I could fully explore my intentions, we stopped outside their gate. Marrok accepted our detour without concern.

"Should I wait here?" he asked.

"Yes. I won't be long." I left Kiki with him.

As I approached the door to their house, Opal came out of the factory. She hesitated, but drew nearer, eyeing Marrok and me with suspicion.

"Can I help you, sir?" she asked me.

I had forgotten all about my hair. At least I knew my disguise worked. I smiled for the first time in days.

She squinted at me. "Yelena?" Then she glanced around in concern. "Come inside! There's a price on your head!" She ushered me into the house.

"Thank goodness you're okay." Opal squeezed me in a quick hug. "What happened to your hair?"

"It's a long long story. Is your family around?"

"No. They went into town. Father received a shipment of sand that was full of rocks so he went to complain and Mother—"

"Opal, I need more of your glass animals."

"Really? Did you sell the bat?"

"No. However, I discovered I can use your animals to communicate with other magicians far away without using my own magic. I'd like to buy as many as I can."

"Wow! I never knew."

"How many do you have?"

"Six. They're in the factory."

She set a quick pace as we crossed the yard and entered the factory. The heat from the kilns sucked all the moisture from my mouth. I followed her through the thick air and roar of the fires. Lined up on a table by the back wall were half a dozen glass animals. They all glowed with an inner fire.

Opal wrapped the animals and I counted out coins. Another idea flashed in my mind when she handed me the package.

"Can you show me how you make these?" I asked.

"It takes a lot of practice to learn."

I shook my head. "I just want to watch you make one."

She agreed. Picking up a five-foot-long hollow steel pipe, she opened the small door to the kiln. Bright orange light and intense heat emanated from the doorway, but, undaunted, she dipped the end of the pipe into a large ceramic pot inside the kiln that was filled with molten glass. Turning the pipe, she gathered a taffylike slug and pulled it out, closing the door with her hip. The slug pulsed with a red-hot light as if alive.

"You have to keep the blowpipe spinning or the glass will sag," Opal said over the noise. She rolled the slug over a metal table to move the glass off the end of the pipe and shaped it so the pipe looked as if it had a clear ball attached to its end.

Her motions quick, Opal then rested the pipe on the edge of the table and blew into the other end. Magic brushed my arm as her cheeks puffed. The glass on the opposite end didn't inflate with air. Instead, a thread of magic was trapped within its core.

"It's supposed to expand, but mine never does," she said as she went back to the kiln and gathered another slug overtop the first. She took the pipe to a bench designed to hold it and other metal tools needed to shape the glass. Buckets of water sat within easy reach.

Opal grabbed a pair of steel tweezers and pinched and squeezed the slug with her right hand while rolling the pipe with her left hand the whole time. "You have to move quickly because it cools fast."

Within seconds the ball transformed into a cat sitting on its back legs. She stood and put the cat back into the kiln, but this time she just spun the pipe above the pot. "You have to keep plenty of heat in the glass or you can't work with it."

Sitting back on her bench, Opal exchanged her tweezers for another set. These were bigger and as long as her forearm. "Jacks, a great all–purpose tool. I'm putting in a jack line so I can crack the piece off the pipe."

When the groove was to her liking, she took the tweezers in hand again and dipped them into the bucket of water. She dribbled a few drops into the jack line. "You have to be careful not to get water onto your piece. So you move from the pipe down." The glass hissed and a spiderweb of cracks spread over the glass on the pipe.

She carried the pipe to another oven close to the kilns. Shelves of trays had been stacked inside and Opal banged the end of the tweezers on her pipe. The cat fell onto the tray. She closed the door.

"If the glass cools too fast, it'll crack. This is an annealing oven." Opal pointed to the tracks underneath the oven. "To slowly cool the piece, the oven is pulled away from the kiln over the next twelve hours."

"Why do you blow into the pipe if the glass doesn't expand for you?" I asked.

"It's a step I have to do." She made a vague motion with her arms as if casting about for the right words. "When Mara does it, she makes beautiful vases and bottles. Mine always ends up looking like an animal and if I don't blow into the pipe it doesn't look like anything at all."

She cleaned up her work area, taking the tools from the water and drying them before replacing them. The bench needed to be ready for the next project, and working with glass didn't give you time to search for tools.

"I love creating things. There's nothing like it," she said, more to herself than to me. "Working the glass. Turning fire into ice."

I thanked Opal for her demonstration and rejoined Marrok. He leaned against Garnet.

"I think your definition of 'won't be long' doesn't match mine," he said by way of a greeting. "Did you encounter another change in plans?"

"Yes. You might as well get used to them."

"Yes, sir!" He grinned.

"Sarcasm? You've been hanging around with Leif too long. What happened to the tough old soldier who mindlessly follows orders?"

His demeanor sobered. "He lost his mind. And when he found it again, his priorities had all been rearranged."

"For the better?"

"Only time will tell."

We mounted and headed to the western edge of the Avibian Plains. Once in the plains, Kiki and Garnet broke into their gust-of-wind gaits and flowed over many miles. We camped outside the plains at night. I hoped our passage wouldn't attract any unwanted attention. My thoughts lingered on Opal's glassmaking skills. Better than giving in to the deep despair that threatened to overwhelm me whenever I thought of Valek.

Our journey to the rendezvous location lasted three days. During that time, Marrok had spotted signs of a large army that had crossed from the Avibian Plains and turned north toward the Citadel. At night, the glow of many fires lit the distant sky and wood smoke tainted the air.

We had agreed to meet Moon Man and the others in Owl's Hill, a small town within the Featherstone lands. According to Leif, the Cloverleaf Inn's owner could be trusted not to report us. "He owes me one," had been Leif's explanation.

Owl's Hill was located on a small rise about three miles northeast of the Citadel. The four towers of the Magician's Keep were visible from the road into town. A bright orange radiance shone from within the Keep's walls. The Fire Warper's home fire?

Still disguised as Krystal Clan traders, Marrok and I entered the town. Situated near the main crossroads, the Cloverleaf Inn's common room bustled with activity, but the stable was only half full. The stable lad suggested we arrive early for dinner as the inn was a popular stop for caravans.

"One less night of road rations," the boy said as he helped me rub down Kiki. "And the merchants prefer camping near here instead of overnighting in the Citadel."

"Why is that?" I asked.

"The rumors have been wild, so I don't know what to believe. But the merchants who do come back say everyone is afraid of these new Daviians and they say the Daviians have convinced the Council to prepare for a war."

"With Ixia?"

"Don't know. They've drafted every able-bodied person. Benn said the Daviians are in league with Ixia, and once a person's drafted they hypnotize him. They plan to use them in the army to turn Sitia into another Ixian Military District. MD-9!"

The boy regaled me with even wilder speculation. I knew the Commander wasn't in league with the Daviians, but the possibility of using the Sitian army against Sitia sounded like a Vermin tactic.

When we finished with the horses, I entered the inn. Marrok had already paid for two rooms for the night.

"We're running out of money," he said.

"Are the others here?" I asked.

"Ari and Janco are in the dining room. Leif and Moon Man haven't arrived yet."

That worried me. It had been thirteen days since we had left to rescue the hostages. Plenty of time for them to discover anything about the Keep's emergency tunnel.

In the back corner of the inn's common room, Ari and Janco held court. Drinking from tankards of ale, they were surrounded by a group of merchants. Serious expressions gripped all their faces and they peered at us with suspicion.

Marrok and I picked a table on the far side of the room. Eventually, the knot of people disbanded and Ari and Janco joined us. Ari had dyed his hair black and both of them had darkened their skin.

"Janco, do I see freckles?" I asked, failing to suppress a snicker.

"Don't laugh. It's this southern sun. It's the middle of the cold season and it's sunny! Bah." He looked at me. "Although, I'd rather have freckles than be bald!"

I put my hand to my hair. "It's growing."

"Enough," Ari said, and the mood around our table immediately dampened. "Were you successful?"

The question stabbed into me as if his words were flaming daggers. I struggled to collect my thoughts; to shoo my emotions away from the black, burning grief that refused to die down. Marrok saw my inability to answer and he told them about Tauno, the rescue and about Valek. To see my pain and shock reflected in my friends' eyes became unbearable. I excused myself and went outside.

Taking deep breaths of the cool night air, I wandered through the town. A few people walked along the dirt streets, carrying lanterns. I felt a tug on my cape as my bat landed on my arm. He stared at me with a sense of purpose in his eyes then flew off to the left. He returned, swooping around my head and again flew to the left. Getting the hint, I followed him until we reached a dilapidated building.

The bat settled on the roof as if waiting. I pulled the warped door open with trepidation, but the interior held a collection of discarded barrels and broken wagon wheels. When I turned to leave, I stepped on a wooden ball. A child's toy. I picked it up and examined it. My bat wanted me to find or see something in here.

I squashed my growing frustration and concentrated on using my other senses. Closing my eyes, I inhaled. The musty smell of decay dominated, but I detected a faint whiff of lemons. I followed the clean and pure scent—not easy as I tripped and banged my shins on the clutter—until I stood in the back corner. There a tingle danced on my skin, raising the hair on my arms. Instinctively I whispered, "Reveal yourself," and opened my eyes.

Gray light bloomed before me and transformed into a young boy. He sat on one of the barrels.

A ghost. A lost soul.

"Where is my mother?" he asked with a thin, tentative voice. "She was sick, too. She went away and never came back even when I cried for her."

I moved closer to the boy. The light from him illuminated the room. The rusted remains of a bed frame and other items indicated the area had been used as the child's bedroom long ago.

My bat fluttered in and circled above the boy's head. I waved it away and muttered, "Yes, yes, I know. I get it."

With a squeal sounding like an exasperated *finally,* he flew out.

I asked the child questions about his mother and family. Just as I suspected, they had lived and died here many years ago.

"I know where they are," I said. "I can take you to them."

The boy smiled. When I held out my hand, he grabbed it. I gathered him to me, inhaling his soul before sending it to the sky.

The true job of a Soulfinder.

Not to save souls and return them to their bodies, but to guide them to where they belonged. My true purposed flared to life finally. Stono and Gelsi should have both been released to the sky. Their personalities changed because they were unhappy at being denied peace.

Death was not the end. And I knew Valek waited for me, but he wouldn't want to see me until I finished finding all the lost and misplaced souls and sent them to their proper destinations.

There hadn't been a Soulfinder in over a hundred and

twenty-five years. Why wasn't Sitia filled with lost souls? Perhaps they were rare.

Renewed determination to find a way to defeat the Fire Warper spread throughout my body. I left the building and stopped. Five souls hovered in different locations along the street. The leathery flap of wings announced my bat's arrival. He settled on my shoulder.

"Did you call them?" I asked the bat. "Or did I?" I guess I should have been more specific when I called to the boy. Either that, or now I'd learned a trick I couldn't shut off.

I gathered and released souls as I headed back to the Cloverleaf Inn. Most went to the sky. One dripped with hate and when he sank into the ground, I worried I might have increased the Fire Warper's powers.

Before I could enter the inn, the clatter of hooves sounded behind me. I spun in time to see Leif stop Rusalka. His panic reached me before his words.

"Moon Man," he gasped. "Moon Man's been captured!"

31

BACK IN THE INN'S common room, the five of us sorted through all the details we had. Moon Man had been captured that afternoon.

"We found no references to the tunnel in the Council Hall's library," Leif said. "We were meeting with an old magician who was hiding from the Vermin. Another had told us he had information on the construction of the Keep, but when we talked to the magician he only had vague details. He knew how to create a null shield and he taught me how to make one. I shouldn't have tried it. The magic called the Warpers and we were attacked as we left his house."

"How did you get away?" Janco asked.

Leif threw his hands up. "One minute we're surrounded by Vermins, the next a group of brawling merchants and screaming children practically rolled over everyone. It was mass confusion. A man grabbed my hand and pulled me out. I hid until dark. One of the children from the Helping Guild told me Moon Man hadn't escaped."

"The Vermin will know we're here," Ari said. "We need to leave now. There's a caravan camping about two miles north of here. We can stay with them."

"Which way is the caravan going?" I asked Ari.

"They have a delivery in the Citadel tomorrow, and then they're going south to the Greenblade lands. Why?"

"Oh no!" Leif said. "She's got that look in her eyes. What are you scheming, little sister?"

"We have to get inside the Keep."

"Impossible. There's a bubble of protective magic around it. We couldn't find the entrance to the tunnel. A few Warpers have gained master-level power. You're powerful, but nowhere near their level. You'll be caught in an instant." Leif crossed his arms as if his statement ended the discussion.

"That's a great idea," I said.

"What?

I ignored Leif's confusion. "Ari, how ready are the people in the Citadel to revolt?"

"They're organized, have some weapons and a few magicians. What I would really like to do is run a few training sessions, but that's not going to happen. They're as ready as they're going to get."

"Would the caravan be willing to lend us one of their wagons?" I asked.

"Something could be arranged."

Comprehension dawned in Janco's face. "If we get you inside, can we keep the five golds?"

"Only if you get us back out again," I said.

"I don't like the odds," Janco said. He brightened. "Gotta love the underdog, though."

"There are *no* odds. It's suicide," Leif said.

"Look at it this way, Leif. It'll put an end to our arguing," I said.

"How?"

"We die, you're right. You don't die, I'm right."

"I feel *so* much better now."

Janco tsked. "Sarcasm is detrimental to the team spirit."

Ari frowned at me. "Don't you mean, *we* don't die, Yelena?"

I didn't answer. Valek waited on the other side. My reward.

We packed our supplies and headed out. The merchants of the caravan agreed to include us in their group and we spent most of the night preparing our wagon. When we finished with the cart's alterations, we stood around it, discussing the plan for the next day.

"Marrok, you'll ride Garnet. Janco can take Kiki, and Ari, you'll drive the wagon. No matter what happens, Ari, make sure we get to the Keep's gate," I ordered.

"Yes, sir."

"What about me and you?" Leif asked.

I grimaced. "We're the cargo." The last thing I wanted to do was get inside one of those crates again, but there was no other way. "Ari is going to use me to get us inside. He'll demand his five golds for bringing me to the Vermin."

"I never thought I'd miss my days as necklace snake bait," Leif said.

"What happens once we're inside?" Ari asked.

"That will be the signal for the Citadel's citizens to riot, which should keep a bunch of the Vermin and Warpers busy."

"But what about all those powerful Warpers?" Leif asked.

"Can you make a null shield?"

He hesitated. "Yes."

"When the riot starts, all the magicians will come to the Keep's gate and help you build and maintain a null shield," I said.

"But it won't last long."

"I just need a little time."

"Time for what?"

"To get to the Fire Warper."

Leif stared at me. "You can fight him?"

"No."

"Tell me again why this isn't a suicide mission."

"I think I can stop him and keep him in the fire world. And in doing so, I think I might be able to pull some of the Warpers' powers from them. If Bain and Irys are still alive, and if you round up as many magicians as you can, then you should be able to counter the Warpers."

"That's a lot of 'ifs' and 'thinks,'" Janco said.

"And there's no 'when,'" Ari said.

"When?" Leif asked.

"When she returns. There's a when, isn't there, Yelena?" Ari asked.

"The only way to keep him in the fire world is if I stay, too." The words tasted like ash in my mouth. Thinking about an event was completely different than stating it aloud. Once said, it was final. But Valek would be there and I *would* find him. No "if," "think" or "when" about it.

"There has to be another way," Leif said. "You always manage to produce ingenious plots."

"Not this time."

Everyone remained quiet.

I was about to suggest we all get a little sleep when Leif asked, "What if we can't counter the Warpers?"

"Then you'd better have a person who's unaffected by magic on your side," a voice said from beyond the wagon.

We all looked at one another. The same question perched on everyone's lips. A ghost voice?

"Although this time I would appreciate it if you didn't leave me behind." Valek stepped into view. He appeared to be solid. His angular face held annoyed amusement. The faint moonlight glinted off his bald head. He wore the brown tunic and pants of a Bloodgood clansman.

Disbelief followed surprise; I reached out to touch him. He pulled me close and my world filled with the sight, smell and feel of Valek.

Seconds, minutes, days, seasons could have passed and I wouldn't have noticed or cared. I clung to him as if my feet dangled over a precipice. His heart beat in my ear. His blood flowed in my veins. I molded my body to his solid flesh, wanting to fuse with him and let nothing—not even air— come between us.

Relief and joy frolicked in my heart, extinguishing the smoldering grief until I remembered my promise to the Fire Warper.

Blazing sadness ignited, flooding my senses. My reward for babysitting the Fire Warper would have to wait. Better to have him here.

I gathered my resolve and calmed myself. The others moved away, leaving Valek and me alone. His lips found mine. Our souls twined. The gaping emptiness inside me filled.

He pulled away, breathless. "Easy, love." His panting turned into a coughing fit.

"How did you survive the fire?" I asked. "The roof collapsed and you didn't…"

"Two things happened at once. At least, I think they did." He gave me an ironic smile. "I was carrying Gale when the roof fell. The force of it sent us through the floor and into a small root cellar." Valek rubbed his ribs and grimaced.

"You're hurt and I can't heal you!" A nasty gash snaked along the side of his skull.

"Just bruised." He ran a hand gently over his head. "A beam knocked me out and I would have probably died from the smoke and heat, but Gale kept us in a pocket of cool air. She had been hit by a piece of the barn's wall when it shattered. But she came to and used her magic. She conjured a cushion of air around us to keep the burning debris from filling our hole."

"Why didn't I see you the next morning? Why didn't you call out?"

"The roof had tented around us, and there was nothing you could do to help until the fire died." His hand went to his ribs again. "I didn't have enough air to yell and Gale needed all her strength to keep us alive."

"Why couldn't she blow the fire out? Or save the children?"

"Her powers are limited. It's all part of her weather dancing thing." He gestured past the wagon. "You can ask her. I've brought her along." When he saw my questioning look, he added, "We're going to need all the help we can get."

I looked on the other side of the wagon. Gale held Onyx's and Topaz's reins. Kiki had already found them and nuzzled Topaz. Garnet stood nearby. Gale's unease about being surrounded by horses was reflected in the queasy look on her face.

"Did you learn anything else?" I asked Valek.

"Yes. Finding clothes when you're half naked is harder than you think. And scared horses can travel pretty far in the wrong direction before you find them." He studied the group of horses. "Onyx and Topaz are fast, but there's nothing like a Sandseed horse when you're in a hurry. And despite your detour to Booruby, love, I had a hard time catching up."

"You could have found a way to tell me you were all right. I've spent the last week in utter misery."

"Now you know how I felt when you jumped into the stable fire. And you know how I'll feel if you don't come back from fighting the Fire Warper."

I opened my mouth then closed it. "You were eavesdropping."

"I had hoped to hear everyone discussing how much they missed my altruistic qualities, my legendary skills as a fighter and as a lover." He leered. "Instead, you're making plans for tomorrow. Interesting how life goes on in spite of itself."

Valek sobered and stared at me with a fiery intensity. "With all that planning, love, I'm sure you can figure a way to return."

"I'm not smart enough." My frustration wrapped around my chest and squeezed until I wanted to scream aloud. "I don't know enough about magic! I don't think anyone does. We're all just bumbling along, using it and abusing it."

"Do you truly believe that?"

"Yes. Although I'll admit to being a hypocrite. First sign of trouble and I fall back on using magic." My ability to guide souls hadn't taxed my energy like using magic. I didn't draw from the power source. It was a natural effort just like inhaling and exhaling. "When I think about magic, all I see is the harm it has done to this world."

"Then you're not looking in the right places."

And this from someone who was immune to magic's effects. I'd seen firsthand the Kirakawa ritual, the blood magic, the corruption of power, the Sandseed massacre and the tormented souls. It had to stop.

Valek studied my expression. "Think about what you said to the Commander about magic."

"I tend to agree with the Commander about how magic corrupts."

"Then why did you mention to the Commander how magic could harness the power of a blizzard and save his people instead of discussing the possibility of using power as a weapon? If magic corrupts, then why hasn't it corrupted you? Or Irys? Moon Man? Leif?"

"We haven't let it corrupt us."

"Right! You have the choice."

"But it's a very tempting choice. Power is addictive. It's only a matter of time."

"Oh yes. Sitia has been battling Warpers for ages. Though you wouldn't know it from all the peace and prosperity hanging around." Sarcasm dripped from Valek's words. "Let's see, how long ago did the magicians use blood magic? I think Moon Man told me two thousand years. Then you're right! It's only a matter of time. A matter of two thousand years. I'll take those odds any day."

"I never realized how annoying you can be."

"You know I'm right."

"I could prove you wrong. I can be corrupt." It was my turn to leer.

Valek looked over at Janco and the others. They milled

about a small fire, trying to appear nonchalant, but I knew they listened to every word.

"Not in front of the children, love. But I'll hold you to that."

The night disappeared in a hurry. We finished prepping the wagon and updating our plans to include Valek and Gale.

The others had taken Valek's return in stride, although Janco made a comment about Valek's lack of hair. "You ever notice how couples start to look alike?" he asked.

In a deadpan, Valek replied, "Yes. In fact, I was just thinking how much you and Topaz resemble each other. It's uncanny."

Ari chuckled at Janco's chagrined expression before saying, "The caravan is leaving soon. What part of the line do we want to be in?"

"Near the back, but not the last wagon," Valek instructed. "When we're out of sight of the gatehouse, head to the Keep."

"Yes, sir." Ari snapped to attention.

I stared at our small group. Marrok eyed Valek with dislike, but he had assumed the posture of a soldier waiting for orders. Leif chewed on his lip, a nervous habit. Gale's face was bleached with fear, but she set her mouth into a determined frown. She told me her power was weak compared to a Stormdancer, but she could agitate the wind and kick up enough dust to impair the Daviians' vision.

"We don't know what we'll encounter inside the Keep. Listen for instructions and follow orders even if they don't make sense," Valek ordered.

"Yes, sir," everyone said in unison, including Gale.

Before we could get into position, I handed three of Opal's glass animals to Leif and the other three to Gale.

"What are these for?" Leif asked.

"Keep one each, but give the rest to Moon Man, Irys, Bain and Dax if they're still alive." I swallowed the sudden lump in my throat. "I think I can use the animals to communicate with you when I'm in the fire world."

Leif peered at me with sad eyes, but I turned away before he could say anything. "Come on, you first." I gestured to the cart.

Leif, Gale and Valek hid in the three boxes at the bottom of the wagon. We put another empty crate and some genuine goods on top of them. Then I lay down inside the top crate.

When Marrok closed the lid, my heart slammed in my chest in a sudden panic. My throat closed when the rugs were piled on top. The wagon lurched. I wanted out. I felt trapped. The others could get out of their boxes through the hidden panels we had installed on the wagon's floor. I could not. This wasn't going to work. The Vermin would figure it out before we could reach the Keep. And then what would happen?

I drew in a few steadying breaths. We would be captured. I would be fed to the Fire Warper just like I wanted. All we would lose was the element of surprise. While helpful, I believed even with it the chances of the others living through the encounter were little to none.

My morose line of thought was not helping my state of mind. So I focused instead on the motion of the wagon. It had been a long and emotionally exhausting night. I fell asleep during the trip to the Citadel.

The sound of an unfamiliar voice roused me from sleep. We had stopped, and I gathered by the voices we were at the Citadel's north gate. The voices came closer and a person banged on my box. I jumped, clamping my lips against a shout.

"What's in this one?" a man asked.

"The finest silk sheets woven by the Moon Clan, sir," the merchant replied. "Perhaps you care to purchase a set? Just feel the fabric and you'll know your wife will be most anxious to try them out."

The man laughed. "I'll not be spending a month's pay for a night with my wife. That's why I married her."

Their laughter trailed away as the guard questioned the merchant on his reasons for entering the Citadel. After what seemed like hours, the wagon began to move. Ari picked up the pace and I guessed we had broken off from the caravan.

When the sounds from the market reached me, the wagon slowed. Ari called out to the stand owners, giving them the sign to prepare to revolt. A network of messengers would fan out to spread the news, then remain in place to deliver the signal for action.

The fighting would erupt when our wagon went inside the Keep. The cart turned around a corner. It stopped with a jerk.

Ari cursed and the jangle of many horses surrounded us. A familiar voice called out, "Oh no. This will not do."

Cahil.

32

CAHIL AND HIS MEN had found us. Trapped inside my crate, I could do nothing but wait for the inevitable. I hoped Valek and the others hiding in the wagon would be able to sneak away.

"I assume you have Yelena hidden somewhere in your wagon?" Cahil asked.

"Have who, sir?" Ari asked, playing innocent. "All I have is goods for the market."

"For the market? The market you just rode through without stopping to unload? I don't think so. Despite your disguises and weak attempts to explain your presence, I know who you are and why you're here. In fact, I was sent by Jal to come and escort you to the Keep."

I heard a creak as Ari shifted his weight and I detected a faint rustling from below me. Probably Valek opening his escape panel.

"Relax," Cahil said. "I'm not here to capture you. I'm here to join you. And I hope for the sake of all our lives you have a decent plan."

I had to let Cahil's words sink in. Had he just said he wanted to join us?

"A plan, sir?" Ari asked.

Cahil snorted with exasperation. "Yelena! Leif!" he called. "Come out and tell your big northern friend I'm telling the truth. Look for yourselves. My men have not drawn their—"

A surprised yelp followed a thud. Then Ari moved off the wagon and the rugs on top of my crate scraped away. The lid lifted. I had my switchblade in hand, but Ari's amused face greeted me. He helped me stand. Valek had a knife to Cahil's throat. He and Cahil were on the ground. Cahil's men remained on their mounts. The men appeared tense and alert but hadn't drawn any weapons. Leif and Janco joined Ari and all three pulled their blades. Marrok stayed on Garnet.

"Tell me why I shouldn't cut your throat?" Valek asked Cahil.

"You won't get into the Keep without me," he said. He kept still and held his hands up and away from his body.

"Why this sudden change of heart?" I asked.

Cahil's gaze met mine. Hatred still radiated from his eyes but the pain of betrayal tainted them. "You were right." He said each word as if it hurt him. "They're using me and…"

"And what?" I prompted.

"The rituals and killings have gotten out of hand. I can't be a part of it anymore." He looked at Marrok. "I wasn't raised to be a killer. I was raised to be a leader. I'll earn my throne the old-fashioned way."

Although the expression on Marrok's face never changed, his body relaxed.

"How do we know you're telling the truth?" Ari asked.

"Yelena knows through her magic."

I shook my head. "I can't use it. It will alert Jal and risk the mission."

"She already knows you're here. You have thwarted her a number of times, although it will be more difficult now, as she has gained an incredible amount of power through the Kirakawa ritual."

"She?" Valek and I asked in unison.

"We thought Jal was Gede," I said.

Cahil blinked at us for a moment. "You didn't know? What else don't you know? You *were* planning an attack at the Keep, right? I thought you had it all figured out."

"You thought wrong," I said, annoyed. "We had to guess about the state of affairs inside the Keep."

"Then here's a way for me to prove my loyalty. I'll tell you what's been going on and will help you get inside. Agreed?"

Valek and I exchanged a glance.

"Do I still get to kill him?" Valek asked.

"At the first sign of betrayal, yes," I said.

"What about after this is all over?"

"Then it's your call."

Cahil stared at us. "Hold on. I'm risking my life to help you. I'd like some guarantees."

"We've come to a point where there are no guarantees. For any of us," I said.

"That's not very encouraging," Cahil said.

"It's not supposed to be. You should know what happens when you play with fire, Cahil. Eventually, you'll get burned. Now, tell us what you know," I ordered.

Valek removed his knife from Cahil's throat and stepped

back. Cahil scanned the area. We had attracted quite the crowd, but I saw to my relief that there were no Vermin among them. Then it hit me—why not? I asked Cahil.

He gave me a sardonic smile. "They're all at the Keep. Roze plans a massive Kirakawa ritual using all the magicians she has captured to empower all her favorite Warpers in one sweep. And you're to be the coup de grâce."

My blood turned to ice. "Roze?"

A superior expression settled on Cahil's face. "Yes, Roze Featherstone, First Magician also known as Jalila Daviian, First Warper and founder of the Daviian Clan."

All color drained from Leif's face. "But how? Why?"

"I had no idea until Ferde was caught. She asked me to rescue him in exchange for the Council's support to invade Ixia," Cahil said. "I thought it was an undercover mission to learn who else was behind his bid for power. Though, when I discovered the truth about her and the other Warpers, I must admit it didn't bother me at the time. She promised to attack Ixia and make me king."

"How many Warpers are inside and who are the victims for the ritual?" I asked.

"Six very powerful Warpers, including Roze and Gede. They have been very careful about who they allow to increase their powers, keeping crucial information about the Kirakawa ritual to a select few. There are fifty Vermin soldiers and ten medium-powered Warpers. Two of those Warpers are scheduled to be given master-level powers during the massive ritual. The victims for this ritual will be the three other Masters, who are incarcerated in the Keep's cells, Moon Man and the Councilors."

"What about the students?"

"The older apprentices have been put in the cells. The younger ones obey out of fear."

"How does Roze plan to control the Master Magicians?"

"She has the power, but I think she does plan to prick them with Curare to save her energy. Once they are tied down, a dose of Theobroma will weaken their defenses."

"They seem to have an unlimited supply of Curare," I mused out loud.

"Gede Daviian has provided the drug for them. He also helped recruit dissatisfied Sandseeds to the Daviian Clan. And having a pet Fire Warper has made him the Daviians' most valued member."

I mulled over the information. "How do you plan to get us inside?"

"As my prisoner. She knows I went to find you. I'll bring you to her and since my feelings for you haven't changed, I won't have to act like I hate you. Sensing nothing wrong, Roze will probably order me to take the rest—" Cahil pointed to Ari and Janco "—to the cells."

"Why would I cooperate with you?"

"Because I'll have Leif, and I'll make a bargain to keep him safe in exchange for your cooperation."

My mind raced through the options and possibilities. For the first time, I felt hopeful about my friends' survival. "Cahil, when you take the others to the cells, can you free everyone inside?"

"As long as Roze is occupied."

Valek smiled. "What's the plan, love?"

We approached the Keep's gate at a slow walk. I sat in front of Cahil on his horse. Ari and Marrok sat on the wagon with their hands tied behind their backs. Valek and Janco hid in the bottom crates, and Leif sat on Kiki with one of Cahil's men sitting behind him armed with a knife.

I didn't have to pretend to be scared and concerned for my friends. We were waved through the gate without hesitation. Ari had informed the Citadel's citizens to wait ten minutes before storming the entrance to the Keep. Ten minutes for Cahil and the rest to free the prisoners and for me to jump into the fire. I hoped it was enough time.

The wagon bypassed the Keep's administration building to where the apprentice barracks formed a ring around an open area. A few students hurried past, keeping their gazes on the ground as they carried out their tasks.

The grassy glen had been transformed. I stared at the wasteland in shock. The bonfire was expected, but the grass around the fire had been covered with sand. Brownish-red stains soaked the sand and stakes had been driven into it.

It was the killing ground for the Kirakawa ritual. And the next victim had already been tied down and prepped.

Bloody cuts crisscrossed his abdomen, legs and arms. Although in pain, Moon Man still managed to smile. "Now we can start the party," he said.

Roze frowned at him and he writhed in agony. She stood next to Moon Man. Gede was beside her. Other Warpers ringed the fire pit, watching with predatory eyes.

"I see you finally managed to get something right, Cahil," she said. "Bring her here."

Cahil slid off the saddle and grabbed me around the waist. He knew he didn't need to help me down, so he must have a reason. I let him yank me from the saddle, and drop me on the ground.

"Where do you want to go?" he asked in a tight whisper as he jerked me to my feet.

"As close to the fire as I can."

"Really?"

"Yes." Although my heart beat a different answer. No! it pounded. Let's go! Run!

He clamped his hand around my arm and pulled me to Roze. We stopped a few feet from the fire. The heat pulsed in waves. Sweat dripped down my back.

Roze gestured to a couple of Warpers. "There are two hiding in the boxes. Take them."

The Warpers and a few soldiers advanced on the wagon. After some banging and cursing, Janco and Gale were hauled out.

"There are three compartments, but one is empty," a Warper called.

Roze looked at me with a question in her eyes.

"For me. So I could get inside the Citadel." The truth. I kept my mind on the task at hand and didn't allow it to wonder about Valek.

"At this distance, Yelena, do you realize your mental defenses are nothing but a thin shell? I will see your lies before you can form them in your mind. Remember that."

I nodded and strengthened my barrier.

She laughed and ordered the soldiers to take the others to the cells. "I'll deal with them later." Once the cart was out of sight, she peered at me and Cahil.

"Your capture was too easy," she said. "You must think I'm a simpleton, but no matter, I've only to expand a sliver of power to find out what you're planning." Her strong magic invaded my mind.

I kept my thoughts on saving Moon Man, Leif and the others as I mentally dodged her onslaught. It failed to work. To distract her, I asked, "Why?"

"Nice try." Her magic crashed through my defenses, and seized my body. "You are in my power now. Sitia is saved."

"Saved from me?" At least I could still talk. In fact, even with her incredible strength, she could only control either my mind or my body. Not both.

"Saved from you. The Commander. Valek. Our way of life is secured."

"By killing Sitians? Using blood magic?"

"Small price to pay for our continued prosperity. I could not let the Commander invade us. The Council failed to see the problem. I created the Daviians as a backup—a hidden weapon for when we needed them. It worked. The Council eventually agreed with me." Smug satisfaction shone in her eyes.

Through our mental link, I sensed she didn't understand the whole truth or she chose to ignore it. "The Daviians forced the Council to agree with you. They had their children."

Extreme annoyance creased Roze's forehead. She shot Gede a venom-laced look. He wisely remained quiet, but his muscles tensed.

"Are you sure you have control of the Daviians?" I asked.

"Of course. And once we choose a new Council we will attack Ixia and free them. They will welcome our way of life." She smiled.

"So you saved Sitia? Tell me, how is sacrificing the Council different than Valek assassinating them?"

Roze frowned and a wave of pain pulsed through my body. My thoughts scattered as an unrelenting torment twisted my muscles. When I regained my senses, I was lying in the sand, looking up at her.

"Isn't *choosing* new Councilors the same as *appointing* generals?" I asked.

Another jolt of pain sizzled along my spine. I arched my back and screamed. Sweat poured from my head and soaked my clothes. My heart pumped as if it ran for its life. I gasped for breath.

"Would you care to ask anything else?" Danger glinted in her eyes.

"Yes. How are your actions different than the Commander's?"

She paused, and I pressed my advantage. "You want to protect Sitia from the Commander, but in the process you turned into him."

Her mouth opened to protest, but I interrupted. "You're worried the Commander would invade Sitia and turn your clans into Military Districts. But you're planning to attack Ixia and turn his Military Districts into clans. How is that different? Tell me!"

She blustered and shook her head. "I'm…he's…" Then she laughed. "Why should I listen to you? You're a Soulfinder. You want to control Sitia. Of course you would try to sway me with your lies."

Gede relaxed and chuckled with Roze. "She will twist your words. You should kill her now."

Roze drew a breath.

"Wait for the ritual! I have something you want," I said.

"What could you have that I can not take from you?"

"According to the ritual, a willing victim releases more power than a resisting one."

"And you will submit to me in exchange for what?"

"For all my friends' lives."

"No. Only one. You choose."

"Moon Man, then." I hoped the others managed to escape.

She released her hold on me. I stood, but she pointed. "Lie in the sand," she ordered.

"Can I ask another question first?"

"One."

"What happens to the Fire Warper after this ritual?"

"Once you're dead, our deal is complete. We have promised him your power and fed him in exchange for knowledge about the blood magic. He will then have enough power to rule the underworld."

A shout reached us and I felt a magical onslaught.

Roze turned to the commotion and gestured to her Warpers. "Take care of them." Unconcerned, she said to me, "You know they will not get close to us. My Warpers and I have enough power to stop them."

"Yes, I know."

"But I don't think you believe it. Watch what I can do. This used to drain me of energy. Now it takes only a thought." Her gaze went to Moon Man's.

His face paled and his body jerked once then stilled. The shine in his eyes dulled as his soul left his body.

33

I DIVED OVER HIS PRONE form and inhaled his soul before crashing to the sand.

Gede gasped. "He was for the ritual."

Roze laughed and said, "Don't worry. She'll now give me two sources of power when I cut her heart out."

"We made a deal, Roze. My cooperation for Moon Man." I brushed the sand off my clothes.

"And you won't cooperate when I press a knife to Leif's throat?" she asked. By the expression on my face, she knew I would. "You're too soft, Soulfinder. You could have raised a soulless army. They would have been undefeatable. Magic doesn't work on them. Only fire."

Another cry split the air, but this time from the opposite direction. A Vermin raced toward us.

"Now what?" Roze asked him.

"The Keep's gates are under attack," he said, panting.

She glanced at the Warpers fighting with the Keep's magicians. A vision of the battle formed in my mind. The ferocity of the combat dwindled. The confusing array of magical images was gone and Gale's whirling dust devils had died. People fell to the ground after being hit with Curare-laced darts. Leif, Ari and Bain lay paralyzed. Janco fought a soldier, keeping the man between him and the blowpipes. His movements slowed as another Warper focused his magic on him.

Roze's Warpers had gained the upper hand; it was only a matter of time.

"There is nobody left to rescue you," Roze said.

Her comments hit home when she called a few Warpers away from the battle to deal with the revolt at the gates.

But there was one person I didn't see and that gave me some hope. "Roze, you haven't figured everything out."

She looked dubious. "What have I missed? Valek? Oh, I know he's here. Magic might not affect him, but Curare will do the trick."

"No. The Fire Warper."

"What about him?"

"You haven't taken into account that he might have different plans than you."

"Don't be ridiculous. Gede and I feed him. We give him his power. Who else would help him?"

"I would."

I ran toward the fire. Roze's yell sounded faint over the roar of the blaze. The heat encompassed me in a loving embrace. Burning pain transformed into pinpricks of pleasure. But this time the world didn't settle into the smooth plain of black. Souls filled my world, writhing and crying with misery. The air stank of decay and infection.

Help! Help! they cried.

The Fire Warper ordered them to be quiet and pushed them away from me. "She is here for me," he said. "She will not help you."

He studied me. "You have brought me a treat. No only a soul for the sky, but Moon Man's bright power will increase my strength."

Moon Man stood next to me. He peered about the fire world with mild interest.

"I'm sorry you're here," I said. "I didn't plan for it to be you."

"Why not? I am your guide, Yelena. In life and in death. That never changes."

"But you said Gede was my new Story Weaver."

"You were looking for an easy road. Which Gede provided. You could have reclaimed me as your Story Weaver at any time."

"How?"

"You just needed to ask. Or rather begged for my return— much better for my ego."

The Fire Warper stepped between us. "How sweet. Now take me to the sky," he demanded.

"No," I said.

"You cannot refuse me. We made a deal."

"I promised to come back. I didn't promise to take you into the sky."

"Then you and Moon Man will stay here in misery and I will use your power to reach the sky." He advanced and grabbed my arms.

My skin boiled as searing daggers of pain spread through-out my body. I screamed, but he didn't have the ability to take what he wanted. I had to give it to him.

He tried another tactic. Waving with an arm, a window opened and I could see Roze and her Warpers. Leif, Bain, Ari, Janco, Gale, Cahil and Marrok all were staked in the sand.

"They lost. There are a few more left, but when they are captured, the fun begins. However, if you lead me to the sky, I will stop Roze and release all your friends and family."

I looked at Moon Man.

"If you do not help the Fire Warper," Moon Man said, "we are stuck here and Roze will send each of them to suffer in this world with us."

This was the one scenario I had hoped to avoid. "Are you saying that's what I should do?"

"No. I am merely pointing out the consequences."

"Then what should I do?"

"Your decision to make. You are the Soulfinder. Find your soul."

I wanted to strangle him, but he was already dead. "Do you think you could give me a straight answer one time?" I demanded.

"Yes, I could."

I gazed out as frustration and futility twisted tightly around me. Sensing I was conflicted, the Fire Warper let the souls draw near to me so I could see the fate of my friends. Their cries grew shrill in my ears and the heat baked my skin, making it difficult to concentrate. The fetid odor assaulted my senses.

"Watch," he said, and pointed to the scene beyond the fire. "Roze has ensnared Irys in a cocoon of magic. She will force her to lie upon the sand and be tied down."

Sure enough Irys walked toward Roze. She knelt before her. Irys's eyes glanced to the side before the other Warpers secured her in the sand. I followed her gaze and spotted Valek.

He fought four Warpers with swords, but I knew they threw every ounce of magic at him. And by Roze's intent gaze, she aimed all her power against him. Even though the magic didn't work, he still felt the presence and it slowed his movements. A soldier waited nearby with a blowpipe, seeking the first opportunity to hit Valek with a dart.

"And Valek will be next," the Fire Warper said. "What do you want to do? Watch your friends and lover die or guide me to the sky?"

I held out my hand to Moon Man and to the Fire Warper. "Come," I said.

34

A TRIUMPHANT GRIN SPREAD on the Fire Warper's face. Moon Man remained unflappable. He held my hand. Even though it appeared to be made of smoke, his hand felt solid in mine. Moon Man looked at me. The oval shape of his eyes matched Roze's. Why hadn't I noticed the resemblance before?

Roze's comments replayed in my mind. Could I reanimate Moon Man's body after I took him to the sky? According to Roze, soulless bodies were unaffected by magic. Could I create a small force to help Irys and Valek?

My bat flew around my head. Odd. How could he be here?

Moon Man sighed. I missed the point. It didn't matter how the bat had gotten here, but why was he here at all. Bats. Opal's glass bat. I reached for my pocket, but the answer halted the motion. Opal's sister. Tula!

When Ferde had stolen Tula's soul and strangled her, I had used my magic to breathe for Tula, but as soon as I had stopped, she had stopped.

I didn't possess the power to raise a soulless army.

The magician born one-hundred-and-fifty years ago wasn't a Soulfinder, but a Soulstealer.

I was a true Soulfinder. And I knew what my job entailed. The Fire Warper grew impatient with my delay and reached for my free hand; I yanked it away. My bat cried out with joy and disappeared.

I sought Roze with my mind, seeing her soul and the souls of all her victims trapped within her. Their blood had been injected into her skin to bind them to her. I pushed at the blood, sweeping and forcing it through her pores, pulling the souls free, sending them to the sky.

She yelped and rolled up her sleeve. Black liquid oozed from her arms, dripping onto the sand. The putrid smell of rancid blood surrounded her like a fog. Each one I removed weakened Roze until only her own power remained.

Then I projected my mind to Gede and did the same to him. One by one I plucked souls from the Warpers, weakening them.

The Fire Warper cried an oath and lunged for me. Moon Man intercepted and fought him so I could return my attention to the Keep.

Roze's magical hold on Irys had slipped when I extracted her power. Freed from the magic, Irys used her own skills to draw a knife close to her and cut the rope. Once loose, she ran to a few others who had not been pricked with Curare but who, like her, had been captured by magic.

Gale and Marrok joined her and they attacked Roze. Valek's opponents had been distracted by the scene around them, giving Valek the opportunity to dispatch them. The man with the blowpipe ran off. Valek turned his full attention to Roze.

Satisfied all was well with my friends, I focused on the Fire Warper. He held Moon Man in a tight grip, compressing Moon Man's soul to bind him to the fire world.

"Stop," I said. "You'll gain no more power today." I pulled at Moon Man with my magic and he popped from the Fire Warper's grasp. "I find souls and ensure they arrive at the proper destination. He doesn't belong here. But you do."

I moved past him. He tried to stop me, but he was a soul just like all the others and I controlled him. Moving through the fire world, I found those who didn't belong and released them to the sky. The Fire Warper screamed at me with each one, but I ignored him. A long time passed as I freed them all, but my energy increased with every rescue.

"Why aren't I tired?" I asked Moon Man.

He smiled. "Think about what you have learned today."

I glanced around. The Fire Warper's power had diminished with each freed soul. Perhaps stealing his power had increased my own?

"No." Moon Man looked a little exasperated, as if he couldn't believe how slow I was. I did take some pleasure from his expression. To alter his calm demeanor required much effort on my part.

The Fire Warper glowered at me. "It is only a matter of time before I regain my strength," he said. "There is always someone who desires more power and I will be waiting for them."

"Not if I can help it," I said.

"Then you will have to spend eternity with me to prevent it. The knowledge is out there now. Another fool will figure out how to contact me through the flames."

He had a point. But I was the Soulfinder. In order to do

my job, I would have to stay in the underworld and send the souls to their proper places. Thinking about my job, I remembered a promise to Moon Man.

"Can you guide me to the shadow world?" I asked him.

"No. But you can lead me."

"And you call yourself a guide?"

He smiled serenely.

"I hate you." I clasped Moon Man's hand.

I thought of the shadow world with its gray plain and sky. The red glow faded and soon the featureless expanse spread in front of us.

"This is only the corridor between worlds, Yelena. Look deeper to see the real shadow world."

Another cryptic instruction. For all my abilities, I still couldn't get Moon Man to give me a straight answer. I pushed away my frustration and focused on who I was trying to find. The Sandseeds who had been killed by the Vermin in the Avibian Plains.

The flat area began to undulate and transform into the plains. Small outcroppings of rocks grew and the smooth gray ground sprouted grass and a few bushes. A cluster of canvas tents popped up and circled a fire pit. The scene before me resembled a Sandseed camp. Yet there was no color. Only black and white and every shade of gray.

Sandseeds huddled together in this camp on the altered Avibian Plain, living in the shadow cast by the real world. They clung to their memories of life, not realizing peace awaited them in the sky.

I walked among them and talked to them. Their numbers grew and I had to stop myself from reliving the horror of the

Vermin's attack and massacre. I made promises to watch over the living Sandseeds who had hidden during the attack. Days and weeks could have passed while I convinced them to move on. I had no concept of time.

Again, as I sent each one into the sky, my strength grew. "There are many more souls clinging to the shadow world," I said to Moon Man, thinking about all the towns and cities in Sitia and Ixia. "Let me return you to your body and you can tell the others my fate."

"I can not return," he said. "My body has died, unlike yours. And even if you heal me, I would be unhappy and would wish for death."

"Like Stono and Gelsi?"

"Yes. Eventually both will find their way back to where they belong."

"Then I will send you to the sky. You deserve to be there."

"Not until you understand."

"I do understand. I'm doing my job. I've resigned myself to living here to keep Sitia and Ixia safe from more Warpers!" I clamped my hands together to keep them from wrapping around Mr. I-know-everything-and-you-don't Man's thick neck.

"Have you truly resigned yourself?" he asked.

"I…" I huffed in frustration. I would rather be back with Valek, Kiki, my parents, Leif, Irys, Ari, Janco and my other friends. I had learned my true job, but there were still many aspects of my magic and others' magic to explore. I thought about Opal's unique ability. Then I remembered my glass bat.

Had it survived the fire? I felt inside my pockets. Odd how my clothing had survived the flames. My fingers touched a smooth lump. I pulled the animal from my cape. The inner core glowed with magic. Staring at the light, I saw Leif's sad face. He peered at me in sorrow, then disbelief when I smiled at him.

"Hello from the underworld," I said.

"Yelena! What the…? Where are…? Come back!"

"I can't. Tell me what has happened?"

He gave me a quick sketch of how the battle had played out after I jumped into the fire. Most of the Warpers were dead, only Roze, Gede and four others remained alive. They were in the Keep's cells, awaiting trial.

"They will be hanged for treason and murder," Leif said. He grew somber. "We buried Moon Man last week."

"Last week? But—"

"You've been gone for weeks. We keep the fire burning, hoping you'll return. Also Valek will not let us quench it. He's been helping the Councilors and Master Magicians recover from their ordeal and to smooth out relations with the Commander via Ambassador Signe. Valek went from the scourge of Sitia to the hero of Sitia." Leif smiled sardonically.

Valek. The one person I wouldn't mind spending eternity with.

Leif continued, "And the rest of us are coping with the aftermath. Many students were killed by the Vermin. We're still sorting out who is left. Your friend Dax is okay, but Gelsi died resisting a Warper."

Moon Man was right, Gelsi found her way back. I hoped Stono wouldn't suffer too much before his soul found the sky.

He paused. "The Sitian army's hunting down the remaining Vermin who escaped. The Sandseeds have moved back to the plains to repopulate." Leif sighed. "You're missed by every-one. Why can't you come back?"

"Someone needs to keep the Fire Warper from regaining power."

Leif frowned as he thought, then looked hopeful. "Bain has burned those old Efe texts to stop someone from learning about the blood magic."

"But there are others who know how to perform the ritual, and, even though you will execute them, they will be here in the fire world and able to communicate to someone who is determined to seek them out."

"You're a Soulfinder, can't you send them somewhere out of reach?" Leif asked.

"They don't deserve to be in the sky."

"Why not?" Moon Man said.

My mind thought over what I knew of the sky, which was very little. "I think they would taint it. It's pure and their vile deeds would soil it."

"Finally. What is the sky?"

What indeed? When I sent souls there, I felt refreshed, en-ergetic even though I used power, which usually caused me fatigue. I added souls to the sky. Adding to the power blanket surrounding the world.

The source of magic!

The world's soul.

Moon Man beamed at me. "Now you can send me there! And then you can return to your life."

He chuckled at my dubious expression. "You will find a way, Yelena. You always do."

"Last piece of cryptic advice?"

"Consider it my farewell gift."

I hesitated for a moment. Once Moon Man was gone I would be all alone.

"All the more reason not to stay," Moon Man said.

"There's one thing I won't miss."

"And that is?"

"You reading my mind all the time and making me figure things out for myself."

"All part of being your Story Weaver. It does not stop, you know. You will hear my voice in your mind from time to time, giving you my unique advice."

I groaned. "And I thought living in the underworld for eternity was bad!"

Before sending him to the sky, I stared at him, trying to hold his features, including his sardonic grin, in my mind. When he disappeared, his absence felt like an icy coating on my skin. I realized I still held Opal's bat, but my connection to Leif was broken.

I wandered through the shadow world and found lost souls. Every so often I checked in the fire world to make sure the Fire Warper remained as he should be. He cursed, taunted and tried to cajole me, depending on his mood.

Irys, Leif and Bain all talked to me through the glass animals. They were the only ones who had the ability to use them. Through them I knew Roze, Gede and the other Warpers would be hanged soon. I prepared to receive them in the fire world.

In the meantime, I stared at my bat, trying and failing to connect to Valek. My desire to talk to him, to hold him, clawed at my body. Frustration at my inability to communi-cate with him caused a window to open to the real world, and

I could view events around my fire. I laughed at my intense feelings of ownership. My fire. But I sobered. I knew after they hanged Roze and the others, my fire would be doused and my window closed for good.

The Council planned to hang Roze and her accomplices on gallows built in the bloodstained sand then burn their bodies in my fire. An insult given only to traitors.

The sand would be cleaned up and perhaps the gardeners would plant grass in the space. Or some trees. Flowers. A memorial? Perhaps a structure similar to one of the Citadel's jade statues or fountains. To remember me and Moon Man.

Now I was being maudlin and dramatic. Next thing I knew, I'd be designing the memorial, sketching its dimensions in the sand. I wondered about what they would do with all the sand. Send it to Booruby to be melted into glass? So Opal could turn fire into ice?

I froze in shock as a wild idea formed in my head. Thinking it through, I found many holes and reasons for it not to work. But success or not, at least I could say I tried. And the effort alone would keep Moon Man from nagging me for a while.

35

CALLING TO LEIF through my bat, I hoped there would be enough time. He seemed eager to help and rushed off to make the arrangements.

Events had to happen in a particular order for this to work. I returned to the fire world. The Fire Warper would be our first test subject. Watching out my window, I waited for Leif to return. I didn't like being in the fire world. The shrill noise drilled through my skull and the putrid smell permeated the air. I preferred the quiet dullness of the shadow world.

The Fire Warper enjoyed my anxiety. "Look at how you long to return. Your suffering is my only pleasure. And I will enjoy keeping you here. Already I sense an unhappy boy who seeks revenge on his tormentors. If his desire grows, I'll be able to talk to him. Unless you prevent it."

Doubt flared about what I planned. Was I being selfish? Could I still rescue souls lost in the shadow world? Yet I had done it before with the ghosts in Owl's Hill. Suppressing all my fears, I ignored the Fire Warper's comments.

What seemed like a couple of weeks to me, but could have been a month or more, passed. By my brief glimpses into the Keep, the cold season had ended and the warming season was in full swing. I received updates from Leif, but now that I had a chance to escape, my impatience grew.

Finally, all the elements were in place. The gallows were built and the needed equipment brought in. My incredible relief at seeing Opal surprised me. Her mouth was pressed in pure determination as she readied her tools.

Another worry crossed my mind. Within the underworld, I hadn't felt cold, hot, hunger or thirst. But if I stepped back through the fire, would it burn me? I would find out soon enough. The Fire Warper hovered near me, his amusement plain.

Opal grasped a long metal pipe and poked it into the kiln. I wondered where they had gotten the glassmaking supplies. She turned the pipe and drew it out. And proceeded to create a glass animal.

When she moved to blow into the pipe, I inhaled the Fire Warper's soul. He yelped in surprise and seared my skin as I sent him through Opal and into the glass. He screamed in panic and resisted. But I controlled him. He was a soul after all.

Opal jerked as if burned, but returned to her task, making the ugliest, squattest looking pig I ever saw.

Placing the animal into the annealing oven, the wait began. Had our experiment worked? If the Fire Warper was truly trapped within the glass, then we could encase all the Warpers who knew how to perform blood magic, preventing them from passing the information along. And I could go home.

Twelve of the longest hours passed before Opal withdrew

the pig and held the statue up for all to see. It was then I noticed
just how many people had come to watch. I expected Leif, the
Master Magicians and Councilors, but it appeared that Fisk and
the entire Helping Guild members were there. My mother and
father lingered at the edges. Perl's hand was clamped to her
throat in dismay, but she looked as determined as Opal.

Cahil and a regiment of soldiers, including Marrok stood at
attention. Ari and Janco waited with Leif. Janco scowled,
showing his extreme dislike of magic.

Valek glowed with his own inner fire. For him, I would risk
the flames' heat.

I turned my attention to Opal's creation. It pulsed with a
muddy red light. The Fire Warper was locked inside.

The audience cheered. Opal placed the pig in the sand, and
gathered another blob of molten glass, preparing for the next
soul.

Roze, under the control of three Master Magicians, was
forced to mount the gallows' steps. The noose was tightened
around her neck and the executioner stepped back. Her face
contorted with rage and she shouted.

Time froze for a moment and I felt what it would have been
like to stand there terrified, waiting for the floor to open and
my life to end with a quick snap of my neck. If I had chosen
the noose instead of becoming the Commander's food taster
two years ago, I wondered if any of this would have happened.

Roze fell in slow motion. Her body jerked at the end of the
rope. Her soul flew. I captured it.

Her hateful thoughts filled my mind. *Guardian of the underworld suits you, Yelena. You belong here. You don't really believe you can
go back? You'll be feared by all and become an outcast in record time.*

If I was a Soulstealer, I would agree with you, I said. *You don't scare me, Roze. You never did and that bothered you more than me being a Soulfinder.*

Opal blew. I sent Roze on her final journey. Then Gede. Then the other four Warpers. Seven in all, including the Fire Warper.

When all the Warpers had been encased in glass, Opal sank to the ground in exhaustion. Now I could leave. I glanced around, trying to determine whether I missed anything, whether a soul who could do harm remained. Roze's words had a bit of truth to them. Regardless of my explanations, Sitians would be frightened of me and the Council's suspicion and unease would linger for a long time.

I welcomed the difficulties. All part of living, and I planned to enjoy every minute.

As I walked through my window to the Keep, sounds reached me first. The roar of the fire. Leif calling my name. Then scalding heat sucked my breath away. Bright yellow and orange stabbed at my eyes. My cape caught fire. I dived to the sand and rolled on the ground to snuff the flames. So much for my grand entrance.

36

I SPENT MY FIRST HOURS back cocooned in an excited babble of all my friends and family. Everyone except Valek. But I knew I would see him when the horde dispersed.

Once my fire had finished its macabre task of burning the traitors to ash, it was doused. Thick smoke boiled from it and clung to the ground until Gale Stormdance created a fresh breeze to whisk it away.

I noted with much interest how fast life resumed. Though glad I had returned, the Councilors left for a meeting, and Fisk and his guild hurried off to work in the market.

Before he left, Fisk flashed me a wide smile and said, "Lovely Yelena, you'll need new clothes for the hot season. I know the best seamstress in the Citadel. Come find me when you're ready."

The hot season? Ari told me it had just started. I had lived in the underworld for seventy-one days, missing the entire warming season. I viewed the time with mixed emotions: glad my perceptions in the underworld didn't match reality, especially if I ever needed to go back; and upset I wasn't here to help clean up the mess left behind by the Vermin.

Ari and Janco grumbled over the hot, sticky weather and confessed their desire to go home to Ixia.

"We had fun rooting out all those Daviians," Janco said. "But I'm sure Maren misses us."

Ari looked doubtful. He had washed the black dye from his hair, and his light skin had burned in the Sitian sun. Janco's skin had tanned, matching his Sitian clothes.

"Oh this?" Janco said, when I mentioned his new coloring. "You missed some beautiful days."

"Janco's been sunning himself every chance he gets," Ari said with obvious disdain. "He claimed he kept the fire going, but I caught him snoozing in the sand a few times."

"Once!" Janco said.

They began to bicker. I laughed and moved away, but heard Ari call out, "Training yard, five o'clock."

Kiki's urgent summons had nagged me the whole time I'd been back. I hurried over to the stable to spend an hour with her. Perhaps Valek would show up and we could get reacquainted in the straw.

I scratched her ears, fed her peppermints and ducked behind a stack of hay bales when the Stable Master came looking for me, probably to give me a lecture about borrowing Garnet for so long.

Lavender Lady not go again, Kiki said in my mind.

I'll try to avoid it. No promises, though.

She huffed. *Next time Kiki go.*

A Horsefinder?

Help Lavender Lady, Kiki said, as if that ended the discussion.

Even though I longed to return to my rooms in Irys's tower, my parents insisted I come to their quarters in the Keep's guest wing after I visited the stables. Leif, Irys and Bain followed me, and the six of us sat in the living room, sipping tea. Wedged tightly between my father and mother on the couch, I was held prisoner. My desire to seek Valek would have to wait.

Bain and Irys were most interested in what had happened in the fire and shadow worlds. After giving them a brief sketch, Bain made me promise to visit him and recite the details for his book.

"You passed the Master-level test," Irys said.

"What?" Caught off guard by this sudden change in topic, I choked on my tea.

"You entered the underworld and returned with a spirit guide. Your encounter with the Fire Warper was your challenge, and his defeat your success."

"But I don't have a spirit guide."

Leif laughed. "Your bat! I thought he was strange. Beside the obvious fact that he wanted to hang out with you."

"Leif. That's not nice, considering all your sister has done for you," Perl admonished.

"Oh, right. How can I forget that she made me bait for a snake, left me under house arrest in Ixia and smuggled me into the Keep in a coffin. And don't forget the time…"

I ignored Leif's rant. I wondered, why a bat? Why not something fearsome like a fire dragon or necklace snake? Irys had a hawk, Bain a wind leopard and Zitora a unicorn. Thinking of Zitora, I reminded myself to go visit her in the infirmary. She had been severely wounded during the fight with the Warpers, and her recovery had been slow.

I kept glancing out the window, hoping to see Valek. My mind circled through various excuses for me to leave everyone to search for him.

Bain interrupted Leif's list of grievances against me. "According to our policies, Yelena is Fourth Magician."

I raised my hand to prevent any more wild speculation. "No. I can't light fires or move objects like the Masters can. I'm a Soulfinder. My job is to find lost souls and send them home, including the souls of Ixia. There is still need for a Liaison between the two countries. I plan to reassume the role."

And the first order of business would be to assess Cahil's intentions. His help in defeating Roze and uncovering all the Vermin nests had proven invaluable to the Council, but I wasn't convinced his new role meant he wouldn't try some way to claim Ixia's throne.

Leif asked, "What do we do with those glass prisons? They're under guard, but we don't want them falling into the wrong hands."

"What would happen if they break?" Perl asked.

They all looked at me. "If the souls are freed, they will go to the fire world, unless there is another Soulfinder to place them elsewhere."

"Elsewhere?" Leif raised his eyebrows.

"Into another body or to the sky." I sighed. "We will have to find a place to protect and to hide them."

"The Keep," Bain said.

"The Illiais Jungle has some deep caves," Esau suggested.

"Under the Emerald Mountains," Irys said.

"Sunken in the deepest part of the sea," Leif said.

"Buried under the northern ice," Perl recommended.

"All good ideas, but the Council will need to debate the issue and decide."

My gaze met Irys's. She gave me a wry smile. We both knew the Council would argue for months, and it was up to me to find a home for them.

I spent the rest of the afternoon with my family. Perl and Esau made me promise to come visit them.

"A nice relaxing visit," Perl ordered. "No chasing Vermin or saving anyone. We'll sit and talk and I'll make you a new perfume."

"Yes, Mother."

She made me eat before I could leave. I hurried to the training yard, hoping Valek would be there.

He was not. The man must be torturing me on purpose. I had made him wait over two months. Perhaps he was returning the favor.

Ari and Janco sparred with swords. And although Janco sang his rhymes and Ari used his brute strength, they were equally matched in skill. They stopped when they saw me.

"Come on," Janco said. "Ari wants to make sure you're in good fighting shape before we leave."

"I do?"

"Yes, you do. Otherwise you'll worry about her."

"I will?"

"Of course." Janco waved away Ari's comments. "Besides, this is just a lull before the next storm. We need to be ready!"

This time I piped in. "The next storm?"

Janco sighed dramatically. "There's always another storm. It's the way the world works. Snowstorms, rainstorms, windstorms, sandstorms and firestorms. Some are fierce and others are small. You have to deal with each one separately, but you need to always keep an eye on what's brewing for tomorrow."

Ari rolled his eyes. "Janco's unique view of life. Yesterday he compared living to food."

"That's because some food leaves you full while others—"

"Janco," I said. "Prepare for *my* storm." I swept my bow toward his feet.

He jumped over it with a nimble grace. Dropping his sword, he reached for his bow and our match began.

Since I had returned from the underworld, I could see everyone with a new sight. With a blink of my eyes, I saw through their bodies and directly into their souls. I knew their thoughts, feelings and intentions as if they were my own. Before I had to pull power for the source and project myself to them. Now the connection was there the second I thought about it.

Janco's comical surprise when I dumped him on the ground in three moves was almost worth my trip through the underworld. Almost.

He huffed and blustered and tried to make excuses. I stopped our second fight to guide a soul to the sky. Many hung around the Keep and I knew I would have to do a sweep of the Citadel.

Janco viewed my magical actions as if they were distasteful to him. "At least you're expending energy. You'll be easier to beat," he smirked.

"Wishful thinking," I said.

After losing the next four matches, Janco finally conceded.

"Am I ready for the next storm?" I asked him, smiling sweetly.

"You *are* the next storm."

Bruised ego aside, Janco and Ari were pleased with my fighting skills.

"You found your center," Ari said with a note of approval in his voice. "You're not afraid to embrace who you are. Now Janco won't have to worry anymore."

"I'll let Ari do all the worrying for both of us. Oh wait! He already does."

"I do not. You're the one who moaned and fussed about Yelena all these weeks."

"I did not."

They launched into another round of bickering. I never thought I would enjoy listening to them, but I did. Until I saw Cahil walking toward the training yard.

He held his long broadsword. I watched him approach, preparing to defend myself if need be. I studied his emotions with my other sight. Hate, determination and anxiety dominated his feelings.

Cahil stopped at the fence. "I didn't come here to fight," he said. "I want to talk to you."

Ari and Janco didn't seem concerned by his presence, and continued their debate. But they hadn't been on the wrong side of Cahil's wrath. I moved closer with my bow in hand, keeping the wooden fence between us.

"What do you want to talk about?" I demanded.

Cahil pulled in a deep breath and let the air out fast. "I wanted to…"

"Go on. Say it."

Irritation flared in Cahil's light blue eyes, but he stifled it. "I wanted to explain."

"Explain why you're nasty, ruthless, opportunistic—"

"Yelena! Will you shut up."

My expression must have warned him, because he rushed to continue. "You bring out the worst in me. Can you listen?" A pause. "Please?"

"All right."

"When I found out that I didn't have royal blood, that my whole purpose in life was a sham, I refused to believe it. Even when Marrok admitted I was just a soldier's son, I didn't want to hear it. Instead, I transferred my anger to you and Valek and decided I would find a way to make the Council support an attack on Ixia to reclaim the throne." Cahil looked down at the sword in his hand. "You know what I did after. I lost my way and swallowed every morsel of Roze's lies."

Cahil handed me his sword. It had been the King of Ixia's sword. Rescued after the King had been assassinated, the sword had been given to Cahil as part of the ruse to make him believe he was the King's nephew.

"Give it to the Commander for me," Cahil said. "By rights, it should be his."

"Have you given up your desire to rule Ixia?"

He looked at me and I saw a renewed sense of purpose in his soul. "No. I still seek to free Ixia from the Commander's strict rule. But I no longer feel I should inherit the throne. I plan to *earn* the privilege."

"Then that's going to make for some interesting discussions between us." I held his gaze.

"You can count on it."

The summons from Ambassador Signe came after a long soak in a hot bath. I exchanged my damaged cape and smoky clothes for a clean pair of cotton pants and shirt. My hair hadn't grown while I was in the underworld. The inch-long strands, though, were long enough to lay flat on my head.

The Ambassador waited in the Keep's administration building. She had the use of a meeting room and an office during her stay. I hurried up the stairs and into the marble building, hoping to see Valek there. My disappointment churned in my stomach and I wondered if Valek was avoiding me.

Ambassador Signe greeted me warmly, inquiring about my health. I studied her face. So similar to the Commander's almost delicate features, yet missing the full force of the powerful spark residing in his gold eyes. With my new vision, I saw the two souls that struggled for dominance. They took turns, but I could see the red spiral of conflict within.

"Irys Jewelrose informed me you wish to resume your duties as Liaison. Is this true?"

"Yes. Becoming an adviser to the Commander is very tempting, but I feel my skills should serve both Ixia and Sitia by keeping relations open and fostering an understanding between the two nations."

"I see. Then your first order of business should be to negotiate a salary."

"A salary?"

"You can not be paid by the magicians or the Council. You must receive equal wages from Sitia and Ixia to maintain your neutrality." She smiled. "For all that you have done recently, I would suggest you barter for a considerable amount."

"Obviously, there are many things I need to think about in my new role."

"I trust, then, your education is complete?"

I laughed. "There will never be a time when it's complete, but I've reached an understanding with my abilities."

"Good. I look forward to our negotiations."

Before the Ambassador could dismiss me, I said, "I have something for the Commander."

She looked at me expectantly.

"It's with your guard. He wouldn't let me bring it in."

Rising from her desk, she opened the door and returned with the King's sword.

"May I speak to the Commander?" I asked.

The transformation from the Ambassador to the Commander happened in a heartbeat. Even the physical features changed from a woman to a man. I had seen it before, but this time I watched with my other sight. It revealed much.

"What is this for?" the Commander asked. He studied the weapon in his hand.

"Cahil is returning it to you. You won the right to wield it over seventeen years ago."

A thoughtful expression settled on his face as he placed the sword on the desk. "Cahil. What should I do about him?"

I told the Commander about his plans. "He could cause trouble for you in the future, although I hope my efforts will change his mind."

"I know Valek would be happy to assassinate him." He considered that scenario. "But he might prove useful, especially in dealing with the younger generation." He saw my confused frown. "It'll give them something to do."

"Or give them someone to rally behind."

"All part of the fun, I suppose. Is that all?"

"No." I gave the Commander one of Opal's glass animals.

He admired the tree leopard and thanked me for the gift.

"The glow you see is magic," I said.

His gaze pierced me and I felt his sense of betrayal as if I poisoned him. He placed the statue on the desk. I explained why he could view the fire.

"I can see two souls within your body. Your mother didn't want to leave you alone when she died so she stayed with you. Her magic lets you see the glow. And it's her fear of discovery that has made you afraid of magic in all its forms."

Commander Ambrose held his body as if any movement would crack it into a thousand pieces. "How do you know this?"

"I'm a Soulfinder. I find lost souls and send them to the sky. Does she want to go? Do you want her to go?"

"I don't know. I…"

"Think about it. You know where to find me. There's no time limit."

I glanced back before I left. He stared at the tree leopard, lost in his thoughts.

Night had fallen while I talked with the Commander. Walking across the silent campus, I inhaled the warm breeze, soaking in the smells of life and the feel of air on my skin. I scanned my surroundings, searching for some sign of Valek.

Irys had lit all the lanterns in her tower. Even though she had given me three floors of the structure for my use, I found myself thinking about a salary, and my mind drifted to Valek's cottage in the Featherstone lands. It would be nice to be close to Kiki and get away from the Council's and Commander's politics each night. The cottage was near the Ixian border, too. It would be neutral territory.

A place of my own. I couldn't claim any room, cell or dwelling as my own. It would be the first time. My excitement grew.

I trudged up three floors of the tower to my bedroom. The sparse furnishings and layer of dust made for an unwelcoming sight, although the bedding was fresh.

I opened the shutters to let in clean air and felt a presence behind me. Without turning, I demanded, "What took you so long?"

Valek pressed against my back. His arms wrapped around my stomach. "I could ask you the same thing." He spun me to face him. "I didn't want to share you, love. We have a lot of catching up to do."

He leaned in and kissed me. I drank in his essence, it soothed my soul.

Eventually, I pulled away, and laid my head on his chest, content to just feel his heartbeat against my cheek.

"That's the second time I lost you," he said. "You would think it would be easier, but I couldn't douse the burning pain. I felt like my heart had been pierced by a spit and was cooking over a fire."

His arms tightened around me as if he worried I would slip from his grip. "I would beg you to promise never to disappear again, but I know you won't."

"I can't. Just like you can't promise to stop being loyal to the Commander. We both have other duties."

He huffed with amusement. "We could retire."

"From being a Liaison, but not a Soulfinder. There are many lost souls to guide."

Ever the analyst, Valek drew back enough to study me.

"How many? It's been a hundred-and-twenty-five years since Sitia crisped the last Soulfinder. Hundreds?"

"I don't know. The Soulfinders documented in the history books were really Soulstealers. Guyan could have been the only one in the last two thousand years. Bain would delight in helping me with that assignment. But I will need to travel around Sitia and Ixia to help them all. Do you want to come? It could be fun."

"You, me and a couple thousand ghosts? Sounds crowded," he teased. "At least you already found one soul, love."

"Moon Man's?"

"Mine. And I trust you not to lose it."

"The only magic to affect the infamous Valek." It reminded me of a question I had. While in the shadow world, I had had plenty of time to contemplate every single facet of him. "How old were you when the King's men killed your brothers?"

I ignored his questioning look. "How old?"

"Thirteen." An old sorrow pulled at the corners of his mouth.

"That explains it!"

"Explains what?"

"Why you're resistant to magic. Thirteen is around the age when people can access the power source. The trauma of seeing your brothers killed probably caused you to pull so much power you formed a null shield. A shield so impenetrable you can no longer access magic."

"After a season in the underworld, you're now an expert in all things magical?"

Although he was quick to dismiss the notion, the shock of the revelation was evident in his wide eyes.

"I'm an expert in all things Valek."

"Analyze this, love." He drew me in and kissed me.

When his hands pulled at the fabric of my shirt, I stopped him. "Valek, as much as I want you to stay, I need you to do a favor for me."

"Anything, love."

I smiled at his loyalty. He agreed without hesitation, without knowing what I needed. "I want you to steal those glass prisons. Hide them in a safe place where no one will find them. Don't tell me or anyone else where you put them."

"You don't want to know. Are you sure?"

"Yes. I can still be corrupted by magic. And if I ever ask you for their location you are *not* to tell me. No matter what. Promise."

"Yes, sir."

"Good." I felt relieved.

"It may take me a few days or weeks. Where will you be?"

I told him about staying on as the Liaison. "I plan to commandeer a certain cottage in the Featherstone lands and declare that parcel of land neutral territory."

"Commandeer?" He smiled.

"Yes. Having safe houses for Ixian spies in Sitia is not very friendly. Spying on each other is not conducive to the type of open dialogue I want between the two nations."

"You'll need to rebuild the stable. Hire a lad," Valek teased.

"Don't worry. I already have a houseboy in mind. A loyal and handsome fellow, who will be at my beck and call."

Valek raised an eyebrow as desire danced in his eyes. "Indeed. I'm sure the boy is most anxious to attend to his duties."

He slid a hand under my shirt and along my skin. Warmth spread across my stomach and chest. I tried to move away, but his other arm snaked behind my back. "You need to finish one job before you begin another," I said.

"The night has just begun." He pulled my shirt off. "Plenty of time to take care of my lady before I run her errand."

His lips found mine, then he nuzzled my neck. "I must." He paused to place a line of kisses down my chest. "Help my lady." He picked me up and laid me down. "To bed."

Then he removed the rest of my garments and all concerns about the glass prisons disappeared as Valek's caress took control of my senses. My entire being focused on the musky smell and smooth feel of him. My lungs filled with Valek's breath. My heart pumped Valek's blood. I thought his thoughts and shared his pleasure.

The feelings of contentment, peace and joy flowed through our bodies. Locked tight together, we owned a piece of the sky.

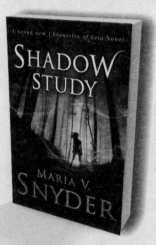

CHOOSE:
A QUICK DEATH...
OR A SLOW POISON...

About to be executed for murder, Yelena is offered the chance to become a food taster. She'll eat the best meals, have rooms in the palace—and risk assassination by anyone trying to kill the Commander of Ixia.

But disasters keep mounting as rebels plot to seize Ixia and Yelena develops magical powers she can't control. Her life is threatened again and choices must be made. But this time the outcomes aren't so clear...

CONFRONTING THE PAST, CONTROLLING THE FUTURE

With an execution order on her head, Yelena must escape to Sitia, the land of her birth. She has only a year to master her magic—or face death.

But nothing in Sitia is familiar. As she struggles to understand where she belongs and how to control her rare powers, a rogue magician emerges—and Yelena catches his eye.

Suddenly she is embroiled in a battle between good and evil. And once again it will be her magical abilities that will either save her life…or be her downfall.

UNTRAINED. UNTESTED.
UNLEASHED

With her unique magical abilities, Opal Cowan has always felt unsure of her place at Sitia's magic academy—but now it's time to test her powers in the real world.

Under threat from a deadly massacre, the powerful Stormdancer clan need Opal's unusual skills to protect their people. And their plea is impossible to resist, especially when it comes from mysterious, mercurial Kade.

THEY DESTROYED HER WORLD. BUT SHE'S THEIR ONLY HOPE...

Avry's power to heal the sick should earn her respect in the plague-torn land of Kazan. Instead she is feared and blamed for spreading the plague.

When Avry uses her forbidden magic, she faces the guillotine. Until a dark, mysterious man rescues her from her prison cell. His people need Avry's magic to save their dying prince.

Saving the prince is certain to kill Avry. Now she must choose—use her healing touch to show the ultimate mercy or die a martyr to a lost cause?

HUNTED, KILLED—
TRIUMPHANT?

As the last Healer of the Fifteen Realms,
Avry of Kazan is in a unique position: in the
minds of friends and foes alike, she no longer exists.

With her one-of-a-kind powers, Avry must now
face an oncoming war alone and infiltrate deadly
King Tohon's army to stop his most horrible
creations yet: a league of walking dead soldiers—
human and animal alike, and beyond any
known power to defeat.

Unless Avry figures out how to do
the impossible...**again**.

SHADOW STUDY

MARIA V.
SNYDER

Published in Great Britain 2015
by MIRA Ink, an imprint of Harlequin (UK) Limited,
Eton House, 18-24 Paradise Road,
Richmond, Surrey, TW9 1SR

© 2015 Maria V. Snyder

ISBN: 978-1-848-45363-0
eBook ISBN: 978-1-474-01318-5

47-0315

Harlequin (UK) Limited's policy is to use papers that are natural, renewable and recyclable products and made from wood grown in sustainable forests. The logging and manufacturing processes conform to the legal environmental regulations of the country of origin.

Printed and bound by
CPI Group (UK) Ltd, Croydon, CR0 4YY

THE TERRITORY OF IXIA

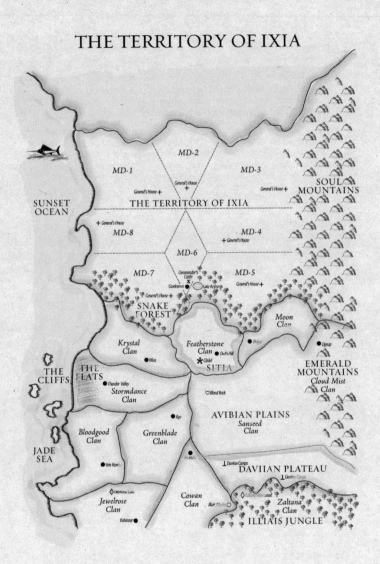

SHADOW STUDY

This book is dedicated to all my loyal readers
who asked for more books about Yelena and Valek.
This one is for you. Enjoy!

1

YELENA

Ugh, mud, Kiki said as she splashed through another puddle. The wet muck clung to her copper coat and dripped
from her long tail. It packed into her hooves and coated the
hair of her fetlocks with each step.

Through our mental connection I sensed her tired discomfort. *Stop?* I asked. *Rest?*

No. Images of fresh hay, a clean stall and being groomed
formed in Kiki's mind. *Home, soon.*

Surprised, I glanced around the forest. Melting piles of snow
mixed with black clumps of dead leaves—signs that the cold
season was losing its grip. Rain tapped steadily on the bare
branches. The light faded, turning the already gray woods
leaden. For the past few hours, I'd been huddling under my
sopping-wet cloak, trying to keep warm. With my thoughts
fixed on my rendezvous with Valek, I'd failed to keep track
of our location.

I scanned the area with my magic, projecting my awareness out to seek life. A few brave rabbits foraged in the soggy
underbrush and a couple of deer stood frozen, listening to the
squishy plodding of Kiki's passage. No souls haunted these
woods. No humans within miles.

That wasn't a surprise. This remote area in the northeastern Featherstone lands had been chosen for that very reason. After Owen Moon ambushed us about four years ago, Valek and I had decided to move to a less well-known location near the Ixian border.

I leaned forward in the saddle. We were getting close and my wet cloak no longer pressed so hard on my shoulders. At this pace, we'd reach our cozy cottage within the hour. Valek's involvement with our friend Opal's rescue from the Bloodrose Clan and the aftermath had kept him busy for months. Finally we would have a few precious days all to ourselves before he reported back to the Commander. He should already be there waiting for me. Visions of sharing a hot bath, snuggling by a roaring fire and relaxing on the couch once again distracted me.

Kiki snorted in amusement and broke into a gallop. Behind the clouds the sun set, robbing the forest of all color. I trusted Kiki to find the path in the semidarkness as I kept a light magical connection to the wildlife nearby.

In midstride, Kiki jigged to the right. Movement flashed to the left along with the unmistakable twang of a bow. Kiki twisted under me. I grabbed for her mane, but a force slammed into my chest and knocked me from the saddle.

Hitting the ground hard, I felt all the air in my lungs whoosh out as pain erupted. Fire burned with each of my desperate gasps. Without thought, I projected again, searching for the… person who had attacked me. Despite the agony, I pushed as far as I could. No one.

Kiki, smells? I asked. She stood over me, protecting me.

Pine. Wet. Mud.

See magician?

No.

Not good. The person had to be protected by a magical

null shield. It was the only way to hide from me. Null shields blocked magic. At least it also prevented the magician from attacking me with his or her magic since it blocked magic from both sides of the shield. But it wouldn't stop another arrow. And perhaps the next one wouldn't miss.

I glanced at the shaft. The arrow had struck two inches above and one inch to the left of my heart, lodging just below my clavicle. Fear banished the pain for a moment. I needed to move. Now.

Rolling on my side, I paused as an icy sensation spread across my chest. The tip had been poisoned! I plopped back in the mud. Closing my eyes, I concentrated on expelling the cold liquid. It flowed from the wound, mixing with the blood already soaked into my shirt.

Instead of disappearing, the poison remained as if being refilled as fast as I ejected it. With pain clouding my thoughts, the reason eluded me.

Kiki, however, figured it out. She clamped her teeth on the arrow's shaft. I had a second to realize what she planned before she yanked the arrow from my chest.

I cried as intense pain exploded, blood gushed and metal scraped bone all at once. Stunned, I lay on the ground as black and white spots swirled in my vision. On the verge of losing consciousness, I focused on the hollow barbed tip of the arrow coated with my blood, reminding me of the danger. I remained a target. And I wasn't about to make it easy for my attacker to get another shot.

Fix hole, Kiki said.

I debated. If I healed myself now, then I'd be too weak to defend myself. Not like I was in fighting condition. Although I still had access to my magic, it was useless against arrows and, as long as the assassin hid behind the null shield, I couldn't touch him or her with my magic, either.

Kiki raised her head. Her ears cocked. *We go. Find Ghost.*

I groaned. How could I forget that Valek was nearby? *Smart girl.*

With the arrow still clutched in her teeth, Kiki knelt next to me. Grabbing her mane, I pulled myself into the saddle. Pain shot up my arms and vibrated through my rib cage when she stood. She turned her head and I took the arrow. It might give us a clue about the assassin's identity.

I crouched low over Kiki's back as she raced home. Keeping alert for another twang, I aimed my awareness on the surrounding wildlife. If the animals sensed an intruder, I'd pick up on their fear. A sound theory, except I'd been in contact with the deer when the arrow struck. I'd be impressed by the assassin's skills if I wasn't in so much pain.

It didn't take long for us to reach our small stable. The main doors had been left open. A warm yellow glow beckoned. Kiki trotted inside. The lanterns had been lit and Onyx, Valek's horse, nickered a greeting from his stall. Kiki stopped next to a pile of straw bales. Relieved to be safe, I slid onto them then lay down.

Kiki nudged my arm. *Lavender Lady fix hole.*

After Ghost comes. I suspected I would drop into an exhausted sleep once I healed the injury and I knew Valek would have questions.

She swished her muddy tail and stepped away. *Ghost.*

Valek appeared next to me. His confusion turned to alarm as his gaze swept my blood-soaked shirt. "What happened?"

No energy for a detailed explanation, I filled him in on the basics and handed him the arrow.

All animation dropped from Valek's angular face. Fury blazed in his sapphire-blue eyes as he examined the weapon. For a moment, I remembered our first meeting when he offered me the job of the food taster. Poisons had brought us together at that time, as well. But I'd never expected it to last. Then I'd wanted nothing more than to escape from him as quickly as possible.

Clear liquid dripped from the hollow shaft. He sniffed it. "Did you expel all the poison?"

"I think so." Hard to tell for sure, but I wouldn't add more fuel to his anger. Valek's hard expression already promised murder.

He smoothed the hair from my cheek. "How bad is it?"

"Not as bad as it looks. Now go, before the assassin gets away." I shooed.

"I'm not leaving you unprotected."

Kiki huffed and flicked her tail, splattering mud on Valek's black pants. I yanked my switchblade from its holder, triggering the blade. "I'm far from unprotected. Douse the light before you go."

"All right. I'll station Onyx outside the stable. Stay here." Valek opened Onyx's stall and the black horse trotted out. After he extinguished the lantern, Valek disappeared into the blackness.

I lay there listening for any sounds. My shoulder and left arm throbbed. Each inhalation caused a sharp stab of pain in my chest. To ease the discomfort, I pulled a thin thread of magic from the blanket of power that encompassed the world. A mental picture of the injury formed when I focused on the wound. My clavicle had been broken. The arrow had sliced through my muscles on impact, and the metal barbs in the arrow's head had ripped chunks of skin when Kiki had yanked it out. Lovely. I used the ribbon of power to lessen the pain—a temporary measure.

Once more sending my awareness into the surrounding forest, I kept a light contact with the nocturnal creatures. Too bad my bat friend was hibernating over the cold season. His unique senses would have helped with finding the assassin in the dark. The wildlife conducted their nightly hunt of food and showed no signs of agitation—not even from Valek. His immunity to magic prevented me from keeping track of him. I hoped he stayed sharp.

As time passed without incident, I wondered who had attacked me. That line of thought didn't go far as all I could deduce at this point was the person was a magician who had the power to form a null shield, who favored a bow and arrow, and who might have an affinity with animals. Either that or he/she was really quiet and had masked his/her smell.

Unfortunately, pondering why I was attacked generated a longer list. As the official Liaison between the Commander of the Territory of Ixia and the Sitian Council, I'd created at least a dozen political and criminal enemies in the past six years. As the heart mate of Valek, the infamous Ixian assassin, for the past eight years I'd been a target for anyone who hated Valek, which included most of Sitia and probably hundreds of Ixians. As a magician and Soulfinder, I made many people nervous, worrying that I'd turn rogue. These people were under the mistaken impression that I could create a soulless army when in fact all I did was find lost souls and guide them to either an eternity of peace in the sky or an eternity of suffering in the fire world, depending on their deeds while alive.

A slight squish jolted me from my thoughts. Careful of my injury, I sat up and swung my legs over the bales of straw. Then I slid off. Better to stand and fight than be caught lying down. The darkness outside was one hue lighter than inside due to the faint moonlight. It illuminated just enough to see shapes.

I kept alert for any movement, peering through the door. When Kiki stepped between me and the entrance, I startled. Even though she was sixteen hands high she could be really quiet. Her back was taller than me and she blocked my view.

Granted, I reached only five feet four inches, but she was a big girl like most Sandseed horses.

A few more squishes set my heart to beat in double time. I tightened my grip on my switchblade.

Ghost, Kiki said, moving away.

I sagged against the bales. A Valek-shaped shadow strode into the stable. He lit the lantern. One look at his grim expression and I knew he'd lost the assassin's trail.

"The guy's a pro," he said. "He used magic to erase his footprints. They just stopped. And without leaves on the bushes, it's harder to track him, especially at night. I'll go out again in the daylight."

"He? How do you know?"

"Big boots, deep prints. We can discuss it later. Let's go inside and take care of you."

"Kiki first." And before he could argue, "She saved my life. If she hadn't moved, the arrow would have pierced my heart."

Valek's shoulders dropped. Knowing I wouldn't leave, he worked fast. He removed her saddle and knocked the dried mud off her legs and stomach. After he cleaned out her hooves, she walked into her stall and munched on hay.

"Guess she's happy enough," Valek said, tossing the pick into a bucket. "Now, let's get you warm and dry, love."

I removed my muddy cloak and left it on the bales before I wrapped my right arm around Valek's shoulders. He wanted to carry me, but I worried he might jar the broken bone out of alignment and I wouldn't have enough strength to heal it.

The sharp pain returned by the time we reached the house. I made it as far as the couch. A bright fire burned in the hearth and a bottle of wine sat on the end table with two glasses and a plate of cheese. Valek must have arrived a few hours before me.

Tilting my head at the food, I said, "That's lovely."

"We'll indulge after you're healed and rested. Do you want to change first?"

Just the thought of moving my left arm hurt. "No."

"Then what are you waiting for?"

"A kiss. I haven't seen you in months."

Valek transformed when he smiled. The sharp angles of his face softened and warmth radiated from him. He leaned forward and pressed his lips to mine. Before I could deepen the kiss he pulled back.

"No more until you're better."

"Meanie."

"Yelena." His stern tone would have made my mother proud.

"All right." I reclined on the couch and closed my eyes.

Reaching for the power blanket, I gathered a thick thread of magic. I wound this ribbon around my broken clavicle, fusing the two pieces back together. A second thread knitted the muscles and a third replaced skin. The effort exhausted me. Drained dry, I passed out.

By the time I woke, afternoon sunlight flooded the living area. Besides the green plaid couch, a couple of oversize nubby brown armchairs and a matching love seat made a semicircle in front of the hearth. In the center, a dark brown deep-pile rug covered the floor—soft on the feet and…other body parts.

All that remained of the fire was ashy coals and half-burned logs. The wine and glasses waited—a promise for later. No sounds emanated from the rest of the cottage, but moving without a sound was second nature for Valek. I called his name just in case. No response.

I opened my mind to Kiki. *Is everything okay?* I asked.

Quiet. Nap time, she said.

If the horses could sleep, then all should be well. *Ghost?*

Out. Woods.

My left shoulder and upper chest ached. The muscles would be sore for a few days. I sat up and examined the wound. Purple bruises surrounded an angry red circle. Another scar to add to my collection. I'd stopped counting three…or was it four injuries ago? Stretching with care, I tested my range of motion. Not bad.

The cold had soaked into my bones. My blanket had fallen to the floor. A hot soak in the tub should cure it in no time.

Stiff with blood and poison, my shirt reeked. All the more reason to bathe. But first a quick check of the rest of the cottage. It wouldn't take long. I palmed my switchblade, but didn't trigger the blade.

The ground floor consisted of a living area, kitchen and washroom. The living area spanned the left half of the cottage while the kitchen and washroom occupied the right half. The hearth sat in the middle of the building so all the rooms could share its warmth.

I peered into the kitchen. A layer of dust covered the table and chairs, but the wash sink, cold storage box and water jugs had been cleaned. Nothing appeared out of place.

The washroom's entrance was to the right of the hearth. I smiled. Valek had filled the large water tank near the back wall. Hot coals glowed underneath—one of the benefits of having a stone floor. I tested the water with my finger. Almost perfect.

I climbed the stairs to the single bedroom in the loft. Our cottage was too small for company, another excellent reason to own it.

My red–silk robe and clean clothes had been spread out on the king-size bed. Valek had been busy. I resisted the urge to check under the bed as I undressed. I'd have to ask my cousin Nutty to repair yet another shirt. Despite a few mud stains, I could still wear my black wool pants. I donned the robe—a gift from Valek. Running my fingers over the smooth material, I verified all my surprises remained in place. Valek always included weaponry with my gifts.

Which reminded me. I removed the lock picks, releasing my long black hair.

After a quick peek outside to check for signs of intruders, I returned to the washroom. Steam floated from the water's surface. I opened the valve and the warm liquid rushed into the sunken tub. Turning off the water, I banked the coals, hung my robe on the hook and settled in, oohing and aahing until only my head remained above water.

Wonderful for about five minutes. Then the door squeaked and I lunged for my switchblade.

"Sorry," Valek said. He leaned against the door's frame as if it kept him from falling.

Had he been up all night? "Did you find anything?"

"He's gone. I found nothing except those boot prints. No doubt he's a professional assassin with magical abilities." He rubbed the stubble on his chin. "That will be the key to finding him. Not many people have that combination of skills. He's probably already a person of interest. I'll have to check my sources."

I resisted correcting him. What he called sources were really Ixian spies in Sitia, which as Liaison, I'd been trying to stop. Ixia and Sitia shouldn't be spying on each other. Instead, they needed to form a relationship based on mutual trust and respect.

"Unless he's a new assassin. Some young hotshot."

Valek straightened. "That's a possibility. And if that's the case, then he chose the wrong target if he wishes to grow old."

"After you find out who hired him."

"Of course. Any ideas who…?" He shook his head. "We

MARIA V. SNYDER

should make a list of who *doesn't* want to kill you, love. It'd be shorter."

I'd be offended, but it was actually a good idea. "Let's not let it ruin our vacation. Join me."

He hesitated, frowning.

Oh no. Bad news. "Tell me."

"I have to leave in the morning."

"Not because of the attack?"

"No. The Commander ordered me to return earlier than I'd planned. He's been very patient. I've been in Sitia for most of the past year and he says I'm needed for an urgent matter. I'm sorry we have to cut our vacation a few days short."

Even though disappointment pulsed, I understood his loyalty to the Commander. And the Commander had been more than generous with Valek's time. Working with Opal and helping to stop the Bloodrose Clan, Valek had done more for Sitia than Ixia.

No sense moping about something I couldn't change. Suppressing my frustration with the time limit, I splashed Valek. "Come on in while the water's hot."

He grinned and peeled off his clothes. Scars crisscrossed his long lean muscles, and a faded C-shaped scar marked the center of his chest. Even after spending seasons in Sitia, his skin remained pale, which contrasted with his shoulder-length black hair.

"Like what you see, love?" Valek stepped into the water.

"You lost weight."

He huffed. "Janco's a lousy cook."

"Did Janco pout when you ditched him to come here?"

"Yes, but it was fake. He's more than ready to return to Ixia." Valek settled next to me. "Do you really want to talk about him right now?" His gaze burned hotter than the water.

"Who?"

"Exactly." He ran his thumb over my wound. "Does it hurt?"

"No." His touch drove the cold away as a fire ignited in my heart.

He closed the distance between us and our lips met. Another perk of stone floors: no worries about water damage.

Morning sunlight and chills woke me late the next morning. Memories of last night replayed and I remained in bed savoring them. We'd gone from the tub to the living area, drunk the wine, tested the softness of the rug, and then up to the bedroom. My lips still tingled from Valek's predawn goodbye kiss.

Another chill raced along my skin. Shivering, I pulled the blanket up to my chin. All my bones ached as if encased in ice. Unease swirled. Something was…off. Wrong.

Without warning, a wave of heat slammed into me. I yanked the blankets off and jumped to my feet. Sweat poured, soaking my nightshirt as dizziness threatened to topple me. I sank to the ground. The heat disappeared as fast as it had arrived, but the cold returned, seeping into my skin, freezing the sweat into a layer of ice.

Before I could pull the blanket over me, another hot flash consumed me. Memories of going through the fire to enter the fire world rose unbidden. The searing pain of my flesh burning all too familiar. I batted at my arms even though I knew my skin hadn't been set on fire.

Fear wormed through my chest. Maybe I hadn't expelled all the poison.

Between gasps of breath, the ice extinguished the heat. My muscles tightened and cramped. My teeth chattered hard enough to cause a headache. I curled into a ball, afraid I'd shatter like an icicle hitting the ground.

When the fire blazed again, I straightened as steam rose from my skin. Then the cold reclaimed me. And it kept going back and forth, hot to cold and hot again. Like I had a super-fast fever, which gave me no time to draw power to counter it.

I endured the waves. Each flip drained my strength. One of two things was bound to happen. I'd either pass out or the attack would stop. There was a third possibility, but I preferred to stay positive.

After hours…days…weeks…the seizures ceased. At first I braced for the next cycle. But as time progressed without an attack, I slowly relaxed. With no energy to stand, I groped for the edge of the blanket and pulled it down, covering me. At this point, even the hard floor couldn't stop me from falling asleep.

Darkness greeted me when I woke. Every single muscle ached as if I'd run here from the Citadel. My dry throat burned and my stomach hurt. I needed water, food and a bath. But first, I needed to ensure that I didn't have another attack. Had the poison run its course? Or was it still inside me? One way to find out.

I drew a deep breath and reached for the blanket of power. Nothing happened. Trying again, I concentrated on pulling a thread of magic.

Nothing.

Fear pushed up my throat. I swallowed it down, determined not to panic.

I opened my mind to Kiki. *What's going on?*

No response. Not even images.

Dead air surrounded me.

My magic was gone.

2

VALEK

He hated leaving her. Memories of last night's activities swirled in his mind, but he suppressed them. No sense torturing himself. Instead, he focused on the attack on Yelena as he saddled Onyx.

Valek had done another sweep of the area as soon as the sun had risen. No one in sight and no signs of anyone. Not much of a comfort, considering the bastard had been able to conceal himself so well. His identity remained a mystery for now. But Valek would find him. No doubt.

Mounting Onyx, Valek grabbed the reins. Kiki said goodbye with a sad little whinny.

"Please keep her safe," he said to Kiki.

She nodded. Her blue eyes shone with intelligence.

"Thanks." Valek clicked his tongue, spurring Onyx into a gallop. Kiki was the only reason he didn't insist on personally escorting Yelena to the Citadel. Yesterday, he'd taken Kiki to the spot where the assassin had waited. She'd sniffed the area and had the man's scent. Combined with Yelena's magic and her skills with her switchblade and bo staff, they made an impressive fighting team. Plus Yelena had assured him she'd recovered from the injury.

Of course, there was the possibility that since the assassin knew how to construct a null shield, he might also know Valek's biggest weakness, which would render him unable to protect Yelena. Valek could never forget that disadvantage. It was like a knife slowly piercing his heart in tiny increments. Each day it dug a little deeper.

Once his greatest weapon against magic, his immunity was now a drawback. If a magician surrounded Valek with a null shield, Valek would be trapped inside just like being caught in a bubble made of invisible steel. Weapons could cross the barrier, but he couldn't. Well, neither he nor Opal, who was also immune to magic. Her adventures last year had uncovered this particularly nasty weakness and, while the magical community promised to keep it quiet, Valek had learned the best way to distribute information was to classify it as secret.

Valek guided Onyx north toward the Ixian border. At this pace, they'd reach the checkpoint in three hours. Their cottage had been in an ideal location. Too bad they would have to move again. He contemplated retirement—not for the first nor the last time. And for a moment, he dreamed of a time when he and Yelena could disappear and never have to worry about assassins, intrigue and espionage again.

Except she couldn't retire from guiding lost souls. Perhaps she could wear a disguise. He imagined them dressed as an old married couple traveling from town to town. For half the year, they'd visit the local sights, try new foods and find souls. The other half would be spent together in a cottage, gardening, carving and going out for daily rides. It was a pleasant daydream.

A mile from the border, Valek stopped Onyx. He changed into his Ixian uniform—black pants, boots and shirt. Two red diamonds had been stitched onto his collar, marking him as an adviser to the Commander. He turned his cloak inside out, revealing the black material with two red diamonds instead of the gray camouflage. In Ixia, he had to wear his uniform with the Commander's colors of black and red. While in Sitia, he had to blend in.

Back on Onyx, he headed to the main checkpoint, hoping the soldiers would recognize him. It'd save time. Valek considered sneaking into Ixia, but the Commander's message said the situation was urgent.

The official border crossing between Sitia and Ixia was a cleared, one-hundred-foot ribbon of ground that stretched from the Sunset Ocean in the west to the Soul Mountains in the east. The border followed the contours of the Snake Forest, which also spanned the area between the ocean and mountains. At one point, Valek had asked the Commander to clear the entire forest. Even with the hundred feet of open ground, smugglers and refugees still managed to slip across the border. But now he found the forest convenient for his network of spies. Not that he'd admit that to Yelena.

The six border guards snapped to attention when he approached. A good sign.

"Welcome back, sir." The captain saluted.

Nice. "Thank you. Any news, Captain?"

"It's been quiet, sir. A caravan crossed earlier this morning, but they were on our approved list. A Sitian delegation is due to come through here in a couple days, but we haven't gotten the manifest for the visitors yet."

Interesting how the man mentioned the delegation as if routine. It was only eight years ago that the border had been sealed tight. No one in or out.

"Do you know why the Sitians are visiting?" Valek asked, wondering if the delegation was the reason the Commander had ordered him back a few days early.

"No, sir."

MARIA V. SNYDER

Ah. He'd have to wait. "Anything else?"

The captain smiled. "*Adviser* Janco informed us that a Sitian spy would attempt to cross this checkpoint today. He claimed this spy would be disguised as you and ordered us to attack first and ask questions later."

Valek suppressed his ire—he needed to have a little chat with Janco. "And why didn't you follow Adviser Janco's orders?"

"I was in basic training with the...er...Adviser, sir."

"My condolences, Captain."

The captain's soldiers all grinned at his deep laugh. "His pranks were endless, but he taught me more than our instructor."

Interesting and not that surprising. "You showed excellent judgment today. While being attacked by six skilled opponents would have been good practice for me, I preferred the friendly welcome."

They parted, letting Onyx through.

"Sir?" the captain called.

Valek turned.

"Papers, please."

Ah. Now the soldiers surrounded the horse. Smart move. Valek pulled a folded sheet from one of his cloak's inner pockets and handed it to the captain. "The Commander's orders."

Valek waited as the man scanned the fake document.

The pleasant expression dropped from the captain's face. His right hand slid to grasp his sword's hilt. Following his cue, his men tensed and grabbed the hilts of their weapons.

"This is a forgery," the captain said.

Valek noted he didn't say *sir*. "Just testing you, Captain."

"Dismount now."

Valek tsked. "What happened to your manners, Captain?"

The captain drew his sword in answer.

Good. The man followed proper protocol. If Valek didn't dismount soon, they'd rush him, yank him from the saddle and unarm him. How far should he push it? Not far. The Commander was waiting for him, after all.

Pulling the real orders from his sleeve, Valek held up his hands. The captain gestured to one of the guards who approached slowly, then snatched the parchment from Valek with one quick motion. The guard delivered it to the captain. So far, so good.

Peering at the letter, the captain relaxed. "This one is real. It was a test."

"And you passed. What is your name, Captain?"

"Broghan, sir."

"I'll make sure to mention this to your commanding officer, Captain Broghan."

"Thank you, sir."

Pleased with the border guard's actions, Valek urged Onyx north. They would reach the Commander's castle by late afternoon. Dirty, hard-packed snow covered the well-used trail. The surrounding forest showed no signs of green—all bare branches and bleak even with the sunlight streaming to the ground. Buds already coated the Sitian trees, and the southern half of the Avibian Plains would be lush with plant life and warm breezes by now.

Not that he missed the south—not at all. Just one specific southerner. Valek scanned the surrounding area seeking signs of an ambush. Memories swirled of the times he'd used the cover of the forest to hide his actions. Valek glanced up. Yelena had also exploited the Snake Forest's tree canopy to escape the Commander's men during a training exercise. It had been the day he learned she was far smarter than he'd thought. And more dangerous, too.

If only the Commander allowed magicians to live in Ixia,

MARIA V. SNYDER

then she'd be working with him instead of being the Liaison. Valek had argued about the benefits of having a magician on staff with the Commander for years, but he remained stubborn. Perhaps Ambrose had changed his mind about magic after Kade's demonstration. Valek had heard the Stormdancer had traveled north during this past cold season to harvest the energy from one of the blizzards that blew down from the northern ice pack. Kade's magic had transformed the killer storm into a regular old snowstorm. The Commander let Kade stay for the rest of the season, but Valek hadn't heard if Kade and his group of Stormdancers would be invited back next year. One thing was for sure: Valek and Commander Ambrose had a lot to catch up on.

When he arrived at the castle complex, Valek stopped at the southern gate. An immense stone wall completely surrounded the castle, barracks, stable and other support buildings.

Once again, he presented his fake orders and was pleased that these guards also followed the proper protocol.

After they allowed him entrance, Onyx automatically headed to the stables near the west gate and next to the dog kennels. Halfway there, they were stopped by a messenger.

"Adviser Valek, the Commander would like to see you in his war room right now. I'll take your horse to the stable and see that your bags are delivered to your rooms, sir."

He'd hoped to wash the travel grime off, but one didn't tell the Commander to wait. Dismounting, he handed the reins to the boy and followed the path to the western entrance.

The only thing impressive about the castle was its sheer size. With four tall towers anchoring the corners of the rectangular base, the palace spanned a half a mile in width. Other than that, the odd layers of squares, triangles, cylinders and whatnot perched atop the base looked ridiculous. Even after all these years, Valek still didn't know why the King had agreed to build a structure that resembled an uncreative child's tower of blocks.

Perhaps the first King of Ixia had thought the asymmetrical design would hinder assassins. It would only confuse the stupid ones. Valek had infiltrated the castle without trouble by posing as a hairdresser for Queen Jewel.

Picking up his pace, Valek cut through the servant corridors to save time. He arrived at the Commander's war room just as the kitchen servers left. They held empty trays. Ah, supper. His stomach growled in anticipation.

Located in the northwest tower, the circular war room was ringed by slender floor-to-ceiling stained-glass windows that spanned three-quarters of the wall. When the afternoon sunlight shone, a rainbow of colors streaked the large wooden table that occupied the center.

Lanterns had been lit, sending sparks of colors in different directions from the windows. Ari and Janco shoveled food onto their plates and the Commander sat at the head of the table, waiting as his food taster slurped and sipped his supper. A small stack of files had been piled next to the Commander's plate.

The food taster, a skittish young man, shot Valek a nasty glare as he slipped past. Valek actually missed the old taster, Star, but she'd been too difficult to work with and keeping track of all her schemes had grown tiresome. So he'd slipped a dose of My Love into the Commander's drink to test her poison tasting skills. Star'd failed the test and paid for that error with her life.

The Commander crinkled his nose at his messy plate, but didn't comment as he speared a piece of beef.

"Well, look who decided to show up—the Ghost Warrior," Janco said. "Have any trouble at the border?" He smirked.

Valek stared at Janco with the promise of retribution.

MARIA V. SNYDER

Unaffected, Janco elbowed his partner, Ari. "See? I told you he'd get through."

While Janco was all lean wiry muscles, barrel-chested and broad-shouldered Ari was solid muscle. About a foot taller and wider than Janco, Ari also had more common sense.

"He told me about it later, Valek," Ari said. "Nothing I could do at that point." His long-suffering tone said more than his words.

"Your prank failed to work." Valek ladled stew into a deep bowl.

"Oh?" Janco didn't sound convinced.

"Captain Broghan recognized you from your basic-training days."

Janco stabbed his fork into the air. "I knew he looked familiar, didn't I, Ari?"

"You said he resembled your second cousin."

"Close enough. So Broghan made captain." Janco tapped the fork against his teeth.

"Is he worth looking into for my corps?" Valek sat on the opposite side of the table from the power twins—Ari and Janco's nickname.

"He's smart and a fast learner, but he has no finesse."

"Not everyone can be a drama queen like you, Janco," Ari said.

"I'm insulted." Janco pouted, proving Ari's point.

"Go on," Valek ordered. "No finesse?"

"Yeah, no spark…imagination. He'll follow orders and protocol, but if a situation goes well beyond the protocols, he'll be stymied."

"Stymied? Who uses that word?" Ari teased.

"Those who know what it means. Please excuse Ari. His vocabulary is limited to fifty words—most of them curse words."

Ari drew breath to counter, but the Commander leaned forward and stopped the banter with a hard gaze from his gold, almond-shaped eyes. Time for business.

The Commander's uniform matched Valek's except he had two real diamonds stitched onto his collar and his was wrinkle-free. His steel-gray hair had been cut close to his scalp.

"I have two matters I wish to discuss," the Commander said. "The first is regarding smugglers. The reports of illegal goods being stopped at the border have slowed to a trickle. However, black-market goods are still in ample supply."

Valek considered. "That means they've found a new way into and out of Ixia."

"Correct." The Commander pushed his plate away.

"Are we still allowing some smugglers to slip by?" Valek asked. Following the caravans of illegal goods to the source was a sound strategy.

"No. The few who are attempting to cross illegally are so inept, they're being caught right away."

"Decoys," Ari said. "To make us think they're still trying to sneak through the Snake Forest."

"Which means they're organized," Janco added.

"Organized how?" the Commander asked.

Janco scratched the empty place where the lower half of his right ear used to be. "If it was just one or two smugglers using the new route, then the others would continue as they have been. But with the decoys, it means all the smugglers have gotten together and figured out a way around the bor-der guards."

"A smuggler convention?" Ari asked with a touch of humor. "Thieves don't usually play well together."

"Maybe a big bad arrived with a new way of doing things."

"A ringleader?" Ari asked.

"Exactly. Some scary dude who has taken over. He's prob-ably all 'do it my way or…'"

"It's a possibility," Valek said while Janco cast about for a proper smuggler threat.

"Regardless. I want the three of you to figure out the new route and the new players. The sooner the better," the Commander ordered.

"What about Maren?" Ari asked. "Will she be helping us?"

Maren had teamed up with Ari and Janco, and the three of them had beaten Valek in a fight, earning the right to be his seconds-in-command.

"She's on special assignment," the Commander said. "You can recruit if you need more assistance."

Unease nibbled on his stomach. Valek knew nothing about Maren's assignment and, from the Commander's closed expression, he wouldn't be learning more about it from his boss.

"Tunnels," Janco said. "They could have dug tunnels underneath the border."

"They'd have to be miles long. Otherwise, they'd pop up in the Snake Forest and someone would have seen them," Ari said. "Who has the ability to build a tunnel like that?"

"Miners," the Commander said in a quiet voice.

No surprise the Commander mentioned them. His family had owned a mine in the Soul Mountains bordering what was now Military District 3 until they'd discovered diamonds. The King of Ixia had claimed ownership of the gemstones and "allowed" the Commander's family to stay and work for him. The King's greedy move had started the rumblings of discontent and turned a brilliant young man into the King's number one enemy.

"We'll look into the possibility of a tunnel," Valek said.

"Boats on the Sunset Ocean." Janco held up his napkin. He had folded it so it resembled a sailboat.

"Not practical," Ari said. "Between the storms and the

Rattles, we haven't had any problems with people using the ocean as an escape route."

The Rattles extended from the coast of MD-7 out to at least a hundred miles into the Sunset Ocean. With submerged rocks, strong and unpredictable currents, and shallow areas that moved, the Rattles were impossible to navigate. Sailing around them took too long plus sailors ran the risk of hitting dead air and being stranded for months.

Valek tapped a finger on the table. "When did the decoys start?"

The Commander flipped through a few papers in the file on top of his stack. "End of the cooling season about sixty days ago."

Valek calculated. "Prime storm season. It's suicide to be on the ocean at that time of year."

"I will leave the detecting to you. As for this other matter..." The Commander pulled a letter from underneath the folders. He scanned it then turned his gaze to Valek. "An unfortunate development, but one that we will *not* get involved in. Do you understand?"

"Yes, sir." Valek kept his expression neutral, bracing for the bad news.

Ari and Janco exchanged a concerned glance.

"Do you remember Ben Moon?"

He couldn't forget the man who had tried to murder Yelena in revenge for the execution of his brother, Owen Moon. Only the fact Ben remained locked tight in a special wing of Wirral Prison for the past three years kept the man alive. So why was the Commander... A sick feeling circled his chest. "He escaped?"

"Yes."

3

YELENA

Don't panic. Don't panic. Don't panic. Clutching the blanket in tight fists, I repeated the words. *Don't panic. Don't panic. Don't panic.* Except it failed to work. Panic burned up my throat. I gasped for breath. The words transformed to *no magic. No magic. No magic.*

The darkness pressed against my skin, sealing me inside my body, blocking me from the warmth and light that was my magic. All my senses had been stolen along with my magic. Sounds, sights and scents gone. A bitter taste all that remained.

No magic. Cut off from the lost souls, disconnected from the wildlife and severed from my colleagues, I'd been rendered useless. No magic.

I stayed on the hard floor of our bedroom huddled under the blanket. My thoughts buzzed with misery. When the sun rose, a bit of relief eased the chaotic terror that had consumed me. My vision worked after all.

A loud bang on the door broke the early-morning quiet and Kiki's piercing whinny cut right through my conviction that all had been lost. Hooves pounded on wood and I staggered to my feet.

I'm okay, I said. No response. My heart twisted.

"I'm okay," I shouted over another barrage.

Kiki stopped. But for how long? I grasped the handrail and eased down the steps. Sharp hunger pains stabbed my guts, but I aimed for the door. Kiki's mostly white face peered through the window. A patch of brown circled her left eye.

As soon as I opened the door, she barged in, almost knocking me over. Not hard to do since I hadn't eaten in over a day.

I wrapped my arms around her neck. "I'm fine." Leaning my forehead against her soft hide, I opened my mind to her. Nothing. I breathed in her scent—a mix of dry straw, cut grass and earth.

"I can't... I don't have..." Why was it so hard to say? "My magic...is gone. I can't talk to you."

Kiki snorted.

"Yes, I know I'm talking to you, but we can't *communicate*."

She pulled away and gazed at me. And while her thoughts didn't sound in my mind, I understood her sarcastic, what-do-you-call-this look. Then she nudged me with her nose as if prompting me to explain.

Her actions snapped me from my scatterbrained panic. Logic wrestled raw emotion aside and I considered. What happened before my magic disappeared? A lovely evening with Valek, but we'd had a number of them throughout the years without consequences.

And before that? I touched the still-tender area on my upper chest. "The poison! How could I be so stupid?"

Kiki nodded in agreement.

"Thanks," I said drily. "Now I just have to figure out what poison blocks a person's magic." Curare fit, except I'd have been paralyzed and I would have recognized its crisp citrus scent. "The arrow." Perhaps a few drops of the poison remained.

Kiki followed me to the stable. Poor girl hadn't been fed grain in over a day. I filled her feed bucket before searching for the arrow's shaft. It didn't take long to figure out Valek must have taken it with him.

Valek. Should I join him in Ixia? It'd be safer. And without the taint of magic, the Commander would welcome me with open arms. Ambrose's aversion to magicians started back in his childhood. Even though he had a female body, he insisted he was male. He dressed as a boy and changed his name. Terrified that a magician would "see through" him, he banned them from Ixia and executed any found within the Territory when he gained power. Plus it didn't help that the corrupt King was also a magician who had abused his power.

When I accepted my Soulfinding abilities, I discovered the true nature of the Commander's dual personality. His mother died in childbirth, but she'd refused to leave her newborn son. She had just enough magic that her soul remained with Ambrose, turning him female. I'd offered to guide her to the sky, but the Commander felt her presence aided, not hindered, him. For now.

The Commander's stance on magicians in Ixia had loosened a bit since he learned of his own magical beginnings, but he still had a long way to go.

Besides, traveling to Ixia wouldn't help me discover what happened. My condition could be temporary and if so I was freaking out for nothing.

Searching my memories, I reviewed the list of poisons Valek had taught me when I'd been the Commander's food taster over eight years ago. None of them had side effects that matched my symptoms. Then again, Valek wouldn't have been worried about a substance that blocks magic. But would he know if one existed? Possible.

How about the Master Magicians? I groaned. First Magician Bain Bloodgood! His knowledge of history and magic was unparalleled, and if he didn't know about this poison, he'd hunt through his stacks and stacks of books until he found it.

Feeling much better, I returned to the cottage to eat and pack. I checked the hearth and coals in the washroom, ensuring all had been properly extinguished. When I closed and locked the door, a pang of regret vibrated in my chest. Because of the attack, Valek would insist on moving. I rubbed my fingers on the stones. Fond memories swirled. The distance to the stable seemed to stretch, growing longer with each step.

Once I reached the stable, I saddled Kiki. We didn't use reins or a bridle and normally, I'd forgo the saddle, but the saddlebags were stuffed with enough food and supplies to last a week. I paused. Had Valek and I ever had a full week to ourselves? No.

Kiki grunted, jarring me from my thoughts.

"What's wrong?"

She jerked the girth's latigo strap from my hand. I'd pulled it too tight. It took me a moment to understand. It was easy to saddle a horse that instructed you on how tight to make the saddle. I wondered how many other things I would need to relearn—a dreary prospect.

I fixed the girth and mounted. "Back to the Citadel as fast as possible, please." That remained the same. I'd always let her find the best way and set the pace.

She galloped through the mud. The bright sunshine of mid-morning failed to lift my spirits. I scanned the forest, seeking predators. A bird screeched and I ducked. I drew my switchblade when I caught movement out of the corner of my eye. And I flattened, hugging Kiki's neck when a thud sounded behind us.

After a few hours, Kiki stopped for a rest. I stayed by her side, keeping my back against her and my switchblade in hand. Invisible dangers lurked in the forest. A whole army of am-

MARIA V. SNYDER

bushers could be waiting for us downwind and I'd have no warning.

Panic simmered. I was weak, vulnerable and an easy target. When Kiki stopped for the night, I didn't light a fire, and the few uneasy hours I slept were spent between her hooves.

By the time we reached the northern gates of the Citadel two days later, I started at every noise. Never had I been so glad to see the white marble walls that surrounded the Citadel reflecting the sunlight. The guards waved us in and I worried. What if the guards conspired with a group inside? What if we were mugged?

I twisted my fingers in Kiki's copper mane as we crossed through the rings of businesses and factories that occupied the center of the Citadel like red circles around a bull's-eye. A bustling market lay at the heart of this section. Skirting the crowded stalls, Kiki headed toward the Magician's Keep, located in the northeast quadrant.

People hustled through the streets, talking, laughing, arguing as they attended to their morning chores. I stared at them. No thoughts or emotions reached me from the crowds. To my senses they had no souls. A horde of walking dead.

I leaned forward and whispered to Kiki, "Faster to the Keep, please."

She increased her pace, weaving through the busy streets. The logical part of me understood that the shouts and curses following our passage did not come from soulless dead people. However, that knowledge didn't stop my trembling hands or rapid pulse.

Shocked, I realized my magic had influenced how I viewed the world. I barely remembered how I had interacted with my world without magic. I wouldn't have thought I relied on my power so much or used it to connect to the people around me in the past six years. Yet, I felt as if I'd been wrapped in a thick black cloth from head to toe. The cloth had holes for my eyes, ears, nose and mouth, but the rest of me remained swaddled.

I eased my tight grip on Kiki's mane when the Magician's Keep's grand entrance loomed. Elegant pink marble columns supported scalloped arches that framed the two-story-high marble doors. The doors were always open, but they were guarded by four soldiers, a magician and a wooden gate.

They straightened as we approached.

"Good morning, Liaison Zaltana. Back so soon?" asked the sergeant in charge.

"Yes, Mally, an urgent matter has cut my vacation short. Is Master Bloodgood in his office?"

She turned to the magician...Jon from the Krystal Clan.

Jon peered at me, questioning. "Can't you—"

"Not right now," I said between clenched teeth.

"Oh...kay." His gaze grew distant. "Yes, First Magician is in his office." Then he met my gaze. "He's with a student right now and says to come by in the early afternoon."

I had no intention of waiting and no desire to tell Jon. Instead, I thanked him. Mally moved aside, but didn't raise the gate. Kiki jumped the heavy wooden barrier in one easy stride, showing off just like she always did.

The Keep's administration building sat directly across from the entrance. A few blocks of peach marble marked the yellow structure and a set of grand marble stairs led up to the first-floor lobby.

Kiki stopped at the base of the steps.

I dismounted and patted her sweaty neck. "I'll catch up with you at the stables and give you a proper grooming."

She butted my palm with her soft nose, then trotted toward the stables located in the northwest corner of the Keep right next to Irys's tower. The Magician's Keep had four towers stationed in each corner. They rose high into the air. Each

MARIA V. SNYDER

Master Magician lived in a tower. Right now, only two were occupied. Second Magician Zitora Cowan had resigned her position to hunt for her missing sister and no other magician had the power to be a master. So far. There was always hope that one of the new students at the Keep would mature into master-level powers.

I raced up the steps and into the administration building. And just like its name implied, the structure housed the administrative staff who handled the day-to-day accounts and bills and the details involved in running a school for future magicians. The Masters all had offices inside and the infirmary was located on the ground floor.

Ignoring the staff in the hallways, I headed straight toward Bain's office. I opened the door without knocking. Not surprised to see me—no one could sneak up on a Master Magician—Bain frowned at my rude intrusion. But one look at my expression and he ushered his student from the room.

Once the girl left he turned to me. He tapped his temple with a wrinkled finger. "Why didn't you answer me?"

"I can't. It's gone. My magic is *all* gone!" Panic spun in my chest. Tears threatened.

His face creased with concern. He stepped closer and spread his hands. "May I?"

"Yes."

Bain grasped my shoulders and closed his eyes. I braced for... What? I'd no idea. However, nothing happened.

His eyes popped open in surprise. "You are correct."

Bain's confirmation hit me like an avalanche of rocks tumbling down a mountain. Unable to keep it together any longer, my body trembled as tears gushed with each sob. First Magician guided me to an armchair, pressed a handkerchief into my hands and muttered soothing words until my bout of self-pity ran its course.

Ringing for tea, he sat in the armchair next to mine and waited for his assistant to arrive. Deep in thought, he smoothed his white hair. Or rather, he tried. The curls resisted and sprang back into their positions, sticking up at odd angles.

I wiped my eyes with his handkerchief and scanned his messy office. Contraptions in various stages of completion or dissection littered the floor, shelves bowed with piles of books, rolls of parchment covered his desk and numerous shades of ink stained…just about everything, including Bain's deep blue robe. The scent of jasmine mixed with a tangy aroma filled the room. I wondered if the large arrays of candles scattered throughout were the source of the smell.

When Bain's assistant arrived, he brought tea and Second Magician Irys Jewelrose, my mentor and friend. Bain must have mentally communicated to her about my arrival. I stood, but she kept her distance as the man poured three cups of tea and set the steaming pot down amid the clutter on the table.

"Do you require anything else, sir?"

"No, thank you."

He left and Irys rushed over to embrace me. "Don't worry. We'll figure this out."

Tears welled, but I calmed as I breathed in her comforting apple-berry scent; more crying wouldn't solve anything. I squeezed her back and moved away. Her emerald-green eyes held concern and a promise.

Bain gestured for us to sit. Two more armchairs faced the ones Bain and I occupied. Irys handed out the cups before settling in. I clasped mine in both hands, letting the warmth seep into my fingers.

Bain gazed at me over the rim of his cup. "Tell us."

Starting with the attack, I told them everything that had happened. They sat in silence, absorbing the information. Then the questions started. I answered them as best as I could.

"Do you know of a poison that robs a magician of her power?" I asked them.

"No," Irys said.

After a few moments, Bain said, "I do not know of a substance that has that ability. If it exists, it would be a formidable weapon against magicians."

"What do you mean *if*? Do you think I'm making this up?" I put my cup down. It clattered on the saucer.

"No, child. I'm merely considering other possibilities besides poison. Perhaps there is another reason for your condition."

"Oh. Like a null shield?"

"Correct. Except it is not a shield."

"How do you know?"

"I can sense your surface thoughts and my magic helped soothe you. Which also means you are not immune to magic."

I sucked in a breath. Bad enough to be without magic, but to be at its mercy… This was just getting worse and worse.

"Perhaps your magic was siphoned," Irys suggested. "Opal no longer has the ability, but there's a chance another magician has learned the skill. There was a gap in time between the arrow strike and your bout of…fever—for lack of a better word."

If that was the cause, my magic was gone forever. Unless there was a vial of my blood around, which I doubted. So far, no one could duplicate Opal's glass magic, but Quinn Bloodrose's magic was also linked to glass.

"What about Quinn?" I asked.

Irys considered. "He's attending classes here. I don't think he's left the Keep. However, we can talk to him. And I can contact Pazia Cloud Mist to see if she has any ideas. Her magic was accidentally siphoned and since then she's been working with glass, making those super messengers."

A queasy unease roiled. "I don't want word to spread about me. I've too many enemies."

"I'll be discreet and won't mention you," Irys said. "I'll check the logbook at the gate. If Quinn left the Keep, there will be a record of it."

The vise around my chest eased a little.

"And I will scour all my books for information," Bain promised. "I am sure Dax will be happy to translate the languages I am unfamiliar with."

I smiled at Bain's word choice. My friend Dax would be *happy* to complain and whine nonstop about the task, but he was trustworthy.

"What can I do?" I asked.

"I suggest you visit Healer Hayes," Irys said. "There's a chance you're sick or he might have some information about what is causing your…condition."

All good ideas. I leaned back, sinking into the cushions as exhaustion swept through me.

"Does Valek know?" Irys asked.

"No. He left before my symptoms started. I don't want to alarm him. I'll message him when I know more."

"We must search for the assassin, as well," Bain said. "I'll contact the security chief. He—"

"No," I interrupted.

"Then who do you suggest?"

I considered. No doubt Valek's spies would be hunting for my attacker, but they didn't have magic or intimate knowledge of Sitia's back alleys. Two people came to mind—one had magic while the other had the knowledge.

"Leif and Fisk. I trust them both."

"Would they be willing to work together?" Bain asked.

"They have before. Remember the gang of scam artists that plagued the Citadel a few years ago?"

"Ah, yes. A nice bit of detecting." Bain tapped his fingers on the edge of his teacup. "However, this assassin may not be from the Citadel or have ties here."

"Fisk has been branching out to other cities." I smiled, remembering the dirty street rat who had begged me for money. I'd emptied my pouch into his small hands, but when he approached me a second time, I'd hired him to help me navigate the overwhelming market.

Eventually he founded the Helper's Guild and recruited other beggar children to help shoppers find good prices, quality merchandise and to deliver packages, all for a small price. His network of guild members also had the unique ability to gather information on the criminal element.

"I didn't know he's expanding," Irys said. "That little scamp. I shouldn't be surprised." She sipped her tea. "Well, he's not so little anymore. It's a good idea to ask them."

If they had time. "Is Leif out on assignment?"

"Not right now," Bain said with a significant look.

Meaning the Sitian Council might have a job for my brother soon, which led to another question. "Should I inform the Council of my condition?"

Bain ran a gnarled hand down his sleeve. Since becoming the First Magician, he'd aged more than just the natural passage of time. His duties included overseeing the Keep and being a member of the Sitian Council—same as Irys. She, too, had aged. Gray streaked her black hair and a few more wrinkles etched her face.

"Not about your lost magic," Irys said. "Not until we know more. However, we should tell them about the attack. They might have intel from their clans."

Each of Sitia's eleven clans had one representative on the Council, and, along with the two Masters, the Council governed Sitia.

Bain straightened in his chair. "I believe we have a plan of attack. I will liaise with the Council and do extensive research. Irys will check the gate logs and talk to Quinn and Pazia. Yelena will visit Healer Hayes and talk to Fisk and her brother, Leif. Did I miss anything?"

"No." For the first time since the morning I'd woken without my magic, my chest didn't hurt. Too bad it didn't last.

"Yes," Irys said. She leaned forward. "Yelena, you need to keep a very low profile. If you interact with the Keep's students, they'll figure it out eventually and then it will be impossible to keep your condition a secret. Plus you're vulnerable. Whoever did this to you knows magic can influence you. What if they use you to get close to one of the Councilors or the Commander and Valek? Or turn you into an assassin? I'd suggest you ask Leif to weave a null shield into your cloak and, once you've talked to Fisk, you need to go into hiding. That's the safest thing you can do right now."

Run and hide? That was so not my style.

4

VALEK

Ben Moon escaped with help? Who could have broken him out of Wirral Prison? Most likely a group of rogue magicians. They'd have to be intelligent, resourceful and powerful in order to get through Wirral's supertight security. Valek dug his fingernails into the chair's armrests, but kept his expression neutral as the Commander relayed the information. His first impulse—to race to the Citadel to warn and protect Yelena—throbbed against his hollow chest.

"As I said, we will not be getting involved in what is strictly a Sitian affair," the Commander said, not fooled by Valek's calm demeanor.

"How long ago did this happen?" Valek asked.

The Commander stilled. "It is not our concern."

Valek chose his next words with the utmost care. "Not directly, but Liaison Zaltana was ambushed and shot with an arrow two days ago."

"What…? How…? Why didn't you tell us?" Janco sputtered in outrage.

Concern hardened Ari's face.

"She's fine," Valek assured them. "Kiki sidestepped and

the arrow missed her heart." He explained what had happened.

"And you think this attack is related to Ben Moon's escape?" the Commander asked.

"It would depend on the timing, sir."

"I see." Commander Ambrose scanned the parchment.

Valek suppressed the desire to snatch it from the man's hand.

"The incident happened ten days ago. Not enough time for Ben to set up the attack on Yelena."

"Unless his buddies planned it and all Ben had to do was show up and hide behind the null shield and wait for her," Janco said.

Good point, except the Commander failed to appear impressed.

"Regardless, we will let the Sitian Council handle the investigation. After all, she was ambushed in Sitia." The Commander gathered his files.

"May I send a message to Yelena, warning her about Ben?" Valek asked.

"She probably already knows, but if you feel it's necessary, then go ahead." He stood. "I expect daily reports on your progress regarding the smuggling routes." The Commander paused. "Valek, stop by my rooms later tonight."

"Yes, sir."

He nodded and left the war room.

Valek stared at the door, wondering why the Commander made a point to order him to visit his rooms. It had been their routine since the takeover to touch base before bed. Valek and the Commander had spent many late nights together discussing strategy and talking through problems, seeking solutions.

Perhaps the Commander thought Valek would skip tonight due to all the work that no doubt piled up while he'd been in Sitia. The stack of reports wasn't nearly as concerning as

MARIA V. SNYDER

Commander Ambrose's indifference over Ben's rescue, which was the opposite of Valek's reaction. Usually they were in sync and the Commander shared all his information. But he hadn't let Valek see that letter, which made him suspect the Commander had lied or hidden something. Why?

If Yelena had been assassinated, the relationship between Ixia and Sitia would be affected. Probably not enough to cause a war, but it would further strain an already uneasy truce. While Valek agreed the new smuggling routes needed to be discovered, the impact of black-market goods on Ixia was minor in comparison.

Perhaps the Commander wished to sever relations with Sitia and he planned to confer with Valek about it tonight.

"You know, the Commander didn't specify *which* messenger you could send to warn Yelena," Janco said.

Valek waited.

"*We* could deliver that message to her," Ari said, catching on. "Then hang around and investigate the *smuggling* operation."

"Oh yeah. The best way to discover the new routes is to infiltrate their operations. In fact—" Janco slapped the table. "I still have a few contacts in Fulgor. They might have some leads to the *smugglers*."

Janco had worked undercover as an officer at the Wirral maximum-security prison, which was located in the city of Fulgor in the Moon Clan's lands.

"I thought you were looking forward to being in Ixia and away from all that 'magical muckety-muck,'" Valek quoted.

Janco pished. "Discovering the *smugglers* is more important."

True. However, rushing off into the unknown never sat well with him. He preferred to gather information, collect data, observe and then infiltrate before making an arrest. Yelena had her magic, and she'd promised to return to the Magician's

Keep after he'd left. No doubt the Masters would inform her of Ben Moon's status and ensure that she'd be well protected.

Anger flared for a moment. He should have killed Ben right away. Valek had slipped inside Wirral once before to tie up a few loose ends. And Ben Moon was definitely a loose end. Too bad Ben hadn't been caught in Ixia like his brother. Owen had attempted to steal the Ice Moon from a diamond mine in Ixia, coercing Yelena to help him by kidnapping Leif. A smart and powerful magician, Owen had almost succeeded, but was outsmarted and executed four years ago. Ben blamed Yelena and, a year later, had tried to cut her throat.

Valek considered. Despite the Commander's orders, he didn't plan to leave it to the Sitian authorities.

"Before we do anything, I'll check with my network in Sitia," Valek said. "One of ours may already have eyes on Ben and his cohorts. Same with the new smuggling routes."

"What do you want us to do in the meantime?" Ari asked.

"Go shopping."

"Shopping?" Janco perked up. "I could use a new dagger and a short sword and a set of sais. I've been drooling for a pair since Opal—"

"Not that kind of shopping, you dolt," Ari said. "He wants us to shop for black-market goods."

"Correct. And see if you can…persuade the sellers into revealing their sources."

"Yes, sir. We'll go first thing in the morning." Ari stood.

Janco groaned. "What's wrong with going in the afternoon? We'll avoid the crowds and I can catch up on my sleep and it's warmer."

Ari ignored his partner and headed for the door.

Janco trailed after. "I've been working undercover for the past two years. It's hard to rest when you might wake up to a

MARIA V. SNYDER

knife at your throat. I should visit my mother. I haven't seen her in—"

The door closed on Janco's prattle. He might be annoying and have a short attention span, but he could be counted on when a situation turned serious. Then he was focused and deadly with his sword.

Valek sat a moment longer, savoring the quiet. He needed to review the piles of reports that waited for him on his desk so he could prepare for his meeting tonight. The Commander's stiff manner during supper warned him it wouldn't be pleasant.

As expected, stacks of files filled every square inch of his desk. Although Maren had kept his office clean of dust while he'd been in Sitia for most of the past year, the room smelled musty and a stuffiness pressed against his skin. Valek wove through the piles of books and heaps of stones that littered the floor, lit the lanterns and candles ringing his desk, opened the window a crack and settled in his chair.

Maren had been in charge during his absence. Again he wondered what mission she'd been assigned and how long she'd been gone. Perhaps he'd find out tonight. Practical as always, Maren had organized the reports into three categories—general updates, important and action required. Notes written in her loopy handwriting accompanied each one. Handy, it would make it easier, but still time-consuming since the reports from his network of spies had been written in code that had to be deciphered.

Sneaking into Wirral and helping the Bloodrose Clan win their freedom was more appealing than sifting through all the files. However, years of experience had taught Valek that golden nuggets of information resided within these piles. He'd just have to dig through them one at a time.

Hours later, a light knocking on his door jolted him from a detailed description of the Hunecker quarry operations in MD-4.

"Yes?" he called, grasping the handle of his sword with his right hand and palming a dagger with his left.

A guard entered slowly.

Smart man.

"Commander Ambrose has retired for the evening, sir."

Valek studied the man's face, committing the guard's features to memory. "Thank you...?"

He straightened. "Sergeant Gerik, sir."

"You're new. How long have you been with the Commander's security detail?"

"Three seasons, sir. I was assigned by Adviser Maren."

Ah. "Has anyone else been promoted in my absence?"

"No, sir."

"Thank you, Gerik. You're dismissed."

Gerik did an about-face and left. Valek added the man's name to the list he'd written of items he needed to follow up on. New personnel in the Commander's detail were not unheard-of, but Valek performed a complete background check on each candidate before he or she was assigned. Perhaps the paperwork for Gerik waited in one of the stacks he had yet to peruse. Those would take another couple of days to complete.

At least Valek had found a few clues that might lead them to uncovering the new smuggling routes. And, even better, he had an action plan to report to the Commander.

Valek swept up a few files, extinguished the lanterns and candles, and locked his office door. The three complex locks prevented most intruders from gaining entry. However, a professional could pop them in minutes.

Heading to the Commander's suite, Valek passed a few servants and soldiers, recognizing them all. He nodded at those

MARIA V. SNYDER

who met his gaze. A few returned the gesture while others kept their gazes on the floor.

Two massive wooden doors guarded by two soldiers Valek knew well blocked the entrance to what had once been the King's royal apartments. The guards opened the doors, allowing Valek to pass into a short hallway.

When the Commander's forces took control of Ixia about twenty-three years ago, Ambrose divided the King's expansive rooms into two suites, one for him and one for Valek. The hall had only two doors opposite each other. Valek knocked on the one on the left and waited.

A faint "come in" sounded. Valek entered the Commander's main living room. The Commander's living space matched the rest of the castle. In a word, utilitarian. After the take-over, Ambrose had stripped the castle of all its opulent decorations. Paintings were removed, tapestries shredded and statues crushed. If it didn't have a specific or useful purpose, it didn't stay.

Instead of sitting in his favorite armchair near the fireplace, the Commander sat behind his desk facing the entrance. He still wore his uniform. A bad sign. Valek approached.

"Sit." The Commander gestured to a hard chair with his quill. "Report."

Valek perched on the edge. "Ari and Janco are going to sniff around the markets tomorrow and see if they can get a lead on the suppliers of the illegal goods. Once we've identified them, we'll follow them and see where they cross back into Sitia."

"A good start. Anything else?"

"No, but—"

"You're dismissed." The Commander returned to his work.

Valek didn't move.

The Commander ignored him. Valek studied his boss. Thin, clean-shaven despite the late hour, and with a couple more wrinkles than the last time Valek'd been in Ixia. They'd been working together for the past twenty-four years. Cold fury emanated from Ambrose, and Valek wasn't going to leave until he discovered why.

The top of the desk resembled the rest of the room: neat, spartan, and no ink stained the wood. However, a single decoration stood out amid the starkness. A ylang-ylang flower crafted from small multicolored stones glued together. Probably a gift from Yelena. Her clan, the Zaltanas, had a number of artists who created those figurines.

"You're disobeying a direct order, Valek. Do I need to call for the guards and have you arrested?"

"Permission to speak freely, sir?" Valek asked.

"And if I say no?"

"Then you'll need to call the guards."

The Commander set down his quill. "You have one minute."

"Spit it out, Ambrose. Why are you so upset with me?"

The silence stretched.

Valek waved a hand, indicating the two of them. "This isn't going to work. If we no longer have an open rapport with us batting ideas back and forth, then fire me or arrest me."

Nothing.

Last try. "Our relationship has always been based on complete trust and—"

"And I trusted you to tell me *everything*."

Ah. There it was. Valek had kept one thing from the Commander. He reported all his adventures in Sitia, and obtained permission to render aid, but he had failed to inform Ambrose about the disturbing fact that a null-shield bubble could trap him. The reason? Initially to keep the knowledge from spreading. But in omitting the Commander from the list of

MARIA V. SNYDER

those in the know, Valek acted as if he didn't trust the Commander, which wasn't true at all. So why didn't he tell him?

"I'm sorry."

How did the Commander find out? Who did know? Those fighting in the Bloodrose revolt—Opal, Devlen, Ari, Janco, Quinn, Kade, Heli, Nic and Eve. Quite the list. Who had opportunity? Anyone could have sent a message, but why would they? Only three people had been in Ixia since then: Ari, Janco and Kade.

"Not good enough, Valek."

"You're right." He stood. "I'll go collect—"

"Sit down."

Valek resumed his seat.

The Commander studied Valek. The force of his gaze had broken many people, rendering them into a quivering mess as they begged forgiveness or confessed to every crime. It was impressive. And Valek suspected the Commander used a form of magic even though Valek had never felt it. To him, magic pushed against his skin like molasses. The stronger the power, the thicker the air around him. The Commander's appraisal certainly held enough weight. The C-shaped scar on his chest burned in response.

"Why?" Ambrose asked.

Digging deep within himself, Valek considered the question. His immunity to magic was not only a part of him, but a protection. Years of practice had honed his fighting skills, and experience with spies, criminals and schemers had given him a sharp mind. To be trapped in a null-shield bubble and encased within an invisible force field of magic galled him. A silly thing to have such dire circumstances. But his weakness meant he could no longer be... What? Invincible? Did he have that huge of an ego? Or was it another thing altogether...?

"Fear," Valek said into the silence. "That once you found

out, you'd no longer need me. I am getting older, and Ari and Janco could—"

"Drive me insane. No, thank you. Do you really think I'd replace you because of one drawback? Actually, two."

"Two?"

"Yelena."

"I think she's an asset."

"Until her life is compromised. That would be the easiest way to hurt you. Or influence you."

True. "I guess I just need more time to…adjust to my predicament."

"Time is an excellent way to gain perspective. I trust this won't happen again."

"Yes, sir."

The Commander pushed away from his desk and swiped a decanter of brandy before settling into the cerulean suede armchair. He waved Valek into the other chair and poured two drinks.

Valek sipped the spicy liquid. Blackberry. A pleasant warmth spread into his stomach and he smiled, remembering when he'd taught Yelena how to detect poisons in various flavors of brandy. She'd gotten drunk at the General's brandy meeting and tried to seduce him. Talk about self-control. Valek had deposited her in her bedroom and bolted before he ravished her. Worry had trumped desire. She might have regretted it when she sobered, and he'd wanted more from her than a drunken one-night stand.

With the tension between him and the Commander gone, Valek asked how he'd found out about the null shields.

"Janco mentioned it before you arrived. He'd assumed I knew and I didn't correct him. And during his monologue of prattle, he remarked that he has a certain sensitivity to magic. Is that true?"

MARIA V. SNYDER

"Yes, he's pretty good at seeing through magical illusions."

"Useful. What about Opal Cowan? After all that training, is she going to join your corps?"

"Not quite." Valek swallowed a mouthful of brandy. "She offered to assist us if we need her." He set his glass down. "And she sent you a present."

"One of her glass animals?"

"No. She no longer is able to make her magical messengers, but what she can now do is far more useful to us."

"Oh?"

"I'll be right back." Valek dashed across the hall and grabbed the package from his saddlebags that had been delivered as promised. He returned and handed it to the Commander.

Unwrapping the cloth, Ambrose uncovered a lifelike glass snow cat. He examined the hand-sized statue. "Her artistic skill has improved, but it doesn't glow with an inner fire." He raised a slender eyebrow, inviting Valek to explain.

"That fire was her magic trapped inside." And only visible to magicians and the Commander. "What's inside that snow cat is a bit of her immunity. What you're holding is a magic detector. When a magician uses magic near that cat, it will flash with light, alerting you to its presence."

"Clever. Is she mass-producing these for the Sitians?"

"The Councilors all have one for protection, and in case a rogue magician tries to use magic to influence them. Regarding mass production, I don't know what Opal plans. The Sitian Council wishes to be in charge of the distribution, but Opal won't give them control. I think she's letting her father handle the allocation of the detectors."

"Wise." The Commander tapped a finger on the glass. "And our spies can purchase more of these for us, evening the playing field a little between Ixia and Sitia."

"They still have those super messengers."

Ambrose frowned. "Those put us at an extreme disadvantage."

Valek agreed. The messenger was a glass cube with a magic-charged black diamond at its heart. The cube allowed magicians to communicate over vast distances instantly. An indispensable tool, and one that would give Sitia a big advantage during warfare.

"We can hire magicians and they would no longer have the upper hand," Valek said despite the Commander's deepening scowl. "You know how versatile magicians are and how many ways they could aid Ixia."

"Better to stop the Sitians from making the super messengers. If we assassinate Quinn Bloodrose, Sitia couldn't produce any more."

The thought of killing Quinn didn't sit well with Valek. "Not quite. They could still charge the blacks with magic and encase them in glass, but once the magic is gone, it'd be useless. Quinn's the only one who can recharge them without cracking the diamond."

"Then we need to steal the diamonds and sabotage their mining operations."

Once they'd won their freedom, the Bloodrose Clan kept dredging the sand for the black diamonds, going deeper into the sea with each sweep. Soon they'd have to use boats.

"It would be difficult." His stomach soured.

"Look into it after you find the new smuggling route." The Commander finished his drink. "I need to write a note to General Rasmussen and have him check his beaches for black diamonds." He returned to his desk.

Valek held up his glass. The light from the fire reflected off the amber liquid. An odd shuffle-step sounded behind him. He jumped to his feet, yanked out his dagger and spun in one fluid motion.

A figure dressed from head to toe in black pressed a knife to the Commander's throat.

5

YELENA

"Other than needing a full night's rest, you're healthy," Healer Hayes said. He'd examined me using both his magic and a mundane physical check. Opening a file with my name on it, he jotted a few notes.

How could good news be bad? I sat up, clutching the sheet to my chest. "Are you sure you didn't detect a poison?"

"All your body systems are working properly. I didn't sense any taint or rot or infection. I'm very sorry."

Frustration grew. "Do you know or have you heard of any substance that would cause my problem?"

I'd explained the entire story to him when I'd arrived at his office in the infirmary an hour ago. Hayes had listened without interruption, then led me to an examination room. Located on the ground floor of the administration building, the infirmary had a number of private rooms for recovering patients as well as an open area of beds for those who needed only a few hours. Unfortunately, I'd spent more time under Healer Hayes's care than most.

"No. I can read through my medical books and see if there is a mention of such a substance. It's a long shot, Yelena. If someone had discovered this poison before, it would have caused trouble and been reported by now."

"Unless it had been forgotten like Curare. That had been mentioned in a history book about the Sandseed Clan and, combined with the knowledge from a Sandseed healer, my father had been able to find it in the jungle." I gasped then groaned over my own stupidity. "My father. He's discovered many medicines and substances in the Illiais Jungle. He might know about this magic blocker."

"A good idea."

I hopped off the table.

"Before you rush off, I need to update your file."

As I dressed, he asked a bunch of questions.

"How old are you?"

"Twenty-seven." Although most people assumed I was younger because of my five-foot-four-inch height. I twisted my long black hair into a bun and used one of my sets of lock picks to keep it in place. Despite being in the Keep, I couldn't let my guard down. Especially not now.

"When was your last blood cycle?"

I paused and glanced at him. He kept his gaze trained on the file in front of him.

"And this is relevant how?"

"Your last dose of Moon potion was close to a year ago. You're due for another, but the timing is critical."

Oh. Since Valek and I hadn't even discussed marriage let alone a child, I needed to take the Moon potion. I thought back. "Twenty days ago or so."

"Here." He handed me a vial full of a white liquid. "Drink this right after your next cycle."

"All right." I put the potion in my backpack and left the in-firmary. Disappointment over his prognosis stabbed. While I hadn't thought Healer Hayes would have the cure, I'd hoped for more. At least I still had other avenues to explore.

Perhaps my father had heard of the poison. Esau had given me a field guide to help me identify plants to use in healing. After I discovered my healing powers, I no longer needed it, but I'd kept it. I would read through it tonight.

Hungry for the first time in days, I headed to the dining hall located right behind the administration building. Remembering what Irys had said about not interacting with the students, I grabbed a couple of sandwiches and bolted, nodding at a few people I recognized on my way out.

I found a quiet sunny spot in the gardens—the green center of the Keep—to eat my dinner. The two apprentice wings bracketed the gardens to the east and west. From the top of Irys's tower, the buildings resembled parentheses. I considered my next move.

Bain wished for an investigation into the identity of the assassin who'd attacked me. I needed to talk to my brother and Fisk. Also Leif had helped our father with his jungle research, and he might know about the poison. I could search for Leif or I could ask the one person who would know where Leif was—his wife, Mara.

When I finished my meal, I strode northeast through the campus. A few students milled about and others dashed between buildings. The sunlight warmed the air and in a few months color would invade the Keep along with the warm season, and the gardeners would plant flowers with vicious delight.

As the manager of the glass workshop, Mara would no doubt be overseeing the student magicians who learned how to work with glass. I wondered if Quinn charged the black diamonds used for the super messengers here or in his rooms. Since he was an older student who'd already learned how to

MARIA V. SNYDER

use his magic, he'd been assigned to the apprentice wing just like I had been six years ago.

Any glass artist could encase the diamond in glass, but only Quinn could charge them with his magic. He was in the same position Opal had been when she'd manufactured her animal-shaped messengers—one of a kind and vital to Sitia. Loads of pressure for the young man to bear. That intensity had almost crushed Opal, but she proved to be as strong and versatile as the glass she loved and now she easily bore the responsibility of being the only person able to create those magic detectors.

If I couldn't reclaim my magic, I'd need to purchase a detector in defense. Lovely. What else would I need? Chain mail and body armor? Bodyguards? I rolled my stiff shoulder. My magic hadn't saved me from the assassin's arrow. Small comfort.

White smoke billowed from the stack atop the glass workshop. When I entered, the heat pushed against my skin like a wet wool blanket. The roar of the kilns rumbled deep in my chest and through the soles of my boots. Students sat at gaffer benches, spinning their iron rods to shape the molten glass gathered on the end. Others blew into pipes and the glass expanded into bubbles.

I scanned the activity, seeking a familiar face. In the center of the bustle stood Mara, instructing a student. A beautiful woman with a heart-shaped face and the sweetest soul. My brother had done plenty of stupid, annoying and crazy things, but marrying Mara had been the smartest thing he'd ever done.

Her tawny-colored eyes lit when she spotted me. A kerchief tied back her golden-brown hair. Dirt smudged her cheek and her apron had seen better days. She gestured to her office and held up two fingers.

Understanding the signal, I wove through the glassmaking equipment and entered the relative coolness of her office. Glass vases, paperweights, bowls and tumblers littered the room. Student efforts or Mara's, I couldn't tell. Did my sister-in-law even have time to produce her own work? The Council hoped another magician would develop an affinity with glass like Mara's sister, Opal, and Quinn, so a steady stream of first years arrived for their mandatory glass lessons. Those who enjoyed it continued to study the art during the rest of their five-year stay at the Keep.

I settled in the chair next to her desk, considering how much had changed since Opal's glass magic had been discovered. It gave me a bit of comfort. Despite Bain's lifelong quest to learn about magic and magicians, he'd never heard of Opal's particular skills. Therefore, there was no reason to panic because he hadn't heard of a magic-blocking poison.

Mara bustled in with a swish of skirts and I stood.

She embraced me. "Yelena! What a wonderful surprise. I didn't expect you back so soon." Then she pulled away and frowned. "Is something—"

"Nothing's wrong. Valek had to leave early. The Commander's patience had finally run out."

"Oh dear, I hope he's not in trouble."

"*In* trouble? No. Causing trouble? Always."

Her musical laugh warmed me.

She closed the door to her office, reducing the noise of the kilns and ensuring privacy. "Would you like some tea?" Mara lifted a glass teapot by its handle.

"Yes, please."

She poured two steaming cups and then sat down.

"Is that—"

"One of Quinn's hot glass pieces? Yes. It stays hot for days. A marvel! He's a darling boy and gave it to me when I cleared two hours each evening just for him. Poor boy doesn't like working

MARIA V. SNYDER

with a crowd drooling over his shoulder. Who would?" Mara sipped from her cup. "And I had to ban the kitchen staff, too. They love his hot and cold glass and had been pestering him for more pieces. Who knew keeping meat cold keeps it from spoiling longer?" Wonder touched her voice.

"Has he discovered any other glass abilities since coming here?"

"He's been concentrating on the messengers and the temperature glass. Opal told me he could attach a null shield to glass and other..." Mara swept her arms out as if searching for the right word. "Emotions. But between his classes and his work, the poor boy hasn't had time to experiment."

Interesting about the null shield. "He's here every night?"

"Except for one night a week."

Keeping my tone neutral, I asked, "Which night?"

Mara gazed at me. "Why? Is it important?"

Shoot. She'd been spending too much time with Leif.

"Just curious."

"Uh-huh." She waited.

"Oh all right. I want to talk to him."

"Better. Let's see..." Mara checked a ledger on her desk. "He was here the last couple of nights... His night off was four days ago."

The timing matched the night of the attack. My heart thumped. "What does he do on his nights off?"

"He has riding lessons."

Oh. Still, he could have missed his lesson. I needed to talk to the Stable Master.

"Is that the reason you stopped by?" Mara asked.

"No, I was looking for Leif." Only after I said it did I realize how it must have sounded. "And to visit you." Weak.

"How nice." Her tone didn't match her words.

"Sorry. It's just…something came up and I haven't been sleeping…" Weaker.

Concern softened the hard lines around her mouth. "And it's probably some political problem that you can't tell me. Between Leif and Opal, I'm used to being in the dark."

From the way her shoulders drooped, I knew she was far from used to the idea, yet she put on a brave front. I drank my tea and reflected. Leif and Mara hadn't even been married a year yet. It had been a lovely wedding and she had glowed with pure joy. She was part of my family. Kidnapped from Sitia at age six, I'd grown up in Ixia believing I had no family. Dreams of a fictional loving family had helped me through the dark times. And now I planned to enlist Leif's help, taking his time away from Mara. Not very nice.

"The reason I need to talk to my brother is…" I filled her in on what had happened.

Mara clutched her apron, gathering the fabric into a tight bunch, but she didn't say a word. When I finished, she slid off her chair and hugged me.

"Oh, Yelena, that's terrible." She squeezed tight then let go. "What can I do to help?"

"Help?" I hadn't thought about it.

"Of course. I'm sure you have a plan of attack. And don't tell me to keep it quiet. I'm not an idiot."

True. "Can you find out if any of the students are able to siphon magic? Opal had done it with glass, but perhaps there is another magician who can do it with another object."

She brightened. "I can. I know all the students and they like to brag about who can do what." She held up her hand. Burn scars marked her fingers and wrist. "Don't worry. I'll be discreet. Are you going to talk to Opal? She might have some ideas."

I groaned. Another possible avenue that I'd missed. "I will."

MARIA V. SNYDER

"Good. Now go get some sleep. Leif's at the Council Hall this morning, but he'll be in the training yard later this afternoon, helping Marrok teach the juniors how to defend against a machete."

"Thanks."

She escorted me out the door and then remained on the workshop's steps, ensuring I headed in the right direction. Another knot in my stomach eased as I skirted the pasture that occupied the space between the glass shop and the stables. Telling Mara had been the right thing to do.

When I entered the large wooden barn, Kiki whinnied a welcome. She looked over the Stable Master's broad shoulder as he bent to clean dirt from her hooves. Her copper coat shone, her mane had been brushed and her whiskers were trimmed. Oh no.

"I was planning on—"

"Yeah, yeah." The Stable Master cut me off. "Always the same. In a hurry with urgent business to attend to. I've heard all the excuses." He moved to her back feet. "She was a muddy mess," he grumbled. "Keep taking advantage of her and one day you'll come out here and she'll be gone."

Not unless he stopped feeding her his famous milk oats. I sighed. The Stable Master lived and breathed horses. To him, nothing was more important. And he had a point.

"I'm sorry." I draped my cloak over a stall door, picked up a comb and worked on untangling her tail. Then I helped him clean tack and muck out stalls until he no longer muttered quite as much. Which was as good of a mood as possible for him.

Before he left to order more feed, I asked about Quinn's riding lessons.

"Strong as an ox, that boy," the Stable Master said. "He

don't look it, but all those years of diving for oysters honed his muscles. See that bay?" He pointed through the window.

A horse with a deep garnet-colored coat and a black mane and tail trotted around the inside of the pasture's fence. "Yes."

"Flann's a son of a bitch—stubborn, spirited and strong. Quinn's the only one who can ride him."

"A Sandseed horse?" Sandseed horses, like Kiki, were picky about who they allowed to ride them.

"Nope. One of those new Bloodgood breeds. I was gonna send him back because he's been a real pain in my ass, but he took a liking to the boy."

"Is Quinn enjoying his lessons?"

"I don't care. He shows up on time and has improved. That's all I care about."

"Did he miss his last lesson?"

"No. Why?"

And there went another lead. "Flann looks like he needs a workout."

"Tell that to the Master Magicians. Quinn's too busy to do more." The Stable Master hooked his thumb toward the bay. "You're welcome to try." He patted Kiki's neck with affection. "I'm sure Kiki here won't mind. Will you, girl?" He slipped her a milk oat then left without saying goodbye.

After he left, I scratched Kiki behind her ears. She closed her eyes and leaned closer. Sadness panged deep inside me, radiating out with pain. The loss of our connection hurt the most. And I cringed at the thought of riding another horse. It would also be an unnecessary risk. Kiki rested her chin on my shoulder as if consoling me.

"I'll figure this out," I promised her.

She nipped my ear playfully then left the stable. I followed her out. She hopped the pasture's fence, joining the other horses. I scanned them. Silk, Irys's horse, and Leif's horse, Rusalka, nickered a greeting to Kiki.

Exhaustion clung to me, but horse hair and slobber coated my clothes and hands. I stopped at the bathhouse to wash up before I trudged to my apartment in Irys's tower.

Each Master Magician lived in one of the four towers of the Keep. Irys occupied the northwest tower and Bain had the southeastern one. The northeast tower belonged to Zitora Cowan, Second Magician, even though she'd retired. We all hoped she'd return. The southwest tower still remained empty. Roze Featherstone, who had been the First Magician, had lived there until she betrayed Sitia. After the Warper battle, she was killed and her soul trapped in a glass prison.

When I was no longer considered a student of the Keep, Irys offered me three floors of her tower to use. A generous offer. My few belongings had all fit on one floor, but I had since expanded to another, setting up guest quarters for visitors. So far, only my parents had used the space.

I lumbered up the three flights of steps. At least I hadn't been gone long enough for my bedroom to be coated with dust. I glanced around. The single bed, armoire, desk, chair and night table all appeared to be undisturbed. My footsteps echoed against the hard marble walls. I hadn't had time to install tapestries and heavy curtains to absorb the harsh sounds. Good thing since now I'd need to hear an intruder in order to wake up in time to defend myself.

Bending down, I checked under the bed and then opened the armoire. Yes, I felt silly and paranoid, but sleeping would be impossible unless I ensured no one hid in my room.

Satisfied, I tossed my cloak over the chair and crawled into bed. The chilly air swirled as I drew the thick blankets up to my chin. If I had any energy, I would light the brassier nearby. Instead, I drifted to sleep.

And for the first time in years, I didn't dream.

★ ★ ★

I woke a few hours later when the late-afternoon sunlight streamed through my window and touched my face. Without thinking, I reached for my magic and encountered deadness. The desire to curl into a ball and remain in bed pulsed through my heart. But I refused to give up. Plus I needed to speak to Leif. I flung my blankets off.

The training yard was located next to the glass shop. I leaned against the fence and studied the various matches. Most of the students held wooden practice swords or wooden machetes since they were only in their third year at the Keep. They wouldn't use real weapons until their final, apprentice year.

Leif sparred with a tall lanky student. I smiled at the mismatched pair. His stocky, powerful build, black hair and square face were the opposite of his opponent—a lean, lithe, blonde woman with a pointy chin. She used her longer reach and sword to stay out of his machete's chopping zone. Moving with the quick grace of a Greenblade, she dodged Leif's strikes.

However, experience won over fancy footwork and Leif ducked low and rushed her, knocking her down while unarming her. He grinned and helped her to her feet, then explained his strategy.

I waited as he wrapped up the session and lectured the group on where to focus.

"Don't stare at their eyes or shoulders," he said. "Watch your opponent's hips to anticipate his next strike. You've seen how a machete can counter a sword with the right moves and tactics. Do you think a machete can fight an opponent with a bo staff?"

A resounding no sounded from the students. Leif's eyes gleamed and he picked up a five-foot wooden staff that had been lying next to the fence.

MARIA V. SNYDER

"Yelena," he said and tossed the bo at me.

Instinctively, I caught it in my right hand.

"Let's show them how it's done." Leif set his feet into a fighting stance. "Unless you don't want to be embarrassed in front of a bunch of juniors?"

His challenge cut right through all reason and logic. It was physically impossible for a younger sister *not* to rise to her older brother's bait. Shedding my cloak, I hopped the low fence.

I faced Leif and slid my hands along the smooth grain of the staff out of habit. The action helped me find that zone of concentration that allowed me to sense my opponent's movements. This time, my fingers rubbed an ordinary piece of wood. No connection flared to life.

Could I still fight without my magic? Everyone had gathered to watch the match—not the best time to experiment. And Irys's comment about keeping a low profile rose in my mind too late. Oops.

Leif stared at me with an odd expression. His nose wrinkled as if he smelled an offensive odor. Great. Guess I'd have to rely on my training, my experience and the thousands of hours of practice I'd sweated through. My magic couldn't be that vital in my fighting. Could it?

Despite my worries, I clutched my weapon at the third points and twirled the bo into a ready position. As soon as the match started, I advanced, swinging the tip of the staff toward Leif's left temple. He backpedaled and blocked my attack. I aimed for his right temple, then left. Right. Left. Feint right. Rib strike. Leif countered with ease.

"Predictable," he said.

"I'm just getting warmed up."

My next series of attacks aimed for his ribs, then temple. Rib. Temple. Rib. Chin strike. Leif jumped back with a laugh. Then he advanced. I scrambled to keep his thick blade from chopping my bo in half. When he swung at my neck, instead of blocking the weapon, I ducked and swept his feet out from under him. He landed with an oomph.

Pleased, I relaxed my guard. Big mistake. Leif grabbed my ankle and yanked. I joined him on the ground. And the advantage of having a longer weapon ended there. From that position, his machete had a greater range of motion, and within a few strikes, he disarmed me.

Far from being triumphant with his win, concern creased his face. I shook my head and signaled for him to keep his mouth shut. Valek had taught us both hand signals to communicate when talking would give away our hidden positions or our plans to an enemy listening nearby.

He sprang to his feet and gestured to me while addressing the students. "See? A machete can defend against a bo staff if you can get in close. Yelena let me take her down in order to demonstrate to you one way to gain an advantage. Normally, she isn't so easy to beat. That's it for today."

The students picked up the training swords and talked in groups as they returned the weapons to the armory connected to the yard. I wiped dirt from my pants.

Once everyone left, Leif turned to me. "Okay, spill it. What's wrong? You smell…"

Leif's magic smelled people's intentions and emotions. He frequently helped with solving crimes due to his unique ability to sniff out criminals. When we'd been reunited after fourteen years apart, he'd proclaimed to our entire clan that I'd killed and reeked of blood. Nice, eh?

"What do I smell like?"

"You smell like death."

6

VALEK

Valek studied the figure standing behind the Commander. Five feet eight inches tall, about one hundred and forty pounds, either a young male or female—hard to tell when the only thing not covered with black was the assassin's light gray eyes. Armed with a dagger, which was currently pressed against the Commander's throat, but Valek guessed the assassin carried more than one knife.

The Commander frowned with annoyance.

"Impressive," Valek said, sipping his brandy. He tightened his grip on his knife, suppressing his anger at the Commander's security detail for not stopping the intruder. He'd deal with them later.

"Move and I'll slit his throat," the assassin said in a gravelly voice.

Not a natural tone, and Valek suspected the person wished to hide his or her true voice. It was an empty threat. If the assassin had wanted to kill the Commander, he'd have been dead before Valek had turned around.

"I'm not the one you should be worried about," Valek said.

Ambrose moved, grabbing the attacker's wrists, yanking the blade down and away from his body. He spun, trapping the assassin's arm. Within a minute the knife clanged to the floor and the Commander had the intruder at his mercy.

"Good show, old man," he said even though Ambrose was only about seven years older than Valek. "You still have the best knife-defense skills in the Territory. Do you want me to dispose of…that for you?" He set his drink down.

"No," the assassin cried in a higher-pitched voice this time. "I have the right to challenge you to a fight!"

"As soon as you climbed through that window, you gave up all your rights." Valek moved closer and yanked the hood off the intruder.

Unafraid, a young woman glared at him. "You know I had the drop on him. How many others have sneaked in here? None. Come on. Let me show you what I can do with a knife."

"Fine by me. Commander?"

The Commander released her. "Don't take too long, Valek. I've an early meeting." He settled behind his desk.

She glanced from him to the Commander and back.

"Don't worry. He won't interfere."

"How about when I'm about to gut you?" she asked.

"If you can gut him, go ahead," the Commander said.

"Such love. I'm touched." Valek patted his chest. "Pick up your knife," he said to the intruder. He switched his dagger to his right hand and turned his body sideways, keeping the weapon close to his stomach. He bent his left arm and held it in front of him to block any incoming strikes.

She mirrored his stance except she held her knife in her left hand. Ah, a lefty. Interesting. They circled and she slashed. He blocked. She shuffled forward and stabbed. He sidestepped. Recovering quickly, she spun and aimed for his throat. He ducked.

Valek remained on the defense as she tried all her offensive moves. She had learned an impressive number of them

MARIA V. SNYDER

and he'd gotten a few cuts during a couple of her combination strikes. He had to admit, she was fast. Her style of fighting seemed eerily familiar.

A slight swirl of unease brushed his stomach. Knife fighters tended to let their guard down when striking, believing their opponent would be too busy protecting himself to counterstrike. Not her. She stayed tight.

Without warning, Valek switched to an offensive series of jabs and kicks, bringing the level of the fight up a notch. She dodged, blocked and kept up with the speed of his attack.

As they fought, he tested her weaknesses and found little. When she executed a perfect feint and lunge, he cursed as the tip of her blade jabbed his gut. Pain burned and blood seeped, but Valek increased the pressure. After she snaked past his defense again in another near miss, Valek recognized her fighting style.

"You're a student of Hedda's, aren't you?" he asked.

"Save your breath." She advanced with a Janco-like flurry of jabs.

He wasn't winded. But if she kept this pace, he'd be sucking air. Concern grew. He'd managed to slip past her blocks a few times, but years of experience showed him how this fight would play out. It didn't look good for him.

As the fight continued, her style of attacks changed. She fought more like the Commander. Perhaps she had two teachers—a deadly combination. He needed to end this match. The sooner the better.

Fortunately, he had a few tricks up his sleeve. Well, not tricks exactly—he yanked another knife from his right sleeve and attacked with both.

She floundered for a bit, backing up. Then she sidestepped and drew a second knife, as well. While competent with two, she didn't have the same precision and speed.

After a few minutes, Valek lunged and slashed at her mid-section, knocking the weapon from her right hand. He pressed his advantage before she could pull another blade, keeping her arms busy. If Hedda had trained her, she would have three or four more daggers hidden in her clothes.

As the fight continued, she managed to grab another knife. By that time, Valek'd had enough. He stepped back, flipped his weapons over, grasping the blades, and threw them. The hilts slammed into her wrists, numbing her hands. She yelped and her knives clanged to the floor.

Then he shuffled in close and punched her. Hard. With a whoosh, she fell back. He followed her to the floor and pressed one of his favorite daggers to her throat.

"That's…" she panted "…not…fair."

"Hedda must have gotten soft in her old age. When she trained me, the words *not fair* were not part of her vocabulary."

She grimaced. Ah, he'd hit a nerve. Perhaps the young assassin didn't agree with all of Hedda's philosophies.

"Did she send you?" he asked.

Clamping her mouth shut, she stared at him.

"Who trained you?"

The Commander stood and yawned. "While that was entertaining, I must get to bed. Clean up the mess, Valek."

"Yes, sir."

The assassin sucked in a quick breath, showing her fear. Hedda hadn't driven all emotion from the young woman. Which made him wonder if this young pup had finished the training.

"Why are you here?" he asked.

"To kill you and take your place."

That would explain why she hadn't slit the Commander's throat. But he couldn't trust her. He yanked a dart from his belt and jabbed it into her arm.

MARIA V. SNYDER

"Listen up. If what you said is true, then I'll lock you in the dungeon. Escape and find me and we'll talk. There's no need to kill me to take my job. Just show that you're smart, capable, resourceful, cunning, trustworthy, loyal, ruthless and are willing to give your life for the Commander's and the job is yours."

She opened her mouth, but instead of words a soft "oh" escaped her lips as the goo-goo juice pumped through her body. Valek stood, gathered all the weapons and pulled her to her feet. She swayed. He grabbed his drink and downed it in one gulp.

What a night.

Picking up a lantern, he led her to his suite so their conversation didn't bother the Commander. She plopped into a chair and scanned the room with a bewildered expression. "So... much...junk! Are you an assassin or a crow?"

Crouching next to her, he asked, "What's your name?"

"Onora. I'm an assassin. Shh...don't tell anyone."

"How old are you?"

"Twenty."

"Which Military District are you from?"

"MD-2. I escaped."

"Escaped from what?"

"The captain. Shh...don't tell him I'm here."

"Captain who?"

"Cap-pa-tain Timmer, thinks he's a winner, and we must all obey," she sang.

"Why are you here?" he asked again since it was almost impossible to lie while under the influence of the goo-goo juice.

"To kill. *You*, of all people, should know that! King killer."

No doubt Hedda had trained her. "Did Hedda send you?"

"Hedda smedda. Crazy old bat. Stubborn. Stupid. Gone. Gone for good."

"You killed her?"

"I...stopped her. No more assassins."

Ice coated his heart. "She's dead?"

"Right-o! Dead to the world."

Valek stood and fingered his dagger. Hedda had taught him the skills that had kept him alive all these years. Anger and sorrow melted the ice inside him and Valek aimed the tip of the knife at her throat.

He buried the blade into the cushion next to her head. Onora jumped. He could always change his mind. Perhaps after he'd wrung every bit of information from her.

"How did you get into the castle?"

Onora explained in a roundabout rambling way how she slipped past the gate's guards, climbed up the side of the castle, jimmied open a window. "Easy as pie in the oven."

"How did you know where the Commander's suite is?"

"Gotta friend working inside. Shh...sweet soul doesn't know."

"Doesn't know what?"

"Doesn't know I know. I tricked. Have to protect... Have to protect..."

"Protect who?"

She shook her head. "Have to... Have to...protect."

Even with the goo-goo juice, Onora wouldn't say the name of her friend. Frustrating. At least it sounded as if the friend had been an unwitting accomplice.

When Valek was satisfied, he pulled her up and towed her to the guards outside the main door.

"I found an intruder in the Commander's suite," Valek said, handing her over.

The guards straightened as the color leaked from their faces.

"Ha," Onora said. "I found him!"

Valek gestured to two of the men. "Take her to the dungeon. Have Lieutenant Abira strip-search her, check every inch of her skin for putty, comb her hair for weapons and dress her in one of our coveralls before incarcerating her. Understand?"

"Yes, sir."

"We will discuss this *incident* in the morning."

"Yes, sir."

Before they left, Valek pricked Onora with another dose of goo-goo juice to ensure she'd remain incapacitated until morning. It would be interesting to see if she was resourceful enough to escape the dungeon.

Returning to his apartment, Valek picked up the lantern and searched the first floor. Aside from being filled with boxes and clutter, the three rooms off his living area were empty of intruders. Valek paused at the threshold of the bedroom that had been Yelena's. He'd kept her close to him with the pretense of protecting her. And while she attracted trouble like a sweet cake drew ants, the true reason had been that he had been fascinated by her and wanted her near.

Back then he couldn't touch her and they were together all the time, but now...they were heart mates and apart most of the time. The dusty air scratched at the back of his throat. What if Onora had succeeded and killed him? He'd never see Yelena again. Unless she visited him in the fire world. He huffed with dry amusement. He'd taken Hedda's teachings to heart. His soul was destined for an eternity trapped in the fire world.

He shut the door and climbed the steps to the second floor. It mirrored the first floor with three rooms to the right of a sitting area. More boxes, books and piles of rocks littered the floor. After a quick peek inside the bedrooms, he retreated down a long hallway to the left of the sitting area. A few more chambers lined the right side of the corridor. A stone wall ran along the left. More packed rooms. Empty of threats. The only organized area was Valek's carving room.

Stone dust covered the grinding wheels, worktable and pyramids of the gray stone he used for his carvings. The lumpy rocks were dull and lifeless, but with a chisel, grinder and sand, they transformed into beautiful black statues with flecks of silver. The hours he spent in here not only honed his artistic skills, but his mind, as well. Many times he'd enter with a vexing problem and leave with a solution.

He unlocked the door to his bedroom, then secured it behind him. No windows in this chamber. Glancing under the bed and in the armoire, he relaxed for a moment. Then Valek stripped off his shirt. The cut in his stomach had stopped bleeding. Good. He changed into his black skintight sneak suit. He wouldn't be able to sleep until he checked the castle walls for spiders.

Alighting on the balcony outside his apartment's first-floor living area, Valek flexed his fingers. The combination of climbing up and down the cold stone walls plus the fight with Onora earlier had stiffened his muscles. He had found no other intruders—the good news—but he'd also discovered how Onora had reached the Commander's room—the bad.

The lapse in security would be addressed in the morning. Valek glanced to the east. The sun would be up in a few hours. He headed to his bed, peeled off the sneak suit and slid under the blankets.

Exhausted beyond measure, Valek still couldn't sleep. He stared at the ceiling, mourning Hedda's death. After his brothers had been murdered, he'd searched for a teacher for two seasons. During that time, many people took advantage of him, selling him bad information, tricking him, or outright knocking him down and stealing the money he'd earned when he'd worked at his father's tannery. A hard lesson on whom to trust. No one.

Hungry, sick and drained, he'd spent his last coin on the

MARIA V. SNYDER

slim chance that the street rat did indeed know the location of a teacher. Valek found the remote complex along the rocky coast of MD-1 at the beginning of the warm season. The gates had been secured for the night and he sat on the stoop and waited in the cold damp air that smelled like salted fish. The irony of having searched all of Ixia for a teacher only to end up within miles of Icefaren, his hometown, was not lost on him.

Eventually he passed out on the hard stone for hours or days—he didn't know nor care at that point. Cold water splashed, jolting him awake. The sun was high in the sky. He blinked, wiping his eyes.

A woman in her midthirties with long red hair peered at him through the gate's bars. "You're persistent, I'll give you that." She set the bucket down.

"Are you the mistress of this school?"

"I am. What do you want?"

He stood to face her. His legs shook with the effort, but he met her hard gaze without flinching. "I. Want. To. Kill. The. King."

She studied him. "Ambitious."

At least she didn't laugh at him. A good sign.

"Can you fight?"

"No."

"Have you killed anyone?"

"No."

"Do you have any family?"

"No." His parents had pleaded with him to stay at home and not ruin his life by seeking revenge. He ignored them. When he left, they told him never to return. He was no longer their son.

"Do you have any skills?"

"No."

"Money?"

"No."

"How old are you?"

"Thirteen."

She shook her head. "Scrawny, penniless, homeless and without any redeeming qualities. Why should I accept you as my student?"

"Because I *will* kill the King. And the claim that *you* trained the man who assassinated the King will be a nice feather in your cap."

The humid air thickened around Valek, pressing against his skin like a sticky syrup. She pursed her lips as she stared at him. "Ten days."

"Ten?"

"To prove yourself."

"Thank you."

"Don't thank me yet. If you don't prove yourself—"

"Save it for the next applicant. I won't fail."

Hedda opened the gate and he followed her up a narrow winding path to a sprawling complex of buildings atop a cliff overlooking the Sunset Ocean. The stone walls resembled the grayish-white rocky outcroppings surrounding the complex. The few people working outside wore subdued tunics and pants that also blended in with the landscape.

She made a grand sweeping gesture, indicating the buildings. "Welcome to the School of Night and Shadows. How many people do you see?"

Valek scanned the area, counting. "Ten."

Hedda whistled. Movement exploded and figures jumped, crawled and slid from various nooks and shadows around the complex.

"Now how many?" she asked.

"More than ten."

"Correct. The best assassins are invisible. No magic needed."

When they drew close to the biggest structure—a four-story-high building with balconies facing the sea—Hedda called to a man. "Fetch Arbon. Tell him to meet me in my office."

"Yes, sir." The man dashed away.

Hedda led him into the main building and to an office on the ground floor. Out of the bright sunlight, Valek studied the woman. She wore a soft gray-green tunic and matching pants. Long red eyelashes framed light green eyes.

Gesturing to a chair, she settled behind a pristine desk. Nothing occupied the surface. He glanced around the room. A few tapestries hung on the gray-white-black walls. The color reminded him of seagull droppings. No fire burned in the fireplace. The sparse furnishings held no warmth and he guessed this wasn't her true office, but a place to conduct business with outsiders.

"What is your name?" she asked.

"Valek."

"Tell me why you want to kill the King."

"Does it matter?"

"Very much."

"His men murdered my brothers." Red-hot agony burned in the center of his heart as an image of their bodies flashed in front of him, but he clamped down on his emotions.

She studied him. "Then why not go after them?"

"Oh, they will die, too."

"But that's not good enough?"

"No." He spat the word out. "They murder in his name. The King's corruption has gone too far."

"Did you know the King is a powerful magician?"

"Yes."

"And that he's well protected?"

"Yes."

"And you still believe you can kill him?"

"Yes."

"How much time are you willing to dedicate to this endeavor?"

"As long as it takes. If my last breath is one second after the King's last gasp, I will die a happy man."

Hedda grinned. "One thing at a time. Let's see how long you last, King Killer." She glanced over his shoulder. "Arbon, come in and meet Valek."

A young teen around Valek's age slipped into the room. His black hair had been shorn close to his scalp.

"Take him to the medic then feed him and show him around. He can have Pyo's cell."

"Yes, sir," Arbon said.

"Valek, I'd suggest you concentrate on getting healthy. Once you begin training, luxuries like eating and sleeping are not guaranteed."

Valek smiled at the memory. He had used that phrase—*eating and sleeping are not guaranteed*—a thousand times with the men and women he had trained for his corps. It was as true today as it had been twenty-eight years ago. Of course, then he'd been a stupid kid and had no idea that lack of sleep and missed meals would be the least of his problems. Ah, youth.

Still unable to sleep, Valek pushed off his covers, dressed in his uniform and ghosted down to the dungeon to check on the newest occupant.

The guards snapped to attention and followed protocol to the letter. Everyone was worried about the consequences of the midnight assassin. As well they should be. Valek planned to demote them to privates and send them to guard the diamond mines in MD-3.

A thought occurred to him. What if the new guy…Gerik, was Onora's friend and he'd inadvertently tipped her off to

MARIA V. SNYDER

the lapse in security? Even if that was the case, the members of the Commander's detail had been chosen for a reason and their system of double checks should have revealed the gap.

Sleeping off the goo-goo juice, Onora sprawled on the cell's metal bed, which had been bolted to the bars. Her brown braid had been pulled apart and her hair fanned around her face like a messy mane.

"Keep a close eye on her, but don't alert her to the extra security," Valek said to the guard.

"Sir?"

"I want to see if she tries to escape."

"And if she does?"

"Let her go. I'll have one of my corps in place to follow her."

"Yes, sir."

Satisfied, Valek swung by the kitchen to swipe a couple of apples before waking up Qamra and assigning her babysitting duties.

"How good is she, sir?" Qamra asked.

"Don't let her get close to you. Bring your darts and blow-pipe."

"Yes, sir." She hopped from her bed.

He left and headed to his office. Qamra had the best aim in his entire corps. He'd put her through the paces, thrown every obstacle and distraction in her way, and she never missed. Valek wished he could say that about all his operatives. Blow in Janco's ear and he'd miss every time. But that was the beauty of training—it exposed the strengths and weaknesses of his corps so he could match jobs to agents.

At Hedda's school, though, she hadn't allowed weaknesses. Every skill had to be mastered before learning another. When Valek had been a student and he'd regained his health, his training began in earnest.

Arbon had shown him the long narrow one-story building then left Valek there without a word. An instructor gave Valek a stone about as big as his thumbnail. The man pointed to a target at one end of the building, then swept an arm out, indicating a series of red marks along the floor.

"Stand on the first mark, closest to the target. When you hit the bull's-eye with that stone at that position ten times in a row, move to the next one. Repeat. When you can hit the bull's-eye from the last mark, you will go back to the first mark and practice hitting the target with a knife. Understand?"

"Yes, sir."

Who would have thought hitting a bull's-eye with a stone would be that difficult? Hours turned into days and, determined to succeed, Valek only stopped when it was too dark to see. Hedda's training methods were simple and effective. No one taught you how to throw the stone. Repetition and practice until calluses coated your hands and you figured out the best way to hit a target.

Valek wished he had the time to train his corps the same way. However, time was always an issue. Back in the days before the Commander's takeover, he had sent promising individuals to Hedda's school to be trained. After the takeover, the Commander wished to incorporate her school into his military. She refused and had retired. Or so she claimed. Obviously she'd lied, and there might be more assassins in Ixia. Yet another detail to investigate.

He unlocked the door to his office. Even with the first rays of dawn creeping in through the square window, it remained too dark to read. He lit the lanterns. Searching through the files, he found the one on Gerik and read through the man's dossier. Nothing popped out at him. Maren had performed a thorough background check.

MARIA V. SNYDER

His door banged open. Valek stood and drew both knives without thought.

"Easy there, boss," Janco said, spreading his hands wide.

"I said to knock. Not to knock the door down." Ari entered.

"I barely touched it. It wasn't latched tight."

Valek returned his knives to their hidden locations and sank into his seat. "Come on in."

They drew closer.

"Is it true?" Ari asked him.

Nice to know the castle's gossip network still worked with lightning-fast precision. "Yes."

"Son of a snow cat!" Janco slapped his thigh. "Did you kill him?"

"Her. And no, I didn't."

Ari and Janco glanced at each other in amazement.

"But she reached the Commander." Janco's voice held outrage.

"He wasn't her target." Valek leaned back in his chair.

Ari smiled. "Possible recruit?"

Or replacement. But Valek wouldn't say that aloud. "We'll see if she escapes the dungeon."

"You want us to hang out near the dungeon, catch her in the act?" Janco asked.

"No. Continue with your assignment, and I'd also like you to nose around and see if you can dig up anything on Sergeant Gerik. He's a transfer from…" Valek consulted the file. "MD-2 about a year ago, and managed to impress his commanding officer enough to be promoted to the Commander's security detail."

"Seems sketchy to me," Janco said.

"Maren approved it. Do you know where she is?" Valek asked.

"No," Ari said. "No one does. She slipped out of here without a word a month ago, leaving Mannix in charge, but all the poor guy's been doing is sorting reports into piles."

"Keep asking around. See what you can discover."

"Yes, sir."

They left and Valek returned to the files. After a few hours, a light tap broke his concentration.

"Yes," he said.

Gerik poked his head in. Strain lined his haggard face, but he kept his voice even. "The Commander wishes to see you in his war room, sir."

"Now?"

"Yes, sir."

Valek straightened a pile of files then followed Gerik out. He locked his door and strode to the war room. Gerik didn't say a word as he trailed behind. The guards waiting near the entrance flinched when Valek approached. White-faced and with eyebrows pinched tight together, he sensed there was more going on than their fear of being reprimanded.

They pulled open the double doors. Valek entered the room.

Onora sat at the table with the Commander, eating breakfast.

MARIA V. SNYDER

7

JANCO

"You know what I can't figure out?" Janco asked. He leaned against the wall despite the grime. They hid in yet another garbage-strewn alley that reeked of piss, tracking potential suspects. Ah, the life of a superspy.

"How to tie your laces?" Ari asked.

"Funny. What I want to know is why sell black-market goods this close to the Commander's castle? Castletown is crawling with soldiers and spies. Why not sell their illegal wares in MD-7 or MD-5 since both are closer to the border?"

"Who says they're not selling there, too?" Ari crossed his arms. "This is a big city full of people. Criminals like to hide in plain sight."

"Yeah. They can be smart until they're stupid."

Ari's mouth opened, but then he closed it. Too bad. Janco enjoyed provoking his partner. It helped pass the time. When they did stakeouts that required silence, it killed him to keep quiet. Worse than magic. No, scratch that—nothing was worse than magic.

"There's the guy with the funky mustache." Janco pointed to a tall man unlocking one of the warehouse doors. "Could be going to get more of those illegal Greenblade cigars."

"Or he's going to warn his boss about the guy who had asked too many questions about those potent cigars," Ari said drily.

"No way. I was smooth. Subtle. More than subtle." He pouted.

"I think you're too recognizable. You should have worn your cap."

"It itches."

Ari sighed. "We'll see what happens next. If they start packing up, we'll know you hit a nerve."

Janco fidgeted. He studied the building. "Why don't we jimmy open that second-story window and slip inside? Better to hear what's going on than guess."

"We've no idea what's inside."

"Exactly."

"What if there're guards?"

"So? Not like we can't handle a couple—"

"And tip them off? By the time we fight our way in, they'll scatter."

"Oh, all right." A few minutes passed without incident. "How about *I* slip inside and you watch for Funky Mustache?"

"No."

Janco groaned. He was a man of action. All this sneaking about… Yes, it was necessary and patience led to results. Usually. But give him a fight over this any day.

Hours, seasons, years must have passed while they watched the door. An ordinary green door with paint peeling from the wood, revealing a yellowish-gold color underneath. Curled chips of paint lay on the ground right in front. Probably from when they installed the lock. A shiny knob and keyhole looked out of place on the weathered wood.

Smart until they're stupid. Install a new lock, but don't bother to paint the hardware to match the age of the building or bother to clean up.

Janco's hair turned gray as another few years passed—or so it felt to him. According to Ari, two minutes equaled two years in Janco time.

Ari touched his arm as the door swung open. They melted back into the shadows of the alley. Two men exited. Funky Mustache and a big burly brute. They parted, with Funky heading back to the market and Big Brute cutting through the alley to the other side.

"I'll follow the new guy," Ari whispered. "Now's your chance to sneak inside. Watch out for guards. If you see anyone, don't engage. We can always come back later tonight. I'll meet you at the Black Cat Tavern."

"Get inside, avoid guards, don't get married, meet at the Cat. Got it," Janco said.

Ari shot Janco his I-don't-know-why-I-put-up-with-you look and followed Big Brute. Giving Ari a few minutes to catch up to Big B, Janco showed considerable sense by waiting a handful of months.

Janco slipped off his boots, tied the laces together and swung them over his shoulder. Not bothering with the door, he scaled the wall, finding finger- and toeholds in the crumbling mortar of the old brick structure—his favorite type. His least favorite—the marble walls of the Sitian Citadel; those buildings were slick as ice.

When he reached the second-story window, he peered inside. The sunlight reflected off the glass and made it hard to see beyond the sill. Clinging to the bricks with one hand, Janco shielded his eyes until they adjusted to the dimness. The room had a few pieces of office furniture, but was otherwise empty.

After a few minutes, he pushed on the window, testing it. The pane slid up without trouble. Rookie mistake, thinking you were safe on the upper levels of a building. No floor was unreachable. All a thief had to do was climb up or use a rope to climb down.

Janco eased into the room. Puffs of dust tickled his nose and he held in a sneeze. Memories of another sneeze that had revealed his and Ari's hiding spot rose unbidden. He'd never seen Ari so angry. No, wait. There was that other time… His eyes watered as laughter threatened to bubble up his throat. He sucked in a deep breath and focused on the task at hand.

After a quick scan of the abandoned room, he put his boots back on, then grasped the door's knob and slowly twisted. The metal creaked. He paused and listened. Nothing. When the latch cleared the jam, he pulled the door open an inch. Beyond the room was a walkway with a half wall on the opposite side, and past that, thick chains hung from pulleys attached to the ceiling.

No voices echoed or footsteps neared, so he poked his head out and glanced to the left. A few more doors led out to the walkway before it ended. To the right, two more offices and then metal stairs. Lantern light from below flickered on the walls. He ventured onto the walkway and peered over the half wall. Stacks of crates lined the space downstairs. A few had been opened and their contents filled tables along the back wall. As he waited, no one appeared. All remained quiet.

Janco then checked the rooms to the left. All had a thick coat of dust and matched the room he'd entered. The same with the first of the two on the right. However, the door to the office closest to the stairs was locked. Kneeling next to it, he pulled his diamond pick and tension wrench from his pocket and popped the lock in seconds.

He slipped inside and closed the door. The dirty window let in enough sunlight to illuminate the desk, chairs, filing cabinet and liquor cabinet. No dust scratched his throat and

MARIA V. SNYDER

an area rug covered the floor. Nice. Invoices, inventory lists and billing receipts littered the desk. Janco scanned them, but nothing illegal was on the list of goods. No surprise.

Checking the drawers and then the filing cabinet, Janco didn't find anything incriminating. Too bad. He searched for a safe. None in this room. Janco read the labels on the whiskey bottles in the cabinet. Expensive. The man had good taste. He left the office, relocked the door and paused. No sounds from below.

Janco crept down the metal stairs. They creaked with his weight. He then explored the warehouse. Crates stacked three high didn't have any writing or labels on them. The big loading doors had been bolted shut. Wagon-wheel marks on the floor indicated where the four-foot-tall crates must be loaded and unloaded onto wagons by using those chains and pulleys. He found the back door with the shiny new lock. Other than that, nothing appeared out of the ordinary.

Time to check the merchandise. Peering into one of the opened crates, Janco saw bolts of Sitian silk. Another crate held small burlap bags filled with coffee beans. The boxes on the table, however, held a dozen Greenblade cigars. Made from dried honey-tree sap, kellpi weeds and crushed abacca leaves all grown in the Greenblade forest, the cigars caused quite a buzz and seemed to be very addictive. The Commander had banned them as soon as it became obvious they weren't your ordinary cigar.

Janco searched the other open crates, but he couldn't find any more cigars. Perhaps there were more in one of the unopened crates. He stared at a stack and again absently scratched at the place where the bottom half of his right ear used to be. Why fill a crate and risk it being opened and discovered by the border guards? Unless...

He returned to the one with bags of coffee and dug down until he reached the bottom. Nothing. Unless…

Measuring with his arm, he estimated how deep it was inside the crate. Then he straightened and compared it to the height of the box. Bingo! False bottom. Small enough to miss and big enough to fit those boxes of Avibian cigars. Janco suppressed the desire to dance a jig. He'd wait until he hooked up with Ari at the Black Cat.

A metallic snap cut through Janco's elation. Oh no. He dived behind a stack of crates as the back door opened. Strident voices quarreled. Janco counted. Two, three, four, five in all. Maybe they'd be so engrossed in their argument they wouldn't notice him sneaking out. Or maybe they'd all go up to the office and shut the door. And maybe Valek'd assign him to spend a season tanning on the beach. That would be just as likely as the other two.

Janco slid into a more comfortable position. He might be here awhile.

"…it doesn't matter whose fault it is," one voice yelled over the others. "Spread out and find him. He has to be here somewhere."

Then again, he might not.

8

YELENA

"I smell like death?" I asked Leif, trying to keep my panic from my voice. "Whose death? Mine? Yours?"

He tapped his chest and crinkled his nose. "No one's. I just…" Leif waved his arms as if trying to pull in the right word. "It's similar to death. It's a…loss. Something is missing. And there's strong grief, as if someone close to you has died."

Oh. That explained it.

"Are you going to tell me what's going on?" he asked.

Guess he hadn't talked to Mara yet. I glanced around at the training yard. A few students still lingered and a couple kept practicing. Some magicians had the ability to listen from a distance.

"Don't worry. It's not that dire. I'll tell you when I tell Fisk," I said.

"Fisk?"

"Yes, I need both of your help and it'd be easier if I only have to explain everything once. Do you have time now?"

Leif looked at the glass workshop with a wistful expression. "Mara knows."

He turned to me in surprise. "She does?"

"Yes."

"Thanks."

Not the reaction I'd expected. I'd figured he'd be put out because I told Mara first.

"I'm not that childish," he said, correctly reading my look. I waited.

"At least not this time. I'm glad you confided in Mara. She always feels left out. She doesn't ever say it aloud or complain, but I can smell the disappointment."

"Must be tough."

"It is, but I've a duty to Sitia, and discretion is a big part of it. You should know all about that. I'm sure you can't tell Valek everything. Right?"

"If I said no, would you have me arrested for treason?"

"No."

"Nice to know you trust me."

He pished. "Trust has nothing to do with it. It'd upset Mara and that would upset Mara's mother and then I'd be cut off from the best food in Sitia."

"Ah, food trumps treason."

Leif laughed. "Every time." Then he sobered. "I need to tell Mara where I'm going and to take a quick bath. How about I meet you at the gate in fifteen minutes?"

I sniffed and crinkled my nose. "Make it thirty."

"Ha-ha," he deadpanned before heading toward the bath-house.

I grabbed my cloak. Since I had the time, I stopped by Irys's office on my way to the gate. She called me in before I could knock. Her office was similar in size to Bain's, but much neater and not as many books.

A red-tailed hawk sat on a perch by the window. He squawked at me in greeting.

"Hello, Odwin. Who's the handsome fellow?"

The hawk flexed his wings, showing off.

MARIA V. SNYDER

"That's right, you are." I stroked his head.

"Don't encourage him. His ego is big enough," Irys said.

"Any news?" I asked.

Irys pushed a strand of black hair from her eyes and leaned back in her chair. "I reviewed the logbooks for the past two weeks, and Quinn hasn't left the Keep. I also talked to him between classes. He said he can't draw magic into the glass. Opal tried to teach him to use the empty glass orbs like she did when siphoning magic, but he couldn't. So far, all he's able to do is make his magic stick to the glass."

"Are you sure he was telling the truth? Maybe Leif—"

"I think I can spot a lie by now, Yelena."

"Sorry." More good/bad news.

"I'm glad he's not involved. And you should be, too. Quinn's a valuable asset."

"I know. I'm being…overly emotional." I huffed. "Do you know at one time I wished I didn't have *any* magic?"

"I'm sure you did. I did, too. We all have. Ask any magician and she will be able to tell you exactly when she wished to be ordinary."

Ordinary. Could I get used to the idea of being ordinary?

"Oh no. Cut that out," Irys admonished. "*You* will never be ordinary. Don't worry, Yelena. We'll find out what happened to you."

"The market closes for supper time. Fisk will probably be at his guild's headquarters," Leif said when he joined me at the gate.

"Is he still at—"

"No. He found a more secure location." Leif glanced around and then lowered his voice. "It's in one of the outer southern rings."

We headed west from the Keep's entrance.

"Let's take the scenic route," Leif suggested.

Ah. Leif wanted to ensure no one followed us.

As we entered the central business district, Leif cut through a couple of alleys and zigzagged through the streets. The sunlight disappeared behind the Citadel's walls and the lamplighters began their nightly ritual.

"Is Fisk still having trouble with that rival gang?" I asked.

"Yes. They're bold and have been trying to put him out of business. Fisk keeps telling me he's taking care of it, but I've heard many shoppers grumbling at the market stalls. Those interlopers cheat, steal and bribe merchants to give them better prices than they give Fisk's members."

A few people hurried past us. Probably heading home for supper. The majority of the Citadel's citizens lived in the northwest and southwest quadrants. However, a number of warehouses had been converted into apartments, which the Keep and government workers had snapped up along with a few business owners who wished to be close to their factories.

"What a shame. That rival gang could have joined his guild and all worked together." Why couldn't they just leave Fisk alone and let his guild operate in peace? Was it jealousy? Greed? Spite? Hate? Probably a combination of all of them.

"I think Fisk is in over his head on this one. Maybe I could ask my brother-in-law for a little favor."

"How can Mara's brother, Ahir, help?" I asked.

"Not Ahir—Valek."

"Valek isn't your brother-in-law."

"Why not? You've been together for… What? Eight million years. And he's, like…eighty by now."

I punched him in the arm.

"Ow!" He rubbed his biceps. "Oh, I see. He hasn't asked you. No wonder you're sensitive."

"Leif," I warned.

He ignored it. "Yes?"

I pressed my fists to my legs. "We've been busy."

"Doing what?"

"Rescuing a kidnapped brother, for one." I gave him a pointed look.

"Uh-huh. Too busy to get married. That's a new one. Does that mean he asked—"

"Drop it."

"Wish I could," he muttered.

And then I understood. "Who put you up to this? Mother?"

He ducked his head. "She just wants you to be happy."

"And why in the world would she think I'd be happier if I was married? If anything, it would make it *harder* to be apart from Valek."

"Maybe she sees how happy I am and wishes the same for you."

Oh.

"And I've been picking up quite a range of emotions from you, sister dear. You're never this easy to read." He turned to me as if he'd just figured it out.

"Wait," I said. "We'll discuss it with Fisk."

By the time Leif was satisfied no one had followed us, we had looped around to the south side of the market. Glancing over his shoulder, he slipped into a narrow alley. I stayed close to him and kept my hand near the hilt of my switchblade. The alley dead-ended.

"Are you lost?" I joked.

Instead of a sarcastic retort, he gaped at me, horrified. Without thought, I yanked my weapon and triggered the blade, turning.

"No one is there, Yelena," Leif said in a tight voice. "You just confirmed what I thought was impossible."

I faced him. He had discovered I no longer had magic. It

hadn't taken him long. Once again, Irys's advice about lying low rose in my mind. Smart woman. Perhaps I should listen to her.

Leif pointed to the side wall. "It's an illusion." He stepped right through the bricks.

Holding my hands out, I followed him. No tingle swept my arms as I entered a dark alcove. Leif rapped a series of knocks on the door and waited. A beam of light shone through a small peephole.

"Kinda late for a visit," a voice said.

"It's never too late to lend a helping hand," Leif said.

The door swung wide, allowing us in.

Momentarily blinded, I stumbled over the threshold.

Fingers grasped my elbow, steadying me.

"Lovely Yelena, always a pleasure to see you," Fisk said, releasing his grip.

My vision adjusted to the brightness. We stood in a foyer. Rooms branched out on three sides. Straight ahead, a fire burned in a small hearth. The enticing aroma of beef filled the air. Leif's stomach grumbled.

I gazed up at Fisk. No longer a boy, he towered over me by a good eight inches. His light brown eyes matched the color of his shaggy hair. Clean-shaven and muscular, he'd filled out quite a bit since I'd seen him last. Except for the impish intelligence in his gaze, he was a far cry from the malnourished, filthy street rat he'd been when we first met.

"Hello, Fisk. How's business?" I asked.

"Never better."

"Are you sure?" I gestured around. "You've moved again."

"That I did. However, we plan to stay here for quite some time. Let me give you a tour."

The room to the right opened up into a large area crowded with bunk beds. Members of the Helper's Guild either sat or stretched out on the mattresses. Others huddled together, playing a game of dice, and some gathered in groups, talking and laughing. They all called a hello to me and Leif.

To the left of the foyer was a classroom.

"We still have weekly meetings and are always training new recruits." He pointed down a hallway on the other side. "There are a few more training rooms down there. Unfortunately, we had to teach everyone self-defense, and a couple of the older members are learning how to fight with swords and knives."

"That bad?" Leif asked.

"It's getting worse."

"We can—"

"No, thank you. I'm handling it. Once I find their leader, there won't be a problem." The steel in his voice ended that discussion.

I peeked down the hallway. "I'm guessing there are classes in information gathering, as well."

Fisk grinned. "Information can be a profitable business. In fact, I'm pretty sure that's why you're here."

Leif's stomach grumbled again.

Fisk laughed. "That and for a bowl of Amberle's beef stew."

My brother perked up. "If you insist…"

The kitchen and dining area filled the room opposite the foyer. Long wooden tables stretched in rows to the left.

"Wow, these rooms are bigger than you think. How much space do you have?" Leif ladled out a big helping of stew.

"My guild occupies the entire ground floor of this facility."

"Nice. Let's hope the owner lets you stay for a while."

"Oh, he will."

A gleam in Fisk's eyes gave him away.

"You own this building," I said.

"Yup. I'm converting the three upper levels into apartments."

"Wow, a landlord at… How old are you?" Leif asked between bites of stew.

"Seventeen."

Leif spat out a mouthful of beef. After sputtering and coughing, he gasped, "I…need a new job. Are you…hiring?"

"Always. Yelena, are you hungry?" Fisk filled a bowl.

"No, thank you. You were right about needing information. Is there someplace private we can talk?"

"Of course."

Carrying his dinner, Fisk led us through the classroom and down the hallway to the very end. He unlocked a door and ushered us into a large living space. The ceiling spanned two stories over half the room. It appeared a loft had been built over the other half. While a couch, armchairs and tables occupied the center, Fisk had converted the space below the loft into an office.

Fisk sat in one of the nubby red armchairs and cradled the stew in his lap. Leif flopped into the opposite chair without waiting for an invitation and I settled on the couch. A glass sculpture of two life-size hands spread out like wings with their thumbs together rested on the table between the armchairs.

"Is that one of Opal's statues?" I asked Fisk.

"Yes. Lovely, isn't it?"

I gazed at Fisk. Was it one of her magic detectors? The Councilors each owned one but, so far, the distribution of the detectors was limited. "Yes. It matches the design of the necklaces your members wear."

Leif grunted in amusement. He stared at the sculpture with a crinkled brow. Inside the clear glass a spark of light flashed in response to Leif's magic. "Handy."

"Yes, it is. And, yes, Opal gave it to me." Fisk smiled. "You've been hanging out with politicians too long, Yelena. No need to dance around a subject. I'll tell you the truth."

"Sorry. Some habits are hard to break." I gestured to the detector. "Are they available on the black market?"

"No. But fakes are showing up, which means the real thing is probably not far behind."

"Will you let me know when that happens?" Leif asked.

"Of course. Is that why you're here?"

"No." I traced the black-and-white diamond pattern of the couch's fabric with my finger. How to start?

"Then how can I help?" Fisk asked.

Might as well just jump right in. "Have you heard of a drug or poison that blocks a person's magic?"

Leif's spoon froze halfway to his mouth, but he kept quiet. Very un-Leif-like.

"You mean something like Curare?" Fisk asked.

"Yes, but without the paralyzing effect."

He rubbed a hand along his chin. "I haven't heard of anything, and considering it would be an effective weapon against magicians, I doubt the criminal element could keep it quiet for long." Fisk met my gaze. "Are you guessing about its existence or do you have evidence?"

Now who was acting like a politician? "I'm speculating." I explained about the attack.

Leif cursed. "It's worse than I'd thought. Are you all right?"

I gave him a flat look.

"Oh, right. Dumb question. Have you—"

Interrupting him, I filled them in on our efforts to discover the cause of my affliction. "…and we were hoping you might have information," I said to Fisk.

"Sorry, but this is the first I've heard about it." He set his half-full bowl aside. Fisk had stopped eating during my story. "I can make a few discreet inquiries."

"That would be great. What about the assassin? Do you know anyone who has those abilities?"

"Not operating out of the Citadel."

He had answered so fast I asked him if he was sure.

"Unfortunately. Assassins make a point to let my guild members know they are available for hire just in case we get a request. Not that we'd ever help a client hire an assassin, but we keep track just in case."

"Are you still expanding to other cities?" I asked.

He frowned. "No. That's on hold until I settle things here."

"I can help—" Leif tried.

"No." Fisk sighed at Leif's hurt puppy-dog look. "Thanks, Leif, but you're too well-known in the Citadel. I've a couple members on the inside and it's just a matter of time."

"You'll let us know if you need anything?" Leif asked.

"Of course."

Leif turned to me. "You should have told me sooner."

"I just arrived today."

He waved away my excuse. "You're vulnerable and unprotected."

I drew a breath, but clamped my mouth shut before Leif reminded me about our sparring match.

"I can weave a null shield into your cloak, but that's a temporary measure. I'll get you something that will work better."

"Than a null shield?"

Leif glanced at Fisk. "It's similar," he hedged.

Fisk grinned. "The new glass magician can probably make you a glass pendant to wear that will kept a null shield around you at all times."

Red splotches spread over Leif's cheeks. "How did you…? Oh, never mind. At least you didn't hear it from me. Right?"

MARIA V. SNYDER

"Right. You're a vault."

I suppressed a smile over Fisk's word choice. "Then who did you hear it from?"

"Ah, Lovely Yelena, I can't give away my sources. Otherwise no one would trust me."

A light tapping sounded. Fisk excused himself and answered the door. "I'll be right back," he called as he slipped out.

Leif stood. "Give me your cloak."

I shrugged it off and handed it to him. He spread it out on the floor. Kneeling next to the cloak, he stroked the fabric with the tips of his fingers, going from the top of the hood down to the hem, then repeating. The glass hands sculpture flashed and flickered as if agitated. Leif turned the cloak over and continued, touching every inch. A sheen of sweat covered his forehead. He sat back on his heels when he finished, pulling off his short cape. Lines of strain etched his face and sweat stains peppered his shirt.

Scanning the room, I spotted a pitcher of water and poured Leif a drink. He downed the cool liquid in a couple of gulps. When his strength returned, he lumbered to his feet, bringing my cloak with him.

Leif tossed it at me. "Use it for a blanket until I talk to Quinn. You also need a bodyguard. Perhaps Irys can assign—"

"No bodyguard."

He set his square jaw and crossed his arms—did they teach this to all the boys at a certain age?

"You're getting a bodyguard. If not one of the Keep's guards, then who do you suggest?" His posture dared me to argue.

Since he was so determined… "How about you?"

I'd surprised him, but he recovered within a heartbeat. "I can't because I'm going to track down the assassin."

"Leif—"

"Don't 'Leif' me. I have law-enforcement contacts all through-out Sitia. One of them has to have heard about this assassin."

"And you're going to travel to every major city in Sitia?"

"If that's what it takes."

So sweet and impractical. "It'll take seasons, Leif. Seasons away from Mara."

His shoulders drooped a bit.

"Perhaps we should wait until we have an idea of which direction to look. Valek promised to check his sources and send me any information on the assassin he finds."

Leif relaxed his arms.

"And in the meantime, you could be my bodyguard. Plus it wouldn't look strange for us to be together so much."

The stubborn line in his jaw disappeared. I kept my expression neutral. If I gloated, he'd insist on assigning me a big bruiser as a bodyguard.

Fisk returned. Concern creased his face. "I think I know who hired the assassin to attack you, Yelena."

But that was good news. Why did he look so grim?

"Spit it out, Fisk," Leif said.

"Ben Moon escaped from Wirral Prison."

Oh no. I sat on the edge of the couch. "How long ago?"

"Eleven days."

Not long enough to stage the attack.

"The authorities believe he had help," Fisk said as if reading my mind.

Leif and I exchanged a glance. We'd had dealings with Ben before. Not only was Ben a powerful magician, but he had inherited notes on magic from his great-great-grandfather, who had been Master Magician Ellis Moon. Perhaps somewhere in those notes was mention of a substance that blocked magic.

"We should inform the Council," I said.

Fisk's expression darkened. "They already know."

"That's good, right?" Leif asked.

A coldness settled over me. "How long have they known?"

"A few days after he escaped."

Ice crackled through my heart. The Council knew before I left to meet with Valek and they didn't bother to warn me.

9

VALEK

Valek's gaze jumped from Onora to the Commander. Ambrose appeared to be relaxed, unlike his guards who stood behind him with puffed-out chests and stiff backs. They glared at the assassin.

She ignored them as she picked at her food. Onora still wore the dungeon jumpsuit. She'd braided her long brown hair, and her feet were bare. Rough calluses covered her toes and scuff marks scratched her toenails.

"Join us," the Commander said to Valek.

Onora glanced at him as he sat to the Commander's right, but she didn't smirk or gloat. His reaction to her presence flipped between impressed and worried. Had the Commander invited her? Or had she escaped and managed to reach the Commander without encountering anyone?

"Relax, Valek. I stopped your agent...Qamra, is it?...before she could shoot Onora with a dart. I figured since Onora made it that far, she deserved breakfast."

"I was on my way to see you," Onora said to Valek. "Unless what you'd told me last night was bullshit?"

The Commander sipped his tea. His eyebrows rose a fraction, inviting Valek to explain.

"Seems this young pup is after my job. I told her if she demonstrates her abilities, shows cunning, resourcefulness, intelligence, and if she proves she is loyal, trustworthy and willing to die for you, then she could have it."

"And why did you tell her that?" the Commander asked.

"She has plenty of raw talent. Another year of training and she would have beaten me last night. But as I said, there's more to my job than winning a fight."

Again, Onora showed remarkable restraint in keeping her emotions under control. If Valek had told Janco he could have won a fight against him, Janco would have jumped on the table and danced a jig.

"Are you thinking about retiring, Valek?"

Was he? He'd been in this business for years. The thought of not having to worry… A nice thought. Of being with Yelena all the time… A wonderful thought. But he wasn't quite ready. "Not for a while. However, if someone comes along and shows he or she can take my job, I'd be content to let that person have it."

"Trust is the biggest issue right now," the Commander said, gazing at the young woman. "Why didn't you join the military and work your way up through the ranks?"

"Valek didn't have to go through all that. Why should I?"

"You've no idea what Valek did to prove himself," the Commander snapped. "A protocol has been put into place since I've been in charge. I see no reason for you to bypass it."

A brief flash of fear rippled her calm. Valek remembered a comment she'd made last night about escaping MD-2. "Captain Timmer," he said.

Onora jerked as if he'd stabbed her with a knife. Her reaction seemed familiar. It reminded him of how Yelena flinched every time she'd heard Reyad's name. The bastard had raped her and Yelena'd killed him. Saved Valek the trouble of hacking the man into tiny pieces and feeding him to a pack of snow cats.

"Tell me," he said.

"No. I'll join the local unit."

"And challenge me again after the first few training sessions? I think not. Plus it wouldn't earn you any trust."

"What can I do to earn your trust?" she asked.

Valek exchanged a look with the Commander. "A series of tests?"

"Do you think she's worth the effort?" the Commander asked.

He studied the young woman. She had been the first to sneak into the Commander's apartment, and she knew how to fight. Plenty of potential. Better to keep her close than risk her making another attempt. Perhaps she'd become a valuable member of their team. Stranger things had happened.

"Yes."

Ambrose dabbed his mouth with a napkin and stood. "I'll leave it to you, then, Valek." He left the war room.

"Tests?" Onora twirled a spoon in her left hand, spinning it through her fingers.

"Yes. You're now an official member of my corps. However, if I find out you haven't been honest about why you are here, you won't be locked in the dungeon. You'll be buried underneath it."

"An empty threat. You said so yourself—it's just a matter of time and I'll beat you."

"True. But if you double-cross us, you won't be fighting just me, but the Commander and a couple of my loyal people. You're good, but not good enough to go against four of us."

"Not yet."

Valek smiled. As Janco would say, gotta love the attitude. "And trust goes both ways, Onora. Something happened to

MARIA V. SNYDER

you up in MD-2. Something traumatic enough to send you to Hedda. I need to know that and how long ago you started your training. How did you convince Hedda to train you? It's all part of what needs to be discussed."

She stilled. "That's none of your business. I'm here to prove what I can do. My past is not relevant."

"Your past is what guided you here. It is your motivation, and I need to know everything."

Onora sprang to her feet. "Why don't you just prick me with that…poison and make me spill my guts?"

"It's called goo-goo juice and it's very effective. Last night you were a criminal. Today you are a new team member. Hard to establish a mutual trust using goo-goo juice."

She stared at him. "And if I don't satisfy your curiosity, you'll use it anyway."

"If this was about mere curiosity, you wouldn't be given this chance."

Lacing her fingers together, she pressed her arms tight to her body. "I'd bet you didn't have to explain everything to the Commander."

"The Commander knows me better than my heart mate. And if I were you, I wouldn't trust rumor and speculation. I didn't beat the Commander in our first fight. He won and could have easily killed me. He still can. With his knife or with an order. That isn't the reason I'm his second-in-command."

"What's the reason?"

"Pay attention and you'll find out. Come on." He strode to the door.

"Where are we going?"

He nodded at her jumpsuit. "To get you a uniform. Nice touch, by the way, hiding lock picks under your toenails." Valek mentally added *check toenails and fingernails* to his growing list of new procedures for the castle's guards.

She covered her surprise. "Thanks."

Valek guided Onora to the seamstress's quarters. Long wooden tables strained under the weight of piles of clothing. Dilana sat in her favorite spot by the window, hemming a pair of pants.

And just like she had done with Yelena, Dilana took the girl in hand and fitted her with the standard plain black pants, shirt and boots the members of his corps wore. After Onora had a stack of clothing, Valek showed her to an empty room in the wing used by his corps.

"Bedding is in the supply closet at the end of the hall," he said. "Meals are served in the dining room. Report to my office right after supper for your first assignment. If you don't know the way—"

"I know the way."

Valek ignored her little dig. "Good."

"What about my weapons?"

"They'll be returned to you tonight."

"And if I take off and disappear?"

"Then you will be considered a criminal again. But I'm thinking you're not the type to run. And besides, what else is out there? Since the Commander's been in power, there hasn't been much work for an assassin, and the few who have survived the takeover have moved to Sitia."

Then it hit him. Perhaps the man who attacked Yelena was an Ixian assassin. Before the takeover, magic was allowed in Ixia. Valek might have the name of her attacker listed in one of his files.

He left Onora and headed straight to his office. The haphazard stacks of files on his desk and the towers of dossiers on the conference table plus the general disarray might give a visitor the impression that he was disorganized. Not so. The mess had been arranged with care and, within the piles, Valek had implemented a system that would help him find the in-

MARIA V. SNYDER

formation he needed without having to search his entire office or suite.

After flipping through a heap of reports under the conference table, Valek located the dossier on known assassins. He settled behind his desk and read. Many of the names were familiar. During his years at Hedda's school, he'd met a few others who'd graduated.

When he'd first started his training, he'd known only Arbon. The boy had shown Valek around the complex and had answered his questions. Arbon had arrived at Hedda's a season before Valek and had been working on hitting the target with a bow and arrow, which came after perfecting your aim with a knife. They'd spent hundreds of hours inside the training building together and a friendly rivalry began.

"The knife is supposed to stick in the wood, not bounce off the target," Arbon said to him during one of their daylong sessions. "Can't kill the King let alone a bunny with that weak throw."

Valek ignored the jab and considered Arbon's comment. His throw had lacked power. He needed to strengthen his muscles. That night, Valek found the weight room. The air reeked of sweat and body odor. A few others worked out in the dim lantern light. He didn't know if the four men and two women were students or instructors and they didn't bother to introduce themselves. They mostly ignored him when he headed toward the barbells.

But there was always one big mouth. "Hey, skinny arms, do you want me to call my mother to help spot you?" he asked as the others laughed.

Valek stared at the man. Taller, heavier and with thick muscles, the bruiser would pound Valek into pulp. He kept his sarcastic retort about the man's mother to himself. But someday, he wouldn't worry about whom he'd pissed off. As he lifted the heavy weights, he focused on that future time.

The teasing stopped after Big Mouth realized Valek wouldn't react to his digs and when Valek continued to lift the heavy weights every night despite his sore and aching muscles.

"Gotta respect the dedication," the big bruiser said.

Arbon scoffed at Valek's efforts. "You'll burn out by the end of the warm season."

Curious, Valek asked, "What happens if someone doesn't complete the training?"

"Why? You thinking of quitting?"

"No. Just wanted to know where to send you my condolences."

Arbon's laughter boomed with a deep explosive sound. "Well, then, you roll up your note of sympathy, stick it into a bottle, seal it and toss it over the cliff. When you hear the splash, consider the message delivered."

Harsh. But that explained why information about the school had been hard to find. Those who failed became fish food. And those who succeeded kept the location of their home base a secret. In fact, most of the students kept a low profile and didn't make friends. Valek had no idea how many students trained here, or the number of instructors or graduates, for that matter. The lack of information intrigued more than frustrated him.

Valek's aim with the knife improved faster than with the stone. Arbon claimed Valek would never catch up to him despite the fact Arbon couldn't finish the requirements with a dart. It just added more incentive for Valek. After working with the weights, he grabbed a lantern and returned to put in a few extra hours of target practice. A couple of weeks later, he started dimming the light a little more each night. It made sense to him. Assassins worked mostly at night. It'd be rare that he'd be aiming at a victim in the bright sunlight.

By the time Valek caught up to Arbon—both working with throwing darts—Valek was sleeping only four hours a day. No one had set a schedule for him, so he slept during the afternoons. Also there were no lessons in fighting or how to be an assassin. On occasion an instructor would arrive to test his aim, but otherwise no one bothered them.

"This is impossible," Arbon said. He stood about thirty feet from the target, but his dart didn't reach.

Valek's efforts to strengthen his muscles showed as he had struck the bull's-eye at thirty feet, but at forty feet the light-weight dart nose-dived five feet short of the target.

"Is this the last weapon?" he asked Arbon.

"I think so. We've done stones, knives, arrows, crossbow bolts and now darts. What's left?"

"Chains, whips, nunchucks."

"You practice with those on a dummy. I've seen the practice area. It's in the building along the edge of the cliff."

Valek hadn't spent too much time exploring the complex. He considered it a waste of time and energy. He'd been given a task and would accomplish it so he could move on.

After Arbon gave up for the evening, Valek continued to throw the darts. No amount of force made any difference. He mulled over the problem. Perhaps there was another way. Valek picked up a crossbow and tried using a dart instead of a bolt.

The force of the string destroyed the dart before it could launch. Valek laughed for the first time since his brothers' murders, and the burning pain that had seized his heart for the past year died down for a brief moment. He returned the weapons to the wall and left the training building, which Valek suspected was only used for the new students to see if the boredom and repetition would drive them away.

A warm breeze blew from the east for a change, carrying the dry scents of pine and earth. Even though it was the heating season, the chilly damp air from the Sunset Ocean kept the temperatures low.

He strode to his favorite spot along the cliff, where large gray boulders jutted over the ocean far below. From this height, the crashing water sounded muted and mild. The white tips of the waves glinted in the bright moonlight.

Smaller gray rocks covered the ground between the path and the outcrop. As Valek crossed them, he concentrated on keeping his weight evenly distributed so the stones wouldn't crunch under his boots. Success was spotty, but tonight he managed only a few cracks.

Grabbing a handful of the rocks, he settled on the edge. His feet dangled and he tossed a bunch of the stones out into the darkness. After a couple of heartbeats, a distant plunk sounded. He absently rubbed two of the rocks together as he pondered the problem with the darts. Nothing sparked. Not even from the heat generated between the stones. However, the action had scraped away the dull gray and revealed a darker color underneath.

Valek pocketed the two rocks and headed back to the target room. On the way, the wind rustled the long green stalks of bamboo that lined the complex's paths. A hollow wooden ring mixed with the shushing of the leaves. He stopped and cursed his stupidity.

After fetching a knife and a lantern from the training building, Valek cut a piece of bamboo from the plant and brought it to his room. Hedda had called it a cell, and if it'd had bars, he'd agree with her. The tiny space held a cot, a table, a chair. It had no windows, a dirt floor and no place to build a fire. By sleeping in the afternoon, Valek stayed warm, but he wondered what he would do in the cold season. Arbon stayed in a

MARIA V. SNYDER

cell two doors down. The other three rooms in the one-story structure that resembled a long shed instead of a building were empty. Again Valek thought isolating the new students had been done for a reason.

He worked on his piece of bamboo until the sides were smooth and straight, and the inside was completely hollow. Sap coated his fingers and the blade of the knife, but he was careful to keep the sticky substance from getting into the center of the bamboo.

Once he was satisfied with it, he returned to the target room to test out his new blowpipe. Starting at the first red mark, he loaded the bamboo with a dart, aimed, then blew out a quick puff of air. He smiled. Much better.

When Arbon arrived after dawn, Valek hid his blowpipe. The boy had once again shaved his hair close to his scalp. White skin shone through the black stubble and looked odd on top of his round face.

"Did you get any further last night?" Arbon asked.

"To sixty feet," Valek said.

"Liar."

"How about a bet?"

"All right. What's the bet?"

They both owned nothing of value. "How about if I hit the target with the dart, you owe me a future favor, and I'll owe you one if I don't?"

Arbon agreed.

Valek stepped up to the sixty-foot mark, whipped out his blowpipe and hit the bull's-eye.

"That's cheating!" Arbon cried.

"No, it isn't. I never specified how I'd accomplish it."

"But—"

"But what, Arbon?" Hedda asked. Clothed in black, she stepped from the dark corner of the room.

Valek wondered if she'd been there all night. Did she often hide there? His heart rate increased.

"The task was to…" He stuttered to a stop as Hedda moved closer to him.

"To what?" she asked.

"To hit the target, sir."

"Exactly. Did anyone tell you *not* to improvise?"

"No. No one told us anything!"

"Are you not satisfied with the training?" A cold flatness settled on her narrow face.

"I'm…I'm…fine."

"I see." She turned to Valek. "So, King Killer, you're still here."

"Yes, sir."

"Let's see what you can do from the last mark."

He grabbed the weapons and demonstrated his skills, hitting the bull's-eye with the stone, knife, arrow, bolt, but not the dart. He didn't have enough air to send the dart that far.

"How would you make it go further?" she asked.

He sensed it wasn't an idle question, so he considered the problem carefully. More air would work, but his lungs only held so much and he doubted he could generate more force. A longer pipe would help improve aim, but again the amount of air remained the same. Then he remembered how his father rigged the water pipes coming into the tannery so the water pressure increased as the diameter of the pipe decreased.

"A longer blowpipe with a smaller exit hole," he said.

"Arbon, does that sound right to you?"

"Uh…I'm not sure, sir."

"Sounds like you need to do some experimentation. See if you can make his suggestion work in hitting the target from a hundred feet."

"Yes, sir."

"Valek, come with me." Hedda strode from the room.

Valek followed, staying a step behind.

"You passed the first test. Let's see how you do with the second." She led him to the main building and up to the first floor, which was a wide-open area filled with mats and people sparring with and without weapons.

Excitement built deep inside him, but he was careful not to let it show on his face.

"You'll start with self-defense techniques and basic moves. When you have mastered them, you will learn how to use a weapon. Tamequintin will be your instructor. If Tamequintin isn't happy, I'm not happy. Understand?"

"Yes, sir."

She called a young man over. He appeared to be in his early twenties. Tamequintin's long black hair had been braided into a single rope down his muscular back. He wore a pair of short black pants and nothing else.

Valek noticed his smooth gait. It reminded him of a snow cat about to pounce. Unfortunately, since he'd lived near the northern ice sheet, he'd seen plenty of snow cats.

Hedda introduced them and left.

Tamequintin studied Valek for a moment. "So you're the wannabe King Killer, eh? Hedda must be getting desperate for recruits."

Valek refused to rise to the bait. Instead, he waited.

The man grunted. "Call me T-quin. Everyone does except for Hedda and only because she earned the right." He scanned Valek from head to toe. "Do you know how to fight?"

"No."

T-quin grunted again. "You will, or..." He shrugged. "You won't. And then you'll be shown the exit. Be careful. That first step's a killer."

Valek remembered T-quin's black sense of humor. Of course,

he hadn't appreciated it when T-quin had beaten him over and over for weeks. Too bad Tamequintin had refused to join Valek's corps after the takeover. And when he'd gone after Yelena, Valek had to kill him.

Reading through the dossier of Ixian assassins, Valek found only one potential suspect. And that was his old friend Arbon. And Arbon still owed him that favor.

10

JANCO

Boots pounded on the floor of the warehouse. Janco pressed against the side of the shipping crate, considering his chances of getting away. Five of them to one of him and they knew he hid somewhere inside.

Not liking his odds, Janco scanned the area. Stacks of crates loomed behind him and the two stacks in front of him blocked him from view. But not for long. He glanced at the metal stairs across an open expanse a few yards away. Should he risk it? One of the men raced up the steps to search the offices. He liked the odds way better against one opponent than five.

"Here," a voice called from the right. Stepping around the crate, the man pulled his sword and advanced on Janco.

The stairs it is. He moved left until another man slid between Janco and escape. The new guy called for someone named Stig, and the guy who'd just been on the second floor clattered back down.

"Come on, buddy," Stig said. "You're surrounded. Put down your sword and let's have a chat."

Janco glanced over his shoulder. Big Brute had joined his friend. If Big Brute was here, then where was Ari? When he turned back to Stig, Funky Mustache stood with the others. Lovely. *Come on, Ari. Where are you?*

He tightened his grip for a moment, then sighed. Sheathing his weapon, he palmed a couple of glass balls. Janco leaned against the crate and crossed his arms. "What would you like to chat about?"

"Why you broke into our warehouse," Stig said.

"Oh that?" Janco waved a hand. "Just testing your security, gents. And I must say it sucks."

"Uh-huh. And why are you so interested in our cigars?"

"I like a good smoke from time to time. Just wanted to make sure the merchandise is genuine."

"He's lying," Big Brute said. "He's that Franco sneak from the castle. Kill him now or he'll report us to Valek."

"It's *Janco*, you moron. And Valek already knows all about your operation."

"He's bluffing." Big Brute inched closer. A pair of nasty-looking hatchets hung from his belt.

The smell of ripe meat assaulted Janco's nostrils. Ugh. Big. Annoying. And smelly. *Anytime now, Ari.* Janco shrugged. "Go ahead and think what you like. But if I'm not breathing when Valek shows up, he'll be extremely put out. I'm his favorite sneak."

"Yeah, sure you are." Stig strode toward him. "We'll let the boss decide." He reached for Janco's shoulder.

A loud crashed echoed. The men jumped. *About time.* Janco spiked the two glass balls into the ground. The chemicals inside the balls mixed and formed a thick white fog. Janco scrambled up the stack of crates, keeping above the cloud. He stood on the top and jumped up, grabbing the chains that hung from the ceiling.

Below him voices shouted. Janco swung from chain to chain, heading toward the exit. Ari guarded the broken door with his broadsword in hand. One of the smugglers staggered from the smoke. Before the man could react, Ari stepped in close and knocked the guy out with the hilt of his sword.

When Janco reached another stack of crates, he dropped onto the top, then climbed down, landing within sight of his partner.

"Playtime is over," Ari said.

Big Brute rushed from the thinning fog.

"Awww, can't I stay just a little longer?" Janco pulled his sword with a flourish.

Yanking a hatchet from his wide leather belt, Big Brute aimed for Janco.

Janco jigged to the side as the weapon whizzed by his ear. "A hatchet? Really? You're taking this whole lumberjack thing way too seriously."

He pulled another, but then stumbled forward with a dart in his neck, collapsing onto the ground.

"Hey, no fair," Janco said to Ari. "He was mine."

"Take your pick." Ari nodded in the opposite direction.

Stig, Funky Mustache and the other man emerged from the dissipating fog. White tendrils of smoke clung to their clothes, and fury burned in their expressions.

"Ooh, I'll take Funky Mustache and Stig. You get that other dude." Janco slid his feet into a fighting stance.

Ari sighed. "Here." He handed Janco a couple of darts.

"You're no fun."

"I hurt my shoulder busting the door down."

Which had given Janco the distraction he needed. "All right. We'll do it your way *this time*."

He aimed the darts and hit Stig in the throat and Funky Mustache in the cheek. Janco backpedaled as the two men continued to charge, ducking Stig's swing and countering Funky Mustache's sword thrust. After a few seconds the sleeping juice kicked in. They swayed on their feet, took a few wobbly steps and plopped to the ground.

"What took you so long?" Janco asked Ari.

Ari gave him a sour look. "They were onto us from the very beginning. The big guy lured me away so you would sneak in. Then he picked up some friends and doubled back. I waited to see if you'd give them the slip, but when you didn't climb out the window, I came in."

"Guess I should have worn my cap." He scratched his head. Just thinking about it made his scalp itch. Maybe Dilana could sew him another one with something…nonitchy.

"I don't think that would have helped. What did you find?"

Janco showed him the cigar boxes and the crates' false bottoms. "There's an office upstairs with lots of paperwork. It looked legit, but I'm not an expert."

"Let's report back and send a cleanup crew." Ari pricked the two men he'd knocked unconscious to keep them from reviving before the crew arrived.

Picking up the pieces of the broken door, Ari leaned them against the wall. It had split right down the middle. They searched for supplies to repair it at least temporarily. No sense having the local thieves clean the place out. By the time they'd left the warehouse and headed back to the castle, the sun had set.

One of Ari's comments nagged at Janco. "How did you know they were onto us from the beginning?"

Ari waited until a group of people passed out of earshot. "I think these guys and that warehouse are all part of the ruse. The smugglers want us to uncover this operation to keep us from finding the *real* operation."

"You think they had us marked as soon as we left the castle complex?"

"Yep."

"We need better disguises."

"And better intel. Let's see if Valek's discovered any new info."

Valek called, "Come," when they knocked on his office door.

Candles blazed, revealing Valek sitting cross-legged on the floor with file folders scattered around him.

"Organizing?" Ari asked, sounding doubtful.

Despite what Valek claimed about his filing system, Ari and Janco were not convinced there had been any logic applied to the piles.

"No. I'm searching for replacements." Valek flipped open a folder. "What do you think of Sergeant Hunter?"

"For what?" Janco asked.

"The Commander's new personal guard."

Ah. Time for the comeuppance. "He's a bit stiff, but dependable," Janco said.

"Smart and ambitious," Ari added. "He won't be content to be a sergeant for long."

"Hmm. I'll add him to my 'maybe' pile." Valek placed the folder on the middle of three stacks. Then he stood and wiped the dust off his black pants. "Do you have news for me?" He scooped up the three piles and carried them to his desk.

"Yes, sir," Ari said. He explained about the warehouse and smugglers. "I asked Deet to send a cleanup crew so we can interrogate them later. But overall, they were too easy to find."

"A fake operation?" Valek asked.

"No. They're selling illegal goods, but it's mostly minor stuff. We can see what the smugglers say, but I'm thinking we need an undercover operative that's not recognizable."

Janco pished. "A good disguise—"

"Won't be enough," Ari said. "They know us too well."

"As in, there's a mole in our operations?" Valek asked.

"That's always a possibility, but this seems more like they've been watching us and keeping track of our whereabouts. Like we do with the minor criminals that we don't arrest, but use to find the more dangerous ones."

"That matches what I've been thinking." Valek drummed his fingers on his desk. "And I may have the perfect operative to work with you. She's a complete unknown. That is, if she shows up."

Janco didn't like the sound of that. Not at all. "Who?"

Instead of answering, Valek picked up one of the files. "What do you think of Private Krist for the Commander's guard?"

Ari and Janco exchanged a glance. Valek would tell them whom he had in mind when he was ready. They discussed personnel and who had the best skills to protect the Commander until a light tapping on the door interrupted them.

Valek tensed before he invited the knocker into his office. Janco's fingers caressed the hilt of his favorite dagger as he turned to see who entered. A young girl approached. Seventeen—maybe eighteen. Her graceful strides seemed familiar. Her gaze flicked between him and Ari, sizing them up. Pretty with light gray eyes. However, no warmth emanated from them. When she neared, Janco changed his estimate of her age to twenty.

"This is Onora. She's going to be working with you," Valek said. "This is Ari and Janco, my—"

"*Current* seconds-in-command," she said.

The challenge in her voice pricked the hair on the back of Janco's neck. "Are we that desperate for recruits we need to hire children?"

She glared but didn't rise to the taunt. Too bad.

"Is she the one?" Ari asked Valek.

"Yes. And she's going to be working with you to find the brains running the smuggling operation."

"Seriously? What's she gonna find? A lollipop and Binky?" Janco laughed at his own joke.

Without warning, Onora palmed a knife and pressed it to Janco's throat in one quick motion.

His smile widened. "Ooh, I like her."

11

YELENA

Anger boiled up my throat as Leif cursed the Sitian Council.

He prowled around the couch and chairs in Fisk's sitting room. "Why wouldn't they warn you about Ben's escape? Are they insane?"

"Perhaps they believed he wouldn't have time to set up an ambush for Yelena," Fisk said. "He's running from the authorities. Even with help, their focus would have been on escaping and not revenge."

"And they promised Valek that Ben would be incarcerated for life in a special wing of Wirral built to block a magician's power," I said. "If they'd told me, I might have informed Valek."

"That's stupid," Leif said. "Why risk Yelena's life? She's valuable."

"Perhaps they thought in the unlikely event she is attacked, she is more than capable of protecting herself," Fisk said. "Plus you were with Valek, right?"

My fury eased a fraction. "Yes, but it happened before I'd reached him. And they wouldn't have known the assassin has this new…poison."

"Are you sure about that?" Leif asked. "They're already keeping secrets and that would be a giant secret. Think about it."

Fisk agreed. "The Council is afraid of magicians. They have been since Devlen switched Councilor Moon's soul with her sister's. They all have a magic detector to make sure no one is influencing them with magic. So it's not a big leap in logic to assume that if they've learned about this power-blocking poison, the group they keep the news from is the magicians."

Fisk's speculation rang true to me. We needed to find out how much they knew.

"Has the Council had any recent closed-door sessions without the Master Magicians?" I asked.

"That's illegal," Leif said. "All members must be in attendance."

"How about an informal get-together?"

"That's harder to determine. The Councilors frequently meet in small groups, but nothing official is supposed to be decided."

"And I haven't heard any rumors about secret meetings," Fisk said.

"What about our Councilman, Bavol Zaltana?" I asked Leif. "Would he tell us?"

"It would depend on how much we're willing to divulge to him," he said. "If he knows you've been poisoned, he'd probably give us any information he has. But if we're vague and ask about a potential substance, he might clam up."

Uneasy about having yet another person know about me, I considered my options. "The attack on me could have been sanctioned by the Sitian Council. They've always been leery of me and my abilities. If they neutralize me, they no longer have to worry about me. Although you'd think they'd've learned to trust me by now."

"Now you're being paranoid," Leif said. "We'll talk to Bavol. But we'll call it clan business."

"And why would it matter what we call it?"

"Loyalty to clan members is important to Bavol. Besides, the Council doesn't need to know about this poison right now as long as the Master Magicians are aware of it."

I'd argue we'd gotten into trouble before by not informing the Council, but the thought of them not warning me about Ben Moon didn't give me any warm and fuzzy feelings toward them.

"All right. Bavol should be back at his place by now. Let's go pay him a visit before we return to the Keep."

We said goodbye to Fisk. He promised to gather any information he could about the assassin and poison.

When I wrapped my cloak around my shoulders, it felt like putting on armor. Just knowing it protected me from magic eased my biggest fear. I resisted the temptation to pull the hood over my head. The night air wasn't that cold.

The lamplighters had finished their nightly task. Bright yellow pools of light painted the streets. Not many people lingered in the central business district after the market closed and the factories reduced their production levels for the evening. We navigated the quiet streets, heading east toward the government quarter, where the Council Hall and housing for the Councilors and their aides was located.

As we neared Bavol's town house, memories of the time I'd had to sneak into his kitchen rose unbidden. The Daviian Vermin had taken over the Sitian Council, there had been a price on my head, and I'd needed Bavol's help.

When we reached his front stoop, I kept walking, pulling Leif with me.

"But—"

"Let's go around back," I whispered.

MARIA V. SNYDER

"There's no one in sight."

I gazed at him.

"Oh, all right, but I still think you're paranoid."

"I prefer to call it being cautious."

He snorted, but followed me for a few more blocks. After a quick glance over my shoulder, I ducked into the alley behind the row of town houses and doubled back to Bavol's rear entrance.

I peered through the kitchen window. Petal, his housekeeper, scrubbed pots. Tapping on the door with my knuckle, I stepped back as she opened the door.

Petal's wide face creased with first alarm then concern when she recognized me and Leif.

"Oh my, you gave me such a fright!" Petal ushered us inside. "Come in, come in. What kind of trouble are you two in now?"

"Seems you have a reputation, dear sister," Leif muttered.

"I believe she was referring to you as well, *dear* brother." I turned to Petal. "No trouble. We just wanted to visit our clan's leader without alerting the entire quarter. You know how nosy the other Councilors and their aides can be."

"That I do. They're the worst gossips. But give an old lady some credit, child. An unannounced visit through the back door only means one thing. Trouble."

No sense arguing with her. "Is Bavol in?"

"He's in his office. I'll go fetch him. Would you like something to eat or drink while you wait?"

Leif opened his mouth, but I said, "No, thanks."

She led us into the front parlor and we settled on a pair of turquoise-and-silver armchairs while she ascended the steps to the second floor.

"You didn't need to answer for me. Petal makes the best jungle soup—even better than Mom's." Leif pouted.

"You ate at Fisk's. How can you be hungry?"

"It's not about being *hungry*. It's about the combination of spices and the explosion of flavors inside your mouth."

My stomach roiled just at the thought of jungle soup. One of the favorite dishes of the Zaltana Clan, it contained leaves and flowers from the Illiais Jungle, where our clan lived. To me, it tasted like pulpy rotten coconut mixed with vanilla and lemons. Yuck.

Bavol followed Petal into the room, his wide smile at odds with her worried frown. She clutched her apron in her hands before disappearing into the kitchen.

"What a pleasant surprise," Bavol said.

Gray had almost covered all his hair, and he was a bit stockier since I'd last seen him.

"Yelena, I didn't know you were back from your vacation already." Bavol sat on the couch.

"There was a change in plans." I studied his expression. Suddenly, I wanted to know if he'd tell me about Ben Moon.

"Oh?" His smile remained, but a slight wariness crept into his gaze.

"I was attacked on the way to our cabin."

"Oh, that." He brightened with relief.

Interesting reaction.

"I've heard. Nasty ambush." Bavol tsked.

"You heard I was attacked, but didn't know I had returned to the Citadel?"

Leif shot me a warning look. Bavol was the leader of our clan and I was cross-examining him like a criminal. Too bad. Bavol should have told me about Ben Moon.

"Yes…well…Master Magician Bloodgood reported the incident this afternoon, but I assumed you remained at your cabin with Valek. Er…how are you feeling?" Bavol asked.

MARIA V. SNYDER

"I'm fine. I wanted to ask you if you had any idea who might be behind the attack."

"No, sorry," he said too quickly. "We discussed this at the Council meeting. And while we listed a number of suspects, we didn't think any of them could have pulled it off."

Leif stiffened, but kept his mouth shut. Even I sensed Bavol had lied to us. Why? And did I call him on it or ignore it?

"Who were the suspects?" I asked.

"Uh…you know…the usual…"

Oh joy, I had *usual* suspects—I should write a letter to my mother. I waited for him to continue.

"You know…Valek's enemies, the relatives of the Cloud Mist men you arrested during that sting operation, and Lyle Krystal, who you exposed as a fraud."

"Oh yeah. I'm good at spotting liars."

Bavol squirmed.

"Okay, Bavol, what's really going on?" Leif asked.

"What are you talking about?"

"Come on. It's *us*. Besides, we already know about Ben."

He leaned forward. "That's classified. How did…? Did you read my mind?" Bavol peered at me. Suspicion narrowed his eyes.

"No." I stared at him. "Why didn't you tell me?"

"The Council—"

"I don't care what the Council decided. I needed to know. Why didn't *you* tell me?"

"I can't go against the wishes of the Council."

Again I waited. He'd gone against their wishes in the past.

Bavol sighed and sank back against the cushions. "Councilor Moon promised he'd be caught and they didn't want anyone to panic."

"And they didn't want Yelena informing Valek, right?" Leif asked.

He didn't answer, which meant we'd been right. The Council still didn't fully trust me despite all I'd done for them over the years.

"I keep Sitia's secrets along with Ixian secrets," I said in a tight voice. "I'd only alert Valek if I had information that Ben planned to travel to Ixia to hunt for the Ice Moon. Do you know if Ben targeted me? Or what he might do now that he's free?"

"We don't think he's behind the attack. As for his plans, he's too busy running and hiding right now."

"Anything else you *can't* tell us?" Leif asked. "Perhaps another escaped criminal? Or a new drug on the black market? Or an attack of rabid Valmurs?"

Bavol shook his head. "We've had an increase in black-market goods and haven't been able to track the source down yet. But other than that…just the usual crises and bickering between the clans."

I stood. "Thank you for your time."

Leif joined me.

"Wait. How did you find out about Ben?"

"Sorry, we can't reveal our sources," I said. "However, I will tell you that Valek probably already knows." I held up my hand. "Not from us or our sources but one of his spies in Fulgor. Despite all my efforts, there are still a few in all the major cities of Sitia. And after finding out the Council had kept vital information from me, I'm glad there's a network of spies that I can tap into."

I strode into the kitchen and said goodbye to Petal, who handed Leif a steaming bowl and spoon.

"You're the best, Pet." He pecked her on the cheek. "I'll bring the bowl back tomorrow licked clean."

She giggled.

I shook my head as we left. "Does everyone feed you?"

MARIA V. SNYDER

"Only the nice ones." He slurped the jungle soup as we headed to the Keep.

Exhaustion pulled on my muscles. My legs weighed a hundred pounds each. It'd been a long day and I wasn't sure if I'd accomplished anything or not. When Leif finished his second supper, I asked about his take on the conversation with Bavol.

"He doesn't know about the magic-blocking poison," Leif said.

"How did you figure that out?"

"When I listed those other threats, I didn't smell a reaction to the one about the new drug or the attack of rabid Valmurs, for which I am grateful—those little devils have sharp teeth."

Ah. Leif had used his magic. "But he did say there were more illegal goods for sale."

"Yes, and I think that's my next assignment from the Council."

Irys had also mentioned he would be needed soon. "Guess that means we need to leave town as soon as possible."

"Field trip to Fulgor?"

"Yes. We can also visit Opal and see if she has any ideas about my problem."

But first to bed. Leif and I agreed to meet at the Keep's stable at noon tomorrow. We both needed to wrap up a few things in the morning.

Irys wasn't in her tower, so I slogged up the three flights of stairs and collapsed into bed, covering my entire body with my cloak. I pulled my switchblade and slid the weapon under my pillow. Not paranoid. Just cautious.

The next morning, I visited Bain and surprised him when I opened his office door without knocking. He started and spilled a bottle of ink. I rushed to apologize and help clean up the mess. Nice to know the null shield woven into my cloak worked against a master-level magician.

He waved my apology away. "I am more glad you are protected than upset over another stain on my desk. As you can see, it blends right in. Now sit and tell me what you have learned."

I updated him on everything except for the news about Ben Moon. "In other words…nothing."

"That is not true. You've ruled out a number of possibilities. We are narrowing down the routes to an answer."

I asked him how the meeting with the Council went.

Bain played with the fraying threads on the sleeve of his robe. "Not as expected."

Good or bad? I waited.

"Of course they were upset and tossed about a few names of suspects. But no one offered to investigate through their clans. Odd."

I studied Bain, his white hair a messy cloud around his head. Did he know about Ben? "Do you think they sent an assassin after me?"

"Oh no, no."

"But how would you know? They're all protected by null shields during meetings. They can lie with abandon."

Bain straightened as if affronted. "My dear child, I can spot a liar without using my magic. And I can also sense when a person is holding information back." He gave me a pointed look.

"So I'm not supposed to withhold information, but you can if you call it Council business?"

"What are you referring to?" His hard gaze slid past my shoulder.

I turned in time to see Irys stride into his office.

MARIA V. SNYDER

Fury sparked in her eyes. "She is referring to Ben Moon's rescue."

"Who?" Bain asked.

As Irys explained, the tight lump in my throat lessened. Always a relief to discover that your mentor and friend hadn't been lying to you.

"The Council has kept this from us, Bain. And this isn't the first time."

He pulled at his sleeve. "No, it is not. But it is the first of this magnitude."

"We should ban null shields from our meetings."

"For what purpose? We are not allowed to rifle through their thoughts. It's against the Ethical Code."

Irys growled in frustration. "We need more master-level magicians!"

"While I agree there is always need for more, why do you think they would help in this situation?"

"They'd aid in changing the sentiment in the Council."

"What sentiment?" I asked.

Irys leaned against Bain's desk. "The anti-magician sentiment." She threw her arms wide. "With all the discoveries about how to neutralize us—Curare, null shields, voids—they believe we're weak and vulnerable and corruptible."

Her comment slammed into me almost as hard as the arrow. "How could...? What...?" Unable to pull together a complete sentence, I shut my mouth.

"The convenience of certain magicians, like healers, has been such a part of their daily life they don't consider them special anymore," Bain said. "And the troubles we have had with other rogue magicians like Owen, Kangom, Roze, Ferde, Galen, Walsh, and Devlen while he was addicted to the blood magic, have tarnished all our reputations."

Wow, that was quite the list. And what did it say about

my life that I knew them all? "What about the ones before I came to Sitia?"

"Oh, we've always had troublesome magicians," Irys said. "But it seems since the border with Ixia has been...opened, for lack of a better word, the incidents have increased."

The trade treaty with the Commander happened around the time I'd returned to Sitia after a fourteen-year absence. Had I been the catalyst?

Irys swatted me on the shoulder. "Stop furrowing your brow. You're not responsible. The rediscovery of blood magic and Curare also matches the timing of the Commander's treaty. So it would have happened if you were here or not."

I gave her a grateful smile. She knew me so well.

"And I suspect the Councilors are frustrated with not being in direct control of the super messengers and Opal's magic detectors," Irys said. "They believe both items should be considered property of Sitia. Two clans, Cloud Mist and Jewelrose, have been very vocal about it. I suspect their richer citizens have been pressuring the Councilors. And there have been rumors about the need to control magicians—to use us like an army instead of letting each be free to do our own thing."

"The problems created by the Council are never ending. That is not why Yelena is here," Bain said. "Did young Fisk have any ideas?"

"No." I filled them in. "Have you learned anything?"

"Not yet," Irys said. "I'll send a message to Pazia this afternoon."

"Where is her glass factory?" I asked.

"In her family's compound near Ognap. Why?"

Ognap was a five-day journey east of Fulgor. "Don't send that message. I'll pay her a visit."

Irys crossed her arms, waiting.

MARIA V. SNYDER

"You told me to keep a low profile, so I'm leaving for Fulgor today."

"My advice meant you should remain in your rooms, reading books, catching up on sleep and avoiding danger. Remember those things?"

"Yeah, well…that's not going to happen anytime soon."

"Do you really think you'll learn Ben's whereabouts when the authorities haven't?"

"Who says I'm chasing after Ben? I'm going to talk to Opal, see if she has any thoughts about my condition. Then I'll visit Pazia and my father."

"Uh-huh."

"I'll be protected. I'm taking Leif."

"The Council has an assignment for him. I'm supposed to tell him."

"Sorry, he just left. Guess you'll have to tell him when he returns."

"Not funny." She huffed. "I should go with you, too."

"You're welcome to come along."

Bain cleared his throat. "That would be ill-timed. We have—"

"Council business. I know. How about taking along another magician for added security?"

"Who do you have in mind?"

Irys covered her surprise. Guess she'd thought I'd give her more resistance. Normally, I would. These weren't normal times.

"Let's see… There's your friend Dax."

"No. I need him to help research Yelena's problem," Bain said. "Plus he's teaching classes."

Too bad. Traveling with Dax would have been fun.

"And Zebb won't leave Councilor Moon's side." Irys rubbed her temples as if she had a headache. "Hale's between assignments. He proved himself when Opal was having all that trouble."

"Does he have a Sandseed horse? We're planning on traveling through the Avibian Plains as much as we can." Plus the Sandseed's magic in the plains would prevent anyone from following us.

"I don't think so, but talk to the Stable Master and see if he'll allow Hale to borrow Garnet."

I gave her a flat look.

"Oh, all right, tell him I sanctioned it."

"I can't believe you're afraid of the Stable Master!"

"I am not."

I laughed at how childish she sounded.

Irys smiled back. "What else do you need from us?"

I sobered. "Just keep searching."

"You got it. And I'll tell Hale about his new mission. When do you plan to leave?"

"Noon." Which wasn't that far off. I said goodbye to Bain and Irys and hurried to finish getting ready for the trip.

I stopped in the message office on the ground floor of the administration building and sent a note to Valek. Using the code we'd developed just for this purpose, I informed him about Ben just in case he hadn't heard and listed my travel plans. There was no need to worry him about my condition. At least, not yet.

After I collected my backpack, I headed to the stable. When I arrived, Leif stood next to Rusalka. He smirked as he watched a man arguing with the Stable Master. The man had close-set eyes, short black hair and a high forehead. Probably Hale.

"...you can't have him, you idiot," the Stable Master said. "I don't care who you are or what you're doing. He's—"

I interrupted them. "Hale's coming with us on an important mission."

Leif made a choking sound. His smirk disappeared.

"Do you have any Sandseed horses he can…borrow?" I asked. "We're going to be traveling through the plains."

"Ah hell." The Stable Master ran a hand through his mane of hair as if smoothing it down. If anything, he made it worse. "Why didn't the…he say so?"

"He just received his orders from Second Magician, so I'm sure he's a bit out of sorts." I shot Hale a significant look.

The Stable Master stomped over to Garnet's stall. "If he'll let you saddle him, then he's up for the trip. If not, then you're out of luck." He scratched him behind the ears. His features softened as he gazed at Garnet. Then he glared at us and continued down the aisle, muttering under his breath.

"Hi, Hale," I said, shaking his hand. "Thanks for coming along. Did Irys fill you in on where we're going?"

"Uh…Irys?" Hale appeared to be a bit flustered.

"Second Magician."

"Oh, she said we're traveling to Fulgor and I was to protect you." His face creased in confusion. "I'm not sure why. You're already covered by a null shield. Plus you're the…Soulfinder." He said the word almost as if it left a bad taste in his mouth.

"I'll explain on the way. See if Garnet will stand for you."

"Okay." Hale approached the horse as if he'd never seen one before.

Leif pulled me aside before I could saddle Kiki.

"What's with the stiff?" his voice hissed in my ear.

"Irys thought I should have more protection. Seemed like a good idea."

"It is, but why Skippy?"

"Skippy?"

"Hale. Let's just say we don't get along."

Oh great. "Irys assigned him. Are you saying he's not trustworthy?"

Leif sucked in a deep breath. "No. He's loyal and has plenty of magic."

"Then what's the problem?"

"He's...annoying."

I laughed. "So are you."

He frowned. "I'm funny and lovable. He's...a snob and thinks our Zaltana magic is impure."

"I don't care what he thinks. Is he good in a fight?"

"Yeah." The word tore from Leif's lips as if it pained him to say it.

"Then we'll let Garnet decide if he's worthy. If the horse rejects him, we will, too. Okay?"

Another huff. "Okay." Leif pulled a thick silver chain from his pocket. Dangling from the chain was a clear glass octopus about the size of my palm. "Here." He handed it to me. "It's from Quinn. There's a null shield attached to it so when you wear it next to your heart it protects your entire body."

"Thanks." I looped the chain around my neck and tucked the lifelike octopus under my shirt. The cold glass sent a shiver through me.

Leif returned to Rusalka. The sorrel-and-white horse nuzzled his neck.

Kiki unlatched her stall with her teeth and stood by her tack. I stroked her neck. A sudden wave of grief rose in my throat, strangling me. Pressing my forehead to her shoulder, I endured the torment. I missed my connection with Kiki the most.

Eventually, she snorted and pawed the ground as if to say, "Stop wallowing in pity and get moving."

I saddled her and attached plenty of feed bags. The plains would have enough water. When I finished, I mounted and glanced around. Leif sat on Rusalka, looking dour, and Hale pulled himself into Garnet's saddle. Hale's expression from atop

MARIA V. SNYDER

the tall horse was a mix of awe and terror. Sandseed horses had a reputation for being stubborn and willful and intelligent.

"Just follow us and you shouldn't have any trouble," I said to Hale.

"No trouble?"

"With the horse. I can't make any guarantees about the mission."

"Yeah, I heard that about you."

"Oh?"

"No disrespect intended. It's just you have a certain... reputation." Hale cleared his throat. "I'm honored to accompany you."

Leif rolled his eyes. "Laying it on a bit thick, aren't you, Skippy?"

Ignoring my brother, I spurred Kiki toward the Keep's gate. If we hurried, we could be in the Avibian Plains by nightfall. We left the Keep, then threaded through the afternoon Citadel traffic. We crossed through the southern exit without a problem and continued south. Once we reached the plains, we'd turn east before cutting north to Fulgor.

I really didn't expect trouble until we arrived in Fulgor. But minutes after we cleared the gate, the rumble of many horses at full gallop sounded behind us.

Leif glanced at me as we moved to the right side of the road. His hand rested on the hilt of his machete. Hale's face pinched tight. A small part of me hoped the riders were just in a hurry and would pass us. But a cold dread churned in my stomach, warning me.

Sure enough, the riders surrounded us. They stopped and blocked our path. Leif yanked his machete out, and in response, seven soldiers pulled their weapons and pointed them at us.

12

VALEK

As Onora threatened Janco with her knife, Ari stood, holding a dagger in each of his massive hands. Even though Janco was grinning, he'd palmed his switchblade.

"Save it for later," Valek said, stopping the inevitable. "You can spar with Onora in the training yard tomorrow." When no one moved, he banged a fist on his desk. "Weapons down. Now."

Ari and Janco returned their knives to various hidden holders without hesitation. Onora waited a few heartbeats before slipping the weapon into her pocket. Valek noted a few other telltale bulges, indicating a number of hidden surprises. She wore the uniform Dilana had given her, but she yanked at the collar as if uncomfortable.

"Onora, you must learn to ignore Janco's taunts. He's testing you. Being quick to anger is not a desirable trait in my corps," Valek said. He gestured to the empty chair. "Sit down."

Ari remained on his feet until she sat. Then he settled next to Janco, who lounged back as if he didn't have a care in the world. Except Valek knew better. Janco was far from relaxed.

"Ari, please update Onora on what we've learned so far,"

Valek ordered. He studied the young woman's body language as Ari detailed their investigation.

Onora perched on the edge of her seat. She listened with her head cocked slightly to the right and her hands clasped in her lap near another concealed knife. He hadn't returned hers, yet she was well armed. Interesting.

When Ari finished, Valek asked, "What's our next move?"

"Interrogate the smugglers, find out who their boss is and where their headquarters is located," Janco said.

"Let one of them escape and follow him," Ari suggested.

"Find another group selling black-market goods and infiltrate them," Onora said.

All good suggestions. "It's doubtful the location of their headquarters is still the same since the arrests. However, learning who is in charge will be a step in the right direction."

Janco puffed out his chest.

"I also liked the other ideas. The three of you will work together as a team and implement them."

Janco no longer looked so pleased. Ari frowned at Onora. They were going to be difficult about working with her.

"Your first team meeting is tomorrow after the morning exercises. We'll meet in the training yard for a workout session. Then you can plan a timeline and task list for finding the smugglers. You're dismissed."

They stood. Ari and Janco left after shooting a couple of glares at Onora. She lingered behind.

"Yes?" he asked.

"You promised to return my weapons tonight."

"I did."

She didn't flinch from his scrutiny. Cocky. He'd never been that cocky even in his prime. Then again…Valek had placed black statues he'd carved on his targets' pillows, warning them just to make it more difficult to assassinate them. Very cocky.

"Well?" she asked.

"You actually want me to check my locked drawer and find it empty? So you can smirk over getting one over on me? Considering that you've already recovered your weapons, it seemed like a waste of time."

Two small splotches reddened her cheeks.

Gotcha. "You shouldn't have threatened Janco. That tipped me off that you were armed."

Keeping her mouth shut, she nodded.

"Experience counts for more than you think." Valek rubbed his chest, remembering when he'd hunted Ambrose, believing it would be an easy kill. "I know you don't believe me. You won't believe me until you're standing here, facing some young hotshot determined to take your job."

"Are you saying you've just realized this now?"

He laughed. "Oh no. I've been facing young hotshots since the takeover twenty-three years ago. You are not the first to challenge me."

"No. I'll be the last."

"That has yet to be determined. Let's see how you do working with Ari and Janco before I turn over my office keys."

She moved to leave, then paused. "How...? What is the best way to work with them?"

Ah progress. "Listen to them. They've years of experience, but don't be afraid to speak up if you have a better idea. They might not like it, but they know a good idea when they hear one. Even Janco. He's used to listening to the voice of reason."

"And that's Ari's voice."

"Yes. Unless Ari's being emotional. Then he can be very unreasonable." Valek watched for a reaction.

Onora pressed her lips together. "Nothing wrong with emotion."

He'd hit a nerve. "Only at the right time and place." Yelena

MARIA V. SNYDER

had taught him that. "But when Ari gets into his protective mode, he will rush into danger without a thought to his own survival."

"Why is that bad?"

"Since you have to ask, I'm guessing that was part of the training you didn't agree with Hedda about."

"Emotion gives us strength."

"At the right time and place."

She shook her head as if he couldn't possibly understand.

"It's the reason you lost last night."

"I lost because you cheated," she said, anger stiffening her posture.

"Keep thinking that. Then I won't have to worry about finding another job."

Onora spun on her heel and left without another word.

Valek returned to his desk. Contemplating their conversation, he dug through the reports. Onora's comment—*emotion gives us strength*—repeated in his mind.

During the second stage of his assassin training, Valek hadn't been able to beat T-quin in hand to hand despite hours of practice and lifting weights until his muscles shook with exhaustion.

In order to move to the next level, he had to win a match against T-quin. Their fights lasted longer and longer, but always ended the same.

"Pinned you, Wanna Be." T-quin pressed his knees into Valek's shoulders, proving his point. He released him and stood. Sweat coated his chest and soaked his hair. He puffed from the exertion, but offered Valek a hand up.

Valek ignored it as anger pulsed through him. He sprang to his feet ready to try again.

"That's enough for now, Wanna Be. I don't want to injure you," T-quin said.

"No. I almost had you. You can't stop now."

"All right, but don't go crying to Hedda if I break your leg."

They faced each other. Both stood in fighting stances. Dark purple bruises stained Valek's knuckles and circles of red, green and black bruising marked his chest, arms and thighs where T-quin had punched or kicked him.

T-quin shuffled forward and snapped his foot out. Valek blocked the blow with his forearm and countered with a round-house kick. T-quin sidestepped and received only a glancing blow. But Valek didn't wait for a counterstrike. He hooked his foot behind T-quin's ankle and yanked. T-quin hit the ground rolling. Valek chased him, but he sprang to his feet and, using Valek's momentum, flipped Valek over his head. His breath whooshed from his lungs as he landed.

T-quin laughed. "So predictable, Wanna Be. You've no imagination."

Fury gave Valek a surge of energy. He scrambled to his feet and rushed his opponent. T-quin once again dipped and threw Valek over his shoulder.

The match continued. T-quin taunted and Valek attacked only to end up on the ground.

"Pinned, again," T-quin said, digging his heels into Valek's hips.

Valek lumbered to his feet. Battered with bruises on top of bruises, he shuffled over to the water pitcher for a drink.

"Lose the anger," Hedda said.

He jerked in surprise. No sound warned of her approach, and he hadn't known she had watched his match against T-quin.

She regarded him with a frankness he'd learned to admire.

"But T-quin—"

"This has nothing to do with T-quin or your vendetta.

T-quin is baiting you on purpose. When you get angry, you make mistakes. Mistakes he can use to his advantage. And you are very quick to anger."

He drew breath to argue, but she had a point. Fury at the King, the soldiers and even his parents had fueled his desire to learn and improve his skills.

"Lose the anger, then lose all those other annoying emotions while you're at it. In order to be an assassin, you must be rational, logical, cunning, ruthless and emotionless. Those soft feelings have no place in an assassin's heart or head. They make you weak."

While he agreed with her, he'd been holding on to his passion for revenge for so long, he worried he'd lose his desire to see the King's blood on his hands.

"Determination, persistence, concentration, focus and drive are not emotions," she said. "Put your emotions aside or you will not succeed in this program. You have ten days." She strode away.

T-quin stood nearby. He raised his hand and then bent it at the wrist as he lowered it while making a whistling sound. "Hope you can fly, Wanna Be. Even if you miss the rocks, the current will drown you. Splash!" He laughed and returned to the training floor.

Arbon met Valek's gaze as he took a break from his match. He'd been working with another instructor for the past few weeks and showed an affinity for hand to hand. Arbon would soon advance to the next level.

Was competition an emotion? The thought of being pushed to his death failed to ignite fear in Valek's heart. The challenge of ten days did more for his motivation than anything else.

However, recognizing a weakness remained easier than overcoming it. Although Valek knew T-quin baited him, the anger boiled inside him, pressing to be released. If anything, his temper shortened. And the heating season's hotter temperatures didn't help, either.

Valek's matches with Arbon and some of the others had gone mostly in his favor until news about his weakness spread. After another frustrating, fruitless day of training, Valek dragged his battered body to his favorite spot overlooking the Sunset Ocean, which was awash in the pinks, oranges and golds cast by the setting sun.

He grabbed a handful of the gray rocks and tossed them one by one out into the sea, wishing he could throw his emotions away as easily. Or rather, evict the anger that had infested him. Valek imagined it as a black, oily rot flowing through his veins, pumping through his heart, twisting around his thoughts.

"Jump, Wanna Be," T-quin yelled. "Save Hedda the trouble of tossing your sorry ass over the edge herself."

Valek's grip tightened. The stones cracked in his hands and the desire to whip them at T-quin's head rose in his chest. He refrained from the action. Instead, he channeled his anger into the unyielding cold rocks cutting into his palms.

"What? No retort? Afraid I'll trounce you again?"

Valek stood and walked past T-quin without saying a word. When he reached his room, he sat on the edge of the bed and opened his hands. Blood covered the stones. The force of his grip had cracked them in half. Inside lurked a sleek blackness with glints of silver.

He reached under his bed for the stones he'd carried back during the first stage of his training. The gray outer coating had been scratched off and revealed the same black-and-silver interior.

Taking out his knife, he chipped away at the dull gray on one of the rocks. He concentrated on carving the stone, letting his rage and frustration disappear for a while. When it was too dark to see, he lit a lantern and continued. Instead of

MARIA V. SNYDER

reporting for training the next day, he remained in his room, working on the stones. Their inner beauty fascinated him and he scraped away the parts that didn't belong.

Odd that he saw a shape trapped within the stone. A figure that had to be released. He worked for hours, neither eating nor sleeping until he finished. Then he collapsed.

The sound of knocking woke him.

"Valek," Arbon called. "Are you okay?" He twisted the knob, but the door was locked.

"I'm fine," he called.

"T-quin's gonna be pissed. He bet Eden a gold you jumped off the cliff."

"I'm happy to disappoint him."

"Are you coming to training? You only have two days left."

Valek rolled over and gazed at his collection of rock statues. The crude figurines stood in a row. One wore a crown, three others held swords and a couple held hands. His father had done nothing to stop the soldiers from murdering his brothers. His mother had disowned him.

"Valek?"

"I'm not going."

"But—"

"Don't worry, Arbon. I'll be there for the test."

"You better. I've two silvers on the line."

"I'm touched you would risk so much."

"Who says I'm betting on you?" Arbon's booming laugh rumbled through the door.

Valek spent the next two days sleeping, eating and recovering his strength. The morning before his test fight, he stood at the cliff's edge holding the statues in his hands.

He whipped the king figure out into the air. Determination replaced anger. The three soldiers went over the edge one by one. Persistence would aid him as he hunted down these three murderers. Tossing the couple holding hands together, he sent the last of his weaknesses out into the abyss. If he cared for no one, then the pain of grief would never touch him again.

When Valek arrived at the training room, he squeezed through a press of people. Trainers, students and teachers had all come to watch the fight. A murmur spread as they spotted him.

As Valek warmed up, Arbon pushed his way next to him.

"Will ya look at this crowd," Arbon said. "I'd call them morbid, but they are training to be assassins or are already cold-blooded killers." He sounded cheery. "Guess there hasn't been anyone tossed over the cliff in a while."

"Your confidence in me is heartwarming."

Arbon slapped Valek on the shoulder and wished him luck.

Valek stretched his stiff muscles. At least they didn't ache as much. The rest had done him good.

"Are you ready, Wanna Be? I want to collect my winnings," T-quin called.

He faced T-quin. The oily blackness inside him had been purged and thrown into the Sunset Ocean. Nothing left but hard silver.

When the match started, T-quin attacked with a series of front kicks. His movements appeared crystal clear to Valek. Rage no longer clouded his vision. He almost felt sorry for T-quin, but sorrow was an emotion. And Valek had taken Hedda's advice to heart.

Valek blocked a side kick and a punch to his head, staying on the defensive.

"Come on, Wanna Be. Fight back or I might fall asleep," T-quin said.

The crowd laughed and cheered T-quin on. Valek ignored the noise, focusing on T-quin's attack pattern, analyzing his strikes for weaknesses. Even though they'd sparred so many

MARIA V. SNYDER

times before, Valek learned more about T-quin's fighting style in these five minutes than in the weeks before.

Valek waited for the perfect opportunity. When T-quin did his favorite shuffle side kick, backhand combo, Valek stepped in close and punched T-quin's exposed ribs. T-quin grunted and backpedaled.

"Lucky strike, Wanna Be."

"You wish."

The fight continued and Valek took advantage of every opening T-quin gave him. After a series of blows to his kidneys, T-quin dropped his guard and swayed on his feet. Valek spun, windmilling him to the ground, and knelt on his shoulders.

"Pinned, Tamequintin," Valek said.

Stunned silence filled the air until Arbon whooped. "Yes! You owe me two silvers, T-quin."

The crowd had recovered and dispersed. Valek had flexed his muscles, assessing the damage—a few sore ribs and a tender spot on his biceps.

Hedda had approached. "Not bad, King Killer. I should have given you the ten-day deadline sooner. You do well under pressure. Now let's see how you do with weapons training."

"Ten days?"

"Of course."

A knock on his office door jerked Valek from his memories. "Yes?"

Sergeant Gerik poked his head in. "The Commander has retired for the evening, sir."

"Thank you." Before the man could close the door, he called, "Gerik, come in here, please."

Strain whitened Gerik's face as he approached Valek's desk. All the members of the Commander's guard knew they'd be punished for letting the assassin through, but had no idea what was in store for them. Once Valek had assembled a new team, this team would be reassigned.

"Sir?"

"According to your file, you're a recent transfer from MD-2. Been here a year. How long did you serve up there?"

"A year, sir."

"Being assigned to the Commander's detail is an impressive accomplishment for someone who's only served a couple years. Most of these guys have ten or more years' experience. What do you credit for your success?"

Gerik hesitated.

"Feel free to speak frankly."

"I'm good, sir. Fighting hand to hand, or with weapons, is easy for me. I've a natural affinity for sparring."

"Fair enough. When you were in MD-2, did you know a Captain Timmer?"

The slightest flinch creased Gerick's face. "I've heard of him, sir."

"And? Again I'm looking for an honest opinion."

"He has a reputation for cruelty, sir."

"Cruelty?"

"The officers believe he's very strict and his troops are the best. No one has ever filed a complaint. It's just gossip among the enlisted, sir."

"If his troops are considered the best, why weren't you promoted to his company?"

Gerik frowned. "I was offered a position, but I turned him down."

Interesting. "Refused because of gossip?"

"Yes, sir."

The man was lying. Valek wondered why, but he wasn't going to push it right now. Some things couldn't be rushed.

MARIA V. SNYDER

"I also wanted to let you know that you're being reassigned, Private Gerik."

He straightened. "Yes, sir." Resignation laced his voice.

"It's a temporary assignment. If you do well, it might become permanent."

"Yes, sir."

"Report to the training yard tomorrow morning after exercise."

"Yes, sir." This time surprise tainted his tone.

"You're dismissed."

"Yes, sir." Gerik left in a hurry.

Probably worried Valek would change his mind. Valek read through Captain Timmer's file, but spotted nothing out of the ordinary. On his way to the Commander's suite, he visited one of his operatives, assigning the man to deliver a message to Yelena, warning her about Ben Moon.

"You give this directly to her. No one else. Understand?" Valek asked.

"Yes, sir," the man replied.

The tension in Valek's shoulders eased as he sent another agent to seek out Arbon and let the assassin know Valek wished to talk to him. Then Valek knocked on the Commander's door. He'd accomplished more than he'd hoped today.

"Come," Ambrose called.

Valek entered. A glass of blackberry brandy waited for him by the empty armchair. The Commander already relaxed in his.

"Did our young assassin show up tonight?"

"She did."

"And how did the boys react?"

"As expected."

Ambrose laughed. "Bared teeth and raised hackles, eh?"

"Tomorrow morning should be interesting." Valek explained what they'd learned about the smugglers.

"Good. Anything else?"

He reported about Captain Timmer in MD-2. "I need more information on him."

"Yes, find out about him. My officers are forbidden to abuse their positions."

Another reason Ambrose held Valek's loyalty. His insistence that his army always behave as professionals. No cruelty, no killing for killing's sake, no drunken brawls and no sexual harassment.

Valek sipped his drink. Molten spices rolled over his tongue, burned down his throat and warmed his stomach. "I'd like to investigate this Timmer personally."

The Commander stilled. "You've only just returned. Why not send an agent?"

"It's too important. He's the reason both Onora and Gerik are here and I suspect they're working together. Besides, an agent would have to infiltrate his squad and earn his trust. Time I'm unwilling to waste at this point."

"And you believe you can get answers faster?"

"Oh yes."

The Commander stared into the fire. "What about *my* safety?"

Good question. What about it? Ever since Onora had appeared in the Commander's suite, Valek had been mulling it over, viewing the entire night from every possible angle. He'd missed something vital. He'd no idea what, but he'd discover it eventually.

"I will ensure that the gap in security has been plugged, and that you have a new detail before I leave. Besides, if Onora has a change of heart, I'm quite certain you can handle her," Valek said.

"Quite certain?"

Valek met the Commander's amused gaze. "I haven't beaten you yet, old man."

"Experience trumps youth?"

"For now," Valek agreed.

"And when it doesn't?"

Valek laughed. "We team up. I'll knock him on the head with my cane and you aim for the groin with your bony feet."

The Commander chuckled and sipped his drink. They sat in companionable silence for a while.

"All right, Valek. Go and take care of this Captain Timmer. You have ten days."

All humor fled Valek. Ten days. Just like the inside joke between Valek and Hedda all those years ago. He'd never told the Commander or anyone about that. Coincidence? Or had the Commander talked to Hedda? And if so, why?

13

JANCO

Janco hated mornings. The bright sunlight, chirping birds and those obnoxious morning people just made his stomach churn. Unfortunately, since he'd been a soldier for forever morning exercise and training had been a requirement. He'd probably be a general by now if training was scheduled for a decent hour of the day.

Ari's white-blond hair gleamed in the sun, making it easy to find his partner in the vast training area. As in everything, Ari was the complete opposite of Janco. He was even one of those obnoxious morning people.

"You're late," Ari said.

"Yeah, well, I got behind a group of newbs while running laps. My grandmother could run faster than them."

"You couldn't just pass them?"

"And miss a chance to taunt them? No way."

"I see you've taken to heart Valek's orders to be a good example to the new recruits."

"Yep, that's me. A shining example."

"Speaking of examples…" Ari tilted his head.

Janco turned and groaned. "Here comes Little Miss Assassin. What have we done to get saddled with her?"

"It didn't help you were caught snooping in that warehouse. Some sneak you are."

"I was far from caught. I was just...biding my time." Janco eyed the young pup sourly.

Little Miss Assassin moved through the groups of soldiers with ease. No discomfort from being surrounded by armed men and women. She joined them without a word and warmed up. Her long brown hair was braided down her back. She wore a light-colored tunic and pants and her feet were bare! And people called *him* crazy.

He stretched and bantered with Ari until he saw *them*.

"Ari, look." He elbowed his partner.

"What? Oh, crap. This can't be good."

"Ya think?"

The Commander and Valek headed toward them followed by some grunt, who looked terrified. Didn't blame him.

Little Miss Assassin froze for a second when she spotted the threesome. Scared of Valek? Not from what he'd heard. The Commander? Ditto. A slight hitch in the big grunt's stride gave him away. She knew him and vice versa. Valek also watched the young pup's expression. Probably testing a theory.

But why was the Commander here?

Valek introduced the grunt—Sergeant something or other. Seemed he might be another member of their team. Oh, this day was just getting better and better. He should have stayed in bed.

"We're going to do some sparring," Valek said. "Janco versus Gerik, Ari versus Onora, then switch."

The Commander leaned against the wooden fence that lined the training yard. Better put on a good show.

"Weapons?" Ari asked.

"Your choice."

Janco sensed a trick. He glanced at his partner. Ari shrugged.

No help there. Janco studied the grunt. Taller than him, but not as broad as Ari. Best to wait until the grunt chose a weapon before he picked his.

Sergeant Grunt chose a bo staff. A surprise. Janco was sure he'd go for the sword. No worries. He'd learned a thing or three from Maren. Picking up his bo, he slid his hands along the wood of the staff and faced the grunt.

Valek refereed the match. "Go."

The grunt swung his bo, aiming for Janco's temple. He blocked and the loud crack of wood hitting wood vibrated in the air. The man meant business. Janco countered and soon all he heard was the rhythmic cracks of the two bos. His opponent was good, but Janco was better. Natch.

"The grunt can swing, but can he sing?" Janco shuffled close and jabbed at the man's groin.

He hopped back. "Hey! No blows below the belt."

"Who says?"

The grunt glanced at Valek. Oh, this was too easy. Janco poured on the speed. Rib strike, rib strike, temple, temple, feint to the ribs and then sweep the legs. Sergeant Grunt landed with an oomph and Janco pressed the tip of his bo just under the man's Adam's apple.

"Gotcha!"

Valek called the match. Janco refrained from smirking.

Ari slapped him on the back and almost sent him sprawling. "Nice."

Janco pulled Ari aside. "Watch out. She almost beat Valek, so she's probably very fast."

"That's why I'm not choosing a knife."

"Use your scimitar."

"Why?"

"No one in Ixia uses it. She'll be unfamiliar with what it can do. Plus it's intimidating as all hell."

"Great idea."

"Don't sound so surprised."

"Ready?" Valek asked.

Little Miss Assassin waited with her knives drawn. Ari approached, holding his scimitar in one hand. The thick, four-foot-long curved blade gleamed in the sunlight. The sucker weighed a ton, but Ari hefted it with ease.

Although she clenched her weapons tighter, Little Miss Assassin kept her cool. This ought to be good.

"Go."

She moved first, rushing Ari. A suicide move, except she cut to the right and sliced at Ari's neck. Ari just blocked her attack. Janco had been right—she was not just fast, but superfast. And she used it to her advantage, snaking inside his strike zone and then dancing back.

Ari adjusted and used his scimitar to keep her from getting close. But she managed a few more strikes. The match lengthened. When Ari grabbed his hilt with both hands, she smiled, probably thinking she had worn him down.

Janco waited, and sure enough, Ari's lumbering swings, slow shuffles and heavy breathing lured Little Miss Assassin within striking distance. She stepped in, and he punched her in her solar plexus. Collapsing with a whoosh, she looked up in time to see Ari placing the tip of his very sharp blade on her neck.

"Gotcha!" Janco yelled, because Ari was too much of a gentleman to gloat.

Ari offered her a hand up, but she ignored it, rising to her feet. Indignation furrowed her brow and her mouth opened as if to protest. She shot Valek a sour look, but then pressed her lips together.

Wiping her hands on her pants, she picked up her knives and faced Janco. He chose the bo staff again.

"Go." Valek stepped back.

She attacked. Boy oh boy her speed was impressive. If he'd held a knife, the fight would be over by now. However, the longer bo staff kept her from getting close, and he was also known for his speedy little jabs. He worked on her ribs as her blades cut chunks from his staff.

"Little Miss Assassin is as slow as molassin," Janco sang.

"*Molassin?* That's not even a word," Ari called.

"Everyone's a critic. I'd like to see you find a word that rhymes with *assassin*." Janco backpedaled as the young pup came after him with a flurry of slices aimed at his throat and stomach.

The tip of her blade nicked his neck.

"This kitten has claws under her puppy-dog paws."

She growled and Janco bit down on a chuckle because her next series of attacks almost knocked him over. Impressive. He endured two more assaults. Then on the third, he planted the end of his bo in the ground and, using his momentum, flipped over her head. He landed, swept her legs, then followed her down, pressing the bo staff against her throat.

"Gotcha."

"The correct term is 'pinned,'" she said, panting.

"That's boring. Besides, we don't do 'correct' around here."

Ignoring his hand, she stood and brushed a lock of hair from her sweaty face. "I've noticed."

"Next," Valek said.

Sergeant Grunt faced Ari without a weapon. "Hand to hand?"

"All right."

"Bad move," Janco muttered.

"Why?" She moved closer to him.

"You'll see."

While the grunt had an impressive array of techniques, Ari

MARIA V. SNYDER

had spent the past ten years perfecting hand-to-hand fighting. In order to beat Ari, an opponent had to have brute strength, speed and to make no mistakes. Grunt gave a good fight, but his inexperience proved his downfall.

"Gotcha," Janco said when Ari pinned the grunt.

"Not bad," Valek said. "Final fight. Ari and Janco against Onora, using knives."

Janco had been about to protest until that last part. He sensed he and Ari were about to get their balls handed to them.

He hated when he was right. Actually, he preened and bragged when he was right, but being soundly beaten by Little Miss Assassin was a huge blow to his ego. And the Commander had watched it! Absolutely mortifying.

Ari wiped the blood and sweat from his arms. "Nice fight."

Janco glared at him. "Nice? That—"

"Oh hush, Janco. Can't you just admit when someone is better than you?"

"Obviously not." He pouted.

"That explains why Valek had such trouble with her. Be glad she's on our side."

He gazed at her. She talked to Valek while the grunt stood nearby. The Commander had left. Probably disgusted by their fight.

"Is she? Her and the grunt know each other."

"Probably why Valek brought him along today."

"He could be the reason she got into the castle without trouble."

"Could be."

"You don't seem concerned."

"I'm sure Valek has a plan."

"Humph." Janco moved closer to eavesdrop on their conversation.

"...obvious you never completed the training," Valek said to the assassin. "You're deadly with your knives. Now you need to be deadly with a bo staff, a sword, hand to hand. These two can help you with that if you let them."

Ha. Not unless Valek ordered him. Or… Hmm. If she shared her knife-fighting techniques, he might be tempted to show her a few moves.

Valek called Ari over. Once they were assembled, he said, "I'm counting on the four of you to work together and find how the smugglers are transporting illegal goods into Ixia. Ari's the team leader for this mission. Keep me updated."

"Yes, sir," they said in unison.

While Janco wasn't happy with the new members, he suspected Little Miss Assassin was annoyed that Ari was chosen as team leader. She stood next to Sergeant Grunt as if waiting for Valek to yell *go*. Two of them against him and Ari would be interesting as long as she didn't have her knives.

"All right, chief. What's next?" Janco asked.

"Team meeting," Ari said.

"Here?" Little Miss Assassin glanced around at the clusters of fighters.

"Hell no. First meeting will be at the Black Cat Tavern this afternoon."

Sweet. "Ari, you the man."

14

YELENA

I scanned the four men and three women surrounding us on horseback. Most of them had drawn their hoods up over their heads. If I'd had my magic, I'd know exactly whom I dealt with and would have clouded their thoughts so we could continue on our way to the Avibian Plains. Instead, I told Leif to put his machete away so we could play nice. For now.

"Is there a problem?" I asked.

One person pushed his hood back and I recognized him as Captain Romas from the Citadel's guards.

"Yes," Romas said. "I'm here because the Sitian Council believes you're in danger."

Leif snorted. "And that's news?"

Romas ignored him. "Seems an assassin is after you, and we are to escort you back to the Citadel so we can provide you with additional protection."

Ah. "Please tell the Council that I appreciate the concern, but I'm quite safe. And I'm not returning."

"We're not here as a courtesy. We have our orders."

"I don't care. The Council cannot order me."

"Liaison Yelena, a word in private." Romas gestured and an opening between his riders appeared.

I considered refusing, but was too curious about what he had to say. Kiki followed until we were far enough away.

"The Council is more than concerned. They know *all* about the danger you're in," Romas said in a low voice despite our distance from the others.

Fear swirled and I gripped Kiki's saddle. Was he implying they knew about my magic? Impossible.

"And considering you're heading straight to the man who vowed revenge on you, it would be wise to return with us."

"Quit dancing around the subject, Captain, and tell me what exactly the Council knows."

Concern creased Romas's brow and he leaned forward. "The Council has recently learned that your magic is gone and you are unprotected."

His words burned into me like a red-hot pontil iron, but I used every ounce of will to keep my face neutral. "Interesting rumor. Who started it?"

He shook his head sadly. "I've my orders. Please cooperate or I'll be forced to take drastic measures."

"Such as?"

"We are armed with Curare."

I shrugged. "Go ahead and waste the Curare." As I glanced back at Leif and Hale, I tapped my fingers on Kiki's neck, signaling her. "Come on, guys. We're done here."

When Romas gestured for his men to stop them, I leaned close to Kiki's ear and whispered, "Ask the others to dump their riders and run home, please."

Seven horses bucked at once, throwing their riders onto the ground, including Romas. They galloped north.

"Let's go!" I yelled.

Garnet and Rusalka joined Kiki as we raced south. Darts whizzed by my head, but I stayed low until we were out of reach. Then we slowed so we didn't exhaust the horses.

MARIA V. SNYDER

"What was that about?" Leif asked, riding next to me.

"Tell you later." I inclined my head, indicating Hale.

"We really should have returned to the Citadel," Hale said when he joined us. His hair was windblown and two red spots spread on his cheeks. "I don't know if I can protect you against an assassin."

"Not to worry, Skippy. Did you see how Yelena gave them the slip? She's more than capable of defending herself. You're just here to be arm candy."

I almost laughed at Hale's pinched expression, but the thought that the Council knew about my condition still burned, sending sweaty waves of fear through me. How did they find out? The only people who knew were Irys, Bain, Leif, Mara, Healer Hayes and Fisk. All trustworthy.

Unless someone tricked the information from Mara. A sweet, lovable woman who was kind to everyone and would never suspect duplicity. Except she kept Opal's secrets and knew how important this was. Unless someone forced the information from her.

I stopped Kiki.

"What's the matter?" Leif asked.

"Give us a moment, please?" I asked Hale as I pulled my brother aside.

"Okay, now you're really worrying me."

I explained about the Council. It didn't take long for Leif to jump to the same conclusions. "I'd better contact Irys. Why didn't you tell me sooner?" He dug in his saddlebags for a small super messenger.

"We were a little busy fleeing the Council's guards."

"Oh, right." Distracted, Leif gazed into the square-shaped glass. After a few minutes he glanced up. "She's checking."

We waited forever. If Mara had been hurt because of me, I'd never forgive myself. Kiki shifted her weight under me as if she, too, worried about Mara. She probably did. Mara fed her apples on her way to the glass shop every morning. As far as Kiki was concerned, a daily apple equaled unconditional love.

Leif's attention riveted on the glass. Then he smiled. I relaxed.

"She's fine and a little angry we didn't trust her to defend herself," he said.

"She wouldn't last against a skilled opponent."

"I know, but she said she'd match her pontil iron against your bo staff any day."

That would be an interesting fight. "Tell her she's on."

We resumed traveling. Once again, my thoughts contemplated the encounter.

Who else knew about me? The assassin was well aware of what he had done to me. Did that mean the assassin worked for the Council, or was in contact with one of the Councilors or aides? A more likely scenario.

After a few hours, we reached the border of the Avibian Plains and headed east. The long stalks of grass had turned brown and brittle. Various shades of browns, grays and tans covered the undulating barren landscape.

"It's dreary during the cold season," I said to Hale. "You should see this place in the warm season. It's bursting with color and life."

"What about the Sandseed's magic?" Hale asked in a small voice.

"Stick with us, Skippy. The protection doesn't attack family. Oh, wait, you're not family. Too bad. Good luck finding your way home." Leif chuckled.

Even after the decimation of a majority of the Sandseed clan members, the protection remained strong, attacking intruders by convincing them they were lost. They'd wander the plains for days until they died of thirst.

MARIA V. SNYDER

"You're not family, either," Hale said.

"Distant cousins. You know that weird magic you teased me about in school? I'll bet you wished you had some of that now."

"Don't listen to him, Hale. Garnet will keep you from going crazy."

"Lovely," he muttered.

Garnet pinned his ears back.

"He didn't mean it, Garnet," I said. "He's just scared." I gave Hale a pointed look.

"Oh…ah…right." He patted Garnet's dark neck. "It's my first time in the plains. I'm a bit…skittish."

Nice word choice. I gave him a thumbs-up. "Okay, Kiki, you're in charge." It seemed weird talking out loud to her after years of silent communication.

"What does that mean?" Hale asked.

"It means Kiki will decide the route we take to Fulgor," Leif supplied. "And she'll stop when the horses are tired or hungry or thirsty. We're just along for the ride. Oh, and hold on tight. It's a ride like no other."

"You mean because of that gust-of-wind gait you talked about?"

"Yep." Leif grinned.

As if on cue, Kiki broke stride and, with a hop forward, launched into the gait I'd dubbed her gust-of-wind gait. It felt as if we rode on a river of wind. That was the easiest way to describe the feeling. Kiki's hooves didn't drum on the ground. I didn't have to match my movement to hers. We flew, covering twice the amount of ground as a regular gait.

The magical gait only worked in the Avibian Plains and only Sandseed-bred horses had the ability. Handy, considering the plains, which were located southeast of the Citadel, stretched east to the base of the Emerald Mountains and south to the Daviian Plateau. A nice chunk of Sitia that we used as a shortcut on many occasions.

Kiki stopped to rest a couple of hours later. We collected firewood and Leif used his magic to start a fire. With Hale in charge of cooking dinner, Leif and I groomed the horses as they munched from their feed bags.

Leif broke the silence. "If the Council didn't find out from Mara about your...ah...condition, how did they?"

"The only possibility that makes sense is the assassin or the person who hired the assassin told one of the Councilors or one of their aides."

"I don't like the sound of that."

"Well, would you like the sound of Irys, Bain, Healer Hayes or Fisk betraying my trust better?"

"No."

"I didn't think so."

"No need to be snippy."

"Leif, word is spreading. Fast. I need to find a cure before all my enemies come after me."

Hale called that dinner was ready.

Leif tossed the currycomb at me. "Good enough."

I caught it, then finished brushing the knots from Kiki's tail. He might be satisfied with "good enough," but my Kiki deserved perfection.

When I finally finished, Leif was asking Hale what he thought of the gust-of-wind gait between slurps of a bread-and-cheese soup.

"It was...incredible," Hale said, smiling for the first time since I'd met him. "Like nothing else."

"Not many people have experienced it. You're in rare company, Skippy."

His smile dimmed and Hale focused on his bowl.

"Leif, how old are you?" I asked.

He creased his brow in confusion. "You know my age. I'm two years older than you."

"Then act like it. Stop calling Hale names."

"Do you know how many names Mr. Hale called me while we were in the Keep together?" Leif asked. "Dozens."

"And you were an annoying teenager who hated the world," I reminded him.

"Doesn't mean I deserved it."

"*No one* deserves it. There just comes a time when you need to forgive and move past it. We're going to be together for weeks. Can you try to be civil?"

Leif pouted, reminding me of Janco. "I guess, but only if I can have another bowl of the soup."

If only smoothing relations between Sitia and Ixia was this easy. I could retire.

"Since we will be traveling for a while, perhaps this is a good time to share with you the extent of my magic," Hale said.

Leif opened his mouth, but I shot him a look and he wisely kept quiet.

"That would be helpful." I encouraged Hale to continue.

"It seemed only fair, considering I'm very familiar with Leif's powers and your…er…current situation, Yelena."

Warning signals rang in my head, and I moved my hand closer to my switchblade without thought.

If Hale noticed, he didn't react. "You see, while I'm able to construct null shields in record time, light fires and communicate with my mind, I'm also able to hear."

"Hear what?" I asked.

"Hear with my magic, meaning I heard your whispered conversation with Captain Romas and your discussion with Leif by the horses."

"Whoa, I didn't know you could do that," Leif said.

"After the Ixian takeover, the Master Magicians decided not to advertise all their students' powers in case the Commander attacked us or another one of our own attempted to overthrow the Council. Since spies are always a concern, it was a sound strategy."

I agreed, but if Hale had this ability, could he be the one who'd informed the Council about me?

"I only use it when necessary," Hale said as if he'd read my thoughts. "I believed the encounter with the captain might not go in our favor, so I listened to be ready to act."

Smart.

"And what he said made sense. I'd already determined something was very wrong. Why would you need to be protected by a null shield? You're the most powerful magician—"

"That would be Bain," I said.

He shook his head. "Who else calls Master Bloodgood... Bain?"

"Uh, Irys?"

"And who calls Master Jewelrose...Irys?"

Only Bain and me. "Okay, you made your point."

"Face it, sis. You're in elite company." Leif bumped my arm.

"You call them by their first names all the time." I swatted his shoulder.

"Not in their presence."

"This is a pointless argument. I'm no longer a magician."

"For now," Leif said.

"How did it happen?" Hale asked.

He had the right to know. We could be attacked again and both Leif and Hale could lose their powers. I explained about the arrow.

"Never heard of a substance with that ability." Hale worried his bottom lip.

"If you wish to return to the safety of the Citadel, go ahead.

MARIA V. SNYDER

I wouldn't blame you. We should have been up-front about it from the beginning, but I was too…" Terrified.

"I think I'm safer with you than at the Citadel," Hale said.

"I'm not so sure about that, Skip…er…Hale. She seems nice now, but wait until you're part of one of her crazy schemes," Leif said.

Here we go.

"One time, I was bait for a necklace snake—"

"What is it with you and that story?" I demanded. "You survived, didn't you? We rescued our father, didn't we? And as I recall, I was the one who ended up wrapped in the coils of an amorous necklace snake."

Leif huffed. "It's a good story if you don't ruin it with all those little details."

I gazed up at the stars, seeking patience with my brother. Moon Man, my Sandseed Story Weaver, was up there in the sky probably laughing his deep laugh. Despite the six years since his death, I missed him just as much now as I had then. He'd probably spout some cryptic advice on how to solve my problem. But this time, I would welcome it.

Two days later we entered the city limits of Fulgor. The city was the capital of the Moon Clan lands and also where Opal and Devlen lived and worked. The bustle on the streets was dissipating as the sky darkened.

"We can stay with Opal. She's like my mother-in-law and loves having company. Plus she can cook."

"Not a good idea," I said. "We might attract the wrong element."

"No problem. Opal's deadly with her sais, and Devlen knows how to swing a sword."

"And Reema, your niece? Or have you forgotten about her?"

"Ah, that little scamp knows how to stay out of trouble. One time she helped me finish a pie, but when Opal discovered us... Poof! Reema was gone. Snug in her bed as if she didn't have cherry juice staining her lips."

"I'm sure Opal won't be happy to see me," Hale said drily.

"True. If you weren't all stiff and haughty and nasty—"

"I wasn't there to be her friend. I had my orders from the Council."

"That's enough, boys." I glanced around at the buildings. Factories mixed with businesses and homes—typical Sitian hodgepodge. "I'd like to keep as low a profile as possible. Let's find an inn for the night and visit your in-laws in the morning."

Leif perked up. "I know the perfect place."

We stopped at the Second Chance Inn. I gave Leif a questioning look over the name of the place.

"Second-best chef in town works here," he said.

Figures.

"Who's the best?" Hale asked.

"Guy named Ian, who owns a tavern called the Pig Pen. We'll go tomorrow. Wait until you taste his beef stew. After a mouthful, you'll never be able to eat another's stew again because the rest will taste like crap in comparison."

I ignored my brother as I helped the stable lad with the horses. The stalls were clean and the air smelled of fresh hay. Happy that they would be well cared for, I joined Leif and Hale in the inn's common room. We rented two rooms, one for me and Leif and the other for Hale.

The next morning, we left Hale to make inquiries about the recent prison break from Wirral as we took a circuitous route to Opal's glass factory.

"It's a nice place," Leif said. "She has four kilns on the ground floor and upstairs are the living quarters. Of course,

MARIA V. SNYDER

it gets superhot in the warmer seasons, but they don't seem to mind the heat. I guess it's because she'd worked in a glass factory almost all her life and he grew up in the Avibian Plains."

Leif continued to prattle on while I kept an eye out for anyone following us. No visible sign of anyone. When we reached the factory, the outer door was unlocked. Inside a young woman sat behind a desk in a receiving area that had been a storefront at one point in time. "Can I— Oh, Leif. Nice to see you again. Go on back." She waved us toward a door behind her that said Employees Only. Fancy.

Leif opened the door and the roar of the kilns slammed into me. He pointed to a thick gray foam coating the inside of the door. "Soundproofing."

Heat pressed on us as we entered. Workers sat at gaffer's benches, some gathered molten slugs of glass, and another cracked a vase off a blowpipe and into an annealing oven. I smiled, remembering Opal's lessons on how to blow glass. That knowledge had saved my life and allowed me to leave the fire world.

I didn't recognize any of the workers, who glanced at us but didn't stop shaping the glass even when Leif said hello to a few.

A shriek pierced the kilns' roar. Leif and I grabbed our weapons, but a small girl with blond corkscrew curls dashed from between the equipment. Opal was hot on her adopted daughter's heels.

"Come on, Reema. You'll be late for school," she yelled as Reema hid behind Leif.

"Uncle Leif, protect me!" she cried.

"After you ditched me with an empty pie pan? No way." He sidestepped, exposing her.

She shrieked again and clutched my legs. "Aunt Yelena, don't let them take me away, please!" Reema implored with her big blue eyes.

Who could resist that? Not me. I picked her up. Technically, I wasn't her aunt by blood or marriage, but Opal insisted I was family. And Valek, too.

"Oh, for sand's sake," Opal said. "It's just school, Reema. You'll be home in time for dinner."

Reema smoothed her beautiful face into an innocent expression. "We have company. It would be rude of me to leave now."

What a con artist. I laughed.

Opal frowned. "Don't encourage her."

Devlen joined us. "There she is!" Most of his long black hair had escaped a leather tie and his shirt was rumpled. He nodded at us. "Come on." He took his daughter from my arms.

She shrieked. "No, Daddy, I want to stay and visit."

"We'll be in town for a couple days," I said. "If you go to school, I'll finish the story about the curious Valmur tonight."

"Promise?"

"Promise."

She pouted, but no longer assaulted our eardrums with that high-pitched squeal. Devlen carried her off.

"Let me down. I wanna walk," she said.

"So you can run off again? I think not," Devlen replied in a tired voice.

Opal gestured to her office. "Come in and let's have a proper hello."

We entered the room, and the kilns' noise and heat dulled. More of the gray foam had been sprayed on the glass walls, but a strip had been left clean. Probably so she could see the factory floor.

"I told you she was a scamp," Leif said, giving Opal a hug.

"And I never disagreed with you. Hello, Yelena." She hugged me next. "Nice to see you."

MARIA V. SNYDER

"What? No nice to see me?" Leif plopped into one of the chairs.

"Talk about a scamp," I said.

Opal laughed. After all of Opal's troubles, it was wonderful to hear the lighthearted sound and see the spark of amusement in her dark brown eyes. Her golden-brown hair had been pinned up in a knot, but strands hung down in a haphazard fashion.

"I'm sorry we came at a bad time," I said.

"Oh no. Don't worry. This is just our morning routine. Reema runs and hides and we search for her, drag her out from whatever hiding spot she's found and carry her to school. You actually helped by intercepting her."

"Ever think of homeschooling?" Leif teased.

"Yes. But she's never been to a school before, and if she wants to join her brother at the Magician's Keep, she needs to learn how to be with other kids her age."

"Do you think she'll be invited to the Keep?" I asked. At age ten, Reema was too young to show any magical potential, but her older brother, Teegan, had plenty to spare. Bain hoped he'd grow into master-level powers by the time he finished the five-year curriculum.

"Yes. She has an intuitive sense that is more than natural. It's hard to explain. She can be so mature and smart at times, acting older than ten, yet at other times, like in the mornings before school, she runs around like a spoiled five-year-old." Opal sank behind her desk. "While I'm happy to see you both, I sense it's not to discuss parenting methods. Unless you have some news about my sister, Leif?" She raised her eyebrows.

Leif blushed bright red. Now it was my turn to laugh. My brother, the prude.

"I'll take that as a no. Yelena?"

My mirth died in my throat. "Not even engaged."

"Too bad. Another wedding would be fun."

"Except we'd be targets. Better to elope like you and Devlen."

"Which worked until my mother found out about it."

I smiled, remembering the big gala Opal's mother had thrown for them.

"Best food, ever," Leif said.

"What about at your own wedding?" I asked.

"I was too nervous to eat."

"Wow, I didn't think that ever happened," Opal teased.

"Not funny."

After a pause in conversation, Opal asked, "Do you want to wait for Devlen to return before you tell me what's going on?"

"Probably a good idea," I said. Bad enough telling my story again. Best to avoid telling it twice.

"Then I'll fetch some tea." Opal left.

I scanned her office. Glass vases, bowls and sculptures decorated the tables and shelves. Stacks of orders had been arranged neatly on her desk.

Opal returned with a tray and poured four glasses. "Devlen's coming." She handed us each a steaming mug.

Devlen slipped into the room. He'd fixed his hair and changed his shirt. He said hello and stood behind Opal with one hand clutching his mug as if it would protect him and the other resting on Opal's shoulder. Leif stared at him as if scenting his intentions. When Opal had first married Devlen, the relationship between Leif and Devlen had been strained. Leif had dealt with Devlen when he'd been addicted to the blood magic, and hadn't witnessed Devlen's change firsthand, only heard about it through Valek.

I had seen Devlen's soul and knew him like no other. Probably why he acted embarrassed around me. Examining a person's soul was a ruthless and intimate experience, and I hadn't

MARIA V. SNYDER

shied away, stripping down the layers to see the good man underneath the childhood traumas and insatiable desire for magical power. He'd lost his way, but had been strong enough to find the right path. And Leif was learning to trust him, as well.

"Is this about the man who escaped Wirral?" Opal asked. "Devlen's been helping the authorities search for him, but the man's a magician and has just disappeared. Has the Council finally sent help?"

"That's one of the reasons we're here," Leif said. "But not at the Council's behest." He glanced at me.

I explained about my connection to Ben Moon and the attack in the woods. "Do you think he could have orchestrated it from Wirral?"

"No," Opal said. "That place is locked down tight. But he did have help, so one of his accomplices could have organized the attack to knock you out of the picture and ensure you didn't come searching for him. The prison break required a ton of planning and skill. Let's just say they'd never get a second chance."

"Do you know who his accomplices are?"

"Only two. A brother-and-sister team of magicians," Devlen said.

"Any clue as to where they are?"

"We tracked them for a couple days. They headed northwest from Fulgor before we lost them." Anger sparked in Devlen's blue eyes.

"Do you think they're hiding in Ixia?" I asked.

"We have searched most of Moon Clan's lands and still have not found them. It is the one place we cannot look."

True. I'd have to send Valek an update.

"You mentioned another reason?" Opal asked.

Here we go. I drew in a breath. You'd think the telling would get easier the more times I recited it, but no, it was even more difficult. At least I knew Opal and Devlen would understand better than anyone else. Each had lost their magic. However, Opal was immune to magic like Valek and Devlen was glad to be rid of the burden.

When I finished, Opal rushed over and embraced me.

"Oh, Yelena, how horrible!"

"I'm hoping it's temporary." I swallowed the fat fist in my throat. "And I'm hoping you might have some information."

"What type of info?" Opal asked.

"I suspect it's a poison, but there was a gap in time between the bolt's strike and my symptoms. What if someone siphoned my powers?"

Opal knotted her hands together. "Maybe Quinn learned—"

"It wasn't him. Unless he could do it from a hundred miles away?"

She relaxed slightly. "No. I needed to be close to the person."

Devlen squeezed her shoulder, giving her moral support.

"And Quinn's a good kid," Leif said. "He smells like the sea—fresh and honest."

"You mentioned being sick for a day. What were the symptoms?" Devlen asked.

I explained about my extreme swings in temperature.

Devlen almost sloshed his tea on Opal's head. "I know what it is!"

15

VALEK

Valek was pleased with the morning's matches. Ari and Janco once again proved why they were his seconds-in-command and Onora revealed quite a bit about herself. Gerik hadn't been lying when he claimed to be good at fighting. He hadn't won a match, but, then again, he'd been fighting the best in Valek's corps. And he'd picked the wrong weapons against those two. Next time, Valek would suggest Gerik choose the bo staff against Ari and hand to hand against Janco.

What impressed him the most about Gerik was the man kept his cool during both bouts. Something Onora struggled with. He'd also confirmed that the two of them at least knew each other. Ah, the plot thickened. And more reasons to take a trip to MD-2.

According to the Commander's detail, they'd followed security protocol to the letter the night Onora attacked and Gerik had not been on duty. Valek was certain the intel Gerik provided to Onora helped her avoid the sweeps.

No. The real problem lay in the protocol and why the security team hadn't noticed the gaps. Valek had read it that morning and spotted the lapses right away. Alarming, since Maren had written the new protocols while Valek had been in Sitia.

And he didn't like where his thoughts led. Perhaps Maren had done it on purpose because of the Commander's request. Perhaps this had all been a test, including Onora's timely arrival. All of which Valek had failed.

As for the reason for the test, the Commander might be feeling vulnerable. Maybe Onora sneaked into the Commander's suite before Valek had returned and they'd worked out a deal.

Regardless of why the Commander had tested him, Valek would not let anyone else write the protocols or assign members to the Commander's detail again. He'd start fresh with a new group. Although he'd still like to talk to Maren. Where was she?

He returned to his office to finish a few things before his trip north. Reviewing personnel files and writing instructions on how to patrol a castle failed to keep Valek's mind from wandering. There had been no clue as to what mission Maren had been given and that irked him. Was finding Maren another test?

Valek was very familiar with tests. When he had moved from hand-to-hand combat to dueling with weapons at Hedda's school, the older students and instructors had tested his new skills at random intervals. He'd learned to sleep with a weapon in each of his hands.

He'd learned how to fight with different types of swords, bo staffs and a number of other sharp implements and nasty-looking devices, but fighting with a knife was his favorite. He loved getting up close and personal with his opponent, despite the drawbacks, like finding out Arbon sprinkled too much garlic in his food. And he loved how the blade was a deadly extension of his hand. Soon no one could beat him in a knife fight.

Hedda's threat hadn't been serious. No way he could master all the weapons within ten days. That would have been impossible. It was closer to ten months, and during that time Valek had turned fourteen.

Near the end of the ten-month span and at the start of the heating season, Hedda led him into a room. Weapons hung on the walls and a mat covered the floor. An unarmed man stood in the center. He wore the same clothes as Hedda, a light green tunic and loose pants. No boots.

Valek turned to her. "Another test?"

She smiled. "Yes." Hedda gestured to the assortment of weapons. "Use as many as you like. The goal is simple. If you can draw Jorin's blood, you win."

Sounded easy enough. Valek pulled two knives from the wall and tucked a couple of daggers into his belt. He faced Jorin. The man remained relaxed with his arms at his sides. Still unarmed. Hedda watched from the doorway.

"Whenever you're ready, Valek," she said.

He suspected a trick and that he was about to get trounced by this man. A lesson in how weapons made you lazy and gave you false confidence. Or something like that.

Valek nodded to the man and assumed a fighting stance. He shuffled close and attacked, slashing at the man's throat with his left hand and stabbing at his stomach with his right. Jorin twisted, grabbed both Valek's wrists and yanked him forward, ramming Valek with his knee before tossing him aside.

Valek scrambled to his feet as pain radiated from his ribs. No doubt Jorin had more training and experience than Valek. Determined, Valek rushed him again and ended up on his back again.

New strategy. Valek flipped his knives over, grabbed the blades and threw one a second after the other. A stickiness brushed his skin as both knives veered, missing Jorin by inches.

Interesting. Valek yanked a sword from the wall. Best to keep away from this guy. He approached and encountered a heavy thickness as if he'd walked into an invisible spiderweb. Odd. But not as odd as the surprise on Jorin's face as Valek lunged with his sword. What else did he expect? It wasn't like Valek hid the weapon behind his back.

Jorin countered in time, but he scrambled to keep ahead of Valek's strikes, which had slowed because of that strange sticky pressure. Too bad his blade couldn't cut through the invisible strands.

Eventually, Valek nicked Jorin's arm and Hedda ended the oddest match Valek had ever fought.

"Jorin, I told you to use magic on him," Hedda said.

The man pressed a cloth to his bleeding cut. "I did."

"All of it?" she asked.

"I couldn't read his thoughts or manipulate them. He broke through the shield and I couldn't stop his charge. Nothing worked."

"Wait, magic?" Valek asked.

"Yes," Hedda snapped. "You need to learn how to fight a magician. How else can you…?" She gaped at him.

Confused, Valek glanced at Jorin. "You're a magician?"

"Yes."

"That's why the knives missed. You used magic."

"Yes."

"Is that why…?" Valek brushed his face. The feeling of cobwebs still tingled on his skin.

"Why what?" Jorin asked.

"Why the air was sticky?"

Jorin exchanged a look with Hedda.

"Try it again," she said.

Turning his brown-eyed gaze on Valek, Jorin's brow creased. A wave of thick air engulfed him, clinging to his clothes.

"Is this how magic feels?" he asked, moving his arms around.

MARIA V. SNYDER

"You shouldn't feel anything," Jorin said. "You should be frozen solid, unable to move a muscle."

The magic pressed on him, slowing him down but not stopping him. He walked toward the magician. The soupy syrup thickened, but he pressed on and reached Jorin.

Sweat beaded the man's forehead. He released a breath and the air returned to normal. "Nothing works on him."

"So that means…" Delight danced in her eyes. "He's immune to magic. And he might be the one to assassinate the King."

"I *will* assassinate the King," Valek corrected. While he was unsure what this immunity meant, there never was any doubt about the King.

"I've never heard of anyone being immune. How long have you had this?" Jorin asked him.

"I don't know. My grandfather was the only magician in my family, but he died years ago. Other than him, I really haven't been around any magicians."

"How about that sticky feeling? Have you felt it before?" Hedda asked.

Valek searched his memory. "Once when I waited on your stoop. During our talk, I felt a brief touch."

"Ah, that's why Colette couldn't get a read on you. We thought it was due to the trauma."

Trauma. What a nice concise word for such ugliness and pain.

Hedda shook her head as if she still couldn't believe it. "And here I thought this would be a surprise lesson for you and contain your cockiness. It was a surprise all right." She blew out a breath. "Well, now, King Killer, more good news. I'm going to personally see to your training."

Uncertain what it meant to be Hedda's student, Valek decided to focus on her inflection instead. Before when she called him King Killer, it was a tease, like calling a small man big. Now her tone implied a matter-of-factness. That he liked very much.

Hedda's training included the usual sparring matches and mind-numbing repetition until he could perform a move in his sleep. However, he finally was learning the art of being an assassin, reading body language, picking locks, studying poisons, climbing buildings and lying without giving himself away.

"Remind me not to play poker with you, King Killer," Hedda joked one night after he'd convinced the cook that Arbon had spilled the soup even though white cream spotted Valek's pants.

When Valek had been at the school for almost two years, Hedda declared he was ready. He was fifteen years old. A mix of pride and unease swirled in his chest as he entered her office. Would she assign him a mark? Hedda not only trained assassins, but she was the go-between for many of her former students, taking half the assassination fees for her services.

However, the bigger question was, could he kill a man who hadn't been a party to his brothers' murders?

"I've a job for you, King Killer," Hedda said. "Think you can handle it?"

He straightened. "Yes."

"Good. You're the new stable boy for the Icefaren Garrison."

Not quite what he'd been expecting. "Who's the mark?"

"No one."

Had he done something wrong? "Then why?"

"A huge part of this job is collecting information. You need to learn this aspect. The actual assassination is the least time-consuming task. First you spend months and months assembling information about your mark. Then you spend days and days planning your attack. The attack itself might take hours at most."

"All right. What information do you need?"

"A precise account of the comings and goings of all the officers in the garrison."

"You could bribe one of the enlisted for a copy of the duty roster."

"I could."

He considered. "But that might tip them off."

"Right. It's always better to have someone trusted inside. And not just anyone, but a person who is invisible. And that would be...?"

Valek recalled his lessons. "Servants, housekeepers, low-ranking staff members and the homeless."

"Correct. No one pays attention to the stable boys. Make sure you act and dress appropriately. There will be a place for you to sleep. If you're arrested, you are on your own. You're to report at dawn. Better get going."

"Yes, sir."

"Oh, and King Killer."

He turned. "Yes?"

"You'll be paid. Not very much, but I expect half of your wages. The other half is yours."

It seemed a fair deal. Hedda had provided food, clothing and weapons for the past two years and had asked for nothing in return. He wondered just how much an assassin earned. From the size of her school, he guessed quite a bit. And in the past two years the local authorities hadn't bothered them once, which meant a large portion of that money had to go to bribing the officials.

Valek packed a couple of knives, a handful of the gray rocks and another set of clothes. Stable boys couldn't afford more than two sets. He changed into his oldest tunic and pants. The clothes he'd arrived at Hedda's in no longer fit. He'd grown taller and thicker. Not barrel-chested, bulging-biceps thick, but a ropy muscular. Valek worried about keeping in shape while mucking out stalls.

After walking for four hours, he arrived at the stable just after dawn. The Stable Master cuffed him on the ear for being late. The desire to stab the guy flared, but stable boys didn't stab their masters if they wanted to stay invisible. He swallowed instead, gazing at the ground.

"Git your ass in there and help Reedy," the Stable Master said.

Valek helped Reedy, a skinny kid barely twelve, groom, water and feed horses. He mucked out stalls, swept up horse hair and cleaned tack. All day. The Stable Master's leftovers were their meals—not enough for one let alone two. And the "place to sleep" was a pile of straw bales under a scratchy smelly horse blanket in an empty stall, unless all the stalls were filled—then it was on a pile in the aisle without a blanket. And since it was the start of the cold season, he needed that blanket.

He kept track of the officers and discovered their names from their companions and the Stable Master. Most went out in the morning and returned in the evening. But groups would leave and be gone for days, doing sweeps of the outer towns.

After adjusting to the hard labor and long hours, Valek used the cover of darkness to climb into the rafters and onto the stable's roof to keep in practice. He also scaled the garrison's main building. A four-story wooden structure with windows.

His pay was a pittance, but he saved half for Hedda. With the other half he bought a few carving tools and a blanket at the market on his day off—the first in a month.

He showed Reedy how to carve. The boy picked it up quick.

"Maybe you can apprentice to a wood-carver," Valek suggested. "It's better than here."

The boy shrugged. "I like it here. Better than starving on the street. And the horses like me."

True. They preferred Reedy's care over his. Even though he'd learned more about horses in the past month than he thought possible. At one point, he thought he had marked all the officers, but then a big group he hadn't seen leave arrived one night from a sweep. Guess one month wouldn't be enough time.

Boredom eventually drove him to attempt to open a window and slip inside the garrison, thinking he'd find a duty roster and copy it so he could return to Hedda's.

Late one night, he climbed up to the third story on the darkest side of the building. The window opened without trouble. He entered an office, but it was too dark to read anything and he hadn't brought a match for the lantern. Voices nearby spooked him and he left.

Some assassin. He'd gone in unprepared and without an inkling of who was around that office or knowing if a light would have tipped them off to his presence or not. Next time, he'd be ready.

"Hey, boy." A boot nudged him in the ribs later that night. "Wake up. Help the riders."

Half-asleep, Valek rolled off the straw and pulled saddles from sweaty horses as the men collected their saddlebags. They laughed and joked and ignored Valek and Reedy.

"There's Fester. What took you so long, Fester? Did you get lost?" The man chuckled as another rider entered the stable.

"Damn horse threw a shoe," Fester grumbled.

Valek froze as ice seized his heart. That voice. He turned as Fester dismounted. The stable's lanterns lit the officer with a pale yellow glow. Beady eyes, bulbous nose, cracked lips—

Valek would never forget this murderer's face. He reached for his knife and paused, closing his eyes for a moment.

Lose the anger. Hedda's words repeated in his mind.

When he opened his eyes, he noticed the details he'd missed before. How many other armed officers crowded the stable. How close the Stable Master stood to him. If he stabbed Fester, they'd be on him in seconds. And what about the two other murderers? They'd be from this garrison, as well. Kill one and it would alert the others. Better to wait.

As he groomed the horses, he had to give Hedda credit. This was more than a training exercise in patience. He'd been so focused on learning to kill, he hadn't spared a moment to consider how he would find the soldiers who'd murdered his brothers in the King's name. She'd been one step ahead of him.

Over the next season, he discovered the names of the other murderers. He learned their schedules, habits, vices, and virtues— none. After he collected enough information, the next stage, planning, loomed over him. Without any prior instruction on how to plan revenge, he returned to Hedda's school on his next day off.

"That's an impressive amount of intel you collected in three months," Hedda said. "You need to find the best way to kill all three without being caught."

"That's why I'm here."

"All right. How do you want to do it? Kill them when they're together or pick them off one by one?"

Valek mulled it over. He doubted he could pull off killing three men unless he poisoned their water. Too easy a death. Only a knife stabbed in their guts or slit across their throats would satisfy him. "One by one."

"It'll take time. Kill one and the garrison will beef up security while they search for the killer. Months might go by before they relax enough for you to get to another one."

"Unless I find a night when they are each alone. I could

MARIA V. SNYDER

kill them all, and by the time they're discovered in the morning, I'll be long gone."

"But what are the odds they'll be by themselves at the same time?"

"Slim. I could follow them when they're out collecting taxes."

"But what if they go in three different directions? That's a lot of ground to cover. And news spreads fast."

"I'm not going to get all three at once, am I?"

"I think you just figured that out."

"Best to get who I can, then wait. There's no rush. I know who they are."

"Now you're thinking like an assassin. And in between, you can earn money and experience doing *other* jobs," Hedda said.

Lieutenant Fester would be the first man Valek assassinated. As he waited for the perfect opportunity, he carved a statue, transforming the ugly gray rock into a black figure with sparks of silver. His chance came a week later. No squads were due to arrive that night and Fester had just returned from a long sweep.

After finishing his stable chores for the night, Valek lay on a stack of straw bales and waited for Reedy and the Stable Master to fall asleep.

The soon-to-be dead man had headed straight to the garrison and, Valek hoped, to bed. The lieutenant frequently complained about the uncomfortable travel shelters and run-down inns the soldiers overnighted in, and each time he returned home, he made a beeline for his own bed.

The ragged snores from the Stable Master's room at the far end of the stable soon joined the soft nighttime noises of the horses. Valek slipped out the window of the empty stall he shared with Reedy. The boy didn't move.

A half-moon provided enough light for him to navigate the compound even though he stayed hidden in the shadows. He wore all black, and once he was well away, he stopped to cover his face and hands with black greasepaint. The air held a chill. However, by the time he reached the main building, he'd sweated through his clothes.

Leaning against the wall below Fester's third-floor rooms, Valek pressed a hand to his chest, willing his heartbeat to slow. Emotions jumbled together, clouding his thoughts. Fear mixed with anger. Hate churned along with trepidation. One thing to think about killing a person, quite another to do the actual deed. Could he?

He focused on the image of his brother Vincent lying in a pool of his own blood and intestines. Vincent's expression frozen in surprised pain as he clutched his stomach. His skin as cold as the snow underneath him. The echo of Vincent's laugh thumped in Valek's heart as the memory of their mother chasing them after they'd knocked down her clothesline full of sheets. Neither one of them could resist the lure of fresh, clean sheets blowing in the breeze. Stealth tag had to be played despite stern warnings to keep away. And that time a rowdy collision led to a collapse. They'd bolted and hid behind the shed until their mother had cooled down.

Vincent had been fifteen when Fester's sword cut him down. Their mother had held Valek back as his brother staggered to the snow. Her fingernails had pierced his shoulders, drawing blood. Small half-moon-shaped scars still marked his skin.

Valek pulled in a breath.

Lose the emotions.

The man murdered his brothers. Justice would finally be done tonight. And experience gained for the ultimate goal—

MARIA V. SNYDER

the King. Pushing the fear, doubt, hate and anger away, Valek drew icy determination into his heart.

He scaled the wall to the third story, slid the window open and paused, listening. The creak of a bedspring and sleep mutterings sounded from the bedroom. Valek eased into the room. The dim moonlight outlined a bulky shape beneath a blanket. He grabbed his knife, advancing on Fester.

By the time Valek reached the bed, his heart rate had returned to normal. With one quick hop, Valek knelt on Fester's chest and pressed the blade against his fleshy throat.

"What the—"

"Shut up and listen," Valek said in a low voice. "Do you remember the tanner's sons? Three boys, Vincent, Viliam and Victor? Ages fifteen and seventeen-year-old twins?"

"Look—"

"Yes or no?" Valek cut into the skin. Blood oozed.

Fester hissed in pain. "Yes."

"You missed one. Sloppy."

"Orders." Panic sharpened his voice. "I was under orders."

"To murder?"

"To make an example out of them. The blizzards had been so bad...no one in Icefaren wanted to pay their taxes." The words tumbled from his lips in a rush. "Boss said the King needed his money and we had to show them what would happen if they didn't pay."

"He targeted my family?"

"No. Just said to pick—" Fester realized his mistake. "I didn't—"

"What's the boss's name?"

"Captain Aniol."

"You should have told your boss to go to hell." Valek sliced deep into the man's throat.

Blood sprayed, soaking Fester's shirt, sheets, blanket and

Valek's sleeves. A hot metallic smell filled the air along with the stink of excrement and body odor. The shine in Fester's eyes dulled as all color leaked from his skin.

Valek stared at the dead man. No regret pulsed inside him. Just a deep feeling of satisfaction.

He wiped his blade and hands on Fester's blanket. Then he removed the statue from his pocket. The figure resembled Vincent. He placed it on Fester's still chest before Valek climbed out the window. Sliding the pane back into place, Valek descended the wall. The compound remained empty at this time of night. The soldiers patrolled only the outer perimeter.

Before he had reached the stable, he had stripped off his shirt and thrown it into one of the still-smoldering burn barrels. Then he had washed the greasepaint from his hands and face. Slipping back into the stall, he had donned a clean shirt and reclaimed his spot on the hay bales.

No sense running away and tipping them off about the culprit. Better to stay and watch and learn all he could about Captain Aniol.

Hedda had called it hiding in plain sight.

A sudden notion jolted Valek from his memories. Maybe the reason he couldn't determine Maren's whereabouts was because she'd been hiding in plain sight all this time? No. Maren had a distinctive stride, and he'd have spotted her by now.

The reason must be because the Commander was up to something. And the only thing that he wouldn't inform Valek about or include him in was something big involving Sitia. Something that would ruin their diplomatic relationship if the Sitians found out.

Valek didn't know what was worse, the Commander not trusting him or the fact that more trouble between the two countries could lead to war.

MARIA V. SNYDER

16

JANCO

The Black Cat Tavern was everything a tavern should be—long bar with plenty of stools and bartenders, big tables for groups of rowdy soldiers, pretty servers who knew how to handle drunken customers, and little nooks around the edges for hosting private conversations. Plus the ale was to die for! Just the right blend of hops and barley and—

"Janco! Are you paying attention?" Ari asked.

"Sure, chief. Me and Little Miss Assassin are going to go undercover, and—"

"Not you—Gerik and Onora."

Janco shook his head. "Not happening."

"Why not?"

"'Cause we can't trust them together. And, as much as I'll miss you, Ari old boy, I'm gonna take one for the team."

Ari rubbed his face. They sat in their favorite nook—the farthest from the door and the deepest in shadow. Onora refused to order a drink. She'd leaned back in her chair with her arms crossed as if they were going to jump her. As if. The grunt sipped his ale, pretending to be relaxed. Except he gripped the glass hard enough for the muscles on his forearm to pop. Impressive pop, though.

"I know better than to ask, but...take one for the team?" Ari set his mug down.

"All your plans are swell, really they are, but they're not gonna work. The same people who recognize us are gonna spot Sergeant Grunt here right away. We need to come at this from a different direction."

Understanding lit Ari's eyes. "Sitia."

"Yup. I'll take the young pup south and you and the grunt do all the typical stuff we do to find information—interrogate the prisoners, follow the leads—so it looks like we're investigating."

"We have to determine a potential location of the smugglers first. The border's over a thousand miles long with lots of small Sitian towns nearby. And you'll need a good disguise. They know you in Sitia."

Janco pished. "The least of my worries."

"And what's your biggest worry?" Onora asked, speaking for the first time.

"My mother. I'm supposed to visit her. It's been forever and she's not gonna be happy."

She huffed in disbelief. "I can kill you in your sleep and you're worried about your mother?"

"You won't kill me."

"Why not?"

"'Cause Valek scares you. While my mother... Nobody scares her."

After their meeting, Ari and Janco returned to their office in the castle. Half the size of Valek's, it contained two of everything—desks, chairs, filing cabinets. One set was neat and organized, and the other set was Janco's. Valek had left a huge stack of reports from his spies in Sitia on Ari's desk. They scanned through the latest ones. Concentrating on the

MARIA V. SNYDER

information from the towns close to the Ixian border, they searched for anything out of the ordinary.

After a few hours, Janco's head ached with all the mind-numbing details. "Listen to this… Forty-three citizens attended the town meeting along with four officials. They voted to install a statue outside the town hall. Seriously? This is what our spies think is important?" He tossed the report on the messy pile with all the other useless data.

"This one dutifully records the entire conversation between two wives of two low-level aides in the Cloud Mist Clan. They talked about a woman named Melinda, who was in labor for three days and had triplets." Ari snapped his shut.

They worked for a while in silence. Janco's vision blurred as he skimmed an inventory list in a factory in the Moon Clan's lands—spare wagon wheels, hitches, nuts, bolts, drying racks, rollers, glass bottles, tubing… As he was about to close the file, an item jumped from the page. A barrel full of leaves.

Why would a factory need leaves? Maybe it was for a medical substance. Yelena's father created all types of medicines and healing salves from the plants he'd collect in the Illiais Jungle. Janco read the rest of the report.

The spies had targeted the place because there had been plenty of activity inside, but as far as they could determine, no products had been produced. They had sneaked in and still couldn't figure out what the factory was manufacturing.

If they'd been making medicine, then the spies would have spotted vials or pouches. What else could be made from leaves? "Cigars."

"What about them?" Ari asked.

Janco handed him the file. "I think this place might be producing them."

Ari flipped through the pages. "It's possible. But there's no way to know if they're manufacturing the illegal Greenblade cigars or regular cigars."

"The building is located in Lapeer near the Ixian border. It's an isolated area of the Moon Clan's lands and far away from the other factories down in Greenblade's forests. It's a place to start."

"We should talk to Valek. He might know what this is."

They found Valek outside his office. He unlocked his door and ushered them inside.

"Did you find something?" Valek asked.

Ari explained about the factory, handing the file to Valek.

He scanned the report, then tapped on a page. "This mentions an amber-colored liquid."

"Could be honey-tree sap used in the cigars," Janco suggested.

"Or real honey or resin or adhesive," Valek said. "There could be a number of different explanations."

"We should check it out since we're going to Sitia anyway."

"You are?"

"Uh…" Janco glanced at Ari for help.

Ari gave him a you-got-yourself-into-this-you-get-yourself-out-of-it smirk. Some partner. Janco told Valek about their meeting and conclusions. "It makes the most sense. We're not going to get far on this side of the border."

Valek studied him for a moment. "Finish reading through *all* the reports first."

Janco groaned. "That'll take days."

"Then I'd suggest you enlist the help of the rest of your team members," Valek said.

"But…"

"But what?" Valek used his flat warning tone.

Janco ignored it. "We don't trust them, do we?"

"I trust you to keep an eye on them." He accompanied

them out of his office. "I'm going to be leaving in a few days, as well."

"Where are you going?" Janco asked.

"North to MD-2."

"Investigating our new recruits?" Ari asked.

"Yes." Valek locked the door and headed in the opposite direction.

As they walked down the hallway, Janco scratched the scar where the lower half of his right ear used to be. "If he doesn't trust them, then why are they working with us?"

"No idea."

"What should we do?"

"We'll do what Valek said—keep them close." Ari shrugged. "Who knows, they might prove useful."

Stranger things had happened.

While Ari rounded up the grunt and Little Miss Assassin, Janco carried armloads of files over to a conference room. Over the course of multiple trips, he filled the long table. By the time the others arrived, Janco had finished writing the cheat sheet to help them decipher the code to read the reports.

Sergeant Grunt frowned at the piles, but Little Miss Assassin sat down and tucked her bare feet under her.

Ari explained what they sought from the reports. "...an oddity or something that doesn't belong. Anything that sticks out."

"Like your bare feet," Janco said to the young pup. "Don't your feet ever get cold?" He couldn't resist asking. Not many rugs covered the stone floors of the castle.

"No." She kept her gaze on Ari.

"Well, when we go undercover, you're gonna have to wear boots."

"Okay."

Janco deflated. He'd hoped for an argument, but she wouldn't rise to the bait. She wasn't the chattiest person, either. At least the grunt asked a few questions as they spent the rest of the afternoon and evening reading reports. How could a person keep quiet that long? Was it part of her assassin training? If so, he'd never pass the test.

When the words blurred together and his eyelids drooped as if they weighed a thousand pounds, Janco called it quits for the night.

The next morning after running laps and training with Ari, he returned to the dreaded task of going through the files. Little Miss Assassin had beaten them there and she had quite a stack of rejects piled on the floor near her seat.

"Have you been here all night?" Ari asked as he sat.

"No." She handed him a couple of files. "These meet your 'odd' criteria."

Janco peered over Ari's shoulder as he flipped through the pages. Most of the information she flagged could be explained.

"Sitians use magic all the time." Janco shuddered. "It is odd, strange, unnatural, weird, crazy—"

"It's a tool," Ari said. "You just don't like magic."

"For good reason! Remember the time—"

"Why did you tag this one from Ognap?" Ari handed her a report.

The pup scanned it and pointed to a passage. "The agent counted sixteen wagons going into the mines, but only thirteen leaving. Doesn't make sense. These mines produce coal and ore, so they'd need all those wagons to ship *out* the product."

"Maybe they were having a slow day," Janco said. "See? The next day they had sixteen in and then sixteen leave... Oh." What happened to those other three?

MARIA V. SNYDER

Ari reclaimed the file. "Looks like there's a pattern. Every three days, more wagons arrive than leave."

"Could this be the smuggling route?" Janco asked. "Through the mines?"

"You tell me. You're the one who spent a few weeks undercover at Vasko's ruby mines."

He scratched his scar. "There are a million miles of shafts under the Emerald Mountains. It's possible that there's a way to cross under the Ixian border and come out in the Soul Mountains. But..."

"But what?" Little Miss Assassin asked.

"The mine owners guard their maps with their lives. They don't let strangers into the mines. For one person to know how all those shafts connect..." He shook his head. "Impossible."

"They don't have to know all of them. Just the right ones," Ari said.

"And you said Sitians used their power all the time. Why couldn't they use magic to find a passage into Ixia?"

The young pup had a point. Unfortunately. A cold dread coated his stomach. Two things Janco despised more than anything—magic and being underground. And it appeared he might just get both at once. Oh joy.

17

YELENA

I gaped at Devlen as blood slammed through my heart. Did he just say…? "You know what the poison is?"

"I believe so. But I am not sure how it will help you."

Relaxing my grip on the teacup before it shattered, I calmed my out-of-control heart rate. "Please explain."

Devlen set his cup down and sat in the other chair opposite Opal's desk and between me and Leif. My brother perched on the edge of his seat and Opal leaned forward. All our attention focused on Devlen.

"Your symptoms of being hot and then cold sounds like the effects of a poison called Freeze Burn," he said. "It is made from the roots of the reedwither plant that grows in the Avibian Plains."

"How come I've never heard of this poison?" I asked.

"Only the Sandseeds know about it, and the plant is so rare, only one was found during my father's lifetime, but the Sandseed who discovered it refused to divulge the location. According to our stories, it is fatal, but before the victim dies, they suffer those extreme temperature swings you described for a full day."

Another near miss. The familiar ache of disappointment panged. "It can't be Freeze Burn. I didn't die."

"That's 'cause it's *you*," Leif said. "You said you expelled most of the poison from your shoulder. Combine that with your healing powers and...voilà! You survived."

Great. How did this information help me? "Is there a cure?"

Devlen shook his head. "Not that I know. In our stories, everyone died."

I considered. "If we can find the plant, then perhaps my father can find a cure. Do you know what it looks like and where it grows?"

"All I know is that it has long thin leaves, resembling blades of grass. In fact, it is often mistaken for a patch of crabgrass until you get closer and see that the blades are attached to a red stem. It is said that the Sandseed horses avoid those plants because the roots poison the water sources nearby."

"Who else knows about the reedwither plant?" Opal asked Devlen.

"The Sandseeds. Not many of them left, though."

"Less people to interrogate," Leif quipped.

No one smiled.

"I don't believe the Sandseeds would share this information with anyone or use the poison to attack Yelena," Opal said. "They view her as family."

"I agree," Devlen said.

My thoughts circled back to Ben Moon and his famous ancestor. Perhaps the knowledge of Freeze Burn had been passed down to Ben in Master Magician Ellis Moon's book. It wouldn't be the first time forgotten information had returned to cause major problems—blood magic and the Kirakawa ritual both sprang to mind. Unfortunately, it probably wouldn't be the last.

"Do you think you can envision the plant so Kiki can pick

up on the image?" I asked Devlen. Perhaps she could find it in the plains.

"I can try."

Devlen accompanied us to the Second Chance Inn. When we left, we promised Opal to return that evening for supper. On the way to the inn, we talked about Devlen's new family.

"It has been an adjustment," he admitted. "I am still in shock that Opal wishes to be with me and the fact she *married* me..." He spread his hands wide. "Plus taking care of two children is a bigger responsibility than I had thought. It is a bit overwhelming at times."

"And then you have to deal with the crazy in-laws." Leif smirked.

"Opal's parents and brother have been very supportive."

I laughed. "Notice he didn't defend *you*, big brother."

"Shut up."

"How is Teegan doing at the Keep?" I asked Devlen.

"I was hoping you could tell us. We have only gotten a few letters from him."

"I haven't seen him. I don't spend too much time at the Keep."

"I thought since Master Jewelrose has taken him on as her student, she would confide in you."

That I didn't know. "She hasn't said anything. Although, I've been focused on my own problems."

He gave me a wry smile. "I understand all too well. When Opal drained my powers from me, I could not think of anything else besides reclaiming my power."

"Do you miss it?"

"Not at all. But it took me a season to adjust to the loss and another to realize I was much better off without it. She freed me from the addiction—I had not realized just how much that craving controlled my actions. I had done nothing but bad

MARIA V. SNYDER

things with my magic and have no wish to return to being that evil man. However, your loss goes beyond yourself. You have done nothing but good things, and if you do not recover your power, the entire world will suffer."

Leif huffed. "I think you're being melodramatic."

"Aren't you like the pot calling the kettle black or something?" I asked.

"Pardon me, oh great one. I forgot my place as a mere footnote in the history of Sitia."

Talk about being melodramatic.

"Is he—"

I cut Devlen off. "Annoying? Yes, all the time."

He studied Leif. "You are more...subdued at our house."

"That's 'cause I'm too busy keeping your daughter out of trouble."

"I take it Reema has Leif wrapped around her little finger?" I asked Devlen.

"Hey," Leif said.

"Yes. He needs a child of his own to learn how to *not* give in to her every demand."

I agreed. "That would certainly mature him. Unless it backfires and Leif regresses. Then poor Mara would have two children to deal with."

"I'm standing right here, ya know."

We ignored him. The late-morning sun warmed my back and I considered removing my cloak. The warming season would officially start in three days.

Arriving at the stable, we woke Kiki from a light doze. She nuzzled my pockets, searching for a treat. I explained to her what we hoped to do. "Can you help?"

She turned her blue-eyed gaze to Devlen and pricked her ears forward. He stared back. I glanced at Leif. Was it working? He shrugged. Leif had told me before he couldn't smell the horses' magic, but I hoped he sensed something.

Kiki snorted and returned to snuffling my pockets. I removed a small apple I had swiped at breakfast and fed it to her.

As she munched and slobbered apple juice on my palm, I asked Devlen about the search for Ben Moon. "Where was his last known location?"

"We had tracked him north to a town about two and a half days from Fulgor. A place called Red Oak. It is a small village—a handful of farms, houses and a couple factories along the Sunworth river. Their main industry is logging the surrounding forest and making parchment from the wood."

"And you lost him in a tiny town where strangers would stick out like a skinny pig in a hog house?" Leif asked.

"He left Red Oak in the middle of the night and disappeared without a trace. From there, he could have gone in any direction, but we circled the town and found no trail signs."

I mulled over the information. "The Sunworth river becomes the border between Ixia and Sitia for a few miles near the Emerald Mountains. Could he have traveled on the river going upstream to the mountains? Or perhaps downstream toward Featherstone lands?"

"We searched the banks for boot prints in the mud or evidence of a boat launch. Nothing for miles in either direction."

"Perhaps they used magic to erase their tracks," Leif suggested.

Logical. Ben was a powerful magician and he'd teamed up with at least a couple of others. "Does Ben have any other siblings?"

"One sister, who is taking care of their parents. They have not been in contact with Ben in years or his brother Owen's wife, who is still serving time at Dawnwood Prison."

Ah yes, Selene. I'd scared her by promising to take her soul to the fire world if she didn't cooperate and release my brother and Valek. "Dawnwood? Not Wirral?"

Devlen nodded. "She is redeemable. Selene cooperated with the authorities. Wirral is for those who are beyond redemption."

Too bad. Everyone deserved a chance at redemption.

Leif and I sat in the inn's common room, eating dinner and discussing our next move.

"We'll leave in the morning for the plains," I said.

"What about visiting Pazia?" He filled his spoon with a huge mass of banana pudding. The portion wriggled on its way to his mouth.

"First we find the reedwither plant and deliver it to Father. If he can't help us, then we'll visit her." I swirled the yellow dessert around my bowl. Unless Bain learned something from one of his old books, Pazia represented my last hope for a solution.

Then what? Find and confront Ben? I shied away from those thoughts. I'd worry about it when the time came. Coward, who me?

Hale joined us and a server arrived to take his order. He studied our expressions for a moment after she left. "I'm guessing the news isn't good."

"It's mixed." I explained about the Freeze Burn poison.

"Not a very original name," Hale said.

"The Sandseeds aren't known for their creativity." Leif finished his dessert and snagged my full bowl. "They call it like it is. It's very refreshing."

"Unless they're doing their Story Weaver thing," I muttered. "Then it's all cryptic and annoying." And hard to describe. "What about you? Anything?"

Hale repeated most of Devlen's information. "The town guards believe there are five of them, including Ben."

Four unknowns. "Are any of the others magicians?" I asked.

"Yes." He scrunched up his face as if sniffing a bad odor. "All of them."

Leif choked, spitting out gobs of pudding. "You mean all five have magic?"

Hale snapped, "That's what 'all of them' means."

Ah. There was Hale's snooty side. But even more disturbing was the news that Ben traveled with four other magicians. Even if I had my magic, I had no chance against them.

Leif ignored Hale as he wiped his chin. "Then it's a good thing we're heading into the plains. Should we leave this afternoon?"

"Why? There's no danger. Besides, we can't. I promised Reema I'd finish the story tonight." I considered as the server returned with Hale's food. "Has anyone spotted them since Red Oak?"

"No." Hale pulled his dinner out of Leif's reach.

Smart man. "Devlen speculated that they're in Ixia. What do you think?"

"Even with uniforms and the proper papers, it's hard to hide in Ixia. If I were them, I'd head east to the Emerald Mountains. There are lots of hiding places in the foothills." Hale cut into his steaming meat pie.

True. But just in case, I would send a message to Valek after we finished. "Did you learn the names of the other magicians?" I asked Hale.

"Yes. Although I only recognize one of them, Tyen Cowan. He was Ben's best friend when they attended the Keep together. Tyen's power to move large and multiple objects is impressive."

"He's from Opal's clan. Do you think she knows him?" I asked Leif.

"It doesn't matter." Leif pulled his glass super messenger from his pack. "I'll ask Irys for more information. Who are the others?"

"Rika Bloodgood, Cilly and Loris Cloud Mist. I'm not sure if they're married or siblings," Hale said.

Leif stared into the messenger as Hale finished his meal. I considered what to do with the information we collected. Best thing would be to give it to Devlen. Perhaps it would help with the investigation.

"Irys said she'll gather information on the prison gang and get back to me later," Leif said. "What should we do in the meantime?"

"Can you talk to your friends in the Council Hall and see if they'll tell you how they broke Ben out of prison?"

"Will do." Leif leaned back. He'd scraped every morsel of pudding from the bowl.

"How will the details of a prison break help you?" Hale asked me.

"I don't know. But there might be something that might seem odd or irrelevant that might give us a clue as to what they're planning."

"Wouldn't the authorities have done that already?"

"Yes, but they haven't been trained by Valek. He taught me to look beyond the standard replies."

"Taught us," Leif said.

"Correct. And in looking beyond, take Hale with you to the Council Hall. He can overhear any conversations you spark."

"Spark?" Hale asked.

"Yeah. You know how sometimes people might not talk to you, but after you leave…"

"They discuss it with a colleague. I get it." Hale paused. "Are you coming along?"

"No. Too many people know me at the Council Hall. And if I'm spotted, the security officers will expect me to aid in the search for Ben Moon."

"But you are helping."

"Yes, *I* am." I tapped my chest. "But the *Soulfinder* is unavailable and they'd rather have her assisting them in capturing five magicians."

"Oh." After Hale finished his dinner, they left the inn and headed into downtown. I sent the message to Valek, warning him Ben might be in Ixia along with his powerful friends. Then I spent the next couple of hours grooming Kiki. The repetitive motion of the currycomb through her coat calmed my mind and centered my thoughts. Valek had his carving rocks, and I had my beautiful Kiki.

Leif and Hale returned a few hours later. They joined me in the stable. Kiki, Garnet and Rusalka gleamed.

"Did you learn anything at the hall?" I asked.

"No one would talk to us," Leif said. "So..." He pulled a thick folder from underneath his cloak. "We helped ourselves."

"You stole it?"

"We borrowed it. Big difference."

"How?"

"Hale put the whammy on one of the secretaries. When she dashed off convinced her boss needed her right away, we... er...appropriated the warden's file, detailing the escape."

"All right. Let's go inside and read through the file. Maybe something will pop."

We spread the pages on the table and each took a section to study, then swapped them when finished. In the late afternoon, Leif stopped to pull his messenger out. He frowned at the glass cube and wrote notes on a crumpled piece of parchment. When he finished, he met my gaze.

"That bad?" I asked.

"Worse. These are powerful magicians that had been operating on their own, but now have teamed up. The Ethical Code means nothing to them."

"Tell us what you learned from Irys."

Leif smoothed the paper flat. "Ben Moon is the most powerful of the group. He can produce a null shield, light fires, move small objects and influence others with his magic.

"Tyen Cowan can only move objects. Unlike Ben, he's not limited in the size and weight of the object. Tyen has been known to move boulders." Leif tapped the file with his index finger. "He's the one who slammed all those correctional officers into the stone walls, knocking them unconscious.

"Cilly and Loris Cloud Mist are siblings born a year apart. They have the strongest mental communication skills of the group. They're the ones who used their magic to force the correctional officers at Wirral to unlock the doors and guide them to Ben's cell.

"Rika Bloodgood's specialty is illusions. Strong illusions that can even fool other magicians. She also has the power to create what's known as mirror illusions that mimic the surrounding area and will remain intact even if you view it through a null shield."

"Will her illusions fool Valek, as well?" I asked.

"Yes, and Opal, too. During the escape, the Wirral officers not in the area of the attacks saw and heard nothing out of the ordinary until it was too late."

"Quite the crew," Hale said into the silence.

I considered the array of talents at Ben's disposal. "Devlen said they lost the gang in Red Oak. With Rika's ability to cast convincing illusions, perhaps they hid behind an illusion. They could still be there."

"Possible, but doubtful," Leif said. "The town's too small. Someone would have said something by now."

True.

"But they could have left clues or a trail to where they went," Hale said. "They'd be pretty confident at that point that they'd given the authorities the slip."

"Good point," Leif said, although he didn't appear happy about it.

I straightened the papers and tucked them back into the folder. "Leif and I will take this along with our information to Devlen. He can bring it all to Fulgor's security forces." I stood. "Hale, we'll be back later. We'll leave for the plains in the morning." Hale nodded and we left the inn. The sun had set while we'd been reading through the file. Leif insisted we stop at the Pig Pen to purchase a container of beef stew to take with us.

"We can't arrive empty-handed," Leif had said.

The savory smell of hot meat and spices teased me the rest of the way to the factory. My stomach growled in anticipation. But as we neared the entrance, Leif slowed.

"Something wrong?" I asked.

"I caught a whiff…" He sniffed the air as if trying to catch a scent. Leif handed me the bag of food. "Go on inside. I'll just do a loop around."

Unease replaced hunger. "We should have brought Hale."

Leif pished. "Nonsense. I'm sure it's nothing."

Devlen answered the door and frowned. "You should not be alone."

I explained about Leif's loop.

He gestured me inside. "Go upstairs. I will wait for Leif."

In the apartment upstairs, Opal helped Reema with her

MARIA V. SNYDER

homework, explaining fractions. But as soon as Reema spotted me, she abandoned her lesson, grabbed the bag and proceeded to unpack the food. By the time she'd ladled out five bowls, Leif and Devlen had joined us.

My appetite returned with a wave of relief.

"Told you it was nothing," Leif said.

"Really?" I cocked an eyebrow at him.

"Okay, it was a family of cats in the side alley." Leif gave Devlen an odd look. "Seems they are…friends and wished to enter the factory."

Opal laughed. "We're having a problem with rodents in the factory and those cats are happy to take care of them for us."

"And in exchange?" Leif asked.

"Food and a warm place to sleep the night," Devlen said. "That big black tomcat has earned his keep many times over. He has taken down rats that are almost as big as him. We named him Valek, the rat assassin."

I laughed. How fitting. "I'll save him a piece of beef, then."

Reema served the stew and quiet descended as we devoured the food. Between bites, Reema talked about school. "Today the class learned about percentages, but I already knew all about them, except I don't call it by that fancy name. It's a cut. No matter what you scored on the street, you always had to give a cut to the bullies or to the so-called landlords or to the officers to look the other way." She scoffed. "I'm not learning anything."

"You learned the word *percentage*," Opal said.

Reema didn't bother to reply. "And the other kids are so… so soft! Crybabies and whiners." She pitched her voice higher. "Teacher, I spilled my milk. Teacher, she pushed me. Teacher, I'm a blubbering baby."

Suppressing a laugh, I kept my expression neutral. Reema had grown up on the streets and survived by dodging the cruelties of that life and, in her mind, that was all she needed to know.

"Reema, that is enough," Devlen said. "School is important."

"For what? When is the history of Sitia *ever* going to be important?"

"I can answer that," I said. "I thought the same thing when I first started my studies at the Keep. Master Bloodgood gave me so many history books to read, I thought I'd be crushed under them. And while reading them, I wished they had crushed me so I didn't have to read anymore."

"This isn't helping, Yelena," Opal said.

"*But* when I was struggling to understand my powers and terrified I was a Soulstealer, it was the information provided in those history books which led me to realize I was a Soulfinder. Big difference. That *knowledge* saved me from execution."

Reema squinted at me as if not sure whether to believe me or not. Her dubious expression aged her and she looked years older than ten.

"It's true," Opal said. "I was there."

"Well, I'd rather learn how to be a spy like Uncle Valek," Reema said. "Do you think he'd take me on as his student?" she asked me.

Opal and Devlen held their breaths. Leif choked on his food.

"Only after you graduated from the Magician's Keep."

"You're lying," Reema said.

"Reema!" Opal and Devlen said at the same time.

I was unable to stop the laughter bubbling from my throat.

Once he caught his breath, Leif said, "Gotta love the honesty."

"Yelena, we are trying to teach Reema manners and respect," Devlen said.

"All right. Reema, you can be brutally honest with *me* and

Uncle Leif at any time. However, you can't accuse someone of lying. You first have to collect proof, and—"

"Yelena!"

This time Reema laughed as her adopted parents scolded me. Her humor died when Opal told her to get ready for bed.

"You'll finish the story, right?" Reema asked me.

"Yes. I'll give you a few minutes to get changed and I'll be in. Where were we?"

"The curious Valmur was hanging from a vine by only one claw and a jungle cat waited below for him to fall."

"Oh yes. Now go." I shooed her away.

Reema hurried down the hallway leading to the washroom and bedrooms. The apartment contained only six rooms, kitchen, living area, washroom and three bedrooms. The office had been converted so each kid would have a room.

Once Reema disappeared into the washroom, I asked, "May I make a suggestion?"

"Of course," Opal said.

"Perhaps Reema needs to be in a higher grade. That might challenge her."

"The problem for her is that no one grade fits," Opal said. "In some areas like math and street smarts, she's well above her peers, but in others like history and reading…she's well below. We thought it best to keep her with the other ten-year-olds."

It made sense.

"And this way she'll learn patience." Opal cleared the table.

"I'm ready!" Reema called from the hallway. "Come on, come on!" She dashed into her room.

"Patience, eh? Good luck with that." I ducked as Opal threw a dish towel at my head.

As I strode toward her room, I glanced at the intricate and beautiful stained-glass murals hanging on the walls. I had never appreciated the versatile aspects of glass until I met Opal. I lingered over one particular swirl of orange that curved into yellow, split into red and looped back, tracing the pattern with a finger. Lovely.

A dim light shone through the small gap between the door and jamb of Reema's room. I pushed it wider as I stepped inside. And froze.

Reema's bed was empty. The curtains billowed as a cold breeze blew in from the open window.

18

VALEK

Over the next two days, Valek read through all the files, discussed the smugglers with Ari's team and assigned a new squad to the Commander's personal security detail.

Happy with Ari and Janco's strategy, Valek watched them depart the castle complex that morning. Janco and Onora headed south while Ari and Gerik went east. Janco had been in high spirits, and by the crease in Onora's forehead, she would either kill him by the time they reached their destination or ditch him. If she was smart, she'd discover how useful he could be when he wasn't driving a person to distraction and when he was—Janco was talented like that.

Valek returned to his office to finish preparing for his mission to MD-2. A light knock on the door interrupted him an hour later.

"Come in," Valek said. He grasped the handle of his knife.

A young page entered. The boy held out a rolled parchment as if it was a shield. "Message for you, sir." His voice quavered.

Valek took the message. "Thank you."

The page nodded and bolted.

Amused, he broke the seal and unrolled the message. His grin widened when he realized the note was from Yelena.

But soon his humor faded as he translated the text. The Sitian Council should be assassinated. He wished Yelena hadn't talked him out of it when the Council had handed Sitia over to those Daviian Warpers. Why wouldn't they warn her about Ben? Valek's fingers twitched. A sharp knife pressed to a Councilor's jugular would certainly help loosen his tongue.

Fear replaced anger when he finished reading the message. Yelena, Leif and another magician were headed to Fulgor—probably there by now. Despite the fact he couldn't go, Valek calculated how fast he and Onyx could travel to Fulgor from here—about four and a half days. The Commander had ordered him to keep out of it, and besides…Yelena was more than capable of defending herself. Plus she had Leif and another magician. At least she was being smart and cautious for once.

Although the desire to assassinate the Council still pumped in his heart. It'd be so easy. He could kill every one of them in a single night. Valek already knew the location of all their apartments in the Citadel, thanks to his alter ego Adviser Ilom. While pretending to be Ambassador Signe's aide six years ago, Valek had had plenty of time and opportunity to explore the Citadel. Time he hadn't wasted.

Assassinating all the soldiers who'd murdered his brothers hadn't been easy. After Lieutenant Fester's body had been discovered, security had increased and an investigation had been launched. Valek had kept a low profile and continued to gather intelligence about the soldiers in the garrison while working as a stable boy.

It took a full season for the guards to relax and lapse back into old habits. Valek carved more statues as he waited another couple of weeks just to let them get comfortable. And when Second Lieutenant Dumin returned early from his patrol the day before Sergeant Edvard left for his sweep, Valek

MARIA V. SNYDER

celebrated. His patience had been rewarded and killing those two murderers in one night would be sweet.

When the sounds of the garrison settled into the nighttime quiet, Valek slipped from the stable and crossed the complex. So familiar with the layout, he could have navigated the way to the officers' quarters blind.

As he scaled the outer wall, Valek remembered his brother Viliam, who had been the prankster of the family and the only one with gray eyes. The others had brown like their father and Valek's blue was inherited from their mother. Dad liked to joke that he would accuse the mechanic of improper behavior, except Viliam's twin, Victor, looked more like Dad. Of course, Dad wasn't laughing when Viliam had booby-trapped a container of leather dye. Their father walked around with black hands and arms for two seasons. Viliam wisely kept out their father's way during that time.

The image of Viliam's shocked and confused expression as a sword pierced his heart replaced Valek's fond memories. The weapon held by the soon-to-be deceased Second Lieutenant Dumin.

When he reached the fourth floor, Valek found Dumin's window and paid the man a visit. Just like he had with Fester, Valek woke him and informed him of the reason he was about to die. And just like Fester, Dumin pointed the finger at Captain Aniol.

"Not good enough," Valek said as he plunged his knife into Dumin's chest, angling the blade so it slid between the ribs and pierced the man's heart.

Cleaning the blood off his hands and blade on the blanket, Valek studied the dead man's face in the moonlight. A sense of rightness pulsed in his chest. Talk about the ultimate prank. Valek believed Viliam would agree. He placed the statue of Viliam on Dumin's chest.

Valek hurried to reach his second target. Sergeant Edvard stayed in the barracks and would be much harder to kill since he roomed with three other sergeants. Victor had shared a room with Viliam and, despite being twins, the two were opposites. Serious and thoughtful, Victor had been born first—a fact he never grew tired of reminding Viliam about every time the other wanted to include him in one of his schemes.

Of all his brothers, Valek had looked up to Victor. Even though his broad shoulders and thick muscles made others believe he'd be the bully of the family, Victor had a calming presence in tense situations. He also could be very protective if provoked, and when the soldiers had drawn their swords that horrible day, Victor had stepped in front of their father without hesitating.

Too bad Sergeant Edvard didn't pause before he sliced the edge of his blade along Victor's neck. Valek would never forget the angle of the blood as it sprayed from Victor's throat like a morbid waterfall.

The barracks consisted of four two-story buildings. The long structures lined the inside of the garrison's walls, one along each side. Edvard slept in a room in the west end of Barrack B on the second floor.

As Valek approached the barrack, he kept close to the shadows. A lesson he learned well—night and shadows were an assassin's best tools. Soldiers patrolled the top of the walls and had a good view of the courtyard if they turned around.

Unfortunately, Edvard's room lacked a window and the closest one opened into a large area full of bunks for the new recruits. Good thing this wasn't the first time Valek had entered the building. He'd been practicing while Edvard had been on patrol.

Grabbing the doorknob, Valek turned it in one smooth motion. Too slow and the damn thing would have squealed.

MARIA V. SNYDER

After Fester's murder all the doors in the complex had been locked at night, which gave Valek plenty of practice in using his lock picks. But their laziness had returned and now he didn't need to waste the time. He slipped inside the building and closed the door behind him.

He waited for his vision to adjust to the semidarkness. A few lanterns remained lit in hallways and the stairwells so if the soldiers were called for an emergency in the middle of the night, they wouldn't break their necks. Listening to the various soft sounds of many sleeping men, Valek ensured no one was awake before moving.

The old wooden steps to the second story needed to be climbed with care. His first attempt up these stairs resulted in a series of loud squeaks, which woke up a few soldiers who came out to investigate. With his heart hammering in his chest, Valek had scrambled up the wall and clung to the ceiling rafters like a large black spider. Too bad he didn't have the spider's eight limbs as his tired at an alarming rate and sweat slicked his grip. Just when he'd thought he'd fall on the men, they returned to bed.

This time, Valek knew where all the noisy spots lurked and he ascended to the second floor with nary a squeak. He ghosted down the hallway to the third door on the left. He pressed his ear to the door. Nothing. Turning the knob, Valek eased into the small room that contained two bunk beds and four trunks. He left the door ajar to let in some light. One of Edvard's roommates was out on patrol, so only three men slept inside. Two on the top bunks, and one on the bottom—Edvard.

Valek wished he could inform Edvard why he was about to die like he had the others, but that was impossible, so he crouched next to the bed and studied Edvard's body position.

He'd have only one chance, otherwise the noise would wake the man's roommates.

Edvard slept on his side, facing the wall. Valek pulled his knife. Stretching out both arms, Valek clamped his hand over Edvard's mouth while simultaneously slicing deep into the man's neck. Edvard jerked and a muted gargle came from his opened throat. Blood splashed against the wall and soaked into the pillow.

Valek pressed his hand to Edvard's mouth until the man stilled. His roommates didn't make a sound, but Valek had forgotten one important detail—the smell. Very soon the stench of blood, feces and urine would wake the sleeping men. Setting the statue of Victor on Edvard, Valek bolted.

He made it halfway down the stairs before the shout echoed on the wooden walls. No longer caring about being quiet, he raced down the steps, heading for the door.

Yanking it open, he dashed out just as another shout cried, "There he is."

Boots pounded, swords rang, voices yelled and called his position with heart-stopping accuracy. In his panic, he'd run right through the courtyard—visible to all. Rookie mistake. More soldiers poured from the other barracks.

Once he reached the far side, Valek slowed and glanced back. A swarm of soldiers followed a half dozen paces behind him. He wouldn't be able to outrun them, but perhaps he could outsmart them. Valek dived into the shadows along the next barracks, then scaled the wall to the roof and lay flat.

He drew in deep breaths in an effort to stifle the desire to gasp for air. As the bulk of the soldiers passed his hiding spot, Valek knew it would only be a matter of time until they found him. He needed to give them a target or a direction.

Valek rolled over and studied the activity on the wall. Soldiers rushed back and forth, trying to spot the intruder below.

　　　　　　　　　　　　MARIA V. SNYDER

They tended to cluster together as if more sets of eyes would improve their night vision. If Valek timed it just right...

Rolling along the roof, Valek traveled to the edge closest to the wall. He peeked over, searching for soldiers before sitting on the edge. Valek rubbed his damp palms along his pants and then reached across the two-foot gap. Running the tips of his fingers over the stones, Valek found small holes and ledges to grasp. Thank fate the garrison was one of the older bases. If it had been a new construction, the wall would have been too smooth to ascend. He stretched out his legs, seeking toeholds and locating secure positions. Well, as secure as this section of wall allowed.

Next was the hard part. Valek needed to transfer his weight to the wall without falling or alerting anyone to his presence. Either would result in his death. He mentally counted to ten, concentrating on steadying his jumpy heart. Valek had to be one hundred percent committed to the action. Any hesitation would result in failure.

Leaning forward, Valek launched. His fingers and arms strained to hold his body against the stones as he dug in his toes. One foot slipped, sending a rain of crumbling mortar to the ground, but he found another toehold before sliding any farther.

Valek pressed his hot forehead against the cold stones. He waited for a cry of discovery or for his abused muscles to give way. But he stayed strong. After he had struggled with clinging to the ceiling of the barrack's stairwell, Valek had worked on strengthening and endurance. Nice to see all those hours of lifting hay bales had paid off.

When no shout of alarm rose above the general noise of the chaos below, Valek climbed to the top edge of the wall. From this angle, only the shadows of the guards were visible. Once again, his next move required decisiveness and no mistakes.

He reviewed each step in his mind, envisioning the actions until he felt confident. Then he waited for the shadows right above him to clear.

His window of opportunity arrived a few minutes later. Valek scrambled onto the top of the wall, startling a cluster of guards five feet to his left. He saluted them, dived for the opposite edge, twisted so he went feetfirst over the wall and stopped his fall by grasping the edge with his hands. Once he found toeholds, he climbed down.

The yells and shouts sounded when he was halfway to the ground.

"Stop!"

"There! He's there!"

"To the left!"

With about ten feet remaining, Valek dropped the rest of the way, landing with a soft thud on the cold earth. An arrow slammed into the ground right next to him. Valek zigzagged as he dashed into the woods. More arrows whizzed past and one burned a line of fire along his thigh. But he didn't stop.

He reached the protection of the forest only to realize soldiers filled the woods. While he'd been clinging to the wall, they must have gone through the gate. And they were converging to block his escape route. Valek found a hiding spot to plot his next move.

What would be the last thing they'd expect him to do? He bit down on a groan. They'd never guess that he'd *return* to the garrison. All his survival instincts screamed at him to ignore that advice and to head for home right now. He wiped his forehead with his sleeve, but the fabric was wet. The thought of being caught soaked with Dumin's blood spurred Valek into action. They'd tear him apart.

Heading away from the guards, Valek neared the wall, but he stayed in the woods as he looped around the garrison. He searched for an empty section, but soon realized that would require a miracle, so he picked a spot with just a few soldiers. And when their attention was elsewhere, he crossed to the wall.

His abused muscles protested as he climbed. When he reached the top, he peered over the edge and waited until the guards were not looking in his direction. Pain throbbed in his leg as fatigue shook his limbs. When the prime opportunity arose, he stayed low as he traversed the wall, moving slowly so he wouldn't attract any attention.

The compound below appeared empty, but Valek eased down the wall and didn't relax until he reached the shadows at the base. He circled around. The bag with his clean stable-boy clothes remained hidden. Valek changed and stuffed the bloody ones into a burn barrel before he washed up.

Lanterns blazed in the stables and a couple of horses were missing. Reedy saddled a big mare while the Stable Master put a bridle on another.

"Where've you been?" Reedy demanded.

"At the latrine," Valek said and helped the boy with the girth straps.

"All this time?"

"Until all hell broke loose. Then a captain ordered me to stay in Barrack A until the ruckus died down. What happened?"

"The assassin struck again. I heard he got two men before they spotted him climbing over the wall." Reedy's voice held a combination of awe and fear.

They worked to saddle more horses as officers left to join the chase. When the flow of officers slowed, the Stable Master questioned Valek on his absence. He repeated his story.

The Stable Master backhanded him across the cheek, spinning Valek to the ground as pain exploded on the right side of his face.

He crouched next to Valek. "I'm your boss, not some captain. Next time you get your ass back here right away or I'll pound on you until you look like raw meat and then I'll feed you to the horses. Understand?"

"Yes, sir." Valek considered adding the Stable Master to his to-be-assassinated list.

Valek worked at the stable for another month. He viewed the effects of his double assassination with amusement. Twice the number of guards traversed the walls, extra locks were installed on all doors, patrols swept the woods surrounding the garrison every night and soldiers patrolled the compound, checking shadows.

Right now Captain Aniol was untouchable. On Valek's next day off, he left and never returned. He had spent a total of three and a half seasons as a stable boy and had learned so much more than he'd expected. Someday, he'd finish the job. No doubt.

He reported to Hedda's office when he reached the school.

"What the hell were you thinking when you killed Edvard?" she demanded. Two red splotches on her cheeks matched the color of her hair.

"I wasn't—"

"That's right, you weren't thinking!" She stood and jabbed a finger at him. "Never kill a target in front of witnesses."

"But they were…"

She waited.

"You're right. It was a disaster."

"You're lucky you weren't caught," Hedda said.

Valek couldn't resist. "Luck had nothing to do with it." He smirked.

A steely glint flattened her green eyes. "And what did?"

"Your excellent training."

She snorted, but she settled behind her desk. "And did my training include leaving clues?"

"Clues?"

"Those black statues. They're calling you the rock assassin."

"Not very original," he said.

"They can be traced back to you."

"How?"

"Asking around at the market, finding the person you bought them from."

He smiled. "I didn't buy them nor did anyone see me carve them."

If she was surprised, she hid it well. "You better make sure no one does. Now, where's my cut from your wages?"

He handed her a small pouch.

Hedda dumped the coins into her palm. "Not much. Talk about slave labor."

Valek shrugged. "I found the experience to be very valuable."

"Did you, now?"

"Yes."

"Are you ready to earn much more than this?" She shook the coins as she studied his expression.

He paused. It was one thing to kill the men who'd murdered his brothers, but to assassinate an innocent...

"They're far from innocent." She gestured to a chair. "Sit down and let me tell you about the people who are targeted for assassination. It's not because they're the pillars of the community or because they do good deeds for their neighbors. No, there is always a reason someone hires us to kill them. Corruption runs deep in this country. The royals are the worst of them. And then there're the drug lords and those exploiting children and forcing women to be prostitutes. Let's just say *no one* mourns their deaths."

"That would make it easier."

"And don't forget the experience alone would be…"

"Valuable." He'd made a big mistake with Edvard. And he still had much to learn. When he went after the King, there'd be no room for error.

"Are you ready for your first paid assassination?" Hedda asked.

"Yes."

Valek had then worked various jobs throughout the next two years. With each assassination, his skills improved and his heart rate steadied. Confidence had come with experience, and a high level of cockiness. Valek had started leaving his black statues for his targets to find, warning them of their impending assassination just to make the job harder. And it had, setting off a series of ruined plans, close calls and mistakes. However, his ability to quickly deal with complications had improved.

Dealing with problems had been a part of his life since he'd vowed revenge on his brother's murderers. And the message from Yelena that lay on his desk was one recent example. Valek tapped his fingers on the parchment, considering if the Commander's order not to get involved with Ben Moon's escape extended to Valek's corps. He could send a few trusted men to Fulgor just to keep an eye on Yelena. That wouldn't be disobeying the Commander's orders.

However, if Yelena found out…she'd probably be upset he didn't trust her ability to defend herself. Logic warred with his heart.

Hedda had trained him to lose his emotions, but Yelena had shown him that there was room for emotion. And he'd learned love trumped logic. He wondered what his life these past eight years would have been like if he hadn't met her. Lonely? Lackluster? Cold?

Truthfully, Valek had been content with his life before she

　　　　　　　　MARIA V. SNYDER

arrived. Would he have woken from his self-induced exile? He'd like to think so, but even though he'd had relationships with women before Yelena, they had always been part of a job he was working and not a true connection. Basically, he'd used them to reach his mark. Not the nicest thing to do, but the King's death had been all that mattered to him at that time. And after he'd assassinated the King, protecting the Commander and Ixia was all he'd cared about.

A sudden thought hit Valek hard. Perhaps it was time for him to be selfish. He should be with Yelena and not up here directing…traffic. The power twins and Maren could take over Ixia's security forces. He'd assumed he'd have plenty of time to retire and enjoy a life of leisure, but at any time, another assassin—one more skilled than Onora—could show up and kill him. Before Yelena, he hadn't cared about his own life, but now he did.

With those thoughts swirling around his head, Valek grabbed his travel pack and headed to the stables. He saddled Onyx in record time, hoping he'd reach a travel shelter before all the beds had been taken. Mounting Onyx, he huffed in amusement. In the past, he'd sleep anywhere—on the cold hard ground, on gravel, in the rafters, wedged under or behind various pieces of furniture. Now he preferred a bed.

The road north had few travelers, and those he encountered quickly moved to the side, giving Onyx a wide berth. Only officers and high-ranking advisers rode horses. All others walked. Valek would rather be on foot—better to spot trouble—and he'd rather be disguised as an ordinary citizen—better to gather useful information. But the travel time to and from the main military base in MD-2 would eat up four days of his allotted time.

The days of unlimited time were, unfortunately, in the past. He remembered spending three months just tracking Captain Aniol's movements. Aniol had ordered his men to kill a bunch of boys to make an example of them, and Valek hadn't been able to get close to the man until Aniol had been assigned a mission with four other soldiers. They'd camped for the night in a section of Icefaren province that was so remote there hadn't been any inns or travel shelters.

Valek waited for Aniol to take his turn for guard duty. After the man that Aniol had relieved fell asleep, Valek baited the captain by making slight noises. As Aniol moved farther and farther from camp to investigate, Valek looped around behind him and pressed his knife to his throat.

"Did you think you were safe, Captain?" Valek asked.

"Safe from what?" The captain's voice remained steady. "A thief in the woods?"

"From the rock assassin who killed Lieutenant Fester, Second Lieutenant Dumin and Sergeant Edvard last year?"

It took him a moment. "*You* killed those men? Why?"

Valek laughed. "I guess they couldn't tell you. I'd hoped the three statues would help you figure out the connection by now."

"I've no idea what you're talking about." His tone no longer held as much confidence.

"Then let me refresh your memory." Valek explained. "Your demonstration certainly worked for the King. No one else in Icefaren tried to ask for leniency or for extra time to pay their taxes. Did the King give you a medal or commendation for your excellent service?"

"No."

"Too bad. I'm sure your widow would have liked to display it during your funeral."

"I have kids," Aniol said.

"How many?" Valek asked even though he knew the answer.

"Two—a boy and a girl."

"My parents had four boys until your men slaughtered three

MARIA V. SNYDER

of them. You should have told them to make a clean sweep of it. Hmm…letting you live and killing your children would be a more appropriate punishment."

"No!"

"Don't worry, Captain. Unlike you, I don't murder innocent children." Valek had sliced his knife deep into the captain's throat. One of the benefits to being behind his victim—not as much blood on his clothes. He left a statue of six people holding hands—a family on the dead man's chest.

When Valek arrived in MD-2 two days later, he found a stable for Onyx a few miles away from the base, changed into a servant's uniform with MD-2's colors of black and tan and entered the compound without any trouble. He located Private Zoel, one of his agents assigned to keep an eye on the occupants of the base. Giving the young man the signal, Valek slipped behind the barracks to wait.

It didn't take long for Zoel to appear. He approached as if he faced a cobra ready to strike.

Valek didn't waste time on pleasantries. "Tell me about Captain Timmer."

"Captain Timmer's a hard-ass, sir, but his company makes all the others look like kids playing solider," Zoel said.

"No signs of him abusing his power?" Valek asked.

"No, sir. His company does train longer and harder than the others, but he doesn't push them past their limits, and if a soldier is unhappy, he can request a transfer." Zoel wiped a sweaty palm on his pants. "If I'd seen anything inappropriate, sir, I would have sent a report."

Valek studied the nervous youth. Zoel's average appearance and build helped him to blend in with the other soldiers. The young man's talent was the ability to make friends with anyone. He'd been a valuable resource, watching the various activities within the base and reporting anything suspicious.

"Why aren't you in Timmer's company?" Valek asked.

"Those extra training hours would limit the amount of time I have to perform my duties for you, sir."

"And in the course of those duties, have you heard anything about the captain?"

"The soldiers don't like him. He scares them in order to make them work hard." Zoel shrugged. "He's harsh and will scream and humiliate a soldier who isn't keeping up, but I haven't heard of any physical abuse."

Valek asked him about Onora and Gerik.

"Gerik wasn't here long," Zoel said. "Talented guy. Didn't cause any trouble. I suspect he'll advance pretty high in the ranks. I don't know an Onora. Is she new?"

"No. She would have been here two or three years ago."

"Doesn't ring a bell."

"Thank you, Zoel."

Zoel nodded and hurried away.

Valek spent the next couple of days observing Timmer's company. Professional and skilled, they performed their drills with uncanny precision. Impressive. The captain yelled and bullied a bit, but nothing that would cause Valek to be concerned. About to agree with Zoel's assessment of Timmer, Valek paused as he realized only a few women stood in the ranks. Not that their low numbers was a red flag, but their reaction to the captain when he neared set off Valek's internal warning bells.

One lady in particular—a tall blonde—flinched and her face set into a mask of fear when Timmer glanced at her. The captain's sly smile was all Valek needed. Timmer warranted a closer inspection.

That night, Valek sneaked into the base's record room to pe-

MARIA V. SNYDER

ruse a few files. It took a bit of digging, but he located Onora's file. She had enlisted four years ago at age sixteen. Her instructors praised her skills and she gained a reputation for her lightning-fast attacks. The glowing reviews and comments stopped when she'd transferred to Timmer's company. After a year of service, she was noted as being absent without leave. Valek didn't need a good imagination to determine what had caused her to go AWOL.

Nothing in Gerik's file contradicted what Zoel had reported. In fact, there was a commendation from Gerik's commanding officer for going above and beyond the call of duty while battling a fire in the barracks. The only thing that caught Valek's interest was Gerik's hometown—Silver Falls. The town was also listed for Onora. Interesting.

Valek woke Zoel and sent him to Silver Falls to investigate and see if there was a connection between Onora and Gerik.

"What about my duties here?" Zoel asked.

"Give this to your commanding officer." Valek handed him a folded piece of parchment. "After you finish in Silver Falls, report back to me at the Commander's castle."

"Yes, sir."

After another day of investigation, Valek learned the blonde's name, Private Wilona, and her age, eighteen. Instead of living in the women's barracks, she had her own quarters. Anger simmered in his chest, but Valek needed to confirm his suspicions before he dealt with Timmer.

Valek followed Wilona to her quarters that evening. He knocked on her door. A faint "come in" sounded. Entering, he noticed her expression first—fear mixed with dread—and then how she'd hugged her arms to her chest, her posture rigid.

Not expecting a servant, she jerked in surprise. "Oh." She blinked as relief softened her pretty face. "Can I help you?" Wilona relaxed her arms, letting them hang by her sides.

"No. But I can help you."

She braced as if for a blow. "Who are you?"

He suppressed a sigh. What was the point of having an infamous reputation if no one recognized him? Removing his cap, he introduced himself.

"Yeah, right, and I'm the Soulfinder. Who put you up to this? Cewen? You can tell her this isn't funny. In fact, it's quite cruel."

Curious. "It is?"

She balled her fists. "Oh come on! She pays you to pretend to be Valek because I… Oh, never mind. Just tell her to stop. She's going to make it worse."

"Cewen's worried about you." He guessed.

"Yeah, well. I can handle it. Goodbye." Wilona made shooing motions.

Valek refused to move. "I disagree. You need my assistance. What time does Captain Timmer visit your room?"

She stepped toward him. "I'm gonna kill her."

"Cewen is not the one you should be concerned about." He laced his words with steel and met her gaze. "I'm not pretending, Wilona."

Whether it was his tone of voice or his expression that convinced her, Valek didn't care as long as she understood he meant business. A range of emotions from fear, disbelief, hope, to relief and back again flashed on her face.

"I'm sorry Timmer wasn't brought to my attention sooner," he said. "A mistake I will rectify tonight."

She sank onto the edge of her bed. "I should have reported him, but…"

"Men like him use fear to control their victims. You had the strength to confide in your friend. A step in the right direction. Did you think she was goading you into more action by sending a servant to pretend to be me?"

MARIA V. SNYDER

"Yes."

One mystery solved. "Would it have worked?"

"I...don't know. The captain is well connected. He has friends who are in charge of transfers, buddies working as messengers and is in tight with the Major. I doubt anyone here would have helped me."

He'd fix that later. For now... "Tell me everything."

Wilona glanced at the door.

"Will he be here soon?"

"He...visits at different times and not every night."

Typical predator behavior—keeping a victim guessing and off balance, Valek thought with disgust.

With some encouragement, Wilona told Valek her horror story. How she'd caught Timmer's eye and, at first, she enjoyed the attention until the flirting turned into threats, intimidation and forced physical contact. Valek wished Yelena was here. His heart mate had been through a similar experience and her magic could soothe Wilona's soul. All he could offer Wilona was the assurance that she'd be safe.

"Don't worry about Timmer anymore. The next time he comes to your room, *I'll* be waiting for him, and if he survives the encounter, he'll be rendered harmless and unable to sire children," Valek promised.

19

JANCO

A person could only listen to the forest sounds for so long before going insane. Janco sighed. Loudly. They'd been hiking southwest through the Snake Forest for hours and Little Miss Assassin had been as quiet as the grave. Her passage through the woods made no noise. Her bare feet padded on the cold hard ground with nary a whisper. Even her short black cape didn't dare flap.

They would stay on the Ixian side of the border until they neared the town of Lapeer, where they would cross over and investigate the suspicious factory before heading east to the Emerald Mountains.

He tried to fill the silence with comments on the case or on the scenery, but he gave up because after a while it sounded inane even to him. And he'd long since stopped asking her questions. Little Miss Assassin was a woman of few words.

This was going to be a long assignment. He sighed. Again.

"Will you stop doing that?" she asked. Annoyance colored her tone.

Janco perked up. "Doing what?"

"That huffing thing. Like you're leaking air."

"It's called sighing."

"Well, stop it."

A very childish "make me" pressed on the edge of his lips. He wisely kept those two words from escaping. Ari would be proud. Instead, he asked, "Why?"

"I can't hear if anyone is following us."

"No one is following us."

"How do you know?"

Good question. He'd known it just as he knew when to stop bugging Ari—by a feeling deep inside him. "The forest is…unperturbed."

"That's ridiculous."

"Do you think someone is following us?"

"I haven't heard any indicators—when I *could* hear." She shot him a sour look. "We need to remain vigilant."

"For what? It's not like they're planning an ambush. If someone is following us, that's good. It means we're on the right track. We're making people nervous. They want to see where we're going, what we're doing. In fact, we should be making *more* noise in order to lure them into coming closer."

Little Miss Assassin stared at him as if he had four eyes and a spike sticking out of his forehead. "How do you know they're not planning an ambush? With all your prattle masking any signs, we'll probably stumble right into a trap."

Janco hadn't realized just how much his friends trusted him until now. Ari would never question him about ambushes. Why not? It wasn't like he had magic. Perhaps years spent in the woods had given him a…forest vibe. If he told her that, she'd really think he was out of his mind. And why did he care what Little Miss Assassin thought? He didn't. Not at all.

"The real danger will come when we're in Sitia," Janco said. "Until then, it's just me, you and the birds."

"What about at the border? Do you expect trouble there?"

"Nope. We're going to slip into Sitia without a fuss."

"You mean without stopping to inform the border guards?"

"That's what I said."

"Sounds like a challenge." A gleam lit her pale gray eyes.

"It's easier than you'd think." Or was it? He'd always walked parallel to the border until he found a spot that was empty of guards. Then he simply crossed into Sitia.

When the Commander had taken over Ixia, he had closed the border to Sitia and had his men cut down all the trees and bushes, clearing a hundred-foot-wide space between the two nations. With the gap, the river and the scattered patrols it wasn't easy to cross the border.

"Now that I'm thinking about it," Janco said. "The crossing can be tricky, depending on who's on duty. I'm gonna let you take point on this one."

"All right," she said. "And just to let you know, I see what you're doing."

"Me?" He attempted to look innocent—a hard expression for him to pull off. Janco hadn't been guiltless since he'd been a baby. Then again…his mother had claimed he'd come into the world feetfirst just to be difficult.

"Save it for someone who has poor vision."

"Ouch." But Janco smiled. She had joked, which meant there might be hope for her yet.

When they stopped for the night, Janco tried asking her questions again, but this time he stayed away from the more sensitive topics. She had donned a pair of well-worn, black fur-lined boots.

He gestured to them. "Looks like Black Angus leather. I hear the people who live near the ice sheet will only wear those boots. Is that why you're not cold? It must feel like the warm season to you down here."

"Yeah. I only brought this cape along for the nighttime. Is Sitia really hotter?"

"Oh yes. During the hot season, it's like swimming in the White Mist Springs up in MD-2. Do you know about them?"

"They're near the place I grew up," she said.

Aha! "Sweet. Did you go there all the time? I would!"

"No. Half the year the snow cats gather around them. And in the warmer weather, it's not as much fun."

"For you." He shivered, remembering being on the ice sheet during a blizzard. Hands down, it was the coldest he'd ever been in his entire life.

She smiled and he marveled at the change. The harsh lines of her face softened, and for the first time since meeting her, he thought of her as truly pretty. Her nose crinkled and two tiny dimples marked her cheeks.

"I guess you didn't grow up in the north?" she asked.

"Nope. I lived on the coast in MD-7. I could have been a beach bum, but I hate sand. Nasty stuff. Gets everywhere. And I mean *everywhere*. My dad tried to make me a fisherman, but I got seasick. Even now the smell of fish makes me gag."

"What does he think of your job?" she asked in a quiet voice.

"Don't know. He was out on his boat when a big storm came through. I was eleven. We never saw him again."

"Too bad. Do you have any siblings?"

Janco laughed. "After I was born, my mother swore off kids. When my dad disappeared, we moved to my uncle's farm and I had to deal with all these annoying cousins! What about you?"

"An older brother. He raised me until he couldn't."

A million questions shoved their way up his throat, but Ari's voice sounded in his head. *Don't scare her off, you idiot.* He swallowed them down. Instead, he asked, "Do you want to take first shift?"

"Won't the forest wake you if someone comes close?" Onora teased.

"Ha-ha. There's no one around. But that can change. Besides, I thought you'd feel more...comfortable if we took turns on guard duty."

She gazed at him a moment. A crease puckered the skin between her eyes as if she couldn't quite figure him out. Janco repeated his comments in his mind, trying to determine what he'd said to cause such puzzlement.

"I'll take the first shift." Onora stood, removed her short cape and boots and tucked them into her pack.

"Won't you be cold?"

"I'm used to it. Besides, the cape's extra fabric can snag on the branches, and it's hard to climb a tree with boots on. Don't you do the same thing when on duty?"

"No. I find a good spot and hunker down."

Alarmed, she asked, "How do you stay awake?"

"If I tell you, do you promise not to tell anyone?"

Instantly wary, Onora bit her lip before nodding.

"That's when I compose my rhymes. Everyone thinks I make them up as I fight, but I have a whole bunch of them ready for my next match." He tapped his temple.

"Oh. Okay." She pinched her thumb and index finger together, touched them to her lips and twisted as if locking her mouth shut. "I won't say a word."

Grinning, Janco set up his bedroll and blankets by the small fire. He squirmed until comfortable. Each year, it seemed to take longer for him to find a position where his muscles and/or joints didn't ache when lying on the hard ground.

Before closing his eyes, he scanned their campsite. Onora had disappeared into the forest. Probably climbing a tree. And then he wondered when he'd stopped thinking of her as Little Miss Assassin.

After a couple of days of hiking, they were close to the Sitian border. Instead of crossing into the Featherstone lands,

MARIA V. SNYDER

they headed east, paralleling the edge of the Snake Forest. Janco thought it best to enter Sitia near the west side of Lapeer. He remembered a river that flowed nearby that would be hard to forge this time of year. Not to mention freezing cold. Brrr. Much better, and smarter, to use the bridge.

They traveled east for another five days and dodged the border patrols performing their sweeps of the forest. When the first squad had drawn near, Onora had grabbed Janco's arm at the same time as he put a finger to his lips to warn her. Without a word, she'd melted into the surroundings, while he'd scouted the patrol's position, tracking them and ensuring he and Onora wouldn't cross paths with the guards.

And soon dodging patrols became routine. His forest vibe would trigger when her assassin senses tingled. She melted while he scouted.

Janco squeezed a few more personal facts from her. The most interesting tidbit was she'd had to join the military when she turned sixteen or she would have starved.

Early in the morning on the eleventh day, pain radiated from Janco's right ear. He pressed his fingers to the scar that had formed after the lower half of his ear had been hacked off. The burning pain spread to his jaw and drilled a hole into his brain. Janco scanned the surroundings while Onora waited.

"Strong magic," he puffed. "Close by."

She drew her knives. He didn't have the energy to tell her the weapons would be useless against a magical attack. She'd discover that lovely little surprise soon enough.

20

YELENA

I raced to Reema's window. A grappling hook bit into the wood underneath the ledge. A rope with knots tied every couple of feet hung to the ground. I looked out in time to see a man hurrying away with a large sack slung over his shoulder. Reema!

Without thought, I swung my legs over the ledge, grasped the rope and scrambled down. Catching sight of his cloak disappearing around a corner, I followed him through Fulgor's alleys and side streets, staying far enough back so he wouldn't see me. There was just enough light from the lanterns to discern his form as he navigated the city.

I debated my next move. Should I rush him before he reached his destination? All I had was my switchblade, which I palmed. I'd left my cloak with its hidden darts and my bo staff at Opal's. Perhaps I should wait until he arrived, then attack? What if he had friends? Maybe I should learn his destination and then fetch help. But what if he left after I did? Argh.

Unable to decide, I trailed him, encountering no one. No security officers. Not even a mugger. After about an hour, he cut down a narrow, dank, foul-smelling alley. Ari's shoulders would never have fit.

He stopped at the halfway point and raised a fist as if to knock on a door.

If he disappeared inside, I might never see Reema again. I yelled, "Hey." Then rushed him.

The kidnapper turned his head and reached for his sword. But I collided with him before he could draw it. We slammed into the ground, landing with me on top and him facing the wall. The sack was wedged behind him.

I pressed my knife to his throat. "Release the girl. Now."

He let go and held both his hands up. "Take it," he said.

"Reema, are you all right? It's me." I pulled open the top, peered inside and stopped as my heart lurched.

The man laughed. "Followed me all this way for a fifty-pound bag of potatoes."

"Where—"

The door swung open. Bright light spilled into the alley, blinding me. The kidnapper grabbed my switchblade as shadows converged and multiple hands yanked me to my feet and dragged me inside. The door banged shut.

A familiar male voice said, "Don't worry. She won't bite. There's a null shield around her."

I won't bite? My eyes adjusted and I counted five people. The man I followed plus another I didn't recognize held my arms. Ben Moon stood in front, gloating with two women beside him.

"Hello, Yelena," Ben said. "So *good* to see you again."

Paler than I remembered, he'd also lost weight. His clothes hung on his tall frame and his sunken cheeks made his face appear skeletal. More gray stubble than black covered his scalp—the officers in Wirral must have shaved his head—but intelligence still shone from his brown eyes along with a gleam of…insanity? Cruelty? Evil? Perhaps all three. Not like the knowledge would improve my situation. Nothing would.

"What? No hello back?" Ben smirked.

"Where's Reema?" I demanded.

"Asleep in her bed. Well, *under* her bed as we didn't want to tip you off. But she's safe and sound."

"You— Oh." Her "kidnapping" had been a ruse to get me here. It worked, except… "Why should I believe you?"

"Because *I'm* not after her. *She's* not the one who is responsible for my brother's execution. *She's* not the one who sent me to Wirral," Ben said.

"Owen is liable for his own execution. He knew the consequences of getting caught in Ixia. And you—"

"Shut up. No one deserves to be in that horrid place. And I'm not going back. You didn't do me any favors by letting me live." A crazed expression flitted over his face before an icy calm replaced it.

"I can rectify that right now." I glanced around. "Where's my switchblade?"

"Are you sure you've got a shield on her?" the man on my right asked. "She's not scared."

Now I was. His comment terrified me. If Ben had a null shield around me, that meant he didn't know about my lack of magical powers. The assurance that I wouldn't bite now made sense, yet I wasn't any closer to an answer. If he didn't send the assassin, who did?

"I'm not going to play around anymore," Ben said. He drew a long dagger. "Hold her still."

Years of self-defense training kicked in and I broke their hold on me, ducked out of reach and ran about two paces before being tackled to the ground. I landed hard and twisted. But the others were on me, trapping my arms and sitting on my legs.

Ben knelt next to me. He raised his knife.

MARIA V. SNYDER

"Ben, stop," a deep male voice ordered from the other side of the room.

"The Boss," the man pressing down on my shoulders said. Fear laced his voice.

Instead of listening, Ben pressed his lips together and brought his arm down. I braced for the explosion of pain, but the blade halted mere inches from my stomach. Ben grunted with effort and his muscles trembled. However, he didn't move.

A hooded figure loomed behind him. "What part of 'stop' don't you understand?"

"She deserves to die." Ben forced the words out as if his vocal cords were pinched tight.

Perhaps they were. No doubt magic was involved in preventing Ben's knife from plunging into my body. A good thing, but the Boss's arrival might just delay the inevitable.

"Yes, she does deserve to die. But what happens when the Council, the Master Magicians, the Commander and Valek find out she's been murdered?"

Ben hissed in frustration. "They'll come after us."

"And your rescue has drawn too much attention already. Besides, Valek won't stop until we're all dead," the Boss said.

"But now she knows where we are."

"Thanks to you." The Boss sighed. "And once again, I'll have to take care of it."

Ben flashed me a look of pure venom. He relaxed back on his heels and lowered his knife. "We're not done," he said to me. "I might not be allowed to kill you, but I can hurt you. Bad."

"That's enough. Ben, go fetch the Theobroma."

"But she's—"

"Go now," the Boss ordered.

Ben left, but my heart rate kept its frantic pace. Theobroma reduced a person's resistance to magic. The Boss believed I still had my magic, and if I ingested the Theobroma, then I wouldn't be able to defend against his power. He had no idea he didn't need the substance.

I scanned the room, searching for a way to escape. Small with only a few benches. A couple of lanterns sat on a table near the door. The unlocked door.

"Not yet," the Boss said, correctly reading my intentions.

"You'll let me go? Yeah, right."

"I plan to, and do you want to know why?"

"Because you're afraid of Valek?"

"For now."

Ben returned. He held a brown lump in his palm.

"Give it to her," the Boss ordered.

I struggled, but the four people holding me down didn't budge. Clamping my mouth shut, I was determined not to open it, but Ben pinched my nose closed until I had to either part my lips or pass out. He shoved the Theobroma into my mouth, then held my jaw tight.

The nutty sweet substance melted on my tongue. I resisted swallowing, but due to my prone position, it dripped down my throat and I instinctively gulped.

The Boss said, "Ben, lift your null shield now."

"Okay."

A pause. Then the Boss turned to Ben. "What are you waiting for?"

"It's off, I swear."

Silence stretched and I braced, but nothing happened.

"A shield remains. Take her clothes off," the Boss ordered.

Renewing my efforts to free my limbs, I bucked as hands grasped my shirt and yanked. Buttons flew into the air, exposing my undershirt and the glass octopus pendant.

"Stop." The Boss held a hand up. He knelt next to me and picked up the octopus. "Interesting. No doubt the work of

MARIA V. SNYDER

the Keep's new glass magician." Tugging the chain over my head, he removed my last defense. "But the real question is why *you* are wearing it."

I kept quiet.

"No matter. I will find out soon enough." He pulled his hood down.

Recognition shot through me an instant before his voice invaded my mind. Without my magic or a natural resistance to his power, I couldn't stop him from delving into my memories. A horrified revulsion flushed through me, but he probed deeper and deeper until I split and shattered, exposing everything.

I stood on the street, blinking at the row of lanterns. How did I get here? It took a few moments for me to recognize the town. Fulgor. And another couple of minutes to remember I'd been on my way to Opal's to read a story to Reema.

Reema. My stomach knotted. I needed to leave Fulgor or an assassin would target her. In fact, if I didn't go now my family and friends would all be in grave danger.

I ran to Opal's glass factory. The place was surrounded by Fulgor's security officers. Their presence increased my panic. I'd been too slow to leave and everyone was dead!

The sergeant at the door smiled when he spotted me. "They've been searching the city for you. You better report in to HQ."

"Reema?" I asked, breathless.

"She's upstairs sleeping."

"Are Opal and Devlen with her?"

"No. They joined the search parties along with your brother. A couple of our officers are watching her."

Search parties? That was the second time he'd mentioned that. Had they been looking for me? It didn't matter. All that concerned me was leaving town to keep them safe. "I'll…just check on Reema and…report in."

He stepped aside and I raced up the steps. The two standing guard relaxed when they recognized me. I waved to them as I confirmed Reema was unharmed. She slept on the couch.

She looked so innocent. No lines of worry or cunning creased her face and her pure beauty shone through. The instinct to protect her burned through me like a sudden fever. Move. Now. Or she'd die.

I gathered my pack, bo staff and cloak and dashed from the factory, heading to the stables at the Second Chance Inn. The knowledge that *they* watched me to ensure I left pressed on my back. No time to waste. Kiki nickered a greeting when I entered. I waved off the sleepy stable boy who appeared while I saddled her in record time. Rusalka poked her head over the wall. Her ears cocked forward.

"Please tell Rusalka not to worry," I said to Kiki. "Tell her we're going…" Where? The urgency to leave didn't specify a direction. I strained to recall elusive details. There had been something about a plant in the Avibian Plains and it had been important…Freeze Burn! "Tell her we're going to the plains and ask her to keep Leif from chasing after us. He needs to stay away from me. It's too dangerous."

Kiki stared at me for a moment. Then turned her head toward Rusalka, doing her silent horse communication thing. Rusalka snorted in either agreement or disagreement. It was hard to tell.

When I mounted Kiki, she twisted one ear back. "We're going to search for that plant Devlen…er…Changed Man showed you. Do you remember it?"

She flicked me with her tail as if insulted that I'd question her memory.

"Good. I'd like to get to the plains as fast as possible." This earned me another long gaze. "I have to leave to keep Reema safe. Okay?"

Just when I started wondering what I'd do if Kiki refused to take me, she trotted from the stables. I let her pick a path through the empty streets. Scanning the surrounding area for potential problems or for anyone following us, I stayed alert until we reached the plains two hours after dawn.

The panic released its vise grip on my heart and I drew a deep breath when we entered the vast grasslands of the plains. My family and friends would be safe. And as long as I stayed away, they'd live. The reason for my conviction eluded me, but just the thought of returning to Fulgor sent waves of fear along my spine. Sorrow weighed heavily on me. I already missed them so much it burned inside me. I imagined it would consume every part of me, leaving behind a hollow husk. And I couldn't even think of Valek right now or I'd collapse in a puddle of misery and never move again.

Kiki broke into her gust-of-wind gait. We sailed on a river of air. I closed my eyes, enjoying the rush of the wind on my face. It banished the sadness if only for a moment. After being up all night, it didn't take long for me to doze in the saddle.

Kiki woke me when she stopped for a rest. The plains stretched in all directions. Clumps of small scrub trees dotted the landscape. A few rocks littered the sandy soil. Kiki sipped water from a narrow depression—all that was left of a streambed.

Despite the desolation, I felt safe. Or was that because of it? When she finished drinking, I fed Kiki grain and then I groomed her. In two days, the warming season would officially start and, halfway through, shedding season would begin. The amount of hair raining to the ground would triple in another month's time. Every year I'd been amazed that Kiki didn't turn bald by the warm season.

After I washed the horse hair from my hands, I ate a quick

meal. Quick because I didn't have much food with me and it would soon be gone. My bo staff and switchblade were useless for hunting, but I might be able to use my Curare darts. Or could I? If I ate the meat of an animal frozen by Curare, would I also be affected? Perhaps I should stick to edible plants and roots. If I found them.

While I waited for Kiki to reenergize, I searched for recognizable vegetation. My thoughts drifted, wondering how Leif and the others had reacted to my sudden exit. Were Leif and Hale chasing after me? I hoped not. Just being near me would endanger their lives. And while my heart ached to see them, I refused to give in to such selfish desires.

I poked around the sparse clusters of greenery. Nothing matched my limited list of safe plants. Perhaps I'd find some at the next stop. Wrapping my cloak tight around me, I lay on the ground near Kiki. The sun warmed the dark fabric, lulling me to sleep.

Kiki nudged me awake a few hours later and we resumed our journey. Did she know where the reedwither plant grew or was she searching for it? For the thousandth time, I longed for my mental link with her. Finding souls and guiding them to their final destination had been satisfying, healing others had been rewarding and even examining a person's soul served a purpose. But my ability to communicate with Kiki, Irys, Bain, Leif and even Valek had been such a deep part of me for so long, I felt disconnected. Adrift. Lost.

Recovering my magic, however, didn't elate me as much when I realized I still wouldn't be able to see them or they'd die. At least I'd have Kiki and I could resume helping souls and others in need. The hardest part would be avoiding Valek. No doubt he'd hunt for me. No doubt he'd find me eventually. I dreaded that time.

We stopped two more times before I located a few edible

MARIA V. SNYDER

berries and roots. At our fifth rest break on the second day, instead of moving away to find water to drink, Kiki pawed at a patch of crabgrass. Odd. I moved closer. Long thin leaves grew from red stems. The reedwither plant.

"Kiki, you're brilliant!" I hugged her and fed her a peppermint. Then I knelt next to the cluster and considered. Should I dig around the plant to harvest the roots or pull it out like a weed?

Perhaps I shouldn't touch the leaves or roots. I dug into my pack for a pair of gloves and returned. I would try yanking out a small section first, and if that didn't work, I'd dig around the base.

I grasped a handful.

"Stop," a male voice commanded behind me. "Let go of the reedwither."

I hesitated. A dagger slammed into the ground near me.

"Let go or my next knife will not miss."

21

VALEK

With Wilona safely tucked into a bunk next to her friend Cewen in the women's barracks, Valek returned to the private's room. Not wishing to alert anyone to his presence just yet, he'd had Wilona tell her friend that she'd decided to take action on her own.

Extinguishing the lantern, Valek stretched out on Wilona's bed. He longed for a blond wig. It would add to Timmer's confusion. However, the captain failed to visit her room that night.

In the morning, Wilona reported to training, acting as if nothing had happened, and Valek spent the day investigating Timmer's network of supporters. The layout of the base matched all the other military complexes in the Territory of Ixia—the Commander insisted the bases and the General's manors be identical, which aided Valek and his corps.

It didn't take long to spot the officers who were truly corrupt, like the captain in charge of personnel transfers, and those that had been bullied by Timmer, like the lieutenant overseeing all outgoing messages. Valek noted each of their names. After he dealt with Timmer, Valek planned to make major changes for the command structure of the base. And he'd retrain the soldiers in spotting intruders. Even dressed as a servant, Valek shouldn't be able to move around the base. with such ease.

Before settling in Wilona's room for the evening, Valek changed back into his adviser's uniform and prepared for a late-night visitor. He lounged on her bed in the dark, considering what he'd learned that day. It had been a couple of years since he'd organized surprise inspections of the bases, and his agents here had missed a number of illegal activities, which probably meant the same lackluster reporting must be going on for the other bases, as well. It was well past time for another shake-up, but the idea failed to excite Valek. He had more important things he'd rather do. Like discover who had targeted Yelena.

A creak of metal interrupted his musings. Lantern light from the hallway outlined the door as it swung inward. A dark figure entered the room and shut the door. Valek smiled as the man banged his shin on a chair.

"Damn it, Wilona, I told you to leave your light on," a gruff voice said.

Valek pulled the metal slide of the bull's-eye lantern open an inch. A beam of light illuminated Captain Timmer. The tall muscular man cut an impressive figure even in his robe. Clean-shaven with short black hair and brown eyes, Timmer held up a meaty hand to block the light.

"That's not funny, Wilona." Menace rumbled deep in his throat. Timmer stepped closer. "Move the light or I'll—"

Valek stood. "Careful, Timmer. You don't want to get into any more trouble." He yanked the slide all the way open, flooding the rest of the room with light.

Timmer grunted in surprise, pulled a knife from the pocket of his robe and froze when he met Valek's gaze. Recognition flashed. He straightened, but didn't put his weapon away. "Sorry, sir. I thought you were an intruder."

Smooth recovery. Impressive. "Since these aren't your quarters, Captain, I could say the same about you."

"I...was invited. Wilona and I have been dating for a couple months."

"You're dating a soldier in *your* company? That's unethical."

"Her transfer—"

"Has been denied by your buddy Captain Maitol twice. Don't lie. I already have enough reasons to kill you, Timmer."

Timmer's grip on the knife tightened along with the muscles in his jaw, but he wisely kept his mouth shut. Good.

"You're going to cooperate," Valek said. His matter-of-fact tone warned there wouldn't be any arguments. "Give me your knife." He held his hand out.

Timmer hesitated.

Valek waited. A part of him hoped Timmer would attack. The feel of his fist ramming into the man's gut would be sweet. Too bad the captain handed his knife to Valek.

"It's her word against mine," Timmer said.

"I believe her. Case closed. Now you're going to tell me about another private who came through here about four years ago. Private Onora. Do you remember her?"

"I've hundreds of privates come through my company." Timmer shrugged, trying to act casual.

"Yet according to the base records, very few who transfer into your company are women. In fact, I memorized all their names and plan to interrogate all of them. Well, the ones who didn't go AWOL on your watch."

"There's not much to tell." Timmer almost growled the words. "Onora showed such promise, but she couldn't keep up with my rigorous training schedule and she left."

"Were you *dating* her?"

MARIA V. SNYDER

Timmer clamped his mouth shut, but his gaze darted to the bed. And that would be a yes. Valek twirled the knife, deciding if this man deserved to walk out of here with his balls still attached or not.

"Do you know where she went after she left?" Valek asked.

"No. We sent the military police to search for her, but they lost her trail in MD-1. Why are you so interested in her?"

"She has reappeared. And she has honed that potential into a new occupation."

"Oh?"

"An assassin."

"Oh." Timmer swallowed. "Is she any good?"

"She managed to reach the Commander's suite. Unprecedented."

The captain relaxed. "You took care of her."

"I did more than that."

"Good. She was willful, disrespectful and unable to follow orders. No one will mourn her."

Valek raised an eyebrow at his outburst and waited.

The captain finally put it together. "You didn't kill her?"

"I recruited her."

"Oh."

"It should be a fun reunion between you two."

"You can't—"

"I can."

Valek escorted Timmer to the base's MPs and gave them strict instructions to transport the captain to the Commander's castle. He reported the lax security and other infractions to the colonel in charge of the base. Valek wished to stay longer, but he had only two days left to return home.

The two-day trip to the castle was uneventful. After Valek unsaddled Onyx and groomed the horse, he washed up and changed into clean clothes. Then he swung by his office and paused.

The door stood ajar. He grabbed his knife and pressed against the wall to the side of the entrance. It'd be stupid to rush inside. The intruder could be armed with a crossbow. Valek slid his small mirror from his pocket. It resembled a lock pick, but with a round reflective surface on the end. Careful not to catch the light from the lanterns, Valek angled the mirror to look inside. A dark-haired man sat at his desk.

"Come on in, King Killer." The man waved.

Valek kept his weapon in hand as he entered. Only a few people could breach the castle's security and then be brazen about it. "What are you doing here, Arbon?"

"I heard you were looking for me." He spread his arms wide. "So here I am."

Keeping a firm grip on his knife, Valek approached his desk.

Arbon grinned and gestured at Valek's hand. "I see you're still skittish."

"Cautious," Valek corrected. "You don't live long in this business without it."

"Ah yes. I've heard about the young chicky who almost took you out."

Leaning back in Valek's chair, Arbon appeared relaxed. Patches of silver painted his black hair, he had filled out a bit in the middle, and wrinkles creased his tan skin, yet he still resembled the young boy who'd trained with Valek at Hedda's school. He wore a servant's uniform with the Commander's colors of red and black.

"You've been hearing lots of things. Does this mean you've been in town for a while?"

Arbon's booming laugh echoed on the stone walls. "I'm surprised you don't know. Or is it in one of these reports?"

Arbon ran his fingers over the stacks of files. "I'd never pegged you for a desk jockey. No wonder you're losing your touch."

Valek stepped closer and brandished his knife. "Care to test your theory?"

"Love to, but this is a *friendly* visit. What did you want to talk to me about?"

He sheathed his weapon. "My chair."

A smile played on Arbon's lips. "You wanted to talk to me about a chair?"

Valek waited.

With a huff of amusement, Arbon stood and made a grand sweeping bow before relocating to the visitor's chair.

Valek settled behind his desk. He pulled one of the files from a stack and opened it. "I'm looking for information about an assassination attempt on Liaison Yelena Zaltana. According to my records, you've been living and working in Sitia."

"Thanks to you and the Commander, that's where the jobs are. The market in Ixia dried up after the takeover."

Ignoring Arbon's jab, he asked, "Did anyone contact you about this job?"

"Of course they did. I'm the best in Sitia. But once I learned who the mark was, I told them to find someone else. Going after your girl would be suicide. I'm not suicidal."

"Do you know who tried to hire you?"

"You know better than to ask that."

Hedda had never shared the names of her clients with her assassins. It had provided protection for both of them. And Valek had been content with that arrangement until he'd met Ambrose.

"Do you know who agreed to take the job?" Valek asked.

"I'm not ratting out my fellow assassins."

"I didn't ask for a name."

Arbon stared at him a moment. "I know a few others who

might have taken the assignment despite the risks, but I don't know which one."

"I'm looking for a male magician. Know anyone like that?"

"Why a magician?"

"He hid behind a null shield."

"Hell, Valek, that could be anyone. These days it's easy to purchase a cloak or even undergarments that have null shields woven into the fabric. What weapon did he use?"

"Bow and arrow."

Arbon laced his fingers together and rested them on his stomach. "That narrows it down to three or four. When did it happen?"

"Seventeen days ago."

"That rules out the Hunter."

"The Hunter?"

"Yeah, the Sitian assassins all have monikers to keep their real identities a secret." Arbon didn't sound impressed.

Valek couldn't resist asking, "What's yours?"

"The Ixian. Original, eh?"

"Accurate. What about the other possible assassins?"

"Sorry, can't do it. I'm planning on retiring soon and don't need some guy with a grudge tracking me down."

"Fine. How about *you* find out who took the job and ask him who hired him? Get me the name of the patron and I won't go after the assassin."

"And why would I do that?"

Time for the ace. "Because you owe me a favor and I'm collecting."

Arbon shook his head. "I waited all these years for you to ask for that favor. I figured after the takeover, you'd forgotten or you didn't want help from me."

"I offered you a position on my staff."

"Yeah, well, I like my freedom."

"I have freedom."

"Do you?"

"Yes." Valek's tone turned icy.

"It doesn't look like it from where I'm standing. From what I've seen and heard, the Commander holds your leash and has since you first met him."

"You know nothing about it. Now, can you get me that name or not?"

"I can, but I'm going to need lots of gold. That information doesn't come cheap. And once I do then we're even."

"As long as the information is accurate. If not—"

"Save it for one of your green recruits. Give me some credit. I've known you longer than anyone else. Do you really think I'd double-cross you?"

"Not if you value your life."

"Exactly. Now, where's that gold?"

"How much do you need?"

"Forty pieces."

Valek waited.

"All right, gimme thirty-five. That should be enough."

"Thirty. I don't think we need to help fund your retirement."

"Too bad. I've a sweet little place picked out on the coast."

"Ixia?"

"No way." He shivered. "Too cold."

"I like the cold."

Arbon laughed. "No surprise. You spent more time hanging out on that freezing-cold rock than in your room at Hedda's."

Valek sobered. "Have you heard about Hedda?"

All humor dropped from Arbon's round face. "No. What happened?"

Surprised Arbon didn't already know, Valek broke the news.

"And you let this chicky live?" Outrage colored his voice. "I would have sliced her into three pieces."

"I need to learn more about her and the situation before I decide on her future."

"What else do you need to know? Hedda took us in, she taught us, she—"

"I'm well aware of Hedda's generosity. However, the girl has made an impression on the Commander."

"So what?"

Valek met his gaze.

"Oh yeah, I forgot." Arbon put his fist up near his neck and pretended to yank on an invisible leash. "He's your master. But he's not mine. If I just happen to run into this chicky, I'll ensure she gets what she deserves."

"Better brush up on your knife-fighting skills, Arbon. She's younger, faster and more skilled than you. In fact, if you do go after her, make sure you get me that name first." Valek unlocked the lower drawer of his desk. He filled a pouch with thirty gold coins and tossed it at Arbon, who caught it in midair.

"That good, eh?" He jiggled the pouch. The coins rattled. "I'll think about it." Arbon stood to leave.

"Would you like an escort, or would you rather sneak out the way you came in?" Valek asked.

"I'll find my own way out." Arbon waved and left.

Valek counted to two then raced to the door. He caught sight of Arbon's back as the man turned the corner. Curious to see how Arbon had reached his office without calling attention to himself, Valek followed. However, the assassin didn't duck down a secret passage or climb out a window or bribe one of the guards. He simply sauntered through the corridors as if he owned the place. Arbon nodded and said good afternoon to the people he passed. No one questioned him

MARIA V. SNYDER

or glanced at him in suspicion. He exited the castle complex without trouble. And when Arbon reached the other side of the gate, he turned and saluted Valek.

No wonder Onora had reached the Commander with ease. Not only had his security detail been compromised, but everyone in the entire castle had relaxed just like at MD-2's military base. Valek had assumed Onora scaled the outer wall and climbed up the castle, but after this little demonstration, she could have waltzed right in the main gate.

Valek pulled the guard who had let Arbon through aside. "Who is that man who just left?" he asked.

"One of the servants," the guard said.

"What's his name?"

"Uh…" The man glanced at his colleague, who pretended to be engrossed in another task.

"Here's an easier question. Where does he work?"

"Um…"

"You've no idea, do you?" Valek demanded.

"He's wearing—"

"A basic uniform that could have easily been stolen. Have you seen him before today? Did he have the proper papers?"

Fear replaced the man's confused expression. "I—"

"You are relieved of duty, Sergeant. Collect your things and come to my office in one hour for your transfer papers."

"Yes, sir." The man hurried away.

Valek turned to the other three guards. White-faced, they braced for his anger.

"Do not let anyone into or out of this complex without checking their papers and making sure their name and position are on the approved list. Do you understand?"

"Yes, sir," they chorused.

"Make sure all of the shifts are following the proper procedures. You will be tested *frequently*. Failure to catch one of my agents will result in immediate reassignment. They're always looking for more workers in the mines."

They blanched. "Yes, sir."

Fuming, Valek strode to the castle. Something had happened to his security measures while he'd been gone. He'd trusted Maren to be in charge, but it seemed as if she'd left long ago and not the few weeks the Commander claimed. Unless she'd been overwhelmed by the job, which allowed the guards to be lazy. Either way, he had to test all the security for the entire castle to discover what else had changed.

Again he wondered if the Commander had orchestrated all this to test Valek. Although he couldn't fathom why Ambrose would put himself at risk. The man had a strong sense of self-preservation. Always had.

Valek remembered when Hedda assigned him what had seemed at the time an easy job.

"It should take a couple weeks at most," she had said. "This young man's been making people nervous with his speeches, and we've been paid a whole pile of gold to make him disappear for good."

"What's the mark's name?" Valek asked.

"Ambrose Diamond. He has all the miners agitated and has amassed quite the following. According to our patron, he has based his operations in Pinchot."

That was on the other side of Ixia near the Soul Mountains. "What's he look like?"

"Black hair, average build, your height, but he's about seven years older than you, around twenty-four. I'm told his eyes are distinctive—almond-shaped and gold in color."

"Does our client want me to give Ambrose a message before I kill him?"

"No."

So this wasn't personal. Probably political. "Anything else?"

MARIA V. SNYDER

"No. This job shouldn't be too difficult. He's been making public speeches. You could probably blend in with the crowd and put a bolt in his heart."

Valek scoffed. "Where's the fun in that?"

"Careful, King Killer. I lose more assassins to overconfidence than to the authorities."

He grinned. "That's sweet. I didn't know you cared."

"Only until you kill the King. That's the only reason I've kept you around."

His humor faded. He'd been working as an assassin for two years, but Hedda kept insisting he get more experience before he went after the King. More like accumulate more money. While he was grateful for the gold he'd earned, he suspected Hedda wasn't ready to give up her best source of income.

"If I kill this guy in public, he might turn into a martyr, and I'm sure our client wouldn't want his successor to gain sympathy and supporters because of the assassination."

"Good point. Just get in and get out. I've more jobs waiting for you."

"Assign them to another. Isn't T-quin back from his southern jaunt?"

She stared at him. "T-quin takes too long."

"Arbon?"

"Is lying low. His last job was a fiasco and he's too hot."

"Sounds like this would be a good time for me to ask for a raise."

"You would think that, but you'd be wrong."

"I see. How about a timeline, then?"

Hedda rested her elbows on her desk. "What do you mean?"

"Don't play dumb. How many more jobs must I complete for you before I can go after the King?"

"It will take a couple years for you to get close enough to him. You're one of my best assassins and, at seventeen, you haven't even hit your prime. You've plenty of time to go after the King. Right now you can earn heaps of gold for your... retirement. Plus once you kill him, you're done. His guards will either kill you or you'll be too hot to stay in Ixia or work as an assassin for a decade."

"In other words, I would no longer be an asset for you."

"Of course. Wasn't that your sole desire? Kill the King? Have you thought about what happens afterward? If you live, that is."

No, he hadn't. Back when he was thirteen, he'd assumed he wouldn't survive. However, he'd gotten quite skilled at this business and he might have a future after all. Hedda had given him much to think about on his trip west to Pinchot.

When he arrived in the city, it didn't take him long to locate his mark. Ambrose made nightly speeches at various taverns around town. Valek kept to the edges of the crowd, listening to the man's propaganda.

"...own a diamond mine, but are we rich? No!" Ambrose sat at the bar, drinking from a mug of ale. "The King confiscates all our product, paying us only enough to keep the equipment running. The King of Ixia claims our taxes go to improve our lives, yet when the south section of the mines collapsed, he refused to send his soldiers to help clear the debris. Twenty-nine miners died, not from the collapse, but from being trapped underground."

Each evening, more people showed up to hear Ambrose speak. Valek recognized many faces from before and it appeared they'd dragged their friends along to listen. He had to admit the man was worth listening to. Valek agreed with him. In fact, the more he learned about the King's crimes in this region of Ixia, the greater his desire to assassinate the King.

Hedda's comments about what happened after the King's death had been in reference to Valek's life. But what about

MARIA V. SNYDER

Ixia? Who would take the King's place? Another corrupt royal? One of his spoiled princelings? Would anything change? Probably not. Yet Ambrose spoke of a new government with clear laws that applied to all. He argued for a fair system where everyone worked and basic needs were provided for by the government.

Too bad Valek had to assassinate Ambrose. The man had good ideas and appeared to be very organized. Valek spotted evidence that this was more than grandstanding at the local bar. Ambrose's loyal inner circle acted more like a military squad, and Pinchot was the sixth major city in his campaign.

After a couple of weeks, Valek pinpointed the ideal location for the assassination. Ambrose always left the taverns by the back entrance with a couple of brutes on his heels. He'd slip through the back alleys to the inn where he stayed.

Valek debated between ambushing him in the alley or in his room and decided on the alley. It seemed more dramatic and those two brutes would be easy to take down in the open versus in the tight hallway. Plus Ambrose had been smart enough to rent an interior room and hire a man to stay inside while he was out campaigning. It made it difficult for Valek to place a sculpted black diamond on Ambrose's bed, but not impossible.

On the big night, Valek followed Ambrose to the Pewter Tavern. He sat in the back until Ambrose hit his stride. Then Valek slipped out and found a dark shadow along Ambrose's route home in which to hide. Pulling on black gloves and a hood with a full face mask, he readied two darts. The hood worked much better than greasepaint. Easier to just yank it off when in a hurry than to stop and wash the incriminating black off his face. Plus it kept his face warm during these cold-season nights.

As Valek waited for his target, he envisioned the sequence of actions he'd need to perform to complete this mission. A slight pang of regret touched him. All of his targets deserved to die, but Ambrose might make an actual difference. He banished the sentiment. Hesitation was lethal in his line of work.

A few hours later, voices echoed off the stone walls of the alley. Three men approached—Ambrose and his bodyguards. As soon as they passed his hiding spot, Valek stepped out and threw the darts. One in each man's thick neck. He silently counted to ten as he followed the group. When the men wobbled on their feet, Valek drew his knife.

Valek slid between them as they thudded to the ground. Ambrose turned to see what had happened. Valek thrust his blade at Ambrose's stomach, expecting to pierce flesh while he met the man's shocked gaze. However, Ambrose shuffled back and a long dagger flashed in his hand.

"Nice," Valek said before engaging him in a knife fight.

Ambrose blocked his first series of strikes with ease. A couple of combinations later, Ambrose went on the offensive. Wow. The man was skilled with the blade. Valek backpedaled long enough to grab another dagger. Now armed with two, he attacked both high and low.

"Feeling more confident?" Ambrose asked.

"Oh yes."

"You won't for long." Ambrose increased the pace. His weapon snaked passed Valek's defenses and slashed his arm. "First blood." He grinned.

Unease stirred. Ignoring the unfamiliar feeling, he switched his strategy, using a more sophisticated series of strikes and blocks that he'd tested against his fellow assassins. Ambrose gave ground, inching toward the wall. Then he quickly stepped to the side and yanked another knife.

It didn't take long for Valek to realize he was outmatched. For the first time in years, fear unfurled and wrapped tentacles around his heart.

"Who hired you?" Ambrose asked.

And this was a great example why Hedda kept that information a secret. Valek's answer was a double thrust to Ambrose's throat, which missed by a hair because the man leaned back, all the while keeping his arms outstretched and dangerously close to Valek's chest. Twin slashes seared into his skin.

Valek shuffled away as Ambrose advanced. He no longer considered this an assassination, but a fight for his life. One that he was losing.

"Did the King send you?" Ambrose asked.

The question took him by complete surprise. Could he be working for the King? It was possible. Distracted by these thoughts, Valek made a critical error. In a blur of motion, Ambrose unarmed him and slammed him into the wall, pressing his blade to Valek's throat. The cold steel burned his hot skin as pain radiated through his skull. Fear squeezed his heart along with outrage—the King would live while he died.

"Who hired you?" Ambrose asked.

"I don't know."

Ambrose ripped off Valek's mask. Cool air fanned his sweaty face.

"Ah hell. You're just a kid."

Valek bit down on a protest. It might work in his favor.

"Just tell me if it was the King or not and I'll let you live."

He considered lying. After all, his life was at stake. But that golden gaze seared right into his soul. "I don't know. I hope not."

"Why?"

"The thought of working for the King makes me ill."

"No love for your King, eh?"

"He's not my King. All he is to me is another target."

"You plan to assassinate him?"

Valek gave him a bitter smile. "I did."

Ambrose laughed at his tone, but then turned contemplative. "*Can* you kill him?"

"Yes."

"He's a powerful magician."

"Doesn't matter."

"Why not?"

A lie sprang to his lips, but he sensed Ambrose would know. "I'm immune to magic."

Surprise and shrewd calculation flashed. Valek expected to be questioned for the details of his immunity.

Instead Ambrose asked, "Can you discover who hired you?"

Strange switch in topic. "I can."

"Would you?"

Ah, there was the right question. "And in exchange?"

"Your life."

"You'd let me go for a name? Just like that?"

"Oh no, not that easy. You see, you're mine now. Live or die, I decide." He slashed his other dagger along Valek's sternum, ripping the fabric of his tunic. Ambrose then carved a half circle into Valek's flesh.

Valek grunted as an intense pain coursed through him.

"It's a *C*. It stands for *Commander*. Meaning, I'm *your* commander. Pledge your loyalty to me and I'll help you reach the King. After all, I want the son of a bitch dead, too."

"And if I don't?"

"I'll slit your throat and leave you here."

Not much of a choice. Valek met his gaze. Deep down, he trusted that this man would keep his promises. Odd. He hadn't felt that way about anyone since he'd witnessed his brothers' murders.

"How soon can I go after the King?" he asked.

"Within the year."

Ambitious. "And when the King's dead?"

"I become the Commander of Ixia, and you can have a position on my staff. But first you need to find out who hired you and then kill him or her."

"What if it was the King?"

"Then assassinate his go-between. A warning to the King not to underestimate me."

"All right. I'm in."

Ambrose stepped back. "Do it right."

A different type of fear gripped him. Dying was a known state—he'd cease to exist—but giving his loyalty to another... one he barely knew...was a new form of terror. Yet his curiosity nudged the uncertainties aside, and his desire to plunge his knife into the King's heart trumped all fear.

Valek knelt on one knee. "I pledge my loyalty to you."

"What's your name?"

"Valek."

Ambrose cut his right palm and held his hand out. Valek swiped his fingers along his bleeding chest before clasping the man's strong grip.

"I accept your pledge, Valek."

They shook hands, linking their fates together.

Valek returned to Hedda's school and reported success. She'd never reveal her client's name, so he followed her when she left to collect the rest of the assassination fee. The man who paid her wore tailored silk clothes and had a half dozen bodyguards around him. Valek recognized him as Prince Theoin, one of the King's four nephews.

Fury burned in his chest. Hedda was well aware of Valek's hatred for the King. To send him on a mission that would benefit the man... He clenched his hands, digging his fingernails into the flesh of his palms in order to calm down. Valek needed to remain emotionless and view the situation with logic.

The King had sent a trusted family member to hire an assassin, which meant he must be terrified of Ambrose. As he should be. Valek looked forward to killing Theoin. It would remove one more corrupt royal.

Valek waited for Hedda in her hidden windowless apartment. The one she thought no one could find. The one where she kept her safe, her personal files, her belongings and her bedroom. It made sense for her to be so well protected. It had to be hard to fall asleep knowing you were surrounded by assassins.

He scratched his chest. Ambrose's cut had scabbed over and the throbbing had been replaced by an annoying itch. Valek decided he'd rather have the pain until his fingernail ripped a scab off. Ouch.

When Hedda arrived, she didn't react to Valek's presence. No surprise she had a warning system in place for when someone breached her private rooms.

Valek lounged in a chair in her living area, giving the impression he was relaxed even though he was far from it.

Hedda held up a pouch. It jingled. "Couldn't wait for your half?"

"Keep it," he said. "In fact..." He tossed a large sack onto the end table. It slapped the wood with a hard rattle. "Here's all my halves, minus living and travel expenses."

"Why?"

"I was never in this for the money."

"But—"

"Consider it payment for all the food, shelter and training you provided. I'm grateful for that." He stood.

"You don't need—"

"Yes, I do, because I quit."

Understanding flashed. She stepped back. Her hand reached for her dagger.

"Relax, Hedda. I'm not going to kill you even though you

knew the King ordered Ambrose's assassination. Have I done his dirty work before?" he demanded.

As expected, she refused to answer. At least she was consistent.

"You'll never get close enough to the King without help," Hedda said.

Nausea swelled as her words sank in. "And you never intended to help me since he's probably your best customer."

Again she kept quiet. Smart.

He clamped down on the anger boiling in his stomach. "Better not spend the fee you collected on Ambrose's assassination. Your King will soon be asking for a refund."

"You didn't—"

"Nope. He's alive and well. And I advise you not to send anyone else after him."

"Why? Are you planning to protect him?"

"I don't need to." Valek left her rooms and hurried from the school's grounds. If Hedda sounded the alarm, he'd be outnumbered and thrown off the cliffs.

Besides, he had a prince to kill.

Valek was jolted from his memories by two border soldiers bookending a young man. The three of them waited for him in front of his office door. The guards' grim expressions warned him to expect trouble. Valek studied the scared man trapped between them. He wore Sitian garb. Ah.

"Report, Sergeant," Valek said to the man on the right.

"This man claims to be a messenger from Sitia, but he wouldn't relinquish his message at the border as required."

"Why not?"

"I've been ordered to deliver it to you directly," the young man piped up.

Interesting. "By who?"

The messenger glanced at the guards. "It's confidential. For your ears only."

"All right." Valek unlocked his office door.

"Sir, he may be a Sitian spy or an assassin," the sergeant said.

Valek stared at him. "And what are you basing this…assessment on?"

"Uh…his insistence on seeing you."

How did this man get promoted to sergeant? "Let me give you a quick lesson on assassins, Sergeant. They don't walk up to the border and announce their plans. Nor do they wear conspicuous clothing. You're both dismissed."

"But our captain told us to stay with the Sitian at all times."

"I outrank your captain. Wait out by the castle's gate."

The messenger wrung his hands as Valek escorted him inside his office. Bad news, or was he just nervous about being alone with the infamous Valek?

Valek leaned against his desk. "What's so important?"

"I'm…er… Second Magician Irys Jewelrose sent me."

His first thought was something had happened to Yelena. It took all of Valek's considerable willpower to keep from shaking the rest of the information from the messenger. "Go on."

"She's very concerned about Liaison Yelena. There's been…"

He straightened. "What happened?"

"The Master Magicians have uncovered a plot to harm the Liaison."

"I already know about the assassination attempt in the woods."

"They're uncertain if this is related to that attack or a new one. And since the Liaison is vulnerable, Master Jewelrose thought you should be informed right away."

"Vulnerable?" Ice rushed through his body. He gripped the edge of his desk. "What do you mean by vulnerable?"

MARIA V. SNYDER

22

JANCO

As the pain in Janco's head increased, Onora prepared for a magical attack. After a few minutes, nothing happened. No one attacked. Yet the agony continued. Janco's vision blurred, and from the corner of his eye he spotted the reason. An illusion. Or rather, a magical illusion right in the middle of the freaking forest.

The pain in his right ear intensified as Janco drew closer to the magical illusion. Onora followed him with her knives drawn. As far as illusions went, this one was rather lame. It matched the forest exactly. Bare trees, bushes, piles of dead leaves—all normal for being in the middle of the Snake Forest.

That meant it hid something important. Janco held his hands straight out as he walked toward the illusion. He grimaced as his head pounded.

"Uh, Janco, there's a tree right— Oh!"

He pierced the illusion and a strange burning sensation flashed through his body. At least the agony in his ear dulled.

"Janco, are you all right?" Onora asked. "Where are—"

He reached through the magical border and yanked her inside. She yelped in surprise, but recovered quickly.

As he caught his breath, he scanned their surroundings.

Wagon-wheel grooves marked the forest floor and led to a mouth of a cave a few feet away. The illusion camouflaged the cave's entrance so the border patrols would walk right by it.

Onora peered inside then entered. She returned with an unlit torch. "Looks like the cave's in use. Could this be a hideout?"

"Was there any evidence that someone is living in there?"

"It's narrow and I couldn't see far. There might be a bigger cavern farther in."

"Then light the torch and we'll go have a look."

"Are you crazy?"

"Define *crazy*."

"Walking right into a trap." She stabbed the tip of her dagger at the cave.

Janco crouched on the ground. "The wagon marks are a few days old. No fresh boot prints. I don't think the cave is occupied at the moment."

"So now you have a cave vibe, too?"

"Okay, Little Miss Assassin, what do you suggest we do?"

"Hide and wait. See who comes out or goes in."

Oh. Actually, that was a pretty good plan. Annoyed he hadn't thought of it, Janco crossed his arms. "For how long?"

"For as long as it takes."

"What about our mission?" And then it hit him. "This could be what we're searching for—a way for the smugglers to cross the border without being seen."

"*If* it tunnels under the border into Sitia, and *if* it isn't just a hideout."

"Killjoy."

"If I was going to kill, it wouldn't be *joy*." Onora gave him a pointed look.

He laughed. "You wouldn't be the first person who wished me dead, sweetheart."

MARIA V. SNYDER

She flinched at the endearment and shoved her weapons into their holders to cover her…anger? No. Fear? Not quite. More like an old nightmare that hadn't faded. He waited for her to threaten him with bodily harm if he used "sweetheart" again, but Onora kept quiet. Smart. If she'd fussed, he'd use it all the time just to goad her. Ari had called it childish, but Janco used it as a tool. He needed to discover just how much tolerance she had and where her breaking point was.

"How did you see through the illusion?" she asked. "Do you have magic?"

"Oh no. Not at all. I'm allergic to magic." He explained about the warning pain. "I had no idea what it hid."

"Since you can sense it, you should find a position outside the illusion, and I'll stay inside," she said.

He glanced around. There wasn't much room. "Where—"

"Not many people look up." She shoved her boots and cape inside her pack, then stashed it out of sight. Onora climbed the rough stone wall next to the cave's mouth until she reached the apex. Settling into a comfortable position, she shooed Janco.

He paused. She appeared to blend in with the gray stones and brown earth that had collected in the nooks of the rock face. Janco glanced away and rubbed the back of his neck. Lack of sleep could do strange things to a guy. He turned to assess her line of vision so he didn't watch the same patch of forest. Except she'd disappeared.

"Get going before someone shows up." Her voice sounded above his head.

Holy snow cats! Did she…? Was she…? He stepped closer to the cave's entrance, expecting his scar to burn. It didn't. Maybe the illusion's magic covered her power. He rubbed the spot as he considered.

"What are you doing?" she asked.

"Uh, just checking something." Janco poked his head into the cave as if it contained all the answers. It didn't. Unless darkness had something to do with the mystery of Onora. Perhaps it did. Perhaps—

"Janco."

Her irritation snapped him from his thoughts. "All right, I'm going." He braced for the pain as he crossed the illusion. It flared to life, stabbing into his head. Janco kept walking until the intense stinging dulled to a tolerable level. Then he found a place to hide.

His thoughts circled back to Onora. In all their time together, Janco had never felt that creepy crawly sensation along his skin, which he'd learned meant magic was in use but not directed at him. Hard to describe. It was like hearing an echo.

She could be one of those One-Trick Wonders who had enough magic to do only one single thing like light a fire or spot a liar. Hey, that rhymed—he'd have to remember that for later. Perhaps her power was blending in with her surroundings like a chameleon. No wonder she'd reached the Commander and escaped the dungeon. For an assassin to have that ability…was pretty sweet! Of course, he could be way off base. The pain from the illusion might have screwed with his vision.

But as he waited for…well, anything at this point. Talk about bored. Janco remembered the times he and Onora had encountered a patrol and she'd melted into the forest. The creepy crawlies hadn't attacked him then, but her ability to disappear seemed…off. He decided to not jump to conclusions—Ari would be proud—and keep an eye on Little Miss Assassin, see if she had any more tricks.

The day dragged, limping toward twilight. Janco's stiff muscles complained about the inactivity. His stomach growled. Wonderful. He'd wait until full dark and then take a break. After all, a man had to eat and sleep and pee.

MARIA V. SNYDER

★ ★ ★

A rumbling creak woke him from a light doze. Darkness surrounded him. It took him a moment to orient himself—Snake Forest—on lookout—with Onora. Check.

A harness jingled and the thud of horse hooves on the ground vibrated under him. Soon two wagon teams rolled into view. The figures sitting on the benches didn't have a lantern, but there was enough moonlight to discern big obstacles like trees. Besides, most horses just needed to be pointed down a trail. They instinctively followed the cleared path.

As they passed his hiding spot, Janco noticed a burlap blanket covering the lumpy contents of the wagon. Intrigued, he followed the wagons as they neared the illusion then slowed.

"Where's that damn cave?" one man asked. "Did we miss it?"

"No, it's a little further," his companion said.

"Just stop here," a woman called from the second wagon. "The horses get too skittish if we get closer. Mattison will meet us."

They unhitched the horses and fed and watered them. They appeared to be waiting for this Mattison. Too curious to stay put, Janco crept up behind the second wagon, noting the long and narrow bed. He lifted the blanket, revealing barrels. Words had been burned into the oak, but it was too dark to read them.

A bright yellow glow pierced the illusion, momentarily blinding him. Three huge men carried torches and pulled a small cart. Another set of three big brutes emerged, but they didn't tow anything. All six men wore some type of leather harness.

The two groups merged. Janco slipped back into the forest while they were distracted.

"Anyone follow you?" one of the big brutes asked.

"You kidding? No one's around for miles," the wagon leader said. "How much did you get?"

"Six golds a barrel."

"Next time ask for eight. It's getting harder to smuggle this stuff out. Valek's got his dogs sniffing around."

An indignant huff sounded next to Janco. He jumped and clamped down on a cry.

"Don't sneak up on me like that," he whispered to Onora. "Assassin, remember?"

"But I'm on your side."

She shrugged. "Habit."

"Did you see what's in the cart from the cave?" he asked.

"Yes. A few small barrels."

They watched the smugglers as they hitched one wagon to the three big men, attaching the chains to their harnesses, and then they hooked up the other three with the other wagon. Odd. Why not use the horses?

"I'm going to crawl under the burlap on that second wagon," Onora whispered. "You track the cart and see where it goes. We'll meet back here once we learn what's going on."

He opened his mouth to protest, but she disappeared. While the others were distracted hooking up the men and horses, the blanket rippled and the wagon creaked under the additional weight. No one but Janco noticed.

After they finished, the smugglers made arrangements for another meeting, then headed in opposite directions. The horses pulled the cart from the cave back into the forest, and the men lugged the two wagons toward the cave.

Ah. The horses either couldn't fit inside the tunnel or were too scared to go underground. Onora's plan had merit, but Janco still didn't trust her. And Valek had ordered him to keep an eye on her.

Janco waited a few minutes before dashing through the

MARIA V. SNYDER

illusion. A brief surge of fire ringed his head before dying down. The circle of torchlight retreated deeper into the cave. He summoned the courage to follow. Janco hoped it was a short tunnel.

After all, he hadn't had time to eat or pee.

23

YELENA

I released the reedwither plant and spread my hands wide. "Good. Now stand and turn around slowly," the man behind me ordered.

Wondering why Kiki hadn't warned me of his presence, I straightened and faced him. A tall and muscular Sandseed warrior watched me. I didn't recognize him. He held a scimitar in his left hand and another dagger in his right. His skin was the color of shadows and he had a green-and-brown-patterned cloth wrapped around his waist. It must be for modesty because the rest of his body was bare despite the cold.

Unconcerned, Kiki grazed nearby.

"You must continue on your journey," he said.

Not a chance. "I need to collect—"

"It is forbidden to harvest the reedwither."

"Why?"

"It is a powerful poison."

"I know. I may have been injected with it."

"Not possible. You are alive."

I stifled a sarcastic retort. No need to upset the well-armed man. "I have healing abilities. I may have stopped the poison from killing me."

He stepped closer. "I sense no magic from you."

All right, time to try another tactic. "I'm friends with almost all of the surviving Sandseeds, but I've never seen you before. Who are you?"

The Sandseed puffed out his broad chest. "I am the guardian of the reedwither plants."

Plants. As in plural. At least there were more.

"Do not think you can steal from another patch," he said. "I watch all."

And that would only be possible if... "There's a magical shield over the plants, and when it's broken, you appear."

"Yes." His eyebrows pinched together, rippling his bald head.

"And you wait in the shadow world."

"How do you know this?" he demanded.

"I've been to the shadow world."

"Not possible. You are not a Sandseed Story Weaver."

"I was the Soulfinder."

"Was?" Confusion gripped his expression. "You cannot undo what is done."

"I wish that was true, but someone poisoned me with reedwither and now my Soulfinding days are over. That's why I need a sample so I can take it to my father and have him produce an antidote."

"Who is your father?"

"Esau Liana Zaltana." Although I had no idea how his name would help.

"I know this Esau."

Then again... Hope rose.

"He will not be able to aid you. This plant cannot do what you claim."

"How can you be so sure? No one has used it on a Soulfinder before."

"True." He tucked his weapons into the cloth around his waist. "But I know I have not been called from the shadow world to protect the plant for many years."

I considered. Some substances remained potent for years. "Did they succeed?"

"No one has since I have been on duty. Before I died, my life threads were woven into the reedwither plant so I could protect it while in the shadow world."

"How long ago?"

"Back when your father, Esau, was a curious young boy, visiting the plains for the first time. Esau asked so many questions, I thought our elders would send him home early."

Sounded like my father. A mix of emotions rolled through me. If the poison wasn't from the reedwither plant, then what had caused my magic to disappear?

The Sandseed moved closer and spread his hands. "May I?"

"May you what?"

"Read the threads of your life."

"You're a Story Weaver?"

"Yes."

Sifting through the logic, I couldn't think of a reason not to let him. Perhaps a ghost Story Weaver would be able to discover what happened to my magic. "All right. What's your name?"

"Midnight Son." He grasped my hand. "There is a…barrier."

I'd forgotten about the null shields. Releasing his grip, I removed my cloak and pulled the octopus pendant from around my neck, setting it down with care. A cold breeze caressed my skin and I shivered.

Midnight Son took my hand in both of his. Heat enveloped my skin and I panicked for a moment, remembering the Fire Warper. Stupid of me to trust so easily. Midnight Son could be from the fire world. And now I was unprotected.

"You do need to be more careful," Midnight Son said, holding tight. "You are very vulnerable." His gaze grew distant. "Your story threads are complex and woven into an intricate pattern." He chuckled to himself. "No wonder my son struggled at times. And why the elders believed he was the only Story Weaver up to the challenge."

"Your son?"

"Moon Man."

I relaxed and wondered why I hadn't noticed the resemblance. The weapons must have distracted me.

"Are you ready?" he asked.

"Yes." My voice squeaked.

"Let us go back."

With a dizzying swirl of color the Avibian Plains spun around us like sand grains caught in a whirlwind. The daylight turned to night and trees erupted from the ground, turning the flat landscape into a forest.

Movement underneath me jerked to the side as pain pierced my shoulder. I relived the events of the night of the ambush in quick succession. My time with Valek and enduring the hot and cold fever sped by along with the trip to the Magician's Keep. Everything I'd done and everyone I'd talked to flashed in front of me. A span of blackness arose after Ben's smug face jumped into view. I flinched as fear pushed me to run and hide, but I had no control over my body or the images.

Midnight Son didn't release me until we reached the present. I sank to the ground exhausted, which seemed strange since I hadn't done anything.

"You did all the work," he said.

Looping the octopus around my neck, I pulled my cloak around my shoulders. The air had turned icy. So much for this being the last day of the cold season.

"Then what did you do?" I asked.

"I watched and learned."

I clutched the fabric of my cloak tight. "And?"

"It confirmed that the reedwither plant is not the culprit."

Another dead end.

"It also confirmed that you did not die."

"What?"

"You are the Soulfinder. You have the ability to bring a person back to life by healing the body and returning the person's soul. You could have kept your soul inside your body after it died, then healed yourself."

I'd returned two souls—Stono's and Gelsi's. Both killed themselves within a year of being saved, and I'd vowed never to do it again. Good to know that, in my panic, I hadn't re-animated myself. A shudder ripped through me.

"If I had done that, would that have caused my problem?" Stono hadn't had magic, but Gelsi had. However, I couldn't remember if she'd still had access to her powers after I brought her back to life.

"That is an interesting question."

"And do you have an interesting answer?"

"No. But it does not matter." His eyes gleamed.

Energized, I shot to my feet. "Do you know what happened to my magic?"

"Yes."

"And?"

"It is blocked."

"Like a null shield?"

"No."

Frustration rose and I tightened my grip on my cloak's rough fabric until my fingernails pressed into my palms. I drew in a calming breath. If Moon Man had learned how to be cryptic and annoying from his father, I needed to choose my words with care. "How is my magic blocked?"

"It just is."

I clamped down on a growl. "You said it was unlike a null shield. Can you explain?"

"A null shield blocks magic from both directions, while this only prevents *you* from using magic. However, you are vulnerable to magic. For now."

Old news. "What is 'this'? A poison? Magic? A virus? A one-way null shield?"

He didn't respond.

I searched his expression. "You don't know!"

No reaction.

Groaning, I plopped back onto the ground, lying back with my arm over my eyes. "You're not going to tell me. Are you?" My throat closed as a hot pressure built. Sheer force of will kept tears from spilling.

"I can tell you this."

I peeked at him.

"You will figure this out, Soulfinder."

"When?"

"When the time is right."

Midnight Son sounded just like Moon Man.

"Did you teach your son how to be cryptic or is it an in-born trait for Story Weavers?" I asked.

"Inborn. We guide, but we do not provide easy answers."

"I'm very familiar with that annoying aspect of your personality." Sarcasm sharpened my tone. I sat up. "Sorry, this has all been…"

"Overwhelming."

"Yes. Can you tell me if my magic returns?"

"No." He held out a hand. "Your future story threads do not reveal the answer. Both futures are equally possible."

That meant I'd have a fifty-percent chance of regaining my magic. Better than zero chance. The black despair that had stained my thoughts since I'd woken without magic receded a fraction.

"What should I do next?" I asked, not expecting an answer.

"You should return and finish what you started."

Ah. "I can't. They'll die."

"How do you know this?"

I searched my memories. A vague image of Ben accompanied the red-hot knowledge that my presence would result in death. "I just…know."

"A powerful magician has altered your memories, planting this fear inside you."

"Ben Moon or maybe Cilly and Loris Cloud Mist?" They might have the talent.

"I do not know."

"Can you fix it?"

"No. You must learn to ignore this fear."

Easier said than done. I huffed. "You know, the longer I spend with you, the less I miss Moon Man."

"Thank you."

Curiosity replaced my apprehension. "Why did you name him Moon Man?"

Midnight Son smiled, revealing big white teeth. "He was conceived during a full moon and born on the night of a full moon, so we named him Moon. Fitting, since the boy never liked to wear clothing. The Man came after his Story Weaver powers manifested. He thought Moon was not…impressive enough." Midnight Son laughed.

I soaked in the sound of his laughter, closing my eyes and imagining Moon Man standing there scowling at his father for embarrassing him. Then again, Moon Man wouldn't be embarrassed. He'd be scolding me for running away without thinking it through.

But what could I do without my magic?

MARIA V. SNYDER

"It is a shame that people without access to the power blanket are so helpless. It is a wonder they do not die at an early age." Midnight Son tsked.

"Don't start that mind-reading stuff."

"I am sorry. You wish to wallow in self-pity. I will leave you to your brooding. But I will say this... You should not feel disconnected from your family and friends nor should you fear for their lives. Their story threads are woven with yours. Even without the strand of magic twisted around your story, the rest of your threads remain strong."

"In other words, I'm not going to unravel."

"Exactly." He grinned and bowed. "A pleasure to meet you, Soulfinder. If you need further assistance, you know how to find me. I will admit, chasing intruders away from a plant is not nearly as exciting as talking to you."

"Glad I could provide some entertainment."

Midnight Son flashed me another toothy smile and stepped into a shadow. He disappeared as he returned to the shadow world. I stared at his boot prints in the sand. His comments spun in my mind. Three main things snagged. Midnight Son had claimed I'd figure out how I lost my magic and he'd given me a fifty-percent chance of regaining my powers. Plus he'd called me Soulfinder, which could have been a slip of the tongue due to something he'd seen in my story threads.

I needed to keep trying to solve the puzzle. What options did I have left? Pazia Cloud Mist might have some answers. She lived in Ognap, which I guessed was northeast of here. Although I'd no real idea where in the Avibian Plains we were. My other choice was going south to the Illiais Jungle to visit my father. He might know about or have heard about a magic-blocking substance. I chewed on my lip, deciding.

Kiki nudged my arm, surprising me. Glancing at her saddle, she turned her blue-eyed gaze back to me.

"Ready to go?" I asked.

Another nudge.

"Okay." Securing my cloak and shouldering my pack, I mounted Kiki. In that instant, I knew the right thing to do despite the terror clamping down on my guts. "Back to Fulgor please, Kiki."

I wasn't surprised by the extra security measures that had been installed around Opal's glass factory. In fact, I approved despite the fact they wouldn't be enough to protect Reema from a determined assassin. One of the many things I'd learned from Valek was that an assassin would sit and wait for days, weeks or even months to find the perfect time to kill.

Looping Kiki's reins around a nearby post, I shouldered my pack and approached the entrance. I tried to ignore the certainty that watchers followed my every move, and the creepy crawly sensation of invisible gazes pressing on my back. The afternoon sunlight had done nothing to dispel the chill in the air, and now that the sun balanced on the horizon, the cold intensified. Or was it the icy glares the guards outside the factory turned on me?

While I waited outside, one man went to verify my claims. He returned with Devlen in tow.

"Have you found the plant?" he asked in a flat tone.

He was probably angry at me. I didn't blame him. I tilted my head toward the guard hovering over me. "Can we talk inside?"

"Opal's not here."

"Opal's not the one I'm worried about. How's Reema?"

Ire flared in his gaze, but he gestured for me to follow him into the factory. Then he stopped. Workers buzzed around the kilns. The heat rolling off the four enveloped me. My numb fingers thawed.

MARIA V. SNYDER

"Reema is driving me crazy." Devlen crossed his arms. He wore short sleeves and pants. "Being cooped up inside is not…ideal for her."

Alarmed, I asked, "Is she upstairs alone?"

"No. Two more guards watch her. Are you going to tell me what happened that night?"

"Where's Opal?"

"In the city, searching for Ben."

"Have they found him?"

"No. You did not answer my question."

"I've no idea what happened that night. They must have lured me away and changed my memories. All I know is if I remained in Fulgor, Reema would be assassinated and the rest of my friends and family would be killed, as well." I held up a hand, stopping his questions. "Even though I think it's just a planted threat, we have to send Reema away or I won't be able to function. She's not safe here."

"She sleeps with us and we have four guards from Fulgor's security forces here at all times."

"Not enough. An assassin might be coming after her."

Fear replaced his anger. "How do you know this?"

I met his gaze. "I don't know, but we can't take the chance that it's one of my fake memories. If Ben thinks his…" I tapped a finger on my temple. "Plan didn't work, he might go after her out of spite."

He nodded. "All right. What do we do?"

"Get Reema. Tell her to pack a bag and don her warmest cloak. You're going with her, so grab your travel kit."

While he rushed off to collect Reema, I pulled my new purchases from my pack and set them aside. They had rested atop my cooking paraphernalia, flint, Esau's field manual and other travel essentials that had all jumbled together. I also kept my valuables in my backpack and I'd tied my bedroll to the bottom.

The heat finally soaked into my bones. I removed my cloak and most of the hidden weapons inside the fabric.

Devlen returned with Reema. They both carried small rucksacks.

Reema raced over to me. "I knew you didn't run away. I told them you were chasing the bad guys, but they didn't believe me. Did you catch them?"

I smiled at her utter confidence in me. "Not yet. I need you to go on a secret mission with your dad. Do you think you can handle it?"

Her cheeks blushed with excitement. "Yes!"

"Good. Do you know how to ride a horse?"

"Yes."

"She's only been on Quartz with Opal," Devlen said.

She shot her father a withering look. He ignored her.

"Can you mount without help?" I asked her.

"Of course."

"That's all you need. Just hold on and Kiki will do the rest."

"Kiki!" she squealed.

"Reema, this is very serious," Devlen admonished.

She settled down, but pure impish delight danced in her gaze. Oh boy, this was going to be…interesting.

"Let's go into Opal's office. Bring your packs." I hefted mine along with the new package.

Once inside the somewhat private space, I showed them the two wigs—one with straight black hair and the other with blond corkscrew curls.

I held up the black one. "Reema, you're going to pretend to be me. If you wear this wig, my cloak, and pull the hood down low, no one should suspect anything. Kiki will take you northeast."

"That's all?" Disappointment laced her tone.

"It is very important. You can't show your face. You need to be serious and stay on Kiki until your dad meets up with you. Kiki will protect you. Okay?"

She nodded. "I won't mess up."

"Good."

Reema exchanged her cloak for mine. The hem dragged on the ground, but not enough to be noticeable in the dark. I hoped. I wrapped her hair into a bun and set the wig on her head.

I showed her where the darts were hidden in the fabric. "These have Curare, and these have sleeping potion. Only use them in an emergency. Don't try to throw them. Just jab into skin if you can."

We walked her to the front door.

"Ready?" Devlen asked, drawing her into a brief hug.

"Where are we going?" she asked.

"It's a surprise. Your dad will tell you when he sees you later. Don't worry. Kiki knows the way."

Reema pulled the hood down low over her face and without looking back strode from the factory as if on an important mission. Which she was. I raced upstairs to a front-facing window and peeked out just in time to see her spur Kiki down the road. Two heartbeats later a couple of shadows detached from the building across the street and followed, proving that not all my memories were false.

Now for part two. I joined Devlen in Opal's office.

He played with one of the blond curls. "I hope you are not endangering her."

"Kiki is going to head straight northeast, pass the town limits, and that should make them happy. And Kiki will not let anyone harm her."

"And this?"

I braided my hair and wound it around my head before taking the wig from him and securing it to my head. "This is to show the other two watchers that Reema is still here." I tied her cloak around my shoulders. It fell to my knees, shorter than I liked, but with my black boots and dark pants no one should notice. Letting a couple of curls escape the hood, I drew the fabric low. "Let's go."

"Where?"

"Where would you take Reema?"

"There's a taffy shop a few blocks away."

"Perfect. Leave your bag. You can catch up with her and Kiki later."

We left the factory. The two guards at the entrance accompanied us as we walked to the taffy shop. The other watchers followed us at a discreet distance. They were professionals. If I hadn't been searching for them, I would have missed them. My heart skittered and urged me to run away. It pulsed a warning that death would befall all if I stayed in Fulgor.

"Where am I meeting Reema?" Devlen asked.

"Just head north. Kiki will find you."

"And then where?"

I twirled one of the curls around my finger. "Kiki can carry you both."

"Yelena."

"You're going to the only place Reema'll be safe from an assassin."

"The Magician's Keep?"

"No. The Commander's castle. Valek will protect her."

He opened his mouth. Probably to protest. Then he sighed. "You are right. As much as I would like to believe I can keep her safe, I cannot."

"Once this mess is settled, you can return home."

We reached the taffy shop. The owner was about to lock up,

MARIA V. SNYDER

but she let us in. Devlen bought a pound of Reema's favorite—peppermint mixed with vanilla. We shared a portion of the confection as we returned to the factory.

"How long should I wait?" Devlen asked.

"When is Opal due back?"

"It depends. Some nights not until late, others…"

"Wait for her and explain what's going on."

"What about Reema?"

"Ben's men should stop following her once they've determined she isn't looping back into the city. Kiki will know and turn west to rendezvous with you. Do you have another way out of the factory?" I peeled off the blond wig.

He smiled. "Of course. Opal insisted we have a few options. Not many people know we purchased the building next door."

"Wonderful." I hefted my pack. "Where's the hidden exit?"

"Where are you going?"

"To find out what really happened that night."

24

VALEK

The poor messenger shrank back.

Valek eased his death grip on his desk and asked again, "How is Liaison Zaltana vulnerable?"

"I...I...don't know, sir. Master Jewelrose said you would know."

Could Irys mean Yelena was vulnerable because of Ben's escape? Looking at the situation from Ben's point of view, Valek would also target Yelena. She posed a dangerous threat to his continued freedom. Plus Ben had to have help in his escape, which meant she was up against more than one magician with a grudge.

"Do you have more details regarding this endeavor to harm her?" he asked the messenger.

"There's been anti-magician rumblings and Master Jewelrose believes someone wishes to make an example of the Liaison as to why the Council shouldn't rely on magicians anymore. Proof to all that magicians can be easily compromised."

Valek wouldn't have used the word *easily*. Curare wasn't available to just anyone and null shields... They might have a point about those. Arbon had said cloaks with null shields were available for sale. Plus Opal's magic detectors had made it difficult for a magician to be subtle. However, he doubted the Council would interfere with the production of the super messengers. They were too vital to Sitia. Valek wondered how they justified the super messengers' existence, but not magicians.

"Does Master Jewelrose know who this *someone* is?" Valek asked.

"Not yet. She just wanted to inform you of the situation."

Remembering the Council had kept the news about Ben from Yelena, Valek asked, "Has she warned the Liaison?"

"I don't know."

Not good. Once again Valek's heart wished to hop onto Onyx and ride straight for Fulgor, but the Commander's order that he remain uninvolved kept him from racing to the stables. Arbon's comment about the Commander holding Valek's leash repeated in his mind. Valek squashed it. Besides, she, Leif, Devlen, Opal and that other magician she mentioned in her message had plenty of protection.

Valek flagged down a servant to escort the messenger to the gate. He returned to his office, but couldn't sit and read reports. Despite all the logic, worry for Yelena churned in his stomach. He changed into his sneak suit and under cover of darkness tested the security measures inside the castle complex.

After a few hours of creeping, crawling, climbing and ghosting, his agitation had diminished. The security wasn't horrible, but the protection in certain areas had gotten lax. Valek understood why as most of the guards probably assumed that a threat from those areas was slim. But it was precisely those particular weaknesses that a shrewd assassin would exploit.

That was how he'd gotten to the King—by discovering that single lapse in security. It had taken Valek months to find. After working for the Commander for a couple of seasons, Ambrose led him to a back corner of the tavern. He carried two mugs of ale and handed one to Valek.

"My supporters are moving faster than expected. We should be closing in on the castle in three seasons. Is that enough time for you to assassinate the King?" Ambrose asked.

Finally! Valek kept his excitement from showing on his face. "Depends if I can identify a way inside. The King—"

"Is well protected. Don't waste time looking for a hole in the security around him. Go through someone else who is close to him. That will be your best shot."

"Like the Queen?"

"Exactly."

Valek sipped his ale. "How will I know when you're ready to attack?"

"By the end of the warm season, I will be in Jewelstown, making my speeches in the taverns. Find me and we'll set a time to strike."

"You're not worried the King will send his soldiers to arrest you?" Valek asked.

Ambrose smiled. "No. By then, he won't have many loyal soldiers. You'd be surprised what the promise of double wages does to loyalty."

"And can you keep that promise?"

"You don't think we gave the King all the diamonds we mined, do you?"

"Ah."

"When the bastard refused to send help to dig out those trapped miners, we decided we weren't going to play nice anymore."

"What happens when the money runs out?"

"The King's coffers are quite full and I plan to close the border to Sitia. Our money has been flowing south, buying imports and making the Sitians rich while our people beg on the streets. Stop the imports and we'll have to manufacture

MARIA V. SNYDER

our own supplies, generating plenty of jobs for everyone and keeping our money here in Ixia."

Valek wondered if it would be as easy as the Commander made it sound. He hoped so. "Speaking of money, I need a handful of gold for expenses."

Ambrose filled a pouch. "I included a few diamonds. They're perfect for big bribes. Ladies find them irresistible." He tossed it to Valek. "Buy yourself a new dagger. That one you carry is—"

"My favorite blade and I plan to sink it deep into the King's heart."

"You do that and you'll become my chief of security. Who better to protect me than one who can get through the tightest security?"

"No one."

Ambrose grinned. "Right."

Valek stood, saluted Ambrose with his mug, downed the contents in one gulp and set it on the table.

"Valek," Ambrose said.

He turned back. The humor was gone from Ambrose's gaze. In its place was a cold hardness like a dagger made of ice.

"Kill them all," the Commander said.

"All?"

"All the royals. King, Queen, princes…everyone with royal blood."

Valek stared at him.

"They're a weed. If we don't get all the roots, they'll grow back. Do you understand?"

He did. It just seemed…heartless despite the logic. "Yes, sir."

The countdown had begun. Six months to assassinate the King and his entire family. Valek traveled to Jewelstown, which was located near the castle's complex. The town had been renamed after Queen Jewel—a wedding gift from the King. Valek spent every night the first week searching for a way inside the complex. The steep and smooth outer walls were not only difficult to climb, but too exposed.

He dressed as a servant and was able to enter the main gates without trouble. However, he soon discovered the servants were restricted to their corridors and quarters and rarely saw the royals let alone interacted with them. Only the trusted servants, who'd worked in the castle for years, were allowed into the royal apartments and kitchen. Smart.

One thing he'd learned at Hedda's was patience. Hired as an errand boy, Valek gathered information about the daily activities of the staff for a few weeks before discovering one way to get inside the royal apartments.

"Where's Darrick?" one of the housekeeping servants asked. "He was supposed to clean the chamber pots hours ago." She twisted her apron.

"He's sick," Valek said. "I heard him in the outhouse." He lowered his voice. "It sounded bad." Thanks to the dose of White Fright Valek had slipped him yesterday morning. "I'm between jobs, ma'am. I could dump them for you."

She chewed on her lip.

"Unless you want to?"

"Heavens no. Follow me." She set off.

Valek hurried to keep up. She led him to a wash station.

"You dump the contents into that bucket." She pointed to a grungy, smelly metal pail. "Then you wash the pot in the soapy water, dry it and return it. When you're done, take the bucket down to the outhouses and dump it. Understand?"

Ah, the glamorous life of an assassin. "Yes, ma'am."

"Good." She escorted him through the royal suites and guest rooms, showing him the location of all the pots. The housekeeper watched him for a while, but soon another servant caught her attention and she hurried off.

As Valek continued cleaning pots, he noted the room locations, guards and who the other servants were. The next day, poor Darrick wasn't any better and Valek filled in for him again. By the time Darrick was well enough to return to work, the housekeeper had assigned the boy to other duties. Darrick didn't complain at all.

Valek learned as much as he could during his twice-daily forays into the royal apartments. Within a couple of weeks, he determined that he wouldn't get close to the Queen or the King by cleaning chamber pots. However, he noticed one of the Queen's women wasn't a lady-in-waiting or a servant. She arrived in the morning and styled the Queen's hair, picked out her gown for the day and applied makeup to Queen Jewel's face. She would return again before dinner and help the Queen get ready for the evening meal. They spent much of the time alone in the Queen's quarters. Her guards were banished to the outer rooms while she dressed.

He made a few discreet inquiries about this woman.

"Oh, that's Parveen," one of the biggest castle gossips said. "She has a little beauty shop in Jewelstown she won't give up. The Queen indulges her because she's supposedly the best." The woman lowered her voice and leaned close. "I personally think the Queen can do better. Did you see her hair yesterday? It looked like a bird's nest." She tsked.

After he cleaned the pots in the morning, he followed Parveen into Jewelstown. Sure enough, she entered a shop along Lowell Street. Valek wouldn't describe it as "little." The place spanned almost a full block. Mirrors covered the walls, and chairs ringed the interior.

Customers filled those chairs as an army of beauticians worked on cutting and styling hair. A few barbers attended male customers. Parveen smiled brightly, calling to her associates. Soon she was braiding a young woman's long copper hair.

Within a few hours, Valek understood why Parveen kept her shop. The women treated her with respect and kindness, unlike the Queen, and Parveen thrived in the homey atmosphere. As soon as Parveen left to return to the castle, her warm smile disappeared.

An idea sparked. This woman may be the key to getting to the King. He just had to figure out the best way to use her. Valek considered romancing her, but there'd be no reason for her to take him to her appointments with the Queen. He could disguise himself as Parveen. Except he didn't have the hairstyling skills to convince the Queen. And while he could kill the Queen before having to fix her hair, he'd no idea how he'd reach the rest of the royals. No. He needed to be working inside the castle for a season at least.

After watching her and the shop for a few days, Valek formulated a plan. He ran his fingers through his hair. Good thing he hadn't cut it in seasons. The black strands fell past his shoulders. Valek bought a long skirt, blouse, female undergarments, socks and a heavy shawl from a used clothing store.

As he worked to hide weapons, money and the diamonds in the skirt's fabric, Valek smiled, remembering the teasing he'd gotten from the other students at Hedda's school when he learned how to sew from the seamstress. He ignored the taunts of "King Knitter" because, unlike them, he understood how useful having skill with a needle and thread would be. Hedda taught them how to apply makeup and create disguises, but didn't see the benefit in sewing.

With a small pack slung over his shoulder, Valek emerged from the inn where he'd been staying to live on the streets as Valma. After a week of scavenged food, sleeping in alleys and no bathing except to shave, he resembled a homeless teen girl.

Valek avoided the dangerous crowd, but befriended a fringer to help him with the next part of his plan.

"Wait, you want me to *pretend* to rob the lady?" Bug asked.

The skinny boy was around thirteen, but he was tall for his age. His light green eyes were the only spots of color on him. His clothing, skin and greasy hair had been coated by multiple layers of gray street grime.

"Yes. Do you have a weapon?" Valek asked, pitching his voice higher so he sounded feminine.

Bug flicked open a shank made from an old razor blade, wood and wires. "I don't know about this, Valma. What if the watchers show up?"

"They won't." Valek had already bribed a few town watchmen to avoid patrolling the area that night.

Bug scratched his neck. "So I jump the lady, demand money, and you come to the rescue, chasing me off?"

"Yes."

"What for?"

"It's better you don't know."

"Yeah? What's in it for me?"

"A couple silvers."

"How about I keep the lady's purse? Gotta be more than two silvers in there," Bug said.

"Do you want the town watch hunting for you?"

"No. All right, but I want four silvers."

"Three or else I'll ask Hoot."

Bug scoffed. "Hoot won't do it."

"He will for three silvers."

"Okay, but if I smell a watcher, I'm outta there."

By this time, Valek knew Parveen's routine by heart. She traveled the same streets to and from the castle unless she was running late. Tonight, the Queen kept her longer than normal, so instead of walking her typical route home, Parveen took a shortcut through a narrow street without lanterns. It saved her a few blocks and allowed Valek to put his plan into motion. Bug blended in with the dark factories facing the street.

When Parveen reached the halfway mark, Bug leaped from his hiding spot and pressed his blade to her neck. "Gimme all your money or I'll slit your throat!"

She stared at him in shock. Her mouth opened and closed, but no sound escaped. Parveen clutched her purse tight to her stomach.

A freezer, Valek thought as he slipped from his place and shouted, "Hey!"

Bug turned his head and cursed right before Valek slammed into him, knocking him down. The shank flew from his hand. Then Bug and Valek grappled for a bit before Bug scrambled to his feet and bolted.

During the entire encounter, Parveen stood blinking at them as if she couldn't quite comprehend what had just happened.

"Are you all right?" Valek asked in a falsetto. "There's no blood."

At the word *blood*, Parveen gasped and touched her neck. "Oh my…he wanted my money… I'd never…"

"He's gone now. You're safe."

"I am…" And then with more animation, "I am, thanks to you!"

Valek shrugged. "Are you going to report this to the town watch?"

"I… Did you get a good look at him?"

"A street rat like me."

"Oh." She peered at him as if seeing him for the first time. "I…don't think so. No harm done and I'm late for…" Parveen

MARIA V. SNYDER

drew in a breath as if to steady her nerves. She opened her purse. "Here, let me give you—"

"No, thanks. That's not why I helped you."

"Surely you could use some money for food?"

"Yeah, but it's..." He glanced at the ground. "You wouldn't understand."

"Try me."

Gotcha. He met her gaze. "I'd rather earn a living then beg for it."

"Then why don't you apply for a job?"

Valek gestured to his shabby and stained clothes—street living was hard on a skirt. "Most people won't let me into their place of business let alone hire me."

"Oh. Well, in that case, you can work for me."

He acted surprised. "Really?"

"Yes. As long as you don't mind cleaning up hair and washing towels?"

"I don't mind."

"All right, then. What's your name?"

"Valma."

"Valma, I'm Parveen. Let's go and I'll introduce you to my staff."

Parveen not only hired him, but let him stay in a small room above the beauty shop and gave him an advance payment so he could buy clean clothes. All in all, a lovely woman. He hoped he wouldn't have to kill her.

Valek worked hard in the beauty shop. Leery at first, the staff welcomed him once Parveen explained how he'd saved her life. He paid attention to the stylists and after two weeks they showed him a few basics. His finger dexterity proved to be useful for braiding hair and soon he learned how to weave the strands into intricate patterns. Then it was only a matter of time before he had his own clients.

"You're a natural," Parveen said one day as she admired his work.

Valek discovered that cutting and styling hair was similar to carving a stone. You started with a formless mass and then you shaped it into a thing of beauty.

After a season of working in the shop, Valek felt confident not only in his ability to blend in as a female, but in his ability to set the next phase of his plan in motion. Getting to this point had taken almost two seasons. He had only about ten weeks left until the Commander arrived.

One morning near the end of the warming season, Parveen arrived to open the shop. Sweat beaded her pale face and she moved as if she walked on the deck of a boat in storm-tossed seas. She pressed a hand to her mouth while her other groped for a chair.

Valek rushed to her side and helped her sit down. "You look awful."

"I feel awful." She hunched forward, resting her forehead in her hands.

"Let me take you home. You should sleep."

"I can't. The Queen—"

"Wouldn't want to get sick."

"She thinks she's immune. That illness only strikes commoners." Parveen pushed to her feet. "I'd better leave now. It'll take me…" She wobbled. "Longer."

"I'm coming with you," Valek said.

"But—"

"Do you want to be alone when you pass out in the street? If that's the case, leave your purse here."

"All right."

It took forever to get Parveen to the castle and up to Queen

Jewel's rooms. Before Parveen collapsed into a chair to catch her breath, Valek pricked her with a sleeping potion.

"Why are you here?" the Queen demanded. "What's wrong with her?"

This was the first time Valek had seen the Queen in person. Known for bewitching the King with her exquisiteness, her emerald eyes, long eyelashes, full lips, high cheekbones, curvy figure and flawless skin were legendary, yet he found no beauty within her. He curtsied and explained.

"Help her stand, then. I need my hair done."

But Parveen had passed out. He made a show of trying to wake her.

Impatient, Queen Jewel strode over and slapped her cheek. Hard. "Wake up, Parveen. I will not be late for my appointments." She reached back to deliver another blow.

Valek stepped close and the Queen's hand slammed into his back instead. It stung. The lady had an arm. He ignored the pain. "If I may, your majesty. I can style your hair for you."

"You?" Her cold gaze swept over him.

"I've been working with Parveen for seasons."

She glanced back at the unconscious woman and sighed. "All right, but if I look hideous I'm sending you to the gallows."

Nice lady. The idea of killing her no longer seemed so heartless.

The Queen settled into an overstuffed chair facing a mirror. Valek gathered her long thick auburn hair in his hands. It reached halfway down her back and flowed like silk. He studied her oval-shaped face and slightly pointed chin, deciding on a style that would enhance her features.

With quick, sure motions, he pinned her hair up, creating rows of curls that gathered into an intricate knot at the back of her head. Then he pulled a few tendrils down to drape over her shoulders. Without being asked, he sorted through her gowns and selected a pale green one trimmed with cream lace. Then he matched her makeup to the colors of the gown and sewed an extra piece of lace onto a barrette, clipping it into her hair. He fished a long pearl necklace from her overflowing jewelry box. It was so long that he looped it three times around her neck to create a cascading effect over her décolletage.

When finished, she surveyed herself in the ring of full-length mirrors for a long time. "Quiet, quick and efficient. What's your name?"

"Valma, your majesty."

"All right, Valma, you can fill in until Parveen is better."

"Thank you. I'll take her home and be right back."

"Back?"

"Just in case you need your makeup fixed or would like a new hairstyle for the afternoon."

"What about your clients?" she asked.

He gave her a puzzled expression. "No one is more important than you. I'll cancel all my appointments."

Her expression grew distant and he saw the wheels turning. Had he hooked her?

"Can you stay overnight, as well?" she asked.

Yes. "If it pleases your majesty."

"It does." She returned to gazing at herself in the mirror.

By the time Parveen felt better, Valek had usurped her. Parveen took the news well. Actually, she seemed relieved and was thrilled with the diamond thank-you gift for her years of service that was supposedly from the Queen. Happy that he didn't have to kill Parveen, Valek settled into his new position. The Queen assigned him a small two-room apartment between the guest wing and her suite.

Between grooming sessions with the Queen, he explored

MARIA V. SNYDER

every inch of the castle. He marked the location of every member of the royal family's sleeping quarters except the King's. Valek avoided encountering the King. He'd seen paintings of the man—tall, broad-shouldered, with graying black hair and rugged good looks, but Valek worried if he saw the King in person, he'd kill him right there.

No. Valek planned to strike in the middle of the night—an assassin's best friend. And the only time the King spent without his entourage of guards was when he visited the Queen's bedroom at night, which wasn't often or predictable. And with the rumblings of revolt in the air, his visits became more infrequent. At least when the King planned to visit her, she received word in the early evening and she'd call Valek to style her hair the way the King liked it.

When the warm season drew to a close, Valek took an evening off to go into Jewelstown. He changed before meeting the Commander. The fabric of his pants chafed against his thighs and calves. He'd been wearing a skirt so long, pants now seemed to restrict his movements—odd and amusing at the same time.

Valek looped around the Black Cat Tavern. A clash of voices and clangs of dishes and mugs poured from the open windows—normal tavern sounds. Too bad the four goons hiding in the shadows around the building were not standard. Assassins? No. They were too easy to spot. Valek waited until a group of people entered and he slipped inside with them.

A mix of patrons filled the bar and occupied the tables. Even without spotting the subtle differences in clothing, the body language marked the soldiers from the civilians. The Commander sat in the darkest corner of the room. Valek wondered how close he'd get before someone tried to stop him. Not many of the Commander's followers knew about Valek.

Sure enough, a wall of muscles inserted themselves between him and the Commander about two tables out.

Valek showed them his empty hands. "I'm just looking to sign up, boys."

"Let him through," Ambrose said.

They parted. He squeezed in between them and sat across from the Commander.

Valek hooked a thumb at the brutes. "Are they here in response to those four waiting for you outside?"

"Four? Hell, Lenny said there were two." He waved a man over and told him about the others. "Do another sweep right before we leave and make sure no more have joined their friends."

"Yes, sir." The man glanced at Valek before moving away.

"They're not the King's men or assassins. Mercenaries?" Valek asked.

Ambrose gave him a tired smile. "Close. They're bounty hunters. Once the King figured out he couldn't reach me with the professionals, he thought if he offered enough gold some untrained hack would get lucky. They're more annoying than dangerous." He swigged his ale. Dark smudges lined his eyes. "How's your pet project going?"

"I'm in."

He straightened. "How soon?"

"The next time the King is feeling amorous."

Ambrose laughed. "And how will we know that?"

Good question. "Do you have anyone else inside the castle?"

"Half the servants and more than half the soldiers."

Impressive. "I'll give a message to one of them to deliver to you. You'll have about five hours' notice. Will that be enough?"

"Plenty. Give the message to a housekeeper named Margg. Do you know her?"

"I've seen her around. Is she trustworthy?"

MARIA V. SNYDER

"Yes. She's from my town. I sent her to work undercover at the castle years ago."

"All right. Do you want me to take care of those annoying bounty hunters lying in wait for you?"

"No. They're potential recruits."

"And if they refuse to join the cause?"

"I haven't encountered that problem yet."

"You certainly present a convincing argument," Valek said. He rubbed his chest as he remembered their first encounter. "Does everyone get a *C* carved into their skin?"

"Only you."

That surprised him. "Why?"

"You're the only one who managed to get close."

"Even the other assassins?"

"Yes. I can sense them coming, while you were a complete surprise."

Funny, it didn't seem that way to Valek. Perhaps the Commander was a magician. "Sense them with your magic?"

Horror creased Ambrose's face. "No. Magicians are vile creatures and we will cleanse our society of them, starting with the King."

We, meaning Valek. He had no love for magicians, but to kill them all...seemed a waste of resources. "They could be an asset to your rule."

"No. They're not trustworthy."

This was the first time Valek hadn't agreed with the Commander. Not that it changed anything. He'd sworn his loyalty to the man.

Valek left the tavern and changed back into female clothing. He rubbed a hand along his jaw, testing for stubble. Sometimes he needed to shave twice a day. Returning to the castle, he checked in with the Queen in case she required anything. She didn't.

Three more nights passed without a visit from the King, but on the fourth night the Queen received a message. Anticipation curled in Valek's stomach. He handed a note to Margg to deliver to the Commander.

That night as he arranged the Queen's thick hair so it fell in waves over her shoulders, he handed her a drink.

"This is called My Love. It's supposed to…ah…greatly enhance the mood," he said. "The cook swears by it and she has six children."

The Queen blushed, but downed the drink pretty quick. Soon after, she complained of being dizzy and he helped her into bed. As Valek fluffed pillows, she died from the poison. A quick death—more than she deserved for being a nasty person.

He closed her eyes and turned the lantern down low. The biggest problem tonight would be the King's guards. Six of them would escort the King to Jewel's suite and they would then wait in her receiving room until morning. Her guards had the night off. Valek had to take the King's men out before the King realized Jewel was dead and raised the alarm.

Valek changed into his black sneak suit and scanned the receiving room, searching for a good place to hide. Dark corner? No. Behind the curtains? No. Under the couch? Not if he wanted to live. He glanced up. The ceiling had shallow wooden rafters. He climbed up the wall and wedged his body between the stone ceiling and the beams that crossed above the room. It wasn't ideal. If the soldiers spotted him, he'd be an easy target. He readied his blowpipe and darts as he waited for the King's entourage. Hesitation wasn't an option.

"…sir? Sir?" One of the Commander's security officers poked his head into Valek's office.

Valek waved him closer. "Yes?"

"The Commander has retired for the evening, sir."

MARIA V. SNYDER

Already? He glanced at the array of candles on his desk. They had burned down a few inches. Absorbed in his memories, Valek had lost track of the time. "Thank you, Lieutenant."

The man retreated. Valek finished writing the notes on the security weaknesses he'd seen earlier. He'd address the issues with the soldiers in the morning. Extinguishing the candles, Valek locked up and joined the Commander.

"Anything to report?" Ambrose asked, handing Valek a glass filled with a dark red liquid.

Valek sat in the soft armchair. He swirled the contents of the glass and sniffed. General Dinno's homemade cherry brandy. Swallowing a mouthful, he savored the sweet taste as it burned down his throat. Then he informed the Commander about the messages from Yelena and Irys, Janco's mission and Arbon's visit.

"I'd like to send a couple agents to keep an eye on Yelena," Valek said.

"Do you really think she needs the help or is sending them a way to make you feel better about the situation?" The Commander studied Valek over his brandy.

"I'll admit, after the first message I wanted to go myself. That was my knee-jerk reaction. But after learning about this new threat from Irys, I'm thinking she'll need added protection."

"From an *unidentified* threat. Could Sitia be trying to get you to do their dirty work for them?"

"I wouldn't put it past the Council, but I think the Master Magicians are sincere."

"We could invade, take over Sitia, and then your loyalties wouldn't be divided."

Valek paused, letting the Commander's comment sink in. Ambrose had put that bit in there about invading Sitia to throw Valek off.

"You believe my loyalties are divided between you and Sitia?" Valek asked.

"Perhaps not Sitia, but between me and Yelena. Am I right?"

Ah. Valek considered.

"Let me put it this way. If she was in mortal danger and I ordered you to stay here and write reports, what would you do?" Ambrose leaned forward. "No need to answer. Your expression gives you away. You'd bolt for the border."

The Commander was right. Valek would. When had his feelings changed? He'd been prepared to kill Yelena for the Commander eight years ago.

"I'm sorry."

"No need to be. You've served me faithfully for twenty-four years. And what I've learned in your absence is that I need someone here who is as committed as you once were."

"I've been trying to train Maren, Ari and Janco."

"Won't work. Maren isn't organized and the boys would rather be playing spy."

Valek had to agree. "You think Onora could do my job? She's pretty inexperienced."

"I hate to disappoint you, Valek, but I'm looking a few years, not a few days, into the future."

"You don't know much about her."

"And I knew nothing about you when I accepted your pledge in that alley twenty-four years ago."

True. "Why did you? You had no idea if my word meant anything."

"You had a hungry determination in your eyes. The same look Onora has now."

"I wanted the King's blood. Whose blood does she want?" Valek asked.

"Perhaps that captain in MD-2?"

— MARIA V. SNYDER

"Perhaps." But Valek wasn't convinced. And if he was going to relinquish his job to her, he would make sure she had more to her than a hungry look in her eyes.

25

JANCO

The clatter of the wagon's wheels echoed off the tunnel's stone walls. Janco followed the glow of the torches while remaining far enough back to avoid being noticed. Not that the six guys would have the energy to look behind them. Each set of three men pulled a heavy wagon through the narrow cave that was too tight for horses.

They had been going downhill, but now the ground slanted up. He wondered if they noticed the extra weight in the second wagon. Onora had sneaked under the burlap. She'd ordered him to follow the cart heading into Ixia, but that was Ari and Gerik's territory. Besides, he didn't completely trust Little Miss Assassin yet.

Janco hoped the incline meant they neared the end. The air seemed thicker in here and harder to draw into his lungs. He'd inspected the walls of the tunnel as he traveled through. The natural cave formation had narrowed then ended. At that point, the smugglers had carved a hole and dug out a mix of dirt and rocks. Shovel marks scored the walls. Janco wondered how long it'd taken them and where all the dirt had gone.

He hunched a bit, half expecting the ceiling to collapse on top of him at any minute. The cool air smelled earthy and a dampness clung to him. Or was that sweat? Being down here was almost as bad as being in the Creepy Keepy.

Finally a fresh breeze fanned his face. The tightness around his chest eased. The tunnel emptied into a forest. It resembled the Snake Forest, which meant they hadn't gone too far into Sitia. And from the location of the entrance in Ixia, Janco guessed they were in the Moon Clan's lands.

A team of horses and four people waited in the forest outside the cave. Janco stayed in the darkness of the tunnel as the men transferred the wagons to the horses. Once they finished, everyone jumped on the wagons. Janco hoped no one discovered Onora. He wondered if she blended in and resembled one of the barrels like she had matched the colors of the rocks earlier.

When the wagons trundled out of sight, Janco followed. Pain pierced his skull as he exited the cave. When it dulled, he turned around. The cave's entrance was no longer visible. Another magical illusion hid it.

Keeping well back from the wagons, he wasn't too worried about losing them. The heavy wagons made deep impressions into the ground. Plus the moon cast enough light to illuminate the wheels' tracks, and dawn was still a few hours away. Janco yawned. Guess it'd be another night without sleep.

He increased his pace when he noticed a faint glow in the distance. There could be a city ahead, and it would be difficult to track the wagons over cobblestones. The smugglers headed toward a town and crossed a bridge. Only one street had been lined with lanterns, which meant calling the place a town was being generous.

The rush and gurgle of water sounded loud in the quiet night. A cold mist hovered over the banks of the river. The temperature dropped as he ghosted over the bridge, keeping low to avoid being seen. The smugglers entered a warehouse on the edge of town.

After the wagons disappeared into the darkness, a big metal door rolled silently down. Someone kept that door well oiled. Considering the moisture in the air, that sucker would have squealed without proper care. The air also held a familiar scent, but Janco couldn't put a name to it.

Janco scanned the streets, but no one was in sight. He cased the building—two stories, flat roof, brick construction and easy-to-break-in windows—his favorite type. Debating if he should sneak in or wait for Onora, he decided to wait—for now. Janco found a perfect spot to watch for signs of activity like lantern light in the windows, which would mean they planned to stay awhile. Noises would also tip him off. Even if she knew he was here, Janco doubted Onora would be the type to yell or scream for help. His spot also gave him a view of all the exit points. Bonus!

When no one left after an hour, Janco figured the windows might be blacked out. And they could have soundproofed the building. It depended on how smart they were. Considering the magical illusion and tunnel, Janco guessed they had a certain level of sophistication. Adding that to the fact that once the sun rose, he'd be stuck until nightfall, he left his hiding spot and climbed to a second-floor window.

Thick curtains had been drawn across it. He eased open the lower pane, listening for…well, anything. Nothing. So far. Counting to ten, he widened the gap and waited. It remained quiet. Janco parted the curtain, peeking inside. Blackness. He pushed the fabric aside, letting in the faint street light to reveal the contents of the room.

Janco relaxed. Crates had been piled in a haphazard fashion, suggesting this was a storage room. He clambered onto a pile, careful to transfer his weight slowly so the wood wouldn't creak. Then he tied the curtain back. He planned to leave before dawn and he'd need the light to find the exit—especially if he was in a hurry.

MARIA V. SNYDER

After navigating over the crates and boxes, he reached the door. The knob turned without trouble. A brief thought—this seemed too easy—flashed, but he ignored it as he opened the door. Peeking out, Janco confirmed that the dark hallway was unoccupied. No light shone under any of the doors, so he kept moving. It didn't take him long to find a stairwell on the far end of the building. Darkness swallowed the bottom of the stairs.

Janco trailed his hand along the railing and descended. When he reached the last step, he groped for the door and encountered a number of spiderwebs—yuck—before finding a handle. He sucked in a breath and pushed it open.

More blackness greeted him, but a slight lightening of his surroundings crept in as his eyes adjusted. That familiar scent overpowered his senses and he stifled a cough. He covered his nose with his sleeve.

Large dark shapes of machinery filled the area around him. They appeared to be big vats of liquid with pipes snaking between them along with mixing tools. Distant light called like a beacon. He avoided the equipment as he crossed the factory, aiming for an oversize entrance. Beyond that, light flickered.

He peered into the other room—a storage area. A bunch of people grouped around a stack of barrels, drinking, talking and laughing. The two wagons and four sweating horses stood nearby. Janco half expected Onora to sneak up to him and demand why he was there, but she didn't.

Moving a little closer, Janco squinted at the words burned into the barrels. Ixian white brandy. Ah, the Commander's special brew, which was illegal to sell to Sitia. That solved that puzzle.

Janco then scanned faces, counting the six muscular men who'd towed the wagons through the tunnel and the four who'd met them on the Sitian side.

And one extra. Maren.

26

YELENA

I slipped through the building next door to Opal's glass factory, exiting into an alley. Letting my eyes adjust to the
darkness, I paused. The acrid odor of rotting garbage filled
the air. Distant sounds from the street reached me, but the
narrow alley remained quiet.

Still wearing Reema's cloak and the blond wig, I walked
to the south end and turned right. Then I pressed next to the
building, waiting. If anyone had been hidden in the alley, he
would have to hustle to catch up and I'd spot him.

No one emerged. After a few more minutes, I continued
down the street. Valek had taught me that trick and a few
others. Without my powers, I'd need to rely on them and the
null-shield pendant. Since Reema had my cloak, only the octopus remained to protect me from magic.

I kept to the shadows and let my fear guide me. When I
turned west, my heart rate increased. Keeping to side streets,
I traveled toward the heart of my terror. I reached a tight alley
and every fiber of my being pressed on me to turn around and
bolt. Death waited for me down this path. This alley must lead
to Ben's hiding place. Before entering, I opened my cloak and
draped the fabric over my shoulders to free my arms. I palmed

a couple of Curare darts in my left hand and my switchblade in my right with my thumb near the button. My hands shook as my heart skittered.

Summoning my courage, I strode down the alley to a door that pulsed with malevolence. I waited for Ben's magic to alert them. But when nothing happened, I returned my weapons to their hidden locations and grabbed my diamond pick and tension wrench.

I knelt next to the door and worked on popping the lock. Good thing light wasn't a requirement for picking a lock. As I lifted each pin, a distinctive click sounded along with a slight vibration through the metal pick. When all the pins were aligned, the tumbler turned, unlocking the door. It swung inward with a creak. I froze as fear burned in my guts.

No other sounds pierced the darkness. Returning my picks, I pulled my switchblade, stood and entered the building. If Ben and his gang had moved on, perhaps they'd left a clue as to where they were headed.

A faint memory of lanterns sitting on a table near the door stirred and drew me deeper inside. I held a hand out, but it failed to warn me as my legs crashed into...something. Sweeping my hand lower, I found a lantern, but before I could dig in my pack for my flint, the scrape of metal sliding along metal rang.

A beam of light from a bull's-eye lantern speared the blackness, blinding me.

Voices shouted. I'd walked right into an ambush. Stupid.

I moved into a defensive stance, but a dark shape tackled me. We hit the ground hard. I landed on my stomach. The impact robbed me of breath. More shouts sounded and someone kicked my switchblade from my hand. Light reflected off the knife as the weapon spun away. Funny, I didn't remember triggering the blade.

I struggled to knock off the person on top of me, but a knee jammed into the small of my back as my arms were wrenched behind. Metal cuffs bit into my wrists. Two sets of hands grabbed me under the arms and yanked me to my feet. The motion knocked my wig to the ground, inciting a gasp, a groan and a couple of curses.

"Yelena, what are you doing here?" Leif demanded.

"Uh…looking for Ben. Did you find him?"

Another lantern glowed to life. I blinked. Hale held up the light. He stood next to Opal. Both frowned. In fact, no one looked happy. Tired, dirty and angry, but not happy.

"Did I ruin your ambush?" I asked.

"Yes," Leif said.

"No," Opal said.

I waited, sensing I trod on very thin ice.

"We're not telling you anything until you explain what the hell you're doing here," Leif said. "And why you ran away."

I'd hoped to avoid all this right now, but they deserved answers. I explained about my memory laspe, my fear, my trip to the plains and my return. "Don't worry," I said to Opal. "Reema's with Kiki and they're on the way to safety as we speak."

"Where?" she asked.

I glanced at the others. "Devlen is waiting for you at the factory. He'll tell you before he leaves to catch up with her."

"All right." Opal turned to Leif. "I'll meet you at HQ."

He nodded and she moved to leave, but paused next to me. "Thanks for protecting her, Yelena."

"Don't thank me. I'm the reason she's in danger."

"This time." Opal gave me a tired smile. "Next time it'll be me or Devlen or her brother."

"Then why not stay far away from those situations?"

"Because we can help and it wouldn't be right not to." She squeezed my shoulder and left.

"Be careful," I called after her, unable to stifle that little voice that threatened all my loved ones.

Hale stared at me with a sullen expression.

"Uh…can you unlock these manacles now?" I asked.

Leif tightened his grip on my arms as if he expected me to make a break for it. A bad sign.

Leif shook his head. "You planned to find Ben by yourself. Don't you think that's really…?"

"Dangerous," Hale supplied.

"And incredibly stupid."

"I wasn't going to attack. I just wanted to locate him for the authorities. I want my memories back," I said. "Besides, Midnight Son—"

"I don't think citing a dead Story Weaver will help you," Leif said.

"Okay, Leif. I get it. I'm sorry for running off, but at the time, I thought I was saving your life and protecting Reema. He might be a dead Story Weaver, but he helped me figure it out and I came back. Doesn't that count?"

"How about a promise to remain uninvolved?" Leif asked.

My stomach squeezed just thinking about it. "I can't. It's just like Opal said. It's—"

"All right, then. Protective custody it is," Leif said.

"What? You can't!"

"I can. I've orders from Second Magician Irys Jewelrose to place you in protective custody if you're too stubborn to see reason—her words, not mine." Leif pulled me from the building. Hale followed with the lantern.

"You can't be serious!" I protested.

Leif lowered his voice. "Irys discovered another plot to harm you, Yelena. The attack in the forest might be connected or this could be a new threat. Either way, she says word is out about you and you're too vulnerable."

"I'll be careful and—"

"Like chasing after Ben on your own?"

I opened my mouth to reply that I'd acted on pure instinct, but that wouldn't go well in my defense. Leif towed me to Fulgor's security headquarters. Nothing I said changed his mind. Citing orders from the Second Magician, Leif explained to the officers on duty that I was under protective custody until the danger had passed. Only orders from him or the Master Magicians should be obeyed.

After transferring me to the soldiers in charge of the jail cells, Leif and Hale left without saying a word. The guards confiscated my cloak, pack and weapons before locking me in a cell with a blanket.

The evening had not gone as expected. Not at all. I prowled around the small cell. Frustration, anger, exasperation, amusement and disbelief churned in my chest. It was one thing for them to be upset with me. But protective custody? This had to be a joke. Or temporary. They'd made their point. Lesson learned. They were bound to be back soon to release me and we'd discuss plans. Right? Right.

Minutes turned into hours and my certainty slowly diminished. I inspected the locking mechanism on the cell's door—all my clothes had lock picks sewn into the hems. But the complex bolt couldn't be opened with standard tools. Only the front side of the cell had bars. The rest of the walls were made of stone. Actually, it appeared as if the builders had dug rough square cubes into the bedrock underneath the headquarters. Dim light shone from the two lanterns hanging on the wall opposite the cells. And from the utter quiet, I guessed I was the only occupant. Lovely.

Hours turned into a day. I pestered the guards with questions when they brought me food, but they refused to answer. Nor did they agree to deliver a message to Irys for me. I pouted. However, with no one there to see me pout, I felt silly. Perhaps I'd get more attention with a hunger strike.

I considered my options for an escape. Inventorying the contents of my hidden pockets, I had two sets of picks and three darts filled with... I wasn't sure. I sniffed the liquid contents. Curare in two of them and goo-goo juice in the other. Too bad. I'd rather use sleeping potion on the guards. Curare seemed harsh for a couple of guys just doing their job. Of course, I needed to get close enough. My aim without a blowpipe was horrible.

During the next few meals, I watched the guards. Only one approached the bars. He slid the full tray through the slot near the floor, while his partner—the one with the keys—stood well away from the cell. Shoot. I'd have to get the second guy to either open the door or stand right by the bars.

One day turned into two as I searched my memory for a way to trick the guards. All my ideas—fake an illness, fake death, fake a swoon—were all unoriginal and I doubted anyone would fall for them.

Huddled under the blanket on the hard metal slab they called a bed for the third night of my incarceration, I stared at the ceiling, plotting revenge on my brother. Just the thought of wrapping my fingers around his thick neck helped ease my frustration and anger. Other more creative tortures came to mind and I almost smiled until the clang of a metal door signaled the first of many nightly bed checks.

Only one guard entered the jail tonight. He peeked in through the bars, confirmed I remained locked inside and retreated. Just then, an idea sparked for a way to escape. I mulled it over. With just one guard, I had a better chance of escaping. A few problems like how I would get past the soldiers in the processing area and the people working the night shift in headquarters might make it difficult. Aside from that, my plan just might work. After all, I had to do something, and getting caught would just land me right back here. Maybe my escape attempt would bring Leif so I could strangle him in person. One could hope.

I decided to wait until the third bed check to spring my surprise, but a ruckus woke me from a light doze. Standing close to the bars, I watched two unfamiliar guards struggle with a prisoner. As he resisted, he shouted slurred curses. The reek of bourbon reached me, and a couple of bleeding cuts marked his face. All the evidence pointed to a bar fight.

They tossed him into a cell and locked it. He rattled the bars, yelling about injustice and how the other guy started it.

"You're wasting your breath," I said. "They don't care."

"Huh? Who's there?"

I hesitated. He might recognize my name, so I used my middle name. "Liana. I'm in the cell next to yours."

"Oh. Whadda ya in for?"

"Nothing. I was framed."

He laughed. "Me, too. Name's Kynan. Anyone else in this rat hole?"

"I don't think so."

He huffed. "No wonder they busted me. It's a slow night. Just my luck." Then he launched into a drunken rambling explanation of his terrible luck.

Eventually, he ran out of story, and from the thump, I guessed he found the metal bed. Soon light snores filled the silence. I returned to my bed and lay down, debating if I should attempt an escape tonight or wait until tomorrow, when Kynan would most likely be gone.

The snap of a lock signaled a bed check. The guard's footsteps paused and he snorted and muttered, "Passed out already." Then he peered in at me before leaving.

I decided to put my plan into action during the next check. First, I flapped the blanket a couple of times, hard, sending a gush of air to blow out one of the lanterns. The shadows in the cell deepened. Then I smoothed the blanket over the bed, letting the edge hang to the floor. From the doorway, it would appear as if I hid underneath.

Second, I needed to test a theory. I kicked off my boots, stashed them under the bed and climbed the bars to the ceiling. The uneven surface had a number of finger- and toeholds. Except I didn't have the arm strength to cling to the ceiling. How did Valek do it? Perhaps if I held on to the bars and tucked my legs up, curling into a small ball. It worked, but it'd be better with my boots on. The rubber soles would grip the metal bars. I slid back to the floor, laced up my boots and waited.

After an hour or so, a metallic clicking sounded. It felt too soon for a check. Regardless, I climbed the bars as the noise continued. Once in position, I peered down the hall. Kynan's cell door creaked open. What was he doing? Was he escaping? He approached my cell and stared at the blanket for a moment. Kneeling, he inserted a strange hooked tool and, after a series of ticks, the lock released.

My heart pulsed a warning and I stayed in place despite my burning arm muscles. Kynan exchanged the tool for a long metal shaft—not quite a blade but an…ice pick? Now would be an ideal time for the guard to return. Should I scream for help? So much for *protective* custody.

Kynan crept toward my bed. He probably believed I slept below. My arms shook. I wouldn't last much longer. Sliding down without making a sound, I palmed a dart.

"Wake up, Yelena," Kynan said. "I've a message for you."

I didn't wait for the message. Charging him, I jabbed the

dart into his neck. He spun and lunged, aiming his weapon at my throat. I backpedaled. The goo-goo juice worked fast and he stumbled forward.

Kynan giggled. "Surprise!" His second lunge went wide.

I stepped in close, trapping his arm. Wrapping my hands around his wrist, I controlled his weapon as I hooked my heel behind his ankle and tripped him. He fell back and I landed on his chest. The pick clattered to the floor, but he made no move to reclaim it.

"Ah, darlin', you just had to ask. I always grant last requests for a quick tumble."

"You have a high opinion of yourself, don't you?" I sat on his stomach and checked him for more weapons.

He grinned. "The ladies love me."

"And your clients?"

"Happy. Happy. The Mosquito never fails."

"Except this time."

Kynan rubbed my arms. "The night is still young, darlin'."

I knocked his hands away. "And you missed me the last time."

"I never miss!"

"Is this your first attempt on my life?"

"Yup. Won't be the last neither."

So this was a separate attack from the one in the woods. Lovely. A number of questions bubbled, but I concentrated on the most important ones first.

"Who hired you?" I asked.

"Can't tell. Big no-no."

The question was too direct. I tried another tactic. "What was the message?"

He perked up. "How's it feel to be at someone else's mercy?"

Gesturing to my position on top of him, I said, "I'm not at your mercy."

Kynan waved a hand. "Details. You're like the rest of us now—slaves to the magicians."

While it was a harsh view of Sitian society, I suspected he knew my secret. "Who told you this?"

"Client. He says you're regular. Unremarkable. An easy mark. No—"

"I get it." Just how far had the news about me spread? If it was common knowledge… Fear tingled along my skin. I drew in a breath. Kynan's client must have learned it a while ago in order to send the assassin. He had to be close to the Sitian Council. "Did the Councilman learn about me from the Council?" I guessed.

"Yep. He gets a pile of gold for nuggets."

I considered. "The Councilman isn't your client."

"Nope."

But his client was bribing a Councilman. I took another guess. "Your client is a wealthy man who is very unhappy with the Sitian Council for not taking control of the magicians. After all, the magicians should work for us and not be setting the rules."

Kynan's mouth gaped open. "How did you know?"

"I had dinner with him last season." I tsked. "He never gave me any indication he'd use such drastic measures to change things."

"Yeah, that's Bruns. He keeps his emotions in check."

Bingo. And now for the clan name. "Which is a good thing. That's how he made all his money."

"Yeah, can't go blabbing about your radical views when you're a respected businessman."

"And he has lots of clients. They all love his…"

"Designs! Man is a wizard with a gemstone."

Aha. Bruns Jewelrose. I didn't recognize the name, but I planned to make his acquaintance. Kynan stared at me in suspicion. The goo-goo juice must be wearing off and I doubted my hand-to-hand fighting techniques would be effective against a trained assassin. I pulled another dart and pricked him with Curare.

While under the influence of the drug, he could breathe and hear, but not move or speak. I emptied his pockets and picked up his weapon. It was shaped like an ice pick, but the metal shaft was hollow. He'd been aiming at my throat. If he'd pierced my jugular, would the shaft speed up the rate my blood would have gushed out? I'd have to ask Valek. I grabbed the device that opened the cell door.

Then I yanked my blanket off the bed and wrestled him up onto the metal so he lay on his side, facing the back wall. I drew up his legs so he looked shorter and closed his eyes before covering him with the blanket.

"Thanks for helping me escape," I said.

Leaving my cell, I pulled the door shut. It locked with a click. Good. I entered Kynan's cell and arranged his blanket like I'd done to mine earlier—smooth on top and hanging over the edge. I left, closing the door. Then I switched the lanterns, so the lit one was farther from the door into the jail.

I stood in a shadow right next to the jail's entrance and waited. The fluttering in my stomach distracted me from my loud heartbeat. To pass the time, I thought about Bruns Jewelrose. I didn't remember crossing paths with him. It sounded like Bruns paid Councilor Jewelrose for information, and Bruns wasn't a magician. Many rich and powerful men in Sitia believed they should control the use of magic like they controlled other resources.

The clang and snap of metal broke through my thoughts. I sucked in a breath. If two guards entered, success was unlikely. One man stepped down, heading to Kynan's cell. He left the door open.

Slipping out, I didn't wait for the inevitable cry of alarm.

MARIA V. SNYDER

No one else was in the processing area, which explained why a single guard performed the bed checks. Instead of crossing through the bull pen to the exit, I headed down a hallway and toward the captain's office. I'd wait for him to arrive and I'd plead my case or I'd threaten to send his soul to the fire world, depending on his response.

His office door was locked. I yanked my lock picks from my pocket and set to work, popping the complex mechanism just as the guard raised the alarm. Dashing inside, I closed and relocked the door. Once my eyes adjusted to the darkness, I spotted a window. Except for the bars, it would have been a perfect escape route. I settled into the captain's chair and, once again, waited.

Muted shouts and pounding boots sounded through the door. A few times, someone tested the knob, ensuring it remained locked. Not much I could do if they checked the captain's office. After an hour, exhaustion caught up to me and I crossed my arms, resting them on the desk, then laid my head down.

An angry male voice boomed, waking me. I straightened. Weak sunlight flooded the room, and streaks of color painted the sky. Keys jangled, metal scraped on metal and the door swung open.

Captain Alden stepped into his office and jerked to a stop. "Yelena! I—"

I put my finger to my lips. "Close the door, please."

He complied, then turned to me. "I'm very sorry about the assassin. It appears we were overconfident in our ability to keep you safe."

"He's a professional. And as you can see, I'm quite capable of handling myself."

"Yes, I know. But I have orders from the Second Magician."

"What happens when the next assassin doesn't fail? How would you explain my death to Second Magician?"

Alden sighed. "This is a no-win situation."

I stood and offered him the seat. "Then tell the Master Magician I escaped. You know I'm safer on my own."

Alden wilted. He removed his cape and hung it on the rack before sitting down. "Can you answer a few questions first?"

"As long as you're willing to reciprocate."

"All right. What happened last night?"

I filled him in on everything except the part where I climbed the bars. No need to give away all my tricks. Besides, there was always a chance I might need it again.

"Do you know who hired him?"

"No, but he called himself The Mosquito." I lied for a good reason. No sense alerting Bruns that I was onto him. Kynan shouldn't remember too much from when he was under the influence of the goo-goo juice.

"How long until he wakes?"

"Curare lasts about a day."

"Okay. Your turn."

"I need an update on the investigation into Ben Moon's whereabouts."

"There's not much to tell. We scoured Fulgor, searching every factory, warehouse, empty building, and found nothing. They suspected you purposely misled them into believing he was in Fulgor."

Which explained some of the hostility from Devlen and the others. "Yet they'd found his hideout."

"Opal walked through every single alley, seeking magic. She discovered an illusion that hid a door. The place appeared to be occupied, so they set an ambush and that's where you came in."

Lucky me. "Did anyone go to Red Oak?"

"No. They concentrated their efforts here. None of Ben's men have returned to the warehouse since our people have found it, but evidence at the scene suggests Ben and his gang are headed west toward Owl's Hill. The task force left for Owl's Hill yesterday."

Too easy. Ben would never leave real clues. He was probably sending them on a wild-Valmur chase. My gut instinct said Ben was in Red Oak or in a town nearby. No logical reason for it, but I'd learned to trust my instincts.

"Task force?"

"A fancy name for Leif, Hale and Opal."

So they planned to keep me in protective custody until they returned. Anger burned, but I kept my voice even. "Can you return my effects and escort me from the building?"

"I can't convince you to stay?" He had a hopeful tone.

"No."

All activity ceased when Alden and I stepped into the bull pen. He glared at his men and ordered them to fetch my cloak and pack. One guard rushed to comply, and in a matter of minutes, I was free.

First stop, a decent meal. I walked to the Second Chance Inn and feasted on sweet cakes. Then I inquired about renting a horse. Red Oak was too far to travel by foot.

"There's a stable a few miles north of here called the Clever Fox," the waitress said. "They lease horses, but they require a pretty hefty deposit."

That wouldn't be a problem. No, the biggest problem I foresaw was what I would do if I found Ben in Red Oak. And I couldn't shake the feeling that Ben and his friends were the least of my worries, but when I focused on it, the memory faded. At least I had a couple of days to think about it. I thanked the waitress and left a big tip.

Before visiting the stable, I shopped for supplies. I'd need the standard travel fare—beef jerky, bread, cheese and tea. Not the most appetizing. I laughed. Leif had rubbed off on me. Traveling with him certainly had its perks. Too bad I still wanted to strangle him.

Once I left Fulgor, no one would know my whereabouts. While desirable for avoiding assassins, Ben's spies and annoying brothers, I thought it best to send a message to Valek just in case I ran into trouble.

The Clever Fox stables offered a number of horses for loan. The tidy barns, neat tack room and the clean earthy smell all pointed to a well-run, well-cared-for place of business. The owner, a man named Ellard, peered at me as if I was crazy when I inquired about Sandseed horses.

"I wish, missy," Ellard said. "Sandseeds won't tolerate multiple riders, but I had one as a boarder here a couple years ago. Ah…she was a thing of beauty she was." His brown-eyed gaze grew distant. "But I might have a good match for you. She's a bit older, but smart like those Sandseeds. Come on."

He led me to a stall in the back of the barn. A gray dappled mare poked her head over the door. Curiosity and intelligence shone in her light gray eyes.

"This here's The Madam. She's strong and steady, unflappable in most cases."

"And what upsets her?"

"Picket fences. Not sure why, but I suspect that scar on her chest might be the reason. It's just a guess, mind you. But if you keep her away from them, you'll be fine."

Good to know. "How much?"

We haggled over a price that included a saddle and tack. When we settled on a price, he saddled The Madam. Then I transferred my supplies, filling the saddlebags with my purchases. The Madam watched me instead of grazing on the grass under her hooves.

I thanked Ellard and mounted. "Let's go," I said to The Madam.

She didn't move.

"Are you sure you have riding experience?" Ellard asked.

"Yes." Just not with a regular horse. I thought back to my riding lessons six years ago.

I tapped my heels against The Madam's flanks and clicked my tongue. She lurched forward into a walk. Ellard waved goodbye as we exited his stables. Once we reached the northeastern road, I spurred her into a trot.

As we passed farm fields, tiny villages and forests, I altered The Madam's gait between trotting, cantering and walking so I wouldn't exhaust her. At least, that was my intention. Kiki always picked her pace and stopped when she was tired.

A few hours after sunset, I searched for a safe place to rest for the night. This route was too remote for travel shelters, and none of the towns had inns. I needed to find a camping site hidden from view.

An hour later, I discovered a small clearing behind a rock pile, which would block us from other travelers. Since we hadn't encountered anyone so far, I risked lighting a miniature fire to heat water for my tea.

While waiting for the water to boil, I removed The Madam's saddle, fed her and groomed her. She stretched her neck and leaned into the currycomb, encouraging me to rub harder. Then she moved around, presenting me with various body parts to comb. The behavior seemed odd to me, but when I thought about it, it made sense. After all, she knew the itchy places on her hide and I didn't.

I returned to the fire and ate a bland supper of jerky and cheese. At least my cinnamon tea tasted spicy. Memories of past campfires swirled—Ari and Janco arguing over the definition of the word *suspect*, Leif cooking up one of his delicious road stews, Valek's gaze meeting mine over the flames as a warmth spread through my body that had nothing to do with the campfire and everything to do with Valek.

Ah, the good old days. As long as I ignored the reasons that sent us on the road and all those miserable nights freezing or being drenched by the pouring rain or experiencing both. Selective recall suited me better—especially when I sat by myself, feeling lonely and skittish.

Plus the alternative, contemplating Ben's reasons for being near the Ixian border, was unpalatable. Except I should develop a plan of action. He might not be in the area now, but he had to have a purpose for going there. Other than leading the posse away from Fulgor.

I decided to snoop around, following the Sunworth river east. If I found him then I'd... What? Deliver a message to Fulgor, reporting Ben's whereabouts.

Report him to whom? Part of me was tempted to send a message to Valek. If he'd had his way three years ago, Ben would be dead and all these problems wouldn't be. Of course, there'd be a whole new set of problems. It never ended. Perhaps I should just travel to Ixia and let Alden and the others deal with Ben and this mystery threat. It was tempting. Very tempting.

But Opal's comment, "Because we can help and it wouldn't be right not to," replayed in my mind. And while I might have lost my magic, I hadn't lost the past eight years of experience in outsmarting the criminal element. At least I could determine Ben's location and possible schemes and then send the information to Captain Alden.

Now that I had a plan of action, I doused the fire and tried to sleep. *Tried* being the key word. Every noise jerked me awake despite The Madam snoozing unperturbed nearby.

MARIA V. SNYDER

There was a downside to unflappable. I worried she wouldn't alert me to danger.

Giving up a few hours after midnight, I packed up the camp and woke The Madam. We'd take our time so we'd reach Red Oak after dark.

It didn't take long to determine the two main sources of income for Red Oak. Between the floating logs and barges, it was easy to guess. The place had a sawmill that misted the air with the fragrance of freshly cut wood and clouds of sawdust. Stacks of lumber filled the wagons trundling south to make deliveries.

Barges loaded with coal bobbed dockside. Men shoveled the black rocks into wagons, emptying the metal boats and paying the tender. Then the barge was tied to a team of horses and pulled back upstream to the foothills of the Emerald Mountains to be reloaded.

By the amount of inns and taverns, I guessed the town benefited just as much from the influx of tenders and merchants as it did from the goods.

I kept to the shadows until I felt safe. A new face probably wouldn't attract attention, but a female one might. The majority of the laborers were men. No surprise, considering the backbreaking labor and strength needed to muscle the logs and shovel the coal.

After searching the entire town, I found no signs or clues that Ben had been here. None of the waitresses in the local taverns remembered serving them. Disappointed, I continued upstream, scouting two or three small towns each night, depending on the size.

Once I determined Ben and his gang weren't in town, I moved on. I had no real strategy for figuring this out. It was a gut instinct based on odd or furtive behavior or unusual interest in my presence. I doubted Ben's men would be working in a mill. After the place settled for the night, I'd visit the tavern for a meal and listen to the town's gossip. Strangers setting up shop or buying abandoned buildings always caused the locals much concern, which they discussed at length.

When it grew too late, I rented a room and pumped the innkeeper for any news. Then I'd be on the road before dawn.

After three nights of finding and learning nothing besides the general grumbling over the price drop of black coal, I approached Lapeer without any expectations. The place matched all the other river towns. But once I neared, a familiar scent jolted me as if I'd been struck by lightning.

Curare.

27

VALEK

"We traced the smugglers to the foothills of the Soul Mountains," Ari said, plopping into the chair in front of Valek's desk. The wood creaked in protest.

"And?" Valek asked.

"We lost them," Gerik said. He stood behind Ari, his posture rigid as if expecting a blow for reporting bad news.

It had been eleven days since Ari and Janco had left for their respective missions.

"Lost them how?" he asked.

"They either vanished over the mountain or under the mountain," Ari said. "The trail signs just stopped, and we suspect magic is the reason for the disappearance, but we can't be certain." Ari shook his head. "I can't believe I'm saying this, but…we need Janco. He's the only one besides you who could see through the illusion."

Valek considered. "It makes sense for them to use the tunnels to enter Ixia and for them to conceal the entrance with magic." Technically, no one in Ixia could sense it except Valek.

"Did Janco report in?" Ari asked.

"Not yet."

"Should we be worried?" Gerik asked.

Valek exchanged a glance with Ari.

Ari shrugged. "Depends. If he's found nothing, he won't bother to send a message, and if he's hot, then he won't have time. I think it's too soon to worry." He turned to address Gerik. "Besides, your girl is quite capable of handling herself."

"She's not mine," Gerik said in a gruff tone.

"So you say." Ari smirked as he leaned back in the chair.

Interesting. "Anything else to report?"

"We did uncover where they're distributing all the black-market goods," Ari said. "There's a warehouse in the factory district of MD-5, a few miles south of the General's manor house."

"Do you think General Ute is involved?"

"Not sure. We didn't do a full investigation, just watched long enough to confirm the transfer of illegal goods."

He mulled over the information. Getting inside the ware-house wasn't as critical as finding the smuggling route into Ixia. Neither Ari nor Gerik had the skills or the size to stow away in one of the wagons heading to the Soul Mountains, and all his best people had been assigned to other missions. Plus if there was magic involved, only he would be able to detect it. Valek would have to go.

After Ari and Gerik left, Valek contemplated the best way to present this new information to the Commander. He outlined a plan, then worked on reports. When the sun set, he lit the lanterns and candles scattered around. He liked plenty of light.

Just as he returned to his desk, the window behind him creaked. In an instant, he was on his feet with his knives in hand. Valek turned. Arbon climbed through the window.

"That's a quick way to get yourself killed," Valek said.

"How else was I supposed to get in here? You've tightened security." Arbon jumped down, landing lightly.

MARIA V. SNYDER

"Apparently not tight enough. You could have sent me a message."

"Where's the fun in that? Besides, I gotta keep my skills sharp." Arbon grinned and made himself comfortable.

Valek remained standing. "How did you get in?"

"Come on, King Killer. You know better than that. How about a pat on the back? It wasn't easy, ya know."

Valek admitted he was impressed. And Arbon had done him a favor by testing his security. Obviously more measures needed to be implemented.

"Do you have the name of the person who put the hit on Yelena?" Valek asked.

"You know how tight-lipped assassins are about their clients, and—"

"Yes or no, Arbon. It's not a difficult question."

"All he would tell me is the client is wealthy and has ties to Councilor Jewelrose."

Valek considered. That narrowed it down to one clan. "Do you know why this person hired the assassin?"

"No. But I will tell you the assassin is called The Mosquito because he keeps a vial of the victim's blood as a souvenir. He also won't quit until he finishes the job. Even if it takes years."

Not good. "Do you know his real name?"

"No. And I don't want to. I plan on retiring soon."

"Anything else?"

"The Mosquito wasn't hired until after that attack on your girl."

Valek sat down. "There's another assassin."

"It's possible, but no one contacted any of the Sitian assassins for hire. Either there's a brand-new player, or it's someone from Ixia."

Or both. Valek thought about Onora. She had the skills

and the intelligence to wear boots sized for a man to throw him off. But why would she?

"Last thing," Arbon said. "The Mosquito mentioned that the only reason he took the job was because his client assured him she is vulnerable." He shook his head. "No. He didn't elaborate."

Valek's stomach pinched with worry. If the rumors about Yelena being weak spread, she'd have more than two assassins after her. "Thanks, Arbon."

"Are we square?"

"Yep."

Arbon left the same way he'd arrived. Valek brooded in his chair, mulling over everything Arbon had said. Onora's arrival the very night he returned from Sitia had seemed rather convenient. Was the attack on Yelena a test to see if Valek would remain with Yelena instead of returning to Ixia? Something had happened to the Commander while Valek was gone. Perhaps Onora had sneaked into his suite prior to Valek's return and surprised him.

Guessing would get Valek nowhere. He needed to find the right time and place to talk to the Commander—maybe after they'd stopped the smugglers. And while Valek's heart urged him to abandon his duties in Ixia and race to protect Yelena, his mind reminded him she was traveling with Leif and another magician, and that many others had underestimated her in the past and all had regretted it.

Valek decided that he'd discover the smugglers' new route and then make a detour to find Yelena.

"You just returned," the Commander said. He swirled pear brandy around his glass, staring at the pale yellow liquid.

"There's evidence that magic is involved with the smuggling operation and only I can sense it," Valek said.

MARIA V. SNYDER

"All right. Go and shut them down. If you find a tunnel, collapse it. If you find a hole in our border defense, plug it. If you find a warehouse full of illegal goods, burn it down. If you encounter anyone who doesn't have permission to be in Ixia, arrest them. If you discover a magician within our borders, kill him."

Oh boy. Valek drank a mouthful of brandy to give him time to absorb the Commander's intent. "You wish to send a message to the smugglers." A *big* message.

"Yes."

"Pull the weed and all its roots so it doesn't grow back?"

The Commander smiled. "Exactly. Take as many soldiers as you need."

"All right, but I'll leave Ari in charge of security."

"Are you worried I'll be targeted again?"

"No. I'm concerned our security forces will revert back to their old ways while I'm gone. Ari will ensure the castle guards and your detail follow the new procedures I've implemented."

"And save yourself some work."

"Exactly."

"When do you plan to leave?" the Commander asked.

"I'll need time to organize my people, brief them and collect supplies. I expect small teams to leave the complex after sunset. Better to travel at night just in case anyone's watching the castle for unusual activity."

"Keep me updated if possible."

"Yes, sir." Valek finished his drink and left.

He crossed the hall to his apartment. Margg had lit the lanterns in his living room. And even though a warm yellow glow coated the furniture, his piles of books and his heaps of carving rocks, an emptiness hung in the air. The challenge and thrill of the hunt had dulled somewhat. Valek paused at the door to Yelena's old bedroom. Maybe if he wished hard enough, she'd appear in the threshold. And probably admonish him for being so maudlin. At least with shutting down the smuggling operation, he'd have an excuse to travel to Sitia and see her.

Before going to bed, he sat at his desk and wrote a list of people for the mission. Then he outlined a few ideas on how to optimize their strike, using the three key ingredients for success—surprise, speed and intensity.

Valek glanced at his collection of weapons hanging on the wall. His favorite knife hung in the center. Those three elements had been vital in assassinating the King.

That night remained crystal clear in his memories. Once he was in position—wedged between the ceiling and wooden rafters of the Queen's receiving room—Valek waited. It wasn't long before the King arrived with his six guards. When the King entered her bedroom, Valek would have mere seconds to disable the guards before the King realized the Queen had been poisoned.

The guards fanned out. Two by the Queen's bedroom, two near the entrance and two by the windows. Valek pressed his blowpipe to his lips. His left hand clutched the other darts. He had a clear shot at four of the guards. The ones by the window would be harder.

As soon as the Queen's bedroom door clicked shut, he targeted the guards by the entrance, hitting them in their throats. Then he hit the two by the door. The guy on the left swatted at his neck as if he'd been bitten.

"What the...?" The first guard held a dart between his finger and thumb, showing it to his partner.

The gig was up. Valek dropped to the ground and spun. He threw his last two darts at the men by the window.

"Hey!" one of them yelled, pointing to Valek.

The others drew their swords and advanced. Valek stood

in the middle of a tightening circle, hoping the sleeping potion would kick in before they skewered him.

The King rushed into the room, his face ashen. "Help me! The Queen is…" He stopped, taking in the situation.

The guards paused. "Orders, my lord?"

"Did you kill my Queen?"

"Yes," Valek said.

"Kill him," the King ordered.

Only one tactic worked when encircled. Valek lunged at the weakest point—the first man he'd hit. The blasted potion finally started to affect the big brute. Valek knocked him down and grabbed the man's sword.

Deflecting the other blades, Valek remained on the defensive while he waited for them to be overcome. The King urged them on. Valek ducked and dodged, earning more than a few cuts before they all collapsed to the ground.

"Are they all dead, too?" the King asked in an icy monotone.

"No. They don't deserve to die." Valek wiped blood from his eyes. A cut on his forehead stung.

"And I deserve to die? You're not the first to think this, nor will you be the last. Who sent you? That young brat from the diamond mines?"

"You sent me." Keeping a firm grip on the sword, Valek stepped over one of the fallen guards.

He laughed. It was a harsh sound. "In that case, you're fired."

"Nice try, but *you* set me on this path. *You* are responsible for your own death." He moved closer.

"I'm sure you have a sob story, but I don't care. And unless you're a master-level magician, you soon won't care, either. Death has a way of eliminating all your problems just like that." The King snapped his fingers.

A bubble of stickiness enveloped Valek. It pressed on his face as if trying to suffocate him. Probably was—the King was known to strangle his enemies with his power because he didn't wish to get his hands dirty. Valek pushed through the magic, advancing on the King.

The King of Ixia frowned. The air around Valek turned to sludge. Drawing a breath took effort; stepping forward was like wading through thick syrup. It was difficult to move, but not impossible. Two more strides and the King would be within striking distance of his sword.

The first gleam of fear shone in the King's eyes as he bent to retrieve a sword from one of his men. If the King had any skills with the weapon, Valek might be in trouble. Hard enough to walk through the magical mire… He couldn't imagine fighting in it.

Another push forward and Valek reached the strike zone. The King of Ixia slid into a defensive position and raised his sword. Not good. However, Valek would not let *this man* walk away from *this fight*. As he had said to Hedda five years ago, if his last breath was one second after the King's he'd die a happy man.

Determined, Valek summoned all his energy and attacked. The King blocked and they launched into a back-and-forth exchange of strikes and blocks. The thin metal rapiers sang with the contact. The monarch knew how to handle a blade and Valek had trained with mostly thicker, heavier swords, which required more muscle than speed. Valek's parries went too wide, leaving his middle exposed. Plus the sticky air dragged at his arms and legs.

The King of Ixia took full advantage of Valek's clunky style. With a flick of his wrist, the tip of his blade snaked past Valek's defenses and cut a path up Valek's right arm. Sharp pain registered for a moment, but he was too busy dodging the

MARIA V. SNYDER

King's next lunge to dwell on it. More cuts followed. Blood soaked his sleeves.

Then Valek miscalculated a strike and parried too late. The tip of the King's blade pierced his flesh near his left hip. Valek gasped as his body jerked. It felt as if he'd run full speed into the edge of a desk. Shock waves rippled through him, sending a cold skittery pulse to his extremities.

The King smirked as he drew back. "You have enough magic to counter mine. It's a shame the same can't be said for your fighting skills. Is there anything you'd like to confess before I kill you? I hear it can be quite...cathartic."

There was no way in hell this corrupt son of a bitch would live to see daylight. Valek envisioned his brothers. Imagining their ghosts standing here watching the fight, he drew strength from them and, it seemed, also advice. Vincent bared his teeth and made a stabbing motion. Valek returned his attention to the task at hand. The pain faded as he focused on what he'd worked so hard for.

"I do have a confession," Valek said. "I'm not a magician. I'm an assassin." Valek threw the sword down and pulled his knives—one for each hand. "I just forgot for a moment."

He surprised a laugh from the King. Then Valek attacked, and the King was no longer smiling. Even with magic pressing down on him, he kept a quick pace, forcing the King to backpedal. The man doggedly blocked the knives.

As the fight continued, sweat ran down the King's face as his responses slowed. Using magic appeared to be as draining as resisting it. The heaviness around Valek disappeared at the same time the King launched an energetic counteroffensive. The man was smart to concentrate his strength on his sword. Too bad for him that Valek's knife-fighting skills had been honed by five years of practice.

Without the presence of magic to slow him down, Valek

disarmed the King within a few moves. Valek pushed him against the wall, pressing the edge of one blade on the King's neck, and the other blade poked into his royal stomach just below the breastbone.

Panic reddened the King's face. "I can pay you ten times what your client offered."

"Not interested."

"I'll make you a general."

"No."

"My daughter! You can marry her and become a prince."

"Aren't you a swell dad. Sorry, but I've met your brat of a daughter. That would be worse than death."

"I'll give you anything."

"Good. After you die, I want you to explain to my three brothers why your soldiers murdered them in *your* name." Valek stabbed his knife up into the King's heart.

The King's magic exploded, propelling Valek back. The King of Ixia stumbled forward clutching the hilt of the knife. He gasped, "My blood...will...stain...your hands...forever." And collapsed.

Valek knelt next to the King and watched the life fade from his gaze. He listened for that last shuddering breath. And once the man died, Valek endured a tumult of emotions. Joy, relief and satisfaction spun around his racing heart. The euphoria rushed to his head. He sat back on his heels, overcome for a moment.

Now he could live his life. If he lived through the take-over, he'd be able to serve the Commander and purge Ixia of the King's rot.

But first, he needed to finish the job and eradicate the roots. Valek stood. All the aches and pains from the fight flared to life, demanding attention. He inspected the stab wound near his left hip bone. Blood oozed from the puncture. It hurt like crazy. At least it wasn't gushing and he could still move.

Focusing on the positive, he climbed out the window. Not much time left for him to visit the King's two children, three nephews, one sister-in-law and one brother before the King's corpse was discovered. While Valek had enjoyed thrusting his knife into the King's heart, he didn't relish this task.

He spidered from one royal's window to the next, easing the panes open and ghosting through bedrooms. Using the same poison he'd fed to Queen Jewel, Valek dripped five drops of My Love into their mouths, or their noses if they slept with their lips clamped shut. If they startled awake, he held his hand over their mouths for a few seconds. The fast-acting poison did the rest.

By the time he finished, the noises from the hallways had increased to panic levels with doors slamming, boots pounding and screams mixing with shouts of alarm. Despite exhaustion settling into all his muscles, Valek slipped out the prince's window and returned to his rooms. The outer door gaped open. Someone had searched them, and his skirts and few possessions were strewn on the floor. He secured the door.

Valek debated changing into Valma's nightgown to continue the ruse, but by this point either the Commander's forces would be successful or not, and in both cases Valma was no longer needed.

Instead, he peeled his blood-soaked sneak suit from his battered body, wincing as the dried patches ripped from his skin and the silky material tugged at the deeper cuts on his arms. He sponged off the gore. Red and purple bruises bloomed around the stab wound in his hip. He'd deal with that later.

Donning a pair of pants, Valek locked the bedroom door and collapsed into bed.

He slept for... He had no idea how long. But way too soon,

a loud crash jolted him from oblivion. In a blink of two very bleary eyes, four big, well-armed goons surrounded his bed. Cuts, bruises, blood spatters, disheveled hair and ripped tunics all evidence these men had been in a fight. But whose side?

"Is this him?" Bruiser One asked Bruiser Two.

"Yup."

"Grab him," Bruiser One ordered the others.

Too tired to resist, Valek allowed them to haul him from the bed. But once he was on his feet, he yanked his arms from Bruiser Three and Bruiser Four. "No need to carry me." He spread his hands. "I'm unarmed."

Bruiser One studied him. "Are you sure this is the guy who assassinated the King and his family? He looks—"

"Hold that insult," Valek interrupted. "If you value your life."

The man snorted.

"Come on. We're to report back to the throne room," Bruiser Two said.

They peered at Valek. He longed to return to his bed, but their postures said they weren't leaving without him. "Who are you reporting to?"

"The Commander."

Good news. "Then give me a minute to change."

After Valek dressed, the four bruisers escorted him to the throne room. He mulled over reasons why they acted as if he were the enemy. They could be recent recruits who had once been loyal to the King's family. While many citizens of Ixia hated the King, they wouldn't automatically be supporters of the Commander. He'd have to win their trust and loyalty. And Valek would be required to do the same with the soldiers. The idea would be more palatable once he was fully rested.

The throne room buzzed with activity. Servants ripped the tapestries from the walls, tearing the fabric with knives.

Groups of guards herded prisoners toward the Commander, who sat on the throne—a large garish chair made from gold. The overstuffed white cushion was reportedly sewn from snow-cat hide. Ambrose talked to the captives. When he finished, most of them knelt on one knee—probably swearing loyalty, while the others were taken away.

Valek approached with the bruisers by his side. The Commander's gaze flashed with joy. Giddy with his triumph, Ambrose jumped to his feet and hugged Valek for the first and only time.

"Well done, my boy. Well done." He thumped Valek on the back. "Where have you been?"

"He was sleeping," Bruiser Two said.

"How can you sleep? You should be celebrating. The takeover was a complete success!"

"He's pretty beat up," Bruiser One said.

"Did that bastard put up a fight?" Ambrose asked.

Valek glanced at his bruiser buddies. "What? No answer this time?"

They stared back.

"It was an intense match, sir. I'll give you a full report later," Valek said.

"Good idea. In the meantime, I have something for you." The Commander gestured to one of his advisers.

The woman picked up a silver platter with a cover. Odd. She presented it to the Commander. He removed the lid with a flourish, revealing Valek's favorite knife. Bright red blood coated the blade.

"We found it in the King's chest. I believe it is yours."

"Guess I need to clean it." Valek reached for the weapon.

"Won't work," Ambrose said.

"Excuse me?"

The Commander grabbed the cloth hanging over the woman's

arm. He picked up the knife and wiped the blade on the material. The blood clung to the metal. Not a drop stained the towel.

"I'm guessing it's magic." Ambrose handed the knife to Valek.

He ran a finger along the flat side. The blood avoided his skin, parting as he skimmed over the blade and re-pooling after his finger had passed. A stickiness pulsed from the weapon.

Valek laughed. "He cursed me with his dying breath. Said my hands would always be stained with his blood. Seems the curse attached to my knife instead." He tsked. "Such a shame. It was my favorite. What should I do with it now?"

"Put it on display in your office. So everyone who walks through those doors knows you are the King Killer."

And twenty-three years later, the King's blood still glistened in the lamplight.

Valek rushed around the next morning, organizing his teams for the mission, assembling supplies and explaining to Ari for the fourth time why Valek was leaving him behind.

"I know where the wagons disappeared in the foothills and where the factory is located," Ari said. "You'll need me."

"I need you here. And you can debrief Janco and Onora when they return."

"Then can we both catch up?" Ari asked in a hopeful tone.

"Not unless I send for you." Valek put a hand on Ari's shoulder when the big man's expression creased. "Ari, the castle's security has been lax, and I'm worried we still have gaps. Hedda trained Onora, but she could have trained more. I need you here."

"Yes, sir."

Valek watched his friend and hoped Janco returned soon. Ari wasn't quite Ari without his partner.

On his way back from visiting the stable, one of the gate's guards rushed up to Valek.

"Sir! There's—"

"I don't have time to deal with another messenger." Valek kept walking.

"It's not a messenger, sir."

He paused. "What, then?"

"It's…well…it's Kiki, sir. She's at the gate."

Did he hear that right? "Yelena's horse is at the gate?"

"Yes, sir. She is. And she brought…er…friends, sir."

28

JANCO

Janco watched Maren as she talked and drank Ixian white brandy with the smugglers in the warehouse. His colleague and friend appeared to be at ease with the others. She wore Sitian clothes and her long blond hair had been pulled back into a braid.

Maren's mystery mission for the Commander was no longer quite a mystery. Janco scratched at the scar below his ear. If Maren was working undercover in the smuggling operation, then why didn't the Commander inform the rest of them? Finding and stopping this gang had been their priority, so why the secrecy about Maren? He wished Ari was here. His partner would have an answer.

Fingers touched his arm and Janco about jumped out of his skin. A black shadow detached from the wall right next to him. Onora frowned. She jerked her head, indicating they should move deeper into the factory.

He retraced his steps, skirting a couple of vats and water pumps to reach the door to the stairwell.

Onora pushed it open, gestured him inside, then closed it behind them, plunging them into darkness. "Did you even discover where the smaller containers were headed?" Her question was hissed in a low whisper.

"Yeah, into Ixia." Before she could explode, he said, "We can learn that later. What if there was a magical illusion on this side, as well? You needed me."

She sighed, sounding a lot like Ari. "Do you recognize any of this equipment? Or what they're producing?"

"No. The smell is so familiar it's been driving me crazy. It's not cigars, that's for sure."

"Why not?"

"They'd be drying out the leaves, not soaking them or pulping them."

"Parchment?"

"Maybe, but what's illegal about that?"

"Nothing. But something's not right here. It feels…off."

Janco agreed. "Perhaps Maren can tell us what's going on."

"Maren, as in the Commander's missing adviser? She's here?"

"Yup. She's drinking with them."

Onora remained quiet for a few moments. "Do you think she switched sides? Who better to aid the smugglers than someone who is very familiar with Ixian security."

That would make sense if the person had been anyone other than Maren. Or Ari, or Yelena, or Valek. "Nope. She's loyal."

"Then why didn't the Commander tell us about her?"

"For a very good reason."

"You have no idea."

"It doesn't matter. I trust the Commander. That's all I need. And all you should need, too."

"All right," she said, but she chewed on her lower lip. "What do we do next?"

"I can see you!" he whispered.

"So?"

He glanced up. A faint light lit the upper level.

She pointed to the small pool of blackness underneath the stairs. They crouched close together. The light brightened as quiet footsteps sounded above. Janco concentrated. Only one person descended. The figure held a tiny metal lantern atop a post. Instead of the lantern hanging down, it resembled a torch, but without open flames.

When the cloaked figure reached the bottom, the person turned around and shone the dim light around the small space, revealing their hiding spot.

"Oh—"

Onora sprang forward. She rushed the intruder. The torch fell to the ground. Janco picked it up. He recognized it. The light was one of those small lanterns built with a long handle underneath to resemble a torch. It was called a lantorch—one of their gadgets. Onora scuffled with the person. They banged against the door and a knife clanged to the floor before Onora trapped the shorter figure in a double arm lock.

"Should I kill her before the others arrive?" Little Miss Assassin asked.

"No." Janco tugged the captive's hood back, revealing a familiar face with a very unfamiliar expression—fear. "Release her. It's Yelena. What are you doing here?"

Onora let Yelena go, but the assassin didn't look pleased.

Yelena smoothed her cloak. "Probably the same thing you are." She glanced at Onora.

"New recruit," Janco said.

Voices sounded on the other side of the door. "…heard something. I'm sure."

Time to go. Janco pointed up and the three of them climbed the steps to the second story. He led them to the storeroom. A grapple had been hooked over the windowsill and a rope hung to the ground. Yelena must have taken advantage of the

MARIA V. SNYDER

open window he'd left behind. He switched the light off as Onora climbed from the room.

They reached the ground and ran for cover. Voices yelled from above, calling out their location. Damn moon was too bright. The other smugglers poured from the warehouse and headed in their direction.

"This way." Yelena took the lead. She raced down the main road and away from the town.

Janco stayed close to her.

"Still too exposed," Onora said, glancing over her shoulder. "They're about a hundred feet behind us."

"There's a sharp bend." Yelena gestured. "Make a right into the woods as soon as we're hidden from view."

"Do you have a boat?" Onora asked.

Yelena didn't bother to reply even though Janco thought it was a really good question. With no leaves on the trees and only about twenty feet of forest between the road and the river, there weren't any hiding places.

Once around the bend, they plunged into the woods and, sure enough, a boat waited at the bank. It was one of those small skiffs with a canvas dome top. However, Yelena pointed to a huge ancient tree. It resembled one of those thousand-legged bugs.

"Climb up as high as you can," she ordered.

He paused. It had at least a million branches, which equaled about a million scratches. "But—"

"Trust me."

She'd gotten them out of a dozen tight spots in the past. He grabbed branches and scrambled higher. Onora had disappeared. Janco assumed she was higher in the tree, but who knew with her and her creepy chameleon power.

Yelena untied the boat and pushed it into the current. Then she swung up behind him. She might have been raised in Ixia, but her Zaltana blood showed as she ascended with ease, passing him with a grin. When the branches bowed under their weight, they stopped. A twig poked in his ear and in a number of unmentionable places.

They didn't wait long before a group of six smugglers dashed into the woods.

"...heading for the river!"

"Look, a boat! Peeti, your crossbow. Quick."

"Light it!"

Bright orange bloomed below them. Then a twang sounded and a burning bolt shot over the water, hitting the boat dead center. The canvas dome caught fire. Peeti shot three more and soon the entire boat was engulfed in flames.

Damn. They meant business. And if anyone glanced up... Old timber burned fast and it wouldn't take long for Janco and his friends to turn into barbecue. He calculated the distance to the ground. If he landed on one of them, he might not break his legs.

"Let's go. We got them," one voice said.

"Not yet. Search the area. The boat could have been a decoy," another ordered.

Great. Janco never liked hiding. He'd rather duke it out, and his companions could each handle two opponents easily.

"No," Yelena whispered. "It's not the right time."

He frowned hard at her. She'd read his mind even though she knew how much he hated magic. Then again, that creepy crawly sensation crossing the back of his neck wasn't quite the same as... A bug! Ewww! Staying still required an immense effort. Janco concentrated on the men below, debated between being killed by smugglers versus being bitten. The bug crawled up into his hair. Okay, smugglers it was!

Yelena flicked the bug away. He smiled his thanks. She shook her head just like Ari did when exasperated with him.

Which was quite often, although he'd no clue why because his logic was undeniable.

Eventually, the search moved far enough away from their hiding place.

"We can't stay here much longer," Janco said. The bug might have friends.

"We should split up," Onora said. She sat on the branch right above him. "They're looking for three people."

Yelena agreed. "Let's meet at the Water Witch Inn. It's in Port Monroe, located about five miles downstream of here."

"See you there." Onora climbed down.

"She's quiet," Yelena said as they returned to solid ground.

Shuddering, Janco brushed off his hair and clothes. "Yeah, and she's good with a knife."

"Hopefully she won't need it tonight. See you at the Witch." Yelena turned to go, but Janco grabbed her arm.

He didn't like how she held herself as if afraid she'd break. And she'd entered the warehouse alone and without backup. That didn't jibe. Something wasn't right and Valek would kill him if he didn't stick with her. Ari, too.

"We'll go together," he said.

"But—"

"They're looking for three, not two."

She smiled. "All right, but we need to get to the other side of the river."

He glanced at the cold churning water. "We're gonna swim?"

"Not if I can help it. There's a bridge back in Lapeer."

"Lapeer? Is that the town we were just in?"

"Yup."

"What about the smugglers?"

"We'll worry about that then."

He released her and she led him along the bank, heading upstream until they reached the bridge. They climbed and peered over the embankment. A couple of smugglers walked along the main street. "Are you sure we need to cross?"

"Yes." She yanked her hood down and unwound her hair, letting the long black strands hang over her shoulders. "Follow my lead." She took his hand, lacing her fingers with his and winked.

Ah. He grinned. "I knew you'd come around eventually."

Yelena tugged him up onto the bridge's walking path. She pressed against his side, walking slow. "It's always been you, Janco. I've just been suppressing my true feelings."

"What about Valek?" He stared at her as if she were the only one in the world even though he longed to check if the goons had spotted them yet.

"Valek, smalek. He's way too serious."

They paused at the center of the bridge, taking in the view. Little diamonds of moonlight sparkled on the water. He pulled her into a hug before they moseyed to the other side.

"You'll leave Valek for me?" he asked.

"Yes. You just have to tell him we're running away together." She smirked.

"Ow." He pressed a hand to his heart. "Doused with ice-cold reality. All loving feelings gone. Sorry, sweetheart, you're not worth dying for."

"Are you sure it's not that pretty new recruit?" She made a left onto a trail, heading downstream.

"It's not. She'd probably rather kill me than kiss me."

"Oh?"

"Long story. I'll tell you about it later." The path cut between the river and the forest. "How many miles is it?"

"About five, but my horse can take us both."

Just as he realized why that didn't sound right, Yelena turned right and entered the woods. She hiked until they reached a grayish horse.

Oh no. Worried, he asked, "Where's Kiki?"

29

YELENA

Despite the near miss at the factory and being chased, my mood had improved. It might have been due to Janco's presence, but I'd never confess that to him. He'd gloat about it forever. Janco held on to my waist as The Madam trotted along the path that paralleled the twists and turns of the Sunworth river.

We reached Port Monroe an hour later. After I settled The Madam in the Water Witch's stable, we entered the common room just as the sun rose. We sat at a table opposite the door, ordered sweet cakes and tea. I needed at least a gallon of tea. Janco didn't seem to be his normal peppy self, either.

"Did Valek send you to investigate the Curare factory?" I asked before he could start with his questions.

"Curare!" He smacked his forehead. "Of course. That's why it smelled so familiar. It was driving me crazy."

I waited.

"Curare. Oh sh—"

"That's what I thought when I caught the scent. It took me a day to hone in on that factory. I waited until the night-time to learn who is responsible, and…well, you know the rest. If you didn't know they were producing Curare, then why were you there?"

Janco told me about tracking smugglers to Sitia. "...using magic to hide their routes. And we also discovered Maren's working undercover in the operation."

"Are you her backup?"

"No. The Commander didn't tell us where she was. Not even Valek."

That worried me. Did the Commander suspect there was an informer in Valek's corps?

Our food arrived and we both shoveled steaming sweet cakes into our mouths. I gulped my tea despite the hot temperature. The liquid burned all the way to my stomach and warmed me.

"Okay, your turn. Why are you here?" Janco asked.

I gave him the short version, which didn't include my lost magic. I'd tell him before we did anything dangerous.

"You think the people who rescued Ben are involved with the Curare factory?" he asked.

"I'm not sure. That's why I sneaked inside to see if there was any connection. But regardless of who is involved, we have to shut that place down."

"Yeah, I kinda figured you'd say that. Do you want to notify the Sitian authorities? Or take matters into our own hands?"

"And what can the two of us do?"

Janco's eyes lit up. "Burn the place down. Totally doable with the *three* of us. You're forgetting Little Miss Assassin, our newest recruit."

This was going to be good. "Little Miss Assassin?"

"She doesn't like to be called that."

"Gee, I wonder why."

"Onora's overly sensitive. But I'm working on her. Anyhoo,

MARIA V. SNYDER

she showed up one night." Janco launched into a detailed story of how Onora made an impression on the Commander. "...and she would have beaten Valek if she'd finished her training. If she wants Valek's job—"

"What does Valek think about all this?"

"He didn't say, but I think he'd be more than happy to let another take over the reins."

"I don't agree. He loves his job."

"He loves you more."

Janco didn't quite understand. For Valek, the Commander would always come first, and I'd accepted that...mostly. I'd admit there were times I'd wished it was different.

As Janco helped himself to my tea, I mulled over the information. With Ben locked in Wirral, he couldn't direct a smuggling operation. We really needed to get inside and find out who was in charge before we informed the authorities. Was it the mystery accomplice I couldn't remember?

The Sitian methods for raiding a place were far from subtle. Plus I didn't have any doubt the smugglers had paid off the town watch. Not with the place stinking of Curare. The watchman would tip them off and all the evidence would be gone before the authorities organized an attack.

"Thinking devious thoughts?" Janco asked.

"Not quite. I'd like to discover who's behind the factory, but after tonight, I'd bet they're scrambling to relocate or hide the evidence."

"Maren might know. We should find a way to contact her."

"Or wait for her to contact us," I said. "She probably recognized us. Either way, we should return to Lapeer and keep an eye on that factory. See who comes and goes."

"They'll be on guard, watching for us."

"Then we'll have to go in disguise. How attached are you to your hair, old man?"

Janco groaned. "How about we pretend to be newlyweds?"

"No." I glanced at the door. We'd been talking for a couple of hours. "Shouldn't Little Miss Assassin be here by now?"

"Maybe she had to make a detour to shake a tail."

"You're not worried?"

"Not at all. The girl was trained by the same lady who trained Valek, and she…"

"She what?"

"She just blends in, but I don't get that icky magic sensation around her. Did you feel it last night? Could she be one of those One-Trick Wonders?"

"Maybe. Did Valek sense any magic?"

"He didn't say. Can't you use your superpowers on her and get the skinny?"

"Uh…about that, Janco. I—"

"There she is."

His voice held more relief than his early comments about her implied. Interesting. I studied the young woman as she approached. Graceful with pretty, light gray eyes and a narrow face. Her lips were pressed together and a crease marked her forehead. She'd be beautiful without that dour expression. I doubted she cared.

"What took ya so long?" Janco asked.

She frowned at me before meeting his gaze. "I don't think it's a good idea to discuss Ixian business in front of a Sitian."

Janco laughed. "Yelena isn't Sitian or Ixian. She's just an ian—neutral."

"No one is neutral," Onora said.

"True. How could she not love Ixia more? She can't. Oh, stop scowling at me, Little Miss Assassin. I'm just gonna tell her everything anyway. This way, I won't mess up the details."

"So you admit you've messed up the details in the past?" I asked.

"No way, sweetheart."

Onora turned to me. "It's amazing he's lived this long."

"He grows on you. Sort of like a barnacle."

"Hey!" He pouted.

"Did you run into trouble?" I asked Onora, ignoring Janco.

"No. While you two were pretending to be lovebirds, I looped back to the factory. Everyone was outside hunting for us, so I figured no one would be looking inside."

Smart. A server came over to take Onora's breakfast order. She ordered eggs, toast and ham.

When the girl retreated, I asked, "Did you find anything?"

"I saw Maren loading up the wagon with those small casks, and I heard two men arguing in an office next to the main factory area. They didn't agree on whether to close the factory down or to relocate it. But they planned to load their inventory on barges and send it upstream to a warehouse in Sunworth. Isn't that the name of the river?"

"Yes, but it's named after a town in the foothills of the Emerald Mountains, where the river starts," I said.

"That jibes with our other intel about the disappearing wagons," Janco said. "Ari and the grunt planned to check it out on the Ixian side."

I considered. "Onora, did you see the men or hear any names?"

"No. When Maren left with the horses and wagon, I followed her."

Janco straightened. "Why?"

"I knew the smugglers' plans, but I didn't know her destination."

"And?" he asked.

"She's returning to Ixia."

"Through the tunnel we found?"

"No. Why would she? She's an adviser to the Commander and can cross the border without trouble."

"Except she's working undercover. That would tip the smugglers off," Janco said.

"Unless—"

"She's not a traitor," Janco growled at Onora.

"*Unless* things have gotten too hot for her."

I suppressed a smile. Onora might be young, but she had plenty of confidence.

"Speculation will only get us so far," I said, trying to break the tension. "If they're planning on moving their inventory then we need to raid the factory."

Janco glanced around the room. "Do you have an army I don't know about?"

"I'll talk to Lapeer's town watch. That might tip the smugglers off, but at this point we need to get a good look inside. There might be invoices and other documents that would indicate who is supplying them with the Curare vine." The vine grew in the Illiais Jungle, my clan's lands, and the Zaltanas were supposed to be guarding it for just this reason. Concern for my family pulsed in my heart. I'd have to send a message to my father, warning him of poachers.

"While you organize the watchmen, we'll keep an eye on the factory," Onora said. "We'll follow anyone who leaves before the raid."

"We?" Janco smirked. "Just can't get enough of my company, can you, sweetheart?"

Onora met my gaze.

"It's best to ignore him."

"Easier said than done," she muttered.

"Hear that, Yelena?" Janco bumped my arm with his elbow. "I'm irresistible."

★ ★ ★

After Onora finished her breakfast, we split up once again. I rode The Madam to Lapeer. The afternoon sun warmed my shoulders. To avoid falling asleep in the saddle, I mulled over all the information from Janco and Onora. What was in those casks Maren loaded into the wagon? Curare, probably. The significance of that hit me. So worried about who'd been producing the drug, I hadn't considered the ramifications of it being available to Ixians. The Sitian Council kept strict control of it for a reason.

If the criminal element in Ixia had access to Curare, then Valek and his corps would no longer have an advantage. My stomach churned just thinking about it. At least Maren managed to take some with her and out of circulation. Or had she? An evil thought popped into my head.

Maybe the Commander was a client. If Sitia ever attacked Ixia, they'd have the upper hand. Sitia had magicians, the super messengers and Curare. It made sense for the Commander to want to even the playing field a bit by importing Curare. Except Janco had said the Commander made finding and stopping the smugglers a priority. Why would he do that if he was benefiting from them? He wouldn't.

The tight knot in my chest eased. I spurred The Madam into a gallop and headed straight for the town's station house.

My arrival was initially met with some resistance, but having a reputation as a powerful Soulfinder pushed past the doubts. Handy. As predicted, it took a while for the captain to organize his forces. We had to wait for off-duty officers to report in and for everyone to be briefed. The delay allowed Janco and Onora to get into position, but it reduced our chances of catching anyone. Hopefully they'd trail whoever bailed. If that was the case, one of them would eventually return to let me know where the smugglers went.

"Speed is better than surprise," I said to Captain Fleming for the tenth time. "They already know we're coming."

Sure enough, the factory was empty by the time we arrived later that afternoon. I hoped Janco had witnessed the exodus. At least I had a couple of hours of sunlight left to search the place. Papers littering the office, drawers hanging open and scuffs on the floor were all evidence of their hasty exit. In the factory, not much remained behind except for the equipment. Not even one of those casks. The rooms on the second floor remained full of storage, and I suspected the boxes had been left over from the previous tenants.

I scanned a few of the documents, looking for information. The captain tsked over the vats of half-pulped Curare vines and insisted everything would be destroyed.

"Didn't you recognize the smell?" I asked.

"Nope. We're not allowed to carry Curare. That's only for the bigger cities." He assigned a man to collect all the papers to bring back to the station to analyze.

I righted an office chair and sat. Hard to believe they managed to empty the place in twelve hours. Perhaps they had a hidden storeroom and after all the commotion died down, they'd return for the rest of their stock. Maybe in a basement?

While the officers cataloged the equipment and inventoried the storage rooms' boxes, I searched for a hidden door. I ran my fingers along the walls in case an entrance had been concealed by a magical illusion. Soon my hands turned black with grime. After encountering a couple of dead ends, I found a small stairwell. At first, it appeared to go to only the second floor. However, an invisible metal seam marked the floor underneath the steps. Feeling my way, I discovered a square metal panel.

I triggered my switchblade and pried the edge of the panel up, revealing a hole of darkness. Another illusion? Digging in

MARIA V. SNYDER

my pack, I pulled out my lantorch and lit the filament, hoping I had enough oil to last awhile.

The light reflected off a metal ladder descending into the darkness. I waited, listening for any sounds from below. All remained quiet. I climbed down. When I reached the floor, I turned, shining the light around the space.

Bingo! Barrels lined the floor along with piles of boxes. Crates had been hastily stacked against the right wall. But no casks. On the far side was an opening into another room. I entered and spotted more barrels. The Commander's white brandy must sell well in Sitia.

A faint click sounded just as I was about to turn around to report my find to the captain. I hurried to the ladder, but the hatch above had been closed.

"I told him it wouldn't work," Ben said.

I spun. What I'd thought was a stack of crates was actually an illusion. Ben, another man, a woman and two goons stood in its place. The lady must be Rika, the magician who created the illusion. They had their weapons drawn, but appeared relaxed. Probably because they'd erected a null shield.

"Tell who?" I asked in a calm voice, although my heart recognized the danger and urged me to bolt.

Ben huffed in amusement. "You don't remember and yet you found us anyway. Amazing."

I bowed. "Thank you."

"How did you find us?"

"I didn't think you could clear out the entire factory in—"

"Not that. How did you know we were in *Lapeer*?"

No reason to lie. "A lucky guess."

"She's lying," one of the men said. "Why didn't you go west with your brother and the others?"

To admit to being locked in protective custody hurt too much. Instead, I said, "Your clues were too obvious. In fact, they all looped north and have surrounded the factory. You might as well surrender now."

Alarmed, Ben asked, "Drey, you said they headed west."

"They did," Drey the goon said. "She's bluffing."

Better than being called a liar. Progress. I acted unconcerned, but I inched toward the ladder. "Believe what you want."

"It doesn't matter. Once the town watch leaves the factory, Rika can hide us with her magic," Ben said.

Uh-oh. Even if Captain Fleming realized I'd disappeared, he couldn't see through a magical illusion. I slid into a fighting stance, keeping a firm grip on my switchblade.

"In the meantime," Ben said, "you're here and so am I. And do you know who's *not* here?"

"Your mother?"

"Cute. The Boss isn't here to save your life this time." Ben tightened his grip on his sword.

The Boss! Memories of being held down with Ben ready to plunge his knife into my stomach surged. But the Boss's identity remained elusive.

Rika touched his arm. "There's a good reason why he doesn't want her dead."

Ben rounded on her. "What else can we do? She won't stay away."

I moved closer to the ladder.

"Incapacitate her," Rika suggested. "Let the Boss decide."

Time for me to leave. I tossed my lantorch at them, grabbed the rungs and climbed.

"Tyen," Ben said.

Oh no. Tyen's magic could move large objects, including me. Except a cold dart pricked my neck. I yanked it from my skin, but it was too late.

"That doesn't work on her. Use one of the barrels."

MARIA V. SNYDER

As the room spun, I knew I was in big trouble. My foot slipped off the ladder and I slid back to the ground. Darkness pressed along the edges of my vision. Not Curare. A sleeping potion? Poison? A heavy object slammed into me, knocking me to the ground, sending me into oblivion.

I woke to the rumbling vibrations of wagon wheels over cobblestones. My head ached, pain ringed my wrists and ankles, and dry cotton filled my mouth. It didn't take long for me to learn the full extent of my predicament. Lying flat on my back in a wagon, I stared at a canvas covering that hung inches from my nose. No light shone through the fabric. Nighttime.

Gagged and tied spread-eagle to the sides of the wagon, I'd been effectively neutralized. Had they figured out the sleeping potion worked or did they assume the barrel had knocked me unconscious? Did it matter? Since I'd been bluffing people based on my reputation alone…yes, it did matter. Very much.

The only thing that kept me from panicking was the hope that Captain Fleming realized I was missing. Also Ben might be taking me to the same location as the other shipments where Janco and Onora should be. A thin hope, but better than nothing.

I marked time by the noise from the wheels. The jarring shake of cobblestones stopped and the crunch of gravel signaled we'd left the main streets of a town. Then the smooth, quiet hum of either a dirt or grass path meant we were in the countryside between towns. Keeping track of the cycles of noise, I'd counted three towns when we slowed after reaching the outskirts of the third town.

We turned left and lurched over uneven ground before hinges squeaked and what sounded like doors clicked shut. Lantern light cast shadows on the canvas covering. Voices talked, but not close enough for me to understand the words. The familiar jingle of a harness indicated someone worked at unhitching the team of horses. This stop could be our final destination. My stomach skittered. Bad choice of words.

The distant voices grew louder as the speakers moved toward my position. Ben and another man argued. The Boss? Something about his superior tone seemed familiar.

"...doesn't matter now. He knows what you're up to," Ben said. "He has plenty of inventory. Cut your losses and run."

"I'd planned to renegotiate, but now you've screwed that up, too."

"What else was I supposed to do?"

"Disappear like I ordered after I rescued you from Wirral," the Boss said.

"I endured three years of hell in that prison," Ben said. "And she put me there. She deserves to die."

"We've discussed this. If she dies, then the Master Magicians, the Sitian Council and Valek will all be breathing down our necks. Even if we're arrested, Valek will still find us and kill us. No. I have a better idea."

A better idea? I didn't like the sound of that. The wagon tilted as someone climbed onto it. The canvas was pulled away and there stood—

"Hello, Yelena. Remember me?"

30

VALEK

"Kiki's at the gate and she brought friends?" Valek asked the guard, just to ensure he'd heard the man right. He kept a tight grasp on his emotions. No sense worrying until he had all the facts.

"Yes, sir."

"Who's with her?"

"Ah...it would be best for you to see for yourself, sir."

"All right." Valek followed the guard back to the castle complex's main gate. Sure enough, Kiki stood on the other side with two riders. The last two people he'd expect, but not unwelcome, either. "Let them in," he ordered.

Kiki didn't wait. She cleared the gate with one leap, then butted his chest with her head. He stroked her neck, but his attention focused on Devlen and then Reema, sitting in front. She wore Yelena's cloak.

"While I'm glad to see you both, I'm curious why you're here," he said.

"It is a long story." Devlen dismounted. He helped Reema from the saddle.

She gazed at the castle with rapt attention. Kiki, on the

other hand, drooped with fatigue. Valek ran a hand down her legs, checking for hot spots.

"She kept a brisk pace and would not stop for long," Devlen said.

"Let's take care of Kiki and then we'll talk." Valek pulled Yelena's saddle from her back and carried it to the stable while Kiki plodded beside him.

Devlen and Reema trailed behind, gawking at the sights. Valek clamped down on the million questions boiling up his throat. The castle's Stable Master tsked over Kiki. He assigned her two favorite lads to attend to her. Satisfied, Valek led the others to his office.

Many of the household staff and soldiers stared at Devlen. Hard to blame them, considering his size and skin color. Unlike the pale Ixians, his bronzed skin stood out. Then add Sitian clothes, a powerful build, a scimitar hanging from his belt and a nasty-looking scar on his neck and he was the definition of intimidating. Devlen ignored the attention. He held Reema's hand.

Valek ushered them into his office. Ari sat at his desk, but jumped to his feet as soon as he spotted Valek.

"I just finished sketching the security around that warehouse," Ari said. Then he grinned. "Devlen! What brings you here?" He shook Devlen's hand. "Tired of beating up those wimpy Sitians and decided to come up here for a real fight?"

"I wish. I have been too busy trying to outsmart a crafty fox who finds new and unique ways to avoid going to school every morning," Devlen said. "Ari, meet my daughter, Reema."

Ari crouched down to her eye level. "Nice to meet you." He took her hand and pumped it once.

"Hello," she said, gazing at him in awe. "Ari as in 'Ari and Janco'?"

"Yup."

MARIA V. SNYDER

"I've heard *a lot* about you two."

Valek fought to keep a straight face.

Ari straightened. "Is that so? What have you been saying, Devlen?"

"Not me. Yelena. She tells Reema stories before bed. Seems the ones with you and Janco put Reema right to sleep."

"Ouch." But Ari laughed.

Yelena's name cut through Valek's amusement. "Ari, why don't you give Reema a tour? Make sure you show her the Commander's war room. She'll love seeing the stained glass."

"All right. Come on, Reema. I'll even show you where Janco likes to hide when he doesn't want to do paperwork."

Reema glanced at Devlen. He nodded and she hurried after Ari, already asking questions.

As soon as the door shut, Devlen said, "Yelena's fine—at least the last I heard."

Relief shot through him. He gestured to a chair. "Sit down. Would you like a drink?"

"Yes." Devlen plopped into the chair.

"Tea? Water? Or something stronger?"

"Stronger. It has been a long four days."

Valek poured two shots of whiskey and handed one to Devlen before sitting down behind his desk. Devlen drank his in one gulp. Valek followed suit and poured them both another.

"What's going on?" Valek asked.

Devlen tossed back the second shot. "Do you know about Ben Moon's escape?"

"Yes. And I received Yelena's message that he and his cohorts might be in Ixia. I dispatched agents to MD-5 but, so far, we haven't seen any sign of them."

"That's because they were in Fulgor. Now the authorities believe Ben and his gang are headed west."

"With Yelena and her colleagues chasing after?"

"No. Yelena is in the holding cells at the Fulgor security headquarters."

Valek stilled. "For a very good reason. Right?"

"To keep her safe."

"That's extreme."

Devlen sighed. "Did Yelena message you about her magic?"

A cold mist of fear settled on Valek. "No. What about her magic?"

As Devlen filled him in on Yelena's predicament, Valek employed every ounce of self-control not to interrupt. His emotions cycled from fear and worry to fury that she hadn't confided in him and then back through them all again at least twice more.

"...understand why Leif had her placed in protective custody?" Devlen asked.

"Yes." Valek was halfway to the door before he realized he'd even stood up. "Come on. She won't be locked in there for long." And she was a sitting duck. The Mosquito would be stupid not to use that golden opportunity to make another attempt to assassinate her. Irys's message about Yelena being vulnerable and the rumors Arbon heard made more sense now. He understood why Irys had been vague. She'd probably assumed Yelena had told Valek about losing her magic.

"Where are we going?" Devlen asked.

"To find Ari and then to Fulgor."

"What about Reema? According to Yelena, they threatened her life, too."

"That's why we need Ari."

He found them in the war room. As expected, Reema stared, mesmerized, at the tall stained-glass windows that ringed the round room.

She squealed when she spotted Devlen at the threshold.

MARIA V. SNYDER

"Daddy! You *have* to see this! It's fantastic!" Reema grabbed his arm and pulled him inside.

Valek gestured Ari into the hallway. He explained what was going on. "Devlen and I are going to Fulgor. You—"

"Are coming, too." Ari crossed his massive arms.

"No. You are going to protect Reema. I don't trust anyone else."

"Why not leave Devlen here to babysit her?" Ari demanded.

"He's Sitian and he's friends with Fulgor's security forces."

"What about the mission to the Soul Mountains?"

Ah hell. Valek had forgotten about it. He'd have to rearrange a number of things. Plus Kiki needed time to rest. She wouldn't let him leave without her. "I'll rendezvous with the teams in the foothills. They'll be on foot, while I'll have Onyx. Can you get Devlen something to eat and find him a place to catch a few hours of sleep?"

"Yes, sir." Ari frowned. "Where should Reema stay while she's here?"

"With you. Don't let her out of your sight."

"Wonderful." Ari's sarcastic tone sounded just like Janco's.

"She'll surprise you. Reema's a smart little scamp." Valek paused. "She reminds me of Yelena at times. They both had difficult childhoods, yet instead of breaking them, it made them stronger. Think of this not as babysitting duty, but encouraging a future recruit."

"Opal won't like that."

Valek grinned. "Opal doesn't have to know."

He left Ari to take care of their visitors while Valek rushed around and updated his team members on the new timeline and rendezvous point. Hopefully, he'd find Yelena, convince her to come with him and then figure out how to return her magic. The Commander would probably not be pleased with Valek's detour, but he didn't care. Nor did Valek plan to inform him of his change in itinerary. As long as Valek completed his mission and stopped the smugglers, the Commander would be happy.

A couple of hours after the sun set, Valek and Devlen mounted Onyx and Kiki and headed southeast through the Snake Forest. With Kiki in the lead, they kept a fast pace and only stopped to feed and rest the horses. As they traveled, Valek searched his memory for a name of a substance or poison that would block a magician's power. Other than Curare, nothing came to mind.

They crossed the Sitian border without encountering a single guard. No surprise. Kiki had an uncanny knack for avoiding the patrols, just like she knew the shortest route to any destination in Sitia and Ixia.

When Kiki veered to the right during their second day on the road, Valek thought she might be overtired. But she cut through the trees and onto another path. Kiki slowed as a wagon appeared, traveling toward them. Odd.

One person drove the team of horses. The driver's hood had been pulled down, hiding his or her face. Yanking on the reins, the driver stopped the wagon.

"What are you doing here?" the driver asked.

"I could ask you the same thing, Maren," Valek said.

"I'm returning from a mission for the Commander."

"What's in the wagon?"

"It's classified."

Valek bit down on a harsh reply. Nothing should be classified for him. But Devlen was with him.

"Are you out here for business or pleasure?" Maren glanced at Kiki.

"We're investigating a smuggling operation."

"Then you want to head east to Lapeer. The smugglers

have dug a tunnel under the border into Sitia a couple miles straight north of the town."

"How did—"

"I was undercover with them, but it got too hot for me, so I bugged out. But don't worry. Janco's there with some chick, and Yelena is sniffing around, too."

Valek tightened his grip on the reins. Why hadn't the Commander informed him of Maren's whereabouts? She had critical information about the smugglers. He kept his tone neutral as he thanked Maren for the intel.

She waved as she spurred her horses forward. Valek's curiosity urged him to follow her in order to take a peek at her cargo, but catching up to Yelena in Lapeer was a priority.

Kiki set off, presumably toward Lapeer. Had Kiki known Maren would have information about Yelena, or had she just smelled a familiar person and decided to investigate? He'd have to ask Yel… Oh. Without her magic, Yelena wouldn't be able to communicate with Kiki. His anger at his heart mate disappeared. Yelena must be devastated. No wonder she'd confided in Devlen and Opal. They'd endured the same hardship.

Valek and Devlen reached Lapeer two days later at midafternoon. Doing a quick recon of the town, Valek noticed guards posted around one of the warehouses and quite a bit of activity around the station house. While Devlen visited the authorities, Valek stabled the horses and then took a closer look at that warehouse.

He found a gap in their security and slipped into the building. While the equipment was unfamiliar, the smell slapped him in the face. Curare. They'd been manufacturing Curare. The smuggling operation, which he'd viewed as an annoyance, had transformed into a high-level threat to both Ixia and Sitia. No wonder the Commander had been so determined to shut it down.

Except…

Why wouldn't he tell Valek that Maren had been working undercover? They could have saved time with her intel.

Unless…

The answer shocked him. He stood in the middle of the room, not caring who might see him. It explained so much. Not everything, but the reason the Commander hadn't confided in Valek became clear.

Maren's wagon was loaded with Curare for the Commander. And now that the Commander had enough of the drug and probably insider knowledge on how to produce more, he'd sent Valek to shut the smugglers down. No point in having Curare if everyone had it—that wouldn't be a good strategy. And since Valek had "divided" loyalties, the Commander kept this part of the operation a secret so Valek wouldn't inform Yelena. He didn't trust Valek.

Not sure how he felt about the Commander's lack of faith, Valek finished scouting the building. All evidence suggested the place had been abandoned. He exited and hurried to join Devlen in the Log Jam Inn's common room for supper. Neither of them had eaten a hot meal in days.

"What did you discover?" Valek asked as he sat next to Devlen.

"That their corn pie is supposedly the best. I ordered one for you, too."

"You sound like Leif."

"I learned to ask the servers what their favorite dish is from him," Devlen said. "It takes all the guesswork out of ordering a meal."

"That is *one* good thing when traveling with Leif. The food is always better."

"True." Devlen scrunched his napkin between his hands. "I learned the smugglers are producing Curare." Guilt creased

MARIA V. SNYDER

his face. "Yelena's father developed the drug to help people in pain, and the Daviian Warpers stole it and misused it. And now… Hell, I was a Warper. I was a part of all that. And just thinking about some street thug using Curare on my children…" He twisted the cloth into a tight rope.

"It can't be undone," Valek said. "It can't be contained. But we can fight it. There is an antidote, and Leif and Esau have been working on finding a way to mass-produce it. And more healers are using Curare to manage pain. A good thing. Besides, from what I hear about Reema and Teegan, the street thug will be the one in danger."

That surprised a laugh from Devlen. "Especially if they're together."

"That poor street thug won't know what hit him." He smiled.

The server arrived with two steaming corn pies and two mugs of ale. All conversation ceased as they inhaled the food. Not bad. The pie had chunks of chicken, potatoes and corn inside a flaky crust.

When they finished, Valek asked, "Did you learn anything else?"

"The smugglers had fled before the raid. But they think Yelena found a clue to their destination and followed them."

"Think?"

"She disappeared after the raid."

Valek wrapped his hands around the mug to keep them from grabbing Devlen's shirt and slamming him on the table. "Why didn't you tell me this sooner?"

"What could you do? They don't know which direction the smugglers headed. The horses need to rest. We need to eat."

He drew in a deep breath. "When was the raid?"

"Yesterday."

Valek considered. "Did they mention if Yelena was with anyone?"

"She was alone, which concerned the captain. He expected the Soulfinder to have an escort and did not believe her story about the factory at first."

Which meant Janco and Onora had kept a low profile. And there was a good chance they'd followed the smugglers. Did they head north to that tunnel Maren had mentioned? One way to find out.

Valek returned to the Log Jam Inn after finding the tunnel. The entrance had been hidden by magic and it had taken him four hours to discover its location. Pure exhaustion soaked into his bones, and he fumbled at the door, waking Devlen when he entered the room.

"Any signs of recent activity?" Devlen asked.

"No. It was last used about three or four days ago."

"That rules out north. And we know they did not go west or Kiki would have smelled Yelena. South?"

"Not with the Fulgor security forces searching for Ben Moon."

"Then that leaves east."

Of course. He groaned. "They have another tunnel near the mountains." Where he planned to rendezvous with his teams.

"You still had to check north just in case they crossed into Ixia and then headed east. Go to sleep, Valek. You will think clearer in the morning."

Except the morning came sooner than expected.

A slight noise woke him. He jumped to his feet with his knife in hand. Onora stood by the open window. Her skin and clothes appeared gray in the predawn light that framed her. She was barefoot and without a cloak despite the cold air streaming into the room.

MARIA V. SNYDER

"Too slow, Valek. I had plenty of time to reach you," she said.

"Why didn't you?" he asked.

"Then I'd have your job and I'd have to deal with Janco all the time."

He relaxed. "He'll grow on you."

"That's what everyone keeps telling me."

Devlen laughed from the other bed. "It would be difficult to find a person who has met Janco and did not wish to kill him right away."

"Who's he?" Onora asked, eyeing Devlen with suspicion.

Valek introduced her to the Sitian. He stood to shake her hand. She stepped back. He wore a pair of pants, but no shirt. And the man certainly kept in shape. Just like Captain Timmer. Devlen sensed her fear—and dropped his hand. Valek needed to have a chat with Onora about Timmer, but now wasn't the time or place.

"Do you have information for me?" he asked.

She pulled her gaze from Devlen and told Valek about her and Janco following a group of smugglers east through a number of small towns before they stopped in what appeared to be one of their hideouts. "A couple of wagons joined them a few hours later. When it was apparent they planned to stay, I left to update Yelena. She was supposed to remain in town. Do you know where she went?"

"No." The worry that had been simmering in his heart boiled over. He explained what they'd learned from Captain Fleming.

"She's either still in the factory, or she hid in one of the wagons that arrived later, or she's a captive," Onora said in a matter-of-fact tone.

"Still in the factory?" Devlen asked.

"Yes. These people have magic and they've been using illusions to conceal things. So why not use it to hide in the factory?"

It made sense. Wait out the raid and leave later. Or even during the raid. If you were hidden from sight, then you just had to make sure you didn't bump into anybody.

Devlen glanced at him. "Did you feel magic in the warehouse?"

"No, but I wasn't searching for it."

"Then we should return and do another sweep," Onora suggested.

"Good idea." Valek changed his shirt.

"What should I do?" Devlen asked.

"Take Kiki and head east. Yelena might be with the smugglers, and that's our destination regardless. We'll catch up."

After Devlen left, Valek stopped Onora.

She frowned at him. "We're wasting time."

"This won't take long. I need to trust you, Onora."

A wary expression crossed her face. "I'm here, helping. What more do you want?"

"Assurance that you won't attack Yelena again."

Onora pressed her lips together to cover her surprise.

"Why?" he asked.

"Orders."

Ah. "How long have you and the Commander been working together?"

"Six months."

"Do you have orders to kill her?"

"I *never* had orders to kill her."

"But the arrow was filled with a poison."

"No. It was filled with a harmless substance to make the attack appear to be more dire."

Powerful relief swept through his body. Nice to know his friend and Commander didn't wish his heart mate dead. Ex-

MARIA V. SNYDER

cept…what had happened to Yelena's magic? "Did you prep the arrow yourself?"

"No. Why?"

"Who gave you the arrow?"

"The Commander."

Everything circled back to the Commander. Damn.

"The Commander said you'd figure it out. I didn't think it'd be this soon."

Valek planned to have a heart-to-heart talk with Ambrose as soon as they found Yelena. He shoved his swirling thoughts and emotions aside to concentrate on her.

Valek and Onora had no trouble entering the factory. This time Valek kept alert for evidence of magic.

"When Janco feels magic it hurts him. Is it like that for you?" Onora asked.

"No. For me, it's sticky. The magic presses against me, but can't penetrate my skin."

"Because of your immunity?"

"Yes."

"Can you see through an illusion like he does?"

"No. I only sense it through touch, and I have to guess what type of magic it is. Very frustrating at times."

Onora remained quiet as they searched the ground floor. Then she said, "If Sitia has all this magic, then why haven't they conquered Ixia?"

"Magic is a strong weapon. But like every weapon, there is a defense. Plus magicians are human. They can be bribed, tricked and coerced. They have their own agendas. Sitia had its hands full with rogue magicians who are more of a threat than Ixia."

"For now."

Valek turned to her. Had the Commander confided in her about the Curare? No emotion shone on her face.

When they entered a small stairwell, Valek sensed power emanating from the floor. He found a hatch. They descended and found Yelena's switchblade lying near the base of the ladder. Valek's heart lurched. She'd never leave it behind, which meant she'd been captured. Determined to return it to her, he tucked it into his belt.

He rushed to finish checking the basement. It was empty of goods and magic. And Yelena. They had taken her with them. Valek needed to find them.

Fast.

31

JANCO

Where was Onora? She should have been back by now. Janco circled the smuggler's farm another time. The place was big and surrounded by a chain-link fence, but he doubted any actual farming went on in there. Lots of barns, people and activity, but no cows, crops or farm equipment. Each hour that passed brought more wagons and sketchy-looking goons. Where was Onora?

Plus Janco thought he'd spotted that Ben Moon guy Yelena had talked about. The man resembled her description, and she'd suspected he might be involved. He thought about the fugitive. That rescue op from Wirral Prison would have cost a bundle. And what better way to raise money than smuggling? Selling Curare. No doubt you could collect lots and lots of gold for Curare.

He watched the compound from a low branch in a tree and kept track of people going into and between buildings, counting heads and guessing their jobs. The sun set and lanterns were lit—a good indication of which structures were occupied. Tired of waiting for Onora, Janco decided to sneak into the compound later and have a look around.

When the activity diminished, Janco ghosted along the

fence until he found a dark area out of sight from the main buildings. He climbed over the ten-foot-high fence. A weird tingle lingered on his palms. Janco rubbed them on his pants. Must be from the cold.

The first barn he explored smelled authentic. Yuck. Moldy straw bales mixed with crates of goods. The second place was even more uninteresting. However, hidden between two buildings was a strange-looking structure. The one-story-high oversize shed had been constructed with glass. Odd. Janco moved closer. Water beaded the glass on the inside. Dark leafy plants filled the interior. He circled it and found the entrance. Locked. But not for long.

Hot steamy air along with the rich earthy smells of the jungle puffed in his face when he opened the door. Janco entered. Various plants and bushes filled the room along with pools of water and two red-hot woodstoves. A thick vine wove through the foliage. The Curare vine.

This was bad. Really bad. If they were growing their own vines here, they could be growing them anywhere. He'd assumed they brought the vines up from the Illiais Jungle. That would be easier to stop than finding these little glass hothouses.

Time to leave. Janco exited the…jungle. He turned to relock the door and a sharp point pricked him in the back.

Three sharp points, actually.

"Hands up," a voice said.

Damn. Not much he could do. He spread his arms, but kept his hands low. They took his sword, knife and lock picks. Well, one set, anyway. Then manacled his hands behind his back. Pushing on his shoulder, they led him to another building. Not the chattiest bunch, either, which meant he'd been ambushed by a trio of grunts. A blow to his ego, for sure.

A number of people were inside the new building. The guy he guessed was Ben was there, but also another man he recognized, who stood inside a wagon. This had gone beyond bad. Janco was screwed.

"Well, well, well. Isn't this just a happy reunion? Yelena, guess who came to visit? Your friend...Janco, is it?"

"Pretty good memory for a dead guy," Janco said. He glanced around, but didn't see Yelena. She must be on the floor of the wagon and under a null shield, otherwise the jerk wouldn't be so cocky.

Owen Moon beamed at him. "I always remember the faces and names of my enemies. I don't want to forget to kill anyone."

32

YELENA

What little hope I had of being rescued shrank even more when Janco's sarcastic voice sounded. He'd been captured, too. And from his comments, he was as surprised as I had been upon seeing Owen Moon alive and well. Despite the Commander's message to the Sitian Council, informing them of Owen's execution four years ago. Why hadn't the Commander killed him? The answer flashed in my mind.

Owen had been busy working *for* the Commander. And it didn't take a genius to guess what he had been doing—learning how to manufacture Curare.

But why would the Commander wish to shut Owen down? Owen smirked at me. His posture like a hunter's, gloating over his kill. Cocky bastard. And I'd bet that particular personality trait of his was what had pissed the Commander off. He'd rescued his brother, alerting the Sitians, and I'd guess he was selling Curare to other interested parties. Yep, I'd wager more than a few gold coins that was what had happened.

Of course, it would have been useful to have figured this out sooner. Before I'd been tied to the wagon and gagged. The knowledge didn't help my situation. Nor Janco's.

"Where is your companion?" Owen asked Janco for the second time.

No answer. Janco would never tell him.

"Loris, jog his memory," Owen ordered.

Janco cried out. A thump sounded. "Nooo…" He groaned.

Helpless, I struggled against the ropes as I listened to Janco's distress increase as Loris pulled the information from Janco's mind. I'd been assaulted the same way when I'd first arrived at the Magician's Keep. Janco had another reason to hate magic. Right now, I hated it, too.

Janco yelped. Then grunted. More than a few moments passed.

"What's taking so long?" Owen demanded.

"His thoughts are…jumbled. Chaotic."

Go Janco!

"Crack a few ribs. That'll give him something to focus on."

I braced for the impact even though I wasn't the target. The thud echoed in my chest as Janco's breath whooshed out.

Another pause and then Loris said, "She returned to Lapeer to rendezvous with Yelena."

"What about Valek? Is he on the way?" Owen asked.

Valek! Reema and Devlen should have reached the castle by now. Devlen would have told him everything. Valek was probably angry at me. No, not probably. *Furious* would be the correct term. Although, keeping secrets was a part of both our jobs. Should I be upset with him for not telling me about Owen? Did Valek even know about him? Hopefully, I'd have a chance to ask him after Owen's arrest. Might as well think positive.

"Last time he talked to Valek, the assassin planned to remain at the castle, collecting information." Loris huffed in amusement. "He didn't have time to send a message to Valek about what he has discovered in Lapeer."

"Good. And the Commander? Any info on him?" Owen asked.

"Nothing new. The Commander is still intent on shutting down our smuggling routes into Ixia."

"Does Janco know how the Commander found out about our...side business?"

"No."

"Take him down to the cellar. Stake him down to the floor spread-eagle. These Ixians have weapons and lock picks hidden everywhere. It's best just to keep their hands and feet far apart."

"Yes, sir."

Sounds of a scuffle reached me along with another thud. Then nothing. Poor Janco.

"Send out a couple patrols," Owen ordered. "His companion will be back and we need to pick her up before she has a chance to send a report north."

"Yes, sir."

Owen looked down. "Now you'll get my full attention." He crouched beside me. "My hunting expedition inside your mind was very educational. While I'm not happy the memories I planted in your head didn't work, I discovered something very interesting about you." His expression was downright gleeful.

I'd panic. But I'd been in a state of ever-increasing panic since I woke up tied to the wagon and saw Owen. I was beyond mere panic and into the realms of mind-numbing terror at this point.

Owen stroked my throat. I recoiled from his touch.

"Oh, please." He pulled on the chain around my neck, tugging my octopus pendant free of my shirt.

Pain bit into my skin as he yanked the necklace, breaking the chain.

"Oops." Owen dropped it over the side of the wagon. It

MARIA V. SNYDER

shattered. He pressed his hand on my chest near the base of my throat.

An uncomfortable burning sensation spread throughout my body. The skin on my scalp crawled. Goose bumps rose despite the heat. A reaction to his magic? The strange conflicting feelings stopped as fast as they started.

Owen laughed. "Too bad I wasted perfectly good Theobroma on you when I didn't have to. You're just a regular girl now. How wonderful." He untied my gag, removing it.

Relief flowed into my cheeks and I worked my mouth and tongue to produce moisture.

He sat back on his heels. "What is blocking your magic?"

"I've no idea." My voice rasped. I told him about the attack in the woods. Why not? "At first, I thought it was one of Ben's cohorts."

"The plan was for everyone to lie low. Until my idiot brother lured you to our hideout in Fulgor. It wasn't us. Seems you're just a very unpopular girl," Owen said. "You shouldn't be surprised. And now someone has gone to considerable trouble to neutralize you with that attack in the woods. Your death will cause too much trouble. So that's a perfect solution—spread the word that you're powerless, and let another person target you. Or rather, dozens of others in your case. Too bad it won't work for me."

"Because I know too much."

"Right. And unless you want to swear loyalty to me…?"

"No."

"Thought so. But not to worry. This time when I erase your memories, I won't make the same mistake."

"Mistake?"

"I only erased a few hours of your life. This time, I'm going to erase everything. You won't even remember your name."

"That's…" Fear closed my throat.

"Clever. I know. Loris and Cilly are very talented with mental communication and the three of us make a great team. How do you think I stayed dead all these years?"

"When?"

"As soon as we catch your colleague. It'll be easier to do all three of you at once."

A momentary reprieve.

"Go ahead, ask," Owen said in his smug tone.

"Was it the Commander's idea?"

"Not at first. He was ready to send me to the noose, but I pleaded for my life. And argued that I could help him by getting him Curare. Actually, I should thank you, Yelena. Your efforts to change the Commander's mind about magicians in Ixia helped sway him."

Lovely. "And he funded your research."

"Yes."

"And you had to screw it up by rescuing your brother."

Anger flashed in his eyes. "I couldn't leave him in that hellhole."

"But you could leave your wife, Selene, in Dawnwood Prison?"

"She's a traitor."

"According to the Commander, so are you." As soon as the words left my mouth, I braced for his reaction.

He curled a fist, but didn't swing. "The fervor over Ben would have eventually died down."

"I was referring to you selling Curare to other customers. That's why the Commander is going to shut you down. You can erase our memories, but eventually, he'll send Valek and his corps after you."

Owen grinned, but the humor failed to reach his eyes. "Oh, don't you worry about me. I've discovered something big that will please the Commander, and all will be forgiven."

MARIA V. SNYDER

I didn't like the sound of that. "And that is?"

"Nice try, but I'm not stupid."

True. Overconfidence and greed would trip him up. If it hadn't already. "The Commander is not the forgiving type."

"I'm touched you're so concerned." Owen straightened. He called to his men. "Take her down with Janco. Secure her in the same manner." Hopping off the wagon, he disappeared from my view.

A couple of his goons untied me, but kept a firm hold. My stiff leg and arm muscles protested the movement as blood rushed to my hands and feet. I considered fighting the two men, but once I stood upright, I spotted a number of other guards in the building. And Ben leaned against the wall, watching with a satisfied smirk.

The musty smell of hay tickled my nose as they escorted me to a hatch in the wooden floor. The high-vaulted ceiling suggested that this building had once been a barn. I glanced out the window. Weak sunlight shone on the glass—early morning. If Owen's men didn't find Onora, we might be here awhile, which was a good thing. More time for… What? Not sure what I could do without my magic.

We walked down a ramp into the semidark dampness below. The root cellar had earthen walls and a hard-packed dirt floor. Two oversize musclemen sat in chairs near the base of the ramp. Daggers hung from their belts. Behind them was Janco.

"Can we gag this idiot?" one of the guards asked my companions. "He won't shut up and is driving us crazy."

Good news. If Janco had enough energy to harass his guards, it meant he wasn't as hurt as I'd feared.

The guy on my left shrugged. "Sure. The Boss shouldn't mind." He handed me off to the guard. "This one can join her friend."

"Yeah?" The guard's expression brightened as a slow smile spread, exposing broken teeth. "Can we play?"

My breath hitched. Fear bit into my guts.

"No."

I relaxed.

"Ah, too bad."

My two escorts left. Broken Teeth tugged me deeper into the cellar. Janco watched us, craning his head up, but he didn't say a word. His wrists and ankles had been tied with ropes. We stopped next to Janco. Four more metal stakes had been driven into the ground.

"Your room is ready," Broken Teeth said.

His partner chuckled. Sections of rope hung from his meaty hands. "Lie down," he ordered.

Broken Teeth pushed on my shoulder. "Come—"

I moved. Spinning and ducking under his arm, I snagged the man's dagger then stepped back. They wouldn't tie me down without a fight.

"Oh, she's feisty. I like that." Broken Teeth advanced. "Give me back my knife before you get hurt."

Broken Teeth lunged. I sidestepped and slashed at his stomach. He blocked my swing late and the blade cut across his forearm.

"Hey! We need help here!" the other guard yelled toward the hatch before he dropped the ropes and drew his dagger. He moved to swing in behind me.

Sparring with Broken Teeth, I countered his attacks and tried to avoid being trapped between the two men.

When boots pounded on the ramp, I knew my time was up. I faked a breakaway to the right, but then cut left, tripping over Janco. He grunted in pain when I landed on him.

"Sorry," I said right before the guards grabbed me.

I struggled, and it took four of them to secure me to the

MARIA V. SNYDER

stakes. When they finished, they nursed their bruises while I puffed with the effort, sweating. Broken Teeth found his weapon lying near Janco. Eventually, the extra guards left, leaving the original two. They returned to their seats. At least they hadn't gagged Janco yet.

"Not bad," Janco said to me in a low voice. "If the guards had manned up instead of crying for help, you would have had a decent shot."

"I tried to cut and run, but that didn't work as planned."

"Not entirely."

I glanced at Janco. He shot me a grin. When I had "tripped" over him, I'd slashed at the ropes near his right wrist, but I'd no idea if it was deep enough to cut through. From the gleam in his eyes and his comment, I guessed my attempt had met with some success. I hoped it was enough.

"Do they have you covered with a null shield? Damn thing screws everything up," Janco said.

The thought of explaining to him how I was even more helpless than he believed while tied spread-eagle to a dirt floor was too depressing. "Yeah. Don't count on my magic. How are you feeling?"

"Murderous. Just give me one minute with that magician and I'll show him how it feels to have things ripped from you."

"And your ribs?"

"Sore. They'll heal. I've cracked my ribs dozens of times. I imagine my bones resemble a messed-up spiderweb by this point."

"I'd prefer a broken bone than cracked ribs," I said. "You can't breathe or laugh or twist or sleep without pain."

"Yeah, but if you break your leg, then you can't walk. And a broken arm makes it harder to fight."

"You can't fight with cracked ribs."

"I can."

"Considering our present situation, I hope you're not exaggerating."

Janco didn't reply right away. "So what's Owen's plan?"

I explained about the memory wipe.

"I'd rather be killed." Janco sounded horrified.

"Oh, I don't know. I've some memories I'd be happy to forget." I mulled over Owen's confidence in regaining the Commander's trust. The Commander already had plenty of Curare. What else could Owen offer him? I mentioned it to Janco.

"Maybe he discovered a new drug from one of his jungle plants."

"His jungle plants? Is that a euphemism for something else?"

"No. He's growing the Curare vine in these…hot glass houses."

"He's growing it? That's…" I searched for a word to describe the magnitude of this news.

"Serious trouble for all of us?"

"To put it mildly."

"Yeah. That's why they got the drop on me. I was still reeling." Janco described what he'd found inside the hothouse before he was captured. "Do you recognize any of the other vegetation?"

"I'd have to see it."

"Maybe Owen will give us a tour before he scrambles our brains."

Trust Janco to put a positive spin on a bad situation. At least he was entertaining. We could be here awhile. "What are the chances of Owen's people catching Onora?"

"No chance. She's probably halfway to Ixia by now."

"Why do you think that?"

"She's smart. And she has no reason to be loyal to us. Ari would charge in here like a bull seeing a lady bull wearing red."

"There are no lady bulls."

"Sure there are. How do you think we get baby bulls?"

It required too much energy to explain about the bulls and the bees to Janco. "Ari would be caught right away."

"That's beside the point. Onora's like Valek—cold and calculating. Well, like him when he's not with you."

At least that meant we had some time to figure out a way to escape. I craned my neck. Janco met my gaze and tilted his head toward the guards, then cleared his throat. The guards kept their attention on the hatch, but checked on us from time to time. I nodded my understanding.

When both guards faced forward, Janco pulled his right wrist free. He dug in the waistband of his pants and withdrew a small knife. I watched the guards and signaled with a cough whenever one turned his head our way.

After twenty minutes or so, Janco called, "Hey, boneheads! I'm hungry. Ya got anything to eat?"

I glanced at him. He appeared to be still tied to the stakes. Janco continued to harass the guards. They threatened to gag him, but he increased his taunting until Broken Teeth stood up with a growl.

He approached and pulled a cloth from his pocket. "I've got a snotty hankie just for you." Broken Teeth leaned over.

Janco slashed at his throat with the small knife. The guard yelled, and then Janco grabbed the man's dagger and stabbed it into his stomach. Broken Teeth's partner raced up the ramp.

"Ah hell." Janco cut the ropes around his ankles, scrambled to his feet and sprinted after him.

I waited. Broken Teeth groaned, cursed and promised to kill Janco, but he didn't chase after him and, eventually, he slumped over. Unconscious or dead, I couldn't tell until the stench of offal reached me. Dead.

Nothing happened for a long time. Then shadows crossed

the hatch and four guards descended. I laid my head back and hoped they hadn't killed Janco. They untied me and marched me back to the main floor. Janco knelt on the ground surrounded by six guards who pointed their swords at him. Blood from a cut on his forehead spilled down his cheek. His hands were laced behind his neck.

"Sorry," he said, looking miserable.

"You tried," I said.

But he tilted his head to the left. Onora stood in the middle of another group of guards. Her pale face and wide eyes gave her the appearance of being nervous, but she scanned the room as if assessing weaknesses. I copied her. At least two dozen of Owen's smugglers filled the area along with Owen, Ben and his three magician friends. Oh joy.

"Take them to the stables," Owen ordered.

We tried to resist, but they dragged us into the daylight and to the stable. The large wooden building had two rows of stalls. But these were fully enclosed, with bars on the top half to prevent horses from jumping. Or to keep a person contained inside.

Pushed into a stall, I tumbled to the straw-coated floor. By the time I gained my feet, the door had locked shut. Janco occupied the one to my left and Onora stood in the stall to my right.

Owen consulted with Cilly and Loris.

I asked Onora, "How did they catch you?"

"Tactical error." She paced the six-foot-square space and twisted the end of her shirt.

If she was digging for lock picks, she'd better hurry. I lowered my voice. "Did you send a message?"

"No time."

"Couldn't you at least lie to me?"

"Oh. Uh…I did send a message, and now the entire Ixian army is camped outside this compound."

"You're a lousy liar."

"My one flaw," she joked.

"One?" Janco choked. "I know at least a dozen. You're terrible at avoiding capture, following orders—"

"I can say the same for you. What part of 'wait for me before you go inside' didn't you understand?"

Owen interrupted them. He approached my stall as Loris stood in front of Janco's and Cilly took up position outside Onora's. Unease swirled. I backed away, until I hit the wall.

"Now," Owen ordered.

I opened my mouth, but a hot knifing pain pierced my head, stripping away my resistance and willpower. It felt as if my soul was being ripped into a thousand pieces. Horror at losing myself welled and built until I could no longer stand the pressure. I screamed.

33

VALEK

Yelena's scream stabbed right through Valek's heart. He moved without thought. Devlen grabbed his arm, stopping him.

"Wait for it," Devlen said.

They crouched in the woods just outside the fence. Town watchmen surrounded the complex. Captain Fleming had gone above and beyond, recruiting as many soldiers from the local towns that he could in mere hours.

When Yelena screamed again, Valek growled. "What is she waiting for?"

"The right opportunity."

Valek had put a great deal of trust into Onora. When the assassin had volunteered to be captured, Valek initially resisted the idea. But then he agreed she had the best chance. However, now he questioned his decision.

Many agonizing minutes passed.

"There," Devlen said. "Smoke."

Valek whistled and the signal repeated on both sides. He waited just long enough for the message to reach all the soldiers. Then he and Devlen and the watchmen all climbed over the fence. Magic clung to the metal links. Hell.

"They know we're coming," he shouted to both sides.

"How?" Devlen asked as he joined him.

"Magic woven through the fence."

"Then we better hurry."

They raced toward the building leaking smoke. It had been a stable. Men poured out, coughing with tears running down their cheeks. The watchmen engaged them, but Valek bypassed them, slipping inside. He crouched low, staying under the cloud. Glass shards from Onora's smoke bombs crunched under his boots.

Through the gray haze, he spotted Onora and Janco fighting a trio of guards.

"Where's Yelena?" Valek asked.

"Owen has her," Janco shouted. "They disappeared. That way." He pointed right as he ducked under an opponent's sword.

"Owen?"

"Ben's not-so-dead brother."

He'd think about Owen's rise from the dead later. Yelena first. Valek followed Janco's directions. At the end of the row of stalls was a corridor. The smoke thinned as he ghosted down the hall and into a training ring.

Owen pulled a hatch open in the center. Yelena lay nearby. She pressed her hands to her head and moaned in pain.

Valek drew his knives and ran toward them. Owen spotted the movement and Valek slammed into an invisible wall. The impact dazed him for a second. A null shield blocked him. Magic couldn't pierce it, but objects could. He flipped his weapons, grabbing the blades, and aimed at Owen. The shield tightened and knocked into his hands just as he threw the weapons. They missed. One struck the soft dirt near Yelena and the other sailed past. The shield pressed around him, trapping his arms.

"Wow," Owen said. "It's true. The infamous Valek can be stopped by a simple null shield. That information was worth every gold coin I spent for it." He glanced at Yelena. "I planned to use her as a hostage, but she'll only slow me down." Owen knelt next to her. "I'll just finish what I started." Touching her forehead with two fingers, he closed his eyes.

Yelena jerked. In a panic, Valek struggled against the invisible force wrapped around him, but it didn't budge. Without her magic, she wouldn't survive. That word, *survive*, sparked a memory. She'd survived before back when she didn't know she had power.

Valek yelled, "Fight him. Come on, Yelena. You don't need magic. You survived Mogkan and Reyad. Come on. Fight. Survive!"

34

YELENA

I'd been torn apart. Pieces of me littered the ground. I felt like a stuffed toy whose stuffing had been ripped out. Owen dug for more. The sharp pain gouged and it hurt to form a thought. Mindless, I burrowed deeper into the tiny bit left, but it crumbled and soon nothing of me would remain.

Valek's strident voice cut through my haze of pain. I didn't understand all the words, but his emotions flowed into me like pure energy. And one word burned brighter. *Survive.* I could do that. I'd done it many times before.

Concentrating on the image of me as an empty toy, I gathered the clumps and crammed them into my mind, body and soul. Owen worked to drag them away, but I collected them just as fast. Survive. All I needed to do was survive. He'd get tired eventually, while Valek's encouragement strengthened my efforts.

The attack increased in intensity, but I persisted, harvesting the pieces of me. My skull ached, and pain seared my skin and burned my muscles. Memories of the agony I suffered when I'd crossed into the fire world surfaced. I'd survived that without the help of my magic. Other recollections of survival rose unbidden. I'd endured Mogkan's torture and lived through Reyad's assault.

Owen yelled and power slammed into me. White light sparked behind my eyelids as pain exploded inside my head. I kept a tight grip on all I'd worked so hard to collect.

Another bolt of agony sliced through me. I fought to remain awake and teetered on the edge, enduring, surviving until the attack stopped. A cool hand touched my hot skin. Safe. I relaxed, letting a blackness wash over me.

I woke to a soft voice and a touch on my cheek. Opening my eyes required effort since my lids weighed a hundred pounds each. The lantern light seemed overly bright, but I squinted and my exertions were rewarded with a wonderful sight. Valek.

He sat on the edge of my bed, holding my hand and stroking my face with his fingers. The small room gave no clues as to where we were. But I didn't really care at this point.

His worried expression disappeared into a smile. "How are you feeling?"

"Like a chew toy for a pack of snow cats." My voice rasped and my throat burned with thirst.

Valek let go and I mewled like a kitten.

"I'm not leaving, love. Here." He handed me a glass filled with a yellowish-colored liquid with bits of green floating in it. "Drink it all."

Raising the glass up to my lips required too much energy. "Is this one of Leif's concoctions?"

"Yes." Valek supported me and guided my hand.

I gulped the lukewarm drink. It tasted like honey grass. "Is he here? And where are we exactly?"

"He's here. Along with Opal and another magician. They arrived a couple hours after the ruckus and have been helping with the cleanup. We are in a bedroom of the compound's farmhouse."

I finished the potion despite the bits of green clinging to my teeth. Leif's restoratives might not taste good, but they worked. "I'm still mad at them. Leif especially."

"I'm grateful Leif's here. Besides the drinks, he aided in your mental recovery. Owen had done considerable damage." All softness left Valek's face. "When I catch up to him, I'm going to personally ensure he stays dead."

Not good. "He escaped?"

"Yes. He dropped down through the hatch and secured it on the inside. It led to a tunnel. By the time we broke in, he was long gone."

"Did you know he was still alive?"

"No, love. The Commander hadn't confided in me about him, the Curare or Maren's involvement."

"Perhaps he thought you'd tell me. It's a game changer."

"Perhaps." Valek didn't appear convinced.

"What are you going to do?"

Pain and betrayal creased his expression and he suddenly appeared to be exhausted. "I need to talk to him. Find out why he's keeping things from me and determine if he still trusts me."

I squeezed his hand. It would be a difficult conversation. "What about the others? Did anyone else escape?"

"We caught Loris, Cilly and Ben Moon. The others got away. I promise Ben won't live for long."

"Don't kill him. We can use him as bait. Owen rescued him before and may again."

"You sound just like the others."

Which reminded me. "How are Janco and Onora doing?"

"They're bickering like brother and sister."

In other words, fine. "Reema and Devlen?"

"Devlen is coordinating with the authorities. Reema is safe in Ixia with Ari. And before you ask, Kiki is impatiently waiting for you in the local inn's stable."

Good. I told Valek about Owen's confidence regarding the Commander's continuing support. "Maybe something growing in the hothouse."

"Leif's already compiling an inventory of the plants."

And what he couldn't identify, our father would know. "There might be more of those hothouses in Sitia. This isn't the end."

"It never is."

Depressing but true. "I'm sorry."

"Nothing you can do about it. It's the way of the world."

"No. I'm sorry for not telling you about...you know. I didn't want to worry you."

Valek pulled the glass from my grip, set it on the table, then took both my hands in his. "When we're apart, I worry about you. Even when I know you're fine and doing some boring research for Bain or visiting your parents, I worry. Even though you are more than capable of taking care of yourself, I worry."

"I *was* capable."

"You still are. Owen couldn't break you."

"If it wasn't for you, he would have. Your voice gave me the strength."

"You used your own strength. I just reminded you that it was already within you."

I didn't know if I agreed with him or not. "Then it's a good thing you showed up in time. How did you find us?"

"Later. You need your rest."

He leaned in and kissed me lightly on the lips then tried to let go of my hands.

I wouldn't release him. "Stay."

"All right."

I scooched over, making room on the bed. Valek kicked off his boots, removed a number of weapons and then stretched next to me. I snuggled against him, breathing in his scent. Safe and warm. My eyes drifted shut.

"Yelena?"

"Hmm?"

"I'd like you to stay with me while we figure out how to unblock your magic. We're stronger together."

"All right."

He laughed. "I thought I'd have more of a fight."

"I'm too tired to argue."

"Then I should take advantage of the situation."

I cracked one eye open. "And?"

"I'd like you to stay with me forever."

My heart jolted with surprise. Wide-awake, I pushed up to my elbow. "Is that a proposal?" I demanded.

"Uh…no. Not at all. Because that would be very unromantic."

"Right."

"Guess I should find a better time and place?"

"There's no guessing about it."

The smell of wet dog intruded on my dreams. They weren't the best dreams, but far better than the stink of damp puppy.

"Go away," I said without opening my eyes.

"No," Leif said.

An image of him crossing his arms and setting his square jaw formed in my mind. It'd be easier to get rid of a splinter driven deep under my skin than my brother. I opened my eyes. Sure enough, that Zaltana stubbornness stiffened his posture. He held a cup of steaming liquid—wet-dog tea.

"If that's your idea of a peace offering, then I'm going to declare war," I said.

"Valek has charged me with your care. Since you haven't been eating, you need to drink this to regain your strength." He handed it to me.

It had been a couple of days since I last woke, but my body still ached, I had no energy and my stomach remained unsettled. The encounter with Owen had left me feeling raw and exposed. Even the blankets chafed against my skin. Sunlight reflected off the window's glass.

I sipped the tea. It tasted better than it smelled. "Happy? Now go away."

Leif stayed by my bed. "Yelena, how many times do I need to apologize? I was following orders and you were going to put yourself in harm's way."

"That's what I do. It's my job so others like Reema are safe."

"I agree. Except now you need to be more cautious and have backup."

I changed the subject and asked about the plants in the hothouse.

"The ones I recognized all have medicinal applications, but there're a few that I can't identify. Father's coming to help."

"Are any of them like Curare, with extraordinary properties?"

"Valek asked about that, too. They're good for fevers and coughs and constipation. Nothing significant. Maybe our father will discover what Owen was talking about."

"Can you ask him about my problem? He might know if a poison caused it."

"Does this mean you forgive me?"

I huffed. "Oh, all right, but only because you're my brother."

"Gee, Yelena, don't get all mushy on me."

"You'll talk to Father?"

"Of course. Now finish your tea."

Holding my breath, I managed another swallow. "How did you know we were here?"

Leif plopped into the chair next to my bed. "After realizing we'd been duped, we trudged back to Fulgor with our tails between our legs. Captain Alden pounced as soon as we arrived, and Hale and I hightailed it back to the Second Chance Inn. I talked to the staff, visited the Clever Fox stables and followed your scent."

"My scent?"

"It's hard for me to explain as it's not really a smell, but rather a primal certainty that you went in a certain direction. Plus Rusalka and Garnet acted as if they knew where they were going. Opal said the Sandseed horses think of us as part of their herd, and they're very protective of the members of their herd."

Leif chatted until I finished my tea. My stomach growled with hunger for the first time in days. My brother jumped to his feet and hurried to fetch me a bowl of soup.

Janco arrived with the promised bowl.

"I see your talents are being put to good use," I teased.

"Real funny." He handed it to me.

I sniffed it. Chicken noodle. Yum.

Janco settled into the chair. "You look better. When Valek carried you up here, I'd thought I'd have to get a shovel and start digging."

"Thanks, I think. How about you? How're the ribs?"

"Tender."

"And your head?"

He scowled. "Other than feeling like my brain has been sliced and diced, fed to a cat and horked out along with a giant hair ball, I'm peachy."

"So back to normal?"

"Normal? I think I've lost track of what normal feels like. Do you know what I want for my birthday?"

"For magic to disappear forever?"

"You know me so well."

"You may have your wish. Whatever is blocking my magic might be the next weapon against magicians. In the hands of the wrong people, they could make magic disappear forever."

Janco stared out the window. "Magic sucks and I hate it, but I wouldn't do that to a magician."

"Really? How about the magicians like Owen? What about them?"

"Tempting. Maybe after they've been tried and convicted of abusing their powers."

"Now you sound like a Sitian."

Janco gasped in mock horror. "Forget I said that! We should kill them all. Every one. Better?"

"Yes, very Ixian."

"Whew!"

Once I started eating full meals, my energy returned after another day.

Valek arrived that evening with my pack slung over his shoulder. "Found this stuffed in the corner of a wagon." He put it on the bed. "And I've been meaning to give this to you." He tossed me my switchblade.

I caught it in midair. "Thanks. I thought I'd lost it." Turning it over in my hands, I examined the handle, running my finger over the silver symbols Janco had etched into it over eight years ago. The symbols meant "sieges weathered, fight together, friends forever." Janco, Ari and Valek had certainly proved this true time after time. And I hoped they'd continue to do so. Which reminded me…

"I found out who sent the assassin after me," I said to Valek.

He stilled. "Tell me."

I detailed my encounter with Kynan, aka The Mosquito. "I still don't know who attacked me in the woods."

Valek's scowl deepened. "Do you think this Bruns Jewelrose is taking advantage of your condition?"

"Probably. My demise could be used as an example. There are a number of Sitians who wish the Council had more power over magicians. The recent ruckus about Opal keeping control of who is given those magic detectors is just one of many skirmishes."

"A visit to Bruns Jewelrose will have to wait until we've figured out how to get your magic back. I doubt the assassin will target you when you're with me. And if he does…" Valek touched the hilt of his knife. "I will be more than happy to take care of him."

"If I don't reach him first."

Valek laughed. "That's my girl. I'd like to leave in the morning. Will you be strong enough to travel?"

"Yes." I opened my pack and sorted through the contents. Ooh…clean clothes. "I need to bathe. Is there—"

"There's a big tub downstairs." Heat burned in Valek's gaze. "I'll be more than happy to assist you."

"Mighty nice of you."

"Not at all. I aim to please."

I laughed. Unable to find my soap and hair wash, I dumped the rest of the stuff onto the bed. My money pouch jingled. Darts and vials of Curare and other potions rolled. And— I gasped.

"What's wrong?" Valek asked.

Holding up a long tube filled with a white liquid, I calculated the last time… Shocked, I stared at Valek.

"What's wrong? Tell me, love." He moved closer.

"This is Moon potion."

"And?"

"And I was supposed to take it after…but, but…it didn't come. I was so busy…I didn't even think…"

"What didn't come? You're not making sense."

My hands shook. "I'm pregnant."

* * * * *

ACKNOWLEDGEMENTS

This book would not have been written if not for my readers.

I was quite happy with how Yelena and Valek's story ended in *Fire Study* and I was excited to move on to new stories and characters. However, my very persistent readers kept asking me to write more. I've been inundated with e-mails, messages, comments on my Facebook page and heartfelt requests at my book signings since 2008. So a gigantic thanks to all of you for pushing me to write more. I had a blast getting reacquainted with Yelena, Valek and the other characters in the Study world! While I was certain my loyal readers would understand the backstory and relationships in this book, I worried a new reader would be lost. However, thanks to some helpful feedback from Joelle Swift, I'm confident the story won't confuse a newbie. Also, a big thanks to Judi Fleming, who not only encourages me to write, but her expertise in horses and a zillion other things has been most useful in ensuring I get 'it' right. And I can't forget Natalie Bejin, who helped me by creating the most wonderful and organised spreadsheet of all the characters in the world of Ixia and Sitia. Thanks so much, Natalie!

I cannot write an acknowledgement without thanking my editor, Mary-Theresa Hussey, and agent, Robert Mecoy. Both have been vital in my career and I can't thank you enough! I also want to thank all the amazing people at Harlequin. Your hard work behind the scenes to produce my books doesn't go unnoticed and I brag about you to my writer friends all the time.

And no acknowledgments of mine are complete without a huge thank-you to my husband, son and daughter. You guys rock!

UNTRAINED. UNTESTED.
UNLEASHED

With her unique magical abilities, Opal Cowan has always felt unsure of her place at Sitia's magic academy—but now it's time to test her powers in the real world.

Under threat from a deadly massacre, the powerful Stormdancer clan need Opal's unusual skills to protect their people. And their plea is impossible to resist, especially when it comes from mysterious, mercurial Kade.

THEY DESTROYED HER WORLD. BUT SHE'S THEIR ONLY HOPE...

Avry's power to heal the sick should earn her respect in the plague-torn land of Kazan. Instead she is feared and blamed for spreading the plague.

When Avry uses her forbidden magic, she faces the guillotine. Until a dark, mysterious man rescues her from her prison cell. His people need Avry's magic to save their dying prince.

Saving the prince is certain to kill Avry. Now she must choose—use her healing touch to show the ultimate mercy or die a martyr to a lost cause?

IN JULIE KAGAWA'S GROUND-BREAKING MODERN FANTASY SERIES, DRAGONS WALK AMONG US IN HUMAN FORM

Long ago, dragons were hunted to near extinction by the Order of St George. Hiding in human form and increasing their numbers in secret, the dragons of Talon have become strong and cunning, and they're positioned to take over the world with humans none the wiser.

Trained to infiltrate society, Ember wants to live the teen experience before taking her destined place in Talon. But destiny is a matter of perspective and a rogue dragon will soon challenge everything Ember has been taught.

WE'LL EITHER DESTROY THEM FOR GOOD, OR THEY'LL DESTROY US

Alice 'Ali' Bell thinks the worst is behind her.
She's ready to take the next step with boyfriend
Cole Holland, the leader of the zombie slayers…
until Anima Industries, the agency controlling the
zombies, launches a sneak attack, killing four of her
friends. It's then she realises that humans can be
more dangerous than monsters…and the
worst has only begun.

www.miraink.co.uk

NIGHT STUDY

MARIA V.
SNYDER

MIRA Ink is a registered trademark of Harlequin Enterprises Limited, used under licence.

First Published in Great Britain 2016
By Harlequin Mira Ink, an imprint of HarperCollins*Publishers*
1 London Bridge Street, London, SE1 9GF

Night Study © 2016 Maria V. Snyder

ISBN: 978-1-848-45448-4
eBook ISBN: 978-1-474-04518-6

Our policy is to use papers that are natural, renewable and recyclable products and made from wood grown in sustainable forests. The logging and manufacturing processes conform to the legal environmental regulations of the country of origin.

Printed and bound by CPI Group (UK) Ltd, Croydon, CR0 4YY

MIX
Paper from
responsible sources
FSC
www.fsc.org   FSC C007454

To my inspiring and awesome writer's retreat ladies—
Nancy Hunter, Mindy Klasky, Jeri Smith-Ready, and
Kristina Watson. Remember. . .what happens during a
writers' retreat *stays* at the retreat!

NIGHT
STUDY

1

YELENA

Valek blinked at me. "You're what?"

I drew in a deep breath and held up the glass vial filled with moon potion. My hand trembled, sending waves through the white liquid inside. "Pregnant... I think."

"Before we celebrate, love, let's go over your logic."

Surprise pierced my growing panic, and I glanced at him. "You want to celebrate? I was taking the moon potion to *prevent* this."

He took the vial from me and set it on the bed. Then he laced his fingers in mine and pulled me close. "Of course it would be a cause for celebration. Well, a *quiet* celebration." Valek gave me a wry smile—we both had so many enemies, it wouldn't be smart to announce my condition to the world.

My anxiety eased a bit.

"Now, why does that vial mean you're with child?" Valek asked.

"Healer Hayes told me to take the potion after I...bled... so I'd be protected for another year. But I haven't yet, and it's been..." I calculated in my head. It'd been six weeks since I'd last had my blood cycle. "I'm two weeks late." My stomach churned with distress—talk about the worst possible time to be pregnant.

"A lot has happened to you in the last four weeks. Maybe you're late because of the stress."

Valek had a point. It had happened to me before during trying times. And recently I'd been the target of an assassination attempt. Twice. The first occurred a month ago, when I was shot with an arrow that I suspected had been filled with a poison that blocked my magic. Or so I'd thought. I tightened my grip at a sudden notion. "Could the loss of my powers be due to being pregnant?"

"If that was the case, wouldn't Irys know that's a side effect? You said she was as baffled as Bain was about why your magic is blocked."

He was right. If magic loss was a common side effect during pregnancy, the Master Magicians would be aware of that. Disappointment deflated my brief surge of hope. I'd been searching for a poison or substance that explained my current predicament without success for the past month.

Correctly reading my expression, Valek squeezed my fingers. "It still might be possible. I'm immune to magic. Maybe Junior takes after his dear old dad."

Ignoring the *Junior* comment, I asked, "In that case, wouldn't I be immune, as well?" That protection would have been more than welcome four days ago when Owen Moon's magic had sliced right through me. If it hadn't been for Valek encouraging me to survive, I'd be a mindless, drooling mess right now.

Valek shrugged. "We've encountered so many different… quirks of magic over the years, this may well be one of them." He grinned. "Time will tell. And during that time, you'll be safe. No assassin would dare target you while you're with me."

I was more worried about Owen Moon. The rogue magician had managed to escape after attacking me. He had been

MARIA V. SNYDER

growing the Curare vine in a hothouse made of glass. When a person was pricked by Curare, it caused full-body paralysis, which was an effective and nonlethal weapon, since the victim could still breathe.

When Owen had been captured in Ixia four years ago, the Commander assured the Sitian Council, Valek and me that Owen had been executed. Instead, the rogue magician had negotiated a deal with the Commander to manufacture and produce Curare for Ixia's army.

A nice little arrangement, until Owen turned greedy. He sold the drug to other interested parties, and it upset the Commander so much he sent Valek to shut down Owen's entire smuggling operation. Too bad the Commander failed to inform Valek of who had really been in charge of the operation.

We'd all had our share of nasty little surprises in the past week.

"What if Owen shows up?" I asked.

The muscles along Valek's sharp jaw tightened as fury flared in his sapphire-blue eyes. "Don't worry about Owen. Janco and Onora will be traveling with us."

I understood his anger. Owen also knew Valek's weakness. Because he was immune to magic, a null shield cast around him would trap Valek as if he'd been imprisoned in an invisible cell. It was just a matter of time before the word spread to other magicians, and those who could erect a null shield bubble would have an easy way to stop the infamous Ixian assassin.

"Speaking of traveling," I said to lighten the mood. "If you want to leave tomorrow morning, I need that bath."

The hard lines on his angular face softened. "I'll show you the way." Valek let go of my hands.

"Uh-huh. Mighty nice of you."

"I aim to please." He leered, but it soon turned into a more contemplative expression.

As I gathered my clean clothes and soap, Valek picked up the vial of moon potion.

"What about this?" he asked.

"If stress has delayed me, then I should drink it afterward like Healer Hayes instructed."

His brow puckered. "How long does it last?"

"A year, but I usually take it about a month before the year is up just to be safe."

"Is it a hundred percent effective?"

Odd questions, but I humored him. "No. For some, it doesn't work, but I've been taking it for eight years now without a problem." Until now.

"Oh." He set it on the top of the dresser. "What if you wish to have a child sooner?"

"Don't you know all this?"

"No. We use different substances in Ixia."

"In that case, there is another potion called starlight that reverses the effects of the moon potion."

Valek stilled. "How fast?"

"I think it's within hours. I'm not sure. Why all this interest?"

"Just curious."

There was something in the taut line of his body that caused me to suspect there was more to it than mere curiosity. But I decided to let it go. Besides, after lying in bed recovering for the past four days, I really needed that bath. And a change of scenery. The bedroom I'd been occupying had bland yellow walls, a single bed, night table, dresser and no decorations.

Valek escorted me down to the ground floor. The farmhouse had plenty of rooms, which was probably why Owen had bought it for his base of operations. The complex of stables, barns and other structures hid his movements from public view while the large chain-link fence kept curious neighbors from stopping by for a visit. Not that there were many people around. The farm was in a remote area in the northern part of the Moon Clan's lands, near the border with Ixia.

"What's the closest town?" I asked Valek. I'd been tied down under a tarp while being transported here, so I'd counted towns by the vibrations from the wagon wheels trundling over the cobblestones, guessing we were three towns east of Lapeer.

"Broken Bridge is just west of here."

I glanced at him. "Interesting name."

"An accurate name. There was a bridge spanning the Sunworth River at that location, but a flood cracked it in half a long time ago. One half floated down the river, but the other remains on the far bank. No one remembers the real name of the town."

"How do you know all this?"

He grinned. "I've been talking to the locals. Mostly to discover how long Owen's been here, if they'd seen any other strangers around town and if they know about other places he might own. Town gossip can be very informative."

When we reached the washroom, I sighed in contentment when I spotted the glowing coals under a large metal tank. Hot water was just an open valve away. An oval tub sat in the middle of the stone washroom. A row of hooks lined the wall above a bench. Towels had been stacked in a cabinet next to it.

Valek filled the tub while I peeled off my sweat-stiffened tunic. The crisp air caused goose bumps to coat my skin. It was just two weeks into the warming season, and while each day would be a bit warmer than the last, it would be another month before I wouldn't need a cloak during the day. Nights would remain cool well into the warm season.

The rest of my clothing soon joined my tunic on the floor. Before I could even shiver, Valek wrapped me in an embrace. Warmth enveloped me and I gazed up into his eyes.

He swooped in for a kiss. I hooked my arms around his neck and laced my fingers in his shoulder-length black hair, deepening the kiss. My worries melted as heat spread throughout my body.

Too soon, he pulled back. "Your water's getting cold."

"I'm not the one still wearing clothes."

Regret flashed across his face. "I've a few things to take care of before we leave tomorrow."

"But—"

He silenced my protest with another kiss. "Tonight. I promise."

After he left, the cold rushed in with a vengeance. I grabbed a towel and my supplies and hurried to the tub, setting the items on a nearby table. Steam curled from the water and I stepped into bliss, sighing as I submerged up to my neck. I closed my eyes and enjoyed the soak until my worries once again solidified. The biggest one pushed all the others to the side, and I rested my hands on my lower abdomen.

A baby.

No. Valek was right. Stress and trauma had upset my monthly cycles before. This time was no different. Besides, the moon potion had worked for eight years; no reason to doubt its potency now.

A baby.

Fear stirred in my chest. I couldn't be pregnant. Not now. Assassins had been hired to kill me, I had no magic and Owen Moon—a dangerous and powerful magician who also wanted me dead—was at large. Plus this new girl, Onora—yet another assassin—was after Valek's job as Ixia's security chief. And he had dozens of enemies.

Then again, I couldn't imagine our lives ever settling down enough for the timing to be perfect. A child of ours would never be safe. But no need to jump to conclusions just yet. As Valek had said, *time will tell*.

And if I wasn't…?

It'd be for the best. Yet a faint pang of disappointment poked my chest at the thought. Silly.

When the water turned lukewarm, I grabbed my soap. Careful of the scabbed-over rope burns and multicolored bruises around my wrists and ankles, I scrubbed off a few layers of grime. Old scars crisscrossed my stomach, ribs, legs and arms. I'd seen more than my share of action. The newest scar, a roundish shape just below my left clavicle, had been made by the first assassin's arrow just a month ago.

I fingered the ridges, remembering the force of the impact that had knocked me from Kiki's back. The shaft had been filled with an unknown liquid poison. My magic expelled most of the drug—or so I'd thought—and healed the wound. That had been the last time I drew from the blanket of power that surrounded the world and fueled a magician's magic. Once I recovered from the injury, Valek and I enjoyed the remaining day of our vacation before he left for Ixia. That morning, the symptoms of the poison began, and I spent the day suffering from intense hot and cold flashes. When they finally ceased, my ability to draw power was gone.

A delay between poisoning and the onset of the symptoms was not unheard-of. Many assassins liked to be well away before anyone suspected foul play. Yet in this case, shooting a victim with an arrow was far from subtle. I considered. The poison may have nothing to do with my blocked magic. Perhaps it was just added insurance, in case the assassin missed my heart. My ability to drain the substance from my wound then turned a lethal dose into a sick day in bed. That scenario implied there was another cause.

Conception? If I was with child, the timing coincided. But

again, if magicians lost their powers while pregnant, it'd be well-known. Unless, as Valek had said, there was some quirk in the magic. Perhaps First Magician Bain Bloodgood would know, or he could search through his history books for a reference to a similar occurrence. It'd be too dangerous to send him a message right now, and it might be a bit premature at this point. Once I had confirmation of my condition, then I'd talk to Bain.

Clean, I rinsed off the soap and dressed in record time. My stomach growled, so I searched for something to eat. No surprise that my brother, Leif, stood at the kitchen's long counter with his hands in a large metal mixing bowl.

Leif was never far from the food.

His strong forearms flexed as he kneaded the dough. About six inches taller than me, his broad shoulders and square jaw gave him a stocky appearance, but despite being obsessed with eating, it was all muscle under his brown tunic.

"You going to stand there all day?" Leif asked without glancing in my direction. His magic sensed a person's proximity, as well as intentions, moods and guilt. He frequently aided the Sitian Council in their investigations.

"I'm still recovering from the shock of seeing you cook."

He grunted. "Who do you think has been feeding you the last four days?"

I stepped into the spacious kitchen. A mammoth stone hearth comprised the entire far wall. Coals glowed red-hot under a large-sized white brick oven, above which hung an assortment of black iron pots. The scent of baking bread filled the air. A long wooden table with seating for at least two dozen bisected the room.

"I know you're famous for your wet-dog tea and rabbit stew, but I thought you'd rather eat other people's cooking."

MARIA V. SNYDER

"It's *corgarviy* tea, and without it, you'd still be drooling on your pillow."

True. Even though it smelled awful, it had helped rejuvenate me. I joined him at the counter. An impressive array of utensils, tools, bowls and equipment lined the shelves.

"Besides, if I had a kitchen like *this*, I'd cook all the time." Leif studied me. "Hungry?"

"Very."

He gestured to the bench near the table. "Sit."

I didn't waste any time, and he laughed. In that instant, he looked much younger than twenty-nine, which was two years older than me. He grabbed a bowl and uncovered one of the pots on the hearth. Ladling a heaping portion into the bowl, he then placed the steaming goodness in front of me, along with a spoon.

After I inhaled a few bites of the beef-and-vegetable soup, I asked him if he'd identified any more of the other plants inside the glass hothouse Owen had constructed to grow the Curare vine. Before this invention, Curare only grew in the Illiais Jungle far to the south, where it was warm and humid all year round. Another benefit of the vine being confined to one area was that the Sitian Council could limit its availability, which it did. The Council kept strict control of who was allowed to carry it as a weapon. A watered-down version was also manufactured and given to healers in order to reduce a patient's pain, which I thought was the best aspect of the drug. It was the reason my father had hunted for the vine all those years ago.

"I know all but four. We'll have to wait until Father arrives to identify the rest." Leif filled another bowl and sat opposite me. He fiddled with his spoon, twirling it around on the table.

"What's wrong?"

"I keep thinking of that factory in Lapeer. In order to produce so much Curare, Owen must have more of those hot-houses. Lots more."

I'd suspected as much. "We'll find them. Has anyone interrogated Ben? He may know where the others are." Owen's brother had been caught, along with Loris and Cilly Cloud Mist. Ben wasn't as powerful as Owen, but he could erect a null shield, light fires and move small objects. The Cloud Mist siblings' abilities to mentally communicate and manipulate a person's thoughts and memories had aided Owen in maintaining the deception of his death.

"No. The three magicians were taken to Lapeer and incarcerated in a cell with a null shield. The authorities won't let any of us near them, although Devlen left this morning to try again. The Captain claims he's waiting for orders from the Sitian Council."

I cursed under my breath. "I hope the Captain's a patient man." The Council took far too much time to make a decision on anything.

"I'd bet they're in a panic," Leif said. "The Commander has Curare, and he won't be afraid to use it. Unlike our soldiers, I'd bet every single one of his soldiers will have darts laced with the stuff in no time. He could be preparing to invade Sitia as we speak."

As the Liaison between Ixia and Sitia, I found that scenario to be unlikely. However, with the Commander keeping secrets from even Valek, I might not know the Commander as well as I'd thought. Still… "Or he could just want to even the playing field. Having both Curare and magicians, Sitia has had the advantage for years."

Leif picked up the spoon. "Which has made me feel all safe and warm. Now I'm wondering what type of uniform I'd have to wear when we're conquered."

Considering the Commander had banned all magicians, ex-

MARIA V. SNYDER

cept me, from Ixia and executed most of those caught inside his borders, I knew that, at best, Leif and the others would be incarcerated in a magic-proof cell for the rest of their lives—or, at worst, they'd all be killed. I decided not to sour his mood any further.

Instead I said, "I'm sure the Commander will find a job that's perfect for your qualifications. You'd look good in a stable boy's uniform, or spiffy as a chamber pot manager."

"Sure, you can laugh. The Commander likes you. And now you…" Leif ducked his head, focusing on the bowl in front of him.

"What? Now I'm not a Soulfinder anymore, the Commander will welcome me with open arms?"

He wouldn't meet my gaze. "Something like that."

"Then say it. I don't want people dancing around the subject or treating me different…or locking me in jail 'for my own protection.'"

"I was under orders from the Council," Leif protested.

It had backfired. The second assassin had found me in no time. "And look how well *that* turned out." Thank fate I still had a few tricks up my sleeves.

"Sorry. Won't happen again," Leif promised.

"Good." I changed the subject. "Are you staying here until Father comes?"

"Yes. I expect he'll arrive in about fifteen days."

That was a long time to wait. Leif's wife, Mara—a real sweetheart—wouldn't ever complain, but she couldn't be happy. "What will you do all that time?"

"We plan to search the surrounding towns and villages, looking for more of those hothouses."

"We?"

"Devlen believes it's a good idea. And he's got a way with the locals. They talk to him."

With Owen at large, Devlen's daughter, Reema, would have to remain with Ari in the Commander's castle until it was safe. Owen had threatened to kill her.

"Have you found any records here? That would make it easier." And so would interrogating Ben. I wondered if Valek had "talked" to him before the authorities swooped in.

"It appears Owen didn't keep any records at this location. Which is why I'm hoping to find another place where he may have left information behind."

"Or you might find him." The thought of the two of them hunting Owen alone caused a queasiness to roll in my stomach. Leif had been kidnapped by Owen before. And while Devlen was skilled with a sword, Owen's magic outmatched Leif's.

"Even better," he said in a low, dangerous tone.

Not good. "At least make sure you take Hale with you." I was glad Hale had been assigned to travel with us for added protection.

"Hale's gone. He was ordered back to the Citadel."

Interesting. "And you weren't?"

"Oh, I was."

"Leif—"

"Don't 'Leif' me." His green eyes sparked in annoyance. "You know as well as I do the Council will debate what to do for months. Meanwhile, Owen's out there—"

"Along with Rika Bloodgood and Tyen Cowan. Two powerful magicians, which brings the total to three against you and Devlen."

He squared his shoulders with that stubborn Zaltana determination.

I tried another tactic. "Owen's smart. He knows both the Commander and the Council will be searching for him, so he's going to lay low for the next few months while he figures out his next move."

MARIA V. SNYDER

"That's why we need to stop him before he can *act*."

Leif had a point. I considered the situation. "Then the best use of your time would be to convince the Sitian Council to let you use your magic to interrogate Ben and the others."

He grunted, but I wasn't sure I'd convinced him.

We ate the rest of our soup in silence. After a few minutes, Devlen entered the kitchen. A deep scowl etched his dark face, and tension radiated from his powerful build.

"Still no luck?" Leif asked him, referring to Devlen's repeated attempt to speak to Ben.

"Yelena, where is Valek?" Devlen asked, ignoring Leif.

"He said he had to take care of a few things. Why?"

Devlen cursed.

"What's going on?" Leif asked.

"Ben, Loris and Cilly have all been assassinated."

2

VALEK

As he prepared for the trip, Valek's mind whirled with the implications of becoming a father, even though he knew Yelena might not be pregnant. Just the thought of a baby sent a giddy, wild happiness mixed with fear pulsing through his veins. No surprise his immediate instinct was the intense desire to protect both his heart mate and the baby. He imagined locking them both in a tower so no one could harm them. Pure fantasy at best.

His second reaction was to plan the logistics. Yelena would stay with him, of course, and they'd raise the baby together. Where would they live? In the Commander's castle? No. In their cabin in the Featherstone Clan lands? No. That location was too well-known. And what if he was on assignment for the Commander?

Valek banished all his crazy thoughts with effort. Yelena needed to be a part of this discussion. And he needed to confirm a suspicion.

When he'd finished gathering supplies, he searched for Onora. She had offered to get the horses ready. Leaning on the side of the stable, Valek studied Onora as she groomed Onyx. The black horse allowed her to inspect the underside of his hooves, lifting each in turn. Kiki and The Madam grazed nearby in the farm's pasture. Their coats gleamed. In order for each member of their traveling party to have a mount, Onora had picked a chestnut-colored Thoroughbred from those Owen had left behind. The gelding displayed a gentle manner and appeared to be strong and healthy. Valek approved of her choice.

Just about everything was ready for their trip east. They would leave at dawn and set a fast pace to catch up to his operatives already in the field. The Commander wouldn't be happy about the delay. Valek straightened as anger rolled through him. If the Commander had confided in him, this entire fiasco would never have happened, and Yelena wouldn't have been in danger. Instead the Commander chose to reveal his plans only to Onora, the twenty-year-old assassin whose sole desire was to take Valek's place.

At this point in time, Valek would be happy to give it to her. The Commander has been using her to test Valek's loyalty for the past month. First by attacking Yelena, to determine if Valek would disobey a direct order, and then with a fake assassination attempt on the Commander. Tiresome, to say the least. Then the Commander assigned him the task of shutting down a new smuggling route into Ixia without informing him of crucial details...

Valek drew in a deep breath to calm the rising fury. No need to waste the energy now. He planned to confront the Commander on his return. In the meantime, he needed to clarify one vital detail with, as Janco liked to call her, Little Miss Assassin.

Onora glanced up as he approached. She continued to comb Onyx's tail, but a wariness crept into her gray eyes despite her attempts to neutralize her expression. Barefoot even in the cold air, Onora had pulled her long brown hair away from her narrow face. A pretty girl and almost unflappable, it was difficult to discern Onora's thoughts.

"The horses are almost ready." She pointed to Kiki. "She won't let me put shoes on her."

Her horse knowledge must be considerable if Onora felt comfortable enough to shoe a horse. "Kiki's a Sandseed horse—they dislike shoes," Valek said.

"Yeah, she made that quite clear." Onora pushed up the sleeve on her right arm, revealing a bright red, horse-teeth-shaped bruise.

Valek suppressed a smile. "That's not for the shoes. Sandseed horses also have a keen sense of smell. That bite is for shooting Yelena with an arrow. Be glad she didn't decide to kick the side of your head in, as well."

Kiki snorted as if in agreement. Onora shifted away from Onyx's hindquarters. She tensed, probably sensing from Valek's tone that he wasn't there to talk about horses. The young assassin had helped rescue Yelena and Janco from Owen, which weighed in her favor, and she had been acting on the Commander's orders when she shot his heart mate. Valek, more than anyone else, understood the advantages and disadvantages of being loyal to the Commander. However, he suspected Onora had lied to him about a few details.

Valek strode right up to her. "The Commander didn't give you that arrow, did he?"

Dropping the comb, she reached for her knives, but Valek already had his pressed to her throat. She froze. Smart girl.

"*You* filled the arrow with starlight, hoping Yelena would become pregnant, hoping I'd be happy to retire from my position to raise a family."

Onora didn't deny it.

"Are you that hungry for my job?" he asked.

"Yes."

"Show me."

She hesitated.

"Show me or I'll slice your tunic open."

Giving him a nasty glare, she yanked down the collar of her shirt. A purple C-shaped scar marked her chest. From his own experience with scars, he calculated that it'd been done approximately six months ago. Probably when she first started working for the Commander. Emotions boiled in his stomach. Betrayal and relief dominated. Betrayal over the Commander marking another without discussing it with Valek or even informing him. Relief that he no longer needed to fear for the Commander's safety whenever Onora was near him, because she had given her life and loyalty to the Commander.

Onora braced for his reaction.

"That scar won't protect you from *me*. Don't lie to me again. Understand?" he asked.

"Yes."

He pressed harder. Blood welled under the sharp blade.

"Yes, sir," she said.

"Hey! What's going on?" Leif asked.

In one quick motion, Valek sheathed his knife and stepped away from Onora. Leif, Devlen and Yelena hurried to join them. Color had returned to Yelena's cheeks. It was much better than the deathly paleness that had clung to her skin over the past few days. Of course, it would be even better if she wasn't staring daggers at him. Probably not a good time to inform her that the Commander and Onora had plotted against her.

"Haven't you assassinated enough people today?" Leif glared at him, then yanked out a handkerchief to dab at the blood on Onora's throat. "It looks shallow, but I should put a poultice on it just in case."

Onora shooed him off. "I'm fine."

Uncertain about what had caused all this hostility, Valek mulled over Leif's question. "Who died?"

"Oh, come on. Don't play the innocent, Mr. *Assassin*," Leif said. "I get that you're all protective of my sister and think anyone who hurts her should die. But they had vital information that could have led us to Owen, you idiot!"

Ah. "All three?"

Leif opened his mouth, but Yelena stopped him. "Yes, Ben, Loris and Cilly."

While not in the least bit upset over their deaths, Valek did regret not having more time to "talk" with them. He'd used goo-goo juice on Ben to learn the location of the escape tunnel's exit point, but by the time he'd returned from his failed attempt to track Owen, the Sitian authorities had arrived.

Valek suppressed the urge to glance at Onora. Was she responsible? And, if so, was she acting on her own or following the Commander's orders? Now was not the time to ask. "How were they killed?" he asked Leif instead.

Leif huffed in annoyance, but Devlen said, "Puncture wound to the jugular. They died of rapid blood loss."

Yelena touched her neck—a gesture her mother often used when feeling anxious or vulnerable.

None of the assassins he knew killed that way. "Sound familiar?" he asked Yelena.

"When The Mosquito attacked me, he aimed an ice pick at my neck. If he'd succeeded, I probably would have died the same way," she said.

Valek vowed to find the assassin and squash him. But first... "Didn't Bruns Jewelrose hire him to target you?" Another whom Valek needed to have a little chat with—he planned to let the sharp point of his knife do all the talking in that conversation.

Her hand remained around her throat. "Yes. Do you think

Bruns sent him after the magicians? That doesn't make any sense."

"You're right, it doesn't. And an assassin rarely works for one client. Owen has the most to lose if they talked to the Council. Plus, he has the money to hire The Mosquito," Valek speculated.

"He wouldn't kill his own *brother*," Leif said. "He rescued Ben from Wirral Prison."

"Which alerted the authorities," Valek said.

"Who would have lost him if Ben had not gone after Yelena," Devlen added.

"Brothers," Yelena said, gazing at Leif pointedly, "can be troublesome and have the tendency to jump to conclusions. You need to apologize to Valek."

Leif crossed his arms as two red splotches spread on his cheeks. "It wasn't a jump. It was a perfectly reasonable assumption. One you made, too."

"I suspected Valek, as well," Devlen said. He towered about six inches over Leif, and his blue-eyed gaze held contrition.

"No need for apologies." Valek considered. "I don't suppose they would let me examine the crime scene?"

"That would be…unwise at this time," Devlen said. "They would not even let me near it or the bodies."

Which meant Captain Fleming suspected Valek and would probably report his suspicions to the Council. "Should we leave tonight?"

"No," Yelena said. "By the time they make a decision, we'll be in Ixia." Her matter-of-fact tone belied her heated gaze. She hadn't forgotten his promise.

Warmth spread throughout his chest. He'd risk being arrested for a night alone with Yelena. Hell, he'd risk his life. Once they left in the morning, there would be no privacy on the road.

Yet there was no sense in taking an *unnecessary* risk. Setting a watch tonight would provide Valek with ample time to escape should the captain decide to arrest him. "All right, we'll proceed as planned. Onora, where's Janco? I thought he was helping you with the horses."

She gestured to a two-story barn to the left. "He's pouting."

Should he even bother to ask?

Yelena did. "About what?" She fed an apple to Kiki, who cleaved the fruit in half with one bite.

Onora rubbed her right arm as she watched Kiki chew. "He wanted to name the horse we're taking with us 'Beach Bunny,' after some stuffed rabbit he had growing up, and I said it was a stupid name for a horse. Then he claimed, if it was his horse, he could name it anything he wanted, and I said he should ride The Madam because she's the easiest to handle, and—"

"You offended his pride and he stalked away in a huff," Yelena finished.

"Yup."

As Yelena scratched Kiki in all her favorite spots, Valek gestured for Onora to follow him to the barn. He stopped outside the oversize doors that had been painted green with white trim.

"Tell Janco to set up a watch schedule for tonight. I'll take the last shift," he said.

"Should he include Yelena?"

"No. She needs her rest."

Onora bit her lip, clamping down on the question dancing behind her eyes—was Yelena with child? Valek walked away without answering. It was too soon to tell, and, as far as he was concerned, Onora would be the last to know. Though a part of him was impressed by the twenty-year-old's ambition and cunning, he also wished to throttle her. But the Com-

MARIA V. SNYDER

mander had chosen her as Valek's successor. And now it was up to Valek to decide if he agreed.

Valek rattled the doorknob so he wouldn't scare Yelena. She lay in bed reading, but she glanced up from her book when he entered. He recognized it as the plant guide her father had given her.

"What took you so long?" she asked, setting the book on the night table with a thump. The low flame in the lantern jumped.

He'd been checking the perimeter, confirming the gates had all been locked and the buildings secured while Janco did a sweep of the surrounding forest. "Ensuring Captain Fleming isn't at the gate with an arrest warrant."

"Good." She peeled back the covers, exposing her naked body. "Join me."

His heart thudded so hard he feared his sternum would crack in two. Breathing became difficult, and the desire to rip the rest of the blanket off and press her to him trembled through his body. Yet he remained rooted in place. She needed to know about the starlight and Onora.

"What's wrong?"

"I need to tell you—"

"Is it important?"

"Yes."

Yelena pulled the blanket up, covering herself. "All right, tell me."

He kicked off his boots and lay down next to her. She scooted closer and rested her head on his shoulder as he wrapped his arm around her. Valek informed her of Onora's nasty little trick.

"I'm going to wring her neck," Yelena muttered after he'd finished.

"You can try. I doubt you'd get close to her."

"Is that why you had the knife at Onora's throat?"

"Yes. She needed to understand that will be the last time she lies to me. And I needed to remind her who is in charge."

"Until the Commander says otherwise."

"True."

"And will you take orders from her?"

"No. By that time, I suspect I'll be taking orders from another woman."

Yelena lifted her head from his chest and met his gaze. "Is that so? What type of orders?"

"You have a dirty mind, love. I'm thinking of orders to change a diaper or rock a baby to sleep. Things like that."

"Not near as exciting as assassinating a criminal."

"Not as dangerous, either. Besides, I think the teen years could be quite exciting. No one is going to mess with my son or daughter."

She laughed. "You can't assassinate bullies or boys who kiss your daughter."

"Pity."

A brief smile flashed, then she grew contemplative. "Since I was hit with starlight, that increases the possibility I'm pregnant. What will we do?"

"I expect we'll do what most people do in that situation—become a family."

"Easier said than done."

"We'll figure this out—I promise." He pulled her tight against him.

She snuggled in and fell asleep. Valek took comfort in the steady rise and fall of her chest, but far too soon, it was his turn on watch. He slipped from her embrace, pulled his boots on and searched for Janco.

A half-moon cast enough light to avoid tripping and walking into tree trunks. Valek found Janco near the glass house.

MARIA V. SNYDER

Condensation misted the outside panels of the structure. Inside, coals burned to keep it warm, and the pans of water added moisture to the air. Leif had been maintaining the equipment in order to keep the plants alive until his father arrived. The whole idea of the house and growing Curare far from the jungle was genius. He wondered if Owen had the original notion, or if the Commander had speculated about the possibility and sent Owen to put it all together.

"Any trouble?" Valek asked.

Janco rubbed the scar where the bottom half of his right ear should be. "Just thinking."

"That could be dangerous."

"Ha, ha. Not funny. What I'm wondering is, if all those plants inside came from the Illiais Jungle, then who brought them here?"

"Owen has been working on this for over three years."

"Yeah, I get that. But wouldn't the Zaltana Clan know strangers were digging around their jungle? Doesn't the Curare vine only grow in a certain section? And isn't Yelena's father the only producer of the stuff?" Janco tapped on the glass. "These are far from seedlings. And then I'm thinking, how many people have enough knowledge of all these plants? Can't be many outside the jungle."

All excellent points. Valek considered. "Tyen Cowan might have the knowledge, depending on where he grew up." The jungle bordered the southeastern and southern sections of the Cowan Clan's lands.

"Or a Zaltana was working with Owen."

Deceit and betrayal were all part of his job; however, Valek had a difficult time believing that one of Yelena's clan members would cooperate with Owen or be involved in illegal activities. Unless they'd been tricked. "Before we leave, we'll ask

Leif to look into it. If Leif finds the expert, he or she could lead him to where the other hothouses are located."

Janco flashed him a bright smile. "See? I have good ideas, too."

"I never said you didn't."

"But you never said I did."

"I don't have to. You're very good at self-congratulation," Valek said.

"I am?"

"Yes."

Janco preened.

"Go get some sleep," Valek said. "It'll be dawn in a couple hours."

At the mention of dawn, Janco's shoulders drooped. "You know, midafternoon is a perfectly respectable time to leave," he grumbled as he headed back to the house.

Valek looped around the complex, testing locks and seeking signs of a disturbance. Satisfied that all appeared secured, he stopped at the stables. Both Kiki and Rusalka, Leif's horse, snoozed in their stalls unperturbed. He'd learned to trust the Sandseed horses. If a strange scent tainted the air, they'd be agitated.

When the sky lightened, he returned to the house. The smell of sizzling bacon reached him. He followed the wonderful scent to the kitchen. Leif filled plates with sweet cakes, bacon, eggs and toast. Everyone was awake and sitting at the table.

Happy to see Yelena tucking into a heaping portion in front of her, Valek joined them, letting the conversation flow over him.

"I'd wake up every morning at dawn if I knew *this* was waiting for me," Janco said, helping himself to another stack of sweet cakes. His salt-and-pepper-colored goatee was sticky with syrup.

"You're going to make yourself sick," Yelena teased.

"Not possible."

"Enjoy it," Leif said. "Tomorrow you're all going to be eating dried jerky, stale bread and hard cheese."

Janco groaned. "Nasty, Leif."

"I'm sure we'll be stopping at a few inns. Right?" Yelena asked Valek.

"We'll see."

"That's Valek speak for 'no way in hell.'" Janco stole a slice of bacon from her plate.

She stabbed him with her fork.

"Owww."

Valek turned to Leif and asked him about other jungle experts.

Leif chewed his food while he thought. "I'll ask my father. Compared to the rest of Sitia, most of the Zaltanas are experts. However, in order to transport plants, you need a higher level of knowledge." He tapped a fork on the table. "And, thinking about it…some of those unfamiliar plants might be crossbreeds." Leif tossed the silverware in disgust. "Of course, that's why I couldn't identify them!"

"Crossbreeds?"

"When you graft one plant onto the other and create a new type of plant. And that's an even rarer specialty." Leif sobered.

"How rare?"

The mulish set to Leif's jaw meant he wouldn't answer without more prompting. "How many people can do it?" Valek asked.

"A few," Leif hedged.

"Two," Yelena said.

Leif shot her a nasty look.

"Do you know their names?" he asked.

"Our cousin Nutty Palm Zaltana, and our Councilman, Bavol Cacao Zaltana."

3

LEIF

Anger boiled. Leif shot from his chair. "There's no way either of them is involved with Owen!"

"Probably not directly," Yelena, his traitor of a sister, said.

"Not at all. They both know how dangerous Curare is." And Leif wasn't going to let anyone cast suspicion on them.

"All right, then prove it," Valek said. "Rule them out of the equation and we'll look elsewhere."

Except all the experts were fellow Zaltanas. His appetite gone, Leif pushed his plate away.

Janco chimed in between spoonfuls of eggs. "It should be easy to do with your lie-detecting mojo."

A queasy expression pinched Yelena's face. "He can't use it unless he has reason to believe they've committed a crime. It violates the Magician's Ethical Code."

"They *follow* a code of ethics?" Janco asked in surprise.

"You should know about it," Yelena said.

"Oh, I know about it. I just figured they all *ignored* it."

"Because, according to you, they're all evil and corrupt?"

"Not all. There are a couple exceptions." Janco inclined his head, indicating her and Leif. "I assumed they ignored it because it's what *I'd* do if I had magic."

"How do you know you don't have magic?" Onora asked, speaking for the first time that morning.

"I don't have magic." Janco huffed.

"But you can sense it."

"And you can sense the cold air, but that doesn't make you a snowman…er…woman."

As they argued over the definition of a magician, Leif collected the empty plates, stacking them in the sink. The thought of interrogating his family sat heavily in his stomach. Maybe a casual visit would work. But then his certainty of Bavol's innocence faded. He remembered how Bavol had dodged their questions when he and Yelena had visited. The man had lied to them, but at the time, Leif had thought it was regarding the Council's knowledge of Yelena's blocked magic.

After everyone finished eating, Leif followed them to the stables. The sun poked from the horizon. Cold air bit through his tunic. He handed Yelena a pouch full of herbal medicines with instructions on how to use them.

She raised an eyebrow at the unexpected weight.

"Just in case you run into trouble," he said.

"I'm traveling with two assassins and a master swordsman. How much trouble do you think we'll get in?"

He gave her a flat look.

"Yeah, okay." She hefted the pouch. "Feels about right." Yelena opened it. "Did you include the ginger tea that helps with nausea?"

"There are a few bags. Why? Are you still feeling sick?"

"Oh, no. Not at all." She tucked the medicines in her saddlebag.

The faint scent of licorice swirled around her. His magic mojo—as Janco called it—sensed she was hiding something. "Are you sure?"

"Yes. I'm healthy."

The sweet smell of truth. "Good. Although you might need that tea after it's Janco's turn to cook."

"I heard that," Janco called. He swung up into Beach Bunny's saddle and shot Onora a triumphant expression.

The quiet woman merely ignored Janco's posturing as she saddled The Madam. Kiki stood head to head with Rusalka, who remained in her stall. Her body language made it quite clear she wanted to go with Kiki and the others. Leif stroked her neck and fed her a peppermint.

Just before the group departed, Leif hugged his sister and made her promise to be careful.

"I will if you will," Yelena said. "If you discover Owen's hiding place, don't go after him with just Devlen for backup. Take Irys and at least another magician with you and about a half-dozen soldiers. Promise?" When he hesitated, she added, "If not for me, then do it for Mara."

Ah, hell. The thought of upsetting Mara always hurt him deep down. And if anything happened to Devlen, their brother-in-law, she'd be doubly upset. Not to mention how devastated Devlen's wife, Opal, and his children would be. "All right. All right. I promise."

"Good. Keep me updated on your progress."

"I will if you will," he said.

"It's a deal." She mounted Kiki.

Leif turned and met Valek's gaze. The infamous assassin had been his best man at his wedding, but Leif still didn't know him all that well. However, he would never question Valek's desire to keep Yelena safe. As if reading his thoughts, Valek nodded at him before spurring Onyx toward the main gate.

He watched the four of them leave. An unsettled feeling swirled in his stomach. Every time he and Yelena parted, one painful memory from his childhood always darkened his thoughts—the time he'd witnessed Yelena's kidnapping and done nothing to help. Each time she left him, he relived his shame and guilt. Fourteen years later, she'd returned and eventually forgave him. But though he'd only been a terrified eight-year-old at the time, he could never fully forgive himself. Instead, he'd made an uneasy peace with his actions. And he accepted that every time she left him, he'd worry that he'd never see her again.

"The horses need to be fed," Devlen said, bringing Leif back to the present.

Devlen mucked out the now-empty stalls. Aside from Rusalka, two other horses remained behind. One for Devlen to use, and the other would be given to the Clever Fox stables as a replacement for The Madam. The unflappable horse was now a member of their herd.

As Leif filled the buckets with grain, Devlen brought fresh water, and together they finished cleaning the rest of the stalls. Valek had invited Devlen to travel with them and eventually join Reema in the Commander's castle, but he'd declined, claiming he'd be more useful aiding Leif with the investigation.

"What is next?" Devlen asked.

"I need to check on the coals in the hothouse." And look for signs indicating crossbreeding to determine the purpose of the unknown plants. They had to have a purpose; otherwise, why take up space that could be used to grow more Curare vines? The factory in Lapeer that they'd shut down had the capacity to process twenty times the number of vines that grew in this one house.

Devlen followed him to the glass building. Using a shovel, Leif spread the glowing remains of the coals while Devlen filled the water pans. A puff of smoke stung Leif's eyes as he added more of the expensive white coals to the fire. They burned hotter and cleaner than the black type. The smell reminded him of Mara and he closed his eyes for a moment to breathe it in. The sugary scent always clung to her clothes after she'd spent the day working in the Keep's glass shop.

"How does the smoke escape?" Devlen asked. The tall man peered at the ceiling.

"Probably through the seams in the panes."

Devlen reached up and ran a finger along the wet drops, leaving a clear line in the condensation. "There are small holes in the glass."

Leif groaned. He'd been so focused on the plants, he hadn't considered who might have constructed the house. Devlen, too, creased his face in chagrin. He'd worked with Opal in her glass factory in Fulgor for the past six months.

The sisters had taught their husbands that making holes in a pane of glass after it hardened would shatter it, but while the glass was molten, holes of any size and number could be added. These panels had been made for this specific purpose. If they found the manufacturer, they might uncover the location of the other houses and, even better, Owen's hiding place.

"Not a word to our wives. Agreed?" Leif asked.

"Agreed."

MARIA V. SNYDER

4

YELENA

Valek set a fast pace and, even though Kiki switched to her smoothest gait, after a few hours in the saddle, I clutched Kiki's copper mane to keep from falling off. My recovery from Owen's attack hadn't been as complete as I'd thought. Lack of sleep didn't help, either.

All morning, we'd pause in a series of small river towns as we headed east, paralleling the Sunworth River. Janco and Valek would dismount and poke around, searching for magic. Or rather, seeking Rika Bloodgood's magical illusions, which may have been employed to conceal the three outlaws. Onora and I would visit the local authorities to inquire about any unusual activities and strange glass houses.

I lost track of the number of towns as the day wore on. We finally stopped for the night in one of the larger settlements. Valek checked us into the Anchor Inn and I collapsed on the bed as soon as he shut the door.

He was next to me in an instant. "Why didn't you tell me?"

"I just need to sleep. I'll be fine. You should be more worried about Janco and Onora sharing a room. One of them is going to kill the other by morning."

"Janco's trying to provoke her."

"And when she snaps?"

"He'll have a bruise and an ego to nurse."

"Are you sure it won't be worse?" Despite Valek's assurances of her loyalty, I didn't trust the girl. And since learning she'd shot me with an arrow laced with starlight, I'd wanted to punch her. Frustration flowed through me. If I had my magic, I'd examine her soul and learn just how dangerous she was. The Ethical Code be damned. She'd started it.

"She won't harm Janco, because it would upset me," Valek said. "And right now, she's still scared of me."

"And when she's no longer afraid?"

"Then it will get interesting."

Typical Valek bravado. If I had any energy, I'd argue.

Sensing my mood, Valek said, "Before you form an opinion of her, I'd suggest you get to know her better. Like you, she's been assaulted and raped. But unlike you, she hasn't killed her demons yet."

"Now you've done it." Regret for my earlier dark thoughts pulsed.

"I've done what?"

"You complicated things. My feelings for her were rather simple. It was nice to just dislike her. Now I want to help her. Too bad my powers—"

"Are not needed," Valek said. "You've overcome your difficulties without using magic, so can she. But I'm sure she'd like a friend to confide in."

"You're sure? Why do you care? She's after your job."

"I've always had people after my job, love. And the Commander's been telling me to find a protégé for years. She's the first to have real potential, and if she can step up, then perhaps she should."

I studied his face, searching for regret or sorrow over the prospect. Finding none, I relaxed back into the pillows. Valek

MARIA V. SNYDER

tucked me in and left to listen to the local gossip. I fell asleep dreaming of our future together.

Morning intruded. I groaned and tightened my grip on Valek as he tried to disentangle himself from me and the blankets.

"A few more minutes," I mumbled.

"I caught a lead last night," he said, pulling my arms off his waist.

Suddenly wide-awake, I let go and sat up. "You found Owen? Why didn't you wake me?"

"Easy, love. It's never that simple. I talked to a man who knew about a strange house made of glass."

"And? Did you go check it out?"

"No. The man claimed he needed his brother's help to find the place again. He offered to get his brother and take me there in the morning, for a fee of course."

"Smells like a classic setup." Instead of taking the mark to the promised location, the journey would end in an ambush.

"Indeed. However, from his comments, I think Owen may have tried to erase his memories, which is why he needed his brother to find the location again."

"Still might be a setup."

He smiled. "There will be four of us."

"And if it's a trap, we'll be facing three magicians." I flung the blankets off and dug through my pack. "Make sure all your darts are filled with Curare."

"Yes, sir."

We dressed and met Janco and Onora for a fast breakfast. The man joined us at the stables. He was in his forties, broad-shouldered and good-natured despite the tension. He introduced himself as Tex. I checked that his shadow matched his physique, ruling out a magical disguise. A short sword hung from his waist, but he might have other weapons tucked in his clothes or boots. I drew my cloak tighter around my shoulders. Or rather, Reema's cloak. We had switched garments when I'd sent her to Ixia and out of danger.

Tex's brother was named Jax—a thick, muscled man the size of Ari, whose shadow also matched. A rolled-up horse whip was tied to Jax's belt. Janco eyed the whip with trepidation, rubbing his arms.

Valek introduced us. He used Janco's and Onora's real names, but changed mine to Elliona and referred to himself as Ilom. The men brought their own horses. Jax mounted a beefy gray quarter horse, and Tex rode a dark brown stallion.

Tex gazed at Kiki. "Is that one of those Sandseed horses?"

No sense lying. "Yes."

"Is it true they can go twice as fast as a normal horse?"

"Only when they're in the Avibian Plains, otherwise, no."

"Huh? I thought no one can go into the plains without getting lost."

"That's true, but if you're riding a Sandseed horse, they never get lost."

"That's handy," Tex said.

We discussed horses as Tex and his brother led us south. From the way Janco scanned our surroundings, I knew he was searching for any magical traces. Valek remained quiet, content to let me chat with the brothers. Onora appeared to be bored, but the stiffness in her movements said otherwise. She also kept well away from Jax and I wondered if the man who had assaulted her had been his size.

As Tex had said, he couldn't quite remember the route through the farmlands and forest. At one point, Tex and Jax argued on the right direction. I asked him how they'd found the place before.

"We've been working the river," Tex said. "Loading and

MARIA V. SNYDER

unloading the barges. Last season, a man hired us to transport these bundles of vines from this glass house you're so interested in to the river. I don't remember picking them up, but Jax does—that house really intrigued him. Apparently we did one trip. I collected the payment, but the man didn't pay enough, so we quit. I guess."

"Do you remember what the man looked like?" Valek asked.

"No. And Jax never met him, so, like I said, I don't remember much. It sounds crazy, I know."

It did, but if Owen had erased Tex's memories, and hadn't known about Jax, then it made sense.

After a few hours we crested a hill and stopped. Down below in the middle of a valley was a large glass house twice the size of the one near Broken Bridge. The afternoon sunlight reflected off its roof. Next to it stood another structure that resembled a barn. No one was in sight.

"There should be a...gardener around here," Jax said. "I think."

"We need to head back for another job," Tex said. "You folks okay with finding your own way from here? We're not in the plains." Concern creased his brow.

Genuine? Or a hell of a good actor? "Yes, thank you. Sandseed horses have an excellent sense of direction regardless of location," I said.

Valek paid Tex a generous sum. The man flashed him a grateful smile and headed back with his brother right behind him.

Janco rubbed his goatee, frowning. "Does anyone else think that's odd?"

"What's odd?" Valek asked.

"Those guys. They were..."

"Nice," I finished for him. "Don't tell me you've never met friendly people before."

"Not in my line of work. Who wants to bet me that there's an ambush waiting for us below?" Janco gestured to the valley.

"Do you sense any magic?" Valek asked.

"No, but we're pretty far. You?"

"Nothing."

A pang touched my chest. If I still had my magic, we'd know for sure if this was a trap.

"How do you want to proceed?" Onora asked Valek.

"You and Janco cut through the woods on the left side, check for any unfriendlies. I'll check right. Meet back here." Valek dismounted.

"And what about me?" I asked.

"Stay with the horses."

Red-hot anger flared. "Kiki can *stay* with the horses. I'm coming with you." I didn't wait for his permission. I swung down from Kiki's back, removed my cloak and yanked my bo staff from its holder on her saddle.

Valek studied me and I prepared for an argument. Instead he nodded. "Let's go." He untied his gray short cape and slung it over Onyx's saddle.

Onora and Janco melted into the woods, and I followed Valek. He wore Sitian clothes—a plain tan tunic and brown pants that blended with the surrounding forest. The trees and bushes remained bare of leaves, but a few buds dotted a number of branches, promising warmer days ahead.

Valek traveled through the underbrush without making a sound, his movements graceful and balanced like an acrobat's. I rustled behind him. My woodland skills had grown rusty with neglect. No need to slink about the woods when I'd already known exactly what creatures lurked inside. Since

I could no longer rely on magic, I suspected many hours of training would be in my future.

Using hand signals, Valek communicated when to stop, wait and go. We encountered no one, and didn't see tracks, broken branches or any other sign that another person had been here.

We returned to the horses and, soon after, Janco and Onora reported the same thing—no ambushers. Mounting our horses, we rode down into the valley. As we neared, Valek asked Janco if he sensed a magical illusion.

"No. I'll let you know if I do," Janco said.

Valek stopped us about fifty feet from the barn. He signaled for us to wait, dismounted and circled the buildings. I peered at the glass house. No condensation coated the panes and no greenery pressed against the sides. From this angle, it appeared to be empty.

When he reappeared he said, "No signs of activity anywhere and the barn door is locked."

"Let me," Janco said with a grin. He jumped off Beach Bunny and hurried toward the barn.

"He does know we can all pick a lock, right?" I asked Valek. Janco had taught me the art, and my set of picks held my hair up in an intricate knot.

"This one's a swivel." Valek drew his sword. "Come on."

Onora and I followed him around the building. Janco knelt next to an oversize door, working on a shiny new padlock. We waited behind him until he made a small sound of triumph. He removed the lock and glanced at Valek, who signaled him to open the door.

Janco yanked it open with a whoosh. We braced for an attack, but nothing happened. Instead a foul odor wafted from the entrance—the unmistakable rancid smell of death.

With a grim expression, Valek ventured inside. After a moment, he returned. "It's safe."

Covering our noses with our shirts, we filed in. From the overturned chairs and scattered trash, it appeared as if they'd left in a hurry. Valek crouched by the body of a man whose throat had been sliced open.

"The gardener?" I asked.

"Probably. He has dirt under his nails. No defensive wounds, which means he knew his attacker."

"Or he was trapped by magic," Janco said. "How long has he been dead?"

"Three or four days." Valek straightened. "Take a look around. See if they missed anything."

We spread out. A small bed and night table lined the far wall. Gardening tools hung near the door. I poked at the ashy remains of the fire, uncovering a half-burned parchment. Fishing it from the pile, I smoothed it flat, revealing a picture of a hobet plant, along with instructions for its care.

My shirt slipped down and the putrid smell filled my nose. It flipped the contents of my stomach and I bolted for the door. Once I reached clean air, the need to vomit slowly disappeared. Shivering with the cold, I retrieved my cloak from Kiki. Once ensconced in its warmth, I strode to the glass house. I peered through the clear walls. Leaves and broken stems littered the dirt floor. It appeared as if plants had been wrenched out by their roots. I spotted something white in the middle of the mess.

Wagon wheel tracks lined up next to the entrance. I guessed they'd loaded everything up that had been in the glass house and didn't bother to lock up. The knob turned with ease and I entered. The air was colder inside. Boot prints marked the muddy spots.

The white object was a sheet of parchment folded in half. When I picked it up, a loud pop sounded. I straightened.

Thousands of cracks raced through the glass like lightning. Fear sliced through my heart just as fast.

"Yelena!" Valek yelled from the doorway, too far away.

I yanked my hood over my head and dropped to the ground. Pressing my forehead to the dirt, I curled up like a turtle, lacing my fingers behind my neck as an explosion of glass roared.

5

VALEK

The glass walls and ceiling of the house shattered with an eruption of sound. Unable to reach Yelena in time, Valek watched in horror as razor-sharp shards and jagged chunks crashed down onto her huddled form. The force of the impact sent glass flying in all directions. He stumbled back, covering his face with his hands. Pinpricks of pain pierced his legs, arms and torso.

"Holy snow cats!" Janco yelled next to him.

When the noise died, Valek yanked his hands down. He raced along the side of the house, searching for Yelena in the heaping piles of broken glass. The gray fabric of her cloak poked through a mound. An ice-cold dread filled his heart when he spotted the blood. Without hesitation, he waded into the ruins. The glass crunched, popped and cracked under his boots.

"Careful," Janco said as he followed.

They reached Yelena's side. She was buried. They removed the big slabs and brushed off as much as possible. She tried to move, but her cloak was still pinned.

"Easy, love," he said, relieved she was conscious. "Let us free you first."

Yelena stilled. Blood soaked her back from dozens of slivers, but the real concern was a large triangle-shaped piece that jutted from her left side, just below her ribs. Janco pointed to it and mimed a yanking motion. Valek shook his head. They'd remove the dangerous one after they assessed where it had hit her.

Working together, Valek and Janco cleared the rest of the glass and freed her. By the time they finished, blood dripped from his and Janco's hands from the numerous cuts they'd gotten.

"Can you stand?" he asked her.

"Yes." She pushed up to a sitting position. All the color drained from her face. "Uh…maybe not. How bad—" She noticed the shard.

"Let's get you out of here first." He helped Yelena to her feet and supported her as they navigated the uneven debris.

Onora waited for them. She had retrieved the first-aid kit from Kiki's saddle. Once they cleared the house, Valek removed her ruined cloak and she sank to the ground. He cut away part of her shirt to expose the worst injury. It looked deep, and he worried it might have pierced her stomach. At least it wasn't close enough to endanger the baby, if she was in fact pregnant.

Yelena inspected the damage. "It shouldn't bleed out when it's removed, but the wound will need to be sealed."

Good thing the first-aid kit contained a jar of Rand's glue. The Commander's late chef had invented an edible adhesive for his cakes that also worked on skin.

"Let's take care of these others first," Valek said. "Do you want me to pour the medicinal Curare on your back?" Yelena's father had supplied them with a watered-down version of the drug for this contingency.

"Save it for when you seal the serious wounds."

Being the only one without cuts on her hands, Onora used a pair of tweezers to remove the slivers from Yelena's back and the back of her head. Onora peeled off Yelena's tunic as she worked. Janco hovered, getting in the way.

"Do a sweep of the area. Make sure no one is around," Valek ordered him. "If it's secure, we'll camp here for the night."

"Yes, sir." Janco dashed off.

"Thanks," Onora said. She continued, creating a pile of bloody pieces next to her. "It could have been worse. The cloak's fabric stopped a bunch." Onora continued to pluck glass from Yelena's skin and then her hair.

Valek hated seeing Yelena hurt. A helpless frustration boiled up his throat, and the desire to murder the person who'd harmed her pulsed with every heartbeat. If she reclaimed her magic, he'd never take her healing powers for granted again.

"Valek, attend to your wounds," Onora said, shooing him away. "You can't help me with bloody fingers."

He stifled a protest—she had a point. And now that she had mentioned them, pain flared to life. Multiple stings peppered his body and blood stained his clothes. Valek pulled glass from his skin, then washed his hands and wrapped a bandage around his right palm, which had sustained the largest gash. He'd save the glue for Yelena.

When Onora finished, he knelt next to his heart mate and met her gaze. "Ready?"

She nodded.

He grasped the triangular shard and yanked it out in one quick motion. She gasped. Blood poured from the wound. Pressing a bandage on it, Valek stanched the flow as she lay on her uninjured side. When the surge eased, he rubbed Curare around and in the injury, then inspected it. It wasn't as

MARIA V. SNYDER

deep as he feared. Relieved, he used Rand's glue and sealed the gash before tending to the others.

In the time it took for Janco to return and build a campfire, Yelena's cuts had been cleaned and wrapped in bandages, and she'd changed into fresh clothes. Despite her protests, Valek tucked her into her bedroll, insisting she rest. The sun balanced on the crest of the hill and darkness would soon fill the valley.

Janco boiled water for one of Leif's healing teas. "I knew those brothers were up to no good. They must have doubled back after they left us."

"Did you see them?" Valek asked.

"No, they were gone by the time I did my sweep. The crossbow must have been hidden somewhere nearby."

"Crossbow?" Onora asked Janco.

"Of course a crossbow. How else could they have shattered the glass from a distance? It had to be a bolt."

It made sense, but Valek had felt a brush of magic right before the walls exploded. "I think it was magic."

"But I thought you checked," Janco said.

"I did." He'd not only circled the building, but touched the glass walls to ensure no magical alarms had been installed.

"It was a booby trap," Yelena said, pushing up to her elbow.

"Then what set it off?" Janco asked.

She gazed at the fire as if in thought. "There was a piece of parchment on the ground. As soon as I picked it up, the glass started cracking. It must have triggered the trap."

"A magical booby trap?" Janco cursed. "Oh, that's just wonderful. The more I learn about magic, the more I hate it."

Valek considered. "Was there a message on the paper?"

"I didn't have time to look," Yelena said. "It's probably still there."

Janco sprang to his feet. "I'll get it." He crunched through the debris. Cracks and pops marked his noisy passage. After a few minutes, he returned with the folded note and a murderous expression on his face.

Janco handed it to Valek. "Read it."

Valek unfolded the parchment. One word had been written in black ink.

"Gotcha."

Fury burned in his chest. Owen would pay for this little stunt the next time Valek encountered him. And he wouldn't allow Owen to catch him in a null shield. Oh no. Valek had no intention of letting the magician know he was in mortal danger. Not even with a note.

"Let me see." Yelena held out her hand. Small cuts crisscrossed her knuckles.

He passed it to her.

She huffed. "Typical Owen."

"How do you know it was Owen?" Onora asked.

"He's the only one of the magicians who can set a trap like this," Yelena explained. "Rika is limited to magical illusions, and Tyen can only move objects."

"What else can Owen do?" She poured hot water into a teacup and gave it to Yelena.

Valek approved of her question. One of the lessons of being an assassin was to know everything possible about your mark.

Yelena crinkled her nose as she sniffed the tea, either disgusted by the smell or the topic. "Owen's quite talented. He can mentally communicate with another magician, which isn't a big deal, but his ability to lie to another when communicating mind to mind is extremely rare."

"He can also lasso one of those null shields around someone pretty quick," Janco added. "They can block magic, but not objects or people, except for—"

"I know what they are," Onora said, glancing at Valek.

MARIA V. SNYDER

Valek hid his amusement. She was worried about upsetting him.

"Owen can also mess with a person's memories, erasing the real ones and inserting fake ones. Or he can just tear your mind apart, leaving you a mindless idiot." Yelena rubbed her forehead, no doubt remembering Owen's attack.

"So that's what happened to Janco," Onora quipped.

Janco tsked. "Nasty."

"Accurate." She shot back.

"You wish. I can think circles around you!"

"I agree. Your mind spins round and round, like a gnat's. A truly dizzying intellect."

Janco squawked in protest, but before he could respond, Valek said, "That's enough."

Janco clamped his mouth shut, but shot Onora a venomous glare. She ignored it. This time. It was inevitable that Janco would push too far and they'd fight, which would be interesting to watch. However, for tonight, Valek didn't want to upset Yelena.

"Is that the extent of Owen's magical powers?" Onora asked.

"No," Yelena said. "He can heat objects. I once held a knife to his throat and he made the handle so hot, I had to drop it, which means he can also start fires. And apparently set traps. That's new to me, so he might have other hidden powers."

"Gee, what a sweetheart." Janco's tone dripped with sarcasm. "Sounds like the creep could be a Master Magician."

Yelena sipped her tea. "He's not that powerful, but he's close. I wonder if he took the master-level test and failed. That could explain some of his...bitterness and antisocial behavior. It's a brutal test." She covered her expression with the cup.

"Have you taken it?" Onora asked.

"Oh, no. Not really." Yelena glanced at the embers swirling in the hot air above the fire.

Probably searching for the bat that was usually her constant companion when it wasn't hibernating during the cold and warming seasons. Valek wondered if the bat would find her or even if it could find her now that she no longer had magic. He hoped the little creature wouldn't abandon her.

The bat had arrived soon after Yelena's first trip into the fire world. Valek remembered being utterly devastated when she'd disappeared into the fire world after the Warper battle. She'd been gone for months. If she hadn't reached out to Leif... He'd planned to join her there.

"According to Irys, when you returned from the fire world you passed the master-level test," Janco said.

"But I didn't meet all the requirements for being a Master Magician. No, it just confirmed what I'd suspected, that I was a Soulfinder and my job was to find lost souls and guide them to either the sky or the fire world, depending on their deeds while alive."

Janco thumped his chest. "I'm sure I'm destined for the fire world. At least I'll be in good company." He gave Onora and Valek a pointed look.

Yelena frowned. "It's not something to joke about, Janco. It's a terrible place full of pain, despair and utter misery. And you're not destined for it."

"Why not? I've lied, cheated, stolen things. I've killed people."

"You have also *saved* people, sacrificed yourself and are helping to keep the peace by stopping the truly evil people from taking over. It's not so much your actions, but your intentions and your choices." Yelena met Valek's gaze. "And it's a matter of balance. Even if you did terrible things, all the good you do will eventually outweigh it, tipping you toward the sky."

A lovely sentiment, but Valek needed a few decades of good deeds to balance out his years as an assassin for hire. He'd killed to learn how to be a better killer. All in order to assassinate the King of Ixia. Granted, the King had been corrupt and evil, but those others had just been marks to him. Except for the men who had murdered his brothers in the King's name. They deserved to die.

Janco's brow creased in thought—a rare expression for him. "Does this mean I have to be nice to Little Miss Assassin?"

"Yes, because I'm no longer a Soulfinder, so I can't rescue you from the fire world."

Now Janco blinked at Yelena. All humor dropped from his face and he pressed a hand to his heart. "You would have rescued me?" he asked in awe.

"Of course, you idiot! I wouldn't let you suffer."

Despite being called an idiot, he grinned. Or was that in spite of? Hard to tell with Janco.

Onora shook her head. "Now you've done it," she muttered.

To forestall Janco's obnoxiousness, Valek changed the subject. "Onora, you have first watch. Janco, take the second shift, and I'll go last."

"That means I have the third shift," Yelena said in a tone that warned of a major battle if he disagreed.

"All right. In the morning we'll stop at the closest town and send Leif a message, informing him of the booby trap."

"Do you think Owen had time to rig all the houses?" Janco asked Valek.

"He has a six-day head start. And he knows we'll be searching for them. Plus the Curare is too valuable to leave behind, so I'd expect him to gather as much as he can. He'll need money to finance his next endeavor."

Owen had claimed to have discovered something big

enough to make the Commander forgive him for his betrayal. It could have been a boast, but Valek doubted it.

"What about the dead body?" Janco jerked a thumb toward the barn.

"We'll inform the local authorities in the morning and let them handle it."

"Does anyone else think it…odd that Owen murdered the gardener?" Yelena asked.

"No," Valek answered. "The gardener probably had information about the operation. It was smart to silence him."

"Yes, but…" She played with the string on her tea bag.

"Owen murdered his brother and the others," Janco said.

"We still don't know for certain who killed them, but assuming it was him, he *hired* an assassin. Big difference." Yelena gazed at the liquid in her cup. "And I'm still not convinced it was him. In all my dealings with Owen, he never acted like a killer. Think about it. He went out of his way to scare me off by *pretending* to kidnap Reema back in Fulgor. Even when he captured us, his solution was to erase our memories. Why not just slit our throats and bury us?"

"Because if he killed you, Valek would hunt him down and tear him apart," Janco said.

True. Valek's fingers itched to grasp a blade just thinking about anyone harming his heart mate. But what Yelena said also had merit. Did she suspect Onora had assassinated the trio? "If Owen didn't do it, then who did?" he asked her.

"It's just a theory, and you're not going to like it."

With that one comment, he knew. And she was right. He didn't like it, but he had wondered the same thing. "The Commander."

Yelena met his gaze. "Owen is proof that the Commander lied to the Sitian Council about executing the magician four

MARIA V. SNYDER

years ago. He'd want to erase all the evidence that connects them, including all Owen's coconspirators."

Janco added another log to the fire. "But the Sitians know Owen's alive and producing Curare for the Commander."

"There's no proof the Commander has Curare and, as long as Owen isn't captured, it's only our word that he's still alive."

"That should be good enough." Janco puffed out his chest.

"The Commander can say we must have mistaken Ben for his brother. He can order you, Valek and Onora to keep quiet. In the political world and without any hard evidence, the Council can't do anything."

Interesting theory. "Are you saying the Commander hired another assassin to kill Ben and the others?" he asked Yelena, wondering if she suspected Onora of assassinating them. Not that she'd suggest it in front of the girl; nor did she glance in Onora's direction.

"I'm not accusing him. I'm just speculating. But if he wishes to keep the relationship between Ixia and Sitia civil, he would need Owen to disappear forever."

"He went to a lot of trouble to get all that Curare," Janco said. "I don't think he's worried about being civil."

The rest of the evening passed without incident. When Yelena woke him for his watch shift, lines of strain marked her face.

Concerned, he sat up. "What's wrong? Do you need something for the pain?" He kept his voice low so he wouldn't wake the others.

"I already dipped into Leif's goody bag," she whispered.

"That bad?"

She waved off his comment, which meant it had been bad and she didn't want to worry him. Too late. He'd never *not* worry about her.

Yelena settled next to him. "I've been thinking about Owen. He's too smart to hire a couple of locals to transport the Curare vine from the hothouse to the river. Locals get curious, ask questions, gossip in the taverns. All things he avoided. Otherwise we would have gotten wind of his operation before."

"You think he paid the brothers to bring us out here? Pretend they didn't remember everything?"

"Yes."

It made sense. "We knew it was a risk coming here."

She agreed, but something was off. He studied her. Her movements were stiff, and she held herself as if she'd break. His own cuts throbbed, so he could only imagine how much more pain she was in. Despite that, he sensed another problem.

"You liked them," he said.

A brief, wan smile. "Yes. And, even though I didn't completely trust them, I relaxed and wanted to believe they were genuine. Did you know they lied?"

"I suspected, but thought finding one of the glass houses was worth the risk."

"I know I should trust no one, but...it's exhausting."

Ah. The real reason for the melancholy. "You've been relying on your magic to assess people you meet and now that's blocked, so you're at a loss and probably second-guessing yourself. Right?"

She nodded.

"Then I'll teach you how to read body language. Most people give themselves away when they're lying."

"Most people?"

"I've only encountered a few who can lie to me." Eventually, he would discover the ruse, but, at the time, they'd convinced him.

"Who?" she asked.

"The Commander. Onora. The others are…gone."

She arched an eyebrow. "Gone?"

"I don't like being fooled."

"And the Commander?"

Valek glanced at Onora. Curled up on her side, she appeared to be asleep. "The Commander's lying is a more… recent event."

"But he didn't tell you about Owen."

"Oh, he's kept things from me before, but he's never looked me in the eye and lied."

"What changed?" she asked.

What indeed? "I suspect a few things."

"Such as?"

"Not here, love. Janco's far more interested in our conversation than his dreams."

"Am not," Janco said, not in the least embarrassed he'd been caught eavesdropping. "Besides, I don't have dreams, I have nightmares."

Before Janco could launch into a detailed description, Valek said, "Then we'll let you get back to them." He stood to allow Yelena to take his place under the blankets.

She untied his short cape and handed it to him. They'd have to buy her a new cloak to use during their trip to Ixia. Once there, she could reclaim her own cloak and give the new one to Reema. Too bad she didn't have it with her before. The special resistant fabric of her garment would have stopped many of the smaller shards of glass.

Valek added a few logs to the dying fire. The air had grown quite cold. Then he moved away from the light, letting his eyes adjust to the darkness. He did a sweep of the surroundings and, when he was satisfied no one lurked nearby, Valek found a spot to watch over the camp until dawn.

When the sun rose, he woke the others. Janco grumbled.

Onora said nothing as usual. Yelena sat up and winced, pressing a hand to her side. Valek insisted she drink a cup of Leif's wet-dog tea. He checked her bandages. With a bit of sleight of hand, he rubbed a couple drops of the watered-down Curare along her injuries before applying fresh bandages.

"I saw that," she said.

"No, you didn't." When she opened her mouth to protest, he said, "We have a long day ahead of us."

They packed up and headed northeast, returning to follow the Sunworth River. At the first decent-sized town, Valek sent a message to Leif, warning him of the booby trap inside the glass houses while Yelena informed the local security forces about the dead gardener.

As they continued east, Janco asked him, "Are we going to keep searching for more of those hothouses?"

"No. Owen's probably cleaned them all out. We'll let Leif and Devlen hunt for the rest of them. We need to rendezvous with my team and locate that other tunnel into Ixia." His team had expected him days ago, and he'd have to eventually report his detour to the Commander. At least they had collapsed the hidden tunnel located near Lapeer. Owen had been making a tidy profit by allowing smugglers to use his tunnels for a fee. Valek loved it when criminals turned greedy. It made his job of catching them so much easier.

"Then we should cross to the north side of the river," Janco suggested. "The other tunnel was on that side near the Ixian border."

"Ari said they traced the smugglers to the foothills of the Soul Mountains. We can travel faster on the road than in the forest." Valek considered. The intel from Ari and his corps had only pinpointed one location. Janco had discovered the Lapeer tunnel by accident. It might be possible there were more. "Actually, you—"

"Don't say it," Yelena said.

Affronted, Janco asked her, "Would it kill you to give a guy a bit of praise?"

"If that guy is you, then yes. Humility is not one of your personality traits."

"You're just mad because now we're going to travel through the woods, which means sleeping on the ground and not in an inn."

"I can handle it better than you. Your joints crack and pop every time you stand up, old man."

"Old man! I'm only seven years older than you."

"Are you sure it's not seven *dog* years? You have a lot of gray in your muzzle," Yelena quipped, referring to Janco's salt-and-pepper goatee.

"Every single one of these gray hairs is directly linked back to saving you or being involved in one of your schemes."

"Oh no, you don't. I distinctly remember the time…"

Valek ignored the rest of their bickering. Usually Yelena avoided verbally sparring with Janco, but, by the glint in her eyes, she enjoyed needling their friend.

Instead, Valek concentrated on the terrain along the northern bank of the Sunworth River. Not far from their location, the waterway turned southeast and became the actual border between Ixia and Sitia near the Soul Mountains. There wouldn't be any bridges along that segment. Plus, the forest had been cut down for a hundred feet past the bank, so anyone attempting to cross the border at that point would be seen by the Ixian patrolmen. Which was why the tunnels worked so well.

When the Commander closed the border after the takeover, he cleared the land from the Sunset Ocean in the west all the way to the mountains in the east. Valek doubted Owen would build a tunnel in the open area between the countries or under the river. Which meant that the only logical place for a tunnel would be in the foothills of the Soul Mountains.

"We'll keep to the road," Valek said, interrupting one of Janco's rants. "Speed is vital at this point."

"And beds," Janco added.

Valek gave him a flat stare.

"Nothing wrong with that." Janco thumped his stomach. "Better sleep means a better response to danger. We've no idea what nasties are lurking in that tunnel."

"Hate to say this, but Janco has a point." Yelena grimaced as he puffed his chest out. "Owen knows you're searching for the tunnels. He booby-trapped the glass house, so it makes sense that he'd rig the tunnel, as well." She gestured to Janco. "We can send him in first since he's the Master Illusion Detector."

Air hissed as Janco's chest deflated. "Me?"

"Yes, you. Weren't you just boasting that—"

Valek spurred Onyx into a gallop. If Yelena had the energy to tease Janco, then she'd be okay for another couple of hours and they could reach the next town by nightfall.

They rendezvoused with Valek's team two days later in a mining camp located in the foothills just a mile inside Ixia. The small unit had spent the extra time searching for signs of the tunnel without success.

"Have you heard from Bravo team?" Valek asked Ivon, Alpha team's leader.

The wiry man snapped to attention. "Yes, sir. Qamra sent a message four days ago. Her team located two warehouses used by the smugglers in MD-5 and burned them to the ground as ordered."

Interesting. Ari had found only one. "And her assessment?"

"At the time of the missive, she was unable to confirm if

General Ute had any knowledge or involvement in the operation. Her plans were to continue the investigation."

"Very good."

Ivon's steel-gray gaze never wavered from Valek's face. Very little slipped past the man's notice. "I'm sorry we were unable to be as effective, sir."

"No need to apologize. Show me where the trail ended."

"Yes, sir." Ivon unrolled a map marked with the place Ari had identified and handed it to Valek.

The spot was about a mile east. The map also indicated the locations Ivon's team had checked. Valek planned to leave Yelena in the camp with Onora nearby, protecting her. Smudges of exhaustion darkened the area under Yelena's green eyes. The fast pace hadn't been conducive to healing.

However, in order for Yelena to agree to his plan, he'd have to choose his words with the utmost care. "No need for all of us to go traipsing around. Janco and I will home in on any magical illusions that might be hiding wagon tracks or the entrance and we'll return once we find it so we can go over options."

"I'm pretty sure there'll only be two," Janco said. "Enter or cover the entrance with a bunch of rocks. Frankly, I'd vote for just blocking the damn thing. No reason to go inside."

"Unless that's where Owen is hiding," Yelena said.

"Even more reason to collapse it."

"Why would he hide inside when he knows we're searching for it?" Onora asked.

Valek met Yelena's gaze. Was she remembering the time they had hidden inside a dungeon? She smiled. That would be a yes.

"Sometimes the best places to hide are the most obvious," she said. "Owen's smart. He knows Valek has orders to put the tunnel out of commission and blocking the entrance is the easiest way. Why look inside? And don't forget Tyen can move those boulders with his magic."

"Lovely." Janco scratched the scar where the bottom half of his right ear used to be. "And what happens if they are hiding there? Let's face it. Between Owen's ability to trap Valek, Rika confusing us with her illusions and Tyen tossing boulders at us, we're fu…er…outmatched."

Valek agreed. Head-to-head, *outmatched* didn't even begin to describe it. However… "The trick is to avoid detection."

"And how exactly do we do that?" Janco asked.

"Carefully. Come on, it's getting late. I want to cover as much ground as possible before the sun sets." Valek consulted the map.

"How can my team aid you, sir?" Ivon asked.

"Talk to the locals and the miners. See if anyone noticed or heard anything that might point us in the right direction."

"Yes, sir." Ivon called to his men.

"What about us?" Onora asked.

"Find a place in the camp where we can set up and make sure the horses have a comfortable spot."

"Busywork," Yelena said. "I know what you're doing."

"You do?"

"Feigning innocence doesn't work on me." She waved a hand. "Don't worry. I'm not going to insist on accompanying you. You're right. I'd be useless for this mission."

"That's not the reason." He tried to explain, but she strode away.

Onora remained. "I'll keep a close watch on her."

"Good."

She hurried after Yelena.

Janco watched her. "You're trusting her?"

For now. "Why do you ask?"

"That hit on Ben Moon and the others."

MARIA V. SNYDER

Valek waited.

"You're gonna make me say it, aren't you?"

"Yep."

Janco scrunched up his face as if in pain. "The Commander ordered you to shut Owen's entire operation down. It makes sense he ordered his shiny new assassin to do the same thing. It'd be dead easy for Onora to make it appear as if The Mosquito was the culprit. And you already know all this, don't you?"

Valek kept his expression neutral, but he was impressed. "I thought Ari was supposed to be the smart one."

"Yeah, well, he isn't here, so I gotta do all the thinking. And I'm not happy about, either. It makes my head hurt."

Valek and Janco spent the rest of the day hunting for the familiar sticky feel of magic in the foothills. They returned late and left early the next morning to resume the search. Another two full days passed before Janco stopped Beach Bunny.

He pressed his hand to his right ear. "Son of a snow cat!"

"You're not thinking again, are you?" Valek drew next to Janco, halting Onyx.

"Not funny. It's gotta be a superstrong illusion."

Valek dismounted. "Which direction?"

Janco pointed to the right. Nothing appeared out of the ordinary. The bare branches of the trees dipped and swayed in a cold northern breeze that smelled of snow, despite it being a couple weeks into the warming season. High, thin clouds filtered the sunlight.

Valek pulled his sword. Janco slid off Beach Bunny and yanked his weapon from its sheath. The rattle and tumble of dried leaves filled the air. This patch of forest grew in a dip in the rolling terrain near the base of the Soul Mountains. To the east, the jagged snowcapped peaks stretched high, like a row of gigantic corn plants reaching for the sun.

The mountain range earned its name from old legends. Folklore claimed the peaks snagged souls as they ascended toward the sky. These trapped souls haunted the frozen heights and sucked the life from anyone who dared climb past the tree line. Valek believed it to be just a story to explain why no one who tried to reach the summit ever returned. The lack of breathable air was the more likely explanation. Although some also asserted that mysterious people who supposedly lived on the other side of the mountains patrolled the upper regions to prevent anyone from crossing into their homeland, keeping their existence a secret.

Pure nonsense. Valek returned his attention to the task at hand. He hadn't expected Owen's tunnel to be this high in the foothills, but the isolated location was ideal.

Janco aimed for an ordinary group of trees and hissed in pain as he disappeared from sight. Increasing his pace, Valek hurried after him and encountered magic. The invisible force pressed against his skin. Pushing through felt like swimming in mud. He found Janco rubbing his temple on the other side. Valek scanned the area for possible threats. Nothing so far.

A mass of oversize boulders was piled next to a hill. At first glance, it resembled a natural rock slide from the mountains, but upon closer inspection the heap was too neatly stacked. It must be blocking the tunnel.

"Looks like someone beat us to it," Valek said.

"No." Janco's voice strained with effort. "Move closer."

He did. The air thickened. Another illusion. "Clever." It would stop the smugglers from using it, but it kept the tunnel open in case Owen needed it again in the future.

"Could be a trap."

"Indeed." Valek tightened his grip on his sword and drew

a knife with his free hand. "I'm just going to confirm there's a tunnel behind it."

Janco straightened. "Then I'll come confirming with you, just in case."

The pressure on his body increased with each step. Janco paled when they reached the authentic-looking rocks. Even knowing it wasn't real, Valek braced for impact as he strode right into the pile. He muscled through the magic.

No one ambushed them. The tunnel's entrance was empty. Valek crept inside a few feet and listened for any noises that would indicate people were farther inside. No sounds bubbled up from the solid darkness.

Wagon wheel ruts warped the ground just past the opening. Janco drew in a deep breath. Relief smoothed his features and he crouched down to inspect the marks, running his fingers along the smooth grooves.

"How old?" Valek asked.

"Eight to ten days."

"Probably the last smugglers before Rika set the illusion."

"Now what?"

"Return to camp and discuss the next step."

"How about we inform the Sitian authorities and let them deal with it? After all, they have all those magicians," Janco suggested.

"That's one option."

They mounted their horses and headed back to camp. It was late afternoon by the time they arrived. Valek slowed Onyx. A number of people milled about the camp. More than he'd expected. Concern for Yelena pulsed in his chest until he rec-ognized Ivon.

"Report," he ordered his lieutenant.

"We've been talking to the other mining camps, sir. Two of them had a significant amount of food stolen from their stores."

"And why is this relevant?"

Ivon snapped his fingers and signaled one of his men, who dashed away. "A witness caught sight of the culprits."

An uneasy sensation brushed his stomach. He met Janco's gaze.

"Can't be good," Janco said.

Ivon's sergeant approached with a grubby teen boy wearing a torn miner's jumpsuit. The all-black material had a row of green diamond shapes down each sleeve, indicating the miner worked for MD-5.

"Tell Adviser Valek what you told me, Lewin," Ivon ordered the teen.

Under the coating of dust, the young man's face drained of color. Lewin stared at Valek as if he peered into the mouth of a dragon just about to eat him. "Um…uh…it was the… the middle of the night and I was on the…the way to the latrine," Lewin stuttered. "I heard voices ar…arguing near the supply shed, so I crept up tr…trying not to make noise, but I couldn't see nobody." He rubbed his chin with his sleeve. "Yet the…the voices kept at it as if there were a couple of invisible ghosts." Lewin glanced around as if expecting them to tell him he was crazy.

No one said a word. Valek's unease turned sharp, jabbing his guts. "Go on," he urged Lewin.

"There's been lots of ac…activity around here and weird… stuff. So I followed the voices to the…the edge of the camp. And…" He shuddered. "Three people step…stepped from the air. Bulging sacks floated behind them. They con…continued into the woods, heading west. I found out later the stores had been raided."

Valek and Janco exchanged another glance.

"I hate it when I'm right," Janco said.

"Can you describe them?" Valek asked Lewin.

MARIA V. SNYDER

"Yes, sir. Two men and one lady."

Valek tightened his grip on Onyx's reins. "Did you see their faces?"

"Yes, sir." Lewin described the thieves.

Janco cursed under his breath.

"Anything else?" Valek asked, almost hoping the answer was no.

Lewin scuffed his boot in the dirt. "Yeah. Their uniforms. They wo…wore the Commander's colors."

The information rendered Janco speechless. However, Valek knew Janco would say *holy snow cats*. If Valek considered the bright side, at least they knew where Owen, Rika and Tyen were. Too bad they were in Ixia and appeared to be heading toward the Commander.

6

LEIF

"Nope, haven't seen anything like that before. Good day." The glassmaker hustled Leif from his shop, closing the door right behind him.

At least he didn't slam it, Leif thought. He wiped the sweat from his brow with the back of his hand. Between the heat pumping from the glass factory's brick walls and the unseasonably hot afternoon sun, his tunic was soaked. Leif returned the small square of glass with the miniature holes to his pack. He'd cut a couple of pieces from the glass house's ceiling for him and Devlen to take along and show to the glassmakers.

He scanned the street. A few people walked along the row of factories and businesses in Whitestone's small downtown. Over the past nine days they'd been checking with every glass factory and workshop in ever-widening arcs from Owen's farmhouse. They hadn't been back there in the past four days, and Leif planned to return after this stop. There hadn't been any messages from Yelena, and that worried him.

Whitestone was located two days southeast and about a half day from the border with the Cloud Mist's lands.

Devlen rounded the corner. Hard to miss the tall Sandseed among the paler Moons.

"Any luck?" Leif asked when his brother-in-law drew closer.

"No. You?"

"Think I've found something."

"Oh?"

"Guy in there showed me the door faster than I could eat a slice of apple pie."

"That is an impressive amount of speed," Devlen agreed.

"And he smelled like black licorice."

"Which you do not like."

"Not at all." He'd always hated it. The candy tasted of fear and deceit.

"Shall we go talk to him again?" Devlen asked.

"Thought you'd never ask."

They entered the thick air. Five kilns roared, masking the sounds of the glassworkers who sat at benches and shaped the molten slugs of glass gathered onto the end of their pontil irons. Assistants scurried, fetching tools, cracking off pieces and filling the annealing ovens to cool the piping-hot glass slowly. The open windows did nothing to dispel the force of the heat.

The older man Leif had spoken with earlier directed the traffic, but once he spotted them he hustled over with a scowl. The spicy scent of red pepper burned the inside of Leif's nostrils. Anger had replaced the man's fear.

"Get out," he shooed. "I've no time for your nonsense. I've orders to fill."

"This will not take long." Devlen projected his voice through the noise. "Your office." When the man hesitated, he leaned closer and said, "Now."

The man bolted for an open door to the left. Nice. And it'd been the reason Leif waited for Devlen before confronting the lying glassmaker. They followed close behind. Leif shut the door on the din.

The neat and utilitarian office lacked personality. No pictures hung on the walls. No decorative glass lined the shelves.

Devlen laid his square sample on the desk.

The glassmaker jabbed a finger at it. "I've told you—"

"Look again," Leif said. "Closer this time."

The man huffed with annoyance and picked it up, pretending to inspect the piece. A fog of black licorice almost gagged Leif. The man was terrified.

"The person who ordered those panels is no longer a threat," Leif said in his most soothing tone, letting his magic mix with the words. "We've halted his operations and are in the process of determining how extensive it is."

"We who?" he asked.

"Me, Leif Zaltana and my colleague, Devlen Sandseed."

The man's fear eased only a fraction. Leif would have been insulted, but unfortunately he'd dealt with Owen and understood just how much of a scary bastard the magician could be. And with the size of this operation, Owen couldn't erase all the staff's memories—too many people.

"Also the Sitian Council and the Master Magicians," Leif added.

"Have you arrested him?" the man asked.

"Not yet. He's on the run, but every city and town has been alerted and he'll be caught soon." Leif hoped.

"Then he remains a threat."

"I'll order the local security forces keep a close watch on you—"

"Not me. My family."

Typical. At least Owen stayed consistent. "Your family, then."

"And in exchange?"

"A list of locations where you delivered those special glass panels."

The silence stretched and Leif sensed a variety of emotions. The bitter tang of fear dominated.

Finally, the man pulled open a drawer and rummaged through the files. He handed Leif a stack of papers. Leif scanned the pages and counted enough panels to construct at least ten glass houses. Delivery dates and locations had been written on the orders. The closest one was about a day's ride west. The others were scattered north and east, up toward the Sunworth River.

"Can I keep these?" Leif asked.

"Yes."

"Thank you. I'll inform Captain Ozma of the situation right away. We talked to her this morning and none of her forces have seen anyone matching Owen's description in this area."

The man's relief smelled of sweet grass. "Good."

They left and stopped by the security offices. Captain Ozma sent a detail to the glass factory to collect more information.

Leif studied the sky. "We won't be able to reach the closest hothouse today, but, if we leave now, we can make it to the town of Marble Arch in time for supper."

"Let me guess, there is an inn there that serves some type of delectable dish that you cannot find anywhere else." Devlen's tone rasped with smugness.

"Wrong, Mr. Know-It-All! It's a *tavern*, not an inn."

"A thousand apologies."

"Can you say that again without the sarcasm?"

"No."

They had stabled their horses in the guards' barn. Devlen had picked a sturdy cream-colored horse with a dark brown mane and tail. She had lovely russet eyes and she watched Devlen's every move. Leif had teased him that it was love at first sight. Devlen named her Sunfire, which was a heck of a lot better than Beach Bunny.

Mounting the horses, they headed east and, as predicted, they sat at a table in the corner of the Daily Grind tavern just in time for supper.

"Lots of stone carvers come here." Leif explained the name to Devlen. "Marble and granite fill this whole area of the Moon Clan's lands. These people earn their living either quarrying it from the ground or chiseling, shaping and grinding it for use."

A server approached and Leif ordered without consulting Devlen. "Two ales and two extra-large portions of pit beef, please."

"Pit beef? Sounds…unappetizing," Devlen said.

"Have I ever *steered* you wrong?"

Devlen groaned. "You have been spending too much time with Janco."

While they waited for the food, Leif spread out the pages they'd received from the glassmaker and they marked the locations of all the glass houses on a map.

"My father will be here in roughly five days." Leif traced a route with his finger. "We have enough time to check three of them on the way back to the farmstead."

Late-morning sunlight glinted off the glass panes of the hothouse. Leif stopped Rusalka before drawing too close. No need to tip anyone off that they were nearby. The long, thin structure sat in the middle of an open clearing along with a small wooden building. Forest surrounded the complex. This was the first of the three they planned to check on their return to Owen's ex-headquarters.

From this angle, it seemed as if the place was deserted. No greenery stained the inside of the glass house and, after an hour of observation, no one appeared.

Devlen returned from doing a reconnaissance. "Nothing. All's quiet."

"Suspiciously quiet?" Leif asked.

"No. Abandoned quiet."

They ventured closer. Leif tasted the wind, seeking the flavors of past intentions. He drew in deep breaths, sensing the echoes of emotions. The trees rustled and the dry grass crackled under Rusalka's hooves. Otherwise, all remained undisturbed.

Peering through the glass of the house, Leif confirmed that nothing grew inside. A crate filled with an assortment of objects sat in the center.

"Perhaps there is information in the box," Devlen said next to him. He strode to the entrance.

Leif followed. When Devlen opened the door, stale musty air puffed out. They entered.

"Looks like they yanked the plants in a hurry," Leif said. He bent to grab a handful of soil, testing the moisture. He freed a root that had been left behind. It was brittle. "It's been about two weeks since this place was in use."

"That fits the timeline," Devlen said. He knelt next to the crate.

"There's...something...off." Leif wiped the dirt from his hands.

Devlen paused. "Off?"

"I can't pinpoint it. It's...subtle." Leif joined his brother-in-law. "Is there anything in there of value?"

Devlen reached into the box.

"Malice," Leif said. "That's what's off. The air is tainted with malice."

"Considering Owen was in here, I am not surprised." Devlen pulled a broken shovel and tossed it aside. He dumped the rest of the contents—mostly old gardening tools.

"Let's check the other building," Leif said, exiting the glass house.

The oversize wooden barn door gaped open.

Leif halted. "The air reeks of death. And there's nothing subtle about that."

"I smell it, too."

They exchanged a glance. Leif yanked his machete from his belt and Devlen brandished his scimitar. Devlen eased the door wider and signaled him. Leif held his breath and crept inside with the Sandseed right behind. Dim sunlight trickled through the dusty windows. The large single room contained furniture and gardening supplies and a dead body.

Leif cursed aloud. Then he gagged on the rotten stench. "Check." He motioned to search the room. "Quick." Covering his nose with his hand, he took the right side while Devlen went left.

Not much to see. An old frayed couch, a couple chairs and a desk. Although the stack of files piled on top might be interesting. Leif sheathed his machete. He opened the first file.

A loud *pop* sounded. The sharp, acrid smell of malice sliced right through death's foul odor. Inside the file was a single piece of paper.

"Run," Leif yelled, just as a whoosh vibrated through the air.

The barn's walls ignited. Flames ripped up the sides, surrounding them.

7

YELENA

One look at Valek's hard expression and I braced for bad news. He didn't disappoint. Unfortunately. "Are you certain it was Owen and the others?" I asked Valek. "It was dark and the boy is very young." The thought of Owen in Ixia coiled like a snake in the pit of my stomach.

Onora and I had been relaxing by the campfire when Valek and Janco returned from searching for the tunnel. They'd found it, but also learned one of the teen miners had reported spotting three strangers that had appeared right out of thin air the same night his camp's food stores had been raided.

"It's not a hundred percent, but it makes the most sense," Valek said, sitting next to me. He held his hands close to the fire, warming them.

"Why did Lewin see them at all?" Janco plopped down between me and Onora. "That Rika chick should be hiding them behind an illusion all the time. That's what I'd do if I were her."

"It's difficult to maintain an illusion when the subject is in motion," I explained. "The magician has to constantly adjust it to match the surroundings. It's exhausting. While something static, like covering the mouth of the cave with an illusionary rockfall, is much easier."

"But what keeps it going?" Onora placed the cook pot on the fire, reheating the beef stew the cook from the miner's camp brought over for supper. "Once the magician leaves, shouldn't the illusion dissipate?"

"In most cases, the illusion disappears," I said. "However, some magicians can loop the magic back to the power blanket. This loop keeps the illusion intact by drawing power from the source. Booby traps work in a similar fashion, except when one is triggered, it connects to the source to fuel the trap and then disintegrates. There's no loop."

"Yeah, yeah, this is all very fascinating," Janco said, "but why would Owen even be in Ixia? The Commander is angry at him for getting too greedy. His best play is to lie low in Sitia."

"Owen claimed he has something that would make the Commander forgive him," I said, remembering that smug, cocky tone he'd used. And now that I thought about it… "Makes sense for him to want to reach the Commander before Valek reports in. He can spin his story, skewing it in his favor."

"Or he can just use his evil mojo and put the Commander under a spell." Janco waggled his fingers.

That wasn't quite how it worked, but Janco had a good point. I met Valek's gaze. "When were they spotted?"

"Three nights ago, and they're on foot," he said.

If they wished to keep a low profile, they would avoid riding horses. In Ixia, only generals and top-ranking advisers rode horses. Merchants used them to pull their wagons, but everyone else walked.

"If we leave now, we can easily catch up," I said, gesturing to Kiki and the others grazing nearby.

"Yeah, but can we stop them?" Janco rubbed his ear. A

queasy expression creased his face. "Leif's not here to make those null thingies that protect us from their magic."

"We have Curare, darts and blowpipes. As long as they don't suspect we're close, we can incapacitate them," Valek said.

"Can we find them?" Onora asked.

Janco huffed in annoyance. "Of course we can track them. That won't be a problem. If they cover their tracks with illusions, Valek and I can sniff out their magic, and I can follow them if they don't. No, the real problem will be if they can sense us coming."

Everyone turned to me. I considered Owen's magical powers. Back when Owen had coerced me into helping him search for the Ice Moon in the MD-3 mines, he had failed to locate Valek's hiding place on the ceiling.

"Owen can't, but I'm not certain about Rika and Tyen," I said. "Many magicians don't reveal all their powers. They like to keep one or two hidden from public knowledge so they have an advantage."

"Not helping, Yelena," Janco said.

"Owen's been one step ahead of us the entire time," Onora said.

"That's what happens when he has a six-day head start," Janco snapped.

She pressed her lips together and shot him a nasty glare. Onora wasn't the type to state the obvious, so I sensed there was more.

"What are you thinking?" I asked her.

"They argued while stealing food and under a cloak of illusion. That's just stupid. Owen's many things, but he's not stupid."

Valek nodded in agreement. "You think he wanted the boy to see them?"

"Yes, so he can lead us into another booby trap," she said.

Sounded like Owen. "Do we follow the bread crumbs or dash ahead and set our own trap?"

"How far ahead?" Valek asked.

"The castle?" Janco suggested.

"That's dangerously close to the Commander," Onora said.

"Yeah, but it's our home territory. Nobody knows it as well as *we* do." Janco thumped his chest. "And there are a gazillion soldiers there to protect the Commander."

"Yet we're just guessing that they're heading to the castle. The red and black colors on their uniforms could be a diversion," Onora said.

As they discussed options, I mulled it over. Why else would Owen be in Ixia? To hide from the Sitian authorities. Possible, but Ixia kept a close watch on its citizens, making it difficult to blend in and disappear. Owen had managed to avoid execution before; he must believe he could do it again in order to risk the journey. I knew Owen the best, so I put myself in his boots and contemplated the problem.

"Owen's heading to the castle," I said, stopping the discussion.

"Then we need to beat him there," Janco said.

"They're on foot. How long will it take them to reach the castle?" I asked him.

"On foot, it would take about ten days to get there from here."

"With their head start, they'll be there in seven days," Valek said.

"And it will take us five days on horseback. Is two days enough time to prepare?" I asked, already worried about it.

"It should be plenty of time. Plus if they're planting booby traps, using magic to cover their tracks and avoiding detection, it'll take them longer than seven days." Valek lifted the pot's lid and stirred the stew with a spoon.

MARIA V. SNYDER

A puff of steamy goodness wafted up. My stomach grumbled in response. It was nice to have an appetite for a change, but I wondered how long it would last before another bout of queasiness swelled. The nausea came and went, but was never bad enough to make me vomit. Thank fate.

Valek ladled stew into the bowls and passed them around the fire. Every day it was harder to ignore my sensitive stomach. By now, I was four weeks late. Hard to pin the delay on stress when I'd just spent most of the past two days resting. And what would I feel if it was confirmed? I shied away from those thoughts. Too scary.

Instead, I decided to wait until we reached the castle to indulge in any more speculation. Once there, I'd visit the medic and seek advice. Lots of advice.

"When do we leave?" But then Janco waved his hands at Valek in a stopping motion. "Don't say it."

"At dawn."

He groaned. "I told you not to say it!"

No one talked while we ate. When we finished the stew, we prepared to turn in early. Valek insisted on checking my cut. The wound remained painful to the touch and throbbed if I made any big movements, but there weren't any signs of infection. He changed the bandage, then pointed to my bedroll. An unspoken order.

Despite my initial annoyance that he'd left me at camp while he and Janco searched for the tunnel, I had to admit the downtime helped restore some of my energy, which I would need for the next five long days in the saddle. I lay down facing the fire.

"What's the watch schedule?" Onora asked.

"I've assigned Ivon and his men to patrol the camp. We all could use a full night's sleep." Valek joined me, spooning in behind and covering us both with the blanket. He draped his arm over my shoulder.

Ah. My favorite time of the day. I snuggled closer. "What are they going to do once we leave?" I asked.

"Continue investigating and track down any smugglers who used the tunnel before Owen and his companions blocked it with the illusion."

A good plan, but what if they found more than they bargained for? I remembered the brothers, Tex and Jax, and how they might have been planted by Owen. What if Lewin was, as well?

"What if Owen is still nearby?" I whispered to Valek, clutching the blanket. Ivon and his men wouldn't stand a chance against the three magicians.

"He's not. Stop second-guessing yourself." Valek kept his voice low, as well.

Easy to say, so hard to do. "I just don't want anyone else to get hurt."

"Unfortunately, that's not going to happen. But it's not your fault or mine. *Owen* is responsible for his own actions," Valek said.

Again the logic made sense, but my heart failed to agree.

Valek smoothed my hair away from my face. "What's really bothering you, love?"

"That we won't be able to stop him. That he teams up with the Commander and…" Horrible scenarios bubbled, but one stood out.

"And?"

"And the Commander orders you to execute me." When the Commander had written my execution order eight years ago, he hadn't given it to Valek. If he had, Valek would have killed me. No doubt. His loyalty to the Commander was absolute. And I understood and have accepted it.

MARIA V. SNYDER

"It's highly unlikely."

I turned to face him. "But not impossible."

He met my gaze with an unwavering intensity. "Then it will be the first time I've disobeyed a direct order." His words a promise.

That was new. Warmth spread throughout my chest, and it wasn't because of the fire.

We reached a travel shelter after three exhausting days on the road. The horses had set the pace and we arrived near midnight—a half day ahead of schedule. Sweat stained Kiki's copper coat and her sides heaved with the effort. She'd adjusted her gait, keeping my ride smooth. Even without our magical link, Kiki had known each stride sent a jolt of pain through my side.

Onora and I walked the horses to cool them down while Valek and Janco checked the area around the small wooden building for magical booby traps. After signaling the all-clear, they entered the structure.

They returned in no time and joined us.

"All's quiet," Valek said. "There's a couple travelers from MD-2 sleeping, but there's not a whiff of magic anywhere nearby."

The Snake Forest surrounded the shelter on three sides. The fourth side faced the wide fields of cotton and flax plants. The rich soil and weather was ideal for growing both, and with their overabundance of sheep, MD-5 produced and dyed all the thread for the Territory of Ixia. The skeins were then sent to MD-3 to be woven into fabric.

"Let's take care of the horses and get some sleep. I'll take first watch. Onora second, and Janco third," Valek ordered.

"And I'll take fourth," I said.

He frowned, but kept quiet.

The stable next to the shelter had room for six horses. The straw smelled musty, and I hoped no critters had nested inside it. We filled water buckets from the well, removed tack and groomed our horses, all in silence. No one had the energy to talk.

When we finished, we headed into the shelter. The one room contained two rows of bunk beds along the walls on the left side, and a large stone hearth with chairs ringed around it on the right. We found three empty bunks next to each other and away from the two occupied ones close to the hearth.

Valek sat on the edge of mine and tucked me in. He'd always been protective, but on this trip, he seemed overly concerned. Perhaps he shared my worries about Owen and the Commander. Right now I was too tired to ask him.

Instead, I wrapped my arms around his neck, trapping him when he swooped in for a quick kiss good-night. Might as well take advantage of the extra attention. I deepened the kiss.

He broke away. "No fair, love."

I acted innocent. "I'd thought you could use a little extra warmth before you went out into the cold night air."

"You mean the cold *lonely* night?"

"You set the watch schedule. I'd be more than happy to work in teams."

He raised an eyebrow. "You would?"

"Yes, you know how much I enjoy Janco's company."

"Ouch. I walked right into that one, didn't I?"

I smirked my best Janco impression. "Yes, love."

My turn on watch arrived in what felt like a matter of minutes. I had a vague memory of Valek sliding under the blanket, but otherwise nothing until Janco poked me on the shoulder. Movement jolted me wide-awake as Valek brandished a knife.

"It's me," Janco whispered, jumping back.

MARIA V. SNYDER

"Sorry," Valek mumbled before turning over and taking the blanket with him. The knife remained in his hand.

The cold air rushed in and I fumbled for the gray cloak we'd purchased at a Sitian market near the border.

I joined Janco outside. "Anything?"

"Nope. It's been quiet."

I peered into the darkness that wasn't as black as it should be. Predawn light seeped in through the edges of the world. "You didn't wake me early enough."

He shrugged. "It's such a beautiful night, I lost track of time."

"Did Valek order—"

"No, but if you're going to take a watch shift, maybe you shouldn't share a bed with a superlight sleeper who has fast reflexes and is well armed."

"You're just jealous."

"Damn right I am. Now, if you don't mind, I need my beauty sleep." Janco slipped back inside.

I checked on the horses. They slept in their stalls unperturbed—a good sign. Looping around the buildings, I ensured no one lurked nearby or had set up an ambush. Although my rustlings and crunchings on dead leaves would have alerted anyone within a mile of my presence. I'd taken my magic for granted. Being on watch had been much easier when all I had to do was scan the surroundings with my awareness.

No sense moping about it; I would just need to learn how to move through the forest without scaring away the wildlife. And instead of doing sweeps, I found a perfect spot to watch for movement and to listen for sounds.

Dawn arrived. I fed the horses and inspected them for cuts or hot spots. Kiki nuzzled my ear and tugged on my braid. I didn't need our mental link to know what she desired.

"I only have a few left, and you'll have to share them with the others," I said.

She nudged me toward the tack room.

"All right." I dug in my saddlebags and removed the sack of milk oats. "You're spoiled."

Kiki sucked hers down in one bite. The others crunched on theirs. Good thing the Keep's Stable Master had given me the recipe for Kiki's favorite treat. I didn't know how long I'd be in Ixia. Could be seasons. Had Irys sent me a reply by now? My message about traveling with Valek to Ixia would have reached her last week. Did she think I stayed with him because I was terrified or because I didn't trust her to keep me safe in Sitia? Did I know the answer?

Why did I agree to stay with Valek when Sitia needed me? The Council was probably panicking over the news that the Commander had Curare. No. Not probably. Definitely.

So why wasn't I rushing to the Citadel to do my job and smooth relations between the two countries? And then there was Owen. What could I do to stop him? I'd actually be safer in Sitia.

I thought about it. I'd been in plenty of dangerous situations without Valek. But this time… This time I was vulnerable. The most vulnerable I'd been since I'd been a lab rat for Reyad.

And every time I'd been in mortal peril, Valek had saved me. Not always physically, but even just hearing his voice gave me the strength to stop Owen. When I'd been trapped in the fire world, the thought of never seeing him again motivated me to find a solution.

Besides, what was wrong with being selfish? Someone else could be the Liaison. Someone else could be a target for assassins. I could just be with Valek.

Except… Yeah, that was the kicker. Except, I couldn't. Even

MARIA V. SNYDER

without my powers, I remained in a position to help, and the last thing I wanted was war between Ixia and Sitia. Not when I might have a child. A country at war was no place to raise a child. Eventually, I'd need to return to Sitia.

My courage had scattered on the ground like leaves fallen from the trees. I gathered my bits of mettle, tucking them into my heart. Each one increased my motivation to learn how to survive without my magic. Bonus that the perfect person to teach me also happened to be my heart mate.

The door to the shelter creaked. I turned. Valek strode out into the sunlight. He combed his fingers through his sleep-matted black hair, but his alert gaze scanned the area. His stiff posture relaxed when he spotted me by the horses.

"Any trouble?" he asked.

"No."

"Good."

"Anyone else awake?" I asked.

"The people from MD-2 are packing their bags. Onora and Janco are still asleep. Since we're ahead of schedule, I'm going to find a local patrol, see if they spotted Owen. Can I borrow Kiki?"

She would sense any magical traps. "You have to ask her. And I suggest you bribe her with milk oats."

He smiled. "Sounds like your brother."

As he offered Kiki the treat, I thought of Leif. One good thing about Owen, Rika and Tyen being in Ixia—I didn't have to worry about Leif running into the magicians. I hoped he'd received Valek's message about the booby traps.

What if he didn't?

A vision of shattered glass piercing his body flashed. My stomach rolled with nausea. I swallowed and dismissed the horrible scene. Just my overactive imagination. Leif would smell the trap and not be skewered as I'd been. I hoped.

Kiki allowed Valek to saddle her. But before he left, he drew me close. "What's wrong?"

"I'm concerned about Leif."

"He's quite capable of taking care of himself. And Devlen is with him."

"I know. It's just…" I fisted my hands.

"Just what?"

"It's been forty days since I woke up without my magic. And just when I think I've come to terms with it, or just when I've mustered enough gumption to learn how to live without it, some comment or some incident sets me back, and I realize just how much I lost and it feels like day one again—all raw and new."

Valek embraced me. Winded from my outburst, I rested my head against his chest and breathed in his spicy musk.

"You're frustrated, love, and that's understandable. We'll figure it out one way or another. We always do."

"But—"

"Tell me one mystery we haven't solved."

I searched my memory. About to concede the point, I thought of one. "Onora. Is she friend or foe?" And another I wouldn't voice—*Am I pregnant?*—because I suspected I already knew the answer.

"Too recent. I'm still working on it, but I'm confident I'll know in time. Just like your problem. The solution may be revealed tomorrow, or not for seasons, but it will be. No doubts."

Wrapped tight in Valek's arms, I believed him. But I expected that my doubts would creep back in. For now, though, I allowed hope and his warmth to sink into my bones.

Far too soon, he released me. Valek tucked a loose strand of my hair behind my ear. "I'll be back soon." He kissed me, then mounted Kiki.

She butted my cheek with her muzzle before heading out.

MARIA V. SNYDER

I wiped horse slobber from my face. The shelter door creaked again. Two men, wearing cloaks marked with tan-colored diamond shapes, exited. They glanced at the horses with worried expressions before heading for the road at a fast pace. I wondered if they'd recognized Valek.

When I entered the shelter, Onora was crouched next to the hearth, poking the ashy remains for a sign of life. A small flame erupted and she added logs until flames danced brightly. Pouring water into a pot, she set it near the fire. A cup with a tea bag rested nearby.

"Have I turned you into a tea drinker?" I asked in a low voice as I joined her. Janco remained asleep.

"It's for you."

"Oh?"

"I noticed you drink that ginger tea every morning, so…"

"That's nice. Thank you." Or was it nice? Was she waiting for confirmation that her little stunt had worked? That I needed the tea to soothe my uneasy stomach? I vowed she'd be the last to know.

Onora sliced cheese and bread, assembling breakfast for us. I regretted my harsh thoughts a little. While Valek and Janco searched for the tunnel, she'd taken care of me, letting me sleep and recover my strength. Perhaps she felt guilty? With her it was hard to tell. She said little and we hardly talked, which seemed to suit her just fine. No wonder Janco bugged her so much. I grinned, just thinking about it.

"What's so funny?" Onora poured steaming water into my cup.

"Janco. He's determined to annoy you."

"He's succeeded. Many times." She handed me the tea.

"He's looking for a reaction and for attention. You're like The Madam, unflappable, and that irks him, so he tries hard to…er…flap you."

Onora smiled. The first genuine one I'd seen. It reached her gray eyes and transformed her. The carefree expression was a glimpse of the young girl she used to be before her life soured and turned tragic.

"And ignoring him is the ultimate affront," she said.

Ah. She'd figured him out. "Which is why you do it."

"Exactly." She sobered. "And I am an assassin. Being quiet and still for hours is all part of the job."

"True." I sensed there was more, so I took a risk. "Why did you decide to become an assassin?"

Onora met my gaze. All animation left her face, but uncertainty lurked behind her eyes. I guessed she contemplated what to tell me. The truth or some offhand comment.

She lowered her voice. "I didn't want to be afraid anymore."

That I understood. "And did it work?"

"No one can touch me."

Not quite an answer. I remembered what Valek had said about her past and how she hadn't killed her demons yet.

"Have you faced your fear?"

She scoffed, "Don't you mean, have I assassinated the bastard I was afraid of?"

"No. I know murdering a tormentor doesn't mean the problem is solved."

"Sorry, but I don't agree. Death is the final solution."

"Then you are luckier than me."

"Luckier?" Her voice rose in anger.

"Yes. When I killed Reyad, my problems didn't disappear with his death. He continued to haunt me."

"That's because you're the Soulfinder."

"I wasn't then. Then I was a terrified nineteen-year-old, fearing I'd lost my soul and would always be a victim. Those doubts clung to me until I faced it. And I'm still learning that running away from my fears is never a solution."

"That's you. Not me." She stood up. "I better do a perimeter check." Onora left the shelter.

I'd struck a nerve. Interesting.

Janco crept from a shadow. "She's a tough clam to pry open. I've a feeling, though, once we do, we'll find a pearl."

"Pearls form in oysters."

"Oysters, clams…" He waved dismissively. "It's all seafood. You know what I meant."

I did. Yet, I wasn't as certain about the gem inside the hard exterior.

Valek and Kiki returned after breakfast. We joined him in the stable. "What's the buzz?" Janco asked without preamble.

"No sign of Owen." Valek swung a leg over and dismounted.

"Is that good or bad?" Janco asked.

"You tell me."

Janco paused. "Bad. They could be anywhere. What about the local patrols?"

"They haven't encountered anything unusual in the last couple of days."

Nor had any of the other patrols we'd encountered the past three days. "Maybe Owen hasn't traveled this far yet," I said.

"That's a possibility," Valek agreed. "Are you ready to go?"

We gathered our supplies and mounted. As we traveled, I considered another explanation for no signs of Owen. Perhaps he had used magic to erase the patrolmen's memories. Could he erase memories without Loris and Cilly Cloud Mist's help? I remembered that the three of them had each picked one of us to restructure our memories so we'd forget. Which meant he could. And then it hit me. He'd also mentioned inserting *new* ones.

Then why would he be careless enough to let that miner see him and the others? Why not erase the teen's memories?

I snagged on an idea. "Holy snow cats!"

The others slowed their horses and turned to me, waiting.

I rushed to explain, "That boy, Lewin, said he saw Owen three nights before we talked to him. What if Owen planted that memory and it wasn't really three nights, but longer? In that case, Owen, Rika and Tyen might have reached the Commander by *now*."

8

VALEK

Alarmed, Valek stopped Onyx. The real possibility that Owen and the others had reached the Commander sent an icy pulse through his heart. "Holy snow cats, indeed."

"It's pure conjecture," Onora said.

"Based on Yelena's knowledge of Owen," Valek said.

Kiki moved closer to Onyx, and Yelena put a hand on his shoulder. "I'm sorry I didn't remember about his ability to plant new memories sooner."

He covered her hand with his own and squeezed. "Trying to outguess your enemy is all part of the fun, love."

"Oh, so that's what we've been doing? Having fun? Who knew?" she teased.

"Gee, Valek, you ought to show your girl a better time if she doesn't even know what fun is," Janco said.

"All right," he agreed, getting into the spirit. "Next time, love, I'll take you along on a raid."

"Oh my." Yelena fanned her face with a hand. "Slow down, handsome, or I might swoon from all the excitement."

Even though she smiled, it did nothing to dispel the dark smudges lining her green eyes and her sunken cheeks. She hadn't been eating or sleeping well. But once they reached the castle, he'd ensure she got plenty of both.

"The castle, Kiki. As fast as possible. Please," Yelena said.

He spurred Onyx, following Kiki. Janco and Onora rode close behind him. On horseback, the trip would take two full days if they stopped to sleep, a day and a half if they didn't. The decision would be Kiki's. She understood their desire to hurry while she also knew not to exhaust or injure the horses.

Kiki stopped for water around midnight, and Valek decided they should get a few hours of sleep. Nothing good would come from them arriving at the castle completely drained and useless.

"There should be a patrol west of us," he said to the group. "We can overnight with them. That way we all can sleep."

"Hoorah." Janco pumped his fist.

Kiki found the patrol an hour after midnight. Their unexpected arrival caused a considerable stir, and Valek had to explain and soothe the nerves of the young lieutenant in charge. Another hour passed before they spread their bedrolls.

Teetering on the edge of sleep, Valek was roused by Janco's voice.

"Just for the record, *holy snow cats* is my line," he said. "You need to find your own."

"And you had to tell us this *now*?" Onora grumbled.

"I thought it was important. I don't like people stealing my lines."

"It's a *compliment*, you dolt. Did you ever think of that?"

"No."

"Not quite the boy genius over there. Make sure to put *that* in the record."

With Yelena sleeping in his arms, and Janco trading insults with Onora, Valek enjoyed a moment of peace. He suspected he wouldn't get many more once they reached the castle.

MARIA V. SNYDER

★ ★ ★

The guards at the castle's east gate reported no suspicious activity in the past two weeks. No surprise. If Owen had breached the walls using magic, no one would have spotted him.

After riding all day, the horses needed to be cared for. Yelena and Janco volunteered to take them to the stables while he and Onora checked on the Commander. At this late hour, he had probably retired for the night, but Valek didn't care.

They raced to the Commander's apartment. Two members of his detail stood outside his door.

"It's been quiet, sir," Private Berk said to Valek. "But he's probably still awake."

Valek exchanged a glance with Onora. She held her hands close to her daggers. He knocked on the door and a faint "Come in" sounded. They entered, ready to fight if needed.

The Commander sat in his armchair by the fire, sipping a glass of brandy and still wearing his all-black uniform. A book lay across his lap. No one else was in sight.

Ambrose set the glass down and studied them with his golden gaze. "Where's the emergency?"

"We're hoping not here." Valek strode into the room, seeking magic and scanning for intruders. "Has anything unusual happened? Has anyone been here? Or tried to get in?"

"There's nothing to worry about, Valek. All is well."

Valek paused and stared at the Commander. "I'd still like to—"

"No need. I'm sure you have quite the story to tell, but it's late and I'm in no mood to hear it. Report to the war room first thing tomorrow morning." He glanced at Onora. "Just you, Valek. You're dismissed."

The Commander's complete lack of curiosity about Valek's mission alarmed him along with the comment that there was nothing to worry about. The Commander never believed *all is well*. Ambrose considered relaxing your guard to be something that would be exploited by your enemy in no time. However, Valek couldn't press the issue. Not with Onora standing there.

"Yes, sir," Valek said.

They left and closed the door. Valek remained in the hallway, considering his next move.

"Magic?" Onora asked him with concern.

"Not that I felt."

"Then what's wrong?"

"Everything."

Valek sent Onora to help with the horses and to instruct Janco to complete a perimeter check of the castle, including the barracks, stables, kennels and training areas, seeking magic. If Owen was here, he'd be hiding behind one of Rika's illusions. Valek concentrated on all the interior rooms and halls inside the castle. The odd-shaped structure had more hidden places than a labyrinth. Starting in the dungeon and working his way up, he searched for a stickiness in the air that meant magic was in use.

The air remained clear until Valek encountered a brief touch near the rooms reserved for his officers. He followed the tackiness down the hallway. One lantern remained lit, casting a sickly yellow glow on the gray stone walls. A door jerked open, and Valek yanked his knives from their sheaths.

Ari's six-foot-four-inch frame filled the threshold. He brandished a long dagger, but relaxed when he spotted Valek. "I'll be damned. You were right."

"I was right about what?" Valek asked.

"Not you." Ari stepped aside. "Reema. She said you were creeping around."

Reema poked her head out from behind Ari. Her blond

MARIA V. SNYDER

corkscrew curls fanned her face like a lion's mane. That explained the magic. While no one, not even Master Magician Irys, could pick up on Reema's magic, both Valek and Opal suspected she used it. But it didn't explain the strength. Before, Valek had to be standing right next to her in order to sense her power. That puzzle would have to wait.

"I wasn't creeping. I'm checking for intruders," Valek said.

Ari straightened. "What can I do?"

"Stay with Reema."

The big man pressed his lips together, but kept quiet.

"Are the others back, as well?" Reema asked. "My dad and Janco?"

"Janco and your aunt Yelena are with the horses." Valek crouched down to her level. "Your father didn't come. He's in Sitia with your uncle Leif. You'll have to stay here a little longer."

"Oh." She stared at him a moment. "Does that mean the bad men who are after Aunt Yelena haven't been caught?"

Valek glanced at Ari.

"I didn't tell her," he said.

She huffed. "I'm not stupid."

No, she wasn't. "Yes. And you're safe here. That's why your father wants you to remain with us." Valek hoped.

"Can I see Aunt Yelena?"

"Tomorrow. Right now you need to get back to sleep." Valek followed her into Ari and Janco's quarters, which included two bedrooms and a large living area with couches, armchairs, tables and desks. No need to guess that the one overflowing with papers, books and files was Janco's.

Ari's bedroom door stood ajar and Reema headed toward it. Valek turned to Ari, questioning.

"You ordered me not to let her out of my sight," Ari said. "I brought in another bed for her."

"Good. Has there been anything strange going on?"

Ari ran a meaty hand over his short, curly blond hair. "You mean other than tonight? No. Why?"

"Just checking."

"Come on, Valek, it's me. What's going on?"

"Not now. We'll have a briefing in my office in the afternoon."

"That gives Janco time to tell me all about it from his... unique perspective. Are you sure you want to risk it?"

Valek smiled. "He'll be too tired to tell stories."

Ari laughed. "Janco is never too tired to tell stories."

Valek finished his search of the castle. Not wishing to disturb the advisers and high-ranking officers sleeping, he didn't check inside the rooms. All was quiet in the guest wing, but he touched each door just in case. None of them were sticky with magic. Valek continued ghosting through the hallways, but encountered nothing alarming.

Janco waited for him outside his office. The poor guy sat on the floor, leaning against the hard wooden door, sleeping. Valek nudged him awake with the toe of his boot.

Janco jerked and grabbed the hilt of his sword. "What? Oh." He released his grip and shuffled to his feet.

"Did you find anything?" Valek asked.

"No. No illusions or creepy-crawly magic." He stretched his arms above his head while yawning. "None of the guards saw anything strange or heard voices. Though there was something I wish I didn't see." Janco rubbed his eyes. "Sergeant Falice hooking up with Sergeant Dallin behind the barracks. Yuck."

"Get some sleep. We're meeting here this afternoon."

"Yes, sir." Janco wobbled away.

Valek glanced out the window at the end of the hallway.

About one hour until dawn. He headed to his suite across the hall from the Commander's. Private Berk remained on duty.

"Liaison Yelena is waiting for you inside, sir," Berk said.

"Thank you." Valek entered and closed the door behind him.

Yelena had lit the lanterns ringing the main living area. She'd sprawled on the couch and was fast asleep. He picked her up. She hardly weighed anything. As he carried her upstairs to his bedroom, she muttered a few indecipherable words. Yelena roused a bit when he laid her on the bed.

"Did you…?"

"Sleep, love. We found no signs of Owen."

She patted the space next to her.

"Wish I could." He pulled the blanket over her as he told her about the afternoon meeting. "I'll have the kitchen staff send up a late breakfast for you. I want you to eat it all. Understand?"

"Yes, love."

"That's my line. You'll have to think of something else." He kissed her and left.

Exhaustion dragged on his body like a sopping-wet cloak. Valek stopped at the kitchen for a few bites to eat and to order the tray for Yelena. Sammy, the head chef, promised to send her a huge stack of sweet cakes.

The combination of the food and a cold shower revived him. Dressing in a clean uniform, Valek combed his hair. The wet strands hung past his shoulders. Valek tied it at the base of his neck with a leather string. The Commander had stopped remarking on the length when Valek explained that he might need to go undercover as a female. Since playing Valma, the beautician, had gotten Valek close enough to assassinate the King, the Commander didn't insist Valek buzz it close to his head like all his other male officers and advisers.

Valek arrived outside the Commander's war room just as the sun rose. No surprise the Commander had beaten him there. The man never slept more than five or six hours a night. The two guards nodded at him, but remained silent.

Bracing for the inevitable argument, Valek knocked and entered.

The Commander sat at the head of the large wooden conference table, eating breakfast. His uniform had two real diamonds secured to the collar. Not a wrinkle or crease rumpled his clothing.

A wedge of strengthening sunlight shone through the stained-glass windows that faced east. Colors splashed on the ceiling. The tall, thin windows covered three-quarters of the round room—the Commander's favorite place.

Valek stood at attention.

"Sit down." The Commander gestured to a chair a few places down the table on the left. "Report."

Perched on the edge of the hard wood, Valek detailed the mission to stop the smugglers, including his detour to Sitia after he'd learned from Maren about another tunnel north of Lapeer. He ended with Owen crossing into Ixia. "And I believe he's headed this way, although we've seen no signs of him."

The Commander's gaze grew distant. Valek kept quiet. He'd learned to let the man absorb all the information. Questions were only a matter of time. After that, Valek had many of his own.

"Why do you assume Owen is coming to harm me? If he claims to have something better against magicians than Curare, wouldn't you think I'd be interested?"

A cold brush of dread swept through Valek. "Owen's a power-hungry magician who can't be trusted. He can erase memories and implant new ones. It's...insane to let him close

MARIA V. SNYDER

to you. With that type of magic, he can influence your decisions. He can make you give up command and appoint him as your successor. Owen is the embodiment of all the reasons you hate magicians."

There was no reaction to Valek's outburst. Instead he said, "The magic detector Opal gifted to me, that—"

"Won't provide protection. It just lets you know there's magic in use."

Annoyance flashed in the Commander's golden gaze. He hated to be interrupted. "I know. And I'm also aware that a null shield provides the necessary protection, which is why I have a null shield woven into all my uniforms."

That surprised Valek. "How? When?"

"Yelena's brother provided the protection for me. I asked him to keep it a secret. And, guessing from your expression, Leif hasn't informed his sister."

Ah. There it was. "Yelena and I do not share classified information."

No response.

"You know I wouldn't jeopardize your safety. I'm thrilled you're protected. I would have suggested it, but I believed you wouldn't be…comfortable with magic that close to you."

The Commander brushed his hand along the sleeve of his uniform. "These are dangerous times."

"Indeed." And it was about to get downright perilous for Valek. He drew in a steadying breath. "Which is why I need to know *everything*. Why didn't you inform me about your… arrangement with Owen Moon and the Curare?"

"Why did you disobey a direct order?" the Commander countered.

Thrown, Valek searched his memory. "What order?"

"The one not to get involved with Ben Moon's escape.

You were heading to Sitia to help Yelena before you ran into Maren."

"How—"

"It doesn't matter how I learned of this. What matters is you failed to inform me of your change in plans."

"An assassin was after Yelena."

"That is the answer to your original question, Valek. Why didn't I inform you about Owen? Yelena."

"I wouldn't—"

"You wouldn't have told her? Truly? He's a dangerous magician, and she's the reason he was caught. She's the reason his brother went to prison. You wouldn't have warned her?"

Now Valek didn't have an answer.

"Your loyalties are divided."

"Yes. They are. But I passed all your tests. I returned even after Yelena was shot with Onora's bolt. I found and shut down the smuggling operation as ordered. It wouldn't have been as successful if I hadn't taken that detour to aid Yelena."

"You had no way of knowing that before you left. And Owen still managed to escape."

Valek bit down on his first retort. If he'd known about Owen in the first place, this whole smuggling mess never would have happened. "You used to trust my judgment."

Commander Ambrose leaned back in his chair. "I did."

"What changed? Was it because I didn't tell you that I can be trapped by a simple null shield?"

"No. Everything changed the night an assassin crept through my window."

"Onora?"

"Yes."

But he'd been there with the Commander. Unless... Onora had said she'd been working with him for six months. "You

MARIA V. SNYDER

mean the *first* time she arrived? Not the second time, when I was there, which was just another one of your tests."

"Yes. The first time played out almost identical to the second. But instead of you fighting her, I recruited her just like I had with you."

She had the C-shaped scar to prove it. Just like his. "It scared you."

"Damn right, it scared me. The fact that she could get in so easily and you were in Sitia, helping Yelena. Helping the Sitian Council. Helping your friends solve puzzles while I was in real danger."

Not quite accurate, but Valek knew not to contradict him. "All sanctioned by you. You know if these people gain power in Sitia, it's only a matter of time before they set their sights on Ixia."

"That is no longer a concern of mine. I've decided that there will be no more helping Sitia with their difficulties. You're staying in Ixia and dealing with Ixian problems. If Sitia has a revolt and the victors attack us, then we will defend ourselves at that time. My army is quite capable, and it will give all those young hotheads something to do. As of now, you no longer have the freedom to assign agents and go off on missions as you see fit. You must clear everything with me first. Understand?"

The Commander's words sliced into Valek as if he'd been stabbed with a knife. In all their years together and throughout all their fights, Commander Ambrose had never spoken to Valek in that tone. Had Owen manipulated him four years ago when the magician bargained for his life, promising the Commander Curare in exchange? It depended on when Leif had woven the null shields for him.

Unable to remain sitting, Valek stood. "I understand that you no longer trust me."

"You need to earn my trust again. I need to know that when I give an order, you will follow it without question."

Fear coiled around Valek's chest. The Commander had never wished for him to be a mindless soldier. "Questioning your orders has been the heart of our relationship. The ability to discuss issues and determine the best way to handle them has been beneficial. It's why I'm one of your advisers. You'll ruin—"

In a heartbeat, the Commander shot to his feet and advanced on him. Valek remained in place, even when Commander Ambrose drew his knife and pressed the tip to Valek's chest. Fury radiated in every one of the Commander's clenched muscles. Valek had pushed too far.

"You've forgotten your place, Valek. You're mine. Live or die, *I* decide."

The Commander cut his shirt open, then traced the twenty-four-year-old C-shaped scar on Valek's chest with the knife. Burning pain seared his skin as the razor-sharp tip sliced through his flesh with ease, but Valek refused to utter a sound.

"Do you remember what you pledged to me in that alley long ago?" he asked Valek.

"My loyalty."

"Correct. See that you don't break my trust again."

"Yes, sir."

"Good."

Valek stared straight ahead. "Your orders regarding Owen Moon, sir?"

"You are to leave him and his companions alone. No more investigating. No more interference in his affairs. Owen is my guest and is staying in the guest quarters. He works for me and will continue to do so until I say otherwise. Understand?"

"Yes, sir." Fear pierced Valek's anger and humiliation. He had to warn Yelena.

MARIA V. SNYDER

"Good. Anything else?"

"Who hired Onora to kill you, sir?"

"It's under investigation."

Meaning, Onora hadn't been able to learn the client's name from Hedda. Which explained why she killed the teacher. "Your orders regarding Onora?"

"No change. She's to continue being your apprentice."

"Will she follow my orders?"

"As long as you clear them with me first. We will meet here at dawn every morning and again right after supper to discuss your assignments."

"Yes, sir."

"You're dismissed."

Valek left. He gathered the two parts of his shirt together, fisting the fabric in his right hand and pressing it against the bleeding wound on his chest. Pain flared, but his swirling thoughts distracted him. Possible explanations for the Commander's behavior bubbled. Had Onora's attack affected him that badly? Or was Owen to blame? No wonder neither Valek nor Janco picked up on magic. No need to hide behind an illusion when you were an invited guest. Valek would have to investigate how much Owen was influencing the Commander, which meant violating another direct order and further ruining their relationship.

Confusion warred with anger, which flipped to fear and then to outrage. Valek no longer knew what to think, to believe, to do. He'd always known what action to take, but not now. Too much had happened.

One thing stayed consistent. Yelena. He needed to protect her, to send her to safety, to ensure that she understood that his loyalties were no longer divided.

Valek arrived at his suite without any memory of the trip. Yelena sat at the table. She'd cleared a section off so she could eat her breakfast. Her forkful of sweet cakes paused in midair when she spotted him.

She dropped it. The metal clattered on the plate. "What's wrong? What happened?"

He strode over and knelt next to her. "The Commander has reminded me of my pledge to serve him." Opening his fist, he let his shirt hang open.

Yelena gasped and reached to touch him. "What—"

Valek grabbed her wrist, stopping her. "Please, just listen. I've no idea what's going on with him, but I do know that you're the one who owns my heart and soul. And this—" he gestured to the C-shaped cut "—is not going to be a symbol of my loyalty to the Commander anymore. It's…" Drawing his knife, Valek cut a backward C shape into his skin right next to the other, linking them so they resembled a heart. "It's a symbol of my love, my loyalty, my respect, my trust and my commitment to you and *only* you. Yelena, will you marry me?"

9

LEIF

The air thickened with heat and smoke. Leif squinted through the flames that surrounded them, seeking a way to escape the barn as the fire's roar pounded in his ears and his heart thudded in his chest.

"...your fire magic?" Devlen's face shone with sweat.

"I can only start fires, not stop them." Leif coughed into his sleeve.

"Any ideas?"

"Window." Leif bent low and raced to the nearest one.

The wooden frame burned scorching hot, but the glass behind the flames remained intact. Shielding his face with his arm, Leif kicked the window. A loud *crack* juddered through the sole of his boot. He kicked again. This time the glass broke, and he used his heel to clear the shards.

"Pants," Devlen yelled.

Leif glanced down. An old childhood taunt played in his mind. *Liar, liar, pants on fire.* Guess he was a liar. He almost laughed. Except a snapping and groaning noise shook the rafters. The roof. Fear pierced his inertia.

"Let's go," he yelled, diving through the flames dancing in the window. Leif slammed into the ground. The force knocked the wind from him, but he rolled to the side to clear the way for Devlen. He kept spinning to snuff out the fire clinging to his clothes as he gasped for air.

A thud and a curse sounded to his left. Devlen also spun on the ground to extinguish his tunic. Another warning screech reverberated.

"Run!" Leif scrambled to his feet and dashed away.

Devlen followed. They raced from the burning structure as its roof collapsed. A red-hot whoosh of air pushed them forward. Embers and sharp bits of flying debris pelted their backs. Leif stumbled. Devlen grabbed his arm and pulled him upright.

They continued for another fifty feet before collapsing onto the grass. Leif checked his body for flames while his brother-in-law did the same.

"What...the hell...happened?" Devlen panted.

"Booby trap."

"You sure?"

"Yep." He drew in a breath. "Owen knew we'd investigate his glass houses. That stack of files was just too tempting. As soon as I opened the top one, it triggered the trap. Bastard left a note, too."

"What did it say?"

"Gotcha."

The horses arrived soon after their narrow escape. They cataloged their injuries. Leif mixed up a poultice for their burns. He bandaged the jagged cuts on his leg from the window's glass and removed the splinters from Devlen's back. Draining half his water skin, Leif wiped his mouth with a soot-covered sleeve.

The burning barn polluted the air with thick black clouds. Yet no one arrived to investigate or to help. Odd.

"Owen must have scared his neighbors away," Devlen said.

By the time they were ready to leave, the structure resem-

MARIA V. SNYDER

bled a pile of scorched lumber. Heat rippled the air above it and an angry orange-red glowed deep inside. Without a water source nearby, they couldn't douse it. Instead, they rode to the nearest town and contacted the authorities.

Once they explained what had happened, they checked into a local inn. After a bath and a large meal, Leif dragged his battered body up to their room. He stretched out on the bed. Devlen plopped onto the other one. The springs squealed under his weight.

Pain pulsed from Leif's right leg despite the healing ointment. His raw skin oozed and his throat burned. He felt like a pig who'd been tied to a spit and roasted over a fire. Leif would never eat pork again. Well… At least not for a couple days.

"Are we still going to check those other hothouses?" Devlen asked.

"No. I can't stop a magical booby trap, and anything could be the trigger." Leif considered. "I'll message the locations to Irys tomorrow. Only she or Bain has the power to remove the trap without springing it."

Disappointment panged. He'd been hoping to discover a clue to Owen's whereabouts. Now it would be at least half a season before one of the Masters arrived.

"You think Owen had time to rig all ten?"

The magician had a six-day head start. "It's possible. Best to assume they're all disasters waiting to happen." And if Owen had enough time for that, then he probably destroyed anything that would indicate his escape plans. Damn.

"What if one of the locals decides to investigate?"

"We can message the various security forces to keep everyone away until one of the Master Magicians clears it."

The next morning, Leif sent Devlen to dispatch the messages to the towns near the glass houses while he communicated with Irys via his super messenger. He tapped into the vast magic stored within the black diamond that had been encased in glass. Using the extra power boost, he connected his thoughts to her thoughts. When she dropped her protective barrier, Leif explained about the booby traps.

I'm not sure when one of us can leave, Irys said. *The Council is still reeling from the news the Commander may have Curare.*

Annoyance colored his thoughts. *He has Curare. It's not a guess. I know, but there's no proof.*

Outraged, Leif countered, *We've seen the factory and the vines growing. Owen boasted to Yelena that he made a deal with the Commander to produce it. What more do they need?*

Evidence, Leif. Not hearsay.

Hearsay? They doubt Yelena's word? Anger flared.

Yelena's been dealing with the loss of her magic and a number of assassination attempts. The Council needs to hear the story directly from her. But she's gone to Ixia instead. Don't you see how that compromises her report?

Unfortunately, he understood the Council's position. They wouldn't accuse the Commander of anything unless they had verification. And it didn't help that Ben, Loris and Cilly had been silenced. The knowledge from Owen's accomplices would have provided plenty of confirmation.

What about the efforts to locate Owen? he asked. *Have they coordinated with the Moon Clan's security forces?*

They're not organizing anything. Aside from Yelena, the people who have allegedly seen Owen alive are all Ixian.

So basically, the Sitian Council has done nothing at all.

They're discussing how to prepare the army if the Commander does indeed have Curare. The first step has already been decided. They agreed that we need to discover a way to mass-produce Theobroma.

Theobroma neutralized Curare, but the substance removed a regular person's resistance to magic and stripped a magician of all protective barriers. Using Theobroma wouldn't be a

MARIA V. SNYDER

concern if fighting Ixia. No, the problem would be growing enough of the trees whose pods provided the main ingredient. The tree only thrived in the Illiais Jungle and it required three to five years of growth before it produced pods. Maybe they could grow them in those hothouses. But it would still take years to manufacture enough for an army.

Who is working on the Theobroma problem?

Bavol Cacao Zaltana has volunteered.

No surprise. However, Leif wasn't sure they could trust his clan's leader anymore. Without anything more substantial than his gut instinct, he couldn't accuse the man.

What can I do? he asked instead.

Find proof that Owen is alive and has committed treason, so we can convince the Council to start a manhunt for him.

Easier said than done. *How about Owen's head on a silver platter?*

That will work, too.

I'll sharpen my machete.

Make sure you treat it with Curare and are extremely careful. Owen's more powerful than you.

Yelena had worried about that as well, which reminded him. *Have you heard from Yelena?*

Not since she left for Ixia. You?

Worry for his sister squeezed his gut. *No.*

Let me know if you do.

I will. You, too.

Of course.

Please tell Mara I miss her and hope to be home soon. A pang of longing vibrated in his chest. *Miss* wasn't a strong enough word for how he felt.

I will. Keep me posted on your progress.

Yes, sir.

Irys laughed. *You've been hanging around those Ixians too long.*

★ ★ ★

Leif and Devlen arrived at the farmhouse two days after he'd spoken with Irys. A young man sat on the steps, but he jumped to his feet when he spotted them and followed them to the stable. When the man approached, Leif rested his hand on the hilt of his machete.

"Are you Leif Liana Zaltana?" the man asked.

"Yes."

"Finally! This is for you." The young man shoved a sealed envelope at him then dashed away.

Devlen joined him. "A message?"

"Or another booby trap." Leif sniffed it, seeking the sender's intentions. It smelled of impatience and boredom—probably from the messenger. Otherwise, there was no malice or magic.

He ripped it open, read the message and laughed. "It's a warning to stay away from the glass houses. Seems my sister also triggered a booby trap."

"Was anyone hurt?" Concern laced Devlen's voice.

"Cuts only. Nothing serious." In comparison to her experience, the fire didn't seem as terrible. Better than razor-sharp glass flying toward your head.

"Does it say anything about locating Owen?"

"They haven't seen any signs of him." And he and Devlen had gotten nowhere with their efforts. Damn. Owen could be anywhere by now.

Devlen decided to return to Fulgor. "Reema is safe in Ixia, and I can tap into my network."

"You mean your band of ex-cons?" Leif asked.

"I prefer to call them friends. And they are able to provide information that the security officials cannot. Perhaps they will have a clue that will lead us to Owen."

MARIA V. SNYDER

"It's worth trying. Plus you haven't seen Opal in three weeks."

Devlen grinned. "Returning home after a long absence is always a delight."

"I hear you, brother."

A touch of envy swirled in his chest when Devlen left the next day. Leif had been away for thirty-five long days, with no set time for his return. Reuniting with his wife, Mara, was the best part of traveling. She was always more beautiful than he remembered. Kinder, gentler, patient—perfect. She filled all the hollow spots inside him, making him a better, stronger man.

Esau arrived three days later. There was no mistaking that the man was Leif's father. They shared the same broad shoulders and stocky yet muscular build. Almost twins, except wrinkles etched tracks across Esau's forehead and laugh lines sprouted from the corners of his green eyes. His father's complexion was also a few shades darker—closer to the color of tea without milk.

As soon as Esau dismounted, he crushed Leif in a bear hug. "So where's this glass house?"

"Don't you want to freshen up first?" Leif asked.

A film of dirt covered Esau's clothes. His shoulder-length gray hair hung in greasy layers.

He waved a hand. "There's time for that later. I've spent the last fifteen days just imagining this invention."

Leif led his father to the glass structure.

Esau exclaimed over the construction as he circled it. "Amazing. Wish I thought of it. The ability to grow the jungle anywhere. Marvelous." Then he sobered. "Too bad it was used to grow Curare." He ducked his head. "Wish I never found that blighted vine."

Leif suppressed a sigh over the old argument. "The good uses outweigh the bad, Father. You know that." No matter how many examples Leif and Yelena cited of the drug helping others, their father clung to his guilt like a child clung to a security blanket.

They entered the house.

Esau paused and drew in a deep breath. "It doesn't quite smell like the jungle. What's that sweet odor?"

"White coal to keep it hot."

"Genius!" Esau walked among the plants, naming them aloud.

The Curare vine with its emerald heart-shaped leaves twisted through the greenery. Underneath the bushy canopy, the Theobroma trees grew. Their thin, brownish-gray trunks blended in, along with their long oval leaves. Tiny white flowers clung to the bark. Once pollinated, these blooms would produce pods filled with beans that would be dried, fermented and roasted, transforming them into Theobroma.

"Nice to see some medicinal ones in here." Esau crawled through the brush with his nose close to the ground.

Memories of accompanying his father on one of his jungle expeditions flashed. Hiking through the underbrush, sweating in the humid air, climbing trees, collecting samples, Leif had trailed after his indefatigable father, who questioned him on the uses and names of every bit of greenery they encountered. And Leif had done nothing but complain of being hot and tired while scratching numerous bug bites. What a brat.

Leif had his father to thank for his knowledge of healing recipes. Those teas and poultices had saved lives and helped others. But he wouldn't tell his father that everyone called Esau's most prized and useful discovery "wet-dog tea."

It didn't take Esau long to find the crossbred plants in the hothouse.

"Odd. Very odd," Esau muttered. He broke off a leaf, sniffed the sap and nibbled on the end.

"Do you know what plants they combined? What they were trying to do?" Leif asked.

"Not yet. It's going to take a while."

"Then I'll see to the horses and fetch you some food."

"Yes...yes...fine." Esau scratched the stem with a finger-nail and peered at the wound.

Leaving his father to his investigation, Leif groomed the horses, filled their water and grain buckets and checked the tack for wear. When he returned with a tray of fruit and meats, Esau sat cross-legged in the middle of the house. He stared in shock at the branch in his hands.

Leif rushed to his side. "What's the matter?"

"This." His father held it up.

"What about it?"

"It's a cross between the Curare vine and the Theobroma tree."

It took a moment for it to sink in. "You mean—"

"These people are trying to create Theobroma-resistant Curare!"

10

YELENA

Shocked into silence, I stared at Valek's bleeding chest. His question bounced around my mind, searching for a place to settle. The deep cut resembled a heart—one half carved by the Commander and the other by Valek, creating a symbol of his love for me. Valek had chosen me over the Commander. A warm sensation swept through my body, turning my insides to goo.

"Yelena?" A hitch cracked his voice. He remained on his knees, waiting for my answer.

Valek's face had paled to bone white. I'd never seen him so vulnerable.

Sliding from my chair, I knelt in front of him. I took his knife—still wet with his blood—from his hand and sliced my tunic open. Then I pressed the tip into the flesh in the center of my chest. Pain buzzed like an annoying fly. I ignored it as I carved a fist-sized heart shape directly over my thumping heart and between my breasts. "Yes, Valek. I will marry you."

His tight expression transformed as joy sparked in his eyes. He wrapped his arms around me, pulling me close as his lips found mine. Red-hot spikes of sensation shot down to my toes. My muscles shivered and my skin caught fire. The need to run my hands over his lean, powerful body pulsated over every inch of my being.

Far too soon he stopped. Before I could protest at the interruption, he pressed his chest to mine. My wound burned with the contact and with the sting of his blood mixing with mine.

"Till death. I do swear, love." Valek whispered in my ear.

"Beyond death. My vow to you," I said.

He drew back to meet my gaze. "So we shall be. Forever united."

"We shall be," I agreed.

This time his kiss vibrated to the very core of my soul. Our pledge solidified our connection, creating an unbreakable bond.

"Clothes…off…" I said between kisses.

The speed of our disrobement took what little breath I had away. But then breathing no longer mattered. My senses filled with the intoxicating smell, feel and touch of Valek as he lowered my shoulders to the floor. Nothing in life compared to being linked with him. Together we were one.

Movement roused me, then cold air hitting parts of my body that should not be exposed to cold air. I groaned in protest.

Valek pushed up to one elbow. "Sorry, love. But I need…"

"To what?" I untangled my legs from his. The cut on my chest throbbed. For the first time in my life, I savored the pain. It meant so much.

"…to tell you—"

"What happened with the Commander?" No doubt the meeting went horribly wrong. When he'd arrived, I'd feared the worst. He appeared so devastated. I had never seen him like that, not even when the Commander had signed the order for my execution and extended the document to Valek.

"Yes."

I waited for more, but he stared off into the distance as if searching for a good place to start.

"Why did the Commander feel it necessary to remind you of your oath?" I asked, helping him along.

"He cited a number of reasons, but it pretty much boils down to the fact that Owen's his guest and he wanted to ensure I didn't assassinate him, Tyen and Rika while they are here."

"Oh." So many thoughts jammed into my head. The first, *we were all dead*, summed up the fear and panic that dominated. Owen must have taken control of the Commander's mind. Ixia and Sitia were both in huge trouble and... *We were all dead*. That one was hard to move past.

"Yelena, I want you to leave this afternoon. Return to Sitia where it's safer. I'll message when it's over."

"No. We just exchanged vows and mixed our blood. Leaving you now would be the same as cutting myself in half. We'll figure this out together. We always do. Remember? No doubts."

He struggled to find a reply. I used his own words, so in order for him to dispute me, he would have to discredit his own logic.

"Don't look so smug. What about Reema?" Valek asked.

That was easy. "We'll send her home with an armed escort. I'm sure Opal and Devlen miss her."

His shoulders sagged. "If anything happens..."

I hugged him. "We're stronger together. And shall always be." The last part set a joyful thrill spinning around my heart.

He leaned back. "We need to keep that quiet for now. And I'm sure your family will want a celebration."

"Yes, they will be disappointed if we didn't."

"After this mess with Owen is finished, we'll arrange a big wedding and get married again."

"Sounds like a plan."

"I wish figuring out what to do about Owen was as easy."

I considered. "He won't do anything overt. At least not yet.

He's a guest for now. We need to determine if he has control of the Commander's mind. And then learn what he is plotting and stop him before he moves."

"We can discuss how to go about it this afternoon with Ari and Janco."

"And Maren?"

He frowned. "It depends on if she knew about Owen's bargain with the Commander."

"What about Onora?"

"I still haven't decided if I can trust her."

"I'll talk to her."

"Then you need to know a few things about her history."

Valek filled me in as we washed and bandaged our cuts. I searched for a clean tunic and finished dressing.

"So the man...this Captain Timmer, who abused her, is in the dungeon and she doesn't know?" I asked.

"Not yet. I haven't had time to tell her."

"And what do you expect her to do once she knows?"

"Kill him."

"I don't think she will."

"Why not? You killed the man who raped and tortured you. I took great satisfaction in assassinating the King and the men who murdered my brothers."

"I killed Reyad to stop him from abusing others. But I still didn't feel better inside. I had to rediscover my sense of self-worth and had to stop thinking of myself as a victim."

Valek rested his hands on my shoulders and squeezed. "Then you're the best one to talk to her. Let me know when I can trust her."

"Just like that?"

"Yes."

"I don't have my magic. What if I get it wrong?"

"You won't."

When I arrived at Valek's office for the afternoon meeting, I paused at the threshold. A few unexpected people sat around his conference table. At least Valek had taken the time to clear it off. The clutter hadn't gone far. Tall piles of books and files wobbled on the floor nearby.

Valek and Maren stood by his desk near the back wall. By their intense expressions and whispered conversation, I guessed he was having his heart-to-heart with her about her involvement with Owen.

Janco waved me over, appearing rather energetic for having had less sleep than I. Sitting between Janco and Onora, I glanced across the table. Another man I didn't recognize sat opposite me. Almost as broad as Ari, he studied me with interest gleaming in his light brown eyes.

I elbowed Janco in the ribs.

"Ouch. What… Oh. Yelena, this is Sergeant Grunt. Grunt, this is Liaison Yelena, the Soulfinder and Valek's heart mate. You do *not* want to mess with her."

Stretching my hand toward him, I said, "Just ignore him. We find that's best for all concerned." We shook hands. "What is your real name?"

"Sergeant Gerik, sir."

The *sir* was a nice touch. I turned to Janco. "Where's Ari?"

"He's—"

"Aunt Yelena!" Reema raced into the room.

I stood in time to get knocked back into my seat by her flying hug. "I've missed you, too." She clutched me tight. "Can't…breathe."

Releasing me, she laughed. "That's my necklace-snake move. I clamp on and squeeze until the person passes out. Do you like it?"

"It's very effective."

She beamed.

"Did you invent it or—"

"Lacole taught me. She said since I'm small, my best defense in hand to hand is to clamp on and not let go."

"Death by hug. I love it," Janco said.

"Which explains why no one wants to date you," Onora muttered.

Stopping Janco's outraged retort, I asked Reema, "Lacole? Hand to hand?"

"Lieutenant Lacole. She and Ari are teaching me how to fight."

"Oh?" I tried to keep my tone neutral, but Janco sensed my concern.

"Hey, Ari. You're in big trouble," he called.

Ari strode into the room. His aimed his scowl at Reema. "Didn't I tell you not to run ahead of me? And to keep in sight?"

She shrugged. "You were too slow."

"I'm not racing through the castle's halls. You need to stay with me."

Reema failed to appear chastised. "Can I take Kiki for a ride?" she asked me.

"We can go for a ride later. And you can tell me all about what you've been doing here for the last month." I glanced at Ari.

"I was following orders," Ari said in his defense. He sat next to Gerik.

"Thanks a lot, Ari. Now I'm in trouble," Valek said as he reached the table.

Maren scraped her chair on the floor as she plopped down, joining us. She had pulled her long blond hair into a ponytail. Her pale complexion stood out against her black adviser's uniform. Nodding at me, she said, "Hiya, Puker. Long time no see. You look soft."

I grinned. "Those are fighting words."

"I certainly hope so. I haven't had a decent bo fight in ages."

"I missed you, too."

Her deep laugh rolled around the room.

"Reema," a woman called from the doorway. "Are you ready?"

"Lacole!" With a quick goodbye, Reema rushed from the room. "Can we do more knife fighting today?"

I glared at Ari and he pointed to Valek, who closed the door after Reema.

"We'll discuss this later," I said to them both.

"That's never good." Janco rubbed his hands together. "Can't wait."

Valek returned and stood at the head of the oval table. I guessed he'd changed his mind about Onora and Maren. He filled Ari, Maren and Gerik in on what had happened in Sitia with Owen. Then he broke the news about Owen and the others being a guest of the Commander's.

Copying Valek, I studied their expressions closely. Onora kept her face neutral. Janco and Ari appeared to be ready to commit murder. Gerik seemed more concerned than Maren, who relaxed in her chair as if this wasn't news to her.

"At least we know where they are," Janco said. "When do we ambush them?"

"We don't," Valek said, then explained about the Commander's orders.

"That's…that's…" Janco was at a loss for words.

"Bad?" Ari supplied.

Janco shook his head. "Beyond bad. Catastrophic. We can't follow *that* order. Owen may have hexed the Commander."

"The order will be obeyed. We will leave Owen alone." Valek's tone left no room for discussion. "Maren, tell everyone what you told me earlier."

Maren leaned forward. "When I worked in the Curare fac-

MARIA V. SNYDER

tory in Lapeer, the Boss… Owen had been working on a secret project with someone they called the Master Gardener. I tried to uncover information. But Owen suspected I'd been sent by the Commander to oversee the production, so it was difficult. During the chaos of shutting down the factory and loading my wagon with all the remaining stock of Curare, I overheard him tell one of his men to gather all the Harman saplings."

Everyone turned to me expectantly.

"I've no idea what a Harman tree is used for. My father might. Did you catch the Master Gardener's name or see who it is?" I asked Maren, thinking this person may have been the one to crossbreed those plants in the hothouse.

"No. All I could discover was the Master Gardener had been key in getting the Curare vines to grow in those glass houses."

"Didn't you and Leif speculate about Zaltanas who may have the necessary knowledge and skills?" Janco asked.

"Yes. Our Councilman, Bavol, and our cousin, Nutty. My father would know if there is anyone else."

"Sounds like your father also has this ability," Gerik said.

"Watch your tongue," Ari growled.

"It's okay, Ari. He has a valid point," I said. "If my father is involved, then he was duped. Or his memories altered. Which I'd like to believe is what might have happened to Nutty and Bavol." Better than suspecting them of treason.

"Would Leif be able to tell if a person's memories were magically changed?" Valek asked me.

"It's possible. I'll messenger him about this Master Gardener and Owen's location. My father should have arrived by now."

"What can we do?" Ari asked Valek.

"You, Janco and Maren keep an eye out for any new construction near the castle. If Owen brought Harman saplings and Curare vines, he'd want to build more of those hothouses.

Also watch for any strange deliveries like ones with unusual materials or odd supplies."

Ari nodded. "What about Reema?"

"She's going home as soon as I can arrange an escort. Gerik, you are assigned to the Commander's security detail again. If you hear or see anything about Owen or the others, let me know."

"Yes, sir."

"Onora, you're to stay by the Commander's side during the day. He has a glass magic detector. If it flashes, then magic is in use. That's when you don't follow your instincts and question all your thoughts, as they might not be your own."

"What about at night?" she asked.

"I'll take the night shift."

I suppressed my disappointment over having the bed to myself at night.

"And if he protests?" she asked.

"He won't. Although he may kick you out for sensitive conferences. In that case, stay by the door."

"Yes, sir."

The meeting ended. I waited until everyone left before asking Valek, "Why did you decide to trust Maren and Onora?"

"Maren convinced me she had no idea Owen was alive. Gerik and Onora showed up with Janco. It would have looked suspicious if I'd dismissed them." He strode to his desk.

I followed. "Which explains why you didn't detail your own plans or mine."

Valek paused before sitting in his chair. "You're sending Leif a message and talking to Onora."

"And?"

"And staying far away from Owen. You're not exactly his favorite person, love."

"Fine. What else can I do?" I half leaned, half sat on the edge of his desk.

"Perhaps a repeat of this morning's activities?" He leered.

"I'm serious."

"So am I."

"Valek." A warning tone rumbled in my voice.

He sobered. "You have training."

Ah. "Spy training?"

"Yes. You need to learn all those skills that you had previously used your magic for."

A daunting task. "That could take years."

"It won't. You're smart and a fast learner. Plus you already have plenty of experience."

"I don't—"

"At the meeting today, who was surprised that Owen's here?" he asked.

"I know what you're doing."

"Answer the question."

Annoyed, I recalled the various demeanors that ringed the table and said, "Ari, Janco and Gerik."

"Very good. You picked up on Onora despite her lack of a reaction."

"That was a guess. How did she know about Owen?"

"You tell me."

I bit down on a Janco-inspired sarcastic response. "The Commander told her. Probably after your meeting with him, since she also didn't seem upset that he'd ordered you to leave Owen alone."

"That's my assumption, as well."

"Okay, I get it. I'm not a total newbie. When do my spy lessons start?"

"Tomorrow afternoon."

That gave me the rest of the day off, which I could put to good use. I needed to check on Kiki. And that reminded me of my promise to Reema.

"Why is Reema learning how to fight?" I asked Valek.

"I may have suggested it to Ari before I left."

I waited.

"She would have driven him crazy if she had nothing to do," he said.

"She's missing school. They could have worked on her reading skills, math, history…" I sighed. And she still would have driven him crazy. "If Opal gets upset, I'm blaming you."

"Feel free. But I suspect her lessons have strengthened her magic."

"No one has been able to confirm she has magic."

"No magicians, you mean? I've picked up on it when I'm next to her, but last night, I felt her power in the hallway."

"Are you sure it wasn't Owen's? She hasn't reached puberty yet."

"Do I need to cite all the examples we've encountered of magic doing strange, unexpected and impossible things?"

"No." It would take too long. "If she's a protégée, then she'll be a target. I just…"

"Want to protect Reema?"

"Of course."

"Then it's a *good* thing she's learning how to defend herself."

I huffed. "Don't be all logical when I want to be irrational and overprotective."

"Now you know how I feel."

"You? Irrational?"

He grabbed my hand and tugged me toward him. I settled on his lap.

Valek pulled me close until I leaned on his chest. "Love trumps logic. And when it comes to you, love, I can be extremely irrational."

"Is that so? Give me an example."

"All right. I've put you in incredible danger by marrying

you now. If my enemies discover the truth along with the news about your magic, which is spreading, they will take advantage of this unique, and hopefully brief, opportunity to target you. The logical thing to do was to wait until your magic returns and Owen is dead."

"Finding an ideal time may have been impossible," I said.

"I'd like to believe we'd find a moment of peace in our future. However, waiting would have been torture. I'm empty without you."

I tilted my head back to kiss him, and my cheek brushed the bandage hidden under his shirt. I wasn't the only one in severe danger. If the Commander discovered Valek's altered scar, he might order Valek executed for treason. I'd already experienced the searing pain of grief that burned me from the inside out when I'd thought Valek had died in that barn fire over six years ago. A horrible time I'd rather not repeat.

Ever.

I checked on Kiki after leaving Valek's office. She munched on the grass in the small pasture next to the stables, but trotted over to the fence as soon as she spotted me. Her coat gleamed.

Stroking her neck, I said, "I see your favorite stable boy has been busy giving you a bath. Did he braid your tail?"

Kiki moved to the side and swished her tail, which now contained a number of thin braids and colorful ribbons.

"Pretty." I patted her shoulder. "Are you rested enough to go for a ride with me and Reema later?"

She dipped her head once, then glanced at the stable, clearly signaling yes. While glad Kiki was able to communicate with me, I wished I could tell her about my union with Valek. My happiness bubbled inside me, pushing to escape, fueling the desire to share it with her. But it was too dangerous to voice aloud.

Kiki snuffled my pockets. I fed her a peppermint before

searching for Reema. The young girl practiced in the north-east training yards with Lacole. Reema had wrestled her long curls into a ponytail and sparred the young lieutenant with a rubber knife. Ari leaned on the fence, watching them. I stood next to him. He tensed.

"Relax," I said. "I'm not going to yell at you. I'm sure you've had your hands full with Reema over the last month."

"You've no idea," he muttered.

"Then explain it to me." I kept my tone neutral.

Ari's broad shoulders sagged. "She's the most exasperating child I've ever met. Not that I know a bunch of kids, but I swear, she's like a mini Janco—just with more focus."

"You do know you're not making sense, right?"

"Yeah." He drew in a breath. "She's smart and learns new skills wicked fast. Faster than anyone I know. Look at that." Ari gestured to Reema. "She has Lacole on the *defensive* and they just started knife fighting last week. The kid's a natural. She's a pro at reading body language. Plus, she's stubborn, fearless and manipulative. Reema can turn on the tears in a heartbeat and suddenly act like a four-year-old. And then she has this…this sixth sense about people, knowing if they're lying or bluffing or sneaking around the hallways."

"Wow." I studied the girl with a fresh perspective.

Intense, Reema didn't hesitate to take advantage of Lacole's weaknesses. The lieutenant dodged a flurry of Reema's strikes that reminded me of Janco.

"Opal is going to kill me," I said.

"But Valek—"

"*I* put her in danger and sent her here. I'm responsible."

"Responsible for what?" Janco asked, joining us.

"Reema's new skills." I pointed to the match.

Janco's eyes lit up. "Holy snow cats! Look at her go. I gotta

MARIA V. SNYDER

get in on that action." He grabbed the top rail of the wooden fence and hopped over it in one smooth move.

Lacole handed her practice weapon to him and he faced Reema with a huge grin on his face.

"Reema's ego is about to be bruised," Ari said.

"Will she get upset?" I asked.

"She'll be sullen for a few hours, but then it turns into determination and I'll have to drag her to bed because she'll practice all night if I'd let her."

Now his comment about her being a mini Janco with more focus made sense. Despite his grumbling, I had the feeling Ari cared for Reema.

"You're going to miss her," I said.

He remained quiet for a while. "Yeah. I am. And I'm sure Lacole will, too. She's been helping me with more than training. There were times Reema needed...er...female supervision, like in the baths." Red splotches spread across his cheeks.

I suppressed my mirth over Ari's embarrassment. We watched Janco run circles around Reema, but I was impressed with her tactics.

"Do you want to join them?" Ari asked. "Get some practice?"

"Not now. I promised to take Reema riding. And I'm going to need to rest before my training starts."

Concerned, Ari turned to me. "What training?"

I searched his expression. "Didn't Janco tell you?"

"All I've heard from him is complaints about Little Miss Assassin and Owen the Bastard. We haven't had time to catch up. Why? What's wrong?"

The desire to let Janco tell his partner about my situation welled, but Ari deserved to hear it from me. So I told him about the morning I woke up unable to tap into the power source.

The crease between his pale blue eyes puckered into full worry. "And you're not immune like Valek and Opal?"

"No. Magic affects me like everyone else." Unfortunately.

"I'm sorry to hear that, Yelena. Will you get your magic back?"

"Hopefully once I figure out why it's gone, I'll be able to reverse it."

"I'm here for whatever you need. Okay?"

"Okay."

He frowned at nothing in particular, his gaze distant. "Well, that explains why Valek asked you if Leif can tell when a person's memories have been altered by magic. I wondered why he didn't just ask you to check with your Soulfinding abilities, but I've learned to ask Valek those types of questions in private."

Interesting. "In case he has a grander scheme in mind?"

"Yeah. He always has a grander scheme in mind. And I, for one, can't wait to see what he has in mind for Owen." Ari punched his palm. Hard.

After Reema finished her lessons and cleaned up, Kiki took us on a ride through Castletown. We stopped in town and I sent a quick message to Leif. Only an hour of daylight remained, and the air held the crisp scent of cold as we trotted into the surrounding farms.

Reema sat in front of me, still in high spirits after her sparring bouts with Janco. I'd found that even when you were being trounced by him, it was hard to get angry at him, and it appeared he had the same effect on her.

However, her good mood didn't last once she heard the news of being able to return home.

"Don't you miss your parents?" I asked in the heavy silence.

"I do, but…"

She had made friends here. "You'll miss Ari and Lacole?"

"Kind of."

"You'll miss training?"

"Yes, and I'll miss being treated like an…adult."

"But you're not—"

"Forget it. You don't understand. Only Teegan and Fisk understand. Besides, it doesn't matter. I can't refuse to go home."

"It's safer."

"It's boring."

Ah. The heart of the problem. I thought about what she'd said, puzzling over why her brother and Fisk might understand. She had lived on the streets for most of her life. First with her mother and Teegan, and then with just Teegan after their mother died. Fisk, too, grew up on the streets, begging. No time for a childhood when you were fighting to survive.

"Can I make a suggestion?" I asked.

Reema tensed. "Sure."

"In order to be treated like an adult, you need to act like one. Make a deal with your parents."

Her ponytail swung as she shook her head.

"Just hear me out. The deal is that you promise to attend school without complaining and to earn high marks, and in exchange they continue your training. Your mom learned from Valek, and your father is an excellent swordsman."

She twisted in the saddle, meeting my gaze. "That might work!"

"Don't sound so surprised." I smiled. "Reema, can you promise me one thing?"

Her excitement dimmed. "It depends."

"Promise to make a friend and have fun once in a while. Stupid kid fun."

"Does stealing pies with Uncle Leif count?"

"No. You need to make a friend who is closer to your age. And Teegan and Fisk don't count, either. Will you promise?"

Reema bit her lip, then nodded. "Yes, I promise."

"Good."

We returned after dark. Reema helped me take care of Kiki

before we entered the castle. I escorted her to Ari and Janco's apartment. We interrupted an argument about cats. Reema immediately took Janco's side. When I gave her a questioning look, she mouthed, *Stupid kid fun*. I laughed and left them to their debate.

Halfway back to Valek's suite, I stumbled over a wave of exhaustion. Leaning against the wall, I considered my day. Nothing should have drained my energy like this, although I hadn't eaten since I woke. Hunger was an infrequent visitor, and the thought of food created another swell—this one of nausea.

As much as I avoided thinking about it and ignoring it, I realized it was time to visit the medic.

Located on the ground level of the castle, the infirmary treated all the castle inhabitants. Another station in the barracks cared for the soldiers unless the injury was too severe. Then the poor soul was transferred here. The main rectangular room contained two rows of beds along each long side. Lanterns blazed from hooks set into the walls. As I strode down the middle aisle, I nodded hello at the few recovering patients who met my gaze. A medic I didn't recognize checked a man's temperature.

The woman in charge of the infirmary, Medic Channa, also affectionately known as Medic Mommy, jumped to her feet when she spotted me heading toward her desk in the far back corner. An examination table waited in the opposite corner. A white curtain hung from a track so it could be pulled around the table to ensure privacy.

A mixture of surprise and concern creased her long, thin face. "The gossips reported you'd arrived last night, but I didn't think I'd see you so soon."

I laughed at the implication that it was only a matter of time before I showed up on her examination table. When I visited Ixia, I avoided using magic to heal the cuts and bruises obtained when practicing with Ari, Janco and Maren. Having a wound magically disappear made the Ixians uneasy, and it gave Janco the creeps.

She tucked her short hair behind her ears. "What can I help you with?"

Scanning the beds nearby, I lowered my voice. "Is there somewhere we can talk without being overheard?"

"Yes. My office."

"But..." I gestured toward her desk.

"That's just so I can do paperwork while on duty."

Channa grabbed the lantern on her desk and escorted me from the infirmary. Halfway down the hallway, she stopped and unlocked a door on the left. We entered a small space crammed with instruments, books and a couple chairs. A desk was buried under the piles. She set the lantern on top of a crate.

Clearing a stack of papers from the one chair, she said, "I'm not in here that much. It's more of a storage space." She sat down. "Now, what's going on?"

I perched on the edge of the seat. "You keep your patients' medical information confidential, right?"

"Of course. I only report cases that involve a crime. But you already know that." She studied my face. "Are you worried I'll tell people you're pregnant?"

Jerking as if she'd struck me, I said, "What... How... I'm not even sure!"

Channa took my hand in hers. "I've birthed all the babies born in the castle complex, Yelena. It's not hard for me to spot the signs."

"But I've been traveling. And been the target of two assassins. I haven't gotten much sleep. It could be stress."

"It's possible," she agreed, keeping her professional demeanor, even though she was probably lying to me. "If you wish, I can test your blood. The results will remove all uncertainty. Of course, time will also do the same."

I hesitated.

"It's best to know. This way you can take proper care of yourself, ensuring your baby will also be healthy."

And there was the Medic Mommy we all loved, laying on the guilt. I allowed her to prick my finger and collect a few drops of blood in a glass vial. She added a yellow powder and mixed the contents.

"It'll take about ten minutes, then we'll check to see if it turns blue."

"Blue for boy?"

"No. Blue for positive," she said, placing the vial inside a drawer and closing it. "Light affects the results." Channa relaxed back in her chair. "Two assassins? Isn't that overkill, even for you?"

Nice. "If you're trying to distract me, it won't work. Besides, those assassins are the reason why I can't be pregnant. It's too dangerous."

"Valek's your heart mate. There will never be a time that isn't risky."

"Exactly my point."

"Don't you want to have children?"

Annoyed, I clamped down on my first response—*it's none of your business*. But considering the reason I was here… "I do, but not now. And before you give me a lecture on how I should have avoided it, I was shot with an arrow containing starlight. Except I didn't know it was starlight at the time."

"Oh my." She tapped her foot. "I thought I'd heard every excuse, but that's a new one."

Lovely.

"If you really don't want the baby, there are—"

"No." The word erupted from my throat before my mind even processed it. "I can't do that. Others can make that choice, but…" I recoiled from the thought. In fact, the entire conversation was uncomfortable, so I changed the subject. "When did you hear I was in Ixia?"

"My assistant told me this morning. He learned from the kitchen staff that Valek asked them to make you sweet cakes."

The gossips worked faster than Valek's intelligence network. I remembered how they had bet money on how long it would take me to be captured while I participated in the Commander's fugitive exercise. Rand, the head chef at the time, had explained it to me: *Gambling and gossiping is all we servants do.*

Perhaps it might work in my favor for once. "Has the staff been talking about the Commander's new guests?"

"Oh yes. They're all abuzz about them."

"And?"

The medic gave me a shrewd look. "And I don't spread gossip. How can my patients trust me to keep their health issues confidential if I'm chatting about others?"

"You can't."

"Exactly."

But that wouldn't stop the kitchen staff or the housekeepers. Perhaps a visit to the kitchens was in my immediate future. After all, I haven't eaten all day. Too bad, the sound of a drawer rolling open ruined my appetite.

As Medic Mommy dipped her hand into the drawer, a strange mix of apprehension, fear and excitement flushed through me, leaving the tips of my fingers tingling. She grasped the vial between her thumb and index finger and held it up to the lantern light.

I stared at the liquid inside.

It was blue.

11

VALEK

After Yelena left his office, Valek tried to concentrate on the piles of reports. But his thoughts kept returning to his heart mate. Or rather, his wife. Amazed, he touched the bandage under his shirt, recalling the intense emotions that had ripped through him mere hours ago. Amid the maelstrom of confusion and betrayal caused by the Commander, one thing had been crystal clear.

Yelena.

Nothing else mattered. No one except her mattered. It was liberating and terrifying at the same time. If she'd said no… He shied away from that horrible thought. Instead he focused on the joy of her reply and the passion of their union. It still hummed in his blood. Along with the desire to keep her safe, which would be difficult because of the current situation.

Valek needed to evict the trio of unwelcome guests permanently. But how to do it? He agreed with Yelena that Owen would lie low for a while. Which was why he hadn't insisted that she have an armed guard by her side at all times. Not that she'd allow it, or that the protector would be effective if Owen attacked. Hell, even Valek couldn't keep her safe, not if a null shield was used against him.

Abandoning the reports, Valek descended to the lower level of the castle. He checked the storeroom that Yelena, Ari, Janco and Maren had used to train back when she had been the Commander's food taster. Except for a thick layer of dust, nothing had disturbed the space. Valek would borrow a handful of rags to clean it. Hopefully, they could keep her new training sessions a secret.

Then he headed to the Commander's office as ordered. The room's entrance was located along the back wall of the throne room. When the Commander had taken control of Ixia, he'd removed all the intricate tapestries, the opulent jeweled throne and expensive decorations. In their place, he brought in desks, chairs and filing cabinets for his officers and advisers. The productive sprawl had no discernible organization or path, but Valek had traversed the expanse so many times, he could navigate it blind.

Onora stood with the Commander's two personal guards outside the open door.

She hooked a thumb inside. "Food taster just brought his supper."

"Any problems?"

"Other than being grumped at, no."

"Good. You're dismissed. Report back for duty at dawn."

"Yes, sir." Onora strode away.

When the taster left, Valek knocked and waited for permission to enter—a new aspect of their changed…shattered?… relationship. He concentrated on expelling all his emotions as the Commander remained silent for twenty minutes before allowing Valek to enter.

He approached the desk and stood at attention, keeping his gaze on the tidy surface. A lifelike glass snow cat glinted with the lantern's amber hues, but the interior of Opal's magic detector stayed dark—a relief. However, the pair of black snow cats Valek had carved for the Commander no longer decorated the desk. He noted the missing gifts without reacting, but their absence was like a slap in the face.

"Report," the Commander ordered.

Valek filled him in on a few new items—reports of thieves using storms to cover their activities in MD-1, and a request for more soldiers in MD-5. The rest were all minor details he normally wouldn't bother the Commander with.

The silence stretched. Finally, the Commander asked, "Have these Storm Thieves been caught?"

"No, sir. They've managed to evade capture so far."

"Do you think magic might be involved?"

"It's possible."

"Then I want you to *personally* investigate this problem."

"That will involve a trip to the coast, sir."

"I expect it will. You have permission to travel to MD-1. However, I did not give you permission to assign Onora as my guard. It is a waste of her time. She is to work with you on all your assignments. Except when you leave for the coast—then she is to be in charge of security. Understood?"

"Yes, sir." Valek fisted his hands. Onora wasn't ready for the responsibility, but he couldn't say anything. This was beyond painful.

"And you are not allowed to skulk about, either, investigating my guests." Papers rustled. "Why is Captain Timmer in my dungeon?"

"He's a sexual predator, sir." Valek explained his abuse of Onora and Wilona. "I planned… Permission to inform Onora about his presence, sir?"

"Granted. Tell her she will have the pleasure of executing him in public. It'll be a mandatory event for *all* my soldiers. They need to understand I will not tolerate such behavior."

"Yes, sir." For some reason Valek thought she'd balk at that order.

"Inform Colonel Qeb to schedule Timmer's execution during the fire festival."

Which was six months away. The festival was held every year in Castletown. An execution during the festival would certainly drive the point home. "Yes, sir."

"Also, I want you to assign one of your agents to collect all information received from Sitia about the Council's reaction to the *rumor* about Owen and the Curare. I want to know if there's any discussion about an attack on Ixia. Do you still have an operative working for one of the Councilors?"

"No, sir."

"Why not?"

"Master Magician Irys Jewelrose discovered him, and he was arrested and extradited to Ixia."

"Was this before null shields were readily available?"

"Yes, sir."

"Send another agent to infiltrate the Council. Have him or her obtain a null shield to block the magicians. I want daily reports."

"Yes, sir." He hoped Yelena wouldn't find out. As the Liaison, she'd worked hard to develop a civil and respectful relationship between Ixia and Sitia.

"When is Yelena planning to return to Sitia?"

An alarming question. And the Commander didn't use her title. "Unknown, sir."

"She is a Sitian and a magician and is no longer welcome in Ixia. Send her home with the Sitian girl."

Surprised, Valek lifted his gaze. He could argue the same thing about Owen and his friends, but the Commander's cold stare sent a warning signal. Was Ambrose in control, or was

Owen directing the man's thoughts? The magic detector hadn't flashed. Yet Valek suspected these orders were from Owen.

Valek sensed he teetered on a dangerous edge. "Permission to speak, sir?"

"Granted."

"Yelena is unable to use magic, sir. She will be a target in Sitia if she returns."

"Why didn't you tell me about her this morning?"

Valek toppled off the edge and landed right in the middle of trouble. He suspected the Commander already knew about Yelena and had been testing him. "At the time, I believed it was more important to warn you about Owen. After that, I didn't have the opportunity."

"I see. Will her magical powers return?"

"Unknown, sir."

"Do you intend to marry her?"

Where had that come from? "Yes, sir."

The Commander tapped his fingers on the desk. "If she agrees and remains here, then she must cut all ties to Sitia and become my Sitian Adviser. If she is unable to do so, or if her powers return, then she must leave immediately. Understood?"

That it was harsh? And that there was no way in hell she'd agree to cut all ties? Oh yes—crystal clear. "Yes, sir."

"Good. You're dismissed."

Valek turned to leave. When he reached the door, the Commander called, "Valek, if I discover you didn't have the *opportunity* to inform me of other important issues, I will add your name to Colonel Qeb's execution list. Understood?"

"Yes, sir." Valek left.

He navigated the throne room with his thoughts whirling from his meeting with the Commander. His threat made it clear that if he caught Valek disobeying orders or taking matters into his own hands, Valek would be terminated. Unnec-

MARIA V. SNYDER

essarily severe. Owen must be influencing the Commander, but the magic detector didn't flash. Valek would have to investigate despite the threat. He'd just have to ensure he didn't get caught.

However, he needed to keep up appearances. He spent the next couple hours doing damage control, informing Gerik and Onora that his earlier orders about Owen were no longer valid.

"Report to my office in the morning to begin your training," he said to Onora. "Gerik, you are to remain on the Commander's detail."

He found Maren doing bo staff drills with a group of young women. She started them on another drill and he called her over to explain.

"We're not to do any investigating. Understood?" he asked.

"What happened?" she asked.

"Commander's orders."

She tapped a finger on her chin. "Little Miss Assassin ratted you out, didn't she?"

The possibility had crossed his mind. "I need you to find an agent who can infiltrate the Sitian Council."

"That's gonna be super hard. The Councilors are all wary of new people. When do you need the agent in place?"

"The sooner the better."

"Even harder. We might have to settle for bribing someone already on the inside."

"As long as the information is accurate. Stop by my office tonight with a couple suggestions."

"Okay, boss." Maren returned to her students.

Valek arranged for Reema's escort. The girl wouldn't be safe until she left Ixia. Then he searched for the power twins. Ari and Janco played cards with Reema in the dining room. From the groans and pile of coins in front of Reema, he guessed the little scamp had won many hands.

Janco threw his cards down in disgust. "That's it! I'm tapped out."

Reema grinned and raked in more coins. "Do you want to play, Uncle Valek?"

"And go broke? No, thank you."

"Awww. You're no fun."

"Did Yelena tell you about going home?" he asked.

Her good humor dimmed. "Yes."

"I've assigned two of my most trusted men to escort you."

She perked up. "Ari and Janco!"

"No, sorry. I need them." Did he ever.

Once again she deflated.

"You'll be leaving in the morning, and you'll ride horses so you can get home faster," Valek tried.

"Horses are fun," Janco said.

"I guess." She fiddled with a coin.

"How about I let you borrow Beach Bunny? She's a hoot to ride and she likes to jump."

"Really?" Reema's eyes lit up.

"Really," Janco said. "She'll jump over logs and streams and stuff."

Valek kept quiet, even though jumping would be prohibited. The object was to get her home safe, after all.

Lacole arrived and announced it was Reema's bath time.

"No." Reema crossed her arms. "I don't need a bath."

"You're grubby. You smell. And your tunic is covered in horsehair," Ari said. "Now go take your bath or you won't get the goodbye present Janco and I bought for you."

"Yes, sir!" She hopped off her chair and pocketed her winnings. "Come on, Lacole." Reema grabbed the lieutenant's hand and dragged the woman away.

MARIA V. SNYDER

"Please don't tell me you bought her a weapon," Valek said.

Janco pished. "A weapon? Who do you think you're dealing with? We got her *weapons*!"

Valek sank into a chair. No need to worry about the Commander ordering his execution. Opal would kill him first.

Ari studied his expression. "Something up?"

Valek glanced around the nearly empty room. Lowering his voice, he said, "Yes. All the orders I gave earlier are void. We will ignore Owen and not do any investigating."

Janco laughed. "Yeah, right."

"I'm serious. The Commander made it quite clear that disobeying his orders will be considered treason, punishable by death."

"Owen must be pulling the Commander's strings," Janco said. "Everything about this situation stinks."

"It's dangerous, and you two will obey his orders." Valek's tone was firm.

"Come on, Valek. It's us," Ari said. "We won't let you do it all on your own."

They knew him too well. "I can't ask—"

"You're not. We're volunteering."

"Yeah," Janco said. "We'll play the good little soldiers. No one will suspect a thing."

"You've never been the good little soldier," Ari said. "If you start now, everyone will know something's up."

"Yeah, well, you know what I meant."

"Who else is in on this?" Ari asked. "Maren? Yelena?"

Valek touched his chest. "Yelena, but not Maren. Not until I know where her loyalties lie."

"Yeah, that whole business with the Curare factory and Owen. She's holding something back." Janco rubbed the scar on his right ear. "It's wonky."

"Wonky? Are you three years old? What kind of word is *wonky*?" Ari asked.

"The fact that you don't know what it means shows your limited vocabulary skills," Janco countered.

"I'll assign you regular, Commander-approved tasks," Valek said before they launched into an argument. "Any extracurricular activities must be done on your own time. Understood?"

"Yes, sir," they both said.

Valek then explained about the Commander's directive regarding Yelena.

"Harsh," Ari said. "But she's not going to stay as his adviser."

"She can't go back to Sitia," Janco said in alarm. "Not with that Bumblebee assassin after her."

Valek didn't bother to correct Janco. "She'll come with me to the coast when I investigate those thieves. The Commander doesn't need to know."

"Risky. Very risky," Ari said.

He agreed, but there was nothing else he could do.

Exhausted from the long emotional day and lack of sleep, Valek considered bypassing his office and going to bed. Then he remembered he'd asked Maren to stop by tonight. He changed course.

Valek slowed when he turned down the corridor to his office. Flames glowed from two lanterns. The rest remained dark. An oversight or blown out? A pool of darkness covered the area in front of his door. Uneasy, he yanked his knife from its sheath and pulled a Curare-laced dart from his belt with his other hand, pinching it between his thumb and finger. He paused, sniffing. No strange cologne or perfume tainted the air. Magic didn't stick to his skin.

He approached the door. Nothing happened. Stopping in

MARIA V. SNYDER

front, he waited, letting his eyes adjust to the darkness. He strained to hear anything that might indicate a person lurking in the shadows. Nothing. The three locks appeared to be untouched. Valek put the dart between his teeth and reached for his key.

An invisible force slammed into him from the blackness, knocking him down. He rolled onto his back as the force tightened around his body, dragging him away from his office and deeper into the darkness. He slid to a stop, but was pinned to the floor. Then it contracted again. He lost his grip on his knife. Breathing turned into an alarming effort.

A black form advanced. Then the shadows shifted and Owen emerged. Rika and Tyen stood behind him. The magician had trapped him in a null shield. A helpless rage built inside Valek as he sipped in tiny amounts of air. Not enough. Light-headed, spots swirled in front of his eyes. Death by hug. He would have laughed if he had the breath.

Owen knelt next to him and the pressure on his chest eased a fraction. "You're not going to obey the Commander's orders despite all your *yes, sirs* and *no, sirs*. And I can't have that. So you're going to have an accident. Poor Valek fell while scaling the castle walls near the guest quarters. The next time you wake, you'll be flying through the air. Enjoy the ride."

The null shield compressed around his chest, squeezing the breath from his lungs. A vision of Yelena flashed. With the last of his strength, he spit the dart at Owen. The magician jerked back, cursing. The force lessened. Valek gasped and tried to move, but he remained immobilized.

"You missed," Owen said, increasing the pressure.

Regret pulsed as Valek fought for consciousness. *Sorry, love.*

Boots clacked on the stone floor as Maren strode down the hallway. Owen, Rika and Tyen froze. Once again, Owen's hold on Valek slipped just enough to allow air to revive him, but not enough for him to warn Maren.

Maren muttered something about lazy servants as she used one of the lit lanterns to light another one closer to Valek's office.

"Rika," Owen whispered.

The woman closed her eyes. "Done."

Valek assumed she'd used her magic to create an illusion to hide them. Since the null shield around him blocked magic, he didn't feel its sticky touch.

Maren knocked on the door, waited and knocked again. Sighing, she leaned against the wall. Valek's three captors glanced at each other. Then Owen stared at Maren.

She yawned. Her eyelids drifted shut. With a grunt, she shook her head and straightened. But it didn't take long for her to slide down the wall into a sitting position. Relieved that they didn't plan to kill her as well, Valek watched as she rested her forehead on her bent knees.

"Okay, I'm here," Janco called from the other end of the hallway. "Although I don't know why you need me." He drew closer. "Valek trusts your judg... Are you sleeping?"

"Mmm?" Maren raised her head as if it weighed a hundred pounds.

"What— Ow." Janco pressed his hand to his right ear.

Don't look. Don't look, Valek chanted in his mind, fearing for Janco's and Maren's lives.

But Janco turned and peered into the darkness. He fingered the hilt of his sword while rubbing his scar with his other hand.

No. Don't. Look away.

Janco turned his attention to Maren. "Guess the servants decided to take off early tonight." He pulled Maren to her feet. "Come on. Valek probably went to bed."

"No." Maren resisted. "He said to meet him."

"Yeah, well, he didn't get any sleep last night. We can talk to him in the morning. Besides, dark hallways give me the creeps."

He guided her back down the hallway and out of sight. Thank fate.

"Let's go, before someone else comes along," Owen said. "Tyen, pick him up. Don't use your magic. Rika will keep us hidden."

"He's conscious," Tyen said.

"But he can't move. Hurry up."

The big man hoisted Valek up over his shoulder. As they traveled though the castle, Valek contemplated his very short future. Was being awake when they pushed him from the window better or worse than waking up in midair?

Worse, because now he had time to think about how easily Owen had captured him. How stupid he'd been to think Owen would wait. How Yelena would react to his death—badly. How he'd promised her forever and he didn't last a day. How he always assumed he'd die fighting and not trapped and utterly helpless, slung over a brute's shoulder like a rag doll, unable to curse or rage at Owen. Or at the Sandseed Clan, for teaching the magicians how to form those blasted null shields in the first place.

A whirlwind of emotions spun, making him dizzy. Or was that the lack of air?

The trip to the guest wing took much longer than necessary. Owen and company made a few wrong turns and wasted time arguing about the right way. Their lack of knowledge reminded Valek of Janco's comment about having the home-court advantage. Too bad it really didn't make a difference for his current situation.

When they finally reached the guest wing, Owen opened

the door and they hustled inside. Rika closed and locked it behind them.

"The window," Owen ordered. He unlatched the shutters. They banged on the stone walls, letting in a gust of coldness.

Tyen propped Valek on the window's sill. A four-story drop loomed below. Valek's heart squeezed in triple time, pumping liquid fear through his immobilized body.

The tightness around his chest eased as Owen put his hands on Valek's shoulders. Valek braced for the shove, but instead, Owen asked, "Any last words?"

Oh, yes. About a million. And all for Yelena, but this might be his only chance to strike a blow. "I'll…tell Ben…hello." Valek panted, trying to fill his lungs.

Owen's grip turned painful. "Did you murder my brother?" Anguish and anger creased his face.

So much for the theory that Owen ordered their deaths. "Not me…another…assassin."

"What about Loris and Cilly?" Rika asked.

"Them…too."

"He's lying. He killed them all. They were a threat to Yelena," Rika said. "Finish him."

"If I'd assassinated Ben…I'd be bragging about it…especially now."

Owen shook his head. "He's just delaying the inevitable. It'll be easy to learn if he's telling the truth. Goodbye, Valek. Oh, and here's something to think about during the few seconds you've left to live. Yelena's next."

12

JANCO

"What's your rush?" Maren asked.

Janco hustled her along the hallways of the castle. The need to hurry pulsed in his veins. "Something's not right," he said.

"What are you talking about?"

"Outside Valek's office. That darkness was…odd…weird. I felt strong magic. And his knife was on the floor. Didn't you see it?"

"No. I was—"

"Too busy sleeping. And that was strange, too."

"Yeah, I guess." Maren remained quiet for a while. "Do you think something happened to Valek?"

Did he? He considered the clues. "Yes."

"But he's immune to magic."

Janco forgot that Maren didn't know about null shields. No time to explain it to her. "Yeah, well, Owen could have shot him with a dart of Curare."

"Where are we going?"

"To get Ari. We need reinforcements."

"You need a couple magicians to fight them."

"Ari's got the best aim with the blowpipe. Curare works on magicians, too."

"But can't that one guy move objects with his magic? A dart wouldn't reach him."

Janco skidded to a stop. "Oh, hell."

"And I'm sure they're gone by now."

They wouldn't wait for Janco to figure it out and return. What to do? Janco closed his eyes. He ejected his chaotic thoughts, suppressed his worry and fear for Valek and concentrated on the logic. If Owen killed Valek, the Commander would be upset, but if Valek disappeared… But he couldn't hide a dead body, it would stink after a few days. They could smuggle the body outside the castle by hiding it with an illusion. Too risky. Maybe they planned to keep him locked up. But where? And would they risk the possibility of Valek escaping? Probably not.

This was going nowhere. He switched his line of thought. Where was the one place the Commander had said was off-limits? The guest suites! Janco opened his eyes.

Maren waited with her arms crossed. "Got something, genius?"

He ignored the insult. "Come on." Janco ran and didn't bother to check if Maren followed or not.

Ari jumped to his feet when Janco burst into their apartment. "What's wrong?"

Janco raced to his room, grabbed his bag of tricks and dashed back. "Reema, stay here. Ari, come on."

"Weapons?" Ari asked.

"Got 'em. Let's go!"

Maren remained in the hall. Janco shot past her, heading to the nearest stairwell. Her and Ari's pounding footsteps sounded behind him.

"Are you going to tell me what this is about?" Ari asked him.

MARIA V. SNYDER

"He thinks Valek's in trouble," Maren answered.

"Thinks?"

Maren explained about the oddness in the hallway outside Valek's office. It didn't take Ari long to reach the same conclusion.

"The three of us can't fight three magicians," Ari said.

Janco reached the stairs and bounded up them three at a time. At the fourth floor, he stopped, putting his hand up to signal all quiet. He peered down the hall. Empty.

Giving Maren and Ari the wait signal, he crept down the corridor until he reached the turn that would lead to the guest quarters. A quick peek confirmed no one lurked in the shadows. But a creepy-crawly sensation brushed his skin.

Magic nearby. Lovely. At least it wasn't the sharp pain of an active illusion. Janco returned to his friends. He explained his plan in a whisper, then dug into his bag of tricks.

Ari raised his eyebrows when Janco handed him a blowpipe and darts.

"Just in case," Janco said. Then he gave Maren the most important item. "Make sure it gets as close to the action as possible."

"What if there's no action?" she asked.

"Then we find it," Ari said. "No stopping until Valek's safe."

Janco flashed his partner a grin. While Maren might doubt him, Ari was all in.

In silence, they ghosted through the hallway. When they reached the door to the guest suites, Janco knelt on one knee. He twisted the knob. Locked. Janco whipped out his lock picks. Using the one with the mirror, he inserted it under the door and confirmed no one guarded the door. A cool breeze blew over his hand and voices murmured from inside.

"A window is open," Janco whispered. "We'll have to move fast."

Inserting his diamond pick and tension wrench into the lock, he aligned the pins in record time and slowly turned the cylinder. Even though every nerve tingled with the desire to hurry, he eased open the door. It about killed him to move that slow.

Owen, Tyen and Rika stood in front of the window with their backs to the door, talking. Strange, but good fortune for him. Where was Valek? He scanned the rest of the room.

"...Valek," Owen said.

Janco's gaze jumped back to the others and he spotted his boss through a gap between Tyen and Rika. Valek sat on the ledge with Owen gripping his shoulders, talking to him. Pushing the door wider, Janco entered the room and signaled Ari and Maren to follow.

Owen said, "...Yelena's next."

"Now!" he yelled at Maren.

The three magicians whipped around just as she threw a glass ball at their feet. It shattered on impact. A knockout gas hissed from the broken shards, fogging the area. But the breeze from the outside would soon clear the air. Then they'd have three pissed-off magicians.

Owen and the others stumbled to the ground. "Ari!" Janco pointed to the prone magicians. "Curare."

But Ari raced through the fog to the window instead. The empty window! Shit. Fear burned in his gut. Janco held his breath and dashed after Ari.

His partner leaned out. Oh no. Janco joined him, preparing to see the worst.

Ari held Valek's arm as the man dangled in midair. The big man's arm muscles strained with effort. Janco reached for Valek's other arm. Together they heaved their boss into the room.

"They're reviving," Maren yelled.

"Go," Valek ordered.

They sprinted for the door and didn't stop until they reached Valek's suite. Valek unlocked the door. Or tried. His hands shook and the key rattled in the lock. Ari nudged Valek aside and finished the task. The housekeeper had lit the lanterns, but the main living area was empty.

Valek called for Yelena. He raced up the stairs, then returned a few minutes later, wild-eyed and frantic. "She isn't here. Owen said she's next. We need to search the castle!"

Ari blocked Valek. "Owen didn't have time to set a trap for her."

"But what if he's looking for her right now?" Valek tried to push past, but Ari clamped a hand on his shoulder.

"He won't just grab her in front of witnesses. He'll have to plan. Let's just take a moment and think. Okay?" Ari guided him to the couch.

Valek just about collapsed onto the cushions. Concerned by his boss's stunned expression, Janco rummaged for the good stuff in Valek's corner cabinet. No one said a word as Janco poured healthy shots of whiskey into four glasses. He handed one to each. They clinked the glasses together and downed the alcohol in one gulp.

Fire burned his throat and warmed his stomach. Janco refilled the glasses.

Valek stared into his, swirling the amber liquid around. "That's the closest I've come to…" He pulled in a deep breath, then raised his glass to them. "Thank you."

"Thank Janco," Maren said. "He's the one who figured it out."

"Yeah, but I couldn't have done anything without you and Ari."

"We're a team. This is what we do," Ari said.

They drank. This time Janco sipped his.

"Now we can concentrate on finding Yelena," Ari said. "Has anyone seen her since she returned from her ride with Reema?"

No one had.

"We'll divide the castle into sections and each take one," Valek said.

"No can do," Janco said. "If one of us runs into Owen or his goons, we'll be in trouble." He scratched his goatee. "We should stay together. Let's list the places she's most likely to be." He glanced at the dark windows. "Supper's over. How about the washroom?"

"Or she could have gone to say goodbye to Reema and found her alone," Ari said.

Valek stood. The whiskey appeared to have steadied him. "Let's go."

They left the suite. As they headed down to the washrooms, Janco asked Valek, "Are you going to report the attack to the Commander?"

"No. Owen will spin a tale about how I tried to sneak into his rooms."

"But we saw—"

"What, exactly?" Valek asked.

Janco recalled the scene in the guest suite. "He had his hands on your shoulders."

"He'll claim he was trying to help me. You didn't witness my abduction. All you had to go on was a creepy feeling in a dark hallway. No. It would be pointless to report the incident to the Commander."

"How did he manage to capture you?" Maren asked.

Valek exchanged a look with Ari. The big guy nodded and Valek explained to Maren about the null shields.

It didn't take her long to understand the danger. "So that means he can trap you at any time?"

"Unfortunately. And he can also suffocate me with that blasted shield." Valek increased his pace.

Janco wished he'd brought the bottle of whiskey along as they checked the washroom, then their apartment, where they found Reema curled up in a chair fast asleep. They searched the stables, the kennels and visited Yelena's friend Dilana, the seamstress. With every stop, Janco's alarm grew twofold.

They visited Valek's office, just in case. Valek's knife remained in the hallway. He picked it up and a murderous expression settled on his face. If Owen had been standing there, no doubt Valek would have rammed the blade into his black heart.

While there were plenty of places left to look, there was no logical reason Yelena would visit them.

"Owen must have her," Valek said in a deadly tone. "I'll kill him."

13

YELENA

Blue. The liquid in Medic Mommy's vial was blue. Blue for baby. I navigated the hallways of the castle without any thoughts on my destination. Lanterns glowed, painting blue shadows on gray stone walls. I clutched a list of foods and drinks that would aid in the baby's healthy growth. The words had been written in blue ink.

Deep down, the news wasn't a shock, but rather a confirmation. Yet the part of me that wanted to automatically dismiss the idea had been a loudmouth, shouting over the quiet knowledge.

Bad time or not, I wasn't able to change the past. Based on my calculations and Medic Mommy's experience, I was about six weeks along, which meant I had a few months before my body revealed the truth to others. The baby was due in seven and a half months and right in the middle of the cooling season. Hopefully by that time, Owen would be turned into a memory. A "remember when" that had a happy ending.

What a crazy day. I wondered if Valek would still consider my news a cause for celebration. So much had happened since I first suspected.

A baby.

I imagined a little boy with bright blue eyes and black hair. The scamp would be causing trouble at every turn. Janco would soon be the favorite uncle, and Junior would probably learn how to throw a knife before he learned how to dress himself. Or perhaps a little girl with curly black hair. She'd be in the midst of trouble and have Valek wrapped around her finger. Ari would spoil her rotten. And she'd learn how to pick a lock before she could read.

I arrived at the kitchen. Laughter and the clatter of dishes vibrated through the double doors. A spicy roasted meat aroma enticed me onward. Steam puffed from buckets of water as the staff scrubbed pots. I'd missed supper while visiting the medic.

Sammy, the head chef, spotted me hovering near the door and waved me over to his workstation. It gleamed, but his all-white uniform sported a number of gravy splotches and other stains.

"Did you stop by to say hello or to scrounge for food?" he asked.

"Both. And to thank you for the delicious sweet cakes. The best you've ever made. You added something new, didn't you?" I sat on one of the stools.

"Yup. Guess what it is." A devilish grin spanned Sammy's youthful face.

At age twenty, he was the youngest person ever assigned as head chef for the Commander. A pang of grief pressed on my heart for the previous chef, Rand. A friend who had betrayed me, and then saved me.

"Lemon juice?"

"Aww, you're no fun." He pretended to pout.

"Then you should ask someone who wasn't trained as a food taster. Why did you add it?"

"The lemon juice reacts with the baking powder, causing

the batter to bubble, and it makes the sweet cakes lighter and fluffier."

"And yummier." I smiled. "Speaking of food, is there anything left over from supper?"

He opened one of the ovens built into the stones above the huge hearth that dominated the center of the kitchen. Grabbing a protective mitt, he pulled a pan out along with the mouthwatering scent of braised beef.

Sammy picked up an oversize metal spoon, ladled two heaping servings and slid one over to me along with a fork. "Nice to have company while I eat."

"Thanks. Do you always wait this late?"

"Yup. This way I know everyone's fed and no one's gonna interrupt me."

The meat just fell apart and melted in my mouth. Sammy chuckled at my unladylike moans.

"This is fantastic. What's the occasion?"

Sammy sobered. "The Commander's guests requested it."

Figured Owen wouldn't be happy with standard fare. And this was the perfect opportunity to learn what the gossip network had discovered. "Does the Commander usually let his guests decide?"

"No. Usually, he lets me plan the menu unless there's a special occasion. Then he orders the meal. But these three have been a giant pain in my ass since they've arrived."

"Really?"

"Yup. They complain about everything. The meat's too hot. It's too cold. Too much bread. Not enough cheese. They also have the poor housekeepers in a tizzy."

"Why?"

"They've taken over the entire guest wing and refuse to let the housekeepers into certain rooms. And they fuss if their beds aren't made early enough and if the chamber pots aren't immediately emptied."

"Has any of the staff complained to the Commander?" I asked.

"No. The Commander gave orders that we were to ensure that their every need was met, no matter what. And no, he's never said that before. Not even when the Generals are visiting."

Not too surprising, if Owen had somehow managed to influence the Commander despite the null shield woven into his uniforms. How long ago did Leif provide the protection? Could Owen have done it four and a half years ago, when he'd first been captured in Ixia? I'd have to ask Leif. But would his answer come in time? Before, I'd contact him through a super messenger and have instant communication. Now it would take a week at least. If my magic ever returned, I'd never take it for granted again.

"Anything else strange going on with them?" I asked.

Sammy chewed thoughtfully. "Yup. They took a bunch of the housekeepers' buckets and filled them with dirt. And they've been burning lots of wood. But not in their rooms, 'cause there's not enough ash."

"Buckets of dirt?"

He shrugged. "Probably in the rooms they blocked from the staff."

Sammy's gossip confirmed that Owen had brought along a few of those Harman saplings and were growing them inside. It made sense if the tree was used to the warmer Sitian climate. Plus, it would take a few weeks for Owen to build a glass hothouse.

As Sammy prattled on about the various hookups among the servants, I wondered if Valek could sneak into the guest suite and steal one of those saplings. Eventually Sammy finished his stories and started yawning. His day started hours before dawn. I bid him a good-night and headed to Valek's suite.

Only a few people traveled the corridors. It was later than I'd thought. By the time I reached the turn into the shortcut through the servant's wing, the halls were deserted.

"Yelena!" Valek called from behind me. He sounded relieved.

I turned.

He ran up to me. "Where have you been?"

"In the kitchen, talking to Sammy. Why? Is something wrong?"

"I've been searching all over for you."

Not quite an answer. "Aren't you supposed to be guarding the Commander?"

"He refused the extra protection."

"Then what—"

"Come on." He grabbed my wrist, tugging me the opposite way. "Janco and Ari found something interesting in the guest wing and want you to look at it."

"Is it a tree growing in a bucket of dirt?"

Valek's grip tightened. "How did you know?"

He sounded accusatory rather than impressed. Strange. "The gossip network. Why else do you think I was in the kitchen?"

"Oh. Well, now you'll get a chance to see it up close."

He hurried through the hallways, dragging me along and going the long way. I stumbled and his nails dug into my skin as he yanked me upright. "Ow. Valek, slow down."

"No time."

I glanced at my arm to see if he broke the skin and I almost tripped again. The long thin fingers clutching my wrist were not Valek's, but a woman's. Yet when I focused on the rest of the body, it appeared to be Valek, which meant...

An illusion! And only one person in Ixia had that ability. Rika.

After a brief moment of panic, I settled my nerves. Illusions couldn't harm me. As long as she didn't have any surprise talents, I wasn't about to let her haul me to her cohorts, where I'd be outnumbered. I dug in my heels, slowing our progress.

"Come on," she said.

Recalling my self-defense lessons, I broke her grip. Then I kicked her in the ribs with a side kick. Rika flew back, and I took off. She yelled, but I ignored her. However, at the end of the corridor, Owen and Tyen stepped into view, blocking my escape. Oh no. My pulse jumped in my throat as fear zinged through me.

I glanced over my shoulder. Rika clutched her side, but she stared in my direction. They wouldn't get me without a fight. Increasing my speed, I aimed for the space between the men, hoping my momentum would allow me to break through.

Except they were also an illusion. I sailed right by them and slammed into the far wall. Pain spiked my shoulder, but I didn't bother to slow or to look back as I ran all the way to the main entrance of Valek's and the Commander's suites. Valek's rooms were the safest place for me.

The guards reached for their weapons when they spotted me. I stopped and gasped for breath. It had been a while since I'd had to run for my life. Guess I'd need to add that to my training schedule.

When no one appeared behind me, I explained about the illusions. "Even if it looks and sounds just like Valek or the Commander, don't let them pass unless you inspect their key for the diamond insignia. Understood?"

"Yes, sir."

"And the same goes for me." I dug my key from my pocket and showed the row of diamond shapes etched into the round, flat section. The Commander's paranoia came in handy from time to time and I doubted Rika would know about the symbols.

"Yes, sir."

"Has the Commander retired for the evening?" I asked.

"Yes."

"Is Valek with him?"

"No."

"Have you seen Valek tonight?"

"Yes. He was here briefly with his second-in-commands. But he hasn't been back since."

"Thanks." I debated if I should search for him, but decided it'd be too dangerous. He'd return to his suite eventually.

When I entered, I spotted four empty glasses and a bottle of whiskey. I considered pouring myself a large portion, but Medic Mommy advised me to avoid alcohol. Too bad.

Instead, I stirred the fire to life and filled the teapot with water. Waiting for Valek proved difficult, so I rummaged through his piles of books for something to distract me. I found one titled *The Art of the Lie*, by Hedda Bhavsar, that instructed readers how to lie convincingly and how to spot liars. Useful information.

Once I had a steaming mug of tea in hand and the book in the other, I settled into a comfortable position on the couch and used my cloak as a blanket. Since it was longer and heavier than she was used to, Reema had been happy to return it to me. She liked the new one I'd purchased, and it fit her much better.

Despite the fascinating subject, I didn't read too long before my eyelids gained weight and the words blurred together on the page. Head nods came next. Giving up, I set the book down and stretched out. After all, Medic Mommy had lectured me on getting the proper rest. I'd finish reading later.

A shuffle woke me, sending fear zipping down my spine.

Valek wouldn't be so noisy. Under the cover of my cloak, I reached for the switchblade strapped to my leg and grasped the handle. I peered between slitted eyelids. Embers glowed from the dying fire. I'd been asleep a couple of hours. No other sounds disturbed the quiet. I waited for an attack, but nothing happened.

Unable to remain still any longer, I jumped to my feet, brandishing my weapon. The room was empty. Or so I thought.

Valek sighed my name. He stood by the door, blending in with the dark wood. He hurried over to me, but I backed up and assumed a defensive stance. His expression of relief transformed into confusion and he stopped a few feet away.

"What's wrong?" he asked.

"What shape did you make with the napkins for Leif's wedding?" I asked.

"Are you—"

"Just answer the question."

Understanding smoothed his features. "Swans, but I can make flowers, as well. Which would you prefer for our wedding?"

I sagged with relief. Closing my switchblade, I stepped into his arms. He hugged me tight. And for a long moment, he said nothing.

"Did they try to trick you with an illusion?" Valek finally asked, releasing me.

"Yes." I explained about the incident with Rika.

"Thank fate you escaped. Seems we were wrong to assume Owen'd wait to attack us."

Alarmed, I asked, "Us?"

"Yes, I had my own run-in with him." Valek detailed his ambush and near-death experience.

"Run-in? He almost killed you!"

Valek didn't deny it or dismiss it with his usual bravado,

which worried me even more. "Is that why you were standing by the door? Did you think I was another trap?"

"No." He paused. "I needed...a moment. The guards said you were in here, but I didn't quite believe them until I saw you. And then..." Valek pulled me close. "We searched half the castle. I thought Owen had you."

"I'm surprised you didn't go after him." And glad.

"I wanted to, but Ari stopped me."

"Did he sit on you?" I teased. That earned me a smile.

"No. He used logic."

"Yay for logic."

"I better go and tell them you're safe. They're waiting with the guards."

"The guards?"

"Yes, I insisted they remain there. It was difficult since Ari and Janco won't let me go anywhere on my own."

"That's good. Stronger together, remember?"

He hesitated for a second, then said, "I need to tell Ari he was right."

"It could be worse."

Valek waited.

"It could be Janco who was right."

"Ah, yes. That would be worse."

Ari and Janco were happy to see me and I gave them each an extra hug for saving Valek.

Maren refused to hug me. "Save that mushy stuff for your boyfriend."

Much to Janco's disgust, Ari limited his gloating. "It's wasted, just wasted on you!"

Ignoring his partner, Ari said, "We'll be back at dawn to escort you to your meeting with the Commander. Then we'll stay with you until you and Yelena leave."

MARIA V. SNYDER

"We're leaving?" I asked Valek in an icy tone.

"Didn't he tell you?" Janco asked.

"There wasn't time." Valek frowned at him.

"That's our cue to say good-night," Janco said, pulling Ari and Maren with him as they left.

I stared at Valek, waiting.

"We're leaving tomorrow."

"Why? What else happened?" The now-familiar throb of fear pulsed in my chest.

"The Commander has given you a choice," Valek explained.

"That isn't really a choice." I couldn't cut all ties with Sitia and my family to be the Commander's Sitian Adviser.

"And since Owen has made his intentions clear, you're safer with me. So you're coming with me to investigate those Storm Thieves."

I drew breath to speak, but Valek interrupted me with a kiss.

"Let's just go to sleep. It's been a hell of a long day," he said.

"That bad?"

He pressed his hand over my heart. "Except for this joy. Yes."

I put my hands over his and then pulled it down so his palm rested on my abdomen. "How about this?"

He stared at me. "Are you sure?"

"Medic Mommy confirmed it."

He beamed. "I've changed my mind. This is the best day of my life! When?"

"Middle of the cooling season."

Valek swept me up in his arms, spun me around, laughing. "We're going to be a family!"

Snuggled together in bed, we exchanged information about what we'd discovered that day and discussed the Commander's orders.

I mulled everything over and found a few troubling inconsistencies. "If Owen is controlling the Commander, then why would he send you to the coast and ensure I'd return to Sitia? Owen wants us both dead. It'd be easier if we remain in the castle."

"But Owen's attempts to kill us failed. Maybe he wants us out of the way so he can work on his plans without us interfering." Valek stifled a yawn.

"You received your orders from the Commander before Owen's ambush."

Valek pushed up on his elbow. "That's right. Are you thinking Owen *isn't* influencing the Commander?"

"No. The Commander has been acting too erratic. Yet…" I struggled to grasp the significance. He'd been horrible to Valek, almost as if he wanted to drive him away. "Did you tell him about the Storm Thieves?"

"Yes."

And that gave the Commander a reason to send Valek away! "I think he's trying to protect us."

"Sorry, love, but I'm too tired to follow your logic. Protect us from what?"

"From Owen. From himself."

"But wouldn't Owen know and stop him?"

He had a point. I speculated further—all I could do without my magic. "Maybe Owen doesn't have complete control yet. Maybe the Commander is hoping we'll get help before he succumbs to the magic."

Valek lay down. "That's a lot of maybes. Although I rather like the idea of the Commander trying to protect us. It's better than the alternative."

I agreed. It didn't take us long to fall into an exhausted sleep. Dawn came way too soon. Valek left for his meeting and I packed my meager belongings. I finished in no time.

MARIA V. SNYDER

Instead of fretting over a dozen different things, I sat on the couch and resumed reading *The Art of the Lie*. The book included instructions on how to read a person's body language by spotting small gestures and tics that revealed a liar.

A shutter creaked loudly. I stood and grabbed my switchblade. Onora climbed through the now-open window and stepped into the room. At least I hoped it was her and not another illusion.

She held her hands wide, showing she was unarmed. "I'm sorry if I startled you, but the guards wouldn't let me in."

"And you couldn't wait?"

"I wanted to talk to you in private before you left."

"Okay, but indulge me first. What is the one thing Janco hates?"

She laughed. "Janco hates many things, but he has a strong aversion to sand. He also despises magic and ants. Did I pass?"

I doubted Owen would know all that about Janco. "Yes." Gesturing to the couch, I asked, "Would you like some tea?"

"Yes, please." Onora sat on the opposite end. "I know you're worried about being fooled by an illusion, but there is no way Rika or anyone else would be able to climb in through Valek's windows."

"That difficult?" I added more water to the teapot.

"Yes, and he has a couple...interesting booby traps." She pulled her sleeve back to reveal a cut along her forearm. "Knives hidden under fake stones being one." Blood snaked to her wrist.

"Let me get you a bandage."

"No need. It's not deep." Onora tugged her shirt down, covering the wound and avoiding my touch.

She wore an all-black, tight-fitting sneak suit similar to Valek's, except it lacked a hood. Plus, her hands, feet and face remained uncovered. Morning sunlight streamed in through the open window.

"Someone may have spotted you on the castle's walls," I said.

"I doubt it. Most people don't look up."

"True." But knowing Valek, he had probably assigned an agent to watch the walls.

I poured two cups of tea and handed one to Onora. "You wanted to discuss something?"

She sipped her tea. "Valek informed me this morning that…" Onora gazed at her lap. "That Captain Timmer is in the Commander's dungeon, and that I would have the honor of executing him at the fire festival in front of the Commander's entire army."

I suspected this Timmer had been the one to assault her, and the Commander wished to make him an example. "Why you? Why him?"

Her foot juddered, swinging back and forth like an excited puppy's tail. "He's the bastard I should have assassinated a year ago."

"Why didn't you?"

"I… Shit." She set the teacup down with a clatter and surged to her feet. "I tried, but every time I got close to him… I just…couldn't. My failure's been haunting me. I was so convinced his death would make everything go away. But then you claimed it wouldn't. And…"

I waited.

Onora stabbed a stick into the fire. Sparks flew and ash swirled. "And I…panicked. What if I can't kill him? What happens if this…" She pounded a fist on her chest. "This hardness inside me doesn't dissipate with his death? What if it spreads instead, turning me as hard and cold as the castle's stones?"

Ah. I drank my tea, stalling for time as I mulled over her comments. "You knew before I said anything that death wasn't the right solution. That's why you couldn't assassinate him."

"But he should die!" She punctuated *die* with a powerful thrust of her branch. The logs shifted, rolling to the back. Her anger spent, she sat on the floor, crossing her legs.

"And the Commander agrees with you. His soldiers are warned of the consequences of abusing their power, and Timmer will be executed, either by your hand or another's. Yet that won't untie the knots inside you. You need to determine what you're afraid of and confront it." I lifted my cup. "I know. Easier said than done, and if I had my magic and your permission, we may have been able to untangle you this morning."

She stared at the flames. They flickered as if agitated.

Memories of my efforts to expel my fear rose to the surface of my thoughts. Terror and pain no longer tainted these memories. Instead I drew strength from them, and Onora needed to know I shared a similar experience. I told her about the torture and rape I'd endured. "Reyad blamed me for the abuse. If only I'd listened better or tried harder, then I wouldn't suffer. He led me to believe that I was no longer a person, but an empty shell to be used. I slit his throat, not to stop him from hurting me, but to keep him from abusing my sisters in the orphanage. I knew murder would land me in the Commander's dungeon, awaiting execution, and I welcomed it."

"How did you get past all that?" Onora asked in a low tone.

"With the realization that I was in control of my life and body. Me. Not him. That I was no longer a victim and should stop acting like one. I also had help from my friends. And I drew strength from Valek's love. I still do."

"I don't have—"

"Yes, you have friends. Janco may be annoying, but he'd drop everything in a heartbeat to help you. You have me and

Gerik—who I suspect cares for you more than he lets on. And the fact Valek hasn't killed you yet is an encouraging sign."

She laughed. "To quote Janco, 'I feel all warm and fuzzy inside.'" Then she sobered. "What am I to do about Timmer?"

"The fire festival is six months away, so you have time to decide. In the meantime, I suggest you visit the captain." Before she could reply, I said, "And I think going to talk to the young women who Timmer abused after you left is a good idea, as well. Valek has their names. Make sure you get them before we leave."

Onora gave me a mulish look, but she said, "Yes, sir."

"Good. I want a report about your progress when I see you again."

"I heard you're leaving for Sitia. Does that mean you decided not to become the Commander's Sitian Adviser?"

Interesting. Valek hadn't trusted Onora with my real destination. I wondered who else knew besides Ari and Janco. "Yes. That shouldn't be a surprise."

"It isn't."

We shared a smile. Then I asked, "Have you noticed a change in him since we've arrived?"

"Yes. He's harsher and no longer wishes to hear advice from me or his advisers. And before you ask, the Commander hasn't confided to me about what Owen is planning."

"Would you tell us if you knew?" I asked.

"Not if the Commander ordered me to keep quiet."

"Fair enough. How about if you knew Owen was using magic on him? Would you tell us then?"

"If you can prove that is the case, then I would, to save the Commander."

"Good to know. Too bad all I know is that Owen is growing those Harman saplings in the guest suite. But I have no idea why."

"How do you know this?"

I explained about the kitchen staff. "They're rarely wrong."

"Would getting a branch of one of those plants help you?"

"Yes, but Valek says it's too dangerous. They probably surrounded them with a magical barrier that would alert them if someone crosses it."

"Do you think they'd relax once you are gone?" Onora asked.

"No. Don't try it. It's too dangerous. I'll ask my father about it."

But Onora's contemplative expression failed to dissipate. She thanked me for the tea and my time. The guards at the main entrance weren't pleased that she'd bypassed their security, but she ignored them.

Valek entered the suite close to noon. He carried a stack of uniforms. When I asked about his meeting with the Commander, he said, "The more I interact with him, the greater my certainty that he's being influenced."

"Even though the Commander has a magic detector?"

"What would happen if Owen put a null shield around it?"

Interesting. "It would no longer flash when magic was used, but it would have sparked when he pulled power to create the null shield."

"In that case, he could just distract the Commander. Owen's rather quick with those bloody things." Valek frowned.

"What about the null shields woven into the Commander's uniforms?" I asked.

"Would that protect his head, as well?"

"Yes."

"Is the shield skintight?"

"I'm not sure. Leif has been experimenting with them. And that glass magician, Quinn, can attach one to a glass pendant."

Valek handed me the uniforms, but seemed distracted. "What would happen if Owen touched your skin while you wore protected clothes?"

I considered. "Are you thinking that once Owen's fingers are past the shield, he could use his magic on a person?"

"Yes. The shield blocks magic, but not physical objects."

And magic would work inside a null shield bubble as long as the magic wasn't directed at something outside the bubble's walls. "He'd have to channel the power through his body and to the ends of his fingertips. Difficult to do, but not impossible. That is *if* the shield doesn't go through his hand, but rather flows around it like invisible water."

"Would Leif know?"

"If he doesn't, it wouldn't be hard to find out."

Tugging his sleeve down, Valek fiddled with the cuff. "Speaking of hands, it was interesting about the illusion Rika tried to trick you with, and how you noticed her fingers didn't match the rest. Do you think it was the physical contact that negated the magical effects?"

With everything that had happened since then, I'd forgotten about that. "If it did, then I would have been able to see her whole body under the illusion and not just her hand."

"Unless it's just the part that is in direct contact with you. Perhaps what's blocking your magic will block others', as well."

Interesting indeed. Could there be a bright side after all? "I can experiment with that when I'm back in Sitia." I'd love to neutralize the bastard with a touch. Thinking about Owen... "What happens after we deal with the Storm Thieves? Are we going to Sitia?"

Valek's expression hardened. "If I leave Ixia, it will be an act of treason."

"You said the Commander is under Owen's influence."

"I know, but I'm still hoping to repair my relationship with the Commander." He stepped close and cupped my cheek with his hand. "It'll never be the same as before, but I don't wish to destroy any chance I have to retire on a positive note."

"Retire?" That was new.

"Someone has to change diapers while you're saving the world, love."

My heart melted over his willingness to retire for me and the baby. "Me? Save the world? So you're a comedian *and* an expert diaper changer. Wow, did I hook a keeper or what?"

He bowed. "You have the total package."

"I'd swoon, except I'm guessing I don't have time."

"No. The boys will be here soon to escort us to the stables." Valek pointed to the clothes I held. "You'll need to change into an Ixian adviser's uniform in order to blend in once we're away from the castle." Valek retrieved his own pack and sorted through the contents.

As I added the solid black pants and shirt with two red diamonds stitched onto the collar to my pack, I mulled over our conversation. "What will I do then? I can't return to the castle and I'm not going to sulk about Ixia, hiding." And do nothing.

Valek didn't answer. And I realized why he remained quiet.

"You don't really need me at the coast. It makes more sense for me to travel to Sitia. Then I can experiment, consult with Leif and my father. It—"

"No. Too dangerous."

"It's dangerous to give Owen time to set his plans in motion."

"We have time."

"How do you know?"

Valek folded his black sneak suit. "We have until the fire festival." Gathering an impressive number of knives, Valek slid them into various pockets in his uniform and into hidden places in his knapsack. "It's not like the Commander to make an execution a public spectacle. Just hanging the man for abusing his power is enough of a deterrent. News would eventually spread to even the remotest post."

A tendril of unease snaked around my heart. "You think the Commander has another reason for requiring all his soldiers to be at the fire festival?"

He met my gaze. "Yes."

"And this reason includes Owen?"

"Yes."

When I considered how close Castletown was to the Sitian Citadel, the tendril thickened and squeezed. "They're going to invade Sitia!"

14

VALEK

"We need to warn Sitia," Yelena said.

"Of what? Our gut feeling? We've no proof, love."

"But the Commander's army might invade."

"And they might not. Besides, I'd hang for treason if I warned Sitia of an attack."

"I won't."

"You wouldn't hang for treason, but the Commander would consider you an enemy of Ixia and send an assassin after you. We'll just have to ruin Owen's plans well before the fire festival."

"How? We need to consult with Leif and my father about those Harman saplings. And the null shields."

Valek loved watching Yelena puzzle out a problem. Her brow crinkled and he suppressed the desire to smooth the ridge with a kiss. "I've a loyal and skilled agent who is going to deliver messages for us. Once Leif responds to your missive, she'll bring it to us in MD-1."

Yelena frowned.

"What's wrong?" he asked.

"Where in MD-1?"

"The northern coast."

"Too far. Once Leif learns Owen is in Ixia, he'll return to the Citadel. Even if your agent had the fastest horse in Ixia, it would still take her twelve days to travel that distance. And messages aren't effective. If Leif doesn't understand something, it will be a twenty-four-day wait until he does. Plus, you can't brainstorm ideas."

"No." The word sprang without thought from his primal core. The place deep down inside him that screamed, *You will stay with me!*

"You know it's logical."

To hell with logic. "We're stronger together. You said so yourself." Ha. She couldn't logic her way out of that one.

"Yes, for when we go against *Owen*. Not against a gang of Storm Thieves. I'll just be in the way."

"Fine. I'm coming with you to Sitia."

"You can't."

"I'll wear a disguise."

"And what happens when the reports keep coming in from MD-1 about those Storm Thieves?"

He crossed his arms, refusing to acknowledge her point.

She answered for him. "The Commander learns you committed treason."

"I'll stay in Sitia."

"And let Owen win?"

Determined to remain stubborn, he kept silent.

"All right. We let Owen win, and he eventually convinces the Commander to invade Sitia, where *we'll* be living. You, me and our child. How long do you think Sitia will last? I guess we could go into hiding, wear disguises and live in constant fear. That's a healthy environment to raise a child." Her tone indicated it would be anything but. "And we both know it's a matter of time before the Commander hunts us down."

Damn it all to hell! Valek growled every single curse he

knew as impotent fury surged through him. At this moment, he hated logic. He wanted to take his knife and stab it through its cold calculating heart. Why couldn't he be selfish and irrational for once? Damn it all to hell!

"I'm not happy about it, either. But I won't be gone long," Yelena said in a soft voice. "We can rendezvous and return to the castle together."

"Have you forgotten there's an assassin after you?" he asked.

"I'll head straight for the Magician's Keep. I'll be safe there."

"Then take Ari and Janco with you. Please."

"Will the Commander agree?"

"I'll make sure he does."

"All right."

He pulled her into a hug as he accepted the inevitable. "This is the last time we say goodbye."

"Don't say that. We have many more goodbyes and hellos left."

"I meant—"

"I know, and that's a sweet sentiment, but even you know it's impossible."

"You mean you won't let me lock you in a tower so you can never leave?"

She gazed up at him. "Tempting...but no."

"You'll promise to be extra careful?"

"Of course."

They finished packing just as the guard knocked on the door to inform them that Ari and Janco had arrived. The man retreated back to his post. Valek slung his pack over his shoulder and grabbed Yelena's.

He grunted. "What's in here? Rocks?"

"Books. And don't you start being all..." She tugged on the handle. "I can carry it."

"Being all what?" Keeping a firm grip on her pack, he strode to the door.

She hustled beside him. "Being all…my-wife-is-pregnant-and-she-can't-do-anything…overprotective."

"Me, overprotective? You must have mistaken me for another man," he teased.

She swatted him on the arm.

"You're the one who had to pack books." Valek waited while she opened the inner door. "What kind of books?"

"Ones about how to spy and stuff."

"Nothing's better than actual training."

"I know, but I can still learn a few new tricks."

"Tricks?" Janco asked as they exited the main entrance.

"Yes. You'll need your bag of tricks," Valek said. "You, too, Ari."

"Why?" they asked in unison.

Valek explained their new mission. "All you have to do is protect Yelena."

"Easier said than done," Janco muttered, then shot her a sweet smile. "What about the Commander?"

"After you pack, we'll swing by his office and I'll obtain permission. I'm sure he'll want to ensure she arrives in Sitia without incident. She may no longer be the Liaison, but he wouldn't risk a diplomatic incident. At least, not yet." He fervently hoped.

As they headed to Ari and Janco's apartment, Valek asked Ari about Reema.

"She left this morning," Ari said.

"Any problems?"

"None."

"She *loved* her gifts," Janco chimed in.

"What gifts?" Yelena asked.

MARIA V. SNYDER

Valek swallowed a groan as Janco listed the various weapons they'd given the girl.

"Opal's going to kill you," Yelena said.

"Not me," Janco protested. "Ari bought them. I just gave her a set of lock picks."

"Ari?" Yelena turned to him.

"Sitian knives are too flimsy. She's going to need a quality set."

"For what? To defend against the other eleven-year-olds in her class?" Anger turned her words sharp.

Ari hunched his shoulders. "To defend against those who would use her to get to you."

Which was the reason Reema was at the castle in the first place. Yelena snapped her mouth shut. Then she exhaled. "You're right. Sorry, Ari."

"And we all know Reema's going into the family business," Janco said.

"Family?" Yelena rested her hand on her stomach.

Before anyone noticed her unconscious gesture, Valek tugged her hand away and laced his fingers through hers. Excitement about the baby tapped a quick tempo in his heart, but a deep bass of worry also played along. He kept his expression neutral.

"Yeah. You know…" Janco swept his arm out, indicating all of them. "Us. She's the next generation of sneak." He grinned with glee. "I almost feel sorry for those future criminals. They won't know what hit them."

"So we're all sneaks?" Ari asked.

"Sneaks, spies, defenders, heroes, masterminds, tenacious bastards—it doesn't matter what you call us. We're the ones who will do whatever it takes to stop those who believe they're entitled to wealth and power at the expense of others."

"The family business," Yelena said, smiling. "I like that. Well said, Janco."

Valek squeezed her hand in agreement. For once Janco didn't preen.

The boys packed in record time. Valek wished his admittance into the Commander's office matched their speed. Eventually the Commander allowed him to enter and heard his request.

The chair creaked as the Commander leaned back, studying Valek. "Granted. Have them collect information on the Council before returning to Ixia."

"Most of the Councilors will recognize them," Valek said.

"They can still get a sense of the Council's mood and look for signs of an invasion. Tell them to look for a possible way to get our agent inside. Perhaps one of the Councilors needs a new adviser."

"Yes, sir."

Relieved expressions greeted him when he exited the Commander's office. "Did you expect him to say no?" Valek asked.

"Yes, actually," Ari said. "He's been giving you such a hard time since you returned from Sitia."

"Yeah, but without us underfoot, there will be two fewer obstacles in Owen's path," Janco said.

Good point, but Valek wouldn't say it aloud and risk Janco gloating. "You might be safer in Sitia."

"Doubtful," Janco muttered.

Yelena flicked his left earlobe with her finger.

"Ow!"

Now she shot him a sweet smile.

"Kids, behave," Valek admonished, but inside the knot of worry for his heart mate eased just a bit. Janco and Ari would do everything in their considerable power to keep her safe.

The four of them left the castle and headed toward the

stables, where Maren and Onora had been waiting for them. On the way, they picked a rendezvous location and estimated a date to meet.

"Don't go back to the castle without me," Valek ordered.

"Same goes for you," she shot back.

When Maren and Onora came into view, Yelena said, "Here are two more members of our family."

The women sat on bales of straw stacked near the entrance. Both Kiki and Onyx had been saddled, and their travel supplies were packed. Valek glanced at Maren.

She shrugged. "We were bored. Where have you been?"

He explained about the change in plans. "Onora is now in charge. The Commander wants reports twice daily."

A subtle flinch of surprise meant Onora hadn't expected that.

"Consult frequently with Maren," Valek added.

"Yes, sir."

When Ari and Janco sought the Stable Master for horses, Valek pulled Onora aside. "Keep a close eye on the Commander. As close as he'll allow. And send me a message if anything odd or strange or bad happens. Also, if you learn of anything that will affect his or Ixia's safety."

"Yes, sir."

"Did you have a nice chat with Yelena?"

Her gaze snapped to him. "Did she tell you?"

"No. The agent who had his crossbow trained on your back as you climbed the wall told me."

"Why didn't he shoot me?"

"He recognized you and once you reached the window, he knew you weren't an illusion."

She touched her arm. A small white bandage peeked from underneath her sleeve.

"Did you visit the medic?"

"It's just a scratch."

"Go see her right away. I treat my blades with scum. You'll get an infection if you don't clean the cut properly."

"Yes, sir."

"I'm quite impressed that when you climbed to the Commander's suite that first time you didn't encounter any of my hidden blades." Valek studied Onora, seeking a reaction. "And it was quite the coincidence that Sergeant Gerik was assigned to cover the wall that evening."

Onora didn't blink, or even breathe, for that matter.

Gotcha. Valek drove his point home. "Gerik must have recognized you, since you both grew up in Silver Falls and you joined the army at the same time. Too bad he was assigned to another unit."

"Why didn't you…"

"Arrest him?"

She nodded.

"And split up a highly effective team? No. You'll need loyal people working with you if you're going to take over my job."

The prospect of being promoted failed to crack her serious demeanor. Perhaps she'd learned enough about his position to realize the danger and constant headaches.

Valek and Onora rejoined the others. The Stable Master had brought The Madam and a thick-chested dark brown horse with a white diamond on its forehead.

"Is it okay to send The Madam along with Kiki?" he asked Onora.

"Yes. She'll help Janco get through his lonely nights without his beloved Beach Bunny."

Janco made a rude gesture at her. As Ari and Janco saddled their horses, Valek warned Maren and Onora to keep away from Owen. He also reminded them of the various operations

MARIA V. SNYDER

in progress. "And select an agent for the undercover job. Ari and Janco will be sending you more information."

"Don't worry, Dad," Maren said. "We won't burn the house down or invite our friends over for a brew party while you're gone."

"We'll probably be at the rendezvous point before you, so message us if you need backup," Ari said to Valek.

"Yeah, feel free to share the fun," Janco added.

"I'll be on the coast," Valek replied.

"Ugh. Forget it. That's not fun."

"I'll bring you back a souvenir. A bag of sand, perhaps?" he teased.

"That would be fabulous. Then I can dump it into Ari's bed so he can experience the joy of coastal living—the unique sensation of sand in your sheets."

"Would it help me understand why you named your horse Beach Bunny?" Ari asked.

"Shut up."

While they finished packing their saddlebags, Valek drew Yelena away from the others. He put his hands on either side of her face and kissed her with the full depth of his love, wishing to communicate the vast extent of his passion and his desire. He'd have gladly given her his magical immunity if it were possible to keep her and their baby safe.

When they broke apart, Yelena gasped for breath. Her green eyes shone. "A few more kisses like that and I might agree to be locked in a tower."

"Then expect many more when you return." He traced her bottom lip with his thumb. "Hurry back, love."

"I will."

Mounting Onyx, Valek exchanged one last smile with Yelena, then spurred his horse forward. He'd already lost more than half the day, and he planned to be at the first travel shelter by sunset. As the distance from the castle grew, the warmth from his kiss with Yelena drained away. Dread, worry and an emptiness rushed in its place.

Instead of brooding, he concentrated on making up time. Traveling in Ixia was different than in Sitia. In the south, even small towns had inns, and the population sprawled from one city to the next. In Ixia, the farmers lived in town and walked to their fields every morning. The town borders were more defined to make it easier for security to patrol the perimeter and ensure everyone remained where they should.

Instead of inns, travel shelters had been built in Ixia when the distance between cities required travelers to stop for the night. Security patrols frequently checked them for unauthorized people. As an adviser to the Commander on horseback, he shouldn't be questioned as much.

Valek headed northwest. As soon as he'd passed the outer wall of the castle, he was officially in MD-6. The Commander governed all of Ixia, but he directly controlled the complex and Castletown. Both were located in the southern point of MD-6, which was ruled by General Hazal.

It would take Valek approximately nine days to reach the coast of MD-1. He'd have to cross the northeastern section of MD-8 to get there. The reports about where the Storm Thieves had hit listed many of the towns along the northern section—a place Valek knew well. He'd learned the assassin arts at the School of Night and Shadows. The complex had been built on top of a cliff facing the Sunset Ocean and near the most northwestern point in MD-1. The terrain to the south smoothed into gentle dunes, allowing fishermen to trap crabs and hook sea cod. A few miles inland, farmers raised herds of bison that thrived in the colder climate.

Valek urged Onyx into a gallop as the irrational part of

MARIA V. SNYDER

him tried to outrun his memories. But the vision of his father's leather tannery rose despite his efforts to quell it. His parents' house was near the area being targeted by the thieves. Valek had left twenty-eight years ago. The sound of his father's voice still remained clear despite the years. He'd never forget when his parents told him never to return. They hadn't approved of his desire to seek revenge on the men who murdered Valek's three brothers. And Valek had honored their request and stayed away.

Of course, he'd assigned agents to watch over them and protect them if needed. But he didn't want a detailed report. All he wished to know was that they were alive and safe. Nothing else was relevant. Details would be a painful reminder of a time he'd rather forget. And soon he'd have his own family— or rather, another addition to his eclectic family, if he agreed with Janco's assessment.

Valek reached the shelter before the sun fully set. The bloated half disk colored the sky with orange and red streaks. A couple horse stalls with a few bales of straw and buckets for water leaned against the structure. He removed Onyx's saddle. It weighed a ton. With only four hours of sleep in the past three days, Valek felt every pound. And when he considered everything that had happened with Yelena, the Commander and Owen, he was rattled, exhausted and overwhelmed.

While Onyx ate, Valek groomed him and filled a water bucket. When he finished, he patted his horse. "If you smell or hear anything, can you please alert me?"

Onyx bobbed his head.

"Thanks." He fed him a peppermint.

No one else was in the shelter. Valek doubted he'd have company, since he'd only seen a few security patrols on the road. The one-room building resembled all the other rest stops in Ixia. Valek tossed his pack onto a lower bunk far from the door. The distance would give him time to react if anyone entered with ill intentions.

After a meal of sliced cheese, nuts, meat jerky and bread—typical travel rations—Valek collapsed on the narrow bed. Already he wished the mission was over. He planned to stop the thieves as quickly as possible and return to the rendezvous location just as fast. If Yelena didn't arrive in a reasonable time, he'd go to Sitia and find her.

Not even committing treason could stop him.

After eight days of hard riding with only brief stops to rest and feed Onyx, Valek arrived at the garrison near the northern coast of MD-1 by late afternoon. He needed to check in with the local patrols in order for them to leave him alone as he conducted his investigation. Besides, a hot meal, a bathtub and a real bed sounded too good to pass up.

The guards at the gate snapped to attention and just about wet themselves when Valek told them his name. High-ranking officers were fetched and a private arrived to take charge of Onyx. Despite the private's assurance to take good care of his horse, Valek followed the young man to the stables to ensure Onyx received the proper attention.

Pausing at the entrance, Valek remembered the first time he'd arrived at this stable twenty-six years ago. He had reported to work minutes late, and the Stable Master had boxed his ear. It had been his first undercover operation, and he learned so much working as a stable boy. Back then, the King ruled Ixia, and all the officers had horses, so he'd not only been busy, but had a perfect spot to keep track of the comings and goings of the soldiers. Best of all, he'd assassinated the three men who had murdered his brothers, and their captain. No one had suspected the stable boy, and it was many years later before the garrison learned who had killed the men.

Satisfied Onyx would be taken care of, Valek allowed the garrison's commander, a Colonel Ransley, to escort him to his private dining room for supper. Four older officers and two younger lieutenants joined them for the meal. Most of the King's soldiers had switched their loyalties to the Commander during the takeover. It hadn't been hard to convince them once they learned they'd earn higher wages and receive better benefits and respect, as long as they followed the Commander's Code of Behavior.

From the occasional scowl directed his way, Valek figured a few of the older men had been stationed here when Valek had caused such panic over the mysterious deaths.

Once they were seated around an oval-shaped table, servers poured them glasses of wine and placed plates filled with steamed cod and salted seaweed. Colonel Ransley swallowed a large mouthful of wine before asking, "What brings you to this remote corner of Ixia, Adviser Valek?"

Conversation ceased as the others waited for Valek's answer.

"I've been getting reports about a gang of thieves that strike when it storms," he said.

Ransley scoffed, "It's just a bunch of kids, stealing for kicks."

"Yet you haven't stopped them." Valek studied their expressions.

"The local security forces can handle it," an older major said. "Besides, they've only stolen petty stuff. When the fleet goes out, the incidents will stop."

"Petty?" Valek asked. "I don't think the weapons taken from the security office in Gandrel are insignificant."

The major glanced at Ransley, who covered his surprise. Ransley cleared his throat. "Are you sure this information is accurate?"

Valek's tone turned icy. "Do you think I'd journey all this way for a mere rumor?"

"No, sir," Ransley was quick to reply. "It's just we hadn't heard about the hit on Gandrel."

"The thieves might be intercepting messages to the garrison," Valek said.

"Wouldn't they block information traveling to you, as well?" the old major asked.

Turning to the idiot, Valek bit down on his temper. "My corps are well trained, Major. They wouldn't make the rookie mistake of trusting the wrong messenger."

"But they couldn't find the Storm Thieves, either," one of the young lieutenants piped up.

The others froze in horror, but Valek pointed his fork at him. "You're right, Lieutenant. My corps couldn't catch them. Every time they set a trap, the thieves avoided it." His gaze met each man at the table. "Someone is providing them with insider information. It could be one of my agents, or one of the local guards. There is also the possibility that the thieves have discovered a way to spy on the authorities. Since my men were unable to determine the source of this leak, I decided to aid their efforts." Valek resumed eating.

"Why do you believe you will have more success?" the major asked, his tone skeptical.

Valek stared at the man with what Yelena called his killer look.

The major dabbed at his mouth with his napkin in an attempt to hide the red splotches spreading on his face. "Er... yes...no doubt you will... My apologies, sir."

Ransley changed the subject. "We have a promising young man that you might wish to recruit into your corps, Adviser Valek. He's a skilled swordsman and smart, too."

Letting the major off the hook for now, Valek made the appropriate inquiries about the swordsman. He wondered if any women had been promoted in this garrison and decided to check into that, as well. The King had frowned on female soldiers, claiming they were too weak to fight. The Commander held the opposite opinion and recruited many loyal and fierce women into his army when he took control of Ixia.

After supper, Ransley escorted Valek to the guest quarters. The two-room suite contained a bedroom and a living room. The lanterns had been lit and a fire danced in the small fireplace. Comfortable and clean. Valek approved.

"Colonel, while I'm investigating I'll leave my horse here, and I'll also need to borrow a couple uniforms." His black-and-red adviser's uniform would stand out among the black-and-white colors of MD-1. Each Military District had its own color combined with black.

"Of course. I'll be happy to provide anything you need."

Valek thanked Ransley as he ushered the man out the door. Changing into his sneak suit, Valek slipped from the guest quarters and ghosted through the garrison's buildings. He found a comfortable and hidden location to watch the back gate. He'd divulged his mission to his fellow dinner guests for a reason. And, after a few hours, the reason approached the gate and talked to the guards, who laughed and waved him through.

Too easy. Valek slid from his hiding spot and followed the man, certain he'd lead him right to the Storm Thieves.

A half-moon peeked from behind a layer of thin clouds, casting enough light to navigate the narrow road. Aside from the occasional glance over his shoulder or the infrequent times he stopped to listen to the night's sounds, the man didn't appear concerned about the possibility of being tracked as he headed straight to the coast.

The familiar cool scent of salt air reached Valek before the distant crash of waves. The expected turn to the southern towns didn't happen. Interested, Valek closed the distance between them so he wouldn't lose his quarry. After a few more hours, Valek guessed the man's destination. Clever. Very clever.

Sure enough, near dawn, the man entered the outer boundary of the School of Night and Shadows. Or what had once been the school. When the Commander took over Ixia, work for assassins in Ixia had dwindled. Hedda eventually closed the school instead of taking the offer to work with Valek and the Commander. But they'd recently discovered from Onora that Hedda hadn't retired, and had actually been training a few students.

Fresh grief for his old teacher rose. Onora had killed Hedda. Probably because she wouldn't divulge the name of the client who had hired an assassin to target the Commander.

Memories stirred as Valek kept the man in sight. When he'd first arrived on Hedda's doorstep, the school had plenty of students. Now the place appeared deserted—although he doubted it was. In fact, this location would be a perfect spot to run another illegal operation, like stealing during storms.

The man disappeared into the main building. In this part of MD-1, cliffs lined the Sunset Ocean, and Hedda had built her school to resemble the rocky terrain, painting all the structures in the complex to blend in with the surrounding grayish-white landscape.

The sky brightened as dawn's first rays chased away the blackness. Valek looped around to a little-known entrance. From the undisturbed and thick coating of salt and rust on the combination lock, he guessed no one had come through here in years. Good thing the corrosive salt air eventually turned metal brittle. Valek broke the lock in two and slipped inside.

He paused, letting his eyes adjust to the darkness. Voices bounced off the stone walls. Concentrating, he detected two speakers, but the words were garbled. Valek tracked the conversation until he understood the speech. He listened next to an open door. Yellow lantern light spilled into the hallway.

"…no one followed me. Stop worrying so much," a man said in a placating tone.

"You're an idiot. You just killed me," a woman responded with a twang that Valek would never forget.

"Relax. Valek's not here for you, but I thought you'd like to know he's in the area," the man said.

Valek stepped into the room, surprising the man, but not Hedda.

"I'm closer than you think. And she's right," Valek said. "You are an idiot." Then he turned to his former teacher.

Hedda stood behind her desk with a knife already in her hand. All but a few fiery red strands of her hair had turned gray. Wrinkles etched her forehead and drew her mouth into a frown.

"Hello, Hedda." Unconcerned about the blade, Valek strode closer. "Nice to see you alive and well."

She inclined her head politely. "King Killer." Her grip tightened on her weapon. "Did the Commander send you?"

15

LEIF

"They're trying to grow Theobroma-resistant Curare?" Leif repeated. "Are you sure?"

"Yes," Esau said. "This…" He waved the thin branch. Its oval-shaped leaves bounced with the motion. "…is a cross-breed of the Theobroma tree and the Curare vine. If this grows pods, the Theobroma seeds might contain Curare. If you press those seeds, you might get a Curare that can't be neutralized by Theobroma."

Sitia's army would be unable to defend itself against the paralyzing drug. The Commander's soldiers could invade without any resistance. The thought of having to wear a uniform and obey his Code of Behavior soured Leif's stomach. "So you don't know if they've been successful?"

"I'd have to wait until it produces pods that are ready to be harvested, and then test it." Excitement raised Esau's voice at the prospect.

Leif studied the specimen. Owen had escaped this compound but was unable to take these plants with him. However, he'd cleaned out his other hothouses. This might be the only sample they had. "How long until the pods are ready?"

"Oh, I'd say about…three, maybe four years."

Somehow, Leif didn't think Owen or the Commander would give them those years. But then again, it would take Owen the same amount of time to supply his men with the resistant Curare.

"What about the other crossbreed plants?" he asked his father.

"One at a time, my boy. One at a time. Is that dinner?" Esau gestured to the tray Leif held.

"Supper, Father. You worked through dinner." Leif set the tray on the ground. "When it gets dark, come inside the farmhouse. I'll have a bath ready for you."

Already chewing on an apple, Esau nodded, but his gaze had returned to the greenery surrounding him. Leif left, knowing he'd have to return and fetch his father or the man would work through the night. When his father immersed himself in a project, Leif's role was simple—take care of Esau's needs.

Esau decided he needed to catalog all the plants in the hothouse, along with the investigation of the crossbreeds. Over the course of a few days he determined that Owen's gardener had crossed a few medicinal plants.

"Very clever," Esau said. "This way one plant will take care of two symptoms. Less to pack!"

"Do you recognize the person who did the crossbreeding?" Leif asked. "Is it someone from our clan?"

"No to both questions. However, I suspect it is someone from the Greenblade Clan. They have forest experts who have been crossbreeding trees to grow a harder wood for buildings."

"But how are they getting the jungle plants?"

"We can't patrol the entire jungle, Leif. Curare and Theobroma grow all over and are just as accessible at the border of the Cowan Clan's lands as well as deep in the interior."

At least it wasn't one of their clan members. Small comfort. He'd hoped his father would recognize the gardener helping Owen.

Esau spent a total of six days working in the hothouse. On the last day, he shouted for Leif, who'd been grooming Rusalka. Leif raced to join his father. Esau had leaves caught in his hair and dirt stained his forearms, forehead and knees.

"Come see what I found!" Esau grabbed his elbow and tugged him inside the hothouse. "Back here. I almost missed it."

Leif crouched down to avoid being smacked in the face by a branch. Near the back right corner, Esau pulled him to his hands and knees, and they crawled the rest of the way.

Esau stabbed a finger at a Theobroma tree. "See that?"

"Yes. So?"

His father pointed to what appeared to be a large knot on the lower trunk "Look! This is where another Theobroma tree has been grafted onto this tree."

"Okay. What's so special about that?"

Esau huffed. "It means that this second tree doesn't need as much time to mature as the first one because the roots and trunk are already established." When Leif failed to produce an appropriate reaction, he continued, "It means that instead of waiting three to five years for the Theobroma tree to mature and produce pods, it will grow pods in just a *year*."

Wow. That meant… "And will double the number of trees growing pods?" Leif asked.

"Exactly!"

"Increasing the production of Theobroma is what the Council has asked Bavol to accomplish."

"Then message Bavol and tell him to come here. He needs to see this!"

And it also implied Owen's stock of Theobroma may be twice the amount they'd estimated. Had he sent it to the

Commander along with the Curare? What if Owen used the grafting to grow Theobroma-resistant Curare? Would they be able to use the Theobroma after they extracted the Curare? Leif asked his father.

"It's possible, but I won't know for sure until the trees mature."

Leif hurried to the farmhouse to contact Irys and ask her to talk to Bavol. Before he reached the porch, a voice called his name. A young messenger stood outside the gate waving a sealed envelope. He thanked the girl and tipped her. The scent of lavender tickled his nose, and the part of him reserved for worrying about his sister relaxed a fraction. He waited until he was inside before ripping it open.

After reading the first sentence, his concern returned, along with fear. Owen was a guest of the Commander, staying at the castle in Ixia. With Yelena! She was supposed to be safe there with Valek. Instead she was in just as much danger as when Owen had captured her.

Leif raced up to his room. He pulled the super messenger from his pack and sat on the edge of his bed. Drawing on the magic inside, he reached for Irys. She allowed him through her defenses right away.

Good timing, Leif. I was just about to contact you. Do you have any news?

Plenty, he said. Leif filled her in on what he'd learned from Yelena. *I'm going to Ixia. Send Hale and two other magicians and have them meet me at Yelena's cabin in the Featherstone lands. Do you know where it is?*

Did she ask for help?

No, but neither she nor Valek can defend against Owen, Rika and Tyen.

I'm sorry, Leif, but I can't spare the magicians. In fact, the Coun-

cil has ordered you back to the Citadel again. *They want your report in person.*

But Yelena—

Must be safe, or else she wouldn't have sent you that message. You need to convince the Council of the danger.

If I return to the Citadel, it will be to gather magicians to travel with me to Ixia. Yelena's helped so many people, I'm sure I'll have plenty of volunteers.

Talk to the Council first, and then I'll help you recruit.

Irys's desperation shrilled in his mind like an out-of-tune violin.

That bad?

Yes. I need your help.

All right.

Thank you. Did your father discover anything useful?

Leif told her about the various plants Esau had identified. Her reaction to the Theobroma-resistant Curare matched his. *And Bavol must come and see this grafting technique.*

He can't leave the Council sessions. Would it be possible to bring your father and the plants to the Citadel?

It's too cold. The plants will probably die before we arrive. But I'll ask him.

Please tell him it's very important.

Now she was scaring him. Leif had known Irys for most of his life, and she'd always been rather unflappable and stoic. *Irys, what's really going on?*

I'll explain everything when you arrive.

A classic dodge. *Come on, Irys, it's me.*

How soon can you get here?

If we leave tomorrow, we'll be there in seven days. But you didn't answer my question.

Be extra careful on your journey. She paused. *We've…lost a number of magicians.*

Lost? Like they're missing, or they're dead?

Both.

Holy snow cats, Irys! Why didn't you tell me that right away?

The Council doesn't want to spread panic needlessly.

Well, if there's a time to be panicking, I think this merits it. Don't you?

She ignored his sarcasm. *Get home as soon as you can.*

Yes, sir.

16

YELENA

My lips still burned from Valek's kiss. The intensity of it seared into my soul like a red-hot iron branding his name right on my heart. The idea of being locked in a tower with him no longer sounded so terrible. If my magic never returned, what else would I do aside from raising our child? I might be content...for about a week.

Valek mounted Onyx. He met my gaze, and his smile promised a reunion worth waiting for. Then he was gone, leaving behind a cloud of dust. The rest of the world returned, appearing duller.

"Yelena," Onora said.

I focused on her. "Yes?"

She held out a roll of parchment. "I drew this for you."

Suppressing my surprise, I took it and unrolled the sheet, revealing a picture of a tree drawn with charcoal. Each oval leaf had been carefully detailed, along with the precise lines and shading of the bark. I half expected it to sway in the breeze.

Why would she— I gasped. "It's the Harman tree, isn't it?"

"Yes." Onora's tone was matter-of-fact.

She'd gone into Owen's suite and sketched one of the saplings, despite the danger. Impressive and brave. "When?"

"This morning. Right after I talked to you."

"Did anyone see you?"

"No. And I didn't touch the trees or go near them, just in case there was a magical alarm."

"Smart. I want to admonish you for taking such a risk, but…" I waved the picture. "This is perfect. You are a talented artist."

She shrugged away the compliment. "Will it help your father identify the tree?"

"Yes. He'll be ecstatic. And then he'll bug me to invite you to the jungle to go on an expedition with him and draw plants. To him, that's the ultimate experience, and he doesn't understand why others aren't jumping up and down at the prospect."

Onora laughed. It was a small burst of sound as it escaped her tight self-control. "I might actually like that."

"When all this mess with Owen is resolved, consider yourself invited."

"Thank you."

I tucked the picture into my saddlebags. Ari and Janco finished readying their horses.

The Stable Master gave Ari's horse a pat on the neck. "His name's Diamond Whiskey, 'cause of that diamond-shaped blaze on his forehead. But we all call him Whiskey for short. Take good care of him and make sure he returns with you. The Commander's partial to him."

Ari paused in midmount. "Why did you pick him, then? I can take another."

"He's the strongest of my lot."

"That's a polite way of saying you're fat, Ari," Janco said.

Ari and the Stable Master ignored him.

The Master pointed to Kiki and The Madam. "I also picked him 'cause he gets along well with the girls."

"Being able to get along is a good quality to have," I said, giving Janco a pointed look.

He batted his eyelashes at me—Mr. Innocent. "Hey, I'm the epitome of a team player."

I suppressed a sigh as I swung into my saddle. Janco in high spirits meant more high jinks. However, no matter how hard I tried, I really couldn't consider that a bad thing.

"Come on, Epitome," I said. "Mount up. I'd like to cross the border before dark."

We arrived at the northern gates of the Citadel late at night on the third day. Since I didn't know Leif's current location, I'd thought to check with Irys about his whereabouts to see if he'd already left the farmhouse.

Surrounding the Citadel was a high white marble wall broken only by four entrances. Janco had wanted to stop at an inn a couple hours ago, but the thought of sleeping in my own bed had given me a burst of energy, and we pushed on.

By the guards' slow response to our calls, I guessed we had woken them. Two men exited the guardhouse to talk to us, but two others headed into the Citadel at a fast pace—so it was a shift change, not a case of sleeping on the job. Much better, considering the Commander's plans.

The guards were members of the Citadel's security forces. Since I wasn't ready for the Council to know I'd returned from Ixia, I'd pulled my hood over my head and planned to give them fake names. I'd inform the Council of my return once I learned of their state of mind from Irys.

"Names?" the taller of the two asked.

"I'm Elliona Featherstone. This is Yannis and Pellow Moon." I hooked a thumb at Janco and Ari. Their pale skin matched most Moon Clan members.

The man asked a number of detailed questions about our

reason for visiting, how long we planned to stay and where we were lodging. He wrote all our answers down with slow strokes of his quill in a ledger. Then he consulted another book before he allowed us to enter the Citadel. The whole exchange took much longer than normal.

Once we were out of sight of the guardhouse, Janco rode alongside me. "That's new. When did they start with the cross-examination at the gate?"

The last time I'd arrived, I'd been waved through. I calculated. "Sometime in the last forty days."

"Do you think it's because the Commander now has Curare?" Ari asked me.

"No. In that case, they would have doubled the guards at the border, but we didn't see any unusual activity on the Sitian side."

"Do they know Owen's in Ixia?" Janco asked.

"Leif may have messaged Irys."

"Is Leif back from Broken Bridge?" Ari asked.

"It's possible. We'll ask Irys once we reach the Magician's Keep."

"I'm *so* looking forward to being in the Creepy Keepy again," Janco muttered sarcastically. "Can't we crash in Leif's apartment? Mara won't mind."

"She will if an assassin climbs through her window," I said. "He might get my blood on her pretty yellow curtains."

"I guess it's the cold, hard floor of your room in Irys's tower, then."

"The Keep has comfortable guest quarters. I'm sure—"

"Not a chance, sweetheart," Janco said. "Valek said 'protect.' We're not letting you out of our sight. Except...you know...when..." He blushed and spurred The Madam into a faster walk.

The Citadel was a large, rectangular-shaped city divided

into six quarters. The northwest and southwest quarters contained a maze of residences. The two middle quarters resembled a giant bull's-eye with an impressive market right at the center. A diverse selection of goods imported from all over Sitia and Ixia were sold in its many stands. Large-scale businesses and factories ringed the market in ever-widening circles. The Magician's Keep with its four towers occupied the entire northeast corner of the Citadel, and the Council Hall, government buildings and Councilor's residences were located in the southeast quarter.

At this late hour, only a couple people hurried through the streets of the Citadel, but I knew various members of the Helper's Guild hid in the shadows cast by the street lanterns. Fisk, the young man in charge of the guild, would be informed of my arrival well before anyone else. Good thing he was a friend and would keep the knowledge to himself.

Firelight blazed from a few taverns where voices buzzed and an occasional burst of laughter tumbled from open windows. We soon passed the outer ring that consisted of inns and taverns and entered the quieter and darker loop of factories.

After a few minutes, the cool breeze shifted and Kiki stopped. She reared up and snorted, signaling trouble. Without conscious thought, I yanked my bo staff from its holder on my saddle just as Ari and Janco drew their swords.

Dark figures rushed from the shadows and blocked our path. My pulse rate increased as I counted over a dozen. Too many for the three of us.

"Ambush," Ari said.

"Ya think?" Janco pulled on the reins, backing The Madam closer to Kiki and Whiskey.

We turned around. More figures stood on the street behind us. There was just enough light to reveal the swords and daggers gripped in their hands. At least two aimed crossbows at us. I scanned the buildings on each side, seeking an alley to escape down. Instead, I spotted more ambushers.

We were trapped. Anger mixed with fear. Those two guards hadn't been rushing home after their shift. Idiot!

"We're on horseback. We can charge them," Janco said.

"And get bolted," Ari said. "I don't think so."

"Drop your weapons and dismount," a deep male voice ordered. He strode forward and into the faint light. Two silver captain bars glinted on his shoulders—Captain Romas.

"They're the Citadel guards," I said to my friends, relaxing. Then, louder, I asked Romas, "Why have you ambushed us? We've done nothing wrong."

"You mean other than giving false names at the gate?" he asked.

Uh-oh. We were recognized. "I don't—"

"Save it for your hearing. Yelena Zaltana, Ardenus Ixia and Janco Ixia, you are all under arrest."

"You can't still be mad at me over that little incident last season," I said, referring to when Romas and a unit of his men tried to stop Leif, Hale and me from leaving the Citadel about a hundred years ago. Or so it felt.

He grasped the hilt of his sword. "It isn't about *that*."

Oops, I shouldn't have reminded him. "Is it for lying to the gate guards? You can't—" I tried.

"No. For conspiring with the enemy, for espionage and for treason. Now drop your weapons and dismount, or my archers will knock you off your horses."

And that answered my question about the Council's state of mind regarding me. Kiki tensed. One word from me and she'd shoot forward and trample anyone unfortunate enough to be in her path. However, I'd been hit by a crossbow's bolt before. If it didn't kill me, it'd still mean an excruciating trip to the infirmary.

"Orders?" Ari asked me.

"It's clearly a misunderstanding," I said, lowering my bo. "No need for bloodshed." I threaded the staff back on my saddle and dismounted. "Do as he asks."

Although they grumbled, Ari and Janco returned their swords to the sheaths attached to their saddles before swinging down.

"Step away from the horses," the captain ordered. "Hands on your heads."

Before I complied, I whispered, "Kiki, once they have us, take The Madam and Whiskey to the Keep, please."

Staying together, we moved a few feet down the road. Romas instructed us to kneel and then his men closed in to secure our hands behind our backs. A shout rose as Kiki lurched forward, scattering guards. The Madam and Whiskey kept pace with her.

"Sir?" someone called.

"Let them go," Romas said. He grabbed my arm and jerked me to my feet. "We've only orders for these three."

"Who signed the arrest order?" I asked him.

"You'll be shown a copy of the arrest affidavit when you're processed. Let's go."

The captain kept his hand clamped around my biceps as they marched us through the streets. I imagined one of Fisk's helpers reporting to him about our arrest. Would Fisk even be surprised? Or had he heard about the arrest warrant through his network?

A list of recriminations spun through my mind. I should have stayed at an inn as Janco had wanted and then visited Fisk in the morning when the traffic through the gates would have hidden us. Too bad I hadn't thought of this sooner. I'd grown lazy, relying on my magic. Being extra cautious, paranoid even, was no longer a habit of mine. At least my stupid mistake didn't get us killed. Not this time.

Instead of leading us to the Citadel's jail, Romas escorted us to the holding cells in the basement of the Council Hall. No surprise that the members of the Council had signed the order to arrest me and my companions on sight. And I probably shouldn't be shocked that they didn't incarcerate me in the Keep's special cells—the ones that blocked a prisoner's magic. By now, news of my condition had probably spread throughout the Citadel and Sitia.

While they searched Ari and Janco and removed a substantial pile of weapons and lock picks, they only performed a quick pat-down on me—an interesting side effect of being considered harmless. They found my switchblade, but nothing else.

We were locked in three adjoining cells, the guards departed and the metal outer door clanged shut, leaving us in utter blackness. I groped for the bed and tried to get comfortable on the thin mattress. The silence didn't last long.

"Ah, just like old times," Janco said. "Oh, wait. What am I saying? It's just like almost every time I'm with you, Yelena. Don't you get tired of being arrested *all* the time?"

"You're exaggerating," I said.

"Oh, that's right. I forgot about our last mission. We weren't locked up, just tied down. My mistake."

"Give it a rest, Janco," Ari said.

"Yeah, well, it seems every time I'm in Sitia, I'm thrown into jail. Do you think they'll stamp my frequent-visitor card? I think I get a prize if I've been in them all."

"What's the plan?" Ari asked. "Do either of you have a set—"

"This place gives me the *creeps*," Janco interrupted, warning us of magic in use nearby.

A magician was probably listening or monitoring us in some way. Lovely.

"Everything gives you the creeps," Ari said, but he didn't sound as exasperated as usual.

"Not everything. There are a few things that don't bother me."

"What about you, Yelena?" Ari asked.

They had switched to talking in code. I replayed their comments in my mind, teasing out the true meaning. Ari was about to ask if we had a set of lock picks and from Janco's recent comment, I guessed he did.

"There are a couple things that give me the willies, but being locked in a cell isn't one," I said. In other words, yes, I had two sets of lock picks on me, but we should stay put. I'd hoped to convince the Council of our innocence, and escaping would be a guilty action.

"Do you think we'll have visitors?" Ari asked.

"I'm sure Master Magician Irys will stop by in the morning to explain what's going on."

"As long as that annoying little bloodsucker doesn't show up, I'll be happy," Janco said.

He referred to The Mosquito, an assassin who'd been hired to kill me. I'd also be happy to never encounter him again. "We've only just arrived. It's doubtful he knows we're here."

"News spreads fast." Concern laced Ari's voice.

"We won't be here long," I tried to assure him.

"Have you been in here before?" Janco asked.

"Yes, to visit Opal when the Council was worried about her glass-siphoning powers." Which meant I knew the layout of the cells and building. "She scared them and they kept her well guarded."

"Do we scare them?" Ari asked.

"Not as much." It'd be difficult to break out, but not im-

MARIA V. SNYDER

possible. However, I hoped to avoid the necessity of escaping. "Just let me do all the talking."

Ari's deep laugh echoed on the stone walls. "Good luck with that."

As I predicted, Irys arrived with our breakfast. My appetite disappeared when her harsh demeanor failed to soften after the guards left. She stood on the other side of the bars and studied me. Deep lines of worry scoured her forehead and dark circles ringed her emerald-colored eyes. Wearing her official purple silk magician's robe, she had pulled her long once-black-but-now-painted-with-gray hair into a neat bun.

"Yelena, why didn't you message me you were coming?" she finally asked.

"I didn't have time." I tapped my ear and gave her a questioning look.

"No one can hear us. I've made certain of that. Now will you tell me the real reason you tried to sneak into the Citadel last night?"

"I wasn't sneaking. I just wanted to avoid a confrontation with the Council before I had a chance to talk to you."

"I see. And how did that work out for you?"

"Wowzers," Janco said in awe. "That's some impressive sarcasm!"

"Zip it, Janco," Ari growled.

"Yes, I realize I made a big mistake," I said. "But Owen Moon is in Ixia, and we need help."

"You mean like the help I needed to convince the Sitian Council of a few impossible things, like Owen being alive despite the Commander's assurance to the contrary, and that the Commander funded an illegal Curare manufacturing facility in Sitia and now has barrels of the drug at his disposal? Like the help I could have used to explain why our Liaison headed to Ixia along with every person who could have enlightened the Council about what had happened in Lapeer? That type of help?"

Her words cut right through me. And the fact they were true gave them a sharper edge. Red-hot guilt welled from the wounds. "I'm sorry, Irys. After the encounter with Owen I…" I tucked my tail between my legs and bolted, yipping in fear. "I felt safer with Valek. I'm sorry I didn't return sooner."

Her anger lessened. "And I must also apologize. The last three weeks have been a nightmare."

No kidding. The formidable Master Magician appeared as if she stood on a crumbling foundation. "Aside from the obvious problems with the Council, what's wrong?" I asked.

"While the Council has been debating how to respond to the Commander's allegedly bold moves with Curare and Owen, the antimagician sentiment, which had been simmering in the background for the past couple of seasons, has now boiled over. Councilor Jewelrose has proposed a new system of keeping track of magicians and overseeing what they can and can't do and when. It's similar to a military structure, but more restrictive." Agitated, Irys paced. "The Councilor claims magicians are dangerous and that we need to be regulated and controlled by the Council."

I glanced at Janco through the bars. If anyone would be happy about keeping a leash on magicians, it would be him. He mouthed, *Too easy.*

Irys continued, "Bain and I and a few other Councilors had enough votes to veto the idea, but…" She stopped. "However, I'm pretty sure another group has decided to implement it. I've been hearing rumors about a cartel."

My relief over the veto disappeared in a heartbeat. "What do you mean?"

She yanked at the sleeves of her robe and smoothed the fab-

MARIA V. SNYDER

ric. I'd known her for eight years and recognized her delay tactic.

"It must be bad," I said.

Lifting her gaze, she met mine. "In the last six weeks, four magicians have been assassinated, and twelve are missing."

The horror of her words hit me with such force that I groped for the bed as my legs lost the strength to hold me up.

"Assassinated how?" Ari asked her.

"Puncture wound to the jugular. We suspect The Mosquito. But the assassin could be using his signature move in order to throw us off."

"Where are the attacks happening?"

"All over Sitia. There's no pattern that we can discern."

I shot to my feet in terror. "Leif?"

"He's fine. I communicated with him two days ago. He's on his way to the Citadel." She relayed Leif's information about my father's discoveries and Owen's whereabouts. "Leif planned to recruit a rescue party to save you from Owen, Yelena." Irys laughed. It was a dry, humorless sound. "I never thought I'd *ever* say this, but our magicians might be safer in Ixia."

"Only if they join Owen," Janco said. "Probably not a bad idea, since he's gonna be our Overlord."

"Your faith is heartwarming," Ari said drily. "Have there been any incidents inside the Citadel, Second Magician?"

"No. And we have sent messages to all our magicians, ordering them back to the Keep."

"That could be exactly what this group *wants* you to do," I said. What was that old cliché…something about fish in a barrel?

"But with the Keep's thick walls and towers, it is almost impenetrable. Not to mention the increase in magicians. Surely they wouldn't attack us there." Her tone failed to match her confident words.

"Who says they're gonna let them *get* there?" Janco asked. "If it was me, I'd set up ambushes on all the major roads to the Citadel and pick them off one by one."

Irys pressed a hand to her forehead and closed her eyes as if enduring a wave of pain.

"Real nice, Janco," Ari muttered.

"What'd I say?"

"You need to warn all of them of the possibility of an ambush," I said to Irys. The desire to add *Leif first, please* pushed up my throat.

Her eyes snapped open. "Of course. I'll do it right away."

"You mean you'll do it after letting us out of here, right?" Janco asked with a hopeful tone.

"I can't. The Council wishes to interrogate you regarding the incident in Lapeer."

"If they just wanted information, why charge us with treason and sign an arrest warrant?" I asked.

"Your actions right after looked suspicious, and when you add in your attempt to sneak into the Citadel with two known Ixian spies…let's just say they're not taking any chances. Not with magicians being assassinated."

Janco huffed. "If we were here on official Ixian business, you wouldn't have caught us."

"Not helping," Ari said.

"Will they drop the charges after I explain what happened?" I asked Irys.

"At this point, I've no idea."

Lovely. "Then what should we do?"

"Talk to the Council. Then escape as soon as you can. It's not safe here."

17

VALEK

Valek considered Hedda's question. Up until five minutes ago, both he and the Commander had been under the impression that Onora had killed Hedda when she refused to name the client who'd paid for a hit on the Commander.

He scanned her office. Spartan and neat—just like when he'd been a student here, she kept her personal effects in a hidden apartment. But nicks marked the furniture, a chair arm had broken off and bald spots littered the area rug. Despite the uniform requirement for all Ixian citizens, Hedda wore a faded gray-green mottled tunic and pants. Patches dotted the threadbare fabric.

Remaining behind her desk, Hedda clutched her knife. Her informant from the garrison sidled next to her. The young pup brandished a sharp dagger. Valek would have been impressed if the man's arm wasn't shaking.

"If the Commander sent me, Hedda, we wouldn't be having this conversation," he said, showing her his empty hands.

She didn't relax. "Then why are you here?"

"I followed your man, hoping he planned to warn the Storm Thieves about my presence."

"I didn't *see* him," the man said in his defense.

"Of course you wouldn't, you idiot. Valek was my best student. The only person to come close is Onora." Hedda's frown deepened as she gazed at Valek. "You killed her." It wasn't a question.

"Actually, no. Do you still keep a bottle of blackberry brandy in your desk?"

Hedda's knife disappeared. "I do."

Valek turned to the idiot. "Report back to the garrison before you're missed."

"Yes, sir." The man paused in the doorway. "Sir, are you…?"

"Going to discipline you?"

He nodded, and his Adam's apple bobbed as he swallowed.

"Let me guess. You've been exchanging information for instruction from Hedda, right?"

His grip on the knob tightened in surprise. "Yes, sir."

"Do you wish to become an assassin?"

"Oh, no, sir. I just wanted to improve my skills. The garrison's master of arms is…old, sir."

"I'm not about to punish ambition, but I suggest you work on spotting a tail."

"Yes, sir." He bolted.

Hedda settled behind her desk and produced a bottle of brandy. She poured the deep red liquid into two glasses as Valek sat in the chair facing her.

"You've changed," Hedda said, handing him a glass.

"Oh?"

"The old Valek would have made him suffer for a few days, waiting to find out if you'd inform his commanding officer or leave him one of your infamous black statues." She downed her drink in one gulp, then poured herself another. "The old Valek would have killed Onora for getting so close to the Commander."

MARIA V. SNYDER

"I'll admit, I was tempted to get rid of my competition, but she's proven to be quite the puzzle. And you know me and puzzles. That hasn't changed."

"Good to know." Hedda sipped from her drink.

"And while I'm truly glad you're alive, I'm wondering why Onora informed us of your unfortunate demise."

"I've no idea."

"No?" Valek swept his arm out, indicating the shabby room. "Perhaps it's because there wasn't a client. You probably haven't had a client since the takeover. And after years of resentment, you finally had a student you could send after the Commander. And what better time than when I was in Sitia."

"You always did have such an active imagination, King Killer."

"Then how about this? When the Commander ordered her to murder this...er...shall we say *mystery client*, she returned. But Onora couldn't kill you. You took her in after she'd been abused, taught her to fight, to stand up for herself, to no longer be afraid. Instead, she reports your death and you agree to go into hiding." He drank his brandy, savoring the burn of the spicy blackberry flavor.

She raised her glass. "That was an entertaining tale, but you of all people should know I don't ever divulge the names of my clients."

"But you are training new assassins, even though you've claimed to have closed the school and retired."

Pressing her lips together, she gave him a shrewd look. "I have to keep my skills sharp."

That was more information than he'd expected. "And if I sent you a promising student or two in the future, would you turn him or her away?"

Surprise flashed in her light green eyes. "No."

"Then I'll add you to my payroll."

"What about the Commander?"

"I'll handle the Commander."

"Are you going to report me?"

"No need."

"You *have* changed."

He quirked an eyebrow. "For the better?"

"I think that your blind loyalty to the Commander is no longer so...blind. And I think the change is due to your heart mate."

"I'll take that as a yes." He finished his drink.

Swirling the liquid around her glass, she stared at it. After a few moments, she met his gaze.

"Since we have an agreement, you should know your story has one error," Hedda said.

"Really?"

"Remember how I helped you find the men who murdered your brothers, but I never sent you after the King as you desired?"

At the time, he'd been making her too much money assassinating targets for *paying* clients, and she believed he'd be caught trying to get close to the King and executed. "Yes. What's this—"

"I also didn't send Onora after the Commander."

Valek kept his expression neutral as his thoughts whirled. He didn't like what they dragged to the surface. Straightening in his chair, he leaned forward. "You're saying *Onora* wanted the Commander dead?"

"Yes."

And you've left Onora with the Commander, you idiot. His heart thumped. But he ignored the panic. Onora had had multiple opportunities to kill the Commander. Plus, she wore his mark, given when she'd sworn to be loyal.

"I found it quite interesting that she changed her mind and

MARIA V. SNYDER

chose not to kill me, even though I was the only one who knew her true mission," Hedda said.

Valek noted her use of the past tense. "Instead she concocted a story of your demise. Risky."

"Compassionate. As you said, I aided her in her time of need."

He tapped a finger on the edge of his empty glass. "The Onora puzzle takes another unexpected turn."

"I'm sure you'll figure her out. You always do." She splashed a generous amount of brandy into his glass. Hedda raised hers and said, "To solving puzzles." They clinked.

The alcohol left a fiery trail down his throat. "Speaking of puzzles, have you heard anything about these Storm Thieves?"

"I may have. It's probably just gossip and rumors," she hedged.

Valek dug a gold coin from his pocket and set it on the desk. "How about now?"

She snatched it in one quick motion. "Damn foolish kids." Jabbing a finger at Valek, she scowled. "I knew they'd eventually attract too much attention."

"They've been rather successful for a bunch of foolish kids."

"That's because no one had linked their petty and seemingly random crimes until recently. Because, like most criminals, they grew bolder and hit bigger targets, and it was just a matter of time until..." Hedda swept a hand, indicating Valek.

"Do you know where they've been operating from?"

"No. No one does. That's why they still haven't been caught."

"Do you know who is involved?"

"Well... I've heard rumors."

Valek understood the hint. He dropped another gold coin on the desk. This one disappeared as quickly as the first.

"They're a group of teenagers—mostly the children of fish-

ermen. The thefts started at the beginning of the cooling season, when the fleet arrived in port waiting for warmer weather
and calmer seas."

So a bunch of bored kids taking advantage of the storms,
but they'd been rather smart. Too smart. Valek suspected a
more experienced person led them. "Anything else?"

"I've lived on the coast all my life. In sixty-two years, we've
never had a cold season like the one we just had."

"What do you mean?"

"I mean, we've always had plenty of snow, rain, wind and
fog. This past year, we've had more storms, but they don't last
near as long and they always rage overnight."

Valek considered. "The Commander has allowed Stormdancers up on the northern ice sheet."

"And they tamed the nasty blizzards sweeping down from
the north, but these others are blowing in from the west."

Ah. "Magic?" He'd suspected it before, but not for the
storms.

She shrugged. "Maybe. You've killed all my magicians, so
I can't say for sure."

He didn't bother to correct her. The Commander had ordered their executions soon after the takeover, but they'd had
more than enough time to escape to Sitia. Valek had made
sure of that.

Thanking Hedda for the information, Valek reminisced
with her for a while before he left. "Keep your low profile,
and when your young idiot is ready, have him request a transfer to the Commander's company."

She smiled. "His name is Gannon."

No surprise he was the one Colonel Ransley mentioned as
showing promise.

As Valek hiked back to the garrison, he mulled over all he'd
learned from Hedda. He concentrated on the Storm Thieves,

MARIA V. SNYDER

putting himself in their place. Bored and physically able to climb ropes and rigging on heaving seas, the young fishermen would have no trouble scaling a wall. They'd also been on boats most of their lives, knew the currents and tides and could spot all the warning signs of approaching foul weather. Valek had no problem believing they were the thieves; however, the fact that his corps hadn't been able to catch them or discover their hideout didn't fit. Magic could explain it. Or an older leader. Or both.

When he returned to the garrison, he checked on Onyx. The black horse's coat gleamed and his tail and mane had been combed. Onyx snuffled Valek's empty hand, searching for a treat. Valek laughed when Onyx's ears dropped in obvious disappointment. He fed the horse a carrot before swinging by the canteen in time for supper.

The loud rumble of voices dwindled and then ceased by the time he'd grabbed a bowl of clam stew, a hunk of bread and a wedge of cheese. He scanned the tables of soldiers. Predominantly male, most of them averted their gazes. However, in the back right corner, a table full of female soldiers ate. Much to their terrified surprise, he joined them. The first thing he noticed was they were all low-ranking, and not a commissioned officer among them.

Once they recovered from their shock and overcame their fear of him, they answered his questions about the garrison's male-dominated leaders.

"Is it true that half of the Commander's personal guard are female?" asked a woman who introduced herself as Sergeant First Class Jaga.

"Yes. And half of his advisers. In fact, the Commander would be upset with the ratio at this garrison. What happened to all your colleagues?"

"Transferred. We stayed because we have family nearby," Jaga said.

"Any inappropriate behavior, Sergeant?"

"No, sir."

She didn't hesitate or exchange glances with her colleagues, which meant she told the truth. Good. He asked her about the higher-ranking officers.

"They've been here for ages, sir. All promoted from within."

"I see." The garrison was way overdue for an inspection. It was partly his fault for avoiding the area all these years. "I think it's soon time for an update and some fresh blood."

They smiled.

"It won't be until after the hot season." And only if the Commander didn't declare war on Sitia.

"It will be worth the wait, sir," Jaga said.

Valek finished eating and returned to his rooms. A pile of MD-1 uniforms waited for him on the small table. He checked for intruders before collapsing on the bed.

The next morning, Valek changed into a basic laborer's uniform. The black pants had a row of white diamonds down the outside of each leg. A row of white diamonds cut across the chest of the black tunic. Throughout Ixia, laborers were men and women who filled in where extra people were needed for a project or job. They had a variety of skills from construction to harvesting crops, and they frequently traveled from one city to another. In other words, the perfect cover for Valek.

He transferred a few things he'd need into a well-worn rucksack, tied his hair back with an old piece of string and altered his appearance just enough to throw a casual observer off. Most Ixians only knew his name and wouldn't recognize him. When he exited the garrison, he stopped and rubbed dirt over the white diamonds on his clothes. Satisfied that he

MARIA V. SNYDER

looked the part, Valek headed southwest to Gandrel, where the most recent and boldest burglary had occurred.

Six hours later he arrived in town. He reported to the local checkpoint and showed them his papers.

"Reason for visit?" the man asked in a bored voice.

"Repairing fishing nets for the fleet," Valek answered. Once the cold season ended, the fishermen spent the warming season readying their boats.

The man grunted, stamped Valek's paper and handed it back all without once glancing at Valek. If the rest of the security personnel matched this man's attitude, then no wonder the Storm Thieves had no trouble stealing their weapons. Pathetic.

Valek visited the Sail Away Inn next. The innkeeper rented him a room, but the few other workers ignored him. Extra laborers usually arrived at the coast at this time of year. Since supper was a couple hours away, the common and dining room were empty. He waited in his room. It didn't take long for a servant to knock. She carried towels and a bath kit for him.

Opening the door wide, Valek stepped aside, letting in Agent Annika, who explained about the amenities of the inn until the door closed.

"Where?" Valek asked.

"Four-fifteen Cannery Road, second floor, sir. There's an entrance in the back, through the alley. Endre's there now. His shift doesn't start until later."

"Thank you."

She nodded and left. He followed soon after. Every town in Ixia had at least one inn and a security office—the two best places to gather information. Valek had an agent in both. Larger cities warranted more agents. And the agents shared a safe house or apartment as a base for their covert operations.

The yellow paint peeled from the wood of building number four-fifteen, which was wedged in the middle of a row of houses. The pungent odor of fish guts fogged the street. Valek looped around to the alley and climbed the metal ladder to the apartment.

Endre yanked open the door before Valek reached it. The burly man held a dagger, but his fierce expression smoothed with recognition.

"Welcome, sir," Endre said as Valek entered the small unit—half of it was living space, the other used for work.

Valek noted with approval the maps of the area covering the table with the thieves' targets already marked. Times, dates and stolen items had been listed next to each.

"Any news, Endre?"

"Since the hit on the security office, no other incidents have been reported, sir."

"Any progress on finding the thieves' hideout?"

"No, sir. Security officers from Gandrel, Krillow and Coral Caye have searched every cove, building, boat, port and wooded area."

Valek studied the map. "Looks like they hit every town along MD-1's coast. I thought the targets were random."

"At first they appeared random, but reports were slow coming in from some towns. They didn't make the connection to the storms right away. But even so, if you look at the times and dates, there's still no pattern."

"And no one knows where and when they'll strike next?"

"No, sir. But Annika is working on finding a few informers. She'll report back here after the supper crowd."

"Tell me about the theft of the weapons."

"They struck in the middle of the night during a nasty downpour. The guys on duty didn't hear a thing and frankly didn't think the thieves would have the gall to rob us. Up until that hit, the Stormers took mostly money, equipment,

MARIA V. SNYDER

tools and food. But they left nothing behind but puddles on the floor."

"Stormers?"

"It's what the officers call them."

Ah. "Any boot prints?"

"No. Just the water."

"Fresh or salt?" Valek asked.

Endre's thick eyebrows smashed together like two caterpillars butting heads. "We didn't check. I'm assuming fresh from the rain. Why would it matter?"

"You tell me."

He ran a hand over the short bristle of his black hair. "Salt would mean they came up from the beach."

"Or waded in from a boat."

"Not this time of year. It'd be suicide."

It would be dangerous for ordinary thieves. But what if one of them used magic to navigate the seas? He recalled Opal's description of how the Stormdancers harvested energy from the storms. They kept a bubble of calm around them as they worked to avoid being swept out to sea. Valek wondered what the Stormdancers did during their off-season. Kade and Heli helped with the blizzards in Ixia, but one of the others might be helping these thieves.

Valek tucked the thought away to investigate later and returned to the break-in. "Forced entry?"

"Yeah, crowbar on the back door and on the weapon lockers."

Not professionals, or they would've used lock picks. Valek considered. "Do you have a complete list of what's been stolen?"

"Yes, sir." Endre hunted through papers lying on a desk and pulled one from the pile. "I copied this from all the reports. After the weapons were stolen, the Gandrel office took the lead on the investigation. All the other offices have sent their incident reports to us."

Interesting. "Where are these reports being kept?"

"In a conference room. The captain formed a team of investigators and we've been working in there, poring over all the information."

"You don't sound too impressed."

Endre grinned. "They're not us, sir. I can only do so much with these guys. Now, if you were on the team with Annika, then…"

Nice to know Endre had such confidence in him. "Then when can I get in there to take a look at those reports?"

"*You* can get in there anytime, sir."

"I'd prefer to remain incognito if possible." And as long as the news of his arrival hadn't already spread to the Storm Thieves. While he'd been following Private Idiot slash Gannon to Hedda's school, another mole could have sent a message to them.

"Oh, then late at night would be best. I'm on the graveyard shift tonight. If you can get into the conference room without being seen, I can make sure no one bothers you. You'll have to leave before the morning shift arrives at dawn."

"All right, then expect me after midnight."

"Yes, sir."

"Do you have any more information?"

The big man gestured to the desk. "Annika and I have been writing down what we've heard and other bits of news." He brandished the list of stolen goods.

"May I?" Valek held out his hand.

"Of course, sir. Here." Endre handed the list to Valek.

Valek scanned the items. Missing money and jewelry were expected, but others like wood, saws, nails, paint and teacups were not. He sat at the desk and read through the other pa-

MARIA V. SNYDER

pers. Endre and Annika had collected a nice variety of facts, including ruling out the initial suspects—a gang of teen troublemakers. Five young men and three young women had had run-ins with the local security for fighting, drinking and vandalism. However, they all had alibis for the storm thefts.

After an hour, Valek rejected the idea of bored teens as the culprits. No. The Storm Thieves were organized and had a precise plan. The building supplies meant their hideout either needed major repairs or they'd built a place. But any new building would have been found during the search.

Repairs? The salt air was corrosive. Each structure in a coastal town needed a new coat of paint every couple of years, and replacing rotted wood was a typical renovation. But why this much wood? Unless both the exterior and interiors had been rebuilt. Would the guards notice this during the inspections? He asked Endre.

"It depends on the person. Some of the officers are more observant than others, sir. The reports on the searches might mention something like that."

Guess he'd have to wait until later. In the meantime, what else needed repairs? Fishing boats. Just like the buildings, each boat needed extensive upkeep, and they'd been searched. Unless the boat was out to sea at that time. Suicide, unless magic was involved. Assuming a magician was on board, Valek mulled it over and found a flaw in his logic. The fishermen would notice if a boat sailed away during the storm season. They'd think the captain was insane and talk about that "damn fool" at all the local taverns.

No. The Storm Thieves couldn't risk such odd behavior. Unless… Valek straightened. Unless they left *before* the storm season and never returned! They'd be considered lost at sea. No one would suspect them because they were all dead. A perfect alibi.

Valek asked Endre if any boats had disappeared during the fishing season.

"There are always a few that don't come back. The Port Master in each town would have those records. Also Annika might know. When a ship is lost at sea, everyone gathers at the inn." Endre paused. "Why is that important?"

He explained his theory.

"That would be a right smart trick. But why go to all the trouble? Living on a ship ain't fun."

"Are there places along the coast only accessible by boat?" Valek asked.

"Yeah. There's a few. Up north there's a couple coves hidden in those cliffs. Do you think they could be there?"

"It's possible. Or they could be stocking up for a journey to Sitia." Which would be a safer place for the magician to live.

"That's too dangerous. Out of dozens of ships, only one has crossed the Rattles intact."

But would a boat with a Stormdancer aboard be able to? Valek considered. The Rattles extended over a hundred miles into the Sunset Ocean from the knob of land jutting from the southern coast of MD-1, which was also the western edge of the Snake Forest. It twisted over underwater rocks, contained pockets of shallow water and created unpredictable riptides and strong currents. The sound of the turbulent water reminded sailors of rattlesnakes when they shook their tails in warning. And it fit perfectly with its location at the end of the Snake Forest.

A Stormdancer influenced the weather and not water, so Valek doubted having one on board would make a difference in an attempt to cross the Rattles. One thing Valek did know—the Storm Thieves must have a grander scheme than stealing in mind. Once he figured that out, they'd be easy to find.

MARIA V. SNYDER

Annika arrived with two steaming containers of seafood chowder for them. Valek's stomach lurched in sudden hunger as the tangy, fishy aroma reached him. She served Valek first, but she gave Endre a sweet dimpled smile with his bowl. Ah. They'd been working together too long. In the past, he'd break them up and assign one to the other side of Ixia. But as Hedda had said, he'd changed. Valek no longer believed love or romance negatively affected an agent's ability to do his or her duty. In fact, he thought it made them a stronger team.

Pah, you've gone soft, old man, Janco's voice sounded in his head. He ignored it. Instead he asked Annika about the boats that had disappeared this year.

"There's always a bunch that wreck or sink or catch fire," she said. "Mostly those have a few survivors, but there were two that sailed from Gandrel and never came back. The *Starfish* and the *Sea Serpent*."

"Do you know who captained the boats and worked on them?"

"No, sir, but the Port Master will have all that information."

"Can you get the names for me without anyone knowing?"

She hesitated, then glanced at Endre. "Do you have any sleeping juice left?"

"Yep."

"Then that would be a yes, sir," she said to Valek. "The Port Master is a frequent customer."

"What about the other towns?" Endre asked him. "There have to be other boats that disappeared."

"The Stormers are from Gandrel."

"How do you know?" Annika asked.

"You tell me," he said. "What's changed?"

She stared at the map in concentration. A section of her long brown hair fell in front of her face, and she tucked it behind her ear with an impatient tug. Her darker skin tone reminded him of Yelena.

Annika tapped on the map with her finger. "Stealing weapons from a security office is a dangerous hit." She met Valek's gaze. Long eyelashes framed lovely brown eyes. "There are a number of offices along the coast, but they picked Gandrel's because they're very familiar with the town. There's no need to worry about getting lost while a storm rages when you know every street, and the chances of encountering an officer are smaller when you know their patrol patterns."

Valek grinned. "Exactly."

After Endre finished his chowder, he left to report to work. Valek asked Annika about the local gossip. "Anyone mention my name?"

"A few noticed you arriving in town, but they all assumed you're here to help with the nets."

Good. "How about speculation over these Stormers?"

"Lots of that, from the ridiculous—ghosts living in the clouds—to the mundane—local kids taking advantage of the weather. A couple folks think the security officers are making a big deal for nothing. So far, I haven't heard anything of value."

Annika returned to her job at the inn. Valek waited thirty minutes before finding a spot at the bar of the inn's common room. He ordered an ale and listened to the various conversations around him.

"...best net caught on the blasted rocks and shredded like wet paper."

"I wanted to ring his bloody neck..."

"I'd bet Nichel's boy is behind all this trouble. Damn kid never did listen."

"...fat cats at the garrison. You'd think they'd help us with these bastards."

MARIA V. SNYDER

When Valek finished his ale, he inquired about work, and one of the boat captains said he needed an extra pair of hands. Then he climbed the stairs to his room, changed into his sneak suit and slipped out the window. He spent the next three hours reading reports. A couple of comments from the searches snagged his attention, and he wrote a list of buildings and shipyards to recheck. Overall, there wasn't any information that challenged his theory.

Good. The sooner he could solve this and reunite with Yelena, the better.

Over the next couple days, Valek helped repair nets. His nimble fingers and skill at tying knots earned him a favorable reputation. The fishermen soon relaxed and Valek listened to their gossip. Eventually he steered the conversation to the lost ships.

"Everyone knows the risks you take when you step on that boat." Pug looped new twine around a tear. His fingernails were black and he smelled like brine. "You expect a few losses, but it's a heartbreaker regardless."

"Yeah," Joey agreed. He was one of the oldest men on the crew. "And sometimes you can guess who's not coming back. I told Nell not to take on such a young, inexperienced crew, but she wouldn't listen. What you get in energy and stamina, you lose in experience and plain old good sense."

"Poor Nell." Pug tsked. "At least those tadpoles didn't leave behind younguns, but I'm sure their parents are beside themselves."

Valek remembered Nell's name from the *Starfish*'s manifest. Annika had copied it along with the *Sea Serpent*'s last night while the Port Master had been slumped over a table at the inn, snoring. The list of names hadn't meant anything to him, but learning the crews' ages helped. A person with children and a spouse wouldn't be as likely to pretend to disappear at sea so he or she could become a thief.

After a few more questions, Valek would have bet money that the *Starfish* was the Storm Thieves' ship. Now the next step would be to find it. There hadn't been a break-in in over three weeks, and most of the fishermen believed the weapon raid was the last one. Only thirteen days remained until the start of the warm season and the first safe day that the fleet could set sail.

Valek figured the Storm Thieves would make one more raid before lying low for the fishing seasons. He needed to review the stolen items again. Once he determined what was next on their list, he could anticipate their destination.

"We better finish this net today," Pug said. He gazed at the sea. "I don't like the look of those clouds."

"Could be a big blow." Joey massaged his stiff fingers.

"Any idea where it will hit?" Valek asked.

"If it's big enough, it don't matter. The whole coast gets punched," Joey said. "If it's smaller, then you follow the waves."

"The waves?"

"Yeah. If the storm's coming right at you, the waves are parallel to the shore, lined up like rolling pins on my granny's table. If the waves are angled to the right, the storm's moving north. Angled left means south."

Valek studied the waves lapping under the dock. Rolling pins.

"Too soon to tell," Joey said. "Look in the morning."

"When will the storm hit?"

Pug squinted. "Tomorrow…maybe tomorrow night."

Valek needed to hurry. He didn't have much time to prepare.

MARIA V. SNYDER

18

LEIF

As he traveled to the Citadel, Leif's thoughts kept returning to Irys's comment about the twelve missing and four dead magicians. And Irys's lack of intel about the attacks gnawed holes of worry in his guts, ruining his appetite. Irys could only speculate why—to regulate all the magicians. As for who, she suspected a group of influential and wealthy people was behind it, but she had no evidence.

The timing of the incidents matched with Yelena's loss of magic. Almost right after she'd been shot with that damn poisoned arrow, the Cartel—Irys's name for them—started their aggressive campaign against magicians. The only suspected member of the Cartel was Bruns Jewelrose, who'd hired The Mosquito to assassinate Yelena and supposedly the other four magicians. And perhaps he'd also targeted Ben Moon and Loris and Cilly Cloud Mist.

Unable to solve the puzzle while traveling, Leif forced his brooding thoughts to a different topic. Too bad yet another worry popped to the surface. Yelena. Through the super glass messenger, Irys told him the good news—that she'd returned to the Citadel with Ari and Janco—and the bad—she'd been arrested and interrogated by the Council.

Irys urged Leif to hurry so he could verify her story. Leif also carried detailed drawings that his father, Esau, provided to show the Sitian Council what Owen had been growing. Esau had refused to leave the glass hothouse until he had finished his investigation and found someone to properly care for the plants while they were gone.

Meanwhile, Yelena waited for Leif's arrival instead of escaping. She wished to regain her positive status with the Council. But every day she remained in the jail, the greater the danger.

Sensing his mood, Rusalka picked up her pace. They rode on the main east-west route in the Featherstone lands. In two more days, he'd be home, but if he pushed it, he might shave off half a day. Of course that meant arriving late at night, when all the Councilors would be asleep, so he'd have to wait until morning to talk to them.

He grinned. Leif knew exactly how he wanted to spend those hours. In bed with his wife, Mara, who made the plainest housedress appear to be the height of fashion. Just wrapping his arms around her would ease the ache pulsing deep in his chest. And he'd breathe in her scent—the light aroma of ylang-ylang flower, combined with the sweet fragrance of the living green—and be home.

Instead of overnighting in an inn, Leif decided to stop to rest for just a couple hours. He'd find a merchant camp to join. The caravans tended to avoid the expense of a real bed and bivouacked along the road. With the warm season a few weeks away, many had started their first deliveries of the year.

A couple hours after sunset, Leif caught a whiff of molasses followed by the bitter tang of fear. Rusalka broke into a gallop as the shrill sounds of a horse in distress pierced the air.

When they turned a corner, a cloud of emotions struck him. Panic and fear the strongest. In the faint moonlight, he identified the black shapes. Horse. Wagon. Person.

MARIA V. SNYDER

As they drew closer, the shapes sharpened. Overturned wagon. Man about to be trampled by a panicked horse.

High-pitched squeals and cries emanated from underneath the wagon. The man shouted at the kids to be quiet. "You're scaring the horse."

Too late. Leif stopped Rusalka fifty feet before the scene. Her presence might make it worse. At least the children quieted to whimpers.

The man lurched forward in an attempt to grab the reins, causing the horse to rear again. Idiot didn't know anything about horses. Leif dismounted, then approached slowly.

"Back away or you're going to get hurt," Leif ordered the man in an even, nonthreatening tone—more for the horse than the idiot.

The man whipped around. "Oh, thank fate! Can you help us?"

"Yes. Stand over there." Leif pointed to a safe spot.

"But my children—"

"Will be fine, if you do everything I say."

The man backed away to the place Leif had indicated. Leif drew in a breath and studied the horse's body language. A wildness shone in its eyes as its sides heaved. Foamy sweat dripped from its body and it blew air from its nostrils. One of the wooden supports of the wagon had snapped in half, but the horse remained tethered. Crates littered the ground behind the overturned wagon.

Leif inched closer, keeping in the horse's line of sight. He projected calming emotions, not sure if it'd work on a horse, but figured it couldn't hurt. Talking to the horse in a steady voice, he approached. The horse shook, but didn't rear. Leif kept his soothing tone and reached for the reins. He grasped them in his left hand. Then he stroked the horse's nose and kept talking.

When the horse's sides slowed and it no longer arched its neck, Leif said to the man, "Move slowly and come take the reins."

The man followed his directions. Keeping his hands on the horse, Leif slid them back to the hitch.

"Daddy, what's going on?" asked a little girl.

"Just wait, sweet pea. We need to free Doggie."

Doggie? Leif glanced at the man.

"We let the kids name him," he explained.

Better than Beach Bunny. Leif unhitched the wagon while keeping contact with the horse so it wouldn't spook again. Then he removed the harness. It was slow and tedious work, but eventually, he freed Doggie. Leif led the horse to a nearby tree, then covered Doggie with his cloak to keep him warm until they could walk him to cool off. He returned to help the man free his children.

They lifted the broken wooden bed and four figures scrambled out as they righted the wagon.

Leif turned. "Is everyone all right? I've bandages and…" The kids were much taller than he'd expected, and the father pointed a loaded crossbow at Leif's chest. Unease swirled into alarm.

Stupid.

"And?" the armed man prompted.

"And I just aided in my own ambush. Didn't I?" Idiotic.

"You're quick. It took that Hale fellow ages to understand."

They have Hale? Why didn't Irys tell me? He swallowed his fear and concentrated on the five assembled before him. No emotions emanated except from the "father." The others must be wearing null shields. "Why go to all this trouble? You outnumber me."

"Where's the fun in that? Besides, if you caught a whiff of an ambush, you'd have been long gone."

MARIA V. SNYDER

If it's fun you want…let's see how fun it is when your clothes are on fire. Leif concentrated.

"Oh, no, you don't. Frent."

A puff sounded right before a prick of pain burned on Leif's neck. He yanked the dart from his skin, but knew it was too late. "Rusalka, go home!"

She galloped by as the woods spun around him. Sinking to his knees, his last thought before the darkness rushed in was of Mara. Their reunion would have to wait. He hoped.

19

YELENA

Five steps. Turn. Five more steps. Turn. I paced along the twenty-seven iron bars of my cell. Even though I had used all my skills as the Liaison and convinced the Sitian Council I hadn't been involved in espionage, treason or conspiring with the enemy, they still required my brother's testimony in order to release us.

Five days. We'd been locked in here for one, two, three, four, five and turn, days. Leif had better hurry.

"You're going to wear a hole in the soles of your boots," Ari said.

I glared at him. He'd taken a philosophical view of the entire endeavor, using the time to rest. He'd claimed we'd need our energy for our eventual escape, which we'd already planned in detail so we could bolt at a moment's notice. Of course it helped his calm attitude that Irys had smuggled in a couple of swords for him and Janco, just in case The Mosquito tried to take advantage of my incarceration.

"Yeah, better to do something constructive with your time," Janco said.

Janco exercised by grasping the highest crossbar with both hands and pulling his body up off the floor. He'd taken his shirt off, exposing long, lean muscles rippling with the effort. Scars crisscrossing his back, arms and chest resembled a street map of a dense city. And he'd named each scar in remembrance of where and when he'd sustained the injury. The healed gash on his stomach and the matching mark on his back, he'd named "Yelena," for the time he'd been run through with a sword and almost died. Janco swore I'd healed him.

"Pacing is also a form of burning off excess energy," I said to Janco.

"I'm not burning. I'm keeping in shape. While Ari's muscles turn to fat, mine will remain strong and ready for action."

Ari shot to his feet. "I'll show you ready for action." He reached through the bars and clamped his huge hands around Janco's narrow waist. With one yank, Ari pulled Janco off the bars and held him suspended over the floor.

Janco sputtered and tried to break his partner's hold. *Tried* being the key word. Without warning, Ari released him. Janco landed with an *oomph*. He recovered, but before he could squawk in protest, a clang echoed.

We turned to the main entrance of the jail. Irys strode in with two guards on her heels. One glance at her pale face and her fingers fretting at her sleeves, and I braced for bad news.

"Unlock the doors, now," Irys ordered the guards.

They moved to obey, starting with Janco's.

Perhaps *bad* was an understatement. I gripped the bars. "What happened?"

"Rusalka showed up at the Citadel without Leif," she said.

I pressed my forehead against the cool metal. Concentrating on not panicking, I drew in a few steadying breaths. "My father? Is he missing, too?"

"No. He remained behind to finish his investigation."

One good thing. I focused on the positive. "What's being done to find Leif?"

"As soon as I heard, I gathered Kiki and your other horses, along with Rusalka. They're waiting for you. Rusalka'll guide you back to where she…lost Leif. Janco, you will be able to track him, right?" The desperate hope in her voice almost cracked my composure.

"How long ago did Rusalka arrive?" Janco asked her.

"This morning. About three hours ago."

"Then we need to hurry." Janco grabbed his hidden sword from under the metal cot.

We joined Irys in the corridor. If the guards were surprised by the sudden appearance of the weapons, they didn't show it.

"Do you think the Cartel has him?" I asked her.

"I suspect they're behind it, but I've no proof."

Sprinting after Irys, we exited the building. Bain Bloodgood argued with a handful of Councilors at the base of the steps. A few shouted at us to stop, but we ignored them and mounted our horses.

"Let's go," I said.

Rusalka turned. We followed. The loud clatter of hooves over cobblestones vibrated in my ears. I let the sound drown out the voice in my head. Being very familiar with that voice, I knew it would list all the horrors that might have befallen my brother, remark on the slim chance of successfully finding him alive and comment on every other terrible scenario. That voice was rather creative when stressed and worried.

After a day and a half of hard riding, we reached the location of Leif's disappearance. A few hours of daylight remained.

Janco dismounted and examined the ground. Ari and I allowed him to do his tracking mojo while we walked the horses. They had set the brutal pace. Patches of sweat stained their coats. Their nostrils flared as they caught their breaths. Once their breathing smoothed, we watered and fed them. By this time, Janco had finished his investigation. He stood

MARIA V. SNYDER

in the middle of a number of scuff marks on the right side of the road, scowling.

"What did you discover?" Ari asked him.

"It wasn't a typical ambush." Janco pointed to clumps of grass and dirt between two trees. "Somebody went to considerable trouble to stage an accident. They overturned a wagon and made it appear as if it was stuck." He strode closer and crouched down. "And here's evidence of a freaked-out horse." Janco straightened. "They knew their mark."

"Janco," Ari warned.

"I'm trying to be dispassionate. Leif's my friend, too."

I concentrated on the information and ignored my emotions, which threatened to let that voice of doom speak. "Why do you think it was set specifically for Leif?"

"'Cause of the elaborate setup. Being a Sandseed horse, Rusalka would have alerted him of people hiding in the woods."

"Unless they were waiting downwind," Ari added.

"Not this time of year. The prevailing wind direction is from the west."

Ari and I exchanged a glance. Impressive.

Janco huffed. "Ya know, it's not all…tracker mojo. There's a lot that goes into it. And there's some good news."

My heart jumped. "You know where he is?"

"I wish. They headed west, but the road's surface is too hard packed and well traveled to distinguish their tracks from all the others."

"The *good* news," Ari prompted.

"There's no blood."

"That makes sense if he was taken by the Cartel. They wouldn't want to harm him until he refused to join them." And my stubborn brother would probably never agree to work for them. Which meant we had a limited amount of time to find and rescue him before The Mosquito bit.

"Another thing about the setup is they knew Leif would be on this road at a particular time," Janco said. "Who else knew his location, other than Master Irys?"

"Bain and the Councilors, who might have informed their aides," I said. Plus all the people who bribed the aides for intel. In other words, too many.

"Janco said they continued west. We didn't pass them on the road, or else Rusalka would have smelled Leif. Is there another road that branches off this one?" Ari asked.

I considered. "There's a shortcut about a day west of here that leads to the main southern road. That route follows the western edge of the Avibian Plains, but they could have veered off into Stormdance or Greenblade lands. And they have a three-day head start." Frustration welled.

"That's also the way to the Jewelrose lands," Ari said.

"*If* Bruns Jewelrose is dumb enough to amass his magician army in his own backyard," Janco added. "I doubt he's that stupid."

"What's our next move?" Ari asked.

Guessing would get us nowhere; we needed reliable information. I stifled a groan. My earlier mistake—the one that had led to us sitting in a cell wasting time for five days—returned for another kick of recriminations. "Fisk."

"But if he knows where Leif and the others are, why doesn't he tell the Council?" Ari asked.

"For the same reason we don't trust the Council," Janco said.

"And the reason is?"

"They're ineffective idiots!"

"He probably doesn't have any proof," I said. "These are wealthy businesspeople who have a great deal of influence and power. Fisk has probably cobbled together bits of information from his sources and determined what's going on." At least I fervently hoped so. "We need to talk to him. Let's go." I stepped toward Kiki, who grazed nearby.

Ari grabbed my shoulder, halting me. "No."

"But time—"

"We haven't slept in over a day."

"We've been resting for five days."

"A few hours is all we need."

"Leif—"

"Leif's clever. He'll play along, knowing we'll come rescue him. But you won't be able to help your brother if you're exhausted."

I peered at him. He'd gone from using *we* to *you*, meaning *me*. "Let me guess. Valek—"

"Doesn't have to order us to protect you. You are family. That goes beyond orders."

When we reached the Citadel two days later, we split up, just in case the guards at the gate had been ordered to look for groups of three. Janco circled around to the southern gate with Rusalka, while Ari and I headed for the eastern entrance. We merged with the early-morning traffic and sidled behind a large caravan of wagons. The guards didn't even glance at us as we passed through.

While the benefit of having busy streets helped us enter unnoticed, the crowded roads slowed our pace. It'd been six days since Leif had been taken, and the desire to scream at all these obstructions clawed at my throat. Then the need to ensure no one followed us to Fisk's headquarters delayed us further as we snaked through the streets.

Fisk's building resided in one of the outer factory loops southwest of the market. By the time we rendezvoused with

Janco near the narrow alley that led to the door, all of my pent-up frustration and worry pressed on my skin from the inside. If Fisk couldn't help, I'd explode. His Helper's Guild members would be cleaning Yelena bits off their ceiling, walls and floor for days.

"Any trouble?" Ari asked his partner.

"None." Janco scrunched up his nose.

"Then what's wrong?" I asked.

"Yet another stinkin' alley. The smell is bad enough, but the place is also reeking with magic. I thought Fisk was a regular kid."

"He is." Although I wouldn't call a seventeen-year-old a kid. "He probably hired a magician to hide the guild's entrance with an illusion."

"Why?" Ari asked.

"Problems with the criminal element. Their cheap labor force, also known as the homeless children and the desperate, have been too busy working and earning money by being a part of Fisk's guild, so the crime bosses have been making it difficult for the helpers. Leif offered to help, but Fisk insisted he'd handle it on his own. The young man's a bit stubborn."

"Stub...born?" Janco sounded out each syllable as if saying the word for the first time. "Gee, I don't know anyone who is stub...born." He stared at me.

"Just for that, you get to go into the stinkin' alley first," I said.

"Yay for me." He rubbed his right ear. "What about the horses?"

"Ari, can you stay with them until we find the door?" I asked.

"What if it's a trap?"

"I'll scream really loud and you run and get backup," Janco said.

"It's not a trap. It's Fisk." I dismounted.

"Yeah, well, Fisk is a businessman, and I'm sure he has other clients who will pay—"

"No. Not Fisk." I kept my tone even despite my anger. "Before you remind me of my…inability to wield magic and how I have to be paranoid and trust no one, it's *Fisk*. Got it?"

"Yes, sir." The big man set his jaw.

"While I'll agree that Fisk wouldn't ever betray or harm you for money, Yelena—" Janco swung down from The Madam's saddle "—I also think Ari has a point, even though he didn't communicate it well. Everyone is vulnerable. If I was a ne'er-do-well, I'd find a person's weakness and exploit it in my favor. Like when Owen found your weakness by kidnapping Leif and forcing you to steal the Ice Moon. Fisk is no exception."

"You're right." Before Janco could gloat, I added, "Ari didn't express it well. My apologies, Ari."

"Just be extra careful," he said. "Janco, if you sense any magic inside Fisk's headquarters—"

"We'll make a super-quick exit." He handed The Madam's and Rusalka's reins to Ari.

Janco entered the alley and I stayed a step behind him. The rank smell of urine and rotted garbage stung the inside of my nostrils, causing nausea to roll in my stomach. Our boots crunched on broken glass. Fist-sized spiders skittered behind heaps of trash. All, I hoped, part of the magical illusion. I kept my hand close to my switchblade just in case.

"You always take me to the fanciest places, Yelena. You really spoil me."

"Anyone who can use *ne'er-do-well* in a sentence deserves every comfort."

Janco grunted, but I wasn't sure if it was over the joke or because of the magic. He stopped, turned to his right, held up his hands and walked through a brick wall, disappearing. I followed, bracing for impact even though I knew it was illusion.

We entered an alcove. Remembering the series of knocks Leif had used during our previous visit, I rapped on the door. If they'd changed the pattern, we might be in trouble.

A small peephole opened. "Kinda early for a visit," a young girl said.

"It's never too early to lend a helping hand," I replied.

The peephole shut with a bang.

"Talk about paranoid," Janco whispered.

Nothing happened. I resisted the urge to pound on the door with the sides of my fists. Then a metallic snap sounded and the door swung wide.

A girl no older than thirteen gestured us into a foyer. "Lovely Yelena, you honor us with your visit." She tucked her long brown hair behind her ears. "Master Fisk has been expecting you."

And probably wondering why we didn't come sooner. I scanned the three rooms that branched off the foyer. On the right, the rows of bunk beds for the helpers were empty, and so was the classroom on the left. The enticing aroma of sweet cakes floated from the kitchen located straight ahead.

"Is Fisk in his office?"

"No. This is our busiest time of day and everyone is at the market helping shoppers. However, I sent Cricket to fetch him. Come and have breakfast while you wait. Amberle's making sweet cakes."

Another delay. I clasped my hands together to keep from shouting at the girl that we didn't have time to eat. With my fingernails biting into my skin, I said, "We have another person outside with our horses."

"Then I will direct him to the stable."

Interesting that she already knew his gender.

"You have a stable in here?" Janco asked, glancing around with a sharp gaze. Probably marking all the exits.

"Not exactly. It's on the other side of our building and is part of the White Rose Inn. However, we have an...arrangement with the proprietor of the White Rose, and there's a convenient door into our headquarters from the stable."

"I'd better go instead. Ari's not gonna trust you." Janco asked for directions.

"Tell the stable boy Hilly sent you."

Janco nodded and left. I followed Hilly to the kitchen. It opened up into an expansive kitchen with rows of long wooden tables to the left of the hearth. Amberle waved hello with her spatula.

Hilly gestured to a table, grabbed a plate, filled it from the stack of sweet cakes next to Amberle and set it front of me. The nausea caused by the odors in the alley transformed into ravenous hunger. I thanked her and dug in as if I hadn't seen food in days. Somewhat true. Cold road rations didn't count as real food, and my appetite had been nonexistent between my worry for Leif and the morning sickness the medic had warned me about.

Once I stopped shoveling sweet cakes and took a breath, I realized that in spite of my concern for my brother, I must ensure the baby remained healthy by eating regularly and getting enough sleep.

By the time I'd finished my meal, Janco and Ari arrived in the kitchen from another direction.

"This place is huge." Janco straddled a bench opposite me.

Ari sat next to me. The wood bowed under his weight and I tipped toward him.

"The horses?" I asked Ari.

"Fine."

Hilly served them and sat down next to Janco. While they ate, I asked her why only a few remained in the building.

"Oh, there are others," she said. Her brown eyes sparkled. "Headquarters is never empty. I'm told it's like a hive with bees flying in and out all day."

Janco paused. "And if you upset the hive, will you get stung?"

She grinned, showing her teeth. "Oh, yes. Many times."

"Nice." He scratched his ear. "But not many people can find this place. There's magic all around the outside, but thank fate the inside is clean."

"These are…uncertain times, Master Janco."

He preened. "*Master* Janco. Did you hear that, Ari?"

Ari and I ignored him. Instead, I studied the girl. Hilly knew his name, and she was here instead of working the busy market.

"You're one of Fisk's information collectors. Aren't you?" I asked.

Hilly smoothed her skirt. "I just answer the door."

"Ha." Janco stabbed a forkful of sweet cakes at her. "Don't try the innocent act, kitty cat. I invented that act ages ago."

"Too bad you never could pull it off," Ari mumbled.

"Zip it, Ari." And then to Hilly, "I spotted you hiding in the shadows the night we were arrested and again when we left the Citadel a few nights ago."

She gazed at him. "You're lying."

"Navy blue tunic and pants, scuffed black boots and the handle of your dagger is patterned with stars."

Her mouth gaped for a second, before she pressed her lips together in annoyance—a typical reaction after dealing with Janco.

"Don't worry about it, kitty cat. You're good—not as good

MARIA V. SNYDER

as me, but no one's perfect." He flourished the fork before sticking it in his mouth.

"That ego is going to get you killed someday," Ari chided.

"Pish." Janco faced Hilly. "After we were hauled away by the Citadel's guards, did you return to Fisk or did you wait to see if anyone else watched the spectacle?"

"What would you have done?" she asked.

"Patience isn't my thing, but a smart spy would stick around and see who the other curious cats are."

Ah, clever. He phrased it in a way to prod her ego into giving us information.

"I may have seen another...cat slinking away," she said.

"Oh? Do you know who this cat belongs to?"

"It depends."

Janco leaned forward. "Depends on what?"

"On how many coins you're going to give me for the intel."

"Gotcha," Ari said.

I laughed at Janco's sour expression. "How about two silvers for the name?" I asked.

"Six, and I'll tell you who also watched you leave to find your brother."

"Three."

"Five."

"Four."

"Deal." She held out her hand.

I placed four silver coins in her palm.

"The cat returned to a well-dressed man wearing a necklace with a large red jewel. The man was staying in the Council's guest quarters. He stepped from the back entrance to talk to the cat."

"Can you describe him?"

"It would be better for you to see him. I can tell you where to find him."

"For a few more coins?" Janco asked.

"Of course. Feeding everyone in the guild isn't cheap," she snapped.

"Well, if it wasn't for Yelena, you wouldn't even have a guild," he shot back.

I held up my hands. "I'm happy to pay. That's the whole point—to provide services in exchange for payment." I gestured, indicating the room. "So those without homes and families have food and shelter." Smiling, I added, "I'd no idea it would expand into a guild, and, for that, you have Fisk to thank." I handed her two more silvers.

Hilly said, "The man sits in on most of the public Council sessions and he's staying in number three-oh-six."

"Do we want to have a look?" Janco asked.

Tempting, but rescuing Leif was my priority. "Let's talk to Fisk first."

"What about the person who took an interest in us when we left the Citadel?" Ari asked Hilly.

"It's the same cat."

I mulled over her comments. Could the cat be The Mosquito, reporting to Bruns Jewelrose? Then why didn't the assassin try to kill me when I was locked in a cell? Probably because his prior attempt in the Fulgor jail hadn't worked. And all he needed was patience. No doubt another opportunity to target me would arise.

Ari touched my sleeve. Concern creased his face. "That cat may have followed us here from the east gate." Ari had chased the same logic as me.

"Unfortunately, Master Ari is correct," Fisk said, entering the kitchen. "A man—or should I say your cat—is keeping an eye on the White Rose's stables right now."

I stood. "I'm so sorry, Fisk!"

"No need to apologize, Lovely Yelena. The man has been

sniffing around here for the last three weeks. Seems he assumed that when you returned to the Citadel, you'd pay me a visit *before* being arrested." A gleam of amusement touched Fisk's light brown eyes. "Kudos to you for doing the…unexpected. It may have saved your life."

"How?" Janco asked.

"Think about it," Ari said.

Janco tapped his fork on the edge of the plate for a minute. "Oh. If we came straight here, he would have surprised us, but now we know his exact location, but he *doesn't* know we know."

"Not bad, Master Janco. I'd hire you if you were available. You could train under Hilly."

The girl smirked at Janco and handed the six silver coins to Fisk. She curtsied to us. "Please let me know if I can be of any more assistance." Then she left.

Fisk pocketed the coins. "Always wonderful to see you, Lovely Yelena, but I fear you bring us bad news?"

"Let's talk in your office," I said.

We trailed him down a long hallway that ended with a door. Fisk unlocked it and ushered us inside. The large two-story room also housed a living area and a loft above his office.

Janco sat in one of the two nubby red armchairs and Ari took the other. I perched on the edge of the black-and-white couch. A glass sculpture of two hands spread out like wings sat on the table between the two chairs. It was one of Opal's magic detectors. Nothing flashed within its core, which meant no magic was in use. Plus Janco appeared to be relaxed.

Fisk remained standing, making him seem taller than his normal six feet. "What happened?"

No way to break this news gently. "Leif's been taken."

He gripped the back of the couch. "When? Where?"

I told him about the ambush.

"Oh, no." Fisk sank to the couch. "I'd thought he'd be safe."

"Why?" Ari asked.

"He has that...smell thing."

"Doesn't matter if they used null shields," I said. They had their uses, but were a big problem when abused. A strange thought popped into my head. What if the Cartel did gain power over all the magicians? They'd be able to regulate those shields, but would they use them for the good of Sitia or for their own plans?

I shook my head. It didn't matter, because we'd stop them. We had to. "Do you have any information about the disappearances?"

Fisk hesitated.

"I'll pay you, of course."

"No. It's not that at all. Leif has aided me so much over the years, and I will do everything I can to help you rescue him."

"Then what it is?"

He took a breath and met my gaze. "Not all the magicians are missing. A few of them are in hiding."

20

VALEK

A storm brewed over the Sunset Ocean, and Valek had a day and a half to prepare. His theory about the Storm Thieves being the crew of the *Starfish*, which was reported lost at sea, meant they'd use this incoming storm to cover their approach to land. But many questions still remained. Which town did they plan to target? Would they use a dock or send a skiff to a beach? And then there was a good chance they wouldn't arrive at all. It'd been three weeks since their last break-in.

Valek returned to the apartment on Cannery Road after supper. Endre snored in the bedroom and Annika worked at the inn. Valek reviewed the information gathered and the list of stolen items. Ignoring the jewelry and money, he concentrated on the others. He considered the basics—food, water, shelter.

Endre had said living on a boat would be difficult. If he assumed they'd found a place to live—a cove hidden in the cliffs, perhaps—then the Storm Thieves had enough supplies to build a couple structures. That covered shelter.

Fresh water was too essential to steal, so Valek figured their location had access to a stream or river that flowed toward the ocean. He checked the map of the coast and discovered that all of the rivers that emptied into the ocean had towns built around them. Which made sense for shipping supplies up the river to cities inland.

He considered the cliffs in MD-1. Would fresh water run under the cliffs and not be marked on the map? Possible. And no one would notice a settlement that was inaccessible by land. However, during the fishing season, they'd be visible to the fleet. Unless they used camouflage. And that would explain the fifty gallons of gray and green paint stolen from Krillow. The hidden cove moved to the top of Valek's suspected location list.

As for food, the Storm Thieves had stolen basics like grain, rice, corn, flour, sugar, but they also took seeds and gardening supplies, which meant they planned to plant crops. No way a cove could sustain plants, unless it was huge. A sandy-rocky soil covered most of the coast, and farmable land started about ten miles inland. So much for the cove idea.

Valek tapped the map with a finger. He chased a memory of a conversation with one of the Stormdancers. Something about islands out in the Jade Sea... They were too small for a settlement because of the unpredictable storms. What if the Storm Thieves built their base on an island in the Sunset Ocean? With their magician keeping the storms at bay, they'd be safe. And no one would suspect they lived there.

Excited, Valek scanned the coastal map. Dozens of small islands were marked on the chart. It'd take seasons to check them all, and news would undoubtedly spread about the search, alerting the Storm Thieves, who could use a storm to keep the searchers from reaching their island. Plus they could have discovered an uncharted island. Deflated, Valek leaned back in the chair. Finding the island would be impossible.

He returned to the list of stolen items. What was missing? What did they need to sustain a settlement? Medical supplies had been taken from an infirmary in Coral Caye, casks of ale missing from a tavern in Lattice Beach, pots and glassware from a inn in Draggan and—

Valek shot to his feet. He flipped through the information Endre and Annika had collected, looking for the report on damages sustained during the storm thefts. Once he found it, he scanned the pages. A henhouse had collapsed during one storm and all the chickens had escaped. During another, a gate blew open and a dozen sheep had run away and had presumably drowned. Four milking cows had disappeared when a storm had knocked down a wall of a barn. What if these animals had been stolen instead? That meant the Storm Thieves still needed beef.

Once again Valek consulted the map. Where was the closest steer farm to the coast? He located one about three miles south of Gandrel and approximately a half mile inland. Gotcha!

When Annika returned and Endre woke up for his night shift, Valek ran his theory by them, seeking flaws in his logic.

"Those cliff coves aren't big enough for livestock and crops," Endre said.

"Are you sure there aren't any missing steers listed in the reports?" Annika asked.

"I checked all the information twice," Valek said. "But I'll read through the ones in the security office again tonight, and tomorrow I'll see what the locals have to say about the islands."

"You think they'll strike tomorrow night?" Endre asked him.

"If not tomorrow, then during the next storm. The Stormers need to have all their supplies before the fishing season starts in twelve days. We need to be in position regardless."

Valek spent another late night in the security office's conference room. With his theory in mind, he scanned the incident reports looking for anything that would dispute his logic.

Finding nothing, he returned to the inn for a few hours' sleep before reporting to the dock to join the repair crew.

The waves no longer lined up like rolling pins. Instead, they titled to the right.

"The worst part of the storm's gonna miss us," Joey said.

"Heading north, right?" Valek asked, tying a knot. Disappointment slowed his movements. More time spent away from Yelena.

"Yup. But the one right behind it might blow over us."

Valek paused. "Two close together? Is that usual?"

Joey cracked his knuckles. "Yup. They're called twins. We get them from time to time. They either follow the same path, hitting the same place one right after the other—those we call identical—or they diverge and go separate ways."

"Let me guess, those are called fraternal."

"You catch on quick."

Pug snorted. "Nothing quick about that, old man. Let's see if he can guess what we call them when they hit the coast at the same time?"

"Conjoined?" Valek guessed.

"Nope. We call them double trouble, and you hope that your boat don't sink and your house don't blow away during one of those nasty buggers." Pug shuddered. "Good thing they're rare."

"I've seen two in my lifetime," Joey said. "That's more than enough."

"Can you tell where the second twin will strike?" Valek asked Joey.

"Not yet."

Valek contained his impatience. He listened to their banter, their mild teasing and fish tales.

"...kid sunk like a stone, I had to fish him out with a net."

"...caught them hiding under the sails, lazy buggers."

MARIA V. SNYDER

"I spotted the wreckage in the water and I thought Smelly drowned, but we found 'im on Hook Island, sunnin' hisself on the beach. He was pissed we got to 'im so fast. Old Smelly thought he'd get a vacation." Joey coughed a chuckle.

"Could he have lived on the island?" Valek asked.

"For a couple days, sure, but he'd run through the food right quick. Nothing grows on them except berries, and you have to be real quick to catch one of them seabirds."

"Do ships wreck on those islands often?"

"Sometimes in a storm, but the fleet avoids them in bad weather. We'll check 'em when a ship's been reported missing, but it's rare we find anyone. Smelly's an exception."

"Yeah, he's an exceptional stinker. The man eats nothing but raw fish," Pug said.

Valek kept a comment about Pug's briny odor to himself. "Do you check them all?"

"Nah. Just the ones in the fishing grounds," Joey said.

"Does anyone use those islands?"

"Are you planning on building a vacation home?" Pug laughed. "If so, I've a deed I can sell you for ten golds."

Valek shrugged, playing down his interest. "Just making conversation."

"Ignore Pug," Joey said. "Those islands are only good for a rest or when you have to make repairs. A few have fresh water, but no one stays for long. Even a mild hot-season storm can swamp 'em and you're swimming."

"Or clinging to the treetops. Remember we found Fawlon tied to a branch?" Pug asked.

"Oh, yeah. Smart fellow, Fawlon. Too bad he died of thirst."

As they traded stories of other poor fellows, Valek mulled over the information. It seemed the Storm Thieves could live on an island as long as they had a magician to keep their settlement from being swamped. A Stormdancer would have to be back in Sitia by the heating season or the dancer would be missed. Was it another magician from Sitia or someone new? Joey said the crew of the *Starfish* was young.

What if one of those teens developed magic? Magic wasn't tolerated in Ixia, so the person had one of two options: escape to Sitia, or hide his or her power from everyone. But then there was the chance the person would grab too much magic and flame out. According to Irys, only those with amazing self-control could prevent that without any training.

If nothing happened during the storms, Valek planned to investigate all the crew members. It was a tiresome, tedious chore, but it might uncover a clue to the Storm Thieves' whereabouts.

After the fishermen rolled up the repaired nets, Joey pointed a crooked brown-spotted finger out to sea. "The first storm's headin' for the cliffs. But it looks like his twin is turnin' toward us. It'll hit tomorrow night, but I'll know better in the mornin'." He patted Valek on the shoulder and lowered his voice. "You catch those Stormers, boy. They're a nuisance." Then he limped across the street to the tavern.

So much for being subtle. Janco's incredulous voice sounded in his head. *An old man saw right through your cover? You're slipping, boss.* Good thing Janco was in Sitia with Yelena.

Valek stopped at his room to grab his pack before returning to the apartment. When Endre woke and Annika arrived, he reviewed his plan with them.

"I'm going north to keep an eye on the storm just in case. I want you both to watch the steer farm tonight. Get familiar with the layout of the barn, fields and the route to the coast. It'd be easier without a storm raging."

"Yes, sir," they said.

Endre rubbed his stomach. "If we want to keep our covers, we need an excuse for leaving work early."

MARIA V. SNYDER

"Not…" Annika covered her mouth with her hand.

"I'm not happy about it, either," he said.

"If it's any consolation," Valek said, "you only need three drops on your tongue, and it'll wear off in half an hour."

Endre rummaged in one of the kitchen's cabinets and removed a small glass vial filled with a brownish-yellow liquid. He crinkled his nose. "It even looks like vomit. Where do you find this stuff, sir?"

Valek grinned. "I've a source in Sitia who makes it for me." Leif always brewed potent concoctions, but he never bothered to improve the taste or smell. "Take the vomit tonic right before you leave. It will kick in once you're at work."

"Kick in?" Annika gave him a pained look.

"Sorry, I couldn't resist."

After the moon disappeared behind the thick bank of storm clouds, Valek headed north along the coast, following the waves. Since it was too dark to see the path, he carried a bull's-eye lantern and kept a small beam of light trained on the ground in front of him. He peered into the inky blackness of the ocean, searching for a ship's light. Nothing.

The edge of the storm reached land. Rain tapped against his black cloak. The castle's seamstress, Dilana, had soaked the material in a liquid wax to help repel water, but Valek had learned from experience that, with enough time, it would become waterlogged.

Gusts of wind blew ashore, flapping his cloak and threatening to extinguish the lantern's flame. Even though he pulled the hood over his head, the salty spray stung his eyes and burned his nose.

The rolling sand dunes along the coast turned rocky and steep. A blast of air from the north meant the cliffs must be ahead, deflecting the storm's wind. Even though he was unable to spot the sheer bluffs in the darkness, their massive presence loomed over him.

Valek retreated, finding a spot that he'd pick if he was on a boat and searching for a place to land. Then he hunkered down, closed the lantern's slide and waited.

He wondered what Yelena, Ari and Janco had discovered about the glass-house plants. It had been thirteen days since they parted. Was she on her way to the rendezvous point? Worry for her and the baby swirled.

At least she hadn't reached him with one of her desperate mental calls. Thrice before, she had been in dire trouble in Sitia and reached for him in a blind panic. Her frantic fear had ripped through him like a giant monster's sharp claws. Each time, he'd opened himself to her, loaning his strength and immunity to her across the miles. It had saved her life, and those times had been the only ones where they magically connected. Except now... His blood ran cold. Without her magic, would Yelena be able to reach him? Probably not.

What the hell was he doing here? Crouching in the rain, hoping to spot a gang of young thieves. Was this important to him? No. Catch these thieves and more would just pop up someplace else. He needed to be with his wife, even if she wasn't in danger. He'd let his job keep them apart for far too long. All he had to do was retire, and once free of the Commander's orders, he'd assassinate Owen.

Valek stood and wiped rain from his eyes. He turned and halted. A sigh escaped his lips. As much as he wished to go, he'd never leave a job unfinished. He revised his to-do list. Catch the Storm Thieves, retire, assassinate Owen. He returned to his position and tried not to fret over Yelena. After all, she was resourceful and smart. Plus Ari and Janco would never let her out of their sight.

Hours later, a light bobbed on the water. Valek watched

it with keen interest. The light broke into two points. The second one appeared to head for shore. As it drew closer, it clarified into four lanterns. The yellow glow revealed a large rowboat with four figures rowing and four others holding the lights. When they reached the shallow water, the rolling waves around the boat smoothed flat. Valek squinted. No rain or wind buffeted the craft, either. Sticky magic pressed on Valek. One of those eight must be the magician. Despite his earlier claims of not caring about these thieves, excitement warmed his chest.

Two men jumped out and pulled the boat's prow onto the beach. There was enough light for Valek to distinguish male and female, but not enough to observe facial features. Three men and two women hopped onto the sand. They carried two of the lanterns. Exchanging a few words with the woman in the boat, the five then strode across the sand, heading inland.

The men pushed the craft into deeper water and leaped in. Picking up the oars, they rowed toward the light still bobbing in the ocean. The water under the boat remained smooth despite the storm surge, which meant the magician had stayed with the rowboat. Valek'd bet a gold coin it was the woman sitting in the stern. Valek moved closer, risking being spotted to get a clear view of the magician. She was young. Sixteen, maybe seventeen years old. Pretty with long dark hair. At least she wasn't one of the Stormdancers.

Unable to follow the rowboat in storm-tossed seas, Valek trailed the group that had been dropped off. If they were a raiding party, then why did the boat leave? Perhaps they planned to rendezvous later at another location. That would be rather smart.

As the Storm Thieves traveled east, Valek recalled the map of the area. No towns or farms had been built here. There was nothing of value to steal. Maybe they'd hidden a stash of goods and were retrieving their stolen supplies. After hiking two miles, the Storm Thieves turned south, paralleling the coastline. The wind eased and soon it stopped raining.

When they bypassed Gandrel, the half-moon shone through a film of wispy clouds. Valek suspected that the Storm Thieves were headed to the steer farm. Instead of relying on the storm, they might be attempting to steal the cattle later tonight when everyone was asleep. An unexpected move. Again, he suspected their leader wasn't an average thief.

But how would they transport the animals? Someone would hear the hooves on the wooden planks of the dock. And he doubted they would bring them back to the beach where they'd landed. That boat was too small unless they carried one steer at a time. In that case, they'd have to make multiple trips, but no one would be searching for them up there. Now the question remained, were the Storm Thieves clever enough to make it work?

A quarter of a mile before the steer farm, they turned east, not west as expected. Curious, Valek closed the distance between them. After half a mile, the five hurried down an overgrown lane and into a barn with a sagging roof and weathered wood. Valek looped to the back of the dilapidated structure. A rusted chain wrapped around the handles of a set of warped doors. An oversize padlock cinched the chain tight.

The barn had only one exit. Good. Scrawny pine trees surrounded the area. There were no other buildings or lights visible. Lantern light glowed through the two dirty windows. Valek peeked inside. The Storm Thieves set up bedrolls. The glass garbled their words, but their tone suggested a relaxed, easy banter. Interesting.

Valek found a hidden vantage point and waited. Nothing happened. They remained inside. Right before dawn, he checked on them again. They slept in a circle around one of

MARIA V. SNYDER

the lanterns. It still glowed. The faint light illuminated their young faces, ranging in age from fifteen to nineteen.

A heaviness pressed on his shoulders. These kids had ruined their futures by being a part of the Storm Thieves. No spouse or children for them. The Code of Behavior didn't give second chances.

He mulled over the reason they hid in the barn. That second storm would hit the steer farm tonight, and these five would already be there to lead the cattle to the ship, saving time. And with the noise of the wind and waves, no one would hear the animals' passage over the dock. Shrewd. Very shrewd. And perfect for him. He knew just what to do.

Valek returned to the apartment. His cloak, uniform and hair were stiff with dried salt and sand. The cold air had soaked into his bones. He stirred the coals in the hearth to life and added logs. Then he washed up and changed into his adviser's uniform.

An hour after dawn, Endre and Annika arrived. They reported a quiet night.

"The owner's not too concerned about a theft," Endre said. "Except the house, none of his barns, sheds or gates are locked up. I guess he's relying on the brands on his livestock."

"Brands don't help when the cattle disappear," Annika said.

"Speaking of disappearing," Valek said. "I've a job for your security force, Endre. How many soldiers are there?"

"Five others beside me."

"We need more. Can you recruit from neighboring forces?"

He shook his head. "My captain can, but she's not going to do it because I ask her to."

"Then I'll ask her. Let's go."

"Now?"

"Yes, I'll explain on the way."

"What about me?" Annika asked.

"Find a seamstress, a bolt of a solid dark fabric and five gallons of sculpting clay. Bring them to the station as soon as you can." Valek didn't wait to see her reaction. He strode from the apartment with Endre close behind.

Detailing his discoveries and his plan to Endre, Valek hurried through the empty streets. Everything had to be in place by the time the storm arrived.

Captain Tahnee scowled at Endre—the newly revealed spy in her domain—but she sent messengers to Krillow and Coral Caye with Valek's orders.

"I'll need Endre and one other to go with me to arrest those kids," Valek said to Tahnee.

"You'll need more than that. There's five of them," she said.

Valek waited.

"Fine. Mikus," she barked.

A slender soldier no more than twenty years old snapped to attention. "Yes, sir!"

"You're with them."

His face paled. "Yes, sir!"

She pressed her lips together for a moment as if swallowing a sigh. "What can we do while you're gone?"

Valek listed a number of tasks. A dubious expression creased her face, but she agreed and organized the rest of her staff. Valek asked Endre to fetch five pairs of manacles, then they headed to the abandoned barn.

"They're young, so you shouldn't have any problems," Valek explained. "You are going to go in first, rouse them, manacle their hands behind their backs and make them kneel."

"Is that really necessary?" Endre asked. "They're just a bunch of kids."

Mikus sucked in a breath, as if he couldn't believe Endre dared to question Valek.

"I want them scared and off balance," Valek said. "I'm going

MARIA V. SNYDER

to make an entrance and terrify them. This way they will divulge all they know. For this age group, it's more effective than goo-goo juice."

"Ah, nice." Endre's tone held approval.

Grabbing the end of his shirt, Mikus twisted the fabric.

"Mikus, I encourage my agents to ask questions so they can understand what's going on. I also value their input. If Endre thought my plan sucked, he'd say so and explain why he believed that without any consequences."

"Oh." Mikus's voice squeaked. "And...would you change your plan then?"

"Depends. If Endre's reason had merit, then yes. If I didn't agree with him, then no." And that had been the same relationship the Commander and Valek had shared until recently. Perhaps Yelena had been on the right track regarding the Commander's unusual behavior. Had Valek missed vital clues from Ambrose? It was something to consider after he dealt with the Storm Thieves.

They reached the overgrown path. Valek signaled for silence, then he motioned for them to wait while he checked the barn. Keeping close to the trees, Valek approached the structure and looked through the window. The teens hadn't moved. He fetched Endre and Mikus.

When they drew close to the door, Valek mouthed, *Go!* The two men yanked their swords and barged into the barn, yelling at the teens to get against the wall. Valek remained outside as shouts and cries sounded. A clang of metal followed a curse.

One young man darted out. Valek tripped him. He sprawled in the dirt, but not for long. He scrambled to his feet and by the time Valek neared, he'd spun with a dagger in his hand. Quick little scamp.

The scamp brandished the weapon. "Don't come any—"

Valek kicked the boy's wrist, sending the knife flying

through the air. He pounced, grabbed the scamp's arm and twisted it behind his back. Valek grasped his shoulder to steady the boy.

"Keep still," he ordered his prisoner, "or I'll break your arm." Valek tugged it higher to emphasis his threat.

The scamp gasped in pain.

When the noise from inside the barn subsided, Valek pushed the boy ahead of him. "Move."

They entered. The other four knelt with Endre and Mikus standing behind them. The Storm Thieves' faces whitened another shade when they spotted their friend.

"You missed one," Valek said.

"Sorry, boss." Endre strode over, snapped the manacles on the scamp and dragged him to join his associates.

Valek gazed at the five with what Yelena called his cold killer expression. "Congratulations, your antics during the last couple seasons have caught *my* attention." He waited a beat. "Do you know who I am?"

They kept quiet.

"Endre, tell them."

"You are Adviser Valek. The Commander's *assassin* and right-hand man."

His name had the desired effect on all but one. Panic flared in four sets of eyes, but the scamp glared—a challenge.

Valek said, "Tell me the plan for tonight."

They glanced at the scamp.

"Don't say a word," he ordered them.

Ah. The scamp was in charge. Valek drew one of his knives from his sleeve with his right hand while palming a dart with his left. He grabbed the closest thief by her arm and yanked her upright, pricking her with the dart. She squealed in fear.

Placing his blade on her neck, he said, "Tell me the plan for tonight."

"You're bluffing," the scamp said. "It isn't a crime to sleep in an abandoned building. You got nothing on us."

Valek stared at him a moment before returning his attention to the girl. "What's your name?"

"Sa...Sadzi." Her eyes glazed.

"You should have picked better friends, Sadzi." He turned and stepped in front of her so he blocked her from the others. Drawing his knife arm back, he stabbed at her, sending the blade into the gap between her arm and side. The other girl screamed. Sadzi buckled as the sleeping potion kicked in. Valek grasped her shoulders, trapping the knife and keeping her upright as he muscled her out the door. He dumped her to the side, but her motionless boots remained visible to those inside.

Valek pulled a bloodstained handkerchief from his pocket. He pretended to wipe blood from his hands when he returned to the others. Mikus's mouth gaped, as shocked as the Storm Thieves.

He waved the cloth at the door dismissively. "She soiled herself. Quite the stink." Valek studied them one by one. The other girl burst into tears under his scrutiny. Yelena's voice sounded in his mind, admonishing him for being mean.

Sliding another knife from his pocket, Valek said, "Tell me the plan for tonight."

Terrified, they started talking at once, rushing to explain the plans.

Back at the station, they processed the thieves. The security officers searched them and gave them coveralls to wear before locking them in the cells.

The scamp scowled at Valek when Endre laid the still-sleeping Sadzi on a bunk. "I knew you were bluffing."

Valek didn't bother to reply. Instead, he checked on the preparations. Annika had arrived with the supplies and a seamstress. The older woman tsked and rubbed the knuckles on her right hand as he explained what he needed.

"I don't know if it'll work," she said.

"That's for me to worry about. Can you do it by supper?"

"Yes." She unrolled the bolt of black fabric on the conference room's table.

Captain Tahnee showed Valek what her staff had found. "They don't look authentic."

"Leave that to me. Annika, did you get the clay?"

"No one had clay, but I brought you quick wood. It's a putty the fishermen use on their boats to plug small leaks. It hardens fast, so it should be good by tonight."

"Wonderful." Valek pried the lid off the bucket. He gave everyone a job and then set to work on his own task.

Around noon, Annika brought chowder for everyone. The spicy scent caused Valek's stomach to cramp with sudden hunger. He hadn't eaten since yesterday. After downing the chowder, he returned to work. The hours sped past.

Endre interrupted Valek at supper time. The soldiers from the other towns had arrived. He gathered everyone in the conference room. Each town had sent five officers, which brought the total number of people available to ambush the Storm Thieves to eighteen—not counting the seamstress, who had finished her part and left. He hoped it would be enough.

Valek explained the plan, picked people to fill certain roles, then set a schedule for small groups to leave for the rendezvous location. Satisfied with the progress, he resumed his assignment, completing the last item around sunset and four hours before the Storm Thieves landed.

His group included Annika and Endre. They were the last to leave the station, leaving only Captain Tahnee to deal with any problems in Gandrel. Valek checked to make sure they

MARIA V. SNYDER

had everything. No one said a word during the trip to the steer farm.

Once they arrived, everyone knew what to do. They prepped and moved into position just as it started to rain.

A thrill of excitement shot through him. The trap was set.

The storm raged, soaking Valek's hair and clothes. The fishing boats banged and screeched against the wooden pilings as they pitched in their docks. Flags flapped in the strong wind, adding to the noise. Waves raced under the planks, sending up salty sprays when they collided with the support beams.

Annika waited at the end of the pier. She watched for the Storm Thieves' ship's light. According to the teens in custody, the ship would appear during the height of the storm. It would tie up to the dock, lower the gangplank and the scamp and his crew would lead five stolen steers onto the ship. Then they'd raise the gangplank and cast off, with no one the wiser until morning.

Valek acknowledged the beauty and simplicity of the Storm Thieves' plan. He looked forward to interrogating their leader. Perhaps Valek would learn a couple new tricks.

Two quick flashes of light pierced the darkness—Annika's signal.

"Get ready," Valek said, and his order was relayed to the others.

The four other teams of two pulled on their disguises. Valek and Endre draped the black cloth the seamstress had sewn around them.

Annika appeared. "They're close." She wore Sadzi's clothes and had styled her hair the same way as the girl. "Where's the rope?"

"Here." Valek handed her the end. The lead was tied around the steer's head. Or rather, the mask of a steer's head that he wore. Not quite an exact replica. He'd done his best to make all five look lifelike, using bones from the butcher shop and the quick wood. Between the darkness and the storm, he hoped no one would spot the deception until it was too late.

"Let's go," Annika said.

Valek and Endre crouched over. Endre grasped Valek's waist and they moved forward. Behind them, the other four teams should be doing the same. The "steers" were each led by a handler who wore one of the captured Storm Thieves' clothes.

Halfway down the pier, Valek spotted the ship. Lanterns blazed from its upper deck. Unlike the other boats rocking on the heavy seas, the Storm Thieves' ship remained steady as if traveling over calm waters. A large commercial vessel, it was under full sail. An impressive sight.

The white fabric of the sails caught a wind that wasn't as strong as the storm's. The magician not only controlled the sea, but the storm, as well. Talented.

Annika slowed, keeping the small "herd" away from the lanterns' bubble of light until the gangplank was lowered. The storm stopped, reducing the noise. The ship approached and four figures jumped onto the pier. Ropes flew over the gap and were secured to the pylons. Voices shouted an all clear and the gangplank eased toward the dock.

"Sadzi, come on! Hurry!" a man called from the top of the gangplank.

Annika kept her pace. When the thud of the plank hitting the pier sounded, she sped up. Two others joined the man. Valek drew his blowpipe. Behind him, Endre pulled his sword.

Stepping into the light, Valek tensed as he encountered thick magic. He scanned the rigging and decks, counting opponents. The magician stood on the bow with her arms stretched to each side.

Laughter reached them. "That has to be the ugliest-looking

　　　　　　　　　　　MARIA V. SNYDER

steer I've ever seen," a man said. "Did you feel sorry for him, Sadzi?"

Annika kept quiet.

"Looks like he's limping, as well," another voice said. "Jibben isn't gonna be pleased."

"They're all walking weird. Did you hobble them, Sadzi?"

"Hey, they're not—"

The jig was up. "Now," Valek yelled, throwing off the fabric and yanking off his mask.

The three men standing at the top of the gangplank stared at him in shock for a few seconds. Long enough for Valek to reach the gangplank. Behind him, he knew the others tossed off their disguises and pulled their swords. He couldn't see it, but by the way the men in front of him blanched, gasped and finally cried an alarm, it must have been quite the sight. Valek grinned. He loved a good surprise.

"Ambush!" one of the Storm Thieves yelled, drawing his sword.

The magician dropped her arms and turned. Valek loaded his blowpipe and aimed at the closest man. Then he shot the other two in rapid succession. He yanked his sword, then rushed them, exchanging a few parries before they wobbled as the sleeping potion took effect.

Yells sounded from the dock. Valek turned. Huge waves of water crashed over the pier, swamping his backup. Annika, Endre and two others had reached the gangplank, but the rest clung to the rope rails as whitecaps slammed into them. Valek had to neutralize the magician and stop the water attack.

Boots pounded on the deck. Four armed Storm Thieves rushed toward him and more poured from the wheelhouse. Valek gestured for Endre, Annika and the two with them to engage the four. He sheathed his sword and raced to the bow.

Two young men dropped from the rigging. Brandishing

daggers, they blocked his path to the magician. Valek tucked the blowpipe into his pocket and drew a knife with a flourish to distract them while he palmed a couple darts. They hesitated for a second, glancing at each other.

"Come on, boys, let's see what you can do," Valek said, sliding his feet into a fighting stance.

The bigger of the two advanced. He held his weapon in his lead hand. Rookie. Valek used a roundhouse kick to knock the weapon from his opponent's grasp, then he shuffled in closer, punched the teen in the solar plexus and pricked him with a dart. The boy fell back on his butt with an *oomph*.

Not waiting for his friend to gain his feet, the second teen charged Valek. The boy's speed made up for his lack of finesse. They exchanged a few jabs and parries and Valek would have liked to test the extent of his opponent's skills, but the sounds of fighting grew louder and, after a quick peek at the ruckus, he saw that Endre and the others were outnumbered.

Valek blocked the next jab with his left hand, grabbed the teen's wrist, stepped back and as he yanked the Storm Thief toward him, Valek kneed him in the groin. The poor boy collapsed to the deck. Not very sporting, but time was critical.

When he neared the bow, another Storm Thief landed in front of him. Valek didn't bother engaging him. He simply bowled the teen over, jabbed a dart into his neck and continued.

The magician faced him. A heavy stickiness engulfed him. The waves pelting the dock disappeared. Good. He guessed she couldn't multitask. Valek waded through the magic, approaching her. Balls of water flew at him, but instead of slamming into him, they veered wide, missing him. She sucked in a breath of surprise. Fear soon followed. The young lady backed up and grabbed the railing.

Valek had a second to wonder what she planned before

MARIA V. SNYDER

the ship lurched violently under his feet. The bubble of calm popped and the storm surged in. Yells and cries of alarm emanated from the fight on deck. He swayed for a moment, teetering off balance, but years of training kicked in and he adjusted to the motion. Smart move, sweetheart.

The magician clung to the wood rail as if her life depended on it. She stared at him with intense blue eyes. When he closed in, her magic disappeared,

She sank to her knees and said, "Please, don't kill me."

In that moment, with her wet hair pressed to her head, she looked twelve years old—someone's beautiful daughter. A vision of Yelena holding a baby girl flashed in his mind. He dismissed the distraction. Valek had no intention of killing her, but what to do with her?

"Stop the storm, and I'll think about it," he said.

"I can't. I only control the water."

"Then restore the calm."

The waves around the boat smoothed and the rain ceased. The ship settled.

"Is someone controlling the storm?" he asked.

She bit her lip and gazed past him. Valek glanced at the battle. All his people had reached the deck, and they had the upper hand. No surprise, considering the ages of their opponents. Experience trumped youth in most cases.

"It's over," he said. "Cooperation is the best way for you to stay alive."

Sitting back on her heels in defeat, she said, "My brother can call the storms, but he's not on board."

"Where is he?"

"On the island."

Valek kept his stern expression, despite the thrill of having guessed right. "You will take us to the island."

Now panic filled her expression. "I…can't."

He waited.

"I… They will kill him."

Not what he expected. "They?"

She swept her arms wide, indicating the boat. "The people who hijacked our ship and forced us to help them."

21

LEIF

A searing pain in his head roused Leif to consciousness. Harsh sunlight waited on the other side of his eyelids, so he kept his eyes closed. He cataloged his woes. The dried-out piece of leather that had been his tongue meant he hadn't drunk any water for a while. The headache meant no food, either. Plus, he suspected a hangover from the sleeping juice. Leif guessed he'd been knocked out for a few days or more. Vague memories rose of being awake for short, blurry snatches to eat stale bread and gulp tepid water.

When the sharp pulses in his temples dulled to a loud throb, Leif opened his eyes. Bright side—not a cell. He lay on a bed in a small, neat room. One window, one night table, no decorations on the white walls and one door currently shut. Dark side—his arms had been pulled up over his head and his wrists were secured. Probably to the headboard, which would match his feet, since his ankles were tied to the footboard. Also a null shield surrounded him, blocking his magic.

A steady hum of unease vibrated through him. Not outright fear. At least, not yet. He still wore his own clothes. The lock picks hidden inside might come in handy. His captors would have to let him up at some point. Right?

As the hours dragged by—each one slower than the previous—Leif worried they'd forgotten him. Or they planned to let him die of thirst. No. If they'd wished him dead, they could have ensured he'd never wake up. This was all part of their scheme to drive the point home that they were in control. Leif kept his thoughts positive. His main objective—stay alive until an opportunity to escape arose or rescued arrived. No doubt Yelena would search for him.

The scrape of metal jolted Leif from a light doze. The knob turned and the door swung inward, admitting a tall man in his late forties. Two bruisers entered behind him. One carried a chair, the other a tray of food. Swords and daggers hung from their belts. The wonderful aroma of beef caused Leif's head to spin. An effective way to torture him would be to withhold food.

The man studied him while Leif assessed his captor. Short black hair combed back with streaks of gray at the temples, and sharp features that would be considered appealing by the ladies. His posture oozed confidence, and, if the jewels in his rings and the monster ruby hanging from his neck didn't tip a person off, then the expensive silk clothes tailored to enhance his muscular build indicated the man had money—lots and lots of money.

Leif waited for the man to speak.

"Aren't you curious about what's going on?" the man asked.

"I am." The words croaked from his dry lips. "But I figured I really wasn't in a position to demand answers."

The man laughed. "Refreshing. You're the first to realize that so soon. The others hollered and blustered, thinking their *status* as magicians had any influence over their situation." He gestured.

Bruiser One placed the chair next to the foot of Leif's bed. Then he pulled a key from his pocket and unlocked the re-

MARIA V. SNYDER

straints around Leif's wrists before stepping quickly back. His meaty paws hovered near his weapons. Everyone in the room tensed, waiting for Leif's reaction.

He sat up and rubbed his arms, working the feeling back into his hands. Weak from days without food or water, and with his ankles still secured, he had no option but to play nice—for now.

The man approached and held out his hand. "Bruns Jewel-rose."

The name sliced through Leif, igniting anger. This was the son of a bitch who had hired an assassin to kill Yelena. He drew in a breath to calm down, reminding himself to play nice and stay alive. He grasped Bruns's hand. "Leif Liana Zaltana."

They pumped once and released—just like a couple of businessmen meeting for the first time. Weird.

"It's a pleasure to finally meet you," Bruns said, sitting in the chair. "Your résumé is quite impressive." He snapped his fingers.

Bruiser Two brought the tray over and placed it on Leif's lap. It contained a bowl of stew, a hunk of bread, cheese, a spoon, napkin and a large glass of water. No knife.

Bruns said, "Go ahead and eat. I'm sure you're starved."

Leif hesitated. "And in exchange?"

"All I ask is that you hear me out. That you don't form an opinion until I'm finished."

Glancing at his bound ankles, Leif said, "What if I've already formed an opinion?"

Bruns inclined his head. "That is an unfortunate necessity. I've learned that a demonstration of my abilities and resources is far more convincing than a discussion. You cannot deny that my network was able to neutralize a powerful magician such as yourself rather easily."

A protest over the word *easily* pushed up his throat, but he swallowed it down. The ambush had been expertly set to appeal to his instincts and bypass Rusalka's abilities. "Did you neutralize my sister?"

"No. My sources say Onora, the Commander's new assassin, did."

He scoffed, "Your sources are wrong."

"Unlikely."

"Why would the Commander do that?"

"That's all part of my explanation." Bruns waited.

Playing nice meant listening to his captor's crazy theories and perhaps pretending to agree with him.

"All right, Bruns. I'll listen to your...pitch." Leif picked up the glass and gulped half the water. Ahhh. Welcome back, tongue.

"The Commander is preparing to invade Sitia. We know this because he has gone to great lengths to secure Curare, stockpile null shields, nullify the Liaison and is harboring Owen Moon, a known rogue magician."

Stockpiling null shields? That was news to Leif. Filling the spoon with chunks of beef and potatoes, Leif shoveled it into his mouth. Not bad. Not the best he'd ever tasted, but up there in the top five.

"The Commander ordered the hit to block the Liaison's magic so she would no longer be an asset to the Sitian Council. Without her magic, the Commander could invite her to be one of his advisers and, with the added appeal of being with her heart mate, it would be a tempting offer. Valek would also be happy. And it's important to the Commander to keep him happy. He's vital to their security. That's also why Onora didn't kill Yelena. That would have sent him on a quest for revenge."

Bruns crossed his legs. "With me so far?"

"One question. Why did you hire The Mosquito to assassinate Yelena?"

"To cause strife in Ixia by sending Valek on that quest for revenge. We hoped he'd assume the second attempt was connected to the first and discover the Commander sent Onora. Plus Yelena has classified information about Sitia. The last thing we wanted was for her to give it to the Commander. We're trying to *protect* Sitia."

Protect Sitia by murdering Yelena? That was very twisted logic. "Who's we?"

"I'm getting to that. Considering the Commander's hatred of magicians, Owen Moon's presence is harder to explain. He must have something rather significant that the Commander can use when he attacks Sitia.

"The Sitian Council has almost all this information, yet they still argue and discuss and get nothing done. Yes, I know they tasked your Councilman to increase production of Theobroma, but that will take years. We don't have years. We have a year at most."

Leif stopped chewing. A year? Even with the grafting technique, they'd never be ready in time.

"Frustrated with the Sitian Council's refusal to accept the facts and act, I contacted a number of friends and colleagues. We formed our Cartel and brainstormed ideas on how to protect Sitia from being invaded. First we listed our assets. Our army doesn't stand a chance—we lack discipline and numbers. But we have magicians and super messengers.

"Except the magicians don't know how to fight or work with an army. Some of them can't be counted on to help because they're selfishly pursuing their own agendas, which is why the Commander can stockpile null shields. It's incomprehensible to me why a magician would create something that can be used against him. It's like giving your sword to your previously unarmed enemy, and then being surprised when he stabs you with it!"

Bruns stopped his tirade. He drew in a deep breath then continued in an even tone, "We decided to stop the randomness and the stupidity. The idea is to gather *all* the magicians into one unit, train them how to fight and use their magic to gain information. Organize them to maximize their efforts during a war and stop them from selling null shields to the enemy. It's the only way we will prevent the Commander from conquering Sitia."

"The Council does use magicians—"

"Only a handful compared to how many there are. And how many like Owen Moon have caused us trouble over the years? Dozens?"

Names sprang to mind, but Leif resisted the temptation to list them. Instead he considered Bruns's idea. He gestured to the bruisers. "And this is your way of gathering all the magicians? Ambush and imprison them until they hear your speech? Then what? Join or die?"

Bruns smiled, revealing a row of straight white teeth, but no humor shone in his gray eyes. "Those who have been recruited by the members of the Cartel had no need for a demonstration of our resources. They recognized the danger and agreed to train."

"And the ones that don't agree?"

"They're persuaded. I can be very convincing."

Leif imagined Bruns's persuasion techniques involved threats, torture and isolation. Good thing he'd finished the food, or he would have lost his appetite. "How about the four who were assassinated? Are they the ones you couldn't sway?"

"No. They were the troublemakers. No amount of logic or appealing to their patriotic sense of duty would ever entice them away from being selfish, greedy problems. We didn't bother to waste our time with them."

MARIA V. SNYDER

Harsh. "And you sent The Mosquito to Lapeer to assassinate Ben Moon and Loris and Cilly Cloud Mist."

"Yes. They were easy–to-solve problems." Bruns's tone remained reasonable, as if they discussed business.

That brought the total number of murdered magicians to seven—playing nice might be harder than Leif had thought. He switched to a safer topic. "Why didn't you try logic and reason on me?"

"I'm doing that right now."

"No. I meant why the ambush, the…demonstration?" At least Bruns hadn't called it a kidnapping. He detested that word.

"Ah. I see. In your case and in a few others, we determined that your loyalty to the Council would make it much harder to convince you. That it would take us some time to demonstrate our sincerity in protecting Sitia."

"A few others? Like Hale?"

"Yes. And those who work closely with the Council and Master Magicians on various operations."

"Is Hale…?" Leif couldn't say the word. He'd grown fond of the stiff—quite the surprise.

"He's fine. Another reason for the extra measures is so you don't warn the Council until we're ready."

"But they already know about the Cartel and the missing and dead magicians."

"Yes, but they don't know *who* is involved or where our base of operations is located."

So The Mosquito hadn't informed his boss about revealing Bruns's name to Yelena when he failed to assassinate her in Fulgor's jail. That little detail might just save Leif's life. "If they do find out who's involved, they'll know to search Jewelrose lands."

"I believe you're fishing for information. And I'm insulted that you'd think I'd be fooled that easily."

"Can't blame a guy for trying."

"If you wanted a tour of the compound, all you had to do was ask." Bruns stood and smoothed his tunic. "First, some safety information. These two gentlemen are armed with blowpipes and darts filled with Curare. Their aim is remarkable, even at a distance. They will be accompanying us. Understand?"

"That they'll shoot me with Curare if I try to escape? Yes, that's quite clear."

Mister Business frowned at him as if he'd used crass language. But he gestured to Bruiser One. The broad-shouldered man unlocked Leif's ankles. Leif noted which pocket the key disappeared into. Valek's lessons on how to pick a pocket just might come in handy. Leif rubbed feeling back into his feet. His boots had been placed beside the bed. He wondered what had happened to his cloak and machete as he tied the laces.

When Leif stood, a brief spell of weakness flushed through him. He'd need more than one meal to return to full strength. Bruiser Two opened the door and, with Bruns in the lead, followed by Leif, the four of them entered a hallway. The null shield remained around him. Too bad. He'd hoped it was attached to the room.

The hallway's white walls held no decorations, just a series of closed doors on both sides. Leif counted a total of forty.

"This is the barracks for the magicians," Bruns said.

Did he expect to fill the entire building? That would be quite an accomplishment. At the end of the corridor, they descended two flights of stairs and walked into the sunlight. Leif squinted until his eyes adjusted. The warm air smelled of wood smoke and leather. A green fuzz lined the tree branches, but he'd have to examine the buds closer to see where in Sitia he might be. Bigger buds would mean he was farther south. Of course, that only narrowed down his north/south location. East/west would be harder to discern without more geographical information.

Bruns strode around the compound, pointing to the various buildings—stables, armory, infirmary, dining hall—with pride. Leif memorized the layout. It resembled a military base and even had a three-story-high marble wall surrounding it. Leif wouldn't be surprised if Bruns had commandeered the Jewelrose garrison.

Soldiers marched in unison, wearing olive-colored fatigues. Others practiced a variety of fighting techniques in a large training area.

Bruns showed him the armory. "We've been developing new weapons." He picked up an oversize bow. "We've discovered the bigger the bow, the farther an arrow will fly, giving us an advantage." Placing it back on the table, he drew Leif over to a pile of leather. "This is going to be made into protective clothing. It resists punctures and will stop a dart of Curare from reaching a soldier's skin!"

When they left the armory, a young soldier ran up to Bruns and handed him a red flag. "They're ready for you, sir."

"Wonderful."

Bruns led him outside the compound. The bruiser brothers closed in on Leif, staying a mere foot away. Unfortunately, the null shield remained. Leif wondered if it had been woven into his clothing. Only one way to find out, but he'd wait until he was alone to strip.

Now the air held the faint scent of the sea. The Jewelrose clan did have a thumb-shaped bit of land that extended into the Jade Sea. And, if he remembered correctly, the area was rather isolated. In fact, just north of it was the Lion's Claw Peninsula, where the Bloodrose cult had lived for years in relative obscurity, until Opal discovered their illegal activities and stopped them.

Reaching a pasture with a wooden fence, Bruns halted. A forest lined the north and west sides. Dozens of soldiers crouched on the southern side.

"Watch this," Bruns said. He leaned against the fence and waved the flag. Gesturing to the soldiers now climbing through the wooden rails, he said, "That's one of our platoons. And in the woods is a mock Ixian army about the same size."

When the platoon reached the halfway mark, arrows sailed from the forest. Instead of slamming into the soldiers, they stopped in midair, as if hitting an invisible barrier, and dropped to the ground. The platoon increased their pace. Two people called enemy positions. Branches shook, dislodging archers.

Within minutes the platoon had penetrated the forest and captured the Ixian soldiers.

Bruns beamed. "See how effective we can be when we have magicians fighting alongside soldiers?"

Leif tried hard not to get swept up in Bruns's enthusiasm. But damn. That was one hell of an impressive demonstration.

MARIA V. SNYDER

22

YELENA

"How many are in hiding?" I asked Fisk. With all the bad news, it was nice to hear something good.

Fisk shot to his feet as if he needed to move. He paced behind his couch. "Five of them. Once the word spread that magicians were disappearing and dying, they came to me to help hide them."

"With that cat slinking around your headquarters, are you sure they're still safe?" Janco leaned forward in his chair.

"Yes. But the requests have stopped, and I fear he's responsible."

I mulled over the information. "So we still have seven missing and four dead magicians."

"Eight, if we count Leif," Ari said.

My heart squeezed. Leif wouldn't become a statistic. I'd make sure of that.

"And they're just the ones we know about," Fisk said. "It's not like they all work for the Council or the Master Magicians. They're spread over the eleven clans of Sitia."

"Who would know if there are more missing?" Ari asked.

"Does it matter how many?" Janco asked. "I'd think the more important question is *where* are they?"

"Not if they've joined forces with the Cartel." Ari gestured. "We wouldn't get a warm welcome if we showed up to rescue them and they have no intention of leaving, and oh, by the way, they outnumber us, so now *we're* captured."

I held up my hands, stopping Janco's retort. "I think we're getting ahead of ourselves. Fisk, do you know how long the Cartel's been recruiting?"

"I heard rumors starting soon after you left for Fulgor eight weeks ago."

Almost a full season.

"But they could have been at it for much longer," Ari said. "We should assume that once the rumors started, they no longer cared if word spread."

Good point. Unfortunately. "Any ideas where they're... gathering?"

Fisk strode over to his desk. He leafed through a stack of papers, pulled one out and returned. "Hilly's been keeping an eye on the people who have been associating with the man who was so interested in your whereabouts, Yelena." He sat on the couch and handed me the paper. "I've been identifying them. This one..." He tapped the blank space next to a description of the man with the large ruby pendant. "I just received confirmation on his name. He's—"

"Bruns Jewelrose?" I guessed.

"Yes. Friend of yours?"

"Hardly. He hired The Mosquito to assassinate me."

"Odd." Fisk's brow crinkled.

Janco laughed. "That's not odd. That's just another typical day for our girl here."

Fisk ignored him, but I scowled at him.

Unaffected, Janco said, "You know I'm right."

Fisk continued, "I mean, why kill you and risk getting

MARIA V. SNYDER

Valek involved? That would be dangerous. Plus, he already neutralized your magic."

Ari and Janco glanced at me. Not many people knew that the first attack hadn't been The Mosquito, but Onora following the Commander's orders to test Valek. Perhaps Bruns had learned this and hoped my death would send Valek after Onora or the Commander.

"Bruns knows that I will rescue Leif, despite not having magic," I said. "And that I have powerful friends to help me." I stood. Time to answer at least one question. "Fisk, do you have a window that faces in the same direction as the stable?"

He grinned. "You want to take a look at that cat hanging around?"

"Yes. Except I suspect he's not a cat."

Fisk led me to the loft above his office. Navy blue curtains covered two long, narrow windows. He pointed. "The glass is tinted, so no one can see you."

"Handy."

"Opal's father made them for me. They're getting popular with people who want extra privacy."

I eased the curtain aside carefully, just in case the movement drew attention. Late-morning sunlight warmed the cobblestones below. The street appeared to be empty. Half a block south, there was an entrance to an alley. Perhaps the cat hid inside the alley's shadows.

"He's good," Fisk said, standing behind me. "Look at the second-floor windows on the third building to the left across the street."

I followed his directions. Sure enough, a figure in dark clothes stood behind the panes of glass.

"Is that your Mosquito?"

"I can't see his face." I considered. Even if he wasn't the assassin, the man still worked for the Cartel and could provide information about Leif's location. "We need to set a trap."

We returned to the living area and I explained my plan to lure the cat from his lair.

"Too dangerous," Ari said. "There's only three of us."

"I can provide as many people as you need. No charge," Fisk offered.

"We can't put a bunch of kids in danger," Janco said.

Fisk huffed in annoyance, but before he could educate Janco about the skills of his people, I said, "That would be wonderful." I calculated how many helpers I'd need. "Six should be plenty. How soon can they be in position?"

"Give me an hour. In the meantime, make yourselves at home." Fisk left.

"I still don't like it," Ari said as he swung up into Whiskey's saddle.

Janco mounted The Madam. "This is going to be fun."

"You said that about the Bejin ambush, and look how that turned out." Ari gathered the reins.

"There's just no way to stifle a sneeze once it reaches a critical level. Besides, no one was hurt."

"No one was arrested, either."

Janco waved a hand. "Details, details."

I helped Hilly into Kiki's saddle. She wore my cloak with the hood pulled down low over her forehead. "Listen to Ari and ignore Janco."

"Hey."

She smiled. "Will do."

The three of them left the stable, heading toward the Magician's Keep. I remained in a dark shadow with a view of the street. Would the cat follow them? It depended on his powers of observation.

MARIA V. SNYDER

"He didn't take the bait," Fisk said, standing next to me.

"Give it a few more minutes. He might have slipped out the back entrance."

We waited. After five minutes, there was still no movement and no signal from Tweet that he'd left the building. It seemed the cat realized Hilly hid under my cloak, even though we were of a similar size and build.

"Time for Plan B," I said. "Shall we?"

Fisk grinned. "We shall."

We peeked from the stable, glancing left and right as if searching for witnesses. Then we strode into the street, going in the opposite direction as Ari, Janco and Hilly. I wore a Helper's Guild uniform and had arranged my hair into a bun similar to Hilly's. We followed a predetermined route that appeared to be random, as if we were checking for a tail, but it allowed Fisk's helpers to relay information to us. The guild members knew every shortcut and alley in the Citadel and could reach certain intersections faster than us.

"Ah," Fisk said, catching sight of one of his helpers. "Smart kitty is following us."

"How soon will everyone be in position?"

"Let's take the scenic route and give them time to prepare."

As we continued walking through the streets, Fisk played tour guide, filling me in on the various buildings and businesses. "A few businessmen have copied me and converted the abandoned factories into living spaces. It has improved the living conditions in the Citadel's two resident quarters, and having four families live in one house is a thing of the past."

"That's wonderful news."

"It is, but there's still criminals and those who prey on the weak. If I can only expel them, then everyone can live in peace."

"It's a lovely goal, Fisk, but I've learned there will always be criminals. You can arrest them and prevent certain crimes, but they'll never be completely gone. They're even in Ixia, despite the Commander's soldiers patrolling the streets and watching the citizens. It's human nature."

"I guess you're right, but I'm still going to try."

I touched his arm. "Just please don't get yourself killed."

He placed his hand over mine and squeezed. "That's not in the plan."

"So that means you'll ask for help when things get too hot?"

His shoulders stiffened with a familiar stubbornness, and he dropped his hand. "Well…"

"Fisk, it's not a sign of weakness to ask for help. We're friends, and that is what friends do. Help each other."

"But then I should pay you like you pay me."

I shook my head. "Not how it works."

"Why not?"

"You need the money to run your business and give your helpers food, clothing and shelter, which is very important. Me, Ari, Janco, Valek and Leif don't need the money. We are paid and have all the necessities in life."

"I still feel like I'm taking advantage of you."

I lightly smacked the back of his thick skull. "Then donate some money to Child Services."

Fisk made a rude noise.

"They're inefficient because they don't have enough staff or resources."

"I'll think about it."

Progress! I let the subject drop. We walked in silence for a while. A few other people strode along the streets Fisk had chosen. Some nodded to him in greeting; others smiled. I spotted one of his helpers lurking in an alley, but she faded from sight once Fisk met her gaze.

"They're ready," he said.

My heart fluttered as my hand rested on my abdomen for a moment. I'd been the bait before. However, this time, I had a baby to keep safe. If Valek ever found out… No. Not going there. I concentrated on the plan.

Fisk took a few turns, then led me to an alley's entrance. He made a show of checking for a tail before we dashed inside. When the alley's rank fragrance turned my stomach, I thought of Janco whining about the stench. The alley dead-ended, but a few doors surrounded us. Fisk produced a key and stepped toward the one on the right.

"Hold it right there," a familiar voice ordered.

I spun. The Mosquito stood about twenty feet away. He aimed a crossbow at us. I wasn't expecting that particular weapon, but we could adapt.

"Hello, Kynan, or do you prefer to be called The Mosquito?" I asked.

"You don't really think Kynan is my name, do you?" He didn't wait for an answer. "Perhaps you did, since you believe I'm not very bright and would follow your Ixian friends."

"It was a good decoy," I said in my defense.

He huffed with amusement. "Maybe at night or if I was half-blind. Her posture on Kiki didn't match yours."

I'd say his powers of observation ranked pretty high. "You need to get a life if you've been watching me that long."

"I told you before. I don't give up, and I always finish a job before moving on."

I glanced at Fisk. He held his hands to the side.

"The boy can go," The Mosquito said, gesturing with his weapon.

Fisk hesitated.

A twang snapped, sending the bolt right between us. I jerked in surprise as the tip struck the building behind us. By the time we returned our attention to The Mosquito, he had loaded another bolt.

"You're not fast enough, boy. Now go on. Fetch help for Yelena."

"Go ahead, Fisk," I said.

Fisk frowned, but he strode past The Mosquito, who kept his weapon aimed at Fisk until he disappeared from view. Then he swung it back to me.

"That's new." I gestured to the crossbow. "What happened to your ice pick?" I asked.

"I learn from my mistakes. I'm not getting close to you until I'm sure you don't have any of those darts hidden in your clothes."

"Then it's in my best interest to keep you at a distance."

He laughed. "Yes, that would be right. But you're in luck. The game has changed."

"Funny, I'm not feeling very lucky." Actually, I was quite confident—one gesture from me and The Mosquito would be squashed.

"Cute. My client has changed his mind about you. Instead of killing you, he wants to talk to you."

"So he can kill me later?"

"All I know is you get a free pass this time. I don't have orders for next time."

I considered his offer. "Does your client have my brother?"

"Yes."

"Will he exchange him for me?"

"No. And if you're thinking you can use your...truth serum on me to get the location of your brother, I've no idea where my client is keeping him. My knowledge is limited just for that very reason." He shot me a sour look.

"I'm guessing Bruns...or rather your *client* isn't happy you blabbed." I couldn't resist needling him.

The Mosquito tightened his grip on the crossbow. "Is that your answer?"

"Where does Bruns wish to meet?"

"I don't know. I'm to inform him of your response, and then he'll tell me the location."

Smart. This way I couldn't detain him until after I'd learned the meeting place. Unless he lied about the extent of his knowledge.

"And I know all about your trap." The Mosquito glanced up at the windows on the second story. "Should I wave to the Ixians?"

Busted.

"You really do think I'm an idiot."

"Not anymore," I said.

He smiled. "Your answer?"

"Tell Bruns I'll meet with him."

"Excellent." The Mosquito backed away. He paused at the entrance, checked for an ambush and disappeared.

I replayed the encounter in my mind, but really couldn't determine a way that it could have gone any differently.

Fisk arrived with a handful of his helpers. "You let him go?"

"I didn't have much of a choice." I explained what had happened.

"I've assigned a team to keep an eye on him," Fisk said. "Maybe he'll lead us to his boss and where they're holding Leif."

"He's intelligent, so I doubt he'd be that careless. But it doesn't hurt to try."

The door into the alley swung open and Ari and Janco arrived. The red splotches on Ari's normally pale cheeks warned me. I braced for his lecture on the dangers of meeting with Bruns. He didn't disappoint, listing a number of horrific and creative outcomes. Janco had rubbed off on him.

"…not listening, are you?" Ari asked.

"I got the point. You're not happy and neither am I, but I see no other way."

"What do we do while we wait?" Janco asked.

What indeed? "We need to update Irys and…" My stomach soured. "And Mara. She needs to know what's going on."

"Can we trust the guards at the Keep not to turn us in to the Citadel's security forces?" Janco asked.

For the first time since I'd come to Sitia, I truly didn't know. "Fisk, can one of your helpers deliver a message to the Second Magician?"

"Yes. In the meantime, you're welcome to stay with me. I've guest rooms."

"Fancy," Janco said.

Pride momentarily eclipsed my anxiety for Leif. Fisk had turned into such a fine young man.

Irys and Mara arrived after supper. Both wore worried expressions. Mara fisted the fabric of her skirt. We settled in Fisk's living area. He had left earlier and hadn't returned. I sat next to Mara on the couch and held her cold hand in mine. Janco leaned against the door and Ari occupied the other chair across from Irys.

"No," Mara said when I'd finished detailing my conversation with The Mosquito. "You can't sacrifice yourself for Leif." She smoothed the wrinkles over her lap.

"It's not an exchange.," I assured her. "He just wants to talk. Plus we can follow him after—see if he'll lead us to Leif."

"And if he doesn't? What if something goes wrong?" Ari asked.

"Then I'll have a *talk* with him," Irys said. Her steely gaze promised results, and the magic detector flashed in response. "Let me know when the meeting is scheduled."

MARIA V. SNYDER

★ ★ ★

While we waited for a message from The Mosquito, my thoughts turned to Valek. It'd been sixteen days since we'd parted. I wondered if he waited at our rendezvous location or if he still hunted the Storm Thieves. Should I send a messenger? I asked Ari and Janco.

"If you do, he won't worry why we're not there, but if he hears about Leif, he'll come here," Ari said.

Not good. He needed to stay in Ixia. "What if I say we've just been delayed?"

"He'll come regardless." Janco crinkled his forehead in confusion. "You act like that's a bad thing. He can flatten that Mosquito."

"The Commander has forbidden him to leave Ixia," I said.

"That didn't stop Valek last month," Janco said. "He disobeyed a direct order from the Commander when he traveled to Lapeer to help you. Valek's never done that before. His loyalties have changed, so unless you're at the rendezvous location soon, expect to see him."

I played with the butterfly pendant Valek had carved for me. If Janco had noticed that Valek's priorities had switched, then it must be obvious to the Commander. No wonder he'd come down so hard on Valek.

"Then we'll have to conclude our business with Bruns as soon as possible," I said.

"No problem. We'll rescue Leif, bring down the Cartel and be home in time for our afternoon naps," Janco snarked.

I stood and slapped him on the back. "That's the spirit!" However, my insides churned with dread. This Cartel might be beyond our ability to stop, and convincing the Sitian Council would require more proof than we currently had. Drawing in a deep breath, I cleared all the things I couldn't control from my mind and focused on the most important issue: rescuing Leif.

Fisk drew on his network of information gatherers to collect any bit of news regarding the Cartel's location. They kept an eye on the businessmen who were suspected of having ties to the Cartel. Irys gave permission to Lindee, Fisk's accountant, to access the Citadel's records room. According to Fisk, she had a sharp mind and was a genius with numbers. Perhaps she'd find a bill of sale for a building that could be traced back to the Cartel.

I organized the intel, searching for clues and weak links, and tried to piece together their plans. Ari and Janco frequented the taverns in the government quarter, listening to the gossip.

The Mosquito's messenger arrived four long days after the encounter in the alley. The young boy waited outside for a reply. The letter said:

The meeting is now. Follow the boy. If you don't arrive in thirty minutes, my boss will be gone.

"No way," Ari said, reading over my shoulder. "We won't be able to have backup on site."

"I think that's the point," Janco said. "It's a trap."

"You can follow me to the meeting place, then send one of Fisk's helpers to fetch Irys. I'll delay as long as possible."

"No." Ari shook his head. "It's—"

"Our only chance to find Leif." I gestured to the papers spread on one of the kitchen tables. "There's nothing here." I stood and wrapped my cloak around my shoulders.

Ari and Janco scrambled to grab theirs, but Fisk stopped them.

"You're too noticeable. Let my people do the honors, and

they'll relay Yelena's position to you. You'll only be a minute behind her. I promise."

Ari straightened to his full height and peered down at me and Fisk. "First sign of trouble and we're coming in. Understand?"

"Yes, sir." I hurried outside and found the messenger. "Where are we going?"

The boy shrugged. "All I know is to go east." He turned right and headed east.

After a few blocks, another boy waited. His instructions had been to lead me south until we reached a third boy. Then a fourth, fifth, sixth and seventh. I had kept track of my whereabouts despite the serpentine route. But once we'd traveled into the southwestern resident quarter of the Citadel, I lost my exact location in the unfamiliar labyrinth of streets. We reached a dilapidated section. Wooden boards covered the windows and doors of the buildings. Broken glass and trash coated the walkways. The air smelled rancid.

The eighth boy led me to a broken-down shack. "Inside," he said.

I hesitated. "Are you sure?"

"Yes." He pulled open the warped door, revealing darkness. "After you."

Bruns hadn't said to come unarmed. I yanked my switchblade from its holder and triggered the blade.

The boy smirked. "Good luck with that."

Bracing for...well, anything, I entered. The floor creaked under my boots. After two steps the door clicked shut, and I stopped, unable to see in the utter blackness. He brushed past me and then swept aside a curtain. We stepped into a room filled with sunlight that streamed in from two skylights high above. I blinked at the expensive furnishings, rugs and solid walls. If I didn't know any better, I'd think I was in the living room of one of the Sitian Councilors and not in the poorest section of the Citadel. The shack must be an illusion to keep the neighbors away.

The boy indicated the couch. "Please have a seat. Can I get you something to drink?"

"Uh, no thanks."

"Mister Jewelrose will be here shortly." The boy disappeared through an alcove on the left.

I peered through the single small window facing a narrow street. A row of houses slumped against one another. A few people sat on porches or pulled wagons over the cobblestones. No familiar faces. I hoped Fisk's people hadn't lost me.

"My estate outside Kohinoor has a much better view," a male voice said behind me.

I turned. A tall, well-dressed man with graying black hair and gray eyes strode toward me. He held out his hand. "Bruns Jewelrose."

Without thinking, I shook it. "Yelena Liana Zaltana."

"Pleasure to meet you."

"Not from what I've heard."

He smiled. "That was just business, Yelena. Nothing personal."

I gaped at him. How could he believe that? I recovered from my shock. "I disagree. You hired an assassin to kill me. That's *very* personal."

"You were an obstacle to be eliminated, but now the situation has changed."

"Yay for me." Sarcasm sharpened my tone.

"Now, now. No need for that. Have a seat and we can discuss my proposal."

I remained standing. "Not until you tell me what happened to Leif. Is he okay? Where is he?"

"You're jumping ahead. Sit down and—"

MARIA V. SNYDER

"Not until I know Leif is alive and well."

Bruns tsked over my stubborn refusal to play nice. "All right." He settled on a leather couch and crossed his legs. "Come on in," he called.

A door opened, and Leif strode into the room. An intense relief washed through me, and I swayed. He rushed to hug me, keeping me upright. I clung to him. Was he real?

"Took you long enough," he said. "Good thing the food is delicious."

Yup. It was him. "Are you okay?"

"I'm fine."

"Good. I'm going to get you out of here." Somehow. I hoped.

"Thanks, but I don't need to be rescued."

I pulled away. "What?"

"I've joined the Cartel."

23

VALEK

"Are you talking about pirates?" Valek asked the young magician.

She knelt on the bow of the ship, soaking wet. "I guess. They pretended to be in distress, and we pulled alongside their ship to help. Except they boarded our ship. They had swords and they killed Nell and our first mate." She closed her eyes for a moment as if enduring a wave of pain. "And then tossed their bodies overboard."

"Did they know about your and your brother's magic?"

"I...don't think so. No one knew except Nell. She taught us how to control it, and then we helped her avoid the storms. Until...they came."

Someone must have known about the siblings. The pirates had targeted their ship for a reason.

The young magician drew in a deep breath. "We tried to use the storms and water to escape, but the...pirates caught and separated us. If one of us doesn't obey, then they will kill the other."

Valek doubted they would have carried out the threat. The siblings were too valuable to the pirates. But the girl was sixteen at most and didn't have the experience to recognize a bluff. Or the confidence to use her magic effectively.

"That's why you can't go to the island. As soon as Jibben sees you, he'll kill Zethan."

"Then we'll make sure he doesn't see me."

Endre arrived. Blood splattered his face and stained his tunic. "All are secured, boss."

"Any causalities?"

"Nah. Minor cuts and bruises. Most are kids, but there are a few adults in the mix." Endre glanced at the girl. "What about this one?"

"She's been spinning quite a tale." Valek told him about the pirates. "What do you think?"

"It explains quite a bit. And we can check the island."

"All right. Find crew who can sail this ship and who are willing to help us for a reduced sentence. Secure the others below. Have Annika find those steer disguises. We're going to need them."

"Yes, sir." Endre dashed away.

Valek studied the girl. Something about her blue eyes and sharp features seemed familiar. "What's your name?"

"Zohav."

"Are you willing to help us?"

"Do I have a choice?"

"It's in your best interests. If your story is true, and you were forced to steal, then you won't be arrested for theft."

Annika arrived with a mass of sopping-wet cloth. "They were all swept into the ocean when the waves attacked us." She frowned at Zohav. "Mikus is fishing the masks out now."

"Wring as much water out as you can and hang them to dry."

"Is there going to be another performance of Valek the steer?" Annika asked with a smile.

Zohav sucked in a sharp breath and scrambled away from

him. She released her control of the waves and the ship bucked on the suddenly rough seas. When her back hit the bow, she huddled in a tight ball.

"What did I say?" Annika grabbed the railing to keep from falling.

He considered. "My name."

"You are the most feared man in Ixia," Annika agreed.

"It can be tiresome."

"Then you should stop eating babies for breakfast."

He laughed. "But they're so delicious."

Annika swatted him on the arm. "Behave."

Valek returned to the problem at hand. The seas remained choppy, but the rain and wind had stopped when the storm moved inland. "Tell the others to prepare to reprise their roles as steers once we reach the island."

Annika nodded and strode away.

Valek approached Zohav and she cried out in terror. He crouched down to her level. "Your magic failed to work on me. Who did you think I was?"

"I thought…you were protected with…with one of those… shields," she stuttered. "You…you're going to kill us." It wasn't a question. "That's what Jibben threatened to do if we ever escaped—report us to *you*." Zohav hugged her knees to her chest. "I'm not going to help you murder my brother."

"Zohav, I'm not going to kill you or your brother."

"You're lying."

"Look at me," he ordered.

With obvious effort, she met his gaze.

"I promise that if your story is true, then I will ensure that you and Zethan are escorted to Sitia." Valek knew that would make Yelena happy, plus it was the right thing to do.

She shook her head. "I don't believe you. You've murdered thousands and are pure evil."

MARIA V. SNYDER

Thousands, eh? His reputation had expanded another order of magnitude.

"You're not reaching my brother." Huge waves crashed over the rails, as if to prove Zohav's point.

She planned to sink the ship. No doubt she loved her brother. Valek pulled a dart from his belt and pricked her arm.

Fury replaced her fear. "Poison! I knew you were going to kill us."

"Sleeping potion. Good night, Zohav." Valek waited until she slumped over, then gathered her in his arms.

He carried her to the main deck. Endre had assembled a crew willing to help sail the ship. In fact, they appeared eager to free their friends.

Valek handed Zohav to Endre. "Find a safe place for her to sleep off the potion while I brief the others."

"Yes, sir."

Valek explained his plan to the ship's crew. It followed the same idea as when they'd ambushed the ship. He and the soldiers would be disguised as the steers. Annika and the other handlers would resume their roles.

"We'll extinguish all but one lantern so it's too dark to see. Once we reach land, my soldiers will attack and neutralize the pirates. The crew will climb into the rigging and keep out of the way," Valek said.

"There are more of them than you," one boy called.

"How many more?" he asked.

"At least thirty."

A little less than double. "I don't expect that to be a problem. Make good use of your darts," he instructed his soldiers.

"What about Jibben?" another boy asked. "He's huge and deadly with his sword. I saw him cut one of his own men in half."

Nice guy. "Leave Jibben to me."

"Please kill him," a teen girl said.

"You think he deserves to die?" Valek asked.

"Yes. He locked my older sister in his room. She escaped twice. The first time they caught her hiding in the woods, and the second time she ran into the ocean and drowned herself."

A heaviness pulled on his heart. He could well imagine what the poor girl had endured. "I'm sorry."

"Why? It's not your fault."

"Ah, but it is. I'm in charge of keeping Ixia safe for all its citizens."

"That's impossible. My ma says there will always be sharks in the water. Nothing you can do about it except be careful where you swim."

"Your ma sounds like a smart lady."

"Yeah, she is. I miss her."

"Then we should cast off and take care of these sharks so you can go home."

The girl saluted him with a bony hand. "Aye, aye, Captain."

The ship rocked back and forth as it crested one wave after another. Some of the soldiers turned green, and a few rushed to vomit over the rail. They raced the sunrise to the island. If the sun rose before they landed, they'd lose the element of surprise. When the boys in the mast signaled that they neared the dock, Valek and the others donned their disguises.

Thuds vibrated through the ship as it bumped against the wooden pylons. The young teens hopped off and tied the ropes.

A gruff voice smashed through the clatter. "Why's the ship moving? Where's that bitch Zohav?"

"She got sick, sir," one of the boys said. "She's down below."

Good thinking. Valek approved.

"What took you so long?"

The same boy said, "One of them steers freaked, sir. Devil to get him on board."

Another smooth reply. The boy had recruitment potential.

"Hurry up with that gangplank," Gruff ordered.

The crew scrambled to comply. The boy paused near Valek. "That's Jibben." Then he hurried away.

Happy that he wouldn't have to chase Jibben down, Valek wrapped his hand around the hilt of his sword and thought of that girl's sister. The gangplank eased toward the dock, revealing a number of men and women. Valek had seconds to assess the enemy before they realized they faced armed soldiers and not a herd of beef. He counted six pirates on the dock and another four on land. The others must be nearby. Perhaps in the woods. They'd want to hide the buildings from the ships that passed by, but wouldn't want to be too far from the dock.

A big brute stood with his thick arms crossed over his chest. Two long braids flowed over his shoulders and a sharp curved blade hung from his leather belt—a cross between a scimitar and a cutlass. The brute had to be the infamous Jibben.

"What in hell? Who picked these scrawny steer?" Jibben asked.

Next to Jibben, a tall man with colorful tattoos along his arms peered at them. "They look…odd, Jib." He pointed. "That one's wearing boots."

And that was his cue. Valek yelled and tossed off the still-damp material. He ripped the mask from his face before drawing his sword. The soldiers followed his lead. They rushed onto the dock in a wedge formation.

The pirates cried a warning, called for backup and drew their weapons in time to meet the rush. While surprised, they didn't panic like the crew of the ship. His men bypassed Jibben, who squinted at the melee, confused, until Valek approached him. He smiled, revealing sharp teeth. Jibben appeared quite calm. So much for Valek being the most feared man in Ixia.

"Ah, the Commander's attack dog. I heard you were in town."

Valek wondered where he'd gotten the intel. "Then why did you send your crew to steal the steers?"

The man kept his smile, but tightened his grip on his strange sword in response.

"Was it greed or stupidity?" Valek asked. "Probably both. You really don't need those steers, but you just *had* to finish your shopping list." He tsked. "Greed and stupidity, the downfall of so many."

"Shut up." Jibben swung his sword, aiming for Valek's neck.

Valek ducked and spun, hooking his heel behind Jibben's left boot. But the man's stance was as solid as a tree trunk. Jibben swiped down at Valek's head. Valek rolled to the right and regained his feet. Okay, time for Plan B.

Jibben pressed his advantage, keeping his longer blade in motion like a pendulum on a clock. Valek backed away until he neared the edge of the dock. Timing it just right, Valek stepped forward and parried Jibben's swinging weapon with his broadsword. The man's curved blade slid right along Valek's, and its tip stabbed right into his abdomen.

Valek gasped as pain ringed his waist.

"Your fancy moves won't save you here." Jibben twisted his wrist.

Before Jibben could disembowel him, Valek jabbed his sword into Jibben's thigh. The man growled, shuffling back.

"At least I know enough to disarm my opponent first, then claim victory." Valek rubbed the fingers of his free hand along the cut on his stomach. Despite the searing burn, the injury wasn't deep. Relief energized him.

Now that Valek had an idea of what that curved blade

could do, he changed the line of his attack from head-on to an angled approach. Jibben was strong like Ari, but also surprisingly quick. Not as quick as Janco, but only a few could make that claim.

This time, when Valek parried Jibben's sword, he deflected the blade down. The tip of the curved sword missed him and Valek was able to cut into Jibben's arm. When he blocked Jibben's blade, knocking it high, Valek nicked the man's thick leg. Each near miss increased Jibben's frustration, causing him to make small but critical mistakes. Blood soon soaked the brute's sleeves and pants. The man swayed.

Valek tried his takedown again, spinning and hooking his heel. Jibben landed with an *oomph* and Valek pricked him with a dart filled with sleeping potion. When the brute relaxed, Valek stood and surveyed the scene.

Most of the soldiers held their own, but a few struggled with their opponents. Valek helped those in need as they advanced inland. The sun rose and the trees cast long shadows. He engaged in a couple fights that ended in a few moves. Jibben should have trained his crew better. Weaving in and out of the other matches, Valek pricked the pirates with darts.

The last pirate fell not long after the sun's arrival. Endre searched the buildings, while Mikus compiled a list of the stolen goods they found. Two other soldiers interviewed the young teens, who had been smart enough to keep away from the fighting.

Annika pointed to Valek's shirt. "You're bleeding."

"It's nothing."

She pulled a first-aid kit from her pack. "Sit."

He recognized that tone. It meant business. He sat on the steps leading up to the door of one of the island's cottages. All the structures but one had been built atop tall pylons, probably in case the island was swamped with water. It would take a fierce storm for the tide to reach the living areas of the buildings.

Annika inspected his wound and decided it needed to be sealed. She pulled his shirt off before he could stop her. If she noticed his still-healing heart-shaped scar, she didn't say a word. Instead, she concentrated on her task by cleaning the cut and applying Rand's glue.

To distract himself from the pain, he studied the structures the pirates had built. Arranged in a circle around a giant fire pit, the one-story cottages appeared to be for housing and storage. One oversize building had a ramp leading up to the first floor—probably for the livestock. All the surfaces had been painted with gray, green and brown paint in a camouflage pattern that blended in with the surroundings. The color combination would probably work during all seasons. Further proof that Jibben was no fool.

The island's trees had been cleared farther out to make room for the crops. Small green shoots poked through the newly plowed dirt.

Valek spotted Endre and waved him over for a report.

"We defeated all the pirates, sir," he said. "The kids have corroborated Zohav's story. There's another ship docked on the back side of the island. It's the *Sea Serpent*."

Ah, the other one that had been lost at sea. "Secure the criminals in the *Starfish*'s hold. And get the names of all the survivors. We'll match them to the manifest and ensure none of the pirates are pretending to be a victim. And find Zethan— he's Zohav's brother and should be among the teens."

"Yes, sir. We also found a few older teens locked in a jail, but we couldn't find a key and the lock is…complex."

"Once Annika is done, I'll open it. Have the soldiers load the stolen goods onto the other ship. Also find a crew for both ships. We'll set sail as soon as possible."

"Yes, sir."

By the time Annika finished, the cut throbbed. "Thanks," he said, donning his ripped shirt.

"What should I do now?" she asked.

"Check the others. Make sure no one else is wounded."

"Yes, sir."

Valek found the jail. It was on the ground floor of the only building not set atop tall pylons. The pirates hadn't cared if the occupants drowned during a storm. Inside, four grubby boys stood on the other side of a row of bars. The rest of the cell had been constructed with thick wooden planks.

Purple bruises marked the prisoners' faces. Their shirts had been torn, and dried blood stained the fabric, as well.

"I take it you're the troublemakers?"

"Who wants to know?" a tall boy with black hair and blue eyes demanded.

The boy resembled Zohav and must be her brother, Zethan.

"The person who is rescuing you," Valek said. He pulled his various lock picks from hidden pockets and worked on the complicated mechanism. After a few minutes, it popped open and he swung the door wide, letting them free. "Give your names to the sergeant. We could also use crew for the ships, if you'd like to help all of us get home."

Three of the boys grinned and took off, but Zethan remained.

"Where is my sister?" he demanded.

Magic swelled around him, pushing against Valek. He held his ground. "She's safe."

"I want to see her. Now."

"You're not in the position to be demanding anything, Zethan."

Zethan jerked back. "How did—"

"Zohav told me. She was worried that I'd kill you."

"Why?"

"Because of that magic you're gathering around you right now."

Recognition was followed by fear. The power disappeared. His control was impressive.

"Are you...?" Zethan asked. His voice barely a whisper.

"Going to kill you?"

He nodded.

"No, and don't call me a liar. I've already been accused of that by your sister. Trust me or not, just keep it to yourself, along with your abilities. Understand?"

"Yes."

Valek waited.

"Uh...yes, sir."

He led Zethan to the *Starfish*. Jibben remained on the dock, but his throat gaped open and blood pooled around him. The pirate's curved sword lay next to him, covered with the bright red liquid. Someone had slit Jibben's throat with his own weapon while Valek was busy. He had wanted to interrogate the pirate, but other than that, he wouldn't mourn the man's death. Perhaps the girl with the bony arms had taken matters into her own hands, meting out justice for her sister.

They boarded, and Valek escorted Zethan below. When they reached the Captain's quarters, the teen gasped and rushed to Zohav's side.

"What did you do to her?" he asked Valek.

"Relax, she's sleeping. Stay with her until I come for you. And if I feel any magic, no matter how small, you'll be joining her. Understand?"

"Yes, sir."

Valek paused at the threshold. With the siblings side by side, he realized they must be very close in age. "Are you twins?" he asked.

"Yes, sir."

"Do you have any other siblings?"

"An older brother."

"Does he have magic?"

"No, nor do our parents. We're the only ones."

Unlikely, but he'd go along with it for now.

They arrived at the port in Gandrel by midafternoon. Anxious to get on the road, Valek put Endre in charge. "Interrogate everyone and have the pirates processed by the security office in Gandrel. Once all the goods are distributed to the rightful owners, you and Annika are to report to the Castle to be reassigned, since your covers here have been blown."

"Yes, sir." Endre gave Valek what Janco would describe as the sad-puppy-dog look.

He suppressed a sigh. "Because you and Annika work so well together, I'll find a post that needs two agents." He'd either gotten soft, or it was just the idea of seeing Yelena soon that made him...nice. Bah.

Endre grinned. "Are you leaving now?"

"Yes. I'm taking the magicians to the Castle."

"Are you going to visit their parents first?"

Annoyed, Valek snapped, "Why would I do that?"

"They believe their children were lost at sea. I'd think it would be a kindness to stop by and let them see their kids for a couple hours."

A refusal pushed up Valek's throat, but he swallowed it down. Endre was right. Valek went to collect the twins, who had remained in the *Starfish* as ordered. Zohav had woken. She leaned against her brother, who had his arm around her shoulders. Good. They could leave right away. He questioned them on the location of their home.

"Our family knows nothing!" Zohav cried. "They have no magic. Leave them alone."

Her fear of him was growing tedious. "Fine. We won't visit them, then. Guess you don't wish to say goodbye."

"We live up near the northern ice sheet in MD-1," Zethan said.

Zohav yanked away and glared at her brother.

At least their home was close to the garrison. "Say goodbye to your friends. We're leaving in ten minutes. I'll meet you on the dock." Valek left.

Instead of going to the dock, he stayed on deck, drew his blowpipe and a couple darts from his pocket, and leaned over the rail opposite the pier. Sure enough, the large porthole in the Captain's quarter's below swung open, and Zohav glanced out. Magic thickened the air around him. Then the water next to the ship flattened and hardened. Interesting.

Valek watched as Zohav then Zethan climbed from the window and stood on the flat water. Impressive. At their age, that level of control was unheard-of. The Master Magicians were going to be thrilled.

"Where are you going?" Valek asked.

Zohav gasped and clutched Zethan's arm as he looked up at Valek. The boy's face creased in chagrin. Valek brandished the blowpipe. "Unless you wish to drown, come up here. Now."

Zethan said something to Zohav. She shook her head. Valek loaded a dart into the pipe and pressed the weapon to his lips. He aimed for the boy. If he shot her, they'd drown for sure. Zohav noticed the motion. She scowled at Valek. At least it was better than terror.

Then the flat water rose, lifting the siblings to the deck. Valek extended his hand and helped Zohav onto the ship as Zethan hopped down lightly next to her.

"Any more escape attempts, and I will knock both of you unconscious and transport you to the Citadel like two sacks of flour. Understand?"

MARIA V. SNYDER

"Citadel?" Zethan asked.

"Yes. I told Zohav I would escort you both there."

"He's lying. He's going to take us to his Commander so he can publicly execute us."

This was going to be a long trip. "Let's go. I want to reach the garrison before dark."

Valek stayed a step behind the siblings. They glanced at him from time to time, but kept quiet. They didn't arrive at MD-1's garrison until well after supper.

Colonel Ransley welcomed him back with a hot meal and an offer to give the siblings their own rooms.

"No, thank you, they stay with me," Valek said. Then he filled him in on how the Storm Thieves were apprehended, but didn't mention Zethan's and Zohav's magic.

"We haven't had a problem with pirates in decades," Ransley said. "No wonder the coastal security forces had a difficult time locating them."

Exhausted from staying up two nights with little sleep, Valek declined drinks with the Colonel. "We're leaving early in the morning. Let the stable boys know I'll need Onyx and another horse saddled and ready to go."

"Yes, sir."

In the large guest quarters, Valek dragged one of the four beds over to the door, blocking it. "I'm a very light sleeper," he warned the twins. "Sounds, movement or magic will wake me." Valek drew two daggers, one for each hand, and stretched out on the bed. "I'd suggest you get some sleep. Tomorrow is going to be a long day."

As he closed his eyes, he wondered if Yelena waited for him at the rendezvous location. Valek calculated how long it would take them to reach it, including the fact that the twins would slow him down. Ten days if he was being optimistic, twelve if he wasn't.

A whispered argument woke him in the middle of the night.

"…not being nice. You're putting our family at risk, Zee."

"Don't you want to see Mother, Father and Zeb? When we were captured by Jibben, I thought I'd never see any of them again."

"Of course I do. But they think we were lost at sea. Isn't that better than knowing we're going to be executed?"

"He said—"

"Don't be a fool. The law is clear. Plus he has executed hundreds of magicians. Why would we be the exception?"

Normally Valek encouraged such exaggerations—fear was a powerful motivator—but this time, it irked him. He pushed up on one elbow. "I've killed twenty-three magicians, and if you two don't shut up and go to sleep, I'll add two more to my total."

He lay back down. The number had been an estimate. When he'd been dispatched to investigate reports of a teen with powers, he'd arrived and soon after, the person with magic disappeared. However, no one knew he'd arranged for him or her to escape across the border. Everyone believed he'd killed the teen. Even the Commander.

Hedda and Arbon had both accused him of blind loyalty. And while he'd been loyal to the Commander all these years, he hadn't been as blind nor as completely obedient as everyone assumed.

When Valek arrived in the stable the next morning, Onyx and a gray horse named Smoke were saddled and ready for travel. Zohav and Zethan kept their distance while the stable boy tied on their bags. They'd acquired fresh uniforms and a few personal items from the garrison's commissary.

Valek petted Onyx's neck, then checked his legs for hot spots. His coat gleamed and the black horse appeared healthy.

MARIA V. SNYDER

"Tell Smoke to follow you," he said to Onyx before mounting. "Zethan, you'll ride Smoke, and Zohav, you're with me."

The girl frowned, but she listened to the stable boy's instructions and soon settled behind Valek. Zethan also received a quick lesson on how to mount and steer the horse. The boy grinned in anticipation. Just like Valek's older twin brothers—Victor had been cautious and protective, while Viliam had rushed headlong into any adventure.

Valek turned to Zohav. "Which way?"

She pressed her lips together, but then told him to follow the road that headed northeast.

Eager for the exercise, Onyx set a fast pace. Valek glanced at Zethan, who bounced in the saddle, but appeared to be enjoying the speed.

When Onyx finally slowed, Valek rode beside Smoke. "How did you end up on the coast?" he asked Zethan.

Zethan glanced at his sister, as if seeking permission to speak. After a brief hesitation, he said, "After we turned fourteen, it became obvious that we both had magic. Our father searched for a teacher to help us learn how to control it before anyone found out. Nell…" He paused and swallowed, staring at his hands, gripping the reins much harder than necessary. "Nell taught us these last two years. She has…had the ability to call the wind, and she used it when sailing or to beat all the other fishing boats to the prime spots."

"What are your abilities?" Valek asked.

"Zee," Zohav warned.

"It doesn't matter now, Zo. Besides, he rescued us from the pirates."

"We're still prisoners."

"She has a point," Valek said. "You should never tell your enemy the extent of your powers, or he'll find ways to counter them." Like trapping you in a null shield, Valek thought sourly.

"I guess," Zethan agreed. "Although I don't know how someone could counter a storm. I can call them and then direct their paths."

"Zee!"

Valek suppressed a smile. "Actually, Stormdancers could turn your storm into a gentle rain."

"Really? What are Stormdancers?"

Valek explained the magicians to Zethan. "The Commander has even allowed Kade Stormdance to harvest the energy from the blizzards sweeping down from the northern ice sheet."

Zethan groaned. "Great. The one year I don't have to shovel snow, and I'm trapped on some island in the middle of the Sunset Ocean."

"I don't believe the Commander would let a magician into Ixia," Zohav said.

Valek twisted in his seat. "That's three. Call me a liar one more time, and you'll be turned into cargo. I also expect an apology when you finally understand."

Zohav stared at him, not backing down an inch. Almost all of her fear of him had been transformed into anger. In the sunlight, the blue in her eyes sparkled like sapphires. He suspected if he flattened his gaze into his killer's demeanor, she'd become frightened once more. But he'd rather have her angry than scared. He faced forward, and their conversation became limited to directions to their town.

They stopped briefly at noon for a quick dinner. The Colonel had provided full travel rations for the three of them.

Zethan couldn't contain his curiosity and asked, "What other types of magicians are there?"

Valek explained about the Master Magicians and the various magical abilities of the others. "Some people have what's called a One-Trick, which is one ability that is more instinc-

MARIA V. SNYDER

tive than learned. They don't have to worry about flaming out or being influenced by other, more powerful magicians."

"Flaming out? Should we be worried?" Zethan asked.

"No. You're in control of your powers, and you have Nell to thank for that. Otherwise, you would have grabbed more and more power until it overwhelmed you. By that point, the Master Magicians in Sitia would have sensed your presence and dispatched an...assassin to end your life before you flamed out. When a flameout happens, you not only kill yourself, but you ruin the power blanket for the other magicians."

Zethan rocked back on his heels. "Wow."

"You know an awful lot about magic and magicians. Is that so you can *counter* them?" Zohav asked.

"Knowing your enemy is always important, but I learned most of this from my heart mate, who has magic."

Zohav gaped at him. "*You* have a heart mate?"

"Who has magic, Zo. Magic! He's not going to kill us or she'll get mad at him. Right?"

"She would indeed."

"What about those twenty-three others you assassinated? Does she know about them?" Zohav asked.

"Yes. In fact, she has neutralized a number of magicians, as well. Just because a person has magic doesn't mean they're good people. Think about what Jibben did using your magic. Can you imagine what he'd do with his own?"

Their queasy expressions said it all. Lecture over, Valek wrapped the remaining cheese, packed it away and mounted Onyx.

Before Zohav stepped up, she said in a low voice, "I'm glad you killed Jibben."

"Me, too. Bastard got what he deserved." Zethan slashed a finger along his neck.

Valek didn't bother to correct them, and it was a quiet ride to—"Icefaren? You live in Icefaren?" he asked.

"I told you it was near the northern ice sheet," Zethan said. "Not many towns up here."

True. However, Valek never considered that they lived in his hometown. In his mind, only two people lived there—his parents, and no one else. According to the reports from his agents, his parents still resided in Icefaren.

Zethan spurred Smoke next to Valek. "I'll take point. If that's okay?" The teen had become comfortable riding a horse pretty quick.

"If you're about to fall off the horse, grab his mane and not the saddle," Valek instructed. "You won't hurt him, and a saddle can move with your weight."

"Mane, not saddle. Got it." Zethan pulled ahead.

Onyx stayed right behind Smoke, and Valek kept his attention on the boy. Falling off a horse at speed could be deadly, but he was glad to see Zethan had a natural grace and good balance.

When the horses stopped at a gate, Zethan jumped off Smoke and cleared the fence in one long stride. Zohav made an *ah* sound, slid from the saddle and took off after her brother. They raced to the house.

It was only then that Valek realized where they were. He stared at the familiar house as ice replaced the blood in his veins. His stomach cramped as visions of his murdered brothers flashed in his memory. With an extreme effort, he reigned in his emotions. Of course his parents had moved. His father was sixty-three by now and must be retired, and his mother was sixty. The five-bedroom house and adjacent tannery was too big for the two of them.

A door banged. Valek grabbed the hilt of his sword and turned. Two men stepped from the tannery. The older man stopped and stared at Valek as if he'd seen a ghost. Valek's heart pushed against his ribs and lungs as if it was a bubble about to burst. The pressure made it impossible for Valek to draw a breath.

The young man glanced between them. "Dad, what's wrong? Who is he?"

24

JANCO

"What do you mean, you *lost* her?" Ari demanded of one of Fisk's Helper's Guild members.

Janco put a hand on his partner's meaty arm. "Easy, big guy. You're scaring her." The poor thing looked to be about eight years old and fifty pounds. He'd seen sand spiders bigger than her.

"I don't care. We shouldn't have let a bunch of kids keep track of Yelena."

"I doubt we could have done any better. That relay system was genius!"

Ari glowered. "Valek charged us to keep her safe. If she—"

"Keeping her safe is almost impossible, and Valek knows it, Ari. Now, let me handle this." Janco crouched down to the girl's eye level. "Can you show me where you last saw her?"

She nodded and turned. They followed her through the busy streets of the Citadel and into the quieter residence quarters. She headed southwest and zigzagged through a maze of alleys and streets. No wonder she'd lost the trail. This place was a tracker's worst nightmare. Well, an average tracker. Janco was far from average.

The girl stopped at an intersection. "I turned this corner and...poof, they were gone."

He glanced around. From this point, there were four narrow alleys that branched off in different directions. He checked each one for any signs of Yelena—a peppermint or dart or bit of milk oat she might have dropped. No luck. Yelena probably assumed they were close behind her. Janco considered the timing and thought they should be nearing the final destination. He checked each narrow path. At the end of the third one, he found a chewed toothpick, as if someone had waited there.

"How many relays did they have?" he asked the girl.

"I counted seven before I lost her."

This one might be the last relay. From this point there were two alleys. Unable to find anything to distinguish one from the other, Janco picked one and closed his eyes. He inhaled, drawing the air slowly through his nose. Nothing but garbage and the typical city stink. He repeated the action in the other road. Same odors, but this time he also detected a faint whiff of lavender.

"This way," he said, hurrying down the tight throughway. It ended in a round courtyard with five different exits.

An uneasy, crawly sensation tickled his skin. Magic. Faint magic. Janco concentrated, seeking that unsettling...substance. Once again he closed his eyes and moved toward the nebulousness that repelled him. The creepy crawlies increased when he faced south.

He led Ari and the girl down an uneven sidewalk. Weeds grew between the cracks and glass crunched under his boots. The broken windows had been boarded over and the houses appeared to have been abandoned and left to squatters.

"I don't think you'll find this area listed in the guide book," Ari said.

"It's a little-known spot that should remain little-known,"

Janco agreed. Plus it hurt his scar. The pain increased, then lessened after he walked past a run-down shack. "You've got to be kidding me."

"What's wrong?" Ari asked.

"The complete and utter lack of creativity. That shack is an illusion."

"Okay, let's go." Ari yanked his scimitar and charged toward it.

Janco stepped in front of him. "Hold on. We don't know what's on the other side. And it might trigger an alarm." He paused as he realized *he* was being the sensible one. How about that? There was a first time for everything. Janco herded them back to the courtyard and out of sight. "Spider Girl, go fetch Fisk and as many of his minions as you can. Pronto!"

She flipped him the finger, but scurried away.

"Now what?" Ari asked.

"The illusion is hiding another building, so we case the joint. See if there are any other entrances. These houses are all jumbled together. They have to be connected."

"All right. I'll loop around back and you take the roof."

Janco eyed the sagging rooftops—some peaked, others flat. "If you hear a tremendous crash, that would be me falling through the shingles."

Ari didn't bother to reply. He slipped around the row of houses without making a sound. Janco sighed and studied the closest dwelling. The drainpipe looked sketchy, and the wooden siding bowed outward as if the house had been stuffed full. The corner of the building might be okay to climb up, as long as the nails hadn't rusted through.

A skittery feeling brushed his back. Janco spun around, searching for the cause. The courtyard was empty. He scanned the windows, but no one watched him. However, he couldn't shake the certainty that someone or something had a keen interest in him. Ignoring the strangeness, he scaled the two-story structure and reached the roof.

Keeping low and testing each step before he put his full weight on it, he headed toward the shack. A number of squeals, squeaks and groans followed his progress. He wondered if any of the residents would investigate the noises or if they'd think it'd be safer to remain indoors. In this neighborhood, he guessed they'd stay inside.

As he drew closer, the quality of the roofs changed. The timber beneath his boots no longer dipped with his weight. The outer layer still resembled a patchwork, but the foundation was strong. His scar tweaked with pain just as he reached a smooth, flat roof with two skylights—quite a surprise.

Janco tiptoed closer, then laid flat on his stomach to peek inside. It took a few seconds for his eyes to adjust to the darker interior. He clamped down on a shout. Yelena lay on a couch below. She appeared to be sleeping, or maybe paralyzed by Curare. Janco fervently hoped it was one of those two, and that she wasn't dead. Before he could move, four men arrived. They carried a wooden crate with them, and then they lifted Yelena and packed her inside it, as if she were a piece of furniture!

He stared in shock as they wheeled the box from the room. *Must. Follow. Box.*

Janco had no memory of his trip back to the courtyard.

"Slow down, you're not making any sense," Ari said. "What's this about a box?"

Fisk and his minions arrived.

Janco explained what had happened. "We need to find that box. Spread out and search."

"Won't work," Fisk said. "This place is a labyrinth, and if you know the layout, you can get from one end to the other without being seen. If she's in a box, then they're not planning on keeping her here."

"Which means they're probably putting her on a wagon along with other goods to smuggle her from the Citadel," Ari said.

"The west gate," Janco said. "It's the closest."

"And the most obvious," Fisk said.

"But they don't know I know." Janco thumped his chest.

"Good point. Fisk, can you show us the shortest way to the gate?"

"Of course." He gave orders to a couple of his minions and then took off at a jog.

"What if we're too late?" Janco asked, keeping pace with Ari. "Or we don't spot it? There was nothing remarkable about that particular box."

"Think positive."

They reached the gate after two lifetimes. Fisk told them to wait while he bribed the guards to let him look at the logbook. Janco fidgeted, unable to endure even a few seconds of delay.

When Fisk returned, he said, "No wagons have left this afternoon. I sent my people to watch the north and south gates while we keep an eye on this one."

The three of them split up so they covered all possible angles. Fisk took the high ground to look down into the wagons. Ari was stationed outside the gate. And Janco waited in the shadow of the guardhouse. If a covered wagon arrived, Janco would peek under the tarp before it left.

In the end, it wasn't a box that tipped Janco off. It was the driver of the wagon. He just about fainted when he spotted Leif chatting with the gate guards. Stunned for a moment, Janco only had time to slip under the tarp before the wagon pulled away.

MARIA V. SNYDER

25

YELENA

I woke with a horrible headache and my mouth as dry as sawdust. Confused, I peered at my surroundings. The simple room had a night table, a single bed, one door and unadorned white walls. Not Fisk's colorful guest room. Something wasn't quite right. I couldn't move. Curare!

Panicked, I thrashed and stopped when I realized my movements were only limited, not paralyzed. Just my hands and feet had been secured. What did it say about my life when I took comfort in that?

Taking a few deep breaths, I calmed my racing heart. I concentrated on the facts. My symptoms matched being drugged with sleeping potion. Concern for the baby burned, and it triggered other worries. And then I remembered. Leif! He'd been captured. Yet that wasn't completely true. He was okay, but not okay. My thoughts spun and I closed my eyes. Perhaps I'd wake a second time and everything would be clear.

The doorknob rattled, and I opened my eyes in time to see Leif enter. He carried a tray of food. My relief at seeing him fizzled when Bruns Jewelrose and a couple goons followed him into my room. My memory jerked to life, and my arm burned where my rat bastard of a brother had pricked me with sleeping potion. I glared at Leif.

"I had to do it," Leif said. "You wouldn't listen to reason, and Bruns was worried Ari and Janco would find us."

"That's because nothing Bruns said was reasonable," I said.

"I thought the same thing at first. But you really need to see what he's done here. It's wonderful." Leif used the same tone he used to describe a delicious stew.

"Do I have a choice?"

"Of course," Bruns said. "Just finish hearing me out, and then decide."

"And if I still think you're a raving lunatic?"

Bruns pressed his lips together and smoothed an invisible wrinkle on his sleeve. "Then we'll discuss your options."

"Options, eh?" My imagination produced a number of horrific scenarios. I quelled my emotions. In this situation, I suspected logic and cold calculation would be required. "All right. I'll listen."

Leif smiled. One of the goons placed a chair near the bottom of my bed while the other freed my wrists. I sat up and resisted the urge to check my clothing for my lock picks and switchblade. Bruns sat in the chair.

Leif placed the tray on my lap. "You'll feel better once you've eaten. The chef is an artist. Everything he makes is divine."

I started with the water, draining half in one gulp. Bruns explained his theory about the Commander's imminent invasion. I half listened as I tried the stew. Leif hadn't been exaggerating. The broth had a nice balance of sweet and spicy. After I swallowed, I picked up on a subtle aftertaste. It tasted familiar. It took me another three bites to identify the substance. Theobroma.

Putting the spoon down, I reached for the water.

"Something wrong with the food?" Bruns asked.

"No. My stomach is still unsettled," I lied. "You were talking about Sitia's assets..." I prompted.

Bruns continued with his logical yet warped reasoning for protecting Sitia. I glanced at my brother. His expression was one of rapt devotion. No surprise, considering he'd probably consumed mass quantities of the Theobroma-laced food. The substance lowered a magician's resistance to magical influence and rendered a person without magic very susceptible to suggestion.

I listened to Bruns's well-rehearsed speech and agreed to take a tour of his facilities. They freed my ankles.

"Before we go, I'd like to talk with my brother. In private," I said.

"Of course." Bruns stood and flicked invisible dust from his pants. "We'll be right outside waiting for you." He left with his goons.

Leif stepped back. "You're not going to get upset again, are you?"

"No. I understand what's going on here."

Relief smoothed his features. "Finally! Isn't Bruns a genius?"

Not the word I'd use, but I had to choose my words with care. "Leif, there's a good reason why you love the food. It's been cooked with Theobroma."

His brow crinkled. "You must be mistaken."

"You know I have a sensitive palate." My survival had depended on it when I'd been the Commander's food taster. "Take a bite."

He did. Concern flashed, then he smiled. "Of course! It makes total sense. The Commander has Curare, and Bruns wants to protect our soldiers. If they're hit with a dart, the Theobroma will keep them from becoming paralyzed. I told you he's a genius."

So close. "But the substance also has other effects. That's why you're helping Bruns."

"No, it isn't. He wants to protect Sitia and so do I." Leif crossed his arms and stiffened into his stubborn stance.

But his gaze held a tiny seed of doubt.

"Come on, Bruns is waiting for us." Leif opened the door. Wrapping his hand around my upper arm, he escorted me out.

Bruns glanced at each of us. "Is everything all right?"

"Yelena is still not convinced," Leif said. "But I'm sure she'll come around in a few days, just like I did." He frowned at me.

I kept my expression neutral, but inside I allowed hope to grow. Perhaps my comments would snap my brother out of it.

Bruns showed me his garrison and demonstrated an impressive mock battle. His ideas and concerns for Sitia's battle readiness were sound; it was his execution that lacked basic morals. Leif remained Bruns's biggest cheerleader.

As we watched a training session, I asked Bruns, "Why did you change your mind about me?"

"My reasons were twofold. Assassinating you always came with the risk your heart mate would trace the hit back to me. When the Commander sent his other assassin after you, I'd hoped he'd think the second hit was also ordered by the Commander, and therefore it'd be a major upset in the Ixian leadership."

I kept quiet about just how much of an upset there was between Valek and the Commander right now. "And the second?"

"Your brother convinced me that your knowledge and intelligence would be an asset, despite the fact you no longer have magic. Also, the Commander has blocked your magic somehow, and we need to learn how he achieved this. If he can do it to you, he'll do it to the others. And while I'm all for no more magicians..." He frowned. "We need them for the upcoming invasion."

What a swell guy. He had a few things wrong, but I wasn't going to correct him.

"And there's also your knowledge of Ixian tactics and their military that will aid us."

Ah. I wondered what Bruns would do if I told him Valek suspected the Commander planned to invade after the Fire Festival a mere six months away. Probably freak out and kidnap every magician in Sitia. We looped back to the magicians' barracks.

"I realize it's quite a bit to take in," Bruns said. "I'll give you a few days to think about it before asking for your answer." He indicated the two goons who had stayed close by for the entire tour. "They will remain with you to answer any questions you might have. Feel free to explore the garrison. The dining hall is open all day."

"What happens if I decide not to join and wish to leave?" I asked.

Bruns's smile failed to reach his eyes. "I don't think that will be an issue."

"And if it is?"

"You're a smart girl, Yelena. You know there are always casualties during a war."

Before I could respond to the threat, Leif linked his arm in mine.

"Come on, sis, you're exhausted. You'll think better tomorrow. I'll fetch you supper."

Leif escorted me to the white room. The goons trailed us, but remained in the hall. Probably taking up flanking positions by the door, which Leif closed.

"Don't bother bringing me any food," I said. "I'll find my own."

"You're being paranoid. Bruns is—"

"Killing magicians, hiring assassins, kidnapping people and committing treason."

He glowered at me.

"You tasted the Theobroma. Come on, Leif, think about it."

"You're wrong."

I almost groaned in exasperation. "Okay, then prove it. Stop eating the food for a couple days and see if you still feel the same way about Bruns."

Leif gasped. "Stop eating?"

"At least find food that isn't tainted by Theobroma. Can you do that for me?"

He met my gaze. "And if I prove you wrong, will you join Bruns?"

"Yes."

Over the next three days, I tested the limits of my imprisonment. The goons bookended me whenever I left my room and kept within two paces of me at all times. Leif brought our meals to my room. It was mostly fruit and raw vegetables—the only edibles not tainted with Theobroma. He ate with me and griped about the food, but he was determined to prove me wrong.

Even with all the various war preparations going on, I spent most of my time in the armory. A number of the new weapons fascinated me, and I practiced with a few at the range. It was amusing to see the goon brothers so tense and ready to tackle me should I aim a weapon at them. Amusing and infuriating, since they completely blocked any opportunity for me to escape.

I also had to fight against the constant barrage of positive thoughts about Bruns and his efforts. Suspecting a magician able to mentally communicate these good feelings to everyone, I asked Leif about it when he brought supper that night.

"I didn't notice it before, but…"

"But what?"

"Oh, for sand's sake! You were right. Since I've been Theobroma-free, it stinks big-time." He speared a piece of broccoli with his fork. "Happy now?"

"Yes!" Relief flowed through me. "What's been going on?"

"There are magicians arriving daily who are already on Bruns's team. I'm guessing his recruiters are using Theobroma to convince them."

That was disturbing. "How is he getting to them?"

"Probably the same way he's doing it here, by spiking their food."

"Do you know where we are?" I asked.

"Krystal Clan's garrison, near the coast."

"Do you know where the other training areas are?"

"No. But I've been Bruns's best buddy, and I'm hoping to be part of his inner circle soon. He's assigned me to convince you to be on our side, so you're going to have to spout the bullshit to keep my cover."

"Can't wait," I said drily.

"I hope you're a better actress than that, little sis, or we're all in trouble."

As we finished our meals, I had an idea. "Is there any way to swap the Theobroma for a substance that tastes like it, but doesn't have the same magical properties?"

"I wish. Theobroma is one of a kind."

"Do you have a plan?"

"I suggest you play nice, show up for meals and pretend to be influenced by Bruns."

"Then what?"

"We gain his trust and find the chink in his armor. Then we send a message to Ari and Janco and Irys."

It sounded easy, except... "We can't eat the food in the dining room."

"But I can't keep coming here. Bruns is getting suspicious." Leif rubbed his chin. "And frankly, I'm sick of eating nothing but fruit and vegetables. I'm friends with Alvar, the chef—let me see what I can do." He stood, squeezed my hand and turned to go.

I made a quick decision. "Leif."

"Yes?"

"Make sure you get plenty of food. I'm eating for two."

He jerked as if I'd slapped him. Then a range of emotions crossed his face—surprise, excitement, worry and then concern. "You shouldn't have risked the baby for me!"

"I couldn't *not* try to rescue you."

Leif wrapped me in a hug. "I'm sorry. I shouldn't have yelled at you. Congrats, sis. Does Valek know?"

"Yes."

"Then we'd better escape before he sends the entire Ixian army to rescue you."

The next morning I met with Leif in the dining room. He had two plates of scrambled eggs and bacon waiting for me. I thanked him before shoveling the food into my mouth. Leif filled me in on how he'd offered to help Alvar with the morning rush and managed to snag a few servings of eggs before they were glazed with a *special* sauce.

"Holy snow cats! There's Dax Greenblade." Leif gazed over my shoulder.

I crushed my napkin in my hands to keep from turning around. Was he captured? "Does he have goons with him?"

"No. Just a goofy smile, and he's heading this way." Leif leaned forward. "Remember, we love Bruns."

"Leif! Yelena! So this is where you two have been hiding," Dax said. "I should have known you'd be where all the action is."

I glanced way up at the tall man with light green eyes. For him, I didn't need to fake a smile. He'd been my first friend when I'd been a student at the Magician's Keep. "Hi, Dax! Did you just arrive?"

"Yup. Isn't this place great? Much better than that stuffy old Keep, where we don't do anything but study. What a waste of time. Now we can contribute to the welfare of Sitia."

"Yes, isn't it wonderful?" The words tasted like ash on my tongue.

"That looks yummy," Dax said. "I'm famished."

I grabbed his wrist before he could leave. "You can have the rest of mine. It's still warm."

"Great." He dug into my plate with abandon.

"So how did you hear about this place?" I asked.

"One of the students, I think," Dax said between mouthfuls. "This is good, but not as good as the Keep's."

"Really?" Leif asked.

"Yeah. We got a new chef and her dishes are...divine!"

Nausea bubbled in my stomach. I met Leif's equally horrified gaze. If Bruns had managed to put Theobroma into the food at the Keep...

"I don't remember a new chef," Leif said. "When did she start?"

"Oh, a couple weeks ago, I think." He shrugged, oblivious to our alarm.

I sagged back in my chair. Everyone at the Keep ate their meals at the dining room, including Irys and Bain, the two most powerful magicians in Sitia.

Leif used a series of subtle hand signals, telling me to stick to the plan.

I replied, *What plan?*

Get Bruns to trust us.

And then?

We stop him.

That's not a plan.

Do you have anything better?

No.

Discouraged, I said goodbye to Leif and Dax. I scanned the faces in the dining room as I left, searching for more magicians from the Keep. I recognized four others. At this point, I thought only the Commander's army could stop Bruns. But what if he couldn't?

I was so preoccupied, I tripped and sprawled on the floor.

Before my goons could help me, another soldier swooped in and lifted me to my feet. "Are you all right?" he asked.

I met Janco's gaze without visibly reacting. Inside, my heart was doing a jig. "Yes. Just a bit clumsy."

"Not your fault—there are *lots* of people in here. It's hard to move."

My depression lifted. Help had arrived! "All the better for when we go to war."

"True. Bruns will lead us to victory."

I took a step, but wobbled and fell into Janco, who caught me with ease. He'd dyed his hair red and wore a fake ear that covered his scars.

"Don't eat the food," I whispered in his good ear before straightening. "Guess I must have tweaked my ankle." I gestured to my goons and let them support me as I limped from the dining room. Ha! *How's that for acting!*

My elation over seeing Janco faded as I realized that even with more people on our side we still didn't have a clue how to stop Bruns.

Bruns joined me in the armory the next day. I'd been practicing using one of the new blowpipes that had scoring in the barrel to improve accuracy and distance. Too bad the dart wasn't filled with poison. That would have been a quick way to solve the problem of Bruns.

MARIA V. SNYDER

"I heard you twisted your ankle. How are you doing?" Bruns asked.

I smiled at him. "That's so sweet of you to ask. It was a minor sprain. Nothing a good night's sleep couldn't take care of."

"Wonderful. Leif tells me you've changed your mind about me," Bruns said.

It about killed me, but I stretched my lips wider and beamed at him. "Yes, I was being so silly. I mean, once I thought about it, I wondered why I would protect the Commander when he fired me as the Liaison."

"Oh? I hadn't heard that. Let's go to my office and have a little chat."

"All right."

With his arm linked in mine as if we were old friends, he led me to the main administration building in the center of the garrison. Before entering, Bruns ordered my goons to remain outside. As we climbed to the top floor, I searched my memory for any bits of information that I could give to Bruns about the Commander.

We arrived at a waiting room, complete with a pretty secretary. She handed him a stack of papers and mentioned a number of people who had been looking for him.

"I'll deal with them later. Can you bring us a pot of tea, please?"

She jumped to her feet. "Yes, sir."

Opening a door behind her desk, Bruns escorted me into his vast office. It occupied the rest of the fifth floor. The sleek furniture was made of ebony wood. My boots sank into lush carpets, and the opulent paintings had gold frames. Floor-to-ceiling windows covered the entire back wall. Unable to resist, I gazed at the view. Sunlight glinted off the Jade Sea in the distance. Right below were the training yards and armory.

"Did you buy the garrison?" I asked, pressing my hand on the glass.

"No. Councilor Krystal agreed that we needed to prepare for war and offered it to me."

"How many other Councilors are helping you?"

"I believe I'm supposed to be asking the questions." Bruns's voice held a dangerous tone.

Uh-oh. I turned. "Sorry! I shouldn't ask such obvious questions. Of course *all* the Councilors support you. You're going to save Sitia."

Bruns relaxed. "Sit down, Yelena."

I sat in one of the leather armchairs. The dark maroon color reminded me of dried blood. Bruns tossed the papers on his desk before sitting across from me.

"Do you know where Valek is?" he asked.

An easy question. "Not exactly. When we parted, he was headed to the coast of MD-1 to deal with Storm Thieves."

"How long ago was that?"

I calculated. "Twenty-three days."

"Do you think that's enough time for him to finish?"

"I don't know. It depends on how smart the thieves are."

"Is it possible that he followed you to Sitia instead of going to the coast?"

"Uh…" That would mean he'd lied to me. Valek might not tell me everything, but he wouldn't lie to me. "It's possible, but not probable."

"Why do you say that?"

"Because you're still alive." Even though it was the truth, I regretted the comment as soon as it left my mouth.

Bruns stilled. "I see."

Thank fate his secretary entered with the tea. She set the tray on the table between us and poured two cups.

"Thank you, Tia."

She gave him a bright smile and left the room.

"Shall we toast?" Bruns picked up his cup.

I grabbed the other and held it up.

"To honesty, no matter how brutal," he said.

An odd toast, but I tapped my cup against his and sipped the hot liquid, which tasted strongly of Theobroma. I set it down.

Bruns questioned me about losing my magic and what I'd learned. Again, I didn't see a reason to lie. "I've no idea what happened."

We discussed potential causes. I'd explored all of them before, but I figured my openness would reinforce my I'm-on-your-side act.

"Is there something wrong with the tea?" Bruns asked.

"It's a little too hot."

"It should have cooled by now."

I picked it up and sipped a tiny bit. "You're right." Holding the cup, I rested my right arm in my lap.

Bruns surged to his feet. "Do you really think I'm an idiot?"

"Excuse me?"

"Your guides are very observant. It didn't take us long to guess why Leif always brought food to your room. I suspected when you first woke. As the Commander's food taster, you must have a sensitive palate. You can stop the act." Without warning, he grabbed my left wrist and pain pierced my forearm.

A dart was stuck in my skin. "What...?"

"I believe you call it goo-goo juice. Leif unarmed you while you were sleeping and gave me all your nasty darts filled with Curare, sleeping potion and goo-goo juice."

My head spun as fear clawed my stomach. I set the tea on the table to avoid spilling it in my lap.

Bruns knelt in front of me. "Now, let's talk."

26

VALEK

Valek stared at his father and then at the young man next to him. The one who resembled his dead brother Vincent. Or rather, how he would have looked if Vincent had lived four or five more years. And it clicked why Zohav and Zethan seemed so familiar. His parents had more children after he'd left.

Strong emotions strangled Valek, rendering him mute. He hadn't seen his father since he was thirteen and left to seek revenge for the murder of his brothers. Since his parents told him never to return.

"Dad, what's going on? Who is he?" the young man asked again.

Valek's father ignored the questions. He walked toward Valek with his brown-eyed gaze locked on him and as paralyzing as Curare. Gray had replaced his once-black hair, and wrinkles lined his leathery face. A part of Valek noted that he wore a tanner's uniform as required, but various colored dyes had stained the white diamonds.

Relaxing his grip on the hilt of his sword, Valek dismounted and stood at the gate. He clamped down on the maelstrom of shock, pain, fear and grief that raged inside him. Instead, he channeled the calm detachment he'd learned to rely on during times of great danger.

When his father reached the other side of the gate, he opened it and said, "Welcome home, son."

Those three words slammed into him. He rocked back on his heels, and only Onyx's solid body behind him kept Valek upright.

"Son? What are you talking about?" the young man asked. His voice squeaked with alarm.

"This is Valek, the Commander's chief of security and your older brother," his father said. "Valek, this is Zebulon."

Zebulon's shocked expression meant his...their father hadn't mentioned Valek before. And he wondered if Father had told him about Vincent, Viliam and Victor.

Just then his mother yelled from the house, "Kalen, Zeb, get in here! The twins are back! They're alive!"

Without a word, both men bolted to the house. Valek sagged against Onyx, glad for the few minutes to collect his wits, which had scattered when his father called him *son*. Completely unexpected, the word woke the small boy who had hidden deep down inside him. The child who craved his parents' love and approval and wished to be held and comforted. And although he tried to shove that young boy back into his slumbering coma, the damage was done. Valek suddenly needed Yelena's touch and her strength. With her support, he could endure this encounter. Without it—he might lose control of everything.

Valek pulled in a few deep breaths, knowing he didn't have much time before the entire family came spilling from the house. No matter what happened, the twins still needed to go to Sitia. However, he suspected leaving after only a few hours would be impossible for all concerned.

As predicted, five people streamed from the house. His

mother led the way straight toward him. She held a large kitchen knife and her expression was not welcoming. Not at all. Anger and determination emanated from her blue eyes— the mother bear protecting her cubs. She'd saved his life. And the nail-shaped scars still marked his shoulder from when she had held him back from attacking the soldiers who'd murdered his brothers.

Valek fought the instinct to grab his knives in the face of her charge. The others shouted after her to stop and think and calm down, but her stride never wavered. She halted on the other side of the open gate and brandished her weapon. The others fell silent, or rather held their collective breaths.

"You will *not* harm my children. You will *not* take them away," she said.

"I have no intention of harming them." Glad his voice didn't shake, he added, "Now that I know who they are, I will ensure they are protected once they're in Sitia."

"What do you mean, *now* that you know?" Mother demanded. "You've known all along." She gestured with the knife. "You've sent your spies to watch us since the takeover."

"I sent them to *protect* you, not *spy* on you. They are only to report if someone comes after you because of me. Not about your personal life." Valek glanced at his three…siblings. "And I take it you didn't tell your new children about your old children?"

"They know about the others, but not you. You're an assassin. The Commander's killer. Everyone hates and fears you— they didn't need to know they are related to an abomination."

The word sliced into him. He encouraged others to feel that way about him, but hearing it from his mother had an unexpected impact. Recovering, he asked, "And how did you explain my agents?"

"We made them part of our family. The kids and the neighbors think we hired them," his father said.

Not a bad idea, except for the fact that his agents' covers had been blown for years and Valek hadn't known.

"I don't care if you've been protecting us," Mother said. "They are *not* going with you."

"Calm down, Olya. Let's go inside and talk about this." Father placed his hand on her shoulder, but she shrugged him off.

"They *are* coming with me," Valek said. "Either we do this the hard way, and you'll have no time to spend with them. Or the easy way, and you'll get...the rest of the day together." A day of pure hell for him. Another day away from Yelena.

"I'll go with him," Zethan said.

"No! He'll kill you. That's what he does. It's all he knows," Mother accused.

That was the breaking point. Valek moved. In a heartbeat, he unarmed his mother. "If I'd planned to kill them, they'd be dead by now." He handed the knife to his father. "Now spend time with your children. We're leaving in the morning." Valek met Zohav's gaze. "You know what I'm capable of. Try anything—"

"And we'll go to the Citadel as cargo," Zethan finished. "Got it."

"Citadel?" his father asked Valek.

"Actually, the Magician's Keep. They need to learn the extent of their magic."

"Why are you doing this?" His father yanked on his shirt with his big calloused hand—a nervous habit that had endured the years.

"Because his heart mate would be angry if he didn't," Zethan supplied.

His father didn't react to Zethan's comment. Instead, he squinted at Valek with his shrewd I-see-right-through-you expression that came from years of raising rambunctious boys. "That's not the entire reason."

"Let's just say it will be beneficial for Ixia. Despite the rumors, I'm not just a killing machine." This he said to his mother. "I do guard the interests of Ixia." *And my family.* But Valek wouldn't voice that aloud. "Go on." He shooed them away. "No sense wasting time."

They shuffled back to the house, appearing a bit dazed. Needing to move, lest his thoughts and emotions ambush him, Valek led Onyx and Smoke inside the gate. He fed them and gave them water. Then he groomed them. Every inch, until they practically glowed.

A door banged behind him. Valek spun and yanked a knife. Standing in the tannery's entrance was Patxi, one of his corp. The man held out his stained hands. Valek relaxed and gestured Patxi over.

The tall man fidgeted under Valek's scrutiny. "Sorry, boss, but this was the best way to protect your family. I'm with your father all day and sleep in the room above the shop. If something happens, I'm right here."

"And Milya?"

"She helps in the house and stays in the guest room."

"How did—"

"Your father discovered the agents long ago. When you assign new agents, we just take over the jobs. You can't be too surprised, sir. You had to get your canny intuition from someone."

Appealing to his ego—nice tactic. "Do you wish to be reassigned?"

"No. I've a feeling your visit today is going to cause a bit of a problem from the locals. I want to make sure Zeb doesn't get into any trouble."

"Is he a troublemaker?"

MARIA V. SNYDER

"He's a fighter. And stubborn. Won't back down ever. I've taught him a few moves to keep him from getting completely clobbered at the tavern."

Interesting. "Recruitment potential?"

"Yes. And now he knows you're his brother, it's probably safer for him to get the full training."

"Okay. Thanks."

Patxi nodded and returned to the tannery. By the time Valek finished cleaning the horses' hooves, the sun hung low in the sky. Now what? Having no desire to see what had changed inside the tannery, Valek looped around it.

The three graves remained in the place that was scarred into his memory. Their names had been chiseled into the black granite headstones lined up in a row—Victor, Viliam and Vincent. At the end sat another, smaller stone without a name. Had his parents put that there to represent him? Perhaps it was better to believe that he was dead instead of an abomination.

But his father's words—*welcome home, son*—didn't match that sentiment. However, the knife in his mother's hand clearly did.

He knelt next to Vincent's grave. Running his fingers over the cold stone, Valek envisioned Vincent's face. Grief surged through him. Valek wondered for the millionth time how his life would have been different if his brothers had lived. An idyllic scene with all of them older, married with children, gathered around the huge dining room table, laughing, teasing, complaining, arguing. His mother spoiling the grandchildren, his father teaching the next generation how to tan and dye leather.

Then the questions would start. Would the King's family still be ruling Ixia? Would the monarch's corruption make that homey scene impossible? Would he have been content to work in his father's tannery? Would he be a different person?

And the most important question: Would he have met

Yelena? The answer to that one was no. When he focused on her and their baby, then all this didn't hurt so much. It still smoldered deep inside him, and he still wished his brothers hadn't been killed. But the promise of having a family again pushed him past all the heartache and grief. Motivated him to find a way to get Ixia and Sitia back on good terms, so his future of laughter, teasing, debates and love would be…not quite assured, but would have much better odds.

"Thought I'd find you here," his father said.

Valek straightened and wiped the dirt from his knees.

"I think of those boys every day." His father tucked his hands into his pockets. Staring at the gravestones, he rocked on his heels. "Those soldiers that were killed about two years later…were they the ones?"

"Yes."

Father lifted his head. "And that Captain who died in the woods?"

"He ordered his men to pick a family to use as an example of what happens when you don't pay your taxes to the King."

"And you lodged a complaint with the King?"

"Everyone knows I assassinated him. Why are you asking?"

"Rumors can't be trusted."

Valek waited.

"I want to hear it from you."

"That I'm a killer, like Mother said? Yes. I am. I personally delivered my complaint to the King, Queen and the entire royal family."

"How did it feel? Once you finished…complaining."

"Satisfying and freeing. But by then, it wasn't all about revenge. I'd seen the rot and the deaths the King and his family were responsible for. I agreed with the Commander's vision for Ixia. He'd never murder a child because his parents couldn't afford to pay taxes."

"True. And my taxes were reduced after the takeover."

"Is that why you had more children?" Valek couldn't resist asking.

"No. We were devastated and lonely. Our house had been full of four energetic and boisterous boys and then...all gone. So quiet. Your mother didn't think she'd conceive, but Zeb was born four years after the takeover, then the twins three years later." He rubbed a hand over his face. "When their magic started causing problems, I'd thought you'd show up and..."

"Here I am."

"Later than expected, and not before we thought we lost them, too."

Dark shadows of grief haunted his expression. More than any one person should be asked to bear. But that was the problem with grief. No one ever asked for it. It arrived with its bags already packed for an extended stay. It settled into your best guest room and demanded to be waited on all day long, and when it finally shuffled out the door, it left behind permanent scratches on your furniture.

Valek wished to ease his father's pain. "They'll be...safer in Sitia. I'll make sure they learn how to protect themselves."

"Thank you. Come inside and get something to eat."

"No thanks. I belong here with the dead." Valek pointed to the unmarked gravestone. "Mother would agree."

"That's not yours. It's for that damn dog Mooch. The twins were so upset when he died. Made me dig a grave and buy a stone. Never did get around to carving his name in it. And do you know what's really galling?"

Amused, Valek shook his head.

"Out of the dozen dogs we've had, that damn dog hated me. Bit me three times, and I couldn't do nothing about it or they'd get upset."

"Which explains why it remains unmarked."

He laughed a deep chuckle. "You always were a quick study of people. I'm sure it helps with your job."

"It does."

His father scuffed his boots in the dirt. "I've thought about you every day, too, wondering if you'd ever come home." A pause. "If you hadn't run into the twins, would you have returned?"

"You made it quite clear—"

"And you've never said something in anger that you regretted later? Never uttered the wrong thing when you were out of your mind with grief?"

Cracks appeared in Valek's calm demeanor. Funny how being threatened by a butcher knife hadn't affected him at all, yet his father's words had the same effect as a blow to his head, followed by a punch to his solar plexus, leaving him dazed and unable to suck in a proper breath.

"Assassins learn to shut off their emotions," Valek finally said.

"That's bullshit. If that was the case, then you wouldn't let the twins stay overnight, you wouldn't be here by your brothers' graves, you wouldn't have a heart mate. Should I go on?"

"No. You've made your point."

"Then what's the answer to my question? Would you have returned?"

He hadn't planned to, but with marrying Yelena, and the baby... "I don't know."

"Fair enough. Now come on inside."

"I... Mother would get upset. I'd ruin her time with the twins."

"Put that intuitive sense to work, boy. How would you

feel in her place? It's a lot to take in, and she's not going to see them again—"

"Why not? You can visit them during the hot season when the Keep's on break."

His father jerked straight. "But they'll be in Sitia. We can't…"

"You can if I help you. In fact, Sitia has tanneries, too. If you want to live there, I can arrange that, as well."

"You can?"

"I can." Even if he no longer worked for the Commander. He gazed at Valek for a few heartbeats. "I'll think about it."

"When you decide, just tell Patxi. He'll get word to me."

Valek's father returned to the house. Movement seemed the best cure for his…confusion. Valek retrieved his pack from Onyx's saddle and built a small fire near his brothers' graves. It might be morbid, but to him it was comforting. The horses moved closer to the heat.

He boiled water and sorted through the travel rations, ensuring there would be enough to last. The crunch of footsteps sounded to his left. Valek jumped to his feet, knife in hand.

"Easy," Zethan said. "Just bringing you supper."

Valek slid the weapon back into its sheath as the young man stepped into the ring of firelight. Zethan handed him a fork and a plate with two slices of roast beef and a pile of mashed potatoes, all covered with a dark brown gravy. The smell alone was intoxicating.

"Did you draw the short straw?"

Zethan laughed. "No, I volunteered."

"Thanks." Valek sat next to the fire.

"I didn't bring you a knife to cut the meat, 'cause I figured you already have about ten of your own."

"At least." Valek smiled.

Zethan took that as an invitation to sit down. "Mother's

coming around to the idea of us leaving. Although Zohav doesn't believe you have the authority to let them come visit us."

Zohav's comment wasn't a surprise. "Consider it one of the perks of my job."

The teen pulled a half-burned twig from the fire. He sketched designs into the dirt with it. "What's it like at the Magician's Keep?"

Between bites of the smoky beef, Valek explained the five-year student curriculum. "You probably won't have to start at the beginning, but I'd guess you'd be there two or three years."

Valek answered a bunch of Zethan's questions before Zebulon arrived with a piece of apple pie.

"Zee, Father wants to talk to you and Zo alone," Zebulon said. "I expect you'll get the same lecture that you got when you left for the coast. Plus, a bonus warning not to get captured by pirates," he teased.

"You mean we weren't *supposed* to get captured? Why didn't he tell us that before?" Zethan brushed dirt from his pants before heading to the house.

Zebulon handed Valek the pie. "Mother said you can sleep in the house."

"Thanks, but I have my bedroll and I'm used to sleeping on the ground."

He shrugged. "Suit yourself." Then he sat on the other side of the fire. He poked at the wood with a twig. Sparks shot into the sky.

Valek waited while Zebulon worked up the nerve to ask the questions he held inside. He studied his…brother—still a difficult concept to accept. Around nineteen years old, Zebulon's personality appeared to be a mix of the twins, cautious like Zohav, but with a bit of a sense of humor like Zethan. Valek wondered if he had Vincent's mischievous streak. Perhaps when the man relaxed, his true personality would show.

Would any of them ever relax around Valek, the King Killer? He doubted it.

"What you mentioned to Father about moving south, does that apply to me, as well?"

"Of course."

"What if we decide to stay here? Can we still visit the twins?"

"Yes."

"Why do you care? You didn't even know we existed until today. You didn't care enough to ask your…agents how my… our parents were doing. How can we believe that you care now?"

Valek imagined Zohav had asked the same questions in the house. "I've many enemies. People who wouldn't hesitate to use my family in order to get to me. But only a handful of trusted people know where my parents live, and I've assigned agents to protect them just in case the information is leaked. If I didn't care, the agents wouldn't be here. As for not knowing about you and the twins…" Valek swallowed. "I…ordered my agents not to tell me anything because…" He gazed at the gravestones.

His father's comments about regret over harsh words repeated in his mind. Had his avoidance really been due to his parents telling him never to return or Valek's own fear that if they became a family again, he'd be vulnerable to the intense heartache of losing them, like the grief he'd experienced when his brothers died? Or was it just pure stubbornness? Or the fear of being rejected if he'd returned? Perhaps all three.

"Because I couldn't handle hearing about their lives continuing on without me and my brothers." Because it would mean they'd moved past the tragedy and grief, while he hadn't. When he'd told his father that killing the King had been freeing, he'd lied. Everything he'd done up to this point had been a result of that day. It was as if he'd been frozen in time.

Yelena had been the only one to reach him through the ice, drilling a small opening.

"What about now? Can you handle it?"

Could he? From the hole, cracks zipped along the frozen surface, creating a pattern. If he let his family through the barrier, would he shatter? Sweat raced down his back as a burning pain bloomed around his heart.

Unable to sit still, he stood and strode to the graves. He'd told his father that he belonged among the dead. That unmarked gravestone could easily be for him. He'd let Yelena in, but it had taken eight years for him to realize just how precious she was to him. The scar on his chest seared his skin. He knelt on Vincent's grave and traced his name with a finger. Valek leaned his hot forehead on the cold, hard granite.

This was what he had been for so long. Cold. Hard. Why was this so difficult? He'd faced assassins, rogue magicians, the Commander, criminals of all sorts, and would gladly face them all a second time rather than watch his family be destroyed again. Yet he saw the murders so clearly in his mind. He relived that day over and over and over and over. Even with all his efforts to keep Ixia safe, they remained dead. The family of his childhood was gone and would never be the same.

Could he handle it? A new family that wasn't just him, Yelena and the baby? A fire suffused him, and then it disappeared. Cold air fanned his face. Just as Janco had said, Valek had found a family despite being surrounded by ice. Yelena and the baby of course, but also a rather unconventional one that included Ari, Janco, Leif, Opal, Devlen and a number of horses.

Could he handle it?

Yes.

The admission zipped through him, and the invisible yet ever-present weight lifted from his shoulders. Breathing eas-

MARIA V. SNYDER

ier, he straightened. Zebulon remained by the fire, watching him with a worried frown, hoping Valek didn't go crazy and kill them all. Odd that Zebulon's thoughts should be so clear to Valek.

As he returned to the fire, the air smelled different. He picked up a number of scents—the ashy smoke from the burning coal, the earthy aroma of leather and the sweet odor of grass from the horses. Tendrils of wind caressed his face. The strangeness continued. He recognized distant sounds and his night vision sharpened, extending his range of sight. It was as if he'd been bundled head to toe in thick furs and had flung them off.

"You okay?" Zebulon asked.

"Yes." He focused on the flames, blocking the extra sensations. Then he addressed his brother. "The answer to your first question is also yes. I can handle it."

"Good." Zebulon laid another branch onto the fire. Then he met Valek's gaze. "I'm not sure I can. I'm pissed at Father for not telling us, but if everyone knew, we'd be targets."

"Which is why you're not going to tell anyone. This little visit—" Valek's hand traced a circle in the air "—is me checking that you don't have magical powers before I drag the twins to the Castle, where they will be executed. Understand?"

"Yes. And you need to understand that just because we have the same parents doesn't make us *brothers*."

"I know. We're strangers." He glanced at the graves. "We haven't ruined the laundry together or planned a prank or snuck out late at night or hidden from Father when he was furious. Those experiences are what forges a relationship."

"Yeah, and I'm too old to hide from Father."

Valek quirked an eyebrow at him. "Really? You don't suddenly find somewhere else to be when he wants to clean out the acid vat?"

Zebulon laughed. "True." He played with the shoelaces on his scuffed and worn boots. "You're not what I expected. Mother had us so worried when Zee's and Zo's magic started doing crazy things. We'd thought you'd arrive with an army and kill us all."

"Reputations are interesting creatures. I've nurtured mine so that most people fear me. They're easier to manipulate that way. However, I don't kill because I enjoy it or get a thrill from it. There was a logical reason for each one, and it was usually after all other options were tried or considered. I've no regrets over anyone I've assassinated. Some criminals just can't be redeemed—locking them in jail just gives them time to plan their next crime and hurt more people. But some can. In fact, a friend of mine was addicted to blood magic and did a number of horrible things in order to feed his addiction, but he pulled it together, turned his life around and is making amends."

"You have friends?"

He gave him a wry smile. "A few brave souls. Being with me tends to put them in danger."

"I bet."

Voices sounded to the left, along with the light bang of a wooden door. Valek sensed the twins and his parents approaching well before he should. Odd. Father fetched more wood and built the small blaze into a larger one while the other three settled around the fire without saying a word. Heat pulsed. Orange light illuminated the ring of faces, the family resemblance clear.

Valek braced for another emotional conversation, but his mother asked about the Citadel, the Magician's Keep, what the twins should pack and how much money they'd need.

He filled her in on what the twins would be doing. "Don't

MARIA V. SNYDER

worry about money. The Keep provides a stipend to the students."

Zohav hugged her knees to her chest during the explanation. She'd rather stay home with her family, but Zethan relished the idea of learning more about his power. If he'd known what he could do, those pirates wouldn't have stood a chance. This insight into both of them hit Valek with such certainty, it was as if he'd read their actual thoughts. His head ached with the ceaseless chatter and emotions.

Mother fiddled with the sliver clasp on her cloak. "Will you tell the Sitians they are your siblings?"

"No. Sitians fear and hate me as much as the Ixians do. They will be safer if everyone believes they are refugees from Ixia."

Mother frowned. "They had to get their magic from my father. No one else in our family has it."

"Yelena speculated that my immunity to magic might be a form of power," Valek said.

"Who is this Yelena?" she asked.

"My heart mate." Best to keep her status under wraps for now.

Zethan asked, "Does she think your immunity is a One-Trick power? Like Nell's?"

"It's possible."

His mother studied him. Her thoughts clear. Valek couldn't be that terrible if another person loved him. Unless she was a monster, too. "Tell us about her."

The pain in Valek's temples increased. Was it due to this strange…sensation…ability? With effort, he concentrated on describing Yelena's wonderful kindness and intelligence, and he ignored the extra thoughts, sounds and smells that threatened to overwhelm him.

"Why isn't she with you?" Mother asked.

"She's in Sitia. I need to catch up with her, which is why we have to leave in the morning."

"Does her family know she's your heart mate?"

Again Valek understood why his mother asked that question. Her desire to find others who didn't hate him might help her see him in a better light.

"Yes. In fact, her brother and father are currently helping me with a problem."

"What problem?" Father asked.

"Identifying a plant. It's important, but we don't know why. It could either be a poison or be used as a potential weapon." Like Curare.

"Would that be something we'd do as magicians? Help you with problems?" Zethan asked.

Both Zohav and Mother scowled at Zethan's enthusiasm, thinking the boy was going to get himself killed if he helped Valek.

Valek rubbed his forehead. What the hell was going on? Why were their thoughts so clear to him? Was it because they were family? Unable to answer any of those questions, he concentrated on Zethan's question instead. "I expect the Stormdancers will be very interested in you, and you'll spend your time with them. Those who help me have a great deal of training and skill. They frequently give up months of their lives to work undercover, and it's a dangerous life."

"Then why do it?" Zohav asked.

His gaze was drawn to his brothers' headstones. "Because evil is out there. We've witnessed its devastation. We know it must be stopped."

"And you're the only ones who can stop it?" Father asked.

"Yes."

"That's rather egotistical," Zohav said.

"It could be taken that way," Valek agreed. "It's still true, though."

"What happens when you're too old to fight?"

Valek noted the use of *when*. Nice to know his father didn't think of him as too old. "By then I hope the next generation will be trained and ready."

"And if they aren't?"

"Evil wins."

Considering the reception of his arrival, Valek's family stayed by the fire longer than he expected. After they left, he lay on his bedroll and stared at the stars. Exhausted, his head throbbed and he couldn't sleep. It was as if his skin had been rubbed off, exposing all his nerves.

So much had happened.

So many emotions.

Thoughts swirled in his mind, bits of conversation repeated, and he replayed his own reaction at Vincent's grave when he'd realized why he had avoided any mention of his family. What had happened to him? His senses had sharpened into a super awareness, and he flinched at every tiny noise.

Giving up on sleep, Valek stirred the fire to life. Perhaps a cup of one of Leif's teas would help soothe him.

It didn't.

By the time dawn arrived, Valek had gotten only a few hours of rest. He packed his bedroll and supplies. Concentrating on the task at hand and not the conversation going on in the kitchen, Valek saddled the horses.

The twins both carried a pack. His parents and Zebulon followed them from the house. While Valek secured their bags on the horses, the others said goodbye.

"We want to visit them at the beginning of the hot season," Mother said to Valek. "Can you arrange it?"

"Yes." If there wasn't a war between Ixia and Sitia by then.

"Good. We'll see how it is before deciding on moving."

"Smart," Valek agreed.

She snorted. "You make sure they're safe." It wasn't a request.

"Yes, sir."

"If anything happens to them, I'm holding *you* responsible."

Mortified, Zethan said, "Mother, he's not going to babysit us. We can take care of ourselves."

"As long as there's no pirates in Sitia," Zebulon said.

"Shut up, Zeb." Zethan punched him on the arm.

She ignored her sons. "And you bring this Yelena to meet us."

Another order, but one that meant so much more. "Yes, sir."

Mother gave him a curt nod, then she hugged each of the twins. Zethan mounted Smoke, and Zohav sat behind Valek. He clicked his tongue and Onyx trotted through the gate. Unlike the last time he'd left twenty-eight years ago, this time he planned to return.

Valek and the twins approached the rendezvous location four days into the warm season and eleven days after they'd left Icefaren. Eleven days of dealing with his super-active senses, the twins' questions, their thoughts and emotions, and worrying about Yelena. Was she there or not?

When they were half a mile away, Kiki's whinny shot right through him. Relief and joy to see Yelena infused him. Onyx broke into a run with Smoke right behind him.

Arriving with a cloud of dust, Valek stopped Onyx. Kiki butted her head against the black horse. Valek peered over her, searching for Yelena. Signs of a campfire and other evidence of camp littered the clearing. But no Yelena, no other horses, no Ari or Janco.

MARIA V. SNYDER

He turned stone-cold. "Stay on the horses and keep quiet," Valek ordered the twins. Dismounting, he freed his sword with his right hand while grabbing a dagger with his left.

One thing kept him from panicking. Kiki. She wasn't agitated or upset. A rustling sounded from the woods. He spun, then relaxed as his new senses spotted Fisk carrying a water skin. Fisk's presence meant bad news, but not immediate danger. By the time Fisk reached him, Valek had sheathed his weapons.

Before the young man could say a word, Valek demanded, "Where's Yelena?"

"She's been captured by Bruns Jewelrose."

A wave of icy fear washed through him, followed by a molten fury that promised Bruns would regret the decision to apprehend her. At least she wasn't dead. Valek focused on that, or else he'd lose the tight control he had on his emotions. "Ari and Janco?"

"Trying to rescue her and Leif. He was captured first and…" Fisk spread his arms.

"Do you know where they are?"

"Yes."

One bit of good news. He hooked a thumb in the twins' direction. "I need to take them to the Magician's Keep, then we can talk to the Master Magicians and devise—"

"You can't go the the Keep."

"Why not?"

"There's no one there."

27

JANCO

Janco touched his smooth chin for the billionth time. Gah. He'd had his goatee for years. He loved it, but shaving it had been part of his disguise. Janco's exposed skin tingled as if the entire garrison saw right through him. Plus his head itched from the red dye, and the fake ear made him sweat. One of these days, he'd impersonate a wealthy businessman for a change. He'd wear tailored silk clothing, expensive jewelry, be surrounded by a cloud of sycophants and... Who was he kidding? Grunts blended in; businessmen with minions did not.

Suppressing a sigh, he picked up a practice sword and sparred with a soldier wannabe. Keeping half his attention on the out-of-shape farmer, Janco watched the armory. Yelena and her thugs had disappeared inside not long ago.

One good thing about the training yard—no magic. Most of the outdoor areas were clean, but magic infected the barracks and canteen. He spent his nights sneaking into the various buildings or reporting information to Ari. The big guy remained on the outside to liaise with Fisk and his people.

Bruns strode toward the armory. By his stiff gait and the short swings of his arms, Janco figured he was either agitated or angry. Bruns entered the building and after a few minutes,

Bruns and Yelena left, walking arm in arm. They both smiled, but Janco didn't like it. Not at all. Something wasn't right.

He let the wannabe disarm him. "Sweet move, puppy dog. You're just too good for me. I'd better go find someone more my speed." His ego shuddered with the blow, but showing off his superior skills would be the opposite of blending in.

Janco slipped away from the training yard and followed Yelena and Bruns to the administration building. The two thugs remained outside. A good or bad thing? He wasn't sure. Finding an inconspicuous spot to wait, Janco kept an eye on the door.

To pass the time, he sized up the thugs and decided he could take them both by himself, if the ruckus didn't cause every wannabe to come running. The problem with this place was not being able to tell the grunts from the magicians. They all wore the same uniform, which was a sound military tactic. No sense letting your enemy know who to target. But his magic mojo failed to work as well here. The power flooded the buildings and he couldn't home in on the magicians.

They needed Valek. His ability to feel magic was more sensitive. Janco hoped Fisk would return soon. Kiki had only allowed Fisk to ride her. She had to be the one to go, since Kiki knew the rendezvous location and was smart enough to avoid the border guards.

Bruns poked his head from the door and barked at the thugs. They nodded and took off. Not good. Janco debated between following the thugs or remaining in his position. Footsteps sounded behind him. He spun, grasping the hilt of his knife and stopped.

"You should give a guy a little more warning," he said to Leif.

"I'm trying to keep a low profile."

"Aren't we all."

"Yeah, well, those two bruisers that just bolted are looking for me."

Concerned, Janco scanned the area for them. So far, so good. "How do you know?"

"We weren't as clever as we thought. Bruns caught on that we weren't eating the Theobroma-laced food. He just tried to use goo-goo juice on Yelena to get her to divulge everything she knows, but when I gave Bruns her darts and told him which ones had Curare, sleeping potion and goo-goo juice, I mixed them up."

"So Yelena is…?"

"Sleeping."

"And you know this for sure?"

"Yes. Hale used his magic to listen in on Bruns and Yelena."

"Then you need to escape. Ari's—"

"I'm not going anywhere without Yelena."

"But—"

"Listen. She'll eventually wake up and then he'll use the goo-goo juice on her.

"She'll blow your cover and tell Bruns about Dax and Hale's involvement. Tonight, the three of you need to leave. This is bigger than we can handle right now. I'll rescue Yelena and join you outside."

"Did you see the size of those thugs? No way you're getting to her without help," Janco said. "Where is he holding her?"

"In the cells under the administration building."

"Damn. There's only one entrance. We'll have to use the windows. It's going to be difficult."

"How about if I let them catch me during a rescue attempt? Bruns might think no one else will try to reach her. Is there a way I can hide lock picks or a weapon where they won't find them?"

"Brunsie is a smart cookie." Without thinking, Janco

MARIA V. SNYDER

scratched his fake ear and almost peeled it off. Aha! "Actually, there is a way that might work, if he doesn't kill you once you're caught."

"He won't. Yelena and I are showpieces. Bruns wants us loyal to his cause. If we're unsuccessful, he'll probably force-feed us Theobroma and blast us until we're mindless Bruns groupies."

"Isn't there an antidote? Can you use Curare to reverse the effects?"

"No. It doesn't work that way." Leif frowned.

"What about something else? Even poisons have antidotes."

Leif stared at him in shock.

"What did I say?"

"Those plants…in Owen's glass hothouses. They… We…"

"What? Spit it out, man."

"We thought the one hybrid plant was Vossen, but it might be an antidote to Theobroma!"

"Too bad you didn't figure this out sooner."

"Once we're free, it'll be a place to start."

"Start what?" Janco asked.

"The revolt."

Janco returned to the barracks and grabbed a few things from the bag stashed under his bunk. Then he met up with Leif in an abandoned storeroom. He mixed the putty, matching Leif's skin tone, and set to work. When he finished, Leif had a couple lock picks and a number of darts hidden under patches of fake skin.

"Don't scratch them. And don't touch the areas when you're being searched," Janco instructed.

"Got it."

They reviewed the plan to rescue Yelena.

"Dax will leave the compound during supper and update

Ari," Leif said. "Hale will meet you on the south side of the administration building unless there are guards. In that case, he'll rendezvous with you outside the magicians' barracks."

"Good. You might as well stay here until midnight. Bruns has increased the muscle searching the garrison for you."

"What are you going to do?"

"I'm going to finish my reconnaissance. There are a few places I haven't checked, and if you think there'll be a revolt, then we're gonna need as much intel as possible."

"Be very careful."

Janco huffed. "I'm Mr. Careful."

"Uh-huh. How many times have you been—"

"I don't count. What's past is past." With a wave, Janco left.

Blending in with various groups of soldiers, Janco explored the infirmary and the stables. Without Leif to secure untainted food, Janco ate a few pieces of ancient jerky from his travel pack. He chewed on it forever.

The canteen buzzed with conversation and magic. Janco's scar tweaked with pain. Despite the power, Janco thought it was a good time to discover where the unmarked door in the back left corner led. It didn't have a keyhole or other evidence of a lock. The knob turned with ease as Janco, acting as if he used the door all the time, strode through and closed it behind him.

He stood on a small landing. Stairs led down into a tight stairwell, ending in grayness. There must be windows below, letting in the last of the daylight. Janco descended, zigzagging from landing to landing until he reached bottom. As he expected, small windows set near the ceiling ringed the basement.

Glancing around, he spotted a collection of chairs, stacks of wooden crates, barrels, a pile of tablecloths and a mound of potatoes—an obvious storage area for the canteen. Footsteps, the scrape of chairs and voices filtered down to him from above. There was another door at the far end of the room. Janco wove through the mess and considered it a win when he only banged his shin once on a broken leg jutting from a table.

This door also opened without trouble. Too bad trouble waited for him on the other side. Big trouble. Pain drilled through his skull.

28

YELENA

Disoriented, dry-mouthed and dizzy—the all-too-familiar aftereffects of sleeping potion. My blurry vision sharpened, along with the ache in my temples. I wished I hadn't opened my eyes, but I couldn't unsee the bars surrounding me or unsmell the wet, mucky dungeon stench mixed with the acrid odor of burned lantern oil—another aspect that I was well acquainted with.

Perhaps it was time to reexamine my life.

Bruns no longer knelt by me, and I no longer sat in a chair, but was sprawled on a pallet of straw. Better or worse? I pushed to a sitting position and groaned as intense pain danced behind my eyeballs. Nausea rolled, splashing up my throat.

Resting my head in my hands, I willed my stomach to settle and hoped the repeated dosing of sleeping potion hadn't harmed the baby.

"It's about time you woke up," Janco grumped.

Oh, no. "I'm not awake. Because you're not in here with me. You're outside the garrison, rounding up the cavalry."

"I hate to break this to you, sweetheart, but the cavalry is hanging with Bruns in the canteen, quaffing down Theobroma and kissing his rich ass." The strain in his voice failed to match his flippant tone.

I swiveled. Janco stood in the next cell. Even in the dim lantern light, a bright red bruise shone on his swollen right cheek. His fake ear was gone, replaced by bloody scratches. His uniform was torn and blood stained the fabric.

"Is it as bad as you look?" I asked.

"Worse."

"Don't tell me." I scanned the small cell, searching for a way to escape.

"I'm all for denial, but it won't last."

"Ignorance is bliss." I ran my fingers through my tangled hair. The lock picks were gone, along with the set I'd hidden in the uniform Bruns made all of us wear.

"He's smart, Yelena. And pissed off."

I spotted a cup of water near the door. At least he wasn't cruel.

"I wouldn't do that," Janco said when I raised it to my lips. "Unless you want Bruns to be your master."

Stopping, I sniffed the liquid. Theobroma muddied the water.

"Can you say *hunger strike*?" Janco joked.

His words slammed into me as I realized that the joke was on me. I had to drink and eat for the baby's sake. If we didn't escape soon, eventually I'd consume enough Theobroma to be turned into one of Bruns's supporters.

"Where are we?" I asked, setting the cup aside…for now.

"I thought you didn't want to know."

"Changed my mind."

"We are in the special holding cells under the administration building." He gestured to the four others—one next to him and three more across the aisle, which were all empty.

"Special how?"

"This place is saturated with magic. I can barely stand it."

"Do you have any of your...toys?"

"No. They took everything, and the building has only one entrance. It's probably surrounded by dozens of guards."

Alarmed, I asked, "What happened? How did you get caught?"

In a rough voice, Janco told me about Leif's plan to stage a fake rescue and his own reconnaissance. "...checking the basement of the dining room and..."

"And?"

He leaned on the bars as if they alone held him upright. Alarmed, I stood, reached through the bars and put my hand on his shoulder.

"And," I prompted again, but more gently this time.

"And I walked right into a nest of nasties. We gotta start confirming dead bodies, 'cause I'd like to avoid being surprised and mind-raped again." He scrubbed a hand over his face.

At first, he didn't make any sense. I repeated his words in my mind, picking up on the significant bits. "Who isn't dead?"

"The brother-sister team of horror who was with Owen and Ben."

A cold knot gripped my insides tight. "Loris and Cilly Cloud Mist?"

"Yeah, them."

That meant Bruns and the authorities in Lapeer had lied. No surprise about Bruns's deceit; I was more concerned about Captain Fleming in Lapeer. Had he been bribed or coerced, and why the ruse? "Are you sure?"

"No doubt," he said drily. "Loris is living below the dining room. He claimed his sister is alive, as well. She's at one of the Cartel's other garrisons."

"Was Ben with him?"

"No. I didn't see him."

I gestured to his bruise. "Did they—"

"Nope. I turned tail and hopped right on out of there like a good little scared rabbit. Made it about halfway through the dining room before he aimed his magical mind mojo onto the soldiers eating supper. At least I managed another couple steps."

I squeezed his shoulder. "You couldn't have predicted they'd be here. They were reported dead by Devlen—a reliable source."

"And Dev trusted the captain. Which ya think would be an okay thing to do, considering all Fleming did to help rescue us from Owen."

"I guess that's a puzzle to be sorted out later." If there was a later.

"Yeah. Too bad I knew *exactly* what was gonna happen when they dragged me to Bruns." He shuddered.

And now his mind-raped comment made sense. "Bad?"

"Oh, yes. They know everything, Yelena. Leif's hiding place, Dax and Hale's involvement, where Ari's located... *everything*." His covered his pained expression with his hand.

While I wished to panic over the dire news, I suppressed the emotion so I didn't upset Janco any further. Pressing closer to the bars, I pried his hand away from his face and held it in both of mine. "Ari and the others are smart, Janco. Plus three of them have magic. They'll be okay."

He stared at our hands. After a long moment, he met my gaze. "What are you doing?"

"Uh...comforting you?"

"The pain's gone."

"See? It's working."

"No, not that." He pulled his hand free, scowled at the air, then grasped my fingers for another moment. Letting go, he signaled, *The magic disappears when you touch me.*

Like a null shield?

"Not quite," he said.

"Then what?"

Switching back to the silent communication, he signaled, *It's like…my ability to sense magic has been turned off. But when you let go, it returns.*

I concentrated, deciphering Janco-speak. *Like something is blocking your ability?*

"Yes, that's it!"

"Lovely." *I'm contagious.* I yanked my hand back and tucked it into my pants pocket.

No, that's a good *thing.* Janco bounced on his heels. *Think about it. If Brother Horror tries to read your mind, you can touch him and stop it!*

"I don't know." I considered. *Owen had no trouble using his magic on me.*

Did you touch him? Skin to skin? It didn't work on me until you grabbed my hand.

The horrific events that I'd been suppressing for the past two months sprang to life. Owen had tried to erase all my memories. Except he'd been interrupted, and the events that followed jumbled together into a blur of being dragged along behind him, then tossed onto the ground. Valek had arrived, and Owen pressed his fingertips to my forehead. His magic had sliced right through me like a bolt of lightning.

Yes, he touched me and almost killed me, I signaled.

Janco rubbed his chin. *Well…your blocking power was new then. Maybe it's growing stronger.*

Jolted by the word *growing,* I placed my hand on my abdomen.

Janco noticed the gesture and he grasped the bars, stiffening in horror. "You're—"

I pinched his lips shut. "Remember where we are."

MARIA V. SNYDER

He used the hand signals to admonish me for risking the baby's life and asked if Valek knew.

"Yes," I said aloud.

He relaxed, grinned and signaled, *Valek will bring an army to rescue you.*

If he can find us.

Not a problem. Fisk went to the rendezvous point to meet up with him.

Which Bruns knows about. Right?

His smile disappeared. "Right. I really screwed up." He flopped onto his straw pallet.

"You can't blame—"

He waved away my efforts to console him. I let him brood. Eventually he'd purge the guilt from his system and return to normal. Well, normal for Janco. Sitting down on my pallet, I mulled over our conversation and what had happened when I touched Janco.

Could the baby be responsible for my inability to connect with the blanket of power? Other female magicians didn't lose their abilities while pregnant, so it couldn't be. But I wasn't exactly like other magicians. Perhaps the combination of my Soulfinder magic and Valek's strong immunity created a void—an area of no magic!

I surged to my feet, unable to remain still. Perhaps as the baby grew, the area affected by the void also expanded. And by touching Janco, I included him in the void. Of course it was all speculation, and I had no way to test my theory right now, but it gave me hope that my powers might return once the baby was born. Considering my current predicament, I held on to that small comfort.

A clang of metal woke me from a light doze. Harsh voices emanated from the far right as a group of figures emerged from the darkness. Janco stood close to his door, his tense posture poised for action. But the group stopped before reaching Janco and unlocked the cell next to his.

The door squealed as it swung wide. The pack pushed Leif into the cell. I winced in sympathy as he hit the floor with a thud. By the time he regained his feet, they had slammed the door shut. And our chances of being rescued narrowed, along with my throat. I swallowed, but it didn't help.

When the group retreated, Janco said, "Welcome to the party."

Leif glared at him. His pant legs were sliced open, his shirt was untucked and torn, and bloody bruises marked his face.

"Are you okay?" I asked.

"I'd be better if it wasn't for Mr. Careful here," Leif growled. "Just couldn't keep out of trouble, could you?"

"I didn't expect to run into—"

"I know. They gloated about it as they tried to puree my brains." Leif ran a hand over his short hair, smoothing the strands down.

I bit down on a joke about his brains already being pureed. In this foul mood, Leif wouldn't appreciate it. Instead, I asked, "Did they get through?"

"No. Unlike Mr. Careful, I have strong magical defenses. Besides, it doesn't really matter. It sounds like he told them everything." Leif waved the ribbons of fabric that had been his pants. "They took my hidden surprises."

"Lock picks?" I asked.

"And my darts."

Janco slouched. "Sorry."

Leif jerked his thumb at the empty cells across the aisle. "Make sure you tell that to Dax, Hale and Ari."

"They're caught!" I sagged against the bars.

"Not yet. Bruns sent trained teams to round them up. It won't take long, since Dax and Hale have no military training."

MARIA V. SNYDER

"Ari won't be easy to catch," Janco said with pride.

"They have highly accurate blowpipes, remember? Ari can be the best swordsman around, but one well-placed dart filled with sleeping potion…" Leif spread his hands.

There's still Valek, Janco signaled.

"They're setting a trap for him," Leif said.

My head throbbed from all the bad news and from dehydration. I picked up the cup of tepid Theobroma-laced water and took a couple sips for a bit of relief. Both Janco and Leif watched me in silence. Their matching resigned expressions said it all.

Over the course of the next few hours, Bruns's hunting parties dragged in first Dax, then Hale and finally an unconscious Ari—one for each empty cell. Janco curled into a tight ball of misery, and I worried about Valek and Fisk, wondering if they'd avoid capture or walk right into Bruns's ambush.

I slept in snatches. Every little noise jerked me awake, convinced Valek had been seized. Ari groaned to life, groggy and surly. Explanations on how everyone had been apprehended were exchanged again. We also discussed escape, but Bruns's men had been thorough and no one had any lock picks or weapons. Rescue might be our only chance.

"No way they'd get Valek," Ari said. "No way."

"They have a dozen magicians that can weave a null shield in seconds," Leif said, shredding that last bit of hope.

When a loud bang signaled the entrance of another group of soldiers, ice coated my insides with dread. But only Bruns and a handful of guards walked in. Relief warmed me.

Bruns surveyed us while his men slid trays of food into each cell and added oil to the lanterns. No one said a word.

"You have a choice," Bruns said, breaking the silence. "Eat and drink the meals we bring, or not." He shrugged. "At this point, I don't care if you die of thirst. You've all been a pain in my side since the beginning. But know that after you've had a few meals here, you'll be welcomed to my team. And you won't be able to fake it, and there's no chance of recovery. I believe you're all familiar with the talents of Loris Cloud Mist." Bruns turned to leave.

"Is that why you didn't assassinate them? So they can work for you?" I asked.

"Yes. Not only does it make them grateful, but no one wastes time searching for the dead."

"You stole that idea from Owen."

"Yes, I did. And why not? The tactic has a little bit of life left in it. Of course, it won't work anymore." He swept a hand, indicating the cells. "But I don't need it to."

"Did you save Ben, as well?"

Bruns met my gaze. His expression remained neutral. "Eat your breakfast, Yelena. I told your heart mate I'd keep you alive if he cooperated. Don't go making me a liar, now."

It took every fiber of my willpower not to react to his comment. Instead, I said in a neutral—I hoped—tone, "Too late, Bruns. We all know not to trust what you say."

A half smile twisted his lips. "Fine. Believe what you will." He left, taking the guards with him.

Leif sniffed the food. "Don't eat it. We can last a couple days without food."

The enticing scent of warm cinnamon tea drifted to me. My stomach cramped with hunger. It'd been over a day since I'd last eaten. I lifted the mug and cupped it in my cold hands.

"Yelena," Ari said. He was in the cell across from mine. "Valek's not caught. I don't care how many magicians and null shields they have. Bruns does *not* have him." Pure conviction vibrated in his tone.

MARIA V. SNYDER

"Have you heard from him?" I asked. If he was close, I could wait.

Ari shook his head, his expression bleak. I calculated the distance to the rendezvous point. If Valek left right now, then it'd take him three days to arrive. Plus he'd need another day or two to figure out a way inside the base. Too long—I'd need to eat by then. I glanced at Leif, looking for guidance. Of all of us, he had the most medical knowledge.

My brother pressed his lips together, clearly unhappy. Then he signaled, *It's your choice. You can probably go another day, but no longer. Think about it. You can save yourself now and have another baby later.*

"No," I said as Ari gasped. He'd been watching Leif. I held up a hand, stopping Ari from voicing his questions about the baby. "I need another option."

"I don't have one," Leif said.

"I do!" Janco jumped to his feet.

The poor man hadn't said a word or moved since they had dragged Dax in.

Janco's hands almost blurred as he motioned. *Wouldn't Brother Horror's power not work on you because of that blocking thing?*

That's just speculation. I can't risk the baby.

You might not have a choice if we're here for a few days.

True.

"Can someone tell us what's going on?" Dax asked.

"It's better if you don't know," Ari said. He sank onto the pallet of straw in his cell. "Did you know about…that before you rushed off to rescue Leif?" he asked me.

"Yes, and don't yell at me. Leif and Janco already have."

Ari grunted, but kept quiet. I sipped the cooling tea. It tasted divine, warming me. However, I planned to wait another day before I ate the food. At this point, I didn't have any other options.

★ ★ ★

The following day passed in a slow trickle of nothing. Without a window, we marked time by the guards' entrance. Trays of hot food arrived, cooled, congealed and were replaced—three per day. I started eating after the fourth delivery. By that time, dizziness made it difficult for me to stand.

Leif made a few obvious gestures to explain to Dax and Hale why I risked being turned into Bruns's minion.

After two days, the others started drinking the Theobroma-laced water. They didn't wish to die. No one voiced what we all thought: *Where's Valek? Will he be here soon? Or has he been captured?*

Four days into our incarceration, Loris and Bruns accompanied the food. They stood in front of my cell.

"You're the only one who seems to have an appetite." Bruns peered at me in suspicion. "Why is that?"

I shrugged. "I don't have as much willpower as the others."

"Uh-huh. Loris?"

Instinctively I glanced at Loris, but wished I hadn't when he captured my gaze. Unable to look away, I fought against a heaviness pressing into my thoughts. I tried to jumble them, keep the answers from his reach like a mental game of keep-away. It worked until he increased his efforts. Then I counted numbers backward as Valek had taught me and recited lists of poisons. It only delayed the inevitable. Eventually, Loris's magic shone on all the corners of my mind, exposing everything. The blocking thing failed to work. Instead, a powerless humiliation spread throughout my body.

"And?" Bruns asked.

"She's pregnant."

While Loris held me, I was unable to see Bruns's reaction. However, through Loris, I sensed Bruns's surprise turn into cold calculation.

MARIA V. SNYDER

"Is Valek the father?"

"Yes, and he knows all about the baby. In fact, the two of them have exchanged marriage vows."

That statement triggered a wave of astonishment throughout the prison.

"Let me be the first to congratulate you, Yelena," Bruns said. "I'm looking forward to learning more about what you've been up to this last year. Is she ready?" he asked Loris.

"Yes. She's mine."

"Good." Bruns gestured to one of the guards. "Unlock her door. We'll take her to my office, milk all the information from her, then scrub her mind clean."

Right now I'd like to scrub the floor with Bruns's face. Loris laughed. "You won't feel that way for long. In a couple days, you'll be his new best friend."

"Gentlemen, say goodbye to Yelena," Bruns said. "The next time you see her, she won't remember you."

The door to my cell swung open.

Loris said, "Come."

The compulsion to obey pushed on my muscles, and I moved to his side. He broke eye contact and I almost swayed with relief. However, my body now followed his commands. Odd.

As we walked by Leif's cell, my brother said, "Remember Mogkan."

A strange way to say goodbye.

"Who's Mogkan?" Bruns asked, stopping.

"Tell him," Loris ordered me.

The strong impulse to divulge the information pressed on me. "Mogkan was a magician who wiped the minds of other magicians in order to steal their magic to increase his own power. He'd attempted to add me to his ring of power, but he failed."

"Ah, a little pep talk from your big brother," Bruns said. "Sweet, but this is very different. I'm sure Mogkan didn't use Theobroma on her, and she had magic then."

We continued to the exit, but Leif's gaze never wavered from mine. I hadn't told them everything about Mogkan, and with good reason. When Mogkan had attempted to turn me into a mindless slave, he could only control one part of me. Either my mind or my body. Never both. And I'd been eating Theobroma, except we called it criollo at that time. As for my magic, it had been a survival instinct that kicked in when I was trapped without options. Mogkan hadn't ever triggered that when we were together.

Could that natural resistance to Mogkan's magic apply to Loris's magic, as well? Leif's pep talk might just save my life.

The questioning spanned hours. It'd been late morning when we started, but now most of the afternoon was gone. I huddled in the leather armchair in Bruns's office as he grilled me on Valek, the Sitian Council, the Master Magicians and the Commander.

There was no need for me to talk as Loris plucked the information from my mind. Each of his forays for details sapped my strength. And the effort to prevent him from my thoughts only weakened my resistance to his probes. I transferred my energy to keeping that bit of free will alive and hiding a few important secrets. However, if this session continued much longer, I'd pass out from exhaustion.

"Yelena and Valek believe the Commander is planning to attack Sitia after the Fire Festival in Ixia. Which is about five months away," Loris said.

"Ah. Good to know," Bruns said. "Did they tell anyone else their suspicions?"

"No. They're waiting for more proof."

"Does she know where Valek is?"

Ha. I knew he'd lied about capturing Valek. Bruns lied with ease. I wondered who else he'd lied to.

Loris shot me a look.

You don't really think you and your sister are safe, Loris. Do you? You're magicians, and Bruns has made his opinion about people with powers quite clear, I thought.

Don't think you can manipulate me. I'm in control here, and I see right through your attempt to distract me. Loris turned to Bruns. "She doesn't know where Valek is. If he's not at the rendezvous location, she can only speculate at this point."

"And?" Bruns asked.

Black-and-white spots swarmed my vision, but I imagined Valek clinging to the ceiling right over Bruns's bed, waiting to drop down and kill him. A guess or wishful thinking? I'd let Loris decide.

Loris studied me. "She thinks he'll come after you."

Bruns considered. "It would be a sound strategy, provided I was the sole person in charge. However, it's a Cartel for a reason. Our plans involve a great deal of people, and my death won't affect it at all." He drummed his fingers on the armrest. "He's going to attempt to rescue her. We'll use her as bait."

I dug my fingernails into the leather as the room spun. Loris's grip on my mind loosened a bit.

"Right now she needs to rest and eat," Loris said.

"All right." Bruns stood and scooped me up in his arms.

I yipped in surprise. He carried me to a small room adjoining his office. No windows or other doors, but there was a single bed, night table and lantern. Bruns laid me on the bed and pulled a blanket over me. No doubt his gentleness was all part of a bigger plan. A bit of energy surged through me as I braced for his threat or warning.

"Get some sleep. I'll have a tray of food sent up along with your favorite tea. You must stay healthy for the baby," Bruns said.

"And a fat, juicy worm works much better as bait."

He smiled, but no humor shone from his gray eyes. "You think I enjoy this? I don't. I value life, Yelena. That's why we're doing what needs to be done in order to save Sitia."

"Your methods—"

"Harsh, I know. But we don't have the time to convince everyone the old-fashioned way. And it's a good thing the Cartel didn't hesitate, because we'll be ready to protect our homeland if the Commander's army invades us in five months."

"You're not the first person to think that, Bruns. Remember Master Magician Roze Featherstone? She believed she was protecting Sitia when she unleashed the Fire Warper and joined sides with the Daviian Vermin. Look what happened to her." Roze had been killed, and I'd confined her soul in a glass prison.

"I'm touched you're so concerned with my welfare. However, the reason Roze Featherstone failed was due to her reliance on magic and magicians. They're an unpredictable, egotistical and selfish lot and can't be trusted unless they're properly…indoctrinated."

"Indoctrinated? That's a fancy word for brainwashed."

"I certainly won't miss these little chats of ours when you've had your change of heart." Bruns glanced at Loris hovering in the doorway. "Command her to stay in bed until you or I give her permission to leave."

A heavy pressure pinned me to the mattress. The compulsion to remain under the covers drained the last bit of vigor I'd summoned. My eyelids drooped as Bruns and Loris left. The door remained ajar mere feet from me. But in my current condition, it might as well have been miles away.

Unreachable.

MARIA V. SNYDER

Voices woke me…later. I had no idea how long I'd slept, but my stomach growled, demanding food. I sat up. A tray of sliced fruit, cheese and ham slices sat on the night table, along with a glass teapot. Heat radiated from the pot—one of Quinn's hot glass pieces.

I wondered how Bruns managed to get one. Had he indoctrinated Quinn, as well? Many of the Keep's magicians had joined Bruns's ranks, but I hadn't seen the young glass mage among them. Perhaps he was at another garrison. It made sense for the Cartel to commandeer as many as possible.

About to pour a cup of steaming tea, I paused as a knock silenced Bruns and his visitor. The other man left and—

"Come in, General," Bruns said.

"I apologize for the road dust and mud, but Tia said you wanted to see me right away," a man said.

There was no mistaking that confident, sly voice. Cahil, or rather, *General* Cahil of the Sitian army. The man who had gone from my friend to my enemy when he discovered he hadn't been the King of Ixia's nephew, and the years he spent planning to retake his kingdom from the Commander had been wasted. Cahil had joined with Roze and the Daviians until the horrors of their kirakawa ritual switched his loyalty back to me, but we'd never regained our friendship. It was obvious why Cahil now reported to Bruns. Cahil hated the Commander and Valek and had been itching for a fight since he was six years old.

I set the pot down quietly, slid from the bed and crept closer to the open door in order to hear them better.

"…new information about the Commander," Bruns said. He repeated all the intel he'd stolen from me. "Seems the Commander might make his move after the Ixian Fire Festival."

"How did you learn all this?" Cahil asked.

"From a reliable source."

Ah. Interesting.

"That means nothing. Valek has spies all over Sitia. I wouldn't trust—"

"Yelena Zaltana provided it," Bruns said with an annoyance that bordered on anger.

"Now I know it's fake. She'd never—"

"She's in my custody." Again the clipped tone.

Silence. "Is it true? About her magic?"

"Yes, and that makes her just as susceptible to Theobroma as everyone else."

Cahil huffed. "She won't *ever* be like everyone else. Don't *ever* underestimate her."

"She is in our control," Bruns almost growled.

And then I realized, I'd left the bed despite Loris's order. His command pulled at me, but it'd been reduced to an uneasy feeling, as if it was starting to wear off.

"Then I suggest you don't wipe her mind."

"Why not? She's dangerous. You said so yourself."

"If she's cooperating with you, then use her. There isn't another person in Sitia with her unique knowledge of Ixia's security and the Commander. I'd bet she'd have good ideas about how the Commander plans to attack. Think about it. She's been working as the Liaison for years. Plus dating Valek." Cahil spat Valek's name as if it tasted rancid in his mouth.

"Not anymore," Bruns said.

A pause. A long pause. "What do you mean?"

"They're married and are going to have a baby."

I bit my thumb, waiting for Cahil's reaction. At one point in our relationship, he'd hoped for more than friendship.

"I see." Cahil's flat tone said more than his words.

"Now there's more at stake than her own life," Bruns said. "Which ensures her continued cooperation."

"Is there anything else?" Cahil asked.

"Yes. Where are we with the other garrisons?"

"We have taken over control of the ones in Moon, Feather-stone and Greenblade. Master Magician Bain Bloodgood and the Councilors have been relocated to safety in the base in Greenblade's lands. Master Magician Irys Jewelrose is at the Featherstone Clan's, along with the stronger magicians. We believe the Commander's army will head straight for the Citadel."

"Have the magicians along the border with Ixia reported any activity?"

"Not yet. They each check in at dawn via the super messengers."

"Send them orders to keep an eye out for Valek."

Another longish pause. "You don't know where he is?"

"He'll be coming here regardless. I'd just like some notice on the timing."

"From my experience, he's probably already here, hidden among your soldiers with a dozen of his corps. And if he isn't, he can cross the border without alerting anyone. If I was you—"

"You're not. We have the situation well in hand."

"All right. Then I'll go check in with the garrison commander."

Boots shuffled on the floor.

"Cahil," Bruns called.

I imagined Cahil looking over his shoulder with his hand on the door.

"Yes?"

"What would you do in my place?" Bruns asked.

"I'd put a big bow on Yelena and deliver her to the Commander. It would keep both her and Valek in Ixia. Plus she'd hinder the Commander's efforts. Yelena wouldn't want war, and she'd do everything she could to stop him from invading."

Actually, that was rather smart. Cahil had matured since I'd seen him last.

"I'll think about it," Bruns said.

The door clicked shut. I returned to the bed, sliding under the covers. After that charged conversation, I suspected Bruns would want to peek in and make sure I'd remained asleep and under his control. I lay on my side, facing the wall with my eyes closed, just in case.

A heel scuffed the stone nearby. I kept my breathing deep and even, only relaxing once Bruns's office chair squeaked under his weight.

I mulled over all I'd learned as I nibbled on the ham. It had a glaze that tasted Theobroma-sweet. It didn't sound as if Cahil was being influenced by Theobroma and magic. He might have volunteered, or he could even be a member of the Cartel. I wondered if Bruns kept a list of the Cartel members in his desk. Probably not—he didn't strike me as someone who made stupid mistakes. No, he was smart enough to ask Cahil what he'd do about me.

And I would be happy to go to Ixia. But Cahil also said to use me first. Not that I really knew the Commander. Other than his secret, I hardly knew him at all. The man was intelligent, cunning and had the brilliant strategy and forethought to plan and then execute the takeover of Ixia.

The takeover of Ixia. I clutched the sheets as I repeated those words.

The.

Takeover.

Of.

Ixia.

MARIA V. SNYDER

Holy snow cats! The Commander wouldn't invade with an army and wage war. No. He'd plan a way to take over Sitia with little bloodshed. Just as he did twenty-three years ago!

29

VALEK

"There's no one at the Keep?" Valek repeated Fisk's comment because it didn't make any sense. "Are you sure?"

"Yes. They've all left, and my network followed them to three different garrisons in Sitia," Fisk said.

"Why?"

Fisk explained about Bruns's Cartel using Theobroma to influence even the Master Magicians to join his cause. The magicians had gone to support the soldiers and prepare for when the Commander attacked.

Valek glanced at Zohav and Zethan, still on the horses but close enough to hear their conversation. Both wore worried frowns, and both their thoughts sounded inside Valek's head. Zethan disappointed they probably wouldn't go to the Keep, and Zohav plotting a way to turn this news to her advantage.

Combined with Fisk's thoughts, Valek couldn't think straight.

"Stop it," he yelled at the twins.

"Stop what?" Zethan asked.

"Stop projecting your thoughts into my head!"

Alarmed, they exchanged a look.

"We're not," Zohav said.

"You've been doing it since we left home."

"No. We've had our barriers in place, blocking magic from our thoughts."

"Then how do I know you wished you brought more books, and Zethan wishes he'd sent a letter to Rosalie before leaving home?"

Again their gazes met. Both bewildered.

Fisk touched his shoulder. "Valek, you're immune to magic. Even if they were sending their thoughts, you should only feel the *magic*."

Fisk was right. Valek drew in a deep breath.

"But I *was* lamenting the fact I didn't have time to write Rosalie," Zethan said.

"Have you ever heard another person's thoughts?" Fisk asked Valek.

"No. Sometimes I can tell what a person is thinking by his body language, facial expression, direction of his gaze…things like that, but not actual thoughts."

Fisk turned to the twins. "You have magic?"

"Yes," Zethan said.

"Can you try it on Valek? Something benign."

Zethan turned to his sister. "Zo can."

She pressed her lips together, dismounted, grabbed the water skin and unscrewed the cap. Zohav stared at it. Water rose from the skin, forming a ball that floated in midair.

Valek would have been impressed, but the fact that he didn't sense her magic, that the stickiness didn't press on him, had him quite distracted. The ball of water approached him and then struck his chest, soaking his tunic.

"Touch the wet spot with your hand," she instructed him.

He pressed his palm to the cold fabric. Zohav's eyebrows pinched together and the water streamed from his tunic and re-formed into a ball.

"Wow," Fisk whispered. "That's amazing."

"What is?" Zethan asked. "That she can manipulate water, or that Valek's immunity is gone?"

"Both."

"Gone?" Valek fingered his now-dry tunic. "That's...that's a big leap in logic."

"Zo."

She glared at her brother.

"We need to figure this out. Besides, he's—"

"Confused," Valek said before Zethan said *brother*.

Stepping toward Valek, Zohav extended her hand as if for a handshake. "It's another test. It won't hurt."

That wasn't why he hesitated. He feared the results more than the pain. But he feared not knowing just as much. Valek grasped her cold hand. A strange tingle zipped through him.

"I sense the water inside your body," Zohav said. "Zee's right. You're no longer protected."

Valek let go of her and stepped back. Unprotected? The desire to draw his daggers pulsed. He craved their tangible weight in his hands. No immunity? The words repeated in his mind, but they failed to find a place to settle.

"What happened to his immunity?" Fisk asked. "Did you two do something to him?"

"No. Even if it was possible, we don't have that ability," Zethan said.

Fisk turned to him. "Did something happen to you? Do you know when it started?"

"I..." Valek pulled his thoughts together with effort. He searched his memories. During the raid on the pirates, he'd been fine. The trip to Icefaren had been quiet. And then... the shock of seeing his parents, the surprise of learning he had three siblings... No. He'd had his share of astonishments over the years without any consequences.

It had happened sometime that night he stayed by his brothers' graves. When he'd talked to Zebulon, and Zeb had asked if he could handle it. Handle the fact his parents had moved past the death of their sons and resumed living. When he realized he'd been frozen in time.

The scene of Valek kneeling next to Vincent's grave flashed in his head. That strange, light feeling that had cracked the cold, hard ice around him. Had it destroyed his immunity? Yelena speculated that his protection was a null shield that he had grafted to his soul when he witnessed his brothers' murder. Did finally making peace with that part of his life release his immunity? And if so, what did that make him now?

"Yes, something happened," Valek said to Fisk in a strained voice. "I can't…" He held a hand up, stopping any more questions. Then he bolted down the road until they disappeared from sight.

Time alone might help.

He needed Yelena. Desperately.

Valek stopped and leaned against a tree. Emotions surged. His world spun as if he'd been set adrift. Was this how Yelena had felt when she realized she couldn't access her magic? Perhaps someone had blocked his immunity? Not likely.

Muted steps sounded, and then a warm, soft nose pressed against his cheek.

Ghost No More upset.

Valek jerked as Kiki's thoughts filled his mind. He stared at her.

She pushed on his shoulder. *Go find Lavender Lady.*

Yes. They needed to rescue Yelena and Leif. *Can you hear me?* he asked Kiki.

Yes. Ghost No More.

The horses called him Ghost because of his immunity. Another confirmation that it was gone, and in its place…

Magic, Kiki said.

Mine? Is that why I can hear you? Or is it your magic?

Both.

When he returned to the clearing, Fisk had packed his bag. All three of them turned to him, waiting.

"Where's Bruns holding Yelena?" he asked Fisk.

"No."

"No?"

"You can't go in there like that."

"Like what?"

"Open to magic. You need to learn how to block other magicians, or Bruns's people will seize you as soon as you get close."

"It's important to block others," Zethan said. "It's the first thing Nell taught us, along with controlling our magic."

"But I can still hear your thoughts," Valek said.

"Yeah...about that." Zethan grimaced. "We think you might be either very powerful or you're pulling too much magic from the blanket of power and could..."

"Flame out and kill us all," Zohav said.

Valek stilled. He hadn't even considered the danger. What else was he missing? "Can you teach me?"

"It's not safe here," Fisk said. "By now Bruns probably learned of this location from Yelena. We need to return to my headquarters in the Citadel and plan our next move."

Fisk was right. No doubt Bruns expected Valek to rescue Yelena and Leif. And he was in no condition to fight Bruns's magicians.

"Can you keep it together until we arrive?" Fisk asked, misunderstanding Valek's hesitation.

"I can explain how to build a mental barrier as we ride," Zethan offered.

He'd have to keep a tight hold on the…magic. Too many people were depending on him. Valek strode to Onyx and mounted. "Let's go."

As the others prepared to go, Valek tried an experiment and sent his thoughts to Onyx, *Go fast to Citadel?*

No response.

Kiki? he asked.

He not Sandseed.

But he understands you.

Kiki speak horse, too.

Valek stifled a laugh. If he lost it now, he wouldn't be able to recover his composure. He was already sure the repercussions from this…turn of events would echo for a long, long time. Mulling it over as they headed south to the border, Valek found a bright side. He'd no longer be trapped by a blasted null shield. Wouldn't Bruns be surprised?

This time, he laughed aloud.

During the two-day trip to the Citadel, Zethan taught Valek how to construct a mental wall that would block other magicians from reading his thoughts and influencing him.

"You tapped into the power source instinctively, which is why you're hearing our thoughts," Zethan explained. "First you need to locate that link, that thread to the blanket of power." He gestured to the sky. "For me, it feels like a current of air, connecting me, which makes sense since I can influence storms. Zo says it's like a tiny stream of water. Block out all distractions and focus. Tell me when you've found it."

Valek concentrated. He smothered his worries, strangled his anxiety and silenced his doubts. In the resulting calm, a river of energy flooded him. "Got it."

"What does it resemble?" Zee asked.

"A…flow of…power, as if spraying from a pipe." Valek

struggled to describe the magic. "Almost like a bolt of lightning that doesn't disappear."

Zethan exchanged a wide-eyed look with his sister. "All right. Imagine a shield made of marble, or something that can block the lightning and protect you. Use the lightning to construct this shield."

"How?"

"Imagine you can grab the lightning and mold it into the shield."

Following Zethan's instructions, Valek closed his eyes, but he couldn't manipulate the bolts of power, no matter how hard he tried. Frustrated, he asked, "What else can I try?"

"I don't know," Zethan said. "It worked for me. What about you, Zo?"

She frowned at her brother, but it seemed more from habit than a real emotion. "I couldn't manipulate the water. Instead, I imagined my shield as a piece of leather and the magic as a dye that I applied to the leather, strengthening it." Another scowl—this one directed at Valek. "I assume you worked in Father's tannery when you were younger. Maybe that might work for you."

A good idea, except his power seared the leather and set it on fire—or rather, it did in his imagination. Leather wouldn't work. Marble didn't resonate with him, either. What could withstand the lightning and was part of him? What had helped him in his time of need? His daggers and sword—both made of steel. Yet that failed to work. The metal melted. What else?

Kiki jigged to the side of the road and a stone flew out from under her hooves, whizzing past his head. He almost groaned aloud, remembering the gray rocks he used for his statues. Envisioning a large hunk of the rock about the size of his head, Valek used the lightning to carve the piece into a black helmet with specks of silver that would protect him from magic. When he finished, he strapped the helmet on and peace descended.

"Better?" Zethan asked.

"Much. Thank you both, and you, too, Kiki."

Kiki flicked her tail, but didn't slow. They were within sight of the Citadel's walls.

They looped around to enter the east side in case Bruns had set an ambush on the west side.

"But remember, if a magician is more powerful than you and he has the ability to read minds, you're screwed. He'll grind that wall into dust." Zethan twisted his fist into his palm, demonstrating.

"You and Zohav don't have the ability to read minds. Right?" Valek asked.

"Yes. I can't reach out to others. But if you send your thoughts to me, I can hear them if I let you past my barrier."

"Unless I'm more powerful and can break through?"

"Right. The same is true for Zo."

"Zee!"

"Relax, Zo. If we're going to help rescue his heart mate, he needs to know our abilities and limits."

Surprised, Valek said, "You're not—"

At the same time Zohav said, "We're not—"

"Nonsense," Zethan interrupted. "Fisk just said all the magicians are gone. Who else is going to help?"

The boy made an excellent point.

"My network of helpers," Fisk said.

"Do they have magic?" Zethan asked.

"No."

"Then how are they going to resist Bruns?"

Fisk looked impressed.

"It's not our fight," Zohav said.

"Nonsense, Valek's our br...er...friend."

Valek would have to teach Zethan how to keep a secret. That was the second time the boy almost slipped up.

"I already know," Fisk said, as if he read Valek's mind.

"How to rescue Yelena and Leif?" Valek asked, hoping to distract Fisk.

"No. That Zohav and Zethan are your siblings. Don't give me that look, Valek. Anyone with a modicum of observation skills could see the family resemblance within seconds. Give me some credit. Besides, I have much more than a modicum of skills. You have to give me that."

"I'll give you credit for knowing the definition of *modicum*."

Fisk laughed.

Valek's attention turned back to the problem of who would help him. The magicians at the Keep had left, but not all Sitian magicians stayed at the Keep. In fact, many lived in other cities. But according to Fisk, Bruns had been either recruiting them into joining his Cartel or drugging/strong-arming them.

"Fisk, do you know if there are any magicians not under Bruns's control?"

"There are a few in hiding, but they're too scared to get involved."

Valek didn't want to risk the twins—he'd promised his mother he'd keep them safe, but they might be his only option. Zethan's storm powers— Ah, of course! "What about the Stormdancers?"

"I'm not sure," Fisk said. "They're on hiatus until the heating season. Maybe Bruns missed them."

Valek hoped so.

They waited until well after dark to enter the Citadel. After they passed the gate, a young boy appeared from the shadows and approached Fisk. Fisk leaned over Kiki's saddle as the boy gestured and made quiet tweeting noises.

　　　　　　　　　　　MARIA V. SNYDER

Fisk's expression turned grim. "What about the escape hatch, Tweet?"

The boy shook his head.

"What's going on?" Valek asked Fisk.

"Bruns has an ambush waiting for us inside *my* headquarters." A hard edge sharpened his tone.

"What about your people?" Valek nodded in Tweet's direction.

"Being forced to feed and take care of the *guests* until we arrive for the big surprise." Fisk's disgust was clear. He held Kiki's reins as if he'd like to wrap the leather around one of the intruders' neck.

"What's the escape hatch?" Zethan asked.

"An alternate way into and out of our headquarters. They haven't discovered its existence yet."

"How many of them?" Valek asked.

Tweet held up ten fingers, then flashed them again.

"Twenty?"

A nod.

He considered. They'd have the element of surprise if they used the escape hatch to get inside. But he still didn't like the odds. "Do you know if any of them have magic?"

Three fingers.

They'd need backup. Or would they? What if he allowed them to capture him? They'd think they were safe if he was contained in a null shield. Then they'd take him to Yelena. He wouldn't have to worry about sneaking in, just getting away.

"Where are they holding Yelena?" he asked Fisk.

"Krystal Clan garrison. About two days west of the Citadel."

"Near Mica?"

"Yes."

And north of the Stormdance Clan's lands. "Can you get null shields for your helpers?"

"No. Bruns stopped the magicians from selling them."

Damn. "What about the magicians in hiding? Do any of them know how to craft them?"

"One or two, but it'll take at least seven days to reach them."

Too long.

"There might be a few of those glass ones that Quinn makes left inside the Keep," Fisk said.

Tweet piped twice.

"The Keep's being watched by Bruns's people," Fisk translated.

"Has the staff left, as well?"

Tweet nodded, but then gestured.

"Most of the staff didn't go to the other garrisons," Fisk said. "Just the magicians."

"Do you know if Leif's wife, Mara, was taken?"

The boy shook his head. He didn't.

Valek considered the information Tweet had provided as he spurred Onyx toward the center of the Citadel. He found an inn with a stable a couple blocks away. After the horses were groomed and settled, he rented two rooms.

Fisk and Tweet followed them upstairs. As soon as they closed the door, Fisk asked, "What's the plan?"

"You tell me," Valek said.

"I'm not one of your corps."

"You could be."

Fisk smirked. "You couldn't afford me." But then he sobered. "I can send a team to check the situation with the Stormdancers and bring them on board if they're able."

"Good. And?"

"And you will visit the Keep and see if you can find anything that will help us."

MARIA V. SNYDER

"What about us?" Zethan asked.

"Stay here for now." He held up a hand, stopping the protest. "I'm going to need you both when we implement the rescue."

"You have a plan?" Zethan asked.

"I'm working on it. First I need to see what resources are available. Tweet, can you find out if Mara is still in the Citadel?"

He nodded in agreement and left with Fisk, who planned to check on his helpers. Fisk promised to return in the morning for another planning session.

Valek instructed Zethan and Zohav to remain inside while he visited the Keep.

"What if you don't come back or are captured?" Zethan asked.

"Fisk or one of his people will take care of you."

"And if Fisk is caught, as well?" Zohav asked, ever the pessimist.

He handed her a pouch of coins. "Then stay here. I will send one of my Citadel spies to keep you safe until I return."

"But—"

"Don't worry, Zo," Zethan said.

She jabbed him in the chest with her finger. "You said the same thing when those pirates boarded our ship."

He spread his hands wide. "And look how it turned out! We're in Sitia!"

"And in the middle of a…whatever this is."

She had a point. As Valek left, he tried to put a name to what Bruns's Cartel had been doing. Recruiting only worked for those who hadn't been coerced, or for those who were too scared to say no. As for those being drugged to obey, they didn't have a choice—more like a hostile takeover.

He paused. A takeover. Under the guise that it was in order

to protect Sitia from the Commander's army. But a takeover all the same.

Valek didn't like where his thoughts led him next. The Commander's hints of massing an army had never made sense to him, and he suspected Owen had influenced that decision. What if that was all a show? What if Owen had made a deal with the Cartel? The Commander's distrust and hatred of magicians ran deep, but what if Owen and Bruns conspired to demonstrate to the Commander that they could control the magicians, make them obey and show that they no longer had any free will?

But they wouldn't be content to rule Sitia. Once they'd earned the Commander's trust, or used magic to hijack him, it'd be just a matter of time before they removed him from power. Then Owen would rule Ixia, and Bruns's Cartel would be in charge of Sitia.

His stomach churned, pushing bile up his throat. Valek tried to dismiss his speculation as nothing but that—an exercise in logic. However, the inner intuitive sense that hadn't ever let him down agreed with his conclusions.

A wave of despair washed through him. He paused in a shadow, leaning against a wall. He didn't have the people or the resources to stop it. Plus, his life had been turned completely upside down. His protection from magic was gone, and he had no idea how to use the power. But Valek knew if Owen and the Cartel won, there'd be no family for him. Yelena, the baby, all the people he cared for would be eliminated, including him. Basic strategy.

He'd find a way to stop it. Or die trying. Giving up was not an option. He pushed the despondency away. Pure determination fueled his steps. He stopped by the safe house and reassigned his agents. They would also aid in the rescue attempt, but for now, he sent them to protect the twins.

Two watchers crouched in the shadows near the Keep. Valek sensed there had to be more. He scanned the buildings opposite the Keep's entrance, searching for places he'd use for stakeouts. Ah. Three—no, four more observed from windows and roofs.

Unfortunately, the Magician's Keep was surrounded by a high marble wall. The four towers at each corner that rose above the walls had also been constructed with the slick stone, which made climbing impossible. And with only one entrance, the place was well protected. However, when the Daviian Warpers had invaded and taken control, that protection worked against the magicians. Which was why the Master Magicians decided to build another entrance known only to them, Yelena and Valek. He'd aided them on so many occasions that they'd grown to trust him. And he'd kept the secret from the Commander.

He ghosted along a row of factories and businesses that faced the west side of the Keep, ensuring no one followed him or was watching. Satisfied, he slipped through a narrow alley, unlocked the third door on the left, entered and secured the door. Torches and flint waited on a table nearby. He lit one and revealed a small landing with steps leading down into blackness.

Valek descended. At the bottom was a tunnel that crossed under the Keep's wall and ended in the basement of Irys's tower. Valek reached it without incident. He climbed to ground level and extinguished the torch.

Letting his eyes adjust to the darkness, Valek waited a few minutes before leaving the tower. A half-moon lit the sky. He passed the empty stables and cut through the overgrown pasture on his way to the glass workshop, hoping a few of Quinn's null-shield glass pendants had been left behind.

The quiet campus felt abandoned and…dead. As if the life

had been sucked away. Perhaps it was his imagination. When he was immune to magic, he would encounter sticky pockets of random magic whenever he visited the Keep. Janco called it the Creepy Keepy because he, too, sensed the power. This time, the name certainly fit.

The door to the glass workshop hung open—not a good sign. He stepped inside and broken glass crunched under his boots. Even the dim light couldn't hide the fact that the place had been ransacked. Scattered tools lay next to overturned gaffer benches. Bent pontil irons and crushed coal littered the floor. Valek hoped the damage had been done after everyone had left the Keep, because worry for Mara grew as he inspected her office—it looked as bad as the rest.

If there had been any of Quinn's pendants left behind, they had been smashed or taken. Valek checked the armory next. All the weapons were gone. No surprise. Inside the administration building, files had been strewn into a chaotic mess. Bain's and Irys's offices had also been searched, along with Bain's tower in the southeast corner.

Disappointed and sick to his stomach over the destruction, Valek headed back to Irys's tower, cutting through the center of the campus. He stopped at the Fire Memorial. It had been carved from stone to resemble a campfire's flames. Valek almost lost Yelena during the battle with the Fire Warper. Many people had died in the fight, and their names had been etched onto a plaque on the front side of the memorial. On another side was a list of the names of those who prevented the Warpers from taking control of Sitia. Valek's name was among them. The one on the back only had two names— Yelena's and Opal's. Without them, the Fire Warper would still be a threat.

Valek touched Yelena's name with a fingertip. *Stay strong, love. I'm coming.*

MARIA V. SNYDER

When he returned to Irys's tower, an impulse to visit Yelena's rooms flared in his chest. Instead of heading down to the tunnel, he climbed up to the third story. And stopped.

A ribbon of yellow light glowed from underneath the door. He pulled a dagger and a small mirror from his pockets. The long, thin handle of the mirror allowed him to peek under the door without tipping off the person or persons inside.

The scent of wood smoke wafted out as he bent to insert the mirror. From this angle, he caught sight of a small fire burning in the hearth and a single pair of boots in front of the couch.

Too curious to leave, Valek straightened, returned the mirror and tested the doorknob. Unlocked. Bracing for an attack, he entered the room. A dark figure stood next to the couch, looking in Valek's direction, but a wavy translucent shimmer hung between them and made it impossible for Valek to identify the person.

"Uncle Valek?" a young male voice asked. "How did you… Oh!"

The veil dropped.

Teegan rushed to him, throwing his arms around Valek for a quick hug. "I'm so glad to see you!"

"What are you doing here?" Valek asked his not-quite-nephew.

"Waiting for you or Aunt Yelena to show up."

"Why? And how?"

"Long story." Teegan raced around and packed up his meager belongings. "Tell you on the way."

"The way?"

"Yeah. On the way to wherever you're hiding."

Valek glanced around, spotting evidence that Teegan had been living here for at least a week. A pile of books teetered near the couch. He couldn't leave Teegan here, even though it was probably safer than the inn. "Tell me when we get there. We need to keep quiet."

"Okay." Teegan poured a bucket of water onto the fire, dousing the flames. Thick smoke boiled up the chimney. Teegan followed Valek's gaze. "It's too dark to see it."

"But not to smell it," Valek said.

"Oh. I hadn't thought of that."

"Remember it for next time. Let's go."

Many questions rose in his mind as Valek escorted Teegan through the tunnel and during the circuitous route around the Citadel. Only when Valek was satisfied no one followed them did he head to the inn.

Teegan stayed with the horses while Valek checked the rooms. His agent waited inside Valek's.

"Report," Valek ordered.

"All quiet. No trouble," the man said.

"Good. Get some sleep. We're meeting in the dining room in the morning. Tell the others."

"Yes, sir."

Valek fetched Teegan. Once the boy was comfortable, he said, "Tell me why you were alone in Irys's tower and spare no details."

"Do you know about the Theobroma in the Keep's food?"

"Yes."

"Then you know why everyone went basically crazy, believing the Commander is going to attack Sitia and they had to help fight. Convinced of the danger, groups of magician and students took off for the garrisons until only a few support staff remained. I didn't feel this compulsion, and I thought it was because I'm a student of Master Irys and she must be protecting me. But when I surprised her by showing up for a morning lesson, she determined that I must be strong enough

MARIA V. SNYDER

to resist the magic, even with Theobroma in my body. Just like her and Master Bain."

Valek jumped on that bit of news. "Masters Irys and Bain aren't affected?"

"No."

"Then why did they follow Bruns's orders?"

"Because they didn't have anyone else but me to help them. Because they thought it better to pretend to be influenced and gather information until you and Aunt Yelena planned a way to stop Bruns's Cartel."

Such trust. Valek hoped not to disappoint them, but his main goal—rescuing Yelena—would come first. And then it hit him. "You have master-level powers!"

Teegan grinned. "I have to take the test first, but this kind of confirmed it."

Great news, except Teegan was only fourteen years old. Which reminded him… "Why didn't you go home and stay with your mother and father?"

"Master Bain thought the Cartel would be watching them, and it would be suspicious if I showed up there. Master Irys destroyed all record of my enrollment here, and she hoped the Cartel would assume they got everyone. Not many people knew I was working with her, and she told me to keep a low profile among the students. She sensed magicians would soon be under attack."

"So when Irys and Bain left…"

"I stayed and waited for you."

"What if someone saw your fire? Or decided to search the Keep?"

"I hid behind an illusion. Didn't you… Oh, that's right, you're immune, so you only felt the magic. If anyone else arrived, he'd see nothing but an empty room."

Valek had seen through the illusion. Did that mean he was

stronger than Teegan or that he was closer to flaming out? This wasn't the time to worry about it. "What if no one came?"

Teegan rummaged in his pack. "The Masters believed you'd come looking for these." He held up a handful of glass pendants.

"Are they—"

"Yup. Null shields. And if you didn't show, I planned to relive my days as a street rat and find Fisk."

Smart. Valek smiled. With Teegan and the pendants, they had a better chance of success. A crazy scheme to rescue Yelena and the others swirled to life. "Besides illusions, what else can you do?"

Teegan gave him a cocky little grin. "It'd be quicker to tell you what I *can't* do."

Oh, yes, this just might work.

Fisk and Tweet returned to the inn in the morning, and they gathered in a private dining room. Valek scanned the people sitting around the table. Two of his corps, Fisk, Tweet, Zethan, Zohav and Teegan. The majority were under eighteen and had no prior experience with subterfuge or fighting.

"I dispatched a team to the Stormdance Clan," Fisk said. "If there are Stormdancers who are willing to help, they'll meet us at the rendezvous location near the Krystal garrison."

Valek filled them in on Teegan's information. Relief touched all their faces when they learned of the Masters' resistance to Bruns's brainwashing.

"How many glass shields do you have?" Fisk asked.

"A dozen," Teegan said.

"Are there any more?"

"Not in the Keep," Teegan said.

Tweet gestured and piped a few notes.

"Good idea," Fisk said to the boy. "He confirmed that

MARIA V. SNYDER

Mara's still in the Citadel. She hired one of my people to carry her purchases from the market to her apartment yesterday. We can ask her if she has some of the glass shields."

"Was there anyone with her or in her apartment?" Valek asked.

"Are you thinking it could be another ambush?" Fisk asked.

"Anything is possible."

Shaking his head no, Tweet wagged his hands and tapped his forearm.

"She was alone."

"Good. I'll visit her tonight," Valek said.

They discussed possible scenarios and ways to infiltrate the garrison. Much depended on whether or not the Stormdancers would assist them, and if Mara had more glass pendants. The twins and Teegan consulted each other on what they could do with their combined magic. It gave Valek a few more ideas, which helped, considering everyone vetoed the plan where Valek walked into the ambush waiting in Fisk's headquarters and allowed them to capture him.

They formulated a basic plan, but more information needed to be collected before they could implement it. Satisfied, Valek ended the meeting, then he returned to his room to catch a few hours of sleep to prepare for another long night.

Under cover of darkness, Valek scouted the area near Mara's apartment building. No watchers lurked in the shadows. Just to be safe, Valek looped around to the back, climbed up to Mara's floor and entered through the hallway's window. Leif had learned how easy it was to open a window and ensured the ones in his apartment had extra security measures installed.

He debated using his lock picks on the lock. But it was late, and he didn't wish to scare Mara. Just to be sure, Valek slid his mirror under the door to check for intruders or ambushers. A small fire burned in the hearth and cast a warm amber glow on the furniture in the main living room. Seeing nothing amiss, he straightened and knocked lightly. After a few seconds, a shadow appeared under the door and an eye squinted through the peephole. He rested his hands near his daggers just in case.

The door swung open. Mara flew into his arms, squeezing him. "Valek! Thank fate!" She stepped back and blushed. "Sorry. Everyone's gone and I've been in a panic ever since. I figured all my friends and family had been caught."

He gave her a wry grin. "I'm not that easy to catch. Are you all right?"

"Fine. Do you have any news?"

Hating to disappoint her, he swallowed the sour taste in his mouth. "We're doing—"

A bang sounded behind him. Valek whirled with both his daggers in hand. The door across the hall gaped open, and armed men spilled from the opposite apartment. Almost twenty soldiers fanned out—ten on each side.

His comment about not being easy to catch had returned to haunt him. With twenty against one, they would have it easy. Valek, on the other hand—not so much.

30

LEIF

Hungry.

So hungry.

His stomach no longer rumbled, it *roared*. It growled and dug its sharp teeth into his gut, insisting, *Feed me!* He lay listless on the straw pallet, trying to ignore the scent of warm sweet cakes a few feet away. It masked the acrid stench of slop pots and body odor. For now.

Torture.

This was torture.

Worse than pain.

With nothing to distract him, he worried about Yelena, wondered how long he'd last before giving in, and wished for his favorite beef stew, and cherry pie, and Mara's pumpkin cake, and...

It'd been four days since Yelena was taken. Four days of sipping water and nibbling on a few bites of food to stay alive. Four days of silent discussions with the others about escaping. Nothing. They failed to find a weakness. A way out. Their one effort to grab the guards when they delivered the food had been a complete and utter flop.

By the fifth day, bouts of dizziness spun his cell, and his

legs shook when he stood. He'd have to decide if refusing to become Bruns's lackey was worth dying for. The scrape of the door roused him. Too soon for supper. He lifted his head.

Mara entered the jail with two guards on her heels.

His own woes disappeared in an instant as a cold knife of horror sliced right through him.

Leif surged to his feet and then grabbed the bars to keep from falling. "Mara..." His voice cracked in anguish.

Alarm and fear flashed in her golden eyes before she gathered her composure. She turned to the guard on her left. "You call this well? He looks half-dead."

"It's his own fault. He refuses to eat," the man said.

An odd exchange. Perhaps Leif was hallucinating. He certainly hoped the bruises on her beautiful heart-shaped face were an illusion.

Mara stepped closer to his cell. "Leif, you need to eat. No more hunger strike. Okay?"

Her sweet scent washed over him. "Mara, what's going on? Did they capture you?" he asked.

"Yes, but I worked out a deal with Bruns. He's really not that bad."

Another jab of pain pierced him. They'd brainwashed her, too.

"If I convince you to start eating, he'll free you. Bruns promised that we'd work together at the Moon garrison. Quinn Bloodrose is there, and I can assist him with his glass creations." She moved and reached her hand through the bars. "It's the best I could do."

He grasped it, twining his fingers in hers. Soaking in her warmth, he savored her touch as if it were the last time. "Sounds like you've given up."

"Bruns's men used the apartment across from us to ambush Valek." She bunched the fabric of her skirt in her free hand. "Valek managed to...kill a couple of them, but they

MARIA V. SNYDER

overwhelmed him. And I was…useless. Bruns is interrogating him now."

The news of Valek's capture slammed into him. Good thing she clutched his hand, or he would've collapsed from the blow. Valek had been their last hope.

"Start eating, please. For me," Mara implored him.

"All right," he said. "For you."

She relaxed, then pressed her face to the bars to kiss him. Her lips opened and he deepened the kiss.

"That's enough," the guard holding her arm said.

She rounded on him. "I haven't seen my husband in months."

"I've my orders."

"Fine." She jerked her arm free and smoothed her skirt. Mara turned to Leif. "At least we'll soon be together." Mara said goodbye and was escorted out.

When the door clanged shut, he sagged against the bars. A thousand emotions ripped through him. Fear dominated. Not for him, but for Mara.

"That was…unfortunate," Janco said.

For once the man didn't exaggerate. Leif glanced up. The rest of the inmates stared at him. No one said a word, but their thoughts were clear in their morose expressions. End of the road.

"Does that mean we're out of options?" Hale asked.

"Can we eat now?" Dax asked.

"Yes to both." Janco wasted no time in stuffing a sweet cake into his mouth.

Soon after, a group of soldiers carried an unconscious and naked Valek into the jail, dumped him into Yelena's empty cell next to Janco's, tossed a uniform onto his prone form and left.

Bloody, battered, bruised and with multiple cuts along his arms, legs and torso, Valek looked near death.

Janco reached through the bars and felt Valek's pulse. "It's strong."

They breathed a collective sigh of relief.

We're dead, Janco signaled.

Relax, Janco. Valek will have it all worked out, Ari said.

Valek didn't regain consciousness until after three meals had come and gone—a full day. He groaned and sat up, pressing one hand to his head and the other to his ribs.

"Welcome to the land of the living, boss," Janco said.

Valek glanced at them, then scanned the jail. "I think I prefer oblivion. It didn't hurt and it smelled better."

"Mara said you took a few out," Ari said.

"Is she okay?" Valek asked.

"Bruised and scared, but she said she made a deal with Bruns," Leif said.

"Good for her." Valek grimaced as he reached for the cup of water.

"Why do you say that?" Leif demanded. He crinkled his nose. There was something...off about Valek, and it wasn't the physical damage. Strange.

"It's a smart move on her part. I'd suggest you all do the same and make a deal with Bruns."

They glanced at each other in alarm.

Ari caught Valek's attention and signaled, *You're just saying that. Right? That's all part of the plan. Right?*

This—Valek gestured to his cell—*was not part of the plan. We were working on one, but it was in the preliminary stages.*

We who?

Fisk, his people and a couple of young magicians.

So we're screwed? Janco asked.

"Yep." Valek eased back into a prone position.

"Can I stop relaxing now?" Janco asked Ari.

31

YELENA

The past three days had been...strange or interesting, depending on the way I looked at it. Bruns had taken Cahil's advice and hadn't wiped my mind. Yet. Once he determined that my knowledge about the Commander was limited, Bruns no longer asked specific questions. In fact, my theory that he was just going through the motions of preparing for war strengthened the longer I spent with him. Which meant Cahil didn't know about it. No surprise, since it appeared Bruns had recruited Cahil and hadn't brainwashed him. So to keep Cahil cooperating, it would have to appear as if they prepared for battle.

I hadn't found any proof of my theory, but I kept an eye out for anything while I worked with Bruns on strategy. He planned to expand to the other garrisons in Sitia, indoctrinating them, as well. I hated helping him, but at the same time, the challenge kept my mind from imagining my brother and friends starving to death in the jail.

I'd been sleeping in the side room of Bruns's office and using the washroom in his suite downstairs. Every morning, Loris arrived and reinforced the magic holding me captive. Funny thing about that—for the next few hours, I couldn't refuse a command and I enjoyed the work, almost existing on an I-love-Bruns high, but as the day wore on, the magic wore off. From what I'd seen of Bruns's other minions, that didn't happen, and from the conversations Bruns had with Loris, it sounded as if once a person had been fully converted, they no longer needed to be influenced unless they had magic.

Perhaps I hadn't been fully rehabilitated yet. Or perhaps what had happened with Janco in the jail—that blocking power—had something to do with it. But I didn't touch Loris. Unless the baby really was a void and was slowly siphoning off the magic. My head ached with the possibilities.

The desire to bolt once the magic released its hold on me was strong, but I wouldn't leave without my brother, Ari, Janco, Dax and Hale. And I hadn't figured out a way to rescue them. Not yet.

On the fourth day, everything changed. Bruns called me into his office. I'd been helping in the armory that morning.

Mara stood on the other side of his desk. I froze in shock for a moment. No guards bookended her, and she appeared healthy, despite a few cuts and bruises on her face. Pure determination radiated from her—a side of Mara I hadn't seen before.

"You see? She's perfectly fine and has joined me. Tell her, Yelena."

"Yes, I'm assisting Bruns now. We have a lot of work to do in order to prepare for war."

"And it will be the same with Leif, if you convinced him to eat," Bruns said.

"He'll eat. As long as we can work together," Mara said.

He gave her a condescending smile. "Of course. I'm a businessman, and that was our deal."

Bruns called for his secretary, Tia, and asked her to escort Mara to the magicians' quarters to wait for Leif.

"It'll take a couple days. In the meantime, please make

MARIA V. SNYDER

yourself at home," Bruns said to Mara. "All meals are served in the canteen, and if you get bored, the cooks are always looking for help."

She nodded her thanks, met my gaze and held it a moment before leaving. Odd. The entire exchange was odd. Did I dare hope this was part of a larger scheme?

"You should be happy, Yelena. Now your brother won't die of starvation."

"I am."

"But?"

"You didn't seem to care if he lived or died before."

"Ah, true. However, working with you these last few days has made me realize why you, Leif and the others locked below have been so successful all these years. The level of intelligence is impressive. Now all I need is for Valek to break, and the Commander won't stand a chance."

"Excuse me if I don't believe you have him."

"Figured you'd say that. When we're done with him, I'll let you visit."

"Mighty nice of you." I gave him a tepid smile, but inside, worry bubbled. Bruns appeared way too smug to be lying.

He laughed. "Return to the armory. The Weapons Master is excited about your ideas. When you're finished, come back here."

Being in the armory had its advantages—access to weapons was at the top of the list. I stole darts filled with Curare and hid them in my clothes and room. Bruns never specifically said I couldn't. He was confident that his order not to escape included scheming, but it didn't.

At night, when the magic wore off, I could sneak down to the jail, disable the guards and free my brother and the others—I refused to believe Bruns had Valek. Denial kept me functioning.

Rescuing them from the jail would be easy. The hard part

would be leaving the garrison. Every entrance was well protected, soldiers patrolled around the buildings and magical alarms had been set on the walls. I could take Bruns hostage, put a knife to his throat and use him to get my friends released. Except it would only take one dart filled with Curare to neutralize me.

I sparked on another plan the morning of my sixth day. Simple, yet it just might work, if I had enough time to prepare. It would depend on when Loris intended to brainwash Leif and the others. I suspected soon. But it was the best plan I had so far.

That afternoon, Bruns ordered me to accompany him to the jail. By the way his chest puffed out and his eyes gleamed with glee, I assumed my days of denial were coming to an abrupt end.

When we entered, the first thing to hit me was the smell. After more than a week without bathing, the men reeked. I met Leif's gaze. He stood next to the door to his cell. He'd lost weight.

"You okay?" he asked.

I nodded. "You?"

"Fine. The food could be better, though."

Ah. They were eating. *Has Loris been here?* I signaled.

Not yet.

One positive. I moved on, and Janco gave me a halfhearted smile. And he might have said something, but my attention focused on Valek. His complexion made the color white look dingy. He clutched the bars, and from the purple bruises on his face and the gash on his forehead, I wouldn't be surprised if they supported his weight, as well. The desire to wrap him in my arms and heal him pulsed deep within me.

Unable to do either, I stood frozen while my heart dissolved. Valek kept his expression flat, but a blast of emotion

MARIA V. SNYDER

pierced me when he met my gaze. I thought his voice sounded in my head, saying, *Sorry, love.* But I dismissed it as just my imagination. He wore a Sitian uniform like the others. Blood stained the fabric in more than a few places.

"Believe me now?" Bruns asked.

"Yes." Time to put on a show. I turned to him. "Why didn't you just prick him with goo-goo juice to make him talk? He has vital information about the Commander we can use."

"I did. It failed to work and so did torture."

It took all my self-control to stay put and not kick Bruns in the nuts.

"Next up. Threats." Bruns turned to Valek, who faced him. "Yelena, tell your *husband* what you've been doing these last few days."

"Helping you."

"Why?"

"Because we need to prepare for the Commander's attack," I said, while I signaled with the hand Bruns couldn't see—but Janco and Leif could. *Because I've no choice, you prick.*

"You follow my orders. Is that correct?" Bruns asked.

"Yes."

Bruns pulled a glass vial from his pocket. "Hold this." He handed it to me. "Don't drop it."

A pretty, deep purple liquid filled the container.

"It's an extract from the amethyst flower," Bruns explained. "It will kill the baby."

My grip tightened. All I could do. It was still early, and Loris's magic controlled my movements. But it didn't stop the panicked screaming inside my head.

"Drink it," he ordered me.

Terrified and unable to resist, I pulled the cork from the bottle and raised the rim to my lips.

"Stop," Valek growled.

"Stop," Bruns echoed to me.

The vial paused a few inches from my mouth. My blood slammed through my body as if I'd run for miles.

"You'll cooperate fully?" he asked Valek.

"Yes."

"Good. Yelena, put the stopper back in and keep that vial with you at all times. Understand?"

"Yes." Happy to comply, I shoved the cursed liquid into my pocket and out of sight. Purple was now an evil color.

"Eat," Bruns told Valek. "We'll have a chat when you've had some more time to recover. Any hint of trouble, and I'll order your wife to drink the extract. If I'm not happy with your answers or if I discover you lied, I'll—"

"I said I'd cooperate." There was a hard edge to Valek's voice.

"You better. The life of your child depends on it." Bruns strode away.

I stepped close to the bars, reached through and lightly pressed my hand to Valek's bruised cheek. He covered my hand with his own. His gaze showed his love as he turned his head and kissed my palm.

"Yelena, come," Bruns barked.

Leaving Valek caused me physical pain, as if my heart had been ripped from my chest. I followed Bruns, but glanced back when we reached the door. Valek watched me, and so did my brother and the rest. Their defeated postures and pained expressions matched. Unable to resist, I flipped them a thumbs-up sign.

No time left. I waited until Loris's magic ebbed, then I rushed to prepare. I could no longer be subtle. Tonight was my only chance to collect the rest of the supplies I needed for tomorrow night's rescue attempt.

Using Bruns's name netted me a number of items I normally would have stolen piece by piece to avoid detection. I hoped no one talked to Bruns.

All the next day, I tried to focus on the tasks Bruns assigned me. If I looked too distracted he'd inquire about my thoughts. That had led to embarrassing revelations, but today a disclosure would be far more than just humiliating.

As I worked in the armory that afternoon, testing the Weapons Master's new ultralight sword for female soldiers, Bruns arrived.

"Put the weapon away. We need to talk," he said.

My pulse skittered through my body. I wondered who or what had tipped him off. Or if he'd spotted the blowpipe hidden in my uniform.

On the way to his office, he said, "Captain Geffers tells me you've been asking questions about the training sessions outside the garrison."

Oh no.

"Why the interest?" he asked.

I chose each word with the utmost care. "They're our first line of defense, and I'm curious how well trained they are."

"Why are you curious?"

"A company of soldiers is trained to fight an enemy army of similar size, and I know from experience that a small group or just one person can cause havoc with a larger group that's not prepared."

"You mean guerrilla tactics? Or someone like Valek?"

"Both."

"And you think our soldiers need this more specialized training?"

"I don't know. That's why I was asking Captain Geffers, to see if we should consider it."

Bruns tapped his fingers on his thigh—a gesture I'd learned

meant he was deep in thought. "Do you think Valek would train our units?"

"Yes."

"But can I trust him?"

"Yes. He'd do anything to keep us safe."

"That's what worries me. With his immunity, he won't be influenced by the Theobroma."

"He gave his word to cooperate. That is more binding than magical coercion."

Bruns studied my expression. "Good to know."

He appeared satisfied with my answers, and I relaxed. When we reached his office, my fear returned in a rush. Ben Moon lounged on the visitor chair, waiting for us.

"I thought Owen ordered you to kill her," Ben said.

Ah, confirmation that Bruns was working with Owen. Being right didn't make me feel any better. In fact, my hopes of stopping the Sitian takeover plunged. Even if we escaped, we didn't have enough people or resources.

Bruns scowled at Ben. "I don't take orders from Owen." Then he glanced at me. "Are you surprised about Owen?"

"No."

"What tipped you off?"

"When I overheard your conversation with General Cahil."

"But Cahil believes we're preparing for a war."

"Exactly, and I know the Commander well enough to know he'd rather come in and take over Sitia the same way he conquered Ixia. There had to be a reason he didn't execute Owen."

"And *that's* why I didn't kill her." Bruns jabbed a finger at me. "She's been an invaluable resource."

"I wouldn't trust her," Ben said.

"She's under my control."

"Yeah, well, Owen thought the same thing, and look what happened."

"Owen didn't take away all her supporters. Besides, he's doing pretty good for a dead man, and soon he'll be in charge of Ixia."

"For sand's sake, Bruns, why don't you just tell her everything? That's another reason she needs to die. We've been successful with this plan because only three of us know what's *really* going on."

"No. I need her and Valek."

"Valek's alive, too? How stupid can—"

"That's enough, Ben. They are my guarantee that you and your brother won't double-cross me."

"Why would we do that?"

"To have Ixia and Sitia to yourselves."

Ben waved it off. "I don't want either. Too much work."

"That's fine, but in case you change your mind, I have two very capable people to send after you."

Ben huffed in amusement. "And they'll obey you? Yeah, right. As soon as they're out of your sight, they'd be gone."

"Yelena, tell him."

I met Ben's dubious gaze with the flat killer stare I'd learned from Valek. In a cold, emotionless voice, I said, "Bruns, it would be our *pleasure* to assassinate Ben and Owen Moon for you." This time, the truth tasted as sweet as my favorite breakfast.

Fear flashed in his eyes for an instant, then Ben grunted and faced Bruns. "Just remember who told you to kill them both. Is this why you wanted to meet? To gloat that you've captured them?"

"No. Valek agreed to cooperate, and I thought you should hear his information firsthand. It should be very helpful."

"If we can trust him."

"We can."

Explaining about the amethyst, Bruns ordered me to show Ben the bottle. I held it up. Then the three of us trekked down to the jail to interrogate Valek. Ben fussed about the stench until Bruns glared at him.

Valek answered every question. The information he provided, while true, omitted quite a bit. Impressive, considering the battered state of his body and mind. The session ended two hours later when Valek passed out. I worried that Valek wouldn't be physically able to escape later tonight, but I couldn't wait for him to recover. Even with Ben's presence at the garrison complicating things, I had to risk it.

Bruns kept me by his side as he played host to Ben that evening. I endured a long supper, an even longer discussion on how they would use Valek's information and then was sent to bed like a child while the "adults" conversed about important matters.

Glad to be released, I lay in bed and reviewed my plan, seeking gaps in the logic and other possible problems. My imagination had compiled quite the list of things-that-could-go-wrong by the time Bruns and Ben finished their conversation and retired for the evening.

I waited a couple more hours. Near midnight, I slipped from my room and crossed Bruns's dark office. I grabbed the doorknob.

"Bruns really is an idiot." Ben's voice pierced the darkness.

My breath locked as fear coiled around my body. I turned. "I was just—"

"Save it. I don't care what you were about to do. The fact that you can do it, despite Loris's magic, should be a surprise, but I've learned my lesson. Do you want to know what that lesson is?" Ben stepped from the shadows.

"No."

"Too bad, 'cause I'm going to tell you anyway. I've learned to never, ever underestimate you. And to never assume anything." He moved closer.

A strange weakness flushed through me.

"You've been consuming the Theobroma," Ben said. "So why isn't the magic working? Let's see…"

The compulsion to sit in Bruns's visitor's chair pressed on me. My body obeyed before my mind gave the command. Panic pulsed and urged me to run, scream or fight back. All was ignored.

"Goody. My magic works on you." He pulled a dagger from a sheath on his belt and stood in front of me. "I've imagined stabbing this knife into you a million times." Ben crouched down to my eye level. He poked my stomach with the blade's tip.

The pain failed to register over the sheer terror that gripped me.

"However, I think it'll be so much more fun watching you slice yourself to ribbons before you cut your own throat." Ben offered me the weapon. "Take it."

Unable to resist, I reached for the hilt. My fingers brushed Ben's as I wrapped my right hand around the hilt. In that instant, the compulsions disappeared. Without thinking, I grabbed his wrist with my left hand and hundreds of hours of knife-defense training kicked in.

I thrust forward, unbalancing Ben. He fell back on his butt as I sprang from the seat and followed him. Turning the knife around, I didn't hesitate to plunge the blade into his stomach, aiming the tip up to his heart, killing him.

It was brutal and ruthless. It was necessary to save myself and the baby. It was just what Ben wished to do to me—erase a problem permanently.

Should I be upset by the warm blood gushing over my

hands? By the final painful exhalation from my victim? By the stench of body fluids pooling under his dead body?

Yes—taking a life was never easy, no matter the circumstances.

But did I regret it?

No.

After I cleaned up, I filled a bucket with water and grabbed the basket full of soap, washcloths and clean uniforms I'd assembled and hidden in a supply closet. I carried them down to the jail. Now wasn't the time to worry about what could go wrong. There were two sets of doors and four guards between me and my family. Now was the time for action.

"What's this?" the soldier on the left asked when he spotted me lumbering toward him with my heavy load.

"Bruns wants the prisoners to wash up before the morning," I said.

"Now? It's the middle of the night."

"I don't question orders," I said. My tone indicated that he shouldn't, either.

"All right, give them here."

I handed the bucket and basket to him as his partner unlocked the door.

"Make sure they all clean up," I said.

"Yeah, yeah. We'll take care of it."

I left, but didn't go far. The second set of guards also grumbled about the time. While they transferred the items to the inner guards, I drew a blowpipe from my tunic and a handful of darts with extra-long needles. Loading the first one, I aimed.

With a sharp puff of air, I shot the closest man. It hit his arm, piercing the fabric. By the time he jerked with surprise, I launched another. Then in quick succession I hit the other two.

The Curare worked fast and, with only a minimal amount of yelling, they toppled to the ground, paralyzed. Sweet.

I tucked the blowpipe back in my tunic. It was a keeper. The rifling in its barrel had improved even my terrible aim. Take that, Janco!

Grabbing the keys, I unlocked the inner doors. I stepped into the lantern light and everyone turned guarded and worried expressions on me.

"You ready to get out of here?" I asked.

Smiles all around and a whoop from Janco. I moved from cell to cell, freeing them. Valek pulled me into a tight embrace. I closed my eyes and allowed myself a moment of comfort in his arms.

"How?" he whispered.

"Later," I promised. "Are you strong enough?"

"Yes." He released me.

"Good."

"What's the plan?" Janco asked.

I pointed to the bucket of water, which remained upright, and to the basket, which had spilled, scattering clothes onto the floor. "Clean up and change quick. Leif, can you and Hale weave null shields into the uniforms?"

"What about Mara?" Leif asked.

"Janco will fetch her. Do his uniform first."

Janco stripped off his shirt. "Where is she?"

I told him. "Tell her you're taking her to Leif. That we're all working for Bruns now and are leaving for an important and secret mission."

Leif found a uniform sized for Janco and concentrated on building a null shield on the shirt. Hale picked up another while Janco washed up. I turned my back when Janco yanked off his pants, giving them some privacy.

They didn't waste any time or energy asking me questions.

Their unconditional trust that I had it all worked out warmed me and terrified me at the same time.

Once Janco was dressed and ready, I said, "Meet us near the entrance of the main barracks. A platoon of soldiers are scheduled for nighttime maneuvers outside the garrison, and we need to join them before they leave."

"Got it." Janco touched his hip. "Weapons?"

"Take one of the guards'."

Janco stripped the men of their swords.

"Give Ari, Leif and Dax the others."

"What about me, love?" Valek stepped into my view. He sponged grime off his neck and bare torso. Large bruises stained his skin. Bright red cuts oozed blood.

Concentrating on the task at hand and not Valek's battered body, I pulled Ben's knife from my boot and gave it to him. His eyes gleamed as he appraised the quality of the blade.

"And me?" Hale asked.

"I hid a few more weapons near the barracks," I said.

Janco left to collect Mara.

"We only need to put null shields on three uniforms," Leif said. "Hale and I can erect ones around ourselves. Plus we can drop them just in case we need to use magic."

"Good, that will save time," I said.

"I need one," Valek said in a tight voice.

I spun around. Everyone stared at Valek.

"Just do it," he said to Leif. "I'll explain later."

"Uh… Yelena," Ari said.

Oh. Half-naked men. Right. I turned, but my mind kept whirling. Why would Valek need a null shield? No logical answer formed, and soon the men were ready to go.

I led them from the jail and along a route I'd scouted that kept us in the shadows. Except for the patrols, the garrison re-

MARIA V. SNYDER

mained quiet. We stopped to grab the weapons before reaching our destination.

Unlike the rest of the garrison, activity and light spilled from the main barracks as soldiers prepped for their training mission and gathered outside. We waited nearby. My heart tapped a fast rhythm in my chest, sending pulses of fear along my extremities. Where were Janco and Mara? If we were caught, there'd be no second chance to escape.

Valek laced his fingers in mine. Comforted by the gesture, I squeezed his hand. But then I remembered what had happened with Ben. My touch had blocked Ben's magic. Would it do the same to Valek and remove his null-shield protection? I let go and shook my head at his questioning glance. If we escaped, we had much to discuss.

A commanding officer called the milling soldiers to order. They formed ranks. Come on, Janco. We needed to join the company soon. Very soon. What if they didn't show? Would I be able to leave without them?

Yes. For the baby, and for the others. This was the last opportunity for all of us.

My stomach twisted with pain as I gestured for us to leave our hiding spot. Leif and Ari refused to move. Stubborn, sweet idiots.

Then Leif faced the wrong direction. About to grab his arm, I stopped. Janco and Mara materialized from the shadows. Leif wrapped his wife in a bear hug.

"Did you take the scenic route?" Ari growled at Janco in a low voice.

While relief pumped through me, there was no time for explanations or hellos. I punched Leif's shoulder and pointed at the company now marching away. We scrambled to join, lining up at the end of the ranks. None of the soldiers in front of us appeared to notice or care about the additional people.

After all, we wore the standard Sitian military uniform. Mara appeared content to march next to Leif.

My heart rate increased as we neared the gate. The guards had swung the barriers wide to allow the company to pass. Just a few more minutes and we'd be outside the garrison.

When the head of the column approached the gate, the commanding officer shouted, "Round up."

The ranks split into two and broke into a run. One side peeled off to the left and the other the right, but neither crossed through the gate. Valek reacted first, drawing his knife as the others brandished their weapons. The soldiers looped back, forming a circle around us.

Trapped.

Surrounded.

Ambushed.

It didn't matter what word I used to describe our current situation, or how Bruns had figured it out. No, what mattered was Bruns's next move. And he was smart enough to conclude that only one option remained.

Death.

32

VALEK

Valek kept tight control of his emotions. He scanned the fifty soldiers surrounding them, assessing skills and searching for a spot where they might be able to break through to make a run for the garrison's gate and freedom. Motioning to Ari, Janco and Leif to form a wedge, Valek pointed to the weak link—a trio of teenagers standing shoulder to shoulder. Must be friends.

Just as he raised a hand to signal *go*, torches blazed to life, illuminating the area beyond their circle. More men flooded into the courtyard, cutting off their escape route. Ah, hell.

He met Yelena's gaze, and his heart lurched to see her so frightened. Something must have tipped Bruns off, and he'd been ready for them. If Valek hadn't been thrown off balance by losing his immunity and gaining magic, he never would have been ambushed at Mara's. Plus, it didn't help that pain still clung to his ribs, chest and back, and the blows to his head clouded his thoughts.

The ring of soldiers parted, and Bruns strode into view. He held a crossbow with a bolt already loaded. Pure fury radiated from every muscle of his body. This wouldn't be pretty.

"I don't know how you managed to disobey my orders, but it stops now," Bruns said to Yelena, aiming his weapon at her.

Valek shifted his weight, preparing to push Yelena out of the bolt's path. He'd gladly be skewered in her place.

"Loopholes," Yelena said with a calm voice.

"What?" Bruns asked.

"That's how. Loopholes in your orders gave me plenty of freedom."

"And you think by telling me this, I won't kill you?"

"You need me. You know Owen will double-cross you."

"No. No more. You'd just find another way to sabotage my efforts." Bruns wrapped his finger around the trigger and squeezed.

Valek tackled Yelena as a sudden gust of wind blew through the garrison. Bruns's shot flew wide and slammed into Dax's chest. The tall man crumpled to the ground with a cry of pain. Yelena struggled to go to her friend, but Valek pinned her down, covering as much of her body as he could with his own.

"Stay put," Valek said to her. "Bruns is reloading."

Another whirlwind hit, kicking up a large cloud of dust and extinguishing a number of torches. Lightning flashed, followed by a roar of thunder that shook the ground. A second blinding flash ripped through the air, sizzling. The main barracks caught fire.

"Hold your positions," Bruns ordered above the noise of the storm and the panicked yells of his men.

They obeyed until the third bolt struck the administration building. The stone wall exploded and sharp pieces bombarded those standing below. Thunder announced the arrival of a deluge. Sheets of cold water rained down, soaking everything and everyone in seconds.

Mass chaos ensued. It was a thing of beauty. One of the best distractions he'd ever seen. With no time to admire the results,

MARIA V. SNYDER

Valek helped Yelena to her feet. She ran to Dax, kneeling by his side. Dax stared at the sky with dead eyes.

Another flashing sizzle. A wooden shed burst into flames.

Valek pulled Yelena away from her friend, despite her protests. If they didn't move, there'd be six more dead. Seven, if he counted the baby.

Leif had his left arm around Mara, holding her close while his right hand clutched a sword. Her confusion was clear, but it appeared her love for Leif overrode Bruns's brainwashing. Ari and Janco crouched nearby, ready to fight off anyone who came too close. Hale had disappeared, but there was no time to search for him.

"Arrow formation," Valek ordered. "Head for the gate."

With Ari, Janco and Leif forming the V shape of an arrowhead, Mara, Valek and Yelena followed in a line. The three teenagers raced up to their group. Janco and Ari raised their swords, but the boys waved their hands, showing they were unarmed.

"This way," the middle one said. "Follow us."

Janco glanced at Valek.

"Fisk sent us."

In that case… "Go, go, go!"

The trio led them to a ribbon of calm. It was a narrow trail where the rain did not pound and the lightning bolts did not penetrate. It snaked through the chaos and Valek wondered if they followed the ribbon or if it matched their movements. Either way, they drew closer to the exit.

Unlike the others in the garrison, the line of guards at the gate held their positions despite the storm. They braced against the now-closed wooden barrier and each one was armed with a crossbow.

Still unnoticed, their group slowed. Yelena pulled out a

blowpipe. That would help, but it wouldn't be enough to incapacitate them all.

One of the teen guides yelled, "These guys don't have the balls to stop us!"

Janco rounded on the boy, ready to berate him for giving away their position, but a loud wet splat sounded nearby. It took Valek a moment to decipher the scene in front of him. Huge balls of water flew through the air and slammed into the guards at the gate, flattening each one.

It clicked. Zohav! His siblings and Fisk were rescuing them! Zethan controlled the storm, and a Stormdancer must be responsible for the calm.

Soon the gate was cleared of defenders and they sprinted from the garrison. They had to get as far away as possible and find a safe spot to hide. As they ran through the dark woods, Valek searched his memory for possible locations, but the effort needed to stay on his feet drained all his energy.

So used to being in charge, it didn't dawn on Valek that the teens continued to lead them.

The night turned into one long slog. Cold seeped into his bones as his wet clothes clung to his skin. At one point, Valek realized Ari's arm was around his shoulders, supporting him. Near dawn, they entered a cave and they all dropped to the ground in exhaustion. Soon after, Fisk arrived with Zohav, Zethan, Heli the Stormdancer and Teegan.

Smiles, hugs and slaps on the back were exchanged. Then introductions were made. Yelena shot him a shocked and questioning look when his relationship to Zohav and Zethan was revealed. He mouthed, *Later.*

"You saved our lives," Valek said to Fisk. "Thank you."

"Except for the jailbreak, it was a combination of a couple of the options we discussed with you back at the Citadel. Plus,

I had lots of help," Fisk said, gesturing to the twins, Teegan and Heli.

"How did you know we needed you tonight?"

"My helpers infiltrated the garrison. They wore null-shield pendants to protect them from the magic. They noticed that Bruns had a man following Yelena, so they followed the man. By his behavior, we suspected something was going down tonight, so we prepared to launch the plan."

Yelena made a disgusted noise. "And here I thought I was being clever."

"You freed us from the cells," Leif said.

"And led you right into an ambush."

"It worked out," Janco said.

"Not for Dax." Yelena's voice quavered. "Or Hale."

Valek pulled her close.

Janco ducked his head. "Ah, I'm sorry, Yelena. I liked Dax. He was a good guy. And we'll find a way to rescue Hale."

The silence stretched as they remembered Dax.

"It's been a hard night for everyone," Fisk said. "There are bedrolls, blankets and supplies in another cavern."

They set up a camp. Valek tried to help, but Janco pushed him down on a bedroll. "Relax, boss. You look half-dead."

"But—"

"It's an improvement from almost dead, but ya still have a long way to go."

Yelena arrived, and all his protests died as she lay next to him, spreading a blanket over them. She rested her head on his shoulder and he hooked his arm around her.

"We have lots to catch up on," she said. "Are there any more surprises you're hiding?"

"Yes, but I'm not hiding them. I just don't have the energy to explain right now."

"All right." She snuggled in closer. "We'll discuss it after we're rested."

But Valek wouldn't be able to truly relax unless… "Janco," he called as Janco hustled past. "We need to set up a watch schedule."

"Already on it, boss."

"Good." But Valek's mind still whirled with all that had happened. And this problem with Bruns and the Sitian take-over was far from over. Oh, no. It was just the beginning, and he had no idea how to stop it.

Despite his dark thoughts, Valek eventually drifted to sleep.

Cries of alarm jolted him awake. Valek jumped to his feet with a knife in his hand before he even deciphered the trouble. Armed soldiers streamed into the cave. Their hiding spot had been discovered.

Yelena stood next to him. She muttered a curse and pulled a blowpipe from her tunic. Ari and Janco met the charge head-on. Their swords cut down the first couple of soldiers. Zohav and Zethan retreated to the back of the cave, along with Heli and Teegan. It would be difficult for them to use their magical powers in the confined space of the cavern.

Fisk engaged the enemy, fighting beside Ari and Janco. Mara huddled by the fire while Fisk's three helpers threw rocks at the soldiers. The melee appeared to be evenly matched, until more of the enemy arrived.

Swiping a sword from a fallen man, Valek moved to intercept the new arrivals. He wondered who'd been on watch and realized Leif wasn't in the cave. A part of him worried about his brother-in-law, but once he reached striking distance, all his energy focused on the matter at hand.

With his first opponent, he sidestepped the man's sword thrust, shuffled in close and stabbed him in the stomach. No time for finesse in this fight. Valek moved to the next soldier without waiting for the first to fall. A successful attack combined surprise, speed and intensity. Valek kept up the pace, but a part of him knew his injuries would eventually slow him down.

The clang of metal, cries of pain and smell of blood soon dominated all his senses, and the fights blurred into one unending skirmish.

Minutes…hours later, it appeared they had the upper hand. And that was when he spotted Yelena and Loris. When had that bastard arrived? And how did he get to her? Fury and fear mixed into a lethal combination and he stalked toward them, stepping over fallen bodies.

Loris held a knife to her throat and was retreating from the cave. He must have also figured out that the surprise attack would eventually fail.

"Don't come any closer, or I'll slit her throat," Loris ordered Valek. He stood behind Yelena, using her to shield his body.

Valek wondered why Yelena hadn't disarmed him. That move had been a part of her training. She even clutched something in her hands. The answer dawned on him when he met Yelena's gaze. Anger and helplessness blazed in her eyes. He stopped.

"Smart," Loris said. "Too bad you weren't smart enough to protect her with a null shield."

Ah, hell.

"Don't let him leave," Yelena said. "He's going to kill me regardless."

"Shut up," Loris said. He backed up a couple more steps.

Valek scanned the cave. Ari and Janco waited nearby. He lifted his eyebrows just a fraction. Then he returned his attention to Loris.

Tapping a finger on the hilt of the sword, Valek gauged the distance to the man.

"You're not getting out of here alive, puppy dog," Janco shouted.

Loris glanced at Janco. In that split second, Valek flipped his knife over and threw it at Loris. The tip of the blade pierced the man's left eye. He screamed and flailed. Valek shuffled close and disarmed Loris, freeing Yelena.

But before he could finish the man off, Loris tackled Valek to the ground and yelled, "Drink it."

As Valek struggled to push Loris off, Janco cried out. Yelena tipped the glass vial filled with amethyst to her lips.

"Don't!" Desperate, Valek finally broke away, lunged and knocked the bottle from her hands, but purple stained her lips. He'd been too slow. His world shattered.

Yelena's face creased in disgust. "Yuck."

How could she be so—

"I never liked grape jam." She wiped her mouth with the back of her hand.

Valek almost fainted with relief. "Was that one of the things we need to discuss?"

"Yes."

Loris moaned. Valek found his knife and slashed the man's throat, ending his ability to bark orders and his life. Then he pulled Yelena to him and held her tight, needing to breathe in her scent and just take a moment before he released her.

Valek scanned the cave, assessing damage. Everyone appeared to be okay, despite their collection of cuts, bruises and bloodstains.

"Pack up," he said. "We need to move to another location. This one's been compromised."

A shout from outside the cave drew his attention. More enemy soldiers already?

MARIA V. SNYDER

He, Ari and Janco raced to the entrance with their weapons in hand, preparing for a fight. The bright sunshine seemed incongruous to the carnage inside. A small group of people huddled over a prone figure. And then Valek remembered.

Leif.

His brother-in-law had been shot with a crossbow bolt. The wooden shaft jutted from Leif's chest an inch from center. Blood pooled underneath him. Unable to stand, Valek knelt beside him, feeling for a pulse. Weak. He sank back on his heels. Ah, hell.

Yelena's and Mara's cries of alarm roused Leif. His eyes fluttered open, focused on Mara. She crouched next to him and grabbed his hand in both of hers. Tears streamed down her face.

"I...tried to...warn..." Leif gasped. "...sorry."

"No," Yelena said with anguish, falling to her knees next to her brother. "You're not leaving."

"Don't think...I...have...a choice. Mara...I...love you." Leif passed out.

Yelena growled in frustration. "I'd give anything to have my magic back."

Magic! "Get Zethan, Zohav, Teegan and Heli," Valek ordered Janco, who hovered nearby.

Janco raced to the cave and returned with the twins, Heli and Teegan right behind him. Valek asked them if they could heal.

"No, sorry," Zethan said.

Heli shook her head sadly. "It's not part of a Stormdancer's power."

Teegan creased his brow, looking queasy. "I tried to heal a squirrel, but I killed the poor thing instead."

Silence followed the bad news.

"We can't," Zethan said. "But maybe *you* can."

"I…"

"Valek? What are you talking about?" Yelena demanded of Zethan.

Wordless, the poor boy stared at her.

The idea seemed ridiculous. He might flame out or end up injuring someone. Plus he'd never used magic before and had no clue how to wield it. But he was intimate with someone who did. He had to try, or he'd never forgive himself.

"Everyone except Yelena go inside the cave," Valek ordered. When they hesitated, he said, "Go now!"

They hurried to obey. Valek stripped off his shirt to remove the null shield Leif had attached, tossing it far away.

"Valek…?" Yelena began, but then she pressed her lips to-gether. "Tell me what you need."

"I need you to imagine you have magic and you're going to heal Leif. Think of each step and how you'd use the magic to repair the damage. I'll follow your instructions. Be very specific."

She drew in a deep breath. "Imagine in my mind, right?"

"Yes. Visualize as much as possible." He reached for her hand, but she pulled away.

"Touching me will block your magic. Tell me when you're ready."

Valek grabbed the bolt in both his hands. "When I yank this free, start."

"Okay. Make sure you press your hand to the wound."

"Got it. One, two, three." Valek tugged the shaft from Leif's chest. Blood welled, pouring out. He covered the hole with his hand and dropped his mental barrier.

Yelena's instructions flooded his mind. He reached for the blanket of power. A bolt of energy pulsed, and power flowed inside him. The temptation to grab it all consumed him. Bruns and the Commander's plans to take over Sitia would be easy

MARIA V. SNYDER

to stop. Nothing could match his power. Nothing could harm him or Yelena or the baby.

"Focus on Leif."

Yelena's voice sliced through the greed. With effort, he extracted a small thread and sent it into Leif's wound. He matched the images in Yelena's mind of stitching skin and bone together with that glowing fiber of magic. One thing Valek did know how to do—sew. The other assassins hadn't called him the King Knitter for nothing. As he worked, pulling thread after thread to repair the damage, the images in Yelena's mind faded. Valek needed to reinforce the connection over and over. It was as if another magician sucked at the magic he used. Odd—but then again, it might be normal. He had nothing to compare it to.

"You got it. Keep going," she encouraged him.

Healing a wound involved more than he'd ever imagined. Broken bones needed to be fused together. Muscles woven back in place. Tissue smoothed. Veins repaired and reconnected.

Exhaustion flirted with him, but he shoved it aside.

"Blood," Yelena said. "He's lost too much. You need to generate more."

"How?"

"Inside the bones." She showed him a mental image.

He seized additional magic from the blanket to keep their link, then drew extra strands to induce Leif's bones to produce blood. And when his own body fatigued, he tugged a few more to energize him.

"The color is returning to Leif's face," Yelena said. "His pulse is stronger."

Valek removed his hand. A livid red scar surrounded with black, purple and green bruises marked Leif's chest.

Relief, joy and pride pulsed through Valek. He'd saved

Leif's life. With magic! The power still rushed through his veins, as if he'd drunk too much whiskey. Valek worked on his own injuries. The cracked ribs gone. The bump on his head erased. The bruised muscles and all the cuts, sewn together. He hadn't felt this good in a long, long time.

"Valek, stop!"

Valek focused on Yelena. Worry and love and gratitude and jealousy swirled in her mind. And that…tug. It sucked his magic, as if he'd sprung a leak. Good thing an unlimited power supply was so easy to reach.

The magic filled him, and he wrapped it around his body, layer after layer after layer, protecting him. Valek ignored Yelena's sharp tone. Her fear grated on him, so he broke their connection. Now he wouldn't lose any power to that leak. He'd keep it safe. And keep it from everyone. Owen and Ben Moon and all those who used it to harm others wouldn't be able to hurt another. No. Valek controlled the magic now, and he wasn't going to share. With anyone.

33

YELENA

Valek gathered too much power. He was going to flame out and kill himself and anyone nearby. I had to stop him, but wasn't sure how. Panic threatened to jumble my thoughts, but I wasn't going to lose him now. I yelled for Ari and Janco. They rushed from the cave.

Pointing at Leif, who stirred, I said, "Take him inside. Tell the twins, Teegan and Heli to come out here now!"

They didn't hesitate. An eternity later, the magicians arrived.

"Oh, no," Zethan said. "He's out of control."

Zohav backed away. "We need to take cover. It's not safe."

"Can you bleed off the magic?" I asked them.

Heli raised her arms and a gust cooled my sweaty forehead. "Some, but he's just drawing more."

I glanced at the twins. "How about you?"

"Are you crazy? You're going to get us all killed," Zohav said.

"Yeah, we can. Zo, that's our brother."

"But you heard Heli, it won't stop him, just delay the inevitable."

"Since I'm still learning control, I've been augmenting Zo's and Zee's powers," Teegan said. "We can bleed off more magic that way."

"Good. Use as much as you can. I'll do the rest." Grabbing Valek's shirt from where he'd tossed it, I put it on and held the material close.

Valek scowled at me as I approached him. The null shield in the fabric must seem like a hole in his cocoon of power. The air grew thick and viscous, and I struggled to get closer. Valek's gaze darted to the magicians, then back to me. He crouched as if preparing to fight, and no glint of recognition appeared in his gaze.

Nothing left to do, I yanked off the null shield. Magic slammed into me. I braced against it as if it were a gale. I concentrated on our love. On the matching heart-shaped scars on our chests. On all our times together. On our baby growing inside me.

He staggered. "I can't…stop."

"Send it back to the sky." I took another step.

"I…can't."

I searched my mind for an image Valek could use. "The magic is an ugly gray stone. Carve it. Shape it into a butterfly and let it fly to the sky."

His black hair clung to his sweaty face. He swiped it from his eyes. His muscles shook with the effort.

"Do it, or we will all die."

That seemed to rouse him. His gaze focused on a distant point. I twisted the fabric of his shirt in my hands. If this failed, I might have to use the null shield to sever his connection to the power blanket. But the magic he'd gathered would be released like a flameout, killing us. Unless he managed to return enough of it.

"It's working," Zethan said. "Keep going, bro!"

MARIA V. SNYDER

Valek sank to the ground. He fisted his hands and his brows creased with pain. I moved to within touching distance.

He met my gaze. Exhaustion and misery etched on his face. "Can't...do...more."

I glanced at Zethan.

The teen shook his head. "Still too much. But he disconnected."

"Go inside the cave," I ordered. And when they hesitated, I added, "Now."

Zohav grabbed her brother's hand and pulled him along. Heli frowned, but she left with Teegan.

When they were safe, I tossed the shirt aside and knelt next to my husband. Perhaps what drained Loris's magic from me would work for Valek. Reading my intentions, he shook his head and tried to scoot away.

"Risky," he rasped.

"I'm not leaving you."

"Go."

"No."

"Yelena, wait!" Zethan ran toward us. "Leif says I can share my strength with Valek. You and Leif have done it in the past."

True. "But we could both control our magic. Valek—"

"Lasted longer than he should."

"No," Valek said.

We both ignored him.

"Come on. Let me try," Zethan said.

"All right, but if he starts gathering more—"

"I'll disconnect."

"What if you can't?"

Zethan gestured to the shirt. "Use the null shield."

A temporary measure, and one that wouldn't save his life, but I agreed. We had to do something. Despite Valek's protest, Zethan grabbed his brother's hands.

"Send the power back," I instructed, imaging how I would release souls into the sky, including the pure joy of it—a feeling I'd missed.

I waited a lifetime. Deep lines of strain scored Valek's face.

"No," Zethan said. "Take the energy from me."

After another couple of centuries, Zethan wilted, but held tight.

"That's it," Zethan encouraged. "Almost there."

Picking up the null shield just in case, I fisted the fabric. It wouldn't be big enough to cover both of them.

"Just a…little bit more." Zethan's head dropped as if it was too heavy to hold up. "Stop." He opened his hands and pulled back, but Valek clung to him. "Stop." Zethan glanced at me with wide eyes. "He's drawing power again."

Dropping the shield, I grabbed both their hands, hoping the blocking effect worked with direct touch. Magic sizzled along my arms and ripped through me. The force pushed me back. Pain exploded in my head and a loud crack sounded. Then it all disappeared in a snap of black.

When I woke, I felt as if I'd been struck by lightning. I groaned, and Heli helped me sit up.

"Not lightning," she said. "I promise. But probably a mini flameout."

"Valek?" I asked.

"Still out," Heli said, pointing.

He lay a few feet away. I scooted over to him. His skin looked almost translucent, and dark smudges ringed his eyes. I smoothed his hair and trailed my fingers down his cold cheek. Someone had put the null shield back on him. Good.

"How long?"

"Four hours."

Not long, but I pressed my hand to my abdomen as a new

worry flared. Did the magical explosion harm the baby? I hoped not.

I glanced around. We were in a small wooden structure. Perhaps a barn or shed. "Where are we?"

"Empty cabin somewhere in the Krystal Clan. We had to find a new hiding place, and the big guy took charge."

"Ari?"

"Yeah."

"Where is everyone?"

"Ari and Janco went to fetch the horses. Fisk and his people left to return to the Citadel. Leif and Mara are in the other room with the twins and Teegan." She quirked a smile. "Leif mentioned something about cooking supper."

Which meant he'd recovered from his brush with death. Thanks to Valek. I checked his pulse. Steady.

"How's Zethan feeling?"

"Probably about the same as you, but he wasn't out as long."

Ah, youth. Ten years made a difference.

"Tea?" Heli asked.

"Please. And could you ask Leif to come?"

"Sure."

Leif brought the tea. Even though he was pale and haggard, he still smiled when I crinkled my nose over the smell of the tea.

"How are you feeling?" I asked him.

He rubbed his chest. "Sore, but I don't care. I'm happy just to be alive! That's the closest I've come to death." Leif glanced at Valek. "He certainly took his role as my best man seriously. Did you know Valek could do that?"

"No." I gazed at my husband. "We haven't had time to talk about anything."

"He'll wake. The man doesn't know how to quit." Leif studied my expression. "How are you doing?"

"I'm not sure." I asked him about the baby.

"I don't know. Let's ask Teegan."

"Teegan?"

"Yeah. Kid's impressive."

Leif fetched Teegan, who was happy to help. The boy gazed at me and said, "Two strong heartbeats."

That was impressive and a huge relief. "Thanks, Tee."

He grinned. "Anytime, but why are you siphoning my magic?"

Surprised and alarmed, I asked, "I am?"

"Don't worry. It's not like you're stealing it from me. It's just when I used my magic to…scan you, something pulled it. When I stopped, it stopped."

"Do you think it's the baby?"

He shrugged. "No idea."

"Hold my hand and see what happens."

Teegan grasped my hand and frowned. "It's like a null shield, blocking my magic." He released me as if I'd burned him. "Sorry, but that's…awful!"

"I know. But it gives me some protection." And perhaps a bright side to losing my ability to use magic.

I remained by Valek's side as one day turned into two. Leif brewed his healing teas, and I dripped spoonful after spoonful into Valek's mouth. My worry grew. What if he didn't wake up? Was this how he felt all those times our positions had been reversed? I think I preferred being oblivious rather than nauseous and on the edge of panic.

At the end of the third day, Ari called everyone into the main room for a meeting. We gathered around the hearth.

"We can't stay here much longer," Ari said. "Bruns has sent patrols to search for us, and we're too close to the garrison. Any ideas?"

"We report back to Ixia," Janco said. "They can come with us as...political refugees."

"You can't," I said.

"Why not? The Commander needs to know what's been going on."

"He already knows." I filled them in on Bruns's and the Commander's plans. "I'm pretty sure once they take over Sitia, Owen is going to kill the Commander."

"Holy snow cats," Janco said. "We're screwed."

Trust Janco to sum it up succinctly.

"We need to stop them," Ari said.

"How?" Leif asked. "There are nine of us, and a million of them."

"Ten." Mara elbowed Leif.

"Oh no, you're staying far away from danger," Leif said. "When I saw you in Bruns's custody, I almost died. I'm not going through *that* again."

"You were shot in the chest and almost died. So by that logic, you're staying away from danger, too." Mara's stubborn expression matched Leif's.

"We can hide on the coast near The Cliffs," Heli suggested. "No one lives there or would dare come there during the storm season."

"Are we really going to hide?" Janco asked. "That doesn't sound like us."

"What sounds like us?" Ari asked.

"Being in the thick of things, causing trouble and—"

"Being captured and thrown in jail," Zohav said. "Have you forgotten that they have magicians, Curare, Theobroma, weapons and garrisons full of soldiers?"

"Fisk and his people would help," Zethan said.

"And Loris is dead," Janco added. "I'm feeling pretty happy about that."

"Ben, too," I said, but unlike Janco, I didn't relish the fact that I'd been forced to kill him.

"Are you sure? 'Cause these guys have a tendency to fake their deaths, and I don't want any more nasty surprises."

"Yes."

"We could try to warn the Commander about Owen," Ari suggested.

"*If* you can get near him, and *if* you can block Owen's magic," Leif said. "And then what? The Commander still wants Sitia."

"The Commander doesn't want Sitia," Valek said from the doorway.

Relief poured through me, cleansing the worry away. I jumped up and rushed to him, wrapping him in my arms. "How do you feel?"

"Like I wrestled a snow cat and lost."

Leif took charge. He made Valek sit down and eat. When Leif was satisfied, he allowed Valek to explain.

"I don't think the Commander has any desire to rule Sitia," Valek said. "But he's probably afraid a rogue magician or magicians will take control of Sitia and invade Ixia. And with all the Sitian resources—magicians, Curare, Theobroma and the glass messengers—he knows he can't win a war with Sitia. Which is probably why he agreed to the Cartel's plan."

"Why does it matter if he wants to or is forced to invade Sitia?" Leif asked. "He's still going to invade."

"It matters because if we give him a good reason not to invade, he won't," Valek said.

"And how can we possibly do that? There's only ten of us," Zohav said.

"For now," Valek said.

Janco straightened. "You thinking of recruiting, boss?"

"Thinking about it, along with a few other…nasty surprises for the Cartel."

"Sweet."

Valek scanned their faces and then met my gaze. "It'll be dangerous."

"Suicidal," Zohav muttered.

Valek addressed the group. "It's your choice. Fisk can find you a safe place to stay until it's over."

"I'm in," Janco said.

Ari nodded. "Me, too."

"And me," Zethan said.

Zohav glared at her brother. "I'll help," she said in a resigned tone.

Leif met Mara's gaze. "We need to discuss it."

She huffed in amusement. "Where you go, I go. It's that simple."

I suppressed a smile.

"No way I'm hiding," Heli said.

"I'm already signed up," Teegan said.

Everyone looked at me.

"You need to think of the baby," Leif said.

"I am. And I don't want to raise our child in a world controlled by two power-hungry megalomaniacs. So I will do whatever it takes to prevent *that* from happening."

"And that would be a yes." Janco grinned.

"What's our first move, boss?" Ari asked.

"You and Janco go scout for a more permanent hideout. I'm going to need time to plan."

Janco jumped to his feet. "We're on it."

Valek recovered his strength a few days later, but we still didn't get a chance to talk about all that had happened while we were separated. Ari and Janco found an abandoned farmhouse inside the Stormdance Clan's lands. We traveled to the site in small groups, each going a different way. Reuniting with Kiki soothed my soul.

We planned to renovate the inside to suit our needs, but keep the outside in its dilapidated state. The horses would stay in a camouflaged structure in the forest nearby.

On the first night, Valek and I arranged our bedrolls and blankets in the largest bedroom on the second floor. We added coal to the small brazier, coaxing a little more heat. Most of the others stretched out by the fire around the central hearth downstairs, but we hadn't had any privacy in forever. Or so it seemed.

Even with so much to discuss, we spent the first couple hours getting reacquainted.

Finally, with our hearts beating in sync and our bodies pressed together skin on skin, we shared the events that had changed both our lives so drastically.

Valek explained about the Storm Thieves and discovering his new siblings. The epiphany by Vincent's grave.

"I had no idea letting go would have such…consequences," he said. "A huge weight lifted off my shoulders, but it took my immunity with it."

"I was right. You attached a null shield to your soul when you witnessed your older brothers' murders. Once you didn't need that protection, it returned to the sky."

"Rotten timing," he murmured.

"I wouldn't say that. Nor would Leif or Mara."

"I lost control and almost killed us."

"But you didn't. Next time—"

"There's not going to be a *next* time." He sounded like a sullen child.

"Yes, there will be. We need every advantage we can get. Leif and Zethan can teach you how to control it."

"I don't have to like it."

Amused by his tone, I said, "Look at the bright side. You reconnected with your parents and gained three new siblings."

"And you gained a mother-in-law."

Oh. Right.

"Not so amusing now, is it? I even promised her to bring you for a visit."

"Fighting Bruns's Cartel doesn't seem that bad now," I joked.

"Ha."

The silence stretched as I considered how much Valek's world had been turned upside down in the past two months. The Commander's mistrust, our marriage, the baby, his family, his lost immunity and the discovery of his magic. No wonder Bruns's men had been able to capture him at Mara's. Anyone else would have been unhinged by just one of those incidents.

"Your turn, love," Valek said. "Why does your touch block my magic? Not that I'm complaining. In fact, I love your touch even more now."

I told him my theory about the baby being a void. "But after my experience with Loris's magic and Teegan's comment, I'm not so sure anymore."

"Something drained the magic when we were connected," Valek said. "Is that what Teegan meant?"

"I think so. But if that was the case, then what did the baby *do* with the magic? I didn't regain my powers. Nothing happened. I don't think so, anyway."

"But this blocking power has grown stronger, right?"

"Yes."

"Perhaps the baby is channeling the power back into the blanket?"

"Perhaps."

"I guess time will tell if the baby's responsible for your lost magic, love. In the meantime, you can neutralize a magician with a touch. That may come in handy over the next couple months."

"As long as it doesn't hurt our baby."

"Of course." Valek rested his hand on my stomach. "That's what the upcoming battle is all about. Protecting our baby, giving him or her a chance for a peaceful life."

"No, it isn't."

"No?"

"It's about giving *all* the babies and *all* the people a chance for a peaceful life."

"You know that's impossible."

"I know, but wouldn't it be nice?" I asked.

"It'd be worth dying for."

★ ★ ★ ★ ★

ACKNOWLEDGMENTS

Even though I spend plenty of hours working alone in my writing cave, none of my books could have been written without the help and support from many people, including my readers. They're a constant source of joy and motivation.

Thanks to my trio of beta readers—Natalie Bejin, Judi Fleming and my husband, Rodney—my stories are as logical and error-free as humanly possible.

My agent, Bob Mecoy, and editor, Lauren Smulski, have been essential in guiding my stories and career. Thanks for all your hard work!

Speaking of hard work, no acknowledgment of mine is complete without a shout-out to all the talented people around the world who are part of Harlequin. Your efforts on behalf of my books are appreciated, and, if you're ever in my neck of the woods, stop on by, I'll buy you a drink.

I don't have a street team, but I do have loads of supporters who help spread the word about my books. They're invaluable and I thank them all, especially Alethea Allarey, Jaime Arnold of Rockstar Book Tours, Michelle Haring of Cupboard Maker Books and Sarah Weir.

Thanks to my family and friends for your continuing support. And thanks to my children, Jenna and Luke, for their patience and for not being too embarrassed by Mom's career and wardrobe choices.

I saved the best for last—my husband, Rodney. Without him, there would be no books. Thanks so much!

Loved this book? Let us know!

Find us on Twitter @MIRAink and on
Instagram @Mira_Ink where you can
share your thoughts, stay up to date on all
the news about our upcoming releases and
even be in with the chance of winning
copies of our wonderful books!

Bringing you the best voices in teen fiction.

www.miraink.co.uk
 @MiraInk

Praise for Maria V. Snyder

DAWN STUDY

MARIA V. SNYDER

ONE PLACE. MANY STORIES

HQ
An imprint of HarperCollins*Publishers* Ltd.
1 London Bridge Street
London SE1 9GF

This paperback edition 2017

First published in Great Britain by
HQ, an imprint of HarperCollins*Publishers* Ltd. 2017

ISBN: 9781848456891

Printed and bound by
CPI Group (UK) Ltd, Croydon, CR0 4YY

MIX
Paper from
responsible sources
FSC C007454

To my husband, Rodney.
You were there in the beginning when Yelena's
story was just an idea. Thank you for enduring the
countless revisions, writing retreats, conferences,
extended travel, bad reviews, strange visitors
and the million other things that come
with living with an author!

1

YELENA

I ghosted through the quiet Citadel streets well after curfew. Dressed in black from head to toe, I stayed in the shadows to avoid detection and lamented the necessity of having to skulk about like a criminal. The row of Councilors' houses appeared to be deserted—we'd received intel that the Cartel had "relocated" the Sitian Council for their safety. Not trusting the darkened windows or the info that the houses were empty, I looped around to the back alley and waited. No signs of movement. Were the houses vacant, or did a professional ambush wait inside?

If I still had my magic, there would be no need to guess. But the baby in my belly was blocking my powers—or, at least, that was the current theory. My pulse skittered with the thought of the baby. Valek's request that I be very careful echoed in my mind. I drew in a breath to steady my heart as I approached Councilor Bavol Zaltana's home, located in the middle of the row.

Without the light from the street lanterns, the darkness pressed around me. A cool night breeze diluted the stink of garbage left too long in the sun. I knelt by the back door and felt for the keyhole, then inserted my tension wrench and diamond pick. Lifting the pins into alignment, I twisted the tumbler and the door swung open into the kitchen that during my previous visits had been filled with heat and light and the scent of jungle spices. Instead, a cold, quiet mustiness greeted me.

I tucked my tools away and stepped inside and to the right. Standing in the threshold, I would have been an easy target. I sniffed the air for any hint of perfume, cologne or shaving cream, or anything that would indicate another person or persons crouched in the shadows.

Only the dry scent of dust filled my nose.

That ruled out the amateurs, but I knew The Mosquito remained a threat and wouldn't make such a rookie mistake. He'd been paid to assassinate me, and he would hunt me until he finished the job. No surprise that Valek wasn't happy about this mission, but due to our limited resources, personnel and time, he'd conceded the need to send me here while he searched Bavol's office in the Council Hall. Since Bruns Jewelrose and his Cartel had moved into the hall, Valek had the far more dangerous task.

We both sought any information on how Bruns's Cartel had been able to procure enough Theobroma to lace the food at the Council Hall, the Magician's Keep and four military garrisons. Their magicians then used magic to turn all those who consumed the sweet treat into compliant and obedient members of the Cartel.

When no obvious dangers materialized, I walked through the house, checking every corner for intruders, including the ceiling. All clear. Breathing became easier as I drew the curtains tight before concentrating on my task. Lighting a small lantern, I started in Bavol's home office, looking in his desk drawers.

Bavol had been given the assignment of determining a way to mass-produce Theobroma for the Sitian military. Once the

MARIA V. SNYDER

Council learned that the Commander had barrels of Curare, they'd panicked. Curare was an effective nonlethal weapon, causing full-body paralysis. The substance that counteracted Curare was Theobroma, which wasn't ideal due to it rendering a person vulnerable to magic, but it was better than being paralyzed. The other problem, however, was that it only grew in the Illiais Jungle, and at a very slow rate.

Or so everyone thought.

Bruns and Owen Moon had managed to increase not only the quantity but also the growth rate, using glass hothouses and grafting techniques. But just how had they learned this technique remained a mystery.

Finished with the drawers, I moved on to Bavol's cabinet. A couple of the files included diagrams of plants, and I stacked them next to me. The last time we visited Bavol, he'd acted… odd. Leif's magic picked up a strange vibe from him, but we hadn't pressed the issue. Now, with Bavol "housed" at the Greenblade garrison and unreachable, I hoped any information we found would help us determine not only where Bruns had procured the Theobroma but also how.

I collected a nice-size pile, but spent a few minutes checking the living area and his bedroom, too, just in case he had hidden files elsewhere.

Satisfied that I'd covered all possible locations, I grabbed the stack and slipped out the back door, relocking it behind me. I waited for my eyes to adjust to the darkness as the air cooled my sweaty skin. I'd left my cloak back at HQ. It was the middle of the warm season. The night air remained a reasonable temperature a little longer each evening. And since I was three and a half months pregnant, I stayed warmer as well.

An extra-deep pool of black appeared next to me. Instinctively I dodged to the side as metal flashed, and a sharp coldness nicked the left side of my neck before striking the door behind me. I dove to the right and hit the ground with a thud. The blackness cursed and followed me. I hissed as a blade seared a path along my left bicep. I kept rolling deeper into the darkness—my only defensive play at this point. Fear pulsed, urging me to hurry.

A narrow beam of yellow light sliced through the darkness. My attacker had come prepared. Lovely. The light swept the ground, searching and then finding me. Caught in the beam long enough to be a target, I somersaulted to my feet as the *thwack* of a crossbow sounded. Debris pelted me when the bolt ricocheted off the ground nearby. Too close. My heart jumped in my chest. Another bolt clipped my right side, the pain a mere nuisance in the grander scheme of things.

I raced for the end of the alley, zigzagging as much as possible and hoping with all my soul that a second ambusher didn't wait for me at the end. A third bolt sailed past. I shot from the alley and increased my pace, no longer caring about staying in the shadows. Glancing behind, I spotted a black-clad figure aiming a crossbow in my direction. Ice skittered down my sweat-soaked back. I changed course, spinning to the left just as the bolt whizzed by my ear. The air from its passage fanned my face. Not stopping to marvel at either my good luck or his lousy aim, I dove for the shadows and ran.

Hours later—or so it seemed to my starved lungs—I slowed and ducked into a dark shadow. Bending over, I gasped for breath. So much for staying in shape. Although running for your life wasn't exactly something you could train for. Plus I'd gained a few baby pounds. The thought sent a new spike of fear right through me. I ran my fingers along the gash on my side, seeking its depth. I sighed with relief—only a flesh wound. Then I remembered my other injuries, and they flared to painful life. The one on my neck was also shallow, but the cut on my arm would need to be sealed. I sagged against the

MARIA V. SNYDER

building for a moment. Not only my life but also the baby's had been in danger.

Once I recovered, I realized I still clutched the files from Bavol's office. I would have laughed, but the sound might have attracted the wrong attention. Dozens more soldiers had been patrolling the streets since the Cartel declared martial law and set a curfew. To avoid them, I took the most round-about path back to HQ, ensuring no one followed me. By the time I tapped on the hidden door, the first rays of dawn lit the white marble of the Citadel.

Hilly, one of the Helper's Guild members, let me in. She raised an eyebrow at my disheveled and bloody appearance.

"I ran into a bit of trouble," I said.

She quirked a smile. "Not as much as when Valek returns."

Oh no. "Did he…"

"Yep. He stopped in about an hour ago, but when he heard you hadn't returned, he took off to look for you."

I wilted.

Hilly took pity on me. "Come on. We'll wake the healer and get you cleaned up before he comes back."

I followed her through HQ. Since the building Fisk had once used to house his Helper's Guild had been seized by the Cartel, he'd found another empty structure tucked almost out of sight in the northwest quadrant of the Citadel to use as a temporary base of operations. Now his people helped us in our efforts to stop the Cartel from taking complete control of Sitia. The so-called resistance.

Sleeping barracks occupied most of the lower level. The members of the guild spanned in age from six years old to eighteen. The kids didn't mind the close quarters, and some happily shared a bed. The extra-large kitchen took up the rest of the level. The two upper floors contained Fisk's room and office, a small suite for Valek and me, and a number of guest rooms for our growing army. Our farmhouse in the Storm-dance lands had been a useful place to plan and recuperate during the last month, but we'd quickly learned that we needed to be closer to Bruns.

The healer was a sixteen-year-old boy named Chale who'd recently developed magical powers. Since all the magicians at the Magician's Keep had been conscripted and sent to the Cartel's garrisons, there had been no one to teach him how to use his power—except me and Valek. Even though I lost my powers over three months ago, I hadn't forgotten my lessons from the Keep. Valek, on the other hand, had freed his power only recently and almost flamed out, killing us all. Now he was reluctant to use it until he learned how to fully control his powers. Not an ideal situation, but we tried.

I sat at the kitchen table in my undershirt as Chale cleaned my wounds. The gawky teen was all thumbs. He peered through a riot of black hair that my fingers itched to trim. As I suspected, the cut on my biceps needed more than just a bandage. At least talking Chale through the steps needed to heal it with his magic distracted me from the pain. As long as he didn't touch me skin to skin, he could use threads from the power blanket to stitch the cut closed.

"I have to keep pulling power to knit the skin together," Chale said with concern. "Something is tugging it away. Is that normal?"

"No. I think what is draining your power is what is blocking mine. At least, I hope that's the case."

"Is it the baby?"

I stared at him. Not many people knew.

He blushed. "Sorry, I just—"

"No, don't apologize. You're a healer. Sensing the baby is a part of your powers."

"It's healthy, if that helps?"

"It does," Valek said from the doorway. He still wore his black skintight sneak suit, which highlighted his long, lean and powerful muscles. "Can you say the same about my wife?"

A dangerous glint lit his sapphire-blue eyes, but Chale failed to notice.

"Of course. It's just a couple scrapes." Chale's light tone downplayed my injuries nicely—perhaps he'd noticed more than he let on. "We're almost finished."

"Good," Valek said, but his gaze seared into mine.

And though his angular face revealed none of his thoughts, I knew he suppressed a whole gamut of emotions. In a few graceful, almost predatory strides, he was by my side. He laced his fingers in mine as Chale completed his work. Bandages were fine for the shallow cuts. I didn't want Chale to exhaust his power on the minor abrasions—one of the guild members might need him tonight.

Valek let go of my hand as I shrugged on my torn and bloody tunic. He studied the garment without comment— another dangerous sign. But by this time, the kitchen bustled with the morning crew, and soon piping-hot sweet cakes were set in front of us. My stomach roared with sudden hunger, and even Valek wasn't brave enough to get between a pregnant woman and food.

Only after I stuffed myself did he reclaim my hand and tug me to my feet.

"Upstairs," he said.

Feeling much better with a full stomach, I trailed after him as we ascended the stairs to the third level and into our rooms. Valek closed the door and I braced for his lecture. Instead, he wrapped his arms around me and pulled me close. I rested my head on his chest and listened to his heart beating, soaking in his warmth, breathing in his musky scent, feeling safe. At six feet tall, he was eight inches taller than me.

I'd known Valek for almost nine years, and the only thing that scared him was the threat of losing me. "What happened?" I asked.

He leaned back and lightly brushed the bandage on my neck with his thumb. "I found out The Mosquito is in town."

Ah.

"Did he attack you?" he asked.

"It was too dark to see, but the first strike was aimed at my throat." The Mosquito's signature way to kill was to stab an ice pick into his victims' jugulars and let them bleed to death. Nice guy.

"Tell me what happened."

I detailed the attack and the reason it took me so long to return. "But I managed to hold on to the files. Did you learn anything else while you were in the Council Hall?"

"I grabbed a few promising files from Bavol's office, but I'm more concerned about what I overheard Bruns and his sycophants discussing in the hallway."

I stepped back in alarm. "You weren't supposed—"

"They didn't know I was there. Besides, the information was worth the danger."

"About The Mosquito?"

"Yes. That, and Bruns knows you're in the Citadel. He's offered a large bounty to the person who kills you."

No surprise. "How much?"

"Yelena, that's not the point."

"It's not the first time someone's put a price on my head." Master Magician Roze Featherstone had offered five golds as a reward for my capture when she tried to take over the Sitian Council seven years ago.

"This time is different. You're..."

I waited.

"Vulnerable without your magic. And it's no longer all

MARIA V. SNYDER

business with Bruns. He took Ben's and Loris's deaths and our escape from the Krystal garrison personally. You need to go back to the farmhouse in the Stormdance lands. You'll be safer there."

"And what about you?" I asked. "As you said, *our* escape. Did he set a bounty for you, as well?"

"No."

"How do you know?"

Valek paced the room. I crossed my arms to keep his lingering warmth close. Plus, judging by the agitation in his steps, I sensed he was working up the nerve to deliver more bad news.

He stopped. "Bruns has offered fifty golds to the person who kills you."

That was a fortune. I whistled, and he shot me a glare. "You didn't answer my question," I said.

Another scowl, and then his shoulders drooped as if in defeat. "Bruns has been in contact with Commander Ambrose, and…" Valek paused. "The Commander has agreed to send Onora to assassinate me."

2

VALEK

Yelena's mouth opened slightly in surprise, and concern flashed in her green eyes over the news. But Valek had expected something like this. If he focused on the logic, the move made perfect tactical sense. The Commander had warned Valek that leaving Ixia would be an act of treason. And acts of treason, no matter what the reason, were punishable by death. Plus, he now had magic, of all things. He'd inadvertently traded his immunity to magic for the power to wield it. And the Commander had a standing execution order on all magicians found in Ixia.

Except he and the Commander had been close friends, and he was unaware of Valek's magic—only a handful of people knew. He'd hoped the Commander would give him the benefit of doubt and not send an assassin after him.

Yelena put her hand on his arm. "He's being influenced by Owen's magic."

"We don't know that for sure." There had been a few inconsistencies, like when the Commander had tried to protect Valek from Owen by sending him to the coast to deal with the Storm Thieves. He was also supposed to be protected from Owen's subversion by the null shields that Leif had woven into his uniforms, but the Commander could have lied to Valek about wearing them.

"He has to be," she said.

He pressed his hand over hers and enjoyed not only her touch but the respite from the constant presence of his magic. With his mental shield in place, it wasn't as bad, but contact with her turned it all off, and he returned to the man he'd been for the last forty-one years of his life.

"Are you worried about Onora?" she asked.

Was he? They had sparred a number of times, and each time he had defeated her. But perhaps she planned to ambush him. "No. She's the best to come along in the last twenty-four years, but unless she catches me off guard, I don't expect her to cause me any trouble."

"And you're never relaxed," she teased.

"I am when I'm with you, love." He picked up her hand and kissed her palm.

"Really? And those knives under our pillows, the swords on the floor, the darts in the headboard?"

"I said relaxed, not stupid. Being prepared is never a bad idea."

"No." Her gaze grew distant as she rubbed her side.

Probably remembering The Mosquito's attack. While Valek was proud she was able to get away, he planned to ensure that would be the assassin's last attempt on her life.

"Speaking of being prepared," he said, "you need to leave the Citadel until I've taken care of any bounty hunters coming after you. Either go to the Stormdance farmhouse, or travel to the Illiais Jungle to visit your mother. Both are safer than here."

She gave him a tight smile. "Nice try, handsome, but I'm not going anywhere. At least not until Leif and Mara return from Broken Bridge with my father, and we've looked over the information from Bavol's."

"At least promise me you'll stay in HQ until they arrive." He leaned close and kissed her neck, then whispered, "Do it for your handsome husband."

Laughing, she said, "I promise to stay in bed for the rest of the morning as long as you stay with me. After that…no promises."

"What if I give you a *very good* reason to stay in bed until I squash The Mosquito?"

She drew back, and desire burned in her gaze. "What's the reason?"

"Me taking care of you until you're out of breath and a puddle in my hands. A service I'll be happy to perform anytime during your…bed rest." He nibbled on her earlobe.

"Oh, my. Someone certainly has a high opinion of himself," she teased.

"Is that a challenge?"

"Oh, yes! Show me what you can do, and I'll consider your request."

He grinned. "Accepted."

Not giving her time to reply, Valek pulled her to their bedroom and made short work of her clothing. A few bloody scrapes marked her back and a number of bruises peppered her arms. Valek suppressed his fury with the knowledge that The Mosquito would soon be crushed.

Valek scooped her up and laid her on the bed, then kissed her for a long moment. She plucked at his clothing, and he grabbed her hands. "This is for you, love."

"Exactly. Now strip."

He peeled off the tight garment, but his gaze never left her. Once divested of his clothing, he joined her on the bed. He trailed kisses down her neck. Valek had been convinced he'd

MARIA V. SNYDER

lost her when she hadn't returned from her mission, and he planned to savor this time with her as if it were the last. His efforts left her gasping, and he gave her three very good reasons to stay in bed.

She stretched like a cat and curled up next to him. Yelena met his gaze. "You're really worried about the bounty on me?"

Valek traced the recently healed cut along her side with a finger. Purple bruises ringed the bright red line. "I know you can handle an assassin." He quirked a smile. "Or two, but with fifty golds at stake…a gang of wannabe bounty hunters could come after you together and split the money."

"All right, I'll stay in HQ until you've dealt with The Mosquito," she promised.

A weight lifted from his shoulders. He pulled her close. She snuggled against him and fell asleep almost immediately. He smoothed her long black hair back from her beautiful oval face. The knowledge that he'd do anything to keep her and the baby safe comforted him, since it required no thinking, no weighing the consequences of his actions and no hesitation.

Valek had once felt the same uncomplicated feelings for the Commander, but not anymore. Even if the Commander's behavior had been caused by Owen's magical hold on him, Valek could no longer return to that place of blind loyalty. His new magic complicated everything, of course. However, that would just be an excuse. No. Yelena meant more to him than his own life and happiness, and much more than the Commander's.

Valek woke a few hours later and slid from the bed without waking his wife. An automatic smile still spread over his lips every time he thought of Yelena as his wife. Not many people knew of their marriage, and even fewer were aware of the baby, but the fact that they had exchanged vows continued to thrill him, as if he'd won the biggest tournament in the entire world.

Going down one level, Valek stopped in Fisk's office. The stark room contained a desk, a couple chairs and a table. The young leader of the Helper's Guild bent over his desk. The fingers of his right hand ran through his light brown hair, leaving behind rows of spikes, while his left clutched a stylus. He frowned at a sheet of parchment spread over the desk.

Valek tapped on the open door, and Fisk glanced up. Dark smudges marked his light brown eyes. The poor boy appeared years older than seventeen.

"When's the last time you slept?" Valek asked.

Fisk blinked at him. "Sleep? What's that?"

"Not funny."

Fisk dropped the stylus and rubbed his face. "Wish I was joking."

"Bring me up to date, and then take a break."

"But—"

"It's not a request. Exhaustion will only lead to fatal mistakes. I'll collect the information from your guild while you rest."

He grinned. "Half of them are terrified of you and won't report."

"Then they can wait until you're awake. What's the latest intel?"

Fisk filled him in. "We think Hans Cloud Mist is a member of the Cartel. He's been spotted at the Moon garrison twice, and we've confirmed Danae Bloodgood and Toki Krystal as members."

Valek considered this for a moment. They were all influential businesspeople who thought their accumulated wealth and business acumen meant they could do a better job of running Sitia than the appointed Councilors. "I'm beginning to sus-

MARIA V. SNYDER

pect there are eleven members, one for each clan, with Bruns designated as their leader," he mused.

"Sounds like something they'd do to justify their actions."

Interesting comment. "What do you mean?"

Fisk leaned back and spread his arms. "They decided that the Sitian Council was not doing a proper job of keeping Sitia safe from the Commander. Plus the Council also failed to rein in the Sitian magicians, letting them go about their business willy-nilly."

"Willy-nilly?"

"Yeah, you know." Waving his hands, Fisk elaborated, "Selling null shields to anyone, using their magic for selfish reasons. I think the Cartel feels they can do better than the Councilors, but they still honor the structure the clans have established long ago. So they're not really usurping the Council—just replacing them."

"And that helps them sleep better at night?"

"Exactly." Fisk rubbed the stubble on his chin. "Why is identifying the other members of the Cartel so important when Bruns has brainwashed them along with everyone else? They've no clue that Bruns is collaborating with Owen and the Commander."

"You tell me."

He huffed. "I don't know, because in order to stop the Sitian takeover, all we have to do is stop Bruns, Owen Moon and the Commander."

Valek suppressed a smile at the "all we have to do" comment. If only it were that easy. "Why are these people members of the Cartel?"

Fisk shot him a sour expression. "Okay, I'll play. They're rich and powerful. Which is why the Cartel has been so successful in getting resources and converting the garrisons—Oh!"

Valek waited as Fisk followed the logic.

"So we identify them all and wake them up to what's really going on, so they can use that influence and power to help us instead of Bruns."

Smart boy. "Or we assassinate them all and take them out of the equation. The added benefit is that we scare their support staff."

Instead of a knee-jerk reaction to the thought of killing ten people, Fisk paused to consider it. "Yelena would never allow that. She doesn't want any of the brainwashed to be killed. Besides, I think they'd be more useful alive than dead."

"And that is why we need to know their identities."

Fisk yawned. "We're getting reports back from the garrisons and will soon have a complete list of personnel at each one."

"Good. I need your people to locate a bug for me."

"The Mosquito?" He straightened in his chair, looking more awake.

"Yes."

"Where?"

"Here in the Citadel."

"Ah, hell. Is that why Yelena needed…" He stopped. "Won't he be with Bruns?"

"From what I heard last night, either he's been fired, or Bruns thinks the competition will compel him to finish the job." Valek told Fisk about the bounty.

"She has to leave now and go some—"

"I already tried that. Best I could do was get her to promise to stay at HQ until I've dealt with The Mosquito." In other words, once Valek plunged his knife in The Mosquito's heart and scared all the others away.

"That's some relief." Fisk ran both his hands through his hair. "But the Citadel will be overrun with assassins, and it's gonna be hard to find the bug. He's smart, and my people aren't as effective in the Citadel. Rumors that they're doing more than helping carry packages for shoppers are spreading. Before, everyone ignored my kids, thinking them harmless and stupid. Now..."

"Just tell them to keep an eye out for him. I only need a general vicinity."

"All right. And now that Yelena is under house arrest, so to speak, she can take over collecting the information from my people, since they trust her, and I can do a bit of reconnaissance on my own." Fisk paused. "Are you sure she's going to be happy hanging around here all day?"

"Don't worry. *I'll* keep her happy."

Fisk shot him a dubious look before heading to bed. Valek settled behind the desk and studied the map Fisk had been marking. The other Sitian garrisons were highlighted. Members of the Helper's Guild had infiltrated them all. Since the Cartel controlled the Citadel and the Moon, Krystal, Featherstone and Greenblade garrisons, they'd put the military soldiers in charge of all the civilian security forces in those lands. Rumors that the Cloud Mist base was also compromised hadn't been substantiated yet.

The garrisons farther south still hadn't been indoctrinated, and Valek had agents working in the kitchens to ensure they remained uninvolved long enough for Valek to recruit them to their side. The agent in the Jewelrose garrison hadn't reported in weeks, and Valek suspected the man had been captured or converted. Heli the Stormdancer was keeping an eye on the base in the Stormdance lands, but the storm season would start at the beginning of the heating season, and he'd need to find another agent then.

Ari and Janco had been assigned to the Greenblade base to keep an eye on the Sitian Councilors and First Magician Bain Bloodgood. Eventually, they would need to be rescued. Meanwhile, his sister Zohav and his brother Zethan—a concept that still amazed him—worked on exploring the extent of their powers with Teegan and Kade on the Stormdance coast. They were safe for now.

Valek reviewed his to-do list—identify the Cartel members, find and cut off the source of the Theobroma, rescue the Councilors, recruit the southern garrisons and free the magicians in the other garrisons. Oh, and find some time to rescue the Commander. Knowing *what* he needed to do was the easy part. Too bad he didn't quite know *how* these tasks would be accomplished, with only Fisk's Helper's Guild and ten others to help. They needed more bodies. More allies. Yelena wished to recruit Cahil, believing the man might be smart enough to see the truth. Valek hoped she was right. Then there were Devlen, Opal and her soldier friends, Nic and Eve. As long as Reema was safe, they might be willing to help. Perhaps when Leif, Mara and Esau returned, he'd send another messenger to Fulgor, the capital of the Moon Clan's lands and ask.

Leif and Mara had left ten days ago to collect Esau and the plants in the glass hothouse near Broken Bridge. They should be at the farmstead where Leif had left his father by now. However, the return trip to the Citadel would take them twice as long since they'd be pulling a wagon.

Fisk's people honed in on a potential location for The Mosquito three days later and provided him with a current description. Valek had been collecting information in the Council Hall in the evenings, much to Yelena's annoyance at the risk he took while she was stuck at HQ. He refused to feel bad. In fact, knowing she was safe after learning Bruns's plans kept him from being overwhelmed with all that had to be done. Plus, when he returned each morning, he woke her with more reasons to stay safe.

"You're going after him," Yelena said. It wasn't a question.

MARIA V. SNYDER

She watched him as he dressed in nondescript Sitian clothing—a gray tunic and charcoal-colored pants—and tucked a number of weapons into the various pockets and hidden holders.

"If you kill him, does that mean I'm no longer under house arrest?"

"Technically, yes. But there's still the bounty," he said.

"What if he kills you?"

"He won't."

"Cocky bastard."

Valek pulled her close and kissed her. "He won't, love."

She melted against him. "I feel so useless."

"Don't. The kids love you, and Fisk is getting better intel by being out in the Citadel."

She managed a half smile. "You're right."

"I'm going to put on quite the show today and attract lots of attention and scare the other bounty hunters off for a while, so if you really can't stand being inside and want to get some fresh air this afternoon, it should be a little safer."

Yelena's face lit up.

"I'd rather you didn't, but if you do, please don't go far or alone. All right?"

"Yes." She hugged him tight.

He nuzzled her neck.

"Tell The Mosquito to enjoy the fire world for me," she said.

"It will be my pleasure."

Once outside, Valek moved through the busy market with ease. He spotted a number of Fisk's guild members working the crowd and darting between shoppers. The market was located at the very center of the Citadel. Factories and businesses ringed it in ever-widening circles and occupied the two center sections of the Citadel. The Magician's Keep encompassed the northeast quadrant, and the Sitian Council Hall and other government buildings were located in the southeast corner. The Citadel's citizens lived in the labyrinth of homes in the northwest and southwest quadrants.

A few of the abandoned warehouses and factories had been converted into apartments, and according to Fisk, The Mosquito lived on the top floor of one of them. Normally Valek would attack at night, but The Mosquito knew that trick and would be ready.

As he crossed the market, Valek noted three people taking an unhealthy interest in him and sensed another, but was unable to locate the fourth—a professional. He considered his options. Lead the three on a merry chase to an unfortunate dead end, or lose them?

When he spotted The Mosquito standing near the entrance to an alley, Valek recognized the setup. Those three worked for the bug. Like a pack of sheep dogs, their job was to herd him toward that alley, where Valek's prey would conveniently dangle like bait on a hook. Then the bait would slip down the alley and draw Valek right into an ambush. Classic.

He judged his odds. The Mosquito plus three—doable with darts, but just how many waited? A brief thought of using his magic to sense the others flashed before he dismissed it. Too many people around. Even though Teegan had taught him to control his magic in order to prevent a flameout back at the Stormdancers' safe house, he was reluctant to use it. According to Teegan, his mental barrier was strong enough that he didn't need to wear a null shield. Besides, he liked being able to detect when magic was in use around him.

Instead of using magic, he decided to take the high ground. Valek returned to the heart of the market and lost his sheep-dogs, then cut down the street next to The Mosquito's chosen alley. When no one appeared to take an interest in him, he climbed the nearest building and reached the top.

MARIA V. SNYDER

When he straightened, he spotted The Mosquito waiting on the roof two buildings down on his left. Fisk did say the man was smart. So how did Yelena get away from him with only a few cuts?

It occurred to Valek that perhaps Yelena wasn't his target.

Valek drew both his daggers and faced The Mosquito as he lightly hopped buildings.

The Mosquito halted six feet in front of Valek. "Please tell me you really didn't think I'd set up such an obvious trap for you."

"You took a contract to kill Yelena. That makes me question the level of your intelligence."

"Fair enough." He swept a hand out.

Sensing movement behind him, Valek angled his body to keep the bug in sight while he glanced back. Four black-clad figures stood up from where they'd been lying on the right side of the rooftop. Nice.

"What about now?" The Mosquito asked.

"It depends on who you brought for backup."

"Well, this is Sitia. Not a ton of trained killers here. But there are plenty of magicians. Four might be excessive, but…" He shrugged. "I'd rather too many than not enough."

Ah. Smart move. Around Valek, the presence of magic disappeared suddenly. The magicians must have surrounded him with a null shield. Valek dropped his arms to his sides, as if an invisible hand had wrapped around his torso. When he'd been immune to magic, a null shield could immobilize him like a rat stuck between the jaws of a trap. Now…not at all. However, he didn't want the bug to learn this fact until the perfect moment.

"Now I'm questioning your intelligence, Valek. Why would you come after me alone when everyone knows how easy it is to trap the infamous assassin?"

"Who says I'm alone?"

The Mosquito opened his mouth, but snapped it closed as his gaze slid past Valek's shoulders. Four thuds sounded behind him. The presence Valek had sensed in the market stood among the prone forms. As usual, Onora was barefoot.

"You do realize she wants the same thing I do," The Mosquito said.

Valek rolled his shoulders as if he'd been released from the pressure of a null shield. "I do," he said. "But she'll wait her turn. Right, Onora?"

"You can play with your bug first," she said.

Valek didn't hesitate. He flipped his dagger and flung it at The Mosquito's chest with all his strength. Shock whitened the man's face as the blade pierced bone and buried deep into his heart. The force slammed The Mosquito to the ground.

Shuffling close, Valek crouched beside the assassin. Valek met the bug's horrified gaze. "I'm sorry we didn't have a proper match, but I need to save my energy for the next fight."

For Onora to show up in broad daylight meant it was going to take all his skills to defeat her. If he even could. She must have downplayed her abilities when sparring with him before. "Oh, and Yelena says enjoy the fire world."

Valek yanked his knife from The Mosquito's chest and stood to face Onora.

3

LEIF

"You can't pack an entire hothouse's worth of plants onto one wagon, Father," Leif said for the billionth time. Sweat rolled down his face as he helped Esau pack the plants' roots into large terra-cotta pots filled with soil. They'd been at it for two days now. "Just collect the important ones and those that you think can survive the trip."

Esau knelt among the greenery. Dirt streaked his face and smeared his coveralls. His tragic expression over leaving any of the shrubbery behind was almost comical. "If Mara makes me glass panels for the wagon, we could construct a hothouse on wheels and—"

"It would weigh a ton and take a team of oxen to drag it to the Citadel. Not to mention draw attention to us, and right now, we can't afford to be noticed." Leif and Mara had to dodge a number of military patrols on the eight-day trip here. Traveling with a full wagon was going to be a nightmare. "We'll probably have to put a tarp over the plants we do take in order to blend in."

Esau gasped in dismay, and Leif suppressed a sigh. His father was the best at identifying and working with plants, but sometimes the man's devotion bordered on obsession.

"We're leaving in the morning, Father. So tell me which ones to pot, or I'm going into the farmhouse and—"

"Take the crossbreeds and the grafted Theobroma trees." Esau stabbed his finger at the plants. Soil filled his nails, which had grown long, along with Esau's wild gray hair.

Leif hadn't wanted to leave his father behind in Broken Bridge when he'd returned to the Citadel two months ago, but that Zaltana stubbornness won out, and Esau had remained at the farmstead. And it appeared that he had practically lived in the glass hothouse and only spent the minimum amount of time on things like basic hygiene, sleeping and eating.

Then again, it was probably a good thing Esau hadn't accompanied Leif. Considering he'd been ambushed, kidnapped, brainwashed and shot in the chest with a crossbow bolt, Leif thought his father had fared better, even with the malnutrition. Leif rubbed the scar on his chest, remembering the pain and the knowledge that he was dying. That he'd never hold his beautiful wife in his arms again. Then, from nowhere, Valek had appeared and saved his life. With magic! A month later, Leif still couldn't get his mind to accept it. Valek, who'd been immune forever, and now…a magician of considerable strength. Weird.

Leif finished potting the plant and several more that Esau gave him, then stood. Stretching his back, he wiped the sweat from his face and headed toward the house to check on Mara. Ever since his near-death experience and seeing her a prisoner of Bruns, he grew nervous when he'd been separated from her for more than a few hours.

The trip to the Citadel was going to be tricky. He planned to let her ride his horse, Rusalka, with instructions to head back without waiting for them. It was safer for her, and she'd have a better chance of avoiding the patrols by traveling alone.

MARIA V. SNYDER

The time apart would be torture for him, but it was much better than letting Bruns capture her again.

Mara was in the farmhouse's large kitchen, cooking supper. He paused in the threshold and watched his wife. Honey-colored curls framed her heart-shaped face. She was gorgeous on the outside and equally as beautiful on the inside. He'd never met a sweeter soul. But he'd learned she wasn't as soft as she appeared. Her run-in with Bruns had brought out her inner strength.

She spotted him hovering and flashed him a huge grin, her tawny-colored eyes shining with love. His heart melted at the sight, and he rushed to gather her close.

Mara nuzzled his neck. "You smell of earth and sweat."

"Does my man-odor turn you on?"

She leaned back to meet his gaze. "You've been spending too much time with Janco."

"I haven't seen Janco in weeks," he protested.

"Doesn't matter. The damage is done," she teased. "Go get cleaned up. Supper is almost ready, Man-Odor."

"Come with me? Father is busy."

"And let the roast dry out?"

"Yes." Food had lost its appeal. Almost dying had a way of rearranging a person's priorities.

"I won't serve a meal that tastes like shoe leather." She squeezed him. "We'll have time later. This house has lots of bedrooms, and we'll probably need to check on the horses sometime this evening."

He laughed. "Is 'check on the horses' going to be our code?" Leif imagined a house full of kids and a future Leif announcing that Mommy and Daddy needed to "check on the horses" and would be back.

"You've no sense of romance."

"That shouldn't be a surprise."

She shooed him away in mock disgust. Smiling, Leif cleaned up and helped her finish cooking dinner. He brought a tray of food outside for his father. After Esau ate, they loaded the wagon and watered the plants.

"Poor things." Esau tsked. "Out in the cold. Maybe I should—"

"No. You're not sleeping here with them. We'll be on the road for—" he calculated "—sixteen days, if the weather cooperates. You'll have plenty of time to coddle the plants. Tonight, you should get cleaned up and have a proper night's sleep in a bed."

But Esau fretted anyway, and Leif offered to put the tarp on that night instead of waiting until the morning. By the time he finished securing the fabric to Esau's satisfaction, Leif really did have to check on the horses. He sent his father into the house with strict orders to wash up and go to bed, then headed to the barn.

He breathed in the comforting scent of hay, horses and manure. Rusalka greeted him with a soft nicker. He topped off her water bucket and added grain to her feed. Then he tended to the other two. Fisk had lent them a hardy sorrel quarter horse named Cider for Mara to ride, and who had also been trained to pull a wagon. Leif had traded in his father's horse for a barrel-chested black draft horse named Kohl. The brute could probably handle the wagon on his own, but, due to the distance, Leif felt better with two.

Mara arrived just as he finished cleaning Kohl's hooves.

"Come to *check on the horses*?" He leered.

She ignored him. "I tucked your father into bed, but I had to promise to tug on the fabric over the wagon to ensure it doesn't come loose."

"Sorry."

"Why are you apologizing?"

"'Cause you're looking at your future. I'm going to turn into an obsessed old man who will demand that each bag of tea I make will have the exact same number of leaves while hair sprouts from my ears seemingly overnight."

She cocked her head to the side and stared at his right ear. "And how's that different than now?"

He growled. Mara squealed and ran for it. He caught her easily and carried her to the piles of hay. "Time to check on the horses," he whispered in her ear.

The next morning didn't go as smoothly as Leif had imagined.

"No." Mara crossed her arms, emphasizing her point.

Leif tried again. "But it'll be dangerous."

"No. Where you go, I go." She climbed into the wagon and sat next to Esau, picking up the reins. "We'll avoid populated areas and keep to the back roads. We'll be fine."

"Do you even know—"

"Leif Liana Zaltana, if you don't mount Rusalka, I'm going to run you over."

Esau covered his mouth but couldn't quite stop a chuckle. Great. This was just great. Didn't she know Leif wouldn't survive if something terrible happened to her? However, her stern expression meant he'd have more luck convincing the Commander to welcome magicians into Ixia.

Leif bit back a childish retort. Instead, he said "Fine" in a peevish tone, then mounted Rusalka and took point. The wagon team followed him from the farmstead.

They stayed close to the Sunworth River and kept to the back roads. Making steady progress to the southwest, Leif decided to remain well north of Fulgor and skirt the edge of the Snake Forest until they crossed into Featherstone lands. A solid plan, until it started to rain.

They'd been traveling about eight days when the skies opened and sheets of rain turned the road into a quagmire, forcing them to go south to access the stone-covered ground of the well-traveled east-to-west route.

Blending in with the other miserable travelers was the one benefit of being on a popular route. However, the presence of more patrols was the downside. But with the three of them huddled under cloaks and the plants hidden by the tarp, no one paid them much attention.

Two rainy days later, they were just about past the outer limits of Fulgor when the scent of burnt sugar stung Leif's nose. Magic. He tightened his grip on the reins but stayed still as the strong aroma swept over him. Rusalka jigged to the side, agitated by the sudden wave of magic. Leif kept his mental barrier firmly in place but was ready to build a null shield if they were attacked by a magician.

Nothing happened, and the scent disappeared. But just in case, Leif pressed on longer than normal, trying to get as far away from Fulgor as possible before they stopped for the night.

The next day dawned bright and beautiful. Too bad it didn't last. Two hours after they set off, Leif spotted a patrol of ten soldiers blocking the road, as if they'd been waiting for them.

Leif slowed Rusalka and opened his magical senses. When Mara caught up to him, he told her to stop the wagon.

"I'll go talk to them. Stay here, but be prepared to jump off the wagon and run into the woods if I give you the signal," he said.

"What's the signal?" she whispered.

His magic detected the sweet scent of her anxiety. It smelled like molasses. "I scream, 'Run.'"

"Clever."

"That's why I'm one of Valek's go-to guys for spy stuff."

She managed a smile. "Just be careful."

Leif nodded and spurred Rusalka into a gallop. Ideally this was just a routine road check and he could talk his way past them. When he rode into a fog of black licorice, his magic detecting deceit, he knew they were in trouble.

Big trouble.

He spun Rusalka around and drew breath to warn Mara, but the words died in his throat. Another patrol stood behind the wagon. Mara spotted them as well, and the bitter tang of her fear stabbed right through him.

Ah, hell. He grabbed the hilt of his machete.

Mara stood up and yelled, "Rusalka, go home."

"No!" But the well-trained horse grabbed the bit in her teeth, cut to the right and plunged into the woods at top speed, leaving Mara and his father far behind.

4

YELENA

After Valek left, I paced from the door to the kitchen and back again. The Mosquito was smart and well aware of Fisk's network. There was no way he'd let them find him unless he wanted them to. He probably had an ambush set up for Valek. At least a null shield no longer trapped him, but he was vulnerable to other magic. An intelligent magician would be able to adapt once he or she realized the shield didn't work.

I really wanted to get some fresh air, but I was trying to be sensible. There was no reason for me to go out. Turning around, I almost walked into Hilly. She blocked my path to the kitchen.

"Lovely Yelena, there are two runners upstairs waiting to report in."

I glanced at the door.

She inclined her head. "Do you think staring at the door will make him return faster?"

"No." In fact, he'd warned me he might not be back until the morning.

"Then why do it?"

"Because emotions don't always follow logic."

"Ah."

"And I'm going crazy."

"That I understand. Perhaps you need something to keep your mind occupied."

"The reports—"

"Not enough. What about all that plant information you and Mr. Valek collected?"

"I'm waiting for my father and brother."

She remained quiet.

I sighed in defeat. "But that doesn't mean I can't take a look at it now. Thanks, Hilly."

Flashing me a smile, she returned to the kitchen as I headed to Fisk's office. The two young boys sprang to their feet when they spotted me. Words tumbled from their mouths before I'd even settled behind the desk. I raised a hand, and they stopped.

Once I was ready, I asked them to repeat the information. Noting it down in Fisk's log book, I thanked them for the good work. I assumed it was vital. Fisk had his members gather an eclectic range of data. And from this variety, he was able to make connections and discover golden nuggets of intel.

I collected the files Valek and I had taken from Bavol's residence. Ignoring the dark brown stains of my own dried blood, I returned to the office. During my initial pass through, I organized them into three categories—useful, useless and beyond my expertise. I marked the third pile for my father.

Getting comfortable, I read through the notes in the useful stack. Bavol had considered the grafting techniques that Leif said Owen's unknown Master Gardener used to increase the production of Theobroma. He had sketches of how to cut into the tree's bark and insert a limb from an older tree and then bind them together. The older limb would produce pods quicker than the new host tree, cutting down on the two-year wait for the tree to mature.

I wondered if Bavol had tried it. There hadn't been any

plants in his home or office. Would he have used another location? Maybe in the Council Hall? No. Not enough light. Perhaps the Magician's Keep? The gardeners who worked for the Keep had an impressive amount of knowledge.

Another hour passed as I continued reading, marking some pages for my father to explain. But one sketch drove me to my feet. I ran to our rooms and hunted through my travel pack, hoping that it was still there after all the insanity of being captured by Bruns.

It was. Thank fate!

Dashing back to Fisk's office, I compared Onora's drawing from the Commander's castle to the sketch in Bavol's file. They matched. I sank into the chair, mulling over the significance. Onora had drawn the saplings that Owen had carried all the way from Sitia. He called them Harman trees, and they had to be important with a capital *I*. Now Bavol also had a picture of them, but there wasn't an explanation to go with it.

I growled in frustration. So close! However, this could be a clue that Owen's Master Gardener might have worked with Bavol at one point. And they needed a place to work close by. Maybe even one of those glass hothouses. I returned to my reading, hoping for another clue.

"What are you scowling at?" I jumped at the sound of Fisk's voice. He stood in the doorway.

"Bavol's notes. Did you have a productive afternoon?"

His light brown eyes shone. "I finally found Lovely Adara the perfect dress for her wedding."

"You're seriously excited about that? At a time like this?"

"Yes. She is extremely picky, and her father promised me double payment if I found her one within the week." He tapped his bulging pocket and coins rattled. "He hated to pay, but once again I proved I can find *anything* in the Citadel."

I grinned at him.

Fisk held his hands up. "Oh, no, what did I say?"

"Have you found a structure made of glass in the Citadel? Or maybe a building with lots of windows? Perhaps with greenery growing inside it?"

"No, but…" Fisk moved to his desk and dug through the drawers. "Tweet mentioned a green glass roof, but I thought I'd translated his report wrong."

"I'm amazed you understand him at all." Tweet's tongue had been cut out at a very young age, so he communicated with a variety of hoots and whistles. Hence the nickname.

"We both grew up on the streets," Fisk said, as if that explained everything. He withdrew a notebook and flipped through the pages. "Ah, here it is. Tweet tried to look inside, but a man spotted him and chased him off with threats of harm if he returned. I figured he'd found a skylight and was peering down into someone's bedroom. People don't like it when you spy into their private rooms." His tone made it clear that the very concept amazed him.

I suppressed a smile. "Where was this glass roof?"

"Not far from here. I can have someone take another look."

"I need to go and see it for myself," I said.

"But Valek—"

"—said I can get some fresh air. Besides, once he kills The Mosquito, the others will be too frightened to come after me. Plus it's close, and you'll be with me. Right?"

"I don't know."

I tried another tactic. "We can bring along a couple bodyguards, if that makes you feel better."

"Bodyguards? You do realize most of my people are underage."

I stared at him.

He fidgeted under my scrutiny. "Well, I do have a few members who are skilled fighters."

"Please, Fisk. I'm going crazy in here. Valek was okay with me leaving as long as we stay nearby."

"If anything happens—"

"It won't."

"—Valek's going to kill me."

"I'll kill you if I have to stay inside one more moment."

"Sorry, but Valek scares me more."

"That's 'cause you've never seen me cranky." I stood.

"All right, but we'll need disguises. And if Valek asks, you forced me at knife point."

"Chicken."

"Damn right."

Our disguises turned out to be a family. Fisk played the father, I took the role of mother and the bodyguards, Lyle and Natalie, were dressed as our children. The irony was not lost on me. With blond curls and chubby cheeks, Lyle was so adorable, I had to resist picking him up and hugging him.

As Fisk and I strolled hand in hand, I asked, "Are they even armed?"

"To the teeth."

"Must take after my side of the family."

Fisk chuckled. "They've been bugging Valek for lessons, and he's been kind enough to work with them when he has time." He squeezed my hand. "He's going to make a wonderful father."

I squeezed back in agreement. We walked for a while in silence. I enjoyed the fresh air and the afternoon sunshine warming my black hair. One of the guild members had pinned it into a sedate bun and used makeup to age my face. My future had stared back at me in the mirror.

Fisk navigated the maze of streets and buildings that comprised the northwest quadrant of the Citadel. Constructed

MARIA V. SNYDER

from a variety of building materials, the once-organized grid of residences was now a labyrinth of homes, apartments and shacks.

"Tweet said he'd meet us near there," Fisk said. "It's a bit tricky to find."

"Good. Is anyone following us?"

"No one has taken the least bit of interest in us."

I considered the speed of his reply. "You have more people shadowing us, don't you?"

"Of course."

"How many?" Or rather, just how scared of Valek was he?

"Two scouts and two sweepers."

"Sweepers?"

"They follow behind and ensure no one is trailing after us."

"Ah."

When we drew closer to our destination, Tweet appeared as if from nowhere. He took my other hand and smiled shyly. We strolled another couple blocks in silence.

"Go with Tweet," Fisk said. "He'll show you and Lyle where the glass roof is, and the rest of us will meet you on the flip side."

"All right."

Fisk released my hand, and I allowed Tweet to lead me. Lyle, the chubby-cheeked blond, trotted at my heels like a lost puppy. We cut through a narrow alley, climbed a rickety series of steps and cat-walked between buildings until we reached a roof. Tweet stopped and pointed to an adjoining roof that was made of glass. Sunlight reflected off the surface, so I was unable to see inside.

Tweet put a finger to his lips and mimed tiptoeing. Understanding the need to be quiet, I crept toward the glass roof. My pulse raced as I drew closer and spotted green shapes. But when I reached the edge, disappointment deflated my excitement.

Algae coated the inside of the glass. All the plants Bavol had been interested in would need sunlight to grow. I peered through a couple clear spots, but dead plants and shriveled leaves occupied most of the room. It appeared nothing but mold and fungus grew inside.

I returned to Tweet, who shrugged as if to say it was worth a shot.

Not about to give up, I crouched down and described the glass hothouse to Tweet. "In order to build it, they would have needed large sheets of glass. Maybe you or one of your friends saw a glassmaker delivering them?"

He met my gaze and nodded. Lyle and I followed him off the roof and joined Fisk. I shook my head at his questioning expression.

"Back to HQ?" he asked.

Tweet piped up with a series of hoots.

Fisk groaned. "Why didn't I think of that?"

"What did he say?" I asked.

"There's a glassmaker with a factory in the fourth ring of the Citadel who has been specializing in sheet glass for windows."

"Great. Let's go talk to him," I said.

"I don't know," Fisk hedged. "The bounty hunters have been watching the market. And you said Valek only approved a short trip."

"We'll avoid the market. Besides, with these snazzy disguises, no one will suspect a thing."

"You're killing me, and not with your humor," Fisk muttered. But he led the way, once again taking up his fatherly role.

We stayed away from the popular routes and avoided the deserted streets. Half the time I didn't know where we were, but I trusted my guides. I smelled the sweet odor of burning

MARIA V. SNYDER

white coal before I spotted the small factory tucked between two warehouses. The sign above the door read Keegan Glass.

A chime announced our arrival. Glass wine goblets, vases and pitchers decorated the display shelves. I gathered the "kids" close and told them not to touch anything.

A middle-aged man glided from a back room. He gave the kids a stern glare, as if daring them to misbehave, before asking if he could help us.

"I hope so," Fisk said. "We are building onto our house, and my wife wanted to put in big windows in the new kitchen. She loves her plants and would really love just a wall of glass, but that's impossible. What's the biggest size you can make?"

Well done. Fisk was flawless.

"Actually, sir, I can make you a wall of glass, if you'd like." Fisk and I acted shocked. "But Crystal Glass said—"

"It's impossible?"

Fisk nodded.

"It is. For *them*. Not for Keegan Glass. *I've* made an entire *house* out of glass."

Yes! Keeping up the act, I furrowed my brow in suspicion. "Surely you jest."

"It's quite simple, actually." Keegan then proceeded to explain how he made sheets of special glass that were used to build a structure. "Mind you, it wasn't very big, but with enough support, it could have been bigger."

"Was it part of a house?" I asked.

"No. It was the size of a large shed, but I can make yours to attach to an existing structure."

Excited, I turned to Fisk. "With all that sunlight, I could grow all my own herbs!"

"You could," the glassmaker assured me. "In fact, the guy who ordered it mentioned something about vines."

Fisk pressed his lips together. "I'd like to see it first. Is it in the Citadel?"

"No. We delivered it to a farm south of the Citadel."

Fisk glanced at me. "Doesn't your cousin own a farm? She's also a plant nut. Maybe…"

But Keegan didn't fall for it. "Not likely. My client prefers that I don't discuss the specifics of his order."

Backing off, Fisk inquired about prices. Keegan wrote down the estimated measurements of the wall and returned to his back room. Fisk waited a few minutes before signaling the kids, who immediately started to bicker and then mock-fight. He gestured for me to intervene. I played the aggrieved mother trying to get her kids to stop. When they knocked over a couple vases, Keegan flew from the back room to admonish us.

I apologized and tried to clean up the mess while the kids continued their argument. As if on cue, the kids settled down, and we paid Keegan for the broken pieces. He was probably so glad to see us go that it would take him a while to realize that in addition to losing a sale, he'd lost an invoice as well. During the chaos, Fisk had slipped into Keegan's back room. Keegan would have used the invoice for the other job to estimate the price of our project. At least, that was the hope.

"Did you get it?" I asked Fisk when we turned the corner.

"Yep."

"And?"

He pulled a folded piece of parchment from his pocket and studied it. "No client name."

I cursed.

"Language, Mother," Lyle scolded.

"Be quiet, or I'll pinch those adorable cheeks of yours."

"Wouldn't be the first time," he muttered sourly.

"There is an address for delivery and a date," Fisk said.

Better. "Where was it sent?"

"A farm right along the border of the Avibian Plains."

Of course. The plains would be the perfect place to hide a glass hothouse. Only the Sandseed Clan and Zaltana Clan could travel across the plains without getting lost, and there were only a couple dozen Sandseeds left. But that meant if Bavol had been working with Owen's Master Gardener, then the mystery person had to be a member of the Zaltana Clan. My clan. My elation died.

"When was it delivered?" I asked Fisk.

"A little over three years ago. Do you think it's still there?"

I told him about my theory.

"Makes sense. No one would accidently discover it in the plains," Fisk said. "Too bad the plains are so huge. It'd be impossible to find."

"No, it wouldn't. Bavol would build it only far enough in to hide it from the roads. No reason to go any deeper."

"There's still a lot of ground to cover."

"Shouldn't be a problem for a Sandseed horse like Kiki."

"You can't go unless you have permission from Valek."

I laughed. "I'd like to see you stop me."

His face creased as if he was about to get sick to his stomach. "Yelena—"

"Relax, Fisk. I'm kidding, and I'm sure Valek will approve of the trip, since I'd be leaving the Citadel and going where only a few can follow."

"You're going to give me a heart attack one of these days. Do you know that?"

"You love all this intrigue and drama. You're the Sitian Valek."

Fisk laughed and started to shake his head, but his expression sobered. He glanced at me. "Do you think if we manage to save Sitia from the Commander, the Sitian Council would hire me as their Chief of Security?"

"They'd be idiots not to. But would you really want the job? You'd have bosses."

"Ugh. I didn't think of that. Hmm… I guess it would depend on the salary."

We walked toward HQ in companionable silence. The lamplighters began their nightly routine, moving from one lamppost to the next like synchronized fireflies. The sun had disappeared behind the Citadel's walls, which meant we'd been gone a few hours. Ideally we would return a few minutes before Valek, so I wouldn't have to worry about him. However, I'd be thrilled if he was already there, waiting for us, even if it meant I'd be in trouble for this extended trip. Although promising to remain in HQ had its…perks.

When we entered the northwest quarter, we caught up to the lamplighters. Amazed by their dexterity, I watched as one woman climbed the post one-handed, holding a lit torch in the other.

Fisk grabbed my elbow and pulled me along at a quicker pace. Concerned, I hurried to keep up and noticed that there were far more lamplighters than this street required, and yet half the lanterns remained dark. I glanced around. We were surrounded by a ring of figures holding blazing torches, and I was unarmed. I'd left my bo staff back at HQ because it didn't fit in with my disguise.

We stopped. I reached for my switchblade as nasty-looking curved daggers appeared in Lyle's and Natalie's hands. Even Fisk pulled a short sword from his tunic. My thoughts flashed to Valek as I slid my feet into a fighting stance. If I escaped, I'd never dismiss his concern for my safety as being overprotective again.

Undaunted by the display of weapons, the ring of fire tightened. My blood sizzled with fear. I shrank back as the lamplighters closed in on us. Even when I had magic, I had no

MARIA V. SNYDER

control over fire. And, although I knew that the Fire Warper had been captured and imprisoned in a glass prison years ago, an irrational part of me expected to see him smirking at me through the flames.

Lyle, Natalie and Fisk formed a protective circle around me. They brandished weapons, but I'd bet all the coins in my pocket that they didn't have any experience fighting against a flaming torch. Neither did I. I held my switchblade, even though its nine-inch blade was inadequate. Fisk had the best shot with his short sword.

One of the lamplighters gestured to a small gap opening in the circle. "Fisk and the kids can go. We don't wish to harm them."

"No," Fisk said.

"Yes, go," I said at the same time.

"No."

I put my hand on his shoulder. "Go and bring back help."

"The sweepers should already be on the way for help." He glanced at me with a grim expression and whispered, "We need to delay as long as possible."

"I'm not worth your life."

Surprised, he said, "Sure you are. Without you, I wouldn't *have* this life."

"Fisk—"

"Time's up," the lamplighter said.

The gap closed, and the lamplighters rushed us. Although the kids showed an impressive amount of skill, the math just wasn't in our favor. Shorter weapons and a dozen against four. My switchblade was knocked from my hand, and it didn't take long for the four of us to be backed against the building.

A torch was thrust at my chest. "Hands up, or we'll set your clothes on fire."

I didn't need any more incentive. I held my arms up as heat

brushed my face. The bright light seared my vision, turning everything behind the fire black. Next to me, Fisk punched one of the lamplighters, but another ambusher swung his torch at Fisk's temple. Knocked unconscious, Fisk collapsed to the ground with a heart-stopping thud. Lyle and Natalie dove through the lamplighters' legs, and four of the attackers chased them. I hoped they escaped.

"Lace your hands behind your head," a voice ordered me.

I did as instructed, not only hooking my fingers together, but through my bun as well.

"Turn around."

I faced the wall. Someone grabbed my wrists. Then each one was pulled down behind my back and snapped into a cuff. These guys weren't taking any chances. But they failed to check my hands. I held two fistfuls of bobby pins.

Dousing their torches, they ignored my questions as they led me through the Citadel without saying a word. I hated to admit it, but posing as lamplighters had been a smart move. No one so much as glanced at us. Six of them kept me boxed in the middle, hidden from casual view. I dropped one bobby pin after each turn, hoping that Valek could follow my trail and I didn't run out before we reached our destination.

I wondered just how long they'd been waiting for me to leave the security of HQ. The ambush must have taken some planning. Did they set it in motion as soon as I was spotted this afternoon? How did they know I'd still be out at twilight?

Did it really matter at this point? No. All that mattered was that it had worked, and I was caught.

We entered the rings of warehouses, factories and businesses in the central area of the Citadel. Looping around to the alley behind a sprawling structure, the lamplighters led me inside. Before I stepped over the threshold, I dropped my last two bobby pins. Piles of crates littered the floor, and we wove around them before stopping at a set of stairs that disappeared down to the dark basement.

One of the group found a lantern and lit it. A skittery prickle coated my skin as we descended. My imagination conjured up visions of a dank cell and being tortured. I slowed. Hands grabbed my arms and pulled me along. At the bottom of the steps was a narrow hallway, and at the end was another door. My insides turned to goo and I braced for the horrors that waited for me within.

5

VALEK

"That's it?" Onora asked, sounding disappointed. "Thought I'd get to see a show. You versus The Mosquito on a rooftop venue."

Valek gestured with his bloody dagger to the four prone forms around her bare feet. "Thanks for the help."

She shrugged. "Trapping you in a null shield wasn't fair."

"Are they dead?"

"No."

"The Commander send you?"

"Yup." Onora studied Valek without emotion. She had pulled her long brown hair into a bun on top of her head. "But you knew that already."

"It never hurts to pretend ignorance."

"Or to have people underestimate you."

"Yup." Valek wondered if that was a hint about her true abilities. He'd expected her to ambush him, not square off against him in a fair fight. That meant she was either crazy, brave or very confident. He'd put his money on confidence.

Onora stepped over The Mosquito's sleeping goons. When she was within six feet, she pulled her daggers. Valek excelled at knife fighting, but Onora had been trained by the same teacher—and she was about twenty years younger than him.

He met her gaze. "Stay in Sitia with us. We need you."

There was a split-second flash of hesitation in her gray eyes, and then it was gone. "I gave my loyalty to the Commander. *I* don't go back on my word."

"The Commander is not the same man I pledged my loyalty to. Even you have to admit he's changed." When she didn't respond, he added, "You're taking orders from Owen Moon now."

"I thought only Janco talked this much before a fight."

Valek shrugged. "Just trying to prevent an unnecessary death."

"Keep it up, and I'm gonna *die* of boredom."

Valek laughed. "Now who's picking up habits from Janco?"

She pressed her lips together and slid into a fighting stance. He waited for her to make the first move. Good thing he didn't blink, because when she came at him, he barely blocked her knives in time. His suspicions were correct—Onora *had* been hiding her skills.

This was going to be…interesting.

At five feet eight inches, Onora was four inches shorter than Valek, but she made up for her height disadvantage with speed and agility. Valek remained on the defensive as she shuffled in close, executed a flurry of strikes and danced back before he could counter. Then she switched tactics, circling him and coming in at an angle. Worry flickered in his chest.

"The Commander's been training you," he said.

"Yup."

A brief stab of hurt and jealousy almost broke his concentration. While the Commander had always been willing to spar, he'd never offered to teach his fighting techniques to Valek.

Fire raced across his neck as her blade skimmed over the

skin, snapping Valek back to the fight. He returned his full attention to Onora. But an impressive number of cuts peppered his arms and ribs by the time Valek had seen enough of her tactics to plan a counterattack. The next time she stepped forward, he also shuffled in close.

Valek launched an aggressive offensive of strikes with not only his blades but also his feet. His longer legs kept Onora at a distance.

She grinned at the new challenge. *Grinned.* Ah, hell.

He kept the pressure on her but knew he wouldn't be able to maintain the pace for long. Already he sucked in breaths, while she appeared unfazed by the exertion. Real fear pumped through his heart.

He changed tactics again, this time trying all his tricks. He hooked her ankle and sent her to the ground. She rolled and regained her feet with ease. Valek poured on the speed and backed her toward the edge of the roof. She dodged and sidestepped.

Then he started fighting dirty. She growled, but countered. In a flash of understanding, Valek knew he wouldn't win unless he used magic.

No.

With the last of his strength, he knocked the blades that had been aimed at the center of his chest, just wide enough to miss his vital organs—he hoped. Valek dropped his own weapons, shuffled in close and grabbed her wrists as she stabbed one blade into his shoulder and the other into his left hip.

Ignoring the explosion of pain, Valek fell back onto the roof, pulling her with him. He wrapped his legs around her torso and squeezed her to his chest. Onora struggled to free herself. He tightened his grip, making it difficult for her to breathe and proving that he'd won the bout. He didn't want

MARIA V. SNYDER

to squeeze the life out of her, but he'd do it to save his own life. Yelena and the baby needed him.

She stopped resisting. "I...wasn't going...to...kill...you," Onora gasped.

"Oh? You sure...looked like you...wanted to kill me," he puffed. The pain and effort of the fight had caught up to him.

"I wanted...to...see if I...*could* beat...you." She relaxed. "I can't."

Valek eased up on the pressure but didn't let her go. "You came closer...than anyone. Only the Commander...has beaten me one-on-one." He considered her earlier comment. "If you weren't going to kill me...then what did you plan to do... when you had your knife at my throat?"

"Make you promise to come back to Ixia with me."

Not what he was expecting. At all. He thought about it as his breath steadied. "The Commander is getting worse."

"Yes. Obviously it's due to Owen Moon, but I can't *do* anything. Your corps won't acknowledge me as their boss, so I've no help except Gerik. I swore to protect the Commander, so I thought if I let you live, you'd return with Ari and Janco and help me free the Commander."

"You'd have to tell him you assassinated me." He wondered if the Commander would be upset by the news. Probably not while under Owen's influence.

"Yeah. Otherwise all Owen would have to do is use one of those shields, and you'd be skewered."

He huffed in amusement at her use of another Janco term. The motion hurt like hell. "Like I am now." Valek released his hold on her.

She extricated herself and sat up. "Sorry. I really didn't expect that last move."

He waved away her apology. "Desperate times..."

"Do you want me to..." She made a yanking motion.

"No." Valek tried to sit up. Pain forced him back down. "Yes. I'll need some bandages." He could heal his wounds with magic, but not on top of a roof without Yelena nearby to give him instructions.

Onora picked up one of Valek's knives. He tensed, but she crossed to The Mosquito's goons and cut strips of cloth off their tunics. It would take a while for Valek to trust her. He'd won, but it had cost him. If they'd fought again, she'd win. Of that he had no doubt.

Returning with the bandages, Onora set the knife aside. "Which one first?"

"Hip." He braced for the pain as she wrapped a hand around the hilt. Even so, a gasp hissed between his clenched teeth as she yanked it free. Blood poured out.

She helped him staunch and bandage the wound. Then she moved to his shoulder, and he experienced a whole new kind of agony. He was too old for this shit. When she finished securing the bandage, Onora let him lean on her as he stood. A moment of dizziness spun the Citadel around him. When the world steadied, he realized the sun balanced on the edge of oblivion. They must have fought for half an hour, at least. No wonder he felt as if he'd been run over by a herd of horses.

Onora picked up his daggers with exaggerated slowness and handed them to him hilt first. Smart. He met her gaze as he tucked them away. Then she cleaned hers and slid them back into their hidden sheaths.

"Can you climb down?" she asked.

He walked to the edge and peered into the dark alley below. The descent was doable, but it was going to be torture. "Yes."

"What about the bug and his people?"

"Leave them. His people will eventually wake and need to decide what to do with his body." Speaking of deciding, Valek glanced at Onora. "What are you going to do now?"

MARIA V. SNYDER

"Go with you, if your offer is still good."

"And if it isn't?"

She didn't blink. "I don't know. I can't go back to Ixia. Guess I'd have to find a job here."

And he was sure Bruns would be happy to employ her. "My offer stands, but it's going to take me a while to trust you again."

Onora looked up in surprise. "Again? I thought you *never* trusted me."

"That's what you were supposed to think."

Crossing her arms, she studied him. "So, to me, nothing's changed."

"Yup. Except when I do trust you, we'll go rescue the Commander."

She smiled, and it reached her eyes. It was that smile that convinced him she'd been telling the truth. However, he wasn't going to let her know. No. He'd let her sweat it out for a while.

As expected, the climb to the alley was a test of his pain tolerance. Twice he clung to the wall and fought off unconsciousness as fire burned along his shoulders and ringed his waist. Thank fate the trip down didn't take long. Onora waited for him below.

Once he recovered, he asked, "Do you know where we've been staying?"

"Yes."

"How long have you been in town?"

"A couple days."

He cursed. "Fisk will need to relocate his headquarters."

She agreed. "There are a number of assassins in town. I don't know if that's normal, but it's a good thing they're not the brightest."

Small comfort. Valek told her about the bounty.

"Yelena needs to leave the Citadel," Onora said, alarmed. "The city is contained by an unclimbable wall and has only so many hiding places. Even those idiots will find her eventually."

He barked a laugh that turned into a hiss. "I tried logic."

"Try again."

He admired her optimism. She followed him as he crossed the Citadel, staying in the shadows. Her passage was soundless, and when he glanced back at her, her skin and clothing appeared darker, as if she was turning into a shadow. Valek remembered Janco commenting on how well Little Miss Assassin blended in with her surroundings. Janco hadn't detected magic, but he didn't always pick up on the more subtle users, like Reema. It was a bad time to open his magical senses so Valek added it to the list of things he still needed to discover about Onora.

When they reached the secret entrance to Fisk's HQ, Valek said, "Here's the story. My injuries are due to a fight with The Mosquito. He used magic and, if you hadn't come along to help, I'd be dead. Oh, and you had no intention of carrying out the Commander's order to assassinate me."

"Except for the fight with the bug, it's true. Why the change?"

"You tell me."

It didn't take her long. "You don't want Yelena to be mad at me." Her brow crinkled. "Why?"

He waited.

Onora shook her head, truly puzzled.

"Because she considers you a friend. Yelena doesn't have many friends. And none who have also been—" there really was no way to say this gently "—raped. You share that in common, and it forges a bond. I don't want to ruin that for her... or you." He sensed she needed it more than his wife.

MARIA V. SNYDER

"Thanks."

He nodded and tapped the code on the door. Hilly opened it. Her gaze slid to Onora.

"This is Onora. She's going to be staying with us."

She stepped aside, letting them in. Hilly took one look at his bloody tunic and said, "I'll fetch Chale."

"Thanks. Can you tell Yelena I'm back?"

Hilly paused and turned around. Her tight expression warned him before the words left her mouth. "She's not here."

He stilled as a number of emotions fought for dominance. Fury rose to the surface, but his battered body couldn't produce the energy to sustain it. Instead, a tired anger laced his voice. "Where is she?"

"She's with Fisk, two bodyguards, Tweet and a four-person surveillance team. They're wearing disguises. She's fine."

"That's not what I asked."

"They went to check a glass roof in this quadrant. They should be back any minute—"

"Not helping."

"I don't know."

Valek tightened his grip on his knives. He hadn't realized he'd drawn them.

"I'll go," Onora said.

"No. She knows the Commander sent you. We'll go together."

"Renée! Innis!" Hilly called into the kitchen behind her. "Report for backup."

"We don't—" Valek tried.

"They know all the problem spots. And they can fight."

Two teens raced into the room. Both were about sixteen years old. Renée was a sturdy-looking girl with pale skin and red hair, but Innis looked like a stiff wind could blow him over. Nonetheless, their determined expressions warned him that arguing would involve too much energy. And he needed every ounce to find Yelena. They tucked daggers into hidden sheaths. Valek figured he'd ditch them if they couldn't keep up.

Without a word, he strode to the door and headed out. It took another minute for his brain to catch up with his body. He had no plan, and therefore no direction and no way of finding Yelena. Valek stopped and sorted through the limited information. Hilly mentioned a roof. A rudimentary plan formed.

"I need to get onto a roof, or the highest point in this quadrant, without scaling a wall. Can you get me there?"

Renée and Innis exchanged a glance.

"Penny's Arch?" Renée asked.

Innis nodded. "Safest bet."

"This way," Renée said before taking off with a ground-eating stride.

Valek, Onora and Innis followed. After ten minutes, he hoped the teens wouldn't ditch *him*. At least the effort to maintain the pace kept his mind occupied. His injuries throbbed with pain, and he didn't have any spare energy to conjure up various dire scenarios for his missing wife.

The street lamps emitted enough light for them to skirt security patrols, avoid busy intersections and cut through an impressive number of alleys. Then it turned tricky.

Renée scrambled up a dilapidated shed and crossed a high fence to get onto the roof that was connected to a row of houses. Innis accomplished it with equal ease. Valek sweated as he climbed and almost lost his balance on the fence. Onora touched his elbow to steady him.

Once on the roof, they stayed on the top of the buildings, winding through the quadrant. The place resembled a maze, and Valek didn't have the strength to track their location.

Penny's Arch turned out to be a thick walkway between

MARIA V. SNYDER

two buildings. It arched high up in the middle, as if the structures had shuffled closer together and bowed it.

Valek scanned the area, noting the brief patterns of the original structures that emerged from the unorganized mess. He didn't know what he'd expected—a giant hand pointing to a specific section? Maybe if he used magic...

Valek lowered his mental barrier and was immediately assaulted with the thoughts of the thousands of people all around him. He raised his shield again, cursing. The entire endeavor had been a waste of precious time.

About to ask Renée to lead them back to HQ, Valek noticed that one area was darker than the others, but there was a bright glow right next to it. As if all the lanterns had decided to huddle together instead of spreading out.

Assassins were creatures of night and shadows, and if they'd set up an ambush, it would be in the darkest part of the city. And if there wasn't a naturally dark spot, then they wouldn't hesitate to create one.

"Renée, can you get us where it's dark?" Valek asked, pointing to the spot.

"Yes. It's near the entrance. There are two routes. Which one?"

"The fastest one."

"There's a wall."

"Up or down?"

"Down."

"I can handle it. Let's go."

Another race through the city. More pain and the conviction that his arm was about to rip from his shoulder. The trip blurred into one test of endurance. He kept his gaze trained on Renée's back, concentrating on the next step.

Shouts pierced his fog. Two more of Fisk's guild members

joined them. Their mouths moved, but it took him a moment to decipher their words. And when he did, they made no sense.

"Slow down. What's this about sweepers and lamplighters attacking?" he asked.

"They're the sweepers for Fisk and Yelena's surveillance team," Innis explained. "They were running for help. Guess the scouts missed the ambush."

The word zipped through him. "What ambush?"

"The lamplighters. Or people dressed like the lamplighters. They attacked with…" He swallowed, afraid to continue.

"With what?" Valek kept his fists pressed to his side to keep his hands from grabbing the boy's shoulder and shaking him.

"Torches."

Cold dread numbed Valek's pain. "Where?"

"This way."

He pulled his daggers and noticed Onora and the others doing the same. They raced after the two sweepers, heading toward the bright spot he'd seen from Penny's Arch.

Except when they arrived, it was no longer ablaze with light. Instead, the dark area had spread, encompassing the entire street. Valek signaled for everyone to slow down. No sense rushing into another ambush.

They found the scouts first. The two young men had been knocked out, but their pulses were strong. Fisk lay crumpled on his side next to one of the buildings. He was unconscious as well, and had a large, fist-sized burn on his left temple. Blood dripped from a cut on his cheek. Valek suppressed his fury, keeping a firm grip on his magic.

"The lamplighters formed a circle around them and forced them up against the building," one of the sweepers explained.

"How many of them?" Valek asked.

"At least a dozen."

Lovely.

"Over here," Renée called. "I found Lyle and Berk."

Valek crouched beside them. Peppered with cuts, bruises and burns, the two...boys looked in worse shape than Fisk. But their chests rose and fell with even breaths. "Are they the bodyguards?"

"Yes."

Incredible.

"They're good," Renée said in their defense. "They were just outnumbered."

"Any sign of Yelena?" he asked the group.

No response.

Onora appeared next to Valek. "A word?"

They moved away from the others. "Did you find something?"

"I've an idea of which direction they're headed."

"Let's go." He stepped past her, but she touched his shoulder and he bit back a scream of pain.

Onora showed him her bloody fingers. "You're in no condition to go anywhere. I'm surprised you made it this long with the amount of blood you've lost."

Valek growled at her, "I'm fine."

She stared at him. "Twelve of them. Two of us. Think you can handle six with that shoulder?"

He sighed. "I'm listening."

"Go back to HQ and take care of your injuries. I'll discover where they've taken Yelena. Then I'll return, and we can plan a way to get her back. Together."

She was right. Yet his heart didn't agree. It slammed against his chest, trying to rally the troops, get the body moving, or else it threatened to break out and go on without him. "What if she doesn't have the time to wait for us to plan?"

"If they wanted her dead, we would have found her body."

She was right. But could Valek trust her?

Onora met his gaze, sensing his hesitation. "She's my friend. My only friend. Ever. I'm not going to let *anything* happen to her."

"What about Sergeant Gerik?"

"He's not my friend. He's my brother."

6

LEIF

By the time Leif wrestled control back, Rusalka had taken them far away from the wagon and its precious cargo— Mara and his father. None of the patrol members had chased after him. Leif dismounted and walked Rusalka, letting the horse cool down. He needed to cool his raging thoughts, as well.

Impotent fury burned in his chest over what Mara had done. She'd commanded Rusalka to go home, and the horse hadn't hesitated. Damn. This was the exact reason why he'd wanted Mara to ride Rusalka. So she'd be safe. But she'd refused, and now she was caught, along with his father. Double damn.

Trying to suppress his fear and anger, Leif considered his next move. The patrol would most likely take them to Fulgor, to either the security headquarters or the garrison. If he could intercept them before they arrived...

No. Too many of them. Plus the soldiers were on horseback, and Leif would need to bring along a couple mounts for Mara and Esau. Doubtful he'd find any extra horses in the middle of nowhere. Leif glanced around at the forest and realized he had no sense of his location. As much as he hated—no, despised—the idea, he'd have to wait until they were taken to a specific place before he could rescue them.

At least he had friends and family in Fulgor. Opal, Mara's younger sister, wouldn't hesitate to help him, and neither would her husband, Devlen. Leif checked Rusalka's legs and gave her water, but his mind was already planning his next move.

Only later, with Rusalka headed toward Fulgor, did Leif grudgingly acknowledge Mara's quick thinking and intelligence. Of the three of them, he had the best chance of coordinating a successful rescue. He had magic, connections and the most experience. It made sense that he'd be the one to escape.

But that didn't mean he had to like it.

Opal's glass factory appeared to be abandoned. No light shone from any of the windows. The sweet smell of burning white coal didn't float downwind. No one had entered or left since he'd started surveilling the place around midafternoon. Leif looped around the building one more time, checking for other watchers, and spotted a couple with a view of the front doors. Interesting.

He ducked down the alley and picked the side door's lock. Inside, he confirmed his suspicions. Dark, quiet and cold—three things he'd never experienced when visiting Opal's factory previously. The four kilns had always remained blazingly hot, day and night. Heating glass to its melting point took too much time and effort to let the cauldrons cool.

Leif lit a lantern and checked the apartment on the second story. Opal, Devlen and their two adopted children, Reema and Teegan, lived above the factory. A sick feeling swirled in his stomach when he spotted the overturned chairs and broken table in the kitchen. The military must have taken them. With Devlen's superior fighting skills and Opal's ability to

MARIA V. SNYDER

make magic detectors, they would be an asset to the Cartel. Once they were brainwashed, of course. And even though Opal was immune to magical subversion, she would do anything to keep Reema safe.

Yelena had sent a messenger to Opal weeks ago, warning them of the Sitian takeover, but Leif guessed they didn't get it in time. Good thing Teegan was currently safe on the coast.

Leaving by the same door he'd entered, Leif headed toward the headquarters for Fulgor's security. Nic and Eve, two officers and friends of Opal, might be able to help him. But once he arrived, the number of uniformed soldiers coming and going at HQ meant the military had taken control of the local security and would likely arrest Leif on sight. No surprise, as martial law had been declared, but it had still been worth checking. Leif watched the flow in and out for a couple hours, just in case he spotted Nic's broad shoulders or Eve's short hair. No luck.

Leif had one last place to go before he ran out of options. Then what?

He pushed down the panic. He'd worry about that later.

The Pig Pen bustled with customers despite the late hour. Leif noted four Sitian soldiers, but he'd altered his appearance as much as he could under the circumstances. It was hard to disguise his square face or his stocky build. No sign of Nic or Eve, and their two stools remained empty. Nic's twin brother Ian owned the Pen and nobody would dare to sit in Nic's or his partner's space. Leif settled on one of the empty stools and waited.

"Those stools are not for you," the man next to him said. "You better find another place to sit."

"I like this stool," Leif said.

"You're either brave or stupid."

"I like to think I'm a little of both. It keeps people guessing," Leif replied. Then he waved at Ian, who was tending the bar. "An order of beef stew and an ale."

His neighbor laughed and muttered, "This ought to be good."

Ian didn't acknowledge Leif's existence. Didn't make a move, as far as Leif could tell, but within a minute, four thugs surrounded Leif.

"You're leaving," Thug One said.

They grabbed Leif under the arms and carried him to the door. Then they tossed him to the sidewalk. Leif rolled on impact and regained his feet.

"Tell the proprietor that I will no longer frequent his business. He doesn't get a second chance."

"Don't come back, Meat," Thug Two said.

They remained in front of the entrance. Leif brushed his pants off, glared at the impenetrable wall of muscle, and walked off in a huff. He took a circuitous route to the Second Chance Inn and found a hidden place to keep an eye on the inn's entrance. He settled in for a long wait.

If Ian hadn't been influenced by the Cartel, he would relay the message to Nic and Eve that Leif was at the inn. Provided Nic and Eve were also free. If Ian had been converted by the Cartel's special indoctrination methods, then Leif expected a number of soldiers to storm the inn, looking for him.

When the sun rose in the morning without either scenario developing, Leif realized he'd have to rescue Mara and his father on his own. An almost impossible task.

Leif wandered the city, reviewing his options. He could return to the Citadel and recruit helpers. Or he could turn himself in and offer his cooperation and loyalty in exchange for Mara and Esau's freedom. The Cartel was run by business people who honored written contracts.

Or he could go in undercover as one of the soldiers. With

a null shield around him, he'd be able to avoid detection for a while. Then Leif remembered Fisk already had people undercover in the garrison. If he could just contact one of them—

"Spare a copper, sir?" a street rat asked him, holding out a grubby hand.

"Uh…sure…" Leif fished a silver coin from his pocket and gave it to…her? It was hard to tell under the grime.

"Thank you, sir. I have something for you in return," she said.

"Oh?" He opened his magical senses, but only the clean scent of honesty reached him.

"A bit of advice. You need to leave Fulgor. Right away."

"I'm not going anywhere."

"You can't stay here. You've been spotted all over town. It's amazing you haven't been arrested already." Her tone was a combination only a young teen girl could pull off—equal parts annoyed, dismissive and incredulous.

In any other circumstance, Leif would have been amused. "Maybe you can help me? I'm—"

"You're too hot, Mr. Leif. You really need to leave."

Ah. She was a member of Fisk's guild. "Not without my wife and father. They were captured and brought to the garrison."

Understanding smoothed her dirty face. "Oh, so you're *trying* to be arrested. No need. They're not here."

7

YELENA

My captors opened the door into the basement of the warehouse. The bright warmth spilling from the entrance threw me off balance. I blinked and, for a moment, thought I'd been transported to the Commander's throne room or a security office. Lanterns blazed from desks. Men and women bustled about or grouped together, discussing what must be important things, if I read their expressions correctly. A few glanced at us but didn't think my arrival all that noteworthy.

Weaving through the people and furniture, our group—now down to four, plus me—headed toward an open doorway, where more light and voices poured out.

Entering the room, my captors stopped. Three men hunched over a blueprint on a table, arguing over the best way to bypass the building's security.

The guy holding my right elbow cleared his throat to catch their attention. "You were right, General, she's terrified of fire."

The man with his back to us turned around, and my emotions seesawed between terror and relief. Cahil. My survival would depend largely on his state of mind, but at least there was some hope when dealing with him.

"Good. Any trouble?" General Cahil asked.

"Nothing we couldn't handle."

"Valek?" He spat the name.

"Occupied with his own ambush."

Worry for him eclipsed my own fears. Did Cahil set up an ambush for him, as well, or had someone else? Was it Onora?

I kept the questions—and my rising concern—to myself. I wouldn't give Cahil the satisfaction.

"Weapons?" Cahil held out his hand, and the lamplighter gave him my switchblade. He shook his head. "Hanni, search her. Be careful. She'll have a number of darts—some filled with Curare—a blowpipe and a couple sets of lock picks. Check her hair, too."

Damn. Cahil knew me too well. Hanni, who had been standing behind me, did a thorough search and found almost all my hidden surprises. She laid them on the table, and the other men stared at the amount in amazement. As Valek said, it never hurt to be prepared. Too bad I hadn't listened to all his advice.

Cahil's gaze, though, never left mine. His blond hair was military short and he'd shaved off his beard, but not his mustache. Amusement lit his washed-out blue eyes. "This reminds me of the first time we met."

That time I'd been ambushed in the woods. Cahil had believed I was an Ixian traitor and planned to deliver me to the Sitian Council in chains. We'd gone on to become friends, then enemies, and finally called a cease-fire when he was promoted to be a general in the Sitian army and I was named Liaison. However, the last time I saw Cahil, he was taking orders from the Cartel. Was he still under Bruns's influence?

"And I escaped."

"True. But you had your magic then."

He had a point. I studied him. Was Cahil aware that the Commander's invasion was just a ruse to give control of the garrisons to the Cartel? That Bruns planned to use the Sitian military to take over Sitia without ever going to war? That Owen Moon practically ruled Ixia?

Now might not be the best time to broach the subject.

"What? No smart comment?"

I shrugged. "Too easy."

He laughed. "Some things never change."

Tired of the game, I asked, "Can we skip all this? What do you want, Cahil?"

Cahil gestured to the wall. "Secure her," he ordered his people.

Resisting netted me a number of bruises, but I managed to knee one of the guys in the groin and kick another in the shin—a small victory, considering they chained my wrists to the rough stones with my arms spread wide. My ankles were manacled together and secured to the wall, as well.

While my situation had gone from bad to worse, I just couldn't contain my amusement. "Are you *that* scared of me, Cahil?"

His cheeks turned red, and he ordered the others out of his office. Closing the door, he turned to me with a dangerous expression. "I know you, Yelena. I know what you're capable of. What situations you've escaped from. This—" he swept his hand at me "—is excessive for a normal person, but you're far from normal."

"Is that a compliment, Cahil?"

"If it makes you feel better, then yes. It is."

"Good to know you wish me to feel better. I was beginning to worry that you meant me harm, Cahil." I kept using his

MARIA V. SNYDER

name to remind him of the time when we were once friends. A trick Valek had taught me.

He rubbed his hand over his jaw and leaned on the desk, as if suddenly tired. A haunted emptiness clouded his expression, and for the first time since seeing Cahil, I feared for my life.

"What do you want, Cahil?"

"To talk with you."

I bit back a sarcastic comment about having to work on his invitation skills. "I'm willing to talk to you, Cahil, but am I talking to *you* or to *Bruns*?"

"That doesn't make any sense. I report to Bruns."

"Does Bruns know you're here?"

"Of course."

Not good. "What is this place?"

"My base of operations." He quirked a smile. "I never felt secure in the one they assigned me in the Council Hall, so I constructed my own. And I took a page from Valek's spy book and recruited a group of loyal people."

"And you used this network to help Bruns and the rest of the Cartel."

"Yes. They wanted to protect Sitia, and the Council refused to see the need."

Old news. "And now?"

"Why are you fighting the Cartel? Don't you want to see Sitia safe for your child?"

A loaded question. "I'm fighting Bruns to keep Sitia safe."

"Yet another statement that doesn't make sense."

"And I won't be able to explain it to you, Cahil."

"Why not?"

"You won't believe me. You've been indoctrinated."

He paced in agitation. "What the hell does that mean?"

"It means that since you've been ingesting Theobroma for

seasons, you're *all* under his control. None of you can think for yourselves any longer."

Cahil shook his head, stopping in front of me. "No. The Commander is a threat to Sitia. And Bruns is a genius. He's combined our resources, and we finally have an advantage over the Commander's army. We don't have to be afraid anymore."

"I agree, he's innovative. But what happens if the Commander doesn't invade Sitia?"

"Our intel says he's planning to attack soon after the fire festival."

"Which Bruns learned from Valek."

Cahil frowned.

"And why did he order you to the Citadel to find me? Aren't you supposed to be leading the Sitian army against a major attack in four months?"

"Because he knew I'd get the job done. You can't argue about that." He gestured to my chains.

"Fair point. But couldn't you have told someone else how to trap me? I'm sure you have more important things to do."

"It doesn't work that way. Can you just tell someone how to find souls?"

Score another for Cahil. I changed tactics. "What happens if the Commander doesn't wage war?" I asked again.

A mulish look settled on his face.

"Nothing happens, right? If the Commander is such a threat to Sitia's safety, then why doesn't Bruns plan to invade Ixia and take care of that threat once and for all?"

"We're not like the Ixians. We value life. As long as we're ready, the Commander won't invade."

I sagged against the wall. He'd been fully brainwashed. Nothing I could say would change his mind. "When is Bruns coming to kill me and the baby?"

Cahil stilled. "I haven't told him you're here."

MARIA V. SNYDER

Oh? I waited.

"The Commander's new assassin is in town. She and Valek were spotted having quite the battle on the rooftops and, I'm not sorry to say, your husband wasn't doing very well."

I kept my expression neutral despite the pain squeezing my heart into pulp.

"Our intel says that after she kills Valek, she'll be coming after you next."

Not a surprise, but still it felt like a kick to my stomach. "You're going to let an Ixian do your dirty work?"

"Yes. You see, despite your current efforts to undermine Bruns, Sitians like you. If Bruns or I were to execute you, it wouldn't be well received. But if the Commander is responsible for your death, the people will be upset and continue to support our efforts."

Ah, hell. A smart move, although I was surprised Bruns agreed. Or had he? "Bruns doesn't know what you plan to do."

"Bruns had his chance to kill you, and he screwed it up because he wanted you as a showpiece."

"What if Valek kills Onora?"

"Then I let one of the assassins in town score fifty golds. Now, if you'll excuse me, I've work to do." He headed for the door.

"Cahil."

He paused without looking at me.

"If Onora comes for me, can you free me from these chains and return my switchblade?"

"You won't beat her."

"I'd rather die fighting than chained to this wall."

He met my gaze. "All right."

Waiting was never fun. However, when I considered what I was waiting for... I forced my thoughts away, but of course they just circled right back around. If Valek won the fight with Onora, I might emerge from this situation alive. If he didn't, I wouldn't. Unless Fisk's people moved in before Onora could. My emotions flipped from optimistic hope to fatalistic numbness and back again.

In order to remain sane, I focused on how I could protect the baby. I concentrated on what I could do. Me, and not any what-if scenarios about being rescued. But after looking at every possibility, I conceded that my chance of survival was close to zero.

Time limped along, and one of Cahil's agents came by to feed me a handful of grapes. The voices in the other room eventually died, and the lanterns were turned down. They must be stopping for the night.

The thought of a night spent chained to the wall produced mixed feelings. The longer I remained alive, the greater the hope of rescue. Besides, stiff muscles and discomfort were a mere inconvenience if it meant Valek lived.

Another agent strode into the office. He extinguished the lanterns and muttered a hasty good-night before bolting. There were a number of words to describe this night, and *good* wasn't one of them. Nope, not even close. I managed to doze briefly, at least until a burning pain in my shoulders woke me.

Cahil returned in the morning, or what I assumed was the morning, as he appeared awake and clean-shaven. He stood staring at me while one of his men lit the lanterns.

Unable to endure the silence any longer, I asked, "What's the verdict?"

"The Mosquito is dead."

"That's good news."

"I'd thought you'd like that."

"What's the bad news?" I braced for his answer.

"Onora was spotted in the Citadel late last night."

MARIA V. SNYDER

My legs trembled with the effort to hold my weight. The chains prevented me from sinking to the floor. Valek would never have allowed her to walk away from a fight. The fact that she lived meant...

"We were unable to locate Valek's body."

"Why would you care about that?" I asked, leaning back on the wall as the rest of my world melted.

"Confirmation. We think she's hidden the body to keep everyone guessing long enough to avoid any retaliation from Fisk and his people."

The body. No longer being referred to by name. I concentrated on Cahil's comment to keep from screaming. My focus narrowed to one thing—keeping the baby safe. "Why would she worry about Fisk's guild? If she can...beat Valek, no one else can touch her."

"Fisk has the numbers, plus Stormdancers."

"Stormdancers?" This kept getting worse. If Bruns suspected the Stormdancers, then they needed to disappear. Fast.

"Don't act stupid, Yelena. A huge thunderstorm roared over the Krystal garrison at the precise moment you needed a distraction to escape. You couldn't have done it without their help."

"We would have figured something out." Eventually. Maybe. Probably not. Bruns had us pinned.

"You know, I was about to disagree, but I'm sure you would have, which is exactly why keeping you alive is a bad strategy."

"Trying to rationalize your decision so you don't feel guilty, Cahil?"

"I won't feel guilty. I'm protecting over a million people. If only you understood that we're doing the right thing—" he gestured vaguely "—none of this has to happen."

"I understand that's what you believe." I straightened as a

sudden notion popped into my head. Perhaps a way to save the baby. "How about a deal?"

"No deals."

"Okay. How about you prove me wrong?"

Cahil gave me a just-how-dumb-do-you-think-I-am look. "Okay, I'll bite. How would I do that?"

"You stop eating the food Bruns's people cook and wear a null shield for ten days. After that, if you still think Bruns's strategy is beneficial for Sitia, then I'll sign up and help you convince Fisk and all his people to join up, as well."

"And why would I trust you?"

"Because I'd give you my word, Cahil. And you know me. I've never broken a promise. Not even to the Fire Warper."

A contemplative purse rested on Cahil's lips. Then he chuckled. "You almost had me, Yelena. But I'm not falling for any of your tricks."

"It's not a trick. I'm serious. Think about it. There's no downside for you."

"Yes, there is. I'd have to let you live for ten days. Plenty of time for Fisk to send in his troops and rescue you."

Good point. "I'll send them home. I'll stay with you."

"Why would they listen to you? You could have been… what's the word you used?…*indoctrinated* to the cause."

I balled my hands into fists. Another valid concern. "It takes more than a few days to be brainwashed. How about if I sign an agreement, so you have written proof that I've given you my word? And we can also leave the Citadel before they try to rescue me. We can go to the Featherstone garrison. Isn't that where you need to be to prepare for war?"

"So you can steal all our secrets."

"Lock me in a cell. I've been in so many, it'll almost feel like home."

He studied my face for a dozen heartbeats. "You are serious."

"Yes."

"And if I write up an accord right now?"

"I'll sign it."

"What if I'm cured, but I still believe Bruns is the best for Sitia?"

"Then I lose. I'll help you and Bruns, like I promised."

"You're that confident of my response once free of the Theobroma?"

"I know you, Cahil. I know that you would be upset by Bruns's methods of robbing people of their free will and ability to make their own decisions."

He strode to his desk, found a clean piece of parchment and wrote up our deal. It was simply worded. I would agree to go with him, without trying to escape or interfere with any of his plans, and to cooperate for ten days. No one but his loyal people would know who I was. In exchange, he would wear a null shield pendant at all times and no longer consume food cooked with Theobroma for ten days.

"How do I know if the food has Theobroma or not?" he asked.

I gave him a wry smile. "I can taste your food like I used to do for the Commander."

He snorted in amusement and continued writing. At the end of the ten days, if Cahil remained loyal to Bruns, I would agree to join their cause, do nothing to sabotage their efforts and be an active participant.

"Like a cheerleader?" I asked.

He was not amused. "More like a spokesperson. And help us with strategy and planning."

If he was no longer loyal to Bruns, then Cahil would join

our side and be as engaged in our efforts. Cahil held up the finished treaty for me to read.

"We'll need witnesses, and you need to release me." Seeing his dubious expression, I added, "If I'm chained to the wall when I sign, then even a bad solicitor can argue that I signed it under extreme duress and that I don't have to comply." Not like I'd ever break my word; signing the parchment was a mere formality and for Cahil's peace of mind. But I really wanted to be free of these chains.

Cahil disappeared and returned with two of his people. He introduced Faxon, and I already knew Hanni. Faxon unlocked the cuffs, and everyone stepped back a few feet with their hands on the hilts of their weapons. Amused by their skittishness, I rubbed my wrists, working feeling back into my fingers.

When the pins and needles ceased, I signed the agreement, then handed the stylus to Cahil. He paused for a moment—probably trying to uncover any loopholes—and added his signature to the document. Hanni and Faxon affixed their names, and it was official. I focused on the fact that the baby would remain alive. At least for the next ten days. If this ended well, we'd have a powerful ally. If not…

Best to focus on one thing at a time.

I drew in a breath. "We need to leave," I said. "Right away."

"Why?"

I told him about the trail of bobby pins.

"Shit." Cahil barked orders to his people, harassing them to hurry and grab their things. We were leaving. Now.

Keeping out of the way, I hoped I'd have a chance to send Fisk a note. One of the agents handed me a cloak to wear, and while everyone was occupied, I reclaimed my weapons and lock picks. Grief threatened to drown me, but I chanted *keep the baby safe* over and over in my mind to block the emotion. Also there was the possibility that Cahil lied about seeing Onora in the Citadel.

Cahil returned. "Time to go." He grabbed my elbow as we headed to the stairs. A number of his people preceded us, and the rest followed. Twelve total.

"Can one of your crew deliver a message to Fisk?"

He slowed. "Why?"

"So when I'm spotted at the Featherstone garrison, he doesn't risk his people trying to rescue me."

"Why would you be…" Cahil's grip tightened, and he muttered a curse. "He has people in the garrisons, doesn't he?"

"There are many public roads to the garrison. We could be spotted at any place en route."

"Nice try, but you're a lousy liar. Do you know who they are?"

Now it was my turn to curse. "No."

"And you won't tell me until the ten days are over."

"No, I really don't know."

I wasn't sure if he believed me, but he remained silent as we climbed the stairs and exited onto the warehouse's ground floor. A few beams of sunlight pierced the blackened windows, providing just enough light to see the words written on the crates. Our group wove through them as if navigating a maze they'd been through a thousand times. I glanced at the floor. The dust was thick between the piles, but underneath our feet, the path was clean. Even I could follow this trail.

"Head to the Council's stables," Cahil ordered when he spotted the entrance. "Yelena will ride with me on Topaz."

The door opened, almost as if on cue. Everyone grabbed their weapons as Onora strode into the building like she owned the place. I stumbled. The dam inside me broke, and grief ripped right through my body. The tiny spark of hope that Valek still lived died.

Cahil's hand steadied me. "Don't worry. I won't let her kill you."

I didn't have the strength or the ability to correct him. Emotions lodged in my throat, cutting off my air.

He faced me. "Breathe, Yelena. We might need you if this gets...ugly."

Right. I focused on Valek's killer. Barefoot, and with her hair tied back, she looked years younger than twenty. Cahil's agents spread out as much as they could among the piles of crates. Two of them held crossbows and they pointed their weapons at her, even though her hands were empty.

No, that wasn't correct. She played with two bobby pins, spinning them through her fingers. Ah, hell.

Cahil strode forward. "You're too late. Yelena's in our protective custody. Go back to Ixia."

Onora cocked her head to the side. "Why isn't she dead?"

"None of your business."

"But Bruns wants her eliminated."

"Bruns? Are you working for him now?" Cahil asked in surprise.

"No. Bruns asked the Commander to send me to take care of Valek and Yelena." She met my gaze. "One down. One to go."

I drew my switchblade and advanced. The desire to plunge it into her heart pulsed through me. Cahil put a hand on my shoulder, stopping me.

"Bruns would never turn to the Commander for help," Cahil said.

"Then maybe you need to have a chat with your boss."

Frowning, Cahil moved his grip to my arm.

Onora noticed. "Unless you've decided to branch out on your own?" She waited. "No? Then give her to me. I'll finish my assignment and be on my merry way."

"No."

"Why are you protecting her? She's just going to cause you trouble."

"Go home, Onora. You're outnumbered, and the ladies holding the crossbows have excellent aim."

Onora grinned, showing two rows of straight white teeth. "Are you sure about your math, General?"

"I count fourteen of us and one of you."

Nice of Cahil to include me in his group.

"You forgot to check the ceiling for spiders." Onora dove to the side.

Everyone looked up, but I stared at her, stunned. She had used Valek's words. I broke free of Cahil's grip and hit the floor as gray figures darted from where they'd been hiding between the piles of crates.

Cahil laughed. "There's nothing up—"

Fighting broke out, and I stayed low. I'd been shot by a crossbow bolt before. Once was enough. Because of Onora's spider comment, I didn't know if the gray fighters were my friends or enemies. Had it been a signal to me, or just something she picked up when she'd been training with Valek? Rather than risk joining the wrong side of the fight, I kept away from everyone, ducking behind a pile of crates to wait.

I listened to the sounds of the scuffle—thuds, grunts, steel clanging against steel, cursing, a hiss of pain. Then, without warning, Onora appeared next to me.

"It's safe," she said.

Reacting without thought, I pressed the tip of my switchblade to her throat. "Valek?"

She held her hands wide. "Fighting Cahil, from the sounds of it."

Surprised, I stared at her. Was this a trick?

"No offense, but if I planned to assassinate you, you'd be dead by now."

Right. I lowered my weapon as relief swept through me. "Sorry."

We returned to the main area. Cahil's people littered the floor, and a number of gray-clad figures stood nearby. But what grabbed my attention was the man in black who had his sword aimed at Cahil's neck. Cahil glared. A bloody cut snaked from his hand up to his elbow. His sword lay on the floor at his feet.

"Onora?" Valek asked without moving his gaze from Cahil.

"She's here."

"Watch him," Valek said, tossing her the sword.

She caught it easily and kept it pointed at Cahil.

In two strides, I was wrapped in Valek's arms—my favorite place to be. After a minute, I whispered, "I thought Onora killed you."

"I told you I could handle her."

"But Cahil said…" I shook my head. "Sorry. I should have stayed in HQ." Should have trusted Valek.

"Doesn't matter now. You're safe."

"And she's still mine," Cahil said. "Yelena, tell your husband about our agreement."

8

VALEK

An agreement? Valek leaned back to meet Yelena's gaze and did not like her pained expression. Not at all. He tightened his arms around her for a second, his instinct to protect her flooding him for a moment. Then, with effort, he relaxed and stepped away. "What is he talking about?"

Yelena explained the deal she had worked out with Cahil. As she talked, Valek kept a tight leash on his emotions. After a hellacious night spent healing his injuries and worrying about her, this was the last thing he wanted to hear.

"...we need Cahil on our side. You agreed. He won't listen to reason while under the influence of Theobroma. This is the only way we'll be able to convince him."

Anger shot through him. "No. You can't go to the Featherstone garrison. Bruns will find out, and then you and the baby will be killed." Valek pressed his arms to his sides as the desire to throw her over his shoulder and bolt from the warehouse pulsed through him. She hadn't trusted him to defeat Onora. Didn't believe she'd be rescued. For the first time in years, he was furious at her.

"You can't stop her. She gave her word," Cahil said, holding up a piece of parchment.

The smug superiority of Cahil's tone grated on Valek's already frayed nerves. He pulled his dagger and advanced on the idiot. "I know a quick way to void that."

"Valek, stop," Yelena said.

"Are you that certain he'll see reason?" he demanded.

"Yes."

"What happens if Bruns learns you're there?"

"I'll protect her. It's a provision in our agreement," Cahil said.

The handle of Valek's knife bit into his palm. He'd never regretted killing anyone in his life, but he'd kicked himself for letting certain troublemakers live, because they always returned to cause more problems. Cahil happened to be one of them. However, Valek's plan to stop the Sitian takeover did include Cahil's assistance.

"Can I see the accord?" he asked.

"Of course." Cahil handed him the accursed document.

Valek read through the terms. A red-hot knot squeezed his chest. He sought loopholes. None. After committing it to memory, he returned it. "In ten days, I will be at the Featherstone garrison."

"What if she loses?" Cahil asked.

"I won't," she said with conviction.

But Cahil could lie or break their agreement or brainwash her or...a million things could go wrong. If Cahil failed to switch sides, Valek would kill him. There was no way he'd allow Yelena to remain with the enemy.

"You didn't answer my question." Cahil stared at him.

"If she loses, then we are enemies."

"And she stays with me," Cahil said.

His heart tore in half. "Yes."

"I want your word that you won't try to rescue her or kill me if her plan fails."

MARIA V. SNYDER

Valek met his wife's gaze. Yelena seemed confident. Not much he could do at this point. "I promise not to attempt a rescue or kill you." The words coated his mouth with a foul bile. Valek hated that he'd been forced to say them. Why hadn't Yelena trusted him?

Cahil relaxed.

But Valek wasn't done. "But I *will* be by her side."

The idiot peered at him in confusion. "You just said we'd be enemies."

"Correct. I won't help your efforts or hinder them. But I'll be with Yelena until the war is over. Consider me her personal bodyguard."

"Valek, no." Yelena protested. "They'll kill you or use you to learn about the Commander. Besides, Fisk and the others need you. Sitia needs you."

"I'm not fighting against *you*."

Her face lost all color as she realized that was what she had promised Cahil. To fight against her friends and family. She clasped her hands together. "It won't come to that."

"I hope you're right." Their future happiness depended on it.

Onora stepped away from Cahil. "What's next?"

With all the emotional turmoil, Valek had forgotten about Fisk's people. They stood awkwardly at the edges.

"Back to HQ," he said. They'd have to relocate and change their plans. Yelena had agreed to cooperate during the next ten days. Cahil might claim that meant revealing vital information. Also, if Cahil remained convinced of Bruns's good intentions, then Yelena would be obligated to reveal *all* their plans.

Then it hit him. He couldn't be part of developing the new strategy, or else he might be forced to divulge the intel if he became her bodyguard while she worked for the Cartel. Ah, hell. They were screwed with a capital *S*.

"What about my people?" Cahil asked. "Are they dead?"

"No. Neutralized," Onora said. "They should wake up in a few hours."

"Cahil knows Fisk has people in the garrisons and that the Stormdancers are helping us," Yelena said.

And just when he thought it couldn't get any worse. Unable to speak without growling at her, Valek nodded instead. It was all he could handle at this time.

"Let's go," Valek ordered. The guild members and Onora headed to the door. Before following them, Valek glanced at Cahil's smug expression, and Yelena's pained one. "See you in ten days." He left.

Valek set a quick pace for a few blocks. Then he told everyone to scatter and meet back at HQ. Onora stayed with him as he leaned against a building, the enormity of the situation catching up to him. And the regret. He hadn't hugged or kissed his wife goodbye.

"Can you shadow her?" he asked Onora. "Make sure Cahil doesn't go back on his word not to harm her?"

"Yes. Meet in the town near the Featherstone garrison in nine days?"

"Yes. Thanks."

"Don't worry. She knows what she's doing." Onora gave him a salute and disappeared down the street.

He'd like to believe that, but ever since Yelena lost her magic, she'd been doubting herself. And now this idiotic agreement with Cahil. She must have panicked last night, believed Cahil's lies and, worried that the baby's life was in danger, come up with what she thought was a good solution. If only she'd trusted him.

Nothing to be done about it now. Valek pushed off the wall and headed to HQ.

MARIA V. SNYDER

★ ★ ★

"Please tell me you're kidding," Fisk said.

Valek wished. "No. You need to relocate the Stormdancers, my brother, my sister and Teegan to a secure place. Recall Ari and Janco. Ari is going to be your best bet for strategy and planning. When Leif, Mara and Esau return, have them go into hiding. And get your people out of the garrisons before they're caught."

Fisk sat stunned. "Wow."

"Do you have any null shield pendants?"

"Yes. Leif's learned how to make them using wood."

"Please send one to Cahil with my compliments. And another for Yelena, just in case."

"Got it."

Valek left Fisk to absorb the bombshell he'd just dropped on him. When he arrived at their rooms, Valek paused. The smell of lavender—Yelena's favorite scent—sucked away all his remaining energy. He sat on the edge of the bed and rested his head in his hands as exhaustion swept through him.

Once Onora had returned with Yelena's location, Valek had spent all last night planning her rescue, and that was after he'd used magic to heal his shoulder and hip. Chale hadn't been strong enough to repair such extensive injuries. The fact that Valek managed to mend the damage and didn't flame out and kill himself had been a source of pride.

Summoning the strength to stand, he packed his and Yelena's saddle bags. Then he carried them down the stairs and headed to the hidden stables behind the kitchen.

Fisk chased him. "Where are you going?"

"I need to leave so I don't overhear your new strategies."

"Where do we find you if everything works out?"

Valek considered. "The Cloverleaf Inn in Owl's Hill. Do you know it?"

"Yes."

"Good." He continued past the ovens.

"It'll work out," Fisk called.

But Valek didn't have the energy to reply. Onyx and Kiki greeted him with whickers, and they nosed his pockets for treats. Giving each a milk oat, he stroked their necks and checked their legs for hot spots. All black, Onyx was built for speed. Sleek and quiet, he matched Valek's personality.

Valek saddled both horses and secured Yelena's bags and bo staff to Kiki's saddle. Leading them outside, he turned to Kiki. White coated most of her face, except for a swirl of copper around her left eye. She had white socks, but the rest of her was copper. Her long ears pricked forward.

He relaxed his mental shield, allowing Kiki's thoughts to fill his mind—one of the perks to having magic. As a Sandseed horse, Kiki used a form of magic to communicate mentally with humans and other non-Sandseed horses like Onyx.

Lavender Lady? she asked, using Yelena's horse name.

With Peppermint Man, he said. *Go find Topaz. He's at the Council's stables. Lavender Lady needs you.*

Needs Ghost No More.

He'd been Ghost, but since he was no longer immune to magic, Kiki had added the "No More" to his name. *Not this time.*

She flicked him with her tail. *Every time.*

He laughed without humor. *Lavender Lady doesn't agree with you.* Besides, he trusted Onora to keep an eye on her.

Smoke Girl part of herd. Kiki approved.

Smoke?

Unable to verbalize, Kiki sent images of Onora sitting quiet and still, blending in with her surroundings and moving with grace, like a wisp of smoke. Kiki hinted at something deeper within the girl. That a fire burned at her core, but she hid it beneath a smoke screen.

A good analogy, Valek thought.

Kiki smart.

Yes, you are.

Come.

I will be there. I just need...time. To cool down? Time to think?

Kiki's blue-eyed gaze peered right through him. He remained still, even though the urge to squirm like a misbehaving child pressed on him.

Come soon. She trotted away.

He wondered how the Citadel's citizens would react to a riderless horse, but then Valek remembered Kiki's ability to stay hidden, despite being so large. Plus, unlike the other breed of horses, Sandseeds refused to wear horseshoes. No clip-clop of hooves on the cobblestones.

Valek mounted Onyx, but he had no idea where to go, except to leave the Citadel. "Let's get out of here, boy."

After they exited through the north gate, Valek let Onyx pick the direction. The steady rhythm of the horse underneath him combined with his exhaustion and it numbed him. His thoughts stilled. His emotions drained. A cool breeze fanned his face. The moist scent of earth and grass filled the air as trees and bushes blurred past, their green buds and blue sky the only colors.

Whenever Onyx stopped, Valek fed and watered his horse. He rested and ate stale travel rations until Onyx indicated it was time to go. The sun set and rose. Twice.

Onyx slowed as the light faded for the third time. Valek roused in preparation to care for his horse. But instead of halting in a clearing, Onyx approached a building. He had his dagger in hand before Valek recognized the cottage he and Yelena had purchased. It was located in the Featherstone lands, near the border with Ixia. Onyx headed to the tiny stable, pushing the door open with his head.

Valek dismounted. "Did Kiki tell you to come here?"

His horse blew a hot breath scented with grain in Valek's face as if to say, *Snap out of it, man!*

Removing Onyx's saddle and tack, Valek groomed, fed and watered his horse before shuffling toward the dark, cold cottage. Horsehair stuck to his sweat-slicked skin and coated his clothes. The warm season should be renamed the shedding season.

He paused in the threshold. It'd been three and a half months since he'd been here with Yelena. This was where their child had been conceived. Memories threatened to push through the fog in his head. Maybe he'd sleep in the stable. No, he was being silly. He entered. The empty rooms held no warmth. A light film of dust coated the furniture. Not bothering to light a fire or heat up the bathwater, Valek washed quickly. The little cottage had been perfect for them. A washroom and kitchen occupied the right side of the ground floor. A large living area filled the left side, and a huge stone hearth sat in the middle, heating all the rooms. The second story loft covered half the building and contained their bedroom.

After trudging up the steps, Valek shook out the blankets on the bed. Yelena's scent slapped him in the face, and he collapsed onto the mattress. All his anger drained away in one gush of misery. Yelena had gone with the enemy, taking all his hopes and dreams with her. Ten days was enough time for Bruns to learn of her presence in the garrison. An intelligent businessman, he'd have informers in all the garrisons. Cahil had been brainwashed like all the rest. There was no way Cahil could protect her, no matter what he promised.

So what the hell was Valek doing here? Pouting. He should

be arranging another rescue. Except he'd given his word to Cahil that he wouldn't do that, and Yelena would never break hers. Until things went sideways with Bruns, Valek's hands were tied.

He breathed in the clean scent of lavender. As he lay on the bed they'd once shared, a realization came to him slowly. He'd been so furious at her for not trusting him that he was doing the same thing—not trusting her. Yelena had been confident of Cahil's ability to see reason, and she'd escaped plenty of tight spots before. And if the null shield pendant was taken from her, the baby created some kind of void, which protected her from magic.

Her comment about Onora finally registered. The idiot had lied to her. Told her Valek was dead. Desperate and upset, she'd made a deal with Cahil to protect the baby. Ah, hell.

He should have picked up on it sooner. Why had he gotten so furious so fast? He could blame his exhaustion on the fight with Onora, the energy needed to heal, and no sleep. But that was just an excuse. No. The Commander had sent Onora after him. Onora, who the Commander had trained and who fought Valek with the clear determination to kill. Considering Owen Moon's influence on the Commander, that betrayal hurt more than it should. Commander Ambrose no longer trusted him after they'd worked together for twenty-four years. When he combined Ambrose's lack of trust with Yelena's, Valek had snapped. However, knowing why he'd been so angry didn't help Valek feel any better now.

Valek pulled the blanket up to his chin. He needed a good night's sleep. And after that? In six days' time, he'd meet up with Onora near the Featherstone garrison. Now that he had time to think about it, a brief amusement flared over Onora's confession that Gerik was her brother. It was one of those things he should have picked up on sooner, but it made perfect sense now that he knew.

But what was he going to do for the next few days? An idea sparked. He dismissed it as too dangerous, but his dreams swirled around the idea, testing it.

In the morning, Valek sat up and knew exactly what to do. Onyx fidgeted while Valek saddled him, turning a twenty-minute task into forty. Then the horse stood rock-still, despite Valek's signal to go.

"I know you were hoping to rest here a few days," Valek said. "We'll be back soon. I promise."

Onyx glanced at the stable with longing. Then he heaved a sigh and broke into a reluctant trot. Valek suppressed a chuckle—no sense upsetting Onyx any further. Valek required his cooperation; walking would take too much time.

Due to the extra time needed to avoid the border guards and keep out of sight, it took them the rest of the daylight to reach their destination—Ixia. Valek found a comfortable spot in the Snake Forest to leave Onyx.

After taking care of the horse, Valek stroked Onyx's long neck and said, "If I'm not back by tomorrow morning, return to the cottage without me. Understand?"

Onyx lifted his head and stared down at Valek.

"I don't like it either, but I need to do this."

The horse snorted. Valek assumed that was an agreement and left. He wanted to be in Castletown before the streets emptied for the night. Due to the small city's proximity to the Commander's castle, Valek was certain there would be extra security officers patrolling the town. If he was spotted, this outing would not end well. His cloak hid most of his advisor's uniform, but he needed to blend in, and there were other uniforms stashed at his safe house in Castletown.

When Valek entered the apartment on Pennwood Street,

MARIA V. SNYDER

he surprised the agents who had been assigned to keep an eye on the city. Adrik and Pasha jumped to attention and saluted. Good to know they remained loyal.

"Report," he ordered.

They glanced at each other. "Uh...there's nothing to report, sir," Adrik said.

Valek raised an eyebrow, inviting them to continue.

"We've been in standby mode, waiting out the storm, sir," Pasha rushed to explain.

"The storm?" Valek asked.

"There's an order for your execution, sir," Adrik said. "All your agents know it's bogus, and we won't work with that... girl because she's with *them*." He spat the word. "We figured we'd lie low until you returned."

"Lie low?"

"We all stopped sending reports to the castle, and all orders coming in have been ignored."

Valek was touched by their rebellion. "You realize that's an act of treason."

"No, it isn't," Pasha said. "The Commander is not in *command* anymore."

"Is it that obvious?"

"As soon as he ordered your execution, we knew. No way you'd do anything against Ixia or the Commander." She flicked a long blond strand of hair from her face.

He wanted to hug them both.

"And there have been a few...inconsistencies with the Commander's orders," Adrik said. "He's never changed his mind before, or given us conflicting orders. It's almost like there are two people in power."

His agents confirmed Valek's suspicions.

"What are your orders, sir?" Pasha asked. "Did you come back to evict the Sitians?"

If only it was that easy. "Not yet. For now, continue to lie low."

Their postures wilted at the order.

"We will evict them at the right time," Valek said. "I need you to spread the word to the rest of my corps that Onora is to be trusted."

Twin surprised expressions.

"Any estimate on a timeline for the eviction, sir?" Adrik asked.

"I suspect things will get hot around the fire festival."

"And if they don't?"

"That means we failed, and they won."

"You didn't train us to fail, sir," Pasha said. "And if we can't fail, neither can you."

Valek laughed. "You're right. Now tell me about the castle complex. What's the word on security?"

"Touch the wall, and you'll have half a dozen guards dropping down on your head," Adrik said.

Owen must have rigged it with a magical alarm. "How about the gates?"

"Only the south gate remains open, and it's tight. All personnel going through it are checked against a list."

Valek considered. "All right. I have a job for you." He explained.

As they headed out with eager grins, Valek rummaged in the supply closet. All his safe houses had the same materials. Soon after the takeover, the Commander had given Valek the freedom to secure these houses and purchase equipment. The addresses hadn't been written down, nor did the Commander know them—the recent orders were probably being sent by Maren. The locations were given to Valek's agents to memorize once they were trusted members of his corps. Each house had its own safe filled with enough money to cover expenses for a year.

It didn't take the agents long to return. They supported a wobbly man between them. He wore a kitchen uniform and muttered nonsense—the effects of goo-goo juice. Best of all, he was about six feet tall with short dark hair.

"His name is Mannix, and he just delivered the castle's meat order to the butcher," Adrik said.

"Good work." Valek dressed in the all-white kitchen uniform with the red diamond shapes on the shirt.

Moving quickly, Valek mixed up putty, matching it to Mannix's skin tone. He then used it to alter his appearance, softening his sharp nose and chin. Tucking his longer hair under his collar, Valek buttoned the shirt up to the top to keep it in place.

"Well?" he asked Adrik and Pasha.

"It should work," Adrik said.

"Should?"

"It's dark. You'll be fine," Pasha said.

He hoped so. If he was caught…

No. Not going to think about it. "Release Mannix in the morning. And stay alert for any news about the castle and the Commander's plans."

"Yes, sir," they said in unison.

"Thanks for the help." Valek left by the back entrance and headed to the castle's south gate.

He strode with confidence and didn't hesitate when approaching the gate. There were six armed guards. Valek recognized them. It was the two others—one man and a woman—standing just inside the gate who he didn't know. The man held a clipboard and the woman stared at him.

"Mannix, cook's aide," she said in a bored voice to the man. Magic brushed his mental shields. Owen had brought in more magicians. Not good. Valek lowered his shield enough for his surface thoughts to be read. At least, that was what he hoped he did. He concentrated on what he needed to do to prep for the morning breakfast rush.

"Mannix, got it," clipboard man said. "Go on."

The gate opened, and Valek headed straight to the castle. His thoughts remained on finishing his work before going to bed. As soon as he entered the castle, he ducked down a little-used corridor. The perks of being in very familiar territory. Valek pulled off the putty and the kitchen uniform, revealing his black skintight sneak suit underneath. While he was tempted to visit his office, he was smart enough to avoid it. Instead, he found a hiding place to wait until the perfect time.

Near midnight, Valek ghosted through the empty hallways. He had written all the security protocols for the castle. As long as they hadn't been changed, he would be able to reach his goal without being spotted. It all depended on Owen's confidence that Valek would never return. Since Owen had easily captured Valek in a null shield and almost killed him the last time they met, the magician had to be feeling pretty confident that Valek would stay far away. And Owen must also believe in Onora's ability to assassinate Valek, or he wouldn't have sent her. Add those together, and Valek was literally betting his life that the protocols had not been changed.

He found a window, drew in a deep breath and then climbed out. He clung to the west wall and braced for shouts of discovery or a crossbow bolt shot through his back. When nothing happened, he scaled the wall.

Avoiding all the booby traps on the roof, Valek reached his target. He opened the window and slipped inside. A bright fire burned in the hearth, and the Commander sat in front of it, sipping his brandy. The other seat was empty. A relief. Valek

MARIA V. SNYDER

had expected to see Owen lounging in Valek's chair, and he had a dart filled with Curare just in case.

"Have you come to assassinate me, Valek?" the Commander asked without even glancing in his direction.

Valek approached the Commander but kept his distance. No doubt the man was armed, and his skills with a knife exceeded Valek's. "No."

He turned his head, and his golden gaze met Valek's. "Why not? I signed your order of execution. I sent Onora after you. Well done, by the way. I didn't think you'd beat her. Pity, though. She had such potential." He paused as if truly grieving. "You know your only chance to leave this room alive is to kill me. If you can."

A big if. "I came to talk."

"Nothing you say to me will change anything." His tone was matter-of-fact, and a bit resigned. The Commander's all-black uniform was pristine as always. Two real diamonds on his collar reflected the firelight, sending sparks of yellow onto the walls.

The faint scent of apples laced the air. "I didn't come to talk to *you*."

"You expected Owen to be here? We're not to that point yet, but he'll be along soon enough."

"Magical alarm?"

"In a way." The Commander tapped his forehead.

"How much time do I have?"

The Commander refused to answer.

Which meant not much. Valek knew the Commander's physical body was female, but Ambrose had always identified as male and lived as a man since puberty. No one else was privy to this information except Yelena. Her Soulfinding abilities detected that the Commander's mother's soul also resided in his body. When Signe had died in childbirth, her magic transferred her soul to her baby. The Commander had trusted Yelena and Valek to keep it a secret.

"I came to talk to your mother," Valek said.

He shrank back in his chair. "She can't talk."

"She can if *you* let her."

"I can't… Owen…" He pressed his fingers into his temples as if enduring a sudden headache.

"Signe's the reason for the inconsistencies. Why you could send me and Yelena away, despite Owen's influence on your mind. Owen doesn't have control of your mother's soul."

"Owen thinks he does, but he can't know…or all is lost."

"I'll be quick so he doesn't find out," Valek promised.

The transformation of Commander Ambrose into his mother, Signe, would have been startling if Valek hadn't seen it before. His features didn't shift, but from one breath to the next, another person peered from his almond-shaped eyes. Even with his bristle-short gray hair, she appeared feminine.

"How did Owen get to Ambrose?" Valek asked her.

"Owen pleaded for his life. He promised my son barrels of Curare for his army in exchange. It appeared to be a standard business deal, but Owen planted a…seed, I think, during that first meeting."

"A seed?"

"A powerful suggestion in Ambrose's mind that Owen was to be trusted."

Ah, hell. That was over four years ago.

"What happened to the null shields in his uniforms?"

"Owen forced Ambrose to lie about them to you so you wouldn't suspect he was being influenced by the magician."

Valek considered. "It worked. Plus, I didn't notice any change in him. Not then."

"No one did. It was subtle. In fact, Ambrose wouldn't believe *me*—he was too focused on getting Curare for his soldiers. Owen kept the connection hidden until he arrived at the castle. By then it was too late."

"When is Owen planning to take over Sitia?"

"Once the Cartel has control of the Sitian military, it's a done deal. They are going to assign military districts and generals to the clans."

"The Sitian people won't accept that." Especially Fisk and his people.

"Owen and the Cartel have a way to change their minds."

"There isn't enough Theobroma for everyone in Sitia."

"They don't need Theobroma. They have something else," Signe said.

A cold wave of fear swept through him. "What is it?"

"I wish I knew. Owen won't tell Ambrose what it is. But it doesn't matter at this point. My son cannot disobey Owen's commands."

"But you can?"

"For now. Owen believes I'm trapped, like Ambrose, and we've been careful to keep up the ruse."

Good to know. Valek focused on the problem at hand. "Do you have any idea what it is?"

"All I know is that Owen learned about it from his ancestor, Master Magician Ellis Moon. It was in the magician's notes."

Valek muttered a curse. "Does Owen have those notes with him?"

"I don't think so. He complained that he could only copy the information, despite being a direct descendant. They're considered vital historical documents and are kept in the Magician's Keep's library. He made an odd comment about how the library wouldn't let him take the files."

Muted voices reached them through the gap under the door. The doorknob jiggled.

"You need to go," Signe said.

9

JANCO

Janco resisted the urge to scratch. No matter what color he dyed his hair, it always caused his scalp to itch something fierce. And the fake ear glued over his scarred one just added to his discomfort. Sweat pooled underneath the putty, driving him crazy. Add in the heat and humidity, and Janco longed for an assignment on the northern ice sheet. At this point, he'd gladly endure frostbite and evade snow cats. Better than dodging deadly Greenblade bees.

The creak of wood and rattle of a harness cut through Janco's misery. From his hiding spot, he craned his neck, peering around a bush. Sure enough, a wagon rode into view, heading west. Two horses pulled it at a fast trot. Janco waited as it slowed. The driver—a tall, impossibly thin Greenblade man Janco had nicknamed Toothpick—must have spotted the tree trunk lying across the road. The tree wasn't big enough to halt the wagon entirely, but in order to continue his journey, the driver would have to roll over it with care or risk a broken wheel.

Janco shifted his weight to the balls of his feet. When the horses stepped over the log, he slipped behind the wagon. As the wheels thumped over the obstruction, Janco climbed in and crawled under the tarp, avoiding the sacks of white coal as he wedged his body between the other supplies.

The wagon increased its speed after it cleared the trunk. Janco grinned and pumped his fist. Toothpick didn't have a clue he'd just picked up a passenger. Not sure how long it would be until they stopped, Janco settled into a more comfortable position.

Janco'd been watching and tracking the deliveries to the Greenblade garrison for two weeks now, trying to identify which wagon brought in the Theobroma for the cook to use in the garrison's food. It had been harder than he expected, since they used a tarp and the schedule was erratic. But once he figured out Toothpick was the delivery man, it didn't take long to plan a way to hop a ride to see just where the Theobroma was coming from.

Janco checked the lump under his tunic, ensuring it remained in place. The null shield pendant kept the Cartel's magicians from brainwashing him and also from detecting him. They'd been rather vigilant about spies, which was why he couldn't simply follow the wagon on horseback.

As the afternoon turned into evening, Janco guessed Toothpick would stop for the night. He remembered General Brazell's Theobroma-producing factory. They had smelled the sweet aroma of the drug miles downwind. He doubted many of the Greenbladers recognized the scent. However, finding an isolated spot to produce the stuff must have been difficult, since the Greenblade forest, which covered two-thirds of their lands, had dozens of tiny settlements all over the place.

When the wagon slowed hours later, Janco prepared to ditch. While certain he could take Toothpick without breaking a sweat, Janco didn't want to ruin the mission. This was an information-gathering endeavor. Ari, his partner, had just about pounded the importance of not being seen into Janco's head.

Slipping out before the horses stopped, Janco dropped onto the road. He ducked into the woods as the wagon continued toward a bright yellow glow. Perhaps Toothpick had decided to overnight in one of the settlements. By the distant brightness, Janco guessed it must be one of the bigger villages.

Janco hurried to catch up, but paused at the edge of the... town? He stared through the trees at the wide array of buildings and factories. People bustled between them even at this late hour. Greenery filled the extra-long glass hothouses lined up like fingers—ten in all. The nutty sweetness of Theobroma fogged the air and mixed with the unmistakable citrus tang of Curare.

Holy snow cats! He'd hit the jackpot.

Or had he? This was blatant, even for Bruns. And judging by the age of the tree stumps and worn paths, this had been here for years. Someone would have noticed it by now. Unless Owen had set it up and scared off the locals?

The answer popped into his head, and Janco almost groaned aloud. Idiot.

He removed the null shield pendant—a gift from Leif—and a dark forest replaced the scene of bright industry. All sounds ceased, and only a moist, earthy scent filled his nose. Pain burned in his right ear.

The town was covered by a massive illusion. Even though Janco hated magic, he had to admit the deception was impressive. The main road curved around the northern edge, so unsuspecting travelers would avoid all the buildings.

Looping the pendant back around his neck, Janco squinted in the sudden light. He spent the next couple hours observing. The activity slowed well after midnight, with only a few people remaining outside. The desire to nose about the complex to learn more pulsed in his chest. Perhaps he'd spot Owen's Master Gardener. The man or woman had to be in charge of

MARIA V. SNYDER

this operation. And Janco even wore the long green tunic and pants that the Greenblade men preferred. His light brown hair and tanned skin matched them as well.

However, Janco remembered the last time he'd pushed his luck. He'd ended up not only getting caught but also causing the rest of his team to be captured. Dax had died, Hale went missing and Leif had almost died.

Being sensible for the first time in his life, Janco left, jogging along the road. He'd report back to Ari and, after they sent the information to Fisk, they'd return and have a good snoop.

Janco arrived in Longleaf late the next morning. Instead of trying to go undercover in the garrison, they'd decided to rent a small house in the nearby town and keep an eye on the flow of traffic going to and from the base.

With a sudden burst of energy, Janco sprinted to the narrow wooden house wedged in the middle of a row. He rushed into the front room and was about to shout his good news, but Ari's tense posture stopped him in his tracks. Ari wore his I-want-to-strangle-someone expression. One that was usually aimed at Janco, but was directed at a young boy. Poor kid.

At six feet four inches tall, Ari loomed over most others. The skinny-mini standing next to him appeared tiny in comparison. Must be one of Fisk's…spies. Hard to call kids under the age of fifteen spies, but the little tykes had come in handy since the Cartel decided to take over Sitia. And the guild members had saved their asses back when Bruns had them. Gotta give them their due.

Sensing trouble, Janco asked, "Something wrong?"

"We're being recalled to the Citadel," Ari said. Frowning, he ran a big, beefy paw—er…hand—over the short curls of his blond hair.

"Who and why?"

"Valek's orders. Tell him," Ari said to the boy.

Janco braced for bad news as Skinny-Mini detailed Yelena's capture and her agreement with Cahil—which explained Ari's murderous glare. Despite the results, using lamplighters for an ambush was a sweet move. He'd never look at them the same way again.

"I need to inform the others. Master Fisk is pulling all agents from the garrisons," Skinny-Mini said.

"Go," Ari said.

"Wait." Janco grabbed his shoulder. "Are you returning to the Citadel after this?"

"Yeah. Why?"

"Tell Fisk we'll be delayed a few days."

"We can't disobey a direct order," Ari said.

"Don't worry, Ari. Valek will forgive us. He'll probably give us a medal."

"Why?" Ari and Skinny-Mini asked in unison.

He told them about the complex. "We can't return without checking it out. It might be the key to stopping the Cartel."

Ever cautious, Ari asked, "How many guards are there?"

"Doesn't matter. We'll be like ghosts—invisible."

"Ghosts aren't... Oh, never mind. We'll check it out, but *I'll* decide if we go into the complex or just watch from a distance."

"Hey, who put you in charge?" Janco asked, outraged.

"Valek."

"Oh, yeah." All his annoyance disappeared. "No problem. I know you'll want to take a closer look. It's irresistible, like candy and babies."

"I know I'm going to regret asking this, but you find candy and babies irresistible?" Ari asked.

"Hell no. They're both sticky."

His partner waited.

"*Some* people find them irresistible. And, you know…" Janco waved his hand. "They're easy to steal…or something like that."

"I was right."

"About what?"

"I regret asking that question."

Janco clapped him on the shoulder. "But you've learned something. Never pick up a sticky baby, 'cause you'll never be able to let go. And I—" he yawned "—am going to catch a couple z's while you go shopping and pack."

As Janco shuffled off to bed, Skinny-Mini said to Ari, "I thought you were in charge."

"Only when it counts."

It was almost sunset by the time they saddled Diamond Whiskey and The Madam. While Janco missed his horse, Beach Bunny—named after a beloved pet rabbit—he had to admit The Madam's calm demeanor was a nice counterpoint to his own fiery personality. Unconcerned, she watched Janco with gray eyes that said nothing could surprise her anymore. He stroked her neck, smoothing the hair on her gray-dappled coat.

Now with Whiskey, Ari had finally found a horse that didn't look like it would collapse under the big, muscular man's weight. The large dark brown horse had a white diamond blaze on his forehead. Strong and quick despite his size, Whiskey shifted, ready to go.

"After you," Ari said, sweeping a hand out.

Janco hopped onto The Madam and retraced the route to the hidden complex. Once the sun set, they'd have to slow down, so he set a fast pace. On horseback, it would take half the time to reach the spot Janco had marked to leave the horses. No doubt there was a magical alarm on the road closer to the facility. He hoped their null shields would prevent them from triggering it.

They set up a base camp deep in the forest. Infiltrating an unfamiliar location took time. While the size of the place was in their favor—an unknown face would not cause alarm—the efficiency with which everyone bustled about was not conducive to blending in. Ari said they would follow the standard three-stage plan.

Stage one—observe. Janco hated this one. For the next twenty-four hours, they took turns watching the facility from different angles, making notes of...well, everything possible. Boring, but necessary. If they planned to go undercover, they'd spend a week or more studying the complex and seeking the perfect place to insert themselves. But for information gathering, this part wasn't that time-consuming—thank fate.

Stage two—forays. More fun than sitting still for hours. Plus, Janco preened because he'd known Ari wouldn't be able to resist. Forays involved making short trips into the complex at different times to clarify their observations. For example, the long rectangular building in the southwest corner could be housing for the workers or a canteen or could contain offices. They wanted to avoid people and find information, so they needed to know where the offices were located.

Since Ari's size tended to draw attention, Janco completed the forays while his partner watched. He strode into buildings as if he belonged there, nosed about the factories, confirming they were indeed producing both Theobroma and Curare, and took a closer look at those huge glass hothouses. Condensation coated the inside of the glass, blurring the contents into an indistinguishable mass of green.

Workers carried long loops of vines from the second hothouse, so Janco headed toward the ones near the end. Checking that no one paid him any attention, Janco ducked into the seventh house and walked into a slice of the jungle. Thick, humid air pressed on his skin with the scent of living green. Insects buzzed around his ears.

A narrow dirt path cut through the plants. He followed it and recognized Curare vines snaked around the trees and hanging from limbs. Underneath the green canopy, pods heavy with beans grew from the trunks of the Theobroma trees. Janco couldn't identify the other plants, so he broke off a few leaves for Leif and shoved them into his pocket.

Knowing Ari was probably having a fit, Janco headed for the exit. The door opened a few feet before he reached it. A middle-age man with dark skin entered. He carried a long pair of pruning shears.

Startled, the man demanded, "What are you doing in here?"

Janco kept calm. "Just looking around."

The gardener peered at him. A shock of recognition zipped through Janco. He'd met this man before, but at the moment, he couldn't recall his name or the place. Bad enough, but if the man recognized *him*, that would be even worse.

Unaware of Janco's turmoil, the man said, "You're not part of the gardening crew or the harvesting crew, so you're not allowed in here."

"Sorry, sir."

"Sorry isn't good enough. Many of these plants are very delicate."

"I didn't touch anything." Janco stepped to go around him.

The gardener held up his shears, pointing the tips at Janco's chest. "Not so fast. You look familiar. What's your name?"

Without hesitating, Janco said, "Yannis Greenblade, sir."

"You'll be docked a week's pay for this little stunt, Yannis. Be glad I don't fire you."

Ah, this man was in charge. Janco lowered his gaze as if in contrition. "Thank you, sir."

"And stay out of *my* hothouses."

"Yes, sir."

The man lowered the shears, and Janco bolted for the door. Holy snow cats, he'd just encountered the Master Gardener. Now if he could only remember the man's name.

10

YELENA

The bang of the door slamming behind Valek echoed in my bones. Shocked and speechless, I stood among the prone forms of Cahil's people in the warehouse. I'd never seen him so angry with me. But he had every right to be. I hadn't believed he'd win in a fight with Onora, or trusted him to rescue me.

Cahil bent to retrieve his sword. "That went better than expected."

I raised an eyebrow. All his people had been neutralized, and a nasty cut snaked up his arm from when Valek had disarmed him.

"When I saw the Commander's new assassin, I thought she'd come to kill us all. And then with Valek… I never thought he'd let you fulfill the terms of our agreement. Although, at the end there, I think he wanted to kill you more than me."

With good reason. I'd ruined all the plans we'd worked so hard to set in motion. The heart-shaped scar on my chest ached. It'd been only two months since we'd exchanged marriage vows and Valek had transformed the Commander's bloody *C* on his chest into a heart, pledging his loyalty to me. In return, I'd cut a heart of my own, vowing to be with him forever.

"Despite your claims, the Commander is not working with Bruns," Cahil said, distracting me from my morose thoughts.

"How did you come up with that?"

"Onora's obviously working with Valek. That fight on the rooftop was probably staged. Her claim that Bruns asked the Commander to send her was just to make me doubt Bruns. Just like you want to do with our accord."

I couldn't argue the point that Valek and Onora were working together. Why hadn't he told me? Perhaps he didn't have time. Did it matter? No. Valek always put my safety first. If he forgave me, I'd never doubt him again. If not...

I shied away from that awful thought.

"Come on," Cahil said, heading to the stairs.

We returned to the basement office. I bandaged Cahil's cut and then sat at one of the desks while Cahil straightened the mess they'd left behind in their hurry to leave. He hummed to himself. The bastard was in a good mood.

"Did you lie about The Mosquito, too?" I asked.

"I didn't lie about Valek. My sources spotted him fighting Onora, and she was seen later. It was a natural conclusion. As for The Mosquito, he is dead. That's been confirmed."

One bright spot in an otherwise miserable day. The sleepless night caught up to me. Exhausted and heartsick, I rested my head on the desk and welcomed sleep.

Voices and movement roused me. Cahil's people had woken, and they filtered into the office area with sheepish expressions. A few sported bruises, and I helped bandage a number of cuts. It could have been worse.

Cahil sent two of them to keep an eye on the door while the rest discussed their next move. A messenger from Bruns

MARIA V. SNYDER

arrived, and I ducked under the desk to avoid being spotted. They went into Cahil's office, but I remained hidden until the man left.

"Good news, Yelena." Cahil smiled. "I've been recalled to the garrison. No need to invent an excuse for our departure."

"Why do you have to go back?"

His grin turned sly. "I'll tell you in ten days."

Bastard.

"We'll leave tomorrow morning for the garrison," Cahil said to his crew. "Hanni, please pick up supper for all of us."

"Not from the Council Hall's dining room," I said. "The Hall's food is laced with Theobroma."

Hanni gave me a wide-eyed stare.

"You don't know that for sure," Cahil said with an annoyed tone.

"How else can you explain the Councilors' willingness to leave and allow the Cartel to take over?"

"They agreed with Bruns's brilliant ideas and strategy."

"Then why not appoint him General and organize the war preparations themselves?" I asked.

"I'm not going to argue with you anymore."

Too bad. It would be a nice distraction from my situation.

"Hanni, buy a bunch of meat pies from the market." Cahil handed her a gold coin.

"Yes, sir." She bolted for the door.

"This place has been compromised. The rest of you pack up all the intel. We'll move the furniture later."

They bustled about, shoving files and various items into boxes and crates. I stayed out of the way.

One of the door guards appeared and gestured Cahil over. "There's a…person at the door. He insists on talking to you and our…guest."

Scowling, Cahil asked, "Valek?"

Excitement swirled in my chest. Did Valek return to say goodbye?

"No, sir. A young man. Says he has a package for you both."

All warmth died.

Cahil belted his sword on and tucked a dagger into the opposite side. He held a hand out to me. "Come on."

Curious and hopeful that maybe Valek had sent me a message instead, I stood. Cahil grasped my wrist tightly.

"I promised to cooperate. You don't need to hold on to me as if I'm going to run away," I said.

He didn't bother to reply. But as he guided me up to the ground floor and through the gloomy warehouse, I remembered he'd done the same thing when Onora appeared. As if the gesture warned her that I belonged to him. Perhaps he worried the young man would attempt to rescue me.

Fisk waited with the other guard by the open door. The fading sunlight lit his light brown eyes. A painful burn shone on his left temple and a raw cut marked his cheek. I shot Cahil a nasty glare. Fisk, though, peered at me in concern. Even though he was seventeen years old, I still saw the small boy that I'd first met over eight years ago superimposed on his tall and lean frame.

"Ah, it's the Beggar King," Cahil said. "Come to check on Yelena, Your Majesty?"

Fisk ignored Cahil. Instead he asked me, "Are you all right?"

"She's fine," Cahil said.

"And she'd better stay that way, or else—"

"What? You'll send your kiddies after me? They're no match for trained soldiers."

Fisk smiled. I marveled that his grin actually lowered the temperature in the room by ten degrees.

"Oh no, General. I wouldn't do something so...overt. There are *so many* ways to make a person's life miserable."

MARIA V. SNYDER

Score one for Fisk.

"Did you just come here to threaten me? I've more important things to attend to."

"I brought you these." Fisk handed a pouch to Cahil and one to me.

Cahil let go of my arm, and I untied the string. Inside was a wooden pendant of a bat hanging on a necklace. Cahil held up an ugly beetle. Leif had been so thrilled when he figured out how to attach a shield to a pendant. His wouldn't stick to glass or metal or stone, but when he tried wood, it had worked. The sudden desire to see my brother pulsed in my chest.

"Null shields, compliments of Valek," Fisk said.

Was this a sign that Valek wasn't angry anymore? I looped it around my neck, even though the baby seemed to be protecting me from magic. When Bruns had captured me, the daily magical brainwashing I endured wore off as the day progressed. And when Rika had used a magical illusion to disguise herself as Valek, I saw through it when she touched my skin. I'd speculated that the baby was stealing the magic, but since I didn't know exactly what was going on or what the fetus was doing with the power, it was a good idea not to rely on the protection it offered.

Cahil gave me a sour look as he tucked the pendant under his tunic, hiding it from sight. "I don't feel any different."

"It's going to take some time for the Theobroma and magic to wear off," I said.

"So you say." He turned to Fisk. "Anything else?"

"I'd like to talk to Yelena in private."

Cahil crossed his arms as if about to refuse, but after a moment he relaxed and motioned for his men to move away. "Stay in sight," he said to me, then strode far enough to give us some privacy if we kept our voices low. But his gaze remained on me.

"Do you have a message from Valek?" I asked before Fisk could even open his mouth.

"Uh…no."

I swallowed my disappointment. It hurt going down and landed in my stomach with a nauseated splash. "How are Lyle, Innis and the scouts doing?"

"Other than pissed about being jumped, they're healing well. I wanted to tell you we're moving HQ and changing all our plans. I'll have the agents out of the garrisons in a few days. If the general doesn't switch to our side in the ten days' time, you can tell him and Bruns what you know and it won't ruin anything."

"But I already ruined everything."

"No. I did. I was supposed to keep you safe. Instead we took you right into that lamplighter ambush."

I shook my head, but his hard expression meant I'd have an easier time convincing Cahil to befriend Valek.

"Is Valek helping you?" I asked.

Fisk creased his brow. "He can't, just in case you get stuck with Cahil."

"Oh." Why hadn't I thought of that sooner? I understood Valek's anger, and now I comprehended the depth of his fury. "Where is Valek?" I held my hands up. "No. Don't tell me."

"I don't know. He left this afternoon." Fisk lowered his voice even more. "I suspect he'll be keeping an eye on you."

A nice thought, but Fisk hadn't seen Valek's reaction.

"Hey." Fisk draped an arm around my shoulder, giving me a half hug. "It's only ten days, and then we'll have another ally. It'll all work out."

I leaned into him. He was as tall as Valek, but he smelled of wood smoke and pine instead of musk. "Thanks."

"Anytime. Stay safe, Lovely Yelena." He gave me another squeeze and then left.

The room's temperature plummeted another ten degrees in Fisk's wake. I hugged my arms and turned toward the stairs. Cahil followed me without saying a word. Thank fate. We returned to the offices and I sat at an empty desk, staring at nothing while I fiddled with the butterfly necklace Valek had carved for me. Would he forgive me?

The smell of beef pies roused me from my dark thoughts. Hanni set one in front of me. Despite my upset stomach, I ate the entire portion. I had to stay strong for the baby. The rest of the evening blurred together. Soldiers returned and left in waves, carrying crates. I noticed that none of the people were familiar. This crew appeared to be close to or younger than Cahil's age of twenty-nine. None of Cahil's old gang—the ones who'd raised him and lied to him about being King Ixia's nephew—were part of this group. Maybe they were stationed at the garrison. Or maybe he no longer trusted them.

Thinking about trust, I almost groaned aloud. Just how loyal were his people? They'd all eaten the spiked food and been brainwashed. What if I managed to wake Cahil, but his agents refused to obey his orders? There was nothing in the contract about his people following the terms of our agreement. I'd have to ask Cahil about it when—or should that be if?—we were alone.

Later that night, Cahil woke me. I'd been dozing with my head on a desk.

"Come on," he said, pulling me to my feet. "Let's go."

"Where?"

"We don't sleep here, and unless you'd rather be chained—"

"No."

"Thought not." He clamped a hand around my arm, escorting me up and out of the warehouse.

Once again, Cahil's crew surrounded us as if they expected an ambush. I pulled the hood of my borrowed cloak up and over my head. No need to tip Bruns off that I was with his general. Few people strolled along the quiet streets. Clouds blocked the moon, but I guessed it was close to midnight. A light breeze blew dead leaves along the road, their rattle the only sound.

"Are you still worried I'll escape?" I asked after a few blocks.

"No. But I'm sure your husband is nearby."

"He promised not to interfere."

"But that won't stop others from trying to get to you. There's still that bounty on your head."

True. We headed toward the southeast quadrant of the Citadel. Before reaching the government's area, Cahil turned right, and we entered one of those old factories that had been converted into apartments.

"You don't live in government housing?" I asked.

"Too many nosy neighbors."

We climbed to the sixth floor, and I waited in the hallway outside number sixty-six with a couple bodyguards while the others checked the apartment and lit the lanterns.

When it was declared safe, Cahil dismissed his crew. "Hanni, Faxon and Sladen, report here at first light. The rest of you, meet us at the stables an hour after dawn."

"And don't eat any of the food at the Council Hall," I added.

Cahil yanked me roughly inside. "*You* don't give my people orders." He locked the door.

"What happens once you know I'm right, but your people are still loyal to Bruns?"

"They're loyal to *me*."

"For now. You and Bruns are on the same page. What happens when you no longer agree?"

"That's not going to happen."

"Use your imagination, then."

He opened his mouth but then closed it.

Not waiting for him to catch up, I said, "They're not bound to our agreement. They can endanger both of us. They should all avoid the Theobroma and wear null shield pendants."

Cahil rubbed a hand along the blond scruff on his jaw. "I'll think about it."

Progress. I glanced around his apartment. Functional and masculine, a deep blue couch and several armchairs occupied the main living area. A few paintings of horses decorated the walls, and I recognized a lifelike portrait of Topaz in one. The small kitchen lined the left wall next to a door to the washroom. Two doors on the right side must lead to bedrooms. The air held a faint stale scent, and I suspected Cahil didn't spend much time here.

Pointing to the furthest door, Cahil said, "That's your room for tonight. I suggest you lock the door, just in case."

"In case an assassin breaks in?" Not a comforting thought.

"Yes, but I highly doubt it. No one followed us from the warehouse."

"I'm not worried about the ones you can spot."

"And I'm certain Valek is ensuring the others won't bother you."

If Valek was actually keeping an eye on my whereabouts. A strange emptiness filled me and I drifted, unconnected and alone. After washing up, I entered the bedroom—a stark, impersonal space meant for guests—and collapsed on the bed.

Cahil woke me the next morning. His people had arrived and brought cheese and bread for breakfast. I longed for a cup of hot tea—more for the warmth and comfort than an actual need. When we left the apartment, I pulled my hood up. Once we exited the building, Cahil grasped my arm again.

The morning bustle filled the streets. Factory workers hurried to report for their shifts and wagons trundled by, delivering goods and supplies. No one appeared to take any interest in us. A gray blanket of clouds sealed the sky, and a chilly, moist wind brushed my cheeks. The prospect of traveling in the rain soured my mood further.

As we walked to the Council's stables, Cahil said, "I thought about your concerns over my unit. And if you're right and Bruns is...brainwashing us, I'd like to have my loyal people free of his influence, as well. Can Fisk get us twelve more null shield pendants?"

I perked up at the good news. "I don't know if he can get that many with such short notice. But you can send someone to the market and ask one of the Helper's Guild members. Make sure your runner mentions my name."

Cahil sent Hanni. If she minded always being the one picked, she didn't give any indication. We continued on to the stables at a slower pace. When we entered the official government district, I scanned faces, seeking anyone I recognized or anyone who paid particular attention to me. I stole glances at Cahil—was he worried about being spotted with me? No. He appeared calm.

We arrived at the stables without any drama. Most of Cahil's unit waited within. I dreaded sharing a saddle with Cahil, but I was looking forward to seeing Topaz again. The familiar sights and smells of the large barn and rows of stalls eased my anxieties. The Council's stables could house over fifty horses—enough room to accommodate each Councilor, his or her aides, and various military personnel's horses. A small army of stable hands kept them all fed and well groomed.

An excited nicker tore right into my heart. Kiki! I broke into a run and found her sharing Topaz's stall. I hugged her, drinking in her earthy scent and soaking in her warmth. Kiki endured my attention for a couple minutes before she nudged me away, snuffling my pockets for treats.

"She showed up yesterday afternoon," one of the stable

MARIA V. SNYDER

hands said. The young boy gestured to the bench next to the stall.

My saddle, bags, bo staff and tack were piled on the wooden seat. Only one person could have sent her. Perhaps Valek wasn't quite as furious with me as I'd thought.

"I recognized her right off," the boy said. "Miss Kiki's not the type to dump and run, so I figured you'd be along sometime."

"Did you tell anyone she's here?" I asked.

The boy gave me a sly smile. "No. I figured it ain't none of their business."

"Thanks." I slipped him a silver coin. "Miss Kiki and I were never here." I added another silver.

He mocked a confused expression. "Who?" He hooked a thumb at Kiki. "Want me to get her ready?"

"No, thank you." Spending time with Kiki was never a chore. Plus I wanted to search my bags. Maybe Valek left me a note inside one of them.

Cahil caught up to me. "I didn't think Valek was the jealous type, but I guess he doesn't like the thought of us sharing a saddle."

I didn't bother to correct him. Valek trusted me. And while he might be overly protective, he was never jealous. Sorting through my bags, I found my travel clothes, personal necessities, cloak, tea bags, three books, weapons and a medical kit, but no note. Disappointment stabbed deep, and pain ringed my scar. I secured the flaps and saddled Kiki. She gave me a wet kiss on the cheek.

"Thanks," I said, wiping hay-scented slobber from my face.

Everyone had their horses saddled and ready to go by the time Hanni returned with a package.

"Report," Cahil ordered.

"As soon as I arrived in the market, Fisk appeared. He had

only seven pendants, but he said one of his members would meet us along the road and give us the rest," Hanni said.

"His kids must be keeping an eye on us," Cahil said, but he stared at me. "It also sounds like they're going to follow us to the garrison." He shrugged. "And thanks to Yelena, I'm sure by the time we arrive, his undercover agents will have left. If not, it won't be hard to find them."

The desire to punch him flowed through me. Would that be a violation of our accord? Probably.

Cahil handed out the pendants to the seven closest to him. A few gave me sour looks as they looped them around their heads, but they all wore them, tucking them underneath their uniforms.

We mounted and left the stables. Fourteen of us on horseback made quite a sight. Even Fisk's newest recruits wouldn't have any trouble following us, not to mention any bounty hunters. I kept my face hidden, and the other horses surrounded Kiki. Hopefully she wouldn't be recognized, even though some of my enemies had gotten up close and personal with her back hooves.

Exiting the Citadel via the north gate, we headed northeast toward the Featherstone garrison. It would take us two days to reach it.

The rain started soon after we left, and it continued for the entire trip. Cahil's crew mostly ignored me, but I enticed Hanni and Kyrie with offers of tea the first morning, and by the second, they joined me without being invited. We encountered few travelers on the road. A handful of Helper's Guild members approached us during the afternoon of the second day and handed Cahil five more pendants without a word. Then they headed southwest, back toward the Citadel.

We neared the garrison that evening. Cahil slowed Topaz so he rode beside me. My stomach knotted. I'd been expecting his lecture about my behavior at the garrison and why I'd spend the next seven days locked in the stockade.

"I'm going to leave you at an inn in Starling's Egg," he said.

Surprised, I gaped at him.

He huffed in amusement. "I've been thinking about it. And no matter what arrangement I come up with, someone is going to recognize you in the garrison. Even if you're locked in a cell, one of the guards will eventually figure it out." He sobered. "Plus, if the cook is using Theobroma, we won't be able to get untainted food without raising suspicions. With you in Starling's Egg, I can join you for all my meals. The town is just outside the garrison."

"A good idea, as long as the chef at the inn isn't using Theobroma, as well," I said.

"You and your sensitive palate will have to let me know. If that's the case, then we'll purchase food from the market stalls."

I glanced at him. He was being very reasonable. A trick? Or was he starting to think for himself? "What about your people?"

"I'm sending the bulk of them on a mission. The rest will stay with you."

"Mission?"

"I'll tell you what it is, if you'd like to exchange information?"

"You already know everything I do, Cahil."

"Oh?"

"Bruns had his magician interrogate me when I couldn't refuse his commands. He relayed it to you when you visited the Krystal garrison over a month ago."

He tightened his grip on Topaz's reins. "Bruns told you about my visit?"

"No. I was in the room next to his office and overheard

everything. And I distinctly remember that you advised him to put a big bow on me and send me to the Commander."

"Bruns should have listened."

"I agree. It would have been a smart move if the Commander planned to attack Sitia."

"Not this again," Cahil muttered.

"But since Bruns knows that there won't be an attack, he knew I'd be more useful to him in Sitia."

Cahil urged Topaz into a canter, pulling ahead. Kiki stayed back. I expected to have that conversation a few times before he was able to accept the logic.

Starling's Egg appeared to be a typical base town with a larger number of taverns and inns for visiting relatives. The market was full of weapon vendors and gear to lure in the soldiers stationed at the garrison. Cahil sent the bulk of his crew to the base, but ordered Hanni, Sladen and Faxon to remain with us.

We avoided the busy downtown district as Cahil led us on a circuitous route to a quieter side street. He stopped at the Lucky Duck Inn. While we settled the horses in the inn's stables, Cahil went inside the four-story wooden building. When he returned, he handed the keys to two adjoining rooms to Hanni. She gave one to Faxon. Guess I was bunking with Hanni.

"Stay out of sight," Cahil said to me. "If you need anything, one of my people will get it for you. Either I'll be here for my meals or I'll eat food purchased from the market. All right?"

"Yes." House arrest was better than being locked in the stockade. Good thing I had a few books with me.

We ordered supper in the common room. Only a few people occupied the other tables and, aside from a few curious glances, they didn't pay us any undue attention. When the server set down five servings of the house pork-and-noodle

MARIA V. SNYDER

casserole, everyone waited for me to taste it. Other than a nice medley of spices, the meal was Theobroma-free.

And that began my daily routine. Meals with Cahil and my guards in the common room, and the rest of the time I either read in the room I shared with Hanni, trained or exercised Kiki. I sent Hanni out for a few things, mostly tea bags and more books. I tried to engage her in conversation a few times. Quiet and serious, Hanni avoided divulging any personal details, but she was happy to read my books and discuss the finer points of self-defense and intrigue. Hanni also sparred with me. About twenty-five years old with short brown hair, she handled a knife and a sword with ease but hadn't trained with a bo staff. I showed her a few basic moves.

Faxon and Sladen preferred to remain uninvolved and kept an aloof bodyguard's demeanor whenever near me. However, on a couple occasions, their laughter slipped through the door between our rooms.

On day four of my house arrest and day seven of the agreement, Cahil joined us for a late supper. He strode to our table with stiff movements, and his fierce expression meant trouble. I braced for an outburst, but he kept silent.

After we'd ordered, I was unable to contain my curiosity any longer. "What happened today?"

"Nothing. And don't start with any of your—" he waved a hand "—speeches."

"All right."

Our food arrived, and we ate in a tense silence.

When he finished eating, Cahil leaned back and let out an audible breath. Dark smears of weariness lined his eyes. He asked me, "Did you know that Fisk's people not only infiltrated all the Cartel's garrisons but also were working in many different areas—some quite sensitive?"

Oh, no. "Yes, except I'm surprised by how...deep they managed to get. Were they arrested?" Poor kids.

"No. They all scattered. Fisk must have quite the communication system in place." He scowled. "Better than ours."

I kept my expression neutral, even though I wanted to beam with pride. "Is that why you're so upset?"

"No."

I waited.

"In order to ensure there are no more spies, the Cartel ordered a complete sweep of all the garrisons for null shields." He banged his hand on the table. The empty bowls rattled. "Don't say it."

Swallowing, I refrained from stating the obvious—why would the Cartel be worried about null shields if they weren't using magic to influence their people? It almost killed me. Instead I asked, "Are you worried you'll be caught?"

The idea surprised him. He straightened. "They wouldn't test me."

"Are you sure?"

Cahil surged to his feet. "I'm the General of the Sitian Army."

"And you follow the Council's—or, in this case, the Cartel's—orders. There are a number of magicians in the garrison, including Second Magician Irys Jewelrose." I didn't add that Irys hadn't been brainwashed, but had been biding her time. As a master-level magician, Irys could ingest Theobroma and still resist the influence. "You need to leave the garrison for the next three days to avoid the sweep."

He grabbed my shoulders and hauled me to my feet. "*You* don't give *me* orders."

"She's right," Hanni said. "We need to leave town. All of us."

Cahil turned to her. "Oh?"

MARIA V. SNYDER

She stood. "A week ago, I believed in Bruns and the Cartel and would have given my life to support them. Now I won't." Hanni met my gaze. "I'm thinking clearly for the first time in seasons."

Sladen and Faxon stood on either side of Hanni in a show of support. I suppressed the desire to pump my fist.

Cahil released me and sank into his chair. "I hate—and I mean *loathe*—having to say this, but…you're right. Bruns has been using magic." He held up a hand. "*But*, I still believe he is trying to protect Sitia and is doing an excellent job of training soldiers and magicians on how to work together."

Being an adult, I did not gloat or act smug or do any of the childish actions my emotions urged me to do. Instead, I said, "That's why we need you, Cahil. There is still a slight chance the Commander will attack, and Sitia should be prepared, but Bruns's methods are unconscionable. Our goal is to stop the Cartel and get the Council back into power. We can best meet that goal with you remaining in your position."

"And spying for you?"

"Yes. And perhaps waking others up so they're loyal to the Sitian Council and not the Cartel."

"Which will be difficult if Bruns's magicians do frequent sweeps for null shields. It took us a week."

"One problem at a time," I said. "Right now, you and your people need to avoid that sweep. Perhaps leave for a training exercise?"

"That would work, except…" Cahil rubbed his face. "I can't believe I'm doing this."

"Doing what?" I asked.

"Switching sides. Betraying Bruns. Working with Valek." He waved a hand. "Take your pick."

"It's the right thing to do, and you know it."

Drawing in a deep breath, he said, "Then I should tell you that your father and sister-in-law, Mara, have been captured. They're on their way here, and so is Bruns."

11

VALEK

The door to the Commander's apartment flew open. Owen Moon strode in as if he owned the place. Tyen, another powerful magician, trotted at his heels. Time to go. Valek backed toward the window, but his connection to the power blanket disappeared suddenly. Owen had surrounded Valek with a null shield. Unwilling to let the magician know the shield could no longer trap him, Valek froze as if caught. Signe vanished, and the Commander returned.

"What did you hope to accomplish with this little stunt?" Owen asked Valek. There was more gray in his short dark hair than Valek had remembered, and he looked older than his forty-four years.

Valek didn't respond.

"Still hoping to save your commander?" Owen laughed. "Trust me, it's too late."

Not quite, but Valek wasn't going to correct him and expose Signe.

"So, what do we do with you now?" Owen asked no one in particular. "You are wanted for treason. I say we arrest you and then publicly execute you."

"That won't work," the Commander said. "He'll escape the

dungeon. It's best to take care of him now. We can display his dead body so his loyal corps will understand who is in charge."

Even though Valek knew Owen controlled the Commander, the comment still stabbed right through him like a hot poker. Owen frowned at the suggestion. Probably because the Commander didn't immediately agree with him.

"Tyen, what do you think?" Owen asked.

The broad-shouldered magician was the same age as Owen. They had attended the Magician's Keep together. "I think we should finish what we started two months ago and push him out the window."

Tyen's ability to move objects would make that easy for him to do. And Valek couldn't use his darts to defend himself, because Tyen would knock them aside with his magic. Fear coiled in his stomach.

Owen grinned. "I agree. And this time, he doesn't have any friends to come to his rescue." He straightened his arm, spread his fingers and thrust his palm toward Valek.

Valek reacted as if a force had slammed into him. He shuffled backward until his legs hit the windowsill. Blood slammed in his heart. He met Owen's triumphant gaze.

"Goodbye, Valek," he said, once again extending his arm.

Seeing no other way to escape, Valek fell back through the window. Twisting at the last moment, he hooked a hand on the ledge to slow his momentum and swing his body close to the wall. But his fingers slipped off. Butterflies spun in his stomach as he hung suspended in midair for a fraction of a second before gravity pulled him down.

Air roared in his ears as he fell. Then the unmistakable *thwack* of a crossbow sounded a second before an iron bolt slammed into the stone right next to him. When a second bolt appeared on the opposite side, Valek realized the significance. He grabbed the shaft as he slid past, slowing his descent. Another bolt materialized, and he seized it with both hands. With a jerk that sent a throb of pain through his arms and shoulders, Valek stopped his fall. He dangled two stories above the ground.

A couple more bolts arrived below him, and he quickly used them to reach safety. The guard assigned to watch the wall must have recognized him. Valek waved a thank-you and then dashed away before Owen could retaliate. Valek hoped the man or woman had a believable story to tell Owen about why he or she shot the bolts.

After Valek reached Onyx in the Snake Forest, the day-long trip to the cottage was easy in comparison. As he groomed and cared for Onyx, his mind whirled with the information he'd gained from Signe. Owen had an ace up his sleeve, and it was vital that the resistance discover what it was. Valek needed to check the Keep's library for Ellis Moon's notebooks. Ideally there would be a mention of something that was more powerful than Theobroma.

Valek had two days until his meeting with Onora near the Featherstone garrison. And then… Valek would either be a prisoner, or he and Yelena would be free to rejoin Fisk and the efforts to stop the Cartel. If the worst happened, he'd give the intel about Ellis Moon to Onora before surrendering.

Exhausted from two nights without sleep, Valek trudged up to bed. After a day of rest, he'd travel to the garrison and find out if Yelena's gamble had worked or not.

The morning of the ninth day since Yelena made her deal with Cahil dawned clear and cool. Onyx trotted into the main district of Starling's Egg a few hours after sunrise and headed for the market. Onora was probably hidden among the stalls, waiting for Valek. He slowed Onyx to a walk once they reached the busy heart of the small town. Sure enough, Onora appeared next to them within a few minutes.

"Report," he said.

She scanned the shoppers. "Not here. Meet me at the Lucky Duck Inn on Cherry Street." Onora disappeared.

Dressed in dark brown pants and a light tan tunic to blend in, Valek dismounted and asked a local where Cherry was located. The woman barely glanced at him as she pointed to the northeast. He led Onyx through the streets, letting the horse cool down. He wondered if Onora had been staying at the Lucky Duck while keeping an eye on Yelena. Had his wife spent the last seven days locked in the stockade? Valek hoped not but wouldn't be surprised if she had.

He found the inn on Cherry and approved of its unremarkable appearance and out-of-the-way location. Onyx headed straight to the small stables behind the building. Valek left his horse with the stable boy but instructed him to leave the saddle on, just in case he needed to make a quick exit.

Onora waited for him at one of the tables in the back corner of the common room. It was a typical inn, with a tavern on the ground floor and rooms on the higher stories. He scanned the other occupants—two men and an older woman. The sweet scent of molasses lingered on the air. When he'd left the cottage yesterday, he hadn't had much of an appetite. The prospect of turning himself over to Cahil had soured his stomach.

Valek joined Onora. A young server appeared and he ordered breakfast, despite still having no desire to eat. He'd need energy to deal with the next step. When the girl left, he asked, "Yelena?"

"She's perfectly fine. She was staying here until yesterday," Onora said.

He straightened. "Not what I expected."

"Me, neither, but it was smart." Onora filled him in on

MARIA V. SNYDER

what had happened. "It took Cahil and his crew a week to wake up, but they all came around, just like Yelena predicted."

Yelena had done it. The crushing pressure around his chest eased.

"You owe her an apology," Onora said.

He owed her much more than a mere apology. While Fisk and Onora had faith in her, Valek had believed her agreement with Cahil had been yet another betrayal and bound to fail.

"While you've been off pouting, she's been miserable. You should have seen the stricken look on her face when she found out *I've* been watching over her and not you."

If Onora wished to make him feel worse, she'd succeeded. "You talked to her?"

"Yes. She stood in the small yard behind the inn where she'd been training and signaled that you should join her and all was well. I thought it might be a trick, but she was alone, and they hadn't ever left her alone before. Still, I waited until Cahil left, then visited her room later that night." Onora grinned. "Scared the hell out of her roommate."

"Where is she now?"

"Setting up an ambush."

Clamping down on his surprise, he said, "Explain."

"Her father and sister-in-law were captured and are being escorted here. Yelena plans to rescue them before they reach the garrison."

Not good. "By herself?"

"No. She has three of Cahil's crew with her."

"And Cahil?"

"Taking a hit for the team."

He waited.

"Cahil remained in the garrison. Bruns arrived yesterday, and he's playing host. He's also unprotected. If Bruns's magicians detect a null shield on him, the gig would be up. According to Yelena, Cahil's pretty strong-willed and should be okay for a couple days."

"So, Cahil has agreed to help us?"

"Yes, but he's not happy about it."

That wasn't a surprise. Valek mulled over the information. "Where's Leif?"

"He escaped when they grabbed Mara and Esau. No one's seen him since."

"He's probably following the wagon."

The server arrived with Valek's order. She placed the steaming plate of eggs, bacon and toast in front of him. His stomach growled with hunger, and he realized he hadn't had a decent hot meal since leaving Yelena with Cahil. Valek dug into the food. Between bites, he asked about the ambush.

"They picked a nice little spot about four hours east of the garrison," Onora said. "They figured by that point, the soldiers will have relaxed, thinking they are almost home. Plus it's better than guessing where the group will stop for the night."

"When are they expected to strike?"

"Tomorrow morning."

"Think they'd welcome a couple extra helpers?"

"Oh, yes. I told them I'd be back, but no one was sure about you."

Ah, hell. He had some major apologizing to do.

After he finished eating, he paid and reclaimed Onyx. The horse glanced at a stall with longing. But when Valek mentioned joining Kiki, Onyx's ears perked up. Valek understood the feeling. The desire to see Yelena energized him, as well.

He mounted and headed west at a moderate pace. The number of buildings dwindled, and fields of corn plants stretched out on both sides of the road. Soon the drumming of hooves sounded behind him as Onora caught up. She rode an unfa-

MARIA V. SNYDER

miliar black-and-white piebald mare with a black mane. Janco had borrowed The Madam since he'd lent Beach Bunny to Reema.

"Who is this?" he asked.

"Horse."

"Original."

She grinned. "I figured the name would bug Janco."

It would indeed.

They rode for a while in silence. After two hours of riding, the fields ended and they entered a forest. Valek worried about Yelena and hoped she'd forgive him. The upside to this whole mess was that the people who'd been under Bruns's influence could be woken. The downside was that a person had to be Theobroma-free for a week—a dangerously long time. At least now they had Cahil's cooperation. The General could begin to wake other high-ranking military officials and perhaps even the Sitian Council members. One could dream.

Onora slowed Horse to a walk as they reached the bottom of a small valley. Ahead the dirt road was rutted from a recent washout. A rustle sounded above Valek. He glanced up in time to spot a net of greenery falling toward him. Valek stopped Onyx right before the heavy blanket knocked him to the ground.

Valek landed hard on his left shoulder. He rolled onto his back and reached for his knives just as a person sat on top of him, pinning his arms, while a thin blade pierced the greenery and nicked his neck.

The blade disappeared, and Valek twisted his hips and bucked the person off. He shoved the net aside, jumped to his feet and yanked his knives. Two figures dressed in green camouflage backed away from him. Onora stood with two others—also camouflaged. She wiped dirt off her pants but appeared unhurt and unarmed. Odd.

Then the trees spun around him. The irresistible urge to sleep liquefied his muscles. He staggered and went down on one knee. His heavy knives slipped from his nerveless fingers. Valek touched his neck. A small drop of blood coated his finger. The blade must have been treated with sleeping potion.

Valek toppled. He'd congratulate them on getting the drop on him, but...

Valek woke but kept his eyes closed. Fuzzy memories of being ambushed swirled. His head ached from a sleeping potion hangover. A dull throb pulsed through his left shoulder. He smelled wood smoke. A fire crackled nearby.

"...too slow. We should use Curare instead. It's faster," a woman said.

"But it won't work. Everyone's been eating Theobroma for months. It neutralizes the Curare. And next time, remember to use a dart and not your knife, Hanni," Onora said. "You have more control and can keep your distance. You saw how quickly Valek freed himself from the net. He could have killed you before the sleeping potion kicked in."

Onora? Was she working for the Cartel now?

"I'm sorry. I panicked. Do you think *he's* going to be mad we did a test run on him?" the woman—Hanni—asked.

No answer, but it explained quite a bit.

"Just don't panic tomorrow," Onora said.

"No problem. Tomorrow I won't be jumping *Valek*," Hanni muttered.

"As long as you all remember that the goal is to rescue my sister-in-law and father without killing the guards. Incapacitate only," Yelena said.

Her voice soothed his soul. Valek opened his eyes. He lay on a bedroll with a blanket over him. Nearby, Yelena and Onora sat around a campfire with two men and Hanni. Darkness

MARIA V. SNYDER

surrounded them. He waited. It didn't take long for Yelena's gaze to find his.

She tensed. Even though he deserved it, her reaction stabbed him right in the heart. The others sensed her concern and turned. He sat up. The men and Hanni hopped to their feet. Their hands hovered near weapons. Skittish lot. Valek would have been amused, but Yelena still hadn't relaxed.

"Onyx?" he asked her.

"Fine. He's with Kiki."

Onora poured him a cup of water and brought it over. "Here."

"Thanks." He downed it in one gulp. "Test run?"

"Yeah. They're young and needed the practice," Onora said.

"We're older than you," one of the men said in protest.

"Sorry. They're inexperienced."

That didn't go over any better.

Valek touched his neck. A dart would have left a smaller injury, but the cut had already stopped bleeding. "Were the darts loaded with sleeping potion as well?"

Onora smiled. "Of course. Although I'm surprised you didn't spot the ambush sooner."

He met Yelena's gaze again. "I was distracted."

"Bad form, old man. Don't worry, I won't tell the Commander." Onora refilled his cup.

"Good, because he believes this old man—" Valek tapped his chest "—killed you."

"Oh?" She stilled.

He glanced at the three others. "I'll tell you about it later." He stood. Cahil's crew stepped back and grabbed the hilts of their weapons.

"Relax," he said. "I'm not upset about the ambush. Onora and Yelena know I encourage training and preparation. Kudos to you for a successful test run." He held his hand out to his wife. "Yelena, a word in private?"

Her hesitation hurt worse than his head. But she slipped her hand in his, allowing him to pull her to her feet. Valek led her well away from the others. As his eyes adjusted to the darkness, the shapes of Onyx, Kiki and Horse formed. They grazed in a small clearing. Weak moonlight outlined them in silver.

"Valek, I'm—"

"No." He pulled her into a tight hug. Surprised, she stiffened, then relaxed against him. He breathed in her scent. "I'm so, so sorry. I overreacted. I didn't trust you. And I threw a tantrum and stormed off to sulk like a child. I'm sorry. *Please* forgive me."

"Only if you can forgive me."

"For what?"

She leaned back. "I believed Cahil and thought Onora had killed you, not trusting that you might have worked out an arrangement with her. I should have just trusted you. And I endangered our child."

"You were right about Cahil. Now we have a powerful ally."

"But I should have believed in you."

"All right, you're forgiven."

"So are you."

Relieved, he kissed her long and hard. When they broke apart, they were both panting. He drew her close and wished they were alone. Maybe if they went—

"Why does the Commander think Onora is dead?" Yelena asked.

"I paid him a visit."

"Are you insane?" She broke away and punched him on his sore shoulder.

MARIA V. SNYDER

He grunted in pain, but she failed to look contrite as he rubbed the sore spot.

"Talk," she ordered.

"Like you, I took a gamble." Valek told her about his visit and what he'd learned. "I hope we can find Ellis's notes in the Keep's Library."

"If they're still there." Then she scowled. "And if we're successful tomorrow."

He glanced at the horses. "Speaking of tomorrow, why aren't there more horses?"

"Hanni and Sladen will commandeer a couple from the guards, and Faxon will drive the wagon."

"Any word from Leif?"

"No. We hope he's following the wagon, but Cahil said they were captured near Fulgor."

Valek considered. "He might have gone to Fulgor instead, thinking to get there ahead of them."

"That's what I thought, too. I hope he wasn't arrested." Concern deepened her voice.

"Would Cahil know Leif's status?"

"Eventually."

"How are you going to communicate with him without the Cartel finding out?"

She peered up at him. "One of his loyal crew will get a message to a member of Fisk's guild."

Not the best situation, but there weren't any other options. "Too bad we don't have any glass messengers."

"That might give us away. The Cartel has a group of loyal magicians who have not been ingesting the Theobroma. The drug makes it too hard for them to concentrate. So they're seeking others who are using magic, and they've been using those glass super messengers to communicate between the garrisons."

Another bit of unwelcome news. If the resistance tried anything at one garrison, all the others would be notified right away.

"What else did you have planned for Cahil?" she asked.

"I hoped he could wake the other military leaders and then the Councilors."

"That would be impossible for him to do without tipping the Cartel off." She explained about the frequent null shield sweeps.

He almost growled in frustration. "We need an…anti-Theobroma. A substance that works faster."

"I agree. Something that works as quickly as Curare would be ideal."

"Now you're dreaming, love. I'd be happy with something that shortens the time to mere days instead of a week."

But her brows crinkled in thought, and she was no longer listening to him. He kept quiet, letting her mull over whatever it was that had snagged her attention. Content to hold her close, he relaxed for the first time in ten long days. She had forgiven him, and right now, that was all that mattered.

"My father mentioned that there were a number of hybrid plants in Owen's glass hothouse. One is a Curare that is resistant to Theobroma. And I read through Bavol's notes. He was working with Owen's Master Gardener, and they experimented with crossbreeding a number of different plants. Maybe they discovered something that could help us make an anti-Theobroma." Yelena told him about Bavol's secret glass hothouse in the Avibian Plains. "Fisk and I had stolen the address of the farm where the glassmaker delivered the sheets, but I never made it back to HQ to follow up."

"Once we rescue your father and find Leif, checking that glass house would be the next logical step. Maybe there will be Harman trees there, as well."

"A logical step for them. I need to return to the Citadel and figure out who the Master Gardener is."

He tightened his grip. "*We* need to. There's still the bounty on your head."

She was quiet for a while. "My father will need extra protection. Onora can go with them. You obviously trust her."

"I do, and I need to tell you why."

"Oh?"

"You remember that fight on the rooftop Cahil mentioned?"

"It was real. I know. Onora told me all about it."

"I'm surprised she confided in you."

"Me, too. But she said *friends* shouldn't keep secrets from each other."

"She's making progress."

"She is. And so are you."

"Because I apologized?"

"No. Because you healed your injuries with your magic. You have control of your power. Now you need to learn the extent of your abilities and start using them. We wouldn't have gotten the drop on you today if you had."

She had a point. "All right. When we return to the Citadel, I'll search for a teacher."

"A Master Magician would be ideal, but since Bain and Irys are occupied, Teegan is the next best choice. And he should be back from the coast by now."

"He's fourteen."

"He has master-level powers and has been training with Irys for a year."

"He's fourteen."

"Valek." She used *that* tone. The don't-be-a-bigger-idiot-than-you're-being-right-now tone.

He sighed. "All right."

She rose onto her tiptoes and kissed him. A jolt of desire swept all his other emotions away. He deepened the kiss.

When they broke apart, he said, "Let's find a more private location."

Yelena linked her hands behind his neck. "Because of the horses?"

"No. The assassin in the trees."

She dropped her arms and stepped away. "Is Onora—"

"Not close enough to overhear us, but keeping an eye on us."

"Why?"

"Like all of your friends, she's become protective of you. And I suspect she wanted to ensure I apologized properly."

"Nice of her."

"Uh-huh. Now give her a wave so I can drag you deeper into the woods and ravish you."

A gleam shone in her eyes. "Those that say romance is dead haven't met you."

"That's right. They don't call me Mr. Romance for nothing." He swept her up in his arms and carried her to a nice spot far away from the campsite. Then he proceeded to follow through on his promise.

Morning arrived far too soon. Valek and Yelena had returned to the warmth of the fire after he proved his remorse over his behavior. As the group ate breakfast, Yelena reviewed the plan. She and Faxon would be stationed in the treetops, Hanni and Sladen on the ground right before the washout and Valek and Onora down the road far enough to come in behind the wagon once it had stopped. They expected the wagon to be escorted by eight soldiers, including two scouts traveling ahead of the team. The six of them settled into their spots a few hours before the estimated time, just in case.

MARIA V. SNYDER

★ ★ ★

Valek had never been on a stakeout with Onora before. Fascinated, he watched as she blended in with the colors of the forest. And it wasn't due to her clothing. Yes, she wore earth tones, but if he had glanced away and looked back at her position, he would have thought she'd moved to another location. Janco had mentioned this to him before, but Valek had assumed it was just Janco's tendency to exaggerate.

Had Onora used magic? Without his immunity, he could no longer detect when it was in use, but...

Remembering his conversation with Yelena, Valek lowered his mental shield. The blanket of power pressed down on him. He drew a thin thread and reached for Onora with his senses. Her surface thoughts focused on the ambush. Onora reviewed the plan and listed what could go wrong. For each unexpected contingency, she calculated a way to counter it. Smart.

However, he didn't detect any magic being used. Either he didn't have that ability, or she wasn't using any at this time. Perhaps she used magic to go camouflage and didn't need any more power to sustain it. He pushed his senses further, stretching them toward Yelena's location on the limb above the road. She squirmed into a more comfortable position and hoped the ambush would work. Worry for Esau, Mara and Leif occupied her thoughts. No surprise. It didn't take long for the baby to yank on Valek's power, draining it.

Valek broke the connection. Drawing another strand of power, he aimed it at the road, seeking the scouts. They would be traveling about fifteen to thirty minutes ahead of the wagon. Their job was to flush out any ambushes or spot trouble before the slower and more vulnerable wagon arrived. Nothing.

Saving his strength for the fight, Valek raised his mental

shield, once again blocking the power. He tried to meet Onora's gaze, but without his magic, she'd disappeared.

"What's wrong?" the tree asked in her whisper.

"Do you do that on purpose?" he asked.

"Do what?"

He gestured. "Blend in. Disappear."

"I'm right here. What are you talking about?"

"Your ability to match your surroundings so well that I can't see you anymore."

Silence. She probably thought he was insane.

"Look at your hands," he said.

"They're hands."

So she was immune to her own talent. He changed tactics. "You must have realized by this point just how well you can hide."

"Janco said something about it, but I thought..."

"He was just being Janco, spouting out a plethora of theories, rants and comments, so you have no idea if he's being silly or serious or if the man's a genius?"

"Exactly." A pause. "Wouldn't you have felt me using magic?"

Onora didn't know about his new situation, and he wondered if he should tell her now that he trusted her. Valek decided to wait until she needed to know the information. "Not if you're a One-Trick."

"One-Trick?"

"A magician that can only do one thing. There are a number of them in Sitia, and I suspect in Ixia, as well. They don't consciously pull power. They just have an instinctive ability that has to be magical in origin. For example, Opal used to work with an old glassmaker who could light fires, but he couldn't do anything else."

She was quiet for a while. "It's not conscious. All I do is focus on the mission at hand."

Sounded like a One-Trick, but only a master-level magician would know for sure.

Onora appeared suddenly. She stared at her hands as she laced and unlaced her fingers over and over. "It didn't work when...Captain...Timmer came for me. I couldn't hide...from him...no matter how hard I tried."

"Because you were afraid. Just thinking about him has made you lose your camouflage."

She glanced up in surprise.

"No need to be scared of him. He's locked in the Commander's dungeon and is scheduled for execution in a little over three months."

"Even if I'm not there to kill him?"

"Yes. The Commander might not be in full control of his mind, but one thing he loathes is sexual predators."

"What if Owen releases Timmer or he escapes?"

"Then, when all this is over, we will hunt him down, strip him naked, tenderize him with a few dozen holes and leave him for the snow cats to find."

Onora grinned. "Good plan."

"I thought you'd like that."

They lapsed into silence. After an hour, the familiar thrum of horses reached them. Valek whistled the signal. Soon the two scouts rode into view and passed Valek and Onora's position. The scouts spotted the rutted road and slowed, glancing to the left and right. Smart enough to know this was an ideal spot for an ambush, but not experienced enough to look up.

Yelena and Sladen released the camouflage nets. They fell at a slight angle and swept the riders from the horses. The victims landed with an *oomph*. Using the net ideally avoided any major injuries. If they'd shot darts filled with sleeping potion, the riders might topple, and falling from a moving horse could be lethal.

Hanni and Faxon jumped on the struggling men and poked them with the potion. In thirty seconds, the soldiers stilled. Yelena and Sladen hauled the net back into position while Valek and Onora caught the two horses. Then they helped drag the two sleeping men into the woods. After Valek led the mounts to Kiki, he returned to his position. They reset the trap.

The next part would be a bit harder. About twenty minutes later, a slower beat of horse hooves sounded, along with the creak and rumble of a wagon. Bantering voices floated on the light breeze. Once again, Valek signaled them to be ready.

Two riders led the way. Two others sat on the wagon's bench, and the final two followed the caravan. A tarp had been draped over the cargo area, and Valek hoped Mara and Esau had been hidden underneath it. As the group reduced speed and lumbered past, Valek shifted his weight to the balls of his feet. He held a dart laced with sleeping potion in each hand.

When they reached the washout, the nets were dropped on the leaders, and Onora shot the two on the wagon with darts. The ones in the back froze upon seeing their companions attacked. Valek and Onora snuck up next to them. He stabbed the dart into one man's leg and yanked him from the saddle while Onora did the same to his partner. The soldier hopped up and drew a short sword. Valek stayed just out of reach until the man wobbled and crumpled to the ground.

The ambush was a complete success. Bodies littered the road, but no one appeared to be injured. Yelena and Sladen climbed down from the trees as Valek pulled back the tarp. Mara and Esau had been bound to the wagon and gagged. Esau's face turned red as he struggled to speak.

Hyper–alert, Valek spun and drew his dagger. The soldiers

MARIA V. SNYDER

they had just neutralized sprang to their feet with weapons in hand. Yelena yipped in surprise as one of the scouts lunged from the woods. The scout grabbed her and pressed a knife to her neck. The desire to rip him apart flowed through Valek, and he gauged the distance to the man.

"Drop your weapons or I'll slit her throat," the scout said.

12

HELI

Heli reread the note from Fisk. While glad she didn't have to watch the rather boring comings and goings of the Stormdance garrison any longer, she wondered why Fisk thought it was too dangerous to remain. It had only been a month, but his other operatives…

She grinned at the word *operatives*. The kids working for Fisk were much younger than her own eighteen years. However, they'd fled the garrison like seagulls before a big storm. Something must have happened and, while she had to be on the coast soon to harvest the heating season's storms regardless, she thought Fisk might be overreacting. Especially when she considered his missive.

He believed Zethan, Zohav and Teegan were in danger and needed to relocate to a safer location. As if there were such a thing. Fisk had never been to The Cliffs, so he had no idea just how difficult it would be for an army or even a person to sneak up on them. With four Stormdancers on the beach, there was no way anyone could traverse the narrow path down The Cliffs without one of the Stormdancers blowing them out to sea. Ridiculous.

Oh, well. She shrugged and abandoned her post by the garrison's main entrance. Stopping at the inn where she'd been staying, Heli packed her knapsack and paid her bill. She considered swinging by her parents' house, but that would add two days to her travel time. And there was no way they'd let her leave after only three or four hours. They'd pepper her with a million questions and insist she stay overnight, bringing the total to three extra days. Fisk was probably being overly cautious, but she had to give the guy credit. He had planned and executed a killer rescue.

Remembering that night, Heli straightened with pride. Zethan had called the storm and Heli controlled it, keeping a safe path open for Yelena and Valek and a bunch of their friends to escape the Krystal garrison. It'd been the hardest thing she'd ever done with her Stormdancing magic, and it'd been both terrifying and exhilarating at the same time. And it had been empowering. When Zethan's twin sister, Zohav, started flattening the guards with giant balls of water, she'd believed the three of them could beat the Cartel on their own. Of course, reality arrived the very next day when they hadn't been able to help anyone because it was dry, calm and sunny.

Heli swung by the stables and saddled her horse, Thunder. The gray-and-white stallion twitched with energy. However, like his namesake, he started out strong but soon faded with distance. She'd been working on his endurance, and riding him was still better than walking, but she wished she had a Sandseed horse like Kade. Moonlight could reach The Cliffs in three days, but Thunder would be lucky to make it in four.

The morning of the fifth day on the road, Heli mounted Thunder. Her bedroll did nothing to soften the hard shale of The Flats and made her cot in the main cavern seem like a featherbed in comparison.

They reached the edge of The Cliffs later that afternoon. A

fresh, damp breeze greeted them. Heli breathed in the tangy scent of the sea far below. The strident call of the gulls interrupted the rhythmic shushing of the distant waves. Sunlight painted the water with diamonds.

Home.

Heli soaked in the beauty of the landscape for a moment. The wind had carved a rippling pattern into The Cliffs, leaving behind wings of stone and arches of rocks. Water had drilled holes into them, and the Stormdancers used the caves for living areas, sleeping quarters, storage and housing the glass kiln. The sweet aroma of white coal and molten glass laced the salty air. Helen, the glassmaker, was probably busy making the orbs for the upcoming storm season.

Thunder refused to move when Heli urged him down the narrow trail. No matter how many times he'd been here, he wouldn't descend unless Heli walked beside him.

"You're a big baby," she said, dismounting. "Come on. If we hurry we might be in time for some of Raiden's seafood chowder." Her stomach rumbled just thinking about it.

Halfway down, she spotted dark gray clouds gathering well out to sea. A storm would be here in a few days. Early, but one of the many things she'd learned about storms was that they didn't follow the calendar. Heli glanced down. Kade stood at the end of a rocky outcropping. Waves rushed past but parted before crashing into his favorite perch.

By the time Heli and Thunder reached the sand, Kade had traversed the rocks and was heading in their direction. She waited. He was her boss, after all. Wearing a cautious expression, he strode over the sand with ease. His shoulder-length brown hair blew in the breeze. Heli tucked her own long brown strands behind an ear. The sun and sea had streaked both their hair with blond highlights.

"You're here early," he said once he'd drawn closer.

MARIA V. SNYDER

"Well, hello to you, too."

"What happened?" he asked.

She suppressed a sigh. Kade was always too serious. And she was only five days early—her Stormdancing shift started on the first day of the heating season.

"I received a message from Fisk," she said, then told him about Fisk's concerns.

He huffed. "They're safer here than anywhere else in Sitia."

"I know. Where are they?"

Kade gestured down the beach. "Zethan is surfing…or rather, trying to, while his sister is swimming."

Heli shivered. "The water's freezing."

"Not to them. They say it's warm in comparison to the waters off Ixia's coast."

"And Teegan?"

"Helping Raiden."

"What should we do about Fisk's message?" she asked.

"Let's wait until everyone is together and discuss it over supper."

Heli led Thunder to the small stables on the beach. When the weather turned nasty, as it frequently did during the heating and cooling seasons, they moved the horses up to the storm cave to shelter them from the elements.

Moonlight whickered a greeting. The black horse had a white moon on his forehead. Smoke, another gray horse, poked his head out. Heli didn't recognize the third horse—a cream-colored mare with a blond mane. The new horse matched the sand on the beach. After grooming Thunder and ensuring he had fresh grain and water, Heli trudged up to the main cavern.

The familiar fishy scent of seafood chowder wrapped around her like a soft blanket. A large fire burned inside the cave.

Teegan cracked open clam shells while Raiden stirred a tall pot bubbling on the coals.

Raiden beamed at Heli when he spotted her. All her fatigue was forgotten as she raced in for a hug. Heli had been dancing in the storms since she was twelve, and the forty-five-year-old camp manager was like a surrogate father. Although he tended to father all the Stormdancers whether they wanted it or not, and he was the voice of reason when arguments sprang up. Even Kade deferred to his experience most of the time.

"You're early," Raiden said when she stepped back.

"I missed your cooking."

He huffed. "What happened to, 'If I eat another fish, I'm gonna grow scales'?"

She waved her hand. "That was last year, when all the meat spoiled. You gotta admit that even you were sick of seafood after eating it for thirty days straight."

"That's a lot of clams," Teegan said as he pried open another one and scooped out the insides.

Heli moved closer and inspected his pile of shells. "You're already a pro. What else have you been doing?"

"We've been practicing our magic, learning our limits and abilities, getting ready for the big battle." Teegan kept his tone casual, but she spotted the tension in his shoulders.

While only fourteen years old, he was well on his way to becoming a master-level magician, though he didn't have as much experience wielding magic yet. When they'd rescued Valek and Yelena, Teegan had kept her safe from the enemies' bolts and arrows that whizzed through the air, since she had to be close to the action to see where to focus the calm.

"Do you have any news?" Teegan asked.

"Not much."

"Anything about my parents or family?"

"No, sorry."

MARIA V. SNYDER

He wilted. It had to be hard not knowing what was going on. She squeezed his shoulder before helping him with the rest of the clams.

Soon everyone except Helen had assembled for supper. According to Raiden, she was at a critical point in the orb-making process. Zethan and Zohav had dried off and changed into plain gray tunics and pants. Their black hair dripped water. There was no doubt the two were siblings, and their resemblance to Valek, their older brother, was uncanny. Both had sapphire-blue eyes and angular faces, but Zethan smiled more, so he didn't appear as...intense as his sister.

Zethan gave her a friendly hello, while Zohav's expression darkened with worry. Once everyone settled around the fire with a bowl of chowder in hand, Kade asked Heli to repeat her message from Fisk.

"That's it?" Teegan asked her. "No reason why we need to move?"

"For your safety."

"We're safe here," Zethan said. "I'm not leaving unless they need us to help."

"The only scenario that makes sense is that the Cartel is aware of your location," Kade said.

"So what? I'd like to see them try to attack us," Zethan said with enough enthusiasm to merit a scowl from his twin.

"I can go to the Citadel and gather more information," Teegan said.

"And walk into an ambush?" Zohav asked. "If they know we're here, then they'll be watching for the perfect opportunity."

"It's not like I'm defenseless," Teegan said, stabbing his spoon into the chowder. White drops splattered onto his tunic.

"Where else would we go?" Zohav asked.

No answer.

"I'm not leaving," Zethan said again. "I'm learning so much about my magic here with Kade, and the storm season—"

"—is our concern," Kade said. "The three of you are vital to Valek's plans to stop the Cartel. They might not be able to get to you here, but like Zohav said, they can wait until you're called to the fight and ambush you up on The Flats."

"But we have magic," Zethan said.

"And they have Curare and null shields," Kade countered.

Now it was Zethan's turn to frown. "But I can guide the storms here."

Kade grinned. "You've brought so many already, Zee. We've reached our quota, and the season hasn't even started yet."

Heli glanced at Kade in surprise. "You shouldn't be dancing on your own. It's dangerous."

"Not with Zethan," Kade said. "He brings them just close enough for me to fill a few orbs with their energy, and then he sends them back out to sea."

That was impressive.

"Which is why you need me," Zethan said, sounding like a petulant child.

"Your brother needs you more right now. Sitia needs you," Kade said.

"Then you should come with us," Zethan said. "I need a dancer to keep the storm from hurting the people on our side."

Heli held her breath. If Kade joined them, she'd be in charge of the other Stormdancers for the season—a big responsibility. But a part of her wished to go with them. They'd worked well as a team before. However, Kade was in charge.

As if he read her mind, Kade met her gaze. "I need to stay on the coast. Since we already have so many filled orbs, Heli can accompany you if she wants. If not—"

MARIA V. SNYDER

"I'll go." A mixture of fear and excitement twisted around her heart.

"When do we leave?" Teegan asked.

"At first light," Kade said. "And don't tell us where you're going, but make sure you send a message to Fisk." He stood and filled another bowl with chowder. "Come on, Ray. They need to plan, and Helen must be starving by now."

Heli's mind raced with possible locations for them to lie low. Also, a couple comments from the conversation had snagged in her mind.

Before Kade and Raiden left, Zethan called out, "Who's in charge?"

"If you have to ask, it isn't you." Kade waved good-night.

Before Zethan could respond, Heli said, "I am."

"Why you?" Teegan asked in a tone more curious than combative.

"I'm the oldest. I know Sitia. And I have the most experience." Heli held up three fingers.

"We just turned seventeen," Zethan said. "Plus we were *all* at the Krystal garrison."

"Heli helped my parents free the Bloodrose clan last year," Teegan said.

Heli flipped up her pinky as those random comments connected like lightning in her brain. "And I've a great idea."

13

YELENA

The knife pressed against my throat. Frustration eclipsed my fear. The soldiers we'd ambushed had just ambushed us. They'd pretended to be knocked out by the sleeping potion that had coated our weapons and filled our darts.

"Weapons down, now," the man holding me ordered.

A thin line of pain seared my skin as he emphasized his point.

Valek glanced at Onora, but she'd disappeared. Cahil's crew looked to Valek for guidance. He held a dart, but the drug hadn't worked on the soldiers. No time to wonder why.

"Easy," Valek said. He placed his weapons on the ground with enough flourish to distract the soldiers while he palmed a new set of darts. I hoped those were laced with goo-goo juice, as it appeared nothing else in our arsenal would work. Valek motioned for the others to disarm.

"Let's be reasonable, gentlemen. What do you want?" Valek asked.

"Let's not," the scout behind me said. "Jone and Nusi, secure them."

The two on the wagon hopped down and reached under the seat for manacles. Jone and Nusi approached Valek first.

Valek waited until they were within striking distance. "Now!" He whirled, kicking the manacles from their hands.

I was yanked sideways so hard, I broke free from the man's grasp. In a heartbeat, he flew forward and landed on the ground. He didn't move. Onora appeared next to me and grinned. She drew her knives. Cahil's crew reclaimed their weapons. I turned, and Kiki's copper face peered at me through the greenery. Happy to see her, I grabbed my bo staff and joined the fracas.

Well... I tried. Valek fought Jone and Nusi. They had some skill but lacked experience. Valek slid past their defenses and disarmed them in a few moves. Onora also took down two opponents, and Hanni, Faxon and Sladen proved very capable of handling themselves in a fight. Soon they had manacled all eight of them—five men and three women—to eight trees. The scout who had grabbed me still hadn't regained consciousness.

"What did you hit him with?" Valek asked Onora.

"I didn't. Kiki kicked him with her back hoof. She has excellent aim. I just tugged Yelena out of the way."

Remembering the knife, I touched my throat, smearing blood from a shallow slice along my skin.

Valek pulled a handkerchief from his pocket and wiped the rest off. "Are you okay?"

"I'm fine. I owe Kiki a few milk oats, though." I gazed at the prisoners. "Why didn't the sleeping potion work on you?"

"We're not telling you," Jone said.

Valek held up a dart laced with goo-goo juice. "You won't have a choice."

Unless they were immune to this drug, as well.

"But first..." Valek strode over to the wagon, and I followed right behind him. He cut Mara and Esau loose, then unlocked their manacles.

Bruises marked both their faces, and raw skin ringed their wrists and ankles. Mara ripped her gag off and collapsed in my arms. Alarmed, I hugged her close as she sobbed into my shoulder. Oh, no. Fear bloomed in my chest, squeezing my heart.

Esau rubbed his hands. Dirt and blood stained his tattered clothing. "Thanks for rescuing us."

"Are you all right?" Valek asked him.

"Minor stuff. I'll be fine. Poor Mara had a rougher time of it, though." Esau glared at the group attached to the trees.

Ice filled my veins. Valek and I exchanged a horrified glance. Was she…? Did they…? I couldn't even think the word.

Mara straightened, jerking from my embrace. Tears streaked her face. She wiped them away with an angry swipe. "I…" Pulling in a deep breath, she continued, "It was terrifying to be tied up, utterly helpless and at their mercy." A shudder shook her body.

"Did they…harm you?" Valek asked the question on all our minds.

"No. They threatened to, and their hands…" Another shudder. "But they didn't rape me."

We all breathed a huge sigh of relief.

She clutched my arm. "Where's Leif?"

"We don't know. We'd hoped he was following you."

"He's not. He would have found a way to let me know he was nearby."

I agreed. "In that case, he's probably in Fulgor."

She nodded. "We need to find him."

"We will, but first I need to interrogate the soldiers," Valek said.

"I know why they're immune to the sleeping potion," Esau said. "Those crossbreed plants…" He waved at the wagon, but only a few dead leaves littered the bed. "They've been working

MARIA V. SNYDER

on antidotes to sleeping potion, goo-goo juice and a number of poisons. So far, they've discovered one for the sleeping potion. And they also have Theobroma-resistant Curare."

"How close are they to finding an antidote to goo-goo juice?" Valek asked.

"I don't know."

"Then let's see what they know." Valek pricked them with the drug, waited a few minutes and questioned them. Unfortunately, they were just grunts following orders. Their knowledge was limited. The only useful information we gleaned from them was that all soldiers on patrol or those escorting officers or prisoners would get enough of the sleeping potion antidote for the length of their mission.

We would need to find another drug that could incapacitate them. I hoped my father would have an alternative.

When he finished interrogating the soldiers, Valek inclined his head and motioned for us to return to our campsite.

Once we arrived, he said, "It's too dangerous for all of us to search for Leif. Yelena, take Mara, your father and Onora to Owl's Hill. Stay at the Cloverleaf Inn until Fisk's people contact you. They will let you know HQ's new location in the Citadel. Stay together until I return."

Not sure I liked this plan, I asked, "Where are you going?"

"To Fulgor, to find Leif."

Torn, I debated whether I should insist on accompanying him to search for my brother. But I decided that Mara needed me more right now.

"What about us?" Hanni asked. "We can't go back to the garrison. The soldiers saw us helping you."

"Go to the Lucky Duck Inn," I said. "That's our rendezvous location with Cahil. He'll contact you there."

Hanni pressed her lips together but didn't voice her doubts.

"We should get moving," Onora said. "Those guys are visible from the road, and I'm sure Bruns will send a patrol when they fail to arrive."

Kiki had kept all six horses calm during the ambush. Cahil's crew mounted three, and Mara and Esau each took one to ride. The wagon and the last horse would remain behind.

"They dumped all the plants right after we were captured," Esau said, clearly pained by the loss.

His comment reminded me of the picture of the Harman tree. I retrieved it and showed it to my father. "Do you know what this is?"

Esau peered at the picture. "This is a beautiful rendition. Did you draw it?"

"No." I pointed to Onora. "She did."

His good humor returned. "Well done, my girl. You'll have to come on expedition with me. The detail is exquisite."

Embarrassed by the compliment, Onora ducked her head.

"Do you recognize it, Father?" I asked again. "It's called a Harman tree, but we don't know anything else about it."

"It doesn't sound or look familiar. Sorry." He handed it back to me.

Oh well, it was worth a try.

Before Valek mounted Onyx, he pulled me close to say goodbye. "If you're not in Owl's Hill, Leif and I will meet up with you in the Citadel."

I tightened my grip. "What if he's been captured?"

"Then I will rescue him."

"But…" What if Valek was caught or killed? I bit my lip, keeping silent.

He waited.

Trust. I needed to trust him. "Please be careful."

"As long as you promise to do the same."

"Do you think Onora would let me do anything dangerous?"

"As if you'd listen to her. I'm not that naive, love."

I laughed. "All right, I promise to be careful."

He kissed me long and hard. I wished that all this was behind us. That we could just be a regular family, dealing with mundane problems. When he broke off the kiss, his gaze seared into me with a protective fire I recognized.

"Thinking of locking me in that tower again?" I teased.

"Of locking *us* in."

"Now you're talking." I claimed his lips for one more kiss. Then I hopped onto Kiki's saddle and, with a small wave, set off south toward Owl's Hill.

Mara kept quiet during the uneventful two-day trip. I filled my father in on what had been going on with the Cartel and me. He was delighted about his soon-to-be grandchild and new son-in-law, although he warned me that Sitia wouldn't recognize the union until we filed the official papers, which might not happen if the Cartel remained in power.

Memories surged to the surface of my thoughts when we checked into the Cloverleaf Inn, which was one of the only two inns in town. We rented a four-room suite on the top floor so we could stay together. The place had been our headquarters while we'd planned a way to defeat Roze Featherstone and her Warpers six years ago. It'd been a long shot, and it hadn't gone as we'd hoped—Moon Man and many others had died—but we'd won in the end and reinstated the Sitian Council.

With a start, I remembered that I'd been unable to use my magic during that time, as well. If I'd pulled any power, Roze would have learned of my location. The situation with the Cartel was on a grander scale than our problems with the Warpers, but not that different.

I mulled it over. Excitement built as new possibilities bubbled in my mind. I didn't need magic. Yes, I missed it; I've relied on my power for years and helped many people. But I didn't *need* it. I was quite capable of dealing with problems without it.

For the first time since I'd woken up without my magic, I accepted my condition. It was time to move on and stop moping about it. My power would either return when the baby was born, or it wouldn't.

Energized, I strode from my room. Esau sat on the couch, reading a botany book, and Mara was curled up in the armchair with a cup of tea. I called for Onora.

She shot into the living area with her knives in hand.

"Sorry to scare you," I said. "But I'd like to resume our training while we wait for Leif."

Onora glanced out the window. "Now? It's almost dark."

"Don't assassins use the darkness to their advantage?"

"You want to be an assassin?"

"No. But I want to learn all the same skills."

"Me, too," Mara said. Putting her cup down with a clatter, she hopped to her feet. "Can you be an assassin without killing anyone?"

Onora shot her an odd look. "I...don't know. I don't think so."

"Is there a name for people who have those skills?" Mara asked.

"Yes. Dangerous," I said.

Mara rubbed her hands together as a gleam lit her eyes. "Oh, I like that. I want to be *dangerous*."

I exchanged a glance with Onora.

"If she's going to hang out with you and Leif, she should learn how to defend herself," Onora said.

True. "All right, let's get started. Father, would you like to learn how to sneak around in the dark?" I asked Esau.

"I've been sneaking around in the dark since before you

were born," he said. "How do you think I get those notte flowers for your mother's perfume? They only bloom in the dead of night, and any bit of light will make them close up tighter than a…er…" He cleared his throat. "If you can navigate the jungle at night without being eaten by a tree leopard or garroted by a necklace snake, then I'd say you don't need any *assassin* training."

"You know, a simple 'no' would have sufficed," I teased.

"Where's the fun in that?"

"I see where Leif gets his sense of humor," Onora said.

While we waited for Fisk's messenger to arrive, Onora taught Mara and me a number of skills she'd found helpful.

"If you're going to be in a lit room for only a short time, then a way to keep your dark-adapted vision is to close one eye when you reach the light. Then, when you return to the shadows, open that eye and you won't be completely blind," she explained.

Onora also showed us how to read body language and to move without making too much noise.

"It's all in keeping your balance and picking up your feet when you walk. Most people are lazy and shuffle. Rubber soles help, as well, if you're going to wear boots," she said.

"Why don't you wear boots?" Mara asked.

"My toes grip better than any sole, and the bottoms of my feet can feel noisy things such as dried leaves or small twigs before I step on them. To me, wearing shoes is like putting gloves on hands. You lose your sensitivity."

We practiced late at night when there were no other sounds to cover our movements. But we kept our boots on. Onora had been going barefoot for as long as she could remember, and her feet were conditioned to withstand the rough ground and cold air.

"I had to wear boots when I was in the army, but I shucked them whenever possible," she said.

We taught Mara a number of self-defense moves, as well. The training kept me from worrying too much about Valek and Leif or from imagining all the dire reasons Fisk's messenger hadn't arrived yet. After two days of practice, Mara seemed a bit more like her old self. And while the time wasn't nearly long enough to learn everything or to be truly proficient in anything, it was a start in the right direction.

After we ate breakfast in our rooms on the third morning, Onora asked, "How long are we going to wait for Fisk?"

Good question. "He's usually reliable, which means something happened at the Citadel and it might be too dangerous for us to return."

"I can scout ahead and see what's going on," she offered.

"Let's wait another day." Mara had benefited from the down time, and the rest had helped my father. The bruises were fading, and the lines on his face had smoothed. Plus I knew that once we returned to the Citadel, he would immerse himself in research and neglect his health again.

As I dozed on the couch later that afternoon, loud voices woke me. Onora stood at the door with both her knives drawn. I pulled my switchblade and joined her.

"What's going on?" I asked in a whisper.

"An argument. Could be nothing. Wait here." She slipped out the door.

I waited about three heartbeats before following her. Onora crept down the stairs, avoiding all the squeaky spots. She frowned at me when I joined her.

The quarrel grew louder as we descended. By the time we reached the second floor, I recognized the voices. Halfway up the steps to the first-floor landing, the innkeeper stood in front of two men, blocking the way. Impressive, considering one muscular man towered over the slight innkeeper and the other man glowered and fingered the hilt of his sword.

"...not allowed upstairs," the innkeeper insisted.

We had asked him to keep our presence under wraps as much as possible. Of course, the locals saw us arrive, and we had to shop for supplies. But he had promised not to tell strangers and soldiers about us. Fisk's people would have no trouble slipping by him, but these two should have known better.

"Idiots," Onora muttered.

"It's okay, Keyon," I said. "They're friends of ours."

"Friends?" Janco asked, placing a hand on his chest. "You wound me. I consider us family."

So happy to see them both, I rushed past Keyon. Ari swept me up into a hug.

Janco beamed. "Fisk and I called it. We knew you'd be here. Ari's such a worrywart."

Onora sheathed her blades. "And now everyone in a twenty-mile radius knows we're here."

Janco held up his hands. "Not my fault. You know how Ari gets when he's in his protective bull mode. I'm surprised he didn't just toss this little fella out of the way."

"Watch it." Keyon jabbed a finger at Janco. "If you're going to rent a room, this *little* fella might charge you double."

"Sorry, sir," Janco said. "But you have to admit, compared to my partner here, even *I'm* considered a little fella."

The man conceded the point.

"Besides, they can stay with us. Come on up to our rooms," I said. Ari put me down, and I led them up to the fifth floor.

Mara and Esau stood in the center of the suite with weapons in hand when we entered. They relaxed as soon as they spotted Ari and Janco.

Janco immediately flopped into a chair. "We've been traveling all night."

"What happened? We expected one of the guild members a couple days ago," I said.

"That was the plan, but things got hot in the Citadel."

"Hot?" Mara asked.

"Bruns has brought in more soldiers to patrol the streets. He closed all the gates except the east gate and doubled security, checking everyone coming into and leaving the Citadel."

Not good. "How hard is it to get in?"

"For you, impossible."

"Even if I wear a disguise?"

"Yes. They're yanking off hoods, checking for wigs and even have a magician scanning for illusions."

"But you managed to get in," I said.

"No. We didn't even try," Ari said. He sank onto the couch. Exhaustion lined his face. "Fisk has people along the roads to the Citadel. They recognized us and sent us here to rendezvous with you."

"Do you know when the extra security measures started?" Onora asked Ari.

"Four days ago."

"The same day we rescued Mara and Esau," Onora said.

"Rescued?" Janco asked.

We explained about Cahil tipping us off, the ambush and Valek's mission to find Leif.

"Valek will find him. No doubt," Janco said with such confidence, Mara smiled.

It was nice to see her happy. I considered the timing of the security. Bruns's magicians must have used a super messenger to communicate between the garrison and Citadel.

"Fisk thinks it's best for all of us to avoid the Citadel right now," Ari said. "He's going to let everything settle down and then find an HQ outside the Citadel, but still close enough that we can observe who is coming and going. It might take a few weeks."

"But—"

"I have a package for you in my saddle bags from Fisk." Ari inclined his head at Esau. "It's all the notes from Councilor Bavol Zaltana, plus the location of that farmhouse those glass panels were delivered to."

Perfect. Fisk knew me so well.

"And Fisk says that Councilor Zaltana owns the farmhouse."

That was interesting.

Janco jumped to his feet. "And we have news! Humongous news!"

We all waited, but Janco needed more prodding. "And?"

"I found where the Cartel's been producing Theobroma and Curare. And I met the Master Gardener!"

Shocked, I glanced at Ari. "Why didn't you tell me this sooner?"

"He *thinks* the man was the Master Gardener, but we were unable to confirm it."

"Who is it?" Esau asked.

Janco took a deep breath and held it, as if about to make a big announcement. Then he let it all out at once, deflating. "He *looks* familiar, but I can't recall his name. It's been driving me crazy for days!"

"What does he look like?" I asked.

"Like half the men in Sitia," Ari said. "Janco's descriptive skills are as bad as his artistic skills. We were hoping to find a magician who could peer into the chaos that is Janco's mind and identify him."

"Ha. Ha. Not funny."

"Is it Bavol?" Esau asked.

"No. I've met him."

"We can travel to the factory and I can take a look at the guy," I said. "And we could also sabotage it, cutting off the Cartel's supply."

"*If* that's their only facility," Janco said. "It was in the middle of the Greenblade forest and hidden by an illusion."

I wondered if that was generated by Rika Bloodgood. Her strongest magical ability was creating illusions, and she was one of Owen's closest colleagues. Her last known location was the Commander's castle in Ixia.

"Plus the place is huge and well guarded," Ari added. "And doing something big like that will need to be included in our grand plans to stop the Cartel. Fisk's messenger said they've changed, but we don't know what they are."

"Regardless, we need more information," I said.

Janco dug into his pockets and pulled out a handful of leaves. "I took these from one of the hothouses." He handed them to Esau.

Esau's green eyes lit up as if Janco had just given him the perfect present. If only we could get my father into one of those glass hothouses.

"No can do," Janco said when I mentioned it. "After I was caught, they put extra security around them. Then we high-tailed it out of there."

I considered our options and remembered the glass hot-house that might be in the Avibian Plains. Explaining the possibility, I said, "We can find that one and see if there's any information of value there before we continue on to the one you found. It'll give us something to do while waiting for Fisk to regroup."

"What about Leif and Valek?" Mara asked. "They'll be caught trying to get into the Citadel."

"Fisk's people can warn them when they get close to the Citadel. Where should we tell them to go?" Ari asked.

"The Stormdance travel shelter across from the plains. Leif knows where it is," I said. "We'll meet them there."

We made plans to leave in the morning. Onora offered her room to Janco and Ari. She moved to the extra bed in my room.

"One of the bounty hunters could have followed them here," she said.

"I heard that." Janco poked his head through our door. "And I'm offended that you think so poorly of our skills."

"After that scene with the innkeeper, I've altered my assessment of your *skills*. Besides, Valek charged me with keeping Yelena safe."

Janco laughed. "Good luck with that."

In order to avoid any more attention directed toward us, we left in shifts the next morning. Esau traveled with Janco, Mara stayed with Ari and Onora kept close to me. No one appeared to take any notice, but a good spy would blend right in with the townspeople.

We met up a few miles east of the Citadel and touched base with Fisk's sentries.

"Is the place still hot?" I asked the young boy.

"Yep. Best to stay well away," he said.

"Can you send a message to Fisk that we're heading to—"

"Is that a good idea?" Onora asked, interrupting me. "It's safer to keep our destination confidential."

"Fisk already knows where we're going," Janco said.

"Then no need to send a message," she replied.

"I'll let him know you passed by," the boy said.

"And if you see Master Leif and Valek…" Ari explained to him where they should meet us.

"I'll inform the others to keep an eye out for them."

"Thank you." I directed Kiki to find us a route heading

southwest. The plan was to ride late into the night. It would be safer to camp near the farmhouse rather than along the road or in a travel shelter.

Kiki set a quick pace, and we arrived a few hours after midnight. We skirted the farmhouse's property and found a small copse of trees wedged between the fields that was perfect for a camp.

"Are you sure no one will see us?" Onora asked. She peered around. "It's not very big or dense."

"The fields around here haven't been planted," Janco said. "I doubt anyone will notice us."

"How do you know?" Ari asked, gesturing beyond the trees. "It's dark out there."

"There's enough moonlight to see there are no fresh grooves in the dirt. And my nose doesn't need light to smell fertilizer. It's the warm season. Any farmer worth his salt would have planted his fields by now."

"Is this from your experience living on your uncle's farm in MD-7?" Onora asked.

"Yeah. How did *you* know about that?" Janco's voice held a suspicious tone.

"From *you*, genius. Am I the only one who listens to you when you talk?" she asked.

"We're *supposed* to listen to his prattle?" I asked. "Who knew?"

"Not funny." Janco mumbled something about checking the area and stalked off.

"Should we light a fire?" Esau asked.

"No," I said. "Just in case there are neighbors."

"I'll take first watch," Onora said.

"I'll take second, and Janco can finish the night," Ari said.

"No." I poked my chest. "*I'll* finish the night. Tell Janco when he returns."

Ari just stared at me.

"Ari," I warned.

"I'll talk to Janco."

A vague response. He could talk to him about the weather and still keep his promise. As I set up my bedroll, I decided to wait for Janco, but once I slipped under the warm blanket, I struggled to keep my eyes open.

Janco woke me at dawn. I growled at him for waiting so long, but he batted his eyelashes at me, trying and failing to look innocent.

"I'm able to stand watch," I grumbled.

"What a coincidence. So am I." He beamed at me, then leaned in closer and lowered his voice. "What I *can't* do is grow a baby inside me. Nor can I hatch an egg by sitting on it. I've the stained trousers to prove it."

"Do you have a point?"

"I thought it was obvious." Janco's expression softened. "Take the rest when you can, Yelena. For the baby. There aren't any guarantees that you'll get a chance later." He gestured to the rising sun. "Besides, it was a short night."

He had a point. I gathered branches and made a small fire. In the daylight, the flames wouldn't attract as much attention. The rest of the group woke and stretched while I heated water for tea.

"I already scouted the farmhouse," Janco said. "It's empty."

"How can you tell?" Esau asked. "It was night, and the occupants could have been asleep."

"No one was in the house, sleeping or otherwise engaged."

Ari shot Janco a look.

"What? I was bored, and now we don't have to tiptoe around."

"Did you find anything?" I asked.

"The place has been abandoned. Not much furniture. Lots of dust and spider webs. Otherwise it was too dark to see."

We ate a quick breakfast before heading to the cluster of buildings in the center of the fields. Weeds and a few small corn plants grew among the leftover brown stubble of last year's harvest. Sunlight glinted off the drops of dew on the leaves. As the air warmed, the earth emitted a fresh scent of grass and dandelions. The heating season started in less than ten days, which meant the baby was about sixteen weeks old. I pressed my hand to the small bulge underneath my tunic. Soon I would start to show, and I'd no longer be able to hide my condition. Not that it mattered at this point. The Cartel found out about the baby when I'd been Bruns's prisoner. And it certainly wouldn't stop them from killing me.

A large porch wrapped around the two-story stone farmhouse. A wooden stable, a barn and two sheds huddled behind it. They all needed repair and a fresh coat of paint.

We split into three teams to search for any information on the glass panels and the location of a glass hothouse. Onora and I tackled the farmhouse. Like Janco had said, it was unoccupied. No squatters had taken up residence while Bavol was gone.

I started in the office while Onora checked the rest of the house. Reading through the files that had been tucked away in the desk's drawers, I only found an invoice for services rendered, made out to Bavol Zaltana. It confirmed Bavol had used this address to send the glass panels. I'd been hoping for more information, but perhaps there would be some when we found the glass hothouse.

Onora shook her head when I asked if she'd discovered anything. Outside, we conferred with the others. Nothing.

"The soil is generative," Esau said when I asked him. "Lots of worms."

MARIA V. SNYDER

"Does this mean we're at a dead end?" Mara asked.

"No. We'll travel into the Avibian Plains and let Kiki sniff out the glass hothouse," I said.

"Why didn't we just do that instead of stopping?"

"There could have been valuable clues or information here. We still don't know who the Master Gardener is or what else the Cartel's been growing." I peered at the horses. None of them except Kiki were Sandseed horses. Would they have trouble with the protective magic in the plains? What about the riders?

"I think I should go into the plains while you wait—"

"No," Ari said. "We stay together."

Janco tapped his chest. "And aren't we immune? Ari and I have null shields, and Mara and Esau are distantly related to the Sandseeds."

"I'm not sure that covers the horses," I said.

"Kiki will take care of the horses," Ari said with conviction.

"What about Onora?" I asked.

"Let her ride Kiki; she'll protect Onora."

I glanced at my horse. She bobbed her head in agreement. Outsmarted, I conceded defeat, and we filled our water skins before mounting and heading south into the plains. It didn't take long to reach the border. The fields with their squat growth ended, and a blanket of long grasses spread over the rolling landscape. The mounds weren't big enough to call hills, but there was nothing flat about the ground under Horse's hooves.

Pulling up beside Kiki, I asked her, "Can you find one of those glass hothouses?" I imagined the structure in my mind, recalling the sweet smell of the white coal.

Unable to use her gust-of-wind gait because of the other horses, Kiki broke into a gallop instead. She set the pace, making wide, curving sweeps over the plains, each one dipping deeper into the interior. After two days of this, she stopped on the crest of a small hillock. In the distance, a glass structure reflected the sunlight.

Janco slid off The Madam's saddle. "Allow me."

"I'll go, too," Onora said.

He crinkled his nose but kept quiet. They melted into the tall grass. I stayed on Horse, straining to track their progress toward the hothouse. The grasses dipped and swayed with the breeze. Time slowed while my impatience increased.

A faint rustle alerted me to Janco's reappearance.

"Well?" I demanded.

"It's full of plants like the ones I've seen in the Greenblade compound. And someone is taking care of them," he said.

Esau leaned forward. "Did you see who?"

"Yes."

"And?" I asked.

"You're not going to like it," he said.

"Tell me."

"It's your cousin, Nutty."

14

VALEK

Yelena's scent lingered on his clothes. Remaining in the middle of the road, Valek watched until she disappeared around a bend. An emptiness ached inside him. Each time they parted, it was harder for him. Instead of giving in to the temptation to chase her, Valek swung up onto Onyx's back. Clicking his tongue, he urged his horse southeast to Fulgor to find Leif.

Four days later, he arrived in the capital of the Moon Clan's lands. Unfortunately, he hadn't encountered Leif, or any sign of him or his horse, during the journey. The afternoon sun warmed his back, reminding him that the heating season would begin in eleven more days.

Valek avoided the busy downtown district. Instead, he rented a small room in a dumpy little inn called Sweet's. After settling Onyx in the dilapidated shed that aspired to be a stable, Valek changed into nondescript clothing and used putty and a bit of makeup to alter his appearance.

His agents stationed in Fulgor had been discovered and sent back to Ixia last season, so Valek spent the rest of the day visiting the places Leif would most likely stay. As the sun crossed the sky, Valek's hopes for quickly finding his brother-in-law faded. Fear stirred in his chest when he spotted guards watching Opal's building. He easily bypassed them and entered. The place was cold and quiet—something he'd never thought he'd equate with the hot glass factory. It was also empty of people. A bad sign.

When he finished checking the obvious locations, he tried to think like Leif. The man was smart and had to know the Fulgor security forces would be keeping an eye out for him. But what about Leif's horse? Valek visited every stable in town, seeking Rusalka. Hours after the sun set, he'd exhausted all his ideas and was starving. Valek entered the Pig Pen for a meal—and to see if Leif was stupid enough to be having supper at his favorite eatery in Fulgor.

The Pig Pen was crowded like usual; however, an undercurrent of tension buzzed through the place. Valek spotted the source of the apprehension. Four soldiers sat at the bar. The stools of Opal's soldier friends, Nic and Eve, were empty, just like their apartments had been. Valek found a table away from the bar and ordered the beef stew and an ale from a server. Despite the name, the tavern was clean. The regulars kept giving Valek the once-over, but he ignored them.

When the server returned with his order, she slipped a note into his hand. Valek glanced up and met Ian's gaze for a brief moment before Nic's twin brother returned to tending the bar.

With a sick tightness ruining his appetite, Valek unfolded the parchment. The note informed him that Leif, Devlen and Reema had been captured and were in the garrison's stockade. And that Nic, Eve and Opal were away on a mission.

Ah, hell.

Since he'd promised to rescue Leif, Valek considered his meager options. Fisk's people had been recalled, and Valek hadn't replaced his own agents. A few of Nic and Eve's colleagues in the security forces might help him, but he doubted they would without Nic and Eve around to vouch for him. Guess it would a one-man operation for now.

Valek spent the next three days watching the garrison and learning the delivery schedule. Each night, handfuls of soldiers headed to town for a few hours before stumbling back. On the fourth night, Valek donned a stolen uniform and joined the group returning from the taverns. The guards at the gate waved them all through, and the magician stationed there barely scanned their thoughts before returning to sleep.

Since this was a reconnaissance mission, Valek stayed in the shadows and poked around, getting a feel for the place. In the morning, he entered the dining hall. He munched on apples to avoid the foods laced with Theobroma while he listened to the conversations around him. Scanning faces for Devlen or Leif, Valek wondered if they'd been here long enough to have been assimilated, or if they remained in the stockade.

Valek left with a small group of guys, but when they headed to the training yard, he peeled off and made a loop around the stockade. An impressive number of guards watched the single-story building, which meant someone important was inside.

He'd bet a dozen gold coins it was Leif, and that the Cartel planned to use him as bait to lure Yelena and Valek into attempting a rescue. Would they expect one so soon? Valek considered. Getting into the base wouldn't be difficult. It would be leaving with Leif and Devlen, who might be brainwashed and reluctant to go, that would be almost impossible. Valek needed time to think and plan. He searched for a spot to hide for the rest of the day.

While checking out the stables for possible locations to wait, one of the kids running errands paused next to him.

"Your disguise sucks, and you're going to get caught," whispered the girl.

Valek glanced at her. Relief warred with concern. "Reema—"

"Not here. Follow me."

He trailed her through a warren of buildings. She entered one of the smaller buildings. Closing the door, she lit a lantern and scowled at him. "Don't you know they've set a trap for you? You need to leave."

He made a stopping motion. "Slow down. Tell me what's going on. Why are—"

"All right. I guess you can't leave until dark anyway. Sit down." Reema gestured to a couple barrels next to a small table. She pulled her cap off, and her blond corkscrew curls sprang free. Drawing in a breath, she said, "My dad and I were arrested a few days after my mom left. He was locked in the stockade, but they didn't think I—" she held up her hands and curled her fingers in mock quotes "—*posed a threat*. They put me with the other street rats they had 'scripted from Fulgor to run errands."

"Conscripted?"

"Yeah, that. I made friends with Fisk's people and was helping them, but they left right before they dragged Uncle Leif in here."

"Where's your father?"

"Still in the stockade with Uncle Leif. They're bait for you and Aunt Yelena and my mom when she comes home."

"That explains the extra guards."

"Yeah, and there are a couple you don't see."

"But you have?"

"Of course. What do you think I've been doing all this time?" she asked in an annoyed tone, sounding much older than eleven.

"You know this place pretty well?"

MARIA V. SNYDER

"Inside and out." Her blue eyes gleamed. "Do you have a plan for rescuing my dad and uncle?"

Did he? Possibilities raced through his mind. "Where did your mother go?"

"To Tsavorite, in the Jewelrose lands."

An odd destination. "Why?"

"She received a letter from Master Magician Zitora Cowan, asking for help."

Did he dare believe there might be some good news? That they might have another powerful magician on their side? "Is it legit?"

"She seemed to think so. Nic and Eve went with her."

"How long ago did they leave?"

"About six weeks ago. She had to dodge the guards on the way out, and I'm sure they've set up an ambush for her when she returns." Reema's pretty face creased in concern, and she bit her lip.

"I trained your mother. She'll spot that ambush without trouble."

Reema relaxed for about an instant. "What about my dad and uncle?"

Valek considered. "Have you made friends with the street rats still here?"

"Yup."

"Will they be willing to help us?"

"Oh, yeah."

"That's a step in the right direction. Do you have any null shield pendants?"

"Yes, Fisk's people left a couple here for us, but we buried them because of the sweeps."

"You know where they are?"

"Yup."

"Good. Now tell me *everything* you've learned while living here."

"Everything? Even the boring day-to-day stuff?"

"*Especially* the mundane stuff. That's where we'll find the golden opportunity."

In the gray light before dawn, Valek stopped the wagon at the Moon garrison's gate. The officer in charge peered at him in suspicion. He resisted the urge to scratch his fake nose or sweep his now dirty blond hair from his eyes. Would the man notice that Onyx and Devlen's horse, Sunfire, weren't the typical breeds used to pull wagons? It hadn't been hard for Valek to convince the manager at Sunfire's stables that Devlen had approved Valek's request to borrow the horse.

"Where's Phil?" the guard asked.

"Broke his ankle," Valek said in a deep baritone. "I'm just filling in. He'll be back next week."

"And you are?"

"Orrick."

"Got any proof?"

Valek grunted and handed him a paper. "The boss said you'd ask for this." He kept his bored expression even when magic brushed him. Then he thought of Phil and his bloody broken ankle and the damn inconvenience to him. Valek kept up a running litany of gripes until the guard returned the parchment and waved him on. He avoided thinking about how he had arranged Phil's "accident" in order to take over his delivery route. Phil's boss had been thrilled to find a cheaper replacement so quickly.

Once Valek was far enough away from the magician at the gate, he raised his mental shields. He could have borrowed one of Reema's pendants, but if he'd worn a null shield, he would have been spotted at the gate. Good thing he preferred knowing when magic was aimed at him. So far his mental barrier has been effective in keeping other magicians from getting too far into his thoughts.

Valek guided the horses to the kitchen. Not many soldiers stirred at this early hour of the morning. Of those, most headed to prepare breakfast for the garrison. He unloaded the crates of fresh meats and cheeses and carried them down into the cold cellar. Then he piled the burlap bags of garbage waiting to be hauled away onto his wagon. Valek kept a slow pace, despite the risk of discovery, taking as much time as possible. However, no one bothered him or looked at him twice. When he left the garrison, the guard at the gate poked a few of the garbage bags with his sword and checked under the wagon.

Not bad for a dry run. The next day, he repeated the routine. By the end of the week, the gatekeepers waved him through both ways without a second glance.

On day four, Reema appeared while Valek unloaded boxes of bananas. "Did you confirm their location?" he asked without otherwise acknowledging her.

"Yeah."

Her dejected tone drew his attention. "I warned you they might be brainwashed."

"It's not that." She bit her lower lip. "My dad...doesn't look good. He's got bruises and cuts. And there are extra guards hiding inside the stockade."

Valek cursed under his breath. He'd bet all the coins in his pocket the bars had magical alarms. The only thing in their favor was the location of the stockade. Unlike the Krystal garrison, the Moon was a one-story standalone structure, and not in the basement of the administration building.

"Stick close. I need to adjust our plan." He continued carrying the boxes, letting his mind run through various plans and dismissing most of them as too dangerous or a quick way for them to get caught. It took him about four trips to the cold cellar, but he figured out a possible way to rescue them. They'd have to move fast.

"Have you found all the guards, even the ones hiding?" he asked Reema as he heaved the garbage bags onto the wagon.

"Yes."

"Can you scrounge guard uniforms for the older kids?"

"For stand-ins?"

He was impressed by how much she knew about subterfuge. "Yes."

She flashed a grin that Janco would be proud of. "Yes."

Good thing she was on his side. "Okay. The plan with the doppelganger is still a go."

"And then?"

"As Janco would say, 'Hit and git.'"

The horses' hooves sounded loud in the predawn air. Valek approached the gate earlier than normal—they'd need every extra second to pull this off. A long list of things that could go wrong repeated in his head, but he suppressed the worries and focused on the job. The guard yawned as he lifted the gate and Valek clicked his tongue, urging the horses into the garrison. Sweat dampened the reins. He wore two layers of clothing. His plain work coveralls covered a Sitian military uniform.

When he arrived at the kitchen, a man the same shape and size as Valek and wearing the same clothes appeared with Reema. The doppelganger began pulling crates off the wagon.

"Take your time. Move like molasses," Valek said to him before ducking into a shadow and following Reema. She led him to an equipment shed, where he pulled off the coverall.

"How many?" he asked her.

"Twelve guards, nine street rats and one cat."

"I'm the cat?"

MARIA V. SNYDER

"Yup. We thought about calling you the big rat, but I thought you'd be offended."

"I'm sure my ego would have survived." Valek handed her the darts. "Be careful. They're loaded with poison."

Aghast, she held them away from her body. "You're gonna kill them!"

"I hope not. It's diluted My Love and should just render them unconscious. I can't use either Curare or the sleeping potion, as they're now immune to them. And I didn't have enough time to find an alternative." Finding the My Love had taken him much longer than he'd expected as it was. The criminal element in Fulgor was very skittish because the city was under martial law.

She nodded and disappeared. He waited for a few minutes. Then he strode through the buildings, heading toward the stockade. He trusted Reema and her young friends to neutralize the hidden guards. No need to waste energy worrying about something he couldn't control.

When he spotted four rats crouched just out of sight of the stockade's main entrance, he drew in a breath. "Hey!" he shouted.

They sprinted, with Valek a few steps behind them. He rounded the corner, and the four stockade guards stared in their direction.

"Stop them!" he yelled when the kids neared the guards.

They grabbed the rats' arms and shoulders. There was a bit of a scuffle, and two of the soldiers yelped in pain while the other two grunted.

By the time Valek arrived, all four were down on the ground, unconscious. None of the hidden watchers sounded an alarm. Reema and her gang had done their part. Good.

Valek swiped the keys and unlocked the main door. The theory was that only the locks to the cells would be warded with magic. If not... Valek didn't have time for doubts. The rats helped him carry the men inside, and the kids pulled off their outer clothes, exposing guard uniforms.

Valek scanned them. If anyone took a close look, their cover would be blown. "Stand tall and try to make yourselves appear bigger," he said as they hurried outside.

He crossed the guard room to another set of doors. Opening those doors, Valek braced as four figures rushed him. He ducked the first swing and stabbed a dart into one of them. Keeping low, he jabbed another in the leg. In the semidarkness, he caught a glint of steel and blocked the strike, but the blade sliced his skin. Fire raced up his arm. He ignored it.

A thud sounded, followed by another as the two guards succumbed to the poison. The third thrust his knife at Valek's throat. Not wanting to harm the man, Valek sidestepped the strike and sent a dart into the man's neck. The fourth advanced with a sword already wet with Valek's blood. Lovely. Valek backed up and tripped over one of the guys on the floor. As he hit the ground, he yanked another dart from his belt. His opponent leaned over, aiming the blade at his shoulder. Throwing the dart, he hoped it pierced skin as he rolled away from the weapon. The tip of the sword cut along his back. He kept rolling until he hit the wall. The attacker advanced, and Valek palmed his knife, but the man wobbled a bit and then toppled, landing with a loud thump.

Valek didn't have time to celebrate or worry if the noise drew any unwanted attention. He hopped to his feet and checked the cells.

They were empty.

A sick dread coiled in his stomach. They had moved the prisoners. Smart. Valek needed to leave. Now.

Except... He paused. Reema said she'd seen them in here. Valek drew in a deep breath and extended his magic. Concentrating on focusing the power, he searched the cells. Power pulsed along the bars. Further in, he sensed the heat from two heartbeats. Leif and Devlen were hidden behind an illusion. Probably gagged.

Valek strode to the entrance.

Reema poked her head in. "What's taking so long?"

"Four guards inside, not two."

"Oops. Sorry."

He gestured her closer. "I need your pendant."

She removed the null shield and handed it to him. "Hurry up."

Valek looped the chain around his neck and returned to the cells. The shield allowed him to see through the illusion. Leif and Devlen slept on metal beds in two different cells. Crouching next to the first one with his lock picks, he hoped the null shield would also keep the magical alarm from tripping, but had no idea if it would work. He popped the lock and swung the door wide.

No audible alarm sounded. Leif wouldn't wake when Valek shook his shoulder. Valek felt his pulse—strong. Probably drugged to keep him quiet. He glanced at Devlen, who hadn't moved despite the noise. This complicated things.

He raced to the entrance. "We need the wagon here. Now!"

One of the boys with Reema said, "That isn't part—"

"New plan. Get the wagon."

"All right." He dashed away.

"What happened?" Reema asked as she followed Valek.

"They're out cold." He opened Devlen's cell, and she raced inside to rouse her father, but the man didn't move.

"Is he—"

"He'll be fine." Valek hoped. By the collection of bruises and cuts on both men's faces, Valek guessed they had resisted.

The clip-clop of hooves and the jingle of the harness announced the wagon's approach. To Valek, a shrill alarm would have been quieter.

"What's next?" Reema asked.

"I need help getting them into the bags."

"Right." Reema dashed off, and soon the stand-in guards and five rats poured into the building. Draping null shields around Leif's and Devlen's necks, the kids wasted no time manhandling the two unconscious men into the burlap bags and loading them onto the wagon with a number of genuine garbage bags.

By the time they finished, the sun threatened to rise. Within minutes, there would be more soldiers up and moving about the garrison.

"Go. Disappear," Reema said to the stand-ins and Valek's doppelganger. They scattered in a heartbeat.

Valek gave her the pendant before she jumped into the wagon and hid in another burlap bag. Valek arranged them so the collection looked like a pile of garbage. He vaulted onto the driver's seat and headed to the gate. Halfway there, he remembered he wore a Sitian uniform rather than his delivery man coveralls. And blood soaked his left sleeve and back.

Valek stopped the horses. He hopped down and, while trying to appear as if he was arranging the bags, he opened Devlen's sack and yanked the man's shirt off.

Glancing around, he noted a few soldiers, but none seemed to be paying attention to him. Valek changed and stashed the torn and bloody uniform shirt under the bags, then closed Devlen's bag.

The sun rose in a burst of color and light. Valek climbed onto the wagon and resumed the journey to the gate. Sweat stung his cuts, and he knew blood would soon stain the green tunic. It felt as if a river of red gushed down his back. Plus his heart seemed determined to pump extra-hard.

The guard didn't move the gate as he had the last few days. Instead, he stood in front of it. Valek kept a neutral expression.

"Took you long enough," the guard said.

"I dropped a damn crate." Valek shook his head as if in exasperation. "Damn apples spilled all over. And then the cook harassed me, yelling that he won't pay for the damaged ones, so I had to count the number that were bruised and write a note."

"Sucks for you."

"Yup. And it's comin' out of my pay, too." Valek spat.

The guard did a loop around the wagon. Then he peered underneath. When he pulled his sword, Valek's heart skipped a beat.

Before he could stab the sword into one of the bags, Valek said, "Hey, can you please not cut into them so deep? Last time one of the damn bags ripped in half when I picked it up. I had a stinkin' mess to clean up, and I stank of rotten fish all day. And I'm already late for my next delivery."

The guard chuckled and sheathed his sword. "Some days are like that." He moved the gate for Valek. "See you tomorrow."

"Thanks," Valek said as the horses crossed through. His back burned as if an archer aimed a crossbow at him, and the feeling didn't dissipate until they were far from the guards' sight. Increasing the horses' pace, Valek guided the wagon to the old warehouse they had rented. It was empty except for Rusalka. She had turned up in a stall next to Onyx one morning, and he'd moved her here as they prepared for the rescue.

"We're here," he said.

Reema squirmed from her bag, jumped down and opened the loading bay door. He drove the wagon inside, and they closed and locked the door behind him. Only then did he allow himself to relax.

He expected Reema to be happy. Instead she frowned at the wagon. Her hands fisted on her hips.

"What's wrong?" he asked her.

"We got away too easy."

Easy? Not according to his burning cuts. But Valek considered. "No one followed us."

"Are you sure? I think—"

"I know how to spot a tail."

"Even one covered by magic?" She rubbed her face with both hands as if suddenly tired. "Ah, I forgot. You're immune and would see right through an illusion." Then she shot him a shrewd look. "But you needed my null shield pendant during the rescue. Why?"

Valek admired her intelligence. Her brother might be the next master-level magician, but she was well on her way to master-level spy. Deciding to trust her, he told her about his new abilities, although he knew that she'd be safer if she didn't know. Plus limiting the amount of people who knew about his magic was a logical strategy, but Leif might have been forced to divulge the information to the Cartel while a prisoner. In that case, all bets were off.

When he finished explaining, she slapped her hand on her thigh. "I thought something was off with you! When we were in the garrison, you didn't spark, but I didn't have time to think about it."

"Spark?"

"Yeah, I see a glow when magic hits a null shield."

Interesting. "Useful."

She shrugged. "Only lets me know who is wearing a null shield. It doesn't really help me."

"But it might help Teegan or Leif or even me."

Reema perked up. "Sweet. Do you like having magic, or do you miss your immunity?"

"Right now I prefer the magic, as I was too easy to capture when I was immune."

"Yeah, I guess my mom has to worry about that, as well."
She sobered and climbed onto the wagon to pull back the
burlap bags, uncovering her father and uncle.

Remembering her earlier comment about possible followers, Valek relaxed his mental shields and drew a small thread
of power. He aimed it at the surrounding area, seeking with
his magic. Sure enough, he picked up two watchers cloaked
in an illusion. Ah, hell.

Even if he still had his immunity, he wouldn't have picked
up on the magic if they kept their distance. Valek needed to be
relatively close to a magician to feel its sticky residue. Common knowledge. However, if they knew he was no longer
immune, then he needed to rely on his magic more often—
something he was reluctant to do. The whole threat of flaming
out put a major damper on things. Valek noted the location
of the watchers and restored his mental barrier.

"When will they wake up?" Reema asked. She sat cross-
legged next to Devlen, clutching his limp hand.

"Depends on how much sleeping potion they ingested."

"Is there a potion that wakes people up?"

"There is something that prevents the effects of the potion."
He explained about the ambush to rescue Esau and Mara.

"Too bad we don't have any of that stay-awake medicine,"
she said. Reema sounded in need of a hug and reassurance.

Valek sat next to her, and she scooted closer to him. He
put his arm around her small shoulders and squeezed. Reema
leaned against him.

He thought of the watchers outside. "We might be able to
learn more about that."

"How?"

"You were right. We were followed."

She jumped to her feet, shaking the wagon. "I knew it!"
Then she scrunched up her face. "Did you use your magic?"

"Yup. And I need your help."

Reema readily agreed to the plan. When she left by the main front entrance, Valek slipped out the back. He kept a light magical touch on the watchers. Otherwise he wouldn't be able to see them. He didn't want to risk using the null shields in case one of the men was a magician. They had taken up positions across the street.

As expected, one of them followed Reema, while the other remained in place. Once she and her invisible shadow were gone, Valek circled around. Then he pounced on the watcher who currently resembled a barrel, pressing his knife to the guy's throat before the man could even draw a weapon. The cuts on Valek's arm and back flared to life from the effort.

"Quiet now," Valek whispered into his ear as he guided his captive inside the building, where he slammed his hilt into the man's temple, knocking him unconscious.

Valek yanked off his cloak, revealing a young man. However, the cloak now blended in with the floor. A mirror illusion must have been woven into the fabric. Interesting. Who had the ability to do that? Rika Bloodgood was in Ixia with Owen. Or was she? He'd encountered two well-crafted illusions in one day.

Valek pushed those thoughts aside for now and wrapped the cloak around his shoulders. Valek hurried outside to take up the watcher's position. A couple minutes later, Reema returned with a paper bag. She glanced up and down the street as if seeking a tail before entering the building.

Her shadow joined Valek.

"Candy run," the man said dismissively. "I can't believe the resistance is using *children*. They must be desperate. She had no clue I was following her."

Valek focused on the location of the voice and lunged. The

MARIA V. SNYDER

man fell back with an *oomph*. Sitting on his chest, Valek placed his blade on the man's neck.

"She knows more than you think. Which is very bad luck for you." Valek hauled the man to his feet and escorted him into the building.

Reema crouched next to the prone man on the floor, making a pile of his possessions, including an impressive collection of weapons.

"Hey!" Valek's captive yelled.

She spun toward the noise, wielding a dagger. "Who's there?"

Valek had forgotten about the cloaks. He yanked the one off his captive and shrugged his own off, as well. Reema relaxed, and Valek noted where her knife disappeared—up her sleeve. Smart.

"Find anything useful?" Valek asked her.

Opening her hand, she showed him a dozen darts. "These, but I don't know what they're filled with. They don't smell familiar."

"We can ask his friend."

"I'm not saying a word." The man clamped his lips together.

"In that case, we might as well let you go," Valek said.

"Really?"

He gave the man his humorless smile. "No. But you said a word. The first of many." Valek pricked him with goo-goo juice and hoped it worked.

Within a minute, the man relaxed. At least the Cartel hadn't found a counter to the goo-goo juice yet. A small victory. Valek sat him down so he didn't fall over.

"What's your mission?" he asked.

"Follow you until..." He spread his arms wide as if that explained everything.

"Until what?" he prompted. Dealing with suspects under

the influence of goo-goo juice had its challenges. And everyone reacted differently.

"You go to ground." The man made digging motions with his hands. "Where all the other rats are hiding."

Ah. No surprise the Cartel wished to learn the location of their headquarters. "And then what?"

"Come home, tell the boss, get a big bonus." His grin lasted for a moment before he peered around in confusion.

"Are the soldiers in the garrison going to chase us?" he asked.

"Yeah. Make it big, but let the rats slip away." He leaned forward and put a finger to his lips. "Shh…they don't know we go, too."

Which meant Valek would have to keep these guys under wraps until they escaped Fulgor. He switched topics. "How do you resist the sleeping potion?"

The man shrugged, but his gaze focused on the darts in Reema's hands.

"Is that the antidote?" Valek asked.

"Yeah. But ya gotta take it before."

"Before what?"

"Before ya think you'll need it."

"So if you're pricked with sleeping potion, and you haven't taken it…"

"Won't work after. And if it's been too long since you took it, it won't work."

"How long?"

"About a day. Guys on special missions get enough to last."

Which explained why his partner had so many. "And your mission was so special you also received these illusion cloaks."

"Yeah. Sweet things, blend right on in."

"Who gave them to you?"

"Boss man. 'Cause we are his two best scouts." He pounded on his chest.

"The best, eh? You were spotted by an eleven-year-old," Reema said.

He growled at her and tried to stand up, but Valek pushed him back down. "Where did the boss get the cloaks?"

"From his boss, who got it from his boss…all the way to the top boss."

"Who is?"

"His name is… Top. Boss."

Which meant the man didn't know. When Valek had extracted all the information from the man, he slammed the hilt of his dagger on the man's temple, knocking him unconscious.

Reema placed the darts into a leather pouch. "Now what?" she asked.

"We need to find a place to stash these guys for a few days. Know anyone in Fulgor who can help us?"

"I might," she hedged.

He waited.

"You can't tell my parents. Promise."

"Tell them what?"

She huffed. "I've made a few friends."

"More street rats?"

"Yes."

"Why is that a big secret?"

"They want me to have friends from school."

"I see. Normally that would be ideal."

"Yeah, but when is my life ever gonna be normal?"

True. With her enthusiasm for subterfuge and intrigue, he doubted she'd ever be far from the action.

"Plus those normal friends would have been useless for rescuing my father."

"I agree. However, those normal friends can be useful from time to time."

She cocked her head. "Like when?"

"Like when you need a cover or information. Their families might have skills or resources you could tap into. You should cultivate as many friends as possible, because you never know when that one person might be vital to a mission."

Her blue eyes practically glowed. "That's a good reason."

"Can you find us a couple babysitters for these guys?" he asked.

"No problem." She headed toward the back door but paused next to the man she'd stripped of weapons. "Too bad we couldn't take them on a wild Valmur chase."

"Yes, too bad," Valek said. "Maybe next time."

"That would be fun!"

Oh boy, she'd really caught the bug.

Valek freed Onyx and Sunfire from the harness and groomed them before settling them next to Rusalka in the makeshift stable. Soon after, Reema returned with three grubby street rats—two girls and a boy. Valek explained what he needed them to do and paid them in advance. The older boy stared at the coins in his palm with a sly squint.

"Don't even think about it, Mouse," Reema said to the teen. "I know where you hang."

"So? I ain't gonna do nothin'."

"Good, because I don't want to tell Pickle about—"

"Yeah, I got it. We'll be here every day."

Valek watched in amusement as they glanced back at Reema as they left. "Pickle is scarier than me?"

"To Mouse, yes."

"I do not know whether to be proud of Reema or petrified," Devlen rasped from the wagon.

"Daddy!" Reema flew into his arms, transforming into a little girl.

Devlen hugged his daughter tight. Well aware of the physical aftereffects of being in a drugged sleep, Valek poured Devlen a cup of water.

The big man downed it. He scanned the room before his gaze settled on Valek. "Thanks for the rescue. How—?"

"Reema can explain it to you. I need to check along our escape route and ensure there's not an ambush waiting for us."

Reema toed one of the unconscious men. "They wanted us to escape. Why would they have an ambush?"

"To keep up appearances. Or there might be more watchers waiting."

"Why—? Oh."

"Oh?" Devlen asked.

"In case we spotted these two. They would be the back-ups," Reema said, as if it was obvious.

"I am leaning toward petrified," Devlen said.

Valek laughed. The motion caused the cut on his back to flare to life. He'd forgotten about his injuries. Blood soaked his right sleeve, and a deep cut showed through the rip in the fabric.

"You will need to change your…or rather, *my* tunic before leaving," Devlen said.

Valek pulled off the shirt with care. Pain burned in his elbow. Showing Devlen his back, he asked, "How bad is it?"

"Bad. It needs to be sealed or stitched up," Devlen said. "Do you have glue or thread with you?"

"No." But he had something better. Magic. Except he couldn't see his back. He needed Devlen's help. "Reema, can you check the route?" Valek held a hand up before her father could protest. "She spotted these guys before I did and can wear one of the mirror illusion cloaks. Even if she's seen, they won't bother her."

Offended, she said, "I won't be seen. And I don't need a cloak."

"Take it, or you cannot go," Devlen said.

Even though she wore an exasperated expression, Reema wisely grabbed one from the floor.

"Go where?" Leif asked in a rough voice. He sat up and rubbed the back of his neck.

"On a mission." Reema gave her uncle a quick hug before slipping through the door.

"Uh…isn't she a little young—"

"Without her help, you and Devlen wouldn't be here." Valek poured another cup of water and handed it to Leif.

"Thanks." Leif surveyed the scene as he gulped the liquid. "Took us out with the garbage, eh? Sweet." Then he straightened in alarm. "Mara and my father—"

"—are safe with Yelena," Valek said.

"But they were—"

"They're safe. I'll explain everything later. I need to heal my wounds first."

"Heal?" Devlen asked.

Valek met Leif's gaze.

"I didn't tell him," Leif said.

"What about the Cartel?" Valek asked Leif.

"No. They wanted to know our plans and where we've been hiding."

No surprise. "And what did you tell them?"

Leif touched a purple bruise on his cheek. "All my best jokes, but they failed to find them humorous."

"I finally have something in common with the Cartel," Devlen said.

"Ha. Ha," Leif deadpanned.

"Are you strong enough to help me?" Valek asked Leif.

"Yes."

Valek turned his back on Leif and relaxed his mental barrier. He pulled a thread of magic and connected with his brother-in-law. "Let me see through your eyes."

Leif focused on Valek's injury. The slash started along his left shoulder blade and crossed over to his right side, ending at the waistband of his pants. Gathering another thread of power, Valek used it to repair the damage, sewing the muscles and skin back together. Then he healed the smaller and deeper wound on his right arm. Exhausted from the effort, Valek leaned on the wagon.

"That is new," Devlen said.

"Leif—" Valek began.

"I'll tell him. Go lie down before you fall over."

Valek shuffled to his pack and spread his bedroll. He collapsed onto it. Leif's voice lulled him to sleep.

Reema was back by the time Valek woke a few hours later. The three of them had made a camp of sorts on the floor of the warehouse.

"No one lying in wait," she said when he asked her about their planned route.

"What's next?" Leif asked.

Color had returned to both men's faces, and they seemed more alert. "We'll leave Fulgor when the workers are going home. The extra traffic on the streets should help us blend in. Then we'll rendezvous with Yelena and the others."

"Opal is due home soon. I am not leaving without her," Devlen said.

"How soon?"

The big Sandseed stiffened as if preparing for a fight. "Any day."

Which meant she was overdue. Valek considered his options. They could remain here and wait, risking capture. He could leave Opal a note explaining their whereabouts. But it might be picked up and deciphered by the Cartel's soldiers. A third option popped into his mind. Yelena wouldn't like it, but it was the safest course of action.

"The three of you will travel to the Citadel and catch up with the others. I'll stay and wait for Opal."

Devlen tried to protest, but the need to protect his daughter overruled his desire to be reunited with his wife. And Reema argued that she'd been just fine on her own, thank you very much, and could gather intel while they waited for her mother. Leif, though, was happy to leave.

In the end, Valek won. When they left the warehouse, he wore one of the mirror cloaks and trailed them, ensuring no one followed them. Reema kept the other cloak.

The cloak came in handy over the next couple days. Guards lay in wait at the glass factory for Opal's return. He figured Opal would dodge the watchers and check inside before leaving. And that was exactly how it played out when Valek spotted her on the first day of the heating season.

Her panicked expression fueled his desire to chase her. But he waited to see if anyone besides him had picked up on her location. Once he confirmed no one had any interest in her, Valek intercepted Opal near Nic's apartment.

"Oh, thank fate!" She grasped his arms. "Do you know where Devlen and Reema are? Are they safe?"

"Yes."

"Where—"

"Not here," he said.

"Right."

Opal stayed quiet as she shadowed him to the warehouse. But she pounced with more questions the second after he closed the door.

He explained what had happened to her family in her absence and why. Guilt, relief and concern crossed her face.

"So this Cartel has control of the Citadel?" Her brown eyes widened in alarm. "What about Teegan?"

"He's safe, too." Another hour passed as he filled her in on their efforts to thwart the Cartel and Teegan's role. "We need to figure a few things out first, but I hope we can stop them before they take over all of Sitia."

"We need to warn Nic and Eve and—" She gasped. "Zitora!"

His heart banged against his chest. "Did you find Zitora?"

"Yes, and she's on her way to the Citadel. We had no clue what's been going on with this Cartel. If we don't stop her, she'll be caught by them!"

15

JANCO

Yelena jerked as if slapped. "My cousin Nutty? Are you sure?"

Janco hated to be the bearer of bad news. He swallowed the sour taste in his mouth. "Yeah. I never forget a face."

"Except the guy you saw in the Greenblade forest," Ari muttered.

Esau leaned forward in his saddle. "Why is that bad news? Nutty is more than capable of caring for the plants."

"It's bad because she might be working for the Cartel or for the Master Gardener," Yelena said.

"She's not working for them," Esau said with conviction.

"We can ask her," Onora said. "She's alone, and there are six of us."

True. Although they only needed two of them. He and Onora would have no trouble sneaking up on her. The tall grass of the Avibian Plains made an effective camouflage.

"What if there are others hiding behind an illusion?" Ari asked.

Janco brandished his null shield pendant. "No chance."

"How about hiding inside the glass hothouse?"

"It's too small for more than a couple. And we can handle more than a couple."

"How small?" Esau asked, sounding disappointed.

Janco opened his mouth to reply, but Yelena said, "All right. Let's go ask."

Janco mounted The Madam and guided her to the clearing in the plains. A small hut sat next to the glass hothouse. The door to the hut creaked open. He rested his hand on the hilt of his sword. Both Onora and Ari also braced for action.

Nutty glanced out. Her maple-colored hair had been pulled back into a ponytail. She scanned the riders, and with a whoop of joy, she sprinted straight for them.

"Yelena! Uncle Esau! I'm *so glad* to see you." Nutty beamed at them. She skidded to a stop next to Yelena and bounced on the balls of her bare feet. "I've been so homesick."

"What are you doing here?" Yelena asked.

Confusion dimmed her smile. "Helping Bavol. Didn't he tell you?"

"No."

"Didn't he send you? He said he would send someone...but that was a while ago."

"No. He's been...preoccupied. Why don't you fill us in?"

She bit her lip and gazed at Onora and then Ari and Janco. The girl—well, not technically a girl, as she was about twenty-three years old—had freckles sprinkled over a small nose, which she crinkled as she peered at Yelena. "Um...they're from Ixia."

Considering both he and Ari had been in Sitia for a while and had tanned in the southern sun, she was rather observant. Janco approved.

"They're trustworthy," Yelena said.

But she still appeared uncertain. Janco didn't blame her.

They all sat on their horses, staring down at her. If it'd been him, he'd have barricaded himself in that hut by now.

As if reading his thoughts, Esau dismounted. "Come on, Nut. Show me what's growing in that fabulous glass hothouse of yours."

Nutty perked right up. "Isn't it grand?"

"Whose idea was it to build it with glass?"

"Bavol's, I think." She shrugged her thin shoulders. "It was already built when I came here to help." Nutty led him to the hothouse and they disappeared inside.

"Should we follow them?" Onora asked Yelena.

"No. Esau will find out as much as possible. Let's take care of the horses."

Esau and Nutty remained in the hothouse while they groomed horses and set up camp. The late afternoon sunlight reflected off the glass, and Janco strained to see any movement inside.

"Do you think she jumped him?" he asked Onora in a whisper. "Should we go in there?"

"Leave them be," Mara said, talking for the first time since they'd arrived. "Esau gets distracted when surrounded by plants."

"And you're not getting out of your turn to cook supper," Onora added.

Janco suppressed a sigh over the lack of action. Filling a pot with water, he set it on a few hot embers to boil for Yelena's tea. He knew how to make one meal—rabbit stew. He sorted through their meager travel rations. Ugh. Nothing even resembling meat. His stomach growled just thinking about fresh, juicy—

"Here." Ari handed him a bow and a small quiver full of arrows. "Make yourself useful."

Janco sprang to his feet. "You know me so well."

"I'll help," Onora said, joining him.

"I'm quite capable of hunting on my own." He slung the quiver onto his back.

"I'll flush prey into the open. It'll go faster."

"The prey in this case are rabbits, not *humans*. Do you even know how to hunt animals?"

Her expression turned flat. "The Commander isn't the only person who has killed a snow cat. I'm sure I can handle a couple rabbits." She strode into the tall grasses without looking back.

Janco met Ari's gaze. "She's kidding. Right?"

Ari shrugged his massive shoulders. "You were rude. Go apologize."

But when Janco tried to catch up, Onora had disappeared. Probably sitting right next to him, blending in with the gold-and-brown stalks that radiated in every direction. The null shield didn't seem to help him spot her when she turned camo.

"Sorry," he said to the clump on his left, feeling silly. "I'm not used to having company when I hunt. It's..." Janco pulled in a breath. "It's one of the rare times I'm alone. I really appreciate your help, though, so if you could—"

"Are you always this noisy when you hunt?" she asked from the right. "You're scaring away supper."

Apology accepted. The strength of his relief surprised him. "Did you really kill—"

"Hush," she ordered.

Soon after, the first of many rabbits bolted across his path. With Onora's assistance, he shot four rabbits by the time it was too dark to see. Much faster than on his own. Not that he'd admit that to her. He'd already apologized. His male ego couldn't handle another confession.

When they returned to camp, Ari had already prepped a couple skewers. Onora and Janco skinned the rabbits, and soon the enticing smell of roasting meat filled the air. Esau and Nutty finally emerged from the hothouse. Dirt stained Esau's knees and elbows and caked the undersides of his nails.

Since everyone was starving, they ate first. Then Yelena turned to her father and invited him to share what he'd learned.

He ran a hand through his thick gray hair. "The plants are all similar to what was growing in Owen's hothouse. Theobroma, Curare and a collection of medicinals. No sign of that crossbreed to produce Theobroma-resistant Curare. But there are a few experimental Theobroma varieties and crossbreeds. Looks like Bavol was trying to figure out a way to counter Theobroma's effects."

Yelena leaned forward as hope gleamed in her eyes. "Did he succeed?"

"Too soon to tell. Damn tree takes years to grow."

"What about that grafting technique? The one that speeds up the growth?" Mara asked.

"That only works when you have a mature tree," Nutty said. "Since none of them have matured, we don't know if it'll work. Once we determine if it will, then we can grow more."

Not the best news. But not the worst, either.

"How long until they've matured?" Ari asked.

"About two years or so."

Janco groaned. By then they'd be reporting to Commander Owen.

Yelena pulled the drawing of the Harman tree from her pack and handed it to Nutty. "Do you recognize this?"

She studied the picture. "No, sorry."

Yelena hid her disappointment, but Janco knew discovering why those Harman trees were so important to Owen and the Cartel was vital to their success.

"How long have you been involved?" Yelena asked Nutty.

"Bavol asked me to help him with some crossbreeding a few years ago, but he said it was a matter of high security and it would be treason if I told anyone." She glanced around as if expecting him to jump from the nearby grasses and yell at her for divulging the information. "Then a couple seasons ago, he asked me come to the plains. He'd built this hothouse as a prototype. He was working with two others, but he wouldn't tell me who they are. Said it was safer for me to not know. The last time I saw him, Bavol suspected he was in danger and told me to stay here and that he would send someone."

"See? I told you she wasn't working for the Master Gardener," Esau said.

Nutty pulled at her ponytail. "Is Bavol all right?"

"As far as we know," Yelena said. "The Cartel moved all the Councilors to the Greenblade garrison."

"The Cartel?"

"I'll explain in a bit, but first, did you discover who was working with Bavol?"

"I saw them. They came for a brief visit soon after I arrived. Bavol told me to hide in the hothouse. I peeked out. I recognized one of them." She hunched down as if afraid of getting caught.

"Who is it?" Yelena asked.

Nutty bit her lower lip.

"We need to know." Yelena's tone held patience.

Janco, in contrast, had to suppress the desire to shake the name from the girl.

"Will he get in trouble?" Nutty asked.

"It depends on whether he knowingly helped the Cartel, or if he was tricked."

"It's Oran," she blurted. "One of our clan's elders."

Yelena clutched her tunic in distress. There could be more

members of her clan involved with the Master Gardener, and that would throw suspicion on her entire family.

"Shouldn't be too big a surprise," Esau said. "He has the knowledge and could arrange the transport of the plants without trouble. Hell, even I've discussed these plants with him many times."

Nutty pressed her hands over her heart. "Have I done something wrong?"

"No," Yelena said. "You were helping Bavol. You had no idea what he was doing with the information."

Nutty didn't relax. "What about Oran? Should I have reported him?"

"To who?" Janco asked, but he didn't wait for an answer, "Bavol's your clan leader, and the Council is under the Cartel's influence. If you said something to them, you could have been arrested or conscripted or killed."

"And Oran could just be helping Bavol, as well," Mara offered. "We're jumping to conclusions. He might not be the Master Gardener. Esau, didn't you think it might be someone from the Greenblade Clan?"

"Yes. They have a few experts with the knowledge and skills, as well," Esau said.

"Have you met Oran Cinchona Zaltana?" Yelena asked Janco.

"Not that I can recall," he said.

"Hold on," Esau said. He pulled a notebook and a thin piece of charcoal from his pack. Drawing a quick sketch of an older man, Esau turned the page to face Janco. "Is this the man you saw in the Greenblade hothouse?"

"Yes! But why does he look so familiar?"

"You've met Bavol, correct?"

"Yes…" Janco wasn't sure where this was going.

MARIA V. SNYDER

Esau drew a picture of Bavol next to Oran. "They are half brothers."

Ah! Finally, they had a name and a face for the Master Gardener. Except the Ixians were the only ones who looked happy about it. Nutty wilted, and Yelena fidgeted with the fabric of her tunic.

"What about the other person with Oran?" Onora asked Nutty.

"Can you describe him?" Esau asked.

"Her," she corrected him. Then, sounding doubtful, she said, "I can try."

"It's just like when you're clinging to the very top of a tree when on expedition with me," he said. "Just describe the parts, and I'll work on putting it together."

"Okay."

As she worked with Esau, Ari leaned close to Janco. "I hope she's better at description than you are."

Janco made a rude noise. "Forgive me for not being perfect at *everything*."

When they finished, Esau showed them the picture. The woman had blond hair and large oval eyes. Pretty and pale like an Ixian, she appeared to be in her late thirties. Janco didn't recognize her.

Yelena cursed. "That's Selene Moon."

"Who's Selene?" Janco asked.

"Owen's wife. She was born in the Greenblade Clan but took his clan's name when they married. I don't remember her file saying anything about her being good with plants," Yelena mused.

Oh. "Hasn't she been incarcerated in Dawnwood prison for her role in Leif's kidnapping a few years ago?"

"Obviously not anymore." Yelena fisted her hands and pressed them into her lap. "She's a powerful magician. That's bad enough, but now I'm wondering who else Owen rescued from prison."

Janco groaned at the prospect of dozens of murderers and criminals helping Bruns and company. Bad enough that they had magicians on their side. Oh, yeah. This just kept getting better and better.

16

YELENA

My heart twisted at the thought of Owen rescuing his wife, Selene, and other criminals from the Sitian prisons. With close to four years to pick and choose who to release, and with Loris's and Cilly's magic to help alter the correctional officers' memories and implant new false ones, he could have recruited a small army of professional delinquents. If Owen hadn't rescued his brother from Wirral's maximum security wing, we might never have discovered he was still alive. Good thing Owen made mistakes. Those would, hopefully, lead to his defeat.

We all sat around the campfire, lost in our own thoughts. The logs snapped and crackled as the flames licked at them with greedy orange tongues.

"Now we know that either Oran or Selene is the Master Gardener. How does that help us?" Janco asked.

I considered. "We could kidnap Oran and find out where all the other glass hothouses are located. Cutting off the Cartel's supply of Theobroma would be a major blow."

"Would he tell us?" Onora asked.

"Unless he's immune to goo-goo juice, he should."

Onora crinkled her nose at the mention of the juice.

Janco rubbed the scar where the lower half of his ear used to be. "Wouldn't that tip the Cartel off to what we're doing? If it was me, and one of my expert green thumbs disappeared, I'd triple the guards around all those hothouses and Theobroma factories."

He had a point. I borrowed one of Valek's tactics. "What do you suggest?"

"I found that complex by following the delivery wagon from the garrison. We could send teams to all the garrisons and locate all the hothouses and factories."

We already knew who supplied the Greenblade garrison, so that left ten garrisons, requiring twenty people. Fisk could probably provide the manpower. Could we locate and destroy them in time? We had guessed the Cartel and the Commander would complete the takeover of Sitia by the middle of the hot season. The Theobroma took at least seven days to wear off. To be on the safe side, all the Theobroma would need to be destroyed by the beginning of the hot season, which was sixty-six days away. It should be enough time, but what if we missed one of the factories?

I voiced my concerns to the others.

"Fisk's kids are good for surveillance, but I wouldn't ask them to attack professional soldiers," Ari said. "Plus, as soon as we hit one compound, all the others will be alerted. We don't have enough people to strike all the hothouses at one time."

Another good point.

Esau squirmed in his seat and ran a hand through his gray hair. He had a pained expression that I'd learned to recognize. "Do you have a suggestion, Father?" I asked.

Unhappy, he dragged his gaze to mine. "I might have a way we can kill off the Theobroma trees without tipping off the Cartel."

MARIA V. SNYDER

Janco glanced at him in surprise. "Why do you look so glum? That's fantastic news!"

"There's a strong chance it would destroy *all* the Theobroma trees in Sitia. Every one."

I understood his reluctance. To Esau, plants, trees and flowers were almost as precious as people.

"Good riddance," Janco said. "It has brought nothing but trouble. In my mind, it's just as bad as magic."

"It counters the effects of Curare," Esau said.

"Until the Theobroma-resistant Curare is ready," Janco shot back.

"That won't be for another three or four years."

"That's based on the plants in this hothouse and the one in Broken Bridge," I said. "Owen's people had more time. There's a possibility that it's ready now." A sobering thought. "What's your idea, Father?"

He stared at his hands, then picked up a twig from the ground. Using the broken end, he cleaned the dirt from under his nails.

"Father?"

Esau sighed. "There's a fungus that grows in the Illiais Jungle. It's called Frosty Pod because it resembles snow. It causes the pods on the Theobroma trees to rot. I've isolated it to one part of the jungle and have been working on a fungicide. But if we were to harvest the spores and spread them, then it would damage all the pods and appear natural."

"Spread them how?" Ari asked.

"With the wind. We'd need to be upwind on a windy day."

"And be in the perfect spot," Janco said. "And hope the wind is strong enough to carry the spores throughout Sitia."

Undeterred, Esau said, "We can travel from city to city, starting at the Illiais Market, then to Booruby and farther north."

"What about through the glass walls of the hothouses?" Janco's good mood soured and he stabbed a stick into the fire. "Besides, we can't control the weather."

Excitement shot through me. "No. But Zethan and the Stormdancers can. Would seeding rain clouds with the spores work as well?" I asked Esau.

"Fungus loves moisture."

"Can the spores get inside the hothouses?" Ari asked.

"There are small holes in the glass panels in the ceiling that allow the smoke from the burning coals to escape," Esau said. "Plus those spores will stick to boots and clothing, so when a worker enters the house, he'll drag them in with him."

"How long until the pods rot?" Ari leaned forward.

"I don't know for sure, as I'm never there right when they're infected, but it's aggressive. The pods shouldn't last more than ten days. Eventually the fungus kills the tree as well, but that takes longer. However, the tree won't produce any more pods."

I glanced at Ari. Judging by the contemplative gleam in his eyes, he was probably thinking the same thing as me. The fungus just might work. I calculated the timing. Ten days for die-off, then probably another twenty before the Cartel ran out of Theobroma—maybe sooner, but it was better to over-estimate—then add ten for the effects to wear off. Forty total. That meant we would have to *finish* spreading the spores by day fifty of the heating season if we wanted to attack the garrisons in the middle of the hot season. So with at least ten days for travel time, our start date would need to be day forty of the heating season, which was forty-six days away. Of course, starting sooner would be even better. I explained my math to the others.

"Father, can you collect enough spores by then?" I asked.

"There are not enough right now for your plan to work. I'll need time to find a dark, moist location to grow more of the Frosty Pod. Given enough nutrients, heat and moisture, the Frosty Pod should multiply like rabbits."

"Then we have to start as soon as possible," Ari said.

I agreed. "After we rendezvous with Valek and Leif, we'll break into two teams—one to go with my father to help with the spores, and the other to arrange for Zethan and a Storm-dancer to meet Esau at the Illiais Market on day forty."

The next morning, we packed up our small camp. The plan was to head for the Stormdance travel shelter. I avoided considering the possibility that Leif and Valek wouldn't be there and instead focused on my stubborn father.

"I need to return home and get started right away," he argued. "We don't have much time."

He had a point. Except... "It's not safe for you to travel alone. The Cartel will be searching for you."

"I'm going with him," Nutty said. "I'm not staying here."

Aghast, Esau asked, "But what about the plants?"

"We'll take a few of them with us, but we *do* have an *entire* jungle full of plants."

He ignored her jab. "It's a shame we can't take the glass hothouse."

I interrupted his musings. "Promise me you'll travel through the plains as long as you can."

"Of course," Esau said.

"All right. Mara, would you like to go with them? I'll send Leif to you as soon as he arrives."

"No, thanks. I'd rather not wait any longer than I have to. Besides, I'm still in training," she said, glancing at Onora.

Janco perked up at that comment. "I can show you this sweet little self-defense move."

"I hope it's not the one you used to fight off Svend," Ari

said drily. "'Cause you ended up in a mud puddle with broken ribs after you tried that one."

"Svend doesn't feel pain," Janco protested. "It would have worked if—"

"Time to saddle the horses," I said, stopping the impending argument.

After everyone was ready to go, I kissed my father goodbye. We arrived at the travel shelter two days later, near sunset. The shelter was located in the Stormdance lands just to the west of the main north-south road. The road hugged the western border of the plains and extended from the Citadel all the way south to Booruby, the capital of the Cowan Clan's lands.

The disappointment and concern was universal when neither Leif nor Valek waited for us inside the small wooden structure. All that greeted us were two rows of uninhabited bunk beds, a cold stone hearth and an empty stable. If all had gone well in Fulgor, they should have beaten us here by two or three days. Perhaps it took Valek longer to find Leif than expected.

Keeping positive despite the heavy weight of worry pulling at my heart, I decided that since we were safer in the plains, we would camp out of sight of the road and check the shelter at random intervals.

Janco looked at the bunk beds with longing before we left.

"The ground in the plains is softer than that thin straw mattress," Ari said to his partner.

"I know. It's just the *idea* of sleeping in an actual bed."

"You can stay. Just remember to scream really loud so we can hear you in the plains and escape," Onora said.

"Ha. You'd miss me. It'd be way too quiet," he said.

"Nothing wrong with quiet," she said. "Unlike—"

"Watch it. Or I'll…"

MARIA V. SNYDER

Onora waited, but when the threat failed to be voiced, she asked, "You'll what?"

"I'll sing every campfire song I know—loudly and off-key."

"So? You sing everything loudly and off-key."

I ignored them as I directed Horse back into the plains and asked Kiki to find us an ideal spot before full dark. Onora teasing Janco was a good sign. Each day she spent with us, she'd relaxed just a little bit more. Soon she'd be a true member of our herd.

Once we set up camp and ate supper, we created a schedule to check the shelter. I planned for the four of us to take turns, but Mara insisted she be included in the rotation.

"I need to practice being dangerous," she said.

"All right, but you'll have to go with Onora a couple times first to learn how to best approach the structure without being seen," I said.

"Okay."

"What about the Sandseed protection?" Ari asked. "Won't that mess up Onora's sense of direction?"

"We're close enough to the border that it shouldn't be a problem. And if they're not back by a certain time, I'll send Kiki to find them."

"Rescued by a horse." Janco snarked. "I can't decide if that's humiliating or just plain sad."

Kiki snorted and whacked Janco on the head with her tail.

"Ow! That stings."

"Be glad she didn't kick you," Onora said.

We soon settled into a routine, taking turns cooking, hunting and checking the shelter. One day turned into two. Then three. The first day of the heating season dawned bright and clear. Not a cloud stained the sky, and the scent of living green floated on the air. Too bad the mood at our camp wasn't as pleasant. A fog of worry tainted all our actions and the few comments.

Four days without a sign of them. Fear and panic mixed and simmered in my stomach. No way it would have taken Valek more than a couple days to find Leif. Unless my brother had gotten captured by the Cartel. To keep Mara occupied and, if I was being honest, to distract myself, we kept training with Onora. Ari and Janco also took turns teaching Mara self-defense as I practiced the skills they'd taught me over nine years ago.

Onora asked me how long we were going to wait.

I clamped my mouth shut before I could snap at her that we'd stay until they arrived. "Fisk knows we're here," I said. "He'll send word if he hears anything."

She drew a picture in the soft ground with a stick.

Drawing in a breath to calm my nerves—an impossible feat, but at least I could say I tried. "If they don't appear by tomorrow night, I'll send Ari, Janco and Mara to catch up with my father and Nutty."

Onora met my gaze. "And us?"

"We'll travel to Fulgor."

"The boys won't like that."

"No, they won't. But my father needs help with the spores. And he'll need protection." I frowned, hating to admit that he might not be safe in the Zaltana homestead. "There could be a few clan members working for the Cartel who might try to stop Esau or sabotage his efforts."

On the fifth day, I couldn't keep still as the desire to move, to do something, *anything* pulsed through my body with a mind of its own. I kept checking on Kiki at various times throughout the day.

This time, she nuzzled my neck in comfort, then glanced at her back, stepping close to me.

MARIA V. SNYDER

"You want to get some exercise?" I asked.

A nod.

I called over to Onora. "I'm going for a ride. Be back soon." I grabbed Kiki's mane and mounted. It'd been a while since I rode bareback.

Onora appeared next to Kiki. "Is this wise?"

"We'll stay in the plains. No one can catch a Sandseed horse in the plains," I said.

"Unless they're riding another Sandseed."

Insulted, Kiki snorted.

"Sandseed horses are good judges of character." I patted her neck. "They wouldn't let a dishonorable person ride them."

Onora's posture remained rigid.

"Do you really think Kiki would let anything happen to me?" I asked.

She blew out a breath. "All right, but don't be gone long."

"Yes, Mother."

"*You* can joke. *I'm* the one who will be in trouble if you're hurt."

I looked at her.

"Yeah, I know. No one would blame me. Ari and Janco keep telling me I'll have more success herding snow cats than protecting you, but that doesn't mean I shouldn't try."

That was actually sweet. Kiki gave her the horse equivalent of a kiss on her cheek. Surprised, Onora touched the wet spot.

"Thank you," I said. "We won't be long." I nudged Kiki with my knees.

Kiki broke into a gallop. Holding on to her copper mane, I enjoyed the fresh air blowing in my face as she raced over the rolling terrain. Without warning, she switched to her gust-of-wind gait. The ground beneath us blurred as her stride smoothed. We flew in a river of wind.

I doubted she sensed danger. Perhaps Kiki had just missed

the speed. She couldn't use the gait when we traveled with the others. And the plains were the only place she could truly fly.

Eventually she reverted back to a canter, then slowed to a walk. Her sides heaved as sweat darkened her coat. We remained in the plains, but I didn't recognize the area until I spotted a familiar clump of stunted pines.

Alarmed, I stopped her and dismounted. "Why did we come so far? Did someone chase us?"

She turned her head to the right. I squinted into the sunlight and spotted a distant brown cloud of dust that meant riders. My first thought was of danger. We needed to hide. Except if they had followed us, why would Kiki stop here? Kiki didn't wait for me to make up my mind. She walked in their direction. I hurried to catch up.

When we crested a mound, all worries melted. Two horses headed our way. I recognized Rusalka and Leif in front, but when I focused on the unfamiliar second horse, my apprehension reappeared in a heartbeat. Not Valek, but Devlen and Reema.

A thousand awful scenarios played through my mind about why Valek wasn't with them. By the time they drew closer, I was all but convinced he'd been captured. Or killed.

Leif shot me a wide grin when he stopped Rusalka next to Kiki. Faint bruises darkened his face. Dirt and blood stained his travel clothes, and he appeared tired.

"I'm so glad to see you." Leif hopped off the saddle and pulled me into a hug. "When Fisk's people said you'd passed by over ten days ago, I worried you wouldn't wait for us." He released me and peered around. "Wait. We're far from the shelter. What happened? Where's Mara?"

"She's fine. She's back at camp with the others." I gestured to Kiki. "We went for a ride, and she must have sensed Rusalka and decided to intercept you."

"Where's the camp?"

Unable to hold it in any longer, I asked, "Where's Valek?"

"He's fine." Leif grabbed my arm to steady me. "He stayed behind to wait for Opal."

"Why?" I glanced at Devlen and Reema. Both looked equally exhausted, although Reema waved and smiled at me.

"Long story. I'll tell you later. How far is the camp?"

"Another day at least."

He frowned. "That must have been some ride."

"We've all been so worried about you. And I would stay with you, but Onora will have a fit if I don't return." Probably too late. We'd been gone most of the afternoon.

"Onora?"

"Valek didn't tell you about Cahil?"

"No, but we were together for only a few hours."

"It's a long story, as well. At least we'll have lots to talk about while we wait for Valek and Opal." And that reminded me. Mara. She needed Leif. "On second thought, maybe you should go on ahead, and I'll stay with Reema and Devlen."

Leif stilled. "Why?"

I led him away from young ears and told him about her terrifying experience.

A cold, hard fury blazed in his gaze. "I'll kill them."

"She might beat you to it."

He grabbed my arms. "What are you talking about?"

I explained how she was training to be "dangerous."

He released his painful grip on my biceps. "Oh, no, she's not. I'm not allowing her to get involved in any more danger."

Remembering Mara's where-you-go-I-go declaration, I asked, "Does that mean you'll stay away from danger, as well?"

He growled at me. "Of course not."

"Then good luck with that."

He huffed with annoyance, then strode back to Rusalka. "Where's the camp?"

"I'm sure Kiki has told Rusalka the location. Please tell Onora where I am."

"All right." Leif mounted and urged his horse into a gallop. They soon disappeared.

"Are we stopping for the night?" Devlen asked.

Kiki grazed nearby. She needed more time to recover. "Yes. You both look like you could use the rest."

"Leif's been setting a fast pace." Devlen dismounted stiffly, then helped Reema down. "Reema, please go find some branches to start a fire."

She ran her hands through her curls, dislodging a few clumps of dried mud. "You know I'll find out what happened to Aunt Mara eventually. No need to send me off so the adults can talk."

"Reema." His warning tone did nothing to discourage her.

She shrugged but did as he asked.

"She is very perceptive," Devlen said. "Although in this case, it does not take a genius to guess Mara is the reason for Leif's dismay."

I filled him in as I helped him take care of his horse, who was introduced to me as Sunfire.

His reaction to Mara's rough treatment matched Leif's. "I shall be happy to assist them both in ensuring those men are punished."

That evening, Reema told me an elaborate campfire tale. I listened without interrupting. By the end, when she finished with how she'd helped Valek rescue her father and Leif, I'd learned quite a bit about Reema. She would be a force to be reckoned with in the future. The very near future, if she had any say in the matter.

"Why is Valek waiting for Opal?" I asked Devlen.

MARIA V. SNYDER

Lines of worry etched his face, but he tried to keep his tone light as he explained her trip to find Master Magician Zitora. While he talked, Reema snuggled closer to her father.

I remained sitting, despite my heart urging me to jump up and down at the possible good news. Instead, in an effort not to get my hopes up regarding Zitora, I asked, "Was Opal successful?"

"I have not received any word from her, but I was incarcerated for most of the time she has been gone. The Cartel may have intercepted a message from her."

That would be bad. Really bad. The Cartel knew enough tricks to capture Zitora, and when the Theobroma didn't work on her, they'd realize it hadn't worked on Bain and Irys, either. I considered. Opal left on her mission when Valek and I were still Bruns's prisoners. Once we escaped, we sent a message warning them, but by then it was too late.

The best-case scenario would be Opal helping Zitora and convincing her to return as an active Master Magician. Since Opal was unaware of the Cartel's existence, Zitora would probably travel to the Citadel. In that case, we would need to stop her. Nothing I could do about it at the moment. Instead of rushing off, I chatted until they tried to hide their fatigue. Then I ordered them to go to sleep. Plus, if we left at dawn, we might reach the camp without having to stop for the night.

As the flames burned low, I stared at the darkening sky. Stars popped into view. More and more of them, until points of white fire glittered from every inch. A strange sensation in my abdomen distracted me from the spectacle. Just a light stroke, as if a fingertip traced a line on my skin. But the touch came from the inside of my body. Odd. After it happened the second time, I had an inkling of the cause. To confirm my suspicions, I reached underneath my tunic and rested my hands on my lower stomach. When it occurred again, I felt the gentle flutter from both sides.

The baby had grown big enough for me to feel its movements. Excited and amazed by the truly unique experience, I kept my fingers splayed over the bulge. The baby was about eighteen weeks along, and I wondered when I'd be unable to hide the telltale bump.

The light touches continued, and I wished Valek's hand rested next to mine. A pang of loneliness and worry gnawed on my heart. I hoped we'd be together soon.

The next day, we arrived at camp late. Everyone was asleep except Onora. She materialized from the darkness as soon as Kiki stopped.

"We need to work on our communication," she said.

"Oh?" I dismounted and stretched. "I told Leif—"

"Your definition of 'not gone long' and mine are completely different."

"Talk to Kiki. She's the one who changed the plan." Unless... I wondered if she had sensed Rusalka before we even left. I'd have to remember to ask her if I ever recovered my magic. Funny how that uncertainty no longer squeezed my heart with anxiety.

Onora frowned.

I chuckled. "It's all part of that 'herding snow cats' Ari and Janco warned you about. You'll get used to it."

"I doubt it," she muttered, but she helped us take care of the horses.

Reema peered at her in between yawns. "Are you the assassin who wants Uncle Valek's job?"

"Eventually, yes." Onora considered the young girl. "Are you thinking of challenging me for it?"

"Oh, no. I'm not skilled enough," Reema demurred.

MARIA V. SNYDER

But Onora was too smart to fall for it. "Uh-huh. From what I've been hearing, you could put the sass into as*sass*in."

Reema's grin erased all signs of innocence. "Ooh, I like! But don't worry, I wouldn't want to limit myself by working for the Commander."

"Free agent?"

"Something like that."

"Reema, it is time for bed," Devlen said. "You can finish your conversation later. Like, ten years later."

In the morning, we gathered around the campfire and exchanged information. Mara leaned on Leif, who sat behind her with his arms wrapped around her torso.

"Time is not on our side," I said. "Leif and Mara, you'll join up with Esau and Nutty in the jungle. I need you to protect him while he cultivates the Frosty Pod. If the Cartel discovers what he's doing, they'll come after him. The rendezvous is at the Illiais Market on day forty."

Leif nodded, then said, "Since we can't use Valek's sleeping potion anymore, I'll brew up my own recipe. It takes longer to kick in and doesn't last as long, but it's better than nothing."

"Thanks." I glanced around. "Ari and Janco, once we learn where Teegan and the twins have relocated, you'll need to join them and escort them to the Illiais Market, along with a Stormdancer. Doesn't matter which one."

"How do we deduce their new location?" Janco asked.

"One of Fisk's people will know."

"What about you?" Ari asked.

"Onora and I will stay at the Citadel—or rather, outside the Citadel—to keep an eye out for Zitora, Valek and Opal."

Ari crossed his arms. "It's not safe for you to be that close. One of Fisk's kids can watch for them, and you can come with us."

"Zitora won't listen to a strange kid. I need to talk to her myself."

"What if you miss Valek? He'll be upset if you're not here."

Janco huffed in amusement. "*Upset* is too mild a word. Try *furious*."

I ignored him. "Kiki can sense other Sandseed horses. If Opal is with him, then Kiki will pick up on Quartz, and if he's alone, then Valek'll skirt the plains. We'll ride close to the western border in case we see him or Zitora."

"That's risking a lot for a long shot," Ari said. "Opal's trip could have been for nothing." He glanced at Devlen. "No offense."

"None taken. There is a chance you are right."

I used a firm tone. "Either way, I need to update Fisk and learn where we are regarding stopping the Cartel." No one argued. This time. "Devlen, you can either wait here for Opal or come with us to the Citadel."

His gaze lingered on Reema before he spoke. "Leif is on the Cartel's most wanted list. They will have watchers on all the roads, and he and Mara might be intercepted before he reaches the jungle."

"Hey, I'm not that easy to catch," Leif protested.

"Oh? What about Fulgor?"

"I…" Leif snapped his mouth closed.

"Devlen, there's not much we can do about that," I said. "The spores are our best chance to cut off their supply of Theobroma."

"I understand. Which is why Reema and I will travel with Leif and Mara. Reema can stay with her grandparents in Booruby, and I will help protect Esau."

"No," Reema said, scrambling to her feet. "I should go with Aunt Yelena and Onora."

I shook my head. "You're—"

"You're gonna need me."

"We are?"

"Yup. You're gonna need to sneak into the Citadel at some point, and *I* can get you in."

"Fisk has an entire network of guild members who can help us," I said. "They know the Citadel inside and out."

"Yeah, but they don't know *people* like I do. And that helper kid we talked to said even they are having a hard time getting through the gate."

"I'm okay with it," Onora said.

"I am not," Devlen said with force. "Reema, you are coming with me."

She sulked, but it was the right decision. Bad enough Devlen and everyone here were risking their lives. I wouldn't be able to live with myself if anything happened to Reema.

Energized by our prospective tasks, we prepared to depart. While Leif mixed some leaves into a pot of boiling water for his sleeping potion, I promised Devlen to inform Opal of his plans.

"How long will Valek wait for her?" he asked me in a low voice.

"Until she returns."

"But what if she…" He swallowed hard, clearly unable to utter the dire words.

I touched his arm. "Does he know where she was headed?"

"Yes."

"Then he will track her down and bring her home."

"But the Cartel—"

"One problem at a time. Right now, we're lying low until we determine how best to attack them. By then, Valek will be back."

He smiled his thanks and strode over to help Reema saddle Sunfire. I fingered Valek's butterfly pendant, or rather, the lump it made underneath my tunic. My confident comment to Devlen left a bitter taste in my mouth. Everyone looked to me for leadership, but I had no idea if anything we were planning would even work. All I knew was that we couldn't give up.

Leif finished concocting his sleeping draft. He distributed vials to everyone, warning us about its limits again.

"How long does it take?" I asked him.

"About a minute or two, depending on how big the person is. For Ari and Devlen, it would take even longer. Oh, and it doesn't affect some people at all, which is why we don't use it for critical situations."

Lovely. "Is there a way to know *who* it will work on?"

"Nope."

I rubbed my forehead. Best to focus on the positive.

Right before Leif and his group left, Reema rushed over to me. She thrust a folded cloak into my arms. "You're gonna need this."

"What is it?"

"A mirror illusion is woven into the fabric. When you wear it, you'll blend into your surroundings."

Amazed, I struggled to find an appropriate response. "How—?"

"The guys who followed us from the rescue had them. I forgot to tell you, sorry!"

Considering all that had happened to her, I wasn't surprised she'd missed a few details. But the implications that the Cartel had these threatened to overwhelm me. I concentrated on Reema instead. "You should hold on to it. It'll keep you safe."

She waved it off. "I'm not gonna need it to hide at my grandparents'. Besides, even if I used it, my grandma would find me anyway. I swear the woman always knows when Teegan and I are doing something we…er… Gotta go. Bye!" She dashed back to Sunfire.

MARIA V. SNYDER

Sitting on Rusalka, Leif laughed. "May I make a suggestion?"

"Of course," I said.

"Don't hire her to babysit."

Two days later, I waited with Ari and the horses while Janco and Onora scouted for an ideal location to make camp. It had to be close enough to the Citadel to keep an eye on traffic flowing to and from the city, but far enough away that we wouldn't be spotted by the Cartel's patrols.

Ari burned off his excess energy by grooming Whiskey. The horse groaned in pleasure over the extra-hard rub. I wondered if Ari would rather be out scouting than babysitting me.

"What's wrong?" Ari asked.

"Nothing, why?"

"That's the third time you've glanced at me with your concerned face. That usually means bad news."

"No. I was just thinking."

"About?"

"Why didn't you go with Janco instead of Onora?"

"She's better." His tone was matter-of-fact.

"Does that bother you?"

"Well, there's always that bit of jealousy when some young recruit is faster or stronger or smarter, but she's part of our herd. And, you know…" He gestured with the curry comb. "Best man for the job, and all that."

"No bruised ego?"

He laughed. "I don't have an ego. Janco has enough for both of us."

True. I fed all the horses a peppermint. Kiki thanked me with a sticky lick. An hour later, Janco and Onora returned.

"We found this sweet little spot at the base of a hill," Janco said. "We can climb the hill and see the Citadel's eastern gate, clear as day."

"So why do you look so glum?" I asked.

He rubbed his right ear. "You know all those rug rats of Fisk's—the ones who've been keeping watch on the roads?"

An uneasiness rolled through me. "Yes."

"They're all gone."

"What do you mean, gone?" Ari asked.

"They've disappeared."

"Are you sure?"

Janco gave Ari a give-me-a-break look. "A couple locals heard rumors that a patrol picked them all up."

"A random sweep, or with intent?" Ari asked.

"They wouldn't arrest kids unless the Cartel had information," Onora said. "The Sitians wouldn't stand for their children being taken, but the guild members don't have families."

They might not have parents and relatives, but they had Fisk. Which meant…

I closed my eyes as the awful news sank heavily in my stomach. "The Cartel has captured Fisk." The words were barely a whisper.

No one corrected me.

"Now what?" Janco asked.

"We have to get into the Citadel," I said, opening my eyes. Reema's comment about needing her help repeated in my mind, but I shoved it down. At least we had the illusion cloak. "Once inside, we'll need to determine what's going on, and then rescue Fisk."

"That's a tall order," Janco said.

"I'm aware of that," I snapped, but regretted my harshness immediately. In a softer tone, I asked Janco to show us the spot they'd found to make camp.

He led us to a small clearing in the forest northeast of the

MARIA V. SNYDER

Citadel, nestled between the road to Fulgor and the road to Owl's Hill. At the base of a hill, the ground was damper than ideal for bedrolls, but as he'd claimed, the view from the top was worth the extra chilly nights and weaker fires.

It didn't take us long to set up and cook supper. Sitting around the sputtering flames that hissed from the moisture in the branches, I outlined the plan. "We'll break into two teams and take turns watching the gate and the road from Owl's Hill. Valek said he'd check the Cloverleaf Inn before traveling to the Citadel. We need to intercept him and Opal before they arrive at the gate. And the same goes if we spot Zitora." That road also led to the Featherstone garrison. If Bruns decided to move Fisk, that would be the closest garrison. "Ideally we'll discover a gap in their security so we can enter the Citadel undetected."

"What if Valek and Opal are already in the Citadel?" Ari asked.

"Then we'll rendezvous with them there."

"Or rescue them, along with Fisk," Janco muttered.

Ari punched him in the arm.

"Ow! Come on. We were *all* thinking it."

"What are the teams?" Onora asked.

"The boys and the girls."

"I suddenly feel like I'm in elementary school again," Janco said.

Onora opened her mouth, but I shook my head. "Too easy. We *all* know Janco didn't graduate from elementary school."

Janco hunkered down. "I'm not feeling the love."

"We'll take the first shift," Ari said, bringing us back to business.

I agreed. "We'll do three shifts a day, alternating teams. Also alternating positions each shift. This way, everyone has a chance to study the gate at different times of the day."

"Smart. What about at camp?" Ari asked me. "Do you want one person to stand watch?"

"No. Kiki will alert us of any intruders. Even asleep, she'd hear or smell them before they can get close. Plus, the person on the hill should be able to hear if there are any problems below, and vice versa."

"What about the person watching the road?" Onora asked.

Good question. "He or she can wear the illusion cloak for extra protection."

"But how do we know if he or she is in trouble?"

"The old-fashioned way," Janco said.

We all waited.

"You don't know?" He acted smug.

"Janco," Ari warned.

"Fine. A high-pitched whistle. Or in the case of the *girls*, a girly scream will do."

This time Onora smacked him on the shoulder.

He rubbed the sore spot and glowered at her. "Definitely *not* feeling the love."

Ari woke us at dawn. Or rather, he woke me. Onora was already making breakfast, and she set a pot of water on the fire for tea. Ahh...the small comforts of life.

I stretched like a cat and then sat up. "Any trouble?"

"No. There were only a few people on the road." Ari rolled his shoulders and neck.

"Janco?"

"They closed the gate for the night. No one in or out." He plopped onto his bedroll. "I did a little exploring to keep awake." He shooed away our protests over the added danger. "There's magic at the gate."

Not a surprise, but it would have been nice for something to go our way. "We have null shield pendants."

"Which may or may not work," Janco said. "If there's a magician stationed there and he can't read us because of the shields, we're caught. And if it's not a magician but one of those magical alarms, we don't know if a null shield will trigger it."

"What about the other gates?" Onora asked. "The Helper's Guild kid said they were closed, but—"

"They're barricaded, with no way through," Janco said. "And they have these nasty-looking spikes."

We all stared at him.

"What? I saved you some time. Sheesh."

We ate a quick breakfast before Onora and I set off for our shift. She volunteered to watch the road.

"Zitora's twenty-eight years old with honey-brown hair and pale yellow eyes. Pretty, with a heart-shaped face," I said. Although it had been almost four years since I last saw the Master Magician. I hoped she hadn't changed her looks too drastically.

Ari tried to hand Onora the illusion cloak, but she waved it off. "I blend in, remember? Give it to Yelena."

But when I donned it, nothing happened.

Janco cocked his head like a puppy. "You look the same. Ari resembled a big fat bush when he wore it."

"That's because I was *standing* near a bush... Oh, never mind. Is it the baby siphoning the magic?"

"Probably." At least, that was the theory—the baby siphoned magic when it was touching me or directed at me. What I couldn't determine was what it was *doing* with the magic. I changed back into my own cloak, which had a number of hidden pockets with nasty surprises, giving me a sense of security. Probably a false sense, but better than being completely vulnerable.

Onora trudged up the hill with me, then headed toward the road. I found a comfortable spot to watch the gate. A few people already waited in a line to enter. The guards allowed only one person through at a time. They alternated sides. One into the Citadel, and then one out. The person stood at the threshold for a few minutes before he or she was allowed to pass. As the day wore on, the line grew longer, but the routine didn't vary.

Halfway though my shift, there was a commotion at the gate. A few shouts reached me as two guards grabbed the man being inspected. They ripped off his cloak and yanked something from around his neck. Forced to the ground, the man was manacled and escorted away. That answered the question of the null shield pendant. It would be a bad idea.

By the end of my shift, I hadn't witnessed any gaps in the security or noticed any way that we could sneak inside. Dejected, I returned to the camp by midafternoon. Onora joined us with nothing to report. Ari and Janco left soon after for the evening shift. I tried to sleep, but my mind whirled.

What if we couldn't get inside? We could rush the entrance, but that would just tip everyone off that we were in the Citadel, and Bruns would probably triple the guards around Fisk. In that case, we'd have to abandon plans to rescue Fisk for now. Instead, we'd endeavor to recruit a Stormdancer and locate Teegan and Valek's siblings. Then what? I mulled over our lack of resources and personnel.

If our plan to kill off the Theobroma pods worked, the soldiers loyal to the Cartel would no longer be under the influence of the drug. They would need trusted leaders to follow.

The Sitian Council. The Council members had to be rescued from the Greenblade garrison before the soldiers woke so they would be ready and able to lead. A good plan. Except it would be Onora and me storming the castle, so to speak. Unless Valek magically appeared with Opal and Zitora. A girl could hope.

The next two…four…six shifts netted the same results. No ideas on how to sneak through the gate and no familiar faces on the road. Then again, would Valek be in disguise? He, too, was on the Cartel's most wanted list.

On the morning of our third day of fruitless spying, it was my turn to watch the road. As I hunkered down in the underbrush, I planned our next move. We'd travel to the Cliffs. Hopefully Kade would know where Teegan and the others were hiding. Not the best strategy, but better than wasting more time. In fact, the more I thought about it, the stronger my desire to leave. It was already midafternoon. I stood and froze.

Walking along the road were two people I recognized—Cahil's scouts, Hanni and Faxon. Which might mean that Cahil and the rest of his men were not far behind.

If that was the case, then we had a possible way into the Citadel. As long as they were still free of the Theobroma. Only one way to find out. Taking a risk, I strode from the woods and hailed them.

"No," Ari said when I explained my plan. "It's insane."

"I gotta agree with the big guy on this one," Janco said.

"It's brilliant," Onora said. "I'm in."

Ari fisted his hands but kept them pressed to his sides. "No. Two of you can't rescue Fisk. You'll get captured."

Onora snorted. I put my hand on her shoulder, stopping her retort before this turned ugly. "This would be an information-gathering mission only."

"Still no." Now Ari crossed his arms, trying to appear more massive and intimidating.

It worked on Hanni, who glanced at me with worry. "If you're going to do it, you should leave soon. General Cahil and the rest of the team are departing Owl's Hill in the morning."

"Then we'll *all* go," Ari said.

"No. Too many unfamiliar faces will trigger suspicion. You and Janco have to go to The Cliffs and recruit a Stormdancer. You only have thirty days to get to the rendezvous point." I outlined what I needed them to do as I rolled up my bedding.

"No."

I sighed. "Ari, I don't need your permission."

"*If* you get into the Citadel, and that's a *huge* if, how are you going to leave?" he asked.

"The same way. We'll get papers from Cahil."

"And the magician at the gate?" Janco asked.

"If we keep our thoughts on our duties for the General, we shouldn't raise any alarms."

"Sounds like your plan might just work," a welcome voice said from the trees.

Everyone except me yanked weapons as they spun toward the sound. Our argument had put them all on edge.

Valek stood at the border of the clearing with his hands wide. "One change, though. *I'm* going with Yelena into the Citadel."

MARIA V. SNYDER

17

VALEK

Yelena stepped into his arms, and he pulled her close. He hadn't realized how much of the painful tightness in his chest had been due to worry. Having her by his side filled a void inside him.

Over her shoulder, Valek studied the expressions of the people gathered in the small clearing. Ari set his jaw and Janco stiffened, clearly preparing to continue to object to Yelena's plan. Onora, too, appeared displeased with the change. Too bad. In the last five days, he and Opal hadn't seen any other way into the Citadel. This was their only chance.

Breaking apart, he kept one arm around his wife's waist. "We need to figure out where they're holding Zitora and Fisk. See if there's any hope for a rescue."

"I knew Opal would find her," Yelena said.

"Except I lost her." Opal emerged from the greenery.

Yelena, Ari and Janco took a moment to greet their friend. However, they didn't have time for lengthy explanations.

"We arrived just as Zitora entered the Citadel," Opal said.

"Was she arrested?" Yelena asked.

"No, but a few of the guards followed her. Bruns is smart

enough to try to recruit her to his cause before using strong-arm methods," Valek said.

"And just how are you and Yelena going to rescue them?" Ari demanded.

"*If* we attempt a rescue, it will depend on a number of factors." Valek used his flat tone, warning Ari.

But Ari was in protective bull mode. Nothing to do but let him say his piece.

"And how are you going to escape the Citadel?" he demanded. "They'll have doubled the guard at the gate."

"I don't plan on taking any unnecessary risks. You should know that better than most." He gazed at his friend. "Besides, Onora will be helping, as well."

"I will?"

"How is she going to get inside?" Janco asked, more curious than combative.

"By doing what she does best—blending in."

Onora's gaze turned distant as she worked it out. The matching sour expressions on the power twins' faces meant they had accepted the inevitable.

"Yelena, where are Devlen and Reema?" Opal asked.

Valek was surprised she'd waited this long to ask.

"On the way to Booruby." Yelena filled them in on the hothouse, Nutty and about Theobroma-killing spores while she packed her bags and saddled Kiki. She also mentioned that Ari and Janco needed to find Valek's siblings, Teegan and a Stormdancer to help spread those same spores.

Opal played with the ring on her finger as she listened. When Yelena finished, Opal glanced at Ari and Janco. "Kade would never let Teegan, Zethan and Zohav leave the safety of The Cliffs alone. He'd either go with them or send Heli."

"That's good to know," Ari said. "Do you know where they might go?"

"Yes. To my parents' house in Booruby."

"Are you sure? We have no time to be wrong."

"Yes. Teegan knows it's a safe place. The Avibian Plains are right next to the glass factory. The Sandseed protection recognizes my family, so they can hide in there if trouble arrives. Which it probably will, because if they messaged Fisk with their new location, the Cartel might already be on the way to intercept them."

Although he'd just learned about the existence of his younger brother and sister a season ago, a protective instinct flared under Valek's ribs at the thought of them being in danger. Plus his mother would kill him if anything happened to them. Valek suddenly understood why Janco feared his own mother.

"Then we'd better get moving," Ari said.

They packed in record time. Opal whistled for Quartz. They had left her and Onyx a quarter mile away, just in case.

"Where do we rendezvous with you once the spores are airborne?" Ari asked.

"Longleaf. It's a town near the Greenblade garrison," Yelena said.

"Why?" Valek asked.

She sketched out her thoughts about the Councilors. "They need to be freed first regardless."

He agreed.

"What if you're not there?" Ari asked.

"If we're not there by..." She drummed her fingers on her pants. "By the first day of the hot season, then you're in charge of stopping the Sitian takeover. Assume the Cartel knows everything Valek and I do when you're formulating a strategy."

Janco glanced at her, then at Valek, then at Ari. "Holy snow cats, she's serious!"

"Of course she's serious," Ari said. "If they're caught, Bruns won't let them escape, and he has the magicians to—" he spun a finger around the side of his head "—steal their thoughts."

Or, in Valek's case, they'd just need to threaten Yelena or the baby, and he would cooperate.

"I know that, but I was hoping for a more upbeat send-off," Janco grumbled.

"We'll always be with you in spirit," Yelena said. "Is that more upbeat?"

"That you'll haunt me? No. That's creepy."

The goodbyes were quick after that, although Ari and Janco paused long enough to obtain a promise from Yelena to not do anything stupid.

"You mean don't do anything Janco would do?" she teased.

"Exactly." Ari nodded.

"Hey! Who's the one who agreed with Ari that it's too dangerous to go into the Citadel?" Janco asked with a wounded lilt to his voice. "Avoiding that place is the smart thing to do."

"It is smart," Yelena said. "I guess there really is a first time for everything."

He pressed a hand to his chest. "You wound me."

She pecked Janco on the cheek. "Be careful. *All* of you."

Quartz and Onyx arrived in the clearing. The horses all rubbed heads in greeting before Opal, Ari and Janco mounted and headed south, planning to ride in the plains to avoid being spotted. Hanni and Faxon returned to the road. They had orders to rendezvous with Cahil and his team before they entered the Citadel tomorrow.

"How does blending in get me through the gate?" Onora asked Valek.

"An hour before dawn, go lean on the Citadel's wall. You'll blend in with the white marble streaked with green. Then move closer to the entrance and wait. Let a few people cross through, then empty your mind of all thoughts and slip in-

MARIA V. SNYDER

side with the next person going in. The magician at the gate shouldn't pick up on your presence."

"How do you know?"

"You're pretty hard to read." He held up a hand, stopping her. "When I saw Yelena earlier, I scanned the area with my magic. I sensed Ari and Janco and the horses, but not you. It's only when I focused on you that I could hone in on your thoughts."

Onora stared at him. "You have magic?"

He met Yelena's gaze. "You didn't tell her?"

"It's *your* secret to share."

Valek turned to Onora. "Here's the short version—I lost my immunity and gained magic. I can heal and read other people's thoughts. I may be able to do more, but haven't had the time or the instruction to find out. But trust me when I say you'll get into the Citadel."

True to form, Onora took the news in stride. "All right. Where should I meet you once I'm inside?"

"The Unity Fountain," Yelena said. "Do you know where it is?"

"No, but I'll find it. What if you can't get through?"

"Then collect as much information as you can about what's going on and leave the same way you arrived," Valek said. "We'll meet you back here in two days. If we're caught, then catch up to Ari and Janco. They'll need your help."

"Yes, sir."

"What about Horse?" Yelena asked.

Onora smiled. "I'll stable her nearby."

"Be careful. See you later." Yelena gave her a quick hug.

Valek clamped down on a laugh. The girl could handle Valek's new magical powers without missing a beat, but a hug from a friend left her a bit shocked. Her hand trembled just a bit as she swiped a strand of hair from her face.

Yelena and Valek mounted their horses and headed to Owl's Hill. They stayed in the forest, letting the horses pick the best path through the underbrush. Only a few hours remained before the sun set, and the warm air held a hint of moisture.

"How did you find us?" Yelena asked him.

He ducked under a low-hanging branch. "By doing the same thing you were, love—watching the road from Owl's Hill." When Yelena had stepped from the woods to talk to Cahil's scouts, Valek thought she was an illusion or a hallucination, as he hadn't slept much since he'd seen the new security measures at the Citadel's gate. He feared the worst after he'd gotten a closer look and knew there was no way to enter without getting caught.

Not at that time. However, if Cahil remained Theobroma-free and was still willing to help, by this time tomorrow they'd be in the Citadel. If not... Best to worry about that later.

Cahil had rented the top story of the Cloverleaf Inn. Watching the windows of the inn, Valek waited in the shadows near the stable. Yelena had stayed with their horses just outside the small town. Not without protesting, but Valek needed to ensure Cahil remained an ally before he risked her and the baby. Besides, scaling walls and sneaking into rooms late at night was his forte.

Once all the lanterns in the suite had been extinguished for a couple hours, Valek climbed the side of the building until he reached a window to one of the bedrooms. He unlocked it and slid it open. As he eased into the room, light from the half moon shone through a layer of thin clouds, giving him just enough illumination to see Cahil wasn't one of the two sleeping men. Two more people slept on the couches in the living area. No one stood watch. Good for Valek, but a misstep for Cahil. Valek checked the next room. Cahil was alone—

MARIA V. SNYDER

another blunder. Too bad they were allies, or he'd give in to the temptation to permanently take care of a big problem called Cahil.

Instead, he stood next to the bed and cleared his throat. Cahil surged awake with a knife in his hand. Impressive.

"Relax," Valek whispered as Cahil scrambled to his feet.

"Who's there?" Cahil demanded, thrusting the blade forward.

Valek sidestepped and pulled the hood of his sneak suit down. But he kept his weight on the balls of his feet, just in case. If Cahil had reverted back to being Bruns's lackey, the young man would likely yell for help.

Cahil kept his guard up. "What are you doing here?"

"No hello for your comrade-in-arms?"

"Let's not pretend we like each other. What do you want?"

"Why are you returning to the Citadel?" Valek asked.

"Orders from Bruns. He didn't specify a reason."

"Does he suspect you're involved with us?"

"Not that I can tell. But with Bruns, you never know for sure." Cahil shrugged, trying to maintain a relaxed attitude about Bruns discovering his deception, but the stiff line of his shoulders said otherwise.

"Tomorrow, when you arrive at the Citadel's gate, will the guards inspect each of the members of your crew or just let you in as a group?"

Cahil lowered his weapon. "Unless they have a reason to be suspicious, they'll just wave us through."

"Will they notice if you have two more?"

"Two? You and…?"

"Yelena."

Cahil cursed. "If they recognize either of you—"

"They won't."

"Why do you want to get inside? You no longer have allies

there. The Beggar King and his minions have been arrested. You can't free them."

"No?" Valek kept his expression neutral, despite the confirmation that Fisk had been captured. He wondered who'd tipped the Cartel off.

"All right, you and Yelena probably can. I've seen you two do some impossible things. In fact, it's better if I don't know your plans. But if you get caught, my involvement will be exposed, and I'll no longer be able to help you or myself."

"We know the risks."

"Fine. What do you need from me?"

"A couple uniforms for me and Yelena. And tell your men that we'll be joining you."

"Done." Cahil strode into the living area and woke his crew.

Valek tolerated a number of sour looks and low grumbles. It wasn't his fault that they didn't have the training to detect an assassin slipping into their rooms late at night. Despite their mood, they dug into their packs for tunics and pants that would fit Valek and Yelena.

Valek dropped the bundle of clothing out the window before he straddled the sill. "Cahil, may I make a suggestion?"

An instant wariness touched his pale blue eyes. "Go ahead."

"Set a watch schedule. Have two guards awake at all times, and don't sleep alone."

"Why? I'm allied with both sides."

"But you're not friends with the Commander. He has other assassins working for him."

"You said it would be a subtle takeover. No war."

"The Commander took over Ixia by assassinating *key* people in power. In other words, those people who might object to the new regime and had the resources to cause problems.

MARIA V. SNYDER

People like the Sitian Councilors and the general of the Sitian army. Besides, it never hurts to be extra-vigilant."

"Noted."

Valek gave him a mock salute and climbed out the window. He doubted Cahil's security would stop a trained assassin, but at least it might slow the person down. Scooping up the bundle, Valek hurried back to where Yelena waited.

She had built a small fire. His comments to Cahil about being prudent rose to mind, but not many assassins could slip past Kiki. Valek paused before his wife noticed him. Over the twenty-five days since they'd been apart, the angles of her beautiful face had softened, while her skin and hair shone. All due to her pregnancy. She might not be showing yet, but to a careful observer, the signs were there.

"Stop skulking about in the woods and come tell me what Cahil said," Yelena called.

He strode into the firelight. "How did you know?"

"Kiki. She raised her head as if she heard something, then relaxed." Yelena pointed to the clothing. "I take it you were successful."

Valek filled her in. "We only have a couple hours to get ready. I'll do your disguise first, and then you can nap while I work on mine." He pulled supplies from his saddle bags. Holding up a pair of scissors, Valek tested the edge of the blades for sharpness.

Yelena made a small *huh* sound and crinkled her nose.

"Sorry, love—the women in Cahil's group all have shorter hair. But with some artful braiding, I can make it appear even shorter without having to cut off as much."

"Not that." She grabbed his hand, pulled up the bottom of her tunic and pressed his palm to her stomach.

"What—"

"Just wait."

The warmth from her body soaked into his skin. He wished they had time for a proper reacquaintance. Perhaps just a nibble on her earlobe. Valek leaned closer, but without warning, a sensation brushed along his fingers. He drew back and met Yelena's gaze. Tender delight shone in her eyes. The light touch repeated, and understanding hit him. Hard. His lungs constricted as if he'd been sucker-punched.

"The baby?" he asked the obvious in a whisper. All he could manage.

"No. Bad indigestion from Janco's cooking," she teased. "Of course it's the baby."

He knew that, so why did the ground soften beneath his feet and the world tilt and spin around him? Because now the baby was tangible. Not just a concept or a belief. Real. Excitement mixed with fear, and the desire to protect crashed through him like a burning hot wave. He staggered to his knees under the weight.

Confused, Yelena held his hand. "What's wrong?"

"You can't go," he said.

She stilled. "What do you mean?"

"Tomorrow. It's too dangerous. Let me and Onora—"

Yelena knelt next to him. "You're overreacting. Besides, *you* argued for it. Remember?"

"Our baby changed my mind."

She grasped both his hands in hers. "You need me. If any of Fisk's members escaped, they won't talk to you or Onora. Zitora also won't trust either of you. And the library in the Keep may not allow you to view Master Magician Ellis Moon's notes."

Her words were all logical. Once inside the Citadel, the risk of capture diminished. Yet the sick fear gripping his insides with its sharp claws refused to let go.

In a softer tone, she said, "There will be no family for us if Bruns wins."

Another valid point.

"And fate might smile on us, and we'll find a weakness that we can exploit, or better yet, that you can use to assassinate Bruns."

Valek's calm detachment returned, cooling his inner turmoil and solidifying his determination to see this through to the bitter end. "You'd let me assassinate Bruns?"

"Oh, yes."

"What about the rest of the Cartel?"

"No. They're pawns."

Pity. "Owen?"

"Yes with a capital *Y*."

Something to look forward to. "How about Cahil?"

"No."

"What if I say please?"

"Still no."

"How about pretty please?"

"Valek." Her tone warned him to stop. She picked up the scissors he'd dropped, wiped off the dirt and handed them to him. "Time to get to work."

In the early morning half light, they waited in the woods along the road to the Citadel. Both wore the uniforms Cahil had provided. Valek's nose itched under the putty that hadn't had time to harden completely. He'd finished Yelena's first, then worked on his own before tending to the horses. After covering Kiki's white patch with a copper color that matched her coat, Valek had darkened her mane and tail. For Onyx, he'd scrubbed off the black dye on his legs, revealing the white socks underneath.

When Cahil's group rode past, Yelena and Valek joined

them. He stayed close to the front, while Kiki merged with those near the back. Cahil nodded in acknowledgment but said nothing. No one spoke much during the rest of the trip.

Hanni and Faxon waited for them a few miles from the Citadel.

Cahil pulled Topaz to a stop. "Any trouble?"

"No. All's quiet," Hanni said. She scanned the riders and, at first, bypassed Valek. "Didn't Yelena— Oh!"

"Hop aboard." Cahil jerked a thumb behind him. "Faxon, share Yelena's mount." At Valek's questioning stare, he added, "The guards at the gate are used to seeing a few doubles, since I like my scouts to remain on foot."

Valek nodded. It was a good strategy.

Cahil urged Topaz into a gallop, and they followed close behind. Valek kept a firm hold on his emotions as they approached the gate. He lowered his mental shield and focused on being happy to return to the Citadel and perhaps having a chance to visit his family.

Riding past the long line waiting to enter, Cahil slowed. The guards scrambled to clear the entrance, and soon the group crossed into the Citadel. A light touch of magic brushed his thoughts. Valek concentrated on his duties for the general and what he needed to purchase at the market. He didn't breathe easy until they were far away. Valek raised his mental barrier again, protecting his thoughts from magic.

They stopped so Faxon could change horses. Before they parted ways, Valek asked Cahil how long he planned to be in town.

"I don't know. It depends on Bruns."

"Will you be using your headquarters?" Valek asked.

"When we can. Why?"

"We'll check in from time to time for updates."

"All right." Cahil frowned. "What happens if you're caught?"

"I suggest you and your crew leave before they have a chance to question us." Valek kept his voice flat, but his heart thudded against his chest at the thought of Yelena being Bruns's prisoner.

"And go where?" Cahil asked.

"South, to Booruby," Yelena said.

Cahil opened his mouth but then pressed his lips together. He gestured for his group to follow him. Yelena and Valek found an empty alley and switched back into their nondescript Sitian clothes before heading to the Unity Fountain.

"We need to keep our disguises on while we're in public," he said.

"What about lodging?"

He gave her a sidelong glance.

"You've got to be kidding." Her tone implied she was far from amused.

"It's secure." Or at least, it *was*.

"That's not the point. I've tolerated all the others, but having an Ixian safe house *inside* the Citadel is..."

Valek waited for her to find the words. Although *smart* was the word he'd use.

Instead she sighed. "It doesn't matter anymore. I'm no longer the Liaison. Why should I care if Ixia is spying on Sitia?"

"Because you want peace between the two countries. Although I think having safe houses helps keep the peace."

"We're not going to argue about this again."

"I wouldn't call it an argument. More of a discussion."

She ignored his comment. "Why didn't you tell Onora to meet us there, then?"

"It's better if we take a more circuitous route, just in case anyone follows us from the gate."

"But the guards—"

"There are still assassins and bounty hunters after you. They're not going to raise the alarm because they want their money."

They reached the Unity Fountain. Eleven waterspouts ringed the huge jade sphere that was the heart of the fountain. Large holes had been carved into the twenty-foot diameter sphere and another smaller sphere, which was nestled inside could be seen through the openings. The holes in the second showed a third and then a fourth. A total of eleven spheres had been chiseled from this stone. One for each of the Sitian clans.

A few people milled about, and a couple kids dashed through the sprays of water, shrieking with delight. Yelena dismounted and removed her cloak. The sun was at its highest point. Sweat dampened her collar. She walked toward the fountain. Valek hurried to catch up with her.

"What are you doing?" he asked.

"It's good luck to drink the water."

"But bad luck to wash off your makeup."

"Good point." She returned for her water skin and filled it with fountain water.

Valek did the same. They could use the luck. The mist from the waterspouts cooled his brow. Glancing around, he searched for Onora. She should have beaten them here. He considered using his magic to locate her. Would it work in the crowded Citadel? And, more importantly, would it alert another magician that he was here?

The sphere chuckled. "Broad daylight. I can't believe you didn't notice me."

Onora hopped down from her perch in one of the outer holes. Her tunic was wet from the spray.

"Wow. You weren't kidding. She's *really* good at blending in," Yelena said to him with a touch of awe.

MARIA V. SNYDER

"I take it you had no trouble at the gate?" Valek asked Onora.

"I kept expecting people to give me odd looks or to point to me and alert the guards. 'Look at that strange Ixian girl standing by the wall!' But no one did." Onora shrugged. "And here I thought my ability to go undetected was due to my mad assassin skills."

Valek kept a straight face. Nice to see her relaxed and joking. "Anyone follow you here?"

"No. But you have an admirer," Onora said.

"The brown-haired boy?" He'd noticed him when they first arrived.

"Yup. Friend of yours?" she asked Yelena.

"Perhaps he's one of Fisk's."

"But would he recognize us?" Valek asked. If a kid could spot them, then they were in trouble.

"Fisk's been training them," Yelena said. "Besides, if they're on the lookout for a couple on horseback, we fit the description."

A good point. "Let's get the horses stabled and see if our friend follows us. Onora, we'll meet you at the Ninth Street stables."

They took a circuitous route to the stables located near the market and the safe house. The boy kept his distance, but also kept them in sight. At the stable, Yelena asked the groom not to get Kiki's face wet, remembering the horse wore makeup as well.

"She hates that and will kick you," she said.

"Thank you for the warning," the young woman said. "Where would you like me to deliver your bags?"

"I'll take them," Valek said. "We're not far."

When the groom removed Kiki's saddle, the horse looked at Valek.

He opened his mind to her.

Home? she thought with longing as an image of the Magician's Keep filled his mind.

Not yet, he answered.

Onora arrived after the horses were settled.

"Anyone else interested in us?" he asked her.

"No."

"Good. Let's have a chat with our new friend. There's a narrow side street a few blocks up. When we enter it, find a spot to blend in and get behind the boy," he instructed her.

"Yes, sir."

Valek hefted their saddle bags, but Yelena kept her knapsack slung over her shoulder. The three of them sauntered along the sidewalk, then turned right. As soon as they were out of sight, Valek and Yelena hurried to the other end, while Onora disappeared. Too focused on them, the boy didn't notice her absence. When they reached the end of the street, they retraced their steps.

Caught in the open, the boy froze for a second before whirling around and running into Onora. He tried to dodge past her, but she tripped him, following him down with a blade pressed to his neck. He immediately ceased struggling.

"Why are you following us?" Onora asked.

"I...thought you were...someone else."

"Lame, boy. Try again."

He sagged as if in defeat. "I thought you might need some help."

Yelena stepped closer. "This is a strange place to offer help."

The boy craned his neck to see her. "Circumstances aren't important when lending a helping hand."

She smiled. "He's one of Fisk's. Let him up."

Onora pulled him to his unsteady feet. "Why didn't you say so?"

He wiped off his pants. "Because it was just as likely that you would arrest me."

"Then why follow us?"

A shrug. "A hunch. I thought you might be part of the resistance, but I wasn't sure since I didn't recognize you."

"How about now?" Valek asked. "Do you recognize us?"

"Not really, but I know Master Fisk was working with a number of adults, and when I saw you two...well, there's not many adults who visit the Unity Fountain in the middle of the day without kids."

Valek had heard enough. It would only be a matter of time before they drew unwanted attention. "Let's continue this discussion at the safe house. Actually, it's the apartment above Alethea's bookshop. Onora, take..."

"Phelan."

"... Phelan, and meet us there."

"Yes, sir."

"Um... I'm not sure..." Phelan tucked his hands into his pockets. "I don't even know who you are."

"It's safer for you if you don't," Yelena said. "But we are friends of Fisk's. And we're hoping to free him if possible."

"Yeah?" He glanced around. "Where did you hide your army?"

Sarcasm, or a sardonic assessment? Valek would discover that eventually. Onora led the boy back the way they'd come.

Valek linked his arm in Yelena's as they headed in the opposite direction.

"Is there food at the apartment?" she asked.

"Probably not."

"Then we should stop at the market and purchase some supplies."

"Hungry?"

She laughed. "Always. Or so it seems. I think that must be Leif's problem, too."

"I doubt he's pregnant, love."

"Ha. No. He must be always starving. Lately all I can think about is Ian's beef stew and the raspberry pie Opal's mom bakes and the sweet cakes Sammy cooks and—"

"I get it. You're hungry."

"Famished."

"Let's get to safety first. I'd like to learn from Phelan how dangerous a visit to the market would be."

"Probably not as dangerous as having a hungry pregnant wife."

Valek hoped she was joking.

A layer of dust coated all the furniture in the cramped two-bedroom apartment above Alethea's bookshop. The agents who had been assigned to this safe house had aided in Valek's rescue from the Krystal garrison and then returned to Ixia. Though small, this was one of Valek's favorite locations. The windows overlooked the busy market. Lots of interesting things happened there. He'd neglected to mention the second safe house to Yelena. That one was near the Council Hall. And while it would be an ideal place to watch Bruns and his minions as they scurried to and fro, it would also be perilous to be that close.

While Yelena checked the cupboards for food, Valek built a small fire in the hearth. A cup of tea would soothe his wife for a while. Onora and Phelan arrived soon after he'd poured her a mug of her favorite blend. She chewed on a piece of beef jerky she'd found in her bags. Valek guessed Ari and Janco had taken the bulk of their travel rations with them to Booruby.

Phelan sat on the edge of one of the armchairs. Onora settled in the other while Valek and Yelena occupied the couch.

MARIA V. SNYDER

Since she was the least intimidating of the three, Valek had asked Yelena to take point on the questioning.

"How did Fisk get caught?" Yelena asked.

The boy gripped the armrests. "Do you know about the Problem Gang?"

"No."

"They are a rival group that formed a couple years after Master Fisk founded our Helper's Guild."

"I didn't know they had a name."

"They dubbed themselves the Problem Gang because they cause problems. It's all the kids who would rather bribe, cheat and steal from people than help them. They also sell illegal goods and services." He rubbed a hand on his leg. "They managed to get a spy inside our guild, and he or she learned we did more than just help and ratted us out to the Cartel." He flashed a scornful grin. "For a price, of course."

Yelena's grip on her cup tightened, but her voice remained steady when she asked, "Was anyone hurt or…killed?"

"Right before the soldiers raided our headquarters, Master Fisk told us all to scatter and disappear. A few of the guild were hurt resisting arrest, but no one was killed. Lots of us escaped, but after Master Fisk was in custody for a few days, the soldiers invaded all our hideouts and dragged in our field agents from outside the Citadel."

Valek hoped the Cartel had used goo-goo juice on Fisk to extract the information. He didn't wish to consider the alternative, but Yelena's rigid posture and clamped jaw meant she'd already envisioned poor Fisk being tortured.

"How did you escape?" he asked Phelan to distract her from her morbid thoughts.

"Luck. I was on a food run when the soldiers attacked our hidey-hole. Ever since then, I've been on the move, living on the streets."

"Where are they keeping everyone?" Yelena asked.

"They sent most of the guild members to the garrisons. Bruns Jewelrose's been telling everyone that he's cleaning up the streets, and instead of begging and taking from the good people of the Citadel, these criminals will be rehabilitated so they can give back by protecting Sitia from the Ixians."

Interesting strategy. Who could argue with that? "And the Problem Gang?" he asked.

"Lying low. I think the Cartel is paying them to keep up the ruse."

"And Fisk?" Yelena asked.

"In the cells under the Council Hall. We tried to get to him, but no one goes into the Council Hall without being questioned. Even the kitchen and housekeeping staff are being searched when they enter. None of our usual methods will work to bypass security."

Onora met his gaze. She raised her eyebrows as if to say, *Challenge accepted.*

"Do you know where Master Magician Zitora Cowan is?" Yelena asked.

"Rumors have been flying that she's back. We haven't seen her, but many of us wouldn't recognize her," Phelan answered.

"She has to be with Bruns," Valek said. "She would head straight to the Keep, and when she saw it was closed, her next stop would be the Council Hall." He considered. "Are there still watchers at the Keep?"

"A few. Not as many as there were before the other gates were closed."

Good to know. "How many guild members are still free?"

"No. We're not going to endanger them any further," Yelena said. "They've risked their lives for us already. Phelan, you and your friends are to find a safe spot to hide in until this is all over."

He glanced at Valek, then Yelena, and recognition shone in his gaze. "Lovely Yelena, we are not going to hide. There are only a dozen of us, but we already have shifts of people watching the gate, the market and the Council Hall. How can we help?"

Yelena huffed in frustration. Valek understood her desire to keep them safe, but if they were determined to help, then he wouldn't pass up the opportunity.

Unable to remain seated, he stood. "How's the market? We need provisions."

"Let us shop for you. There are too many soldiers in the market, and they are all looking for new faces."

"All right." Valek paced. It helped him think. "What is the status of the Council Hall?"

"Guards inside and outside all entrances. Shift changes every four hours around the clock."

"Where does Bruns sleep at night?"

"The Council Hall."

Valek clamped down on a curse. So much for targeting the man between locations. He mulled over the information from Phelan and developed a plan for the next couple of days. Giving the boy a few coins, Valek listed the items and food they needed.

After Phelan left, Valek sent Onora to observe the Council Hall. "I'll relieve you later tonight. While there, watch for Zitora."

"Yes, sir." Onora prepared to leave.

"Aren't you going to eat first?" Yelena asked.

"I'll get something on the way."

"But Phelan said—"

"No one will see me. Queen of blending in, remember?" She swept her arms wide in a dramatic fashion.

Yelena laughed—one of Valek's favorite sounds. "Just wait until I tell that to Janco."

"Go ahead. He'll just argue with you that *he's* the queen," Onora shot back.

"Don't you mean king?"

"Janco doesn't worry about the details."

"True. He'll just wave it off and say it's all royalty."

The girls shared a smile.

When Onora left, Yelena asked, "What's my task?"

He hesitated, knowing if he ordered her to eat and rest, she'd probably punch him. "I need you to go to the Keep's library to search for information about those Harman trees and find Ellis Moon's notes. But…"

She leaned forward. "But what?" Her tone held an edge.

"I'd like to check the security at the Keep first." No response. "Please," he added. "You can go in the morning."

Yelena relaxed back on the couch. "On one condition."

His heart paused in mid-beat. "And that is?"

"That you tuck me into bed properly before you leave to-night." Heat burned in her gaze.

Desire shot through him. "As my lady wishes." He bowed. "Perhaps you'd like to retire early? Like right now?"

"Nice try, but food first."

Undaunted, he settled next to her on the couch. "Phelan will be a while." Valek cupped her cheek, turning her face toward him. He ran his thumb over her lips. "Let me distract you from your hunger."

"When you put it *that way*, how can I resist?" she teased.

He pulled her close and kissed her with the full depth of his love. It was a long time before he broke away. "Still hungry?"

A pink flush spread over her skin as she gasped for air. "Oh,

MARIA V. SNYDER

yes. But not for food." Yelena laced her fingers behind his head and claimed his lips.

They never made it to the bedroom.

Yelena was curled up asleep on the couch when Phelan returned with the supplies late that afternoon. However, the spicy scent of the still-warm meat pies woke her.

She wolfed down two while Valek questioned the boy. "Do you know where General Cahil's headquarters is located?"

"No. Why?"

"I want you to assign a few people to keep an eye on it and let me know when the general is there."

"All right."

Valek told him the address of Cahil's safe house. After Phelan left, Valek ate and then tucked Yelena into bed. The lack of sleep caught up to him, and he curled around his wife and slept for a few hours.

It was full dark by the time he reached the Council Hall. Onora signaled him with a faint whistle. Blending in a hidden corner, she was impossible to see. The lamplighters had finished their duties, and the air smelled of lantern oil. Heat pulsed from the buildings as the air cooled.

"What do you think of their security?" he asked, staring at the Hall's front entrance. The large square structure had multiple tiers and resembled a wedding cake. Constructed from the same green-streaked white marble as the city walls, it also sported jade columns at the grand entrance on the first floor. No windows or doors had been installed on the ground floor, and steps led up to the well-guarded double doors.

"It's tight."

"Can you get in?"

"Yes, but I couldn't get anyone out."

"Have you seen anyone significant?"

"There's a fair amount of traffic, but I haven't recognized anyone."

"All right. Go get some sleep. Tomorrow night we'll take a peek inside."

She grinned. "I'll let you tell Yelena."

"Chicken."

Onora gave him a wave before ducking out of sight. Valek remained in place for another hour, but it appeared as if the Hall was closed for the night. Ghosting north to the Magician's Keep, he checked for watchers and found a couple stationed near the main entrance, which was the only way in if you weren't aware of the underground passage. A wall also surrounded the Keep, and four towers, one at each corner, rose high into the air.

Satisfied that no one else lurked nearby, he traveled to the west side of the Keep. He slipped down a narrow alley and counted doors. The third one on the left was unremarkable. Valek pulled his lock picks from their hidden pocket and opened the door. Bracing for an attack, he entered the darkness.

Nothing. All remained quiet. He drew in a breath. The dry scent of dust tickled his nose. Closing the door, Valek then groped for the torches and flint that had been set on a nearby table. With a quick strike, a spark flew, igniting the torch. The light burned his vision for a moment. When his eyes adjusted, he descended the stairs and used the tunnel to cross under the Keep's wall. The passage ended in the basement of Second Magician Irys Jewelrose's tower.

Once Valek ensured the tower remained empty, he left the torch in a holder near the tunnel and did a sweep of the campus. It had been abandoned only about three months ago, but a cold, lifeless feeling permeated the air. After the Cartel had managed to position their cook in the Keep's dining room, they laced most of the food with Theobroma. When all the students, staff and magicians had ingested enough of the drug, Bruns's loyal magicians brainwashed everyone into believing that Ixia was going to invade Sitia. Determined to stop the Commander, the Keep's personnel traveled to the garrisons and joined the Cartel. Valek had to admit it was a brilliant plan.

Valek stopped in the library. It appeared as deserted as the rest of campus, but he searched for an ambush just in case. Happy to see it remained as desolate as the rest, Valek hurried to the exit tunnel.

Back at the quiet Council Hall, Valek considered his options. Built to withstand invaders, the building had few places to enter. The tall, narrow glass windows of the great hall stretched three stories high but didn't open. Valek wondered if a magical alarm had been attached to the slick marble walls. Only one way to find out.

Looping around to the back, Valek stood close to the hall and lowered his mental barrier. No magic buzzed, other than from the power blanket around him. He pressed his palm to the cool stone.

Nothing. Or so he thought. A…consciousness sought him, as if drawn by his magic. Valek quickly raised his shield, but distant shouts cut through the quiet night, and the unmistakable sound of drumming boots echoed. He cursed.

18

HELI

When they arrived at the gate, Heli halted Thunder. "Are you sure your grandparents won't mind?" she asked Teegan, who stopped beside her. "There are four of us."

"For the twenty-third time, no. My grandparents will be thrilled." Teegan dismounted to unlock the gate.

"Until you tell them we're being hunted by the Cartel," Zohav muttered darkly.

Everyone ignored her. Zohav had an annoying tendency to exaggerate the direness of every situation, and Heli was too hot and tired to correct her. Yes, the Cartel sought them, but the Cartel had no idea where they were—unless they'd intercepted the message to Fisk, informing him of their new location. Which she doubted, since Fisk's people were ignored by most adults. No, the missive would have reached Fisk by now.

It had taken them *forever* to reach Teegan's grandparents' home in Booruby. They had traveled a circuitous route to ensure no one followed them, which added more time to the trip, so they reached the city on the fourth day of the heating season. And it was confirmed that Thunder was the slowest horse in Sitia. The cream-colored horse in the Stormdancer's stable turned out to be Teegan's mount—a sweet mare named

Caramel. Plus Smoke showed no signs of fatigue, even with the twins riding together. Meanwhile, Heli could have walked behind and pushed her horse faster.

The hinges squealed as Teegan swung the gate wide. He led them up to the large stone farmhouse. Instead of a farm, there was a glass factory, a few sheds and a small stable that looked new. Puffs of light gray smoke blew from a chimney atop the factory. The Avibian Plains surrounded the small complex on three sides, leaving only one direction open for an attack. Heli approved.

A short woman with graying hair opened the door to the house. She put her hand up to block the sun from her eyes.

"Hi, Grandmom!" Teegan gave her a quick hug. She peered at them over his shoulder. If she was surprised by their arrival, she hid it well.

"What are you doing here?" she asked him. "Aren't you supposed to be in school?"

"Oh, yeah, she sounds *thrilled*," Zohav said in a low voice.

"Hush," Zethan scolded her.

"The Magician's Keep is closed. Haven't you heard?" Teegan asked.

"No. Why didn't you go home, if that's the case?"

"Uh, Grandmom, can we discuss this inside?"

Her demeanor changed in an instant. "Of course! Where are my manners? Your friends must be thirsty." She gestured to the stables. "Please feel free to use our facilities. There's grain and hay, but I'm not sure how fresh it is. It's been a while since we had equine visitors."

Teegan trotted over to Caramel, but Heli waved him off. "Go explain things to your grandmother. We'll take care of the horses."

Not wishing to intrude, the three of them took their time grooming and settling the horses. When they finished, Heli grabbed her saddle bags and headed to the house with the twins. The door opened before they arrived. Teegan stepped to the side to allow them into a large, comfortable kitchen. A fire burned in the vast hearth. Pots of delicious-smelling edibles bubbled on the coals. Heli's stomach growled but, unsure of their welcome, they remained by the door, standing awkwardly. The older woman finished stirring one of the pots and wiped her hands on her apron.

"Grandmom, this is Heli, Zethan and his sister, Zohav," Teegan said.

"You're welcome to stay here with us until you're needed." She gripped the stained fabric of her skirt in a tight fist.

"Thank you, Mrs. Cowan," Heli said.

"Please, call me Vyncenza. Teegan will show you to your rooms. Supper will be ready soon."

Teegan led them through a living area and up a set of stairs. The air smelled of anise and cinnamon.

"What did you tell her?" Zethan asked.

"She'd already heard rumors about the Cartel but didn't know what was really going on."

"No, I mean about *us*?"

"Oh, that." Teegan shrugged. "I told her we were helping Aunt Yelena and Uncle Valek, and they told us to lie low until they needed us."

Which explained why the woman fretted with her skirt. Yes, Teegan was a powerful magician, but he was only fourteen and her grandchild.

"Does she know that we're Valek's...you know," Zethan said.

He flashed a grin. "Didn't have to. She's quick, but she thought you were his children and was worried about Aunt Yelena's reaction."

Zohav choked. "Bad enough being his sister—"

MARIA V. SNYDER

"I wish I had a sister," Heli said to distract her. "Being an only child, I didn't have anyone else to play with, and I had my parents' attention *all* the time. It would have been nice to share that pressure with another sibling."

"I always wanted an older brother," Teegan said in a quiet voice. "Especially when we were living on the streets and I had to take care of my sister."

Heli felt foolish for complaining. Even Zohav remained quiet.

On the second floor, Teegan pointed to a room down the hall. "That's my mom's old room. Heli and Zohav can sleep there. Zethan and I can share my Uncle Ahir's room." He jerked a thumb at the door behind him.

"Will he mind?" Zethan asked.

"Nope. He grew up with *three* older sisters."

Zethan made sympathetic noises. Zohav swatted him on the arm.

Teegan grinned. "Yeah, he says he needs his *man time* when I visit."

Having heard enough, Heli hefted her bags and entered Opal's childhood room. She dumped her stuff on one of the two twin beds. A couple of colorful pictures hung on the walls, but it was the collection of glass animals on the shelves that drew her attention. Some of the statues glowed with an inner fire. Beautiful.

Soon after they unpacked a few things, Vyncenza called them downstairs for supper. Teegan had regaled them with stories about his grandmother's cooking while they traveled. Heli had considered it a form a torture, but now…now, she practically drooled with anticipation. The heady scents of roasted beef and garlic made her almost dizzy with hunger.

An older man with short gray hair and dark brown eyes was already seated at the long table. He introduced himself as

Jaymes, Teegan's grandfather. Heli noted his resemblance to Opal—tall and thin, while her mother shared the same heart-shaped face as her other daughter, Mara.

The small talk ceased when a young man—probably Ahir—blew into the room. Around her age, he was as tall as his father with the same eye color, but a mop of black hair flowed to his shoulders.

Ahir whooped when he spotted Teegan. "How's my favorite nephew?" He high-fived the boy, who beamed at him.

"I'm your *only* nephew."

"For now. Wait until Mara and Leif start popping out the babies." He puckered his lips and used his hand to make popping sounds.

"Ahir, manners," Vyncenza scolded. "We have guests."

"Ah, so we do. Tee's friends from the Keep?" Ahir sat down next to his nephew.

"Close," Teegan said. He explained their adventures over the last couple months.

Judging by the increasingly alarmed expression on Vyncenza's face, Teegan must be giving him more details than he'd given his grandmother earlier. Heli hoped the woman didn't insist they go hide in the plains or hire bodyguards.

When Teegan described the big rescue at the Krystal garrison, all color leaked form Vyncenza's face. Ahir, though, peered at Heli with a contemplative purse.

"Do your parents know what you've been doing?" Vyncenza asked in a strained voice.

Teegan hesitated. "I'm sure Aunt Yelena or Uncle Valek sent them a message."

"You don't know?" Color returned to his grandmother's face in a flush of red.

Oh, no. Heli came to his aid. "Because Teegan's been safe at The Cliffs, we haven't gotten much news."

MARIA V. SNYDER

"And Reema's safe in Ixia," Teegan added.

Even Heli knew that was the wrong thing to say. Vyncenza exploded. Heli understood her reaction—no one appreciated being kept in the dark about the status of their loved ones. Poor Opal would have a lot of explaining to do once this was over.

Ahir interrupted her tirade. "Relax, Mother. It's obvious they can handle themselves." He poked his fork in Heli's direction. "She's the other Stormdancer who helped free Opal and her friends from that Bloodrose cult."

Heli was surprised Opal had told him, and that he remembered her name.

"And," Ahir continued, "Tee might be younger than them, but I'd bet he's more powerful. Right, Tee?"

"Uh…" He glanced at his grandmother, who still seethed, then at his grandfather, who hadn't said a word. "Master Jewelrose did say I should be able to pass the master-level test. But I'm—"

"—helping to stop the Cartel right now, along with the other Master Magicians," Heli said. While that comment wasn't well received, it was better than informing his grandparents he was still learning how to control and use his magic.

It took a while, but his grandmother settled down, and they finished supper. The twins cleared the table without being asked. Heli suspected it must have been their job at home. She wondered if they missed their parents. Heli had grown used to being away from home for months at a time once her Stormdancer powers developed at the age of twelve. However, the other Stormdancers filled in for her family.

Vyncenza refused to let Heli wash the dishes but allowed her to dry them. After she left the kitchen, Heli slowed down, enjoying a moment of solitude. It didn't last long. Ahir arrived to put everything away.

"Was Kade at The Cliffs?" he asked as he shoved a stack of plates into a cupboard.

"Yes. He was working with the twins." Although she doubted that was the reason for Ahir's interest.

"Why didn't he come here with you?"

"It's the beginning of the heating season. Lots of storms are expected, and he's the strongest." Not that there were many dancers left. Heli hoped more Stormdance children would develop the power. When Ahir didn't respond, she added, "Our priority is to our clan. Those storms can kill, and we rely on their energy to fuel our factories."

Ahir scooped up the utensils and sorted them. "Is he... okay?"

Confused, Heli said, "He's fine."

"I mean...about Opal. I...really liked him. I like Devlen, too, but..."

It had been a shock to Heli when Opal chose Devlen over Kade after they had almost died at the Bloodrose compound rescuing her. "He sulked and was grumpy for a few months, which isn't that big of a change in his personality, trust me. He was happier when he was with Opal, but lately he's been better." She lowered her voice and said in a conspiratorial whisper, "I think he's starting to like Helen, our new glassmaker. She's a real sweetheart."

Ahir smiled. "Good."

Heli agreed. They worked in companionable silence for several minutes. She dried the pots and handed them to Ahir, who hung them above the hearth.

"What about you?" he asked. "Do you have a boyfriend back home?"

Her heart thudded. She focused on the towel in her hands. "No."

"That's a surprise. Unless you and Zethan..."

MARIA V. SNYDER

"No." Heli met his gaze. "He's not my type."

"Really? He's a good-looking guy—a young Valek." A pause. "What is your type?"

Heli considered. No one had ever asked her before. Everyone just assumed she'd eventually get married and have Stormdancer babies. Was he just making conversation, or was he interested in the answer? Her pulse sped up. "Zohav would be more my type if she wasn't so sour all the time." She held her breath, waiting for his reaction.

"Oh." Ahir clutched the pot to his chest. He blinked a few times, as if it helped him sort her comment into its proper pile, like the silverware. "She's pretty, but you're right. She's far too serious."

Heli relaxed. She knew of a few other same-sex couples, and most people were accepting, but there were always a handful who found the idea to be objectionable, so she'd never told anyone before. Not like she had any time to date anyway.

"You want me to keep it between us?" Ahir asked.

"I'd rather you didn't gossip about me. But if someone asks, don't lie. It's not a secret."

"All right." Then he laughed. "I advise patience with my mother. She thinks she's a matchmaker and will try to hook you up. If you want her to find you a match, just tell her your type, and she'll try to find you a heart mate."

Heli grinned. "Did she send you in here?"

"No. I volunteered." He held up a pot. "Don't worry. I wanted to ask you about Kade in private. However, my mother thinks otherwise, so when she starts singing my praises to you, just know that they're all true."

"Your modesty is staggering."

He mock-bowed. "That's me. Actually, I'm looking forward to hearing what she says. I haven't done anything remarkable. Not like Opal and Mara."

She wished to reassure him, but she didn't know him well enough to do so. They finished putting away the pots and joined the others in the living area.

Zethan sprawled on the couch with a hand pressed to his stomach. He groaned. "That was the best meal ever. I'm stuffed to the gills and will never eat again."

Vyncenza leaned forward. "There's still a slice of cherry pie left."

Zethan hopped to his feet. "Mine."

After two days of eating, resting and more eating, Heli grew bored. Teegan had given them a tour of the glass factory. Helen's little kiln at the coast looked like a toy compared to the massive machinery and quantity of equipment needed to run eight kilns. Not to mention the number of workers scurrying about. Intrigued by the scale of the operation, Heli followed Ahir and Jaymes into the building on the third morning, hoping she could lend a hand.

The hot air pressed against her like a physical force as the kilns roared in her ears. Without thinking, she used her magic and pulled the moisture from the heat. It condensed into tiny water droplets, which she blew out the door with a light wind. The temperature in the factory dropped twenty degrees.

All the workers paused and stared at her. Oops. "Sorry, I…"

"That was amazing," Jaymes said. "Will it last?"

"Until the heat from the kilns builds up again." Glass melted at twenty-one hundred degrees, so it wouldn't take long.

"Too bad."

"What are you doing during the hot season?" Ahir joked.

Jaymes showed Heli how to gather a slug of molten glass from the kiln, spinning it onto a metal rod called a pontil iron so she could help the glassmakers who sat at their gaffers' benches crafting bowls, vases, goblets and decorative statues.

MARIA V. SNYDER

It was hot, tiring work, but she enjoyed being useful. At the end of the day, Ahir taught her how to shape a ball of glass into a flower by using a pair of large metal tweezers.

He inspected her daisy. "Not bad for a first effort."

"How do you get it off the iron?" she asked. Helen usually had all the glass orbs ready by the time Heli arrived.

"You put in a jack line, like so." He spun the pontil iron on the bench as he pressed another metal tool into the soft glass, carving a groove. Ahir then carried the rod over to a box filled with sponges. Tapping the pontil with the end of the tool, the daisy cracked off right at the line and fell into the box. "Now we have to wait until it cools."

"I can cool it." The air was unstable and easy to push with her magic. A breeze sprang to life.

"No, don't." Ahir made a stopping motion. "If it cools too fast, it will crack. Instead, we'll put it in an annealing oven to cool slowly." He donned a pair of heat-resistant gloves and carried the daisy to a metal cabinet. A few other pieces were already inside. "It'll be ready tomorrow."

"Working with glass takes a lot of patience."

"And skill. These glassmakers—" he gestured at the empty benches "—they make it look easy, but they've spent thousands of hours to get to that point."

It was difficult to imagine working that hard. Her ability to connect with the weather and harvest storms had always been a natural extension of her. Sure, it took some practice to funnel the energy into the glass orbs, but no longer than a couple hours.

A brisk wind blew the next morning, and a sheet of dark clouds threatened rain. Jaymes muttered about the weather at breakfast.

"What's wrong with the wind?" Zethan asked him, digging into his pile of bacon.

"It blows the sand around, making the glass gritty."

"And it cools the kilns, so more coal is needed to keep them at temperature," Ahir added.

"I can move the storm for you," Zethan offered. "It won't be hard."

"That might attract the wrong kind of attention," Zohav said.

Heli hated to agree with her. "I can keep a bubble of calm around your factory, Jaymes."

"No need to exhaust yourself for us. It's a minor inconvenience."

"It doesn't take that much energy. I do it all the time when I'm dancing in a storm."

Ahir stroked his chin. "You know, having a Stormdancer around is handy. When everything is resolved with the Cartel, you should consider going into business."

Surprised, she asked, "Doing what?"

"Weather stuff. Couples could hire you to ensure they have a sunny day for their wedding. Kade gave us beautiful weather for Leif and Mara's day. Or farmers could engage your services to water their fields when it gets too dry." Ahir sat up straighter. "You and Zee could work together when you're not needed on the coast. You'd be rich in no time."

"I never thought of it that way," Heli said.

Vyncenza beamed. "That's my smart boy. Always thinking." She tapped her temple with a finger.

"Yeah, always thinking of ways to avoid work." Jaymes stood. "Come on, Mop Top, the glass doesn't gather itself."

Their days fell into a routine. During the day, Heli helped in the factory while Zethan and Teegan practiced their magic.

MARIA V. SNYDER

Zohav preferred to stay with Vyncenza, learning how to bake pies, crochet and cook, which had surprised everyone, including Zohav. At night, Zethan sprawled on the couch, groaning about eating too much, Zohav read a book next to the lantern, and Heli, Ahir and Teegan played cards or dice.

Heli should have recognized it for what it was—the calm before a storm—but she was having too much fun. When Ahir woke her a few hours before dawn on the ninth morning, she shouldn't have been startled.

"What's wrong?" she asked, sitting up in bed.

"Dad says we have company. And it's not our distant cousins coming for a visit."

Alarmed, she scrambled to her feet. "Are they in the house?"

"No. He spotted them outside the gate. Looks like they're waiting for something…or someone."

Her first impulse was to run and hide in the plains.

Zohav pushed her covers back. "How many are there?"

"Dad says six or seven, maybe more."

"What do they want?" Heli asked.

Ahir shrugged. "I don't know. But Tee might. He's downstairs."

Heli almost smacked her forehead. Of course. They rushed to join Zethan, Teegan and Jaymes in the dark living area.

"Mom's asleep. It's better if we don't wake her unless we absolutely have to," Ahir whispered.

Teegan peered into the night.

"Robbers?" Heli hoped.

"No," Teegan said. "The Cartel. They know we're here."

"All of us, or just me?" Heli asked. Bruns had learned that one of the Stormdancers had helped with Yelena and Valek's escape, but he shouldn't know about the twins or Teegan.

"All of us."

Damn. Something must have happened at the Citadel. "Are we surrounded? Can we slip out the back?"

Zethan turned to her. "There are only seven—"

"Ten," Teegan corrected him.

"—only *ten* of them. Between the four of us, we can easily blow them away."

"Yes, we could, but they'll just come back with reinforcements." Heli mulled it over. "What are they planning?"

"A sneak attack while we're still sleeping." Teegan flashed a grin. "Good thing they didn't know Grandpop checks the kilns at night." Then he sobered. "They have Curare and null shield nets with them. No magicians, though."

"They won't be able to use their weapons because they'll be too busy flying through the air, and so will their reinforcements," Zethan said.

Heli touched his arm. "We still can't stay here. We're putting Teegan's family in danger. We need to leave. Jaymes, you and your family also need to find a safe place to go. The Cartel won't be happy when we escape, and they'll question you or use you to get to Teegan."

"*When* we escape?" Zohav asked. "You're that confident?"

Heli resisted snapping at the girl. Instead, she glanced at Zethan and Teegan. "Escaping won't be the hard part."

"What's the hard part?" Teegan asked.

"Making them *think* they have a chance to catch us."

Except for Zohav, there were answering grins all around. Heli explained her plan, and the four of them slipped through the back door to their positions. There wasn't much light, so they moved with care. The twins hid behind the well while she and Teegan sidled up to the stables. All three horses were awake, with ears pricked forward and nostrils flared.

Since Heli needed to know where the soldiers were, Teegan updated her on their positions.

MARIA V. SNYDER

"There are twelve of them now," he whispered. "They're climbing over the gate. Huh. Someone must have told them it squeaks." A few long seconds passed. "They're moving to surround the house. Two of them know how to pick locks."

Heli gathered her power. "Let me know when they're close." Aiming a powerful and narrow wind gust took a great deal of concentration and energy. She hoped to loop it around the house and strike them all with one mighty gust.

"Almost there…"

The gate squealed open.

Teegan gasped. "Father. Reema."

19

YELENA

The bright mid-morning sunlight woke me from a dreamless sleep. I yawned and reached for Valek, but his side of the bed was empty. Alarmed, I sat up. It was a few hours past dawn; he should have returned by now. Shoving the blankets off, I dressed quickly and hurried to the small living room.

Onora stood by the window, staring down at the busy market. A pot of water steamed on the stone hearth.

"Has Valek reported in?" I asked her.

She turned. "Not yet."

"Shouldn't he be back by now?"

"It depends." Onora didn't appear to be worried. "He might be following a lead." She strode to the hearth and nudged the pot closer to the burning coals with the toe of her boot. She must have been out early, because she only wore her boots when pretending to be a normal citizen.

Her lack of concern only increased mine. "What if he was caught?"

"Not much we can do about it right now. If he's not back by this afternoon, I'll visit the Council Hall and see if I can learn what happened."

I'd planned to go to the Keep today, but I'd promised Valek

to wait until he checked it out. Perhaps he ran into trouble there. Too many possibilities. I strode to the window, hoping to spot him among the shoppers.

"Have some tea." Onora poured a cup. "Sit down. I'll make you something to eat."

"Are you bribing me?"

"Would you rather fret until you're sick?"

"Yes," I said peevishly.

"And will that change anything?" She answered for me. "No. And it isn't good for the baby."

Fine. I flopped down on an armchair like an adolescent and dust puffed up, making me sneeze. My emotions had been erratic lately. I'd accused Valek of overreacting, but I guessed he wasn't the only one. "Sorry," I said when she handed me the tea.

"No problem. Besides, you're doing better than my aunt."

Strange comment. "What do you mean?"

"My aunt sobbed through her entire pregnancy. Or so it seemed. She'd cry when she couldn't find matching socks or when a bird flew into the window pane."

"So I can blame the baby for my mood swings?"

"Yup. And she was absentminded and really goofy at times. She called it baby brain."

That explained quite a bit.

"And swollen ankles. Hers blew up like melons." She spread her hands to demonstrate the size.

Lovely. I wondered what other effects the baby would cause. "You know more than I do about this. Were you close to your aunt?"

"I…" Onora focused on slicing an apple. "She raised us after our mother died."

I realized I didn't know much about Onora's past. I knew that she'd trained as an assassin, and she'd been abused by her commanding officer. Valek's news that Sergeant Gerik was her brother had been a complete surprise. "Do you have other siblings?"

"No. Just the two of us." She paused. "When my aunt and the baby both died in childbirth, my uncle kicked us out, so we joined the military." She shrugged. "You know the rest."

"Sorry to hear that."

"It's all in the past." Her tone remained flat.

She wasn't fooling me. I'd spent a couple years running from my traumatic past, and I recognized the signs. It would catch up to her eventually. I just hoped I'd be there to help her get through it once it did.

Onora set a plate full of ham and apple slices for us to share on the table between the armchairs. The table had been wiped down.

"You dusted. Thanks."

She bit into a piece of ham. "I was bored."

We ate the rest of the meal in silence. I kept glancing at the door, as if my will alone would cause Valek to appear.

"My aunt also had strange cravings for food," Onora said. "One time, she sent me to the market for eggs—dozens of eggs. We ate omelets and scrambled eggs for a week straight." She laughed at the memory.

"How long did you live with her?" All humor fled her face, and I wished I hadn't asked the question.

"About six years. My dad left us a year before my mom died. She sickened with a lung infection, and by the time the medic determined the source, it was too late." Onora stared into the past. "Same with my aunt. We lived too far from help, and my uncle wouldn't let her travel to town when the baby was due. He said the midwife would do fine, even though both the midwife and my aunt thought the baby was breech." Her shoulders stiffened, but then she drew in a quick breath as if she'd realized something. "Not that it will happen to you! Valek will have you surrounded by healers and medics. You don't have to worry."

I hadn't thought that far ahead. Right now my priority was for Valek and me to survive the Cartel's takeover. Once that happened, then I could focus on our future.

I checked the door. Still closed.

When Valek failed to show up by midafternoon, I decided I wasn't waiting any longer. I touched up my disguise.

"Where do you think you're going?" Onora asked.

"While you check the Council Hall, I'm going to visit Cahil's headquarters. Maybe he has some information on Valek."

"No. It's too dangerous."

"I'm not asking permission." No way I'd sit here another minute.

"Cahil might not even be there."

"Then I'll find Phelen, see if he's seen or heard anything."

"What if Valek shows up before one of us returns? You know he'll panic when no one's here."

"Nice try. We can leave him a 'be back soon' note."

Onora muttered under her breath, but then said, "I'm coming with you."

Not like I could stop her. "Fine."

We looped around the Council Hall just in case Valek had stayed there to watch the traffic.

"Do you want me to go inside?" Onora asked. "See if they've caught him?"

I considered. Valek wasn't easy to catch. "Not yet. If there's no sign of him, that'll be plan B."

Our next stop was Cahil's headquarters. A shudder rumbled through me when I stepped inside the abandoned warehouse. The time I'd spent here hadn't been pleasant.

No one guarded the entrance. I followed the dust-free path through the stacks of dirty crates that littered the floor. The place smelled of grease, rusted metal and mold. When we arrived at the top of the stairs that led down to Cahil's underground offices, we spotted a faint yellow glow. At least one person was here, probably more.

Onora pulled her daggers and slid off her boots before signaling me to follow her down the stairs. I grabbed my switchblade but didn't trigger the blade.

The light brightened, and the murmur of a distant conversation floated on the air. By the time we reached the bottom, I recognized Hanni's and Faxon's voices. Onora eased into the room so quietly, they didn't hear her.

"...going to be hard keeping silent when—" Hanni jerked to her feet with her sword in hand when I entered. Faxon followed a second after.

Guess I wasn't as stealthy as Onora. No one moved. They blinked at us for a moment before relaxing.

Hanni sheathed her weapon. "No need to sneak up on us. We're on the same side."

Onora shrugged. "Habit." She scanned the area. The room was filled with desks, and a door in the back led to Cahil's office. "Are you alone?"

"Yes. I guess you heard about Valek."

My pulse jumped. "No. What happened?" My tone was sharp and squeaked in panic.

"Then why—"

"What happened?" Must. Not. Shake. Her.

"Master Magician Zitora Cowan detected him near the Council Hall, and they've been hunting him all morning."

I sank into a nearby chair. They didn't have him. Yet. "Hunting?"

"Yes. General Cahil was summoned to the Hall an hour

MARIA V. SNYDER

ago to help with the efforts. Master Zitora can track Valek within a few blocks, so they are setting up an ambush and plan to steer him into it."

"Where?" Onora asked.

"The messenger said they spotted him on the roof of the third ring."

Onora glanced at me. "Third ring?"

"It's one of the business and factory rings that are located around the market," I said. "Hanni, do you know his position on that ring?" Otherwise, it'd be miles of ground to cover.

"Northeast."

Still a rather large area, but it was better than nothing. I thanked her. We dashed up the stairs. Onora snagged her boots as we crossed the warehouse.

"The intel's an hour old," Onora said, pausing at the door to put on her boots. No need for stealth. Not yet.

"I know, but it's a place to start."

When we exited the building, I took a few seconds to get my bearings. Cahil's headquarters was in the southeast section of the fifth ring. Heading north at a quick pace—not fast enough for me, but if we were seen running, it would draw unwanted attention—we scanned the streets, alleys and rooftops as we cut through to the third ring. Once we reached the northeast section, we slowed, seeking any signs of an ambush. Trying to appear as if I wasn't frantically searching for my husband, I resisted the urge to yell his name.

At one point, Onora leaned close to me and said, "Have you ever heard the term 'looking for a snowflake in a blizzard'?"

"No, but there are millions of snowflakes in a blizzard."

"Exactly."

"That makes no sense. It'd be easy to find a—"

Onora touched my shoulder. She drew me into a side street.

"There are a number of soldiers ahead. Stay here while I go check it out."

My protest died in my throat. Valek was more important than my ego. I nodded. She left her boots with me and then disappeared. It took all my self-control not to poke my head around the corner to see where she was going.

Instead, I inventoried my weapons just in case I needed them. Then I compared my boots to Onora's—hers were two sizes bigger. I paced while trying to ignore the various horrible scenarios that threatened to play out in my mind. Counting the buildings on both sides of the narrow street—there were eight—I tried to guess what type of industry went on inside them. One had to be a garment factory, judging by a delivery wagon outside full of bolts of colorful cloth. Although they could also be manufacturing bedding.

Without warning, Onora appeared at my elbow. I jumped a foot into the air. "Well?" I demanded.

"They know he's nearby, but not exactly where. Soldiers are blocking the streets and alleys, and a group of eight is search-ing buildings. I think Zitora is with that group."

Not good. I mulled it over. "Where?"

"A few blocks north of here."

"Can you show me?"

She scrunched up her face. "Why?"

"I'm not sure."

"Okay." She said the word as if placating a crazy person. "Stay right behind me."

The deserted streets felt strange in the middle of the day. Onora stayed in the shadows and slowed once we'd crossed two streets. She stopped next to a wagon that had been aban-doned. The soldiers must have chased the driver off while they searched for Valek.

"They're another block north," Onora said.

I scanned the area. It was familiar, but I couldn't remember why. If I was Valek, where would I hide? Onora might know. She'd had the same training. But this was the Citadel. Fisk would know best. Fisk!

"Come on!" I said. Turning around, I hurried a block south, then found the alley that led to Fisk's first headquarters. I hadn't been there in years, but I remembered the deceptive entrance. Unlike the other doors in that alley, this one only appeared if you stood in a certain location. I hoped Valek also recalled this little quirk. It took me a few minutes to find it. Being with a jittery assassin who thought we were too exposed didn't help.

Finally I popped the lock, and we entered the semidarkness. Dust motes floated in a beam of sunlight from the single window. A thick coat of dust painted the broken furniture. Cobwebs filled the corners. Empty, but another chamber was further inside. It had beds for the Helper's Guild members. Keeping my disappointment at bay, I moved deeper into the shadows.

"Yelena," Valek said behind me. It was Onora's turn to jump.

I turned and stifled a gasp. Dark smudges lined his eyes. Already sharp-featured, Valek now appeared almost skeletal. I opened my arms for a hug, but he grabbed my hands, lacing his fingers in mine instead.

"Ahh." Valek sank to the floor. "I hoped you'd find me here."

Alarmed, I knelt next to him. "What's wrong? What happened?"

"When I was checking the Council Hall with my magic, she picked up on me and latched on with her incredibly strong powers. My barrier is barely keeping her from discovering my location. Otherwise, she would have found me by now."

"Why is she chasing you?"

"Because she doesn't believe me about Bruns. I tried to explain, but Bruns has already convinced her that the Commander is planning to invade Sitia. She thinks I assassinated the Councilors, Irys and Bain, and that I'm coming for Bruns next."

I sat back on my heels. "Does she know about your magic?" That would be bad.

"No, she thinks it was only because I was so close that she was able to reach me. And that my immunity allows me to lie to her." He gave me an exhausted grin. "She and a contingent of soldiers are hunting me."

"They also set up an ambush for you," Onora said.

"I figured they would try to flush me into a trap."

"Why didn't you return to the apartment right away?" I asked. "I could have talked to her."

"I couldn't risk Bruns discovering our location."

"What about now?" Onora asked. "Can Zitora find us while you're holding Yelena's hand?"

Valek's strained face was grim. "Yes. It's just a matter of time."

"I thought the baby blocked magic," Onora said.

"The baby drains it," I said. "Are you using your magic?" I asked Valek.

"No. I stopped using mine to block her as soon as I held your hands, but the baby is siphoning her power through me. Being the second most powerful magician in Sitia, *she* can follow that drain of magic."

Which explained his exhaustion.

"Is she close?" Onora asked him.

"Yes. They're a block away and heading for the mouth of the alley."

"How many are with her?" She pulled her daggers.

"Eight. Best to ambush them. Do you have any darts with sleeping potion?"

"Yes."

"Good. Find a hiding spot in the alley. When they come, hit as many as you can."

"What if they're resistant, like the ones who were guarding my father?" I asked.

Valek cursed.

"Wait," Onora said. "We have that new draft Leif cooked up for us."

So much had happened, I'd forgotten about that. Or was it baby brain?

"Thank fate," Valek said. "Give some of them to Yelena and then get into position."

"Yes, sir." Keeping ten, Onora handed me six darts. Then she disappeared through the door.

"Yelena, do you have your blowpipe with you?" he asked.

"Always." I loved that weapon. Stolen from Bruns's armory, it had a rifling pattern on the inside to improve even my terrible aim.

"Stay here and hit anyone who comes through that door."

"And you?"

He pushed to his feet, pulling me up with him. "I'm the bait." He let go of my hands.

I clamped down on my protest. "What is she planning to do once she catches you?"

"Take me to Bruns for interrogation. I considered letting her so I could see where they're holding Fisk, but..." He rubbed his ribs, probably remembering the last time he was Bruns's prisoner and had almost been beaten to death.

"Better to get Zitora on our side first. You need to convince her, love." He sat down on the floor next to the door. If anyone entered, the open door would hide him from view.

I moved to the deepest shadow that had a clear shot to the entrance. Careful not to prick myself with the sharp tips, I laced the darts in my tunic for easy access. Then I loaded a dart into the pipe and waited. My stomach did flips—or was that the baby, energized by all the magic? Easier to blame him or her than my nerves.

After a moment, Valek said, "They're in the alley." He closed his eyes. "Onora has engaged."

A few shouts and sounds of a scuffle reached us.

"Right outside." Valek's voice strained with the effort to speak.

I raised my blowpipe and aimed. The door flew wide. Spotting the guard's neck, I puffed, then loaded another dart. People tumbled into the room. I shot at anyone I didn't recognize until I ran out of darts. However, many of the guards remained on their feet, and while I managed to hold my own with my switchblade for a minute or so, the small confines of the room limited my maneuverability. Two guards disarmed me and grabbed my arms, pinning me between them.

"Yelena! Figures I'd find you here." Zitora's tone turned deadly. "Traitor, where's that killer Valek?"

Flabbergasted by her anger and hatred, I stared at her. Words refused to move past my lips.

"Behind you." Valek pressed a knife against her throat. She didn't make a sound or move, but he tightened his grip on her and said, "Don't."

Zitora glowered at me. Finally the sleeping draft kicked in, and the men holding me swayed and collapsed. Wow. Leif hadn't been kidding when he'd said it would take longer. Onora entered and, in a few quick moves, disarmed the other two before they also succumbed to the drug.

"Is that all of them?" Valek asked Onora.

"For now. When they don't return, the others will come investigate."

"Yelena." Valek met my gaze. Lines of strain showed on his face.

Oh, right. I approached and grabbed Zitora's hand.

She cried, "You? You're the one draining my power?"

"Not me. The baby."

She glanced at my abdomen, and for the first time, I wished I had a baby bump.

"It's hard to explain, but if you stop aiming your magic at me, it won't…er…collect it. At this point, we don't really know what it's doing with the magic."

"You're not making any sense," she said.

I figured she might be distracted by the deadly weapon at her throat. "Valek, put the knife away. Why don't you and Onora go guard the door?"

"Are you sure?" he asked.

No. "Yes."

He stepped away from Zitora, and I released her hand. When she didn't move, he titled his head at Onora, and they left the building.

She crossed her arms. "My magic might not affect you, but I still can escape at any time. All I have to do is set this place on fire."

"You can, but you won't. There are innocent people living on the upper floors." Before she could respond, I held up both my hands. "Give me five minutes of your time. Please."

"And what if I don't agree with what you have to say, Traitor?"

Oh, boy. "Then you can go."

"Just like that?"

"Yes. I'm not the enemy."

She glanced at the prone forms scattered on the floor.

"Those men are asleep. Not dead."

"Fine."

Where to start? "The Councilors, Bain and Irys are not dead either. And you don't have to take my word for it. Try contacting Irys or Bain."

"How? There are no more super messengers. Your Commander had them all destroyed."

One thing about Bruns—the man was smart and a smooth liar, which Zitora should have picked up on. Unless... "Bruns wears a null shield pendant, doesn't he?"

"Of course, or you'd attack him with your Soulfinding magic."

"I can't access my power right now. The baby is blocking it." I hoped.

"That's ridiculous."

"Read my thoughts. See that I'm not lying."

She scrunched up her face as if smelling a rotten egg. "I can't."

Shoot. Valek had been able to read my thoughts a month ago. The baby's ability must be getting stronger as he or she grows. "That's the baby."

Zitora failed to appear convinced.

I tried another tactic. The truth. "Bruns has lied to you. His Cartel is planning a takeover of Sitia and is working with the Commander, who is under Owen Moon's control."

"He said you might try to twist things around. Besides, Opal never said a word about this Cartel to me."

"That's because when Opal left to help you, we didn't know the extent of their reach. They've been feeding everyone Theobroma and using magic to brainwash everyone. At least tell me you noticed the taste in the food at the Hall."

"I did, but Bruns said the new chef likes to use it as seasoning, and it's harmless in small quantities."

MARIA V. SNYDER

Bruns had an answer for everything. I needed to try yet another angle. "You don't even know Bruns. But you know me and what I've done to keep Sitia safe. Do you really think I would do anything to harm it?"

"You're married to Valek and are having his child. You could have been sent here as a spy."

She had a point. Although it'd been years since anyone had accused me of being an Ixian spy. Which reminded me of Cahil. "Do you trust General Cahil?"

"Yes."

"Talk to Cahil before you report this to Bruns. Ask him about Bruns. He'll say the man's a genius and is going to save Sitia, but use your magic and you'll sense he's lying."

"Why would he lie?"

Time to take a gigantic risk. My heart fluttered. "Because he's working with us. And you know how much Cahil hates me. So if he's helping us, that's because he understands Bruns is dangerous and must be stopped."

Her expression softened just a bit. "If you're telling the truth…am I in danger?"

"Not if Bruns thinks you still believe him. He's waiting for the Theobroma to build up in your system so he can brainwash you, too. He hasn't learned that it doesn't work on the Master Magicians. Both Irys and Bain have been playing along until we're ready to fight back." I took a deep breath to steady my voice—I'd just dug us in deeper. "If you tell Bruns what I just said, he will kill them, and you, as well as Cahil. And then it's only a matter of time before the rest of us are all dead." I rested my hand on my stomach. "When you believe me, tell Cahil. He'll get a message to us and we can arrange for you to escape."

"And if I don't believe you?"

"*That* message won't be hard to miss." I called for Valek and Onora.

They returned and we hurried into the back room. A grimy window let in enough light for us to find the exit. Fisk always ensured there was a back door in his headquarters, just in case. Once we stepped outside, I grasped their hands so it would be harder for Zitora to track us to our apartment.

"Did you convince her?" he asked.

"I don't know."

He slowed. "We need to leave the Citadel right away."

"Bruns already knows we're here. And I may have doomed us all anyway, so there will be no point in trying to leave. It will only delay the inevitable."

It was a sign of his exhaustion that he just squeezed my hand.

After a few blocks, Onora said, "I'm gonna swing by the Council Hall. If I'm not back by midafternoon tomorrow, worry. Otherwise, don't." She aimed that comment at me as she released my hand.

"Sorry, but I'm *gonna* worry anyway. Get used to it."

"Yes, sir."

"That's nice, but it would be better without the sarcasm."

She flashed a rare smile and ducked down a narrow side street. Valek and I took a winding path back to the apartment. He towed me to the bedroom.

"Is the Keep safe?" I asked, thinking I might have a couple hours to check the library.

"Yes, but I need you, love. Zitora could find me again, and I don't have any energy to block her."

He released my hand long enough to strip off his shirt and pants. The heart-shaped wound on the center of his chest had healed, but the scar hadn't faded. I traced it with a fingertip.

MARIA V. SNYDER

The mark on my chest matched his—symbols of our marriage vows.

He caught my hand and kissed my knuckles. Then he swayed with fatigue, so I pushed him down on the bed. "Sleep." I shucked off my boots and tunic before joining him. Although he pressed against my bare back, he reclaimed my hand just before falling asleep.

Onora woke us...later. Outlined by the lantern's yellow glow, Onora stood at the threshold. Valek was already sitting up and clutching a knife—where did that come from? Darkness streaked with lamplight flickered against the windows. My stomach roared with hunger. We must have slept for hours.

"I've news," Onora said a bit awkwardly.

"We'll be out," Valek said.

She nodded and closed the door. We disentangled, reaching for clothes. Once we were dressed, Valek claimed my hand as we joined Onora in the living area.

She sat in one of the armchairs with her bare feet propped up on the table. I wondered what she'd been climbing—the walls of the Council Hall were too slick. Valek and I sat on the couch opposite her.

"Report," he said.

"It was pretty quiet at the Hall," she said. "If Zitora had informed Bruns about us, there would have been lots more commotion."

So far so good. "Fisk?" I asked.

"Down in the cells, with layers of security around him." She flexed her fingers as if stretching the joints. "I didn't know you'd taught him the hand signals."

Valek tensed next to me. "You talked to him?"

"Yup. I scared the crap out of him. Poor kid."

"Is he...healthy?" I asked, bracing myself for the answer.

"Yes. He was mostly pissed off and upset about being caught, but when I explained you were safe for now, that calmed him down. He says he's sorry that Bruns knows everything."

Poor kid, indeed. The desire to hug and comfort him pulsed through my chest.

"Have they been feeding him Theobroma?" Valek asked.

"No, but they used magic to extract all the information from his mind."

Oh, no. That was a horrible experience. Now tears threatened, and Valek rubbed his thumb on my hand.

"Can you free him?" Valek asked.

Onora pursed her lips in thought. "If there was a major distraction in the Hall, I could rescue him from the cells. Not sure if we'd escape the Hall, though."

I tightened my grip on Valek's hand.

He squeezed back. "What about Bruns? Did you see him or Cahil?"

"I did a sweep and found where he set up his office. He's staying in one of the guest suites on the third floor. Cahil wasn't around."

"Are there layers of security around him, as well?"

"Yes. Not as many, but I think a few are magicians. I recognized Cilly Cloud Mist." She frowned, probably remembering when Cilly tried to erase her memory.

No surprise Bruns was keeping Cilly close.

"Can you reach Bruns?" Valek asked.

Onora sat up, setting her feet on the floor with a thump. "You mean…?"

"Yes. Assassinate the bastard."

Her already pale face whitened as she pressed her arms on her lap. "I…" Onora stared out the window.

When she didn't say anything, Valek asked, "Could I reach him?"

MARIA V. SNYDER

"No. You'd never get inside the Hall without blending in. But if he leaves…"

"I'd rather we target him while he's asleep. That would give us more time to get away. And I doubt he'll venture outside knowing I'm in the Citadel. Ideally, we'd kill him at the same time we make our move in the hot season, but this might be our only chance to reach him. You'll have to do the honors."

She dragged her gaze to him. "I…"

"Never killed anyone?" he asked, but it sounded more like a statement than a question.

"Yes."

20

VALEK

Onora confirmed what he'd suspected for a while now. She'd never assassinated anyone. Talk about bad timing for this revelation.

"How can you call yourself an assassin, then?" Yelena asked in surprise.

"I have all the training and skills. I just haven't…couldn't… can't…"

Yelena reached over and grabbed the girl's hand. "That's not a weakness. That's a strength."

Onora gave her a grateful smile.

"What about with the Commander?" Valek asked. "Do you hide your full fighting abilities like you have with me?"

"No. But like you, he stopped me by doing something unexpectedly desperate. And I was glad, because I already knew I couldn't finish him."

That explained why the Commander had been so freaked. She'd gotten closer than Valek, and it had terrified him. "What about now?"

She quirked her lips in an ironic half smile. "We've sparred a few times, and I've identified his weakness."

So had Valek, or so he'd thought. Ambrose liked to dangle

the bait and see if you'd bite. But if he'd been forced to do something desperate, then maybe she truly could beat him. Not like any of this helped them now. He considered their meager options.

Rescue Fisk, or assassinate Bruns. There was no way they could do both. Either would bring instant attention to them. Plus there was Zitora to consider. She could expose everything. A bone-deep ache of exhaustion throbbed through him. He hadn't had nearly enough sleep.

"Now what?" Yelena asked.

"Tomorrow we'll go to the Keep's library and touch base with Cahil. After that…" He shrugged.

"We rescue Fisk," Yelena said in a tone that dared anyone to argue with her.

He glanced at her. "You have a plan?"

"Onora said she needed a distraction. So we're going to provide one for her."

"Go big or go home?"

"No."

"No?" he asked.

"Go big *and* go home."

They woke late the next morning. Onora returned from her mission while they ate breakfast.

"How did it go?" Yelena asked.

"After I did a reconnaissance of the Hall, I met with the Helper's Guild and explained our plans to them." She huffed in amusement. "Bets are already being made. We're not favored to win, but I put a silver coin on us."

"Only silver?" Yelena raised an eyebrow.

"No need to break the bank."

Yelena laughed. "As Janco would say, 'Gotta love the confidence.'"

Onora smiled, but it failed to reach her eyes. Valek wondered if she worried about Janco's reaction to her not being quite the Little Miss Assassin he'd always believed her to be. It hadn't changed Valek's opinion of her. She hadn't lied. Everyone had just assumed and never asked her directly. Killing a person was not easy in any situation. Some people couldn't do it even to save their own lives. Valek, on the other hand, recognized the need to eliminate certain people to ensure the safety of others, but he'd never done it lightly or for no reason. Which was why he had no regrets.

Focusing on the problem at hand, Valek asked Onora if she'd talked to Phelan.

"Yes. The General visited his headquarters late last night. He might be there again tonight."

"Good. Any signs of trouble?"

"None so far, but Bruns might be biding his time, hoping to draw us out."

In that case, Bruns would succeed.

When they finished eating, Valek escorted Yelena to the Keep, despite her protests that he was being overprotective.

He was, but this time he had a legitimate reason to tag along. "While you're checking the library, I'll search Bain's office. He might have had the same idea as us, and since he's the First Magician, the library might have allowed him to borrow Master Magician Ellis Moon's notes."

"That's a good idea."

"Don't sound so surprised, love. I might start to think you're only interested in me for my body."

"Did you say something? I was too busy staring at your muscular chest."

"Nice."

They crossed the tunnel into the Keep without trouble. Yelena clutched her hands together while she scanned the

MARIA V. SNYDER

empty campus. Valek squeezed her shoulder in support before she headed to the library. Without her touch, he needed to reinforce his mental barrier. Zitora might not be searching for him, but he wasn't going to risk opening his mind at this point.

He looped around to the back entrance of the administration building that housed the Master Magician's offices, along with the Keep's clerical staff. Valek ghosted down the hallway to Bain's office. Halfway there, a muffled cry sounded. Drawing his knives, he paused to listen. A bang and a thud echoed. Valek tracked the noise to Irys's office. The door stood ajar. He peered inside and cursed his rotten luck.

Zitora faced the back wall, but before he could retreat, she said, "I know you're there. I shouldn't, because of your immunity." She turned. "But you're no longer immune. Are you?"

"No." Valek eased into the room.

She held up a hand. "Stop right there."

He did as instructed and slid his daggers back into their pockets. They wouldn't help him in this situation. Nothing would. Her power could rip through his barrier like tissue paper. The only reason she hadn't done it before was because he'd surprised her. Now she'd had time to think about it.

"You have magic. How did it happen?" she asked.

No sense lying. His and Yelena's future rested in what happened next. "I made peace with my brothers' murders. Seems that released the null shield I'd unknowingly grafted onto my soul when I'd witnessed their murders. Once the shield was gone, my magical powers were freed." That was Yelena's theory, and the timing confirmed it.

"Did you come here to kill me?" she asked.

"Do you think I can?"

"No. You're strong, but not as strong as me."

"Then why are you worried?"

"I wouldn't call it worry. More like curiosity. Indulge me."

"You have nothing to fear. You fall under the category of a Sitian who has been duped or brainwashed, and therefore are not to be killed or harmed if possible. Yelena's orders."

"Then what are you doing here?"

"Investigating. I hope Bain has some information to help us counter the Cartel." He was growing tired of her suspicion. "Have you talked to Cahil yet?"

"No. We haven't been able to talk privately. In fact, unless I'm in my room, I'm never alone. That magician, Cilly, is always hovering nearby. Bruns says it's for my protection from you." She frowned. "She's tested my defenses a number of times, trying to get a sense of my loyalties. Don't worry, she doesn't have the power to get through. And I haven't told Bruns what Yelena said or that she's here."

One good thing. "You're alone now."

"Master Magician, remember? I'm done with being *protected*."

He approved. "This is a good place to hide."

"I'm not hiding." Zitora hooked her thumb toward the wall behind her. She stood in front of a large safe. The painting that had covered it rested on the floor. "Can you open it?"

Janco was the expert, but Valek had some experience. "Maybe. It depends on the model."

"Will you open it for me?"

Ah, there was the right question. "If I can."

She stepped aside. Moving slowly so he didn't startle her, he crossed the room. He inspected the safe. Made of thick steel and with a complex lock, it would be difficult to crack. He spun the cylinder, feeling for that subtle vibration. It took him multiple tries, but finally the door opened.

He backed away. "What are you looking for?"

She dug into the contents, pulling various things out and

setting them onto Irys's desk. "Ahh." Zitora removed a glass super messenger. "I thought she'd have one in case of an emergency."

Smart. "Now you can contact Bain and confirm our story."

"That's the idea." Yet she hesitated.

She still didn't trust him.

"I'm going to Bain's now. If you have time, ask him if he has any of Master Magician's Ellis Moon's papers." He left.

Bain's office was only a few doors down from Irys's. Unlike Irys's neat organization, a mess sprawled on every surface. Valek would have thought someone had searched the place if he hadn't known Bain so well. The most powerful magician in the world loved researching little-known historical details when he had time. But as a member of the Sitian Council, he rarely had time.

Valek started with his desk and scanned the various piles of parchment. He found a list of missing magicians, and Valek wondered how many of them remained alive. Then he remembered Fisk had helped hide a few, which meant Bruns likely knew their locations. The desk drawers were crammed with…well, everything. Valek slid them shut without digging deeper. If Bain had gotten the notes, they would be on top somewhere. He strode over to the table. Flipping through the files, he searched for anything that appeared old.

"They're in Bain's tower," Zitora said.

Valek spun around.

She cradled the messenger like a baby. Her eyes shone with unshed tears. "They're both alive!"

A relief. While the intel on the status of both the masters was fairly recent, there had been no guarantee that they remained alive.

"You were right," she said. "I'm so sor—"

"Don't apologize. Otherwise I'd have to apologize for not

getting to the Citadel in time to stop you from entering in the first place, and a whole list of other transgressions."

She laughed. It was a light, sweet sound.

Bain's tower was located in the northeast corner of the Keep. As they trudged up four flights of stairs to the living quarters, he asked Zitora what she'd told Bruns about the chase.

"I told him I'd lost you. That it was pure luck that I'd sensed you in the first place. He has watchers stationed all around the Citadel now, but they aren't aware that you're wearing a disguise."

Good to know, especially considering their plans for tomorrow night. They retrieved the thick file of Ellis's notes from Bain's night table. Then they crossed the campus to the Keep's library.

Yelena sat at a table in the middle of the reading room. Sunlight streamed in from the skylight above, illuminating the open book before her. Two piles of tomes were stacked on both sides of her.

She glanced up when they entered and shot to her feet. "What—"

"Relax," he said. "She contacted Bain."

She blew out a breath. "How?"

He filled her in, then pointed to her book. "What are you reading?"

"When I didn't find Ellis's journals, I pulled books that mentioned plants, hoping to find a reference to the Harman trees." She swept her hand over the piles to her left. "Nothing so far."

"Keep looking while I read through the journals." He placed the file on the table. They were safer here than in the apartment. Valek turned to Zitora. "You can stay in the Keep until the big rescue. We're going—"

"I'm not leaving."

"Why not?" Yelena asked.

"I'm going to stay with Bruns and play along, like Bain and Irys. I'll be in the perfect position to help you when you stop the Cartel."

Such confidence.

"How will we contact you?" Valek asked.

"Here." She gave him the super messenger.

Magic pulsed inside, and the vibrations traveled up his arm.

"You can contact us all," she said.

"I don't—"

"It's not hard to use. I can teach you." She took back the glass cube. "Let down your mental barrier and reach out to me with your magic."

He did as instructed. At first, he hit a solid brick wall. *Zitora?* he thought.

An opening appeared. *Welcome to my mind,* she thought. *Sorry about the mess. I've had an interesting couple of days.*

Same here.

She smiled. *All right, now you know how to knock on another magician's shield. Now I want you to reach out to Irys and tell me when you've hit your limit.*

He sent his awareness to the northeast, toward Irys in the Featherstone garrison. A few people traveled on the road outside the Citadel. Then he picked up on the thoughts of those living in Owl's Hill before he was unable to go farther—although he was shocked he had managed to even reach that far. *I'm at the end.*

Zitora placed the messenger in his hands. *Use the magic inside to propel you further.*

It was like a concentrated piece of the power blanket. As the extra magic infused him, he flew over the miles, seeking Irys. Then he slammed into a stone barrier. Dazed, he needed a moment to collect his wits before knocking. *Irys?*

Valek? What are you doing here?

Long story, but I can access the power blanket now, and Zitora's teaching me how to use your super messenger.

A pause. *Ah, good. Contact me again when I'm needed. Remember those messengers have a limited amount of magic. Once used up, it can only be recharged by Quinn.*

How can I tell how much has been used?

I could send a dozen messages before it's depleted. Since you aren't as strong, it would be less for you. Maybe eight total.

He calculated. It'd been used three times—twice by Zitora, who was stronger than Irys. *Six left?*

Yes. That's probably right. Good luck. Give Yelena my love.

He retreated, returning to the Keep's library. Not that he'd ever left. Odd. Both Yelena and Zitora stared at him expectantly.

"Irys sends her love," he said.

They both grinned.

Yelena gestured to the messenger. "That's a game-changer for our side. I told you your magic would come in handy."

"Yes, love, you were right."

Zitora slapped him on the back. "If you keep using those words, you're going to have a long, happy marriage." Then she sobered. "I'd better head back before Bruns gets too suspicious. Good luck with the big breakout." She turned, then stopped. "Oh, I almost forgot." She pulled a locked wooden box from her pocket. It was about six inches long and two inches wide. Zitora handed it to Yelena. "Give this to Opal when you see her."

"What is it?" Yelena asked.

"Opal will know what to do with it."

They spent the rest of the daylight hours reading. Valek quickly realized that his knowledge of magic and all things magical was rather limited, despite his years countering it, so they swapped tasks. Now he scanned pages of text and botanical drawings, seeking any sign of the Harman tree.

At one point, Yelena glanced up and said, "Ellis was a genius, but he had a warped way of thinking. Now I know where Owen Moon gets his crazy ideas. Owen must have read through these when he was a student at the Keep." She tapped a page with her fingernail. "Ellis believed that only the very strong and master-level magicians should be able to keep their powers. He thought all the others were just a danger to themselves and others. He wanted to start a magicians' guild to keep track of everyone."

"That sounds like Bruns's philosophy." And Bruns was close to Owen's age. "I wonder if Owen and Bruns knew each other before—" A thought popped into his head. While the Commander had financed most of Owen's glass hothouses in order for the man to produce Curare, Owen would have needed funds prior to that endeavor. Money to pay for his failed effort to recover the Ice Moon from the Commander. Had Owen and Bruns been planning this takeover all along?

"Before?" Yelena prompted.

He explained his theory. "The Ice Moon would have accomplished their goal of limiting who has access to magic." Once activated, the huge blue diamond could have stored the entire power blanket within its depths. But that would be too much power for one person to wield, so the Master Magicians sent the Ice Moon to the Commander for safekeeping. Believing it was a dangerous weapon, he had sliced it into thin sheets and incorporated them into the stained glass windows of his war room. Had he known what it had been capable of, the Commander might have been tempted to use it. He'd never trusted magicians and would have been happy to strip them of their powers.

Yelena fingered the edges of a book as her forehead crinkled in thought. "When the attempt to retrieve the Ice Moon failed, they came up with a plan B to control the magicians."

"For now. The Theobroma is just a short-term solution. Eventually they will need to weed out the magicians who are not dedicated to their cause."

"By killing them all?" she asked with a horrified tone.

"I doubt they would risk upsetting Sitians with such an extreme action. They need another way to neutralize them."

"Like me?"

He considered. "If they had succeeded in blocking your magic, I'd think they would have used that substance on the other magicians by now. Perhaps they're experimenting with null shields. They can be attached to objects. Maybe they found a way to inject a shield into a person's body or bloodstream."

Color leaked from her face. "Do you really think...?"

"I've no idea if it's possible. But I'm pretty certain they're working on something. Bruns and Owen want control of who keeps their powers and who doesn't. Since the magicians are all in Sitia, the Cartel must be leading the efforts. Maybe the answer is in Ellis Moon's notes."

They kept working.

Yelena finished before Valek. "Is this everything you found?"

"Yes. Why?"

She pushed the file away. "It's missing a few journals. Ellis mentions experimenting with various substances, but he keeps referring to a lab book for more details."

"It might have been passed down through the family. Owen is Ellis's great-great-grandson."

"Or it could be shelved under a different topic."

They searched through the rows and rows of bookshelves

MARIA V. SNYDER

for the lab notes but found nothing. Then Yelena helped him look through the rest of the botany books that she had collected earlier. Nothing. And the last of the light was fading. He hefted half the stack to return to the shelves while Yelena grabbed the rest. They all belonged in the same section of the library. When he slid in the last volume, another book title caught his eye. *Ixian Horticulture.* The image of the trees in the castle flashed. Could it be?

He grabbed it and brought it to the brightest spot in the library. Yelena followed him and leaned over his shoulder as he flipped through the pages. Unlike all the other books, he recognized many of the plants and trees. Funny how he'd never known most of their names.

Valek paused at a drawing of a familiar circular leaf.

"The Cheeko tree," Yelena said with a laugh. "The leaves are good for camouflage. Remember?"

"That is one of my favorite memories." When they'd first met, he'd suspected she was intelligent, but when she had glued them onto her bright red uniform in order to blend in with the forest, it confirmed his assessment. Plus she'd looked adorable, even with mud on her face and her hair covered with leaves.

Valek continued to turn pages, scanning each one as the light dimmed.

"There!" Yelena stabbed a page with her finger.

Excitement pulsed as he spotted the Harman tree with its distinctive leaves. He read through the description, but it focused on planting the tree for shade and listed the ideal growing conditions.

"Why can't anything be easy?" he asked.

"Were you hoping for a footnote that tells us why Owen is so interested in it?"

"Yes."

She patted his shoulder. "At least we know it's grown in

Ixia. That's more than a few minutes ago. And maybe there's something here that my father will find useful."

He gripped the page to rip it free from the book.

Yelena stopped his hand. "The library won't like that."

Since so many student magicians had spent long hours in here researching over many years' time, magic had infused every inch of this place—the library was very protective of the books.

"Will it let us take the book?"

"I don't know."

Feeling silly, he addressed the walls. "This book might help us solve a problem, and if we do, then the students will return and study here again."

Yelena covered her mouth with a hand and her eyes shone, but she didn't laugh.

"Come on," he said, tucking the book under his arm. "We need to check in with Onora."

They left the building without any shelves crashing down on them—a good sign. Crossing under the Keep's wall, they ascended and slipped into the alley. No one appeared to notice as they joined the flow of day shift workers hurrying home. The streets buzzed with conversation. The sun had just set, leaving behind a flat gray twilight that would soon turn black. Valek held Yelena's hand, keeping her close. Zitora had warned that watchers sought him. They would be on the lookout for a lone man versus a couple. He hoped.

They talked on the way back. Yelena said she was craving sweet cakes.

"You're always in the mood for sweet cakes, love."

"But this time it's because of the baby." She told him about Onora's aunt.

"Anything else you plan to blame on the baby?" he teased.

"Actually…" Yelena explained about baby brain. "So it

MARIA V. SNYDER

wasn't my fault that I forgot about my disguise when I was going to drink from the Unity Fountain's water spout."

"It was due to baby brain?"

"Exactly!"

He laughed. "I thought I'd heard every excuse possible, but that's a new one."

She glared at him. Oops.

"However, since I have *very* limited experience with pregnant women, I'll defer to your expertise in these matters from now on." He brought their clasped hands up and kissed her knuckles.

"Was that an apology? Am I supposed to swoon now?"

"Yes it was. And I believe swooning is required. Don't worry, I will catch you."

"Men," she muttered, shaking her head.

Onora waited for them in the apartment. She had purchased supplies for the rescue and bought half a dozen meat pies. Yelena groaned in pleasure as she devoured the warm, spicy beef. So much for sweet cakes. Onora and Valek shared an amused glance.

"Everything should be good to go," Onora said after they finished eating. "However, the timing of your distraction is going to be crucial. So far, most of the activity in the Council Hall occurs in the late afternoon, when everyone is leaving for the day."

"When do the guards change shifts?"

"About an hour before."

Smart. They'd still be alert during the afternoon rush. "What about the mornings? When do the guards switch?"

"An hour before dawn. But I can't get in until there's activity. Unless I go in the afternoon before."

"No need. We'll stage the distraction in the middle of the

rush. But if Yelena doesn't get in, abort the rescue. The rest of the plan will remain the same."

"Yes, sir."

"I'll get in," Yelena said with confidence.

And that was half the battle. Most often, if you acted like you belonged, no one questioned you. However, the magician at the door would be their biggest obstacle. They were already on high alert for Valek, so Yelena was their best bet. But that didn't stop the anxiety from gnawing on his stomach. His ability to shut down all his emotions has been shot to hell since he lost his immunity. Or had it been since Yelena confirmed her pregnancy?

Phelan arrived with a few more supplies and an update. "General Cahil's in his headquarters."

They reviewed the plan with Phelen before Yelena and Valek left to visit Cahil. His headquarters was located in a warehouse that was no longer in use to store goods. Instead, the large piles of crates served as obstacles for anyone trying to sneak in. Cahil had converted the basement into an office space for his crew of loyal people. Similar to Valek's corps, but on a much smaller scale.

The guards at the entrance allowed them to pass, but their sour expressions deepened. Yelena led the way through the crates to the stairway. Cahil was hunched over a table in his office, discussing tactics with two of his men. He scowled when they entered, but he ended the meeting.

Cahil closed the door and turned around. "You do realize every soldier in the Citadel is hunting for you. Right?"

"Do they suspect Yelena is here, as well?"

"No. Master Zitora said she scanned the entire Citadel and didn't sense her." He glanced at Yelena. "Are you using a null shield pendant? Because she fell hard for Bruns's lies and

MARIA V. SNYDER

is looking for blood. At least there is no need to worry she'll expose the other Masters."

Valek decided not to enlighten Cahil about Zitora. Not just yet. "Why did Bruns summon you here?"

"To escort Master Zitora to the Moon garrison. He wants her trained and ready. Bruns is certain the Commander will invade right after the Ixian fire festival."

"We know that's a sham. What happens when his soldiers don't show?" Yelena asked.

"I don't know. He's making plans for all the northern garrisons to march to the Ixian border and be in position by midseason. He's transferred Master Bain to Krystal so each garrison has a Master Magician in the lead, and all our magicians will be accompanying our army."

Valek kept his expression neutral, but his mind whirled. They had guessed wrong. The Commander's forces would invade, and there would be a battle. There would be casualties on both sides. In the chaos of the battle, no one would realize who had specifically targeted the magicians to neutralize them, but they would all know who to blame.

The Commander.

21

JANCO

Janco sensed the ambush before he reached the edge of the Avibian Plains. Which was kind of amazing, considering the house wasn't even in sight. He'd left Ari and a very reluctant Opal behind so he could scout the premises. Smart move. As he crept from the tall grasses, he counted at least four crouched figures in the dim moonlight.

With Opal's horse setting a break-neck pace—he now understood why they called it break-neck, 'cause if you fell off at that speed, you'd break your neck for sure—they'd arrived at Opal's parents' place in just four days.

Once this was over, he planned to sleep for a week.

Janco looped around the house and, sure enough, ambushers covered all the doors and windows. Twelve total. Shoot. Too many for them to fight. And he doubted he could fetch his partner and Opal in time. It appeared things were about to go down. The air felt…unsettled. Then he remembered. A Stormdancer might be sleeping inside. If he could wake—

The gate squealed. The noise sliced through the heavy silence like a sharp blade through flesh and had the same effect. The figures whipped around to advance on the poor sod.

Janco cursed. What the hell were Devlen and Reema doing here now?

No matter. Janco straightened from his crouch and drew his sword. A high-pitched wail sounded, followed by a whoosh. One after the other, the ambushers were slammed to the ground. And for once, Janco wasn't exaggerating—an invisible force had literally picked them up and slammed each one into the ground so hard that they didn't get back up.

A smaller figure darted from the shadows of the stable and launched at Devlen. The big man caught him in midair and hugged him. Ah, sweet. Janco sheathed his sword. Another person also materialized from the shadows, but she moved at a much slower pace. After that display of power, Janco was surprised Heli still had the energy to stand.

All four of them whirled around when he approached. A knife flashed in Reema's hand. Nice.

"It's me. Janco." He spread his hands wide.

Teegan peered at him, but his forehead creased with suspicion. "Null shield. That's why I didn't sense him. Can you take it off?"

About to ask why, he answered his own question. He could have been brainwashed by the Cartel and turned into a spy. Janco pulled the pendant off. "Hope you're not too traumatized by my thoughts." A prickly, unpleasant sensation invaded his mind as his ear tweaked with pain. It disappeared just as fast.

Teegan grinned. "Tell my mom we'll be joining you in the plains as soon as we pack up."

Good. "Are Zohav and—"

"We're here," Zethan said. "Just enjoying the show. Since Heli hogged all the fun."

"Next time you can do the honors," Heli said in a tired voice.

"Sweet."

Zohav frowned.

"Don't worry, Zo," her brother said. "I'll let you in on the action."

Which just caused her expression to deepen. But Zethan laughed, clearly not discouraged by her reaction. Janco approved. The boy had potential.

While they gathered their things and saddled the horses, Janco returned to Ari and Opal.

"Well?" Opal asked immediately.

"Relax, Mama Bunny, your family is safe. They'll be here soon."

"Here? What happened?"

He explained how Heli had stopped the ambush. "…that air blast of hers was a thing of beauty. If I was the Cartel, I'd be shaking in my boots right now."

"It's better if they underestimate us," Ari said. "And don't you mean Mama *Bear*?"

"Nah, female bears got nothin' on bunnies when it comes to protecting their young. I once saw this—"

"I should have known better than to ask." Ari walked away.

"Do you want to hear my story?" Janco asked Opal.

"No."

"Fine. But the next time you get bitten by an overprotective mama rabbit, don't come crying to me." He pouted, but no one paid any attention to him, so he checked The Madam's legs for hot spots. After all that hard riding, he hoped to give her a couple days' rest, but they would need to travel further into the plains to avoid the Cartel's next attempt. 'Cause they certainly weren't going to stop, and it appeared that they'd upped the stakes.

He grinned. *We scare them.*

Within the hour, a group of nine people and four horses

MARIA V. SNYDER

trudged into view. Opal whooped and raced to meet them. She scooped up her kids and hugged them both to her as if they weighed nothing. Devlen wrapped his arms around them. A hollow pang of longing ricocheted in Janco's equally hollow chest, surprising him. He'd never considered settling down before. All this drama with the Cartel was getting to him. Pah. Janco looked away.

Ari interrupted the family reunion. They needed to put a few miles between them and Booruby.

"Where are we going?" Opal's dad asked.

"South. We'll find a medium-size town where you can stay," Ari said.

They had a total of twelve people and seven horses, so most had to double up. Janco shared The Madam's saddle with Opal's father. Ahir joined Teegan on Caramel. Opal rode with her mother on Quartz, the twins shared Smoke, and Devlen and Reema stayed on Sunfire. Ari and Heli each rode alone, but Whiskey and Thunder carried additional bags.

Quite the posse. With all the extra weight and baggage, they moved slower than Janco's grandmother—and he'd seen snails lap her.

Traveling through the plains as long as possible, they stopped near the Daviian Plateau's border to make camp. There were still a few hours until sunset, but everyone drooped with fatigue. While they made camp, Janco hunted for a few rabbits. The fresh meat would help revive everyone. When he returned, Opal's mother took the skinned rabbits and turned them into the best campfire meal he'd ever eaten.

Zethan brandished a forkful of meat. "This is why I gained ten pounds in the last week. Ahir, it's a wonder you don't weigh five hundred pounds."

"I sweat it all off in the factory." Ahir glanced at his dad. "Did you warn our employees about the Cartel?"

"No. I just left a note for my assistant saying we had a family emergency. She'll take care of filling orders while we're gone," Jaymes said.

"Uh, what about the ambushers lying on the ground?" Janco asked. "They're not going to be happy when they wake up." Considering how hard they'd hit, they might still be out cold.

Teegan grinned. "No worries. We cleaned up the mess."

"How— No, never mind," Opal said. "I don't need to know. I'm just glad we're all together and safe." She put her arm around Reema, who leaned into her.

Which reminded Janco. "Devlen, did something happen to Leif and Mara? You should have dropped Reema off a while ago."

"They reached the Illiais Market without any trouble. Reema stayed with us because…" He glanced at Opal.

Janco straightened. This ought to be interesting.

"I'm good at spotting places to avoid," Reema said.

"What do you mean?" Ari asked.

She shrugged. "We didn't want to draw attention. And I know where to travel so we didn't get noticed." Then she crossed her arms. "Which is why we should have stayed with Uncle Leif and not wasted time coming up here. You're gonna need me."

Devlen ignored that comment. "Once the others continued into the jungle, we returned to Booruby. I wanted to arrive before dawn, just in case there were watchers on the house."

"I was asleep, or else I would have warned him about the ambush," Reema said. Then she beamed at her brother. "But Tee took care of it!"

"Heli did all the work," Teegan said. "I just directed traffic."

Janco glanced at Heli, but the poor girl was curled up, fast

MARIA V. SNYDER

asleep. It wasn't long before the other kids joined her. Ari, Janco, Opal and Devlen took shifts guarding the camp.

Two days later, they entered the town limits of Kerrylee. It was smaller than desired and hugged the western edge of the Daviian Plateau. But according to Reema, the place had no watchers working for the Cartel. How the girl knew this, Janco hadn't a clue, but he'd learned to trust the little scamp. They found a nice inn for Opal's parents and brother to stay at, and for the rest of them to spend the night. Devlen and Opal were having a family discussion about Reema's future.

Janco caught a few words as he passed their room on the way down to the common room. He smiled as Opal kept repeating, "She's only eleven," with Devlen reminding his wife how Reema had aided in his and Leif's rescue. Should be an interesting conversation, but Janco wasn't about to listen at the door. No need to spy on his friends.

The warmth and bright lights of the common room wrapped around him like an embrace. He scanned the occupants. Banished from the discussion upstairs, Reema played cards with Teegan, Zethan and Heli, but she shot dark looks at the stairs, as if her unhappiness could travel up to her parents' room. Ari sat nearby, drinking ale. Janco joined him and ordered a pint.

When the drink arrived, he took a long pull. It wasn't half-bad.

"What do you think?" Ari asked him.

"It's a little sour, but I like the lemony flavors."

"Not the ale. Our next move."

Oh. He scratched his ear. "I think the others will be safe traveling to the Illiais Market without us."

"You think they'll take Reema with them?"

"They'd be stupid not to."

"Thank you," Reema said.

"Hey, it's rude to eavesdrop on people's conversations," Janco said.

"Oh, sorry. I wouldn't want to be *rude*. Is it rude to talk about someone when she's sitting right here?"

Janco opened his mouth to reply, but Ari shook his head. Instead, they moved a few more tables away. However, due to her sly smile, Janco suspected the scamp had rabbit ears.

"I agree that there will be enough people and magicians to spread the spores," Ari said. "We can leave for the Green-blade garrison tomorrow. I want to gather as much intel about the place as possible before we rescue the Councilors. Do you think Opal will let Teegan come with us?"

"Do you think Teegan will listen to his mother if she says no?"

"Some kids actually listen to their mothers."

"Really?" Janco blinked at Ari. "What a concept."

"Your poor mother. She should get a medal for not killing you."

"Oh, she tried. Many times. That's how I learned the fine art of duck and cover."

Devlen and Opal joined them four ales later. From the shine in Opal's eyes, he guessed they'd done more than discuss their daughter. Understandable, considering they'd been apart for months. Reema showed remarkable restraint by not pouncing on her parents right away. It also helped that the scamp was soundly beating her brother at cards. Good. It would keep the boy humble.

Ari told Opal and Devlen their plans and asked them about Teegan. "I think you'll have enough protection. Plus a bigger group of people will draw more attention."

"I agree," Opal said. She glanced at her children. "As much as I want to keep them safe from harm, I know we won't be safe until this is over. Teegan can decide."

"What about Reema?" Janco asked.

"She coming with us."

"Woo-hoo!" Reema said. When they all looked over at her, she slapped a card down. "I win!"

Smooth recovery. Janco'd been right. Rabbit ears.

Teegan chose to accompany Ari and Janco. They picked a rendezvous location near the Greenblade garrison.

"When you're done spreading the spores, meet us there," Ari said. "I think Yelena and Valek are planning the big counterattack to commence during the first month of the hot season."

"And if they don't escape the Citadel?" Janco asked.

"Then we'll implement the other counterattack."

"Oh, the *other* attack. I feel so much better now."

The next morning, as they were saying goodbye and eliciting promises to be careful, Heli pulled Janco aside.

"You're going to rescue the Councilors?" she asked.

"We're going to try."

"I have something that might help you. Come on."

Surprised, he followed her. She opened her bulging saddle bag. He had wondered what she'd packed in there. Heli pulled out a wrapped bundle and handed it to Janco. It was shaped like a small watermelon and about as heavy.

"What's in here?"

"A glass orb. Be careful. It's filled. And you do *not* want it to break."

Confused and alarmed, he asked, "You mean there's a storm inside it?"

"Not quite. The energy from a storm is trapped inside. And if you shatter the orb on...let's say, the garrison's wall...the energy released will bring that wall crashing down."

"Holy snow cats! That's…" Janco couldn't find the proper words for just how awesome it was.

"I couldn't carry more than two, but Kade and Zethan have filled lots of extras. They're storing them at The Cliffs. Just make sure you're a safe distance away before you use them. Maybe they'll come in handy for the big counterattack." She grinned.

"Sweetheart, there's no *maybe* about it."

22

YELENA

I paused halfway up the steps to the Council Hall. Leaning slightly forward, I pretended to huff from the effort of the climb, resting a hand on my huge fake belly. My five "children" bounced up the stairs. Then, when they realized "mom" wasn't keeping up, they hopped back down. The two oldest supported me as I waddled up to the landing.

"Thanks, ducklings." I patted my "sons" on their shoulders.

The guards at the entrance watched us with amusement. I kept my thoughts on the task at hand, suppressing the doubts and million worries about what could go wrong deep into my subconscious. Free Fisk first. Then I'd fret over the next task.

There were a few other people entering the building, and I followed them with my children in tow. "Sir, can you direct me to where I obtain permission to leave the Citadel?" I asked one of them.

"Second floor. Can't miss it. There's a line."

"Thank you." Out of the corner of my eye, I spotted the magician turning her attention to me. I signaled my children. They started bickering and it escalated into fighting. Then they knocked into the magician as they wrestled. I swooped in and scolded them, apologized and made them say they were sorry before we all trundled off.

As I waddled, I kept expecting her to call after me or sound the alarm, but nothing happened. The stairs to the upper floors were visible from the open lobby. According to Onora, the queue for the permits stayed long all day, and it trailed down the steps. I joined the line with a sigh, rubbing my lower back. My ducklings pretended to get bored and wandered off. The magician at the entrance scanned the people exiting and didn't appear to be interested in me.

Onora had left the safe house earlier this afternoon. I assumed she'd entered without trouble. Now it was just a matter of waiting for the signal. I rubbed my back with a little groan.

"Maybe you should sit down, dear," the lady next to me said.

"It's worse when I sit. This duck is just being difficult." I patted my stomach.

She nodded knowingly. "I had one like that. Are you due soon?"

"Not for a week, at least."

"Not a good time to travel."

"Oh, no, I'm not leaving yet. Once the new duck is born, I'm going to visit my mother. Let her wrangle the others while I rest."

"That's a good idea."

We stood in companionable silence as the line inched along. I scanned the flow of people crossing the lobby and using the other set of stairs. Valek's theory about Bruns's plans to target all the magicians tried to sabotage my thoughts. We needed to stop that battle and find a way to protect them. How we would accomplish this monumental task had so far failed to materialize.

Instead of worrying about it, I switched my concern to

MARIA V. SNYDER

Valek. His part of the plan was just as dangerous as ours, but he'd downplayed it with his usual bravado. Then, out of the corner of my eye, I spotted Onora on the far end of the lobby. She nodded at me—our agreed-upon signal—before disappearing.

"Oh, my!" I clutched my bulging stomach.

"Is it the baby, dear?" the lady asked, her voice shrill with alarm.

"It's just a cramp—oooohhh! I'd better…" I waddled down the stairs. "Ducks, come on, we're—aaaahhh!"

The kids joined me in the middle of the lobby, which had grown quiet. Everyone stared at the pregnant lady making noises. Good. I took a few steps toward the exit. "We need to get ho—oooohhh, no!" I gasped, stopping and bending over as if in extreme pain. "The baby is coming!" Squeezing my stomach, I ruptured the seal on the water skin that was hidden under my tunic. Except it wasn't water that splashed onto the floor.

The people closest to me jumped back, but the guards at the door stepped forward to render aid. However, it was the guards streaming up from the cells under the building that scared me.

"Now!" I covered my nose and mouth with a cloth just as my ducklings threw small glass spheres onto the liquid. They shattered on impact.

An angry fog hissed and spread. My kids swarmed out of the way of its gray tentacles, making a beeline for the exit. Breathing shallowly through the fabric, I remained in place as the people around me stumbled to the ground. Then I, too, bolted for the door.

Outside, the kids had already disappeared. Kiki waited at the bottom of the steps. I mounted, and she took off for the Citadel's gate, weaving through the government quarter. Once we were safe, she slowed so I could remove the deflated water skin and allow the others to catch up.

Time for part two. We rendezvoused with Onyx and the guild members a couple blocks away from the gate. Valek's horse was saddled and ready.

"Is everyone here?" I asked. We would leave no one behind.

"Yeah, except for Master Fisk," Phelan said with a worried frown.

"He's not on horseback," I said. "Fisk and Onora should be here soon." Along with Valek, unless he was unable to ditch his pursuers.

Kiki pricked her ears back and turned. Onora and Fisk raced into view. She waved us on. "Go, go! The guards are right behind us."

Damn. I hesitated. Valek hadn't appeared. Where was he? I glanced at the kids and at Fisk's pale face. We couldn't wait.

"Fisk, mount Onyx. You take Valek's role."

Onora helped him into the saddle.

"All right, let's go," I ordered. The words sizzled on my tongue and seared down my throat.

The kids raced ahead of us. Just before we turned the last corner and would be in full view of the gate's guards, we all paused. I hooked my right foot through the stirrup and swung my left leg over. I dropped the reins so they dragged on the ground and shifted until I clung to the side of the saddle, as if I was about to fall.

I signaled. Showtime. The guild members ran straight at the armed soldiers, screaming about a runaway horse just before Kiki burst into view. Onyx followed close behind, with Fisk bravely trying to grab Kiki's reins and save the damsel in distress. I played my part by screaming for help and carrying on.

There were only a few guards at the gate. Valek had suc-

MARIA V. SNYDER

cessfully drawn off the extras who had been stationed there. Did they catch him?

The men and women dove to the side when it became obvious they would be trampled by the horses if they didn't. I tightened my hold and braced as Kiki broke through the gate in one powerful stride. A loud crack split the air, and splinters flew in all directions. Pinpricks of pain peppered my hands and face. I glanced back. Onyx and the kids poured from the Citadel like water breaking through a mud dam. The plan was to scatter once we were free and meet up later. Kiki slowed, and I pulled myself back into the saddle.

While elated that we'd rescued Fisk and the guild members, my heart burned for Valek. I tried not to get too upset. He might still be free but unable to leave the Citadel. Once I rendezvoused with Fisk and the others, I could wait for when Cahil and his group left to escort Zitora. He would have information on Valek's whereabouts. Or Valek might even be hidden in his posse. A girl could hope.

The trip to Bavol's farmhouse seemed to take an eternity. Since it was close to the plains, it would be an ideal hideout for a couple of days. Fisk and his people would need to move on in case Valek had been captured. The bitter taste of ashes coated my mouth at the thought.

It was dark by the time we reached the farm. Fisk and Onyx had beaten us there. Since the kids were on foot, it would take them longer to arrive. In the meantime, I lit one of the stable's lanterns and tended to Kiki's injuries. Cuts crisscrossed her chest, and thick wooden splinters protruded from her neck and legs. Blood ran down her front legs. Poor girl.

I rubbed a little of the watered-down medical Curare into her wounds first. Finding a pair of tweezers, I carefully tugged the pieces free from the cuts. Fisk groomed and settled Onyx before he joined me.

Limping slightly, he leaned against a beam. Lines of exhaustion etched his young face. Purple bruises stained his skin. His defeated posture said more than his haunted gaze.

"I'm sorry," he said.

"Don't be. It's not your fault."

"It is. I should have—"

"Stop right there. Should haves are a complete waste of time and energy. They can't change the past. It happened. You learned a lesson. Now you know what not to do. That's what you focus on for the future."

He didn't reply. After a while, I glanced at him. He rubbed his arm but stared into the night as if deep in thought.

I pulled the last splinter from Kiki's copper coat, then washed her wounds before smearing on one of Leif's healing salves. Thinking of Leif, I calculated the timing of his trip. My brother should have reached the jungle by now. Had our father started cultivating the spores?

The pain in my chest, which had died down to a smolder while I'd been distracted, flared to life once more. Would Valek divulge that information to the Cartel? He was resistant to goo-goo juice, but not to magic. And Cilly would take great delight in scrambling Valek's brains as she searched for information. Revenge for killing her brother.

"Thank you." Fisk interrupted my morose thoughts. "For…" He swept a hand wide. "Rescuing me, and getting my kids to safety. Despite the danger."

"You're welcome. Besides, it was my turn." I touched his shoulder. "Tag, you're it."

That surprised a laugh from him. "I don't know if I can top today. When I saw you hunched over, screaming about the baby, for a moment I actually worried you were going to squat down and pop the kid out right there in the lobby."

MARIA V. SNYDER

Pop the kid out? If only it would be that easy. "Don't worry. I've about two seasons to go."

We shared a look as we both acknowledged the unspoken— if I survived that long. If any of us did.

Fisk wrapped his arms around his stomach. "I'm sorry about Valek."

"Me, too, but he knew the risks. And he's escaped worse situations. The man doesn't know how to quit. And we shouldn't, either." Energized, I grabbed my saddle bags and headed for the house. "Come on. Your people are going to be hungry and thirsty when they arrive."

The place was just as dark and empty as it had been the last time I'd visited. Just to be safe, I did a sweep of all the rooms. When I returned, Fisk was building a lattice of branches for a fire. I moved to help him, but he waved me off.

"Go get cleaned up or you're gonna scare my kids." He pointed to his cheek.

I touched mine. Ow. My fingers came away sticky with blood. So worried about everyone else, I'd forgotten about my own injuries. In the washroom, I plucked splinters from my face, neck, hand and arm. Just like with Kiki, I cleaned the wounds and rubbed a healing ointment into the stinging cuts. By that point, my disguise was ruined. I scraped off the putty and untangled my black hair. At least Valek had left the strands long enough for me to collect them into a single braid. It reached just past my shoulders.

A fire roared in the hearth. Fisk huddled next to it, soaking in its heat.

I sat next to him. "Bad enough to be locked in a cell, but then the cold dampness seeps into your bones until you believe you'll never be warm again."

"Yeah, I hadn't experienced it before." He watched the flames as they danced. "I've been hungry, poor, homeless, alone and afraid, but I've never been so helpless and terrified. So…"

"Exposed?"

"Ripped apart." He rubbed a hand over his short beard. "All my thoughts and memories laid bare. All my secrets. My kids who depend on me…taken. Nothing I did made a bit of difference."

"I know. It's rough, and it leaves you feeling raw. But you walked away with your personality and memories intact. You're still Fisk. They could have taken that, as well."

"So, I should be grateful?" His tone was bitter.

"Not at all. Just think about it. As bad as it feels right now, and when all you want to do is curl up in a ball and ignore the world, remember—you are alive, both body and soul. You didn't die, so don't act like it. There are a lot of others who can't say the same thing."

"Is that your idea of a pep talk?"

"Yup. Mind you, it's just plain old Yelena's words of wisdom from her own experiences, and not the Soulfinder talking."

"That's okay. I've heard the Soulfinder is a bit of a drama queen anyway," he teased—a good sign for his recovery.

"Tell me about it. Plus, she's always in the middle of trouble."

His small smile widened suddenly. "Cilly didn't get everything."

It took me a moment to follow his shift in topic. "No?"

"No. She doesn't know about your deal with Cahil, thank fate!"

"Why not?"

"She didn't know to ask or to look. Bruns is confident that his people are loyal."

Thank fate, indeed.

As Fisk warmed up, an unpleasant odor emanated from

MARIA V. SNYDER

him. Unfortunately, I was well-acquainted with the reek of dungeon. I sent him to get cleaned up before his kids arrived.

Around midnight, they started trickling in, either alone or in pairs. All were tired and hungry, but still had enough energy to give their leader a hug or a high-five. We fed them and sent them to bed. The farmhouse had plenty of bedrooms.

"Not many helpers left," Fisk said in a dejected tone.

"Phelan said none of your guild were killed. They've been sent to the other garrisons, which is a good thing for us."

"They've been brainwashed and forced to work for the Cartel. How is that a good thing?"

I'd forgotten that he didn't know about the spores. Without telling him all the details, I said, "There will come a time when they'll recover their senses, and then they'll be in the perfect position to help us stop the Cartel."

Fisk shook his head. "My guild has gone in well over our heads. It's too dangerous for them."

"I agree it's dangerous. I didn't want them involved in your rescue, but they refused to lie low. Even with the Cartel rounding them up, they still gathered intel."

"Are you saying that even if I order them to stay uninvolved, they'll ignore me?"

"Yes." I patted his arm. "You did a good job raising them."

He huffed.

A few more members arrived by dawn. Fisk refused to go to sleep, even though I promised to man the door. Instead, he dozed on the couch.

Phelan showed up in the morning. Mud coated his pants, and rips marked his sleeves. "I picked up a tail and couldn't shake him. Tenacious bastard. I hid in the briars for a few hours until he gave up."

"Is anyone else coming?" Fisk asked him.

"How many have arrived so far?"

"You make thirteen," Fisk said.

"That's everyone."

A sad relief shone on Fisk's face, but the comment sliced through me. Onora was still missing. I didn't panic right away. Knowing her, she was probably waiting for everyone to be safe inside before joining us. But just to be sure, I asked Phelan if he'd seen her.

"No."

"She told me she was staying in the Citadel," Fisk said.

"What? Why didn't you tell me?" I demanded.

"I thought you knew. She made it sound like it was part of the plan."

A sick dread swirled in my stomach. "What did she say?"

"That she needed to stay behind and keep an eye on Bruns."

Oh, no. She planned to assassinate Bruns.

I couldn't sleep. I paced around the living area while Fisk and his guild slept. The midafternoon sun painted a sheen of brightness on the trees and grasses. Yet to me, the colors resembled mud.

Onora and Valek remained in the Citadel. Perhaps they would team up and Valek would kill Bruns to save Onora from doing it. But what should I do? Should I assume they wouldn't reveal our plans to the Cartel and proceed as arranged, or should I change everything? There were forty-five days left in the heating season. I needed to be at the Greenblade garrison before the start of the hot season.

Kiki whinnied. I froze for a moment. She repeated the sound. Distressed, and definitely trying to get my attention, I yanked my switchblade and triggered the blade. Peering through the windows, I studied the land between the house and stables. Nothing. Kiki jumped the stall door and ran to the house.

I bolted outside. "What's wrong?"

She spun and returned to the stables. I followed her. Onyx thumped at the walls. Was he injured? Perhaps one of the splinters from the gate had struck him and festered. I ducked inside and stopped. Valek slumped over a bale of hay. A knife jutted from his back.

An ice-cold lance of fear shot right through me, pinning me in place. He looked...

Dead.

Racing to his side, I paused. His magic might be able to heal him, but not if I touched him. I crouched next to him and called his name. His eyelids fluttered, as if he needed every ounce of energy to open his eyes, but he didn't wake.

Alive. For now.

I ran into the house and woke Fisk and Phelan. They carried Valek into the house and lay him on his stomach in the master bedroom downstairs. Valek moaned.

"Should we pull the knife out?" Fisk asked.

"No. He might bleed to death if it pierced his heart." My thoughts jumbled into a swirl of panic. No healer. No magic. No way he'd live without one or both.

"One of us could fetch a healer from... Where's the closest town?" Phelan asked.

"No time," I said. The words repeated in my mind. No time. No healer. No magic. Think! There was magic in the Avibian Plains, but could Valek access it? No. Kiki had magic. Who else had magic? No one. What else?

Holy snow cats! I sprinted to the stables and into the tack room. Valek's saddle and bags rested on a pile of straw bales. I yanked open the pouch and dug deep, flinging items left and right. It was down deep at the bottom, rolled in one of his tunics. Racing back to house, I dashed into Valek's room, gasping for breath.

Fisk and Phelan hovered near him.

"What's that?" Phelan asked.

Wrong question. No time to explain.

"What do you need us to do?" Fisk asked.

Right question.

I handed the bundle to Fisk. "Unwrap it." Then I instructed Phelan to move Valek's arms until his hands were over Valek's head. Pointing to the knife, I said, "Phelan, when I say three, you yank the knife free in one quick motion."

With an "ah" of understanding, Fisk dropped Valek's tunic on the bed.

I picked it up and folded into a square. "Press this to the wound right after you remove the knife," I instructed Phelan.

When he gave me an odd look, Fisk said, "She can't touch him."

"You know what to do?" I asked Fisk.

"Yes."

"Be quick."

"I know."

"On three. One. Two. Three."

Phelan yanked. Valek jerked awake, gasping in pain. Fisk thrust the glass super messenger into Valek's hands while Phelan staunched the wound.

It was a gamble. A long shot. If Valek wasn't conscious enough to tap into the magic stored inside… I hovered nearby, completely useless.

Fisk pressed Valek's hands to the glass. Valek's head dropped back onto the mattress. His eyes drifted shut.

23

VALEK

A hot poker of pain speared him with unbelievable agony. His eyes watered, and sweet oblivion beckoned as his body shut down to protect against the onslaught.

"No, you don't!" Yelena yelled. Her voice was distant, but the panic and fear were clear. "Come on, Valek. Use your magic."

Magic? He'd tried. Before. It worked. For a while. But... not strong enough.

"Come on, you bastard."

The bastard was the guy who'd stabbed him in the back. Except he couldn't remember which of the five did the deed.

"Heal yourself. Use the super messenger."

Messenger? His hands tingled and pulsed with magic. But he couldn't see his injury. It hurt to think. It hurt to breathe. It hurt.

As if reading his mind, Yelena said, "Reach inside. Like when you reach out with your magic, but this time, reach inside instead."

Black-and-white spots swirled as energy drained from his limbs.

"Do it now. That's an order!"

Conditioned to following orders, Valek gathered the magic and concentrated on the pulsing fury of pain in his chest, projecting his awareness into his body, sensing the injury. His heart struggled to beat as blood spurted from an inch-long tear. Fear gripped him. The injury was too severe to repair.

"Valek, do it for your child."

The memory of the baby's movements caressed his mind as gently as the baby inside her had caressed his fingers. Using the magic in the messenger to strengthen him, Valek pulled a thread of power and stitched the tear in his heart.

Lightheaded with the effort, he drew in a deep breath. He wasn't done. Blood had pooled in his chest. Too much. He guided it back through the cut arteries in his back before working on repairing the muscles and tissues, looping tiny, neat stitches. He rested for a moment. Yelena's voice roused him again, goading him into action.

Feeling a bit stronger, he drew more power from the blanket, since a part of him knew to avoid draining the messenger. By the time he finished knitting the skin together, he shook with fatigue. The temptation to pull in more power throbbed.

Resisting the lure of unlimited energy, Valek let go. He hoped he'd done enough to quiet that insistent voice, so he could rest in peace.

He woke in snatches. Faces came and went. Fisk. Phelan. Yelena. Valek reached for his wife, but she wouldn't touch his skin. Liquids burned down his throat, and he shivered under a thousand pounds of blankets until fire raced over his skin and he flung them off. Pulling in a breath became a struggle. Oblivion was far easier.

But the voice returned. "You missed something. Look again," it ordered. He tried ignoring that voice. It demanded too much. However, it refused to give up and it sawed into

MARIA V. SNYDER

his mind, cleaving its way into his core. "Fight or die," it challenged him.

And that voice saved him. Again. He'd never backed down from a fight. Valek connected to the blanket of power and sought the injury with his awareness, seeking what he'd missed. A sliver of metal was lodged in his rib. Red inflammation and green pus hovered around it. A hole in his right lung leaked air. Sewing the hole was second nature. Once completed, his breathing returned to normal.

The shard, however, would have to be removed. He needed help and another pair of hands. When he built up enough strength, he asked for a volunteer who wouldn't faint at the sight of blood. And who would allow Valek to invade his or her mind.

Fisk volunteered. Yelena's strained face softened with surprise. Valek wondered why, until he encountered the damage in Fisk's thoughts. Another had invaded, and she had a heavy touch. Like a bully, she had taken what she wanted and left a mess behind.

Valek kept a light connection with Fisk, being a mindful guest. He showed the young man what Valek needed him to do.

Fisk cursed. "I've gotten some strange requests from clients before, but this one beats them all." He glanced at Yelena. "He wants me to cut into his back."

"Why?"

"Metal shard left behind."

"Oh. No need, Valek. Push it from your body. It will cut through muscles and skin, but you can repair the tears as it travels. That will cause much less damage." She frowned at him. "Why didn't you just ask me?"

He gave her an apologetic smile. "Baby brain."

She relaxed. "No. I'm sorry. I'm just not used to you

being…" Yelena drew in a breath. "Let me do the thinking for you until you're recovered. Okay?"

"Yes, love." He rolled onto his stomach and worked on evicting the unwelcome visitor. Pain once again sliced through his back, but he managed to wiggle it out. Blood and pus poured from the new wound. He let the pus drain before stitching up the cut. Yelena wiped the fluids up with a towel, being careful not to touch his skin with her own.

Too exhausted to move, Valek closed his eyes, but he vowed to get better just so he could hold his wife again.

The days passed in blurs of activity. Waking, eating, talking and sleeping. He explained to Yelena and Fisk how he'd drawn the bulk of the guards away from the gate. A smile at the memory. Janco would be proud of the taunt he'd used to goad them into action. Valek had led them on a merry chase throughout the Citadel and well away from the distraction at the Council Hall.

Then the smile faded. They'd been harder to shake than expected. A magician had accompanied them, and she'd tracked him with her magic. By the time he looped back to the gate, the soldiers had recovered from their surprise. And behind him, the Council Hall guards had arrived, charging toward the exit, trapping him between the two.

He'd faced ten. Nothing left to do but surrender. Fear was a pale shadow compared to the regret that pulsed in his heart for failing to rejoin Yelena. Except Onora had appeared from nowhere. She ambushed a couple guards, and Valek couldn't let her have all the fun.

He ignored Yelena's squawk of protest and continued the story. It hadn't taken long to realize five armed opponents exceeded his fighting skills. "A blow to my ego."

When the knife had sliced into his back, he'd yanked power,

MARIA V. SNYDER

flinging his magic away from him in a blind panic and flattening the guards to the ground.

"A mini flameout?" Yelena asked him.

"No idea, love. By the time I came to my senses, Onora was gone. I clutched magic to my chest and ran until I couldn't." He reached for her. And since he no longer relied on his magic to heal, she laced her fingers through his. "Then the nagging started."

She huffed and tried to yank her hand from his grip.

He tightened his hold. "It saved my life. Thank you." Valek kissed her knuckles.

Fisk laughed. "Power nagging. I love it." He paused. "Don't tell my mother."

"Where's Onora?" Valek asked. "I need to thank her, too."

Both Yelena and Fisk sobered. He braced for bad news, but Fisk's report wasn't all doom.

"She's quite capable of avoiding capture," Valek said.

"What if she tries to assassinate Bruns?" Yelena asked.

"She'll probably succeed. Why are you upset? It would derail the Cartel's plans."

Yelena sat on the edge of his bed. "I'm worried about her soul." She looked down at their clasped hands. "Killing another changes a person."

He squeezed her fingers. "I know. Onora will have to decide what to do. If she kills Bruns and manages to escape, then it's a good thing most of her friends understand exactly what she sacrificed in order to save others."

Yelena's expression grew thoughtful. He wondered what she mulled over. Before he could ask, she released his hand and stood.

"You need to rest." Yelena pulled the blankets up to his chest. "You have to regain your strength."

"I sleep better when you're with me, love." He patted the bed beside him.

"And that's my signal to go." Fisk paused in the threshold. "My kids are bored and want to help. What should I tell them?"

Valek exchanged a glance with Yelena. She nodded.

"Send them to the three northern garrisons. When the Theobroma starts to wear off, they'll be in position to help spread the word," Valek said.

"Spread the word about what?"

"To listen to the Master Magicians and follow their orders."

"What will be their orders?"

Valek tried to shrug, but it still hurt too much. "I don't know. We haven't figured that out yet. Let me know if you have any ideas."

Fisk just muttered as he left.

"Can you contact the Masters?" Yelena asked.

He touched the super messenger. It sat on the bedside table, just in case he needed it. Magic hummed inside, but how much was left? "I hope so." Valek considered. "Bruns told Zitora that all these had been destroyed, but we know he's been using them—and he has Quinn, who can recharge them."

"You want to steal one?"

"Or two or three or—"

"I get it." She perched on the edge of the bed and pulled off her boots. "We can see if there are any in the Greenblade garrison when we free the Councilors."

That reminded him. "How long have I been out of it?"

She stripped down to her underclothes. "It's close to the middle of the heating season. We've been here for ten days."

Shocked, he sat up. "Ten…" But his head spun, and his muscles shook.

Yelena tsked and pushed him back down. "You almost died.

Even with using magic, you can't recover that fast." Sliding into bed with him, she snuggled close.

"We need to leave soon." There wasn't much time left.

"When you're healthy." Her tone implied it was not up for discussion.

He lay there, staring at the ceiling. A few dusty cobwebs hung in the corners. Depending on how well-guarded they were, it could take days or weeks to plan and then execute the Councilors' rescue. Then they would need at least a week for the Councilors to recover their free will.

"Stop fretting," Yelena said. "Rest."

When he didn't relax, she took his hand and placed it on her slightly bulging belly. Even through her undershirt, he felt the baby's movements. Amazing.

"A little over halfway," she said.

That scared him. So much to do before they were safe. He tensed again.

"What do you think? Boy or girl?" she asked.

Ah. A classic distraction technique, but he played along. "Girl."

"Why?"

"Because she already takes after you, love."

"How's that?"

"From the very beginning, she's been in the middle of the action, causing trouble."

"Ha. I think it's a boy, because of all your brothers. Your parents had six boys and one girl. The odds are good for a boy."

"And for twins," he said.

She pushed up on her elbow, looking a bit panicked. "No. Teegan said 'two healthy heartbeats.'"

"Are you sure he wasn't referring to two babies?"

"I…" Yelena swallowed. "I thought he meant me and the baby. Can you see?"

"I can try."

She lay back down, and Valek slid his hand under her shirt, resting it on her warm stomach. Reaching with his magic, he sought the baby...or babies. But his power was taken from him before he could sense anything. The more he tried, the greater the drain. He stopped. "Sorry, love. Guess we'll have to find out the old-fashioned way."

"Easy for you to say," she muttered.

"If it helps, the baby has grown in strength as well as size. You're even more protected from—" Struck by an idea, he mulled it over.

"Magic?"

He chased the logic. Excited, he turned to her. "Do you think you could wake those under Bruns's influence with a touch? The Cartel uses magic to manipulate their loyalties, so if you drain that magic away, wouldn't they wake up?"

Yelena gaped at him. "I'm... But Loris was able to control me."

"That was three months ago. And even then, you said you were able to shake off his magic after a few hours."

"What about Cahil?"

"What about him? Did you touch him skin to skin? Or his crew?"

"No." Her face lit up. "It might work."

And if it did, that might just be the break they needed. Valek snaked his hand up her stomach. "This calls for a celebration." Desire purred in his voice.

She grabbed his wrist and plucked his hand from her body. "No. You are to rest, recuperate and recover."

Right. "If I follow your orders, will I get a reward?"

"Yes."

The future had just brightened even more.

MARIA V. SNYDER

Five days later, Valek was finally declared healthy enough for travel. He received his reward the night before they left.

Breathless, and with their heartbeats in sync, they lay together. Valek wondered aloud if their bedroom exertions endangered the baby.

"No. Medic Mommy said we can have relations—those are her words, by the way, not mine—up until the last couple of weeks. However, I'll be huge by then and probably resemble a turnip with legs. I doubt that you'd even want to have relations."

He cupped her cheek. "You are more beautiful to me today than yesterday. Each day, when I think I can't possibly love you any more than I already do, you prove me wrong. So I'm very confident that even if you turn into a turnip with legs, I will love and desire you."

She turned and kissed him on the palm. "I love you, too."

He nuzzled her neck, then nibbled on her ear. "Besides, turnips are my favorite vegetable."

"Am I supposed to melt in your arms after *that* comment?"

He pretended to be confused. "Turnips don't melt." Which earned him a hard smack on his arm. "Ow." He rubbed his bicep.

"Any other comments?"

"You're even beautiful when you're annoyed."

"Nice save."

"The truth is easy, love." He pulled her closer and breathed in her scent. Contentment filled him as he drifted to sleep.

Morning came too soon, but Valek refrained from complaining as Yelena studied his face for signs of fatigue. They said goodbye to Fisk. He'd reluctantly declared the farmhouse his new headquarters until the Cartel was gone.

"It's too quiet. It smells weird. And it's dead boring," Fisk said. "How do people survive out here?"

"Some people like dead boring," Yelena said, smiling at him.

"Well, I don't. Better hurry up and evict those bastards."

"Glad you're feeling better," she said.

He grinned back at her. "Me, too."

Carrying their bags to the stable, Valek and Yelena saddled their horses. When Valek mounted Onyx, the big black horse pranced underneath him, energetic and ready to go.

Fisk followed them. Before they left, he asked, "How will I know if you rescue the Councilors?"

"When we knock on your door," Yelena said.

"Oh."

"If we're not back by the beginning of the hot season, we failed."

"And you're in charge of taking down the Cartel," Valek added.

"Lovely."

"You're the best man for the job," Valek said.

"Yeah, yeah. I'm the *only* man for the job. Better not get caught, or I'm gonna be stuck here and might have to…gasp… farm."

"Well, if that's not incentive to survive, I don't know what is," Valek teased. "Thanks for the pep talk."

"Yeah, yeah." Fisk headed back to the house.

As soon as Valek tapped his heels, Onyx exploded into motion. Kiki ran right beside him. Even with a few detours to avoid patrols and using extra caution when entering Longleaf, they arrived near the Greenblade garrison in three days.

The town was mid-size and had a number of inns. Ari and Janco had a safe house nearby, but Bruns had probably plucked that location from Fisk. Valek doubted the Cartel would be

MARIA V. SNYDER

actively searching for them here, but he ensured they wore disguises when then rented a room at the Thermal Blue Inn for one night. Since they couldn't plan a rescue in a public establishment, Valek would find another dwelling tomorrow while Yelena chatted with the locals. The horses remained in the forest surrounding the town.

They ate a late supper in their room, but they joined the other guests for breakfast the next day. The common room was about half-full. Conversation buzzed and the smell of bacon filled the air. Yelena dug into a huge pile of steaming eggs, but he picked at his, pushing the yellow clumps around his plate. The trip had worn him out more than he'd expected. He'd thought getting pushed from a window by Owen twice was the closest he'd ever come to death. That crystal-clear moment when gravity tugged was forever etched into his mind. The first time, Ari's strong hands had snatched him from that fate, and the second, an unknown rescuer provided handholds. Escaping death a third time had been much harder. He doubted he'd survive a fourth.

A man and his son entered the common room. They strode over to their table. Valek reached for his dagger, but then he recognized the man's swagger.

Janco and Teegan joined them. They both wore disguises.

"You gonna finish that?" Janco asked, sitting next to him.

"Here." Valek slid his plate over.

Janco flashed him a surprised grin before he grabbed a spoon.

"How did you find us?" Valek asked.

"I've been doing daily sweeps since we arrived," Teegan said, tapping his head.

Interesting. Valek hadn't felt any magic. "I didn't pick up on it."

"You're not supposed to." Teegan smirked.

"Can you teach me that?"

The question startled the smirk from Teegan's face. "I don't know."

"Can you try?"

"Yeah, sure."

"Good. I need to keep working on my control and learn what I can and can't do before we take the next step." The boy's presence meant Ari and Janco had caught up to the twins and a Stormdancer. Valek glanced at Janco. "How long have you been here?"

Talking around a mouthful of eggs, Janco said, "Two weeks."

"What about my father?" Yelena asked in alarm. "Did something happen?"

"No. He's fine." He waved his spoon. "Opal, Devlen, Reema and the twins are all fine." Janco lowered his voice. "I'm sure they're making heaps of spores by now. There were just too many rabbits in the stew, and we thought we'd get a head start on things."

"Does that include securing a safe place for all of us?" Valek asked.

"Of course."

"Then we'll finish our discussion there."

After breakfast, Valek and Yelena grabbed their bags from the room they'd rented. They followed Janco and Teegan to a small building a few blocks over. The place had once been a tailor shop. Bolts of moth-eaten cloth, cloudy mirrors and dusty mannequins decorated the first floor. Black curtains covered the large display windows in the front.

Alerted by the noise, Ari came downstairs. After the hellos, he carried Yelena's bag to the second floor, despite her protests, and showed them the living quarters. Teegan and Janco followed them.

MARIA V. SNYDER

"There are three bedrooms," Ari said as he deposited her pack in the unoccupied room. "Janco and I are in there, and Teegan has the little one." He gestured to a door on the left.

Valek set his bag next to Yelena's. There was a living area with a couple couches and armchairs. A few bolts of cloth and parts of a sewing machine littered the floor. The tailor must have lived here.

Janco picked up the top half of a broken mannequin. "This place went bust."

Everyone groaned at the bad joke.

"Come on, guys. That's a classic."

No one agreed.

Ari turned to Valek. "Please tell me you need Janco to travel far away from here for a dangerous undercover mission."

"Let me guess," Yelena said. "He's been driving you crazy."

"Janco and boredom don't mix well."

"That's 'cause the boy genius here has taken all the fun out of everything." Janco pressed his fingertips to his temples. Talking in a falsetto, he said, "They're doing another sweep in town. We'd better hide."

"I do *not* sound like that," Teegan protested.

"Report," Valek ordered before they started to bicker. He settled on the couch next to Yelena. The others sat, or in Janco's case, plopped.

Janco gestured to Teegan. "I'll let the boy genius fill you in."

Teegan gave Janco an indulgent look, as if Teegan was the adult and Janco the child. "I've been spying on the garrison with my magic. I know where the guards are stationed, where the Councilors are housed and, most important, who the magicians are and what they can do."

"That's impressive," Yelena said.

He shrugged off the compliment. "Most of them have been

eating Theobroma, so their thoughts are dripping from their heads."

"Are the Councilors together?" Valek asked.

"Yeah. They're all staying on the second floor of the barracks. Although Master Magician Bain is not there."

"He was moved to the Krystal garrison." Valek considered. "Can you reach Bain from this distance?"

"It's probably too far for us to connect. Why?"

"We're going to need to coordinate with the Masters."

"With your help, we might reach him," Teegan said.

Good to know. "What's the status at the gate?"

"No need to worry about the gate," Janco said. "We have another way into the garrison."

The man appeared mighty pleased with himself. Valek took the bait. "Oh?"

"Heli gave us a storm orb. When you're ready, we'll blast a hole into one of the walls. Ka-boom!" Janco threw his arms wide.

Smart. With that much energy at their disposal, the possible uses were endless. If they had more—

"Way ahead of you, Boss. While Boy Genius and I were scoping out the garrison, Ari paid Kade a visit on the coast and picked up a few more."

Yelena jumped up and hugged Ari. "That's fantastic!"

The big man actually blushed.

"But once we set one of those babies off, there's no more sneaking around," Janco said. "We're committed, big time."

"Hit and git," Yelena said.

He grinned. "Exactly."

"We need to find a location that will limit casualties but is close to the barracks," Valek said.

"Done," Teegan said with a flourish reminiscent of Janco.

"What we don't know is what happens after all hell breaks loose."

Yelena frowned at Janco.

"He didn't learn that from me!"

"Uh-huh."

"The next part is easy. We round up the Councilors and escort them to the farmhouse," Valek said.

"How are you going to convince them to leave?" Teegan asked. "There are eleven of them. I can only influence three or four people at a time."

Impressive. "We'll wear uniforms to blend in and tell them we're taking them to safety."

"And when they realize we're not Bruns's minions?" Janco asked.

"Yelena will convince them to stay with us." Valek explained his theory.

"I thought babies only sucked their thumbs," Janco mumbled.

"Our child is exceptional," Valek said, daring Janco to disagree.

He held up his hands. "Easy there, Papa Bear."

Yelena laughed. "If it doesn't work, we'll fall back on plan B."

"Plan B?" This was new.

"They're sure to drink water that first day, so we'll tell them they've been poisoned. They'll have a week to live unless they get the antidote, which is at the farmhouse. By the time they arrive there, the Theobroma will have worn off."

"Brilliant plan," Valek said with a smile. "Wherever did you get that excellent idea from?"

"Shut up."

"I love you, too."

Janco glanced at Teegan. "I think we're missing something."

"It's probably one of those lovey-dovey things," Teegan said. "My parents do it all the time, and it's gross."

Laughing, Janco said, "Give it a few years, puppy dog."

Valek considered. Once they rescued the Councilors, the Cartel would step up their attempts to find them. They would surround the garrisons with soldiers and be extra-vigilant. Therefore, they couldn't move too soon, or else they'd give the Cartel more time to prepare. If all went well, they needed to rendezvous with the rest of the team by day fifty of the heating season, which was sixteen days away. It would take them at least six days to escort the Councilors back to the farmhouse. What to do in the next ten days?

"Are you up for a field trip?" Valek asked the power twins.

"Always," Janco immediately replied.

"Yes, sir," Ari said.

"Good. I think it's time to have a talk with the Cartel's Master Gardener." He listed a number of questions they'd need to ask. "Think you can handle it?"

"Is sand the most horrid stuff in the world?" Janco asked.

Ari swatted his partner on the shoulder. "He means yes. We can. What's our timeline?"

"Be back here in nine days."

"Got it."

"Am I going with them?" Teegan asked.

"No." Valek glanced at Yelena. "You're going to work with me."

The next day, Ari and Janco set off for their mission. Valek and Teegan rode Onyx and Kiki through the woods north of Longleaf while Yelena remained in town. The scent of pine increased as the air warmed. Birds darted between limbs, cutting through the shafts of sunlight that speared the tree canopy.

When Teegan thought they were far enough away from the magicians at the garrison, they stopped and dismounted.

"What can you do?" Teegan asked.

"I can heal and communicate with other magicians." He described what had happened with the soldiers.

"Not a flameout," Teegan said. "You would have been unconscious for longer than a few minutes. Remember when you healed Leif? You were asleep for days afterward."

True. "Then what was that?"

"You probably overloaded their minds, and they passed out. If you'd knocked them down, they would have been conscious. But we'll soon discover the extent of your abilities. What do you want to start with first?"

"It doesn't matter."

"All right." The boy searched the ground and picked up a thin branch. "Let's see if you can start a fire." He held it up. "Concentrate and direct your magic at this. Think heat and fire. I have to get a little angry at it for it to work for me." Teegan furrowed his brow. Flames erupted on the end of the stick. He extinguished it. "Your turn."

Valek dropped his mental shields. Gathering a thread of power, he aimed it at the branch as Teegan instructed. Nothing happened.

"Try again. It took me a couple times. Think of Bruns. That might help to *inflame* you." Teegan chuckled.

Fueling his magic with rage, he hurled the power. Nothing. Not even a wisp of smoke. A third, fourth and fifth effort had the same results.

"That's a no for fire. Let's see if you can move the branch. Using magic is all the same, really. It's an invisible force that you can manipulate... Well, that's how I imagine it, anyway. To move an object, I picture the magic in the shape of a hand

and reach out and—" the stick flew from Valek's fingers to Teegan's "—take what I want." He grinned. "Your turn."

Valek envisioned a hand, a spoon, shovel, pitchfork and a strong wind, all to no avail. The branch stayed put, but a wave of weakness crashed into him. He leaned against a tree to keep from falling over.

"And that's a no for moving objects." Teegan dug into his pocket, withdrew a small paper bag and tipped a piece of hard candy onto his palm. "Here, this will help."

The sweet taste of strawberries filled Valek's mouth as he sucked on it. After a few minutes, he felt better.

"Okay. Let's see if you can influence me." He gave Valek a cocky grin. "I'll let my defenses down. It's similar to reading a person's thoughts, except you're taking over, giving the orders, and they have to follow them. Just don't have me jumping around like an idiot."

Connecting with Teegan's mind was almost second nature for Valek—a scary prospect. The boy's curiosity dominated.

You're sending too much magic, Teegan thought. *Use the same touch as if you were sneaking into someone's room to assassinate him.*

Valek adjusted the flow.

Better. Now, let's see what you've got, Teegan challenged.

One thing Valek excelled at was giving orders. *Sit down.*

The boy plopped onto his butt, surprising them both.

Keep going, Teegan encouraged him.

Hands up.

Stand.

Come here.

Teegan obeyed each command.

Now I'm going to resist. Let's see how strong you are.

Jump around like an idiot.

The boy grinned but didn't move.

Valek increased the pressure, but Teegan's feet stayed on

the ground. Valek ramped it up a bit more. Still no response, but the boy's cheeky demeanor disappeared as he concentrated on countering the order. With a final burst of energy, Valek threw everything he had at Teegan. Nothing.

Sagging with exhaustion, Valek sank to the ground.

Teegan breathed in deep, wiping sweat from his brow. "That was impressive. Not master-level strength, but I doubt there are many magicians who could withstand that." He pulled a water skin off Onyx's saddle, gulped down a few mouthfuls and handed it to Valek.

"Thanks." The cold water soothed his throat.

"Most magicians have one skill that dominates and maybe a couple others, but those aren't as strong. Like Aunt Yelena has…had…the Soulfinding thing. If she told me to jump, I couldn't resist her. Not even Master Bain can. And then she can heal…in a strange way, but it works. But that's it. I'm guessing your major thing is going to be influencing others, but we'll see." Teegan studied Valek. "I think that's enough for today. We can try again tomorrow."

"I just need a few more minutes, and I'll be ready for more."

"Oh, no. I've strict orders."

Ah. He had Yelena to thank for that. But she was right to limit their session, because by the time they returned to the tailor shop, it took every bit of his energy just to climb the stairs and collapse onto the bed.

The next morning, Yelena wouldn't let him work with Teegan. He had to promise to eat a hearty breakfast, or she would have refused to let him get out of bed. Not that he minded a day in bed as long as Yelena joined him, but her stubborn gaze froze all his desire.

"You're whiter than the Citadel's walls," she said in *that* tone. "You're rushing your recovery and will wind up having a relapse if you're not careful."

He pouted until she agreed to at least snuggle with him. A small but crucial victory—he always slept better with her in his arms.

Finally allowed to do more experiments, Valek and Teegan traveled to the clearing the next day. They worked for a few hours but were unable to discover any more of Valek's talents.

"Try calling the wind," Teegan said. "You might be half Stormdancer, like Zee and Zo."

An interesting thought. Valek reached for the…air. Unlike with living creatures, he couldn't make a connection. Water, too, proved to be unresponsive.

"What about null shields?" he asked.

Valek stilled. "What about them?"

Most of Valek's friends would have recognized the warning tone, but Teegan failed to heed it. "You obviously created one when you became immune to magic. I can teach you how—"

"No." Just the thought of them turned Valek's blood to ice.

"But it could—"

"We have plenty of other people who can create them." Valek stared at the boy. The subject was closed.

Teegan, however, refused to drop it. "We do. To me, magical abilities are like weapons. The more talents you have, the bigger your arsenal." He gestured at Valek. "As an assassin, you have quite the variety of weapons at your disposal. But I'm sure you wouldn't refuse to add another just in case you need it."

Boy genius indeed. "What if I end up…stabbing myself?" And grafting the blasted thing onto his soul again.

"You won't. You have control of your magic now." Sensing a change in Valek's opinion, Teegan continued, "I'll link with you to ensure you don't."

"You're going to make a heck of a Master Magician," Valek said.

Teegan's face lit up at the compliment. "Does that mean you'll try?"

"Yes, but I'm not happy about it."

"An understatement," Teegan muttered. "All right." He explained how to build the shield.

The steps reminded Valek of the fishing nets he'd helped repair on the coast of MD-1. First he wove a web of magic threads coated with...oil was the only way he could describe it. The oil repelled magic. Then he tightened the strands until they formed a sheet, which could be shaped into anything. Valek's napkin-folding skills transferred over to creating shields. By the end of the afternoon, Valek had it down and even managed to impress the boy genius.

"That's all for today, or Aunt Yelena is gonna kill me."

An exaggeration, but Yelena did insist Valek take another day off, which became a pattern—one day of rest, followed by a work day.

On the sixth day, Teegan said, "I think we've explored all the magic talents that *I* know. We could test the extent of your skills with mental communication. You might be a Story Weaver."

Doubtful. "Will that help me when I'm fighting Owen?"

"Not unless you want to heal his mental anguish."

"I'm pretty sure I'll be *causing* him anguish." And pain and death. His fingers twitched at the thought. "We can determine that later." Valek mulled over his plans for stopping the Cartel. "Let's see if the two of us can reach Bain from here."

"All right." Teegan grasped his hand.

The boy's power surged northwest, seeking Bain. His ability to bypass all the other people along the route impressed Valek. He would have skimmed their thoughts, looking for the master magician.

Reading his thoughts, Teegan said, "Master Bain and I have

linked before. It's super easy to find someone once you've done that. It's like spotting a yellow dandelion in a grassy field."

However, even with their combined strength, they were unable to reach Bain. Disappointed but not surprised, Valek strode to Onyx, who napped in the mid-afternoon sunlight, and retrieved the super messenger. "Do you know how much magic is left in this?"

Teegan touched it with his finger. "Not much."

"Do I have enough to contact all the Masters?"

"Not you, but I might be able to, if I keep the conversations short."

Valek guessed that would have to do.

On the ride back to town, Teegan grabbed Valek's arm, stopping him when they were a couple blocks away from the tailor shop.

Instantly alert, Valek scanned the surroundings. "Trouble?"

"Yes."

24

JANCO

All this creeping around could wear a man down. Good thing Janco loved sitting still for hours and pretending to be a bush.

Not.

The compound in the middle of the Greenblade forest hadn't changed too much since Ari and Janco's last visit, when he'd run into Oran Zaltana, who might or might not be the Master Gardener. Ten glass hothouses remained lined up in a row, the sweet aroma of Theobroma mixed with the sharp tang of Curare was still polluting the air as the factories pumped the stuff out by the barrel...or so it seemed.

Yup, if he didn't count the ring of soldiers guarding the place, he'd swear nothing had changed.

They'd crept as close as they dared and had been observing the place for days. Ari and Janco were dressed in green tunic and pants to blend in with the Greenblade workers who buzzed about the site with far more energy than Janco had ever had in his life. Pah.

The best time to approach Oran was when he was alone in his room at night. Otherwise, the man spent all his time inside the hothouses. They'd identified which building he slept in, but not which room. For that to happen, Janco needed to get past the ring of guards.

The soldiers stood within sight distance of each other. If one of them were to suddenly collapse or disappear, his neighbors would know right away. Even if Ari and Janco neutralized half a dozen, there would still be soldiers left standing to raise the alarm.

Well away from the compound, Ari and Janco discussed their pitiful options as the sun set.

"Why can't we use that fancy cloak?" Janco asked.

Ari arranged the kindling into a lattice. "If you had bothered to listen, Teegan explained that since the compound is already covered by an illusion, the mirror illusion would cancel them both out. As soon as we stepped through the barrier, we would be visible."

"Great, just when I was thinking magic might be good for once," Janco muttered.

"At least you're thinking." Ari patted Janco on the head as if praising a well-behaved dog.

Janco growled.

Ari ignored him. "What else can we do?"

"We can create a distraction," Janco said.

"Only if you can create a distraction that won't alert them that something *else* is going on. As soon as the ruckus dies down, you know they'll search the place," Ari said.

"We can start a fire. That'll keep them busy for a while."

"And risk it getting out of control and harming innocent people? No."

Janco flopped onto his bedroll. They'd set up a small temporary camp that could be quickly abandoned without too many tears.

Ari settled next to him. He dug a piece of jerky from his pack and chewed on it. "Let's face it. We can't complete this

MARIA V. SNYDER

mission. The risk of getting caught is too high, and even if we did manage to escape, we might tip our hand, ruining Valek's plans."

Janco disliked failing. Very much. He lay back and stared up at the darkness. However, he agreed with his partner. They lacked recourses. Nothing here but dirt, leaves, bushes, trees—

An idea popped into his heat. What an idiot!

He jumped to his feet. "Ari, do you still have that rope?"

"Yes. Why?"

"'Cause I have a plan."

"The guards—"

"Won't suspect a thing."

"Why not?"

"'Cause I'm not gonna try to go through them. I'm gonna go over their heads." He pointed up to the tree canopy.

"Nice."

The plan was simple and easy, which should have clued Janco in that it wouldn't be as simple or as easy as he'd thought. First, using a rope to climb a tree required a lot of upper body strength. The darkness complicated things as well. Hard to find handholds when you couldn't see your hands.

Once he reached the upper limbs, he didn't need as much muscle. He wound the rope around his waist. However, in order to keep the noise of his passage from tree to tree as quiet as possible, he inched along the branches, which meant he probably sounded like a fat, out-of-shape Valmur. At one point, he imagined the soldiers below having a great laugh as they took bets on how far he'd get before plummeting to his death.

Good thing he wasn't afraid of heights. Or was he? A limb dipped with his weight. He clutched another while his heart swung from rib to rib. Easy there. When his pulse returned to—well, not normal, but not thumping as if his life depended on it—he transferred his feet to a thicker perch. Whew.

When he'd moved far enough away from the ring of protection, Janco unwound the rope and tied it to a sturdy trunk. Going down was easier on his arms but burned his palms. Once on solid ground, Janco paused, listening for sounds that he'd been discovered. All quiet.

Ghosting through the forest, Janco kept to the shadows as he aimed for the building they'd suspected housed the officers and other important people. Not many windows had been installed, probably for security purposes. A few people hustled between the structures even this late at night. Since he was dressed for the part, Janco strolled into the open as if he belonged there.

No one even glanced at him. Janco entered the building and paused. Lanterns lit the corridors, illuminating closed doors. Now what? He couldn't knock on each one and inquire where he might find the Master Gardener…or could he? Maybe pretend there was an emergency?

No. Too risky. He'd just have to do it the old-fashioned way. Once he'd checked all three stories—same design as the ground floor—Janco retreated outside. A few hours remained until dawn. Ari knew not to expect Janco back until the next evening. Janco snooped around a bit but, finding nothing interesting, he returned to Oran's building. Locating a hidden spot with a view of the entrance, he settled into a comfortable position to wait.

Good thing Oran was one of the first to leave, which confirmed he resided there. Now Janco just needed to occupy himself for the rest of the day. He followed a few people to a canteen. He stole a couple apples and a banana. Then he joined a team hauling vines from the hothouses to a factory.

MARIA V. SNYDER

No one questioned him. Everyone looked stressed and harried, so he fit right in.

He kept an eye on Oran as the day turned into night. The man worked inside the hothouses almost nonstop. Late that night, he swung by the canteen, ate supper and headed to his quarters. When Oran reached the door, Janco was a few steps behind him. Oran climbed to the third floor without realizing he had a tail. Only when Janco followed him down the corridor did the man become suspicious.

"What are—"

Janco placed the tip of his knife on Oran's throat. "Quiet. I don't want you to wake your neighbors."

Oran swallowed.

"Your room," Janco ordered. When he didn't move, Janco pressed a little harder. "Now."

The man led him to the last door on the left. Fumbling for a key, Oran finally managed to unlock it. The light from the hallway illuminated a spartan room. Janco pushed him inside.

Oran stumbled a few steps, then spun to face him. "I recognize you."

"Good, that'll save time on the introductions, Oran Zaltana."

Alarmed, the man straightened.

"It took us a while to discover that you're the Cartel's Master Gardener."

"I'm not—"

Janco held up a hand. "Save it." He pointed to the lantern on the night table. "Light that, and then sit down."

Oran hesitated until Janco stepped closer. Then he hurried to strike a spark. Once yellow glowed from the element, Oran settled on the unmade bed. Janco closed the door. The man fisted the blanket in fear when Janco advanced.

"You'll never—"

Janco didn't wait for the rest of the warning. He jabbed Oran with a dart filled with goo-goo juice. Many people had tried telling him he'd never get away with it or that he'd never leave the place alive. And those same people were always wrong. Just once, Janco would love to hear a truly unique threat.

Oran slapped a hand over the tiny wound. "What the hell was that?"

"A truth serum."

"That's…" He gazed around the room as if confused about why it had started to spin.

"Cheating?"

"Yes."

"Who says I have to play fair? The Cartel certainly isn't. Now tell me about your work as the Master Gardener."

"Not me. Nope. I'm…going to be sick." Oran heaved, vomiting onto the floor.

Janco jumped back just in time. Great, a puker. It happened from time to time. A nasty smell invaded the small room. Lovely.

"Who is the Master Gardener?" he asked.

"Bavol doesn't know."

Talking to a person under the influence of goo-goo juice required a certain level of patience. "Know what?"

"He's working for us." Oran giggled. "Shh. Mr. High and Mighty is really a traitor."

"Who's us?"

"The Cartel. Although I suggested *Alliance*…it's a stronger…" He swept a hand out. "You know."

"Word?"

"Yep."

Janco tried again. "Who's your boss?"

"Uptight know-it-all."

MARIA V. SNYDER

"Really? I heard…"

"Don't listen. She thinks she knows it all, but really…nothing."

Ah. "But she's Owen's wife."

"So she says."

"Were the hothouses Selene's idea?"

"No. Bavol's. He built…little bitty one." Oran spread his thumb and index finger about an inch apart. "Clueless to the potential."

"What about the Harman trees? What do they do?"

"Oh…that." He made a dismissive sound. "Uptight know-it-all's pet project."

"But it must be important."

"Not to me. It's a weed."

"You don't know."

"It's Ixian. Not my area of expertise."

He was getting closer. "It's Selene's area of expertise."

"It's unnecessary. I provide plenty of Theobroma."

"Always good to have a backup plan."

"She's killing people." Oran stood up.

Holy snow cats. Janco kept his expression neutral, although his heart danced a jig in his chest. "That's to be expected."

The man wobbled on his feet. "Bavol and I…we…never, not…ever experimented on people. She…" He sank onto the bed. "She's gone now. Took her poison and left."

"Where's she been doing this?" Janco asked.

"Plot behind…" He gestured to the window.

It took Janco a while, but he learned the location of Selene's lab. He pricked Oran with Leif's new sleeping draft and waited for Oran to succumb.

With his time running out, Janco sought the garden plot Oran described. He found rows of young trees stripped of their bark. A small building next to it appeared to be empty. Janco picked the lock and slipped inside.

The smell almost knocked him off his feet. No mistaking the acrid stench of death mixed with bodily fluids. He held his breath and lit a small lantern, planning to do a quick search of the room. Cages filled with dead bodies lined the back wall. Their open, lifeless eyes didn't reflect the light.

The place had all the paraphernalia of a laboratory—beakers, burners, containers and hoses. Nothing else remained that might help them discover what exactly Selene had been doing. Would it be too much to ask for a journal filled with notes?

Sick to his stomach, he turned to leave and spotted another door. Also locked, but he fixed that in seconds. More cages, but this time, people stirred awake inside them. He froze.

"Isn't it a bit early for breakfast?" asked a woman, pushing up on her elbow as she squinted in the light.

Janco debated. There were four of them. He should bolt, but he couldn't. What would Yelena do?

"I'm not with them," he said.

All four scrambled to their feet.

"Are you here to rescue us?" asked an older man. The skin clung to his skeletal face and gaunt arms.

"I...can't," Janco admitted. "I'll be lucky to escape myself. Please tell me what's going on."

"Why should we?" spat the woman. "You're not going to help us."

"Not now. But I promise I will do everything I can to return and free you."

They appeared doubtful. Given their circumstances, Janco didn't blame them. "Look, I'm working with Yelena, the Soulfinder, and we need to know what Selene's been doing so we can stop her. We've been doing everything we can to upset the Cartel's plans."

"I doubt you'll be able to stop them, young man, but if you piss them off, I'd die a happy man." The older man gestured to his companions. "We're the survivors. Selene's been injecting people with sap from the Harman trees. With each batch, she adjusts the concentration. By the time it was our turn to test the sap, she had determined the right dose, and it didn't kill us."

"It did something worse," the woman said bitterly. "We can't use magic anymore. It's all dead air."

Holy snow cats just didn't seem strong enough for this news. Janco stared at her, speechless for the first time in his life. His mind processed the information, turning it over. A small part of him thought magic had caused nothing but trouble, and he'd be happy to see it gone for good. But one thing his friendship with Yelena had taught him was that it wasn't the magic that was evil, but the person who used it to do evil. He finally found his voice. "Do you know if there is a cure?"

"No."

Yikes. "How long have you been here?"

"We *volunteered* a year ago." The woman gave him a humorless smile. "Bought into the entire 'save Sitia' propaganda, until it was too late. Now they don't even bother to feed us the Theobroma or waste magic on us."

"No offense, but why are you still alive?" Janco asked.

"Just in case the poison wears off," the older man said.

That would ruin Bruns's plans. "Has it?"

"Not yet, but I'm hopeful."

"It's been a season, Rurik. It's not coming back," the woman said.

"How long has Selene been gone?" Janco asked.

"Once she found the right concentration, she produced gallons of the stuff. I think she finished with the last batch a couple weeks ago and left soon after," Rurik said.

"Thanks."

When he turned to go, Rurik said, "Remember your promise."

"I will." But right now, he needed to deliver this information to Yelena and Valek.

25

YELENA

The market hummed with activity. Late afternoon was a busy time for the merchants as workers stopped for supplies before heading home for the evening. Dressed in a light green tunic and tan pants, I blended in with the crowd of mostly locals. A few soldiers from the garrison shopped, but they were more interested in the vendors selling roasted pork than in me. I kept an eye on them, though, just in case their focus shifted.

The enticing aroma of fresh baked bread drew me to a popular stand. I was on a mission. We needed more food. Not a surprise. Valek expended a great deal of energy practicing his magic, Teegan was a teenage eating machine and I was pregnant. Mass quantities of bread, meat and cheese were being consumed on a daily basis.

As I lugged my bags toward our hideout, the nape of my neck tingled. I turned right at the next street and glanced back. Two soldiers strode down the street at a brisk clip. They weren't carrying packages, and their gazes were trained on me. I hurried to the next intersection and turned left. Sure enough, they followed me. Unease churned, ruining my appetite. Had someone recognized me at the market? Or had a magician used magic to find me? Either way, I needed to shake the tail.

Recalling my lessons from Valek, I found a short street. I turned down it, and, as soon as I was out of their sight, I dropped my bags, sprinted to the end, bolted left, crossed the road, ducked down an alley and hid behind a row of trash cans. My heart banged against my chest, urging me to keep going. Instead, I pulled out my blowpipe, loaded a dart while palming another and waited.

Boots drummed on the cobblestones.

"This way," one man yelled.

Shadows crossed the mouth of the alley. I counted to ten, then crept deeper into the alley, hoping there was an exit. Avoiding the piles of rotting leaves and puddles of a foul-smelling muck, I encountered a locked gate at the end. Swapping my blowpipe for my lock picks, I popped the lock and eased into the street. A few people lingered near a fruit stand and a horse pulling a cart trotted by, but there were no soldiers in sight.

I drew in a deep breath and took a long, circuitous route back to our hideout. We would need to leave Longleaf right away and camp in the woods until Ari and Janco returned.

Circling the tailor shop, I sought watchers before entering through the back door. The sun hung low in the sky. Valek and Teegan should—

Large shadows broke from the walls and rushed me. I reached for my switchblade, but it was knocked from my hand before I could trigger the blade. Fear shot through me, increasing my pulse to triple time. A sword flashed just as my arms were pinned. I braced for the thrust, but the tip hovered mere inches from my neck. This explained why I'd lost my tail so easily, but not why I'd had one in the first place.

"Search her," a female voice ordered.

MARIA V. SNYDER

The four goons closed in, hands searching and removing most of my weapons.

"She's clean," one goon said.

"Put her in the chair," the lady said.

I was shoved into the old armchair. Dust puffed up in a cloud. The goons moved, making a tight semicircle around me, revealing Selene Moon, Owen's wife. Her long blond hair shone almost white in the sunlight. Normally as pale as Valek, she appeared as if she'd been spending time in the sun. Worry for Ari and Janco flared to life. Had she captured them while they tried to sneak into the compound and learned our location from them? If so, all was lost.

"I see prison's been good to you," I said.

"I wouldn't think you'd be so smug, considering you walked right into our trap." She gestured to the corner. My bags of food were slumped against the wall. "You thought you were safe once you'd ditched the tail." Selene tsked. She had me there. I refrained from commenting. Instead, I dropped my gaze as if dejected, but I scanned the floor for my switchblade and spotted it near her left boot.

One of Selene's goons came down the stairs, increasing the total to five. "Nobody is up there, but there's evidence of at least three others living here," he said.

Selene turned her silver-eyed gaze on me. "Who are they?"

I considered giving her the silent treatment, but I needed to stall for time. Once they dragged me into the garrison—if they didn't just kill me here—it'd be harder to escape. "My Ixian friends. The people who helped stop you and Owen from getting the Ice Moon." Ah, the good old days. Reminding her of the past had the desired effect.

A flush of red painted her cheeks. "Where are they now?"

"Gone on a mission."

"What mission?"

I smiled. "To hunt you down, of course. We know what you've been up to, Selene," I bluffed.

"Is that so?" Her icy tone promised pain.

I ignored it. "Yup."

"Are you having fun?"

Not at all. I gripped the armrests to keep my distress from showing on my face. "Yup."

"Not for long. You have no powers, Yelena. You're not even wearing a null shield. There is nothing to stop me from taking the information from your mind."

Except the baby. But I wasn't going to tell her that. "So why bother with all these questions?"

"I thought I'd give you the option to cooperate."

"How nice, but would you believe anything I told you?" I paused long enough to see her doubtful expression. "No. So why go through all this? Unless…"

Selene arched a nearly invisible eyebrow.

When she failed to take the bait, I continued. "Unless you're still terrified of me."

"Don't be ridiculous. You're no longer the Soulfinder."

Had she done something to ensure my fate? We'd thought it was the baby blocking my magic, but it was just a theory. I could have been targeted around the time of conception. Swallowing my alarm, I bluffed, "How do you know my powers haven't returned?"

"In my experience, once they're gone, they are gone." She smiled, showing a row of straight white teeth. "But just in case, I'll make sure you're never the Soulfinder again."

I lunged, grabbing her wrist. "Too late."

Her goons rushed to her aid, and multiple hands seized me. When I spotted the terror in her eyes, I knew she'd tried to use her magic against me and failed. They broke my grip and shoved me down into the chair.

MARIA V. SNYDER

She rubbed her wrist and stepped back, but then stopped. A cold calculation slid into her gaze. Oh, no.

"That was...interesting. But if you truly had your powers, you wouldn't need to touch me." Selene dropped her hands. "Something else is going on. Care to tell me?"

"No."

"That's okay. We'll find out soon enough. Let's go." She gestured to the goons bookending me.

They seized my upper arms and hauled me to my feet. I struggled and managed to break free for a second before goon number three stepped in. Pinned between all three of them, I gasped for breath from my exertions.

"Don't be ridiculous, Yelena. That baby in your belly won't prevent me from hurting you."

"That's because *I* will prevent you," Valek said from behind her as his knife appeared at her throat.

Everyone jerked with surprise. I silently cheered. My delay tactics had worked.

"Tell your thugs to unhand my wife," Valek ordered.

"Do it," Selene hissed as blood welled under the blade's sharp edge.

They released me. I smoothed my garments, making a show of it as I scanned the room for Teegan. No sign of him. Good.

"Now tell them to return to the garrison."

An odd command. The goons looked at each other in confusion. I met Valek's gaze. He winked at me. Ah.

"Go." Selene waved them off. "Bring reinforcements."

"Please do," Valek said.

Now I was confused, but I trusted my husband.

After the goons left, Valek pushed Selene away. "Let's talk."

She touched the cut on her neck, then glanced at her hand. Blood coated her fingertips. "Big mistake."

"Oh?"

"Owen isn't the only one who knows how to build a null shield."

Valek froze with his hands and knife pressed to his side, acting as if trapped. Not sure of my role in this, I dove for my switchblade. Sweeping it up from the floor, I triggered the weapon. The blade shot out with a distinctive *snick*. Selene faced me.

"I can squeeze the life from him," she said.

"Not before I stab you." I advanced.

Fury and frustration creased her beautiful face. She bolted for the door. I moved to give chase, but Valek caught my arm.

"No. Let her go."

"Why?"

"Because if she and her men went missing, there would be a manhunt."

"But there's still going to be a manhunt once they all return to the garrison and report they've seen us."

"Yes, but the Cartel won't think we've gotten information from Selene and change their plans."

Oh. That was a good point. "It still would have been nice to discover what she knows."

"Who said we didn't?" Teegan asked. He stepped from the back room with a huge grin on his face.

"What if she sensed you in her mind?" I asked in alarm.

"Uncle Valek had her quite distracted. Besides, I'm smooth." He swiped his hand through the air.

Teegan has been spending too much time in Janco's company. Before I could move, Valek wrapped me in his arms. "Thanks," I said into his neck. He smelled of the forest.

"Anytime." He released me and we shared a smile.

"Enough with the kissy face," Teegan said. "They'll be back soon."

Right. "Okay, Mr. Smooth, time to pack up."

MARIA V. SNYDER

We rushed around and grabbed our belongings and the food. Dashing through the streets of Longleaf, we made quite the sight. Eyewitnesses would report that we'd fled town and disappeared into the forest, heading northwest. In reality, we looped around to the south side of the garrison, but far enough away from the reach of their magicians. We hoped.

"What about Ari and Janco?" I asked as we set up camp. "Were they captured at the complex?"

"No," Teegan said.

"How did Selene find me, then?"

"She received a tip from one of the merchants."

So much for my disguise. "We need to warn Ari and Janco not to return to town."

"We're pretty close to their return route. The horses will alert us when they're close," Valek said.

"Are we still going to rescue the Councilors?" Teegan asked.

"Yes. In fact, tonight would be ideal. The garrison commander will send extra patrols into town to search for us, which means not as many guards in the garrison."

"Yeah, but there will be more chance of us running into all those extra patrols," Teegan said.

"And they might find Ari and Janco instead." I paced.

"Don't worry, love. Those two know how to avoid patrols. But you're right. As Janco would say, 'There are too many rabbits in the stew.' We'll hang tight until everything settles down."

Valek spread his bedroll, even though it wasn't full dark yet. Although he tried to hide it, I recognized his fatigue. Normally so graceful and fluid, his movements jerked, as if every action required a great effort.

I sat next to him, and he draped an arm around my shoulders, pulling me closer. "What did you learn at your magic lesson today?" I asked him.

"That he can make an *awesome* null shield," Teegan answered, pumping a fist in the air.

"And how to recognize them." He smiled. "Selene was so pleased with herself, thinking she'd trapped me."

Which reminded me. "And what did you learn from Selene?"

Teegan's humor faded. "She confirmed that the Cartel plans to target all the magicians during the Firestorm—her words, not mine."

"Firestorm?" Valek stared off into the distance. "Which matches our guess that the Commander plans to attack around the time of the fire festival."

"It does. But I don't think they intend to kill the magicians. She took great pleasure in the fact that we were going to be hit with some kind of substance."

"Do you know what the substance does?" I asked, hoping we'd finally learn what exactly the Cartel was planning.

"No, sorry. I only had time for a brief glance into her rotten thoughts. But—" Teegan glanced at the forest.

Both Valek and I reached for weapons.

Teegan shook his head. "It's Ari and Janco. Kiki's leading them here."

Sure enough, two men and four horses appeared from the forest. Dirt and mud splattered their clothing, and their stiff dismounts indicated they'd spent too much time in the saddle.

Janco pulled a leaf from his hair. "I was really looking forward to sleeping in a bed tonight."

"Look on the bright side—if we'd stayed in the tailor shop, you'd be sleeping in the garrison tonight," I said.

He grunted. "So I gathered."

We filled them in on Selene's visit. Ari and Janco exchanged a glance.

"What did you discover?" Valek asked.

MARIA V. SNYDER

"That substance she mentioned is called Harman sap. And it can block a magician's magic."

We all stared at Janco in shock.

"Are you sure?" Valek asked.

"Unfortunately."

"Is there a cure?" My voice was barely a whisper. Perhaps that was what had happened to me. If that was the case, at least it hadn't affected the baby. It was no longer a theory that he or she had some form of magic.

"No one knows," Janco said.

"You haven't been hit with it, Yelena," Ari said.

I clamped down on my emotions. "How do you know?"

"Selene didn't discover the correct concentration until a season ago."

A rush of relief swept through me. I grabbed Valek's arm to steady my wobbly legs. However, the good feelings died when I considered that the Cartel could still target me with the sap, and perhaps block the baby's powers, as well. And the rest of our herd was at risk, too.

"Does it wear off?" Teegan stood as if rooted to the ground.

"They don't know." Janco explained what had happened to the volunteers.

Valek was the first to recover. "It doesn't change anything. We assumed the Cartel planned to target the magicians. This is...kinder, and they can still blame the Commander."

"No wonder the Commander invited Owen in with open arms," Ari said. "He'd jump at the chance to get rid of *all* the magicians."

Janco was the only one not horrified by the prospect. "Maybe we can snag a few vials and use it on Selene, Owen and their sycophants."

We all stared at him.

"What? If they use it on us, then we'll be able to level the playing field. No magicians on either side." He shrugged. "Seems fair to me."

"Fair?" Teegan choked, truly appalled by the prospect of losing his magic forever. "It's—"

"An issue to be discussed later," Valek said, ending the discussion.

Two nights later, we prepared to rescue the Councilors. As the strongest of us, Ari volunteered to throw the storm orb at the wall, but Teegan thought he'd still be too close and might be killed.

"I've watched the Stormdancers. Those things are packed with energy," Teegan said. "I can use my magic to deliver the orb."

Janco shook his head. "According to Heli, it's gotta hit with some force or the glass won't break."

We rigged a slingshot instead, with Valek aiming and Teegan on hand to nudge the orb in case it went off course. Not like we could practice.

I crouched with Ari and Janco about two hundred yards away from Valek. Teegan promised he'd be able to protect the two of them from flying debris, and there was no reason for the rest of us to be with them.

The faint twang of the slingshot reached me a few seconds before a roar of sound dominated all my senses. Wind and pressure flattened me to the ground. Leaves, dirt, branches and a fine white powder blasted over me. My skin felt rubbed raw. The cacophony ended as suddenly as it began. Unless I'd gone deaf.

Janco pushed up to his knees. "Holy snow cats!" His voice sounded very far away.

Glad my hearing still worked, I turned to see what he gaped at. The storm's energy had cleared a path in the forest. And in

MARIA V. SNYDER

the distance, a huge hole replaced the garrison's wall. Then it hit me. There was no sign of Valek or Teegan. Panicked, I jumped to my feet. Ari was right behind me as we waded through the debris, calling their names.

A small hand poked up from a pile of leaves. Ari and I cleared the branches and bits of the wall from the mound. Underneath, Valek covered Teegan's body. His shirt was streaked with bloody rips, but he rolled off the boy with a groan.

Teegan sat up. "Wow. That was…incredible!"

"What happened to protecting the both of you with your magic?" I asked Teegan. My voice was sharper than I'd intended.

He jerked as if slapped. "Didn't expect…so much…power."

I touched his shoulder. "Sorry."

"Not his fault," Valek said. He struggled to stand.

Ari pulled him to his feet as if he weighed nothing. "Let's go before they regroup."

We trudged through the rubble and climbed over the broken edge of the wall. Soldiers milled about in shock, some of them sporting bloody cuts and gashes. A few helped others who lay on the ground. Cutting through the chaos, Teegan led us to the nearby barracks. Chunks of the wall were embedded in the sides of the building, and the glass had shattered in all the facing windows. People streamed from the building, gaping at the damage. A number of them milled about, unable to act, while others looked as if they were waiting for orders.

I pointed to a group of people. "There's Councilor Cowan."

Teegan nodded, then called the Councilors to him with his magic. They shuffled toward us as if sleepwalking.

Ari, Janco, Valek and I guided them to the wall and encouraged them to climb over. All the while, we assured them they would be safe as long as they kept moving away before the rest of the garrison collapsed. When we entered the forest, Councilor Tama Moon resisted.

I clasped her hand and murmured comfort and reassurance in her ear. After a minute, she met my gaze.

Confusion swirled in her eyes, but also recognition. "Yelena, you're here."

"Yes, I am."

"For us?"

"Yes."

"Good."

I hoped that was a sign that the baby had drained the magic brainwashing her, but I didn't know for certain. When she steadied, I moved on to Councilor Bloodgood. I made sure to touch them all during the long trek through the forest. It lasted until dawn, when it became obvious we all needed a break.

"Do you think we're far enough away?" Janco asked. He gulped a mouthful of water before handing the skin to Ari.

"Teegan?" Valek asked.

Valek's injuries looked worse in the daylight. But he wouldn't let me tend to them or use his magic to heal them, claiming they were minor.

"We have a good lead on them. Plus those tracks Janco made earlier have led half of them in the opposite direction," Teegan said.

"Good." Valek studied our traveling companions.

The Councilors huddled in pairs. Their expressions still remained a bit stunned. But none complained or demanded to be returned to the garrison. They thanked Ari as he shared a water skin and strips of jerky. However, I suspected the questions would soon start.

"We need to split up," Valek said.

No one appeared to be happy about this—quite the oppo-

MARIA V. SNYDER

site. And while I trusted Valek had our best interests in mind, the Councilors still believed he worked for the Commander.

"Why?" I asked him.

"We're too big a group. It will slow us down and attract unwanted attention."

"Shouldn't we be *seeking* help?" Councilor Greenblade asked. She spread her hands wide, indicating the trees around them. "My clan will be more than happy to render all of us aid and shelter."

"We can't endanger your clan," I said.

"Endanger them, how? The Commander is our enemy, not our own people," Bavol said, speaking for the first time.

Hostile glares focused on Valek. He met my gaze. "Time for plan B?"

I shook my head. Not yet. Instead, I explained to the Councilors about the Cartel, Bruns, Owen and the Commander.

"No, you're wrong," Councilor Cloud Mist said. "The Cartel is *helping* us defeat the Commander."

"Then why are you in the garrison and Bruns is at the Citadel?" I asked.

"To protect us from assassination." Councilor Cowan pointed at Valek. "To protect us from him."

"If I'd been sent to kill you, you'd be dead by now," Valek said in a flat tone.

Not helping. I held up my hands. "Trust me, please. You need time for your heads to clear. Look beyond what you've been told and form your own opinion. You all know me. I've helped you with various problems in the past. Just give me seven days. After that, if you wish to rejoin Bruns and the Cartel, we won't stop you. I give you my word."

As the silence lengthened, Janco jiggled the water skin, reminding me of plan B.

"I'm willing to wait," Bavol said. "Yelena's risked her life for Sitia many times. She deserves our trust."

Tama Moon said, "Without Yelena, my soul would be forever trapped in another body."

"She saved my wife and your children from the Daviian Warpers," Councilor Stormdance reminded everyone. "We can give her seven days."

Only Janco appeared disappointed that we didn't need to resort to plan B. Relieved that they had decided to trust me, I shook each of their hands to thank them, and to draw off any magical influence that might remain. I wasn't sure if it had worked, another touch certainly couldn't hurt.

Valek split the Councilors into two groups. "Teegan, Ari and Janco will lead Councilor Moon's group. Yelena and I will escort the rest." Valek gathered the five of us together for some instructions. "Teegan, keep scanning for trouble. Head east and then north to the farmhouse. Yelena and I will go north, then east. We'll meet you there."

The trip back to the farmhouse took us longer than expected. Many patrols swept the forests and the roads heading north. It didn't take a genius to guess we'd be traveling toward the Citadel. I hoped no one had discovered Fisk's new headquarters, or else we'd be finished. In order to defeat the Cartel, we needed everyone, including the Councilors, who had finally shaken off the effects of the Theobroma. By the time we neared the end of the journey, our group fully supported us and I hoped Teegan's group felt the same. Bavol and Valek even walked together, debating various courses of action and devising ways to counter the Cartel.

We drew close to the farm on the afternoon of the eighth day, which was also day fifty-two of the heating season. Valek scouted ahead while we waited. He returned with good news.

MARIA V. SNYDER

The place was still safe from the Cartel, and we had visitors. Lots and lots of visitors.

Leif met us at the stables. "Teegan and his group showed up late last night," he said, helping me remove Kiki's saddle.

"How did your mission go?" I asked as I combed the nettles from Kiki's tail.

"We encountered some troubles. At first, the spores wouldn't reproduce, and then Father almost killed the ones we had, but the spores are all blowing in the wind now. Heli, Zohav and Zethan made an effective team. It was kinda scary, actually."

"Did you run into any difficulties returning to the farmhouse?" Valek asked. He groomed Onyx in the next stall.

"The number of patrols has increased the last couple days, but Reema kept us from having any unfortunate encounters with them."

"Reema? What's she doing here?" I asked in alarm.

"Same as us. She's good. We're going to need her." Leif set his jaw. Clearly not happy about the necessity of endangering a child, but determined to defend the decision.

"Does Opal—"

"Yes. She's in the house with Devlen." Leif frowned. "Father's here, too. He won't go home where it's safe *either*."

"Must run in the family," Valek muttered.

We ignored him. I sensed the tension rolling off Leif's stiff shoulders, and his emphasis on the word *either* was a big giveaway. "How's Mara doing?"

He crossed his arms. "She's mad at me. I tried to get her to stay with Mother in the jungle."

Even I knew that wouldn't work.

"What am I supposed to do?" he demanded. "She's been dragged into the middle of all this. She's been captured, beaten and terrorized. I can't *not* try to stop her."

"But you can trust her," Valek said. "She understands the danger and chooses to be here. Respect her wishes, even when it feels like your insides are on fire." His gaze burned into me.

And I'd increased his pain by endangering our baby. But to me, there was no other option. There would be no happily-ever-after for any of us unless we defeated the Cartel. We needed every able-bodied person. And if that meant including a magic-sucking unborn baby, then so be it.

Leif sighed and relaxed. "You're right. I know that. It's just hard. And at times, she's like a stranger to me. She's changed so much."

I touched his arm. "Patience, Leif. Just be there for her. It takes time. But she'll never return to the same woman you married. She can't. None of us can. No matter if our experiences are good, bad or in-between, we all change and grow as the years build up."

He rested his hand on mine. "Thanks. But I'm not going to apologize for wanting to keep her safe."

"You don't have to," Valek said. "You need to apologize for not trusting her."

Again I felt his gaze on me, and I wondered if he was thinking about our problems with trust when I'd been captured by Cahil.

"Apologizing can be quite enjoyable if you do it right," Valek said.

And that would be a yes. Heat swept through me as I remembered just how he had sought my forgiveness.

"I'll take that into consideration," Leif said.

When we finished settling the horses, Leif hefted my saddle bags to carry them into the house.

"Careful. There's a storm orb in there." I tried to tug them away from him. "I can carry them."

"I *trust* that you can." He shot Valek a smug smile as if to

MARIA V. SNYDER

say, *See? I learned something.* "But it would put undue strain on your body. Which is bigger than the last time I saw you."

"Did he just call me fat?" I asked Valek.

"Oh, no. I'm not getting in the middle of this."

I huffed. "I'm six months along, and think I look pretty damn good."

They both rushed to assure me.

The house was stuffed full of people. I counted twenty-six total, including the Councilors. It was a bit overwhelming when Valek and I first entered. Everyone was talking and hugging and laughing, and Leif wasn't the only one to notice my baby bump. Opal and Mara took turns feeling the baby kick, both squealing like two teenage girls when the baby obliged. Eventually we focused on the reason that had brought us all together, and the mood turned serious.

Councilor Bavol Zaltana stood in the middle of the living area. He'd been appointed the spokesperson for the Sitian Council. "I'm glad you all made yourselves at home. I had bought this property in the hopes of developing a way to increase our Theobroma and Curare production. I built the first glass hothouse here four years ago, and it was a success. Worried that it was too visible to Ixian spies—" he smiled at Valek "—I moved it into the Avibian Plains." Then a sadness pulled at his face. "I believed I was helping Sitia. That everything I did would help keep us safe from the Commander. I trusted Oran and had no idea he was giving all my information to Selene. The Cartel played me like the fool I am."

"You can't blame yourself," Tama Moon said. "They played us all using the Theobroma."

"And their plans were brilliant," Valek said. "Even the Commander was caught in their trap."

"How do we stop them?" Councilor Stormdance asked.

He gestured at the people sprawled around him. "This is it, right? The resistance."

Fisk stood up. "We have a few other helpers in the garrisons."

"Onora is in the Citadel, and we have General Cahil's support," I said.

"And don't forget the Master Magicians," Valek said.

"But they have the army," Tama said.

"We hope that won't be for long," I said, and explained our efforts to destroy the Theobroma pods.

"Sorry, Bavol," Esau said, responding to Bavol's horrified gasp. "There was no other way to reach all the hothouses."

"The soldiers will follow the Cartel's orders, even if they're no longer brainwashed," Councilor Bloodgood said. "The threat of an Ixian invasion has always been very real. It's the reason for their very existence."

"But the magicians and those in charge will be able to think for themselves," I said. "That will help."

The mood lightened considerably.

"There is a new problem, though," Valek said.

He explained about the Harman sap, which destroyed the optimistic feelings in the room. Silence followed. Then came the questions.

"The best we can do is warn the magicians," Valek said, cutting through the buzz of alarmed voices. "They can wear extra layers of clothing to keep the darts from reaching their skin and can guard against an attack from both sides."

Bavol gestured to Valek. "We've been discussing the situation on the trip here. Valek has a plan that I believe will work. It'll be dangerous, and we're going to need everyone's full cooperation. If you're not willing to help, please leave now so that if you're apprehended, you won't endanger the rest of us."

No one moved.

Bavol nodded. "Good. Valek, you're in charge."

He stood and gazed at us. I marveled at the situation. The Sitian Council had appointed Valek, who had once been the most feared man in Sitia, to lead them. And he'd accepted it without a moment's hesitation. If he pulled this off, he would save both Sitia and Ixia. And if he failed… I clamped down on that line of thought and listened to my husband with pride swelling in my chest.

"We're going to form four teams," Valek said. He held an open notebook. "The first team is assigned to the Krystal garrison and includes Ari, Janco, Zohav and Zethan, as well as Councilors Krystal, Stormdance and Bloodgood. Second team is stationed at the Featherstone garrison and includes Leif, Mara and Esau, plus Councilors Featherstone, Cowan and Jewelrose. The third team consists of Opal, Devlen, Teegan and Reema, and Councilors Moon, Cloud Mist and Sandseed. They are assigned to the Moon garrison." He looked at me. "The Citadel team will include Yelena, Fisk and Heli, plus Councilors Zaltana and Greenblade."

Valek then explained what he needed all of us to do. "Timing is vital. You must strike at the exact same time on day twenty of the hot season. I want to attack before they march to the Ixian border."

Silence once again dominated the room. I calculated. That was twenty-eight days away. If the spores did their job, then there would be just enough time for the effects of the Theobroma to wear off. Conversations started as people discussed logistics. Most wanted to leave soon so they could be in position well before the date. I considered my part of the plan to breach the Citadel and realized there was one name Valek hadn't included in any of his teams.

I pulled my husband into the room we shared with Leif,

Mara and Esau for a private chat. As soon as he closed the door, I asked, "What are *you* going to be doing?"

"I'm going after Owen."

No surprise. "By yourself?"

"No, love. I'll have help."

"Who? There's no one left!"

"Not in Sitia," he agreed.

Oh. "You still have loyal people in Ixia."

"That's the hope. It's been a while, though. The Commander might have gained their trust." He reached up and rubbed my forehead with a thumb, smoothing my crinkled brow. "Don't worry, love. I'll be in familiar territory, and Owen doesn't know I have magic."

"He might be stronger than you."

"That's possible." Valek grinned. "But I have better aim."

"That cocky attitude is going to get you into trouble."

"*Get* me? I think it's safe to say it's *already* gotten me into trouble more times than I can count."

"Don't look so proud of that." I swatted him lightly on the arm.

He grabbed my wrist and pulled me close. His touch sent spikes of heat through my body.

"Do I need to apologize?" he asked in a husky whisper.

I glanced at the door. There were twenty-four others in the house.

"It locks, and this will be our last chance for a while."

He had me at *it locks*.

The next day, I sorted through my saddle bags. Each of the garrison teams would be armed with one storm orb, and the Citadel team would take the other two. My team would remain at the farmhouse longer than the others, since we were only a few days south of our destination. My knapsack was a

MARIA V. SNYDER

complete mess, so I dumped the contents onto the bed. Weapons, vials, darts and travel clothes in desperate need of a wash tumbled out, along with the box Zitora had given me for Opal.

I'd completely forgotten about it. Picking it up, I searched for her. She sat with her family in the living area. When I caught her attention, I gestured for her to join me in the kitchen.

"That girl is going to be the death of me," Opal said.

"Valek is quite impressed with her." I set a pot full of water near the fire. With so many people in the farmhouse, we kept the hearth burning so there was enough hot food for everyone.

"Reema's proved herself, but I worry she's too confident."

Laughing, I put a tea bag into a mug. "That's always my concern with Valek." I considered. "But it's that confidence that makes them so successful."

"I know. Did you want something?"

I'd forgotten again. Was this another symptom of baby brain? Pulling the box from my pocket, I handed it to Opal. "Zitora said you'd know what to do with this."

Opal stared at the box in shock.

Not the reaction I'd expected. "What's wrong?"

"This is..." Her hand tightened around it.

"It's locked, but you shouldn't have a problem with that." And if she did, there were at least seven of us who could open it in no time. Eight, if I included Reema, who I suspected probably had lock-picking skills by now.

"That's not it." She drew in a deep breath. Her brow creased as if she was conflicted. "I need to talk to Devlen."

"I'm sorry, Opal, I didn't mean—"

"Not your fault. You didn't know."

I waited.

She pressed it to her chest. "There's a syringe full of my blood inside the box."

Of all the things that could have been inside, I'd never thought that would be it. "That's…well, kinda gross, but… why is it significant?"

"You remember the whole nasty business with the blood magic and the Bloodrose cult?"

"Yes." Blood magic was illegal. Those who used it became addicted to the magic and did terrible things in order to increase their power.

"What isn't well known is that after all was said and done, there was still one syringe full of my blood left. The blood was drawn *before* I lost my magic. Basically, if I inject this blood into my bloodstream, my siphoning magic should return."

Now it was my turn to stare in shock. Opal's magic was very powerful. She could siphon other magicians' magic into a glass orb, forever robbing them of their powers. "Who else knows about this?"

"Devlen, Irys and Zitora. But Yelena…" Opal's voice broke. "I don't know if I can… I have no desire to reclaim my powers. But my family is in danger. I should…"

I clasped her hand. "It's your decision. I will support you either way. And I won't say anything, so no one will pressure you."

She nodded, looking a bit more relieved.

Then I remembered the blood Roze Featherstone had injected into her skin to increase her powers. When I'd drained the blood from her, it'd turned black and rancid. "Besides, it might not be…potent anymore. Blood spoils."

"Magic is keeping it fresh. I can feel it through the box," Opal said.

"Oh." Then it hit me. "Oh! I'm glad the baby didn't take it." That would have been terrible. However, it appeared the baby only siphoned the magic aimed at us.

Opal shrugged. "Then I wouldn't have to make a decision."

MARIA V. SNYDER

She peered through the window, deep in thought. "You've lost your magic, too. What would you do in my place?"

"Reclaim my power. No doubt." If only I had filled a syringe with...

I gasped.

"What's wrong?" she asked.

"Opal, you just saved all the magicians in Sitia!"

26

VALEK

"Slow down, love. You're not making any sense," Valek said to his excited wife. Opal stood next to Yelena with a wide grin on her face. They had pulled him away from a meeting with the Councilors for a private chat.

"We have a way to protect the magicians," Yelena said.

"I understood that part. It's the next bit I'm having trouble following. How does extracting a syringe full of blood save a magician's power?"

Yelena glanced at Opal. "I'll let Opal explain. She has more experience."

"Unfortunately," Opal said dryly. "Don't you remember what happened at the Bloodrose cult? With me and Galen?"

"I thought that was specific to you two because you shared blood."

"That was part of it. But in essence, a person's ability to use magic is in the blood. I don't know why, but it's been proven. This magic ability remains in the blood even when it's drawn into a syringe. The power can be transferred to another magician by injecting it into his or her bloodstream, or it can enhance a magician's power by tattooing it into the skin." She rubbed her arms. "But it can also be used if something happens to a magician's magic. As long as it was drawn *before* the ability to wield magic is lost."

It didn't take him long to make the leap in logic. "So, basically, if all the magicians draw a vial of blood and then are hit with the Harman sap, they could theoretically reclaim their powers?"

"Yes!" Opal said.

No wonder they'd been so enthusiastic. He thought through the logistics. "When I contact the Master Magicians, I'll warn them about the sap. They'll have to find enough syringes for everyone and someone who isn't squeamish to draw the blood."

"They only need a few syringes," Opal said. "The blood can be stored in glass vials."

"How do they preserve the samples?" he asked.

"The masters can do it," Opal said. "And I believe Teegan will be able to do it for you and the others who are here."

Valek hadn't even considered his own magic. It was so new, and he hadn't had time to come to terms with it. The thought of being hit by the Harman sap didn't upset him, but he would take the steps needed to preserve the ability, just in case.

When news about the Harman countermeasure circulated, the mood in the farmhouse was positively buoyant. Valek spent the next few days reviewing the plan with his team leaders in the small office. Since Teegan and Leif had the ability to mentally communicate with the Master Magicians, they'd been assigned as the principals. Even though Zethan could only receive a mental communication, he was also picked to be a lead.

"Don't try to contact the masters when you first arrive," Valek instructed them. "There are other magicians in the garrisons who are seeking magic, and we don't want to tip them off that you're nearby."

"Shouldn't the magicians be on our side by then?" Teegan asked.

"Assume they aren't until it's *confirmed* that they are no longer under the Cartel's influence. There are also messengers who are Theobroma-free, so don't take any unnecessary risks. Contact them right before all hell breaks loose."

Smiles all around. Although Zethan's didn't last.

"Zee, Bain will reach out to you," Valek said. "He will know you are coming, and of all the masters, he can bypass anyone who is trying to snoop."

"Just don't be offended when he calls you 'child,'" Leif said. "He calls everyone that, even the Keep's bursar, and that man is only a few years younger than Bain."

When they finished the meeting, Valek asked Teegan to stay. He uncovered the super messenger and handed it to the boy. "Time to contact the masters and let them in on our plans. Start with Bain, then Irys. If there's enough power left, reach out for Zitora. If not, you'll be close enough when you arrive near the garrison."

"And I have a light touch," Teegan bragged.

"There's that."

Then the boy sobered. "I don't know Master Zitora. She might not let me in."

A valid point. Valek considered. "She knows me."

Teegan tapped on the glass. "We should do this together. We'll have more power, and you can answer any of her questions that I don't know."

"Good idea."

"Boy genius, remember?"

"How could I ever forget?" Valek's voice dripped with sarcasm.

Teegan grinned. "Baby brain."

He mock-growled at the boy but couldn't keep a stern ex-

MARIA V. SNYDER

pression. Now that everyone had heard it, the phrase was quickly becoming the excuse for everything. Teegan grabbed his hand, and they contacted Bain, Irys and then Zitora. The magic in the messenger died before they finished their session with Zitora, but Teegan now had a connection to her.

Tired from the effort, Valek considered resting—perhaps Yelena needed a nap—but Ari and Janco entered the office soon after Teegan left. They stood in front of the desk.

"We're not happy about you facing Owen alone," Ari said.

"I don't expect to go toe-to-toe with the man," Valek said.

"What do you expect? 'Cause there are three of them and one of you," Janco said.

"I expect to assassinate them. If I do it correctly, they will have no idea what hit them."

Janco grinned. "Way to go, Boss."

Ari elbowed him. "We still think you should take—"

"There's no one *to* take. And you know it." Valek understood their concern, but there was nothing he could do about it.

"Little Miss Assassin would have been perfect to act as your backup." Janco's expression turned somber.

"Don't worry about her," Valek said. "She's more than capable of taking care of herself."

He brightened a bit. "Yeah. I bet she's driving Brunsie crazy."

"Hanging out with Janco, she certainly had enough experience with the fine art of pestering someone to distraction," Ari said.

"Hey!"

Valek studied his two friends as they bickered. They had saved his life, protected Yelena, and done so much for him over the years, including committing treason by being here instead of with the Commander in Ixia.

And now, he needed to ask them to do one more thing.

Interrupting them, Valek said, "When you breach the garrison, please keep an eye on the twins. They're powerful, but they're still young, and my mother would be upset if anything happened to them." He already had more of an understanding of this parent-child bond, and his own baby wasn't even born yet. Valek could only imagine how much worse it would be once the child joined the world and faced all the dangers and hazards associated with living.

"Will do, Boss," Janco said. "I understand all about keeping mothers happy."

"You do?" Ari asked with a doubtful tone.

"Yes. Just because I *ignore* it doesn't mean I don't *understand* it."

After Valek ensured everyone understood what they needed to do, he planned to leave the next morning. Having the most experience with syringes, Devlen drew a vial of Valek's blood, which Teegan preserved. Valek would find a safe place to hide it on his way to the castle. Each magician would decide where to hide his or her own blood. This ensured that the vials weren't stored in one location and would protect them from being sabotaged by the Cartel.

When he joined Yelena in their room, the desire to lecture his wife about being extra careful and staying alive boiled up his throat with searing bubbles, but he kept it in check. She understood. And he was sure she was biting back on her worries as well.

Instead, they locked the door and spent the evening being together. When they'd exhausted their bodies, they lay intertwined and talked about everything but the upcoming Firestorm.

"If it's a boy, we could name him Valek," Yelena said.

MARIA V. SNYDER

"Then we'd both respond when you called," he said. "No. Too confusing."

"What do you suggest?"

He decided to have some fun. "Rock. That's a strong name."

"It's also an inanimate object. Try again."

"Steel. Another powerful name."

"That's not a name."

"Storm?"

"Valek." She'd had enough.

He considered. "How about Vincent? After my brother." Grief bloomed in his chest for a moment. Valek and Vincent had gotten into a lot of trouble as boys.

Yelena squeezed his hand. "It's perfect."

"But we both know the baby's a girl," he said.

"We do?"

"Yes, we do. What should we name her? Sweetie Pie?"

She elbowed him. "How about Daddy's Little Girl?"

"I like that."

"Figures."

He chuckled, but then thought of their future daughter. She'd be beautiful and strong and smart and stubborn, just like her mother. No doubt about that. "How about Liana?" It was Yelena's middle name, but it also meant *vine*. "She's already wrapped around both our hearts."

"That's lovely."

Morning arrived far too soon. The garrison teams prepared to leave, and the Citadel team gave them a hand with packing. After saying goodbye and good luck to everyone, Valek kissed Yelena.

He refused to say goodbye to his wife. Instead he said, "I will see you in a few weeks."

"You'd better."

Swooping in for another kiss, he cupped her cheek. "Yes, sir."

Valek mounted Onyx. They headed northwest. The Commander's castle was about a three-day ride north, but Valek planned to approach it from the west. He found a stable for Onyx a few miles south of the Ixian border. The horse would draw too much attention and be hard to hide from the Ixian patrols. Realizing that the vial of his blood would likely be safer here than with him in Ixia, Valek hid it in Onyx's saddle. He then packed a small bag and slung it over his shoulders.

When he reached the border, he expected an increase in the number of patrols guarding the edge of the Snake Forest. What he didn't expect was the sheer number of soldiers in the forest. He suspected the Commander—or rather, Owen—planned to have the army in position well before the fire festival. But did that mean they would strike sooner? He hoped not, or all their plans would be ruined.

With so many bodies to avoid, Valek needed to use his magic to enter Ixia undetected and to steal a patrolman uniform. He arrived in Castletown late on the fourth night. Ghosting along the quiet streets, he kept to the shadows. When he neared the safe house on Pennwood Street, he slowed. The place appeared empty, but he extended his magic to search the rooms, just in case. The good news—no ambush waited for him. The bad news—no one else was inside.

Valek waited until late, hoping his agents would return. When it was obvious they weren't coming back, he debated his next move. His agents might have left a message for him, explaining their whereabouts. Or there could be a magical alarm set to go off if he entered the building. Not willing to take any chances, Valek searched for another place to lie low.

He found an empty house that had seen better days. Wedged between two others, the narrow three-story building was

MARIA V. SNYDER

one strong windstorm away from collapse. Cracks scarred the stone foundation, and the wooden beams sagged. The smell of mold permeated every empty room, and a hole in the roof allowed entrance to a variety of birds that nested on the top floor. Valek set up his bedroll in the only dry corner on the ground floor.

The next day, Valek poked around the town, hoping to get a sense of what had been going on in his absence. He noticed the population of the town had dwindled, and the mood was glum, despite the warm sunshine. Also, it was the first day of the hot season, which meant the fire festival was only a month away. There were only two festivals celebrated in Ixia, and both were always highly anticipated.

Valek widened his explorations and discovered the source of their…discomfort. Soldiers filled the festival field outside Castletown. Instead of brightly colored tents, rows of camouflaged military bivouacs lined the ground. He worried that this meant they planned to march sooner. Valek needed a way to confirm their intentions. Perhaps he could mingle with the soldiers in the mess tent? Too risky. What else?

He almost groaned aloud. He could target an officer and read the person's thoughts. Valek wondered when using his magic would become second nature.

He watched the activity from a hidden location for the rest of the day. A few people looked promising, but Valek didn't want to rush it, nor did he wish to rip the information from someone's mind. He'd rather coax it out, so the person would have no idea Valek was ever there. But he doubted he had that light a touch. After a couple days of observation, he found a potential mark—a male captain. The man wasn't ranked high enough to be making decisions but should be aware of the details of the attack.

A few hours after the captain retired to bed, Valek crept to the man's tent—which was rather easy, since no one had bothered to station guards around the encampment. He crouched behind the shelter. Since he wasn't sure of his magical range with this many people around, he preferred to err on the side of caution. Valek hoped the captain would explain Valek's presence in his mind as strange dreams.

Lowering his shield, Valek extended his awareness. The captain was alone. And awake. Damn. Valek floated on the very surface of the man's thoughts. Captain Campbell reviewed all the tasks he needed to do on the morrow. The list was quite long—probably why Campbell couldn't sleep. Most of the items could be taken care of by a lower-ranking officer in the captain's unit, but this man liked to be in control and refused to delegate. Good for Valek, because he sensed the man housed a deep well of information.

Valek used his magic to encourage the man to fall asleep. Once Campbell drifted into a deeper slumber, Valek nudged the captain toward considering the future. Campbell longed for the festival, especially the pit beef and cream cakes.

No sweets once it's over, Valek thought.

No, but something important. Images of soldiers fighting with swords flashed in Campbell's mind. *So much training…better pay off.*

Valek picked up on the man's worry. *Sitia'll be ready for us.*

Yeah. Columns of soldiers formed. They marched right into rows of Sitian ranks. Sadness darkened Campbell's thoughts over the imagined battle. *Casualties can't be avoided in the initial attack.*

Picking up on the word *initial*, Valek gently prodded.

Second attack from the rear. Surprise, surprise, Sitia.

An icy chill ripped through him, but he kept his emotions in check. *How?*

Slow leak over the last couple of seasons. Use the tunnel.

Valek stifled a curse. Owen had been using the smugglers' route under the border to sneak soldiers into Sitia. While the Sitian army fought off the Ixians, another Ixian force would move in behind them. The Sitians would be trapped between the two and forced to surrender. At least the Commander wasn't planning a slaughter.

Hard to hide so many, Valek thought.

Best of the best. Kept out of sight. Assassins in first, to target the leaders.

Even the Cartel?

All *leaders.*

No surprise Owen planned to double-cross Bruns. Good riddance. It was the others that concerned Valek. Without any leaders, Sitia would be easy pickings.

When?

After the Sitian army leaves the garrisons.

That made sense. They'd no longer be protected. Valek needed to warn them, just in case his mission failed.

Before breaking his connection with Campbell, Valek pulled on a bunch of random thoughts so the captain wouldn't suspect he'd been interrogated. The man might, regardless. It was hard to tell. A few sessions with Teegan hadn't given Valek enough experience. He suspected it would take years to fine-tune his skills.

Tired from the exertion needed to read Campbell's mind, Valek returned to his hideout. He lay on his bedroll and pondered the information. At least the timing of the attack remained the same. However, he wasn't sure how to get a message to the resistance. Perhaps he could reach Irys. The Featherstone garrison was the closest to Castletown. But would his fumbling efforts do more harm than good? Another magician could pick up on his attempt, exposing Irys or bringing unwanted attention to his whereabouts.

He decided to wait. If his mission appeared to be headed toward failure, he would endeavor to warn Irys and the others.

Once he'd rested, Valek spent the next three days monitoring the traffic through the castle's gate. The security personnel just about tripped over each other in the narrow opening. And he counted at least three magicians—they stood out due to their lack of visible weapons. Plus Valek recognized Tyen, Owen's chief minion, who spent most of the day glaring at everyone. Probably upset about being assigned to guard duty.

Not a single person touched the compound's walls, which meant the magical alarm remained. And without his agents to help, Valek's chances of getting inside undetected dwindled to zero. If he had a storm orb, he'd be able to breach the castle without any trouble, but that would certainly alert them.

There was only one way to get inside—as a prisoner. But he had to do it right. If he was spotted in Castletown or caught trying to sneak through the gate, Owen would suspect Valek had done it on purpose. Basically he needed Owen to believe he'd outsmarted Valek. That line of thought led to the safe house. It had to be rigged with a magical alarm. Owen would know exactly when Valek entered.

Valek spent the rest of the day and evening preparing for his capture. After midnight, he packed up his things and headed to the safe house. No one lurked inside. Before unlocking the door, he paused. Once he touched the knob, there would be no turning back. If Yelena knew what he was about to do, she'd be very upset. But she'd understand. No one was safe until this was done.

The door swung open without a sound. The dark interior appeared the same. Valek closed the heavy black curtains and then lit a small lantern. He lowered his mental shield but didn't sense any magic. If he'd triggered an alarm, it was beyond his ability to detect. He checked all the rooms and found noth-

MARIA V. SNYDER

ing of note, except for a faint layer of dust. Back in the main living area, he scanned the table. Files had been left behind, and he wondered what Adrik and Pasha had been working on.

When he opened the top file, a pop sounded. The ever-present weight of magic around him disappeared. A single small piece of paper had been tucked inside. It read, Gotcha.

Valek laughed. Owen had set a booby trap for him. There was a null shield around him, which would have effectively trapped him here until they arrived to collect him. Nice. He tested the boundaries of the shield. It circled the table, allowing him some room to move, but not much. He wondered how long it would be before they arrived. Just in case there were other booby traps in the apartment, Valek stayed close to the table. If he set off another one, Owen would think someone else was here. Playing the part of ambushed victim, Valek sat on the table and waited.

They took their sweet time. Probably to rub it in. Fine. Valek's assassin training included patience.

The rasp of a key in the lock roused Valek from a light doze. He pulled his daggers. As soon as the door swung wide, he threw his knife. It thunked into a wooden shield. They'd come prepared. He waited for a clean shot, but as the shielded man advanced, Valek spotted Tyen behind him. To keep up appearances, he tried to hit Tyen with his second throw. But it veered off course as Tyen's magic deflected the blade. The darts Valek had lined up along the table flew off with a single gesture from Tyen.

"Do you have anything else?" Tyen asked with a bored tone.

Valek gave him his cold killer gaze. He spread his arms wide. "Why don't you check my pockets?"

"Cute. Boys." Tyen stepped aside as four thugs fanned to the sides.

They held a net. Ah. He'd wondered how they would contain him without Owen to adjust the null shield. He assumed a null shield had been woven into the rope. Once the net was around him, it would allow them to move him without a struggle. Not about to make this easy for anyone, Valek circled behind the table, keeping it between him and the advancing men. All he could do with only a small space to maneuver.

A needle of pain pricked his neck. Focused on the thugs, Valek hadn't kept an eye on Tyen.

The magician shrugged. "You were screwed either way."

True. Valek pulled the dart from his skin. A heaviness flowed through his body, pressing him toward the ground. His arms felt as if they'd turned to stone. The thugs threw the net over him, and the weight of the ropes knocked him down as the sleeping potion knocked him out.

Dry-mouthed and with a killer headache, Valek woke in one of the cells in the dungeon underneath the castle. Lying on a pallet covered with vile-smelling straw, he rubbed his forehead as he took stock of his situation. No magic surrounded him. Valek concentrated, sensing that the shield had been woven around all the bars of his cell.

His uniform had been replaced with a standard-issue jumpsuit. A faint glow of lantern light flickered on the damp stone outside the bars. He wasn't in one of the deeper levels, which meant he'd probably get visitors. He was alone in his cell for the moment, but multiple forms occupied the cells next to him. When he pushed to a sitting position, the others stood and shuffled close to the bars separating them. Valek recognized all of them—his agents.

"Are you okay?" Adrik asked. Faded purple bruises marked the man's face.

"Yes," Valek's voice rasped. There wasn't any water in the cell.

A shuffle sounded, and then Qamra's hand appeared between the bars. She held a metal cup of water. Valek took the water and downed it, despite the unidentifiable bits floating on the surface.

"Thanks," he said. He scanned the people. A few had cuts and bruises in varying stages of healing. Most were grim-faced, but a couple smiled in anticipation. "Report."

Adrik gestured. "We refused to follow orders and are here awaiting execution. They plan to...burn us alive...during the fire festival." His voice hitched.

Valek didn't blame him. Burning someone to death was cruel and horrific. "The Commander prefers hangings."

"Well, we all know *he's* not making the decisions anymore. That magician thought fire was a more fitting execution."

"And my other agents?"

"Are following the Commander's orders." He pointed to his ear, then signaled. *We have a friend in high places.*

Advisor Maren?

Yes.

Smart, but dangerous. If Owen and the Commander discovered she was only pretending to be loyal, they'd milk her for information before killing her.

We're hoping you have a brilliant plan, Adrik motioned.

He wasn't sure of its brilliance. And he couldn't tell them, either. If a magician read their thoughts, Valek's plan had no chance. *No, sorry, I don't.*

His agents reacted with dismay. Worried, strained expressions replaced the smiles. He hated lying to them, but he hoped they'd forgive him later, once they'd managed to escape.

"That magician, Owen, did something to your bars with his magic," Adrik said, then signed, *He's under the impression that will keep you contained.*

"Then I'm stuck here like the rest of you," Valek said in a defeated tone.

Really? Adrik gestured, still hopeful.

Really.

The mood turned downright ugly.

Valek's expected visitors arrived a few hours later. Owen, Tyen and Maren stood on the opposite side of the bars. The Commander was smart enough to avoid endangering himself by entering the dungeon. The Commander also wasn't the type to gloat—unlike Owen, who looked mighty pleased with himself. Maren kept her expression neutral, though, even when she met his gaze. Standing, Valek moved closer to the door and sized up the enemy. A short sword hung from Owen's waist. Tyen had Valek's daggers tucked into his belt—a nice little dig at besting Valek. Maren was unarmed, as far as Valek could tell, which said quite a bit. Owen might not fully trust her yet.

"I knew you wouldn't be able to resist returning to Ixia," Owen said. "Did you like my trap at your safe house?"

Valek considered keeping quiet, but the man had an ego that Valek planned to manipulate. "It was clever."

Owen preened. "I've been two steps ahead of you this entire time. In fact, I'm quite happy that your resistance is going to use those storm orbs on the garrisons. It'll help me tremendously."

Valek acted surprised, but it just confirmed what Campbell had told him about the attack from the rear.

"No sarcastic comeback?" Owen asked.

Now was the time for silence.

"I guess you've realized you're out of luck and options. You're up first for execution."

"Is it scheduled for tomorrow?" Valek asked.

"No. You'll be going up in flames as part of the grand opening ceremonies for the fire festival. It'll be quite the show."

"Too bad I'm going to miss it," Valek said.

Owen tapped the bars with his finger. "A null shield will be around you at all times. And *I* control that shield. Right now, it's as big as your cell. But all I have to do…" Owen held his hands wide and then brought them slowly together.

Valek stared at the magician, but he kept his senses open to determine the exact location of the shield. If he didn't react properly, it was the end of the road. Owen's lips quirked just a bit as the shield closed around his body. Valek stiffened, pretending his arms were pinned to his sides. A glint of cruelty shone in Owen's eyes, and Valek held his breath as if his lungs were being squeezed. Valek's gaze promised pain and death, but Owen merely laughed at Valek as he held the shield for a very long minute before spreading his hands apart again. Valek sucked in deep breaths, trying not to gasp, which just amused Owen even more. Good.

"Face it, Valek. You can't escape," Owen said.

"I've heard that before. And it wasn't true then, either."

"Is that so?" Owen jerked the door to Valek's cell open. "It's not even locked. Go on, then. Escape."

Unbelievable. Owen had just given him an unexpected gift. Valek strode up to the opening but jerked to a stop just shy of breaking the threshold. While Owen and Tyen delighted in the action, Valek signaled Maren. If she wasn't on board, Valek was done. Maren, however, didn't react at all.

"You're a relic," Owen said. "Your weakness is well known, and any magician who can erect a null shield can beat you. Considering your immunity served you so well all these years, it's ironic, isn't it?"

Valek dropped his shoulders a bit. "I'm well aware of the irony."

"Good. You have lots to think about before I return to escort you to the pyre."

Owen turned to leave.

"I do have one question," Valek said.

The magician paused. "Yes?"

"Any last words?" Valek moved. He stepped through the door, grabbed Owen's short sword and stabbed it deep into the man's stomach. Hot blood gushed over his hands, adding to the satisfaction of seeing the shocked expression on Owen's face.

Maren had a knife on Tyen, but she yelled as the man's magic slammed her into a wall. She crumpled to the ground in a heap as the weapon clattered to the floor. Tyen gestured, and the knife flew at Valek.

Valek dodged the blade, but soon both daggers were sailing through the air and there wasn't enough room to maneuver. He put his back against the wall and waited to grab the weapons when they came close, risking a nasty slice. However, once Tyen caught on to his plan, the man just pinned Valek in place with his magic. Shit.

Pulling power, Valek projected into Tyen's mind. A strong barrier prevented Valek from getting inside.

Tyen stared at him. "Never thought you'd stoop to using blood magic, but that's the only way to explain your magic."

Valek didn't bother to correct him.

"You can't be as strong or as skilled as I am." Tyen spun the knives in the air until their tips aimed at Valek's throat.

"If you stop now, I'll let you live," Valek said.

"I'm a dead man regardless. You know that. Least I can do is take you with me." The blades shot toward Valek.

Desperate, Valek yanked a big chunk of magic. With no time to knit a null shield, he shaped it into a spear and drove it into Tyen's mental barrier with all his strength. It punched a hole right though, flooding Tyen's mind with Valek's magic.

Stop! Valek commanded. *Sleep!*

The man and knives dropped to the ground. Valek peeled away from the wall. The dungeon reeled under his feet as his muscles turned to goo. Collapsing to his knees, Valek scraped his remaining energy together to fumble underneath the jumpsuit. He clawed the flesh-colored putty away from a set of lock picks. He managed to toss them to Adrik before the world spun around him, sending him into a whirlwind of blackness.

Valek woke up in the infirmary. His wrists were cuffed to the metal bars of the bed's headboard, and his ankles were cuffed to the footboard. He would have laughed at how utterly ridiculous it was to secure him, but he didn't have the strength to even produce a sound. At least he wasn't in the dungeon. Small mercies. The next time he woke, Medic Mommy tsked over him. Every single muscle in his body ached, and just the thought of moving sent him back into oblivion.

The third time he roused, he wondered if this was how a newborn felt—unable to do anything but suck liquids. He stopped counting after that. His moments of wakefulness blurred together. Maren's visit eased his worries for her. She reported that both Tyen and Owen were dead. He wished to know how Tyen had died, but that required too much effort.

Instead, he asked, "Rika?" in a whisper.

Maren frowned. "You need to rest. As near as the medic can tell, you're suffering from a complete, full-body exhaustion." She stood to leave. "Was all that about the null shield just a ruse this entire time? If so, it was a pretty damn good one."

So why did she act so unhappy? Was she upset to be left behind when everyone else had gone to Sitia?

Summoning the strength to talk, he said, "No."

She huffed as if she didn't believe him, then strode from the room without answering his question about Rika. Maren didn't return, and over the next few days, Valek regained some of his vigor. Enough so that he longed to sit up and move around, but Medic Mommy also dodged his questions about why he'd been secured.

When he woke next, the Commander stood at the foot of his bed.

"Interesting scar," he said, pointing to Valek's bare chest.

The blanket only covered the bottom half of him. He would worry, but the altered scar was the least of his problems at the moment.

"A wedding present for Yelena," Valek said.

"Ah, yes. I heard about that. And you've a baby on the way, too. Congratulations."

Nice words, but the tone was flat and...dangerous. "Thank you."

The Commander pulled a chair over to the bed and sat down. "I should thank you for killing that bastard, Owen."

"Are you—"

"Yes. *I'm* in full control." Fury blazed in his gaze for a moment. "Just when I start thinking that magicians aren't *all* corrupt and power-hungry, along comes proof that I'm right not to trust them."

"You agreed to work with Owen," Valek said. "If you'd executed—"

"I made a mistake," the Commander snapped. "And I paid for it." He smoothed an invisible wrinkle from his pant leg. "You saved me yet again. I should thank you for that, as well."

Should didn't mean he would. Valek rattled the cuffs. "Not the best way to express your gratitude."

"You're a traitor, Valek. You're helping Sitia, and you were a *magician*." He spat the word as if it tasted vile in his mouth.

But it wasn't the *m*-word that snagged Valek's attention.

MARIA V. SNYDER

Were. He reached for the power blanket. Nothing. Exhaustion or Harman sap? Did it matter?

Yes, it did. The answer surprised him.

"How long did you hide it from me?" the Commander asked.

"I didn't hide it. It happened on my return trip from the coast." He explained what had occurred by Vincent's grave. "All those who said my immunity to magic was a form of magic were right. No one was more astonished than I."

The Commander showed no emotion. "You still should have reported back to me."

"You were under Owen's influence, and I'm well aware of your views. It would have been a death sentence." The conversation had drained his energy. Valek wouldn't last much longer. "My corps?"

"Pardoned."

That was a relief. "Am I still first in line to be barbequed?"

A faint smile. "Hanged."

"Much better." And he meant it.

"The invasion of Sitia will continue as scheduled."

Valek closed his eyes as a wave of crushing dismay swept through him. Even though he'd killed Owen, he'd failed to stop the war.

"Magicians need to be neutralized," the Commander said. "The Sitian Council has proven to be ineffective at keeping them in check. It won't be a bloodbath, Valek. You know that's not my style. The Sitian people will be well taken care of, just like the Ixian people."

He wished it was that easy. Valek opened his eyes and met the Commander's gaze. "It'll be impossible to target all the magicians."

"A few will slip through the cracks," he agreed. "But what

I find very telling is that you didn't ask me *how* we planned to neutralize the magicians."

If he'd had more energy, Valek would have cursed.

"The Sitians know we have the Harman sap," the Commander said, more to himself than Valek. "That'll complicate things, but I'm confident once we target enough magicians, it will be easier to get them all. At least Owen delivered on his promise to produce an effective substance. He never fully trusted me, so he kept the details secret until recently. I suspect he'd just managed to get it to work." His cold smile failed to soften his expression. "Excellent timing for me."

Valek ignored the jab. "What about Rika?"

"She's been in Sitia, helping the Cartel."

Ah, that explained those illusion cloaks.

"Don't worry. She's on my list to be neutralized by the Harman sap," the Commander added. "You were the first, by the way."

"I'm honored."

A flash of amusement crossed his face before the Commander turned somber. "I've missed our conversations." He stood to leave. "I'm going to need a new assassin and security chief. Do you have any recommendations?"

"Onora."

Valek had managed to shock the Commander. He gaped at Valek, speechless. First. Time. Ever.

"I forced her to work for the resistance," Valek said. "She's not a traitor."

"I see."

And the Commander did—he was smart that way. A pang of grief rolled through Valek. Too bad he would have to assassinate the Commander.

27

LEIF

Leif opened his senses and waited for Master Magician Irys Jewelrose to contact him. His team hid in the woods near the back wall of the Featherstone garrison. He reached for Mara's hand and squeezed, reassuring her. The weak moonlight lit her face with a soft white glow. Strain etched lines of worry in her forehead, but if he'd suggested she remain at the inn, where it was safe, Mara would have growled at him.

The growling was new. And while he longed for the sweet woman he married, Valek's comments repeated in his mind. Trust. And perhaps with time, some of the sweetness would return.

Nearby, his father cradled the storm orb in his lap. Leif had constructed a null shield around Esau, Mara and the three Councilors—Featherstone, Cowan and Jewelrose. They also crouched in the underbrush. The buzz of insects was the only sound.

Leif glanced at the moon again, estimating its position in the sky. The attack was scheduled for tonight. They needed to launch it at a precise time or risk ruining the resistance's chances of success. What if Irys didn't contact him? What if she was compromised?

It didn't matter. Leif wouldn't miss the deadline.

He sniffed the air, seeking emotions or any signs that a patrol was close by. Refraining from reaching further, he drew back to avoid alerting the garrison's magicians that he was outside their walls.

The moon refused to move, or so it seemed to Leif. It clung to that one spot, just to annoy him. He suppressed a sigh and squirmed into a more comfortable position.

Leif, Irys's voice sounded in his mind. *We're ready.*

Cooling relief flowed through him. *The soldiers?* he asked.

They're regaining their senses, but a few are stubborn and insist they have to defend against the Commander's army. They might try to stop you.

Leif checked his tunic. Darts loaded with his sleeping draft had been threaded through the fabric. The rest of his team was similarly armed. *Let's hope by the time they figure out what's going on, it'll be too late.*

He signaled the Councilors to secure the slingshot. *Keep well away from the wall*, he told Irys.

Will do. See you on the flip side.

He clamped down on a chuckle.

Once the slingshot was strung between two trees, Leif took the orb from his father. Councilor Featherstone pulled the rubber sling back and angled it. Leif hoped the man's aim was as accurate as he'd claimed. A few other hopes followed in quick succession: hope that they were far enough back to avoid being flattened by the blast. Hope that no one was killed on the other side. Hope that they reached the main administration building before one of Bruns's magicians could warn the other garrisons.

Leif shoved all those worries deep inside. He placed the orb in the sling. The others moved deeper into the woods.

He held up a finger, signaling to the Councilor. One. Two fingers. Three.

Featherstone let go. The orb sailed through the air. Moonlight sparked off the glass, and for a heart-stopping moment, Leif thought it would fly over the wall. But then it smashed into the marble. Lightning exploded, blinding him two seconds before a roar slammed into him.

The force of the storm picked him up, carried him a few feet and hurled him to the ground hard enough to knock the air from his lungs in one whoosh. Bits of greenery floated in the clouds of dust while dirt and pieces of stone rained down on him. When he caught his breath, he sat up. Every muscle ached, and small cuts peppered his arms and legs.

Then he remembered the others. Panicked, he stood on shaky legs, searching for Mara and his father. She materialized from the fog. Blood streamed from a gash on her shoulder, but she waved away his hand.

"I'm fine," she said, reassuring him. "But your father's been knocked unconscious."

She led him to Esau. A nasty gash marked his temple. Leif felt his pulse. Strong. Thank fate. He rolled his father into a more comfortable position and covered him with foliage. "He should be fine. We need to go, or we'll lose the element of surprise."

They assembled and did a quick injury check. Councilor Featherstone and Leif had gotten the brunt of the blast, but nothing serious. The others had minor cuts and bruises.

"Stay close to me," Leif ordered.

Every one grabbed a dart, and the team raced for the ragged hole in the garrison's wall.

Bits of marble crunched underfoot as he led the others. Dust clouded the air, but fuzzy yellow dots marked the location of the torches and lanterns. Shouts and sounds of confusion echoed off the parts of the wall still standing. They climbed over the mounds of debris. Figures rushed toward them.

Leif aimed at the closest man, but Irys yelled, "He's one of ours." She strode into sight with a number of armed soldiers trailing her. Her long hair had been pulled up into a bun. Irys wore a generic Sitian uniform, but there was no mistaking the power in her emerald gaze, nor the commanding posture that only a Master Magician could pull off. She gestured to her men. "Provide cover."

Her soldiers surrounded them in a protective formation. Sweet.

"This way," she said, breaking into a jog.

His team chased her. They headed straight for the administration building where the garrison's high-ranking officers and magicians lived. A thick ring of guards two deep waited for them outside the building. They slowed to a stop. The defenders remained in position despite seeing Irys leading them.

Surprised, Leif asked Irys, "Is Cahil no longer on our side?"

"He sent his men on a mission, but Bruns ordered extra security, and he had to comply or risk being discovered." She glanced at him. "Bruns suspects something is going to happen, but I didn't tell Cahil which night, just in case."

Smart, but it didn't help with this obstacle. He looked over his shoulder, ensuring Mara remained right behind him.

Before he could stop him, Councilor Featherstone strode through their front line and approached the guards. "I'm Councilor Drake Featherstone. This is my garrison, and I'm in charge. Stand down at once."

No one moved.

"What now?" Leif asked Irys. "The noise of a skirmish will alert the magicians inside, and they'll send a message to Bruns."

Irys smiled. "I've a null shield around the building." She

MARIA V. SNYDER

gestured to the guards blocking them. Two of them flew through the air and crashed to the ground. They lay still. "I've been wanting to do that for months."

Ah, yes, so nice to be fighting with a Master Magician again. "Engage," Leif ordered.

The soldiers surrounding them surged forward. He glanced at Mara. "Stay with me."

"I've got your back," she said in a firm tone, even though she trembled.

Irys remained beside Leif as they fought through the chaos. Using the darts, Leif jabbed them into arms and legs while ducking blades. It worked, at least until he faced an aggressive opponent intent on skewering him. Irys's attention was elsewhere, so he pulled his machete to defend himself. Unwilling to inflict any major harm, Leif stayed on the defensive, searching for an opportunity to jab the man with a dart. Except the guard was smart enough to avoid getting too close.

Out of the corner of his eye, he spotted Mara. Distracted, Leif blocked left instead of right, and the man disarmed him. He backed away as the guard advanced. So focused on Leif, he didn't see Mara until she'd stabbed a dart into his neck. The man cursed and rounded on her, but she kicked him in the groin. Hard. He crumpled to the ground.

Mara grinned. "Told you I had your back."

Leif hugged his wife. "That's my girl!"

Working as a team, they wove through the clumps of fighters. Eventually they reached the entrance. Irys joined them soon after with two others.

"The null shield won't stop the magicians from using magic inside the building. I can't tighten it and keep the guards off balance." She hooked a thumb at the melee.

"I have a null shield around Mara, and I can construct another pretty fast if needed."

"Good. They'll be in the main command center on the third floor. Let's go."

Irys led the charge up the stairs. No one tried to stop them. When they reached the landing, the door was closed, but faint lantern light shone underneath.

Booby trapped? Leif asked Irys.

No. They're too busy arguing.

How many?

Four.

Leif turned the knob, opening the door into a large area filled with tables, chairs, desks and file cabinets. Beyond that was another door. It stood ajar, spilling a yellow glow.

Inside, four people gestured over a glass cube sitting on a pedestal. Their voices were clear. "...null shield, you idiot. We need to take this to the roof."

"And risk being shot by a bow and arrow? No thanks."

"Bruns needs to know!"

Leif gestured for Mara and the two soldiers to wait. Weaving through the furniture, Irys and Leif crossed the room without tripping over anything. They paused by the door.

Allow me, Irys thought.

Go right ahead. This was going to be good.

Irys swept into the room, surprising them. They turned and then froze, held immobile by Irys's magic. A number of big, comfortable-looking couches ringed the room, along with a few windows and doors.

"It's safe," Irys called to the others. "Leif, prick them with the darts, please."

Happy to oblige, he yanked a couple darts and approached. The air smelled like black licorice. Deceit. The four magicians were an illusion. He spun, crying a warning just as four people seemed to step from the walls. Another illusion? One swung a mace at Irys, catching the Master Magician on the temple.

MARIA V. SNYDER

She crashed to the ground and didn't move. Not an illusion. And now the null shield surrounding the building was gone.

The three others attacked Mara and the soldiers with such speed that by the time Leif yanked his machete, they were unarmed. Realizing his options were dwindling to nothing, Leif swiped the glass super messenger off the pedestal. Thank fate it was real. He hefted it in one hand.

"Stop, or I'll smash this into a million pieces." Leif hoped they didn't have another one nearby.

Rika Bloodgood pressed a knife to Mara's neck. "Put it down gently, or I'll slit her throat."

He met Mara's gaze. She mouthed the word *no*. But Leif couldn't sacrifice her life. Not even to stop a war. It was selfish, and they'd probably die regardless. His heart twisted with anguish as he set the messenger back on the pedestal.

"Now drop your weapon."

Leif released his machete. It clattered to the floor, making the same hollow sound that echoed in his chest. He gestured to the walls. "Nice trick."

"Not a trick, but skill and talent. I fooled a Master Magician with that illusion."

Modest, too.

"Now move away from the messenger."

He obeyed.

28

YELENA

Crouched near the Citadel's southern gate, I waited. After twenty-three days of fretting, we finally moved into position after the sun had set. In a few short hours, we would launch the orbs and storm the castle…er…Citadel. Valek had decided a strike in the middle of the night would be more effective. Roused from sleep, the soldiers would be disoriented and disorganized. It had worked for the Greenblade garrison, but this time the garrisons had some warning and wouldn't be as scattered.

Fisk's helpers reported that the supply of Theobroma to the garrisons had trickled to a stop. But was it in enough time? A list of worries cycled through my mind. Had Valek reached Owen? Would the other teams be successful? Would the blood really work? Opal had assured us it would, but maybe the Harman sap would be strong enough to overpower the blood. It wasn't like we could experiment. I envisioned everything that could go wrong, and I was quite imaginative.

By the time we traveled to the Citadel, my desire to just get it over with pressed on my skin from the inside out. And I was about to burst. In this mood, I could bring down the walls with my bare hands—no storm orb needed.

Fisk strung the slingshot between two tree trunks. Bavol and Councilor Shaba Greenblade watched for patrols. They'd increased in frequency the closer we traveled to the Citadel. However, Shaba's magic was just strong enough to sense them, giving us enough time to avoid the soldiers. Hopefully Phelan's crew had also avoided the patrols and was now getting ready to target the northern gate.

When the appointed hour arrived, Heli placed the storm orb in the slingshot and, together with Fisk, drew it back and aimed at the Citadel's south gate. It had been barricaded closed, and no one should be around it at this time of the night. It was also the second-closest gate to the Council Hall. Remembering what had happened to Valek's back when we blasted the garrison's wall, I tried to get Fisk and Heli to scoot back a couple...okay, more like twenty feet. Heli assured me she'd be able to direct the storm's energy around them.

I crouched behind a tree as Fisk and Heli launched the orb. The moonlight reflected off the glass as it sailed through the air. The impact rattled my teeth as sound roared to life, ripped through the barricade and blew chunks of the Citadel's walls in every direction. Bits of marble and dust rained for a few minutes. However, a bubble of undisturbed vegetation surrounded Heli and Fisk.

"Wow. Teegan wasn't kidding," Fisk said in a hushed whisper. "That's...the coolest thing I've ever seen! Is anyone else's ears ringing?"

"Move now, marvel later," I said. "Those patrols are all making a beeline straight for us."

"Right."

The five of us dashed through the hole and into the Citadel. Businesses and factories occupied most of the area, but a few had been converted into apartments. People were already peering through the windows and coming to investigate the damage. Fisk led the way, and soon we disappeared through the alleys that he knew so well.

We arrived down the street from the Council Hall. Sliding into a shadow, we watched the main entrance. Soon after, a man raced up the steps and disappeared inside to report the blasts. After a few moments, guards streamed into the street. They split into two teams and raced off, leaving only a few behind at the entrance.

Bavol, Shaba and I stepped from the shadows. We climbed the stairs at a stately pace. By the time we reached the door, the four guards pointed swords at our chests.

"At ease, men," Bavol said in a commanding tone that promised pain if disobeyed. Impressive.

"You don't give orders," one man protested.

"I am *Councilman* Bavol Cacao Zaltana. This is *Council-woman* Shaba Greenblade. We do indeed give the orders. Stand down. Now."

The tips of their weapons wavered.

"Fetch Bruns Jewelrose," Bavol ordered. "Tell him we await his immediate presence in my office." Bavol strode into the Council Hall without waiting for an acknowledgment.

Shaba and I followed him. We made it as far as the middle of the lobby. Bruns stood on the stairs amid an impressive array of armed soldiers, Cilly Cloud Mist and a few other magicians. A sly smile spread on Bruns's face.

I sucked in a breath. Showtime.

Cilly met my gaze. She pressed her lips together, and I sensed a light touch of magic in my mind before it was swallowed by the baby. Confusion creased her expression before she smoothed it out.

Baby, one. Cilly, zero.

"Ah, there you are, Bruns," Bavol said.

"Bavol, what a...surprise. You shouldn't have come. It's much too dangerous for you here."

So he was going to act civilized. At least, for now.

"Nonsense. This is where I and the rest of the Sitian Council *should* be. Don't you agree?"

"No. The Commander has spies and assassins everywhere."

"We accepted that risk when we were *voted* by *our people* to oversee Sitian affairs and protect our citizens. Thanks for stepping in, Bruns, but you're dismissed. Councilwoman Greenblade and I will take it from here until the others arrive." Bavol swept a hand out, indicating the crowd. "Everyone, report back to your stations until further notice."

No one moved.

Bruns clapped. "Bravo. A very convincing performance. However, you don't know your audience very well. All of them are loyal to me. No Theobroma needed."

It made sense, but we'd hoped at least a few had been coerced and were beginning to wake up. Time for plan B. Glancing over my shoulder, I confirmed that all the guards were focused on the action happening inside the hall. Then I reached under my tunic and withdrew a glass storm orb. My baby bump diminished by half the size.

Holding it high above my head in both hands, I said, "Surrender now, or I'll blow us all to bits!"

Many of the soldiers took a step back, but Bruns said, "She's bluffing. She wouldn't kill herself or her baby. This is truly pathetic, Yelena. What do you hope to accomplish?"

"Aww, shucks, Bruns, you saw right though me. You're right. I'm not going to kill us all. I just wanted to distract you." I tossed the orb at the staircase and grinned when they all flinched.

It shattered and released a thick white fog. The smoke swirled without direction for a second, but then raced up and down the steps with enough force to knock people down as they tried to flee. Heli stood near the door. She focused on controlling the air while Fisk and his helpers entered.

"The gas won't last long," I said over the roar of the wind. "Prick them with the Curare. It should work."

The kids moved like scavengers over the bodies. But there were two missing—Bruns and Cilly.

They hadn't come down, so they must have gone up to one of the upper floors.

"Bavol, stay here with Shaba. When the reinforcements arrive, you need to convince them you're in charge," I said. "Heli and Fisk, come with me."

Fisk pulled his knives, and I loaded my blowpipe. We sprinted up the steps, being careful not to step on anyone.

"How do you want to do this?" he asked. "Room by room?"

"Is there another exit?" Heli asked.

"The Masters' entrance," I said.

"This way!" Fisk cut down an empty hallway.

Why was I surprised Fisk knew about it? Little scamp enjoyed ferreting out little-known facts like that. At the end of the hall was a stairway to the ground floor. I paused a moment to listen. Not a sound. Not even the pounding of boots. Good or bad?

"Are you sure they went this way?" Heli asked me.

"No. But they can't escape, so if they didn't, they're still in the building."

We descended two stories. The stairwell ended in a large room where the Masters changed into their formal robes before attending Council meetings. The expensive silk material swayed in the breeze blowing in from the open door.

Fisk cursed and crossed the room at a run with Heli on his heels. Magic brushed my thoughts.

MARIA V. SNYDER

"I see them!" Fisk pointed outside.

"There they are," Heli said.

Before I could stop them, they raced into the empty street. The door slammed shut behind them, plunging the room into darkness.

I yanked my switchblade but wasn't quick enough. A knife poked my stomach with its sharp tip. I froze.

"Drop it," Bruns said on my left.

Could he see in the dark? I released my blowpipe. It clattered to the floor.

"And the knife."

Damn. I let go of that as well.

"I'd love to gut you right now, but I need you. Later," he promised. "Cilly, search her for weapons."

The woman was quite thorough. Too bad she didn't prick her finger on one of my darts. Once she'd collected most of them, Bruns instructed her to lead the way.

He grabbed my upper arm, but his knife remained in place. "Move." He pushed me up the stairs.

"But I thought—"

"You thought wrong," Bruns interrupted me. "My men will wake as soon as that gas wears off. Did you really think I wouldn't protect them against *all* your potions? Just because I didn't need Theobroma to convince them doesn't mean they don't consume it. And I was smart enough to stockpile it, just in case."

He dragged me to the lobby's staircase. Below, Bavol and Shaba waited for the reinforcements, but it didn't take them long to notice us.

"Don't do anything stupid," Bruns said to them. "Or I'll kill your Liaison. Cilly, take care of them."

They remained in place as the magician descended. She held a couple of my darts. She jabbed one into Bavol's arm and pricked Shaba with another. They both stiffened and toppled to the ground.

Feeling sick to my stomach over the turn of events, I stumbled a bit as Bruns led me to his office. Cilly lit a lantern as he pushed me into a chair. His weapon remained pressed against my skin.

"Secure her," he ordered.

Cilly picked up a pair of manacles and yanked my wrists through the wooden slats of the chair's back. The metal cuffs bit into my flesh. I could probably still stand, but my seat would come with me. When Bruns finally moved the blade away from the baby, I took my first deep breath since he'd jumped me.

"Go downstairs and wait for the others to wake," Bruns ordered Cilly. "Then take the Councilors down to the cells before returning."

She nodded and left. Bruns pointed to a glass super messenger on his desk. "I received word from Owen that he captured Valek. The Commander is going to execute him for treason at the opening of the fire festival."

I tried to keep my expression blank, but tears filled my eyes as grief crashed into me. Unable to stop them, they ran down my cheeks and dripped off my jaw.

Bruns studied me with a quizzical expression. "You stayed dry-eyed through far worse. Being forced to cooperate with me, seeing Valek after he'd been beaten…you never blinked. How do you even know I'm telling the truth?"

If I wasn't sobbing, I would have laughed at Bruns's attempt to console me. He actually appeared…upset. He'd had no trouble threatening a pregnant woman with a knife, but making one cry must have been one of those things his mother taught him was not nice. I took a few shaky breaths, trying to control my emotions. No doubt the baby was responsible

MARIA V. SNYDER

for my outburst. Valek might have been caught, but he was a hard man to keep.

Bruns cleared his throat. "And through my magicians, I'm also aware of your attacks on the garrisons. They failed, by the way. And I'll blame the incidents on the Commander. So thank you for your help."

A gamut of emotions rolled through me. I bit down on my lip to keep them in check.

Bruns leaned back and tapped a finger on his chin. "In fact, those gaping holes in the walls won't be easy to defend. Especially with the enemy also on the inside. The Commander's forces should have no trouble conquering the Sitian army. You should be happy about that. Fewer lives lost."

"Thrilled," I said with plenty of sarcasm.

He grunted in amusement, but then turned serious. "There will be casualties, of course. You're not going to leave this room alive. I've learned my lesson and will not take any more chances with you."

"Then what are you waiting for?" I asked.

"Cilly. I promised her she can enact her revenge for her brother's death." Bruns frowned at the door. "How long until the gas wears off?"

Not long. However, the sleeping draft we gave them would keep them asleep for a couple more hours. But Bruns didn't need to know that we hadn't used Curare on his men. In fact, there were lots of things Bruns didn't know.

I shrugged. With my arms pinned behind me, it was harder than expected.

Cilly burst into the room. "They're...coming." She panted. "From all...directions."

Bruns was on his feet in a heartbeat. "Who?"

I answered for her. "The Sitian army." I savored his confusion. Getting caught wasn't part of the plan, but at least I had a front-row seat to his downfall.

He rounded on me. Pressing his knife to my throat, he asked, "What did you do?"

"Me? Other than tonight, not much. But my friends attacked the garrisons a few *days* ago. The Master Magicians were never under your control, Bruns. They've convinced your magicians to report the attacks tonight, instead of when they really happened."

"How? My people are loyal!"

"It's amazing how quickly the magicians switched sides once they learned about the Harman sap."

Bruns growled. "Die."

The blade burned through my skin. Pain ringed my neck. Guilt and grief over the baby dominated my thoughts.

Then a figure slammed into Bruns, knocking him away from me. He recovered and spun, aiming his knife at his attacker, but Onora blocked it with ease. She held a dagger in each hand. Bruns lunged and, while he had a bit of skill with the blade, it wasn't near enough to counter a well-trained assassin. In one smooth move, she sidestepped the attack and stabbed her knife right into his chest.

Cilly screamed and dove for Onora. The magician should have used her magic. Onora disarmed her in two moves and knocked her unconscious with the hilt of her weapon.

Everything had happened so fast that my heart was slow to catch up, but now it banged in my chest and made it difficult to breathe.

Onora stared at Bruns's corpse. An angry flush painted her cheeks. "He was going to kill you."

"Yes, he was." My throat throbbed, and the top of my tunic was wet with blood. My muscles trembled with shock.

Onora met my gaze. "Not on my watch."

MARIA V. SNYDER

29

VALEK

Valek's strength returned in bits and pieces. He'd have a good day, only to relapse the next. They moved his bed into a windowless room with one door. Medic Mommy cared for him, and she informed him he'd been her patient for ten days. The attack on the Citadel would happen in two days' time, and the Commander would invade in twelve days—unless Valek stopped him.

The next time Medic Mommy checked on him, he asked, "Why bother?"

"Excuse me?" She tucked a short strand of hair behind her ear.

"I'm going to die. Why bother to nurse me back to health?"

"Orders." Meeting his gaze, she asked, "Would you rather be tossed into a cell to fend for yourself?"

"Actually, yes." He grinned. "Better chance to escape."

She snorted. "Which is why I also have orders not to release you."

Pity. He tried another tactic. "At least you know the orders are coming from the Commander and not Owen Moon."

"It's better, that's for sure. No one is going to mourn that bastard."

"I'd hoped the Commander would be more grateful."

"You know his stance on magicians."

"But I'm no longer one." He considered. "Do you know if that's what happened to Yelena's magic?"

"I don't know." Medic Mommy glanced at the infirmary's door with a worried frown. "Did Yelena come with you to Ixia?"

"No. She's in Sitia."

The woman visibly relaxed. Valek remembered they were close friends. Time to capitalize on that sentiment. "She's not any safer there. Once the Commander takes over Sitia, she'll be executed, as well."

"He wouldn't do that." But the words lacked conviction.

"He has to. She's trouble." He gave her a wry grin. "Always has been. In order for the Commander to rule the Sitian clans without resistance, he needs to assassinate the Sitian Council, the Master Magicians, Yelena and a few other influential people."

"He'd wait until the babe's born," she said, as if trying to reassure herself.

"He can't risk the baby growing up and plotting revenge for the death of his or her parents. Plus, we both had magic at one point—the baby might turn out to be a powerful magician."

Medic Mommy's face creased in concern. She was all about saving lives. He played his final card. "Before I left, we picked names for the baby. Vincent for a boy and Liana for a girl. What do you think?"

"They're..." She swallowed. "Nice names. I...better get back to work." The medic bolted.

Valek hoped he'd planted a seed. At this point, he had no other options. But the next couple times she checked on him, she avoided all conversation, keeping focused on her duties.

Before she left the next day, he asked if she'd let him stand

MARIA V. SNYDER

up. "Just for a few minutes? Otherwise, you're going to have to carry me to the noose. I give my word not to do anything."

But she shook her head and dashed from the room. When the door opened, he counted four guards outside. The Commander wasn't taking any chances. Valek tensed and relaxed his muscles. Straining against his bonds also helped to keep his body limber. It passed the time. Once he'd flexed each muscle, he started over again. He feared the only chance he'd have to escape was the trip to the noose.

Time dripped by, leaving Valek with nothing to do but think. He didn't like where his thoughts led. The only scenario in which his friends and family didn't perish was if Sitia won. A possibility, if they weren't reeling from the attacks by the resistance. No. Valek doubted Sitia had the skills to beat the Commander's army.

Two, maybe three days later, a muffled sound woke Valek. The door swung open. He blinked in the lantern light as a couple dark figures entered. Only their eyes showed, but Valek recognized Adrik's broad build.

"Vacation's over," Adrik said. He unlocked the cuffs and helped Valek stand.

The world tilted, and he leaned on the bed for a moment.

"Here," Pasha said, thrusting a uniform into his hands.

Getting dressed required some help. But once he could stand on his own, he asked, "Weapons?"

Adrik handed him two knives. Not his, but Valek would rectify that as soon as he was able.

"Time to go." Pasha peered out the door. The four guards lay in a heap in the hallway.

They hurried through the silent and empty corridors. Adrik and Pasha moved as if they'd planned the route in advance. Soon they were outside.

"The gate?" Valek asked. The effort to keep up the pace had winded him.

"Taken care of," Adrik said.

Sure enough, there were a few prone forms on the ground. A handful of Valek's agents waited in the shadows. Most of them had been in the dungeon with him.

"About time, Boss," Qamra said. "Come on. We have reservations for dinner in Sitia, and I don't want to be late."

He scanned his loyal corps. "Thank you."

"Anytime. Now, come on." Adrik headed for the gate.

But Valek remained in place. "You go on without me."

Everyone stared at him.

"But—" Pasha started.

"Stay together and act as if I'm still with you. I'm going to need a couple days, so lead them on a merry chase."

Understanding smoothed her features.

"What do we do when we arrive in Sitia without you?" Adrik asked.

"Find Yelena. She'll make sure you're not arrested or harmed."

"You can't beat him," Qamra said.

"No, but I have to try. It's Sitia's only chance."

"What should we tell Yelena?" Pasha asked.

"That I'm doing this for a peaceful life. She'll understand."

Valek returned to the castle. He knew every inch of the building, from the dungeon's abyss to the rooftops. First he needed a place to hide. He had regained some of his strength while recuperating in the infirmary, but he had to get back into fighting shape before he faced the Commander.

Five days later, he was ready. Well, as ready as it was possible to be, considering his circumstances. Plus only four days remained until the Commander attacked Sitia. To conserve

MARIA V. SNYDER

his energy, Valek decided on a frontal assault versus climbing over the rooftops. Stealth was no longer needed.

After the Commander retired for the evening, Valek strode up to the two men guarding the entrance into his apartment. He hoped his reputation would scare them away, but he was prepared to fight dirty to save energy.

When he approached, he cursed under his breath. Just his luck—Sergeant Gerik was on duty. Valek wondered if the Commander had informed the man that Onora still lived. Gerik growled and pulled his sword when he spotted Valek. That would be a no. The second man also brandished his weapon, but he appeared a bit shaky.

"I should have let you fall to your death," Gerik said, sliding his feet into a fighting stance.

Gerik had been covering the wall the night Valek had visited the Commander. "Onora is alive and well."

That deflated some of the menace from Gerik. Not all, but it was a start.

"How do I know you're not lying?" the sergeant asked.

"Because *your sister* trusts me."

He jerked in surprise. "She told you?"

"Yes. Thank you for saving my life. Now get lost."

The other man took a step back, but Gerik put a big hand on his shoulder, anchoring him in place. "We can't," he said. "The Commander would hang us as traitors. And, no offense, Valek, but if Onora couldn't kill him, you can't, either."

"Gee, thanks for the vote of confidence." Valek drew a knife with one hand while he yanked a couple darts with the other. Before the men had a chance to react, he hit them both in the neck with Leif's sleeping draft.

Gerik yanked his out. "What's this?"

"It's supposed to make you fall asleep," Valek said.

An awkward silence ensued. Finally, Gerik's companion

swayed on his feet and leaned back on the wall. The guard struggled to keep his eyes open and failed. He toppled to the ground.

Showing no signs of drowsiness, Gerik glanced at his companion. "Supposed to?"

"Leif warned us that it doesn't work on everyone." And it was just his luck that he'd found someone who was immune. Valek didn't have the time or energy to spare to fight Gerik. Perhaps he should hit him with a second dart.

Shoving the dart back into his neck, Gerik stretched out on the floor.

Touched by the big man's gesture, Valek said, "Thank you again."

"It was nice knowing ya." Gerik closed his eyes.

Valek unlocked the door into the short hallway that contained only two doors that faced each other. Valek's suite was on the right and the Commander's on the left. He paused as sorrow swelled. Twenty-four years together, and they ended up right back where they started.

The Commander's door was unlocked. Keeping the knife in his hand, Valek entered without knocking, then drew the second blade. Ambrose sat in his favorite armchair by the hearth, sipping brandy. Valek's knives rested on the table in front of him.

Not surprised to see Valek, the Commander smiled instead. "I've been waiting for you." He gestured to an empty glass. "Drink?"

"No, thank you."

"All right, then." The Commander set his drink down and snatched the daggers from the table in one fluid motion. He stood. "Shall we?" He inclined his head toward the right side of the living area. The Commander had cleared away all the furniture.

MARIA V. SNYDER

"Can I convince you not to invade Sitia?" Valek asked.

"No."

"Then we shall." Keeping the Commander in sight, he moved to the cleared area. "I wish to reclaim my knives."

"Oh, you'll get them back soon enough." The Commander attacked.

When they had sparred before, the Commander preferred to remain on the defensive for the first series of exchanges, testing Valek. Not this time. Ambrose lunged, aiming for Valek's throat with the intent to kill in his cold hard gaze.

Valek shuffled back and blocked. The impact reverberated through Valek's bones. The grim knowledge that this fight wouldn't last long coiled around his heart and tightened, evicting the fear and doubt that had been dwelling there. Pure determination pulsed inside him as the Commander increased the pace, striking with unrelenting quick jabs—a brutal street style that Valek hadn't expected.

Unable to match the superfast speed, Valek scrambled to block but remained a hair too slow. The edges of Ambrose's blades sliced the skin on Valek's arms. Pain burned, but he ignored it. Valek had a much bigger problem. He was running out of room to maneuver. If that happened, Valek would leave a smear of blood on the wall as he sank to his death.

Deflecting the Commander's double thrust up instead of to the side, he kicked the Commander in the stomach. The solid impact pushed Ambrose back a few steps, giving Valek a little more room.

Valek sidestepped and dropped to one knee, thrusting his knife toward the Commander's thigh, aiming for the femoral artery. Ambrose dodged the attack and once again Valek was on the defensive. As the fight lengthened, Valek's energy ebbed. He sucked in air and his throat burned with the effort.

Valek rallied and tried a number of offensive techniques.

Familiar with each of them, the Commander countered with ease. The man wasn't even sweating.

After a few more exchanges, Valek sensed he was about to reach the limit of his skills. The certainty of failure brought desperation, which reminded Valek of his rooftop fight with Onora. It was clear there was no way he'd beat the Commander. Not with his knives. And not using conventional fighting tactics.

Bracing for pain, Valek blocked a double jab to his midsection, then dropped his weapons. He grabbed the Commander's wrists and found the pressure points. The tip of a blade pierced Valek's left bicep, but he clamped down hard, pressing his fingers and thumbs on the points.

Ambrose yelled as the all-consuming pain traveled up his arms. Using a pressure point created a unique sensation that dominated the entire body and scattered all thought and reason in the victim. Devlen had taught them to Valek a year ago. In any other fight, Valek would never have resorted to using them, because in any other fight, Valek wouldn't need them to save his own life and ensure his family's safety.

The Commander's weapons clattered to the floor. Valek kept his hold until the Commander sank to his knees. Then Valek released one wrist. He picked up the closest knife and rested the sharp edge on the Commander's neck. Valek let go of the man's other wrist. The fog of pain cleared from Ambrose's golden gaze. He stared at Valek, waiting for death. No fear shone in his eyes. No requests for mercy. No promise to stop the invasion of Sitia in exchange for his life. Not his style.

Valek tensed, preparing to end the Commander's life. But he was unable to execute that final move. Valek couldn't kill him. If he slit the Commander's throat, Valek would regret it. They'd shared too much history, friendship and even love. Ambrose was a part of Valek's family. Owen had ruined everything between them, but Valek wouldn't let the dead magician force his hand.

"Finish it, Valek," Ambrose said. "If you let me live, I'm going to invade Sitia."

And Valek would have to live with the consequences. War and death and no hope for a peaceful life. Or was there hope? Valek's comments to Leif about trust came to mind. Perhaps he should trust the Sitians. They'd certainly proven their resourcefulness in the past. Valek released the Commander. "You can try. Sitia will surprise you."

"Then why the assassination attempt?"

"Because I forgot."

"You forgot what?"

"That *I'm* a Sitian now, and we don't solve our problems by assassination." Valek found his knives and sheathed them. "I'm retiring as Chief of Security. Effective immediately." Valek headed for the door. He only had a few days to warn Sitia.

"I can't let you leave," Ambrose said.

Valek spun with weapons in hand.

The Commander stood and smoothed his uniform. The other knives remained on the floor. "You can't leave without having a drink with me."

Valek stared at Ambrose in confusion. The Commander strode to the chairs by the fire and poured two drinks. Was this an attempt to delay Valek long enough for the security guards to arrive?

"I—"

"Relax, Valek. I'm not going to invade Sitia. You're not going to be executed." He sat in his favorite chair, waiting for Valek to join him.

This seemed too good to be true. "Is this because I spared your life?"

"No. Once I learned Sitia knew about the Harman sap,

I figured that they would have already discovered a way to block the darts. An invasion would be a waste of time and resources right now. But if the Sitian Council loses control again, I *will* invade. They won't get another chance, and I can assure you that the magicians will be a casualty. But for now, I'm betting that when you're hired as Chief of Security for the Council, you will do a much better job of keeping the rogue magicians in check."

Valek tucked his knives away as he sorted through the Commander's comments. "Why did you let me believe you planned to invade?"

"Because I wanted to see what you would do."

Shocked, Valek searched for a proper response. All he managed was, "I almost killed you."

"But you didn't. And now I can trust you again."

Anger boiled up his throat. "Another test?"

"Partly. It was also for peace of mind. I know you won't be coming after me in the future. I'm not getting any younger, and don't wish to be constantly worrying about assassination."

"I'm not the only assassin."

"No. You're the only assassin that can beat Onora, and now me. In my mind, you're the only one who is a threat."

Valek had used two very desperate moves to win both fights. Moves he would be unable to utilize again against either the Commander or Onora, because they would be ready for them. His upper arm throbbed, and a dozen or more stinging cuts seeped blood that soaked his sleeves. Plus his magic and immunity were gone.

Valek certainly didn't feel like a threat.

Now that he didn't need to rush off to warn Sitia of an impending attack, Valek walked over to the armchairs. The Commander's comments had generated a number of unanswered questions. "Have you heard any news from Sitia?

MARIA V. SNYDER

There's no guarantee the Sitian Council and the others will defeat Bruns and his Cartel."

The Commander gave him a flat look. "Who planned the attack?"

"I did."

"Who did you leave in charge?"

"All right, I get it. There's a pretty good chance of success *if* everything goes well."

"I've received a report that the Sitian Council and Master Magicians have regained power and are rallying the troops to counter our invasion. I suspect they'll have a number of soldiers disappointed over the lack of action."

Valek gripped the back of the empty chair as relief threatened to turn his legs into mush. "Yelena?"

"She's been spotted in the Citadel, aiding the Council."

Unable to remain upright, Valek sank into the chair and rested his head in his hands for a moment.

"Onora was seen in her company. Please tell Onora to report back to Ixia immediately."

Valek lifted his head. "Ari and Janco?"

"If they wish to return, they'll be welcome. No charges will be filed against them or the agents who helped you escape a few days ago."

Good to know. "And if Ari and Janco want to stay in Sitia?"

Smiling, Ambrose raised his glass. "Good luck." He drank.

Valek laughed as six months of worry, tension and fear melted away. He grabbed his drink and took a long swig. The smooth white brandy slid down his throat, trailing fire. "The good stuff?"

"I thought the situation warranted it."

"You were that confident I wouldn't kill you?"

"Not at all. If this was going to be my last night, I didn't want to drink inferior brandy." He raised his glass again. "Here's to your new life in Sitia."

Valek clinked and took another swallow. He considered his future. Being with his family would be a highlight, but what else would he do? The vial of his blood might not return his magic. "I'm not sure that the Sitians trust me enough to put me in charge of security, or that I would even accept the position if they offered. My priorities have shifted."

"They'd be fools not to." The Commander sipped his drink. "Would they trust you more if you still had your magic?"

"Probably." Valek leaned back in his chair as fatigue washed through him. If not for his injuries, this could have been any night during the past twenty-four years. He realized with a pang that he was going to miss this.

"I'm not sorry for injecting you with the Harman sap," Ambrose said. "As far as I'm concerned, I've done you a favor."

"I know. I'm well aware of your views on magic." They shared a smile. It was an old argument.

"And you know I've been a hypocrite about it ever since I've learned my mother's soul shares my body. Something that is only possible because of magic."

Valek straightened. This was new.

"If Yelena's powers return, and she doesn't hate me, can you ask her to visit me? I'd like her to send my mother to the sky."

"I'm sure Yelena would be happy to help you if she's able." Valek tapped a finger on his glass. "What if her powers don't return? Would you be more accepting of magicians?"

"In that case, I will use the Harman sap on myself."

It seemed drastic. "That might kill your mother."

"She's already dead."

"No. That might destroy her soul, and she won't find peace in the sky. She'll cease to exist."

MARIA V. SNYDER

"Is your soul dead because of the Harman sap?" Ambrose asked.

"I…" Valek recalled Yelena's description of souls and how she influenced them. A body without a soul was like an empty cup—it lived, but had no awareness or emotions or personality. "No. I'm still…me."

"Exactly. The Harman sap will remove the magic that is holding my mother here." He tapped his chest. "That's the theory. But I'd rather Yelena do it, so I know for sure my mother is at peace." He smoothed a hand over his pants leg. "Speaking of peace, do you think Yelena will be willing to be the Liaison again?"

Good question. "I don't know, but I'll ask her. What if she says no? Who else would you accept?"

"You."

Valek's laugh died in his throat—it would be an interesting job. "I doubt the Sitian Council would agree."

"I'll also work with Ari, but if Janco is assigned the position, I'm declaring war."

Amused, Valek imagined Janco pouting from the insult. "I'll make sure to include that in my report."

They talked late into the night, healing the rift that had grown between them. The Commander then insisted Valek see the medic, and even escorted him to the infirmary. On the way, they stepped over the still forms of Gerik and his partner. Valek wondered what Gerik thought, seeing the two of them together. He guessed Gerik would pretend to sleep until the other man woke.

Medic Mommy's professional demeanor didn't alter when the Commander roused her from sleep and explained.

"I'll leave you in good hands. Good luck, Valek. You and your family are welcome to visit at any time." Ambrose shook his hand and left.

As soon as the door closed, Medic Mommy grinned. "I'm glad you two are friends again." Almost gleefully, she peeled off his shirt and cleaned and then sealed the cuts on his arms. But when she finished and Valek stood to leave, her jovial manner changed in a heartbeat.

She jabbed a finger at a bed. "Sleep." When he hesitated, she stepped closer. "Do I need to secure you?"

An empty threat, but Valek decided right there and then that his future would *not* include being captured, chained, manacled, jailed, beaten, stabbed or knocked unconscious ever again. And while he was dreaming, he included a future in which he spent his days locked in a tower with Yelena and their children. "No, sir."

"Good. Give me eight hours, and then you can leave."

His stiff and sore muscles protested the movement, but he managed to lie down and pull the blanket up before he fell into an exhausted sleep.

When he woke, Sergeant Gerik stood next to his bed. Valek reached for his knives, but the big man held up his empty hands.

"I'm here to escort you to the Citadel," Gerik said. He tried to keep a stern expression, but a glint of cheerfulness shone in his gaze. "The Commander's orders."

Ah. Gerik would see his sister sooner. "And escort the new Chief of Security home?"

"Yes."

The cuts on his arms flared to painful life as Valek pushed into a sitting position. His entire body ached. "Do your orders include carrying the ex-chief to Sitia?"

"If that's what it takes, sir."

"Good to know." Valek stood, although his body threatened to revolt and send him reeling back into bed. He needed at least a couple more *years* of sleep.

Medic Mommy hurried over to inspect Valek's injuries before she discharged him from her care. "Send me a message with your new location. I'll come to deliver the baby."

He was about to remind her of Sitia's capable healers, but remembered the baby's magic-sucking abilities. If anything unexpected happened, they couldn't use magic to heal Yelena or the baby. "I will. Thank you."

They swung by Valek's hiding spot. Valek retrieved his pack and changed into a clean shirt. Then they left the castle.

"Horses?" Gerik asked as they crossed the complex.

"Not this time. Getting into Sitia is going to be tricky, even without horses. The Sitian army is prepared for an invasion, so they will attack anyone or anything exiting the Snake Forest."

A crowd of people waited by the southern gate. The guards on duty saluted Valek as he approached. Pasha and Adrik stood with Valek's other agents. Smiles shone in the bright morning sunlight. It appeared the Commander had orchestrated his rescue. Figured.

"We would have busted you out regardless," Adrik said.

"What if I decided to go to Sitia instead of remaining here?" he asked.

"Then we would have escorted you to Sitia," Pasha said. "But Adrik would have lost a couple of golds to the captain of the watch."

No surprise they'd been betting on him. He shook hands with everyone, thanking them for their years of loyal and excellent service. "Onora is more than capable. I'm sure she'll earn your respect in no time."

Maren waited for him outside the gate. She stood with her arms crossed, blocking the path. Gerik rested his hand on the hilt of his sword, but Maren ignored him.

Instead she asked Valek, "So this is it? You're done?"

"What do you think?"

"I think you broke your pledge to the Commander."

Valek considered. Was she trying to force a reaction? He kept his tone neutral. "I retired."

"Onora's not ready."

"Do you think *you* should be in charge?"

Maren dropped her arms. "Hell, no. No one can do that job."

"I'm flattered."

She huffed. "You're leaving all of us vulnerable. Onora's bound to make mistakes."

Gerik gripped his weapon. Valek put a hand on his arm, stopping the man from drawing the sword. Maren's comment explained quite a bit. "Yes, she will make mistakes," Valek said. "Just like I did when I first started. Just like I did a few days ago. You're right. No one can do the job on his or her own. Not even me. I built a support network to help me, and she will, too. She's already learned how valuable even Janco can be. And you'll be here to help her." Unless… "That is, if you want to stay. You're always welcome to come with me to Sitia."

"Not interested. I pledged my loyalty to the Commander."

Okay, then. "If you change your mind—"

"I won't." She stepped aside. "Tell Ari and Janco to get their asses back up here. Their vacation is over." Maren strode away without saying another word.

Gerik watched her go. "Does Onora need to worry about her?"

"No," Valek said. "Maren has a temper. She'll settle down."

"And if she doesn't?"

"Onora can handle herself." Valek met Gerik's concerned gaze. "Right now, your sister is the best in Ixia and Sitia."

MARIA V. SNYDER

"Right now?"

"There will always be a young hotshot eager to prove himself or herself. Part of the job. Someday, one of them will best her, but I don't think you need to worry about that happening anytime soon."

Gerik smiled. "You lasted twenty-four years."

"Exactly."

Valek calculated. He and Gerik would arrive at the Citadel right at the hot season's midpoint. The day the Firestorm had been scheduled—and a day longer than it should have taken, because he was unable to avoid the Sitian army. The soldiers had blanketed the land south of the Ixian border. The only way to get through without causing an incident was to creep into the encampment at night and find an officer to explain things to. The fact that the Snake Forest had emptied of all but a few border guards helped support his news of the canceled invasion. However, the unit he'd surrendered to didn't have a magician who could communicate with the people in charge.

Since they still didn't quite believe him, the captain sent him and Gerik to the Citadel with an armed escort. Valek longed to retrieve Onyx and reclaim his vial of blood, but as soon as he spotted the white marble walls of the Citadel in the distance, his focus and energy and thoughts all turned to one goal—holding Yelena in his arms.

30

YELENA

"What do you mean, the forest is empty?" I asked Ayven, sure I'd heard wrong.

"The Ixians withdrew all but a few patrols," the magician said.

Ayven stared into a glass super messenger, mentally communicating with Master Magician Irys Jewelrose on the front lines. Or what had *been* the front lines. We expected Ixia to attack in two days' time.

I glanced at Bavol and then at Onora, who'd stayed by my side as much as possible since she'd saved my life. We stood in Bavol's office in the Council Hall. Most of the other Sitian Councilors had joined their regiments in the field. We hadn't received any information or news from Valek since he'd left thirty-two long days ago. Many people assumed he was dead when the Ixian army remained in the forest.

Dare I hope?

"Perhaps Valek was successful after all," Bavol said.

The baby kicked as if in agreement, but I wasn't going to jump to conclusions. By concentrating on the impending invasion, I'd been able to function. And I avoided the dark thoughts that threatened to ambush me late at night.

"Ayven, please contact Master Zitora and ask her about that unit she and Teegan sensed hiding behind our front lines," I said. "See if they know where they are now."

"Okay." He focused on the messenger. A few minutes later, he looked up. "She says the unit has disappeared. She sent Devlen and Teegan to track them, and she's waiting to hear from Teegan."

Good or bad news? Hard to tell.

"Let me know if you learn anything new."

"Will do," Ayven said.

Over the next two days, more reports of the Ixian withdrawal arrived. It was the day of the planned Firestorm, and nothing happened. My emotions swung from confused to concerned to relieved, and settled into a general feeling of unease. Was this a trick? Perhaps the Commander had found a way to get all of his troops behind ours.

Zitora relayed a message from Teegan that the unit was headed east toward the Emerald Mountains. We had positioned a battalion near the tunnel the smugglers had used to get into Ixia. Perhaps we'd moved them too late—not that we'd had a ton of time. We'd only had ten days since we regained control of Sitia and the garrisons.

I sat at Bavol's desk that afternoon, staring at the map of Ixia and Sitia. Was there another tunnel beneath the border? Or another way past our defenses? Onora had left to fetch me some tea, but the baby's rhythmic hiccups made it difficult for me to concentrate. Poor little soul suffered with the hiccups at least once a day. I put a sympathetic hand on my mound. Calling it a bump no longer applied, I'd lost sight of my toes and couldn't touch them without great difficulty. And I still had ten weeks to go! If I grew any larger, I wouldn't be able to fit through the door.

A knock roused me from my musings. Fisk stood at the door with a pleased grin on his face as if he'd scored a good bargain.

"Don't tell me," I said, raising a hand. "You found the perfect hat for your latest client. What's her name?"

"Mrs. Catava." The glow dimmed just a bit. "Not yet. Soon—it's close, I can feel it. However, I found something better than a hat."

"Oh?"

"I found a husband." Fisk stepped aside with a flourish.

Valek stood in the doorway, and the rest of the world disappeared. The next thing I knew, I was wrapped in his arms. Not as close as I would have liked, though, because of the mass of baby between us.

He laughed and rested a hand over my girth. "You're—"

"Watch it," I warned.

"—more beautiful than I remembered," he said.

"Nice recovery."

Cupping my cheeks with his hands, he met my gaze. "I mean it."

Then he kissed me and proved he wasn't lying. By the time he broke away, I was gasping for breath and thinking of continuing our conversation in my bedroom.

A polite cough reminded us that we weren't alone. Fisk stood nearby with Sergeant Gerik.

"Do you know where Onora is?" Gerik asked me.

"The kitchen. She'll be ba—"

He disappeared.

"He thought she was dead," Valek explained. Exhaustion lined his face, and he was too thin. His hands slid down my arms, and he laced his fingers in mine. "I heard you defeated the Cartel. Did anyone... Are there any..."

MARIA V. SNYDER

I understood his reluctance to hear bad news. "Bain Bloodgood had massive heart failure during the attack on the Krystal garrison."

"Ah, sorry to hear that."

"Everyone is still reeling. And now Zitora is First Magician."

"That's a heck of a homecoming." Valek braced for more bad news. "Anyone else?"

"A few soldiers were killed by the blasts from the orbs. It couldn't be avoided. And we can't find Hale in any of the garrisons. I suspect Bruns killed him soon after we escaped the Krystal garrison, but I can't ask him." I explained how Onora had saved our lives.

Valek squeezed my hand. "I owe her a debt of gratitude. How is she doing? Any problems with guilt?"

"I don't think so, but she's been acting like a mother bear protecting her cub. Guess who is her cub?" I tapped my chest.

"That's normal."

"Says the man who wants to lock me in a tower."

"That's normal, too."

"For *you*, maybe."

"Well, I'm glad she's been protecting you. Were there any… incidents at the other garrisons?"

"Other than a few injuries, none of our herd died. Thank fate."

"Injuries? How bad?"

"Janco has a couple of new scars to name. No doubt he'll be boasting about them when we see him. Mara cut her hands pretty badly. Seems Rika Bloodgood had a knife at her throat, but Mara wasn't going to let Leif surrender, so she took matters literally into her own hands."

"Good for her."

"She saved us all. If Rika had warned Bruns…" We all knew the consequences if that had happened. "Irys has already healed Mara, and Irys is talking about giving her a medal for her bravery."

"My siblings?"

"Fine. However, Zohav almost drowned Zethan, or so your brother claims, but I suspect he's exaggerating." I smiled, but sobered when I remembered Bain. We'd all miss him. "Now it's your turn. Owen?"

"Had a very bad case of overconfidence and died in my arms."

"I'm not sorry to hear it. I take it that's when the Commander woke up and recalled his army."

Valek tensed. "Not exactly."

"What happened?"

He sighed. "It's a long story. The short version is the invasion has been canceled, and Sitia can return to normal." He put his fingers on my lips. "I'll fill everyone in on the details once they're all back. Fisk?"

I'd forgotten he was there!

"Yes?" Fisk asked.

"Can you spread the word about the invasion? And please ask Ari and Janco to return to the Citadel with the twins."

"All right."

"Thanks." He returned his attention to me as Fisk left. "Do you have any plans for this afternoon?"

"Not anymore."

"Good." Valek tugged me into the hallway. "Have you been staying in the guest suites?"

"Yes. Are you tired?"

"Not anymore." His gaze met mine.

Heat flushed through me. "My room is this way."

MARIA V. SNYDER

★ ★ ★

Hunger woke me a few hours later. Valek didn't stir when I slipped from the bed. Exhaustion? Or was he finally able to relax?

I dressed and visited the kitchen—again. I imagined I'd worn a path in the rug, since I spent more time eating than sleeping these days. I grabbed a few extra pieces of fruit and cheese for Valek. At least, that was the plan. Since he didn't wake up until the next morning, I felt justified in eating his share.

Onora and Gerik visited us soon after we returned from breakfast. The guest suite had a living area, but they stood instead of making themselves comfortable. I suspected Onora had unwelcome news.

"The Commander has ordered me back to Ixia," she said.

I studied her. She tried to keep a stoic expression, but she appeared a little green, as if she was going to be sick to her stomach. "Are you worried he thinks you're a traitor?"

She glanced at Valek.

He shook his head. "I didn't have time to tell her."

"I'm the new Chief of Security," she said.

Surprised, I turned to Valek.

"I retired," he said.

Clearly we needed to catch up, but that would have to wait until later. I focused on Onora and was happy for her. "Congratulations."

She hesitated. "Thanks."

"Isn't that good news?" I asked, because she still looked queasy. "That's what you wanted. Right?"

"Yes. No. I don't know."

Ah. "The Commander would not have given you the job if he thought you couldn't handle it."

"I know. It's just…overwhelming."

"That'll pass in about five or six years," Valek said.

"Thanks," she said dryly.

"Just remember that you're not alone. And that I owe you one."

Onora peered at him in confusion.

"You saved Yelena's and our baby's lives. If you get into trouble and need help, send me a message, and I'll—"

"—*we'll* come and assist you," I finished for him.

He drew in a breath. I waited for overprotective Valek to frown at me, but instead he amended, "We'll come. And if it's bad, then we'll bring the whole herd with us."

"Herd?" Gerik asked.

Onora smiled in relief, and the color returned to her face. "He means his family and friends."

"*Our* family and friends." I corrected her. "You and Gerik are now part of the herd."

Shocked, Onora glanced at Valek. "We are?"

"Yes. The horses have named you Smoke Girl, but I don't know Gerik's horse name yet."

"Thanks." Another smile, this one with genuine warmth. She then asked Valek for advice on how to make the transition from his leadership to hers go smoothly.

He suggested she rely on Maren for guidance. "She's had years of experience, and my agents trust her. They'll trust you, too, once you've proven that you can handle difficult situations. Don't try to be their friend. Ask their opinions, listen to them, but once you've decided on a course of action, don't let them change your mind. Never show them you're uncertain. Issue orders with confidence, despite how you feel."

"Is that what you do?" I asked.

"Not at all."

"Uh-huh."

MARIA V. SNYDER

He flashed me a grin.

"Anything else?" Onora asked.

Valek sobered. "When you return to Ixia, you'll have a chance to show everyone what type of leader you'll be by how you deal with Captain Timmer."

She stiffened. I didn't blame her. Timmer had sexually abused her when she'd been a young solider in his unit.

"I thought the Commander…" Onora swiped a hand along her throat.

"He's waiting to see if you'd like to execute the captain yourself or if you want him publicly hanged. Or…if you wish to spare the man's life. What you decide will send a message to everyone in Ixia."

"No pressure," she muttered.

I grasped her hand. "You're protecting the citizens of Ixia now. They're in your care. Keep that in mind, and you'll do fine."

She hugged me. Or at least, she tried. Her arms weren't as long as Valek's. We laughed.

"Take care of the baby," Onora said. "If you need some extra protection or a dozen babyguards, just let me know."

I mock-groaned. "A dozen *baby*guards? Don't you start. I get enough of that overprotective nonsense from him." I jabbed my thumb in Valek's direction.

She gave me a smug Janco smile. "Too late."

"Go." I shooed her out the door.

Gerik shook our hands before following her.

After they left, I glanced at Valek. "What happened with the Commander?"

"I'll tell you on the way."

"To where?"

"To fetch Onyx."

We set off that afternoon. Valek borrowed a horse from the council's stables and I rode Kiki, who kept her gait as smooth as possible so I didn't go into premature labor. During the two-day ride to the farm where Valek had left Onyx, he filled me in on his adventures in Ixia. When he told me about the Commander's orders to execute him and still proceed with the invasion, I focused on the fact that Valek had survived and was with me. Otherwise, I'd plot a way to punch the Commander. Hard.

But then his next comment about being poisoned with the Harman sap turned my desire to punch the man into wanting to stab him.

"I hid the vial of my blood in Onyx's saddle," Valek said. "I'm…surprised that I'm anxious to find it. I never wished for magic, but once it was gone…"

"I understand completely."

"I know, love. There's still hope for you, as well."

However, there was no guarantee for either of us. Valek finished his story, and I mulled over the Commander's request to free his mother's soul. "If I can, I'll help him, but I can't promise not to punch him afterward."

Valek chuckled, but then he sobered. "If I do recover my magic, we shouldn't tell the Commander."

"He'll eventually learn about it. Plus, then he won't bother using the Harman sap on anyone."

"That's true. Of course, there's always the chance he'll find another way to neutralize magicians."

"Or someone else might discover a way. There's always going to be another problem to solve. We'll just have to tackle it when the time comes."

"We? I'm retired, love."

I stared at him. "*You'd* let someone else solve the problem?"

"I already have. Onora has my job."

"What about Sitia?"

"I'll help for now, but Teegan, Reema, Zethan, Zohav, Heli and Fisk are all poised to take over, and I'll be happy to let them."

I wasn't convinced that he could remain uninvolved. But only time would tell.

We retrieved Onyx, and Valek's vial remained hidden in the saddle. Both of us relaxed. However, we waited until we returned to the Citadel to inject his blood back into his body. If I missed his vein, it would ruin Valek's only chance to recover his magic.

When we arrived, we headed straight to the infirmary in the Council Hall. To our surprise and relief, Healer Hayes was back and helping at the Hall until the Keep was ready. Hayes instructed Valek to lie down on the bed while he filled a syringe with Valek's blood.

"Why lie down?" Valek asked.

"Just in case you pass out. Unless you want to hit your head on the floor?"

"I'm not the fainting type," Valek muttered, but he settled on the mattress.

"Have you been injected with your blood after losing your magic before?" Hayes asked, knowing full well Valek hadn't. "I don't know what's going to happen." He tied a band around Valek's bicep, right below a cut that had been sealed but still remained bright red. Hayes traced his thumb over the injury, and Valek sucked in a quick breath. "This is getting infected. Do you want me to heal it now or after?"

"Later. If my magic returns, I'll be able to heal myself."

"That's good to know. I can always use help in the infirmary."

"Walked right into that one, didn't I?"

"Yep." Hayes pressed the needle into Valek's arm and pushed the plunger. Red liquid disappeared into his vein.

I suppressed the impulse to hold his hand. The baby's magic-sucking ability might interfere. Instead, I hovered nearby.

Valek stiffened. He squeezed his eyes shut as his fingers curled into fists.

"Talk to me," Hayes said. "What's going on?"

"It burns." He arched his back. "Too hot..." A red flush swept over his pale skin, leaving beads of sweat in its wake. Valek jerked again. Then his head lolled back.

I dug my fingernails into the palms of my hands as I stood there, utterly useless. Glancing at Hayes's calm expression didn't help. "Is he all right?"

The Healer touched Valek's neck. "The toxin in his body is fighting the clean blood. It has overwhelmed his system."

"And that means?"

"He lost consciousness."

I bit back a sarcastic reply about stating the obvious. Instead I asked, "Will he wake up?"

"I hope so. Time will tell."

Must. Not. Strangle. Healer Hayes. Once I clamped down on my panic, I dragged a chair closer to Valek's bed and sat down to wait. There was nothing else I could do. As I watched my husband thrash about as if in the grip of a fever, I alternated between sitting and standing. Each position eventually caused my lower back to ache.

The hours added up. One day turned into two. I slept in the next bed, close but not touching. Visitors came as our friends and family returned from the various garrisons. Leif mixed his sustaining teas.

I paced around Valek's bed. After everything he'd gone

MARIA V. SNYDER

through—being knifed in his heart, being captured by Owen, fighting Onora and the Commander—to be taken out by his own blood? The desire to scream at fate clawed up my throat.

On the third day, Healer Hayes suggested I touch Valek. "The baby might neutralize the magic, and he'll wake up."

Without his magic. Better than without his life. But it was the "might" that caused me to hesitate. When I heard that Ari and Janco had returned, I asked Fisk to bring Janco right away.

I pounced on him as soon as he entered the infirmary. "You saw those survivors in the Greenblade forest. Did they say anything about the Harman sap that might help Valek?"

Janco's movements lacked his customary grace. He appeared tired and was probably in pain. The mischievous spark didn't flash from his gaze as he stood next to Valek's bed. "Wish I could help, but all I know is Selene reduced the concentration of the sap until it stopped killing her test subjects. She would know. Did she survive?"

"I don't know."

Energized, Janco squeezed my shoulder. "I'll find out."

"I doubt she'll cooperate."

"Oh, I don't think that will be a problem." A fierce expression gripped his face.

For the first time in days, I had a reason to hope. However, the next day Janco returned with Ari, and they both looked glum.

"Sorry, Yelena," Janco said. "The survivors of Selene's experiments were freed, and they managed to find and kill her."

There was nothing left to do but try Hayes's suggestion. I stood next to Valek's bed and cupped his sweaty cheek. He stilled and sighed. But he didn't wake.

"He might be exhausted," Hayes said. "Give him some time."

★ ★ ★

While we waited, there was a succession of meetings in the Council Hall. At one point, everyone who had been involved in stopping the Cartel, plus the two Master Magicians and Cahil, all assembled in the Hall. Twenty-eight people total, if you didn't include the three scribes who took turns writing everything down. Each of the teams reported what had happened at the garrisons. Fisk and I explained what had occurred at the Citadel. Then I related Valek's adventures in Ixia.

"Do you think the Commander plans to invade Sitia in the near future?" Councilor Tama Moon asked me.

"As long as the Sitian Council remains in power, he will not get involved or attempt to take control of Sitia. However, if you are compromised again, the Commander will act."

"Noted. And you say he's open to having a Liaison again."

"Yes."

"Yelena, would you be willing to resume your duties as the Liaison?" Councilor Featherstone asked.

Would I? I rested my hand on my belly. Hiccups vibrated against my palm. "Not at this time. I'm going to be busy with *other* duties the next few years."

Smiles ringed the room, but I couldn't share their good humor while Valek remained unconscious.

"All right. Please add that to the list of items the Council needs to discuss."

It took all day for everyone to report. The Council spent another day addressing the most immediate concerns. Cahil was charged with rebuilding the garrisons. The Master Magicians had already started clearing the Keep of debris, and the Council allocated a couple dozen soldiers to help them. The Masters aimed to reopen the school on the first day of the cooling season—twenty-three days away.

Opal, Devlen and their children returned to Fulgor. Teegan

MARIA V. SNYDER

would be back to continue his studies with the rest of the students, which now included Zohav and Zethan. They planned to fast-track Teegan's master-level training since they were in dire need of more masters. Reema had to wait a few more years before she could attend. The news didn't go over well with her, to say the least.

Heli returned to the coast, where Zethan would join her and the Stormdancers for the next storm season. Leif was asked to be the new Liaison. He accepted the job, as long as Mara could accompany him on all his missions. She beamed. I couldn't stop a twinge of jealously over their happiness. Once I acknowledged it, I moved on and was able to congratulate them both with genuine love and warmth in my heart.

I spent every night with Valek, sleeping pressed next to him. I talked to him, relating what had happened at the garrisons. Ari and Janco visited and told him how they'd attacked the Krystal garrison. Each took a turn telling their version of the story. Of course they kept interrupting each other to protest a comment or argue over a particular detail. I thought Valek would wake just to order them to shut up. He didn't.

That night, it took me a long time to find a comfortable position to sleep. My bulging belly made lying on my back or stomach impossible. It didn't help that my thoughts swirled with worry. I'd been avoiding making any decisions, since I couldn't face a future without Valek. I finally drifted into an uneasy sleep a few hours past midnight, but a cold touch jerked me from my nightmares. I yelled and almost punched the dark shape next to me until I realized it was Valek.

I struggled to sit up. "Valek?"

"Hmm?"

All the emotions I'd been holding in broke through my barrier. Clinging to Valek, I sobbed. He wrapped his arms around me. My cries were loud enough to bring Healer Hayes.

He carried a lantern. "What's wrong?"

Valek blinked in the bright light.

"About time. How do you feel?"

"Hungry."

"I bet. I'll be back." Hayes set the lantern on the night table and left.

Valek turned to me. He wiped the tears off my jaw with a thumb. "Thanks."

"For what? I took your magic."

He shook his head as if that didn't matter. "For guiding me home. I was lost in a world of fire and didn't know how to leave." Valek picked up my hand and rested it on his stubbly cheek. Then he covered it with his own. "You showed me the way."

Was he in the fire world? Or just lost in fever dreams? "That was days ago."

He frowned. "How long?"

"About a week."

Valek groaned. "I've spent most of the hot season lying in a bed." He threaded his fingers in mine. "There's only one good reason for being in bed. And it's not sleeping." He gave me a tired leer.

"I brought soup and some bread. Be careful not to eat too much," Hayes said, carrying a tray into the room.

Valek let go of me to sit up. Then he grinned.

"It's just chicken broth. No need to get that excited," Hayes said.

But I understood. "Your magic?"

"Looks like I'll be helping Healer Hayes after all."

A few days later, Valek was released from the infirmary. We returned to the guest suite, but eventually we would move to the apartment over Alethea's bookshop until classes started at the Keep. Then we would stay in Irys's tower while Valek explored what he could and couldn't do with his magic. Irys speculated that Valek had gone into the fire world while he was unconscious, which was very similar to the master-level test. Because Valek couldn't leave without my help, his magic wasn't strong enough to be a master.

Soon after, my father left for home, but not before promising to be back with Mother when the baby was born. "I'll warn you now," Esau said to me in the living room of the guest suite. "Your mother will want to discuss plans for your wedding celebration."

"Even with a grandchild distracting her?" I asked.

"This is your mother we're talking about. She can be very persistent and stubborn."

Valek burst out laughing, and we both looked at him in confusion.

"Sorry," he said, wiping his eyes. "It's just I have a feeling that I'll be saying that very same thing to our son or daughter in the future."

"Hey," I said in mock outrage.

Esau clapped him on the back. "Just remember it's those qualities that made us fall in love with them in the first place."

"Really? I thought it was because she said I looked stunning in my dress uniform. Love at first compliment," Valek joked.

I marveled at my husband. I'd never seen him so happy and carefree.

Ari and Janco stopped by later that night for a visit. I'd relayed Valek's information to them about the Commander welcoming them back, but they'd wanted to wait for Valek to wake up before they decided anything.

"You certainly took your sweet time," Janco said to Valek as he plopped into one of the armchairs. He propped his feet up on the ottoman and sighed.

Ari shook his head. "The boy has no manners."

"What? I'm supposed to wait for an invitation to make myself comfortable?" Janco pished.

Sitting in another armchair, Ari made it appear small in comparison to his large frame. "You both look better," he said.

I opened my mouth to thank him, but Janco waved a hand. "Pah. Small talk. We're beyond small talk."

"True," Valek agreed. "You're here to say goodbye."

Janco straightened. "How did you know?"

Valek waited.

"Yeah, well, I guess we spent a lot of time working together." He frowned. "But we think we'd be bored here in Sitia."

"We?" Ari asked.

"Well, Ari is too polite to use the word *bored*, but we realize that you are going to build a nest and settle down."

"Nest?" I asked.

"Home, nest, you know what I mean. You don't need us getting in the way. And Little Miss Assassin needs us more."

I wasn't surprised by their decision. "I'm glad. Onora has a rough road ahead of her, and having friends will make it easier."

"We'll visit, of course. Someone has to teach the kid how to get away with stuff that you won't let him or her do."

I glanced at Valek. "Remind me to never leave Janco alone with our child."

"Hey!"

We all ignored him.

"And we'll drop everything and come if you need us," Ari said.

"Unless you need us to change diapers. Then forget it." Janco waved a hand under his nose.

MARIA V. SNYDER

"Just remember, we also can offer aid if you need it," Valek said to them.

"Will do." Janco saluted. "Our herd may roam, but we all know where is home."

The students returned to the Magician's Keep on the first day of the cooling season. The New Beginnings feast was a highly anticipated affair. I hadn't been to one in years. But this year's feast represented so much more than the start of a new school year. Everyone needed a night of celebration and fun after being under the Cartel's influence.

Before the party, Valek stood in front of the mirror in our rooms in Irys's tower. He wore a silver silk tunic with black piping, black pants and a silver belt—formal Sitian dress clothes—and they showed off his athletic physique. He'd regained weight and muscle tone since he'd recovered from the Harman sap. And I'd gained about a hundred pounds in baby weight...or so it seemed. He was sleek and sexy, and I was the size of a heifer.

"I feel ridiculous," he said, yanking at his high collar. "I'm the oldest student ever to attend the Keep. Can we skip the feast?"

"No. It'll be fun. Don't worry, you'll be working with Irys and Teegan and won't have to attend classes with the first-years."

"Thank fate."

We entered the dining room and wove through the clumps of people, stopping and talking as we headed for the buffet. Food first, dancing second. After we ate, Valek pulled me to the dance floor. He twirled me around as the music vibrated through the air.

Zethan mingled among the students and faculty with ease, but Zohav stayed on the edges of the room, frowning at anyone who approached her. Valek coaxed her onto the dance floor, while I partnered with Zethan.

"Don't worry about Zo," he said when he noticed the direction of my gaze. "She'll thaw eventually. It always takes her a while to adjust." Then he laughed. "And this has been the craziest year in our entire lives."

"I'd say. You've experienced a lot of changes. But you seem to have made friends already."

"Compared to being captured by pirates and then arrested by the scariest man in Ixia, who ends up being your older brother and involved in a dangerous plot to overthrow an evil Cartel? This is easy."

I laughed. "When you put it that way, I see your point."

"And it all worked out. I'm learning about my magic. I have a sister-in-law, and I'm gonna be an uncle!" He beamed at me.

His resemblance to Valek was unmistakable, and I hoped it didn't cause him trouble in the future. Many Sitians still feared Valek, despite all he'd done to save us. At the end of the song, I said, "Just remember, we are here if you and Zohav need anything."

"I know. There's only one thing I'm worried about."

Concerned, I put my hand on his arm. "What is that?"

"That after all the excitement of the past couple seasons, school will be boring in comparison."

I swatted him. "You're just like your brother."

"Thank you."

Boys.

After the feast, life slowly returned to normal. Valek kept busy attending sessions with Irys, and with helping to teach the students self-defense and fighting techniques in the training yard. I spent my time reading through Bain's history books. I hoped to find some mention of another magician who might have had the same magic-sucking power as the baby.

I was propped up in bed scanning a book on the clans that traced the lines of magic in families when pain ringed my stomach. My first thought was that I'd been poisoned by White Fright again. Memories flashed of being locked in General Brazell's dungeon while it felt as if someone shredded my insides with a rusty knife. But that was nine years ago. My confusion cleared when another contraction hit, stronger than the last. It was the middle of the cooling season, and the baby was coming. Now.

Terror and panic mixed with relief—I'd gotten to the point where I couldn't stay in one position for long before something on my body hurt. Lumbering from bed, I put on my robe. Valek worked at a table in the living area. He concentrated on a wooden stick.

"Valek."

"Hmm?" He scowled at the thin branch. "Looks like lighting fires is truly beyond me. Pity. That would be a really useful skill to have."

Another contraction rolled through me. I sucked in deep breaths like Healer Hayes had instructed. Medic Mommy had arrived yesterday morning, but she hadn't thought I'd go into labor for another week. When I could speak again, I said, "Valek."

The strain in my voice caught his attention, and he was beside me in a heartbeat. "Is it time, love?" He remained calm. Typical.

"Yes."

"Almost there, Yelena, one more push. You can do it," Medic Mommy said.

She and Healer Hayes had taken turns soothing me while

I clung to Valek's hand as the contractions grew in frequency and severity.

"That's it. Breathe."

I grunted instead. After all these hours—I had no idea how many, except it was a lot—I thought I'd earned the right to grunt.

"Another push for the shoulders," she instructed. "The rest is easy."

And it was.

"The baby's a girl," she said, holding up a squirming little worm covered in goo.

Relief and joy pulsed through my tired body. Valek cut the cord, and I collapsed back on the bed, sweaty and achy. But all my woes disappeared when the baby cried. I lifted my head in concern. Was something wrong?

"Relax, Mom," Hayes said with a grin. "She's healthy." He weighed her. "Almost eight pounds. What's her name?"

"Liana Zaltana Icefaren," Valek said, leaning over and kissing my forehead.

Our gazes met and his eyes shone with unshed tears. *Even with her hair a mess, Yelena's still beautiful.*

Wait. I blinked at him.

"What's wrong?" he asked.

"Give me a minute." I reached for the blanket of power and concentrated. Magic flowed through me like a fresh, cool breeze. My magical senses awakened, and the world came alive around me. One of the best days of my life just became better. I met Valek's questioning gaze, then projected my thoughts toward him. I hit a solid barrier. Hard. Irys wasn't kidding when she'd said he was strong.

Valek straightened in surprise, but then he grinned. The wall disappeared.

Hi there, handsome, I thought.

MARIA V. SNYDER

Welcome back, love.

I smiled. Reaching out further, despite my low energy, I sought another.

Kiki?

Lavender Lady had foal. Approval flowed over our connection. *Better?*

Yes, I can hear you again!

She snorted as if she knew this would happen all along. *Bring foal.*

We'll visit soon.

Bring apples.

I promised to bring an entire bushel.

Healer Hayes cleaned Liana, wrapped her up so all that showed was her round pink face and handed her to me. Long black eyelashes arched from blue-green eyes, and dark hair covered her head. It was long enough to curl slightly. She was perfect. Liana stared at me for a moment, gazed at Valek for a few seconds, then promptly fell asleep. Unimpressed? Bored already? Or was it a sign that she'd be a good sleeper?

"We'll leave you alone now," Hayes said. "When she starts to fuss, that means she's hungry. Let us know if she has trouble latching on, and we'll come back and help."

Latching on sounded painful, but I nodded as if confident it would work. We marveled over our daughter for a while. It was love at first sight for both of us.

Valek touched her cheek with his finger. "She's so soft." His voice held awe. Then he crinkled his brow. "She's also blocking my magic." He pulled his hand back. "Is she blocking yours?"

I focused. "No." Then I placed my thumb on her chin. Her skin was soft, and my connection to the power blanket severed. "Yes, when I touch her."

"What happened to her sucking power?"

I thought about it. "Maybe since she didn't have direct contact with you, it seemed like she was sucking your magic, when in fact she was not being very effective in blocking it? You know, like when you build a dam of rocks, but water still leaks through?"

"Possible."

I laid my fingers on her forehead. "Try using magic on me."

Valek stared at me, but his voice didn't sound in my mind. "Now she's pulling my magic."

Unaffected by the magic around her, Liana remained asleep.

"What if you use magic, but don't direct it at us?"

He glanced at the door. "Healer Hayes and Medic Mommy are having a celebratory drink in his office." Valek laughed. "He's wondering if she'd consider moving to Sitia."

"I'd like that, especially if magic won't work on Liana."

"Do you think she's immune?" he asked in concern.

A good question. "Can you build a null shield around us?"

"Probably not without difficulty." He scanned the room. "I'll put one around the bassinet. Then I won't be able to lay her in there if she's immune."

The impulse to protect her surged through me—hot and fierce. I held her closer, "I don't want to hurt her."

His face softened. "Neither do I, love. But we need to know if she'll be trapped by a null shield."

True. He moved the bassinet to the farthest corner of the room. After a few moments, he returned to me. He lifted our daughter from my arms. Valek held her as if she'd break. "Wow, she's pretty solid. No wonder you were—"

"Watch it."

"—so uncomfortable."

"Nice."

But he wasn't listening. Valek gazed at Liana as if he held a precious jewel in his arms. He cuddled her a little longer be-

MARIA V. SNYDER

fore heading to the bassinet. Slowly, and with great care, he lowered her to the small mattress. I held my breath.

Valek straightened with his arms empty. "She popped the null shield and didn't even wake up." He grinned.

Was she a void? Did that mean she had no soul and would never find peace in the sky? I projected my awareness toward her and was blocked, but I sensed the spark of life that was her soul. I sagged back on the bed in relief. Did it really matter what she was? Not at all. As long as she was happy and healthy and safe from harm. We could determine the extent of her abilities when she was older.

Valek rolled the bassinet back beside my bed, then kicked off his boots and slid under the covers with me. Wrapping his arms around me, he pulled me close. I snuggled against him, listening to his heartbeat while breathing in his unique musky scent.

We'd survived so much, and I would never take moments like this for granted. I savored the peace, knowing full well that once the rest of the herd learned of Liana's arrival, we'd be inundated with visitors.

I was on the edge of sleep when Valek said, "I'm sorry I didn't keep my promise sooner."

I opened one eye. "What promise?"

"That we'd be together."

"I know I just had a baby and might not be thinking clearly, but I'm pretty sure we've been together for nine years."

"No. We've been living two different lives. I worked for the Commander while you were the Liaison. We were lucky to spend two weeks together at one time. If you add up all the days, it wouldn't fill two years."

He had a point. "And now?"

His arms tightened. "Now we're truly together. Body, mind and soul."

Liana hiccupped and started crying.

"And baby," I added.

"And babies," he amended. "She's going to need a brother."

EPILOGUE
VALEK

Valek watched as Yelena set Liana in the sling, securing the baby to her stomach before she mounted Kiki. Yelena's bat flew over and grabbed the edge of her hood. It hung upside-down from the fabric as it settled in for the trip. Much to Yelena's delight, the little creature had shown up mere hours after Liana was born. She hadn't seen it since the baby was conceived.

He checked the sling's straps, looking for weak or frayed spots. "Are you sure she'll be warm enough?" Valek asked his wife. The warming season had just ended, but the air was crisp despite the morning sunshine. Plus Liana was only five months old.

"Yes, she'll be fine."

"Are you sure you want to ride? I can get a wagon," he offered.

Kiki and Yelena stared at him. He didn't need to use magic to know what they were thinking, but he thought he'd asked a legitimate question.

"All right," he said. Valek checked through the saddle bags on Onyx. "Did you remember to pack—"

"Valek, get your butt in that saddle before we leave without you," Yelena said in exasperation, but then she relented. "It's my fault. I've spoiled you."

Confused, he asked, "What do you mean?"

"You've gotten your wish for the last five months. Other than trips to the market and Council Hall, Liana and I have been safe in Irys's tower while you've been learning about your magic. You're out of practice."

"Practice?"

"Yes. You haven't had to squelch your overprotectiveness during that time."

"It's not..." Well, that was part of it. "Sorry, love." He secured the bag's flap, then swung into the saddle.

Setting off at a walk, Onyx followed Kiki to the Keep's main entrance. The guards waved them through the gate. The horses navigated the busy Citadel's streets. A few Helper's Guild members waved to them as they hurried on their various errands. Fisk had rebuilt his guild, but he was also helping the Sitian Council. After regaining control of Sitia from the Cartel, the Councilors had realized their security measures were woefully inadequate. They hired Fisk to develop and implement new protocols. Fisk, in turn, hired Valek as his primary consultant. He'd enjoyed working with the young man. Plus it kept his skills sharp. Their first task had been to apprehend and arrest the members of the Problem Gang—a task Fisk had relished.

Valek and Yelena exited the Citadel through the northern gate. "Do you think we should keep this pace?" Valek asked her. "Trotting or galloping might jar the baby too much."

She peered at him as if he had two heads. Then her expression smoothed. "Why are you so nervous? *I'm* the one meeting them for the first time."

And there was the other part. "I...don't know." Which

MARIA V. SNYDER

was the heart of the problem. He had no idea what to expect. The last time he saw his parents, he'd been blindsided by the existence of his three younger siblings. With a storm of emotions raging inside him, Valek had stood next to his three older brothers' tombstones and finally come to terms with their deaths. That released his immunity and freed his ability to use magic. What might happen this time?

"Then again," she said, "they did spend a few days with Ari and Janco when they moved down to Sitia. Who knows what stories Janco told them about you?" She grinned.

"About *us*, love. Janco has just as many Yelena stories."

"Oh."

"Not so funny now, is it?"

"Maybe we should stay at a walk. It's such a lovely morning."

Kiki flicked her tail and broke into a smooth gallop. So much for that idea. At this pace, they'd be at his parents' new tannery by the afternoon. Wishing to be near their children, they had decided to move to Sitia without visiting first, as they'd originally planned. Valek had located a small complex that had been for sale. It was just outside Owl's Hill. It had a four-bedroom house, a storage shed and a building big enough to be used for his father's business. The Commander had approved the move, but it had taken a few months to transport the equipment, their furniture and dozens of crates full of their belongings. They'd lived in that house in Ixia for over forty-five years.

Valek could commiserate. The Commander had sent all of Valek's things, including his carving tools, soon after Liana was born. The boxes filled two entire floors of Irys's tower. Once Valek had completed his magical training, they would purchase a home somewhere in northern Sitia. It didn't matter where, as long as it was quiet and hidden. The Commander had given him a very generous retirement bonus, so they would be able to keep the apartment above Alethea's bookshop as their public address and for when they had business in town. Plus the Council planned to pay Yelena to resume her Soulfinder duties once he finished his training at the Keep.

His parents' tannery was on the northwest side of Owl's Hill. The path from the main road wove through the budding trees before it ended at a white picket fence that surrounded the complex. The house dominated the clearing. Valek's mother had insisted on at least four bedrooms so there would be plenty of room for her children and grandchildren to visit.

Kiki hopped the fence with ease, and Valek heard giggles. When Onyx cleared the barrier, he joined Yelena. She smiled at him. "Liana likes jumping."

Sure enough, his daughter's happy face peered from the sling, her blue-green eyes alight with glee. Figured. So far, she'd been a joy, easy to put to sleep and entertain. But Valek suspected that might change when she was older. He wondered if Liana would develop magical powers, or if her blocking skill was the extent of her abilities. Time would tell.

They stopped outside the main door of the house. Valek dismounted and helped Yelena down from Kiki. The squeal of a screen door alerted him. Yelena squeezed his arm. He drew in a deep breath and faced his parents.

His father strode toward them with a welcoming grin, while his mother hung back, uncertain. They both still wore their Ixian uniforms.

"About time you came to visit," Kalen said, slapping Valek on the back. "The twins were here two weeks ago. And you must be Yelena. Nice to finally meet you." He shook her hand with both of his. "Valek didn't exaggerate when he said you were beautiful. Ahh! There she is. Can I hold her?"

MARIA V. SNYDER

"Of course." Yelena removed the baby from the sling and handed her to Kalen.

His father's face lit up with an amazed joy as he gazed at Liana lying in his arms. She peered back, studying him with interest. Years of grief seemed to melt from Kalen's lined skin, and his brown eyes shone.

"Oh, she's a beauty. Olya, come see. She resembles your mother." Then he lowered his voice. "Let's hope that's as far as it goes."

"I heard that, Kalen," Olya said, joining them. She nodded at Valek and said hello to Yelena. But her reserved demeanor changed when she saw her granddaughter. "She's lovely." Olya plucked the baby from her husband's arms.

"Hey," he protested, but it was weak.

"Aren't you a sweetie!" She marveled at the baby, letting Liana clutch her finger.

Kalen gestured with a hand. "Let's get out of this sun. Come on into the house."

"Go on," Valek said to Yelena. "I'll take care of the horses."

Yelena gave him a don't-you-dare-leave-me-alone look. He suppressed a grin.

"No need," Kalen said. "Zebulon!"

Valek's brother exited the tannery, then strode over to them. He wore plain brown pants and a cream-colored tunic. Zebulon's black hair flopped about his head, and his brown-eyed gaze scanned them. With the same distant manner as their mother, he greeted Yelena and Valek, but warmth flashed when he spotted Liana.

"Zeb, can you take care of the horses?" Kalen asked.

"Uh." Zeb glanced at the horses with a queasy expression.

"Groom and feed them like the twins showed you, and then join us inside," Kalen said.

"All right."

Valek skimmed Zeb's surface thoughts. The twenty-year-old had only watched Zohav and Zethan care for the horses. Zeb had no idea what to do. Valek met Yelena's gaze, and she nodded.

Hurry up, she thought.

"I'll be right there," Valek said to his father. "I'll help Zeb—it'll go faster."

As they headed to the house, Kalen asked Yelena, "Is it always *this* hot here? I'm roasting."

"No."

"Thank fate!"

"It gets hotter."

He groaned. Yelena would be too polite to tell him he needed to wear Sitian clothing, but Valek would find some way to mention it. In the meantime, he showed Zeb how to remove the horses' saddles and tack. Then he handed his brother a curry comb and demonstrated how to use it. Zeb groomed Kiki. They worked for a while in companionable silence.

"What do you think of Sitia so far?" Valek asked.

"It's okay. I guess I need to learn how to ride, right? Isn't that how everyone gets around in Sitia?"

"Not everyone. You can walk, and there are travel shelters between cities." Valek sensed that wasn't what Zeb wanted to hear. "Although it's faster on horseback. Especially if you're going farther than Owl's Hill."

"There's not much to do in Owl's Hill."

Ah. "Would you like me to teach you how to ride?"

He hesitated. "Did you teach the twins?"

"I showed Zethan the basics when we traveled to Sitia, but they're learning the finer art of horsemanship at the Magician's Keep." Along with a number of other things, like fighting and self-defense techniques. Things the Ixian schools didn't cover unless it was required for your job. Since Zebulon didn't have magic, he wouldn't get this extra education. And since he was already twenty, he was too old to attend the Sitian schools.

"Yeah, they seem to be fitting right in at the Keep," Zeb said.

"Do you plan to stay here and work for Father?" Valek asked.

If the question surprised the young man, he didn't show it. "I don't know. Before, I sort of had to. I didn't have any other options in Ixia. Now…"

"Too many."

Zebulon laughed. "Yeah."

"What do you like to do?"

He shrugged, but then said, "I like working with my hands."

That was a start. As they groomed, fed and watered the horses, Valek asked a number of questions. By the time they finished, he had a better idea of Zebulon's interests, which didn't include the military, law enforcement or spying. Basically, not going into the family business.

"What about working with glass?" he asked Zeb as they brushed off all the horsehair from their clothes and washed the grime from their hands. "I've friends who own a glass factory in Fulgor and would be amenable to taking on an apprentice."

Zeb appeared interested. "It would be someplace to start. Is Fulgor like Owl's Hill?"

"No. It's much bigger. It's about a four-day ride west of here."

"I'd like that. Thanks."

They entered the house. It was cooler inside. Despite the fact that the family had moved in only a few weeks ago, all the crates and boxes had been unpacked. The familiar furniture and decorations from his childhood filled unfamiliar rooms, and the effect was disconcerting. Voices emanated from deep within, and Valek followed Zeb to the living area.

"...planned for the beginning of the hot season in the Magician's Keep," Yelena said. "You're all invited, of course."

"Invited to what?" Zebulon asked. He sat next to their mother on the couch.

Liana remained in Olya's lap. The baby chewed on her favorite yellow horse-shaped rattle. The number of gifts she'd gotten just for being born had been astounding. Janco had brought her what he called "baby's first set of lock picks." And the Commander sent her a pink diamond the size of Liana's fist.

Despite everyone's relaxed postures, an awkwardness thickened the air. Yelena sat in an armchair with a cup of tea on the table next to her. Kalen occupied the other chair.

"Our wedding celebration," Yelena said.

Valek hid his grin. Yelena's mother had refused to leave the Keep until plans had been set into motion for the celebration. And after a month of having her mother underfoot, Yelena would have agreed to anything to speed Perl's departure. Which was why the party was scheduled for when the Keep's students were gone. Perl's guest list was so long that they would need to use the student barracks to house them all.

"I thought you were already married," Olya said. She bounced Liana on her knee. The baby squealed in delight.

"In Ixia," Valek said. "Sitia has different rules."

"And they'll use any excuse to throw a party," Yelena joked.

Olya frowned at that. Valek suspected it would take his mother the most time to adjust to the Sitian way of life.

"Hot season, eh?" Kalen wiped his brow. "We'll come, but I can't guarantee we won't melt into puddles."

"We've invited a couple Stormdancers who will make sure

MARIA V. SNYDER

clouds block the sun and a cool breeze blows," Valek said. "Their powers are similar to Zethan's."

The tension increased with the mention of magic. Oh, boy.

Kalen cleared his throat. "Zethan mentioned you're working for the Sitian Council. What are you doing for them?" He adopted a casual tone, but the tightness in his shoulders said otherwise.

"I'm helping with security. What they had in place before the Cartel was not very effective."

"You mean like guarding the Councilors?"

Valek didn't need to read his father's thoughts to understand the real question. "More like setting up protocols, ensuring the guards are trustworthy and helping with training." He glanced at his mother's pinched face. "*Not* assassinating anyone." Unless they threatened the safety of his herd.

"Of course not," his father said too quickly. "I'm sure all that's behind you now that you have a beautiful wife and daughter."

Smooth recovery. Valek approved.

Kalen hopped to his feet. "How about a tour of the tannery? Yelena?"

She hesitated, glancing at Liana.

"Oh, she'll be fine. Olya's raised seven babies."

"All right. A tour would be nice."

Valek laced his fingers in Yelena's as they trailed his father. The equipment in the tannery remained the same as he'd remembered. The smells of the vats and the hides stretched over the drying racks brought many of his childhood memories bubbling to the surface of his mind. He and his brothers had devised many creative excuses to avoid working.

Kalen led them back outside. Three mounds of dirt marred the grass behind the tannery. The headstones of Valek's older brothers marked each one—Vincent, Viliam, and Victor. Yelena's grip tightened in his. Valek glanced at her in concern, but she shook her head. *Later.*

"I wanted to let you know we brought them with us," Kalen said. "We couldn't stand the thought of leaving them behind."

"Thank you." Valek swallowed the wedge of emotion in his throat. "I see you left Mooch behind."

Kalen laughed. "Yeah. The twins were upset, but I wasn't digging up that damn dog."

They returned to the house and spent the rest of the afternoon making awkward conversation. Valek offered to hire a couple of trustworthy people to help his parents.

"The tannery is smaller than the one in Ixia," his father said. "Zeb and I can handle it."

Valek exchanged a glance with Zeb, but his brother pressed his lips together, signaling it wasn't the right time to mention the glass apprenticeship. "They would be able to do more than work. They can advise you on the local customs, ensure you're not being cheated or taken advantage of and tell you where to purchase certain goods, like a fabric that breathes in this hot weather. Those wool uniforms are far too warm for the Sitian climate."

"We'll think about—" his father started.

"That would be nice," Olya said in a tone that warned her husband not to argue with her.

Wow. He hadn't expected his mother to agree so easily. Valek kept his expression neutral. "I'll make inquiries at Owl's Hill before we return to the Citadel tomorrow."

"Thank you." She stood with a sleepy Liana in her arms. "The baby needs a nap, and I need to start dinner."

"Would you like some company?" Yelena offered.

"Yes." Olya transferred Liana to Valek's arms. "You had those same long eyelashes when you were a baby. Everyone

MARIA V. SNYDER

thought you were a girl, despite the fact that you wore your brothers' hand-me-downs." Then she went into the kitchen.

Yelena flashed him a grin before following his mother.

Do not *tell Janco*, he thought.

Sorry, I can't hear you. Too busy cooking.

Zeb and his father left to check on the next batch of hides, but Valek was content to remain on the couch and hold Liana as she napped. He drank in her clean, powdery scent and gazed at her. She was so precious to him. The urge to protect her burned in his veins, and he wondered if he'd survive her childhood. Just the thought of her learning how to walk and run and climb the stairs and sleep in a big bed and ride a horse already made him anxious with worry. If only she could remain a baby forever. Then again, forever's worth of dirty diapers was incentive enough to trust his daughter to reach those milestones without hurting herself too much.

After dinner that night, his mother escorted them to a guest room. "Zeb put your bags inside already and lit the lantern." She stood outside the door. "Kalen assembled the crib, so you might want to test that it's sturdy."

"I heard that," Kalen called from down the hall. "It wasn't my fault the legs broke off. The twins were too big to be in a crib, anyway."

A brief smile flashed. "Let us know if you need anything."

"Thank you," Yelena said.

Olya nodded and retreated to her bedroom.

When Yelena and Valek entered, he froze.

"What's wrong?" Yelena asked.

"It's…" He crossed to the armoire and opened the door. Scratches marked the inside, appearing random at first, but upon closer inspection, they were code words that Valek had etched into the wood when he'd spied on his older brothers.

Shock rolled through him. Valek scanned the rest of the room. The sloppy boat paintings Vincent had done in school hung on the walls, and the wooden toys Valek had carved lined a shelf—he'd forgotten all about them.

Except for the larger bed, nothing had changed. "It's *my* room. The one I shared with Vincent." It made sense that they'd kept the furnishings and Vincent's paintings, but he hadn't expected them to save his toys or leave the marks he'd made on the armoire alone.

Yelena tested the crib with one hand and then laid Liana down on the mattress. The baby sighed in her sleep. His wife took Valek's hands in her own. "They never stopped loving you."

He shook his head. "I'm no longer that boy. And my mother is still terrified of me."

"Despite her fear, her soul knows you." Yelena released his hands. She pressed her palm over his heart. "Her soul knows who you are right now, and she loves you. Your reputation has colored her thoughts, but she just needs time to adjust to all the changes in her life. Then she'll see what I see every day."

He pulled her close. "What do you see?"

"I see a loving husband and father who will do anything to protect the people he loves. A man worthy of love in return."

Unable to put his emotions into words, he kissed his wife with all the passion she stirred in his soul.

When they broke apart, she gazed at him. *It's time.*

To make love all night? I'm in. He tugged her toward the bed. She resisted. *No. Time to say goodbye to your brothers.*

He stopped as all the colors in the room drained away, leaving behind only shades of gray. *Is this—*

The shadow world. Yelena twined her fingers in his. *Look.*

Valek's three brothers stood in the room. So young and so... perfect. No wounds marked them. They grinned at him, but

MARIA V. SNYDER

he couldn't smile in return. He glanced at Yelena in horror. Instead of finding peace in the sky, they'd been trapped in the shadow world for the last twenty-nine years.

No. She tapped his chest. *They've been with* you *for the last twenty-nine years.*

But wouldn't you have seen them?

They were locked inside you. Don't worry, they have no memories of that time. According to them, they remember being murdered. Then they woke standing next to their graves in the shadow world. They were confused to see you much older and kneeling in front of Vincent's gravestone.

You've seen them since your magic returned? You've been talking to them? A sense of betrayal pulsed in his heart. Why hadn't she told him?

Of course not. I saw them for the first time this afternoon, by their graves. They've been waiting for you to come back. Your parents said goodbye when they moved here, and now it's your turn.

He thought he had made peace with them back in Ixia, when he'd lost his immunity to magic. Valek looked at Yelena. *Can I talk to them?*

Only through me. She squeezed his hand. *Go ahead.*

He turned to his brothers. *I'm sorry.*

For what, Little Brother? Vincent asked. *Marrying the prettiest girl in the world? Of course, if I'd been alive, she wouldn't have even looked at you.*

I'm sorry for being alive, when you… The horrible image of them lying dead in the snow flashed before him.

Stop that, Victor said. *Look at me.*

Valek focused on him. As the oldest of the four of them, Victor tended to take charge and calm everyone down.

We were beyond relieved that you weren't killed, as well.

Phantom pain spiked in Valek's shoulders where his mother had held him back. *But I should have—*

What? Gotten killed, too? Vincent asked. *Come on, Little Brother, we thought you were past all this.*

So did I. But seeing them again brought all those feelings back.

Well, I'm sure your lovely wife and beautiful daughter are happy you're still sucking air, Viliam said. He was younger than Victor by two minutes, but they were complete opposites in personality. He also had a good point.

Valek sensed Yelena's agreement.

Victor gestured to the three of them. *Remember us this way. No blood or gore.*

Good thing, since I faint at the sight of blood, Viliam said.

His twin frowned at Viliam. The gesture reminded Valek of Ari and Janco. How could he not see how much their personalities resembled his older brothers'? Again, Yelena's agreement pulsed inside him.

You can't change the past. We can't change it either, Victor said. *We're content and are ready to embrace peace in the sky. Are you ready to say goodbye?*

I... He'd have liked more time, but he had let them go back in Ixia. This goodbye shouldn't be any harder than the last. *Yes.*

Three matching grins.

Live for us, Vincent said.

I will.

They faded. Color returned to the world, brighter than before.

Yelena leaned against him. *Now, where were we? Oh, yes, you mentioned something about making love all night?*

He swept her off her feet and carried her to bed, savoring every moment with her. While spending all night engaged in intimate relations would have been a very romantic interlude,

MARIA V. SNYDER

the realities of their life—little Liana—made that quite impossible. They fell into an exhausted sleep after the first round.

Liana's hungry cries woke them a few hours later. Valek slid from the bed and carried the baby back to Yelena to nurse. He hoped Liana hadn't woken anyone else. Valek lowered his mental barriers and checked. His father and brother remained sound asleep, but his mother sat in the kitchen, sipping a cup of tea despite the late hour.

What's wrong? Yelena asked.

My mother is downstairs. I…need to talk to her.

Yes, you do.

Lovely. Her Soulfinding abilities didn't seem to be rusty after the long hiatus, he thought dryly.

I heard that, she said.

You were supposed to.

Uh-huh. Go on. We'll be fine.

He padded down the stairs soundlessly, but Valek made a little noise before reaching the kitchen. He didn't want to scare his mother. She turned her head as he entered. Fear flashed as she stiffened, but then she relaxed her grip on the cup she held.

Valek ignored her reaction. "Did the baby wake you?" he asked, knowing full well Olya was here before Liana had cried.

"Not at all. I…couldn't sleep."

Valek didn't need to read his mother's thoughts to know it was his presence in her house that was keeping her awake.

"Does Liana need something?" she asked.

"No, but I do."

She stared at him for a moment. "What do you need?"

He knelt next to her and took her free hand in both of his. "I need to thank you."

"You're always welcome to come visit us anytime."

"Not for your hospitality, although that's appreciated. I'm

thanking you for saving my life that awful day. I never did." He drew in a breath. "Thank you."

She put her cup down and rested her free hand on his shoulder, still marked with the scars from her fingernails. "You're welcome."

★ ★ ★ ★ ★

ACKNOWLEDGMENTS

I began this journey with Yelena and Valek twenty years ago, when the idea to write a fantasy novel about a food taster popped into my head. Little did I know that the characters in my first novel, *Poison Study*, would resonate with readers worldwide and be the impetus for eight more novels. It's been quite an adventure to chronicle their lives and acts of bravery, to cry with them and laugh over Janco's antics, to grieve and celebrate with them. I'm so honored and proud that my characters have inspired so many readers and have touched their lives. Their emails are the best reward for all the hard work.

This was a beast of a book, and not only is it longer than my others, but it was also difficult to write. To all those who provided feedback and guidance to help calm the beast—my agent, Robert Mecoy; my editor, Lauren Smulski; and my beta readers, Judi Fleming, Kathy Flowers, and my husband—thanks for all your help. You make me look good.

Speaking of looking good, I need to thank all the talented people at Harlequin who work behind the scenes. Your efforts are appreciated. And an extra-big thank you to the Australian team—I had a fantastic time when I visited! You made me feel right at home—you guys rock!

I'd also like to give a special shout-out to my Aussie friend, Natalie Bejin, for her help in keeping me organized and for finding all the inconsistencies—you're the best Chief Evil Minion an author can have.

Thanks to Meili for her expert advice on rabbits—Janco's glad you backed him up. And thanks to Abby, who gave me permission to use her quote in the book: "You put the *sass* in as*sass*in." Also thanks to Mike Farrar, who came up with the idea for the title.

This journey would never have happened without the following people in my life: my husband, Rodney; my parents; my sister, Karen; her husband, Chris; and my children, Luke and Jenna. Thank you all so very much!